CHILDLESS

CHILDLESS

A Novel

DR. JAMES DOBSON
AND KURT BRUNER

New York Boston Nashville

FaithWords
Hachette Book Group
237 Park Avenue
New York, NY 10017

www.faithwords.com

Printed in the United States of America

Originally published in hardcover by Hachette Book Group.

First trade edition: April 2014

10 9 8 7 6 5 4 3 2 1

FaithWords is a division of Hachette Book Group, Inc.

The FaithWords name and logo are trademarks of Hachette Book Group, Inc.

The Hachette Speakers Bureau provides a wide range of authors for speaking events. To find out more, go to www.hachettespeakersbureau.com or call (866) 376-6591.

The publisher is not responsible for websites (or their content) that are not owned by the publisher.

The Library of Congress has cataloged the hardcover edition as follows:

Dobson, James C., 1936-
Childless : a novel / Dr. James Dobson and Kurt Bruner. -- First edition.
   pages cm
  ISBN 978-1-4555-1315-4 (hardcover)—ISBN 978-1-4555-7605-0 (large print hardcover)—ISBN 978-1-4555-1314-7 (ebook)
1. Christian fiction. I. Bruner, Kurt D. II. Title.
  PS3604.O24C47 2013
  813'.6--dc23

                                                2012051320

ISBN 978-1-4555-1313-0 (pbk.)

In memory of the late Dr. Francis Schaeffer who warned us of the perilous future depicted in this book.

AUTHOR'S NOTE

When I was young my father gave me a poem presumably written in the sixteenth century by a woman named Ursula Southeil, better known as Mother Shipton. It contained a series of predictions about future events that have proven remarkably accurate. One of those predictions seemed to prophesy some of the present-day trends that inspired this book.

Then love shall die and marriage cease,
And nations wane as babes decrease

Nations wane when the old and feeble outnumber the young and productive. The best demographers tell us the growth in global population will soon end and then reverse due to an unprecedented drop in fertility taking place throughout the developed world. Places like Japan and Russia are already experiencing the economic turmoil caused by too few children trying to support a growing pool of aging citizens.

In *Fatherless* we explored one of the causes: men neglecting the honor and responsibilities of paternity. In *Childless* we'll ask what happens when sex is severed from the life-giving joys of maternity. Be forewarned, such questions require depicting ugly realities that come when we disregard the beauty and sanctity of the marriage bed.

As we said in Book One, a happy home is the highest expression of God's image on Earth. Marriage and parenthood echo heaven, something hell can't abide. This series is a fictional account of where the battle against human thriving is heading in the not-too-distant future. But it is also a celebration of God's design for families, which retains a resilient beauty and redemptive power the most ardent forces of hell cannot destroy.

James C. Dobson, PhD

CHILDLESS

September 1, 2043

Victor

The faint sound of doorbell chimes prompted Rebecca Santiago to click off the hair dryer. That's when she panicked. The oven timer! Her gown somewhere out of reach, she hastily grabbed Victor's gangly bathrobe while darting toward the kitchen in a futile effort to rescue her forgotten pumpkin scones.

Balancing the hot cookie sheet with her hand in an oven mitt, she opened the front door with the other hand. She rolled her eyes at the sound of an overnight delivery truck hastily speeding away from the driveway.

"You call that friendly service?" Rebecca shouted to the fleeing license plate before bending down to retrieve the thin package. It was small and flat like any of the countless legal documents that required her husband's attention. She tossed it aside before hurriedly disposing of the dozen smoldering lumps no longer suitable to serve with tea. As on every other Tuesday, the bridge club gals would arrive at eleven o'clock sharp. She had less than fifteen minutes to make her graying strands wavy and refurbish a face banished from makeup-free appearances decades ago.

The envelope sat ignored until four thirty that afternoon, when it caught Rebecca's eye. As she waved goodbye to Shelly, who, as usual, had overstayed her welcome by ninety minutes, she noticed it balanced conspicuously on the dining room table right next to a legal brief Victor had forsaken seven hours earlier.

"Gotta run," he had mumbled through a half-eaten piece of toast wedged between his teeth on his way out the door. "Lost track of time."

Rebecca sighed at the reminder of her husband's chief short-coming. She knew what few others could guess. The esteemed Victor Santiago, presiding judge in the Tenth Circuit Court of Appeals, was a man severely allergic to multitasking. Sipping coffee and reviewing legal opinions were two simultaneous activities that had squeezed checking the time out of his morning routine. She marveled that Victor managed to survive while away from her attentive hovering, let alone that he'd earned a notable reputation. But he had, thanks in large part to their thirty-two-year arrangement. The day Victor married Rebecca his formidable mind had entrusted all nonjudicial matters to his better half, and she had gladly assumed them.

Finding a pair of scissors, Rebecca slit the seal and let the contents fall onto the kitchen counter. A smaller envelope shaped like a greeting card displayed handwritten script.

To: Mrs. Rebecca Santiago
From: A Fan of the Judge

She smiled, anticipating another note expressing admiration for her husband's growing influence. She had a pleasant habit that had begun with her scrapbook of news clippings from Victor's years as prosecuting attorney. She loved saving mementos from key career milestones. Her favorite was the framed picture taken at the press conference announcing his appointment to the federal bench. Victor had protested when she placed it so prominently on display in the living room. But household décor fell within her jurisdiction. No matter how brilliantly worded his opinion on the matter, hers remained the deciding vote.

Rebecca hoped that no one, especially Victor, would ever suspect her least becoming custom: she routinely sorted through the office wastepaper basket to retrieve notes her husband might have discarded after dismissing thanks or a compliment from a client or colleague. Part of her role, she told herself, was to relish the accolades her husband considered irrelevant or undeserved.

Rebecca assumed this note came from yet another character witness offering evidence that her lifelong lover was also the most important legal mind on the planet. She slid the contents free and noticed a slight bulge from the folded letter inserted between the elegant panels of a card that must have been purchased from an upscale stationery store. She removed the page before reading the card's inscription.

Dear Rebecca:

I apologize for troubling you at home, and I regret any distress the enclosed may cause you. But I desperately need your assistance in what has become a most pressing, delicate matter. Thank you, in advance, for your cooperation.

Warmest regards,
A Manichean

She stared at the signature for several seconds, trying to place the name. Nothing came. Then she began unfolding the longer note to read the details of the mysterious request. Her mind raced ahead of her hands to offer possible scenarios, each seeming less plausible than the last.

A practical joke by her ornery brother? Keith hadn't even bothered fixing himself a sandwich since losing Kay. He wouldn't waste the little energy he had left concocting an elaborate gag. And even if he had, his hands shook too much for such graceful penmanship.

Perhaps some surprise Victor had arranged for her sixtieth? Of course her birthday remained weeks away, and Victor wasn't the type to plan such things. Then again, he could have received prods and help from his ever-thoughtful assistant Jennifer. Possible, but not likely.

Could it be a legitimate request to get involved with a case? Victor had presided over hundreds of decisions during his years on the bench. At his insistence, none had ever invaded the sanctuary of their home. On the one occasion he'd seemed tortured over a particularly challenging case she'd asked if he wanted to talk about it. But he had slammed the door on the possibility with a grateful kiss on her forehead.

Having dismissed all three alternatives Rebecca felt a rush of vague panic as she began reading the double-creased page.

Dear Victor:

Please forgive my sending this note to your wife Rebecca. Prior attempts to correspond through your assistant have proven unfruitful. I have yet to receive a single response to any of my previous letters regarding the wrongful death appeal involving NEXT Transition Services. As you know, many lives hang in the balance in this matter. That's why I was pleased the case fell to a man with the kind of wisdom and restraint you have demonstrated throughout your distinguished judicial career. But this case is far too important for any hint of ambiguity. That's why I must know where you stand before the scheduled ruling deadline of September 4th. Please consider Rebecca's future as you contemplate the following alternatives:

- *Option One: Assure me that you will indeed decide in favor of NEXT.*
- *Option Two: Bid your sweet wife farewell since you will die before issuing an opinion.*

Once again, I apologize for alarming Rebecca. But she deserves to know about the increasingly tense situation in which we find ourselves. I could not allow any of what might transpire to come as a surprise, and I trust that her intervention will motivate you to do what's right for everyone.

As always,
A Manichean
P.S. Kindly post your response at the following private forum address: ANON.CHAT.4398

Rebecca felt her legs weaken as she steadied herself with a dining room chair. She had always known that important work like Victor's came with certain risks. "So does driving a car or boarding a plane," her husband had always said reassuringly. He'd never bothered to mention possible assassination.

She took an overdue breath as her eyes returned to the only sentence on the page that mattered. *Bid your sweet wife farewell since you will die before issuing an opinion.*

The letter fell to the floor in union with Rebecca's sinking heart. She cradled her face in shaking hands, then closed her eyes to preview the scenes of a coming-soon nightmare.

Act One. She would plead with her husband. Beg him to cooperate.

Act Two. He would say no, stubbornly refusing to fear the same menacing threat that promised to keep her on edge for several fretful days and sleepless nights.

Act Three. A faceless stranger Rebecca might never detect would kill the man she could never live without.

PART ONE

Three Weeks Earlier

CHAPTER ONE

August 15, 2043

Tyler Cain drove through several blocks of boarded-up homes and vacant apartment buildings before reaching the familiar street. The neighborhood could have been any of a hundred half-abandoned sections of town. Denver had begun following in the footsteps of once-thriving cities like Detroit, Philadelphia, Chicago, and Boston. The national population had officially tilted downward only eighteen months earlier, but some regions had already transformed into empty havens of life free from the burden of kids.

Neighborhoods don't hide the signs of aging any better than the people who desert them. Decades earlier these homes had likely bustled with the sights and sounds of children heading off to school. They now served as rickety remnants of a bygone era. Few of the single-family dwellings appeared in use beyond the occasional crack dealer, palm reader, or senior citizen too poor or stubborn to leave an area the underfunded police no longer patrolled.

Tyler pulled his unwashed '28 Ford Mustang behind what he guessed to be an abandoned '22 Lexus. Two unrepaired flat rear tires suggested the vehicle had been pronounced dead after the prolonged torture of owner neglect. Tyler's car fit right in, providing the perfect camouflage for yet another mind-numbing stakeout.

With the flip of a tiny switch on the left rim of his sunglasses he looked toward the residence in question. He could have parked closer. But four hundred yards gave him a reason to use the vision-magnification feature that, he had convinced himself, would be well worth the extra expense. Tapping the lens twice, he zoomed in enough to confirm drawn draperies and a solitary car in the driveway.

Absolutely nothing was happening, as during most of his billable hours.

Tyler glanced at the clock while reaching for a slightly crumpled bag containing today's indulgence: two bacon cheeseburgers with extra pickles. Renee would not have approved, but he needed sustenance beyond the bird food she called a sensible diet. His girlfriend had always been a health nut. It was one of the things that had attracted him to her when they first met. Her fit forty-one-year-old figure remained the best part of an otherwise exasperating relationship. Daily jogs and calorie counting looked great on her, but they cramped his style. Besides, he was in better shape than most guys pushing fifty.

He looked in the visor mirror to inspect a face she had once called boyishly cute. No man wants to be either, so he had grown a slight goatee that now contained more gray than he had allowed his thinning hair to display.

Renee disapproved of facial hair almost as much as bacon burgers. "It itches me when we kiss," she had teased. "Itchy kissing can spoil the mood."

Fortunately she never followed through on the veiled threat.

So he continued ignoring her appeals to restore the aging baby face she had fallen in love with three years earlier.

While downing a final beefy bite with a sip of strawberry shake Tyler noticed a vehicle approaching from behind. He watched it grow in the driver's-side mirror as it slowed to a wary crawl. As the car crept past he recognized the woman's face from the photograph his client had provided. Her car continued rolling forward as she strained to find a legible address before pausing in front of the house Tyler had positioned himself to observe.

She remained seated inside for several minutes, apparently adding finishing touches to her makeup. When she finally opened the door Tyler tapped his lens for a closer look. Nearly attractive, she appeared old enough to be helping grown kids pack for college or spoiling her grandkids rather than getting dolled up in such a pleasantly inappropriate outfit.

Why do they care how they look? he wondered. The man waiting inside, Tyler assumed, would act out this week's sexual fantasy regardless. To guys with made-up names that change daily, the risk of getting caught was a bigger turn-on than high heels.

Tyler quickly grabbed his camera to snap five pictures of the woman, the first as she walked from the car and the fifth as she looked back from an opening front door to confirm secrecy. That's when he caught a glimpse of the man's face. He appeared a bit younger than the woman, his tentative eyes darting to and fro as if checking for a stalking lover who might catch him in the act. Five seconds later the door closed as the pair secured themselves within a renovated slum house far less attractive and sanitary than it had appeared in the online ad for this particular House of Delights.

So began Tyler's Monday-through-Friday afternoon routine of sitting outside this or some other den of iniquity to glean the scraps of a booming arranged hookups industry. It was all part of a predictable sequence for securing clients and earning a steadily mediocre income.

- Step One: Follow home whatever man or woman left one of the sordid establishments
- Step Two: Trace his or her address to identify a potential partner
- Step Three: Leave an anonymous note to plant a seed of suspicion and recommend a "trustworthy investigator" named Tyler Cain
- Step Four: Wait for the phone to ring

The process had kept Tyler so busy he no longer bothered asking his former supervising detective for legitimate investigation leads.

Business is great, he would boast when asked. *More work than I can handle paying me more than I deserve.*

In truth he felt like a crawdad bottom-feeding on the city's sludge to barely earn enough to match his former salary. He wondered how much longer he could muster the self-assured grin that masked the greatest regret of his life. Tyler should have never abandoned the force. He should have swallowed his pride when passed over for a promotion, rather than leave a job he loved.

Tyler swiped through the images he had captured to make sure the woman's face could be clearly identified and that the time marker didn't obstruct any important details. Satisfied, he smiled in anticipation of invoicing another heartbroken client. Receiving payment was the only part of the business Tyler still enjoyed. Years earlier he had imagined himself catching murderers and foiling international conspiracies like the handsome secret agents on television. But then he'd stumbled into a lucrative niche in the private detective business. A steady stream of insecure partners gladly paid his hourly rate to determine whether the loves of their lives were cheating.

Placing the camera aside, he settled in to await the woman's departure. He guessed it would be at least thirty minutes before he could snap the all-important exit photos, ample time to listen to a few weepy client recordings. They always phoned after receiving his invoice, because he included a personalized invitation to call if they needed a listening ear. Clingy lovers always trap and smother the next partner, so Tyler's business could thrive for many years on repeat business alone. In the early days he had scheduled face-to-face closure meetings, a touch of humanity that had earned him several word-of-mouth referrals. But he quickly ran out of time and patience for that routine. So he began offering to talk on a phone he rarely answered, resulting in a steady stream of extended messages. Ten minutes of listening to whiny, emotional bleating followed by quickly typing a message of condolence had proven nearly as productive with far less effort.

"Hi, Mr. Cain, this is Naomi Wilkerson." The voice broke, and there was a long, sniffling pause. Tyler rolled his eyes in recognition of a weakness he had come to despise in the people who paid him so well.

"I can't stop looking at the photographs you sent," she finally continued.

He recalled three sets of pictures taken over a span of six days.

"I showed them to Davey like you suggested. But when I asked him to explain he just ignored me and went back to sipping his beer and watching the game.

"I started kissing his hand and asked him if he still loved me, then I said I don't feel like he wants me the way he did when he first moved in. I tried to be strong because he gets mad when I cry. So I took a deep breath before asking him if he had slept with other women.

"He didn't get mad. He didn't react at all. He just turned slowly toward me and said, 'It's none of your business who I sleep with. And no, I don't want you like I did before.'

"I felt like a knife went into my heart. I ran to the bedroom and cried myself to sleep.

"Well, you can imagine my surprise when he woke me a few hours later to say he wanted to make love. I was so happy. When we finished he began to fall asleep. I cuddled in close and whispered in his ear that I will always love him, no matter what."

Same song, hundredth verse, Tyler thought, *a needy woman grasping for an apathetic man like a drunk caressing an empty bottle.* Tyler saw what Naomi refused to accept. Davey didn't love his partner the way she hoped for or deserved. He merely enjoyed their living arrangement and the on-demand sex afforded by a girl sleeping twelve inches away. But Naomi had invested too much of herself in the relationship to let him go. Better to keep a small part of Davey than lose all of herself.

"Anyway," the message continued, "I paid your invoice and I thank you for your hard work. I suppose it's possible that Davey made a mistake, possibly even slept with someone once. But I still think we have something special and I'm choosing to hope for the best. I don't know what I'd do without him. You're a very nice man, Mr. Cain. Your girlfriend is a lucky gal."

The comment reminded Tyler that he hadn't yet made dinner plans to celebrate his girlfriend's good fortune. She insisted they do something special every August seventeenth, the day they had met, in lieu of a nonexistent wedding anniversary.

Three years with one woman, he marveled.

Two more than I intended, he thought with a sigh.

This relationship, like his prior three, should have ended after a sensible nine or ten months, when infatuation wanes and daily habits annoy. Both happened with Renee after fifteen months, about the same time he found himself short on capital and scrambling for clients.

"I'll cosign," she had offered supportively when Tyler confessed his inadequate credit. Renee would have done anything for her man. Still would. So the relationship expanded from that of while-love-lasts lovers into that of until-the-loan-gets-paid business partners.

What made him most nervous was Renee's recent comment about her biological clock. As if afraid of a ticking bomb, the thought made him want to get away. Despite cutting corners and pinching pennies, however, he had only managed to pay down the outstanding balance on their joint loan by a few thousand dollars. It would be two more bottom-feeding years before he could retire the loan, before he'd feel right easing out of the relationship.

After tapping the DELETE MESSAGE icon Tyler typed and sent a brief note.

Hi Naomi:

I just got your message and wanted to wish you well. Thanks for sending payment. While I hope it won't be necessary, I am available if you or any of your friends find yourself in need of investigative services in future days.

Warm regards,
Tyler Cain, PI
P.S. Davey is lucky to have you.

Tyler felt a sudden urge to stretch his legs. He hesitated, concerned the distraction could cause him to miss the woman's exit. Checking the time, he noticed twenty minutes had passed. He had always called arranged hookups the illicit counterpart of drive-through fast food. Transaction and consumption occur quickly. But he figured the two would spend time getting acquainted before going through the motions of awkward foreplay, hesitant passion, and the rest. Perhaps another fifteen or twenty minutes. Tyler decided to take a chance. He exited the car to cool in the shade of a nearby tree.

That's when he received a call from Greg Smith, the one man able to rescue Tyler from self-imposed exile.

CHAPTER TWO

"Smitty!" Tyler shouted with too much enthusiasm, leaning against the white bark of a full-leafed aspen. "How's my favorite former partner doing?"

"Fine, Cain. Just fine." Detective Smith had never been the most gregarious officer on the force, content to let his partner cover rituals like disingenuous backslapping for the both of them. He was even less inclined toward empty chatter now that he held the post of assistant chief.

"Great to hear from you," Tyler continued. "How's life at the top?"

He regretted the dig immediately. It wasn't Smitty's fault Tyler had been passed over. Greg Smith was a solid officer and a good man. He had earned every promotion, unlike the conniving Kory Sanders, who actually deserved snarky comments about maneuvering his way into a higher rank.

"To be honest, stressful," he replied. "But I won't bore you with my headaches."

Tyler paused for a fraction of a second. Would Smitty finally nibble on the line? Tyler had never actually asked his former partner to hire him back onto the force. But Smitty must have known.

"Can I do anything to help?" Tyler asked, trying to sound indifferently willing rather than desperately eager.

"Actually, you can."

Tyler jerked forward as if standing at attention. "Really?"

"That's why I called," Smitty continued. "The chief got an odd message from a staffer over at the Tenth Circuit this morning."

"Over on Stout Street?" A dumb question. The Federal Court of Appeals had been housed in the same building for more than a hundred years.

"I'm forwarding you the message."

Tyler instantly heard the ping of arrival in his ear.

"I know you have a full dance card, but could you squeeze in a quick call between cases? I think you're the right man for this one."

Tyler smiled. "What's the issue?"

"Can't say. The message is pretty cryptic, the kind we would ignore if it came from the average citizen. But this came from the courthouse to the chief's in-box."

"Say no more. 'When it comes from the top...'" Tyler began.

"'...we get to the bottom.'" Smitty finished the familiar mantra. "Probably just needs a courtesy call that will go nowhere. But I can't let this one fall through the cracks. You never know, it might generate some business."

Disappointed that Smitty hadn't called about an opening on the force or a juicy case like the ones they'd solved together in the glory days, Tyler resumed his leaning posture. "I'm on it. I'll call today."

"Thanks, Cain. I owe you one."

Tyler smiled at the notion of being owed anything by Smitty, the same man who'd sent one strong lead after another during Tyler's early, starving days as a private detective. What's more, his former partner treated Tyler with a respect that nearly made him feel legitimate by pretending not to know what kind of work kept Cain Investigations LLC above water. This call was yet another ploy to feed Tyler an assignment much more respectable than his usual fare. Captain Greg Smith was a very good man.

"Play message," he said.

"Greg, the chief asked me to forward you the attached for handling per the usual." Tyler couldn't place the voice. Perhaps the chief's office assistant? "Please close the loop with me and I'll let him know it's done. Thanks."

He continued listening until the forwarded portion began.

"Good morning. This is Jennifer McKay from Judge Santiago's office in the Tenth Circuit. We've encountered a sensitive situation and find ourselves in need of a private investigator that can be trusted with highly confidential information. I wonder if someone from your office could recommend a name or point us in the right direction. Thank you for any assistance you can offer. I will be available at this number all day."

Tyler felt a twinge of self-esteem while tapping his phone to pursue such a mysterious, potentially important case. It's not every day a federal judge calls the chief of police requesting a private detective recommendation.

"Jennifer McKay," a voice answered.

Her abruptness told Tyler he had reached a very busy person who skipped pleasantries to squeeze additional seconds into an overloaded schedule.

"Yes, Ms. McKay, my name is Tyler Cain. I'm following up on a request that came from the chief of police. I was told you were looking for a reliable private investigator."

"If such a thing exists." A sardonic laugh told Tyler she

ranked his profession only slightly above that of used car salesman. "Do you have a recommendation for me?"

He allowed a momentary silence while considering the
most advantageous posture in reply. "Actually, Assistant Chief
Smith asked me to offer my services. I made no promises, but
said I would give you a call. I'm very busy, but I owe him a
favor."

"I'm so sorry," came the suddenly embarrassed answer. "I
didn't mean to…" She paused to redirect. "I appreciate your
call, Mr.…?"

"Cain. Tyler Cain," he said, glancing toward the house of ill
repute to check for motion. Nothing.

"Listen, Ms. McKay, I stepped out of an important meeting to
make this call. I can only give you a few minutes. Can you give
me the gist of your situation quickly, or should I try you again in
a day or two?"

A sense of apologetic urgency overtook the woman's voice.
"Of course. I'm sorry. I'll make this brief."

He smiled at the results of his favorite tactic. He who cares
least controls the conversation.

"Judge Santiago has received three letters that I consider
threatening. We need someone to help us turn sparse details into
meaningful clues so that we can decide next steps."

"Next steps?"

"Specifically, I need to decide whether to share the content of
the letters with the judge."

"He hasn't seen them?"

"He won't let anything compromise his objectivity. I read all
of his mail and screen out anything directly or indirectly touching a case on his docket. He trusts me to handle them as I see fit
until after he issues an opinion."

"And these letters touch an open case?"

"They do," she explained. "A pretty high-profile case."

The comment piqued Tyler's curiosity, but he continued feigning indifference. "Why not ask the police to look into it?"

"I'd like to avoid that if possible."

"Because?"

"It might force the judge to recuse himself from the case. If either lawyer learned of the threats they could claim his self-interest trumped their oral arguments."

"So you're certain the threats are credible?"

She hesitated. "Not certain. Quasi-worried. I've read a lot of messages sent to the judge over the years. Nothing like this before. It feels, I don't know, both quirky and diabolical. It's probably nothing. But it might be for real. I don't trust my gut on this one, so I'd like another set of eyes."

He appraised the voice. She seemed unaccustomed to qualms.

Tyler jumped when he noticed the front door of the house starting to open.

"Let me check my schedule and call you back," he said, scurrying toward the car. "I might be able to move an appointment to squeeze you in late this afternoon."

"That'd be perfect," Jennifer said gratefully.

Tyler ended the call while retrieving his camera. He pointed the lens in the general direction of the house to capture whatever images he could before the pair moved out of range. Luckily a few proved useful. The first revealed a smeared trace of lipstick on the man's earlobe that matched the color the woman had applied before entering the house. The other showed smeared streams of dark mascara on the woman's face, as if the fantasy she had anticipated had turned into a shameful nightmare.

The tearstains prompted a sudden burst of anger that caught Tyler by surprise. He reached for the source, remembering a frightened, shame-ridden victim from his last year on the force.

Raped by a lowlife who got his kicks defiling somebody's mom. It was Tyler who had placed the blanket over her slumped shoulders and brought a Dixie cup of room-temperature water for her to sip while waiting. It took thirty minutes to get a female officer to the station to console the woman toward a lucid statement. He spent the time gathering other evidence for the lab. He recalled a queasy repulsion at the lingering scent of the rapist's sweat and fluid on the back of the woman's torn skirt. It had proved useful in nailing the culprit.

Tyler watched the car pulling out of the driveway carrying a different kind of lowlife: one who had traumatized a woman *with* her consent. He wanted to follow the car to the man's home. He wanted to whip out the handcuffs he no longer carried and frighten the guy, possibly teach him a lesson about true manhood. But he restrained his temper and turned his car in the opposite direction. Tyler Cain was no longer a police officer authorized to right the wrongs of a world filled with ugly realities that, for now, helped him pay the bills.

CHAPTER THREE

Matthew Adams's steps felt lighter as he strolled toward the Campus Grinds coffee shop. He reread the words that lifted a weight his shoulders had been bearing the entire academic year.

> Congratulations on maintaining a cumulative GPA of 2.30, more than adequate to release you from probationary status at the University of Colorado.

He had done it. The late nights memorizing study sheets and drafting essays had paid off. Matthew's dream could now shift from a remote possibility to a "more than adequate" pursuit. Sure, he still had three years of undergraduate to complete before applying for a master's and then a PhD program. But he was one important step closer to becoming a college professor, the aspiration his mom had died to make possible.

The money hadn't actually arrived yet. It remained in an interest-bearing account while the estate trustee resolved a few legal technicalities. But it would come, an assurance he had given the registrar's office when he learned it required tuition and other fees up front. The idea of making minimum payments on an academic loan did not trouble Matthew in the least. After all, his financial prospects looked every bit as promising as his burgeoning academic career.

Entering the coffee shop, Matthew accepted Sarah's bright greeting with a nod before slipping into the same chair he occupied whenever he arrived early for his scheduled shift. Placing his tablet on the table he began typing, eager to share the news with his favorite professor.

Dr. Vincent,
    Yahoo! See attached. I guess this makes me legit. Thanks for all the encouragement.

Matthew looked up from the screen to think of others who might share in his excitement. None of his fellow students knew he had barely cleared the admittance hurdles, nor would they care. Most college freshmen still had pimples. Matthew had thinning hair. The few who knew his name weren't likely to admire his triumph. Thirty-five-year-old men should be teachers, not students. They should assign and grade papers, not barely escape academic probation.

Matthew pushed past a momentary sense of isolation to find Sarah's smile. He tried to curtail fantasizing about his wholesomely gorgeous shift manager now that she had a formal long-term partner. Sarah and the steroid-enhanced Ian had been living together for nearly a year, enough time to seriously dampen any hope that Matthew's unspoken admiration might blossom into something more. Still, he enjoyed any splash of her attention—the closest thing he felt to the feminine nurturing his mother could no longer give.

Mom would be excited, he thought. On a good day she would

have beamed with pride over the accomplishment, over a son she just knew would be a professor someday. On a bad day she would have been confused, would have asked what it meant only to misunderstand his explanation. Despite her hazy grasp, however, she would have placed her lean hand on his arm to offer a well-deserved squeeze.

But Janet Adams was no longer part of Matthew's life beyond warm recollections mixed with a diminishing regret. He told himself she had died a hero, that he hadn't forced his mother's decision. She had made a willing choice. His urgings had only bolstered her timidity and given her the reassurance needed to do what was best. For both of them. Why cling to a decaying body when the freedom of pure spirit could be achieved with a simple, painless procedure?

What a bodiless existence entailed seemed more mysterious now than it had eleven months earlier when Matthew had escorted his mother into an Aspen House transition room. That was part of the reason he looked forward to spending more time with a man who could shed light on the subject. As a freshman he hadn't been able to register for 200-level classes. As a sophomore, however, Matthew would sit under the formal instruction of Dr. Thomas Vincent. The recollection prompted a second brief message.

I plan to take METAPHYSICS 202 during fall semester. See you in class!

"Big news?"

He looked toward the voice to see Sarah clearing a nearby table. He relished both the view and the question.

"Actually, yes," came his mockingly smug reply. "You have the great honor of speaking to a world-renowned scholar."

"You got the 2.0?"

"Blew past it," he said. "Just got notice from the dean's office. She practically begged me to consider an associate professor position."

"Yeah, sure."

"But I said I want to finish my sophomore year before committing myself," he continued.

They shared a laugh as Sarah slapped him playfully with her towel.

"Seriously, Matt, that's great. Congratulations!"

He felt a single pat on his arm as she rushed back toward the counter. He wished she had added a slight squeeze.

"Thanks," he answered over his shoulder. "I'm pretty excited."

Celebration ended, Matthew glanced at the clock. Ten minutes until his shift began, enough time to let others in on the exciting news. But who? He considered his mom's former sitter. Donny would certainly act enthused. He might even genuinely admire his pal's accomplishment. But his occasional buddy had barely graduated from high school. Probably didn't even know the difference between a freshman and a faculty member. Donny hadn't read a book in forever. No. A moment like this required someone special, someone at or above his rising station rather than beneath it.

He thought for a moment longer. No one came to mind because, as he had told himself repeatedly, Matthew Adams lived in a relational Siberia.

"Maria Davidson," he whispered to himself, tapping the name on his screen. He had been sending her anonymous notes for months. Wasn't the occasion of his academic validation a perfect excuse to cross the line from secret admirer to high school classmate hoping to reconnect? Didn't people do such things? Sure they did, all the time. Would it be so wrong to send a message suggesting coffee or dinner? Of course it wouldn't.

He thought about the invitations he had received to attend their ten- and fifteen-year class reunions—where, he assumed, people went to learn whether the homecoming queen still turned heads and whether the geeky valedictorian had made millions. More to the point, people who never spoke to one another during high school had been known to hook up. Sixteen years can humble the most rigid caste systems, even those defending the popular elite from invasion by mortals like Matthew Adams. So while Maria Davidson declined Matthew's invitation to the senior prom in 2027, she might give him a chance in 2043.

Back then Maria had been the hottest girl at Littleton High School, while Matthew had little swagger and even less muscle mass. She had received nine invitations to the prom before Matthew's. He knew of at least five other guys who wanted to ask her but didn't have the confidence. He gave himself credit for at least taking that risk. He remembered that she wore a short, dark-blue, open-backed dress. Matthew went alone and spent the entire evening watching her from afar, seething whenever her date's groping hands touched her barely concealed body.

Sixteen years later he continued watching from afar, a pleasure that had become significantly easier nine months earlier when she'd accepted his anonymous request to join her "secret admirer" network. Every picture she posted told Matthew she remained amazing. Unlike those of the other former cheerleaders, her photos did not appear doctored. Even if they had been touched up here and there, you couldn't make here or there look that good unless you started with something great.

Mustering every ounce of his newly bolstered confidence, Matthew decided to do something he had imagined doing since the day he and Maria threw their graduation caps in the air. Alphabetical seating had put them only ten rows apart, the A's in row one and the D's in row eleven, but the distance between them couldn't have been greater. Today he lived within an easy drive, a gap he could quickly close by sending a note revealing his identity, asking her out, and, he let himself hope, receiving her "I'd love to" reply.

He opened her unique page and clicked the LET'S CHAT icon just below her smiling image.

> *Hello Maria:*
>
> *It's me again. Thank you for your latest post. You get lovelier by the day!*
>
> *I've never mentioned it in my prior messages, but I thought you would be interested to know that we have met. You and I attended Littleton High together. Class of '27. More than met, I asked you out. You probably won't remember me, but I certainly remember you. Who doesn't?*
>
> *Anyway, I have recently experienced a bit of success . . .*

He stopped typing. Was it unwise to suggest his success had been recent? Yes, women probably liked guys with a longer track record than two semesters of college. He deleted the last sentence to replace it with something better.

> *Anyway, I plan to be back in Littleton on business quite a bit in coming months and wondered whether you would be open to reconnecting. Perhaps we could meet for coffee or dinner? I promise I'm safe, although I'm not so sure how safe you are after reading your latest entry. But I'm willing to risk it.*
>
> *I look forward to hearing back.*
>
> *Matthew Adams*

He sat back to review the draft. His message needed to strike the perfect balance between sincere admiration and playful flirting. Maria Davidson liked, and deserved, both. Pleased, he reached toward the SEND icon. But he paused for one last scan. Then he moved the cursor over the last two words and bounced thirteen taps on the DELETE key, clearing his real identity to replace it with his favorite pen name.

I look forward to hearing back.

A Manichean

CHAPTER FOUR

When his shift ended, Matthew logged into the registrar's system to confirm his fall schedule, something he had done at least a dozen times before. Like pinches to make sure he wasn't dreaming, Matthew enjoyed reminders of his good fortune. With only fifty openings in Dr. Vincent's class he had rushed to secure a spot two minutes after student access to the online registration system was opened. An hour later fifty other students, including three seniors, found themselves on a growing waiting list. He worried those seniors might do some last-minute jockeying to bump him out of his spot. That's why he went online to check his status often.

Matthew entered his student identification number followed by a password. An error message appeared. Assuming a typo he reentered the information. Another error message. This time he bothered to read it.

ACCESS DENIED DUE TO OVERDUE BALANCE.
CONTACT STUDENT FINANCIAL SERVICES TO SETTLE YOUR ACCOUNT.

Matthew cursed at the screen and the reminder of the university's student loan policy. It would carry an outstanding balance within a single academic year, but not into the next. He hadn't given the matter much thought back when he requested a loan, because he assumed the transition money would be freed up within a few short months. He'd fully intended to pay off the loan by winter break, then by the end of the spring semester, then by midsummer. With less than two weeks until fall classes began, however, he still hadn't received a dime.

Matthew quickly phoned the number on the screen.

"You have reached the Office of Student Financial Services at the University of Colorado." The recorded voice went on to offer Matthew more options than he could follow, none of which seemed promising. "If you wish to wait for the next available student assistance representative, please remain on the line. The current estimated wait is approximately ten minutes."

He swore again, then considered his options. Perhaps he should call back in the morning. No. Some senior might have snagged his slot in Dr. Vincent's class by then. He decided to wait, enduring the musical selection that sounded like a cross between a traditional Celtic folk song and a sleazy lounge-lizard ballad. Some music major must have landed a big break by convincing the university to use his laptop-produced album for hold music. Not a bad angle. What better way to reach a large captive audience?

Midway through the third near-identical song Matthew reached for something to occupy his numbing mind. He landed on a recollection that made his stomach tense. With all the excitement over planning his fall schedule, learning he had passed probation, and contacting Maria Davidson, he hadn't even considered the possibility he might not return to school. He had convinced himself that all would be well. But what if it wasn't?

Would he be stuck in a pointless job for another year, waiting for his money to clear? What if it never cleared? How would he endure the embarrassment? How could he continue to justify his mom's transition?

"Transitions are nothing more than suicide by a different name," Father Richard had said. He called it a mortal sin, Satan's attack on the very image of God. But Matthew refused to believe it. Matthew preferred the enlightened spirituality of Manichean philosophers to dogma he, like Dr. Vincent, had rejected. He reminded himself, yet again, that death brought freedom from the prison of the body. Spirit was pure and good. The body was bad. It decayed. So even if his mother's money remained beyond reach it would take nothing from the majesty of her choice.

As much as Matthew hated to think her heroic sacrifice might have been in vain, he refused to accept the possibility that it had been a sin.

"Thank you for holding, Mr. Adams. My name is Juanita. How may I help you?"

The interruption rescued Matthew from his quandary.

"Hi, Juanita," he began. "I just tried to sign in to confirm my fall schedule and got a notice that says—"

"I see that your account is past due," she interrupted. "Do you want to settle the balance today?"

"Actually, I was hoping to get a short extension."

"I'm afraid I'm not authorized to grant extensions into the new school year."

As he'd expected.

"I understand. I'm sure I'll have the money in hand shortly. But I'm concerned about losing my scheduled spots in several key classes. Is there any way to—"

"We don't reopen scheduled slots until ten days before the start of the semester."

Matthew felt a brief flood of relief followed by a rising panic. Classes were scheduled to begin on August twenty-seventh.

"So I only have a day?"

"Two days, actually," she offered generously.

"Two days, then. Will my schedule be locked until, let me see...August seventeenth?"

"That's correct."

"Thanks." He ended the call before she could recite her closing script and immediately dialed the number of the only man who could get him the necessary funds that quickly.

"Cedillo and Associates, how may I direct your call?"

It always impressed Matthew how professional Carol Cedillo seemed when answering her husband's office number. She sounded just like an efficient assistant sitting in the downtown law office Benjamin Cedillo didn't occupy and handling an appointment schedule he couldn't fill. You would never know Carol was standing in her kitchen, walking through the aisle of a grocery store, or in any of a hundred other locations speaking into a tiny microphone affixed to her earpiece.

"Hi Carol. It's Matthew Adams."

"Oh, hi, Matty."

Matthew grimaced, then smiled. He hated the nickname Carol Cedillo had given him while he was in diapers. A name he let only her get away with using.

"Is Ben around?"

"I think so. Hang on a second and I'll check. He might be watching television."

"Sorry to bother him this late in the day but it's kind of urgent."

"No worries," she said. "I'm sure he would love to talk to you."

Not likely, Matthew thought. It had been nearly six weeks since the two last spoke. The conversation had gone badly.

"There's nothing else I can do, Matt," Benjamin had insisted. "Aspen House says they refuse to take any action until the NEXT appeal is settled."

"Why can't you pressure Chuck Kohl?" Matthew had pushed. "He told me he would be happy to co-approve Mom's procedure."

"Which you didn't get in writing."

"Can't you say we had a verbal contract?"

"Sure, I can say it. But that would be next to impossible to prove. Your word against his."

That's when the conversation had turned ugly. Matthew questioned Benjamin's competence before suggesting he hoped to pocket the money himself.

"Watch yourself, young man," Ben had snapped back. "You know I won't get and wouldn't accept a penny of your mother's estate."

"Then you're holding things up out of spite. You're still upset over her decision."

"You're sure it was *her* decision?"

Matthew had resented the implication. "Of course it was her decision."

"Charles Kohl told me he isn't so sure about that."

"He's just covering himself. He signed off on the transition, for Pete's sake!"

"He signed off on her mental competence, not on whether he thought she felt coerced."

"I told you a hundred times, I didn't coerce her!"

"I know you believe that. But I can't prove it, nor could I get anyone at Aspen House to corroborate it."

Matthew didn't remember the rest of the conversation, only the cloud of anxious fury he'd felt when he left Ben's home office. During the six weeks that had passed since the encounter Matthew had tried to remain optimistic. He'd chosen to believe the man responsible for his mother's estate would find a loophole of some sort that would release enough money to pay off Matthew's freshman loan and fund his sophomore year.

He'd also tried to urge things along on two fronts. First he badgered the receptionist at Aspen House, a process he stopped after the third visit because Aspen House threatened him with a restraining order. His second effort was much more creative and far less sensible. He delivered several handwritten letters to the federal judge overseeing the NEXT appeal. It couldn't hurt to let the man who seemed to control his economic fate know the real-life ramifications of the court's decision.

"Hello, Matthew." Benjamin's voice lacked its customary warmth.

"Hi, Ben," Matthew said hesitantly. "How've you been?"

"Oh, you know, I've been out back rolling in the pile of money I'm earning from your mom's estate."

Matthew winced at the dig before swallowing his pride. "Look, Ben, I apologize for losing my temper, OK?"

He took Ben's silence as permission to continue.

"Listen, I only have about a week left before fall semester starts and they tell me I can't officially enroll until the balance from my freshman year is paid."

More silence.

"Anyway, I was hoping we could figure out a way to release some of Mom's money before—"

"Not gonna happen, Matt."

"Look, Ben, I said I'm sorry."

"Fine. I accept your apology. But this has nothing to do with what happened between us. Aspen House won't budge. End of story."

"So my money just sits in an account forever?"

"Not forever. Just until sometime in September."

"What happens in September?" Matthew asked.

"Opinions on the NEXT appeal will be issued."

"By Judge Santiago?"

Ben seemed surprised by Matthew's recall. "That's right. Judge Victor Santiago is the presiding judge. I forget the other two judges' names."

"Coates and Howatch," Matthew reminded him.

"Right again. I'm impressed."

Matthew decided not to tell Ben about the letters he had sent to Judge Santiago's office. "It's an important case to me."

"I bet it is," Ben said wryly. "Nothing gets people interested in the law like the risk of losing cold, hard cash."

"I'm not just interested because of the money," Matthew lied. "This case could determine the future of the whole transition industry."

"It could. Probably won't, though. I'm guessing they'll overturn the ruling against NEXT and everything will go back to normal."

"Including my inheritance?"

"If the Tenth Circuit Court decides in favor of NEXT I'm confident Aspen House will come around. Until then they're like every other transition clinic in the country, worried about an avalanche of wrongful death lawsuits."

Matthew found the whole legal mess confusing. How had a voluntary transition turned into a wrongful death case anyway? Why had a judge ruled against NEXT? Why had the court granted some dead debit's brother so much money? And what had made that case prompt so much debate in Congress over the president's Youth Initiative?

Whatever the reasons, the director of Aspen House had gotten nervous when Ben requested a digital copy of the neutral consent form after Matthew's mom transitioned. One day Chuck Kohl said he would send it. The next day Aspen House said he was no longer an employee. The request should have enabled Ben to tie up a last-minute detail for Matthew's inheritance. It had instead generated dozens of delay tactics and one large unpaid student loan.

"I can't keep waiting for some court's edict," Matthew said tensely. "The semester starts in a few weeks."

"I don't know what to tell you, Matt. Until that case gets resolved I simply can't release the money."

"And if it doesn't?" Matthew hated to ask. "What happens if they decide against NEXT?"

"You don't want to know."

"Yes, I do."

"If they uphold the decision against NEXT then all bets are off. The state of your mother's estate will most likely be decided by some judge using criteria on which I won't even try to speculate."

"Wait," Matthew said. "Are you saying I might not get the money at all?"

"It's a possibility. Remote. But possible."

Matthew suspected Ben took silent pleasure in the prospect, his voice betraying a hint of smug condemnation. The eighty-one-year-old lawyer had never liked transitions. He mocked the idea that snuffing yourself out just because you'd passed your prime was in any way noble or heroic. A devoutly nonreligious man, Ben never called transitions a sin as Father Richard had. He just resented them for making anyone over seventy-five feel guilty every time he enjoyed dinner at a nice restaurant or took a leisurely vacation. He intended to live as long and comfortably as possible, blissfully callous to the growing economic crisis facing the younger generation.

He seemed even more callous to Matthew's personal economic crisis.

"Selfish jerk," Matthew said after ending the call.

Three heads turned in his direction.

"Sorry. Not you," he said toward the trio. "I was talking to a stubborn old debit."

Each nodded in knowing solidarity. The young, after all, must stick together in a world increasingly plagued by aging parasites.

CHAPTER FIVE

It was late. Jennifer McKay had wanted it that way—to avoid... notice.

Tyler Cain stood between the massive white pillars of the Byron White United States Courthouse. He'd entered much taller buildings in downtown Denver, but none that evoked such grandeur. An echo of pride accompanied the clack of his heels as they ascended the massive marble stairs that led to the public entrance. Tyler had once been part of the justice system. He had a legitimate claim to the sense of satisfaction he should never have taken for granted or traded away for spite or easy money.

"Only a few minutes to closing time, sir," the security guard said as Tyler removed his belt and shoes before entering the body scanner.

"I'm meeting with—" He stopped himself. *Utmost confidentiality.* "I have a meeting on the third floor."

"You'll need to sign the register."

No paper trail.

"Could I just leave my wallet instead?"

"Mr. Cain?"

"Why, yes. How did you—"

"Go on through. Ms. McKay said she is expecting a confidential guest."

"Great. Thanks. Have a nice evening."

The guard nodded. "You too, sir."

After slipping into his shoes and fastening his buckle Tyler turned left down a marble hallway. He noticed a large portrait of an impressively dignified face. He didn't recognize the name of the person who had no doubt played an important role in the 150-year judicial history housed within these walls.

Tyler continued walking until he noticed a sign marked COURTROOM TWO. He stole a peek inside, letting his eyes adjust to the darkness enough to admire an impressively manicured trinity of judicial benches elevated loftily above a duo of wooden tables and chairs. This room, like four others located throughout the building, was a theater that hosted some of the best and brightest attorneys who had ever practiced law. Each of them received a mere fifteen minutes to make oral arguments that might sway the court. Tyler considered the human drama that took place whenever the trio of shadowy benches held a federal judge who must decide whether to uphold or overturn some lower court's ruling.

Moving past the clerk's office on the right he found a spiraling stairwell that led to the second-floor conference rooms. He took the time to peruse a hallway nearly as long as a football field, where he read dozens of forgotten names on portraits too far down the pecking order of historic significance to warrant main-floor exhibition. He then climbed the final flight of stairs to locate the office of Judge Victor Santiago.

He pushed through the large doors and was greeted by a series of polished walnut desks, their occupants now missing in action.

Even during his days on the force Tyler had never worked in such an opulent environment. He thought of his own "office" back home, a cluttered, secondhand desk that shared a corner of the extra bedroom with a box of old clothes destined for charity. He breathed in the rich aroma of importance he had never attained. Never wanted to attain. At least that's what he told himself now.

"Hello?" he called out, glancing at a clock on the wall. Ten minutes later than agreed, part of his plan to appear disinterested. Now he worried the strategy might have backfired. Perhaps Ms. McKay had thought Tyler unprofessional and given up on him.

"Mr. Cain?" a voice said from behind.

Tyler spun around to see a thirtysomething woman, her tightly bound hair and crisp clothing working hard to conceal an otherwise natural beauty. She appeared to be the kind of woman bent on achieving success through no-nonsense precision rather than good looks. Tyler made a mental note: *Driven, but...insecure.*

"Tyler Cain?" she asked.

He nodded. "Ms. McKay?"

"I'm so sorry to have kept you waiting." She ushered him past her vacated desk while retrieving a series of white business envelopes. Then she hurried through a nearby doorway. He followed her into the adjoining conference room. "Please, have a seat. Would you care for something to drink?"

Straight to business. Perhaps his plan hadn't backfired after all.

"No, thank you. I'm good."

She sat across from him, opened one of the envelopes, and slid the contents across the desk: one handwritten letter.

"This was the first letter Judge Santiago received."

He glanced to the bottom.

"A Manichean?"

"No idea. I can't find a record of the name in anything re-motely associated with the NEXT case. Possibly an alias."

Tyler scanned the letter, trying hard not to seem terribly inter-ested. He picked up the gist, however. Whoever this A Manichean was, he—or she, Tyler reminded himself, although the handwrit-ing didn't exude femininity—seemed terribly concerned about the outcome of the NEXT Transition appeal, as though his or her own well-being hinged on the outcome. Tyler tossed the letter back onto the table. Jennifer slid him a second, then a third. In all three cases the writer asked the judge to correspond.

"I look forward to hearing from you soon," Tyler read aloud. "Please post your response at the following private forum ad-dress: ANON.CHAT.4398."

Tyler recognized the link format. ANON.CHAT sites were littered with titillating posts from illicit lovers trying to stay con-nected between trysts. The perfect forum to remain anonymous. The posting party controlled whether and how to reveal his or her identity. Very few ever did.

He rescanned the text of the final letter but found no explicit threat. All four of them could have been written by anyone in-terested in the case; possibly a snooping reporter or religious activist.

"It just sounds to me like a person worried the judge will make the wrong decision."

Jennifer visibly bristled at the remark. "And which decision would that be?" she said accusingly.

Defensive. Or maybe…protective.

Tyler shrugged. "You tell me what the wrong decision would be."

"Even if I knew Judge Santiago's opinion on the case," she said with brash self-importance, "I'm certainly not at liberty to tell you."

"Ms. McKay, I don't really care about where Judge Santiago lands on the specifics of"—he glanced back at the letter to jog his memory—"The specifics of the NEXT appeal. But you must suspect someone dangerous does care. Isn't that why you asked for the best private investigator available?"

"I'm sorry. You're right." Jennifer seemed to welcome Tyler's condescension. She seemed eager for someone to relieve her from an exhausting posture of strength. He sensed control moving to his side of the table.

"Listen, Mr. Cain. You've taken time out of your busy schedule to help, and here I am...well, I'm the one who asked you to come. It's just, usually we receive this kind of letter and forget about it. People send hastily written notes crafted in a moment of anger or frustration or even praise. End of story. But this feels different."

"You mentioned that on the phone."

"This case has serious implications for a lot of people no matter which way the judge decides."

"I thought appeals required three opinions. What about the other two judges?"

"I checked. No letters."

"What's your theory?"

"Both have published opinions in the past in transition-related cases. One leans for, the other against. I assume whoever wrote these letters knows enough about the judges to figure Judge Santiago's opinion will be the tiebreaker."

Tyler frowned at the unhelpful but likely theory. "Perhaps you can tell me who has the most to lose and gain from Santiago's decision."

"Well..." Jennifer hesitated. Tyler understood. He hadn't officially accepted the case. She couldn't risk saying much more. But he wouldn't commit to this case, no matter how great the opportunity, until they reached an agreement on compensation. *Keep playing it cool*, he told himself.

"Listen, Ms. McKay..."

"Jennifer."

"Fine. Jennifer. You don't know me from Adam. I get that. But if you want me to help you, you'll need to trust me."

"I understand. I'm sorry. It's just—"

"You don't like private investigators?"

"I don't have to like them, Tyler."

"Mr. Cain."

Her face reddened at the rebuff.

"Listen, Jennifer. I don't have to be here at all. You called asking for help, and I'm only here because I owe someone a favor. But we can end this now, if you prefer."

"No." She took a deep breath. "But please be advised that everything I tell you must remain confidential."

"Absolutely."

Jennifer gathered up the three letters, setting them in a neat pile before continuing. "Jeremy Santos, the plaintiff. He has the most to gain or lose. He received a very large award in punitive damages."

"For what?" Tyler preferred admitting ignorance in order to speed up the discovery process.

"He lost both his brother and his mother during a transition."

"A double transition?"

"No. It was his disabled brother's transition. The mother tried to stop the procedure and fell. Very sad."

"A transition and an accident. Then why the large settlement?"

"The boy scheduled the appointment while a minor."

"Oh. Let me guess. The mother hadn't approved?"

"That's right. The bottom line is that Jeremy Santos will lose a large sum of money if NEXT wins on appeal."

"What about NEXT?"

"They have even more to lose. And not just the settlement

money. Losing this appeal could force them to institute far more stringent approval requirements for all transitions."

"Is that so bad?"

"It could cut deeply into their business. The more hurdles volunteers face, the more likely they will change their mind. Even a twenty percent decline in transitions would mean nearly a billion-dollar hit per year."

"A billion? I had no idea," Tyler confessed.

"There is a lot of money at stake in this case. Especially when you consider the impact on President Lowman's Youth Initiative."

"Such as?"

"Fewer transitions mean higher senior-care costs and a drop in transition estate taxes," she explained. "Not a good time for either."

"So the White House may be worried about this case?"

"To be honest, Mr. Cain, you're the first person I've met who isn't concerned about this case." She seemed to enjoy the jab. "As you can see, the implications are enormous. Sooner or later this case will impact the household budget of anyone caring for an aging or disabled loved one."

Tyler raised his finger pausing the conversation to steal a moment. He retrieved his tablet and pretended to type a few notes while absorbing the scope of the case.

"I don't suspect NEXT incorporated itself. They're too big to risk open retaliation. But I suppose it could be some rogue individual within the company with something to lose. Maybe a person who slipped up on the Santos case who fears losing their job."

Tyler glanced at his empty page of notes before asking whether Jennifer could think of anyone else.

"Who knows? There are religious nuts all over the place who would love nothing more than to see NEXT take a serious fall."

"Religious nuts?"

"Sorry. I shouldn't call them that. But you know what I mean. There are people who would love to see the transition industry come to a screeching halt."

"Do you think that might include murder?"

"Murder?" Jennifer's gaze fell to the letters. "Do you think Judge Santiago's life is in danger?"

"I don't know what to think. I'm only exploring what you think, and what might be at stake."

Tyler found it difficult to continue feigning disinterest in a case infinitely more important than jilted lovers and forbidden sexcapades.

"When we spoke over the phone," he continued, "you seemed worried. Like a person fearful over something potentially... dangerous."

"I'm sure it isn't. At least..." Jennifer took another deep breath. "I don't know. The tone in the letters is—"

"—disconcerting?"

"Yes. As I said, in the past, the judge has received many letters on various cases. Some of them from wackos and religious diehards. He's maintained a strict policy of ignoring those letters. So it falls to me to decide what to do about them, if anything. Nothing's ever come of any of them in the past. But this one seems less nuts and more... calculating."

"I tend to agree with you," Tyler said. "But the motive behind these letters isn't clear. There's no way we can come up with concrete conclusions without further investigation. As you indicated, it's probably religiously motivated in some way, and perfectly harmless. But you never know."

Tyler felt himself leaning forward to again scan the mysterious content of the letters. He imagined himself tackling a case far more intriguing than anything he'd seen since leaving the force. For the first time in years he felt a hint of excitement over what tomorrow might bring. But he still couldn't appear eager. He flashed a purposeful glance to the clock on the wall above the door. Jennifer gathered the letters.

"So, do you think you can help?" she asked.

Tyler shrugged, then slipped a Cain Investigations, LLC business card from his jacket pocket. He jotted a number on the back and slid it across the table. "I'd be willing to do some preliminary investigation. My usual daily rate applies, of course."

A daily rate he had just doubled.

She took the card, glanced at it, then switched back into professional mode. "Fine. But once again I must insist that you keep this completely confidential. I don't want the police involved. No publicity at all. It could completely undermine perception of Judge Santiago's neutrality when rendering his opinion. I can't let anything happen that might force him to recuse himself from the case."

"I understand. Now, I do have one request. I'd like to take a copy of each of these letters."

"Of course. I've already made copies. You can take these. But please don't make any additional copies, electronic or otherwise. I wouldn't want anyone to get wind of their content until we know what... or who... we're dealing with."

—⁓—

As Tyler made his way out, he paused again to admire the building's classic architecture and the inscriptions that made him wish he knew more judicial history. Then he noticed the massive bronze plaque displaying names of the former postmasters general. This building must have served as a major post office in early years.

Post office. A thought came to him. He pulled out the three letters and examined the postmarks. They seemed archaic in a day when nearly all communication took place through electronic tablets. Archaic, but in this case important. The postmark on all three letters indicated that they originated from southern Colorado. Which meant whoever sent the letters lived...here.

CHAPTER SIX

The ringtone blared through the car's speakers. Tyler checked the time on the dash, cringing. Renee was probably worried sick. Any deviation from the normal schedule required a call, a daily reality when you mixed private detective work with a somewhat paranoid girlfriend.

He ignored the melody as he eased his Mustang across the freeway and into the AutoDrive lane, north on Interstate 25. The vehicle accelerated quickly to cruising speed as he relinquished control. He had exactly seven minutes before his exit, just enough time to update his financial plan spreadsheet.

Tyler slid out his tablet and pulled up the calculator. He figured the Santiago case would entail a boatload of billable hours, every one of them moving him closer to his goal. The extra cash and a bit more scrimping should enable him to pay off the business loan in eighteen months—allowing him to escape the shackles of Renee's cosign. After...who knew how long? Three years plus another eighteen months? Practically married!

The phone rang again. No use putting off the inevitable. He sighed while tapping his earpiece.

"Hi, beautiful," he said in a pretty convincing tone.

"Don't 'Hi, beautiful' me," she chided. "You should have been here hours ago. Or at least called!"

"I'm sorry. It's just…well, I actually have some good news!"

"Are you almost home?"

She clearly had no interest in his good news. He felt a pail of chilly water soak his excitement over landing the Santiago case.

"Listen," he started, shifting into damage control mode. "I'm sorry about not calling, but when you hear why I think you'll—"

A slight sniffle on the other end of the line cut his words short. Something wasn't right.

"What's wrong?" Tyler asked, rising above his aggravation to sound genuinely concerned.

There was a pause, then, "It's nothing. We can talk about it when you get home. Just…can you pick up a few things at Bulrich's on the way? I'll forward you a list."

"Sure. I'll be home in fifteen." He was about to end the call, but decided to earn a few extra points. "Then we can talk."

"Fine."

Two minutes later his car signaled the Longmont exit ahead. He eased out of the AutoDrive lane, off Interstate 25, and onto the street that led to Bulrich's Organic Market. He pulled into the parking lot and then confirmed Renee's list had made it onto his tablet. He walked inside and moved straight to the liquor aisle to pick up an item she hadn't requested. Whatever the problem, he thought, a few glasses of wine could only help matters.

—◆◇◆—

Tyler struggled to shove open the door to the house from the garage. Something was in the way. He managed to create enough of a gap to squeeze through, then stepped over the overstuffed box of used clothes sitting on the floor.

"Renee?" he called out, then placed the bag of locally grown veggies and bottle of wine on the kitchen counter.

Her voice hailed him from upstairs. "I'm in the guest room."

Guest room? They didn't have a guest room. Not really. There was a bed in there, sure. But it had been officially declared his "office" when he bought the rickety old desk Renee refused to allow anywhere downstairs. She called it a monstrosity. She wanted it out of sight, along with the mess typically strewn across its surface. So the desk and its owner were both relegated to the spare room.

A stack of clean blankets and two pillows sat like lumps in the hallway just outside the room. Not the old worn-out blankets, either. Tyler had grown accustomed to those from being banished to the extra bed, usually because Renee had caught him staring at another woman. These were the nice blankets, usually reserved for company.

He peeked inside. Renee's petite, fit form stood, motionless, dressed in a tight-fitting athletic top and spandex shorts, as though she were ready for an evening run. She was just standing there, staring.

"What are you doing?" he asked.

"Here," she said, startled into action. She pointed to the end of his desk nearest the wall. "Help me move this."

He obeyed, lifting the heavy end as they dragged it across the room. They set it down at an angle that would make it impossible for him to use, comfortably or otherwise.

"Is someone coming to visit?"

Renee turned her gaze toward Tyler's, then stepped forward, grabbing his arms and wrapping them around her waist in a hug. She caressed his stubbled jawline, then kissed him long and hard before pulling back and resting her head against his chest.

He drew her face to his and kissed her back. This wasn't about his being late and not calling. She was clearly upset about something. He slowly ran his fingers up her back to her long, dark hair. Then she pulled away.

"I can't," she said, a tear forming in her eye.

He kissed her nose, then her forehead. "Why not?"

"My dad called."

This time Tyler pulled away, seating himself on the edge of the desk. "What happened?"

Renee brushed away the tear, blinking several times before saying anything. Tyler felt momentarily awkward. He hated this kind of stuff. Renee's parents were always calling about something. Usually it was her mom complaining about Renee's dad and his crazy nonsense, or going on and on about their latest health woes. But rarely was it her dad who called.

"My mom fell. The ambulance came and, well, they're at the hospital now. They thought she might have broken her hip."

"Again?"

She nodded. "But I got through to my dad after I called you and apparently the doctors think she'll be OK. A bit bruised. She sprained her arm trying to catch herself."

Another tear.

"And you know my dad. He can't take care of himself worth anything if she's not there to cook and pick up after him."

Tyler tried to inject a bit of levity. "I don't think he'd remember to change his underwear if she didn't lay out his boxers for him."

"Exactly." She smiled, slightly. "So now I have to figure out what we're going to do."

"We?" It came out before Tyler could check himself.

"I was thinking they could come and stay with us. Just for a while."

"Here?" He glanced around the room, looking for any reason that wouldn't work. "They can't stay here. Imagine if your mom falls again while climbing the stairs? And this room...it isn't big enough for them! I can hardly squeeze around the bed! There's gotta be somewhere else. Somewhere better."

Renee perched herself on the edge of the bed. "I know, I know. But there is nowhere else. They certainly can't afford one of those rehabilitation centers right now. So I was thinking—and this is just for a week, two tops—that they could move in here and stay in our room."

Our room. That's what had come of living together three years. He missed the days when there was just *his* room. When any overnight guest was there for a short, no-strings-attached frolic. And now he was being asked to give up the master suite in exchange for this room. This very small room.

"It's downstairs," Renee stated over Tyler's silence. "No steps to manage. And there's a shower instead of a tub. It's perfect, really."

"But...it's *our* bedroom."

"I know. I'm sorry, Ty baby. But don't worry. We can celebrate our anniversary in here just as well as downstairs." She patted the mattress reassuringly.

He half-smiled, but that wasn't what he'd been thinking. In fact he'd forgotten, once again, about their upcoming anniversary. He'd been thinking that this wasn't what he had signed up for when Renee suggested moving in with him. At the time he'd naïvely thought it would make sex easy. No special dates or grand gestures required. Living together would mean that anytime he wanted it, all he had to do was roll over. And that's how things had been...at first.

But the longer they lived as domestic partners the more tension he felt over the increasingly intertwining and interdependent realities of their lives. Especially the business loan. And retiring that debt would require at least another eighteen months, a year and a half more of near-marriage.

He looked into the same eyes that had drawn him so deeply into the longest serious relationship he had ever endured. Her eyes were pleading while her lips formed an alluring pout. Truth was, he did care about Renee more than he wanted to admit. He couldn't throw her out in her time of need—especially over something like her mother falling.

Tyler reached out toward her. Their hands met, and he sighed. "You're right, of course," he heard himself say. Then he cursed silently.

Renee beamed. "You mean it?"

He shrugged.

She tugged him off the desk, kissing him again.

Tyler glanced around the still-disorganized room. "I guess we should finish getting this room in order."

"Later," Renee said. "I've got a surprise for you first."

~

He tried to like it. Or rather, he tried pretending to like it, but it was no use. Leeks and asparagus hardly made for a hearty dinner. Where was the meat? Where was the protein? This meal quite possibly ranked as the worst ever.

"So, you mentioned good news," Renee said over dessert: apple slices with honey and cinnamon.

"I did?"

"On the phone."

"Oh, right." He gladly set down his fork, shoving away his plate. "A new client."

Renee reached across the table with her fork and stabbed one of his apple pieces. "Another rich and jealous lover?"

He took a sip of wine, shaking his head. "No, no. Not like that. This one's different. Kind of a big deal, actually. Should be interesting. A bit of a mystery."

"Mystery sounds good."

"It is. Only...I don't know. My client doesn't want the police involved, and I'm a little uneasy."

"Police? Sounds serious."

"It is. I'll probably stop by to see what Smitty thinks...just in case."

His eyes landed on a frame on the mantel cycling through a series of pictures. He saw himself standing proudly alongside his old partner, both dressed to the hilt in their formal uniforms. Tyler hated that picture—a constant reminder of the life he'd traded away. But Renee loved it because, in her words, it made him look "hot," whatever that meant in reference to an almost-fifty-year-old guy. The rest of the photos held far less significance.

Standing with Renee at some ski lodge.

A solo shot of Renee making a cheesy smile, holding up a fish she'd caught during a tent camping trip they took together when they first met.

Then came Renee's family. Her father, his head mottled with age. Her mother, fragile and lean. Tyler had never really known his own father, and his mother had died before reaching such an advanced age. Ambushed at fifty-four by pancreatic cancer.

"So, when are they coming?" he asked, still staring at the picture frame.

"Hmm," Renee mumbled while finishing the last bite of apple off his plate. She swallowed hard. "Well, as soon as possible. Tomorrow would be good, but..."

She hesitated.

"But what?"

"Well. You know how much I hate the drive through the mountains alone and—"

"Renee," he said warily. "You do remember that I have work to do, right?"

"I know, I know. But…it will only take a few hours. Can't you come with me?"

Tyler felt anger in his throat as the afterglow of their earlier romp dwindled back to annoyance. Renee seemed eager to fit Tyler into the mold of her father, a man who had spent forty-some years of marriage doing anything his wife asked at the drop of a hat and sacrificing his dreams and desires for an existence Tyler would have found smothering. He told himself he had no intention of spending his life catering to the whims of a needy woman and, God forbid, potential kids.

He looked back toward Renee's relatively youthful face smiling beside his own from the picture frame. Would she end up as gaunt and decrepit as her mother? Would he end up like her father, sidelined by life with no real reputation to speak of or even hobbies to enjoy? Would he be stuck eating leeks and asparagus for the rest of his life?

"I…don't want to."

"Oh." Renee cast her gaze downward, then grabbed the dishes from the table and started toward the kitchen. "I understand. You're busy. I'm sorry to bring it up. I can manage. Somehow."

"Renee, don't be like that. I just got this case. It's important."

The dishes clattered into the sink. "No, really. I get it. Sometimes things are more important than…family."

"Renee!" he said, hoping to stand his ground. But it didn't matter. No further conversation would take place between the two of them for the rest of the night.

CHAPTER SEVEN

Julia Simmons watched her nephew jerk himself away from his mother's reach and then scan the mall parking lot for potential witnesses. No twelve-year-old boy likes to be surprised by a hug his friends might see. He huffed away as Maria Davidson wilted back toward the car, her dejected stroll in stark contrast to the hurried sprint she'd used to deliver Jared's forgotten backpack.

"Let me guess," Julia said as her sister slunk into the passenger seat. "He didn't say thank you."

Maria flashed an exaggerated pout. "I guess I'm off the cool list."

Julia laughed while putting the car into gear. "I don't think either of us is on Jared's cool list anymore."

Maria extended her arm as if to pause the car's forward movement. "Wait! What movie did he say they were seeing?"

"The one about micro-robots gone wild."

"That's right." Maria reached toward the dashboard to tap in the title *Micro-Predators II*. "Here it is. The movie ends at twelve thirty. Add an hour for them to get pizza afterwards—"

"—and that gives us until one thirty." Julia completed the

sentence. "We should go downtown. When was the last time we ate at Vesta?"

"Perfect!" Maria flashed a predatory grin. "Nothing like an upscale dipping grill to cheer up a mom banished from the domain of cool."

As they pulled out of the parking lot Julia considered the idea of her sister falling out of style. At thirty-five, Maria Davidson remained a remarkably attractive woman, her blond hair and effortless spunk creating a feminine charm other women couldn't help envying. She had never been shy about wearing the latest designer fashions. The outfit selected for today's sis lunch outing, for example, would turn every male head in the restaurant. While it was too risqué for Julia's taste or comfort, Maria enjoyed flaunting curves even her son's adolescent buddies found impossible to ignore. Regardless of Jared's attitude toward his mom, Maria Davidson would never be totally banished from the popular class.

"So, how's Troy?" Maria asked while checking her hair and makeup in the visor mirror.

"He's doing fine. A bit stressed lately. But fine."

"How was your night at the Omni?"

The question prompted a slight blush from Julia as she remembered celebrating six months with Troy.

"It was very nice." A smile lingered on her lips.

Maria's eyes shot in her sister's direction. "Julia Davidson," she said. "You naughty girl!"

"The name is Julia *Simmons*," she protested. "I'm his wife, remember? There's nothing naughty about it."

Both tried to suppress a sly grin.

"Well, I'm jealous. It's been a long time since I've been naughty."

Julia rolled her eyes. "You've got to be kidding. You just broke up with what's-his-name three or four months ago."

"Jonathan. And it's been six months."

"Right, Jonathan."

"Don't act like you forgot his name. He liked you first, remember?"

"And then he saw you and I became yesterday's news."

Maria looked out the window to avoid her sister's *I told you so* rebuke.

"I warned you about him," Julia said.

"You warn me about everyone I date."

Julia decided to retreat. "Anyway, Troy and I had a great time."

Maria softened. "Marriage looks good on you, Sis."

"Thanks. It feels good."

"I guess I was wrong about Troy."

"How's that?"

She hesitated. "You know. I said I thought you needed someone more...well—"

"More hip?"

Maria nodded uncomfortably. "You have to admit, he wasn't someone who would have shown up on my hot list. He was kind of, I don't know, peculiar."

Julia gently slapped her sister's arm. "He was not peculiar. He just got a bit tongue-tied around me. 'Smitten beyond words,' he used to say. I thought it was sweet."

"That's what I mean. He uses words like *smitten*. Who says things like that? I bet he still calls you *my lady*."

"Not anymore. I insisted he cut the noble-gentleman shtick."

"Good."

A brief silence passed between them.

"I remember what else you said," Julia reflected aloud. "You said I should find someone less religious."

Another nod. "I still think he needs to ease up a bit in that arena. You'll end up like Angie. Mark my words, the elegant Julia Davidson—"

"Simmons!"

"Sorry. The elegant Julia Simmons will become infamous for wearing frumpy sweat suits while pushing a double stroller through the neighborhood."

Julia winced at the reminder of a caricature her sister still couldn't shake. A caricature Julia herself had helped embed in the popular imagination throughout her award-winning career with RAP Media Syndicate.

"I seem to recall you also saying marital sex would put me to sleep." She turned toward Maria. "Trust me. You got that one wrong too."

They shared another sly smile.

"How are Kevin and Angie anyway?" Maria asked. "She looked so adorable at the wedding in her maternity bridesmaid's dress."

"I'll let you know next week. I'm flying out tomorrow afternoon with Troy to see them. Kevin has an important presentation he wants Troy to attend."

Maria lifted a single brow. "Really? You're going to DC?"

"Troy said he thinks it's time to release myself from self-imposed exile."

"Wow."

"I think I'm ready," Julia said.

"You don't sound convinced."

"I'm ready," she said. "I guess I'm just a bit apprehensive going back to the place where I nearly destroyed my best friend's marriage and ruined Kevin's political career."

"You didn't destroy or ruin anything," Maria objected. "You simply did your job."

It was the same thing Julia had told herself a hundred times before. She hadn't known her editor would play fast and loose with the *Breeders* story or that the pictures of Kevin with another woman had been staged. Still, she felt guilty about the wave of journalistic success the story had propelled.

"A job you quit, by the way," Maria continued. "You made it very clear you disapproved of what happened."

Julia accepted the reminder with a thin smile.

"Angie and Kevin are fine. You shouldn't worry."

"I know. I just wish—"

"Hush," Maria interrupted. "It'll be fine. You'll see."

Julia did her best to agree. "How's work?" she asked to change the subject.

"Oh, you know. Every other day we get another prediction of ruin."

"I thought things were turning around."

"Like I said, every *other* day."

"I'm sorry." Julia empathized with her sister's growing sense of insecurity. "Still looking for something better?"

"Who isn't?"

The question prompted Julia to make a mental note: *Finish the story on unemployment.* She had pitched a unique angle: a year-in-review feature that would connect the dots between twelve months of layoff and closure announcements and the dramatic spike in anxiety-induced depression. Nearly everyone who still had a job worried about losing it. When would the next shoe drop? Would there be another market crash? What if the government made another cut to the unemployment fund? Every news syndicate included a regular feature speculating about how the economy would change in the wake of what the *Wall Street Journal* now labeled *The Meltdown of 2042.* Every economist had a different viewpoint. None seemed to have a clue.

Julia had recently warmed to Troy's opinion. The crash had occurred after revised revenue projections confirmed the economy was chasing fertility rates over a steep cliff. The ratio of dependent seniors to younger workers was simply unsustainable. The pyramid had flipped, leaving too few productive young straining under the economic burden of an aging population. The past decade had brought a net decline in the number of households for the first time in the nation's history. Fewer households led to empty, unsellable homes. Lower property values led to lower consumer confidence, further reducing spending on goods and services. The resulting decline in corporate profits dried up most of the business capital necessary to invest in growth or innovation. Dominos fell in a predictable sequence. They would continue to fall.

Even shrinking the social safety net, while inevitable, hadn't helped. Some said the cuts might have deepened the crisis because business leaders had followed the government's lead. Nearly every sector of the economy took a hit, with the notable exception of the senior-care industry. That's why millions of former engineers, architects, manufacturers, sales managers, retailers, builders, and journalists found themselves giving baths and fixing diabetic meals for a living. The old still had access to the cash they hadn't spent raising kids.

Julia considered herself lucky. She had never had more work. One assignment after the next flowed to her independent writing business, most of them lucrative feature stories for a variety of online journals.

Maria was feeling the pinch more than her sister. But at least she had work. Only five employees at her salon remained full-time. A dozen others had had to leave without severance or accept a downgrade to part-time status.

"Dark zones," Julia whispered.

Maria strained to hear. "What's that?"

"Oh, something Troy mentioned the other day. He said we have so many dark zones in this economy that it makes the bright spots stand out more."

"Bright spots? Remind me."

"Kevin's proposal for stimulating the economy. Find pockets

of growth to copy their patterns. You know, bright needles in an otherwise dismal haystack."

"Oh yeah. I thought that proposal got killed."

"Not killed. Just ignored. Senator Franklin's austerity committee set it aside when the crisis hit. But Troy and Kevin seem to think there may be a window to resurrect the idea, especially since Franklin needs something positive to offset his slash-and-burn reputation. People won't support a presidential candidate whose chief accomplishment has been further pummeling a battered economy with one draconian cut after the next."

Maria appeared uninterested in matters so far removed from her own world.

"Anyway," Julia added quickly, "Troy suggested I should write stories on both."

"Both what?"

"Both dark zones and bright spots. You know, sections of the country in decline contrasted with those on the rise."

"Are any on the rise?"

"Troy says there are," Julia explained. "He thinks I should publish a series of features that would show how current policies touch everyday life. But I can't imagine who would pay me for the stories, and my plate is pretty full right now with the column and paid assignments like the series I owe Bing Media."

Julia shifted her concentration while easing the car onto the interstate, allowing Maria to steer the conversation to more pressing matters.

"I got an interesting message this week."

Julia recognized the lilt in her sister's voice. "Did you?"

"A guy. He seems interesting. Kind of mysterious."

"How'd you meet?"

"The usual."

"Not another one of your secret admirers! I thought you swore off—"

"I said I was taking a break, not that I'd sworn off exploring possibilities."

Julia stared straight ahead while motioning for Maria to spill the juicy details.

"He says we knew each other in high school."

"They all say that."

"Stop it."

"Sorry," Julia said sincerely. "I just worry about you, Sis. There are a lot of nutcases out there. And the sane ones could be driven nuts by the images you post. You need to be careful."

"I *will* be careful," Maria said glibly. "Besides, I haven't agreed to anything yet. But I am thinking about meeting him."

"When? Where?"

"Haven't decided yet."

"Promise me it will be during daytime and that you'll meet someplace besides your apartment or office. A public location in a different part of town."

"Of course."

"And bring a—"

"Can I please finish telling you about him before you knit my straitjacket?"

"Sorry," Julia said. "I'm listening."

"He said we knew each other in high school and that he asked me out."

"Who didn't?"

"Julia!" Maria shot daggers in her sister's direction.

"OK, I'll stop. But you do still hold the record for prom invitations at Littleton High."

Maria's glower morphed into a self-congratulatory smile. "Anyway, he has business in Littleton and wants to connect while in town."

"What kind of business?"

"Didn't say. But any man who has managed to keep a business going in these times must have his act together, right?"

Julia thought of her husband Troy. Difficult times had forced him out of Washington back to Denver to try salvaging his own business. He had been working day and night to keep things afloat.

"I guess he gets points for that," she said. "Would I have known him?"

"I think he signed the note with an online handle rather than his actual name. I checked the class annual. It wasn't in there. The closest I found were Mansfield and Manchester."

"Hip Manchester?" Julia asked with a laugh. "I remember him. What a goof!"

"I think that was our exit." Maria pointed to a passing Colfax Avenue sign.

"I'm taking Speer," Julia said. "It's a bit early for lunch so I thought we could stop by Troy's office to say hi. He could use the interruption. Do you mind?"

"Not at all. As long as you promise he won't call me Lady Maria. It makes me feel old."

"I told you. I outlawed the chivalrous lingo."

"Good."

They took the next exit onto Speer Boulevard, five minutes away from Troy's office, where Julia intended to grace her gallant gentleman with a much-needed kiss.

CHAPTER EIGHT

"Floor?" asked a thirtysomething gentleman, appreciating Maria's skirt and heels. His tailored suit and silk tie made the perfect package for a visible confidence.

"Ten, please," Julia replied.

"Me too," he said, tossing a wink toward the younger sister.

"Are you here to see Troy?" Julia asked.

"Yes, ma'am. Troy Simmons of TS Enterprises. You?"

"I'm Julia, Troy's wife." It felt good to say it when standing beside Maria. Her kid sister still turned heads like few other women. But Julia had managed something even less common, a committed relationship.

"Nice meeting you." A slight nod in Julia's direction finally acknowledged her presence. "Robert Wilkie."

"Hi, Robert. This is my sister."

Maria offered her hand to formalize the handoff from married to available woman. "Maria Davidson. A pleasure."

Julia marveled once again at the subtle movements and voice inflections that made her sister irresistible to the opposite sex.

In less time than it took an elevator to climb ten floors she had turned a complete stranger into a promising romantic prospect.

"What time is your meeting?" Julia asked as the doors slid apart.

The man glanced at his watch. "Eleven thirty. I'm a bit early."

Maria's eyes met Julia's. Both seemed to imagine the same scheme.

"Listen," Julia began. "I need to pop into my husband's office for a quick conversation. Do you mind keeping my sister company in the lobby for a few minutes? I won't be long."

Robert smiled at Maria, releasing Julia to approach a vacant assistant's desk in front of her husband's closed office door. She paused before entering at the sound of muffled conversation within. After a few moments she discerned a solitary, agitated voice.

"I understand you took a big hit last month, Marcos," Troy was saying. "Times are tough for all of us. But we moved forward in good faith assuming you would deliver your part of the funding."

Julia turned the handle to peer inside. She found Troy's eyes. He eagerly motioned her to enter but seemed a bit embarrassed by her sudden presence, as if she had stumbled upon a messy room in his otherwise tidy life.

He moved toward Julia to position himself for the expected embrace. Both waited impatiently while Troy listened to a voice apparently making more excuses or offering inadequate apologies.

"Listen, Marcos." He broke the silence. "All I need you to do is buy us both a few more days. I'm meeting Wilkie from Peak Capital for lunch in five minutes. I can't ask him to invest in a deal you plan to abandon or the conversation will end before we order appetizers. It'll be better for both of us if you hit the pause button until I can raise more cash. Two days."

Troy resumed listening while Julia reached for his left hand to pull it down from his forehead and place it around her waist. Then she removed the chewed-up pencil from his right hand to place it on the desk before forcing clenched fingers open onto her other hip. His frame seemed to welcome the soft distraction from beleaguered tension.

Julia didn't like or recognize the look in her husband's eyes. Troy's habitual confidence appeared shaken. Whatever deal he had made seemed very important. It also seemed to be unraveling.

"Fine," he said curtly. "I'll talk to you after three."

Troy took a deep breath after ending the call. Julia rose on tiptoe to offer her lips. He accepted them less enthusiastically than she had expected.

"Let's try that again," she ordered. "Only this time imagine I'm your wife rather than your sister."

He released a reluctant smile before accepting the invitation.

"Much better," she responded afterward. "Do you want to talk about it?"

She knew he did even as his head shook from side to side.

"No, thanks. I'm good. Especially now. This is a pleasant surprise."

She slid his hands upward until they cupped her face as if to frame a message she wanted him to hear.

"Troy Simmons," she began. "It's me, Julia, your wife. Talk to me."

He appeared reluctant, as if ashamed at her discovery of a chink in his masculine armor.

"A big deal?"

"One of the biggest," he explained. "I've called in every favor on this one. I've also met with most venture capitalists this side of the Rocky Mountains. They all like the concept but seem skittish. Everybody's nervous about another dip."

"I'm sure you'll make it work," she said reassuringly.

He fixed intently on her eyes while gently caressing her cheek with his thumb. "Don't worry your pretty head, my lady. Everything will be fine."

He gave her another quick peck on the lips that told her he didn't buy his own propaganda.

Julia let a momentary silence linger between them. Then she hesitantly asked a question he wouldn't like. "Have you talked to Kevin about it?"

She braced for impact. Troy took pride in his ability to navigate complex situations and in protecting his longtime partner. Kevin Tolbert had too much to worry about already, he insisted. That's why Troy had volunteered to move back to Denver in the first place. He missed the excitement of Washington DC and the influence of serving as Kevin's chief of staff. But somebody had to shore up what remained of their business holdings.

"No need," he lied. "Besides, I can update him in person tomorrow."

She decided to retreat.

"Are we still meeting at the Beltway Bistro?" He seemed eager to turn a corner. "I could use a good power-broker steak."

"Afraid not," she explained. "I got a message from Angie saying the baby is sick and asking if we mind coming to the house instead."

"Leah's sick?" he asked with concern.

"Not Leah...Ricky. Nothing serious, just a cough. Angie doesn't want to take any chances. I said we'd come over after we settle in at the hotel."

"How old is Ricky now?"

"Let's see. He was born about six weeks after our wedding." Julia began tapping fingers while running a mental tabulation. "Almost five months old."

Troy moved back toward the desk, his mind clearly someplace

else. Capitol Hill, Julia assumed. She knew that Troy loved his visits to Washington DC, where he breathed the air of an influence he'd held before the economic crisis forced him to re-assume the reins of TS Enterprises. The company he and Kevin had birthed and grown together had been hit hard during the prior twelve months. They had majority interests in seven distinct small businesses. Two had since gone under. A third was starting to sink. The money that had enabled Kevin to run for Congress and that allowed Troy to serve as his friend's loyal general was drying up. Now, rather than help steer the ship of state, Troy Simmons seemed to spend his days bailing water from leaky budgets.

"Earth to Troy," Julia teased.

"Sorry, babe," he replied. "Five months old. Wow."

She drew closer. "Are you sure you're OK? You seem worried."

"Just tired."

"Do you want to skip tonight's session? We fly out pretty early in the morning."

"Not a chance."

Troy definitely liked their Exploring Christianity class more than Julia. The weekly ritual took place in Reverend Ware's living room, where a half dozen lapsing pagans tried to understand the fine print before buying faith. Troy had insisted they attend together. Julia had reluctantly agreed, unsure whether she was ready to dive deeper into the religion she had recently come to admire from a safe distance. Christ appeared far less demanding from the sixteenth row on Sunday mornings than he did when she read his specific words. She wouldn't have minded skipping now and then, but Troy refused to miss a single session.

"I'm fine, babe, really." He reached for a blue blazer hanging on the arm of the desk chair. "I'm expecting a lunch appointment to arrive any—"

"Robert Wilkie," Julia interrupted. "He's in the lobby with Maria."

"You're kidding. He knows Maria?"

"No. Well, he does now. We met him in the elevator. He seemed smitten."

"Good." He chuckled. "I need every angle I can get with him. Maybe he'll make a deal if I offer to set him up with my sister-in-law."

"I think she's probably beating you to that punch right now."

They shared a laugh.

"Eating at Panzano?" Troy asked.

"Vesta."

"My next guess."

Troy retrieved his tablet from the desk and placed it in his jacket pocket. "Did you finish your column?"

"Nearly," Julia said, tightening her husband's tie. "It needs a few tweaks. I'll get it done after lunch. I might even have time to outline the Bing Media story they requested about—"

Julia cut herself off when a hint of tension returned to her husband's torso. While Troy had often said how proud he was of her journalistic resurgence, she feared it also spawned other feelings. Her rising notoriety highlighted his descent into obscurity. He had done the right thing by voluntarily leaving the circle of power to mind the shop. But such things could emasculate even the strongest male ego. Even though Troy hid it well, Julia felt his struggle.

"Oh, never mind about that. You have far more important things to think about right now. What do you say we go rescue your lunch partner from mine."

They left the office hand in hand. Julia noticed the still-vacant assistant's desk.

"Where's Maggie?"

"She left the third week of July."

"You haven't had an assistant for over a month?"

"Nope."

"No wonder you're feeling stressed. Any prospects?"

"I haven't really tried to find one," he admitted. "Can't afford the salary just now. I'm doing all right."

He placed his hand on her lower back to usher Julia away from another uncomfortable conversation. She refused to take the hint, pausing to glance at the adjoining office.

"Wait a minute," she said. "Wasn't that Steve Reynolds's office, your controller? Is he gone too?"

A sheepish nod. "Since late June."

"Then who's been managing the books?"

Troy bowed his head while raising his right hand like a schoolboy caught cheating in class.

"So you're doing Steve's job on top of everything else, and all without an assistant?"

"Look, Julia—"

"Why haven't you told me about this?" she interrupted. "No wonder you've been working such long hours and feeling so stressed!"

"I didn't want to burden you with—"

"Burden *me?* What about you?"

"I can handle it, babe. It's only temporary. You'll see."

She crossed her arms like a girl threatening to hold her breath.

"Please," he said. "I might be just one lunch meeting away from the solution. Let's talk about it later, OK?"

Julia forced herself to soften, unwilling to further upset Troy before an important meeting. "OK. But I want us to talk about it tonight."

"Deal."

As they rounded the corner Julia saw an all-too-familiar sight. Her sister sat cozily close to a man she had met minutes earlier, who was now enthralled with chatter about nothing in particular.

Julia smiled at the couple, then halted her advance and faced her husband to cut a different deal.

"No, I don't want to talk about it tonight," she whispered. "I want you to tell Kevin what's going on when we see the Tolberts tomorrow. You shouldn't have to carry this by yourself. I don't care how busy he is, Kevin is still your partner."

"Don't worry. I'll discuss everything with him tomorrow."

"Promise me," she insisted.

"I promise," he said in a hushed voice. "Now can we go? I really need the time with Robert if I'm going to make this deal work."

Satisfied, Julia squeezed her husband's hand. Then she turned toward the lobby to greet the potential investor with the most charming voice she could muster.

CHAPTER NINE

"We're gonna miss you," Sarah said while Matthew placed a chair on top of the table she had just finished cleaning.

"Thanks," he replied, forcing an upbeat grin. "Back at'cha."

The thud of the last wooden stool settling onto the flat surface created a disquieting sensation in Matthew. He had volunteered to stay and help Sarah close up shop, buying him a few extra minutes in a job he had never really liked but that had given him a place for nearly ten years.

Campus Grinds was where Matthew had voiced his frustration back when the University of Colorado rejected his first attempt to enroll, still one of the most disheartening moments of his life. His dream had died. Or so he'd thought at the time. His coworkers might not have cared all that much, but at least they offered a semblance of sympathy.

Watching Sarah clear the last bit of clutter from the counter prompted a twinge of grief. Matthew would miss her, his favorite of the many part-time employees who had come and gone over the years. He would miss waxing eloquent on a range of academic-sounding topics while she nodded with varying degrees of interest. The tiniest possible audience, she had given him a sense of validation the enrollment office seemed unwilling to bestow.

Sarah had been most thoughtful during his mother's worst years. A willing shoulder if he had been inclined to cry. But his mother's decline had fueled anger, not tears. So he never took her up on the offer.

"I'm not sure I ever told you how much I appreciated your kindness during my mother's illness." He paused to watch her reaction before saying more. She appeared momentarily puzzled, as if reaching to recall any sympathy she might have offered.

"Oh," she muddled, "don't mention it."

They both moved toward a small closet door in the corner behind the counter, where Sarah retrieved a broom and dustpan while Matthew grabbed a small garbage bucket he had filled and emptied hundreds of times before.

"How is she?" Sarah asked while maneuvering the broom into a corner.

"Who?" he asked.

"Your mom."

Matthew's brow furrowed. Then he remembered that he had never told Sarah about the transition. He'd told her about getting accepted as a full-time student. He'd sought and received her smiling approval when he said he could finally pursue his dream. But he hadn't mentioned his mother's death. Why would he? The money that would have freed him to quit his job still hadn't been released. Had that happened he might have told her about the inheritance. So, with the exception of a few shift-change requests to accommodate Tuesday and Friday classes, nothing was different about Matthew from what Sarah had observed over the prior four and a half years.

"My mom is…" he began, then stopped. "Actually, she's doing great. Never better."

He almost believed it after months of telling himself his mom was now free from the limitations of a decaying body.

"Glad to hear it." Sarah seemed eager to change subjects. "Remind me again why you're moving to Denver."

She knelt and positioned the dustpan in front of a freshly swept mound of dirt while handing Matthew the broom.

"Littleton, actually," he said.

"That's right. Littleton then."

He hadn't had time to invent an impressive reason for the change, so he told her the embarrassing truth. "I need to pay down my loan before I can fund another semester."

"I see," she replied, emptying the dustpan into the bucket. Then she stood and waited for the rest of a story he hadn't intended to tell.

"I grew up in Littleton. Lived there until about ten years ago when my mom retired."

"What brought you to Boulder?"

"Naïveté," he said, laughing. "I assumed living close would improve my chance of getting into the university. Mom agreed. Of course, she never went to college herself, so knew even less than I did about what it takes."

Matthew took two steps forward to accompany Sarah, who had inched her way toward the front of the shop for one last inspection of the floor.

"It took me seven years to get accepted, one of them driving to Front Range Community College to prove I have what it takes."

"Uh-huh," she said robotically.

He kept talking despite losing her attention. Closing duties completed, she appeared eager to lock up and head home.

"Anyway, there are more jobs in the Denver area. Besides, I

still have a few high school friends living in Littleton. I figure
I'll hang there to save for ten or eleven months and then come
back to school next fall."

Matthew was glad she didn't ask what job he had lined up.
The only thing less impressive than cleaning coffee mugs was
taking care of old people. But senior-care services paid a premium wage. Short of receiving the inheritance, he knew of no
other way to get the kind of money necessary to enter his sophomore year.

They returned the cleaning supplies to the closet before
Sarah retrieved her purse from behind the counter.

"Well," she began, "I guess this is goodbye for a while."

"For a while," he said with a tentative smile. "Thanks, again,
for being a great shift boss. And for being a friend."

"You bet." She extended her free arm for a side embrace, less
than he wanted but all he could expect.

"I'll miss you," Matthew heard himself say.

"Ditto," she said awkwardly. "So I'll see you in about a year?"

"For sure," he agreed. "In a year."

Matthew stood outside in the warm August air watching Sarah
enter the locking code on the front door. They walked silently
in the same direction, the space between them widening as each
veered onto diverging paths.

He gradually slowed his pace until he found himself standing
still on the university lawn while Sarah continued toward the
parking lot. He waited for her to move out of visual range before
turning back. Matthew needed to say one more goodbye before
loading up the U-Haul and moving back to Littleton.

~~~

Three hours earlier Professor Thomas Vincent had popped
into the shop for his daily Brazilian coffee and invited

Matthew to stop by the office whenever his shift ended. He said he would be working late, code for an evening tryst with one of the female students eager to impress her teacher. Matthew smiled at the former priest fully recovered from a vow of chastity.

While approaching the philosophy building Matthew recalled the professor's instructions. He glanced up toward the outer window of the second floor. Drawing near he noticed light shining through opened blinds, his cue to climb the stairs.

"Hello, Matthew," Dr. Vincent said after opening the door. "Come on in."

The professor moved toward a dark wooden cabinet. "What are you drinking?"

Matthew shrugged. "Beer, I guess. Thanks."

Matthew walked toward a small sofa nestled between the professor's desk and bookshelf. Just before sitting he noticed the faint aroma of perfume only slightly more pungent than the lingering scent of Dr. Vincent's cologne. He moved to a different chair.

"Here you go." Dr. Vincent offered a cold bottle to his guest before raising his own. "To a successful freshman year."

Matthew mirrored his host with a nod before joining in a celebratory swig.

"And to your one year sabbatical before returning as a sophomore," Dr. Vincent said, repeating the ritual.

"'Sabbatical,'" Matthew mocked. "I like the sound of that. Although it's more like an exile."

"I'm sure everything will work out. You got this far. You'll find a way to keep going."

Matthew pressed his lips into a weak smile. "I guess."

Both men sat in silence for thirty seconds.

"So, tell me about the job. You said something about better pay but didn't mention what you'll be doing."

Matthew looked toward the bookshelf to avoid the professor's eyes. "I accepted an elder-care position."

"Really?"

"My first client lives in Littleton."

"East of Denver?"

"Right. A few blocks from my old high school."

"Friends?" Dr. Vincent asked.

"A few. There's a girl." Matthew left details of the relationship to his host's imagination rather than explain the pathetic reality.

"Anything serious?"

"Not yet." The truth. "But things seem to be progressing nicely." A stretch.

Another thirty seconds without words.

"Pretty lame, isn't it?" Matthew asked.

"What's that?"

"If you think about it, I'm right back where I started. No. Worse than where I started."

"How so?"

"Last year I couldn't go to school because I was broke and taking care of my mom. Now I'm in debt and will be taking care of a complete stranger."

"True. But you have a year of school under your belt."

"Right. And the loan to prove it," Matthew scoffed.

"Big accomplishments come through small moves, Mr. Adams."

The comment struck Matthew wrong. He felt anger rise as he recalled a year-old conversation with this same man. A conversation that had fueled a very *big* move.

"Do you consider it suicide if someone volunteers to transition?" Matthew had asked while wrestling with the most difficult quandary of his life.

"There's no such thing as a mortal sin," Dr. Vincent had assured him. "Just hard choices."

"Would you help your own mother transition, you know, if she asked you to?" Matthew had pressed further.

"Yes. I believe I would have helped her."

Matthew looked up from the bottle of beer toward his host. "I'm willing to make small moves. But I made a big move last year and I'm not sure it was the right thing to do."

"By helping your mom transition?"

More than help, he didn't confess.

"Listen to me, Matthew," Dr. Vincent insisted. "Your mother was in severe decline, am I right?"

A single nod.

"And she wanted to fund your dream?"

"She did," he acknowledged.

"Then you did the right thing by confirming her choice. There's no way either of you could have known the transition money would get held up in a legal mess."

"I guess you're right."

"Of course I'm right," Dr. Vincent decreed. "And it won't do either of you any good to second-guess the decision. Your mom's death wasn't a sin. Nor was it a waste. Even if the money never comes, the procedure put her out of her misery."

Matthew's stomach tensed. *Mom wasn't miserable, just forgetful.*

"What was the phrase you borrowed from that journalist?"

"Julia Davidson?"

"Davidson, right."

"'Free to thrive.'" Matthew recalled the title of a column that had eased his conscience. "She said something about using genetic prescreening to prevent defective babies. I thought it applied to people like my mom who deserve freedom from disease now."

"Your mother couldn't thrive while trapped in a decaying body."

Matthew pushed aside thoughts of his mother's smile and

touch to recall her failing memory, bathroom mishaps, and fits of anxiety. "I suppose not."

"There's no supposing about it," Dr. Vincent insisted. "You did the right thing, Matthew. I'm sure your mother would be proud of all you've accomplished this year."

He lifted his bottle for another toast. "To her heroic sacrifice." They shared a drink.

"And to your hard work," he added.

"Thanks, Dr. Vincent," Matthew said. "I appreciate your encouragement."

"Just promise me you won't let this girlfriend in Littleton distract you from your goal. I expect to see you back here as soon as you resolve the transition money mess."

"I promise."

The host ushered his guest to the door, where both said their goodbyes before Matthew descended the stairs and began walking toward the parking lot. He felt much more at ease than he had when the day began, even allowing himself a hint of self-respect. A playful ping came from the device in his left pocket. Retrieving the source he tapped the tablet screen, where a brand-new image of Maria Davidson appeared. She had apparently posted it seconds earlier as another treat for her anonymous admirers. As usual, she looked amazing.

The moment prompted a satisfied smirk. In less than twenty-four hours Matthew would pack up his few possessions and move them to the home of an elderly client who lived a few short miles from the woman of his dreams. A woman Matthew hoped might become the kind of sweet distraction Dr. Vincent had warned him against.

CHAPTER TEN

Tyler waved his tablet over the police station parking meter until it acknowledged payment with a beep. Straining his left ear toward his shoulder he tried working out the kink in a neck that resented sleeping on the couch. After a series of comforting pops he stretched in the other direction. Renee had said he couldn't sleep in the master suite since she had cleaned the sheets for her parents. And joining her in the guest room would have required groveling, something he refused to do.

He approached the door in grumpy silence with a slight anxiety. He couldn't quite pinpoint what it was that troubled him about asking Smitty's advice. His old partner would keep the conversation completely confidential. But he still felt uneasy.

Tyler felt his pocket to confirm that he had remembered to bring the Santiago letters. Then he swallowed hard while crossing the threshold to reenter a former life.

A minute later Tyler found himself standing outside a window of bulletproof glass, behind which an unfriendly face eyed him skeptically. She said nothing while waiting for the day's first interruption to identify himself.

"Cain," he offered. "Tyler Cain. I'm here to see Smitty."

A disapproving scowl caused him to wonder what had happened to the perky brunette who used to occupy the receptionist station.

He nervously cleared his throat. "Or, I mean, Assistant Chief Smith."

A familiar voice called out from behind. "Cain?"

He spun around to see Kory Sanders, annoyingly happy to see him.

Tyler forced a smile in return, nodding. "Kory."

Kory slapped Tyler on the back, as if they had once been great friends.

They hadn't.

"What's happening?" asked the man who had weaseled his way into the post Tyler had deserved. "It's been a while. I haven't seen you since, oh, let me think, right after I became captain. Am I right?"

Kory smirked.

Pull out your gun and shoot me in the heart now, why don't you? Tyler thought.

"Uh. Yeah," he heard himself say.

"How's PI work treating you?"

"Great!" he lied. "Couldn't be better!" Which was almost true, given the new case.

Kory wore a doubtful smirk. "Riiiight."

Tyler suppressed an urge to slug his former nemesis.

"So, still with, oh, what was her name? Courtney?"

"Heck, no." Tyler snorted awkwardly. "Escaped that relationship years ago." Another forced laugh. "How about you? Anyone keeping you warm at night?"

"Off and on. You know how it is...I'm game if they're willing with no strings."

"I hear you," Tyler said. "My current live-in is a nice-enough gal. But it's about time I ended it."

The officer behind the glass glanced up, rolling her eyes.

"It's just getting, you know, complicated. She wants more from me than I—"

He stopped. Why in the world was he telling Kory Sanders about his relationship with Renee? Kory Sanders was a jerk. But Tyler found himself on the speeding train of a conversation heading nowhere good.

He lied again. "I think she wants a kid."

"Whoa, man," Kory said. "You gotta nip that one soon. That's why I have a strict policy: never live with a partner. Way too many expectations I'm not willing to meet."

Change the subject, Tyler thought. "I'm here to see Greg. Running an important case by him."

"Really?" Tyler could almost see the gears churning away in Kory's head. "Anything I can do to help?"

Tyler shook his head as he went for the dig. "Nah. Really needs someone...higher up."

Kory sniffed. "Gotcha. Well, you know where to find me if you change your mind." He rapped his knuckles twice on the counter before sliding two fingers across the entry scanner. The door buzzed open. "Don't be a stranger."

Tyler knocked assertively on the door with the sign that read GREGORY SMITH, ASSISTANT CHIEF OF POLICE.

"Smitty?"

His former partner glanced up from behind several stacks of

files and offered a wry smile. "Tyler Cain. To what do I owe the pleasure?"

Tyler set one foot over the threshold, waiting for an official invitation. "Got a few minutes?"

Smitty hesitated. Then he leaned back in his chair to wave him in. "You bet," he said, closing the folder in front of him. He tossed it onto one of the piles. "We've been in the computer age for nearly a century, and there's more paperwork now than ever!"

Smitty stood and moved to the front edge of his desk. Then he leaned back and crossed his arms. Tyler recognized the "keep it brief" stance, so he turned a chair around and leaned back to mirror his host's posture.

Their reunion felt awkwardly cordial, another reminder that Greg Smith was no longer Tyler's partner. The two had once trusted each other with their lives. They had been fairly close confidants who felt a bond forged patrolling neighborhoods, sipping doughnut-shop coffee, and enduring the boredom of more stakeouts than either cared to recall. But diverging streams of time's river had created an expanse Tyler could no longer pretend away.

He reached deep for something to restore their former amity. He found a useful memory: Smitty confiding in his partner during a rough spot in his relationship with Carol Anne. Were they still married?

"How's Carol Anne?" He felt his way lightly.

"Fine," Smitty said. "She's fine. We're fine, actually."

"Really? So you're not—"

"No." Smitty chuckled. "We're not apart. Actually, quite the opposite. We got some help, worked through our issues, and then, well..." He paused, reaching back to spin around a frame. "There's the result!"

A little girl who looked about two years old smiled cheesily at the camera, her hair decorated with ribbons and pigtails.

"Wow," Tyler said, not sure if Smitty considered fatherhood a coup or a curse. He'd never wanted children back in the day, one of many tense spots in the marriage. He had called kids conceived in the heat of passion "unplanned monkey wrenches thrown into the gears of life."

But the adoring grin Smitty flashed while displaying the photo suggested a change of heart.

"But I gather you're not here for a social visit," he said, spinning the frame back into place. "Is this about the case I sent your way?"

"Yes...and no."

Smitty frowned. "Well, which is it?"

"The judge's assistant insisted I keep the police out of this for now. Until I know more, at least. Officially speaking."

"But unofficially?"

"Unofficially, the whole thing makes me uneasy. There's a lot at stake, and I'm nervous the judge could be in danger."

"Which judge?"

"Can't say."

"Fine. So, unofficially, what's going on with this nameless judge?"

Tyler slid the letters from his pocket, holding them up but not quite offering them. "So far I've got three letters. Each mentions a big case on the nameless judge's docket. He or she also makes a request for direct communication, hoping to dialogue about the pending decision."

"He or she? No name?"

"Just a first initial and a last name."

Smitty lifted his eyebrows in a silent request for more.

"A Manichean," Tyler explained. "Might be a pen name. I found some information about an ancient religious sect called Manicheans, but nothing that seemed relevant to the case. Probably a coincidence."

"Has the judge responded to the sender?"

Tyler shook his head. "Not so far. I'm not even sure he's aware the letters exist."

"So what's the problem?"

"Each letter sounds more desperate than the last. Possibly more threatening. The first reads like a simple request to correspond anonymously. The second hints about unwelcome consequences of a wrong decision. The third expresses annoyance that the judge has ignored the sender's requests to dialogue."

Smitty stroked his clean-shaven chin in thought. "Any criminal record?"

"Nothing listed on my usual sources. Of course, they're always a bit out of date." Tyler hesitated before floating his first request. "Any chance I could run the name through the department database?"

"Done," Smitty said, uncrossing his arms, his standard end-of-meeting gesture.

Tyler didn't move, prompting Smitty to reluctantly resume an attentive stance.

"What else?" he asked.

"Scan the envelopes to see if forensics can find anything useful?"

"Also done."

"I've got a hunch about this one, Greg," Tyler began. "The same hunch I got on the Gilbert case."

As their eyes met, Tyler noticed Smitty's jaw begin to clench.

"Gilbert?" he asked.

Tyler nodded slowly as both minds regurgitated the details. The brutal murder of a young girl could have been prevented had the two disobeyed orders. The chief hadn't trusted Tyler's gut. He had wanted something concrete before approving an arrest. One anonymous lead wasn't enough to risk the embarrassment and backlash of hauling Travis Gilbert into custody. The respected businessman had donated generously to the mayor's campaign. But Tyler knew his low-life source had told the truth. Sure, it would have been risky acting on the word of a twenty-eight-year-old drug dealer. But it was even more risky, Smitty had argued, to sit back and do nothing while Gilbert committed murder to prevent a public scandal. The girl had gotten in over her head trying to blackmail Gilbert. They had met at a party. He enjoyed her for a while, then discarded her like a disposable toy. So she threatened to expose his "discreet habit" of using recreational drugs. But Gilbert figured it would save hassle and money to take her out of the picture. The girl's body disappeared until police uncovered her shallow grave behind a condemned suburban crack house six months after Tyler and Smitty were taken off the case.

"That's why I wanted to get another opinion," Tyler added. "You know, from the one person I trust on this kind of thing."

Smitty half-smiled, appreciatively. "Well, I think you're probably right."

Tyler frowned at the validation.

"Unofficially, I'd trust your instincts."

"But officially?"

"Officially, you already know what I'm going to say."

Tyler nodded, sighing. "No crime has been committed."

"We can't invest time or resources on someone who, from all appearances, simply wants to exchange words with a judge. Even hostile words." He waved his hand over the stacks of folders on his desk. "Look at this. I can't get on top of the pile as it is."

Tyler glanced down at the letters in his hand. He had anticipated Smitty's response, the same one he would have given had some private investigator shared the scenario back when he was a detective. The police can't get involved in a case based entirely on a hunch something *might* be wrong.

"I understand," Tyler responded.

"But I'll ask someone to run the name through our database for any additional leads."

"I appreciate that."

Smitty moved back around the desk to retake his seat. Recognizing the hint, Tyler slid the chair back into place before offering his hand across the desk.

"Thanks for the help, Smitty," he said. "And for the lead. You're a good man."

Smitty shook firmly, then retrieved a folder from the pile.

"Listen, Ty," Smitty said as Tyler moved toward the open door. "I miss working with you."

Tyler turned back toward his former partner to accept the badly needed sip of camaraderie. "Me too," he said.

"I gotta tell you, when you left the force, I thought you were crazy and…maybe even a little selfish."

"Ouch."

"No. Listen. I know there was bad blood between you and Kory, but it bothered me when you left. I won't lie, it hurt a little."

Both men blushed as honest sentiment invaded the conversation.

"But now I think it's exactly what needed to happen."

"What's that supposed to mean?" Tyler asked.

"It means losing my favorite partner forced me to reflect, you know, about what was happening at home."

A puzzled stare sat on Tyler's face.

"Carol Anne and I were a train wreck waiting to happen. And the truth is, all my venting to you wasn't helping matters. While I appreciated your encouragement it actually made things worse."

"Good to know," Tyler said self-deprecatingly.

"Oh, it wasn't your fault. It was mine. I heard what I wanted to hear. I mean, it's not like you had any experience with marriage. A married man has no business seeking advice from a carefree single buddy."

They shared a laugh. Tyler's less enthusiastic than Smitty's.

"I guess I wanted what you had."

Tyler nodded silently.

"But after you left I had to turn elsewhere. Long story short, Carol Anne and I got help. I learned to view love as a choice, not a feeling. That's when things improved."

Tyler shook his head, unsure of himself. "I'm not following you."

"I think someone up there used your departure for good even though it didn't make sense to either of us at the time."

"Someone up there?" Tyler asked callously. "You mean God?"

Smitty shrugged. "Perhaps."

A momentary silence lingered between them.

"Well, I'm glad my absence proved so helpful," Tyler ribbed as he turned back toward the door.

"Ever read the story of Esther?" Smitty asked.

"Esther who?"

"Just Esther. Look it up."

"OK. Because?"

"Because I think events can be orchestrated for purposes beyond our own intentions. The story of Esther describes a girl who had no clue that her crummy situation was being used to prevent an ancient holocaust."

"You don't say." Tyler tried to follow.

Smitty chuckled. "Just read the story. Bottom line, I disagreed with your decision to leave the force. I was ticked off. But that decision ended up salvaging my marriage." He reached for the picture frame. "And now I have this precious little girl."

"I see." Tyler finally connected the dots.

"Maybe something like that is happening for you. What if

God wants to use your gut to prevent something awful from happening to this judge?"

"A nice thought. But I seriously doubt God has anything to do with it."

"We'll see. Meantime, both officially and unofficially, I'm confident you'll figure it out. Come see me if things escalate to the point we can actually intervene."

"Gotcha." Tyler moved to the door. "Well, congratulations on your little girl there, I guess."

"Her name is Esther."

"Right." Tyler smiled. "Esther."

"It was good to see you, Ty. Don't be a stranger."

PART TWO

CHAPTER ELEVEN

Julia glanced toward her husband seated on the sofa across the room. He seemed more at ease than he had been in months. Spending time with Kevin had a calming influence on Troy, as did the escalating rivalry between the two older Tolbert children.

"It's my turn," six-year-old Tommy demanded, yanking his little sister's pajama hem.

"No!" Joy tightened her squeeze around Troy's torso to weather Tommy's assault.

Adult conversation paused yet again while Troy tried brokering a peace accord.

"I promised you each fifteen minutes," he said, checking the watch Tommy had been impatiently eyeing for eight minutes and forty-seven seconds. "Joy still has about seven minutes to go. Don't worry, buddy. I won't forget about you."

Tommy huffed, recrossing his arms to resume his leer at Joy's beaming face.

Two miniature tongues pierced through pressed lips toward one another.

"Tommy," Angie said sternly as the boy retrieved his tongue with lightning speed.

"She started it," he protested.

"You're the oldest," she replied before sealing his fate with a momentary glare.

Julia restrained a laugh at the childish dread only disapproving mommies can engender.

Angie looked back toward Julia. "How's he doing?"

"Good." Julia tried to believe it.

"Julia…" Angie flashed another motherly glare. "Really. How's he doing?"

"He misses Washington," she began. "No. He misses Kevin."

They both looked back toward their husbands.

"And the kids," Julia added.

Angie offered a knowing nod. "They miss him too."

"The business has struggled, of course. But he doesn't talk to me about it. I get the feeling it makes him feel…I don't know…inadequate or something."

Angie's eyes smiled over her sip of tea.

"What?" Julia asked.

Angie tilted her head toward Kevin while cupping a hand to the edge of her mouth. "Sounds like someone else I know," she whispered. "When things get the worst he says the least."

Julia lowered her voice to match her friend's. "Why do they do that?"

Angie grinned widely before taking another drink. She looked like a woman eager to invite her friend into a secret society otherwise closed to newlywed brides.

"What?" Julia prodded again.

Angie looked back toward the men to confirm neither was listening.

"They *do* feel inadequate."

The revelation momentarily stunned Julia, then morphed into an elusive puzzle piece suddenly found.

"Why? I mean, both have accomplished so much at such a young age. Why should they feel inadequate?"

"Not should. Do. And I don't mean just Kevin and Troy. I'm talking about all men."

Julia thought of the men she'd dated before meeting Troy. Most carried themselves with a swagger that hid any hint of uncertainty. She remembered rebuking herself for craving their admiration and affection. *A successful and intelligent woman shouldn't need the attention of some egocentric man.* It's what she had written in her column and shouted at the mirror after countless disheartening dates. But watching her sister's romantic roller coasters and reading her readers' posts had convinced Julia that every woman struggled with a nagging insecurity just like her own. It had never occurred to her that the same might be true of men. Some men, perhaps. But Troy? And Kevin?

"Do you mean when things go wrong?" Julia asked.

"I mean almost always," Angie explained. "While brokering business deals and walking the halls of Congress my husband appears bold and self-assured."

Julia agreed. Kevin Tolbert came across as even more confident than Troy.

"And he is," Angie continued, "as long as he knows I respect him. But one look of disappointment or word of criticism from me and he becomes a different man. A smaller man."

"Smaller?"

"Less than he is when he senses my admiration."

Julia felt a familiar sense of indignation. "So we're supposed to stand on the sidelines wearing cheerleader outfits so they can win the big games. Is that it?"

Angie smiled disarmingly. "Something like that. But I hope

you wear something a bit racier than a cheerleader outfit now that you're married." She added a mischievous wink.

Julia suppressed a reluctant grin while marveling at her friend's unflappable confidence. Rather than take the bait Angie had redirected the potential quarrel like a seasoned mom distracting a child from a tantrum.

"You know what I mean," Julia snapped playfully.

"If there's anything I've learned about men during a decade of marriage it's that they desperately need their woman's admiration and respect. Why shouldn't they? I mean, God made two halves of a whole. Doesn't it make sense that men need us as much as we need them?"

"I guess I don't like thinking of it as a need," Julia admitted. "I love Troy. I want him. But *need* him?"

"That's right," Angie mocked. "I forgot. No man is an island. But a woman is different. She can go it alone."

Julia absorbed the rebuke. Probably even deserved it, she thought, after years of columns peddling an ideology that must have seemed shallow or silly to her newfound mentor. Angie would, of course, resent being called a mentor. The two had been high school friends reunited after a season of estrangement. Slowly drifting apart was the cowardly route Julia had chosen while falling in love with a world far removed from the kind of life Kevin and Angie Tolbert had built together. The kind of life, as Troy had hoped, she found it easy to admire.

But it remained difficult to choose.

"Point taken," Julia said, raising a hand of surrender.

Angie winked at her friend before lifting the mug back to her lips. "So," she began over the brim, "how's that discussion group with your pastor going?"

Julia sighed before glancing at a clock on the wall. "A new record," she said.

"Record for what?"

"For how soon you slipped into evangelist mode." She paused to calculate backward from her and Troy's arrival time. "Less than two hours."

In truth, Julia had hoped to avoid the subject. Yes, she had agreed to join Troy in the Exploring Christianity class. And yes, Pastor Alex had answered most of her toughest questions during the past few months. But Julia hated admitting to her hopeful friend that she hadn't yet decided to go as far as her husband. He had become an official follower of Jesus a few months earlier. Kevin had flown to Denver for the baptism, beaming with delight at his best friend's decision. Despite Angie's prayerful prods, however, Julia remained a straggler: open to the possibility, but hesitant. At times she felt an inexplicable yearning mixed with fear, as if nervously eager about her own likely plunge. But no decision as yet.

"I'm sorry." Julia regretted causing Angie's blush of unease. "I shouldn't have said that. The class is going well. Thanks for asking."

Angie smiled forgivingly. "You know I'm praying for you."

Julia nodded, then swallowed discomfiture at the idea of heavenly intervention. The thought of needing anyone, be it her husband, a dear friend, or even her Maker, stirred unwelcome but instinctual feelings. Might they explain her spiritual foot-dragging?

"I guess Pastor Alex is right," she confessed.

"About what?"

"He said the greatest barrier to becoming a Christian isn't any question or doubt."

"No?"

"No," Julia continued, "it's our pride."

Angie's brow lifted in surprised reaction to the admission. "Julia Simmons, proud?"

They shared a knowing laugh.

"Anyway," Angie said while gently touching her friend's arm. "They need us more than we realize."

Julia nodded to acknowledge Angie's return to the subject of husbands.

"I guarantee Troy needs you more than you think he does," Angie added.

"Then why doesn't he talk to me about what's going on?"

"Like what?" Angie asked.

"Like yesterday morning. I stopped by his office to say hi. He seemed happy to see me, but he also seemed nervous, like I had caught him in a secret."

"What kind of secret?"

"Like letting go of a few key staff members. And like failing to attract the kind of capital they need for a big deal he's trying to put together."

A look of concern invaded Angie's face. Julia regretted saying too much.

"I'm sure everything is fine," she added. "He plans to talk to Kevin about the situation tomorrow."

"He probably already has," Angie said. "Like I said before, when things are going the worst Kevin tells me the least."

Julia hesitated before deciding to say more. "Actually, he hasn't told Kevin yet. I insisted he do so."

Another look of apprehension from Angie.

"I think the business is struggling, Angie. Troy has been doing everything he knows to do without bothering Kevin with the details."

"Sam Gamgee," Angie mused aloud.

"Sorry?"

"From *The Lord of the Rings*," Angie added.

Julia recalled Troy's description of his relationship to Kevin. Sam Gamgee was the loyal companion of Frodo Baggins, bearer of the Ring. Kevin had been called to play a part Troy gladly supported, as Sam Gamgee eased the Ring-bearer's burden.

"That's right," Julia said. "Troy seems reluctant to saddle Kevin with bad news. He's trying to handle it himself."

Angie seemed reflective. "Did he say how bad it is?"

"You know how they are. Always putting the best spin on the situation."

Angie nodded silently.

"I didn't get a sense of imminent doom or anything like that. Just some tough decisions."

"Good." Angie seemed relieved. "I'm sure they'll sort it out together."

"I hope so," Julia said. "I think the whole mess has been wearing Troy down."

"Into a lesser man?"

Julia smiled at the reminder. "I suppose."

"Which means?" Angie directed.

"He needs a cheerleader?" Julia asked.

"I think you're catching on, girl!"

———

"My turn!" Tommy shouted from across the room. Protesting whimpers followed from three-year-old Joy. Both women watched in amusement as Kevin tried prying his daughter loose from Troy's lap.

"I'd better intervene," Angie said, moving toward the commotion.

Thirty seconds later Julia joined her husband on a tour of Tommy's bedroom, where he was eager to show "Uncle Troy" his collection of dead bugs and pricelessly worthless rocks. She then dismissed herself at Tommy's not-so-subtle insistence. He said it would be a violation of a soldier's honor to open his secret stash of battle supplies hidden in a box under the bed in the presence of "the fair maiden."

Troy knelt down before crossing his legs to mimic his mini comrade. Pausing at the bedroom door, Julia turned to enjoy one last look at her husband's face. The stress lines around his eyes so evident only hours earlier had vanished, like wrinkles on a crumpled shirt freshly ironed flat. Troy relished time with Kevin's kids. He would probably make a wonderful father.

The thought formed a knot in the pit of Julia's stomach.

CHAPTER TWELVE

It was nearly midnight when Julia and Troy stepped onto the hotel elevator. As the doors slid closed he pressed the top button, then took a step backward.

She noticed the illumined number. "Aren't we on floor seventeen?"

He nodded silently.

"Then why thirty-five?"

He turned and slipped his hands around her waist. "Twice as much time for mischief," he said, moving in for a kiss.

Julia put both hands against her husband's chest and gave a weak shove while punching the correct button. "Troy Simmons! I'm a respectable woman."

"You're also a beautiful woman," he said, drawing her body closer.

The kiss began about floor three and continued until briefly interrupted by a voice announcing their arrival.

She grabbed his hand and led him into the hallway, where they tiptoed quickly toward a door both yearned to enter and lock behind them.

Moments later, Julia sensed what little tension remained ebbing out of Troy's body as she removed his shirt. Then she heard a sound that halted their advance. Troy's sigh of pleasure and anticipation triggered the memory of another moment, another man. A wave of guilt slowed her throbbing pulse. It was not the first time Troy's touch had resurfaced old passions. She pulled back, then tried to resume. But a bewildered look told her he had noticed.

"Is something wrong?" Troy asked between winded breaths.

She pressed her lips to his, hoping the present reality could overpower the intruder from her past. No good. The taste of Troy's kiss only fueled the memory of the nameless encounter her body refused to forget. She pulled back again.

"I'm sorry." She sighed.

He placed his hand on hers, joining her on the edge of the bed. The two sat silently while Julia considered what to say.

"I forgot to bring protection." A lie. Claiming forgetfulness seemed better than admitting memories.

The comment clearly bothered him more than the interruption.

"Don't worry," Julia added. "I'm sure you can run down to the lobby to buy some. I'll shower and slip into—"

"I don't want to buy protection," he interrupted. "I just want to make love to my wife."

The comment startled Julia. "You know I'm not on the pill right now. And we don't like using—"

"I don't mean it like that."

"What then?" she asked, hugging a pillow to defend her body from the chilly air of an overhead vent.

Deep lines of stress reappeared on Troy's face. She knew he wanted to say something that he couldn't put into words.

Then it struck her. "You don't mean..."

She paused.

He nodded.

She swallowed back a sense of panic. "Troy. Be sensible."

"I'm tired of being sensible."

"We've only been married for six months," she reminded him. "We agreed we would consider kids after a few years."

"I know what we agreed. I was just hoping…"

He didn't need to finish. Julia recalled the look on her husband's face when Angie let him hold the new baby before dinner. He stared at little Ricky for at least five minutes, marveling at his fingers, earlobes, and toes. Then he volunteered to sit next to Leah to help her eat. Leah had held a special place in Troy's heart ever since Kevin told him about her genetic disorder. Tiny signs of fragile X syndrome had begun to appear, nearly indiscernible previews of her coming life filled with limitations and stares. They were nothing that would mark her as particularly unusual to the uninformed eye, but enough to cause Troy to hold her more tightly than he had the others.

Julia had said she was open to becoming a mom someday. She even had started to believe it. But she knew that Troy wanted to be a daddy now.

"Listen, babe," she said softly. "I think I'll be ready to talk about having kids soon, OK?"

"Why not talk about it now?"

"While in a romantic hotel room?" she asked playfully. "Not a good idea."

"Some people would call it the perfect time."

Julia felt her anxiety rise. Was Troy suggesting a blind conception? Did he honestly think she would consider such a risky option?

"Be serious." A nervous laugh.

He didn't respond.

"People don't do that anymore, Troy."

"Kevin and Angie do that," he retorted. "And they have four great kids."

Julia felt momentarily ashamed of her gut reaction, words that might have appeared in one of her columns a year or two earlier: *They have too many kids. Their irresponsibility brought an unproductive debit into the world.*

But Angie rejected the sensible approach to impregnation. She viewed kids as a gift to receive rather than a product to design. So she refused the common practice of screening out genetically defective embryos and letting a doctor implant the best and brightest. While Julia would no longer think of calling Angie a breeder, her friend fit the label.

"Listen, Troy, I want to give you children. I really do. But I can't imagine myself going that route. Making love is making love. We can do that here or anywhere you like. But making babies belongs in the clinic. I know you admire Kevin and Angie, but the thought of a blind conception scares me."

His shoulders slumped at another lost negotiation.

"I tell you what," she said with forced enthusiasm. "I'll make an appointment with the in vitro selection clinic as soon as we get home. We can start exploring options. OK?"

Troy seemed somewhat heartened by the suggestion as he moved slowly toward the minibar. He looked inside for a moment before retrieving a bottle of water.

"Do you want something?" he asked.

She removed the pillow from her body and spread her arms toward her husband. "Yes I do."

He looked away and opened his bottle to take a sip, suddenly immune to her advance.

"So, do you want to go to the lobby while I—"

"We have a big day tomorrow," he interrupted, passing two fingers across her cheek. "What do you say we get some sleep?"

Julia swallowed back the sting of rejection, trying to own the blame. "Are you sure?"

"I'm sure." He offered an affectionate smile.

She reached for the pillow to cover herself again.

CHAPTER THIRTEEN

Troy settled into the chair located immediately behind Kevin Tolbert's seat at the conference table. He felt at home, as if he had never left his role as intelligence officer and adviser to his friend. It was from this very location that he had fed Kevin talking points and supporting statistics on the day the congressman first introduced the concept of *bright spots* into the congressional vocabulary.

He leaned toward Julia, sitting nervously in the adjoining seat. "All's well," he said with a slight squeeze of her hand.

"So he doesn't mind?"

"Not at all. Kevin explained the situation. Anderson knows you no longer work with RAP Syndicate. You're attending as my wife rather than as journalist Julia Davidson."

"Julia Davidson Simmons," she corrected with a smile.

"Who were you talking to in the hall?" Troy asked.

Julia pointed toward an elegant fortysomething woman seated at the other end of the long conference table. "Trisha Sayers recognized me and made a fuss," she explained. "Wanted to catch up."

"Does she know you've gone over to the dark side?"

Julia laughed. "We only had a few seconds. The topic of marriage didn't come up."

Troy looked toward the clock on the wall: a few minutes before ten. If he knew anything about the host of this meeting, the discussion would start right on time. Brent Anderson, Senator Joshua Franklin's right-hand man, was a stickler for both punctuality and productivity. Troy had come to admire Anderson's efficiency back when he led the austerity coalition toward consensus. They debated and decided on a package of proposals in a matter of weeks, a monumental task that should have taken months. But they had been racing against time. Franklin knew that revised budget projections from the census would create panic in the markets. He wanted to strike quickly to position himself as a proactive leader in the midst of crisis. And while his timing did little to ease the economic collapse, it did propel him even higher in national polls.

Troy sensed that a similar urgency would likely characterize this discussion. Why else would Franklin have insisted that Anderson chair the meeting?

Kevin leaned back in his chair toward Troy, who leaped forward in response to a summoning motion.

"What's up?" Troy asked in a hushed voice.

"Look here." Kevin pointed to a page on the screen embedded in the conference table. "You were right."

Troy read quickly, trying to beat the countdown to meeting launch.

Comeback Coalition
August 2043 Agenda
ITEM A: NEXT Appeal Update (Anderson)
ITEM B: Youth Initiative Expansion Strategies (Florea)
ITEM C: Bright Spots Relaunch Proposal (Tolbert)

ITEM D: Projection Adjustments (Journeyman)
ITEM E: Press Relations Strategy (Sayers)
ITEM F: Broad Policy Framework (Anderson)

"Prime placement on the agenda," Kevin said with enthusiasm. "Who'd have thought?"

Troy cleared his throat in mock offense. "A certain former chief of staff would have thought," he jabbed. "I owe you a head-rub for questioning my instinct."

Kevin patted his head protectively as Troy retreated back to his chair.

"I nailed it," he whispered to Julia. "They're taking the bright spot approach much more seriously this round."

"They would have taken it seriously last year if I hadn't written the *Breeders* story," Julia said with regret.

"If you hadn't been assigned to that story you wouldn't be Mrs. Troy Simmons," Troy reminded her. "Besides, the timing is better now."

"How's that?"

"Everyone's nervous about how the NEXT appeal will land. They can't bank on growth in transitions to fund a recovery. A loss for NEXT could turn Kevin into Churchill."

"Winston Churchill? The chubby Brit?"

"The chubby Brit who everyone considered a nagging crackpot until his warnings became their reality."

"Got it. Kevin is the nagging crackpot warning them about trends they don't want to face."

"They'll have no choice but to face them when the transition industry takes a hit."

"*If* it takes a hit," Julia corrected.

"My gut tells me it already has. That's got to be the reason Franklin formed this coalition."

The sound of opening doors drew their eyes to the far end of the conference room, where Brent Anderson entered with an entourage of aides. He took the chair at the head of the table as the others settled into seven of the nine empty chairs that lined the walls.

The assembly complete, Troy looked at each face gathered, to identify potential allies and opponents. He recognized nearly every attendee. Several had served with Kevin on the austerity coalition in 2042. Others had participated in a long series of floor debates defending specific cuts that had been pieced together for a larger proposal. No one had liked the details he or she was defending. But they had no real choice. It was considered political suicide to oppose the only viable plan for preventing an economic free fall. In the end even liberals joined the fiscal conservatives, holding their noses while voting for what became commonly labeled the Franklin Austerity Plan. With his eye on the White House, Franklin now hoped to make another strategic move.

"Franklin's Comeback Plan," Troy whispered.

Julia eyed him inquisitively.

"That's what they'll call it," he continued. "They'll call whatever comes out of this dialogue Franklin's Comeback Plan. Ten to one says he'll use it as his calling card for the 2044 campaign. No politician wants to be known for cuts. He wants to offer a positive plan to rebuild the economy."

Troy hushed himself as Brent Anderson launched the meeting.

"I'd like to begin by thanking everyone for accepting Senator Franklin's invitation to participate on the comeback coalition," Anderson began. "As you no doubt read in the advance briefing I sent last Thursday, we've been asked to craft a viable strategy our party can rally around to restore this nation's economy back toward some semblance of health."

Troy typed and sent a note to Kevin's screen.

RESTORE HEALTH? MORE LIKE RAISE THE DEAD!

Kevin nodded slightly in inconspicuous agreement.

"The few of you who served on the austerity coalition last year," Troy heard Anderson continue, "will be familiar with the process I intend to use for this assignment that, I hope, will help us move quickly through what could otherwise become a daunting agenda. We must discuss very important and complicated matters in short order. Not an easy task. But it can be done if you will allow me to enforce a few simple rules of order."

Troy remembered the process well. Each agenda item would begin with a fifteen-minute fast-fire presentation followed by another fifteen for questions to clarify or enhance rather than debate. Anderson would have already leveraged his tough-minded tenacity to cull through the clutter of a million possible options to find the most promising ideas. He was the master of keeping committees focused on productive ends rather than wasting time on grandstanding or speculation about what might or even should be done. Under Anderson's direction this coalition would discuss only those items that met three simple criteria.

1. Was easy to explain in a sound bite.
2. Had solid data showing it would work.
3. Served Franklin's political agenda.

Kevin's backstage efforts to sell the idea of resurrecting the Bright Spots proposal must have convinced Anderson it satisfied all three.

"As the first item on the agenda suggests, we'll explore comeback options in anticipation of the decision scheduled to come out of the Tenth Circuit a few weeks from now. Senator Franklin has asked that we craft a proposal that can play well regardless of where things land on the NEXT appeal."

"Early indications?" asked Trisha Sayers, seated to Anderson's immediate right.

"Could go either way. Judge Coates leans for and Judge Howatch against. That makes Santiago the deciding vote. He has no track record of similar cases so we have no idea where he'll come down."

"Who appointed him?" came a question from the other side of the table.

"Obama."

"Must be an old bugger," someone said.

"Over thirty years on the bench," Anderson replied.

"Not good," added Sayers. "The older demographic leans against the Youth Initiative."

"By a two percent margin," Anderson responded. "A practically even split. Like I said, we have no idea where he'll land. That's why we need a plan that assumes either possibility. Remember, even if NEXT wins the appeal the case could go higher."

"The Supreme Court?" someone said. "They'll never accept the case."

Troy moved his head to get a better look at who had made the comment. Congresswoman Nicole Florea of Nevada.

"Why do you say that?" Kevin asked.

"It's a wrongful death case alleging inadequate approval measures." Her tone betrayed irritation at Kevin's question as well as his presence in the room. "Hardly worthy of our highest court's attention."

"I disagree." The comment came from a disheveled-looking gentleman leaning forward in his chair. "The NEXT case has major implications for the entire industry and the president's signature initiative. Every new hurdle people are required to jump creates a corresponding drop in transition volunteers. Hundreds of billions of dollars are at stake. I think the court will want a say on whether—"

"Rather than waste time in speculation," Anderson interrupted, "I'd like to ask each of you to read the executive briefing on the NEXT case after the meeting. It should arrive in your inboxes momentarily. Now, I'd like us to move on to the second item on the agenda. Nicole."

DID SHE BRING THE WITCH'S BROOM? Troy typed to Kevin, prompting a gently scolding slap from Julia.

"Stop it," she whispered. "Let him concentrate."

Troy leaned toward Julia to explain but decided he could defend his tactics after the meeting. Part of his role had always been to help Kevin keep things light. While his friend had an impressive mind, it was Congressman Tolbert's beguiling charm that usually won the day. An occasional quip deflected rising tensions and might help his performance during the Bright Spots portion of the agenda.

Nicole Florea had already thanked the committee for the opportunity to speak when Troy received a printed copy of her briefing delivered by a young man the congresswoman must have hired for front office décor. Printed pages meant it contained highly confidential information. The same young man would likely collect and shred the handouts after the presentation.

Florea burned five of her fifteen minutes reliving her glory days as leader of the Western States Conservative Coalition. She took credit for garnering the support necessary to help President Lowman pass the Youth Initiative over what she labeled the "sentimental qualms" of the religious wing of the party. Then she burned another five minutes trying to make the case that any serious attempt to drive an economic comeback required expanding the initiative to recruit a wider circle of volunteers.

Brent Anderson glanced at the clock. "Forgive me for interrupting, Nicole," he said impatiently. "But we have only allocated fifteen minutes. Did you want to explain the details of your proposal before we open up for questions?"

She appeared indignant at the idea that Anderson's rules of order might apply to her, apparently considering her autobiographical self-tribute and policy remix mere preliminaries before the meat of her presentation.

"Well, I did plan to walk us through details of the plan found on page three where I—"

"If I may," Anderson interjected, clearly eager to spare everyone another ten minutes of listening to the obvious. "I suggest you move us right to the bottom of page ten. I'm pretty sure most of us are familiar with the economic trend lines justifying your plan. It might be a better use of time to dive right into details of the proposal."

The redirect flustered the congresswoman more accustomed to giving speeches than to receiving direction. "Yes. Of course," she said, flipping pages of her own copy of the document.

Troy half listened to Nicole Florea's clumsy explanation while his eyes scanned ahead to her supposed solution. Kevin would be doing the same. Nothing new. She made yet another call to expand the president's Youth Initiative; to create greater incentives for potential transition volunteers. He had seen the language before. "Greater incentives" meant increased pressure. Make it easier to say yes so it would be harder to say no. America needed more of the elderly and disabled to get with the program. They were, after all, debits. They cost more than they produced. They spent personal wealth on themselves rather than releasing it to the younger, healthier generation. That's why so many had come to label them "selfish parasites" draining rather than fueling the economy by requiring time and attention from otherwise productive workers and entrepreneurs; those who contributed. Those who paid taxes.

Troy looked up from the page to cringe at the congresswoman's efforts to sell financial projections she clearly didn't understand. "So as you can see, a mere five percent volunteer rate among unproductive segments of the economy during the next three years will dramatically reduce the deficit while stimulating private sector growth."

Troy did the math. Depending upon where you drew the line between "productive" and "unproductive," 5 percent could mean between four and eight million new transitions on top of the roughly five million since the Youth Initiative began.

Kevin's daughter clearly fit within the "unproductive" classification. Little Leah would never live an independent life. She might always require care, placing her at the top of Nicole Florea's list of fitting volunteers for a simple procedure at one of the many conveniently located NEXT transition clinics.

Troy noticed a rising crimson hue on Kevin's neck.

So much for helping my friend keep things light, he thought.

CHAPTER FOURTEEN

"Any additional questions before we move to the next proposal?"

Brent Anderson appeared eager to get Nicole Florea back to her seat. Her presentation had run ten minutes longer than allocated.

"Good," he said before anyone could reply. "Congressman Tolbert."

Kevin finally had the floor.

"He still looks upset," Julia whispered to her husband.

A slight nod told her Troy agreed.

Kevin had managed to hold his tongue during the entire presentation. He had even resisted the urge to point out glaring mistakes in the projections. He must have needed the time to will himself calm. At least as calm as could be expected from a man listening to someone disparage his daughter's existence along with eight million other "unproductive" lives.

"Thank you, Mr. Anderson," he began after taking the kind of breath Troy recognized from their high school soccer days. His friend was determined to score. "Rather than review every de-

tail in the briefing we just forwarded to your tablets I'll simply
state the bottom line and invite questions."

Anderson chuckled at the jab against the long-winded Florea.

"You can review the charts on page six to see two trend lines
that, on the surface, will seem counterintuitive," Kevin continued. "But I can assure you, the data is solid."

Two dozen hands began swiping their tablet screens to find
the page.

"The first graph shows the economic trend lines we've all
been reviewing with dismay these past few years with a deepening free fall over the past twelve months. Despite the brief
flattening immediately after instituting the austerity measures
approved in January, the month-to-month spiral shows no sign
of slowing.

"The second chart, the one labeled 'Bright Spots,' shows a
stark contrast. Most of the lines have been moving steadily in
the other direction during the same period."

"Bright spots?" The question came from a voice Troy didn't
recognize.

"That's what we call the communities showing sustained
growth."

Anderson interrupted to suggest Kevin give a brief recap of
the concept "for those who weren't part of the austerity coalition."

Troy smiled in admiration of a vintage Kevin Tolbert tactic.
Keeping it short so they ask for more works better than droning
on until they glance at their watches.

"If you insist," Kevin said. "We took the concept from a case
I studied back in grad school. About fifty years ago a nonprofit
group was given six months to solve child malnourishment in
poor Vietnamese villages. A crazy deadline, since experts had
identified a complex range of systemic problems intertwining to
cause the epidemic. One guy cut through the complexity that

had been paralyzing the experts. He asked what the mothers of the few healthy kids were doing differently from everyone else in the village. He figured if some kids thrive despite identical poverty, then there might be hope for the other kids. To make a long process short, they discovered a few simple habits among those families that made a huge difference."

"Give an example," Anderson said.

"Well, the mothers of the healthy kids divided daily rations into four small meals instead of two larger meals. They also snubbed cultural norms by feeding their kids foods widely considered low-class."

Anderson jumped in to add the punch line. "The relief agency called those families *bright spots* and used their success as a model for large-scale solutions."

Kevin stood silently as the eyes in the room shifted toward the front. Brent Anderson appeared embarrassed by his own outburst, which betrayed enthusiasm for Kevin's proposal.

"That's right," Kevin said with increased confidence. "And we did the same. We culled the data to find common characteristics among economic bright spots in this country. Every region has suffered the same downward pressures. But some seem to fare much better than others. We wanted to know what makes the difference and whether those differences can be encouraged elsewhere."

"And?" asked another voice. All eyes were back on Kevin.

"As the detail on page eight explains, these pockets of economic stability and growth match areas with the highest rates of fertility and the lowest percentage of transition volunteers."

"I thought we dealt with this nonsense last year," came an objection from the woman seated to Anderson's right.

"Please, Trisha," Anderson said, raising a hushing hand. "I'd like us to hold reactions and questions until Mr. Tolbert has finished explaining his proposal."

With a delegating gesture from their host Kevin picked up where he had left off.

"As these charts show, I propose that we find ways to incentivize growth. Look closely at the breakout on page seven labeled 'Dark Zones' and you'll see why expanding the Youth Initiative as Congresswoman Florea recommends would add to the long-term problem. Any short-term savings we might glean will only intensify the downward spiral. Ask any first-year MBA student worth his salt and he'll say a business can't just cut its way into prosperity. It must drive new innovation and reach new markets. The same is true on a national scale. Our nation can't transition... no, *kill* its way into health."

Nicole Florea shot to the edge of her seat, clearly aghast at Kevin's unnuanced word selection. But she said nothing. She just leered quietly while Kevin summarized his proposal three minutes ahead of schedule.

"In short," he said, "our economic woes stem from these dark zones. That's why we need more bright spots like those shown in the first graph. We need to make it easier for young people to marry and raise children and foster a society that welcomes the wisdom and support of our elderly rather than pressures them toward the grave. Take a long, hard look at the numbers, ladies and gentlemen. Our problem is not that we have too many old and disabled. Our problem is that we have too few young and healthy."

The room fell silent. Troy's eyes raced from one face to the next, trying to gauge reactions. He guessed a third might be modestly warm to Kevin's rationale. The rest looked like cougars frozen in position, awaiting Anderson's permission to pounce.

Which they did.

The next fifteen minutes brought a barrage of thrashing claws in Kevin's direction, each masked as appeals for more realistic, sensible strategies than the one presented by the young congressman from Colorado.

How would the Treasury Department absorb the massive hit if, as Kevin seemed to suggest, Congress made it harder for people to transition? The Youth Initiative had generated a trillion dollars in entitlement spending savings to date. The present budget assumed another two trillion over ten years. Where would those savings go if Grandma and Grandpa Citizen suddenly decided to stick around for another decade?

And even if committee members trusted the bright spots data, which few did, how could they advocate the notion of the federal government calling parenthood preferable to childlessness? That was a lead balloon that couldn't possibly pass Congress or be sold to the public. Dead on arrival.

But the cruelest swipe of all, the one that made all others seem tame, came from Trisha Sayers, when she asked a question so ugly it was hard to believe it had come from such a lovely mouth. The supermodel-turned-fashion-industry-tycoon might have retained her glamorous beauty despite the dog-eat-dog battles of business and politics, but she had apparently lost all tact.

"Excuse me?" Kevin asked across the table.

"I asked whether this isn't some sort of personal therapy," Trisha repeated, this time with less humor in her voice.

"Ms. Sayers," Brent Anderson said in an effort to intercept the confrontation. "There's no need to—"

"It's all right," Kevin said. "I'd like to answer the question if I may."

The tone of his friend's voice brought Troy back to ninth grade at Littleton High School. Kevin had confronted a kid named Eric who had been poking fun at an autistic eleventh grader named Edward. Eric had labeled him Ed the Sped.

Anderson paused momentarily. Then he nodded.

Kevin leaned down and swiped his tablet screen to find and

open a different file. He looked toward Troy, who shook his head slowly from side to side, hoping to dissuade his friend from saying something he might regret, then relaxed at Kevin's wink.

"I'm sending a photograph to your tablets now," Kevin began. "For those of you who don't know my family, I'd like to give you a bit of context for Ms. Sayers's question."

Trisha's mocking sneer softened to an embarrassed blush.

"This is my daughter Leah," he continued. "She'll turn two years old in a few months."

Several female attendees sighed in reaction to the child's toothy grin.

"Leah is what Ms. Sayers might call a debit."

"I never—" Trisha began.

"I know you wouldn't use the slang, Ms. Sayers. Nor would Congresswoman Florea. Nor would any of us in this room. But Leah has something called fragile X syndrome. I won't bother you with the details of her prognosis other than to say she will likely have severe intellectual disabilities her entire life. She may never be capable of living on the credit side of the ledger. So I guess that makes her a debit."

"Mr. Tolbert, there's no need to—"

"Please, Mr. Anderson, this will only take what remains of the time you've allotted my presentation."

A reluctant nod.

"I take it from Ms. Sayers's question that she thinks I have been advocating the bright spots idea out of some kind of guilt complex."

Trisha said nothing but gave a half nod of consent.

"You see, Ms. Sayers knows that my wife and I skipped the genetic screening process when we conceived Leah, just as we did with our three healthy kids. And despite her disability, we love and accept her as a gift. I suppose we should view her as defective. But we don't. And yes, we know we will be responsible for her the rest of our lives. We know that one or more of her siblings will accept responsibility for her after we're gone."

Kevin paused to take a sip from the glass of water sweating on the coaster in front of his place at the table. Three others followed suit in nervous solidarity with the successful congressman turned loving dad.

"I can assure you, Ms. Sayers, that I do not bring forward these ideas out of any sort of guilt. Nor do I advocate parenthood because I have more than the sensible one or two kids."

Several joined him in a self-deprecating laugh.

"And I don't show you Leah's picture to gain sympathy for my proposal. If the numbers make sense, vote with me. If they don't, move on."

Julia reached for and took Troy's hand as if anticipating Kevin's next words.

"I show you this picture to illustrate why I believe advocating bright spots will bring light to our darkening situation. With all due respect to Ms. Sayers and the honorable congresswoman from Nevada, those of you who have kids know what I mean when I say parenthood compels different choices than you would otherwise make."

Half of the room, including Brent Anderson, nodded in unison.

"Dads take extra shifts and second jobs. Moms cut coupons and launch home-based businesses. Grandparents buy birthday presents and watch grandkids, providing cheaper and better childcare while giving them something better to do than rot away in retirement villages.

"Take my family as a case in point. How much more do you think my wife and I save now that we have Leah?"

"Don't you mean spend?" asked Anderson.

"I mean save," Kevin explained. "We spend less on the things we would like to do for ourselves in order to invest in a long-term care fund for Leah. My colleague and I are in the process of buying another business I hope will create an income stream to cover my daughter's long-term needs."

Troy felt Julia look in his direction.

"Believe me. My love for Leah will motivate me to do everything I can to grow that business. And if the business grows, it will hire more workers. And if we hire more workers... well... you know the rest.

"Ladies and gentlemen, when we encourage bright spots we tap the most powerful natural resource on the planet. Families, not governments or businesses, motivate hard work and innovation, frugality and investment. They also provide the social safety net government can no longer afford."

"Trying to buy another business?" Troy heard Julia whisper. "Is that why you've been feeling so stressed?"

Troy raised a single finger to his lips as he strained to hear Kevin's final comment.

"But I've said enough. You can review the numbers for yourselves. All I ask you to do is open your minds to positive strategies that will spur growth rather than settling for defensive measures you think will diminish losses. Thank you for listening."

—◆—

Brent Anderson appeared relieved as he received the handoff to regain control of the meeting. He also seemed pleased, as if he had secretly hoped Kevin would win the day.

Troy leaned forward as Kevin retook his seat. He pretended to pass a note as an excuse to offer his friend an affirming squeeze on the shoulder.

"You made us proud, Mr. Congressman," he whispered.

Kevin's nod seemed appreciative, if unconvinced.

The next agenda item burned about ten minutes in reviewing the impact of a slight decline in transition volunteers. The wrongful death decision against NEXT, Paul Journeyman explained, had prompted extreme caution in the industry. Every transition provider in the country had suddenly started requesting what no law required, co-approval by a neutral party. The seemingly commonsense safeguard added one more hurdle for nervous volunteers to overcome. So the past year had seen fewer volunteers enroll than any year since the Youth Initiative began in 2036. As a result, higher-than-anticipated senior-care expenses would further drain public coffers while lower-than-projected inheritance capital would flow in the private sector.

"In short," Journeyman summarized, "the uncertainty created by the NEXT case has added tremendous downward pressure."

There were no questions beyond those swirling around Troy's head about faulty assumptions beneath the analysis. He decided he would review the data more closely later.

Trisha Sayers was given fifteen minutes to discuss how they might manage the media when Senator Franklin released the Comeback Coalition's proposals. She described the importance of timing, carefully worded spin, advance access to friends at RAP and Bing Syndicates, and about a dozen other steps she called "smart" and "proactive."

Troy rolled his eyes toward Julia.

"She's good," his wife whispered, to Troy's surprise. "Exactly the approach I would recommend to work the system in Franklin's favor."

An idea popped into Troy's head that he tucked away for later.

Anderson suggested a short break in an uncharacteristic show of mercy. Half the group hurried out to find a restroom. The other half, including Anderson, found isolated spots to make calls.

Kevin approached Troy and Julia. "Well?"

"You did great," Julia said with enthusiasm.

He smiled gratefully in her direction before looking Troy in the eyes. "Give me the body language numbers."

"I figure about a third are with you," Troy began. "But Anderson is one of them, so I'd call it about even."

"You think?" Kevin said with a trace of optimism.

"I'd bet your golden locks he's on the phone with Franklin right now for approval to railroad your proposal into the final plan."

"Not likely."

"Very likely," Troy argued. "Didn't you hear what Journeyman said about the decline in transitions?"

"I did. Good news from our perspective."

"It is. But it's also a mandate to find alternative solutions."

"A mandate from?" Kevin asked.

"A mandate from Franklin. Surely he's known about those numbers for weeks. He must have assembled this coalition because he anticipates trouble."

"What kind of trouble?" Julia asked.

"If NEXT wins the appeal you know Franklin will push full steam ahead on Nicole Florea's proposal."

Kevin gave a nod of annoyed agreement.

"But if NEXT loses…"

"He'll hold a press conference to pitch an alternative plan," Julia interjected.

"Exactly," Troy said to punctuate his wife's intuition.

"But two-thirds of this coalition want to throw me and my proposal out of the room," Kevin reminded him.

"Which is why I seriously doubt Anderson plans to call for a vote."

All three sets of eyes looked toward the front of the room. They saw Brent Anderson nodding into his phone in deferential agreement with, Troy presumed, a direct order from Senator Josh Franklin.

CHAPTER FIFTEEN

Irritation clawed up Tyler's spine at the man's voice calling from downstairs. Renee had roped Tyler into "keeping an eye" on her father while she took her mother to a follow-up appointment, "just for an hour or two." The moment she was out the door, he locked himself in his office—no, make that his new bedroom-slash-office-slash-closet space.

"Tyler?" Gerry called again.

Tyler squeezed out from between the desk and the wall and trotted down the steps, dismayed to find a stark-naked old man dripping water all over the floor.

"Geez, Gerry!" Tyler exclaimed, averting his gaze to his now-sopping carpet.

"I can't find any towels. Do you have any towels?"

"Did you try under the sink?"

Gerry pondered for a moment, then shook his head, splattering the walls like a wet dog.

Tyler nabbed a dishtowel from the kitchen and tossed it at his...well, what was he? Not father-in-law. No relation in any way whatsoever, and here Tyler was, being subjected to—this! "Use that in the meantime. And cover up, for Pete's sake," Tyler said.

Gerry smiled, then began drying off his hair.

"Listen, Gerry," Tyler said. "I've got a lot of work to do. So why don't you go put on some clothes and watch television or something."

A few minutes later Tyler was back at his desk, banging his head against the wall behind him in frustration before typing in his next search.

NEXT TRANSITION APPEAL.

A whole slew of search results popped up, although most were variations of the same. Antonio Santos's mother had died accidentally in a NEXT facility during Antonio's transition—trying to stop him, since he was, apparently, a minor at the time he volunteered. Jeremy Santos, Antonio's brother, filed a wrongful death suit and won. NEXT appealed, and now the case sat pending.

"With Santiago," Tyler murmured to himself.

He scrolled to the next article. Second verse same as the first. Then a third, and fourth. Nothing useful other than what he already knew—until he found Julia Davidson, RAP Syndicate. The name rang a bell. He poked at the title.

Jackpot! It appeared Ms. Davidson had already done a lot of legwork on this case, including an interview with Jeremy Santos, as well as the transition specialist involved. That could be interesting.

Name withheld on condition of anonymity.

Tyler swore under his breath. Still, a lot here, including connections to the government's Youth Initiative with potentially billions of dollars on the line. This case might actually be even larger than he had first believed. Jennifer McKay had already suggested Jeremy and NEXT as the most likely suspects to have written the letters. But there was a whole industry involved.

For now, however, the conspiracy theories would have to wait.

Back to Julia Davidson. He pulled up his Privacy Search account and found all her personal information, including direct contact accounts for both phone and messaging. For a few hundred bucks a year he had access to more private information than he could ever have accessed legally on the force. Everyone was afraid of the government butting into their lives where it didn't belong, but no one seemed to mind revealing anything and everything about themselves to the civilian population through cell phone records, social media, and the rest. Security scanners now knew and could report when someone walked into a store, what he bought, and in what size, all in the name of "targeted marketing" and "price reductions."

As for Julia, she was apparently married now with a different last name, and as luck would have it, living right here in the Denver area. He clicked the ESTABLISH CALL button and waited as the other end rang. With any luck he could meet with her today to learn everything she knew about the Santos case.

Less than thirty seconds later her auto response came back indicating she would be unavailable until after the weekend. No way to know whether she was actually gone or screening requests. He left a message indicating his desire to meet.

Julia Davidson would have to wait, which put Jeremy Santos on deck. Tyler looked up his info and placed the call.

"Hello?" the voice answered on the other end.

Within five minutes he had set up a meeting with Jeremy for that afternoon. Tyler glanced at the time, then grabbed his keys and headed downstairs, ready to escape the very moment Renee returned. She gave Tyler the evil eye in reaction to finding her father watching some old war movie in nothing but his underwear.

—⁓—

Tyler hadn't expected to find Jeremy living in such a run-down apartment complex. Then he remembered. Winning an enormous case doesn't translate into cold, hard cash until after you survive the string of appeals. Jeremy's sofa was threadbare. The rest of the décor? Deteriorating bits and pieces showing neither a girlfriend's nor a mother's touch. The kid appeared broke, alone, and into who knew what kind of trouble.

Did desperate need motivate desperate measures? Tyler wondered as he fingered the threatening letters.

"Sorry about the mess," Jeremy said, indicating the piled-up dishes strewn around the room. "Haven't had much time to clean up lately."

"Working a lot?"

A nod. "Making a buck more than minimum wage." A shrug. "It pays the bills." A pause. "Barely."

Tyler smiled encouragingly, unsure if Jeremy's final statement was meant to inspire levity or compassion. "I read Ms. Davidson's article about the NEXT case," he said. "And I know about the ongoing appeal. I'm confused about something, though."

"Shoot." Jeremy tossed the bangs from his eyes. He appeared unkempt, like someone wearily trying to find his way in life. Stuck in post-adolescence.

"I thought it was a wrongful death case."

"That's right."

"So, why haven't you at least received your"—Tyler hesitated, unsure of the correct wording—"inheritance?"

Jeremy laughed weakly, then gestured a wilted hand across the room. "You're lookin' at it."

"So, you got very little from your mother and brother's estate?"

Jeremy looked around with a sigh. "Less than little."

"I hope you don't mind me saying, but this appeal has to be pretty important to you, to your future. Financially speaking."

"You could say that. At the moment, I'm on a fast track to nowhere. I essentially work to live. Although I was able to pay for exactly two classes at Denver Community College. Passed both of them."

"Congratulations," Tyler said with a smile. "Any friends?"

"Nah. I burned through my few friends when I was still angry about what was happening to Antonio. Or more like what *wasn't* happening with me because of Antonio."

"Family?"

"I've got a dad. Somewhere. Maybe. Who knows? Other than that, I've got no one. Not even a girl." He laughed, uncomfortably.

Tyler pulled out the letters and spread them across the coffee table. "Have you seen any of these?"

Jeremy slid one close, glanced it over, then shook his head, his expression turning to one of concern. "No, I haven't. But...where did you get these? Are they for real?"

"Are you sure? Do you recognize the writing, maybe?"

He shook his head again, then locked his gaze on Tyler. "Wait a minute. You think I wrote these?"

Tyler shrugged, figuring there was little point in not being honest. "I don't know what to think. I'm still trying to investigate this whole mess. But the fact is, you're prime suspect number one. Let's face it, until this appeal is over, you're living in squalor. So I have to ask: did you write these letters?"

"No!" Jeremy shouted defensively. "Absolutely not!"

Tyler closely watched Jeremy's eyes, the poor man's lie detector. This was the moment of truth for a quick and easy investigation. *Bam, case closed.*

No such luck.

Jeremy returned Tyler's stare.

Both men realized the question of Jeremy's innocence had been resolved.

"Listen, kid," Tyler said, "as much as I'd like to discover who wrote these letters, I imagine you'll want to find out even more."

Jeremy settled back into his chair, nervously running his fingers through his hair. "It's got to be NEXT."

Tyler waited.

"They're trying to derail Judge Santiago's decision. They must think they're gonna lose the appeal. Oh man, this is intense."

Jeremy stood and walked toward the tiny kitchen. He came right back and sat. "What if these threats work? I can't keep going on like this. Hoping this whole thing will eventually end gets me through right now."

"I understand," Tyler said sympathetically. "It must be hard, having lost both your mother and your brother on the same day."

Was this going to turn into a counseling session? Years of holding weepy clients' hands had qualified Tyler more than he cared to admit. He'd consoled countless lovers through grief over cheaters. Was a death, or even two deaths, any different? Reassuring the boy might be as simple as inviting him to open up and talk about...his feelings.

"What was it like?"

Jeremy continued staring as if trying to decipher an algebra problem.

"Son," Tyler said more loudly.

"Sorry?"

"I asked what it was like. You know, losing them both so suddenly?"

Jeremy looked deeply into Tyler's eyes as if trying to gauge the stranger's heart. Then he stood again, this time walking toward the bedroom. He returned carrying a tablet. He placed it on the coffee table in front of Tyler's seat. "Watch this."

An icon labeled SANTOS BODIES awaited Tyler's initiating tap.

A video commenced playing. He realized immediately what it was. He had recorded countless others himself while investigating murder scenes. Someone had made a video record of the bodies in hopes of identifying clues to what had actually occurred on the day Jeremy's brother and mother died.

The first image was a small sign outside of what appeared to be a medical office complex. The large print read NEW DAY TRANSITION CENTER. Much smaller letters beneath said A SUBSIDIARY OF NEXT INC. just above an address, a contact code, and office hours.

A quick blink of the screen brought Tyler into a room containing about two dozen chairs and a few end tables with stacks of cheap tablets, the kind dentists and hospitals made available to occupy waiting patients.

"This is the reception area where Ms. Santos would have been sitting with Antonio before his procedure?" Tyler didn't recognize the voice. Female. Most likely a videographer contracted by the police department to document the scene.

A long silence followed as the woman awaited an answer to her question. The camera shifted, focusing on a slumping male form offering a silent nod in reply. Jeremy, twenty-four months earlier. He looked pale and shaken.

"Were you waiting with them?"

"No, ma'am," he said weakly.

Another blink and a new image. A narrow hallway with a series of doors bearing tiny signs indicating TRANSITION ROOM #1, TRANSITION ROOM #2, and so on. They stopped at room number four, where the woman invited Jeremy to step in front of the camera and open the door.

"Do you really need me to go back in?" he asked. "I already identified Mom's...I mean...I already identified the victim bodies. And I told the police officer everything I know. Can't you record without me in there?"

"I'm sorry, son," the woman said in a frail attempt to sound sympathetic. "But I don't have the authority to change the assignment. You'll be fine." She spoke like a woman who had grown callous to human loss, a hazard of her line of work. Get in, record the facts, and move on to the next case in your queue. Tyler remembered fighting the same tendency after being assigned to the homicide division.

"Can you call someone?"

"Not at this hour," the woman replied.

Tyler noticed a small time stamp in the bottom left corner of the shot:

[7:37 PM—AUGUST 17, 2041]

Less than five hours after Jeremy lost the two most important people in his life.

Tyler saw Jeremy's back obscure the scene. Then Jeremy opened the door inward, the camera following closely behind until he stepped out of the way.

The woman's voice assumed a more official diction, like that of a news anchor reporting live from the scene. "We've entered the room where Antonio Santos and his mother Sylvia Santos died within minutes of one another at approximately three o'clock mountain time."

The screen zoomed onto the body of the boy, starting with his face. All color had drained from the lips, cheeks, and ears. Tyler recognized the familiar, vacant stare of death.

"This is the cadaver of the late Antonio Santos, his body identified this afternoon by his biological brother"—the camera moved to Jeremy, his head bowed in awkward reverence—"Jeremy Santos."

The camera lingered for a moment, then returned to the corpse, this time offering a full-body review. A catheter remained unremoved, one end attached to a needle in the boy's arm and the other to an empty plastic pouch, the slight residue of yellow serum still clinging to the bottom of the bag.

That's when Tyler realized he had never actually been inside a transition room, or even a transition clinic. Like everyone else, he knew they existed. He even placed himself in the 68 percent of the population in favor of the president's Youth Initiative. Had probably parroted the common rationale about redeploying scarce resources rather than wasting them caring for debits. He imagined craggy, drooling seniors opting for a merciful release from dementia. An eighteen-year-old boy lying dead on a gurney didn't fit the picture of an industry he had always admired from the safe distance of opinion columns and political speeches.

Neither did the next image to appear on the tablet screen. A pool of drying blood escaping from its source, a woman's skull with matted hair splayed onto the floor and over her lifeless face. An assortment of male and female footprints had spread the dark redness throughout the room, evidence of a flurry of activity immediately following the fall.

"And this," the woman's voice explained, "is the body of Sylvia Santos, identified at three o'clock this afternoon by her biological son, Jeremy Santos."

Another shot of the wilted boy offering the faintest possible nod of confirmation.

"As you can see," the woman said, pointing the camera back toward the floor, "Ms. Santos died shortly after a fall that appears to have crushed the occipital bone on the bottom posterior of her skull. According to an attending nurse who checked for a pulse at three oh-seven, Ms. Santos died within seconds of the injury. That assumption will be confirmed by the coroner in due course."

The camera scanned the full length of the body. Other than signs of the nurse's efforts to confirm death, it appeared no one had touched the body. Few of the crime scenes Tyler had recorded while on the force had been so well preserved. No one had even bothered to reposition Jeremy's mother's legs after her death. They seemed postured to receive a husband, or birth a child. Tyler felt a rare blush at a sight less graceful than a mother would want to appear when identified by her grieving son.

He noticed a scalpel lying beside the woman's open palm. The alleged weapon the distraught mother grabbed at the last second to interrupt Antonio's procedure?

Having seen enough, Tyler tapped the screen to halt the video. "I'm sorry for your loss," he said inadequately.

Jeremy bristled. "I don't need your pity, you know. I'll be fine."

Tyler waited. Eventually Jeremy sighed.

"It was hard," he began. "Not just that day. All of it. You don't realize how incredibly dependent you become on someone depending on *you* until they don't need you anymore."

"Your mother?"

"Antonio."

"I see." Tyler glanced at the time, then sat back in his chair. The boy obviously needed to talk.

"Near the end, every minute of every day, everything revolved around Antonio. Of course, it hadn't always been that way. At first it was just little things. You know, like helping him get from one room to the next when he didn't have his crutches. No big deal.

"Of course, Mom worried about every little thing. I think that's because she could see, even early on, how things would eventually end. Me? I was too self-absorbed to realize that this was only going to get worse over time. And as it did, I'd lose more and more of myself."

"So, you felt bitter toward your brother?" Tyler asked.

"Yes and no. I wasn't bitter at *him*, really. I mean, how could I be? It wasn't like he chose his disease or could do anything to stop it. I mean, what teenaged brother really chooses needing his mommy or his only sibling to wipe his butt for him?"

Tyler thought of Renee's parents. He thought of Gerry dripping water all over his carpet. In some ways it didn't seem so different.

"But I guess I was bitter. What brother wants to do the wiping? It shouldn't have been just me and Mom. It should have been my dad, too. No. It shouldn't have been any of us. But I guess sometimes life deals you a crummy hand.

"Anyhow, eventually I had no life. Just helping take care of my brother. Even when I was at school, I felt guilty that I wasn't there for Antonio. I could barely concentrate. It was ironic, really. Me, the one who had every hope of becoming somebody, of making something of myself...I was the one who started failing. And Antonio, the one who could do less and less almost every day, never ever gave up trying. He was an inspiration, really."

Jeremy paused, choking back emotions. Tyler, however, was confused by his last statement. *An inspiration*? How could a helpless debit be an inspiration? Already, after just a few days, Renee's parents were wearing him down. Wearing both of them down. Renee was too exhausted for sex, and her parents were sucking away any and all free time. Even now Tyler felt the resentment festering.

He thought of Renee's face. Tired as she appeared, he had

never sensed resentment. It was as if she was immune. As if she took pride in caring for her parents.

Tyler saw an echo of the same baffling pride on Jeremy's face, now accompanying the salty puddles of moisture trying to escape the boy's eyelids.

"I'm sorry," Jeremy finally said. "It's just I never told him that. I never told him that he was an amazing brother. Maybe if I had, none of this would have happened."

"I'm sure he knew." Tyler was still trying to comprehend how one drew inspiration from suffering.

Jeremy seemed to read Tyler's mind. "I guess you couldn't understand. Antonio made the most of each day he had. Even when he could barely communicate, when he had to struggle for each and every syllable that came out of his mouth, he would always find a way to make everyone else feel better. He'd tell a joke, or type an encouraging word. Sometimes that's all he could do. One word."

Jeremy wiped the embarrassment from his cheeks with manly verve.

"And I had the audacity to feel sorry for myself," he said with a recovering snort. "I was such an idiot."

"But you have nothing to feel guilty about. I mean, you gave up your life to take care of your brother."

Jeremy shook his head. "No, Mr. Cain. Antonio is the one who gave up his life…for me. Or at least that's what he wanted to do."

"And would have done," Tyler surmised, "if NEXT had accepted the court's verdict."

Jeremy nodded silently while Tyler reached for his own tablet, knowing this investigation had only just begun.

CHAPTER SIXTEEN

"Holy...!" Donny groaned across the room, his voice stretched from an unexpectedly heavy load. "What on earth's in this one?"

Matthew glanced up from disassembling an upturned kitchen table. "Sorry, man. My books. All seven of the boxes in that corner are pretty heavy."

"Books? You have seven boxes of books? Ever hear of a digital reader? They've been around for something like a million years. Don't you think it's time to upgrade?"

"I have a digital reader, wise guy," Matthew said. "Those are collector copies. You know, print classics."

"Whatever," Donny said, rolling his straining eyeballs. "I'll send you the chiropractor bill."

They shared a forced laugh as Donny took his tenth jaunt through the front door toward the small U-Haul trailer latched to the back of Matthew's car.

"You sure that piece of junk is gonna make it all the way to Littleton pulling this load?" Donny teased upon returning.

"You let me worry about that," Matthew replied. "You just worry about trying to find a new guy-flick buddy."

"Already figured that one out," Donny said smugly. "We're gonna meet in the middle, Broomfield Virtual Cinema."

Matthew paused his wrench to glare in Donny's direction. "Broomfield isn't in the middle. That's about fifteen minutes from your place. I'd have to drive through Denver traffic. It would take me at least forty-five."

"I'm not the one moving. You should have to drive farther than me."

"I'm not the one who can't find another friend." Matthew realized it was the first time he had ever used the word to describe their relationship. "You're the pathetic hermit."

"Welcome to the club, buddy."

Matthew winced at the jab, knowing he had lost the banter. It was true that he had joined the club of live-in senior-care workers. He, like Donny, could easily sink in the social quicksand of a job that entailed watching television or scanning porn sites while providing what his employer described as "caring attention for that aging loved one who wishes to remain in the comfort and privacy of his or her own home." Matthew shook the image off by reminding himself the job was temporary. One year. Less if Judge Santiago decided the NEXT appeal as he should.

"Talk to your client yet?" Donny asked.

"In the morning," Matthew replied. "They sent me a keypad code so I could settle in my stuff tonight. They'll bring him over after breakfast."

"Name?"

"I forget." He felt slightly embarrassed by the admission. He remembered Donny's thoughtfulness while caring for Matthew's mother. Donny had always been careful to use her first name. He never called her Ms. Adams or ma'am. Always Janet.

"What's wrong with him?"

"Dunno. I think he's just old and ornery. The daughter said

they put him in a pretty nice senior home but that he keeps offending the residents and staff."

"A dirty old man?"

"Who knows? I guess I'll find out tomorrow."

———

Thirty minutes later they loaded the final piece of furniture into the trailer. Donny followed in his car as the two drove the hour to Matthew's new temporary residence. Turning east off Santa Fe Drive onto Church Avenue, Matthew saw the familiar campus of Arapahoe Community College, the one his favorite high school academic counselor had said Matthew should attend. A good idea in retrospect, since he could have completed his freshman and sophomore years with little hassle or expense. But the suggestion had offended him at the time. Way beneath his aspirations, even if fitting for his grade point average.

Turning left onto South Curtice Street he watched the campus shrink in the side-view mirror. Two hundred yards later a dashboard voice announced his arrival at the intended destination.

"What a dump!" Donny said as he folded his arms across his chest while leaning against the hood of his car.

It was. Brownish strands of thirsty grass had succumbed to invading weeds now claiming territorial rights. Faded mulch infested with stringy, naked vines filled flowerbeds that might have once displayed annual and perennial colors. Part of the gutter above the dented garage door hung loose. The exterior paint, a deep green that had been quite popular two decades earlier, offered glimpses of wood siding that should have been replaced back in the mid-twenties.

"Home sweet home," Matthew said with a sigh. "For now, anyway."

After tapping the keypad code Matthew eased the front door open like a man worried about waking a sleeping child. But the house was empty. His client had been away for months. The HOUSE FOR SALE sign leaned against the wall just beneath the entryway light switch, remnant of an abandoned plan A. According to the job notice, the old man was leaving a senior center to move back into his own home the following morning.

"What's that awful smell?" Donny muttered, holding his nose.

"Whew! Something must've died." Matthew opened both front windows to invite fresh air into the room. "The guy's daughter said she checked on the place every couple of weeks."

"Well she hasn't checked lately."

They spent the next ten minutes searching for the source of the foul odor. A small stream of dark blood on the kitchen floor led them to a jellifying rat hidden behind the refrigerator, an apparent victim of the small mousetrap still clinging to a rear claw.

"Must have tried dragging itself to shelter," Donny surmised. "Not a good omen for you, my man!"

Two hours later a dusk-lit breeze blew away much of the smell while the two men emptied the U-Haul trailer of the few belongings Matthew had decided to keep. The furniture, appliances, and decorations had met his mom's needs while she was alive. Now they entombed her memory. Matthew had decided to give most of them to charity.

"What do you say we order a pizza?" Donny said, looking up from a horizontal posture on the floor. "I'm starved and exhausted."

Matthew scanned the room to confirm the job had been accomplished. His new pillow sat on top of a floral bedspread that must have belonged to his client's daughter when she was a teenager. Beneath that was a mattress he feared would further stress his already aching back. But buying a new bed was out of the question, since he intended to save every penny possible to pay down his loan. Whether the inheritance money came or not, he had no intention of making live-in senior care a long-term career.

His books sat stacked along the wall that would have to double as a shelf. Most of his clothes hung on a dozen hangers in the closet or had been folded and placed in two open drawers. The rest of his belongings remained in a large box labeled "miscellaneous" on top of a dresser, where Donny had placed it compliantly.

"I guess I've gotten enough work out of you for one day," Matthew said with a grateful smile. "You've earned a meal."

Donny raised his head from the floor. "And a movie?"

"Can't," Matthew replied. "I need to shower and take care of a few things tonight and then get a good night's sleep. Gotta rest up. You know, first impressions and all."

"Do I ever," Donny said with a reluctant push against the floor. "And you might want to learn your client's name before he arrives in the morning."

"Good tip," said Matthew.

As Donny pulled away from the house, Matthew offered a single wave before clearing the empty pizza box and soda cans from the porch. They had decided to eat outside rather than defile the scent of pepperoni with the lingering stench of rat decay.

He showered away the grime of heavy lifting in the August heat, then moved into the front room to try enjoying his last evening alone by settling into what must have been the old man's favorite chair before the daughter moved him into an assisted living facility. Beside the chair was a small table on which sat a familiar icon. His mother had kept something similar beside her favorite chair. But her cross had been attached to rosary beads; this cross appeared on the cover of a book. Matthew flipped to the title page.

THE HOLY BIBLE
AUTHORIZED KING JAMES VERSION

He turned the book on its side and noticed dozens of dog-eared and worn pages in the last third. The Bible appeared quite old, possibly even from the glory days of early-twentieth-century publishing. Matthew recognized it as a leather-bound classic like one he had removed from the box Donny had complained most about carrying. Probably a collectible more valuable than the old man realized. Certainly too valuable to leave lying around in an empty house.

Matthew closed the Bible and placed it back on the table with gentle care, then tapped his tablet awake to find something that might distract him from a sinking feeling that had engulfed much of his day.

One message appeared. He glanced at the sender's name. It jolted him out of despondency.

Hi there!

OK. Your last message piqued my interest. I even went to the school annual to find your name. No A. Manichean listed. I assume you're using a handle. Here's the deal. We can meet on one condition. Send me your real name and a current picture, which is only fair since you seem to have been ogling my pictures for some time! (I'm glad you like them, by the way.) Then we can set a date. I get to pick the place. You get to pick up the check!

Your turn,
Maria Davidson

Matthew stood while rereading the note for a second opinion. After validating his good fortune he realized that he was standing. He sat back down to shoot back what he hoped would be a cleverly perfect reply. Before he could type a single word, however, he felt a slight panic. Did he even have a picture to send besides his license and student ID photos? He could shave and dress to take a shot with his tablet camera. But he felt like a goof when taking his own picture, and it always showed.

He quickly tapped his FAVORITES folder. He found several saved images of Maria and about a dozen other smiling beauties, but nothing of himself. He cursed. Then he remembered adding a headshot to his social network site about three years earlier. Two taps on the screen brought him to his home page. He smiled at the satisfactory image. But there was too much hair on his head. Maria would immediately peg him as insincere for posting such an outdated shot. He quickly replaced it with one of the stock cartoon images people used to conceal their own faces.

He considered sending a reply with no picture. But he didn't want to risk refusal, banishing him to the eternal torture of what might have been.

The seed of an idea rescued Matthew from total defeat. He set the tablet aside and walked to the bedroom to search through the unopened box filled with last-minute junk. Two minutes later he found what he'd hoped hadn't been discarded. Charles Kohl had taken a picture on the day of his mother's transition. He looked at his own face first. Not bad. Modest digital doctoring might even make him look ruggedly handsome. A relief!

Then he looked at the other face. He had never really examined it before. The photo had been hidden away in a drawer since the day it fell out of the envelope containing a thank-you note from Aspen House, which had included the picture as a memento of his mother's heroic choice. He saw it as a reminder of the burden he had borne and didn't care to recall.

Her eyes were more downcast than he remembered. Matthew had worked hard to make it a special day, to avoid any hint of what was really happening. He had told her they were visiting Aspen House so she could spend more time with the nice gentleman they had met earlier. A date, not an appointment. A chat, not a procedure. But the eyes staring at him through the photo now seemed to tell a truth he had refused to consider.

"I knew, Son. Sure, I went along. But I knew."

Matthew felt his hand start to tremble. He forced his gaze away from hers, then flipped the photo over. He walked to the living room, where he placed it on his tablet's scanner. Dragging the image into a photo-editing application, he isolated his own face. Moments later it looked like the kind of man he hoped Maria would want to meet, but enough like him to appear genuine.

He attached the picture to a note he decided to keep short but sweet.

Hi Maria:
  Here you go. I'll be in town this week. What do you say?

Matthew Adams

CHAPTER SEVENTEEN

The stream of unwelcome light inched its way across Matthew's eyelids but failed to rouse him, his aching lump clinging to the much needed haven of slumber. It was a different interruption that finally forced motion, the creaking swing of the door hinge followed by a gentle thump and high-pitched breathing. Someone had entered his room.

Matthew rolled over with great effort. He opened one eye, then the other. To his disorienting surprise he saw a ponytailed intruder sitting Indian-style beside his bed, looking up at his disheveled head with childlike wonder.

"Hello sir," she said, extending a hand and standing. "I'm Isabelle Gale. What's your name?" She looked no more than five or six years old. Her cheeks retained a pudgy cuteness left over from toddlerhood. But her mannered diction gave off an air of confident authority, like that of the de facto leader of her kindergarten reading circle.

Maneuvering his aching back and stiff legs, Matthew managed to achieve a sitting position on the edge of the bed.

"Matthew," he answered over the sandpaper sounds of a chin-scratch. "Matthew Adams." He cleared his throat of morning phlegm before accepting her offered hand. "Pleased to meet you, Miss Gale."

She giggled. Whether at the respectful title or Matthew's disheveled appearance was unclear.

Out of the corner of Matthew's eye he noticed movement near the foot of the bed. He turned to see a small forehead peering over the rumpled pile of blankets spilling off the edge onto the floor.

"And who's this?" he asked.

"That's Peter."

"Your little brother?"

"My older brother," Isabelle corrected.

"Really?" Matthew took a second look. Peter appeared timid. No, more than timid. Weak. And frightened.

"Hi there, Peter," he said to calm the boy's qualms. "Nice to meet you."

The boy froze, glaring at Matthew's extended hand as if it were an aimed rifle. Matthew pulled it back.

"He doesn't talk," Isabelle explained.

"How old is Peter?" Matthew didn't know whether to look at the boy or his proxy.

"Six and a half. Same as me. We're twins."

"You don't say."

"I was born two minutes after Peter. That's why Mommy calls him my big brother even though I'm taller by almost an inch."

"I see—" Matthew began before an adult voice interrupted the conversation.

"Isabelle!" Mom appeared flustered, and embarrassed. "I'm so, so sorry. I had no idea they were in here. I'm Marissa, Hugh Gale's daughter. I was distracted helping Dad with his oxygen tank. I apologize if they woke you."

"No worries," Matthew said to allay concern. "I'm Matthew Adams. We were just getting acquainted."

"You two come into the kitchen this instant," Marissa ordered as four little feet scurried obediently.

"Bye, Matthew," Isabelle said from the doorway.

"Mr. Adams," Marissa corrected, prompting another girlish giggle.

—⁓—

Five minutes later Matthew entered the kitchen to find Isabelle and Peter sitting at the counter. A scrumptious aroma told him they were eating some sort of toasted pastry. Both pairs of lips sipped from tiny straws protruding out of half-collapsed apple juice boxes. The table held several bags of groceries patiently awaiting their promotion to the pantry and refrigerator.

"Hi guys. Where's your mom?" Matthew asked.

"In there," Isabelle said after swallowing. She pointed toward the front room. "With Reverend Grandpa."

"Reverend Grandpa?"

"That's what we call him."

"Interesting," Matthew said, moving toward the doorway. He paused to take a deep breath before entering.

Father and daughter sat in silence. Marissa Gale was perched on the edge of the sofa with legs crossed at the ankle, her folded hands resting on her lap in polite impatience. She shot to her feet like a three-tour soldier noticing the arrival of her replacement. "Mr. Adams."

"Call me Matthew," he replied, stepping into the room.

"Matthew then. I don't believe you've met my father."

To Matthew's relief the man appeared modestly robust, his stout frame reclining comfortably in the chair Matthew had occupied twelve hours earlier. Hugh Gale looked more like

a recently retired trucker than the death-courting skeleton
Matthew had imagined. His forearms were particularly impressive, suggesting Hugh Gale had lifted weights in earlier
life. It wasn't until Matthew repositioned himself in front of
the man's seat that he noticed signs of disability: mechanical
braces on his legs and a tiny oxygen tube protruding from his
lower neck.

Matthew extended his hand. "Hello, Hugh. Pleased to meet
you."

The man scowled. "Hugh?"

Matthew looked to the daughter to confirm he had heard the
name correctly. Her eyes said he had, but that he had blundered
nonetheless.

"Did I say you could call me Hugh?"

"Oh, I'm sorry," Matthew backpedaled. "Mr. Gale then."

Another scowl. "Mr. Gale?"

"My father prefers to be called *Reverend*." Marissa appeared
embarrassed by the expectation.

"Reverend Grandpa!" the old man insisted.

Matthew searched the man's face. Was he testing Matthew's
sense of humor or revealing an idiosyncrasy requiring careful
navigation?

"Reverend Grandpa it is then," he decreed good-naturedly.
"But only if you tell me where you got the title."

"I don't negotiate," Reverend Grandpa barked.

"Neither do I," Matthew said without blinking. Then held his
breath.

The man slapped the armrest of his chair with a laugh. "Ha!
I like this kid." A slight wheezing sound overtook his breathing
before he continued. "Take no guff! That's always been my
motto too."

Matthew and the daughter shared a sigh of relief.

"I got the title from little Pete."

"Peter," Marissa corrected. "How many times do I need to tell you, he wants to be called Peter?"

"You want to call him Peter. He prefers little Pete!"

Marissa shook her head. She seemed exasperated, as if she had lost this same argument on countless previous occasions.

"You mean the Peter sitting in the kitchen with Isabelle?" Matthew asked.

"One and the same. My favorite grandson!"

"Do you have other grandkids?"

"No sir," Reverend Grandpa said through a faint chuckle. "Just the twins."

"So he does talk?"

Marissa shot a surprised look at Matthew. "No, he doesn't speak. Hasn't said a word in the three years since his father died. But how did you know about that?"

"Isabelle told me. I'm sorry about your partner...or was it husband?"

"They weren't married," Reverend Grandpa said disapprovingly.

Marissa smiled dismissively at her father's quaint reaction.

"Thank you," she said to Matthew. "We were partners for three years. It was hard. I'm doing fine, but I worry about Peter since—"

"Little Pete will be just fine," Reverend Grandpa interrupted.

Matthew looked back toward his client. "So if he doesn't talk, when did he give you the title?"

The old man raised a hushing finger to his lips, then winked a smile at his new caregiver. Clearly the answer involved some secret grandpa/grandson pact.

"My father was a minister," Marissa explained.

"I'm still a minister!" came the gruff correction.

"A priest?" Matthew wondered aloud. He had never met a Father who was also a dad.

"Heaven forbid! Do you see me wearing a dog collar?" Reverend Grandpa touched the edge of his open-necked shirt. "I'm a Baptist preacher. I rely on this here book. I don't submit to some Roman pope!"

Matthew didn't know much about Baptist preachers, but it sounded as if Reverend Grandpa shared his own aversion to Catholic dogma. "Me neither," he said.

"That's good." The old man caressed the classic Bible Matthew had been admiring the prior evening. "We don't need a bunch of highbrow traditions or creeds. We have the word of God right here in black and white!"

Marissa rolled her eyes. "How about if we hit the pause button right there. I've heard this sermon before. You two can get acquainted later. I need to talk Matthew through instructions and then get Isabelle and Peter to school. I open today, so my shift starts in about an hour."

Reverend Grandpa raised a hand in surrender to his daughter's wishes while she moved toward the kitchen.

"I look forward to talking to you about religion, Reverend Grandpa," Matthew said as he started to trail Marissa. "I've been studying spirituality at college. We can compare notes."

"Anytime, my boy. Anytime."

―――

Matthew helped organize the groceries before joining Marissa at the kitchen table to run through her list of instructions. They quickly covered mundane matters like emergency and doctor phone numbers. Then she told him which foods not to prepare "no matter how much he shouts." He smiled at the daughter's attempts to change the diet of a man who must have spent all eighty-two of his years eating pretty much whatever he liked.

"Got it," Matthew said deferentially.

The most important instructions centered around managing and changing the oxygen tanks she called "vital to his daily survival."

"What happened?" Matthew asked. "I mean, your dad appears to be in pretty good shape. Why so much trouble breathing?"

"He had what should have been a mild heart attack a few years back. The old fool tried driving himself to the hospital. He got into an accident on the way. Ran off the road. No seat belt. His legs slammed into the dash pretty hard."

"I noticed the braces."

"They don't work as well as he had hoped. They help him stand, but he still needs the walker to get anywhere."

"No wheelchair?"

"I put it in the garage. Be warned. He hates it. Only lets us take it to places like the zoo or airport. You know, long-distance uses only. He says it makes him feel like an invalid."

"But he—"

Marissa raised her hand to interrupt. "I know, I know. But being an invalid and seeing yourself as one are two different things. You'll soon find out what I mean."

Matthew nodded, appreciating the heads-up.

"Anyway, the real damage of the accident was pulmonary. The extra strain on his heart from the internal bleeding and the time it took to move him caused some pretty serious damage. His ticker only pumps in first gear now. He needs more oxygen per red blood cell than his lungs can generate."

"Wow."

"That's why he needs someone around most of the time. A few minutes without oxygen and his system will start shutting down."

Matthew looked down at the list of instructions to confirm every detail.

Marissa placed her hand on Matthew's and said, "I want to thank you for accepting this job."

Looking into her eyes, Matthew tried to hide any of the discomfort he felt over the unexpected attention from a woman ten years his senior. Was her touch the affirming pat of a grateful daughter or the suggestive advance of a lonely woman?

"You bet," he said guardedly while trying to think of something to change the subject. "So the senior center didn't work out?"

She removed her hand. "A minor disaster!"

"Why? What happened?"

"In less than a month he had set a facility record for complaints from residents and staff."

"Anything I should know about?"

"You've already had a taste."

"The preacher stuff?"

"He figured God had placed him in the senior facility to rescue every lost soul from eternal damnation."

"I see."

"The straw that broke the camel's back happened last week. Dad decided to pull the fire alarm in the middle of afternoon naps as an illustration of Jesus's second coming."

Matthew flashed a quizzical look. "I don't follow."

"He thinks Jesus is going to blow a trumpet at any moment and come back to redeem his chosen people."

"Ah. So the fire alarm was—?"

"The closest thing he could find to a trumpet in order to wake unsuspecting heathens."

Matthew laughed at the image of Reverend Grandpa watching an unnerved crew of attendants frantically wheel groggy residents into the nursing home parking lot.

"I'll be sure to hide my trumpet."

Marissa joined Matthew's smile at an incident she seemed to

find amusing now that a solution to her father's care had been found. "You'll have your hands full, that's for sure," she said.

"We'll be fine," he said reassuringly. "Now you better get moving. I don't want to make you late for work."

—◦◦◦—

Matthew finally closed the door to his bedroom ten hours later. Other than a few relatively harmless verbal jousts while he served meals to his client and helped him change into his bedclothes, the two hadn't talked much. Reverend Grandpa seemed eager to enjoy his freedom from sterile smells and white walls with the simple pleasures of a good book and a long siesta. So, refusing to become the stereotype, Matthew kept himself busy with a list of self-assigned chores like watering dying grass and familiarizing himself with appliance dials.

As he crawled into bed he felt a surprising sense of usefulness. He'd almost forgotten what it was like to sink into a well-earned sleep after a particularly exhausting day caring for his mother. Despite resenting the work, he had always relished the satisfaction.

Just before turning out the light he remembered that it had been several days since he'd last checked his anonymous forum. He typed in a twelve-character pass-code to access what he hoped would be a thoughtful response from Judge Victor Santiago agreeing to dialogue on the NEXT appeal. But the forum listed no messages.

Then he heard the ping of a new message. He quickly tapped the bouncing icon.

Hi Matt:

I do remember you. And yes, I'd like to meet. How about 10 a.m. Monday at Enchanted Coffee near I-470?
Maria

Matthew stood, clasping his hands tightly together while pacing the tiny space between the bed and closet door. He moved back toward the tablet lying on top of the disheveled covers and reread the message. He spent the next thirty minutes suppressing an overwhelming urge to say a prayer of thanks.

CHAPTER EIGHTEEN

"**Ooh. Let's** pop in here," Angie blurted like a child startled by a candy store. "Their stuff is adorable!"

Julia glanced up at a sign that read TINY THREADS.

"Angie," she protested. "Kevin said to find something for you, not shop for the kids."

Too late. Her friend had already escaped into the treasury of infant and toddler apparel.

The time had been a gift from their husbands, a pleasant surprise since Julia had assumed she would spend the morning at the house with Angie watching the kids. Ricky still had a sniffle Leah seemed eager to mimic, which had killed their plans to dine at Tommy's favorite fast-food playland. A major disappointment since, he complained, McDonald's would soon renovate the space into a "stupid coffee lounge for grown-ups!" Made sense, Julia thought, in light of shifting demographics. But hard on a five-year-old losing his Neverland complete with burgers, shakes, and fries.

"You two go shopping," Kevin had suggested. "Buy yourself something nice. We can work here just as well as at my office."

Angie offered an obligatory refusal until Tommy cheered Uncle Troy's presence as a terrific consolation prize. That's when she gladly accepted.

Part of Julia liked the idea. Troy needed time with Kevin to discuss problems with the business. But he also loved hanging around the kids. Their exhausting demands seemed to charge rather than deplete her husband's batteries. Which worried another part of her.

She reluctantly followed Angie into the store, where she was confronted with the pleasing aroma of baby lotion innocence. Julia positioned herself next to a rack of pink newborn outfits and nervously fingered a pair of tiny booties half the size of the socks she had seen Angie drape over Ricky's pudgy toes. She felt out of place watching Angie scurry from one darling outfit to the next in a continued quest to coordinate Joy and Leah for their upcoming family photo.

Two hours earlier Angie had fled her home in eager anticipation of a morning away from the relentless demands of kids. "I really need the break," she had said. "I wanted to kiss Kevin when he suggested we go." No wonder the fifteen-minute drive to the outdoor mall had turned the car into a confession booth where Angie unloaded a series of hesitant complaints.

"This is the fifth week in a row one of the kids has been sick. I can't remember my last full night of sleep."

"Kevin tries. But he's been too busy to notice that I'm drowning."

"I hate those fund-raising dinners. I still haven't lost the last ten pounds of baby weight. I gave up trying to keep up with the trophy girlfriends."

"We got the results last week. Leah isn't progressing as well as we'd hoped. I cried myself to sleep Thursday night."

"Confidentially, there were days I hoped Kevin would lose his reelection bid."

"Some days I feel utterly alone."

Julia remembered her sister's warning. "You'll end up like Angie...wearing frumpy sweat suits while pushing a double stroller through the neighborhood."

Placing the booties on a nearby display rack, Julia watched Angie move toward the checkout counter. A bit of self-doubt notwithstanding, she was not frumpy in the least. Just a woman needing the kind of pampering a shopping-and-lunch outing might provide; perhaps splurging on a stylish new outfit would make her feel as beautiful as she remained. Yet there she was, cute as a button, standing in line to buy matching dresses for her little girls. How does a woman so eager for a break from Mommyville miss her children only hours after escape?

The sight made Julia aware of her growing unease.

"What do you think?" Angie asked, holding up the purchases.

Anxiety retreated in the glow of her friend's delight. "Perfect," she confirmed with a wink.

Julia heard Kevin's voice coming from Angie's phone.

"Hi, beautiful. Sure would like to talk to you." They were the identical words Troy's voice spoke when he called Julia.

"Is she OK?" Angie asked.

The look on Angie's face told Julia something had happened back at the house. The fingernail between her friend's teeth suggested the possibility of something serious.

"We can leave now if—" Angie paused in reaction to an apparent interruption from Kevin.

"Are you sure?" she asked, her face showing signs of uncertain compliance.

"Joy?" Julia asked when Angie ended the call.

"Leah," she replied with concern.

"Sniffles?"

"Diarrhea."

The word alone seemed to vanquish any baby lotion smell.

Julia frowned at the thought of yet another Mommyville reality she couldn't imagine herself handling.

"He said she's in the tub," Angie explained. "She likes taking a bath to get rid of the yucky feeling."

"Who doesn't?" Julia said tepidly. *Does it ever stop?* she wondered.

They spent the next thirty minutes finding distractions from thoughts of the mini-crisis their husbands might mishandle. They found three outfits Julia insisted Angie try, all of them flattering but none of them leading to a purchase.

They decided to enjoy the late-morning sunshine with a stroll toward the food court, where they saw a man proactively cooling lunchtime customers by opening a series of large umbrellas in the outside seating area.

"OK. Time to fess up, girl," Angie said abruptly, surprising Julia. "What's bothering you?"

"Bothering me?"

"Yes, you," she insisted. "I can tell there's something on your mind."

"I'm just worried about you," she lied. "I mean, the last thing you needed was another sick child."

"Comes with the job," Angie teased. "Besides, Kevin will muddle through."

Julia offered a thin smile.

"I upset you with what I said earlier, didn't I?" Angie continued. "I'm sorry. I didn't mean to dump on you like that. I just needed to tell someone what I'm feeling."

Julia slipped her arm into Angie's and bumped hips. "Don't worry about it. I understand."

She didn't want to say more. Angie's guess seemed an easier explanation than the truth. "But it's not what you said," she heard herself say.

"No? What then?"

Julia hesitated. *How to tell the mother of four kids that you resent your husband's push for a baby?*

"It's Troy," she began. "He wants more than I'm ready to give."

Angie stopped, her face seeming to flip through ugly possibilities that didn't fit what she knew of her husband's lifelong friend.

"Really? Like what?" she asked blankly. "He acts like he adores you."

"He does," Julia admitted with a tint of shame. "He's been wonderful to me. It's nothing like that."

"Then what's wrong?" Angie pulled them both toward a nearby bench. They sat.

Julia looked away from her friend's anxious eyes.

"Before we got married we discussed children," she began. "We agreed we would consider kids after a few years together."

She paused to watch a final umbrella rise in the distance.

"Troy wants kids now, doesn't he?" Angie said what Julia couldn't.

A single confirming nod.

"I'm not surprised. That scares you?"

Another hit, followed by a comforting stillness.

"I know how you feel."

Julia's head swung back toward Angie. "You do?"

"Of course I do." She took Julia's left hand in her own. "How do you think I felt when I found out I was pregnant with Ricky, that I was going to have a fourth child?"

For some reason Julia hadn't considered the question until that moment.

"One of my first thoughts was that you'd probably think I'd gone off the deep end!"

The comment prompted a nervous laugh. Then a prick of guilt.

"I'm so sorry," Julia said. "I must have made it more difficult for you."

"You and nearly everyone else on the planet. If I hadn't been thrown into a tailspin over the accusations against Kevin I would have been pretty upset about how you characterized people like me. Or should I say breeders like me."

The reminder of her feature's title made Julia blush. "Please forgive me. I know I hurt you and Kevin and I—"

"Stop it," Angie interrupted. "We've been over that ground a dozen times before. You're forgiven, OK? No more asking."

"I know, but—"

"Enough," Angie commanded.

Another single nod.

"I only mention the article because it put into words what I feel when people look at my life, my family."

"You have a beautiful family."

Angie smiled. "I think so. But it frightened me when I found out I was pregnant again. Did you know we had just received Leah's diagnosis a few weeks earlier?"

"It must have been scary."

"It was, for a few days. But then it became wonderful, just like my other three pregnancies."

"How?" Julia asked.

"How what?"

"How did it become wonderful? What changed your feelings?"

Angie seemed to wrestle within, as if reaching for words that didn't exist.

"When did you get past the fear?" Julia pressed further.

The question prompted a smile of realization. "I didn't."

"But you said—"

"I didn't say the fear disappeared. I said it became wonderful." She looked away, then back as if she had found a cue card on the horizon. "I guess the fear kind of lost itself in the wonder. Like leaning over the railing at Niagara Falls. Does that make sense?"

"I've never been."

"Go. It's a deafening force rushing over the edge and crashing on the rocks below. When you get close it looks and sounds like a million thunderous explosions per second. The second-most frightening, awe-inspiring experience you'll ever encounter."

"Second-most?"

Angie smiled silently while raising a single eyebrow.

Julia understood. "Oh, right."

"It's OK to be afraid, Julia."

She received Angie's squeeze with gratitude.

"Just don't let the fear keep you from the wonder."

"I think I get that part," Julia began. "But what about the rest?"

"What rest?"

"Today, for example. You couldn't even spend two hours away from the kids without a new worry to pull you back."

"I can't argue with that." Angie sighed.

"Do you ever resent the constant demands? Or giving up your career? I mean, be honest. What about your dreams? Your needs? Who looks after Angie?"

Angie started to say something, then held her tongue.

"What?" Julia asked. "Tell me."

"I'd rather not. Too holier-than-thou-sounding." She paused, seeming to gauge Julia's reaction before continuing. "You know, too religious."

Julia blushed at the nakedness of the comment. Then she joined Angie's lead by stepping over a line of candor. "Not too religious. Just religious. And I don't know about anyone else, but you've definitely lived holier than me."

They shared what seemed their first authentic laugh in years.

"Go ahead," Julia continued. "You were going to say?"

"I know I did a bit of whining earlier about the frustrations of motherhood. Forgive me for that. Being a mom often feels like one long string of sacrificial moments."

"Especially with so many. Does it ever stop?"

"Ask me in twenty years. Until then, I try to remember what Jesus said. 'If you want to find your life you must first lose it.'"

Julia nodded, remembering the sentiment from one of the Christianity classes she had attended with Troy. "I know that quote."

"He also said that unless a seed goes into the ground and dies, it can't give life."

"Meaning?"

"To me it means we find our true purpose and joy when we follow his example, when we give our lives away to others. It helps me view all of my little sacrifices for Kevin and the kids as my way of losing my life." She paused to lock eyes with Julia. "But I wouldn't trade the life I've found for anything in the world."

Kevin's voice interrupted the moment. "Hi, beautiful…"

"Speaking of the life I've found," Angie said before accepting the call. "I think it's time to rescue our men before they go over the Falls in a barrel!"

CHAPTER NINETEEN

The ancient world had conspired to create such architectural marvels as Rome's Coliseum, China's Great Wall, and India's Taj Mahal. Modern man had raised the stakes with the Panama Canal, Empire State Building, and Golden Gate Bridge. But none of them had outdone the genius on display in Tommy Tolbert's bedroom.

"This is it!" Troy announced as Tommy added a final Lego piece to a three-foot-high replica of the tallest building on the planet. "Ladies and gentlemen..."

He paused to make eye contact with both members of the audience. Kevin stood in the doorway with Joy at his knee. The official count might number three spectators, but little Ricky never actually lifted his head from Daddy's shoulder.

"...I proudly present the tenth wonder of the world, a three-hour construction effort that, according to the box, should only be attempted by individuals twice the age of our construction foreman. Please join me in congratulating an engineering genius, Mr. Tommy Tolbert!"

Joy clapped riotously while Kevin quietly raised his thumb in a show of fatherly pride. Tommy relished the moment, bowing deeply in self-congratulation while keeping the secret: Uncle Troy had helped him. A lot.

"What do you say we celebrate with sliced apples and peanut butter?" Kevin asked while confirming the baby's slumber. "I'll put Ricky in his bed and then we'll start the party."

Six minutes later the gang tapped milk cups in response to Daddy's congratulatory toast. Before he could sip, however, Troy leaned toward Leah's high chair for a second inspecting whiff.

"Keep her diaper fresh," Angie had coached Kevin on the phone. "Otherwise the diarrhea will cause a painful rash."

Troy was not going to let that happen. "I'll get this one."

The sound of the front door opening interrupted Kevin's grateful nod.

"Mommy!" Joy squealed in delight.

"Aunt Julia!" Tommy said, rushing from the table. "Come see what's in my room!"

Kevin and Troy insisted they could have handled the job. They even pretended offense at their wives' early return. But Angie had been right. The men hadn't found time to talk about any of the pressing matters each was eager to discuss.

"You two go for a walk," she commanded.

Four blocks later Troy halted their advancing footsteps. "Wait," he interrupted. "Are you saying what I think you're saying?"

Kevin flashed a triumphant grin. "Twenty percent."

"So a fifth of potential voters would support a Bright Spots platform?"

Kevin slapped his friend's back. "What's wrong, pal, didn't believe your own numbers?"

Troy's eyes followed a passing car while his mind tried to process the implications. Elections were won and lost on single-digit margins. Political fortunes were made and lost because of catering to voting blocs much, much smaller. His friend would likely become an important player in the minds of party leaders. They needed Kevin's influence to garner support among an important segment of the electorate.

Troy looked back toward Kevin. "What else did Anderson say?"

"He said Franklin thinks the Bright Spots proposal, properly positioned, could help his campaign."

"Properly positioned?" A yellow light. "What's that supposed to mean?"

Kevin resumed walking. "In a second. You said you wanted to hear the good news first."

"No I didn't," Troy said, trotting to catch up with Kevin. "I said I wanted the bad news but you overruled me, as usual."

"Oh yeah." Kevin laughed. "You need to understand the good news to help me think through how to react to the bad."

"React to what?"

"Brent Anderson ran his own version of our numbers. He said we were right about bright spot regions as the primary engines of population and economic growth. He said Franklin needs to attract votes and donors from these segments of the population if he's gonna win the election. Social conservatives still resent his support for the Youth Initiative."

"Yes, we do!"

A momentary silence while Kevin seconded Troy's motion with a nod.

Troy's yellow light shaded toward red. "Why do I get the feeling there's more? And that I won't like it?"

"Anderson said it would be political suicide to move quickly," Kevin explained. "Nicole Florea's crowd already fumes anytime Franklin even mentions the Bright Spots proposal. Imagine how they'll react if and when he makes it part of his platform."

"Let me guess," Troy groaned. "They want to take a 'balanced' approach."

Kevin halted his advance. "I can't believe it," he said, extending his arm toward Troy's chest. "That's exactly what he said."

"It's what they always say, Kevin!" Troy sounded angry. "But you can't make a balanced choice between east and west. If you're heading in the wrong direction you turn around. You don't stop and admire the view! Bright spots shine because they go against the flow of the majority. How on earth do you take a balanced approach to a one-hundred-and-eighty-degree turn?"

"I hear ya, buddy." Kevin took a deep breath as if trying to lower Troy's rising volume. Then he looked his friend in the eyes. "Listen, Troy. I don't agree with any of this. OK? I don't like it any more than you do. But I need to figure out how to play the hand I've been dealt."

Troy understood. "I'm sorry. Go on. I'm listening."

Kevin pulled his friend into the deep end by repeating what he had been hesitant to share. "Franklin says we need more transitions in light of the deepening economic free fall."

"More transitions? Has he even read...?"

"He's read our proposal, Troy," Kevin said sternly. "Anderson told me Franklin agrees with our long-term analysis. But he worries our approach could deepen the short-term crisis. That we need the cash infusion and savings generated by Youth Initiative policies."

"But—" Troy cut himself short. He couldn't argue. It would take a long time to reap the benefits of a pure Bright Spots agenda. Even in the unlikely event every family in the nation started having more kids immediately, the corresponding economic growth wouldn't outrun the soaring costs of an aging population for decades.

Resignation swept over Troy's face. "So what's the plan?"

Another deep breath released Kevin's reluctant explanation. "Franklin hopes to sell a big goal that he thinks will strike a positive, forward-looking tone."

"Why doesn't that make me feel better?" Troy mocked.

"He wants to increase fertility at twice the rate we increase transitions." Kevin held his tongue while Troy absorbed the news.

"Two births for every killing?"

Kevin remained silent a moment longer. "I said the rate of increase, not the raw number."

Troy did a mental calculation to correct his misunderstanding. "That's even worse!"

"I know. But the average voter will make the same mistake you just made. Speeches and sound bites will leave the impression he hopes to solve the long-term population crisis twice as fast as he wants to reduce the elderly population."

"An all-around swell guy!" Troy spat.

"I told you we wouldn't like it. But think for a second. What opportunities would such a policy present?"

Troy reluctantly obeyed, closing his eyes as if concentrating to calculate a restaurant tip.

"Well," he began, "in light of current trends, it would require some pretty aggressive incentives to motivate couples to have kids."

"My thoughts exactly," Kevin replied.

"But they'll probably also increase incentives for seniors to transition. Those trends have flattened. Most of the early adopters and sickly have already opted in, or rather out. Whatever you call it when they die. Anyway, the low-hanging fruit has already been plucked and destroyed. You know the snakes will want to expand into healthier, younger markets."

"I know," Kevin confessed. "But I don't think we can win that battle in this round. But we might be able to win on the other front."

Troy placed both palms on his head while filling his chest with air, his way of replacing hotheaded passion with a brainstorming cap.

"Besides," Kevin continued, "NEXT might lose their appeal. The Tenth District Court might give us a bigger victory than we could possibly hope to achieve in Washington."

"Let's hope," Troy said with a nod.

"Meanwhile, let's address the root of the problem." Kevin turned back toward the house, where they could pull out some scratch paper and pens to record whatever brilliance might transpire. "We can make a strong case that as fertility rates continue to drop the problem will get worse. I'll show pictures of Tommy, Joy, and Ricky, then your ugly mug. I'll say my kids will each have to work a second job just to cover their Uncle Troy's share of senior-care costs."

"Hey, don't toss me into the freeloader bucket yet. I still have time to have my own brood of kids."

The comment distracted Kevin's train of thought. "Really?"

Troy grinned awkwardly. "Well, a guy can hope."

"Have you and Julia been trying?"

Troy chose to divert. "I can't answer that. A gentleman always protects a lady's reputation." He flashed a thin smile.

It worked. Kevin returned to his point. "Anyway, I've been thinking. What if we started a privately funded research and capitalization organization?"

"Like a foundation?"

"Sort of. But more directive, like a venture capital operation.

A not-for-profit version of TS Enterprises. You know, do what we do well."

Troy winced. "To be honest, we're not doing it that well at the moment. In fact, we need to discuss a few pressing matters before I head back to Colorado."

"Fine," Kevin said dismissively to resume vision-casting. "We'll need an official-sounding name."

Troy thought about that for a moment. "How about something like the Center for Economic Health?"

"Perfect!" Kevin snapped. "The Center for Economic Health will exist to discover what's working in bright spot communities and provide seed funding for promising innovations that can help other regions foster bright spot habits."

"I like the sound of that," Troy added. "Although Nicole Florea will say we're subsidizing head-in-the-sand choices and creating a culture filled with environmentally irresponsible breeders."

"We'll worry about people like Nicole Florea later. First things first. Someone has to find, fund, and highlight what works so our nation doesn't advance the kind of failed strategies they tried in places like Russia and Japan. We can do better than just throwing money at single mothers to have another kid. We need married couples raising families."

Troy sensed a tinge of optimism in his friend's words. "Wait a minute," he said suspiciously. "You've already scripted this, haven't you?"

A sheepish grin.

"We aren't brainstorming from scratch, are we? You've given this some serious thought already."

"So?"

"Spill it!"

"Spill what?" Kevin asked defensively.

Troy threw his right arm around his friend's unsuspecting

neck and positioned his left hand for a torturous head-rub. "Don't make me do it, Kevin. You know I will."

"All right! All right!" Kevin pleaded while trying to rescue his face from an armpit moist with August heat. "Man alive, Troy!" Kevin used his shirt to wipe the stink from his face. "Ever hear of Speed Stick?"

"Spill it," Troy said calmly after releasing his victim.

"I think Franklin plans to give me a platform to present the Bright Spots policies."

"Anderson said that?"

"No. But I can read between the lines."

"Wow," Troy heard himself utter. "What kind of platform?"

"Who knows? But whatever it is, we'll need an organization that has my back. At this moment all we have is a bunch of spreadsheets showing bright spot communities have more kids and fewer transitions. We need more. We need to show how these communities make those trends easier and more likely. And most importantly, we need to find out what can be done to replicate those patterns in other regions."

The conversation reminded Troy of what he loved most about spending time with Kevin Tolbert. His friend's contagious enthusiasm had managed to find a silver lining despite very bad news. He smiled, reminiscing about times spent together finding turnaround potential in a failing business, selling investors on a plan neither fully knew could work, and garnering support for a congressional campaign both considered a long shot. He missed these moments feeding one another's creative juices and fanning the flame of a shared dream.

Despite the excitement of the present dream, however, Troy knew that it would be tough to turn it into reality while TS Enterprises remained short on cash.

Against every instinct within him, Troy forced himself to toss the wet blanket. "I gotta be honest, Kevin. I'm not sure we'll be able to bankroll this one. That's one of the things we need to discuss. I'm coming up short on investors for the Westar deal."

"What about Peak Capital? Didn't you meet with Wilkie?"

"He said he'll present it to the board."

"In other words, not a chance."

Troy's nod confirmed Kevin's conclusion. "All of our usual sources came up short. I don't know how we're gonna fund the Westar project, let alone pursue a whole new venture. Especially something as big as this."

They slowed their pace from blue-sky dreaming to rainy-day prudence.

"I'm sorry, Kevin."

As they eased toward the house, Troy felt a familiar squeeze on his shoulder. He tilted his eyes down toward his friend's earnest gaze.

"So, what do you say?" Kevin asked.

Troy knew what it meant. He had seen the same look of dogged determination on countless other occasions. *Damn the torpedoes, full speed ahead!* Kevin Tolbert would find a way to make the Center for Economic Health a reality. And when he did, the organization would need a leader, someone who could be trusted to implement Kevin's vision, someone who knew how to clarify and organize, but who also had the political instincts to smell the smoke of trouble long before it burst into flames of destruction. Someone who would rather die than disappoint or betray his best friend.

A few hours earlier a bewildered Tommy Tolbert had stood beside a mound of unassembled Legos. Now a second Tolbert genius needed Uncle Troy's help. A lot.

CHAPTER TWENTY

Julia's eyes landed on two passing images, as if a spotlight had selected each from the faceless herd of travelers rushing across her path. Troy had suggested she wait with the carry-on bags while he spoke to the airline boarding agent, the perfect occasion for a bit of people watching. Both scenes conspired to answer an unspoken question her day with Angie had posed.

The first spotlight framed a gentleman talking to no one, or rather someone out of sight, apparently using one of the new phone implants popular with techies. But he didn't look like a techie. He was strikingly handsome. A rugged shadow on his face suggested he had risen early, possibly for a power breakfast with a congressman or foreign ambassador. He wore a dark-gray suit, a deep-blue tie, and a casual grin that suggested an intimate chat rather than any kind of official conversation. *Of course*, she thought. *His office would be closed at this hour.*

Julia mentally filled in details. He was talking to a beautiful wife or partner back home in—what city? Phoenix. The man's smile was in reaction to a playful flirt from the woman he loved.

Both anticipated a passionate reunion after their long week apart.

Before she could complete the script, however, Julia noticed a different sort of smile as the man's eyes followed a passing woman clearly dressed to attract attention from the opposite sex. Not a quick, discreet glance. A long, hungry gaze that began the second he caught her approaching wink. It continued until she sashayed around a corner that took her beyond his line of vision. He stopped his advance, checked the time, then hastily wrapped up the phone conversation. He turned to follow the woman's path, presumably in pursuit of contact information for a possible rendezvous during his next trip.

Julia wondered if her husband had ever ogled other women while talking to her on the phone. She scowled at the man's back as the spotlight moved her eyes toward a second scene.

A heavyset woman, perhaps in her mid-forties. Too wide to be called glamorous, but pretty in the face. She shifted a purse from one shoulder to the other. That's when it became clear that she wasn't overweight, but pregnant. Julia guessed seven or eight months along. Seconds later the woman vanished from sight, slipping into the unisex restroom facilities after nearly colliding with a man rushing out the same door.

Julia again imagined the details. The woman appeared exhausted from a business trip that would have been much less taxing when she was young and skinny. Did she have a husband, like Troy, eager to become a dad? Or had she swallowed the same myth Julia had once advanced in her weekly columns? *Better to go it alone to defy outdated social constructs.*

She thought of Angie while sighing at her former folly. Of course things worked better when a man and woman partnered to raise kids. She thought of Kevin's Bright Spots presentation. Married couples with kids, for whatever reason, were much more likely to thrive than solo women. Even those bravely bearing kids without a partner ended up dependent upon someone, usually parents or the government. Or a sibling, like her own sister Maria who would have never made it without Julia's help during Jared's early years.

Julia scanned heads in a crowded line to find Troy standing at the counter. He appeared to be wearing down the defenses of an overworked agent. Then she looked back toward the restroom door. The pregnant woman exited, then checked her tablet for some urgent detail. Gate change information, Julia guessed. The woman shifted the weight of her purse from the side of a protruding belly.

Julia thought of what that belly meant for a woman midway between forty and fifty. Her child would get its driver's license when Mom turned sixty. If the baby was a girl who followed in her mother's footsteps she would have her own child in four decades, making the woman a grandmother at the age of eighty. Unless, of course, Grandma had already passed away or volunteered.

Julia felt her own tummy. Flat. Firm. Lifeless.

She noticed Troy walking in her direction. He winked at Julia, eyes so fixed on his bride that he failed to notice a passing miniskirt.

"I did it!" he announced triumphantly.

She smiled. "Did what?"

"I got us upgraded to first class."

"Nice."

"Only the best for my gal."

The achievement had augmented her husband's already excellent mood. The time spent with Kevin had lifted his spirits, as Julia had hoped.

She couldn't wait to cap off his day with the news now forming in her heart.

—◊◊◊—

Thirty minutes later the flight attendant refilled Troy's glass while Julia pretended to read a novel. Despite a Pulitzer-winning journalism career, she found herself losing a battle to find the right words for such a big moment.

Are you ready to become a father? Not quite right. He'd always been ready.

I think it's time we moved toward parenthood. Way too prim. Besides, you didn't "move toward parenthood." You got pregnant.

Let's make a baby! Fun, but too abrupt.

"You OK?" Troy asked after sipping his soda. His voice betrayed concern.

She looked up casually from her tablet. "Fine," she said, reaching toward his torso and offering a slight squeeze. "Why do you ask?"

"You've been staring at the same page for about ten minutes."

She blushed. Time to fess up. "Yeah. I'm not all that interested in the story."

"And?" he pressed.

"And I've got a lot on my mind."

He shifted his weight to face her.

"I've been thinking about last night," she began. "I'm really sorry for shutting you down so quickly. You know, about having a baby."

"Me too," he said eagerly. "I shouldn't have pushed like that. Will you forgive me?"

She nodded silently, not sure whether she felt relief or disappointment.

"You're right," he continued. "We should wait a little longer."

"But I thought you wanted—"

"I did," he interrupted. "I do. But there's no need to rush. We have time."

He offered a supportive smile to seal a decision made on her behalf: another heroic gesture by the noble Troy Simmons.

Julia opened her mouth, but no words came.

"Which leads to the other thing I wanted to tell you." He looked like a boy eager to tell his mommy he had made a touchdown.

She felt a vague dismay, as if something important was rushing past them too quickly. She leaned forward to sort through feelings she had not known possible. Not for her, anyway. Her mind screamed words she had never spoken. Could never speak.

I want us to have a child.

Let's make love tonight, as soon as we get home.

No more caution.

Just spontaneous, abandoned love!

"Julia," his voice interrupted, "did you hear me?"

"Sorry," she returned. "Yes. You said Kevin needs something."

"He needs our help."

"Help with what?" she asked without interest.

"Things are moving fast with the Bright Spots proposal. It looks like Franklin wants to include it as a major emphasis during his campaign. Figures it will help him with a growing segment of the population."

She forced her full attention back into the conversation. "To raise money?" she asked.

"And votes. But yes, his campaign needs to raise money. I think he's struggling in dark zone regions where the austerity cuts hurt most. He needs bright spot support if he hopes to win."

She reached for her glass and sorted her thoughts while sipping cherry Fresca.

"Do you really think he'll back away from the Youth Initiative?"

"No, I don't. He'll speak out of both sides of his mouth, saying he wants to expand the economic potential of bright spots while continuing to glean the savings transitions generate."

"How does Kevin feel about that?"

"Same as me. He hates it." Troy borrowed Julia's tablet and began tapping the screen. "But we think it creates a window of opportunity."

"What are you looking for?" Julia asked.

"Here it is." He shifted the screen in her direction. "Kevin and I spent the afternoon outlining the framework for an organization he wants to launch called the Center for Economic Health." He gestured for her to read his draft document.

"You talked about a new project?" she said without noticing the words. "What about getting you some help with the business you already run?"

"If we don't help turn things around our business will sink along with the rest of the economy." He said it as if he was quoting Kevin. "Anyway, take a look."

She read the screen displaying a classic Troy Simmons template summarizing an organizational mission, strategy, and high-level budget.

"What does this mean?" She pointed to the fifth item listed under the Strategy section.

TELL THE STORIES (Julia via RAP Syndicate)

"It's one of the things I wanted to talk to you about," he replied. "The most powerful weapon in the battle for public opinion will be the media. And we don't have a prayer of getting a fair shake with any of the syndicates."

She knew what he would say next. Julia's journalistic star had been rising ever since the *Breeders* feature nearly destroyed Kevin Tolbert's reputation.

"You can't be serious," she protested. "You actually think RAP

Syndicate will let me advance the Bright Spots agenda? The current editorial board would kill any attempt to—"

"They would kill any attempt by the average journalist," he interrupted. "But there's a certain managing editor who might be open to a series of stories from a former columnist who resigned on his watch."

"Paul Daugherty?" she nearly shouted, then softened her voice to a vicious whisper. "Give me a break! I have no intention of asking Paul Daugherty for any favors. The man can't be trusted."

"No, he can't. But he owes you big. And he happens to work for the second-largest media empire in the nation."

"In case you've forgotten, I quit my job with RAP last fall. I haven't spoken to Paul in nearly a year. And I don't intend to talk to him for at least a few more decades!"

Troy held his tongue to let Julia's simmer cool.

"Listen, babe, you're one of the most widely read feature writers in journalism." Troy began stroking Julia's arm as if to caress away her tension. "Imagine the impact if RAP ran a series of features that put human faces on bright spot trends."

"But they won't. I know these people, Troy. They have editorial directives a hundred-eighty degrees opposite of Kevin's agenda."

"And the last feature you did for them hit very, very big," he reminded her. "I'm sure they'd love to snag a series with the famous Julia Davidson."

"Julia Simmons!"

"Not to them. They don't know or care that you're sleeping with the enemy."

He was right. Media syndicates didn't like it when a writer with a huge following suddenly started working for the competition. And since Julia remained an independent journalist, she could accept contracts from anyone.

"What would I say to Paul? 'Remember me? I'm the gal who

knows you stole my work on the *Breeders* feature to violate every rule of journalistic integrity. I don't trust you any farther than I could throw you. Wanna hire me back?'"

Troy smiled wryly. "Actually, yes."

She flashed a puzzled look.

"Think about it, babe," he continued. "Daugherty knows one word from you could end his career."

She didn't argue.

"And landing a series with you would be a feather in his cap."

It was true.

"But even Paul can't override the editorial board," she said. "The new owners of RAP Media are even less breeder-friendly than when I was on payroll, in part thanks to my feature."

"Which can serve our purpose. Imagine approaching Paul Daugherty with a series that explores the tension between economically disadvantaged neighborhoods and neighborhoods on the rise."

"Go on." She felt her creative juices begin to flow.

"The features could tell human interest stories highlighting the downward spiral of dark zone choices and the upward momentum of bright spots."

"I guess that could work," she confessed flatly.

"Not to mention leveraging your influence to sway public opinion on Kevin's proposal. All while maintaining the highest journalistic ideals."

"By implicitly blackmailing the editor?"

He laughed. "No. By presenting the reality of both sides. Communities with fewer kids and more transitions are in decline. That's a fact. Communities with higher fertility and lower transition rates are doing relatively well. A good journalist will put a face on both realities."

He leaned in to give her a peck on the forehead. "And you, Julia Simmons, are a very good journalist."

As Troy pulled back from the kiss Julia breathed the echo of his scent. Despite the two hours before they would arrive in Denver, the aroma made her feel at home.

"What do you say, babe?" he asked. "It *is* a key bullet on my strategy outline."

They shared a smile as Julia looked deeply into her husband's eyes. She thought of the man in the airport who pretended fidelity while chasing skirts. Troy would never do the same. She hoped it. She knew it.

She remembered another airport spotlight cast on a pregnant woman only five or ten years older than Julia. Had that woman's partner also agreed they had plenty of time, that they shouldn't rush into parenthood? Would accepting this assignment be the first of many postponements that might put Julia in the same boat a decade hence?

"You really think it would help?" she asked apprehensively.

"I do," Troy assured her. "And so does Kevin."

A *fitting penance*, she thought while pulling his hand toward hers to intertwine fingers. A tender squeeze gave the answer he wanted.

"Thanks, babe," he said, kissing her palm.

Julia reached for her glass and lifted it slowly to her lips. She didn't sip, distracted by the gentle, lingering presence of Troy's forearm on her abdomen. Flat. Firm. And lifeless.

CHAPTER TWENTY-ONE

Matthew spun the cap back onto a newly opened bottle of mouth-wash while swishing the sting from cheek to cheek. He counted seconds toward the recommended sixty, but gave up at the half-way point. "Blah," he complained, spewing the clear liquid into the sink, wishing he had bought the mild, minty variety. But today was too important to take any chances. The stronger the better.

He ran a still-tingling tongue across his teeth while admiring the man staring back from the bathroom mirror.

Trimmed hair? *Check*.

Clean shave? *Check*.

Ironed shirt? *Check*.

Fresh cologne? *Check*.

Fresh breath? *Double check*!

Matthew wondered whether Maria Davidson was standing in front of her own bathroom mirror nervously anticipating their reunion. *Unlikely*, he guessed. She had probably sug-gested ten o'clock coffee because she could squeeze in a quick, cordial hello and be done with it. Maria had always been kind, even to the unpopular boys. Today's meeting was, for him, a shot at happiness. For her, he feared it was an act of charity.

He felt the abrupt jolt of three firm raps on the door.

"Matthew?" The slightly muffled voice sounded young and familiar. Isabelle?

"It's Mr. Adams!" came the faint sound of Marissa Gale correcting her daughter.

Matthew pulled the door open. He was greeted by two six-year-old faces, the first smiling boldly and the second dodging the scene.

"Hello there, Miss Gale," Matthew said.

She giggled while extending her hand for a proper greeting. "Hello, Mr. Adams. I told Peter you were probably in the bathroom."

"Hi, buddy," Matthew said to the pair of eyes peering around a protective corner. The boy then darted across the hall toward Reverend Grandpa's bedroom. The door quickly opened and closed to swallow his escape.

"My mother asked us to let you know we're here," Isabelle explained. "She said to say sorry for being late."

"Did she?"

"Yeah. It was Peter's fault."

"Isabelle," came another distant correction.

"OK. It was my fault too. We were playing Battleship and I only had one more ship to sink."

"I can understand that," Matthew said, glancing at the time. Thirteen past nine. "No worries. I wasn't going to leave for another few minutes anyway."

Isabelle surprised Matthew by grabbing his hand and leading him into the kitchen, where Marissa was unloading the dishwasher.

"You don't need to do that," Matthew protested. "I was going to—"

"Don't be silly," Marissa interrupted him. "From the looks of the place you've been keeping busy enough. This is your day off. Go and enjoy yourself. You deserve it."

She seemed overly grateful.

"You don't mind?" he asked, still feeling bad about requesting time off so soon after accepting the job.

"Are you kidding?" she said. "I half expected your message to say you wanted to quit. Wouldn't surprise me after two full days with Dad." She laughed nervously.

A brief silence.

"You won't, will you?" she asked timidly.

"Won't what?"

"Quit." She seemed a bit pale. "I mean, you'll give me a chance to find someone else if he gets to be too much to handle, right?"

He recognized the anxiety in Marissa's eyes. Matthew had felt it often the year his own mother crossed a fuzzy line from parent to dependent. He recalled a vague, persistent panic over a reality he hadn't been ready to accept.

She's getting worse, not better.

How much of my life will her illness put on hold? And what will it cost?

I'm not so sure I'm cut out for this.

Is anyone?

"Don't worry about it," Matthew reassured her. "Your dad's not so bad."

Marissa seemed relieved by the upbeat evaluation, honest or not.

"I think he might be a bit depressed, though," Matthew continued. "Stays in his room most of the time. I only see him when he rings the bell to let me know he needs help."

"Does he?" she asked.

"Ring the bell?"

"Yes. I mean, no. I mean, does he need very much help?"

"Only a few times a day. Otherwise I just bring his food and change his oxygen tank when it gets low. You know, like you showed me."

She nodded distantly.

"I mainly help him maneuver his legs when he wants to use the walker to get to the bathroom. He doesn't let me go in with him, so I assume he does fine on that front."

Marissa seemed reassured. "Good."

A brief pause.

"Good," she said again. "Well, I appreciate all you've done."

"Don't mention it," he said, feeling his empty pockets. "Oops. Forgot my tablet." He took a step toward the doorway. But he noticed Marissa positioning herself on the kitchen counter stool looking intent, as if she wanted to say more.

He waited. "Everything OK?" he asked.

She nibbled one side of her lower lip. "Fine. I'm fine."

"You sure?"

"It's nothing. I don't want to make you late."

The comment reminded him of the time. "OK," he said, starting toward the bedroom.

"It's just," she began, pausing his advance. "I worry. I wonder how long this is going to work. You know, a live-in arrangement."

The comment unsettled Matthew. He had just moved in. Just started this job.

"I know you don't mind him right now," she said. "But it's still the honeymoon period."

Matthew failed to connect any dots between the prior seventy-two hours and his images of a honeymoon.

"He always behaves at first. Even seems docile. He creates a false sense of security. Then, out of the blue, he goes in for the kill."

"The kill?" Matthew repeated nervously.

Marissa chuckled at Matthew's expression. "Sorry, bad choice of words. I mean he climbs onto his religious high horse. He'll start preaching at you soon. If he hasn't already."

Matthew shook his head. "Nothing yet. But I wouldn't sweat that. I'm kind of a spiritually oriented person myself. I've taken a few religion classes and plan to take more when I get back to school. Who knows, we might hit it off on that front."

"I doubt it." Marissa placed both hands, palms open, onto the counter. "But we can hope," she said in rebuke of her own pessimism.

Matthew sensed something else might be bothering Marissa. He waited a moment longer. Nothing came. "OK, then. I'll just go grab my tablet."

He moved swiftly down the hallway toward his open bedroom door, passing Isabelle en route. Her eyes were glued to some educational television program.

He searched the usual places, dresser top and side table. Nothing. Then he remembered. Reverend Grandpa had asked to borrow his screen to read the day's news.

While approaching the main bedroom Matthew heard a child's voice. *Peter?* He waited before knocking, pressing one ear against the closed door.

"And then the lady gave me this!" the boy said in a hushed tone, presumably raising some mysterious prize.

Isabelle was wrong. It seemed Peter could speak after all.

"My goodness!" came Reverend Grandpa's enthused voice. "Let me take a look at that."

Momentary silence.

"Looks like the genuine article," the old man continued. "Twenty dollars is a boatload of dough. What are you gonna do with it?"

"Hide it with the rest," Peter whispered. "I'm not telling

Mommy about it. She said we're running out of money. But she doesn't know about my secret supply."

Matthew heard subdued laughter, an intimate moment between conspiratorial masterminds. He pulled his ear away from the door and positioned his knuckles to knock, an intention halted when he heard Peter continue.

"I don't want you to go away, Reverend Grandpa. I want you to live at our house."

A brief gasp suggested the old man had been caught by surprise.

"Don't worry, Pete," Reverend Grandpa forced out after a hard swallow. "Your mommy and I discussed the money already. I'm gonna live right here, real close, for at least six months."

Six months? Is that what Marissa hadn't been able to say? The job ended in six months?

"Why not longer?" Peter was asking. "Why not always?"

"It's difficult to explain," the elder admitted. "But like I said, don't you worry about that right now. I need to stick around long enough to train my favorite apprentice, don't I?"

Another silence. Peter nodding?

"You still plan to take my place in the pulpit, don't you, buddy?"

Matthew chuckled at the thought of a boy who never spoke becoming a preacher. Or rather, a boy who spoke only to his grandfather.

Three gentle knocks on the door silenced the conversation within.

"What do you want?" came an unwelcoming bark.

Matthew hesitantly pushed the door open. "Excuse me Hugh...er...I mean, Reverend. Do you still have my tablet?"

"On the bed," came the terse reply, the old man's index finger pointing.

The smaller mastermind was crouched near the bedpost,

glowering with a look of disgust. Highly classified conversations should not be interrupted by such small concerns.

"Thanks," Matthew said apologetically, scooting out of the room.

He closed the door, then paused to listen. He smiled, anticipating more clandestine scheming. Then he remembered the time. Less than thirty minutes before his rendezvous with Maria Davidson. And nothing, not wild horses or the top-secret chatter of a mute child, could make him late.

CHAPTER TWENTY-TWO

She looked incredible.

Matthew had pulled into the parking lot a few minutes early, so he should have been the one sitting at a table watching for a semi-familiar face. But he instead parked his car twenty yards from the entry and slumped down in the seat to peer over the steering column until he spotted his, what? Date? Not really. Maria had only agreed to catch up with a guy from high school whom she would have described as an old acquaintance at best.

But she agreed to meet, he reassured himself. *And she actually came. So far, so good.*

He drank in one last look before approaching the entrance. She probably hadn't noticed his gaze, his face obscured by the words *Enchanted Coffee* stenciled on the glass. Maria only looked up from her tablet whenever the stir of the opening door prompted a brief glance. No extending neck. No hope-filled eyes. No pumping her ankle like a woman wondering if that special someone will arrive. Maria Davidson was, unlike Matthew, at ease.

Why wouldn't she be? The years had been very kind. Her face retained the frisky allure that had ensnared every fifteen-year-old boy during ninth grade. She wore a white sleeveless blouse and mid-length blue skirt that lay gently over her crossed legs. The tip of her foot peered out from the thin cotton edge as if offering his eyes the tiniest hint of those familiar, feminine limbs. Matthew had been admiring Maria's playfully provocative pictures for years, her online images searing themselves into his imagination. But now, moments away from their first real encounter since high school graduation, all he could think about was the trickle of nervous perspiration threatening to stain his new shirt.

Get out of the heat, you idiot, he chided himself. *Just go in and say hello.*

So he did.

"Maria?" he said, pretending only vague recognition.

After a slight hesitation she lifted an eyebrow of recognition, then stood to offer a cordial embrace. "Matt Adams," she said with a perky voice that matched the fragrance of her perfume. "How've you been?"

How to answer? *I'm flat broke. My mom's dead. And I quit college to take a job changing an old debit's oxygen. You?*

"Never better," he lied. "Let me take a look at you."

She turned to her side and lifted one leg while touching an index finger to her cheek like Betty Boop. He laughed at the same pose she'd used to flirt with boys back in high school. This was the first time the gesture had been intended for him.

"You look wonderful."

"You too," she said, reaching toward his neck.

He felt a flush of embarrassment as he realized she was fixing his right collar. "Thanks," he said sheepishly.

"Same old Matthew." She smiled while patting his shoulder like a puppy's head.

His heart sank. The last thing Matthew wanted was for Maria

to recall the awkward boy who'd had no business inviting her to the senior prom. He wanted her to see him as a new man. A successful man. Possibly even an attractive man.

"Can I get you something?" she asked, beating him to the punch.

"My treat," he insisted.

"OK, Mr. Big Spender!" she teased.

It took him a moment to react, wondering whether to make light or take offense. Her good-natured pat on his chest told him to play along.

"You know it," he chuckled. "Just got a bump in my allowance!"

She offered a polite but seemingly sincere laugh that boosted his confidence.

"I might even let you order a large," he said with a wink.

They spent the next few minutes dancing between questions about their ancient past and the sexually charged teasing they had started online. But much of it felt forced and out of place. That's when she eased the conversation toward Matthew's recent history.

"What sort of business are you in?"

He felt an immediate panic. He hadn't practiced how to answer questions about the supposed business that had brought him into town. He tried forcing his mind to offer options, but it refused to cooperate.

"You first," he said with relief. "Tell me what you do."

She appeared embarrassed by the question.

"I'm sorry," he added quickly. "I shouldn't make assumptions in this economy. So many people out of work."

"No, it's fine. I have a job, most days anyway."

He waited.

"Guess," Maria said with a gleam. "What do you think I do? No. Wait. What do you think I *should* do? That's more fun."

Matthew hesitated. Then he grinned. "Is this a game?"

A mischievous smile.

"OK," he began. "What should a woman with your charm and beauty do for a living?"

The mug paused in front of her lips as if she anticipated playful flirting or the perfect compliment.

He felt another panic. What did she hope to hear? Should he say something naughty, like lingerie model, or flattering, like teacher?

"A truck driver?" He chose funny.

Maria slapped his leg playfully.

"No?" he continued. "OK, give me another shot."

She lifted the mug back to her lips before lowering it again. "I style and color hair."

It fit. "Really?"

She nodded timidly.

"I bet you're really good at it," he said, refilling her sail with air.

"I am, actually," she confirmed. "But I'm looking for something better."

"Why?" he asked. "I mean, don't you like what you do?"

She seemed pleased by the question. "I do, actually. But unemployed people don't spend money on beauty. And those who do don't tip like they did before the crash."

Matthew understood. He had noticed a gradual shift in the appearance of middle-aged women, those who would have been salon regulars in better days.

A brief hush reminded Matthew that he still needed to answer Maria's question. He felt a bit less anxious knowing she had been self-conscious about her own career. Might he risk telling the truth?

"My turn," she said, filling the silence.

"OK," he said eagerly, realizing she intended to make the quiz multiple-choice. "What do you think I do?"

She uncrossed her legs and scooted to the edge of her chair. She began peering deeply into his face like a movie director deciding which angle to use for his close-up shot. Matthew waited as she pretended to gather clues from his blank stare.

"I've got it," she finally announced.

"Oh really," he said skeptically. "Just like that?"

"You're in the pharmaceutical industry."

He liked the option. He had managed so many of his mom's prescriptions that he could probably bluff without too much trouble.

"Close," he said. "But not quite."

She offered an irresistible but fleeting pout. "Don't tell me," she said, placing her index finger over his lips, her face contorted in concentration. "You drive a truck for a pharmaceutical company."

She laughed at her own effort to even the score, then pulled away from Matthew's finger as he tried to poke his revenge.

Another quiet moment as he thought about how much more impressive driving a truck would be than his real job.

"I don't want to bore you with the details"—a picture of Reverend Grandpa's wheelchair and oxygen tank invaded Matthew's mind—"but I work with medical equipment."

"Oh," she said with a hint of surprise.

He recalled the leg braces. "Mostly new mobility technologies."

He sensed intimidation in her rising brow.

"Sounds more impressive than it is, actually," he added. "But it pays the bills."

To his relief, she didn't ask any specific questions about his alleged field, allowing Matthew to imply and evade rather than outright lie. By the time he managed to change the subject Maria probably imagined him as a modestly successful businessman making a profit selling his wares to hospitals and senior-care facilities. Good enough, he thought.

Matthew noticed the sound of smooth jazz above the silence as they sipped their drinks.

"I guess Julia does pretty well," he said to keep the conversation alive. "I've read a few of her columns. My favorite is the one called *Free to Thrive*."

She nodded evasively. Was she trying to recall the specific column or ignore her big sister's ubiquitous presence? It must be odd for a hairstylist, living in the shadow of her sister's journalism career. He quickly tried to think of another subject.

Maria did it for him. "This is my son Jared," she said, sliding a small tablet toward Matthew's side of the table.

"Wow," he said with genuine surprise. "I didn't know you had a kid."

She had never mentioned a child in any of her online posts. But then, why would she? Secret admirers want airbrushed girls, not diaper-changing moms.

Matthew recalled a column written by Maria's sister that seemed down on kids, so he'd assumed Maria felt the same. Apparently he'd assumed wrong.

"Looks like a great kid," he said. The look on Maria's face told Matthew this was the moment when other men had backed away. He shifted his eyes toward the boy's face. "How old?"

"Twelve, going on twenty," she said with a concise laugh.

He wondered about the rest of the story. The father? The circumstances? He decided not to pry.

"Would you like to meet him?"

"Really?" he erupted, realizing she had just said yes to a second date.

"Sure. If you want."

"I'd love to," he said in stunned delight. It had never occurred to Matthew that the Maria Davidson of his fantasy world might have real-world needs. Perhaps she longed for a man who admired her for being a mom. A man who might even like her kid.

She smiled broadly. "Great. When will you be back in town?"

He bobbled the question in his mind. Then he remembered. He had implied he was in town on business. She had no idea that he lived right up the road.

"Actually, I'll be here for a while…" He paused while reaching for more. "I have sort of a big deal in the works that needs a lot of my attention."

"Go big or go home," she said farcically, pretending a masculine voice.

"Excuse me?" he asked with confusion.

"Go big or go home," she repeated. "It's something one of my clients says all the time."

"What's it mean?" he asked.

"I guess it means don't waste time chasing little opportunities," she explained. "I thought of it when you said big deal."

The look in her eyes told Matthew that Maria found the idea of pursuing big deals rather than small matters attractive in a man. Attractive in Matthew. Or rather, in the Matthew he had let form in her mind.

—⁓—

Twenty minutes later Matthew sat in his car unable to wipe an ecstatic grin from his face. His reunion with Maria Davidson had gone better than he could have hoped. And a second date was already on the calendar!

"Go big or go home," he repeated to himself, a new life slogan for a new Matthew Adams. Or at least a Matthew determined to become worthy of the kiss Maria had planted on his cheek before they parted.

He touched his fingers to the spot and savored the lingering hint of her perky scent.

"Go big or go home," he whispered while starting the engine. Peering into the rearview mirror he saw his own face frowning back at him.

Who are you kidding? it said accusingly. *You're not going big at all. In fact, you're dithering away time on a small opportunity. Changing oxygen tanks for Reverend Grandpa might earn enough extra to pay down part of your school loan, but it will never position you to seriously impress Maria or any other potential lover.*

Only his inheritance money would do that.

"I will go big!" Matthew shouted at his withering confidence while cutting off the engine. He opened the glove compartment to retrieve a pad of paper and a pen before walking back into the coffee shop. He sat down at the same table he and Maria had just left and began writing a letter.

Dear Judge Santiago:

Greetings once again. I apologize for sending yet another letter. But I have yet to receive any response to my earlier communications. Very important decisions have been placed on hold and I would appreciate input on your opinion in the case involving NEXT Transition Services. I realize you cannot correspond at length, but a simple, anonymous post would be greatly appreciated. I continue to await your response at the following forum address: ANON.CHAT.4398

I hope you will see fit to comply with my request.

Cordially,
A Manichean

Matthew reread the note. It lacked urgency.
Bigger!

He took a second sheet of paper to rewrite the note, this time with a revised ending.

I must insist that you comply with my request to avoid more drastic measures.

Respectfully,
A Manichean

CHAPTER TWENTY-THREE

Tyler plopped himself on a rotting park bench, tearing open the paper sack overflowing with fat and flavor: two bacon double cheeseburgers, extra mayo, large cheese fries, and a chocolate shake. Inhaling the lovely smell he realized he risked contaminating his clothes with an aroma that would sicken Renee. But he couldn't last another day without eating something that could make him smile.

A robin landed, curious enough to hop within a few feet before giving up and flying off. It was peaceful here. A great place to get things done. The rusting play structure had long been abandoned, the neighborhood possessed by those beyond childrearing years or those lacking any desire for the task. Vacant swings served as little more than a reminder of a quainter time when young mothers would bring their even younger children to play. Women who worked hard at pretending to enjoy themselves. At least, that's how Tyler had perceived it. He couldn't imagine his own mother actually enjoying places like this. Duty, that's what it was, not pleasure.

So why on earth Renee still hoped to have a kid escaped him. Worried him.

Tyler dug a floppy fry from the bag, shoved it into his mouth, then pulled out his tablet with his other, non-greasy hand. A small icon strobed subtly to indicate a new message. Julia Simmons. At first he couldn't place the name, then remembered—he had tried to contact the journalist who'd written the feature about Jeremy Santos. Tyler tapped to open the message full-screen.

Dear Mr. Cain:

I'm not sure if I'll be able to help you beyond what I wrote in the article. But I'd be happy to meet now that I'm back in town. Late Monday or early Tuesday, perhaps? Send me a few time options.

Regards,
Julia Davidson Simmons

He sent back a quick reply suggesting late afternoon.

The pounding of a man's running shoes approached. Tyler glanced up in time to see an elderly but fit jogger frown self-righteously at Tyler's half-eaten burger. The man passed by down the sidewalk.

"Yeah, well…which one of us is happier?" Tyler called out smugly…after the man was out of earshot, of course. Then he remembered, he was only here eating this sack of junk food to escape his live-in girlfriend and her parents. Not exactly the poster child for happiness.

Just then his tablet flashed and began to beep. He tapped his earpiece. "Tyler Cain," he slurred through a mouthful of burger.

"Mr. Cain?" the voice of Jennifer McKay said hesitantly.

Tyler forced a hard swallow and wiped his face. "Ms. McKay! I was just thinking about you."

"Why do I seriously doubt that?"

"Thinking about your case, I mean. I have a few leads, and so—"

"Mr. Cain. We have a problem. Can we meet?"

"Problem? What kind of a problem?"

"We received another letter. Hand-delivered to the security guard late yesterday, and...well. This one seems like an overt threat."

"Can you forward me a copy? I can take a look."

"No," Jennifer said firmly. "Once you go digital, you lose control. If this information gets in the wrong hands...well, we just can't chance it."

Tyler resented the thought of an unnecessary drive downtown. He could work the case just as easily from where he was with the tap of a SEND button. Jennifer McKay was being much too uptight about the whole thing.

He reminded himself that another meeting would translate into more billable hours.

"OK. Where should we meet?" He hoped it could be someplace far less...antiseptic...than before.

At least Tyler managed to finish his second burger, the fries, and the shake on his drive back to the Tenth District Federal Courthouse.

———

Jennifer's desk looked even more expansive now that Tyler's home desk sat nestled into a cramped corner. He slid his hand enviously across its surface, then noticed his own greasy fingerprint trail. He immediately wiped it away with his sleeve, an instinctive reaction against leaving Renee any potential "evidence."

"You mentioned having some leads," Jennifer said, turning

away from him to locate the most recent letter from the bottom filing cabinet drawer.

She stood upright, spun abruptly, and handed him the letter. He scanned it quickly. On the surface it wasn't much different from the others. Same signature. Same request for the judge to post an anonymous reply. But this one, unlike the three prior, had a greater sense of urgency. And the final line about "more drastic measures" caused concern.

Something has changed, thought Tyler. Whoever was writing these letters was becoming impatient to know the judge's decision. But who, he wondered, would benefit from a decision against NEXT besides Jeremy Santos?

"You're right," he said in Jennifer's direction. "This is a problem."

She sat down. "What do you think he means by drastic measures?"

"No idea. But it concerns me."

Tyler glanced around the office to find signs of adequate security. There was the check at the building entrance, of course. But after that, what would stop some crazy person like Mr. or Ms. Manichean from coming in here and creating a scene... or worse?

Jennifer apparently followed his gaze as it drifted to Santiago's office. "His office is locked at all times, even when we're working. Only he and I can get in during regular business hours."

"What about after?"

Jennifer frowned. "Mr. Cain, I can assure you Judge Santiago is in good hands here. There hasn't been a single violent incident in this building in over twenty-five years. I need you to focus on finding the person writing these letters. Let our security team handle things at the office."

"But I think—"

"We hired you to be a private detective," she said abruptly, "nothing more."

Tyler recalled Smitty's comment about being the right person for this job. He shoved the thought aside. "Ms. McKay, I need to be blunt. I get the distinct feeling you're more concerned with protecting yourself than protecting the judge."

"What?" The word erupted from Jennifer's lips, her gaze piercing. "Protecting myself? How dare you suggest that I…"

She paused to regain composure while lowering herself back into her seat, her manicured nails pressing firmly into the surface of the desk. "I would like an apology for that, Mr. Cain."

Tyler shrugged, trying to see how far she might go. "I just call it like I see it, is all."

"Really?" she answered, her eyes pinched into a condescending glare.

"Yes. Really. Listen, I don't get paid to be nice."

"You won't get paid at all if—"

"If what? You hired me to protect the judge."

"No. I hired you to look into these letters and find out who sent them."

Tyler decided to call her bluff. "Is there a difference?"

He let the question settle, then added another dig.

"You seem too afraid of losing your own job to look out for the judge's best interest."

She glared back, her arms crossed defensively. "The judge's best interest?" she began. "You have no idea what you're talking about, Mr. Cain. This is a federal appeals court, not a traffic court. Major issues are decided in this building. And Judge Santiago plays a very important part in that process."

"Why can't he let another judge handle this one?"

She rolled her eyes as if the question revealed inexcusable ignorance.

"This isn't like popping into a local magistrate's office and requesting a search warrant," Jennifer said derisively. "Let me educate you, Mr. Cain."

Tyler held his tongue. He knew next to nothing about federal appeals. But he was loath to let it show.

"There are three judges who render opinions in this court," she continued. "In this case, one of the three leans left, the other right. That leaves Judge Santiago as the only judge really open to the merits of both sides. So his is the opinion that truly matters. It also means there's no way on earth he'll ever allow anyone to influence his decision. He has asked me to shield him from that. So, yes, that is my job, if we're talking about jobs. And Judge Santiago is well aware of the risks. But he trusts me. And I admire his integrity, a rare quality in this day and age. Frankly, I'll do anything to make sure I don't let him down."

"Even if it gets him killed?"

A look of dread replaced the air of superiority on Jennifer's face. "Killed? Do you really think it could come to that?"

"I don't know what it could come to, Ms. McKay. But as a precaution—"

"Precaution is what we're paying you for," she snapped angrily, as if trying to balance her earlier show of fear. "Just find out who is sending these letters, and make sure they stop. Can you do that?"

He hesitated, looking toward the window to consider options. Part of him wanted to walk away from the whole mess. He was getting too old for lectures from self-important assistants, even ones as attractive as Jennifer McKay. But he also knew blowing this case was not an option. He might never get another lead from Smitty or anyone else on the force. Swallowing his pride in this instance might just get him back in the game. Besides, it was Santiago's business if he wanted to risk his life for some higher good.

He turned back toward Jennifer, who seemed to have softened.

"Listen," she said conciliatorily. "I wasn't going to tell you this so soon..."

"Tell me what?" he asked, upset that something had been withheld.

"That I'm authorized to pay beyond your daily rate on this case."

Tyler's head jerked toward her with a start.

"I can offer you a bonus of thirty thousand if you actually find the culprit."

Tyler tried to suppress a stunned reaction. A grin on Jennifer's face told him he'd failed. Thirty thousand dollars was more than enough to pay off the loan cosigned by Renee. With this one case he'd be able to return to bachelorhood a year and a half earlier than he had hoped.

Jennifer's smile grew. "Who's concerned more about his job now, Mr. Cain?"

He beamed in her direction, abandoning any pretense of indifference.

She stood and held out her hand. They shook.

Control had shifted unmistakably back into the hands of Jennifer McKay.

"Excellent," she said. "I look forward to a quick and tidy conclusion to this mess. I have the utmost confidence in you."

She's good, Tyler thought. *Very good.*

CHAPTER TWENTY-FOUR

"Mr. Cain?"

The woman extending her hand toward Tyler seemed assertive, like Jennifer McKay, but less forged. Comfortable in her own skin. Little wonder. Julia Davidson was a rare sight. Stunning but effortless beauty. Perfectly styled hair fell midlength to merge feminine chic with a refined elegance. Her outfit was tasteful, implying rather than flaunting a lovely figure.

"Ms. Davidson," he said, accepting her greeting. Her left hand brushed a black strand from her face to return it to its proper place. That's when he noticed a ring. He remembered she had a new last name he couldn't recall.

"Call me Julia," she insisted.

He matched the offer. "Tyler. Thanks for meeting."

"Not a problem. I only hope I can help."

The hostess escorted them to a table situated next to a large window overlooking an outdoor parking lot. The same lot Renee frequented whenever she shopped at Bulrich's Organic Market.

"Would it be all right if we sat away from the window?" Tyler asked. He didn't need the agitation of defending an innocent lunch with a beautiful woman.

The hostess raised a surprised brow, then moved them to an inferior spot.

They made small talk while perusing menus. He learned about her recent marriage to Troy Simmons, who, it turned out, had spent time in Washington DC working with Congressman Kevin Tolbert. "I voted for Tolbert," Tyler boasted, claiming his share of credit for the newcomer's victory.

"I didn't," Julia said with a laugh. "But his wife and I have been friends since high school."

Tyler gave a curious glance.

"Don't ask," she said preemptively. "Let's just say that if you told me a few years ago I would end up married to a man like Troy Simmons, I would have said you were crazy."

"A hard marriage?" he heard himself ask. The same question he posed to potential clients. "Sorry," he added quickly. "None of my business."

She smiled at his embarrassment. "I guess every marriage is hard sometimes."

Tyler's phone vibrated, a welcome interruption. He glanced at the message.

FROM RENEE: CALL ME RIGHT AWAY

He begged Julia's pardon and tapped the RETURN CALL icon.

"Hi," he said with professional distance. "What's up?"

"'Hi'? 'What's up'?" Renee scolded. "Not 'Hi babe' or 'How are you?'"

"I'm in a meeting."

"Oh, sorry," she replied, a touch of warmth returning to her voice. "My tracker app says you're at Bear Rock Café. I'm just around the corner. I thought we might meet up for lunch. What time will you be done?"

"Can't do it," he said abruptly. *Why not?* "I'm, uh, booked up the rest of the day. I think I found an important lead in the new case."

"The case you won't tell me about?" she asked suspiciously.

He sensed hurt and paranoia overtaking the conversation. "I told you, I can't reveal—"

"I know what you told me," she interrupted. "Not much. That's what you told me. For all I know the case is a cover for a secret rendezvous with another woman."

Was she teasing or accusing? He looked at Julia nervously. Their lunch was completely innocent. It *was* about the case. He wasn't cheating on Renee. Granted, Julia was the kind of sharp, confident woman he found irresistibly attractive. And yes, he had wondered whether a marriage that was "hard sometimes" might mean she was open to advances. But he hadn't done anything wrong.

"Can we discuss this later?" he asked, aware of Julia's failed attempt to ignore the conversation.

"I'd rather not wait…" she said. Then the call ended.

"Renee?" he asked into the phone. No response. Had they lost a signal? Or had she hung up angry? Was she on her way over right now?

"Everything OK?" Julia asked as he returned the device to his pocket.

"Fine. Fine," he said while motioning toward the waitress, who took their orders and retrieved their menus. That's when Tyler got down to business.

"I read your story on the Santos case," he began. "I found it while doing research for a client."

"You mentioned that in your message. May I ask what type of client?"

He hesitated. But she needed the detail. "A federal official." He offered no title or name. But she was smart enough to connect the dots herself. "Confidentially, someone has been writing letters. It appears they're worried about the NEXT appeal decision. Now they're making threats."

"What kind of threats?"

"We can't be certain," he replied. "But I fear the worst."

"I see," she said with alarm. "How can I help?"

"I met with Jeremy Santos the other day," he began. "I figured him to be a prime suspect. You know, eager to get at the money tied up by the appeal."

Julia took a sip of water, her eyes offering a knowing smile. "And?"

"Dead end. That kid's no threat."

She nodded in agreement. "I felt bad for him. Very sad situation."

The sentiment offered a window into a tender side of the hard-hitting journalist. Tyler admired the sweet sympathy in her eyes.

The restaurant door opened. Tyler yanked his gaze away from Julia, expecting to see Renee charging in their direction. To his relief he saw an elderly couple shuffling toward the hostess desk.

"How's he doing?" Julia asked.

"The kid? Oh, he seems to be surviving. Just." He took a sip of water. "Anyway, I was hoping you could suggest other suspects. Did you come across anyone associated with the Santos story eager for NEXT to lose their appeal? Maybe a religious zealot trying to bring down a big transition provider? Or some other family with a wrongful death case waiting in the wings?"

Julia sat back to consider the question. She seemed to reach for details long forgotten. "Holly?" she asked herself. "No, not Holly. Hannah."

"Hannah who?"

"I'll need to find her last name. She's the transition specialist who was injured during the incident."

"I see," he said, jotting down the name while stealing another glance at the door. "Mad about the injury?"

"Not about the injury," Julia explained. "About the industry."

"But you said she works for NEXT."

"*Worked* for NEXT. She quit after the Santos deaths. A month later she contacted Jeremy and encouraged him to sue."

"Really?" Tyler said. "What's her piece of the pie?"

"None. At least that's what she told me."

"Then why tell Jeremy to sue?"

"She said she wanted to see more restrictions placed on the practice because it's easier to schedule a transition than to book a flight."

Tyler recalled the video images he had seen in Jeremy's apartment, including the lifeless stare of Antonio Santos's cold cadaver. He tried to imagine what it must have been like for Hannah or any other person to bear such sights as a routine part of the job.

"She called them sheep," Julia added.

"Called who sheep?"

"Transition volunteers. She said they aren't heroes but sheep going to the slaughter."

"How's that?"

"You should ask her yourself. I can find her contact information if you'd like."

Tyler knew he could just as easily find the information in the case file. But he preferred the opportunity for further correspondence. "That would be helpful. Thank you."

"I didn't get the impression Hannah was the type to do anything violent or rash," Julia added. "But she did mention struggling with depression. You never know."

"Right," Tyler responded.

The door opened again, this time with aggression. Tyler's head jerked. Another false alarm.

"You seem a bit jumpy. Is everything OK?"

"I'm good," he said apologetically, offering no explanation.

The food arrived. Tyler watched Julia as she bit into a potato chip. Not a baked veggie crisp as Renee would have forced him to order, but a greasy one with ruffles. He smiled in her direction. "You like potato chips?"

"Who doesn't?"

The perfect woman, he thought.

They both ate a few mouthfuls while Julia tried to recall other potential suspects. None came to mind.

"That's OK," Tyler said. "Give it more thought over the next few days. I'll start with Hannah. She sounds like a promising lead."

The phone vibrated again. Another call from Renee. The location tracker told him she was not in pursuit, but had driven home, probably in a huff. He ignored the call, then looked back toward his lovely lunch partner.

"So," he said, feeling more at ease. "What are you writing?" He had never really cared about journalism, but Julia seemed a good reason to start.

She swallowed down a bite of chicken salad sandwich. "I just got the green light from RAP for a series of features. Stories about dark zones and bright spots."

"The power grid?"

She laughed. "No. Economic regions. Dark zones follow general trends of financial decline. Bright spots show signs of growth. I plan to paint real-life portraits that embody the larger trends."

Tyler sensed an opportunity. "I don't traffic many light spots."

"Bright spots," she corrected with a charming grin.

"Right. Bright spots. But if dilapidated buildings and crack houses are any indication, I can probably introduce you to a few of my clients living in dark spots."

"Dark zones."

"Right."

"What kind of clients?" she asked.

He had made a misstep. Working with a federal official sounded impressive. Spying on cheating lovers sounded pathetic. Was pathetic.

"I can't reveal specifics for obvious reasons," he recovered, "but I serve a niche in the private investigation field that keeps me in touch with the lower classes."

Julia scrunched her nose at the slight.

"I mean, dark zone residents," he corrected himself.

"Well, I have a few bright spot families lined up already," she said. "They seem open to talking. But I'll have a harder time finding willing victims on the other end of the spectrum."

"Like?"

"Like people living in areas with higher concentrations of transitions."

Surprised, Tyler asked, "Don't you mean lower concentrations of transitions?"

"No, higher."

"But I always thought the point was to transition wealth to younger families."

"So they say." She paused. "Which reminds me. I'll also need households with few or no kids."

"Why's that?"

"Something about the combination of low fertility and high transitions correlates to economic decline."

"Hmm."

"Childless adults who've transitioned their parents would be the ideal interviews. Do you know any?"

Tyler tried reconciling the question with reality. Or, rather, with the reality he had always assumed.

"I know," Julia said to his bewildered stare. "It sounds counterintuitive. But the numbers don't lie. Trust me, my husband is an expert on this stuff."

Tyler frowned at the mention of a husband. Then he silently rebuked his imagination for entertaining possibilities.

"I can send you a list of dark zone streets and zip codes. Maybe you could look it over to see if you know anyone who'd be willing to chat. That would really help me out."

Her voice carried an appreciative detachment that made him feel like a guy hearing "We can still be friends."

"Sure thing," he agreed with a sigh. "I'll do what I can."

The phone vibrated: Renee calling, probably semi-distraught and eager to apologize for the earlier tiff. Tyler smiled at his girlfriend's predictable pattern.

"Excuse me," he said. "I need to take this call."

CHAPTER TWENTY-FIVE

Matthew sighed as he scraped half of Reverend Grandpa's lunch into the garbage can. It was something he had done a thousand times before while caring for his mom. He tried to recall when she'd begun leaving more food on her plate than she ate. Was it about the same time she'd started forgetting to take her medications? Or when the spark of determined strength in her eyes had surrendered to befuddled fear? Either way, he recognized diminished appetite as a sign of something wrong. Disease? Depression? No. Decay.

His client, like his mother, must be crying out for help. Why else would he specifically request a bean-and-cheese burrito for lunch and then shove it aside after a few pitiful bites? Why else would he keep himself cooped up in his bedroom like a man condemned to solitary confinement? During the five days Matthew had lived with Reverend Grandpa he had seen only one brief sign of passion: the covert scheming with his grandson. Even that, come to think of it, had sounded more like an effort to convince himself than an effort to cheer up Peter. Did Reverend Grandpa really intend to stick around for a long time?

Matthew finished the cleanup process and mentally checked off the third of five daily chores. Then he walked toward the laundry room, where a clump of damp towels awaited transfer from the washer to the dryer. He halted, trying to recall what the old man had told the boy. *Your mommy and I discussed the money already. I'm gonna live right here, real close, for at least six months.*

Of course!

Abandoning his to-do list, Matthew gave himself a much more important assignment.

——⁓——

"Free to thrive?" Reverend Grandpa said with a snigger. "Is that what they taught you up there in Boulder?"

Matthew couldn't quite read whether his client was intrigued or incensed.

The old man put both hands on his left leg brace, the first of three sequenced steps before standing. Matthew instinctively moved toward him, then remembered the rule: *Only assist when asked.* Afraid of another rebuke, Matthew reminded himself that his client was not, in Reverend Grandpa's words, "some helpless invalid!"

"Actually," Matthew answered, "the wording came from a column written by my girlfriend's sister." Mostly true. Maria Davidson might not yet qualify as his official girlfriend. But Julia was her sister.

"Oh, I see," Reverend Grandpa mocked. "So you got this entire cockamamy philosophy from a blogger?"

"Not the philosophy," Matthew corrected. "Just the *free to thrive* part."

The old man placed his right hand on the arm of his chair

while the other reached toward the top of his leg brace. Step two of three. Then he paused to look up, unimpressed, toward Matthew's face.

"Uh-huh," he said. "And the rest?"

Matthew wanted to mention the mountain of ancient sources, academic articles, and recent books he knew existed that would substantiate his philosophy. But in the moment only one touchstone of credibility came to mind.

"I've been studying under the chair of religious studies at the university. His name is Thomas Vincent." Matthew let the name linger in the air, waiting for his client to recognize the renowned scholar.

No raised eyebrow. No reaction at all.

"Dr. Thomas Vincent, PhD," Matthew added.

"Never heard of him."

Reverend Grandpa appeared distracted by the small icon affixed to the top of his leg brace. Despite repeated pressing, the hydraulic lift moaned without movement.

"Probably a low battery," Matthew said. "I better add recharging your brace to my daily routine."

"You do that," the man barked, reluctantly waving Matthew in his direction. "Don't just stand there like a worthless college boy. Help me up."

He bent down to receive Reverend Grandpa's weight.

Look who's calling me worthless, he thought while loaning the man his own limbs.

Five minutes and thirty-seven laborious steps later Reverend Grandpa settled into the front room recliner, inhaling rapidly through a suddenly stingy oxygen tube.

"You good?" Matthew asked.

A single nod.

Both men sat quietly until the deprived lungs were replenished.

"There." Reverend Grandpa sighed with some comfort. "So, what was it we were talking about?"

"Manichaeism," Matthew resumed. "Saint Augustine embraced it before he submitted to church dogma. I'm surprised you didn't study it in seminary."

A hint of vague familiarity appeared on the minister's face. "Fourth-century Augustine?"

"That's right," Matthew said eagerly. "You've heard of him?"

A laugh. "Of course I've heard of him. Bishop of Hippo. Wrote *Confessions*."

The title didn't ring a bell. "*Confessions?*"

"You know, his testimony."

"Testimony?"

"Good gravy, boy!" Reverend Grandpa exploded. "You haven't spent much time in church, have you?"

"Plenty. I went to parochial school."

The old man waved off the comment. "I'm not talking about catechism classes." His speech took on a melodic rhythm. "I'm talking about Bible-preaching, song-singing, amen-shoutin' church where people give a testimony of how God saved 'em from hell and damnation by his grace-givin' love!"

Matthew met the statement with a puzzled stare. Was he serious? Or was this another effort to pull the college boy's leg?

A smile on the minister's face told him it was both. "You'd need to be my age or older to remember what church was like back in the day."

"In what day?"

"Sunday!" he said as if delivering a punch line, laughing weakly. "At least, Sunday where I grew up."

Matthew watched his client's eyes enjoying a moment of reminiscence. They suggested deep bonds to a world quite different from the one Matthew inhabited. A universe far away, he assumed, from the one Reverend Grandpa's daughter had chosen.

"Did you raise Marissa in that kind of church?"

"I tried," he said dimly, placing his hand reverently on a book sitting beside him on the end table. It was the same vintage Bible Matthew had perused on the night he arrived at the house. "But times change, my boy. Times definitely change."

Matthew sensed the dismal cloud reclaiming Reverend Grandpa's disposition. He remembered his mission.

"So, Manicheans taught that the spiritual realm is good and the material world evil."

The comment seemed to pull Reverend Grandpa out of his descent. "And the incarnation?" he asked perceptively.

"A great question," Matthew said. "Church dogma says Jesus was God, a spirit, who became a man by taking on a material body."

"Amen!"

Matthew froze at the abrupt interruption.

"Sorry, old habit. It means I agree."

"OK. Well, anyway, some of his followers also created the myth of Jesus's bodily resurrection. The Manicheans, by contrast, understood that Jesus's resurrection was spiritual, not physical."

"They understood that, did they?"

"They did. And they saw Jesus as one who helped show us the way to God."

"Oh really. How?" Reverend Grandpa sounded as if he were humoring a child rather than engaging a foe.

"How what?"

"How'd he show us the way to God?"

"By transcending the prison of an evil, smelly, decaying body."

"So you think he died to escape stubbed toes and mosquito bites for some out-of-body existence?"

"Exactly."

"God didn't become flesh?"

"Didn't need to. Nor would it make sense. A perfect spirit wouldn't contaminate himself with an evil, material body."

"I see," the minister said. "And no bodily resurrection from the dead?"

"What for? The body decays. Only the spirit matters."

"Go on," Reverend Grandpa said, as if loosening a fishing line. "You say Augustine believed this?"

"He did. At least until he blindly accepted church dogma that condemned Manichean teachings as heresy."

"Those nasty church dogma guys!" Reverend Grandpa seemed to suppress a smile.

"Are you mocking me?"

"Not at all, my boy. I would never—" A bouncing torso interrupted the minister's explanation.

"You're laughing at me!"

The old man regained his composure with a snort. "I'm sorry, son. I'm just playing with you."

"But I'm serious!"

"I know you are." He suppressed another laugh. "If you only knew how many times I've heard some version of this same nonsense.

"Jesus wasn't God, just an exceptional man.

"Jesus didn't rise bodily, he showed us the path to enlightenment.

"Same song, two thousandth verse!"

"Have you ever asked yourself what it would mean if the Manicheans got it right and the Church got it wrong?" asked Matthew.

"They didn't get it right."

Matthew thought of Dr. Vincent. "Some very smart people think they did."

"I'm sure they do. But a lot of very smart people think and do some very dumb things."

"But if the Manicheans were right it would make a big difference, you know, in what you need to do six months from now."

Reverend Grandpa glowered at Matthew. "What do you mean, six months from now?"

Matthew swallowed hard at the realization he had said too much. "I didn't mean to hear."

"Hear what?"

"I overheard your conversation with Peter."

"Little Pete," he corrected. "What part of the conversation?"

"The part where you talked about money, and how you would be around for another six months."

The old man appeared confused. "And?"

"And, well, I assumed you were depressed because you plan to"—Matthew groped for the best word—"volunteer."

"Volunteer for what?"

"To transition. What else?"

The minister's face turned a furious shade of red. "So you brought up all this Manichean nonsense because you thought I was planning to commit suicide?"

"Not suicide. Transition."

"Same difference!" he barked. "Why in the world would I kill myself?"

"Well," Matthew scrambled, "you seemed a bit depressed. And then I heard you talking about money and a change in six months. I just assumed you wanted to help your daughter and grandkids."

The old man took a deep breath as if trying to submerge his rising ire.

"I do want to help Marissa and the kids," he began. "I've sat in that room thinking about little else. But, other than going back in time"—he slapped his leg brace and pinched his oxygen tube—"there aren't any good options."

Matthew sensed an intense self-doubt. No, self-condemnation. That would explain the depression.

"It was an accident," he said sympathetically.

"A stupid accident. And an avoidable accident if only I hadn't been too stubborn and cheap to add the accident anticipation package when I bought that car."

"Package?" Matthew wondered aloud. "I thought accident anticipation came standard on every vehicle."

"It does now. But not in the late twenties when I bought it."

"The twenties? Wow."

"Vintage, my boy. Vintage. Anyway, a measly thousand dollars then would have saved us a boatload of medical costs now. Plus I could've kept working for at least another decade. As it is, I'm probably gonna end up living with her and the kids."

"Is that so bad?"

"You tell me," Reverend Grandpa said. "Would you want the burden of me if you were my child? A child, incidentally, who's spent her whole life trying to get away from her religious nut of a father?"

Matthew held his tongue. He, too, had rejected a parent's religion. He knew what it was like to dread and then endure days on end managing doctor appointments, medication doses, overdue bills, and bathroom mishaps. The time and expenses of caring for a sick parent strangled dreams and killed options. They had reduced Matthew from budding professor to live-in caregiver.

"Six months is how much we have left on my reverse mortgage," he explained. "After that, no more income."

"What happens to the house?"

"The bank will own it. I can still live here until I die, but without the monthly check I can't afford utilities, upkeep…" He paused, glancing back toward Matthew. "Or help."

"I see."

"Either I'll move in with Marissa or she and the kids will

move in with me. We need to pool resources." A faint, humorless laugh. "Correction. We'll live off her paycheck."

Reverend Grandpa looked around the room as if scanning a gallery of better days. "Olivia and I bought this place when she was carrying Marissa. Seems like yesterday. Three hundred and sixty payments later it was all ours." He stopped, another reminiscent gaze sweeping over his eyes.

"How'd you lose her?" Matthew asked gingerly.

He cleared emotion from his throat. "Her ticker quit. Seventy-one years young."

"I'm sorry."

"Anyway, I've been living off the house's equity ever since the accident."

Matthew tried to imagine how it would feel, a proud father knowing he would soon be dependent on his little girl.

They sat silently, two men living in the wake of different misfortunes.

The elder finally spoke. "I should have listened to Olivia."

Matthew didn't follow.

"She wanted to give Marissa a sibling. Maybe two. I didn't think we could afford a houseful of kids on a preacher's salary."

"Sounds sensible to me," Matthew said reassuringly.

"Now I'd give anything if she had someone to share the burden. A brother maybe."

The minister put his hand on Matthew's shoulder like a wounded marine explaining how to disarm land mines. "Marry that girlfriend of yours, Matthew Adams." He moved his hand back to the side table, where his fingers gently caressed the book's leather binding. "And once you do, take some ancient advice."

"What's that?"

"Be fruitful and multiply."

Matthew smiled politely. "Forgive me," he said. "But you

could leave what little is left in your estate to Marissa, Isabelle, and Peter by doing the same thing millions of others in your situation have done. Volunteer."

"I can't do that," Reverend Grandpa insisted. "Never could."

Matthew heard a hint of hesitation and saw a touch of self-doubt in his client's eyes before they looked away. He decided to drop what was clearly an uncomfortable subject.

For now.

CHAPTER TWENTY-SIX

Tyler peered through the glass wall at three sleeping babies: two girls and a boy, judging from the colors of their caps. He knew he should think they were cute; but in all honesty, they looked a bit like misshapen aliens with oddly colored skin. Sights only their mothers could love.

Hannah Walker stood in the corner, hovering momentarily over a fourth baby, her stethoscope pressed against the child's chest. A boy, he noticed when she shifted her stance to perform some sort of test. The child suddenly let out a raspy, quavering scream of pain or irritation. Tyler sympathized with the little guy. One minute you're floating comfortably to the rhythmic echo of Mom's beating heart, the next you're being poked in the bottom by a colossal stranger with chilly hands. Next stop? Who knows? Spying for jealous lovers? Investigating obscure death threats?

"Welcome to the asylum, kid," he whispered through the glass. He sniffed his cup of lukewarm coffee before tossing it in a trash can next to the nursery entrance.

Hannah exited the hospital's newborn nursery, giving Tyler a quick smile.

"Sorry about that," she said, indicating down the hallway. "Where were we?"

"You enjoy your work?" It was more an observation than a question.

She smiled again, bigger this time. More genuine. Laugh lines formed to nearly obscure the slight scar along her lower jaw. "I really do."

"Quite a change from your previous line of work."

"Well, Mr. Cain, that's about the biggest understatement I've heard in all my life."

Tyler chuckled at himself. Hannah Walker had gone from helping push seniors out of this world to helping smuggle newborns in.

"It's OK, though," she went on. "I needed to find something positive if I was going to stay in the medical field. For over a year I kind of wallowed in self-pity after leaving New Day. This job came along, and it was serendipity." She paused. "I have this neighbor who believes in reincarnation. And sometimes I think that maybe, just maybe, these little ones are the souls of my former clients."

"You believe that?"

She pursed her lips with a slight shaking of the head. "No, not really. Wish I did, though. It would probably ease a bit of the guilt."

"Guilt for what?"

Hannah stopped their advance and turned partially toward Tyler. "One thousand, four hundred and twenty-three deaths," she said, her eyes still fixed down the hallway. "I stayed more than two years at New Day." The words dripped with disdain.

He said nothing. They resumed their stroll, rounding a corner under a sign that read BIRTH AND DELIVERY.

"Why did you? Stay, I mean."

She shrugged. "I don't know, honestly. At one time I thought I did."

A brief silence.

"At the time I think I had convinced myself I was helping heroes fulfill their destiny." A single laugh scoffed. "It took leaving to realize."

Tyler looked toward Hannah, waiting for the rest. Nothing came. "Realize what?" he asked.

"That I believed a lie. Wanted it to be true."

She met Tyler's eyes.

"No one likes to admit that about themselves, Mr. Cain. Especially when you're still living in the lie. So you go on, swallowing back sour bile while telling yourself you're part of some greater good."

She glanced upward, noticing the sign that summarized her new reality. She pointed toward it. "'Birth and Delivery,'" she read aloud. "Back then I sneered at breeders. Can you believe that? I actually made fun of the women who are helping me climb out of the pit."

"What pit is that?" he asked curiously.

"The one I helped dig. As of this morning it was eleven hundred and sixty-four graves deep. That little boy you saw me with in the nursery moved me one closer to the surface. Only eleven hundred and sixty-three to go."

"Sounds like a steep climb," Tyler said, from not knowing what to say.

"Believe me," she replied. "It's much easier climbing up than digging down. Like I said, I love my new job. Nine months now."

She paused, as if surprising herself with the comment.

"Nine months," she repeated. "Kind of ironic, isn't it?"

Tyler offered a weak smile of agreement before steering the conversation back.

"I see why you're *not* a fan of NEXT Transition Services."

She grimaced at the possibility. "Not in the least."

"You'd be pretty happy if they lost the appeal?"

"I wouldn't shed any tears if they lost. Other than possible tears of joy."

"Can you think of anyone else who would benefit if NEXT lost the appeal? Other than Jeremy Santos, that is?"

"Benefit?" Hannah Walker began, but an urgent ringtone erupted from the phone stuffed in her nursing scrubs pocket. She held a brief conversation on where to be for her next patient: a baby being born by C-section in just a few minutes. She ended the call, then glanced at Tyler, quite intently. "I'm sure there are plenty who would benefit, Mr. Cain. But why do you assume the person you are dealing with is *opposed* to NEXT? Does it say that explicitly in the letters?"

The question confused him. *Of course it does. Wait. Does it?* "Why do you ask?"

"Well, I'm sure there are many who want to see NEXT lose the appeal. But others would have far more to gain if they won."

Tyler had been so focused on Jeremy or some other lawsuit beneficiary he had barely considered the possibility. How stupid of him! *Losing my edge,* he thought with a sigh.

"The transition business is just that: a business. It's about making money, and a lot of it. Certain people will go to great lengths to make a buck. And when it comes to the old and afflicted, death pays handsomely."

"So you think it's NEXT?"

"Maybe. Or maybe someone with more to gain than NEXT."

"Like?"

Hannah shook her head as her phone beeped, then started down the hallway backward while finishing her thought. "I haven't a clue. That's for you to find out. But might I suggest you visit the clinic where I worked? See for yourself what goes on. You might find a lead or two. Goodbye, Mr. Cain."

And with that, she scurried off.

—ᴡᴠ—

New Day Transition Center seemed considerably smaller in person than it had in the video tour, at least from the outside. The brick exterior blended seamlessly into the surrounding establishments. It would be easy to miss unless you were looking. Probably on purpose. Despite the overall popularity of transition clinics, Tyler imagined there were still a few crazy zealots around eager to bomb the place if given half an opportunity. But here, nestled neatly between a pediatrician's office and that of a gynecologist specializing in reproductive screening, it felt rather harmless. Tyler laughed at the grouping.

It did seem odd, though. For a business set up to make lots of money, as Hannah Walker supposed, the interior seemed rather lackluster. Tyler wasn't even sure what he hoped to find here. He'd already seen the place, virtually, through the police recording. Maybe he needed to actually experience it for himself.

He glanced around the waiting room, where two elderly men sat with their fiftysomething children beside them. One was in a wheelchair, and the other had a canister of oxygen attached via clear plastic tubing to his nose. It was disturbingly quiet.

The receptionist smiled brightly. "Welcome to New Day, may I help you?"

Tyler was caught off guard, momentarily unsure of what to say. He glanced again at the man in the wheelchair. Probably the same age as Renee's father, or a few years beyond. A fleeting thought crossed his mind. What it would be like to see Gerry or

Katherine here, Renee holding his or her hand as they prepared to say their final goodbyes? She would never do it, of course. But the image gave him the needed reply.

"Yes," he said, bringing his gaze back to the young woman's. "It's my father-in-law, really. He's...well..."

"Oh, I understand. Hang on one moment." She stretched to check on the clients in the waiting room, as though fearing they had escaped, then handed Tyler a series of papers. "I'll have you meet with a counselor. In the meantime, you should read through this, making sure you, your partner, and his or her father understand everything fully."

Tyler continued playing the part as the receptionist leafed through the first several pages of legal mumbo jumbo. She stopped on the final page.

"This is the official application. The front is just basic personal information. You know. Name, date of birth, that kind of thing. On the back is a series of questions you—I mean your father-in-law—will need to answer after meeting with one of our counselors."

Tyler flipped the page to the back, scanning the list. On the surface they all seemed quite reasonable questions to ask oneself before deciding to die. But then Tyler realized how pointed some of them seemed. Like "Have you pre-identified allocation and distribution of your estate via a legal will?"

At the bottom, in barely legible fine print, was a revision number and date. It was recent, less than six months old. This was the eighth version of the form, in fact.

Ten minutes later Tyler sat on faux-wood-grained furniture across from a male counselor. A cheaply framed lithograph hung crookedly. The hint of fresh-breeze-scented air freshener wafted from a small plug-in behind the man. His nametag read LEO, probably short for Leonard.

Tyler had dutifully filled in the first page with Gerry's personal information, but held off on the questions targeting Gerry himself. Leo glanced at the form, then leaned forward, hands prayerfully folded.

"I know this must be a difficult time," he began.

Tyler nodded, then feigned an appreciative smile. "To be honest, I'm not even sure this is what he wants. But Renee…I mean, my wife, she's a bit overwhelmed right now."

"That's to be expected. No one should have to go through the process of having to see their parents slowly deteriorate to the point that they can't even take care of themselves. But we see it so often. And it doesn't have to be that way."

"But when's the right time?"

Leo leaned back too quickly, as if checking *Show compassion* off a mental list. It must have seemed Tyler didn't need convincing, just the proper motivation. "That's the tricky part," he said.

"Tricky?"

"Yes. See, transitions must be completely voluntary. We can't have overburdened children making decisions on behalf of their mother or father without absolute certainty that the parent understands and agrees to the process. That's the point of the second page. See there?"

"Yes."

"And so, assuming your wife is in agreement, the first step will be helping your father-in-law understand what kind of burden he has become to your wife. Sometimes that takes time and a little bit of patience."

"A little bit?"

Leo chuckled. "Or a lot. One of the volunteers sitting in our waiting room now had his first consultation nearly six months ago."

"Six months?" Tyler had spent less than ten days of hosting Gerry and Katherine in his house and already felt burned out.

"I know, but don't worry. Those are exceptional cases. If your father-in-law is already aware of his worsening condition, which is...?"

"Uh. Mild dementia."

"Oh, I'm so sorry," Leo said, briefly returning to a posture of pity, then continuing. "If your father-in-law can be made to see the toll his dementia is taking on your wife he'll be more open to volunteering. You can help that along some."

"Help it along?"

"Not that you want to push him into something he doesn't want to do."

"No," Tyler heard himself say.

"Like I said before, the decision must be completely voluntary. But sometimes the person less emotionally tied to the situation, such as yourself, can help them see the situation from a more clearheaded perspective. You know, help them focus on the benefits rather than just grieve the potential separation."

"Benefits?"

"Such as freeing resources for your wife, any grandchildren—"

"No kids."

"I see. Does she have a career, then? In a very real way, your father-in-law is probably holding her back."

Tyler's mind filled in other motivations. He and Renee hadn't had sex since the day her parents moved in. "I hadn't thought of it that way."

"Here," Leo said, handing the forms over to Tyler. "Take these. Discuss them with your wife. Look over the questions. And when you're convinced that your father-in-law is ready to answer them honestly, then you'll know the time is right."

Tyler folded the forms and slid them into his pocket before standing and offering his hand in thanks. Leo returned the gesture, escorting Tyler back toward the lobby. On the way Tyler caught a glimpse of the man in the wheelchair being

moved through an open door. The sign overhead read TRANSI-
TION ROOM #2.

In the waiting room Tyler noticed the man's daughter sitting
quietly, dabbing a mascara-stained tear from each eye. She returned his glance. He sensed both relief and regret.

Hannah Walker had been right. He *was* surprised. Not because he had found any useful lead. He hadn't. He was surprised
by the efficiency of the process. It had taken the NEXT staff
less than thirty minutes to move him from a vaguely curious
inquirer to a convinced salesman of their product. One or two
sentences had emphasized that volunteering must be "completely voluntary." But they had seemed like legally required
fine print, not sincere attempts to dissuade. Under other circumstances the encounter might have convinced Tyler to seriously
explore a step he had never really put much thought into before.

Was Antonio Santos as easily convinced? he wondered.

Tyler forced the question out of his mind. Private detectives
don't have the luxury of rabbit-trail thoughts. He got paid when
he delivered. He put his Mustang in reverse, matching the direction of his case. The interviews with Julia Simmons and
Hannah Walker had brought him no closer to finding the author
of Judge Santiago's threatening letters. Nor to pocketing his
thirty-thousand-dollar bonus.

CHAPTER TWENTY-SEVEN

Julia took a third glance at Tyler's text message to confirm the address.

> Austin Tozer said he would talk to you.
> Definite dark zone guy. His mom volunteered recently.
> Owes me a favor. Expecting you at 10 a.m. tomorrow.
> Address: 2210 Kingston Street in Aurora

She had the right place, unlikely as it appeared. What had she expected? A half-abandoned apartment building? A yard filled with knee-high weeds? A broken-down washing machine on the front porch? These were the images that came to mind whenever Troy mentioned dark zones. But Austin Tozer, whoever he was, lived in what appeared to be a modestly respectable neighborhood within jogging distance of the University of Colorado–Denver School of Medicine. Only peeling trim and graying roof shingles offered hints of the home's concealed age.

She felt a mild vibration from her tablet, a reminder that the scheduled time had arrived. Julia moved toward the recently painted front door, shaking her head in disbelief. Troy's scheme had actually worked. Paul Daugherty had jumped at the chance to present her concept to the editorial board, just as Troy had predicted. She frowned at the thought of Paul's likely pitch. *You'll never guess who I landed for the next weekend feature*! Julia hated the thought of Paul once again leveraging *her* work to increase *his* stature at RAP Media Syndicate. But it had to be done. Kevin needed this story. And many more.

When she reached the second of three porch steps Julia noticed a slight movement from the front window drapes. Had the man been watching her? For how long? Admiring eyes usually flatter a girl. But when hidden behind shadowy curtains they give her the creeps.

Before she could knock Julia noticed the door inching open. A partial face appeared from behind. Not a man. A woman? No. A girl. She looked Julia up and down as if eyeing an intruder before deciding whether to call the cops.

"Hi there," Julia said through the gap. "My name is Julia Sim—Julia Davidson. I'm here to see Mr. Tozer. Austin Tozer."

"Austin!" the girl shouted toward the back of the house. Then she disappeared, leaving Julia standing on the porch like a pizza delivery guy waiting for his tip.

A moment later the door fully opened. The man, like the house, caught Julia by surprise. She had, for some reason, expected a gruff, unshaven face and protruding beer belly. His thin torso and lean biceps lacked enough muscle tone to justify a tank top intended for less boyish forms. Patches of auburn whiskers splotched a face that could have used a shave but couldn't produce a beard. At first glance she assumed Austin was barely beyond adolescence. But his eyes and thinning hair said mid- to late thirties. Possibly older.

"Sorry," he said, motioning for Julia to enter. "Amanda never learned manners."

She stepped into the front room. "Your daughter?"

He laughed. "Nope. Childless by choice. She's my kid half sister. She lives with us."

They stood for a moment while Austin looked around the room, scratching his neck. He seemed nervous, as if he had expected someone different.

"Is this still a good time to chat?" she asked.

"Yes," he said quickly, glancing at the clock. "Perfect. Can I get you something? Water? Soda?"

Julia wasn't thirsty, but she accepted the offer anyway.

"Back in a flash," he said as if relieved by the opportunity to regroup. "Please, make yourself comfortable."

She moved to a chair situated across from the sofa, ideal for a face-to-face interview. When she sat, however, the cushion sank like a deflating balloon. Too many years had met too little padding. She scooted herself forward to find a patch of support while searching her tablet screen for a specific icon.

"May I record our conversation?" she asked as Austin re-entered the room.

His face was hit with embarrassment. "I'm so sorry," he said, offering his hand to rescue Julia from the wrong chair. "I should have warned you about that." He quickly moved a pillow from the left side of the adjoining sofa. "Please. Sit here instead."

Finally settled, she repeated her question. "May I record our conversation?"

He nodded. "Do you plan to use my real name?"

"Would that be a problem?" she asked. "I prefer it when possible."

His eyes darted nervously at the other spot on the sofa, then back toward Julia. "Depends on what kinds of questions you ask," he said, taking the open seat. "I'll let you know when we're done."

Julia shifted her posture to face Austin, who was crossing and uncrossing his legs as if trying to assume the best position for an interview that suddenly felt like an awkward blind date.

Julia tapped the RECORD icon and placed the device on the space between them.

"Tyler Cain says the two of you are friends."

Austin appeared surprised by the comment.

"He said you owed him a favor." She smiled.

He didn't laugh. "More like I owe him money."

"Detective work?"

Austin chuckled. "That's what Tyler calls it. Did me more harm than good."

"I see," Julia said without curiosity.

"I hired him a few years ago when I thought Gwen was cheating on me. She still gets irate every time I get an outstanding invoice reminder."

"Gwen?"

"My partner. Been together nearly ten years." Austin pointed up and back to a picture hanging on the wall behind his head. "That's her there."

Julia stood to take a closer look. The woman in the photograph appeared older than Austin. Peering beyond the artificially blond hair and an outfit more suited for Austin's manners-deprived kid sister, she figured Gwen to be around forty. A self-conscious smile suggested a woman hoping to conceal teeth that had lost their former symmetry. There was a blotch on the right side of her neck just below the earlobe. A birthmark? Perhaps. But more likely a now-distorted tattoo applied to younger skin.

"She's lovely," Julia said generously.

"Thanks. I like her."

Julia smiled at the mystery of human attraction as she reclaimed her spot on the sofa. "How'd you connect?"

"The seventh tier of Virtuality."

"Virtuality?"

"A gaming universe. All my clan buddies made the switch to NuLIFE TREK. But I stuck with Virtuality. Call me old-school. Anyway, that's how we met. It's like we were meant to find each other. I'd probably still be living alone if Virtuality hadn't brought us together."

Julia smiled politely.

"Yep. Gwen and I hooked up online long before meeting face-to-face. Our avs were so hot together we just had to take it to level eight, if you know what I mean."

"Avs?"

"Avatars. You know, our other selves."

"Ah," Julia said with a nod, pretending to follow.

"Sorry she couldn't join us. The store called this morning offering a half-day shift."

"I understand," Julia said. "Take work when you can get it."

"You know it."

"How about you? Are you employed?"

Austin's sunken chest appeared to expand slightly. "I actually just started a new job last week."

"Congratulations."

Julia waited for details. None came.

"Nothing much, but a lot better than sitting around here all day waiting for Gwen to get home. You can only play so many solo levels before you need your av-mate to advance. Plus, we need the cash. Mom's estate was smaller than I expected. And the house still has a mortgage."

"Did the house belong to your mother?"

"Yep. Lived here with Amanda."

"Your sister?"

"Half sister."

"How old is Amanda?"

"Twelve. No. Eleven." He cursed. "I should probably keep better track of that now that I'm her legal guardian."

"So you and Gwen moved into your mother's house after her...passing?"

Austin shifted uncomfortably in his seat. "Before, actually."

A moment of silence.

"Go on," Julia prodded.

"Gwen and I moved in to help with Amanda after Mom got sick."

He lifted his eyes to meet Julia's. She held a sympathetic stare. He looked back toward the carpet.

"Well, not exactly sick. But she was pretty depressed."

"That's not true!"

Both looked toward the accusing feminine voice.

"Mom wasn't depressed. You were!"

Amanda stepped around a hallway corner that must have led to three bedrooms and a bath. Her appearance startled Julia even more than the outburst. She was darling, possessing a natural beauty diligently buried beneath the common trappings of a girl trying to look like a woman. Dark mascara hid a noticeable innocence that reminded Julia of her nephew Jared. Both kids inhabited that awkward age when children yearn to escape carefree-ness for the prison of forbidden knowledge. Her clingy top revealed the promise of breasts not yet blossomed. A short skirt flared suggestively, the latest design of fashion moguls hoping preteen girls would join their mothers as eye candy for hungry males.

"We were perfectly fine before you and Hen started mooching off Mom."

Austin frowned. "For the thousandth time, her name is Gwen. I hate it when you call her Hen!"

Julia resisted the urge to smile at Amanda's "henpecked" insinuation as the girl stormed out of the room. A door opened, then slammed.

Austin shook his head in a blend of anger and humiliation. "Like I said. She never learned manners." He breathed deeply. "Where was I?"

"You were telling me about your mother."

He looked as if his mind remained fixed on the accusation. He stood up and took a single step in Amanda's direction. Then he stopped.

"Right. My mother," he said, reclaiming his seat.

"She volunteered?" Julia already knew the answer thanks to Tyler's text.

"She *was* depressed," he insisted. Then he looked Julia in the eyes, as if realizing he had mischaracterized his mom's decision. "But that's not why she transitioned."

"She must have been fairly young," Julia suggested.

Austin reached for a tablet sitting on the table beside the sofa. He tapped the screen and handed it to Julia.

"That's her a few years back," he said as Julia studied the picture.

"I see where your sister gets her beauty."

"Half sister," Austin corrected.

Brother and half sister had clearly inherited different ends of the gene pool. Austin must have come from sperm lacking rugged good looks. The man who had partnered in Amanda's conception, by contrast, had merely jump-started a process that resulted in near-perfect transmission of feminine elegance from mother to daughter.

"Were they close?"

The question appeared to confuse Austin. "Was who close?"

"Amanda and her mother."

"Oh. I guess." He gave his answer another thought. "Actually, I'd say they oscillated between friends and enemies. Like a lot of mothers and daughters, I suppose."

Julia absorbed the comment. "It must have been tough to lose her mom at such a young age. Ten?"

"Yep. Wait." He cursed again, then started tapping fingers like a boy doing arithmetic. "Eleven. My mom volunteered a month after Amanda's eleventh birthday."

Julia tried to imagine the motivation for such a decision.

"In fact, Amanda's birthday played a role."

"How's that?"

"Gwen and I had been living here for about a year. That's when we noticed a growing sense of apathy in my mom. Some days it felt like despair."

"A year after you moved in?"

"Yes."

"Not before?"

"Before what?"

"Earlier you said you moved in to help with Amanda due to your mom's depression."

Austin's eyes shifted toward the wall. "That's right. We did," he said pensively. "Of course, that wasn't the only reason for the move."

Julia reminded herself that Austin's neighborhood officially qualified as "economically deprived."

"Was money a reason?"

"Both Gwen and I lost our jobs during the meltdown. Couldn't pay the rent. You know the rest."

Julia nodded.

"Anyway," he continued, "we thought it would be good for everyone if we pooled our resources."

"What kind of resources?"

A blank stare.

"You mentioned that your mother's estate was smaller than you thought."

"Actually, I didn't realize how small until later. Mom said her transition would provide more than enough to pay off the mortgage and establish a college nest egg for Amanda." He gave a single laugh. "Hardly."

Julia took a sip of soda. "What happened?"

"Bad math. She underestimated the transition service fees and inheritance tax rates. We barely got enough to pay off the mortgage."

"I thought you said you still had a mortgage."

"We do. The money would have been enough had I landed a steady job, which I didn't."

"So the money has been paying your monthly bills?"

He nodded.

"Even the portion intended for Amanda's college fund?"

Another, slower nod.

"Anyway," he continued, "shortly after Amanda's eleventh birthday Mom and Gwen did a bit of number crunching. Gwen's always been good with that sort of thing."

Julia looked up at the picture of Gwen, then at the elegant face smiling on Austin's tablet. "So your partner helped your mother decide to volunteer?"

"Yes and no. She helped her work through a decision tree I brought home from Aspen House."

"The NEXT clinic?"

"You know it?" Austin asked. "A really classy place."

"I've driven past it. Looks...nice."

"Anyway, it was clear we needed to do something drastic. I think Mom was the first one to say so."

He looked at the ceiling as if trying to recall his mother's precise words.

"'We can't continue like this.' That's what she said. 'We need to make a major change.'"

"Why didn't you sell the house?" Julia asked.

"Impossible. She wouldn't even discuss it. A move would have been too unsettling for Amanda."

More than losing a mother? Julia thought.

"How did Amanda and your mom make it before you moved in?"

"Barely. That's how they made it," he said defensively. "Mom's paycheck covered their monthly expenses. No more. She wasn't saving anything for Amanda's future."

"What about after your move?"

He scowled. "We weren't moochers, if that's what you're suggesting!"

"I'm not suggesting anything," Julia said softly. "I'm just trying to understand what led your mother to volunteer."

"I had nothing to do with it," he insisted.

"Nothing to do with what?"

"With her decision. Gwen and Mom did all the talking. I kept myself out of it."

"I thought you said you brought a decision tree home from Aspen House."

He blushed. "I was just curious about how it all worked. You know, whether it might be a good option to consider."

"Was moving out one of those options?"

"I told you, Amanda—"

"I mean did it occur to you that it might help if you and Gwen moved out? If your mom and Amanda barely made it before you arrived, it must have been worse with three adults and a child living on one modest salary."

Austin began pinching uneasily at a patch of facial hair. His eyes appeared to be assessing what more, if anything, to say.

"Look, Ms. Davidson, I'm gonna shoot straight with you." He paused. "Mom drank."

"I see," Julia said sympathetically.

"She drank a lot. I found that out after we moved in."

Julia began assembling the pieces in her mind. A functional alcoholic stretched beyond what her frayed edges could handle. Drinking away the disappointments of a go-nowhere job, a do-nothing son, and a daughter increasingly at odds. A girl whose maturing features served as a daily reminder of her own waning beauty.

"Mom told Gwen she wanted to do something decent for her kids."

"Decent? As in leaving you the house?"

"Mainly the house. There were other assets. But the house mostly."

Austin looked as if more needed to be said. Julia waited.

"And we nearly lost it."

"Lost the house?"

A single nod. "Would have if Gwen hadn't got pregnant."

Julia looked up with a start. "Pregnant?"

"Twice in the past twelve months," he said with a curious enthusiasm.

"But I thought you said you and Gwen were childless by choice."

"We are," he replied matter-of-factly. "We sold them."

"Sold them!" Julia felt her right palm pressing against her abdomen.

"Two grand each. The embryotics market is booming."

A blank stare joined Julia's queasy feeling. She glanced at her tablet to make sure it was still recording what she was hearing. Then she willed herself back to a journalistic posture.

"Of course. Embryotics," she said, trying to connect the label.

Austin must have perceived her confusion. "You know. The

organic material used in everything from surgical attachment tissue to those skin rejuvenation ointments used by rich old ladies."

"Right," she heard herself say. "So you sold your girlfriend's fetus?"

"Yep. Wish we'd discovered the market earlier. Prices have been steadily rising for years."

"Who buys them?"

"Who doesn't? We responded to an ad that said elder cosmetic innovations have overwhelmed traditional suppliers, or something like that. I don't recall the exact wording. All I know is that they pay top dollar for a two-month fetus."

Julia swallowed hard as she recalled late-night commercials for creams promising to "miraculously reverse your skin's aging process" using "cutting-edge organic materials." The ads had clearly targeted well-off women worried about age spots. Snake oil priced high enough to seem legitimate.

The sound of an opening door forced Austin to his feet. He appeared nervous, as if worried about how Gwen would react to discovering an attractive woman sitting beside him on the sofa.

Austin relaxed, then scowled, when he realized it was just Amanda.

Julia felt strangely warmed by the girl's arrival. "Hello," she said enthusiastically.

Amanda smiled and offered a single wave. Then she scrunched her nose at Austin.

"Where'd you go?" he demanded.

"Out." Nothing more.

"I'm glad you're back," Julia interjected, hoping to draw the girl into the conversation. "I want to ask you a few questions as well."

Austin's head spun toward Julia with a look of incredulity. "But—"

"I was just wrapping up my interview with your brother," Julia interrupted.

"Half brother," they corrected in unison.

"You don't mind if Amanda joins the conversation, do you, Austin?" Julia asked, eager for the girl to confirm or correct Austin's version of events.

He looked at Julia, then at Amanda, then back at Julia again. "Actually, I'd rather she didn't."

"Please, Amanda, will you join us?" Julia continued over Austin's protest.

"Sure," Amanda said proudly, moving toward the sofa.

"I said I'd rather she didn't," Austin repeated with conviction.

"What's the matter?" said Amanda. "Afraid I'll expose more of your bull?"

"Ms. Davidson, I must insist."

"I could really use her perspective for the story."

Austin stood in place for several awkward seconds, shifting his weight from side to side as if trying to decide a next move.

"Ok, I'll let you talk to her," he said. "But don't plan on using my real name," he said, as if threatening to take his ball and go home.

Julia considered the threat. "Actually, that might be best anyway. You know, more authentic knowing you had no reason to hide anything or embellish."

He continued standing for several silent seconds. "Tell you what," he finally said. "You two have a chat. I'm gonna go in the other room to…check in at work."

"Check in at work?" Amanda mocked. "What are you gonna check, whether you'll be on the grill or running the milkshake machine tomorrow?"

Austin's neck turned shades of both anger and humiliation on his way out of the room. He paused at the hallway to shoot Amanda a daggered glare before disappearing around the corner.

The girl flashed a triumphant grin before plopping herself Indian-style on the floor. Lines of obstinacy melted on her face as she offered Julia an admiring smile.

"You're really pretty," she said.

"Thanks. So are you."

The girl blushed. "Hen says I look like a tramp."

"A tramp?" Julia said, recalling the tart-like appearance of the woman in the photograph. "Well, you know better than that, don't you?"

Amanda appeared entranced by the graceful sophistication of Julia's clothes and the stylish cut of her dark, unbleached hair. She even seemed to admire the way Julia sat, which prompted a self-conscious glance at her own contorted posture. The girl repositioned herself on her knees while pulling a tiny skirt over her thighs with one hand and finger-combing her disheveled strands with the other.

"You look a lot like your mother," Julia said. "Your brother... I mean Austin showed me her picture."

Amanda smiled at the truth of it.

"She's dead. Killed herself last year."

"Yes, I heard that from Austin. Were you close to her?"

A shrug. "Sometimes."

"She went through a rough spell?"

Amanda looked toward the hallway, then back. "Yeah. Ever since the day Henpecked moved in with his Hen."

Julia let herself smile at the alias.

"Where'd you get that blouse?" Amanda asked, leaning in for a closer look. "Mmm. And that perfume? I like it."

"The blouse came from Standout."

"I love that store!" the girl said. "Mom let me order shoes from the clearance bin once."

"I don't remember where I got the perfume. It might have been a gift from my husband."

"You're married? For real?"

Julia laughed at the girl's astonishment. "For real. His name is Troy. He likes this perfume on me too."

Amanda giggled, prompting Julia to do the same.

"Can I see his picture?"

Julia complied by touching her tablet screen. "That's him."

"Oooh," Amanda sang. "You look good together. Where is this?"

"We were on our honeymoon in San Francisco."

"Your honeymoon? Nice." Amanda giggled again. "Kids?"

"No. Not yet."

"How come?"

"We've only been married for six months."

The girl appeared confused by the explanation, as if it had never occurred to her to associate marriage with having kids.

"So, Amanda, would you let me ask you a few questions for my story?"

"Your story?" she asked warily.

"I'm writing a feature about families that struggle financially. It's for RAP Syndicate."

The name didn't ring any bells for the girl.

"They own several online media channels."

"Do you ever write for *Gal Style*?"

"I don't. But RAP owns that one."

"Really? Cool."

Julia waited a moment while the girl considered.

"Why not?" Amanda said.

"Great!"

Julia again checked the tablet's recording status before diving in.

"Do you know why your mother volunteered?"

"Volunteered for what?"

"To transition."

"Oh. You mean why did she kill herself?"

Julia found the lack of nuance refreshing, and disturbing. "Yes. Why did she kill herself?"

"Austin." She said no more, as if her half sibling's name said it all.

"Why Austin?" Julia prodded.

"He moved Hen in with him. She took over the nest, if you know what I mean."

Julia nodded vaguely. Then she shook her head. "Actually, I don't know what you mean."

"Before Austin and Hen moved in Mom and I were doing fine."

"But Austin said he moved in to help when he realized your mom had been drinking."

"That's a pile of bull!"

"He said she wanted to…" *How to say it?* "To do something that might give you a better life."

"He's a liar!" she shouted toward the hallway before hushing herself. "She did it because Hen kept whining about her own crummy life. She convinced my mom to commit suicide so Austin could get the house."

"Didn't the house go to you?" Julia wondered aloud. "I mean. Wouldn't your mother have put the house in trust for your future?"

Julia knew what Amanda couldn't: that Austin would have hit obstacles trying to cosign for his mother's transition. More clinics were requiring confirmation from a neutral party, someone who would not receive any of the inheritance. At least not officially.

"Gwen!" Julia realized.

"What about her?"

Julia covered her mouth, suddenly aware she had spoken the name aloud. "Nothing. Sorry," she said.

"It doesn't matter now anyway," Amanda continued bitterly.

"Why's that?"

The girl searched her internal vocabulary list. "Moreclosure. Is that the word?"

"Do you mean *foreclosure*?"

"Foreclosure. That's it."

"The bank is foreclosing?"

"If that means we lose the house, yes. Although I guess Hen made enough fuss at the bank that we'll get to rent it back. We won't have to move out."

A few seconds of stillness passed between them.

"I wish *I* could move out," Amanda finally added. "I hate it here."

Julia looked into the girl's eyes. Resignation. And the acid of resentment.

"So you blame your brother for your mom's decision?"

"My half brother. Yes, I do."

"And Gwen?"

A nod. "Her too. But mostly Austin. He could have stopped it."

"Could he?"

"One word from him and Mom would have changed her mind. I know she was depressed. And yes, she drank. But who could blame her? Hen was making this place a living nightmare. I hate her!"

"Do you have anyone else? Relatives? Other siblings?"

"Nope. Just Austin and Hen."

A brief silence.

"I might take the school counselor's advice."

"What kind of advice?"

"She told me if things get bad enough I can request protection from the state."

The comment troubled Julia. "Protection? From what?"

A shrug. "Don't know. Misery? Depression? I just know she said kids without parents can go to live with the Foster family."

"I think you mean a foster home."

"That's it. A foster home. Believe me, I've thought about calling them more than once."

"For protection?"

"For a home. At least more of a home than this place."

"I see," Julia said softly.

"Anyway," Amanda sang while leaping to her feet. She took the seat beside Julia on the sofa and moved in close. "Got any more pictures from your honeymoon?"

Julia smiled at the girl's hand resting on her own. They spent the next few minutes swiping through photo album files, Amanda grilling Julia for details about Troy's business, her sister's wardrobe, her nephew's school, and the nickname of each child in the Tolbert clan.

Fifteen minutes later Julia said goodbye to a pouty Austin and accepted Amanda's invitation to walk her to the car. She sat in the driver's seat watching the eleven-year-old wave goodbye from the porch, then vanish behind the front door of her dark zone address.

As Julia pulled away from the curb she ran through scenes of a story now captured on her tablet's recorder.

An alcoholic single mother struggles to make ends meet.

An estranged son manipulates her into an early transition, then squanders away his sister's financial future.

An oddly matched couple sell their potential offspring for cash to a snake-oil salesman promising youthful vigor.

And a beautiful orphan girl awaits rescue, starving for attention and dreaming of the day she might escape the shadowy realm of 2210 Kingston Street to find a brighter life.

CHAPTER TWENTY-EIGHT

The refrigerator shelves held some hormone-free, antibiotic-free, pesticide-free, and, most importantly, flavor-free milk, fruits, and vegetables. Tyler clung to the door, hunched over, and rearranged a few items. Hope rose within him at the sight of a reusable plastic container. Leftovers. Some forgotten remnant of a meal he must have thought worth keeping. Then he remembered the mashed potatoes from four nights ago.

Renee never saved anything since, to her, only fresh foods deserved the honor of consumption. Tyler wasn't so picky. Anything that hadn't gone rancid or turned into a moldy science experiment should be given a sporting chance.

He pulled out the container and flicked off the lid excitedly before disappointment sank in. Add "Gerry's dentures" to the list of disqualified entrees. They sat balanced atop the pile of mashed potatoes like Noah's Ark on Mount Ararat, condensation flooding the valleys. They'd been missing for several days, forcing Gerry, Renee, Tyler—and the disembodied voice of Katherine calling out from the bedroom—to conduct a mad, unsuccessful hunt. Until now.

"Found your dad's teeth!" Tyler called out, tossing the container onto the counter and slamming the fridge closed. He was still hungry.

"What?" Renee said, arriving with a laundry basket on her hip.

Tyler pointed at the evidence. Renee leaned in close, barely glanced at it, then sniffed, wrinkling her nose at Tyler.

"Gross, huh?" he said.

"Yes," she said, pulling away with the back of her hand protecting her nose to prevent gagging. "But not that. You. When's the last time you changed? Your clothes stink."

Tyler sniffed at his underarm, shrugging. Cologne de Burrito Supreme from lunch.

"Give me your clothes."

"I'm kind of using them at the moment."

"I'm about to put a load in, so hand them over."

Tyler stripped off his shirt and pants and tossed them with a smile.

"You want these as well?" he asked, pulling at, then snapping the waistband of his boxers.

Renee rolled her eyes and stuffed his clothes into the basket before disappearing around the corner to head upstairs.

Drat! He glanced back at Gerry's teeth.

"Ty?" Renee called from the top of the steps. He rushed to the foot of the staircase and glanced up. "Take a shower, and then maybe we can meet up in the bedroom."

"Nice look." Gerry's voice smacked from the hallway, complete with grinning gums. His skimpy attire mirrored Tyler's.

Tyler looked down at himself, then back to Gerry, shaking his head. He suddenly worried Gerry had heard Renee's obvious come-hither call. "I thought you were in bed."

"Katherine can't sleep."

"Is her back hurting again?"

Gerry nodded. "Just came to get some water and Vicodin for her. Then I'll be out of your pants." He sniggered. "I mean out of your hair!"

"Very funny. I was just heading upstairs, so help yourself. Oh, and you might want to rescue your dentures from the potatoes."

With one towel wrapped around his waist, Tyler dabbed moisture off his hair with another as he pushed open the bedroom door hoping to find Renee in next to nothing. Instead he found her on the bed, dressed in the same jeans and T-shirt she'd had on earlier. She was surrounded by several pieces of paper, tears on her reddened cheeks. She clutched one page tightly, her blank gaze moving up to meet his, saying nothing.

He blinked once, hard, then instinctively took a single step backward. What was this? A trick? Had she lured him up here just to yell at him? For what? He ran through a quick mental list of all the infractions he might have committed in the past couple of days, but came up empty. This couldn't be about the burrito, could it?

Renee said nothing as her glare shot piercing daggers. He wondered whether she intended to hold it all in, passive-aggressively, or let it rip. In the past, entire nights, days, even weeks could be ruined by one wrong word at a moment like this. So he stood in paralyzed silence. Then he imagined what could happen if he ignored her obvious distress. He chose the lesser risk.

"What's the matter?" he asked, forgoing any attempt to mind-read the problem and abandoning the fantasy he had indulged in while showering.

She waited, the tear on one cheek dripping to the page in her hand, drawing out the moment like a knife sliding slowly across taut skin. Finally she gathered herself enough to speak. "You want to kill my dad?"

Tyler squinted in confusion. Kill her dad? Why would he want to kill Gerry? Sure, he had flipped Tyler's life upside down, but any fleeting thoughts of murder were harmless catharsis. Nothing even remotely serious.

"Don't play dumb with me," she said, sitting up more bravely. "You want him dead. Probably both of them. Am I right? And you seriously thought I'd be OK with it? They're my parents, Ty! My flesh and blood!"

The final comment came out as a definitive jab. *They* were her flesh and blood, whereas he…wasn't. She had put Tyler in his place, and to his surprise, it stung. It was one thing for him to view Renee as expendable, but quite another for her to do the same to him. Out loud.

"Renee. I don't know what—"

"Don't deny it. I found the evidence in your pants pocket!"

For the first time Tyler examined the pages scattered about. They were the legal documents and partially filled-in application from New Day Transition Center.

"No, Renee, you don't understand!" He took a step forward to defend himself from what, he realized, might be the perfect way to end this relationship. Let her think it. Give her a reason to leave his house. His life.

No! he thought to his own surprise.

Renee held up the application, positioning it so Tyler could read it clearly. "What's not to understand?"

He wasn't sure what to say, how to explain it. She didn't know about the case with Judge Santiago. At least not specifically. He'd mentioned a new opportunity, that he was finally doing some real detective work with a real detective paycheck. But she didn't know how big it was, nor that it involved the transition industry. He wished now that he'd at least said that much. She would never believe he had just pretended to enroll her father to transition as part of a case.

"It doesn't mean anything," he heard himself saying. *Great! Now you sound like every one of your clients' cheating lovers.*

"Doesn't mean anything? You can't be serious. They're my parents!"

"No, listen. I'm working on this case. Remember, the one I told you about? There have been threats, and I need to make sure that…" He hesitated. What *was* the reason he'd gone to New Day? He really didn't know. A lead from a guilt-ridden former transition specialist that had gone nowhere?

"Make sure that what?" Renee pressed.

"You see, the entire transition industry hangs in the balance on this lawsuit appeal that—"

"I don't care about the transition industry."

"I know, but…a lot of people do and—" Suddenly Tyler wasn't sure he was talking to Renee. *A lot of people* included those who had nothing to do with the NEXT lawsuit or the Santiago case. He forced aside the hazy form of an emerging idea and brought himself back firmly to Renee. He stepped forward again, this time reaching to grab her hand. She jerked it away, but relented on his second attempt. "I needed to find out for myself what actually went on inside one of those clinics."

"I don't understand. Why my father?"

"It was the best I could come up with in the moment. I'm sorry. I never meant for you to even see these." He shoved aside the documents and climbed onto the bed, one knee at a time. "I just had to make it seem like, to them, I was serious."

Renee wiped a tear from her face, then sighed. "And were you?"

"Was I what?"

"Serious." Her gaze rose to his. "Because I know you hate every moment of them being here."

Tyler shook his head before looking away. She was right. He did hate it. The moments. But not them.

"I don't hate your parents," he finally said. "It's just…I interviewed this guy. His mother died, and his invalid brother transitioned. He had given up everything for his brother, including his own future. And after he was gone, Jeremy—the brother—he told me that even though he hated the situation he had been in, he missed his brother dearly. And that's how it is with your parents."

This time Renee was the one who appeared confused. "You missed my parents?"

"No. I mean, even though I don't like the situation we're in—and I'm just being honest—even though I don't like it, I know it's the right thing to do. Otherwise I never would have agreed to it to begin with."

"Do you mean that? Really?"

Tyler pursed his lips. Did he mean it? The words had just kind of fallen out of his mouth without much thought. Perhaps he'd become so accustomed to smoothing things over with Renee he was lying without even realizing it. But then again, maybe it really was how he felt. That taking in Renee's parents had been right. Katherine was practically bedridden. Gerry had managed to lose his own teeth in a container of mashed potatoes. They clearly could no longer manage by themselves. They needed Renee. He smiled. "Of course I mean it," he finally said to her, and to himself.

"Thank you." She took both his hands in hers, pressing his palms against her cool, wet cheeks. "But I need you to understand something. My parents are my priority right now. I mean, I love you. I want you. But they're my flesh and blood. If I'm ever forced to make a choice…"

She couldn't bring herself to say the rest.

He leaned forward and kissed her. "Don't worry. I get it."

She pulled back, smiling, then leaned her head against his chest before squeezing tightly. He returned the embrace, kissing the top of her hair tenderly. It felt nice, making up.

A voice came shouting from downstairs.

"Renee? Are you up there?"

Tyler tried to ignore Gerry's call, tried to distract Renee by kissing her neck just behind her ear. It didn't work.

"It's my dad."

"Ignore him. Five minutes."

"Renee? Your mother needs you. She needs to use the bathroom and I can't do it by myself."

Tyler tossed himself to the bed in defeat. "Fine. Go."

"I won't be long," Renee said with a wink. "I promise."

He knew better. Bathroom duty was a choreographed endeavor that took at least thirty minutes from start to finish. Tyler slipped under the covers, questioning his fleeting sense of love for Renee. Perhaps he'd confused his desire for passion with a willingness to continue this relationship indefinitely. He needed to regain control. This could be his life for a very long time if he didn't solve the Santiago case.

He drifted off to sleep, vaguely aware he was still hungry.

CHAPTER TWENTY-NINE

"Very nice," Dr. Vincent said as he watched Sarah walk away after delivering two steaming mugs to the table. "A friend of yours?"

"Sarah and I worked together," Matthew said, still enjoying the lingering scent of her *good to see you again* embrace. "We got pretty close."

Campus Grinds looked as it had every day of every year that Matthew had started and ended a shift. But it *felt* different sitting across from his mentor enjoying conversation instead of rushing to clear used napkins and empty mugs.

Both men took a first sip.

"How close?" Dr. Vincent asked with a wink.

Matthew's first instinct was to confirm the professor's suspicion with a bluff. But he had already exaggerated his progress with Maria, so decided to tell the truth. "Nothing like that. Just coworkers chatting to pass the time."

Dr. Vincent pulled out his phone, pointing and zooming toward the counter where Sarah was taking an order, and clicked a photo. Then he began voicing letters as he tapped "S. A. R. A. H." He paused, looking back at Matthew. "How do you spell her last name?"

Matthew recognized the professor's pattern. "She has a partner," he said protectively.

Dr. Vincent frowned like a wine connoisseur shaking an empty bottle. He hit the DELETE key.

"So, this girl in Denver," he said, getting them back to the conversation interrupted by the arriving drinks. "Any chance she'll keep you from returning to school next year?"

"Maria, from Littleton. And no, I don't see her keeping me from school. Although I do face other obstacles."

Dr. Vincent glanced at the time. "What do you say we spend twenty minutes overcoming your obstacles and leave the last ten for you to tell me about Maria?"

If only his financial problems could be solved so quickly.

"Actually, I wanted to discuss a different topic if that's OK with you."

The professor smiled. "You made the drive and bought the coffee so I suppose I should let you set the agenda. What's on your mind, Mr. Adams?"

"I'm working with a man who should transition," he said abruptly. "But he thinks it's wrong. And his daughter, who really needs him to volunteer, is scared to talk to him about it."

Dr. Vincent enjoyed a second drink while waiting for Matthew to say more.

"Well, not scared. More like perplexed. I think she likes the idea but vacillates between what she knows would be best and what she thinks would be wrong."

"So you've discussed this with both the father and the daughter?"

"I have. I raised it with my client after lunch a few days ago.

Then I spoke to his daughter yesterday. That's when I decided I needed your advice."

Dr. Vincent seemed pleased by Matthew's deferential regard. "I'm glad I was available. Tell me about the conversation with...what's the daughter's name?"

"Marissa. She's a bit older than me. Has two young kids."

"No partner?"

"Died a few years back. That's part of the reason the old man should transition. If he doesn't he'll need to move in with her and the kids."

The look on the professor's face told Matthew he didn't entirely see the problem.

"They don't get along," said Matthew.

Dr. Vincent continued to stare.

"And he's about to run out of money."

Finally an understanding nod. "I see. And his health?"

"Pretty bad. He can't walk. Breathes through a tube. Can't really be left alone."

"We decay," the professor said. They were the same words he had used when Matthew asked about his own ailing mother. And the words he used to explain Manichaeism to students and readers.

"Exactly!" Matthew said. "He's in decay and plans to make himself a burden to Marissa, Isabelle, and little Pete."

"The kids?"

"Yeah. Twins. About five or six years old."

"Hmm. Do they get along with their grandpa?"

The question carried weight, as if the professor thought affection might trump pragmatics.

Matthew recalled little Pete's secret conversation in his grandfather's room. "They get along," he replied. "But they've never had to live with Reverend Grandpa."

"Reverend Grandpa?" A chuckle.

"Don't ask," Matthew replied with a roll of his eyes. "He's sort of eccentric."

"I bet."

"He insists everyone call him Reverend. So the kids call him Reverend Grandpa." Matthew matched his mentor's smile as he thought of the comical man. "He used to be a preacher of some sort. Loves to read and quote from a vintage Bible he keeps in the front room."

The description flattened Dr. Vincent's grin into a disapproving sneer. "A literalist?"

Matthew didn't understand the question. "A what?"

"Does this Reverend Grandpa read the Bible as if it were literally true?"

"Seems to. Why?"

"What about the daughter?"

"What about her?"

"Does she share the old man's beliefs? You know, does she read the Bible literally?"

"I don't think she reads it at all. Like I said, she and her father don't get along."

"So she doesn't object to her dad volunteering for religious reasons?"

"I don't think so. She never mentioned any religious reasons. She just seemed afraid to talk to him about it."

"What did she say exactly?"

"Well," Matthew said, trying to recall. "I told her that I had asked Reverend Grandpa whether he had ever considered volunteering. She seemed both surprised and intrigued, especially when I explained your 'spirit good, body bad' concept."

"It's not entirely my concept," Dr. Vincent said with a reluctant hint of modesty. "Did Marissa seem open to transitions in theory?"

"I think so."

"So she didn't dismiss the process as immoral out of hand?"

"No."

"But she got nervous when you suggested a transition could help her specific situation?"

"Exactly! How'd you guess?"

"I've been teaching about enlightened spirituality for a long time now. The easy part is getting students to accept ideas in the abstract. It's much harder getting them to connect the dots to concrete realities like life and death. Humanity is hopelessly addicted to the embodied-personhood paradigm."

Matthew pretended to follow. "I guess," he said, returning to his dilemma. "One thing's for sure. Marissa Gale will never suggest a transition to Reverend Grandpa."

"But you did."

"Yes. I sensed he was depressed and assumed he had been considering volunteering. Boy, was I wrong!"

The two shared a laugh.

"Bit your head off, did he?"

A nod. "Yep. But I also sensed a tiny crack in the door, as if I had raised an option he would only consider under dire circumstances. That's why I mentioned it to Marissa. I even offered to help."

"Help? How?"

"I said I'd raise the topic with him again at the right moment. Possibly when he's feeling depressed or when he asks me to deposit his reverse mortgage check."

"Reverse mortgage?"

"He's been living on the house equity."

A nod of recall. "Right."

"Anyway, I said I could raise the subject at a time when he might be open to a different solution than burdening his daughter and grandkids. That's why I called your office. I was hoping you could help me come up with a few arguments that he might hear."

"I take it he doesn't like Manichean philosophy."

"Not at all. Dismissed my best points without a thought."

"I'm not surprised," the professor said. "Bible-thumpers aren't exactly known for their ability to think." He chuckled derisively.

"I guess. But he seems pretty smart. He's even read a book by Augustine."

"*City of God*?"

Matthew didn't recognize the title. "No. The book where Augustine described his religious conversion."

The former priest grimaced. "*Confessions.*"

"So you know it?"

"All too well."

"Should I read it?"

"No."

The answer surprised Matthew. "No?"

The professor corrected himself. "I mean, yes, of course. But Augustine wrote *Confessions* after ditching Manichaeism for Christianity. His books won't help you convince an old literalist that it's OK to escape a decaying body."

"I see."

A brief silence.

"Let's get back to the daughter," the professor said. "Did she accept your offer to talk to the father about volunteering?"

"She didn't say yes. But she didn't say no either."

"Then you need to do it."

"Really?"

"Absolutely." Dr. Vincent appeared to have overcome any concerns about affectionate grandkids. "Does the family have money?"

"Not much. Like I said, he's burning through a reverse mortgage. Why do you ask?"

"I just wondered whether the daughter would be willing to pay down your school loan if you convince the old man to go through with it. You know, sort of like a finder's fee."

"Would that be, you know, ethical?"

Dr. Vincent rolled his eyes. "Why wouldn't it be? Anyone can donate to a university."

"I don't know. It feels sort of—"

"In fact," the professor interrupted, "I have a research project that's been on hold since the end of last semester when I lost my grant. If you can find me a donor I could easily create a full-scholarship intern position."

"Wait. You mean if Marissa donated to your research project you could get me back into school?"

"Not just Marissa. Anyone."

Matthew considered the possibilities.

"What about my mother's estate?"

The question seemed to confuse the professor. "I thought your mother's estate was held up until the NEXT appeal gets resolved."

"Yeah. But it's only held up because I'm the direct beneficiary. What if the money got donated to the university instead?"

Dr. Vincent smiled at the idea before showing a look of concern, as if trying to figure out how to avoid getting into trouble with the IRS. After a few seconds he appeared to imagine a loophole, or possibly a cheat. "We might just be able to make that work."

Ten minutes later Matthew sat alone at the same table staring at the bottom of an empty coffee mug. His breath quickened with excitement as he considered his next steps.

First, call estate trustee Benjamin Cedillo to relinquish his inheritance money to the University of Colorado.

Second, ask Maria Davidson on a date in order to celebrate his pending return to college.

CHAPTER THIRTY

Troy looked at Julia from his side of the sofa without saying a word. He had seemed distracted while reading the first draft of her story. It had made her nervous watching facial expressions and hearing sighs that she couldn't quite decipher. Was he impressed? Confused? Did he love it? Hate it? Perhaps the pause meant he was trying to think of what to say without hurting her journalist ego.

"Be honest. What do you think?"

Another, deeper sigh. One that she recognized.

Troy was agitated.

"Say something."

"They sold their babies on the black market?"

Julia felt relieved knowing she had appalled her first reader. That was the purpose of the feature, after all. To put a human face on dark zone trends. Although, in the case of Austin Tozer and the woman Amanda called Hen, *inhuman* might be the more fitting word.

Troy continued. "The guy convinced his fifty-eight-year-old mom to transition just so he could avoid getting a job?"

"I didn't say he said that, did I?" Julia asked, fearing she had misrepresented Austin's rationale.

Troy glanced down at the tablet to rescan a section of the article. "No. I guess I read that between the lines."

Good, thought Julia. The story had accomplished both of her goals. First, give the facts as presented. Second, show the truth as observed.

"And I didn't call what they did 'selling on the black market' since it's legal to sell a fetus. Right to privacy."

"But I specifically remember a provision in the Ethical Embryotics Act stating companies can only accept *donated* embryos from unsuccessful in vitro implantation."

"True," Julia said. "But that law only applies to companies supplying materials for medical uses. It never mentioned cosmetics, health supplements, or a dozen other product categories."

"Health supplements?"

"Embryotic-enhanced protein powder. Bodybuilders add it to shakes."

Troy's face took on a greenish hue. "We ingest human embryos?" he whispered as if asking forgiveness.

"*Soylent Green* come to life," Julia said.

"*Soylent Green?*"

"An old movie where human beings became part of the food supply due to overpopulation. Too many people for too little food."

Troy winced, then sighed. "Too *many* people? Oh for the days we worried about *that* problem."

"Austin Tozer and his partner fit the dark zones themes to a tee," Julia said. "They took two thousand dollars per potential kid to spend on video games and Pop-Tarts, clueless to how badly we will need those kids a few decades from now. How badly *they* might need them. I thought their story was poetically appropriate."

"Tragic poetry," Troy scoffed.

Julia waited for more.

"You did good, babe," Troy said as he kissed her forehead. "It captures the ugly side of dark zone trends. I can't imagine anyone reading this piece without questioning common assumptions behind the Youth Initiative."

"Thanks," Julia said. She sensed he wanted to say more. "And?" she asked.

He hesitated before speaking. "Well. I also can't imagine RAP Syndicate publishing this story as is."

"I have a deal with Paul. He promised to run what I deliver. No changes that I don't approve first."

"That's good," Troy replied. "But can we trust him?"

Julia knew what was behind the question. Paul Daugherty was the same editor who had radically altered Julia's *Breeders* feature a year earlier. He had merged Julia's work with a smear piece by Monica Garcia, a rising star at RAP thanks to great legs rather than winning prose.

"No, we can't trust him," she said. "But that's a risk we take."

He nodded in reluctant acceptance of the gamble. "Regardless," he said, "it's one of the most powerful things you've written. I'm proud of you." He gave her another kiss, this time on the lips. "And I'm grateful to you. I think this will help Kevin."

"Wait till you see my second story. Polar opposite of this one. My first bright spot family."

She began describing an interview she had done the prior afternoon: a couple married almost twenty years, with three kids, running a software support business they operated out of their home. The oldest son, seventeen years old, worked in the business part-time after school. The grandparents lived in the same house. Or rather in an apartment that adjoined the main structure and provided easy access so the younger kids could get

Grandpa's help with homework or assist Grandma chopping vegetables. Her favorite part of the story, she explained, was how the older and younger couples had pooled their resources after the crash, an ideal arrangement that enabled the younger pair to launch the business.

Midway through her description Julia realized Troy was nodding his head without really listening. She stopped talking, folded her arms with a huff, and waited the ten seconds it took for him to notice.

His distant stare finally saw her scolding face. "Sorry, babe," he said. "I'm listening."

"No. You're *trying* to listen. Not the same thing."

She was right.

"You might as well tell me what's on your mind," Julia insisted. "You'll find out what I was saying later when you read my second story."

He smiled sheepishly before he groaned. "I'm not sure you want to know."

Her mind jumped to Troy and Kevin's business. Another setback? Had the needed venture capital deal fallen through? "Now you *have* to tell me," she insisted.

"I spoke to Kevin about an hour ago. He said it seems like Senator Franklin may be up to something."

"Something bad?"

"Not necessarily bad. More like calculated. Franklin encouraged Kevin to approach a guy named Dimitri to help us fund getting the Center for Economic Health off the ground."

"Evan Dimitri?" she asked. "Isn't he the brains behind the Saratoga Foundation?"

"The brains and a big chunk of the cash," Troy said. "He's a major player behind Franklin's campaign. He even gave a large gift to Kevin's reelection PAC last year. That's why Franklin suggested Dimitri as a potential source of seed funding."

"Makes sense. So why the concern?"

"There's more. Kevin said Franklin is acting all chummy again, like he did before…"

Troy stopped.

"Say it. Before my *Breeders* story tarnished Kevin's reputation?"

A faint nod.

"Anyway, rumors are floating around that Franklin sees Kevin as a key ally to win the White House next year."

"I thought Franklin had been trying to distance himself from Kevin."

"He was. It appears that's changing."

"Isn't that a good thing?" Julia asked. "I mean, it can only help Kevin to gain access and influence, right?"

"Perhaps," Troy said warily. "But Franklin isn't known to do favors for other party leaders, even young up-and-comers like Kevin, unless he sees how it will advance his agenda or bolster his poll ratings. I can only think of one reason Franklin would start courting Kevin now."

Troy paused, giving Julia a moment to fill in the punch line.

"He wants Kevin's endorsement?"

Troy appeared confused by the suggestion. "No," he said. "Kevin's endorsement wouldn't mean much at this stage of the game. He's only a second-term congressman from a medium-size state."

"What then?" Julia asked impatiently.

"I think he might be considering Kevin for the ticket."

Julia gasped. "As in, *Tolbert for vice president* ticket?"

"Exactly. Think about it. The *Breeders* story tapped the disdain of a large swath of the population against people like Kevin Tolbert."

"Don't remind me," she said.

"But it also forced the party to face facts. They now acknowledge the existence of a sizable voting bloc that seems to be growing and that can afford to donate more than dark zone citizens."

"Franklin wants support from the breeders."

"Which Kevin's smiling face and family photo would embody better than anyone in the party. Traditional marriage. Four kids. All he needs is some platform to give voice to and garner support from a constituency no one else has tapped. A large influx of cash to establish the Center for Economic Health as a credible voice would position Kevin well."

"But you worry it would make Kevin beholden to Franklin."

"I'm not as worried about Franklin as I am about the guy funding Franklin's rise."

"Dimitri."

"Do you know what he did during the lunch meeting with Kevin? He flashed a two-million-dollar check in his face like a puppeteer dangling strings. The recipient line was blank. Then he placed the check in front of Kevin and handed him a pen. 'Fill in the name of your new organization,' he said."

"Two million dollars?"

"Twice what we had hoped to raise in seed funding."

"What did Kevin say?"

"He thanked Mr. Dimitri for the support, wrote 'Center for Economic Health' onto the check, and slid the pen back across the table."

"So you have two million to work with? That's terrific!" She noticed Troy's frown. "Isn't it?"

"It would be if not for what happened next. Dimitri slid the pen back toward Kevin and handed him another document. Kevin read it, then tore up the check."

Julia's eyes widened. "He tore up a two-million-dollar donation?"

"The document Dimitri wanted Kevin to sign would have

made us promise that the Center for Economic Health will only advocate policies that encourage increased fertility while leaving the second bright spot trend alone. 'I'm fine with you rallying support among voters who love kids,' Dimitri told him. 'That'll help us. But if you do anything to undermine the core of the Youth Initiative I'll drop you faster than a bowling ball!'"

"Meaning?"

"Meaning hands off the transition industry. No research showing it causes harm. No suggesting there have been abuses. No proposals that would curtail its growth."

"Did Kevin explain to him that transitions aren't bringing the promised growth?"

"He knows. He doesn't care."

"Why would a fiscal conservative like Dimitri support a practice that stagnates the economy?"

"Because he doesn't believe the evidence."

"But—"

"Correction," Kevin continued. "He doesn't *want to* believe the evidence because his company makes a fortune as the exclusive supplier of PotassiPass, the key chemical ingredient used in every NEXT transition."

No wonder Troy had been so distracted. So agitated.

"I'm sorry," was all she could think to say.

"Me too," he said, squeezing Julia's hand. "I've had a bad feeling about Evan Dimitri ever since...well...since the first time I saw his name."

"When was that?"

"A large donation check from out of the blue last year. No prior relationship. No connection whatsoever. Kevin met him for lunch alone and later with Franklin."

Troy paused as if watching wheels turn in his head. Then he turned back toward Julia. "It took guts for Kevin to tear up that check. But he may also have turned one of Franklin's most reliable friends into one of our wealthiest enemies."

"Let's hope not," Julia said as she reached for a silver lining. Nothing came. She instead placed her hand on Troy's tensed jaw. "Hey," she whispered sweetly. "Where's the man I married? The one who makes a living figuring out how to turn declining companies into thriving enterprises?"

She sensed his anxiety ease at her touch. She moved in closer, teasing his lips with her own.

"The man who discovered bright spots in an economy everyone else saw as a dark, mucky swamp?"

She wrapped both arms around Troy's neck while sliding from her side of the sofa onto his lap. She began nibbling his earlobe.

"The man who brightens my life every day and"—she tasted his upper neck—"the man with whom I plan to join the bright spots movement."

They kissed deeply for several seconds. Then Troy pulled his head back to look Julia in the eyes. "Wait. What did you just say?"

A sly grin followed by a fierce nod.

"So you want to? Now? Not in a few years?"

"Now," she said eagerly, recalling Angie's description of pregnancy and motherhood. It was like leaning over the railing at Niagara Falls, the fear overwhelmed by the wonder.

Her husband's fingers slid around her torso. Her body tingled with anticipation. Julia knew she was about to enjoy the first unprotected sex of her life.

And it surprised her to realize nothing had ever made her feel so safe.

CHAPTER THIRTY-ONE

Tyler sat in his car rereading the partially completed application he had taken from the New Day Transition Clinic. It stubbornly refused to give him even one additional clue. He took a first bite of his second doughnut before wiping the side of his mouth on a glaze-smeared napkin. He would have used the fresh napkin sitting on the passenger-side seat had it not held notes that, sadly, summarized his entire investigation.

The Facts

- 4 letters from "A Manichean"
- 3 polite. 4th seems a threat
- Jeremy = most to gain from NEXT loss
- Hannah hates them—possible suspect?
- New Day Clinic a bit pushy but legit

He needed more. He crammed the rest of doughnut number two into his mouth before attempting to speak a command.

"Please repeat," the device said in response.

Tyler swallowed without chewing and tried again. "Association search for A Manichean."

"Three thousand relevant results. Please specify to narrow."

"Within one hundred miles of Denver," he said while licking glaze from his thumb.

"Please repeat."

He sighed as he reached for the tablet. "I'll just type it in!"

"Thank you," the device said politely.

Two quick taps left a sugary smudge that reminded Tyler he still had four deliciously sticky fingers. He sucked the glaze from each while trying to clean the mess. Then he groaned at the streak left on the keyboard by the used napkin.

These notes are useless anyway, he thought while grabbing his case summary document. Seconds later the screen was legible again.

The phone rang in his ear.

"Tyler Cain," he answered.

"Good morning, Mr. Cain." He recognized the voice, but couldn't immediately place it. He glanced at the dash screen: JULIA DAVIDSON, JOURNALIST.

"Oh, hi, Ms. Davidson," he said with surprise.

"Simmons."

"Right. Ms. Simmons." *Probably calling to thank me*, he thought. "How'd it go with Austin?"

"Actually, quite well. I'm including his story in the series. Thanks for making the connection."

"Like I told you, Austin's definitely a dark zone kind of guy."

"The story won't use his real name, but you'll recognize him. It should run in the next few weeks."

The comment reminded Tyler to subscribe. "I look forward to reading it. Glad I could help."

"I'd like to return the favor," Julia began. "Something came up I think might prove helpful in your investigation."

"Really?" he said as if spotting a sliver of light through an overcast sky. "Let me hear it."

"During our chat you said the judge had received three letters, is that right?"

"Four, actually."

"Four letters then. And you said the person seemed urgent to know Santiago's opinion on the appeal?"

"That's right."

"Did the writer indicate whether he or she hoped the judge would decide for or against NEXT?"

Tyler glanced at the notes on his now-crumpled napkin and decided to play the odds. "Against."

"You're sure about that?"

He remembered Hannah Walker asking the same question. "Well, actually, the letters don't indicate one way or the other. But we've assumed—"

"Don't," Julia interrupted. "Don't assume the writer wants NEXT to lose the case. There are some very powerful people who need NEXT to win that appeal. Some of them might even go to extreme lengths in order to protect their interests."

"What kind of interests are you talking about?"

Tyler waited. Why the long silence? Was she trying to convince herself to say the rest? "Mrs. Simmons?"

"Please, call me Julia."

"OK, Julia. What kind of interests?"

She hesitated, then spoke. "It's probably totally unrelated to this case, but my husband learned of a conversation that took place in Washington that sheds light on the importance of the NEXT case."

"Go on," Tyler said.

Julia told him about the large check Kevin Tolbert had declined to accept from a man named Evan Dimitri.

"So this Dimitri guy has the exclusive supplier contract with NEXT?" Tyler chewed on the revelation for a moment. "And he threatened Congressman Tolbert?"

"Not exactly threatened. But he was clearly upset by Kevin's refusal."

He let the additional information settle. "I don't get it," he finally said. "I imagine those kinds of lunch conversations happen every day in Washington. Why did you think to mention this one? I don't see what it has to do with the Santiago case."

"Maybe nothing," she said. "But for whatever reason it made me think of you. I remembered you saying you thought those letters came from someone like Jeremy. Someone who has a lot to gain if NEXT loses its appeal."

"And you think I'm on the wrong track?"

"I do. I think you need to consider who has something to *lose* rather than something to gain. Evan Dimitri, among others, could lose a fortune in sales if anything undermines the transition industry."

"Like a wrongful death victory against NEXT."

"Exactly," she said.

Tyler's mind began racing as new possibilities breathed life into a dead-end investigation.

"Anyway," Julia was saying, "I wanted to mention it in case it could help you find the culprit."

"Thank you, Julia," he said. "It certainly can't hurt."

They ended the call. Tyler remembered his search and grabbed his tablet.

"Association search," he began. "Evan Dimitri and A Manichean."

"Please repeat."

He cursed, then began tapping the revised query onto the screen.

"No results," the tablet said disappointingly.

He deleted A MANICHEAN and hit SEARCH again. A string of results surfaced, most of them press releases about quarterly profits, emerging innovations, and recent acquisitions. Tyler tapped the most promising. To his surprise it didn't bring him to a company site, but rather to the news posting page from a political action group called the Saratoga Foundation.

Saratoga Foundation chairman Evan Dimitri recently announced the addition of fashion industry mogul Trisha Sayers to the board of directors. Ms. Sayers brings a wealth of experience to the team derived from more than a decade running one of the nation's largest retail chains and from serving on a variety of presidential commissions including the Youth Initiative coalition that helped the president craft what became a sweeping plan to address the nation's steep economic decline. Mr. Dimitri said he considers Ms. Sayers an excellent addition to the board because she will bring...

A musical ping interrupted Tyler's reading. He looked at the dash screen. A short text message.

FROM: JULIA DAVIDSON, JOURNALIST
Be careful, Mr. Cain. This case might end up carrying you into the deep end of the pool.

CHAPTER THIRTY-TWO

"For Pete's sake!" Reverend Grandpa shouted from his perch. "Shut the door!"

Matthew should have knocked. He had been too eager to take one last peek at his freshly ironed collar and swish one last shot of mouthwash before leaving. He apologized at the mutually embarrassing intrusion and pulled the door closed as quickly as he had opened it. Then he heard the old man's voice mushroom from a slow, deep chuckle into a leg-brace-slapping roar of laughter.

"You should have seen the size of your eyeballs!" Reverend Grandpa said between guffaws, his voice slightly muffled by the bathroom door. "You looked like a little boy accidently skipping into the ladies' locker room!"

If only, Matthew thought. That would have been much less disturbing than the image now trapped behind his still-closed eyelids.

"Sorry, son," the old man said after one last snigger. "Thought you had left already. I shouldn't be long."

Matthew knew better. Besides, he had no desire to use the room now. "It's all right. I'm good. See you tonight."

"Have a good time, my boy."

Matthew walked back to the bedroom to grab a gift he had finished wrapping moments earlier. The box contained a framed picture of a photo he had clipped and saved from the Littleton High School annual; a little something he hoped Maria Davidson would appreciate. Maybe even like.

"I'm off," he said, shooting Donny a wave.

"You're still here?" Donny said. "I thought you left."

"So did the Rev. I needed to wrap a little something." Matthew displayed the package.

Donny grinned and nodded.

"Thanks again for covering for me. I owe you one."

"No problem, man." Donny's eyes were fixed on a television screen mounted on the kitchen wall. "Sure you wouldn't rather hang out with us boys to watch the rest of the game?" He chuckled at his own dumb question. Of course Matthew didn't want to watch baseball instead of go on his first official date with the most amazing woman on the planet. Still, he sweetened the deal by holding up a partially consumed bag of cheese puffs. "I brought your favorites."

"Tempting. But I'll pass."

Matthew started toward the back door, then looked back toward his in-a-pinch pal with a twinge of guilt. Should he have warned him about Reverend Grandpa's evangelistic fervor? Should he suggest steering clear of religious topics?

"Forget something?" Donny asked.

Matthew shook his head. "Good luck, buddy."

Donny shrugged, then looked back toward the game while tossing a single puff in the air to nearly catch it in his mouth.

As Matthew slipped out the door his phone rang from his front jeans pocket. He glanced at the screen and realized he needed to take the call, much as he hated any delays. "Hi, Ben," he answered. "Thanks for getting back to me."

"Hello, Matthew." Just as distant as the last time they'd spoken.

"How's Carol?" Small talk might help thaw the chill.

"How should she be?"

Matthew could tell Ben intended to make him work for every syllable of conversation.

"Give her my love."

"I will. Right after we get back from wasting another five hundred or a thousand dollars of your mom's estate on a romantic dinner and bottle of wine."

"Very funny. I never said you were—"

"What do you need, Matthew?" Ben asked as if speaking to a disruptive child raising his hand for yet another trip to the bathroom.

Matthew swallowed back contempt. Further antagonism in an already tense relationship wouldn't help matters.

"Did you get my message?"

"I did."

"Did it make sense?"

"It didn't."

Matthew inhaled deeply. "Well, I need to know whether I can redirect a portion of my mother's estate to the University of Colorado."

A brief silence told him wheels were turning in Ben's head.

"Ben? Did you hear me?"

"You can't do that," Ben said decisively.

"Why not?"

"I already told you, the money can't be released until—"

"It can't be released to *me*," Matthew interrupted. "But I'm asking if some of it can go to the university. You know, as a donation. I wouldn't get a penny."

Another spell of silence.

"Ben?"

"Why?"

Now Matthew went silent to consider options. Should he tell Ben the whole story? It might help if he knew Dr. Vincent had suggested the idea. Or would it be better to feed Ben information on a need-to-know basis?

"Matthew? What kind of scheme are you up to?"

"It's not a scheme," Matthew snapped as he placed the wrapped gift on the hood of his car to free a hand. He opened the door while admiring the package that symbolized his real goals. *Get back to school and become a professor. Do something with your life worthy of a woman like Maria Davidson.* "I just need to know if it can be done, OK?"

Matthew sensed the lawyer's subdued chafing. He didn't care.

"All right, Matty." Matthew hated when Ben used Aunt Carol's nickname for him. "I'll look into the possibility. Seems like a long shot, but I'll check it out."

Matthew had hoped to know before his date with Maria. A simple question, he assumed, with a quick yes-or-no answer. No such luck.

"When will you know?" Matthew pushed.

He heard Ben's familiar put-out sigh. "I'll see what I can do."

Each waited for the other to speak next.

"Thanks," Matthew relented. "I'll expect a call tomorrow."

He ended the call before Ben could respond.

Matthew knew Maria's eyes were trying to read his reaction. He had to say something, anything, now.

"Of course I don't mind."

He sensed her gaze sinking. Say more!

"In fact," he added quickly, "this is great!"

He hoped to sound convincing despite the shock. So much for a romantic dinner alone followed by, what had he expected, a trip back to her apartment? His first glance at her incredible outfit had said, *Yes.* Her son's sulking presence said, *Not a chance.*

Matthew recalled Maria's asking if he wanted to meet Jared on the day they'd had coffee. He had assumed she meant later, after the two of them spent time together. After they had hit it off. Not on their first real date, if that's what this was. Did she want the protection of a third wheel? Did the boy lack friends, someone to hang out with during his mom's date? Or maybe, he hoped, his presence meant Maria really liked Matthew, that she wanted him to see the full package sooner rather than later.

He realized he had been silent for a few seconds. "Put 'er there, buddy," Matthew said hastily, shoving his hand toward the boy.

Jared crossed his arms while turning to glower at his mother.

"Come on, man, don't leave me hangin'."

Which is exactly what the boy did.

Maria gave Matthew an embarrassed smile. "Sorry," she said.

Her eyes seemed like a plea for Matthew's help, triggering in him a curious sense of purpose. He tried to imagine the relationship between Maria and her twelve-year-old son, a boy who must be leery of the countless men hovering around his flower of a mom. Some of them, perhaps, had hurt her. Or him.

"Listen," he said, lowering his extended hand. No point in pretending with the boy. "I get it. You don't want to spend time becoming best friends with some old guy just because he likes your mom."

Maria seemed pleased by the comment.

Matthew looked at the restaurant hostess, who had already retrieved a pair of menus in anticipation of seating the "party of two" reserved under his name.

"And I'd be shocked if this young lady even has a table for three available."

The hostess looked toward the half-empty dining area, then back toward the trio. She followed Matthew's lead. "I'm afraid I only reserved a table for two, sir," she said with a complicit grin.

"So we have two choices," Matthew continued. "We can either call off the whole thing or"—he paused for dramatic impact—"we can jump in my car and head over to Conroy's to grab some burgers and shakes and then play a few rounds of Battalion Call."

The boy's brow lifted slightly at the mention of the vintage virtual warfare game. Then he forced his expression back to a frown, followed by a shrug.

"Sounds fun," Maria chirped. "What do you say, Jared?" She bumped him with a hip.

An hour later Matthew was sitting at a booth in front of empty burger wrappers and milkshake cups and a smattering of cold, neglected fries. He was listening to a grateful Maria confirm his suspicions. She did indeed have a rocky history with men.

"After that I promised Jared no more surprises. And I figured the best way to keep that promise was to bring him along."

"Makes sense to me," Matthew said as he glanced around the room to make sure the boy remained out of earshot. "He seems like a pretty good watchdog to keep away the wolves."

An embarrassed giggle. "Actually, too good. You're only my second date in the past six months."

Matthew dropped his jaw. "Not possible."

She blushed at the embarrassing secret and at the admiration in Matthew's eyes.

"How about you?" she asked. "I bet you've had a long line of women in your life."

He laughed awkwardly. "I wouldn't say a long line."

"What about Molly? I thought for sure she would pursue you after graduation."

The name didn't ring a bell at first. Then he remembered. "Jolly Molly Carson?" He blushed at the recollection. Maria had suggested Matthew ask Molly to the senior prom. It was the excuse she gave for rejecting his request. Said she couldn't go with a guy Molly crushed on. Molly Carson had a pretty face, but a heavy figure. Her quick wit made her good for a laugh. But not for a prom date.

"We never went out," Matthew said with a touch of offense. "I didn't even know she liked me."

"Who then?"

"Nobody you'd know," he said limply.

She seemed to sense her mistake. "Well, I'm glad."

His eyes met hers. "Glad? For what?"

"I'm glad you haven't been serious with many girls."

The comment surprised him, and pleased him. "Really? Why's that?"

Maria turned toward the gaming machines as if looking for Jared. "I don't know. I guess because it can include complications." She appeared reflective, as if wondering what life might have been had she made different choices. Then she turned back toward Matthew with what seemed a smile of sincere admiration. She slid her hand toward his. "You look good, Matthew. I'm glad you got in touch."

Feeling Maria's softness, he considered slipping to her side of the booth. But he stayed put. Maria Davidson had offered herself to many men over the years. Each, he assumed, had eagerly tasted a small piece of the delicious creature touching him now. But he wanted more than a fragment, more than a short-term fling. And getting what he wanted meant heeding the warnings of a wary watchdog named Jared.

His hand retreated tenderly to retrieve the gift he had placed on the bench beside him. "I brought you something."

A look of surprise. "What is it?"

"Open it and find out."

She did. A picture frame. She flipped it over to view the image.

"Do you remember this?"

Watching her eyes, he saw she clearly did not. No matter. "I've kept that picture framed in my room ever since high school."

She looked closer to examine the younger versions of them both. "Where did you get this picture?"

The question bothered him. She must have purchased their senior annual. Maria appeared in dozens of posed and spontaneous shots. But only one, this one, included Matthew Adams.

"It was in the annual," he explained. "That was us in the lunch room on February twelfth of our senior year."

"Right," she said guardedly. "I guess I missed this one."

A brief, awkward silence passed between them. What was she thinking?

"You know the exact date?" Maria asked.

"I sure do," he said proudly.

She shifted uncomfortably in her seat. Her soft allure seemed to harden, as if she were suddenly in the presence of a pesky stalker. It was the same look, he now remembered, she'd given him the day he asked her to go with him to the senior prom.

"That was great!" Jared shouted as he approached the booth. Both sets of eyes turned in the boy's direction, grateful for the interruption. Matthew forced a smile, still wondering what was on Maria's mind.

Jared slid into the open space beside his mom. The same space Matthew now thought he should have taken when he'd had the chance.

"Level eight!" the boy bragged in Matthew's direction. "I hit level eight that time!"

Matthew offered a thin smile of congratulation. "Whoa. You rock, dude!" he said like the dinosaur he felt himself becoming.

Had the picture reminded Maria that the mysterious Matthew Adams was not an overlooked gem from high school sweeping back into Littleton after building a successful business? He was the pimple-faced geek who had dared violate class system boundaries by crushing on the most desirable girl at Littleton High. A guy who, it turned out, had been obsessed with her since February twelfth of their senior year.

Maria pulled Jared close, a motherly embrace that seemed to double as a human shield protecting her from whatever danger Matthew suddenly posed.

"Geez, Mom!" the boy said while pulling away. He scanned the room for potential witnesses. Coast clear, he relaxed enough to notice the picture frame.

"Is that you?" he asked his mom, looking closer at the picture. She nodded. "Uh-huh."

He continued examining the image. "Who's the dorf?"

Maria's eyes met Matthew's. Both blushed at the embarrassing nature of the question. And at the truth of it.

"He wasn't a dorf." She gently slapped her son's arm. "He was a friend."

Not a *boy*friend. Not a long-lost love. Just a friend.

Maria quickly gathered the torn wrapping paper and bundled it around the frame before placing the gift beside her on the bench.

"Matthew brought it as a reminder of the good old days, didn't you, Matthew?"

He nodded as the boy exclaimed, "So you're the dorf?"

Another slap, this time less playful than the last.

Matthew smiled weakly until Maria broke the momentary

silence. "Why don't you two play another round together? You know, see if you can reach level nine."

Matthew started to object. Time to throw in the towel.

"I'm in!" Jared announced.

"I don't know," Matthew began before stopping himself at the thought that he might have been misreading Maria's body language. She wouldn't have suggested another round with Jared unless she wanted the two to continue bonding. Maybe the picture hadn't given her the creeps after all. Perhaps she was just reacting to an embarrassing reminder of her own age. Unlikely, he thought, but possible. Most women, even those as gorgeous as Maria Davidson, struggle with self-doubt.

"Come on," Jared prodded. "Just one more round."

"Why not?" Matthew said with a smile of renewed optimism.

"And then we should go," said Maria.

Jared frowned indignantly. "But you said I could order a dessert if I came along."

"Yeah, Mom," Matthew added. "We can't leave before I buy you two an ice-cream sundae."

She smiled at the label, and the offer. "All right," she relented. "We'll stay long enough for dessert."

"Great!" the duo said in unison, prompting another smile from the beautiful woman Matthew hoped was open to giving him another, less creepy, chance.

CHAPTER THIRTY-THREE

"I'm sorry, Mr. Cain," a pleasant female voice said through Tyler's earpiece. "Mr. Dimitri will be with you in a few minutes. He's wrapping up his other meeting now."

Tyler continued staring at his tablet screen. It displayed a still-vacant chair behind what looked like an empty news anchor desk. He'd seen countless nearly identical sets on television, with this or that pundit commenting on the latest White House decision, international incident, or celebrity hairstyle change.

"Like I said, I don't mind rescheduling if it would be more convenient." He half hoped the assistant would accept the offer, still a bit unnerved by his sudden inclusion in Evan Dimitri's "very busy schedule." Tyler's idea of a power lunch would be meeting Smitty for a sub sandwich. Dimitri, by contrast, routinely dined with senators and corporate titans. Tyler's greatest accomplishment had been putting a low-life murderer behind bars. Dimitri, from all appearances, had put presidential hopefuls in the White House.

"That won't be necessary, Mr. Cain. But thank you." The

woman spoke with more respect than Tyler deserved. He hadn't, after all, been entirely forthright when requesting the meeting.

It was true, he reminded himself, that he was investigating a case of suspected murder. Never mind no killing had yet occurred.

He actually had been a Denver detective…once upon a time.

And he did want input on the case from a well-respected businessman with unique expertise on the transition industry. And, he'd failed to mention, a strong motivation to intimidate Judge Santiago. Or kill him.

"Nice set," Tyler said to make small talk.

"Oh, yes, thank you," the woman's voice replied.

"I suppose Mr. Dimitri does a lot with the media?"

"Actually, not as much as you'd think. Necessary evil, if you know what I mean."

Tyler answered with a polite, unseen nod.

"He mostly uses it for board meetings, conference calls, and such. He prefers it over face-to-face meetings, which he considers an *unnecessary* evil. Except when it includes lunch." She laughed.

Tyler joined her chuckle. "I see."

A few more minutes of dead air.

"Sorry I'm late," Dimitri finally said while taking his seat, an obligatory comment that sounded more like an irritated bark. A ten-minute conference call with some detective named Tyler Cain was not, it seemed, on the top of his priority list.

Evan Dimitri appeared every bit as intimidating as his net worth. A solid frame matched a strong, determined jaw. His thick gray hair implied experienced maturity. And a four- or five-thousand-dollar suit fell awkwardly on a body more bruised rugby player than cultured CEO.

He barked again: "What do you want to know?"

Tyler had prepared himself for a few pointless pleasantries such as a comment about the weather or the latest major league rankings. But clearly Evan Dimitri disliked wasting time.

"Thank you for your time, Mr. Dimitri," Tyler began. "My name is—"

"Tyler Cain. I know. Denver police?"

"Yes," Tyler said instinctively. "I got the case from the assistant chief."

"Why didn't *he* call me?" A fair question from a powerful man.

"It's a somewhat unique situation requiring arm's-length handling. That's why it was assigned to me."

"Who are you?"

"A former officer now on special assignment."

"Former officer?" Dimitri glanced down, presumably at notes compiled by the executive assistant Tyler had convinced to schedule the meeting. "So you're not"—he paused to reread—"a homicide detective with the Denver police?"

"Retired to launch my own private investigation agency."

"Hmm," he said, clearly unimpressed. "So, what do you want to know?"

"I understand your company owns the patent on the Potassi-Pass serum."

A single nod.

"And that you have an exclusive supplier contract with NEXT Transition Services."

Dimitri huffed impatiently. "Do you plan to waste my time telling me what you already know or do you have a question?"

Tyler heard annoyed arrogance in Dimitri's voice, the same kind he had heard a thousand times during criminal interrogations. Apparently felons and power brokers felt a similar self-importance. Tyler knew how to respond. "Look, Mr. Dimitri," he said sternly, "I have no interest in wasting your time any more than my own. This will only take a few minutes."

Dimitri's smile suggested a respect for tough-skinned adversaries. "All right, Mr. Cain. I'll give you five."

Tyler realized he had acquired a measure of respect, but had lost half of his scheduled time.

"What do you know about the wrongful death decision appeal involving NEXT?"

"Same as anyone else. A greedy kid hopes to land a big payday from his mom's accidental death."

"Do you know the judges reviewing the appeal?"

A scowl. "Know them? Personally?"

Tyler hesitated. He had planned to feel his way through the conversation to find a less direct angle. But there was no time for tact.

"I mean have you corresponded with any of them?"

The question appeared to confuse Dimitri. "Corresponded? About what?"

"The case."

A caustic laugh. "Of course not."

Tyler watched Dimitri's eyes. He appeared to be telling the truth.

"Mr. Cain, I was told you wanted to discuss a murder case. Why are we talking about appeal court judges in a wrongful death lawsuit?"

Tyler wished he could hit pause and then rewind to restart the conversation on a less adversarial footing. He needed to gain Dimitri's confidence quickly. An idea came.

"I must ask you to keep what I'm about to share completely confidential," Tyler said, already regretting what he had decided to do.

"Of course."

"One of the federal judges issuing an opinion on the NEXT case has received letters that appear threatening."

Dimitri's eyebrows rose, but his face offered no indication of guilt. "Really?"

"Yes, sir." Tyler's tone changed, as if he were speaking to an ally helping with the case. "I was hoping you could help me think through who might be behind them."

For the first time since the conversation began Dimitri's eyes met Tyler's image on the screen. "Help you think it through?"

"That's right."

"So you can identify potential suspects?" He sounded, what, flattered?

"Exactly. I would really appreciate your opinion."

"Would you?" he asked flatly.

"Yes, I would," Tyler replied warily.

"Why me?"

"Excuse me?"

"Why me, Mr. Cain? You don't know me from Adam and I've certainly never heard of you. Yet out of the blue you decide to seek my advice solving a case involving NEXT."

Dimitri reached to accept a glass of something on the rocks from a feminine hand. He sipped, then smiled derisively. "What do you take me for, some kind of naïve fool?"

"No. Not at all. I just—"

"Who gave you my name?"

Tyler froze. *What to say?*

"Who told you to talk to me, Mr. Cain?"

"Two different sources suggested you could help me," he lied.

"Name them."

"I can't do that."

"Then this conversation is over. I don't have time for a goose chase prompted by anonymous leads. I'm a very busy man."

"Davidson." The name spilled from Tyler's lips before he could stop it.

Dimitri stared blankly. A good sign. Tyler sensed an opening window.

"Julia Davidson suggested I show someone like you the letters."

"Someone like me how?"

"Someone who understands both the business significance and the political significance of the NEXT appeal."

"I see," Dimitri said, appearing and sounding a bit more receptive. "Kim," he said into the air.

"Yes, Mr. Dimitri."

"Track down any communications or meetings I've had with a Julia…" He paused, shifting his eyes back toward Tyler.

"Davidson," he said, reluctantly filling in the blank.

"Julia Davidson."

"Yes, sir," the woman replied obediently.

Tyler knew Dimitri would connect the dots from journalist to husband to congressman. But he couldn't worry about that now. He had less than two minutes of Dimitri's attention left. The moment of truth had arrived. *Show him the letters and watch his eyes like you did with Jeremy Santos*, he coached himself.

A different voice protested within. "Once you go digital, you lose control," Jennifer McKay had warned. He pushed past the objection.

"Would you be willing to take a look?"

"At what?"

"At the letters."

Dimitri seemed intrigued. "What? Now?"

"Yes, sir. I can forward copies. All I need is a secure in-box and the assurance you'll destroy the files after our conversation."

Tyler waited as seconds chipped away at his remaining minutes.

"Any insight you can give would help. To be honest, we don't have many leads at the moment."

Dimitri smiled like a man accepting a stick of his favorite gum. "Kim will send you an in-box address, same one we use for confidential legal documents," he said, standing. "Send them while I take a leak."

The man disappeared from view while his voice trailed off. "Then you'll have another five minutes."

Glad for the restored time, Tyler quickly unfolded the letters to snap and save copies. Seconds later a link arrived on his screen. He hesitated, then hit SEND to complete the transfer.

He waited two minutes. Then he waited three more.

"Mr. Dimitri?" he said apprehensively.

No response.

He tried the woman. "Um, Kim? Is everything OK? The files should have arrived."

"They arrived, Mr. Cain," she responded matter-of-factly. "Mr. Dimitri is reading them now."

Tyler cursed within. He needed to watch Dimitri's pupils and decipher facial movements in reaction to the letters. How else would he be able to gauge guilt, surprise, confusion, or any other emotion?

"I don't see him. Where is he?"

"I'm right here," Dimitri said, resettling himself in the chair and lifting his eyes from the tablet in his hand. "I read the letters. Odd."

"Yes, they are," Tyler said. "Any other reactions?"

"Seems pretty straightforward to me," Dimitri offered.

"Really? How's that?"

"Judge Santiago needs to resign from the case. He's been compromised."

Tyler swallowed hard. *How much to say?*

"The judge hasn't been compromised because he hasn't actually seen the letters. I got them from an aide."

Dimitri waved his hand at the fact as if swatting an annoying insect. "No judge should issue an opinion on a case when some religious nut has made threats."

"Religious nut? Did you see something in the letters to suggest—"

"Isn't it obvious?" Dimitri interrupted. "Who else would want NEXT to lose the appeal? It's always the same people."

"The same people? Who?"

"Do you have any idea how many hostile letters come to my company every week, Mr. Cain? Ever since we landed the supplier contract with NEXT we've been targeted by every wacko on a mission to keep debits from ending their misery."

"Do you keep them?" Tyler asked, an idea forming.

"Keep what?"

"The wacko letters?"

"Beats me," Dimitri said. "Kim, do we keep the wacko letters?"

"I'm sure we have them on file somewhere, sir," she replied.

"Can I take a look?" Tyler asked. "You never know. I might find one with matching handwriting."

"Not likely."

"All the same, I'd like to try."

"Be my guest," Dimitri said curtly. "Kim..."

"On it, sir."

"Can I give you a bit of advice, Mr. Cain?" Dimitri continued.

"Please."

"I suggest you ignore these letters."

Was he offering advice or issuing a threat? "We can't just ignore them, Mr. Dimitri."

"Why not? You already said the judge is ignoring them."

"I didn't say he's ignoring them. I said he hadn't read them. He has a policy of delegating any messages related to an appeal to his aide until after issuing an opinion. So he won't even know these letters exist until September fourth."

"Why the fourth?"

"It's the day after the case will be decided and opinions released."

"I see," Dimitri said, his eyes shifting quickly toward a woman's hand appearing on the screen. He reached to receive a slip of paper. He read it aloud. "Julia Davidson is married to Troy Simmons, Congressman Tolbert's former chief of staff."

Needles of panic stung Tyler's neck and shoulders.

"So Congressman Tolbert gave you my name?"

"No, sir. I've never met the congressman."

"But you've met Troy Simmons?"

Tyler shook his head defensively.

Dimitri swore. Then he swore again. "What exactly are you trying to pull here, Mr. Cain?"

"I'm not trying to pull anything. I'm doing a job that—"

"You said your job was to investigate a possible threat, not to accuse honest citizens without a shred of evidence."

"I haven't accused you of anything."

"Oh no?" Dimitri's face flushed a furious red. "Why else would you have started this conversation by asking whether I had corresponded with the judge? And why didn't you tell me right up front that you were friends with Congressman Tolbert?"

"I told you, I've never met any congressman."

"Right. You've never met him," Dimitri scoffed. "I think you're lying, Mr. Cain. I think you know Tolbert and that you're trying to concoct a plausible story that will throw the trail off of a much more likely suspect."

Likely suspect? Tyler wondered.

"You got my name from the only congressman who has an ax to grind with the transition industry. The man who came crawling to me for reelection money last year but now thinks I'm too dirty to fund his Bright Spots crusade."

Tyler only vaguely recalled the term, something Julia had mentioned. No matter now. He racked his brain for a way to recover the moment. Nothing came but the realization his Hail Mary pass had been intercepted. Evan Dimitri now had the identity of a confidential source. Worse, he had digital copies of the documents Jennifer McKay had insisted Tyler protect.

"This conversation is over, Mr. Cain," Dimitri said after downing the last of his drink. "And you can assure Mr. Tolbert that I intend to speak to Josh Franklin about this little stunt."

Tyler reached deep to forge an intimidating tone. "I wouldn't do that if I were you. This is a highly sensitive investigation that—"

It was too late. The screen had already gone black, leaving Tyler wondering what, exactly, he had done. One thing was certain. He had stepped in something messy. And it smelled pretty bad.

CHAPTER THIRTY-FOUR

As far as Tyler could tell, Jennifer McKay's preoccupied gaze fell somewhere between the digital calendar of events hanging on the wall and whatever was beyond, as though she possessed X-ray vision. A desk phone handset was wedged firmly between her left shoulder and ear while she poked mindlessly at salad leftovers with a fork. The conversation seemed unimportant based on the brief utterances she made every few seconds.

"Hmm."

"Right."

"I see."

After nearly two minutes she was still completely unaware he was standing there. Finally Tyler rapped his knuckles hard on the desk surface to announce himself.

Startled, Jennifer simultaneously juggled the phone and spun around to locate the intruder. Seeing Tyler, she held up one finger, then ended the call with a curt "Let me call you back in a few minutes."

At this, Tyler plopped himself into one of two guest chairs.

"What are you doing here?" she said accusingly, nervously glancing around the otherwise empty office.

"We need to talk."

"Mr. Cain, I wish you had called first. Now's not a good time. Judge Santiago is in his chambers right this very moment. If he were to see you here—"

"Tell him I'm your long-lost cousin, then."

"I don't have any long-lost cousins."

Tyler hoped to gain the upper hand to head off a repeat of their last encounter. He leaned forward with an air of importance. "Does it matter?"

Taking a long deep breath, Jennifer finally relaxed enough to lean back in her chair. "I'm assuming this is about the letters."

Showing up unannounced had served his purpose. Tyler glanced around the office. Aside from the guard at the building's entrance, he hadn't been approached by anyone asking why he was there, nor had anything stopped him from walking right into this office without Judge Santiago's personal assistant even noticing. What would prevent someone from breaking through into Judge Santiago's chambers? Above the doorway a metal conduit led up through the ceiling. Probably wiring for an alarm system of some kind, but too little too late to stop a potential killer with a grudge.

As he'd hoped, she followed his gaze around the room.

"You're completely unprepared, Ms. McKay."

"Excuse me?"

"What if I had been a gunman?"

"There are metal detectors. No guns allowed."

He nodded toward a decorative lamp sitting on the edge of her desk. "Blunt-force trauma to the head is just as deadly."

Jennifer instinctively raised her hand to the back of her head protectively, combing her fingers through her hair in a vain attempt to seem unfazed. "Are you trying to scare me, Mr. Cain? Because as I already told you, safety is not a concern here. Unless you have information to suggest we *should* be concerned..."

This time it was Tyler who eased back into his chair. Mission accomplished. Jennifer McKay was on the defensive. He had the upper hand. A little fear was a powerful way to hook a listening ear.

"I *might* have information," he said, dangling a proverbial carrot.

Jennifer glanced toward Santiago's chambers again, then back to Tyler, her demeanor sharpening. "You *might*? Is that short for 'I don't have a single lead'?"

She was onto him already.

"No," Tyler lied, hoping to recover. "It's code for 'I have a potential lead, but I need something to help smoke out the author to know for sure.' Something from you."

"From me?"

"I need you to reply to the letters."

She shot up immediately. "I already told you I can't—"

"You can't do that. Yes, I know. But the stakes on this case might be higher than either of us originally imagined. Much higher."

Which was true. Maybe.

"Really?" Jennifer said doubtfully, then turned and slid open one of her desk drawers, pulling out a photograph. She laid it out on the desk and shoved it over for Tyler to see.

It was a picture of a little girl in pink pajamas holding tightly to a rag doll. It reminded him, vaguely, of the photo Smitty had shown of his daughter, with her larger-than-life innocent smile. But aside from that slight resemblance, the photo seemed unremarkable.

"Is she...yours?" Tyler asked.

Jennifer shook her head. "Gosh, no! I'm far too busy to have a partner, let alone a family! No, this little girl represents the outcome of an eight-year battle her parents had in the court system, fighting for the right to adopt the frozen embryo of the mother's brain-dead sister. An auto accident prevented implantation, and there was no legal precedent in allowing such an adoption without a parent's written consent. In fact, the sister had left instructions to donate any unused embryos to science. But here she is, almost twelve years after the legal battle began. She's four."

Tyler glanced at the little girl one more time, then slid the photo back. "She's cute. But I don't see how this matters to this case."

Jennifer sighed. "It matters because you still seem to underestimate the importance of Judge Santiago's work."

"What are you talking about? I've never said his work wasn't important."

"Not directly. But I need you to understand. This little girl—Hope is her name—she's a reminder. She's alive today because of an opinion Judge Santiago issued several years back."

"And?"

Jennifer frowned as if Tyler had missed her obvious point. "The stakes in Judge Santiago's cases are always higher than we know, Mr. Cain. Not just in this case."

"Fine. But hear me out, please."

"I'm listening," she said grudgingly.

"There just aren't enough useful clues in the letters themselves. And if I try to approach the suspect directly, there could be dangerous ramifications."

"Such as?"

"Such as…retaliation."

"Retaliation against whom? Santiago?"

"Perhaps."

She shook her head, clearly frustrated. "There you go with

the suppositions again. Perhaps. Might. Possibly. I need more than that."

For a moment Tyler considered mentioning his conversation with Evan Dimitri. But he stopped himself. He just couldn't be certain. Yes, Mr. Dimitri had something to lose—a lot to lose, actually—but Tyler had been unable to watch his eyes, leaving him no choice but to believe Dimitri when he said he knew nothing about the letters. Besides, he couldn't tell her about the conference call without mentioning that he had violated her insistence that no one see the letters. Worse than see them, Tyler had scanned and sent digital copies!

"I can't give you more. Not yet. But what if you contacted the author on *behalf* of Judge Santiago? It doesn't have to be the judge himself. He doesn't even have to know about it. You can do it. I just need you to establish actual communication. I'll coach you on what to say."

Tyler stopped talking when he realized Jennifer was not even pretending to consider his suggestion.

Just then the door to Judge Santiago's chambers opened, and out came an impeccably dressed man with thinning gray hair. He closed the door behind himself and double-checked to see it was locked by rattling the handle. When he spun around, he looked surprised.

"Oh!" he exclaimed, then took a step forward. "I didn't realize we had any further appointments today, Jennifer."

Tyler rose respectfully. "It's an honor to meet you in person, sir."

Santiago smiled, then said, "Well, I'd say the honor is mine, but I have no idea who you are!"

"Oh, right. I'm…" Tyler searched frantically for an appropriate ruse.

"—the caterer," Jennifer finished for him, "for your wife's surprise birthday party."

"Ah, yes! Then it is an honor to meet you," Santiago said more enthusiastically. He accepted Tyler's outstretched hand and shook it vigorously before frowning. "Although I must admit you don't fit the part."

Tyler tried to release his grip, unsuccessfully. "Excuse me?"

"Caterer. You don't fit the part. Handshake's all wrong. Clothing choice. If I had to guess, I'd say you worked as some sort of public servant. A fireman, perhaps?"

Tyler smiled at the suggestion.

"Or maybe a security guard," the judge added.

Tyler furrowed his brow then went with the judge's first guess by playing the part of caterer. "It takes a lot of strength in the hands to properly prepare hors d'oeuvres!"

Both men laughed politely.

"Oh, don't worry about that," Santiago reassured him. "The trick will be pulling it off without anyone other than myself and Ms. McKay here knowing. My wife always has a way of finding out about any surprise. I think she has my office bugged or something!"

Tyler smiled. "I see."

Then Santiago pulled his coconspirator in close, glancing at Jennifer before whispering in his ear. "I don't care what she says...you just make sure to serve something men like us can really sink our teeth into. I'm tired of all those delicate finger foods with names I can't even pronounce. Got it?"

Tyler liked the judge already. He quickly pulled back and winked.

Santiago freed Tyler's hand. "Well, I must be off. My beautiful wife Rebecca awaits my return!"

And with that he turned and rushed out the door.

"Caterer?" Tyler said to Jennifer as he sat back down. "Well, he seems like a nice guy. Good judge of character."

"Yes, Mr. Cain. Exactly. He pegged you in three seconds flat." After several moments of silent tension she added, "Are you finished, then? Because as I told you I can't risk compromising his role."

He pursed his lips in frustration, then blurted out, "Doesn't a death threat compromise his role?"

"Please. A request for dialogue is not a death threat, Mr. Cain. You aren't hearing me on this. It doesn't matter if Judge Santiago merely knows about the letters, if he actually reads the letters, or if he opens dialogue with the person who wrote the letters. Even if I were to dialogue with the author on his behalf, there would be the appearance of impropriety. The appearance. That's all it takes for someone to declare Santiago unfit to render an opinion."

"Well, then, it might be time we convinced the judge to resign from the case. For his own protection."

"Protection from what?"

Tyler ran his hand over the back of his head, staring up at the ceiling, tired of this game. What else could he say? He had vast experience in these matters. She should just trust his expert opinion.

Then he remembered the forensic report; a small detail that might mean nothing. But he needed something, anything, that would imply progress.

"I think the author of these letters is on the move," he finally said, taking a completely different tack.

"On the move?"

"It appears the first three letters were sent from outside the area. In the vicinity of Boulder, actually. While the most recent letter was probably sent locally."

It was no more than a possibility. The envelopes showed microscopic traces of DNA from staff members who work at a Boulder postal processing facility. But that only meant the letters had *been* there, not that they had necessarily been sent from there. Still, it seemed a plausible theory.

"And?" Jennifer McKay continued staring, waiting impatiently for some juicy revelation.

"And I think it's an indication of the author's obsession with this case. His next move might be to confront Judge Santiago in person."

"I'm sorry, Mr. Cain," she said. "But Judge Santiago pays me to make hard calls. I simply can't tell the judge about these letters until you have some shred of evidence that tells me he is in real danger. I need more than hunches and assumptions."

"But I just told you…"

"People move all the time," she interrupted. "They also drop letters off at different post boxes. Boulder and Denver are not that far apart. What you have is circumstantial at best."

"It's just…a gut instinct I have. And when my gut tells me something, I find it's best not to ignore it!"

"Then don't ignore it. Find out who sent these letters, like I hired you to do in the first place."

Tyler felt a rising sense of desperation. He was going nowhere fast with this conversation. He feared Jennifer's stubbornness might be Santiago's undoing. Not to mention his own. He decided to appeal to her one last time. *Less confrontational*, he told himself.

"Just think it over," he began. "Message me if you change your mind. Ultimately, it's your decision."

"Yes. It is," she agreed. "And I don't need to think about it since I'm certain I won't change my mind."

The words of Julia Simmons crossed Tyler's thoughts. *Be careful, Mr. Cain. This case might end up carrying you into the deep end of the pool.* And it had. Deeper than he'd imagined.

This case had begun as a much-needed distraction from his usual pathetic clients. Then it escalated into a high-stakes gamble. Now he feared he had bet too many chips. Perhaps it was time to fold.

While the car carried him toward home in the AutoDrive lane Tyler made a decision.

"I'm done with this case," he told the windshield, resolutely. "I'll bill for time served. Then I'll resign."

The car responded by saying, "AutoDrive disengaging. Switching to manual mode."

"My thoughts exactly," he said. He took the steering wheel, the small measure of control it afforded a welcome change of pace from the unruly mess he had made during the past twenty-four hours.

CHAPTER THIRTY-FIVE

Julia noticed three brochures lying on the table beside an unoc-
cupied waiting-room chair. She selected the middle one, titled
Genetic Screening: The Loving Choice. She took a seat and began reading. The opening paragraph seemed familiar. It could easily have
been paraphrased from one of the many columns on the subject
she had published during her years working for RAP Syndicate.

> For as long as women have had babies they've been asked
> the same question.
>
> "Do you want a boy or a girl?"
>
> And they've given the same answer.
>
> "We just want a healthy child."
>
> But there was little they could do besides taking prenatal vi-
> tamins or avoiding drugs, alcohol, and cigarettes.
>
> Thankfully, today's parents can take steps to dramatically
> increase the likelihood of delivering a healthy bundle of joy.
> And when it comes to the child's sex the choice is literally
> yours!

> This office is a proud member of HEALTH ASSURANCE,
> an alliance of caring gynecologists who serve the needs of
> women opting for genetic screening and physicians partnering
> with families to radically reduce lifelong medical expenses by
> accepting only prescreened pediatric patients.

Julia recalled praising the insurance companies and physicians who had created the Health Assurance network. It made sense to give parents who had opted for genetic prescreening lower rates, since their offspring showed dramatically fewer incidences of disability and disease. Within a few years nearly half of all new mothers paid lower premiums and deductibles than their "blind conception" counterparts. Doctors would only accept new patients who had been prescreened, an easy way to cut costs for everyone. Before long it became difficult to find a pediatrician unless you had prescreened. Only a handful of older doctors on their way to retirement were willing to treat the higher-cost kids. Even they began demanding cash payments up front, since, they discovered, healthcare authorities questioned every treatment before delaying or denying payment. So in less than a decade, Julia recalled, financial prudence had pushed nearly every woman away from blind conception toward what the brochure called *the loving choice*.

> What better way to show your child love than to give her or
> him all of the advantages that come with prescreening?

Julia noticed her hand cradling her tummy. Had the passion she'd enjoyed with Troy made today's visit more than research for another dark zone story? She had felt a bit queasy before breakfast. Did morning sickness occur within twenty-four hours? If so, would a urine sample even detect pregnancy this early?

She shook off the questions, reminding herself she had always felt slightly nauseated when preparing to deceive.

The first lie had occurred when she went online to make an eight a.m. appointment for Troy and a ten a.m. appointment for herself. Julia tried to imagine the look that must have been on her husband's face when a nurse handed him the sample container a few hours earlier. He must have turned bright red. The thought prompted a quiet snigger.

The second lie had taken place a few minutes earlier when Julia checked in for her own appointment. "My name is Julia Simmons," she had said. "I'm here for my preconception consultation."

The process was pretty straightforward. The male partner submitted a sample so the lab could test the viability of his sperm. The potential mother then received an examination to determine whether she was a good candidate for implantation. What exactly that entailed Julia didn't know; probably checking to confirm the woman wasn't already pregnant, her ovaries still produced healthy eggs, and her uterus could maintain a pregnancy. Assuming all was well, the woman would be scheduled for some sort of ovarian stimulation to harvest as many eggs as possible for fertilization. The more embryos produced, the brochure explained, the more options from which to choose the best possible offspring.

"Julia Davidson?"

The voice didn't sound familiar. Nor had Julia given her maiden name. She looked toward an open door where a cute, thirtyish woman stood as if inviting her to enter. Julia stuffed the brochure in her purse to finish reading later.

"I'm Julia," she said with an inquisitive smile. "Have we met?"

"No. But I'm a big fan of your column."

Of course.

"Oh, um, thanks," Julia muttered while glancing around the room. Two of the five women seated in the waiting room were flashing warm grins in her direction. So much for undercover research.

She walked toward the woman and glanced at her name tag. "Hello, Lynette. Very pleased to meet you."

A lie. She hadn't wanted to meet anyone while trying to stay under the radar. No matter, she reassured herself, as long as she avoided hinting at the real reason for her visit.

As soon as the door closed behind them Lynette became as giddy as a teenage girl suddenly face-to-face with her favorite pop star. She caught Julia by surprise with a hug. "I can't tell you what an honor it is to have you visit our office," Lynette was saying over Julia's shoulder.

"Oh my," Julia said with a gentle pat on Lynette's back. Rather than taking the hint to separate, however, the woman tightened her squeeze. Julia finally pulled herself away.

"Sorry," Lynette said with a wink. "My partner tells me I get a bit over-enthusiastic."

Julia smiled weakly. "No worries."

They stood for a few more seconds until Lynette finally remembered her role. "This way," she said, extending her arm toward a scale.

Julia went through the motions as if planning for an in vitro selection pregnancy with her husband Troy.

"I must confess," Lynette said while taking Julia's pulse, "I was shocked when I recognized your face. Julia Davidson is the last woman I would have expected to go with Troy Simmons."

She knows Troy?

"I met him this morning. He seemed..." she paused as if trying to find a different word.

"Uptight?"

"Well, yes." Lynette appeared embarrassed. "But very handsome," she added as a consolation.

Julia felt suddenly protective. "We've been married for six months."

"I understand," Lynette said with consequence.

"Understand what?"

"The six-month bug. Pretty common here."

Lynette seemed to notice Julia's puzzled expression.

"We get quite a few couples in here trying to seal the partnership."

"Seal? What do you mean?"

"You know, making a kid together. Nothing bonds two people like a mini-us."

"Right," Julia said.

"I could tell right away Troy was different than most of the guys we see."

"How's that?"

"He didn't accept the stimulant aids for starters."

"Stimulant aids?"

"A gentle term for porn. He said he would be fine without it. Seemed a bit embarrassed by the offer."

Julia smiled at the description of her noble gentleman. Memories of their recent love-fest would have been more than adequate to aid Troy's contribution to the ruse.

"When I realized who you were I assumed there must have been some mistake. Julia Davidson married?"

"I guess wonders never cease," Julia offered.

"You can say that again." Lynette was shaking her head while jotting down the last of Julia's stats. She handed her a cup. "I'll need a urine sample, then we'll draw some blood."

Julia nodded.

"I almost got married once," Lynette said as Julia was turning the doorknob.

"Is that right?"

"Yep."

"Why almost?" Julia asked.

Lynette flashed a wide grin. "I guess I discovered your columns in the nick of time!"

The woman was shaking her head as if amazed by the irony as Julia slipped into the hallway toward the designated bathroom.

After capturing a urine sample Julia stood in front of the mirror. The same mirror, she assumed, Troy had looked into two hours earlier. She wondered how she would feel if this had been a real appointment rather than an act. It felt unseemly standing in the same spot where her husband had donated half of the required ingredients; as if they were two workers on an assembly line rather than participants in an intimate, one-flesh union.

"So this is how babies are made," she said to the woman in the mirror.

Two quick raps on the door followed by a muffled voice. "Ms. Davidson? Is everything OK?" Apparently she had fallen behind the usual assembly time line.

Julia took a deep breath in anticipation of the next scene of her performance. Then she opened the door. "Everything's fine. Please, call me Julia."

Lynette smiled at the invitation. "OK, Julia. Let's go to the consultation room to discuss next steps and options."

Julia's phone, the one she was supposed to have turned off in the waiting room, rang. Lynette looked at her with playful condemnation. She apologized while retrieving the device from the bottom of her purse and then glancing at the screen.

Tyler Cain.

She started to tap the IGNORE icon but hesitated while trying to recall what might have prompted the call. Did he have another dark zone contact she might interview? Another question about the Santiago case?

"Do you need to take that?" Lynette asked thoughtfully.

"Do you mind?" she asked while tapping the ACCEPT icon.

"Second door on the left," Lynette whispered while pointing down the hall. "I'll join you there in a minute."

Julia nodded at Lynette while turning her attention to the voice on the phone. "This is Julia."

"Hi, Ms. Simmons," Tyler began. "Can you talk?"

Julia began walking in the direction of the consultation room. "For a second. What's up?"

"I just wanted to bring you up to speed on the Santiago situation."

Situation?

"I've decided to end the investigation."

"Really? Did you find out who—"

"No I didn't," he said as if mad at the question. "But the judge isn't taking my advice; or rather the judge's aide. Either way, I don't like to waste people's money. If they won't listen to me, I can't help them."

Julia waited for more. Tyler remained quiet. Was that it? If so, why call Julia about the decision? If he had more, why not just say it?

"And?" she prodded.

"And, um..." A hesitation. "And I just wanted to say thanks for your help."

Julia sensed the call was about more than wrapping up the loose end of thanking a source. What wasn't Tyler saying?

"Are you sure there isn't more?"

"Like what?" he said too quickly. And too defensively.

"I don't know." She recalled their last conversation. "Did you identify any other potential leads?"

"Like Evan Dimitri?"

"Well, not him specifically. But yeah, people who might want to protect NEXT rather than harm it?"

Another long silence. Julia sensed Tyler struggling with an internal tug-of-war. Why? What had he really called to tell her?

"Mr. Cain? Is there something else you want to—"

"Like I said," he interrupted. "I wanted to thank you for your help and let you know I'm off the case."

"OK. Thanks for the update," she said in puzzled deference.

"And I appreciate your keeping our conversations strictly confidential."

"Of course."

"Good luck on your dark zone story. I'll let you know if I think of other leads on that front."

"Please do," she said before realizing the call had ended.

After a few seconds Julia noticed she was standing in the doctor's consultation room, the place where she would learn about next steps and options. Julia walked toward one of two seats positioned before a modestly cluttered desk. Her eyes landed on a small grouping of photographs on the wall that depicted what appeared to be a ski trip with friends; an older couple, possibly Lynette's parents; and Lynette sitting with two other women toasting the photographer with glasses filled with a dark wine: a celebration of some sort, possibly her graduation from medical school?

Then she noticed the diploma. UNIVERSITY OF COLORADO was stenciled boldly across the top, followed by smaller text she couldn't read, presumably the same congratulatory script used on countless other certificates ending with "has conferred upon" before the graduate's name; in this case, LYNETTE ROSE WRIGHT. Then more small text followed by DOCTOR OF MEDICINE.

As if on cue, the graduate entered the room. Julia felt old as she watched Lynette remove her doctor's smock. Stylish and pretty, Lynette reminded Julia of Maria a few years back. She appeared to be in her late twenties, thirty tops. More like the unattached, childless girlfriend with whom you would go shopping than an MD to whom you would go for pregnancy advice.

"All set?" Lynette asked.

"Yes, thank you. Nothing urgent."

"Good." Lynette sat beside Julia rather than occupying the seat behind the desk. Then she tapped her tablet screen and held it between them for shared viewing: a checklist of steps followed by a series of questions.

"We've completed most of the pre-consultation items."

Julia glanced at the list. Only a few boxes remained unchecked.

"I need to review the lab results to confirm what I've seen today," Lynette explained, "but on the whole I'd say you shouldn't have any problems." She looked to Julia with a congratulatory smile.

Julia felt herself tear up in response to the gesture. The reaction embarrassed her. "I'm sorry," she said while reaching for a tissue.

"Don't be," Lynette replied while touching her famous client's forearm. "This is very good news for a woman of your age."

A woman of my age?

"Half of the women I see past age thirty-five aren't good candidates."

"Half?"

"More maybe," Lynette explained.

"So only half of the women my age can have a child?"

"Half of the women your age who make appointments with my office. The rest don't want a child."

"Of course," said Julia.

"Of those who do, less than half are good candidates for in vitro implantation. There are a dozen reasons."

"Are there other options? You know, for the women you can't help?"

Lynette appeared to be recalling clients who had hit the snooze button on their biological clock once too often. "Not really," she finally said despondently. "But you look good. I think we'll be able to harvest a good selection of eggs. So, barring any surprises, I expect you'll be choosing a child within a few short months."

The comment reminded Julia of her agenda. "Tell me how that works. You know, the actual screening process?"

"My lab does most of the work," Lynette replied. "In the typical case we fertilize between five and eight eggs. About half of those will meet specs."

"Meet specs?"

"Sorry. Standard specifications. We analyze the genome sequence of each zygote to screen out any with likely defects or chronic diseases. The process has become remarkably precise. A recent batch detected propensities for both bipolar and attention deficit hyperactive disorders." She said it like a proud mom bragging on the accomplishments of her genius kid. "Anyway, we eliminate those zygotes before presenting you with the good options."

Julia suppressed an urge to grab her tablet to capture notes. Today she was a patient exploring motherhood, not a reporter conducting research.

"Assuming you have both possibilities you'll select the child's sex, unless of course you want it to be a surprise. Then we get to pick."

"How often does that happen?"

"Not very. Most people know what they want. Usually a boy, come to think of it. But I like to make a big deal about it when we do. I call the office staff together and we hold hands in a circle."

"To pray?" Julia guessed.

"To flip the ceremonial coin. Heads a girl. Tails a boy. At last count we had a pretty even mix of the two. I guess random chance would improve the odds for us gals."

Lynette laughed at her own quip while Julia wondered which sex she and Troy might select. Then she felt her suddenly queasy tummy. Had random chance already beaten them to the punch?

The doctor looked back at the list. "I should get the results from your husband's sample later today. After that we'll get you scheduled for your first infusion of a fertility stimulant and, if all goes well, invite a few of your eggs to the dance."

Julia forced a thin smile.

"Any questions?"

"Just one," Julia said after a slight hesitation. How to say it? "You mentioned eliminating some of the zygotes. Can I ask what happens to them?"

Lynette gently slapped her own cheek as if suddenly recalling a skipped step. "Oh yes," she said. "I almost forgot." She drew Julia's attention to the tablet and pointed beneath the action items toward a column of unasked questions.

"We need you to provide direction on how you want us to handle the embryotic material."

The comment reminded Julia of the conversation with Austin Tozer that had prompted her decision to make the appointment. He had gotten two thousand dollars per embryo. Would she receive a similar offer?

Lynette began reading a script from the tablet. "In order to respect the ethical sensibilities of our clients we request input on the preferred method of disposal for any excess embryotic materials resulting from your treatments."

Julia braced herself for the first of three questions.

"Are you undergoing this process with the intent of carrying and delivering a full-term baby?"

Julia tried to imagine another reason to schedule an in vitro selection consultation. "Yes I am," she answered. "But may I ask what it would mean if I said no?"

"We'd assume you plan to donate."

"Donate? To what?" Julia wasn't sure she wanted an answer.

"To the embryotics supply."

"Is that like the blood supply?" Julia blushed at her own ignorance.

"Sort of," Lynette explained. "But more like an organ donation to a specific beneficiary. Usually a family member asks relatives for donations when they schedule any kind of surgery that might require tissue repair or mild regeneration of internal organs. Embryos from close relatives make the best donors since the body can better assimilate organic material with a similar genome sequence."

Julia nodded, a look of vague comprehension triggering Lynette's second question.

"Would you like the attending physician to decide the best means of disposal for any unused zygotes?"

Julia considered how to reply. "What does that mean?"

"It means you give us permission to choose the best course of action depending upon a variety of factors."

Julia knew a dodge when she heard one: lots of words with no real answer. "What factors?"

Lynette seemed suddenly hesitant to say more, perhaps remembering that she was talking to a journalist. "Oh, you know, the usual. Which field of study would benefit most from access to the material? Things like that."

"For money?"

"Excuse me?" the doctor sounded offended.

Pull back, girl, Julia told herself. She had begun sounding like an antagonistic reporter rather than a curious client.

"I mean," she said in the least threatening voice she could muster, "are there any financial incentives for selecting one disposal strategy over another?"

"Incentives for whom?" Lynette asked indignantly.

Julia decided to change course quickly. "For me."

The doctor's tension seemed to dissipate. "Oh, that," she said with a relieved smile. Lynette looked back to the tablet to read the final question.

"Do you wish to dispose of excess embryotic materials in any of the following manners?" She looked toward Julia before reading off a menu of fifteen or twenty official-sounding organizations requesting targeted donations. Each needed a specific variable. Male or female. Caucasian, Asian, African-American, or mixed-race. One requested embryos that would have red hair. But none of them offered money.

"I'm curious," Julia said after Lynette completed the list, "whether there are any organizations willing to—" She stopped herself.

"Yes, there are," Lynette volunteered. Then she tapped a small icon located at the very bottom of the screen before handing it to Julia.

The tablet displayed a long list of businesses. Julia quickly scanned to identify names associated with health supplements and cosmetics. None appeared clearly marked.

"I'm not allowed to recommend any specific companies," Lynette was saying, "but I can tell you that some offer more compensation than others."

Julia felt a wave of shame. Not for her lies. For her discovery.

Dear God, she thought. Or perhaps prayed. *What have we become?*

"Would you like a copy of the file to review with your partner?"

"Husband," Julia said.

"Right, sorry. Would you?"

"Please," Julia said while handing the tablet back. She thanked the doctor for the information as she stood to leave the room.

"You can stop by the front desk to make a next appointment," Lynette said warmly. "I look forward to seeing you again."

Julia nodded while extending her hand. Lynette ignored the offer, opting instead for another demonstrative hug.

It took Julia a split second to return the gesture. It was more physical intimacy, she mused, than Lynette's clients experienced while conceiving a child.

The thought reminded Julia that nothing had been said about her urine sample. Wouldn't they know immediately if she was pregnant?

"So, I guess I'm not expecting?" she asked as if checking a minor detail. "I assume we couldn't proceed if I were."

The question seemed to startle Lynette. "Oh," she said while reaching for her tablet, apparently to check Julia's pregnancy test results. "Yes, we would recommend a different approach in that case. Could you be?"

Julia nodded guiltily, knowing Lynette probably frowned upon spontaneous, unprotected marital sex. "A small chance," she confessed.

The doctor tapped and swiped the screen until she found the tidbit of data needed to answer Julia's question. "Let's see here."

Julia held her breath.

"Congratulations!" she said after one final swipe. "You're clear."

"Oh," Julia replied with a weak smile. "I see. That's good. A relief," she lied. "Thanks for checking."

"You bet. See you soon."

"Yes. See you soon."

Julia walked past the receptionist's desk, then through the lobby and out the door. A door she hoped she would never have to enter again.

CHAPTER THIRTY-SIX

Julia lowered the music and dimmed the dining room lights. The table looked exquisite beneath two lustrous flames dancing to the smooth sounds of romantic jazz. She smiled in anticipation of inviting her husband to do the same as soon as he arrived home from the office.

She had considered sending Troy a text message suggesting they meet at his favorite restaurant. She would have spent the last part of the meal rubbing her foot against his leg while they took turns feeding one another spoonfuls of his favorite dessert.

But she changed her mind. A candlelit dinner at home would be better: less time between suggestion and action. Rather than whisper during dessert she would *be* the dessert.

Julia went to her closet and flipped through the possibilities. Which was Troy's favorite? Short teddy or lingering gown? How could she know when he seemed equally pleased by all of them? She finally chose. White. The perfect color for a night that she hoped would move their union from two people in love to one flesh in partnership.

Since the day Julia met Troy Simmons she'd known he wanted to be a father. It was in the lobby of Apostles' Church in Washington DC. She had accepted Angie's invitation to attend a service while in town. She should have known Angie would use the occasion for matchmaking. Troy clearly loved the Tolbert kids, especially when they called him "Uncle Twoy." But he also seemed to love the dream of little feet running into his arms and hearing his own child shouting, "Daddy!"

Julia never would have imagined herself going on a date with a man like Troy, let alone accepting his hand in marriage. Marriage itself, she had believed, was an archaic institution. What a difference a year can make! Here she was now, planning an intimate evening with a man she'd never intended to marry, hoping to conceive a child she never wanted to have. Or so she had thought. Apparently our deepest desires eventually trump our most persuasive objections.

A sudden noise startled Julia. Troy arriving home early? No, a timer alerting her that the crescent rolls were ready to remove from the oven.

While placing the last roll into a basket on the table, Julia checked the clock. Troy should be another twenty minutes, plenty of time for her to shower and slip into his surprise. The phone rang. She glanced at the television screen to read the caller's identity. Not Troy calling to say he would be late. Just Dr. Wright's office, probably calling to give her the detailed results of fertility tests she assumed were fine. She decided to ignore the call, instead rushing into the master bathroom for her most important preparations.

Fifteen minutes later Julia found herself moving from one spot to another, trying to decide which location best fit the occasion. She imagined Troy's face when he walked through the door to delicious smells, dim lights, and an alluring bride lounging on the sofa or waiting invitingly at the table.

Only one unfinished detail remained. She reached for her tablet to restart the programmed sequence of Troy's favorite jazz artists. She noticed a bouncing icon reminding her of the ignored call, now a waiting message with an attachment. She tapped it to pass the remaining moments, expecting Lynette's assistant to say she had forwarded the formal test results and ask when Julia wanted to begin the in vitro process. She instead heard the doctor's voice.

"Hi, Julia. I've attached results of the full range of tests we ran today. As expected, you look healthy."

Julia smiled at the surprising feeling of relief.

"But I wanted to explain the results on page six of the attached summary so you will understand your options," Lynette continued. "Don't worry. I've helped plenty of couples in the same situation. Call my office when you can and we'll set up a consultation. OK? We'll talk then."

Options for what? Julia wondered. *I thought she said I looked healthy.*

Even though Troy could walk through the door at any second, Julia had to know what was on page six. She tapped the attachment icon to open the document. She tried her best to decipher the medical jargon, including two "possible causes" with labels that meant nothing to her; *epididymitis* and something called *Young syndrome.* She looked at the top of the page for any clues that might inform what she was reading. That's when she realized this was a summary of Troy's sperm sample. But what did it mean? Was it something bad? Lynette mentioned she had helped other couples in the same situation. What situation?

She moved toward the door to peek outside. No sign of Troy's car. She went back to her tablet and quickly entered the unfamiliar words into a medical terminology search engine. All five of the top results carried the same disturbing label.

Causes of male infertility.

She began scanning the first article. Apparently epididymitis was some sort of blockage preventing sperm from releasing to its fruitful destiny. But that included a list of symptoms Troy had never experienced such as fever and pain. The only other potential culprit, *Young syndrome*, was described as having "no known effective treatment or cure."

Did this mean she and Troy couldn't conceive naturally? Could they conceive at all?

Julia heard the familiar sound of the opening garage door announcing Troy's arrival. She quickly swiped out of the screen and tossed her tablet beneath a throw pillow. She had never decided whether to stay on the sofa or move to the dining room. She chose the latter, buying a few extra seconds to absorb the news and decide whether and how to tell her husband.

The thought of telling Troy prompted unwelcome grief. "Not now!" she said aloud, grabbing one of the perfectly placed napkins to dab her moistening eyes.

The last thing she wanted was for Troy to see her in tears. This was supposed to be a romantic evening of thrilling intimacy, not a cry-fest over possible bad news.

But she knew in her soul that it was more than *possible* bad news. Why would the doctor call unless the results suggested her husband could never be a daddy?

Another wave of sorrow invaded, this one too strong for Julia to swallow back. She heard the doorknob turning. What to do? She darted from the dining room back into the master bedroom. Better for Troy to enjoy the surprise and anticipation of a candlelit room than wonder what had triggered his wife's uncontrollable tears.

She rushed to the bathroom and closed the door before splashing cold water onto her puffing cheeks. She would let Troy assume she was still getting ready to greet him with an alluring smile. A smile she commanded her disobedient face to produce.

Julia reached deep to summon the strong, controlling woman she had been before falling in love with Troy. The girl who had maintained a cool demeanor during a year of nightmarish dreams. The journalist who had confronted Washington power brokers with prudent diplomacy. The woman who could use the same iron will to finish what she had started a few hours earlier. She had planned a night of bliss with her husband. So a night of bliss is what she intended to give.

"Hi, babe," she heard Troy saying from the dining room. "What's all this?"

She took a deep, restorative breath before replying. "A little surprise. I'll be out in a minute."

She used the time to reapply a bit of makeup. Troy would never guess she had been crying, even if his eyes managed to peel themselves away from her gown. Then she opened the bedroom door to find her husband nibbling on a crescent roll at the dining table, his shoulders slumped as if he was contemplating his own brand of dispiriting news.

She moved toward Troy, glad the music covered the sound of her approach. She slid her arms around his chest to offer an embrace both needed.

She whispered into his ear, "Welcome home, Mr. Simmons."

Her touch and voice prompted a smile. He pulled her hand to his lips and gently kissed her soft skin. Julia sensed he was trying to push past exhausted discouragement to receive her wonderful but poorly timed gift.

"This looks terrific," he said while rubbing her arm.

She moved to the chair beside him. His eyes turned to saucers. She blushed, then giggled.

"You look terrific!" He gasped to recover his stolen breath.

They kissed. Then they kissed again.

"I hope you're hungry," Julia said.

His eyes sank as if the comment reminded him of a lost appetite. Then he looked back at the candlelit arrangement. At the enormous effort his wife had gone to for him. "Starved," he said with forced enthusiasm.

She placed a single finger on his chin to move his eyes back in her direction. "Troy Simmons. Tell me what's wrong."

His eyes sank again. "Is it that obvious?"

"I'm afraid so. But thank you."

"For what?"

"For trying to enjoy my surprise."

He leaned toward her for another kiss, which she refused to accept.

"No food or dessert until you tell me what's wrong."

"There's dessert?"

She stood and then turned to give him a full view of her sheer outfit. "Yes, there is." Both smiled as she sat again. "Now, what happened?"

Troy released a lengthy sigh. "I got a call from Brent Anderson today."

"Franklin's right-hand man?"

"He called to warn me. No, to scold me."

"For what?"

"That's just it. I have no idea what he was talking about. He accused me of seriously undermining Kevin's opportunity for broader influence in the Franklin coalition. I asked what I had done, but he accused me of playing dumb as if I knew what I'd done. Then he told me to back off with Dimitri."

"Evan Dimitri?"

"I suppose. But I haven't had any contact at all with Evan Dimitri."

A prickly thought entered Julia's mind. She pushed it aside and said, "That's odd."

"Very odd. I can only assume he's upset about the refused donation check. But that was Kevin. I was a thousand miles away minding the shop."

"Maybe he thinks you put Kevin up to it."

"Unlikely. I'm nothing to Dimitri and Anderson: an invisible gofer who runs reports and accepts assignments."

"You're a lot more than that!" Julia protested. "Kevin relies on you for, well, for everything."

He touched her cheek in appreciative acceptance of the reassurance. "I know that."

"And Kevin knows it!"

He smiled at her resolve. "And Kevin knows it. But I can't imagine why Anderson would call me."

"Maybe he called Kevin too."

"He didn't. I checked."

"What did Kevin say?"

"Not much." Troy's shoulders slumped again. "Just that he would follow up with Anderson."

A prickly thought Julia couldn't dismiss. Had Tyler Cain contacted Evan Dimitri in response to her call?

"What if someone else used your name?" she asked.

"Used my name for what?"

"To gain access to Dimitri."

"Who would do that? And why?"

Julia dismissed the possibility again. "Never mind," she said. "I'm just thinking out loud."

A brief silence as both tried to imagine what would suddenly turn Anderson against Troy. Against Kevin.

"It must be the donation thing," Troy finally said. "Nothing else makes sense. Kevin refused Dimitri's check, meaning he rejected the attached strings. That must have upset Franklin."

"I guess," Julia agreed. "Which means you did nothing wrong."

He looked up as if relieved by the verdict.

"It also means there's no reason I shouldn't reheat our dinner." Julia stood and reached for the serving dish.

Troy's hand caressed the thin fabric that barely concealed her thigh. "And dessert?"

"The dessert is still warm," she said, sitting on Troy's lap. Her lips moved toward his ear, the breath of each whispered word seeming to deepen his desire. "Would you rather skip dinner?"

She sensed the tension releasing from both husband and wife with each escalating touch.

Thirty minutes later Troy was sitting at the table, a new man.

"I made it to the clinic today," he said casually while spreading a slab of butter onto a freshly heated roll.

Julia's body stiffened. "Did you?"

"Talk about awkward. I had to go into a bathroom and…" He stopped short, then fast-forwarded. "I had to hand my sample to an office aide who looked young enough to be my daughter. Embarrassing."

"Thanks for doing that," Julia said. "It will help my next story."

"How about you?" he asked.

"What?"

"Weren't you supposed to go today as well?"

"Oh, that." A slight hesitation. "I had a consultation appointment. Learned quite a bit." *Keep it short. Don't elaborate. Change the subject.*

"And?" he said, preempting her strategy.

"And I found out there are a bunch of businesses that buy unused embryos, just like Austin Tozer said. They try to get you to donate as the preferred disposal method for what they call excess embryotic material. But I asked one question about financial incentives and the doctor showed me several options for selling instead."

Troy huffed angrily in her direction. "Are you serious?"

Julia nodded.

"No wonder I got a bad feeling the second I walked into the place," he continued. "Their process gave me the willies. A father should be more than a nameless, faceless cog in the wheel. They handed me a dirty magazine and said, 'Have at it'!"

"Troy!" Julia blushed while slapping his shoulder playfully.

"Well, it's true," he said. "And dehumanizing."

She had to agree. "Having a child should be beautiful, not mechanical."

As she placed another roll on his plate Troy put his hand lovingly on her waist. "You're beautiful," he said. "Thank you, Julia."

She smiled, knowing he meant more than the roll.

"That's how babies are supposed to be made." He winked while placing his hand on her abdomen. "And you never know."

A wave of guilt. *Should I tell him?* she wondered. *No. Not now. Why spoil a beautiful moment? Tell him in the morning.*

Troy buried his head in Julia's bosom. "You're a gift," he said. "I love you."

She placed her hands on his head and began caressing his hair. "I love you too," she said, swallowing back a returning sorrow, an emotion that she would try to hide but that she knew would keep her awake late into the night. "I love you too."

CHAPTER THIRTY-SEVEN

"Hello, Mr. Matthew," little Pete said, extending his hand forcefully.

Reverend Grandpa beamed as he smiled at Matthew, who accepted the gesture with delighted shock.

"Hello, Mr. Peter," Matthew said, shaking the boy's hand. "Great to see you again."

It must have been the longest conversation Peter Gale had had with anyone besides Reverend Grandpa since his father's death. For sure the only words Matthew had actually seen coming out of the kid's mouth. And the happiest he'd ever seen the old man appear.

Little Pete looked toward his grandpa like a private waiting for the sergeant to say, "Dismissed." A congratulatory wink released the boy to flee the room in embarrassed gratification.

"I'm impressed," Matthew said.

"I told you he's a smart kid," the old man bragged.

Matthew didn't recall being told any such thing. He nodded in agreement anyway.

The reverend continued. "All he needed was a little time. Next stop, the pulpit."

"The what?"

"The pulpit. You know, a preacher's podium."

"You call it a pulpit? Why?"

Reverend Grandpa rolled his eyes and waved a hand to bat away Matthew's ignorance. "Never mind."

"So you want Peter to be a preacher when he grows up?"

"Not really."

The answer surprised Matthew. "But I thought—"

"Little Pete is the one who wants to be a preacher like his granddad. I figured I could use his goal to help him start talking again."

Matthew remembered overhearing his client's earlier conversation with Peter. "He's been secretly talking to you for a while, hasn't he?"

Reverend Grandpa nodded. "Welcome to a very exclusive club, my boy."

"I'm honored."

"You should be," he said matter-of-factly. "It took an hour of coaching to get him to say those three words to you today."

Matthew smiled at the accomplishment. He tried to imagine how the death of a father might traumatize a little boy. What kind of pain had forced the child into such a self-imposed cone of silence? Having never known his own father, Matthew couldn't relate to the loss. But he had occasionally sensed himself grieving the absence.

Reverend Grandpa inhaled deeply as if accepting well-deserved congratulations. Then he inhaled again, unnaturally. The third attempt alarmed Matthew, prompting him to bend down and check the gauge on the old man's oxygen tank. The usually green light was bright red. He had seen yellow before, but never red. Wasn't there supposed to be an audible tone when the tank fell below the minimum safe level? No matter now; Matthew had to move fast.

The old man continued gasping for air as if suffering a heart attack while running a marathon in the summer heat. Matthew hurried toward the closet to retrieve a replacement tank. He panicked at the sight of one already depleted container, then darted out of the room toward the kitchen pantry, where they kept an emergency backup tank.

By the time he returned Peter and Isabelle were on either side of their grandpa, each holding a hand while frantically patting the old man's back in a useless effort to help.

Thirteen seconds later Matthew turned a knob to release the life-sustaining gas into Reverend Grandpa's lungs. A few replenishing breaths later the old man appeared to calm. The children, however, remained visibly shaken.

"What the—" Matthew stopped short, remembering the presence of children. "What on earth happened? I never heard the caution tone. This tank shouldn't have dropped into the red zone that fast!"

"My fault," Reverend Grandpa confessed after relishing a few more oxygen-rich breaths. "I hit the silence button to stop the racket while coaching Pete. We were so close to a breakthrough I didn't want the interruption."

"Dropping dead would have been a whole lot more of an interruption than asking me to change tanks!" Matthew scolded.

"Drop dead?" Isabelle shouted. "You mean he could have died?"

Matthew hesitated as post-panic anger arrived. "Yes, he could have died. Stupid old man!"

Peter jerked his head toward the mouth that had dared utter such an offense.

"He's not stupid!" the boy said. "You are!" Peter ran out of the room.

Isabelle's jaw dropped. "Grandpa," she said while her eyes fixed on the spot where she'd last seen Peter. "Peter said a whole sentence. Out loud!"

"Actually, two sentences," the old man said with a chuckle that quickly escalated into a roar of amused relief.

Isabelle ran after her brother.

"You've been honored again, my boy!" Reverend Grandpa said between guffaws.

"Great," Matthew replied, still irritated by the old man's carelessness.

He spent the next fifteen minutes rounding up every oxygen tank in the house. Four empty containers went into a box next to the front door to be put in Marissa's car as soon as she returned from her errands to get the kids. He found one additional full tank in a corner of the garage and placed it in his client's closet where it belonged for easy retrieval during the next stupidity-induced incident.

An hour later Marissa drove away with the box and the kids. Isabelle remained true to her pledge not to mention the little scare to Mom who, Grandpa had insisted, would make a big fuss over nothing. Matthew had calmed himself enough to speak to the old man, determined to say things he needed to hear whether he liked them or not.

"Did you see the look on Peter's and Isabelle's faces today?" Matthew began. "You nearly scared them to death when you were wheezing for air."

"It was a silly mistake. I'm still alive, and the kids are fine."

"What if I hadn't been nearby? What if you had died?"

The question seemed to anger the old man. And bother him.

"It wasn't my time to go yet."

"Thanks to me," Matthew said.

"Thanks to God," the old man countered. "You were just his instrument. If he wanted me home, I'd be there."

Matthew didn't follow. "What are you talking about? You are home."

Another look of exasperation. "I mean my home beyond the clouds."

A continued blank stare.

"Heaven!"

"Oh," Matthew said, finally understanding. The comment prompted an idea. "Speaking of heaven, I need to talk to you about something."

The reverend motioned Matthew in his direction. "Well, if we're going to chat about something important, let's do it in the living room. Help me up, will you, son?"

Matthew loaned the old man his arm as he stood to position himself in front of his walker. Then Reverend Grandpa firmly squeezed Matthew's shoulder as if acknowledging a debt of gratitude.

"Thanks, my boy," he said with what sounded like sincere affection.

A few minutes later the two sat side by side in the living room, Reverend Grandpa in his favorite chair and Matthew on the sofa. No eye contact, just as Matthew preferred for this particular conversation.

"I think God wants me to tell you something."

The old man seemed pleasantly surprised by the comment. "He does, does he?"

"Yes."

"Which God?"

Matthew turned toward the question. "What?"

"Which God told you to say something to me? The one I believe in or the one you believe in?"

Matthew didn't know how to respond, prompting the old man's playful sigh.

"Look, son, my God speaks through the Bible, not through

a college boy." The sting of offense quickly dissipated as Reverend Grandpa added, "Even a college boy I've grown fond of."

"I still need to say something to you. Promise me you'll listen and at least consider what I've got to say. I think I've earned that."

A deferential nod. "OK. Take the pulpit."

Matthew tried to remember the reference.

"I'm all ears," the old man added.

Matthew swallowed hard before diving into his hastily planned speech. "I think Marissa wants you to volunteer."

He paused to let the words sink in.

"And I think that you want what's best for her and the kids, so I think you need to consider the option."

There, he'd said it.

"Marissa told you that?" Reverend Grandpa asked with injury in his voice.

"No. She didn't say she wants you to transition. But I can tell."

"How?"

"By the look in her eyes when I suggested it. I can tell she feels the same way I felt when facing a similar situation with my mom."

"You lost your mom?"

"Long before she died." Matthew sensed the old man looking at him as he kept his own eyes fixed on the wall.

"What happened?" Reverend Grandpa asked gently.

"We decay."

"Excuse me?"

Matthew looked at his client. "It's something my religious studies professor told me. It was certainly true of my mom. She had been deteriorating for years before she finally volunteered."

"She killed herself?"

Matthew turned back toward the wall. "No. She didn't kill

herself. She sacrificed herself. For me." He felt the admission moisten his eyes. He swallowed back the growing lump in his throat. "She wanted me to go to college in order to become a teacher. But her medical expenses were burning through our savings." He looked at his client. "Just like you're burning through yours."

Reverend Grandpa looked away. He was either ashamed of himself or angry at Matthew. Probably both.

"So she decided to escape."

"Escape?"

"Escape the decay. Transcend the limitations of physical existence to follow in Jesus's footsteps."

"Jesus's footsteps?"

"That's what I wanted to tell you. I think God wants you to know you've misunderstood. You see Jesus as someone who rose from the dead like a death-conquering hero. But he was actually showing us the path to our true destiny."

"Which is?"

"Which is to transcend the limitations of a decaying body by becoming a death-embracing mystic. To escape the body."

Matthew noticed Reverend Grandpa reaching at an awkward angle as he twisted his torso while shoving a hand deep into his pocket.

"What are you doing?" Matthew asked. "Do you need some help?"

"No need for help. I'll have it in just a…ah…here it is."

The old man held up a small pocketknife. Matthew wondered why on earth he had been carrying a tool used by campers and hunters. Perhaps a keepsake preserving bygone memories?

"I had planned to wrap this as a gift for little Pete," Reverend Grandpa began, "to celebrate today's big accomplishment."

What did a celebration gift have to do with Matthew's speech? Was the old man even listening?

"But I think you need it more." Reverend Grandpa pulled open what appeared to be a dangerously sharp tip. He flipped the knife around to hold it by the blade. "Here you go."

Matthew accepted the gift with a confused gaze. "Thanks, I guess. But why do you think I need this more than Peter?"

"So you can slit your own throat."

"What?" Matthew asked, covering his Adam's apple protectively with his other hand. "Slit my throat?"

"Or should I say, set yourself free?" A scathing laugh.

Matthew handed the knife back, rejecting the ridiculous notion.

"What's the matter, my boy? Don't believe your own philosophy? Or is it just something you believe when it applies to old debits like me?"

Matthew stood to leave the room. "I was trying to be serious," he said with disgust. "My mom's death isn't something to joke about."

"No, it isn't," Reverend Grandpa agreed. "Nor is it something to compare to Jesus's sacrifice on a cross!"

Matthew sensed his client's rising indignation.

"Death-embracing mystic? Nonsense! You have no clue what you're talking about, boy. Jesus Christ was not showing us the way to some harebrained enlightenment. He was giving his life as a payment for sin. My sin. Your sin. Even your mom's sin."

"What's that supposed to mean?"

"Your mom committed suicide, Matthew. No matter how much you try to dress it up as a heroic act, it was taking the most precious gift God gives us. Not to mention adding another coffin to the bonfire of human dignity."

The words made Matthew too furious to speak. How dare the old man call his mom's transition a sin! Even if it had been wrong, she hadn't done it. Matthew had. He was the one who had convinced her frail mind to volunteer. He was the one who had put the sword of guilt into her back as she walked the plank of "heroic sacrifice." He was the one who had chosen to heed the advice of Dr. Vincent rather than the warnings of Father Richard.

It wasn't a sin! Matthew tried to believe. *It was the right decision.*

"You're the one who has no idea what you're talking about!" Matthew finally retorted. "My mother was a good woman. She did what you're too selfish and cowardly to do. She's better off today because of it. And so am I!"

Matthew stormed out of the room, ignoring Reverend Grandpa's effort to coax him back.

"Sit down, my boy…" The bedroom door slammed to shield Matthew from noisy words he had no interest in hearing.

He spent the next few minutes trying to quell an irrational desire to grab the old man's knife and silence him for good. He instead grabbed his tablet from the top of the dresser and searched the PICTURES folder to find a portrait of his mother. He found one taken in her better days, when she still retained an echo of girlish beauty, a reminder of what she had been before dementia started stealing her away.

"I'm sorry, Mom," he heard himself whisper. "I thought it was for the best. But now I can't even get to the college money you left me."

He closed his eyes. Then he cursed.

When he opened his eyes he noticed a bouncing icon at the bottom of his digital screen. An unopened message from Maria Davidson! His mood lifted immediately as he tapped.

Hi Matt:

It was great catching up after so many years. I'm afraid I'm entering a pretty busy season of life, so it probably isn't a good idea to try getting together again before you head back to your mysterious life. But I had a wonderful time and appreciated you taking an interest in Jared. Thanks for reconnecting. Be happy and be good.

Maria

Matthew read the letter twice before the meaning finally sank in. Maria Davidson had just said goodbye. Or rather, good riddance!

He cursed again as he let the tablet fall to the floor.

I won't let this happen, he thought. Then he frantically searched his dresser drawers to locate some stationery and a pen.

CHAPTER THIRTY-EIGHT

Sitting at her dining room table, Rebecca Santiago tried to push past her fear. Her weakness. She picked the letter up from the floor and read it one last time.

Dear Victor:

Please forgive my sending this note to your wife Rebecca. Prior attempts to correspond through your assistant have proven un-fruitful. I have yet to receive a single response to any of my previous letters regarding the wrongful death appeal involving NEXT Transition Services. As you know, many lives hang in the balance in this matter. That's why I was pleased the case fell to a man with the kind of wisdom and restraint you have demonstrated throughout your distinguished judicial career. But this case is far too important for any hint of ambiguity. That's why I must know where you stand before the scheduled ruling deadline of September 4th. Please consider Rebecca's future as you contemplate the following alternatives:

- *Option One:* Assure me that you will indeed decide in favor of *NEXT.*
- *Option Two:* Bid your sweet wife farewell since you will die before issuing an opinion.

Once again, I apologize for alarming Rebecca. But she deserves to know about the increasingly tense situation in which we find ourselves. I could not allow any of what might transpire to come as a surprise, and I trust that her intervention will motivate you to do what's right for everyone.

As always,
A Manichean
P.S. Kindly post your response at the following private forum address: ANON.CHAT.4398

Rebecca walked into the kitchen, where a small stack of dirty teacups and saucers reminded her that she had been plunged into a different universe from the one she had inhabited only a few minutes before. Hadn't she just waved goodbye to Shelly, the last straggler from a chatty afternoon with friends? Hadn't she intended to complain to Victor about the tragedy of burned pumpkin scones? It was part of their daily ritual over dinner to share the high points and low points of their day. She suddenly had a new, dreadful low to report. And it couldn't wait until dinner.

She found the phone and pressed the image of Victor smiling back at her. She heard his recorded voice begin the custom greeting made for her ears only.

"Hi, Rebecca. There's two things I want to do at this moment. First, answer your call. Second, tell you how much I love you. Unfortunately, I'm probably in session at the moment. So I'll have to settle for saying that I love you. I'll call back as soon as I can."

She smiled. Then she panicked. What if he could *never* talk to her again? What if the crazy killer had been impatient and decided not to wait until September fourth after all?

She quickly tapped another image. A live voice answered. *Thank God*!

"Jennifer?" It was all she could say, her fear and sorrow surfacing at the relief.

"Rebecca?" Jennifer responded to the sound of crying. "What's wrong? What happened?"

Jennifer McKay had been like a daughter to the Santiagos. There was no one Rebecca would rather have called, short of Victor himself.

"Rebecca? Are you hurt?" Jennifer was asking through the phone with urgent concern.

She finally regained a semblance of composure. "I'm all right, Jennifer." Then she swallowed back another ocean of moisture and took a deep breath. "But I'm afraid for Victor. We need to do something to protect him!"

She had never said anything like it before. Victor had always been the sentry in their relationship. It was his job to worry about his frail bride. Rebecca knew herself to be weaker than she wished. She relied on Victor's strength. But in this moment she would settle for Jennifer's.

"A letter arrived today," she continued. "Somebody wants to kill my Victor!"

No response.

"Did you hear me, Jennifer? I said—"

"Did the letter specifically mention killing?"

"Yes, of course. Why would I make something like that up?"

"Is the letter signed?" Jennifer asked.

Why doesn't she seem alarmed?

"I'm afraid, Jennifer. I'm so afraid."

"Listen to me, Rebecca. I need to know if there is a signature."

Rebecca walked back to the dining room to find the letter and search for a name. "Someone named Manichean," she replied. "Why, what's going on?"

Before Jennifer could respond Rebecca saw a line in the letter she hadn't noticed before.

Prior attempts to correspond through your assistant have proven unfruitful.

"You've received other letters, haven't you?"

"Yes, we have. But don't worry. We have a detective investigating the situation."

A detective? Situation? Rebecca felt her fear becoming anger. "What situation? And why didn't you tell me about this? Why didn't Victor tell me?"

A long, torturous silence. Jennifer finally answered. "Rebecca, Victor doesn't know about the letters."

She couldn't believe her ears. Why would Jennifer keep such an important secret from her boss? From Rebecca's husband? "What do you mean?"

Jennifer explained everything: Victor's policy of ignoring any correspondence related to an open case, her role of deciding how to handle each situation, and why in this instance she had chosen to hire a private investigator rather than go to the police.

Rebecca looked back at the signature. *A Manichean.* "Do you have any idea of his identity?"

A two-second delay. "We have a few leads."

Rebecca sensed the truth. They had no idea. "I want to talk to Victor immediately," she insisted.

"I understand," Jennifer said. "But, please, can you read me the letter? Word for word."

She did, her voice breaking again when she reached the ultimatum.

"He's going to kill my Victor!" she said, the panic recoloring her voice. "We have to tell him now!"

A momentary hush meant Jennifer must have been assessing her dilemma. If she did as Rebecca suggested she would be violating Victor's policy. A policy Rebecca both admired and suddenly hated.

"Listen, Rebecca," Jennifer began. "The judge will be in session for at least another ninety minutes. Security is on high alert due to the earlier letters, so nothing can happen to him here."

"Nothing can happen to him? Come on, Jennifer. *Anything* could happen!"

"Please, Rebecca. I promise we'll protect him. But I need to come over and see that letter right away. I'll call the detective and we'll meet you there. Then we'll decide. One hour, that's all I ask."

Rebecca considered the request. What would Victor want her to do? She knew the answer immediately.

"OK," she said reluctantly. "One hour."

The call ended. Rebecca felt light-headed. She sat back down at the dinner table where her living nightmare had begun. Then she refolded the note, slid it back into the envelope, and wrapped her arms around a delicate frame now home to the consuming demon of terror.

PART THREE

PART THREE

CHAPTER THIRTY-NINE

Jennifer McKay was sitting on the living room sofa beside a distraught woman who was downing the last swig of a drink that was not, Tyler presumed, her first. Although he had never seen her before, Tyler knew the woman immediately: the judge's wife, understandably shaken.

He glanced toward the dining room table, then groaned at the sight of Assistant Chief Greg Smith. Tyler had hoped to arrive in time to read the letter first and then debrief his former partner rather than the other way around. Jennifer had said she'd phoned the police before calling Tyler. He had raced through downtown Denver in slow motion behind rush-hour traffic hoping to beat Smitty to the house. No such luck.

Tyler heard the clack of a dead bolt latching behind him as an officer closed the front door. The sound prompted a glance from Smitty, who looked up from the letter to offer a summoning wave.

"Tyler," he said in a hushed voice.

"Smitty," Tyler replied with a nod. "What've we got?"

It was the same question he'd asked a hundred times before, back when he and Smitty had investigated everything from petty burglary to serial homicide. But this time it felt impertinent. They were no longer partners. Tyler wasn't on the force. Nor was he an effective private investigator—he had failed to prevent whatever threat Smitty was reading.

He quickly corrected himself. "I mean, what have *you* got?"

Smitty handed Tyler the page. "Take a look for yourself."

He did. Then he glanced in Jennifer's direction. She was rubbing Rebecca Santiago's forearm to offer comfort. Their eyes met. His shot an *I told you so* rebuke. Hers stubbornly refused any *I should have listened* regret.

"I was afraid of this," he said while following Smitty around the corner to speak in private. Tyler wanted his former partner to believe the letter hadn't been a surprise. And in a way it hadn't. Tyler's gut had told him the situation could escalate. He had told Jennifer she should write back to smoke out the culprit. That she should alert the judge so that he could resign from the case to protect his life. "Maybe now Ms. McKay will take my advice," Tyler continued.

"What advice is that?"

"Tell the judge about the letters."

"You mean he doesn't know?"

"No sir. He has a strict policy against paying attention to any correspondence related to an active case."

Smitty sighed. "Of course."

Tyler waited a moment to let Smitty appreciate his dilemma. "I have a few potential suspects," he lied. "But I need the judge to write back so we can spring the trap."

Smitty looked at Tyler questioningly but said nothing. Then he glanced back into the living room.

"Ms. McKay, may I speak to you for a moment?" he asked. "That is, if Mrs. Santiago doesn't mind."

The woman shook her head deferentially while reaching for the bottle of brandy sitting strategically beside her now-empty glass. "Go ahead, Jennifer. I'll be fine."

Jennifer appeared grateful for the promotion from comforter to collaborator. She clearly disliked the thought of Tyler and Smitty discussing next steps without her input.

She joined them in the dining room, where Tyler still hoped to control the situation. He spoke first. "Smitty and I were just discussing the need to show this letter to the judge—"

"No!" she interrupted. "This is a very important case and he's only a few days away from issuing an opinion. The judge would be very upset if we—"

"Come on!" Tyler said, too loudly. He hushed himself before continuing. "You can't be serious. The man's wife is sitting in the next room so alarmed she's drowning her fears in booze. I think it's about time you woke up to what's happening here, Ms. McKay."

"I know exactly what's happening here, Mr. Cain! And I know exactly what Judge Santiago would want."

"You're just too stubborn to admit I was right!" Tyler added before Smitty raised a hand to silence the whispered spat.

"Ms. McKay is right," he began.

Tyler's head jerked in Smitty's direction, then back toward Jennifer, who appeared equally startled.

"What?" Tyler said.

"I don't think we need to show Judge Santiago this letter."

Jennifer grinned in triumph as Tyler weighed his response. How to save face? More importantly, how to protect the judge? Then it struck him.

"We don't have a choice," he said. "His wife will tell him the second she sees him."

"No, she won't," Jennifer said with surprising confidence. "I explained the situation. She knows the judge better than anyone. She knows he would want us to wait until after he issues an opinion."

Tyler peered back around the corner toward the shaken woman. "Look at her, for Pete's sake! Even if she managed to keep her mouth shut, which seems highly unlikely, the judge will know by looking at her that something's up." He turned toward Smitty. "Imagine the fallout if it gets out that the police knew about this threat and didn't try to stop it."

"I didn't say we wouldn't try to stop it," Smitty said. "I said I don't think the judge needs to see the letters. We can inform him of a threatening situation without specific details. If we do our job properly, there's no reason we can't let the man do his."

If we do our job properly. A dig at Tyler's failed investigation?

"We'll tell the judge that we have evidence he may be the target of an assassination attempt," Smitty continued. "Then we'll tell him it's related to a court case without saying which or what decision the suspect demands. The judge can make his own decision on whether he wants more detail or not."

"He won't," Jennifer insisted as Tyler seethed.

"We'll see," Smitty replied. "But for now, tell me everything either of you knows so that we can determine the best course of action."

Jennifer reminded Smitty that she had called the chief of police to request a recommendation for a private investigator. She sounded like a disappointed customer complaining to the store manager.

Then Tyler shared what little he had learned from the earlier letters. He decided to leave out the part where he called Evan Dimitri. No need to further sully his reputation by describing the blunder. A mistake that had gotten him nowhere and, he told himself, was probably irrelevant to the case.

Smitty sighed reflectively after listening to Tyler's debrief.

"So," he began, "our only real clues are the postal facilities in which the letters were processed and an odd pseudonym."

"A Manichean," Tyler inserted in an attempt to prove useful.

"Right," Smitty said without interest as he considered options. "Here's what we're going to do. Ms. McKay, I want you to inform the judge of a threat."

"Of course," she said, obviously pleased by Smitty's wise tactic.

"Tyler, I want you to further analyze this new letter."

Smitty handed the note to his former partner, who accepted it eagerly and with relief. "You got it, boss," he said, grateful to still be on the team.

"I'll assign an officer to guard the judge's house and another to his chamber until he either resigns from the case or issues an opinion."

"Only two officers?" Jennifer asked, like a still-disgruntled customer.

"It's two more than I can afford, Ms. McKay," Smitty explained.

She huffed. "We have security guards at the courthouse already. Would it be possible to assign both officers to the house? I'm sure it would make Mrs. Santiago feel much more secure."

A single nod. "Done."

Tyler joined Smitty in offering reassurance to Mrs. Santiago before heading to his car. He closed himself in and breathed deeply the sun-warmed air. As the engine engaged, the date and time appeared on the dashboard. September 1, 2043. Only three days until Judge Santiago was scheduled to issue an opinion on the wrongful death appeal initiated by NEXT Transition Services.

He had less than seventy-two hours to find the culprit. And, he hoped, to prove himself worthwhile to his former partner.

CHAPTER FORTY

The bartender reached for the empty glass. "Another round?"

The question interrupted Tyler's concentration. "What's that?"

"I asked if you need a refill."

"Oh, yeah, thanks. Diet cola."

The man smirked at an order more suited to a fast-food joint than his establishment. "You sure you don't want something stiffer? You look like you could use it."

"Not tonight." Tyler pointed to his open tablet. "Still on duty."

The man went away for a moment and returned with a fresh glass of ice. He slid it forward along with an unopened can of soda. "Enjoy."

Tyler nodded, then resumed his digital doodling, jotting down each new clue found in the latest letter.

WANTS NEXT INC. TO WIN THEIR APPEAL
CLEAR DEATH THREAT
DIFFERENT HANDWRITING?

Tyler deleted the last line when he realized the differences were too slight to suggest another author. It was probably the same hand more nervous due to rising stakes. He continued reviewing the list.

SENT BY COURIER VS. POST

The first three letters had been sent from the Boulder area. The fourth from Denver. This one had no origination postal code or any other mark suggesting a location. It had come on a delivery truck Rebecca Santiago hadn't been able to describe.

VERY RESPECTFUL TONE

As in the earlier letters.

WRITER KNOWS WIFE'S FIRST NAME

Easy enough to find with a simple online search of news clippings.

In short, nothing useful.

Tyler took a sip of his soda to cool a rising anger at Smitty's decision. At this very moment Jennifer McKay was informing the judge of a vague threat rather than insisting that he correspond with the writer or resign from the case.

He scanned the letter again, resting his eyes on the postscript.

P.S. Kindly post your response at the following private forum address: ANON.CHAT.4398

Why not send a short note promising to decide in favor of NEXT? It would neutralize the threat and, perhaps, provide a few additional clues. The judge could ignore the promise and decide the case as he saw fit. By then they might even have caught the culprit.

But Tyler knew the suggestion would fall on deaf ears. Judge Santiago would rather risk his life than undermine his integrity, a fact Tyler found both exasperating and laudable. He wondered what, if anything, he himself would risk his own life to protect. Certainly not his integrity. That was already in the toilet.

Tyler glanced again at the signature line.

A MANICHEAN

It must mean something. But what?

He quickly typed the name into a search field for what must have been the tenth time since taking the case. The same useless list of results appeared.

That's when it struck him. Maybe the words weren't a pseudonym at all. Maybe they were a description. Not a first initial and last name, but a title, like A CANADIAN or A DENVER BRONCOS FAN.

He looked at the list of links again to spot any group or organization that might accept members. Perhaps a religious order, or a club, or an online chat association with dues. Nothing fit.

He narrowed the search criteria to anything near Boulder. Twenty results: two of the top five included the name Dr. Thomas Vincent, chairman of the Religious Studies department at the University of Colorado.

"Bingo!" Tyler said aloud.

"Nope," the bartender responded while wiping the counter. "But we host a poker match every Monday night."

Tyler chuckled at the misunderstanding, then tapped the first link. Apparently this Dr. Vincent fellow taught a course on ancient religious controversies in the very city from which the first letters had been sent.

He tapped the second link and learned Dr. Vincent had also written a book about Manichaeism. The author's biography said he was a leading authority on a wide range of philosophies that had been largely rejected by the early Christian church.

Tyler launched another search, this time typing the name Thomas Vincent in conjunction with Boulder, Colorado. A long list of results surfaced: video highlights from prior lectures, free downloads from an upcoming book about something called Gnosticism, and a whole string of spicy photos posted by college-age girls to his personal attention. Tyler pulled up several of the pictures before ordering himself to focus on the task at hand.

He dialed the number listed on the university's website. A recorded female voice answered, accompanied by a pleasant musical selection. He glanced at the time. Past office hours.

He tapped Smitty's image to ask for help. Within ten minutes he had Dr. Vincent's private number compliments of a citizen-watch database law enforcement agencies could access with a proper warrant. A warrant Jennifer McKay had gladly procured from the judge.

He dialed the number. A voice answered. "Thomas Vincent."

Tyler found himself at a loss for words. What to say? He couldn't mention the letters. After all, the professor was a possible suspect.

"Hello," Tyler began hesitantly. "Forgive me for the intrusion, but is this the same Dr. Vincent who wrote the famous book on a religious movement known as Manichaeism?"

A brief laugh from the other end of the line. "I'd hardly call it famous. Academic works don't sell many downloads. But yes, I'm the author. To whom do I have the pleasure of speaking?"

A nice-sounding man. Very respectful. Just like the letters.

"Tyler Cain. I'm doing research on a project and was encouraged to call you for help. I'm told you're the most respected voice in your field."

A bit of flattery couldn't hurt, especially when talking to an academic who seemed more distinguished than famous.

"Well, I'm happy to do what I can," Dr. Vincent said. "Who recommended me?"

Tyler felt a slight panic. What to say? "I'm embarrassed to say it, but I forgot the person's name. We met on a plane and struck up a conversation."

"A student of mine?"

"I think so."

"Hmm. A young woman?"

Tyler thought for a second. Play the odds. Other than in the movies, killers tend to be male. "A man."

"Really?"

"Is that surprising?" Tyler asked.

"I don't give this number out to many of my male students."

Tyler glanced back at the spicy pictures. *What a life*! he mused.

"Well, no matter," the professor continued. "How can I help?"

"I was hoping you could point me in the right direction on something."

"I'll do what I can."

Should he risk mentioning the signatures? Without eye contact Tyler would have no way of sensing the professor's reaction. What if Dr. Vincent had written the letters? Or delivered them? Would this call ruin any hope of cornering the culprit? Maybe. But Tyler was running out of time and options. He decided to chance it.

"Do you know anyone who would call himself a Manichean?"

"A Manichean?"

"Yes, sir."

"Well, yes. Of course."

"Really? Who?"

"Well, the most notable would be Augustine."

Tyler quickly grabbed his tablet. "Could you spell that name?"

The professor laughed at the request. "Certainly you're familiar with Saint Augustine."

"Saint?"

"Fourth century. Bishop of Hippo." Dr. Vincent's voice sounded suspicious; he had been tipped off by Tyler's appalling ignorance.

"Truth is," Tyler began, "I don't know much about ancient religions or philosophy or anything of the sort."

A brief silence. "What's this about? Who gave you this number?"

"The police."

"The police?" Dr. Vincent said with alarm. "Why would the police give you my private number? Come to think of it, why do they even *have* my private number?"

Tyler couldn't see the professor's eyes, but his voice carried no hint of guilty avoidance. Tyler decided to come clean by telling Dr. Vincent about the letters.

"I see," the professor responded after listening in silence.

"Do you have any idea who would be eager for NEXT to win its appeal and describe himself as a Manichean?"

Dr. Vincent thought for a moment before mumbling something beneath his breath. Possibly a name.

"What's that?" Tyler asked.

"I had a student this past year who seemed particularly interested in Manichean philosophy. As it happens, he also has a transition inheritance tied up with his late mother's estate. I think he might have mentioned something about the NEXT lawsuit, but I couldn't say for sure."

"What's the student's name?"

The professor hesitated. "I can't imagine this young man doing anything so stupid. He wants to be a teacher. And he's worked very hard."

"You'd be surprised what people will do when they get desperate," Tyler said. "I just want to ask the guy a few questions. Can you please tell me his name?"

Another pause. "His name is Matthew. Matthew Adams."

"Thank you, Dr. Vincent. Does Matthew Adams live in student housing on campus?"

"He's no longer a student. He plans to return to school next year if he can—" The professor stopped short.

"If he can what?" Tyler pushed, sensing the professor knew more than he wanted to reveal. "If he can get the money?"

"Yes."

Double bingo!

"Which will happen if the transition inheritance is released?"

"I suppose," Dr. Vincent agreed grudgingly.

"Do you have any idea where we might find Mr. Adams now?" Tyler asked. "Please, Dr. Vincent, this could be a matter of life and death."

The professor explained that Matthew had left Boulder to take an elder-care job in the Denver area.

"And when did you last speak to Mr. Adams?"

"Last week. He came to me for advice on dealing with his client."

"Did he mention an address? Give you a phone number? Anything like that?"

"I'm afraid not," Dr. Vincent replied, as if relieved by his own ignorance. "Like I said. Somewhere in the Denver area."

Tyler thanked the professor and left the door open for a follow-up inquiry before ending the call.

He had a name.

He had a general location.

And he still had two days.

Tyler smiled in self-congratulation as he reached for the soda can to refill his glass. Then he paused, motioning toward the bartender, who was refilling a collection of empty nut bowls.

"I think I'll have that stiff drink now," he said. "I'm suddenly in the mood to celebrate."

CHAPTER FORTY-ONE

It felt good to receive Maria's long embrace, the sorrow Julia had managed to conceal from Troy for the past thirty-six hours finally erupting into her sister's nurturing arms. It had only taken three gently spoken words.

"I'm sorry, Sis."

Despite her embarrassment, Julia thanked Maria for listening, for caring, and for promising not to say anything to Troy.

The two now sat on a large rock in silence, holding hands as they had when they were little girls during a thunderstorm. A streak of early-morning sunlight peered over the nearby mountains, brightening the stony trail they intended to hike.

Maria spoke first. "Are they certain? No chance at all?"

"Not much. The doctor mentioned a surgical option. But that rarely helps." Julia paused to swallow back another flood of tears. Then she continued. "She said most couples in our situation use a sperm bank."

"Would Troy be open to that?"

"He wants a child badly." Julia wiped her nose with a tissue she had retrieved from her jogging suit pocket. "But he wants *our* child. How would he feel about a baby that was half me and half some other guy? Could he love that child like he would his own flesh and blood?" She shrugged. "I don't know. And I'm afraid to ask."

Maria placed her hand on Julia's shoulder. "What are you afraid of?"

"Afraid he'll say yes. You know Troy. He'll do whatever he thinks would make me happy. But would it make *him* happy? I'm afraid I'd never really know how he felt about a child that his wife had with a complete stranger."

"Julia!" Maria said sternly. "You make it sound like you're contemplating a one-night stand. It's not like that. Couples use sperm donors all the time."

Julia laughed self-consciously. "I know, I know," she said with a sigh. "I'm probably being silly. Of course it's not wrong. But it still doesn't feel quite right. At least not for Troy. Or for me."

Maria nodded quietly, waiting a few seconds, then stood up. "Do you still want to go?"

Julia nodded, glad to move beyond self-pity. She loved nothing more than a brisk walk along Bear Creek Lake to help clear her head and regain perspective.

Neither said anything for thirty or forty paces. Then Maria asked, "Have you thought about adoption?"

The question raised a different cloud over Julia's demeanor. Not personal grief, but the memory of a disturbing discovery. While researching dark zone trends Julia had learned there was a five-year waiting list for adoptable infants. Five years!

"There aren't any babies available," she said without explanation.

"You can't be serious. There must be some babies in need of a good home."

"Very few. It seems harvesting pays better than delivery."

The comment appeared to startle Maria. She stopped walking and turned toward her sister. "What did you say?"

"Fetus harvesting. It's become a fairly large industry supporting the embryotic supply chain."

"The what?"

"You know: surgical repair material, cosmetics, health supplements. That sort of thing."

It took a moment for Maria to connect the dots. "Wait. You mean that's what they mean when they say 'embryotics'?"

Julia nodded. "You can sell a two-month-old fetus for a few thousand dollars. So, unless you want to raise a child, what's the motivation for women to invest nine months getting fat, visiting doctors, and buying prenatal vitamins? It's illegal to sell a live baby due to human trafficking laws. But embryos can be sold without hassle or questions."

Maria appeared every bit as troubled as Julia had been when confronted with the naked facts. But the process had never been a secret. It had just remained hidden in plain sight thanks to naïve indifference, or perhaps willful ignorance. In the back of Julia's and Maria's minds they must have known that someone, somewhere had been harvesting embryos. Like everyone else, they had chosen not to ask where the raw materials fueling the public's enhanced appearance and extended years came from. The look on Maria's face reminded Julia of her own earlier epiphany. They were like two children stumbling upon a suspicious dog kennel beside their daddy's butcher shop.

Eager to move beyond the depressing and dark, Julia raised a lighter subject as they continued their walk. "So, tell me about your date. How was the reunion with the high school mystery suitor?"

Maria smiled, then frowned. "Well, despite your worst fears he didn't turn out to be a mass murderer hoping to rape and strangle me."

Julia laughed at the reminder of her overprotective warnings. "That's good news. So, what's his name?"

"Matthew."

"And?"

"And we met for coffee."

"A public place. Very good. You listened to me. Did you meet during daylight hours like I—"

Maria slapped her sister's arm.

"Ouch! What was that for?"

"Love pat," Maria said playfully. "Yes, Julia, we met in the daytime. Now will you quit with the hovercraft questions?"

"Sorry. Tell me about him."

"I didn't remember him at first. But he sure knew me. He could tell you what I was wearing the day we sat together in the cafeteria, what I said when I refused his invitation to the prom, and how many pictures I've posted online in the past year."

"Sounds creepy to me."

"It wasn't like that. At least not at first. I thought it was kind of sweet. Flattering."

"Maria," Julia said severely. "That's how it always starts with you. They look. They like. They flatter. They enjoy. And then they leave."

"Not this time. I ended it before reaching the 'enjoy' phase."

Julia was genuinely surprised. "Really? Just like that? What happened?"

"He didn't pass the Jared test."

"The what?"

"Jared made me promise I would introduce him to any guy I liked enough for a potentially serious relationship. So he came with me on my second date with Matthew. It didn't go well."

"What happened?"

"Nothing really. Jared just got bad vibes. He wants me to marry someone like your Troy. This guy didn't come close."

"Was he mean?"

"No. Quite nice actually."

"Then what?"

Maria appeared to be searching for the right word. "Needy. No, weak. That's the word. He didn't seem like the kind of guy who would put me before himself. At least that's how Jared read him."

"I see. Disappointed?"

"A bit. He was cute. And it was my first real date in six months. But I'm learning not to trust my own first impressions."

They walked another quarter mile before either spoke again.

"I'm proud of you, Sis," Julia finally said. "I bet it made Jared feel good knowing you respected his opinion enough to end the relationship."

"It did." A sigh. "I'm OK with the decision. There was something odd about Matthew anyway. It kind of gnawed at me but I couldn't put my finger on it. At least not until after Jared gave him the thumbs-down. Then I remembered feeling something was off-kilter when he first contacted me. He used a really weird online handle."

"A lot of guys do that when using online connection services."

"I know. But most use something fun like 'Lover Boy' or 'Dream Man.' Matt used something pretty strange. I can't remember it exactly. *A Manichu* or *A Mannequin*. Something like that."

Julia stopped in her tracks.

Maria took several steps before noticing, then turned back. "What?"

"Was it *A Manichean*?"

"That's it!" Maria said with surprise. "How on earth did you know?"

Six minutes later both sisters were sitting in Julia's car.

"That's the same name I got from a Dr. Vincent I called last night," Tyler Cain's voice was saying through the stereo speakers. "He's a professor on ancient religions in Boulder who said Matthew Adams recently moved from Boulder to Denver to take an elder-care job. Triple bingo!"

"An elder-care job?" Maria said. "He told me he was in town on business."

"Did he mention an address?" Tyler asked.

"No. I assumed he was staying in a hotel."

Tyler cursed. "Well, I already tried the address change information service. They list the Boulder address he left but nothing on this end."

"No mail-forwarding mailing address?" Julia asked.

"One of those rental box places. I had planned to try tracking it down this morning."

"But there must be a hundred of those places in the Denver area."

"Three hundred and twenty-seven, actually. Smitty said the police have no record of credit card use since Matthew moved from Boulder. He seems to have gone underground. No address. Cash purchases. So I have to start with what I've got."

"Who's Smitty?" Maria asked.

"My former partner with the Denver police."

"Did you check for an active bank account?" Julia suggested. "Surely that would have his new address."

"I couldn't get any information over the phone. My call routed to somebody named 'Jeremy' in one of those foreign call centers in North Korea or Vietnam. You know how they talk. Anyway, I plan to stop by the major bank branches when they open this morning, right after I get a compulsory cooperation document from Smitty."

"Wait a minute," Julia said while looking at her sister. "Maria was in touch with Matthew last week."

"A few days ago, actually. But I told you. I sent him a Dear John message. It's over between us."

"I bet you said goodbye in a way that would keep the door open in case you ever changed your mind."

"Julia!" Maria reacted with offense.

"I'm right, aren't I?"

A nod.

"I thought so."

"That's perfect!" Tyler interjected. "Maria, I need you to send Matthew Adams another message."

"Saying what?" she asked. "Matt's not likely to respond if I tell him the police want to talk to him."

"No," Tyler agreed. "But I bet he'd respond if you told him you would like to see him again."

"That you'd *love* to see him again," Julia corrected as she shoved her tablet in front of Maria.

She reluctantly accepted the device. "I'm not so sure about this. What if he—"

"Please, Maria, just type whatever Mr. Cain suggests."

She did, carefully following Tyler's wording to request a rendezvous later that afternoon.

Just before Maria hit SEND, Julia placed her hand on her sister's arm, then suggested one last action. She reached for the tablet and pointed. "Wink."

"Excuse me?"

"I said wink at the camera. We're attaching a snapshot."

Maria glowered at her sister. Then dutifully obeyed.

CHAPTER FORTY-TWO

Nothing was going to keep Matthew from getting to Bear Creek Lake by six. Not even Reverend Grandpa's ill-timed attempt at making amends. Feeling bad for what he had said about Matthew's mother, the old man suggested the two might grab a burger together. "My treat!" he had said with a sheepish grin.

But even if Matthew had wanted to accept some lame apology, he wouldn't have gone. Maria Davidson had made that impossible by retracting her rejection note. Why else would she suggest a picnic dinner and say she would love to see him again? Reverend Grandpa could fend for himself for a few hours, even if it meant Matthew abandoning his post. Or losing his job.

He triple-checked the destination to confirm the precise location suggested in Maria's mischievous note.

I'll be waiting near the trailhead wearing white shorts and a bright yellow sleeveless blouse. (Easy to spot from a distance and enjoy up close!)
Go to coordinates 39.653182,-105.148349.

I'll wait exactly ten minutes. If you don't arrive I'll figure you aren't coming.
But I really, really hope you do!

He looked urgently at the dashboard clock for the eighth time in as many minutes. Assuming a hundred-yard walk from the parking area he should make it with time to spare. He took a deep breath while turning left onto Kumpfmiller Drive. One turn later he saw Maria in the distance. She was, as promised, easy on the eyes. Her blond hair was pulled back, revealing a lovely neck that matched lightly tanned limbs. She looked even better than he had imagined, her upper legs partially concealed behind a small picnic basket dangling from her coupled hands. She appeared to brighten when she spotted Matthew's approaching smile.

As he slammed the car door, Matthew waved in Maria's direction. She lifted the basket slightly as if offering evidence of her intentions, then turned onto the trail and began walking into the trees. He laughed to himself, still stunned by his sudden good fortune, before starting toward her. Then he stopped and turned back toward the car to grab the love note he had planned to send. Now he could watch her read it and, he hoped, relish her reaction.

"Maria," he called into the trees. "Wait up. I've got something for you."

No answer.

He trotted to the trailhead, where he found a path beneath the shade of unwieldy tree branches.

"Maria," he repeated, half hoping she would continue the game of hide-and-seek.

But this time she called back. "I'm over here by the lake."

He turned left toward the voice.

"Just beyond the clump of trees."

Matthew's mind raced through the possibilities. Would he find her lounging on a blanket beside two freshly poured glasses of wine? Or perhaps in a bikini with her bare toes caressing the water's edge? Or, dare he hope, taking a plunge wearing nothing but an invitation for him to join?

"Mr. Adams?"

The male voice startled Matthew. He looked left toward an approaching stranger who somehow knew his name.

"Have we met?" Matthew asked while instinctively extending a cautious hand.

The man matched the offer with a firm shake. "My name's Tyler Cain. I've been trying to track you down."

Track me down? Matthew thought while scanning the shore for signs of Maria. He noticed a trace of yellow and white moving quickly on the other side of a tree-lined path.

"Ms. Davidson won't be able to join us," Tyler explained.

"Us?" Matthew said with confusion. "What are you talking about? Maria and I arranged to meet here for…a…picnic. Who are you?"

"I'm a private investigator working with the Denver police. I've been investigating threats made against Judge Victor Santiago."

Matthew cursed, once in alarm and again at Maria's apparent betrayal. But how could she have known about the letters? Had he accidently mentioned them during their first date? No, he hadn't.

"Threats? Against a judge?"

"That's right."

"What does that have to do with Maria? Or me?"

The detective reached into a backpack he had placed onto the path. Did he have a gun? Bounty hunter handcuffs? No. He pulled out a small stack of handwritten notes Matthew recognized immediately.

"What are those?"

"I was hoping you could help me figure that out," Tyler said while offering the papers. "Like I said, I've been investigating a case involving the judge. But I need your help piecing together some of the clues."

"*My* help?" Matthew felt himself start to panic. "Why me?"

"Two different people suggested I talk to you."

"Who?" he demanded.

"Dr. Thomas Vincent from UC–Boulder, for one. He's an expert on this word here." Tyler pointed to the signature line at the bottom of the first note. "I'm not entirely sure how the professor pronounced it."

"Manichean," Matthew read without thinking. He quickly feigned ignorance. "Is that how you say it?"

"Sounds about right," Tyler confirmed.

Matthew looked up. What to say? "Who else suggested talking to me?"

"Maria's sister, Julia Davidson. She's been helping me on the case and said you had signed notes to Maria using this same word."

Of course! Sisters always share intimate love-life details. Maria must have shown Julia his messages. Matthew hated to imagine what Maria must think of him now.

But he had an even more troubling concern. What did the police believe? And what did this private investigator know?

"Listen, Mr. Cain—"

"Call me Tyler, please."

"Tyler then. You've gotta believe me. I never meant any harm. I just wanted to communicate with the judge. I thought maybe—"

"No, Mr. Adams," Tyler pounced. "You didn't think. A thinking person doesn't send death threats to a sitting judge. A thinking person doesn't sign those threats with the same screwball name he uses to woo women."

"Death threats? I never sent any death threats."

Matthew quickly unfolded and reread the first note he had sent to the judge. Then he read two more. "I just asked the judge to correspond with me about the case. To consider the real-life impacts on people like me if he—"

Tyler took the stationery pages back from Matthew. Then he retrieved another from his pack. This one photocopied since, Matthew assumed, the original was sitting in a protective plastic bag at police headquarters. "This letter arrived yesterday, Mr. Adams," Tyler said. He began reading aloud. "Bid your sweet wife farewell since you will die before issuing an opinion." He stopped and looked into Matthew's eyes. "Sounds a heck of a lot like a death threat to me."

Matthew appeared startled as he quickly yanked the page from Tyler's hand. He felt the color draining from his face as he read.

"I've never seen this letter before in my life," he said in a voice that sounded every bit as guilty as the detective had assumed him to be.

"Yeah. And I'm the Easter bunny," Tyler mocked.

"I'd never kill—" The image of his mom's slumping corpse interrupted Matthew's defense. "I'd never *murder* anyone! You've got to believe me."

CHAPTER FORTY-THREE

Tyler glanced at the page, then back at the ball of anxiety standing before him. "Save it for the police, Mr. Adams," he said. "My job is to follow the evidence trail wherever it leads and then hand everything over to the authorities. I'm just glad I tracked you down before you did something *really* stupid."

"Wait!" Matthew grabbed Tyler's wrist as if trying to keep him from leaving. "Listen to me. I didn't write this letter. I admit I wrote those." He pointed at Tyler's pack. "But not this one. Look here, even the writing looks different."

It did. A little.

"Please, Mr. Cain, I just wanted to get the judge to seriously consider the impact of his decision. I admit it was stupid. But I never intended to hurt the man. I swear I'm no assassin."

Tyler reached into his pack to find and retrieve the letter Jennifer McKay had shown him only a few days earlier. He scanned the page until he found the damning line.

"Even if you hadn't written this last letter," he said, "you still threatened the judge."

"No I didn't!" Matthew protested.

"Then how am I supposed to interpret this line, 'comply with my request to avoid more drastic measures'?"

A look of surrender came over Matthew's face, as if he had forgotten about the earlier threat.

"I shouldn't have said it like that," he confessed.

"But you did say it like that."

"I know," Matthew said. "I was trying to go big."

Tyler didn't follow.

"Forget it." Matthew's head was hanging in defeat. "It doesn't matter now anyway."

Tyler noticed moisture forming in Matthew's eyes. Liquid fear. As much as he wanted to believe the clear, indisputable evidence, something inside told him the guy was harmless. Dumb. Rash. Perhaps even conniving. Matthew Adams certainly fit the part of an uptight coward who would send anonymous, threatening letters. But he looked nothing like the sort who could walk into a federal courthouse and shoot to kill. With so many actual murderers walking free thanks to high-paid defense attorneys, and knowing what happens to weak men thrown in with hardened predators, Tyler would have hated to see Matthew spend a decade in a federal penitentiary.

"Do you have a lawyer?" Tyler asked.

Matthew wiped his face, then looked up self-consciously. "Not really. Just my uncle Ben. He handles my mom's estate. We don't get along."

"You'll need a good defense lawyer," Tyler said while rummaging through his backpack. He pulled out a pad and pen, then jotted down a name and number. "Call this guy," he said.

Matthew read the scribbling. "A friend of yours?"

"More like an enemy," Tyler replied. "But he's good at his job. Got several guys off I tried to put behind bars. You'll need someone like him. Expensive. But effective."

"I can't afford expensive." He looked Tyler in the eyes. "I guess I'm sunk."

Tyler shrugged. "Maybe not. They'll go easier on you if you come clean. You never know. You might even get a good plea bargain."

"What's that?"

"They'll charge you with plotting to assassinate a federal judge. A conviction would carry a long minimum sentence. If you admit to something less, perhaps violation of federal postal regulations, the judge could be much more lenient."

"I see," Matthew said into the air.

Tyler suddenly realized he had no script for the next scene of this drama. He had been 100 percent focused on finding and confronting Judge Santiago's potential assassin. It hadn't occurred to him what to do if the threat proved innocuous. Should he offer to drive Matthew to the station and hand him off to Smitty for questioning? Or should he show compassion? Let him go home to wrap up details of a life that was certain to change for the worse?

He decided to pull out his phone and point it at Matthew's face. Matthew frowned in reaction.

"I need to know where you'll be and how to reach you," Tyler said. "I'll send the information with this picture to a friend on the force. They'll want to talk to you. Tell them what you've admitted to me and you'll be OK."

Matthew gave the information. "Do you really think they might go easy on me?"

"I do."

But he didn't. Courts weren't likely to show much mercy to a guy who had threatened to murder a sitting judge. They might go light on someone who had threatened a congressman or senator. Possibly even the president. But a fellow judge? Not a chance.

"Go home, Mr. Adams," Tyler said. "Call a lawyer and wait for the police."

———

He had probably made the wrong decision. Smitty would have told Tyler to bring in the suspect personally. Immediately. "Don't let him out of your sight!" he'd have ordered. But Tyler wanted to give Matthew time and space to think through a plausible excuse for his folly. Which is exactly what Tyler knew it had been, a series of idiotic decisions by a desperate fool. Still, to be safe, Tyler shadowed Matthew's car from a discreet distance. He followed him to the house, then parked several hundred yards away to observe. The same routine he had used in countless stakeouts for jealous clients. As an added precaution he also placed a tiny observation camera on the rear porch. He could watch both through his car's windshield and tablet's screen.

Several hours of inaction gave Tyler time to think. Part of him rested comfortably in the knowledge that he had found the culprit, solved the case. But another part of him felt uneasy, as if one or two pieces of the puzzle didn't fit. The look on Matthew's face, for one, when Tyler showed him the final letter. He appeared genuinely surprised, as if he had no recollection of writing it. And the handwriting. There were differences, no matter how slight. Was it possible Matthew hadn't sent the final note after all?

No. Not possible. Who else would have sent it? Matthew must have intentionally altered the script. That's why he had been so eager to draw attention to the differences.

Tyler tapped an image on the dash menu. Three rings later he heard Smitty's voice message accept the call.

"Hi Smitty, it's Tyler. Great news. I found the guy who wrote the letters to Judge Santiago." Hearing the words prompted a swell of self-congratulation. He had solved the case. He had saved the judge from possible assassination. A job well done. "He's no real threat. I'm sending you the suspect's picture and the information on where you can have him picked up for questioning. I would keep the security detail at the judge's home for a few days to play it safe, but I think we can rest easy on this one."

He ended the call. No need to mention any doubts. Smitty would trust Tyler's assessment that it had been a one-man operation. The same man who had driven home in the still-parked car and entered the still-closed front door Tyler had grown tired of watching.

His stomach rumbled as Tyler eased away from the curb. He frowned, then smiled at the thought of rewarding his investigative genius with a double cheeseburger and a chocolate shake. A few minutes later he pulled up to the drive-through window of the only burger joint still open. He ordered value meal number six. Then he imagined Renee's disapproving gaze.

Renee!

In all the excitement over finding and confronting Matthew Adams he had forgotten to call her to say he wouldn't make it home in time for dinner. He quickly tapped her image on the dash.

"Tyler Cain, I'm very upset with you!" A recording made for his specific number for this specific occasion. "I don't ask for much. Just a bit of courtesy. I made a very special meal tonight. I also bought a new nightgown. But you won't be enjoying either. There's a pillow and blanket in the den. I hope you get a major crick in your neck!"

The message ended abruptly. He imagined her slamming a vintage phone receiver onto the cradle in a huff.

Banished to the sofa! So much for celebrating success with his gal, his first meaningful accomplishment since, well, since too long ago to remember.

"Did you want to add a hot cherry pie to that order?" the drive-through voice asked, short-circuiting Tyler's pity party.

He looked at the clock. Much too late for a deep-fried indulgence sure to trigger middle-of-the-night heartburn.

Renee would definitely not approve.

"Sure!" he answered defiantly. "And top it with vanilla ice cream."

CHAPTER FORTY-FOUR

Julia snuggled in close to caress her husband's chest while enjoying the gentle movement of his fingertips up and down her bare shoulder. Exactly what she needed after a long, eventful day. She had connected the dots between her sister's mysterious suitor and Tyler Cain's elusive suspect, helped orchestrate a seductive bait and switch where Maria was the bait, and then tried to calm her kid sister's nerves while driving away from the scene. Maria had finally gone home with Jared after a very late dinner that included giving Troy a play-by-play description of the whole fiasco.

"Are you sure she'll be OK?" Troy asked while staring up at the ceiling. "This Matthew guy won't come after her, will he?"

"She'll be fine," Julia said. "Tyler told me he decided to follow the car home to keep an eye on the house until the police arrive. But he wasn't concerned. He said the guy was no real danger to anyone but himself."

"Good."

A moment of tender silence passed.

"Kevin called this afternoon."

"He did?" Julia said while sitting up to wrap herself in the disheveled sheet. The day's adventure had dominated all conversation to the point that she had neglected to ask about Troy's day.

"He told me to tell you he liked your first feature and that he's eager to see the second."

"Does he think they might help?"

"Can't hurt."

She waited for more. Nothing came. "Has he heard any more from Franklin?" she asked.

"He has. It seems the whole Dimitri thing blew over. Anderson said they managed to convince him I wasn't behind whatever made him so mad."

Julia remembered Brent Anderson's earlier threat, "Back off with Dimitri."

"If they don't think it was you or Kevin, who do they think *was* behind it?"

"No clue. Doesn't matter. They've moved on to the next potential scandal and we're back on their 'useful' list."

Julia sighed. "Doesn't it bother you?"

"Doesn't what bother me?"

"The whole game. You know. They consider Kevin an asset one day and a liability the next. They call you a brilliant player on Monday but try to distance themselves from you on Friday. It's not fair. It's not right."

Troy leaned on his side to mirror Julia's posture. "No, it's not right. But it is what it is. Neither Kevin nor I expected politics to smell pretty. Cleaning up a mess sometimes means working around garbage. But it's part of the price you pay when trying to do something significant."

"I'd call it a pretty big price."

One shoulder gave a half shrug. "Maybe. But someone needs to be a voice for the weak and vulnerable. Might as well be us."

"I guess. I just wish…" She stopped when she noticed Troy fiddling with the edge of the silk sheet she had turned into a toga. He lifted the edge, pretending to steal an indiscreet peek. Julia slapped his hand playfully. Then she smiled. "Again?"

"Aren't you ovulating?" he asked with a wink. "How 'bout doubling our odds?"

Julia's smile melted as the grief her sister's adventure had interrupted mounted another invasion.

"What do ya say?" Troy began moving his lips toward hers.

Julia's head slid slightly back before she could overrule the motion. Hoping he hadn't noticed, she willed her arms around his torso to hold him tightly. But it was no good. She knew that he sensed something was wrong. She sat up again, revealing a single tear disobediently falling onto her cheek.

His finger touched the moist insurgent. "Hey there now. What's this about?"

The sweet, clueless tone of Troy's voice opened another breach in the dam. A second tear fell, then two more. She knew that if she spoke a river of sorrow would drown her explanation in a flood of misunderstood emotion.

Julia wanted to tell her husband how much she loved him, that she wished with all her heart a second round of intimacy could double their chances. But she knew what she couldn't say. That their union would never conceive the blessing of a child. Never give Troy what he wanted more than anything in the world.

"Oh, it's nothing," she finally managed. She kissed him gratefully, then inhaled a breath of composure. "I'm just tired. Do you mind waiting until morning?"

He appeared to believe her. "Of course," he answered while grabbing a tissue to wipe final remnants of wetness from her face. "Let's wait until morning."

Troy kissed her forehead before rolling onto his side of the mattress.

Julia slipped into the bathroom to wash her face and find an oversized T-shirt to wear. That's when she noticed a woman she barely recognized staring back at her from the mirror. Was this the same woman who had once celebrated the drop in global fertility? The girl who had disregarded marriage as an outdated institution and motherhood as the valley of the inept? The journalist who'd fed a mountain of myths to nine million approving readers? "The fewer carbon footprints polluting the planet the better!" she'd once scoffed. Now she would give anything to conceive, deliver, and nurture one into a son or daughter of her own. Troy would have wanted a boy. Or would he have? He loved hanging out with Tommy. But he seemed smitten with Joy and Leah. He might want a girl after all.

Julia let her imagination carry her into an alternate future. She envisioned dressing her toddler in frilly dresses. She saw herself shopping for a new outfit with a preteen daughter eager to look pretty when Daddy took her to the symphony or father-daughter dance. She pictured a cute, precocious girl as she had been herself during adolescence. Sort of like Amanda, Austin Tozer's half sister. She and Julia had seemed to hit it off the way she might have with her own child.

Another tear began to form at the thought of what a wonderful daddy Troy would have made. Unlike her own father, Troy would never have abandoned his family. He would have modeled loving strength and heroic sacrifice. He would have shown their little girl what a man could be. What a man should be.

But that day would never come. Troy couldn't produce a child of his own. And the prospect of finding a baby to adopt was, at best, remote.

Julia wiped away the tear while turning off the bathroom light. She walked back to the bed and slid gently under the covers. Then she leaned in close to Troy's ear. "Good night, darling," she whispered.

His undecipherable grunt told her he was asleep. She smiled, patting his back while settling onto the billowy comfort of her pillow.

That's when it struck her. Amanda! She sat up with a start.

If Troy could be such a wonderful adoptive uncle to the Tolbert kids, why couldn't he be a wonderful adoptive father to a girl with no parents of her own, a girl who hated living with her self-centered half brother and embryo-selling wife?

"Troy," Julia said, shaking her husband awake.

"What? What?" he said in dazed confusion while his hands felt around the bed as if swatting bugs.

Julia clicked on the lamp, causing Troy's eyelids to scrunch tightly together at the sudden, blinding brightness. She bolstered her courage by lifting his hand to her lips for a reinforcing kiss.

"Troy, honey, we need to talk."

CHAPTER FORTY-FIVE

A sudden surge of fear forced Rebecca Santiago awake. When had she dozed off? She looked at the bedroom television screen. Credits were rolling from the movie she had hoped would help keep her awake until her husband got home. She looked at the clock. Half past midnight! Three hours earlier Victor had promised he should be home soon.

She felt herself breathing faster. It was the start of a panic attack like the one she had endured during the blizzard of 2037 when Victor decided to drive home instead of stay at the office as she'd asked him to. "The roads are too slick," she had said. "You'll slide into a ditch and freeze to death." It took him more than an hour, but he made it home safe and sound. Her panic was for naught then. She tried to believe it was equally pointless now.

She got out of bed, clicked off the television, and found her gown before moving to the window to open the blinds. The police car was still parked out front. She squinted for a better look. It appeared the officer's head was leaning against the glass in sound sleep. Not much comfort.

Rebecca opened the bedroom door and moved into the kitchen, where she hoped to find Victor sitting in front of a bowl of cereal enjoying a late-night snack after a longer-than-expected day in his chambers. But the room was dark. She rushed to the back door to check for Victor's car in the garage. Empty!

She told herself to stay calm, that he was probably in his office sipping a cup of cold coffee while tweeking a written opinion on that big case. He had said it needed to be finished by morning. It wouldn't be the first time he had burned the midnight oil to hit a deadline.

But he had never done so while a death threat hung over his head!

She tapped her husband's image on the phone, then heard his recorded voice.

"Hi, Rebecca. There's two things I want to do at this moment. First, answer your call. Second…"

"No!" she shouted at the phone.

She dialed again. The same result.

The phone fell to the floor as Rebecca raced toward the front door. Seconds later she was sitting in the passenger side of the police car pleading with an officer whose name she couldn't recall to drive to the courthouse as fast as possible.

—⁓—

Rebecca felt both overwrought and foolish standing outside the courthouse. She hadn't thought to grab the latest entry code. Victor always left it for her in an envelope sitting in his sock drawer. She rarely used it, relying on Jennifer or a guard to open the door whenever she came to meet Victor for lunch or surprise him with a fresh-baked afternoon snack. Of course, neither his assistant nor security was in the building at such a late hour.

And since her telephone lay on the floor back home she couldn't call Jennifer for help. It took nearly fifteen minutes for the officer to track down someone who could help him gain access to the judge's private chambers. The delay was agony for Rebecca, who spent every second imagining one awful scenario after another. The patient young officer tried comforting her by suggesting it would be even more difficult for a potential assassin to reach the judge than it had proven for them. That didn't make her feel any better.

As soon as they reached the third-floor office wing Rebecca noticed the outer door was slightly ajar. Would Jennifer have left without locking the door behind her? No, not when Victor remained inside working. She was almost as protective of Victor as Rebecca. Something was wrong.

"Please, ma'am, let me go in first," the officer insisted.

Rebecca ignored the suggestion, rushing through the door, past Jennifer's desk, and into Victor's now-dark office.

The light came on in reaction to the motion. She looked toward the chair where she had imagined finding Victor slumped over his desk in a pool of blood. It was empty. She rushed past a row of bookshelves to peer into his conference room, where she had imagined her husband dangling by the neck from a noose suspended from the ceiling. But the room was empty.

Rebecca heard the sound of the officer's footsteps finally catching up with her frantic search.

"He's not here!" she shouted while grasping both of the officer's arms. "Where could he be? Dear God, where is my Victor?"

The officer gave her a blank gaze. "Perhaps he left before we arrived. He might be at the house looking for you right now."

But she knew better. She knew they would find Victor's car parked in his private space. And she knew something dreadful had happened to her husband.

"No. He must be here somewhere," she insisted while running back out the front office door. "Victor!" she shouted to her left, then to her right. "Where are you, sweetheart?"

She heard the officer's voice utter a muffled obscenity, drawing her back into Victor's chambers.

She entered the office again. No sign of anyone. A moment of dread passed before she saw the open door of Victor's private bathroom.

The officer stepped toward her without a word.

"What?" Rebecca asked urgently.

"Ms. Santiago, please, stay right where you are."

"Why? What is it?"

He lowered his head like a rookie trying to recall the official protocol for nightmares.

"The judge."

"You found him?" she asked, rushing past his protective blockade.

"Please, ma'am..."

It was too late. She saw what the officer had cursed. Victor, lying on the floor with eyes wide open as if staring at her from the realm of the dead. No blood or hangman's rope. Just her husband's empty form.

She fell onto his lifeless body, then tried lifting him to her breast. His corpse spurned the effort like a steadfast bag of sand. It was the first show of affection he hadn't returned in three decades. And the last, Rebecca suddenly realized, that she would ever attempt.

CHAPTER FORTY-SIX

As soon as Tyler entered the detective wing of headquarters he came face-to-face with the last person he wanted to see.

"Cain," Kory Sanders said with a solemn nod that carried a hint of derision. Tyler's old rival clutched a mug of java while leaning against the wall beside a pretty young detective Tyler didn't recognize. She added her own nod, then gave the once-over to the fumbling private investigator who had failed to prevent Judge Santiago's assassination.

"Sanders," Tyler responded flatly. "Seen Smitty this morning?"

Sanders tilted his head toward a hallway without a word before resuming whispered speculations about how badly Cain had botched the job or how dumb it had been for Smitty to assign such a big case to a washed-up former detective.

"Thanks," Tyler said, lowering his eyes. If only they knew the whole embarrassing truth. He had actually found the suspect, had confronted him and followed him home. But rather than have Matthew Adams arrested Tyler pitied the guy and handed him the name of a defense attorney. Maybe the chief had been right in promoting Sanders instead of Tyler after all. Had Sanders ever made such a fatal miscalculation? Had anyone?

Tyler walked toward the conference room where he knew Smitty would be waiting.

As he approached the row of glass-walled offices Tyler spotted Jennifer McKay, who had already arrived. Of course she had. She must have been up much of the night trying to console a grief-stricken Rebecca Santiago. She looked even more exhausted than Tyler despite his aching back and stiff neck, compliments of the sofa. His only consolation was that Renee had felt bad after he told her about Smitty's call.

"Oh no!" she had said. "When did it happen?"

"Last night," Tyler explained while hurriedly zipping his pants and buttoning his shirt. "The judge's wife and a cop found the body around one o'clock this morning."

"That's seven hours ago. Why didn't they call sooner?" she asked.

Tyler was still asking himself the same question. Shouldn't Smitty have had someone phone him immediately? No one knew more about the suspect. But then, Tyler reminded himself, he was no longer part of the force. Gathering evidence after an assassination was the domain of public officials, not private investigators who ranked one step above anonymous tipsters. Besides, obtaining an arrest warrant in the middle of the night and tracking down Matthew Adams would have been Smitty's all-consuming priority.

As he approached the closed door Tyler noticed a third person in the room with Smitty and Jennifer, probably the officer who had been with Mrs. Santiago when they found the judge's body. He looked even more spent than Jennifer.

Smitty waved Tyler in eagerly, as if he had been impatiently waiting to take an important next step in the process.

"Sorry it took so long to get here," Tyler said. Of course he had come faster than anyone should have expected, his crumpled shirt and morning breath offering sufficient evidence of a mad rush. "I just got the call twenty minutes ago."

"Close the door," Smitty ordered.

Tyler obeyed. "Any trail yet?"

Smitty seemed confused by the question. "Trail?"

"On Matthew Adams's location."

Smitty looked at the other two, who must have already known what Tyler didn't. "Didn't they tell you on the phone?"

Tell him what? All Tyler knew was that Judge Santiago had been killed and that Smitty had wanted him in the conference room as soon as possible. He had assumed Smitty wanted help tracking down the fugitive. Not because Tyler was the best man for the job, but because he had been the last person to see Matthew Adams before letting him roam free for a midnight murder.

"We found Mr. Adams right where your message said he would be. He was at the home of an elderly gentleman named Hugh Gale. Of course, he claims to know nothing about the killing."

"You questioned him already?" Tyler asked in stunned surprise. "Wait. You found him sitting at the house?"

"Yep. Not too bright, I gather. I mean, who commits murder and then returns to the same address he just gave to a guy investigating death threat letters?"

Tyler felt the rebuke. "Look, Smitty, I'm really sorry about—"

Smitty raised his hand to silence Tyler. "Not now."

"I parked outside his house for several hours after—"

"I said not now."

Tyler's gut tightened at the realization he had let Smitty down. But his apology would need to wait. "So what was Matthew doing when you picked him up?"

"He told my guys he had been sitting in the front room reading most of the night."

"Reading? Reading what?"

"An old Bible," Smitty said. "Claims he was trying to find something to calm his nerves after meeting with you."

"He told you we met?"

"He did. Said you suggested he wait at the house and expect our arrival. He seemed pretty calm until the officer said he was under arrest for the murder of Judge Victor Santiago. That's when the guy went into a meltdown, claimed he knew nothing about any murder and that he never intended to hurt anyone. You know the litany."

Tyler said nothing. Something didn't fit. Why would a killer wait for the police to arrive, knowing a mountain of evidence existed to pinpoint him as the murderer? He had seen the letters. He had even confessed to writing most of them.

"Did you get much out of him?" Tyler asked.

"Not since he made his one phone call."

"Defense lawyer?"

"Yep. Clammed up after that. I'm getting ready to go in and try again. I need more. All we have is circumstantial evidence right now. I'm hoping he'll slip up and say something we can use in court. I need you to listen for anything that might feed the right line of questioning."

"Certainly."

"I'm especially interested in these," Smitty said, handing Tyler two clear plastic bags. "We found them stuffed in a trash container just outside the judge's chambers."

Tyler examined the first bag. It contained a needle and a catheter about two feet long. The second held one of those clear bags hospitals use to hold IV fluids. It was empty except for small traces of a yellow liquid. The label read "PotassiPass."

"I know this chemical," Tyler said, remembering the brand

name from the summary he had read of the Santos wrongful death case. "It's the chemical NEXT Transition Services uses with clients."

Smitty and Jennifer eyed one another as if the comment had confirmed their hunch.

"Who could get that for him?" Smitty asked.

"Who couldn't?" the other officer said. "All you would need to do is find a transition clinic employee willing to swipe a bag for you."

"Or take one out of a clinic yourself," Smitty suggested.

Tyler didn't follow.

"The suspect's mother transitioned about a year back," Smitty explained. "I bet he stole some of the serum then."

Plausible, Tyler had to agree. But something still didn't seem right. Why would Matthew have stolen transition chemicals months before he even knew Judge Santiago would be assigned the case?

He followed Smitty to the next room. Jennifer and the other officer joined him as they took their seats behind a two-way mirror. On the other side sat a clearly shaken Matthew Adams, who was fidgeting with a pencil. Tyler remembered the routine. Hand the uncooperative suspect a pencil and paper as you leave the interrogation room and suggest he write down a confession "for his own good" so the judge might go easy on him. The page appeared blank.

As Smitty walked out of the room Jennifer turned toward Tyler. "I owe you an apology," she whispered.

He turned toward her dark form. "For what? I'm the one who blew this case."

"I should have listened to you." Tyler sensed tears of regret in her voice. "If I had warned the judge he would still be alive."

"And you'd have lost your job," Tyler said generously. "You did what he ordered you to do."

She sighed. "Still." A pause. "I'm sorry."

"Me too," Tyler said faintly while reaching to pat her slumping shoulders. "Me too."

They saw Smitty closing the door behind him as he entered the brightness beyond the glass.

"There's a sick irony in all of this," Jennifer whispered in Tyler's direction while awaiting Smitty's first question. "The same drug used to transition Antonio Santos ended up killing the man who was about to decide in favor of the plaintiff."

"What?" Tyler said. "He was going to come down in favor of NEXT? I thought he was leaning the other way."

"So did most people," Jennifer replied. "But I proofed his draft opinion. He was going to say NEXT did nothing wrong. The boy was an adult when he transitioned regardless of what day he applied. The law doesn't require parental approval after eighteen."

"So NEXT is off the hook?"

"Would have been. Now the appeal will get assigned to a new trio of judges. Could be months before that happens."

Tyler looked through the glass at the nervous suspect. A few more days and Judge Santiago would have freed up Matthew's urgently needed inheritance money. His mother's estate would have been released thanks to NEXT's successful appeal.

Then Tyler thought of Jeremy Santos, who wanted the court to confirm the malevolence of a system that had caused his brother's and mother's deaths. NEXT should pay for what it had done to the two people Jeremy loved more than anyone on earth. Ever since watching the gruesome footage taken at the clinic on the fateful day of their deaths, Tyler had unconsciously hoped the same.

"Do you have anything else to tell me?" Smitty was asking.

Matthew sat silent while biting the end of his pencil.

Smitty took the sheet of paper from in front of the suspect. Blank. "Nothing to write?"

"I told you already," Matthew said in exhausted desperation. "I didn't kill anyone."

"Well, someone did," Smitty said. "Someone who, like you, goes by the pseudonym Manichean. Someone who, like you, wants to see NEXT win its appeal. And someone who, like you, had access to these." Smitty tossed the plastic bags onto the table in front of Matthew. "Do you want to tell me where you got them?"

Matthew bent closer to examine the bags. He seemed to recognize the contents but appeared alarmed by their presence.

A sudden knock on the interrogation room door drew Smitty's attention. "Sir," a male voice called into the room, "I have the autopsy report."

Smitty moved away from the table. Matthew seemed relieved by the momentary interruption, as if he needed time to figure out what was going on or how to spin his story.

Then Smitty reentered the room, reading what must have been a summary of key details from the autopsy. At the same moment the door to the observation room opened to receive a man holding what appeared to be an identical page.

"What's he reading?" Jennifer asked in the man's direction.

"Here," he replied, handing the report to Jennifer. "Read for yourself."

Tyler leaned toward Jennifer and squinted to make out the words.

CAUSE OF DEATH: Heart attack triggered by potassium chloride poisoning
    TIME OF DEATH: 6:35 p.m.

Tyler jumped up from his chair with a start. All three pairs of eyes darted in his direction, then turned toward the sound of

Smitty's voice. "Where were you between six and eight o'clock last evening?" he was asking.

"We have the wrong man!" Tyler shouted toward the glass.

"What?" Jennifer said in unison with both officers.

"I said we have the wrong man."

"Why do you say that?"

"Because I was questioning Matthew Adams near Bear Creek Lake at the time of the assassination!"

CHAPTER FORTY-SEVEN

Evan Dimitri approached the same black limousine that had carried him to his corporate jet earlier in the day. A man wearing a cap stood beside the open door extending a much-needed glass of brandy that he accepted without a word before slipping inside. Then the driver trotted to the front of the vehicle and awaited instructions.

"Home," Dimitri grunted.

It had been a long day meeting with a board of directors he neither needed nor liked. More of the same claptrap, fretting about matters he had completely in hand. Yes, profits had dipped slightly as a result of the NEXT appeal. Yes, the pending Tenth District ruling could sink all hope of hitting revenue targets. And yes, he did agree it would be wise to develop a short-term contingency plan while considering diversification options.

Dimitri hated the thought of how much time he had wasted addressing the board's concerns. They needed to trust him. He knew exactly what had to be done. In fact, he had already set solutions in motion.

He glanced at the time. Might there be news so soon? Or had the police done a better job than usual of avoiding leaks? He tapped an icon embedded in his armrest to wake a flat screen positioned over the bar. Then he kicked off his shoes while taking a sip of his favorite post-nonsense drink. A query box appeared.

"Find any news about the NEXT appeal or Judge Victor Santiago," he said. Almost instantaneously the two most recent stories appeared.

4:34 PM Breaking News

- FEDERAL JUDGE FOUND DEAD IN DENVER CHAMBERS

6:21 PM Breaking News

- PERSON OF INTEREST QUESTIONED IN SUSPECTED JUDICIAL ASSASSINATION

He watched the first clip. It revealed that one of the judges hearing the NEXT wrongful death case had died suddenly of an apparent heart attack. The same judge many political and corporate titans feared would tip the scales against the transition industry. Dimitri knew that Judge Santiago's death, while tragic for the family, could be a boon to company stock when markets opened the following day. He smiled at the realization that profits, for now, remained safe from the unpredictable actions of a crusading judge.

The second clip revealed that someone "close to the case" said police had questioned an unnamed man with some connection to what they now feared might have been an assassination. No mention of any accomplices or a conspiracy. A probable lone killer.

Dimitri gave an approving nod in response to the sparse details before tapping an icon that prompted the voice of his ever-available assistant Kim.

"Yes, sir."

"Get me Dean Myerson."

Moments later another voice came on the line. "You saw the news?"

"I did. Any surprises?"

A long silence. "Actually, yes. The suspect walked after questioning. I didn't see that coming."

Dimitri cursed. "He walked? Did they charge him?"

"Murder. But something happened during the interrogation that made them drop it down to suspected mail fraud. The Manichi guy's lawyer demanded they release him to his oversight."

"It's pronounced *Manichean*," Dimitri said, feeling a shade of concern. "What about our letter?"

"As far as I can tell they still think the guy wrote it."

A look of reassurance came over Dimitri's face. "Good. That's perfect." He took another sip of brandy.

"I guess," Dean replied.

"Keep me posted if anything changes."

"Will do, sir."

Dimitri ended the call before summoning Kim back onto the line.

"I'm here, sir," she said.

"I need you to draft a message to the board of directors. Tell them we've received word that a decision in the NEXT case will be delayed until they can assign a new team of judges. We can expect business as usual for the rest of the fiscal year."

"Got it."

"Send me a draft to proof later tonight."

"As you wish," she said before being cut off.

His short-term problem had been resolved, buying him time to finalize a longer-term growth strategy he had been considering for months. He felt a sudden surge of creative energy demanding he flesh out the concept further.

"Driver?"

"Sir?"

"I've changed my mind. Take me to the office."

CHAPTER FORTY-EIGHT

Renee slid a covered plate in front of Tyler. He had offered to serve, but she had insisted he join her parents at the table and seemed excited about whatever gourmet bird food she had been preparing. He was trapped. But he didn't mind. Not really. He had never found her more attractive.

Perhaps it was because Renee had spent every waking moment of the past few days trying to lift him out of the dumps. She had apologized at least a dozen times for banishing him to the sofa on the night before the terrible day. And then there was the refrigerator surprise. He found an unopened Hostess snack sitting on the shelf right next to a gallon of soy milk. Never mind that he hated soy milk. It was the thought that counted.

But that wasn't the reason. Something else had made Renee more appealing.

Tyler reached for the mystery plate to peek under the makeshift lid before feeling a slap at his hand.

"Not yet," Renee said playfully. "Wait until I serve everyone."

He grinned sheepishly toward Gerry and Katherine. Neither paid him any attention. Gerry was enamored with the spoon that doubled as a mirror he was using to peer up his left nostril. Katherine sipped her glass of water, staring in blissful contentment as usual.

Tyler continued watching Renee in search of what had changed. She had the same perky face, cute hairstyle, and slight figure. A guilt-induced cupcake notwithstanding, she maintained the same obsession with all things healthy and tasteless. And her nonstop hovering while trying to cheer him up, while appreciated, had started to make him feel claustrophobic. He almost wanted to go back to work. Almost, but not quite. He couldn't bear to take on another jealous-lover case. Not after coming so close to doing something important again.

Tyler noticed Renee sitting down to join them at the table. Then she smiled in his direction.

"Smells delicious," he said. "What is it?"

"You'll find out in a minute."

Despite low expectations Tyler prepared himself to react with delight. He'd love to find a pile of garlic-and-bacon mashed potatoes next to a pecan-crusted chicken breast. But he knew it was more likely he'd discover steamed cauliflower with a tofu garnish. Either way, Renee deserved an enthusiastic response.

He looked across the table at Gerry and Katherine. Then he looked back at their daughter, now placing a napkin on her lap.

"Ready?" she asked like a giddily excited girl.

"I'm ready," Tyler replied in the most energetic voice he could muster as Gerry finally placed the spoon back on the table.

"Then take a look."

It was worse than Tyler had imagined. Some sort of green slimy base possibly made of boiled spinach beneath what appeared to be a baked slab of…what? Certainly not any kind of meat he had ever eaten.

"Baked eggplant!" Renee announced proudly. "I've been trying to find a good recipe forever. This one said it tastes just like fried chicken but with less than half the calories and much, much less fat."

"Mmm," Tyler said in anticipation of a meal he was sure to hate. "Sounds wonderful."

He took a big bite. The texture felt more like warmed squash than crispy chicken. He chewed, slowly at first. He considered saying something but realized a second and third mouthful would mean more to Renee than the most perfectly worded compliment.

"Do you like it?" her eyes asked.

Tyler recalled a comment from Smitty. "Love is a choice, not a feeling."

"I love it!" he willed himself to say.

Renee leaped from her seat to hug Tyler's neck. Startled at first, he moved his arms around her waist and invited her to sit on his lap.

"Tyler Cain!" she pretended to protest. "Not in front of the children."

Renee's parents smiled at the comment. That's when it struck him.

Gerry and Katherine!

"I need you to understand something," Renee had said a few days before. "My parents are my priority right now. I mean, I love you. I want you. But they're my flesh and blood."

With a single gutsy declaration Renee had transformed herself from a weak, clingy lover into something else. Something better. She had made a choice to do what was right by her folks even if it meant losing the man she loved. Losing him! And rather than pushing Tyler away, the resolve had drawn him toward her like nails to a magnet. He knew that Renee loved him. But he also realized that she didn't *need* him. The subtle change made her someone he wanted to pursue rather than flee; someone strong enough to expect him to do what was right, and to become his best. A woman who deserved better than she had received. Better, perhaps, than he could possibly ever give.

For the first time in a while Tyler felt lucky to have her in his life. Possibly because he realized he had almost driven her out of it.

Tyler had taken the Santiago case hoping for a high-paying gig that would inch him closer to freedom from what he saw as Renee's needy, demanding presence. Had he successfully prevented the assassination he would have received a handsome bonus. He could have paid off their joint loan. Today might have been the day he sent Renee packing and returned to the carefree existence he thought he wanted. Instead, he was starting to realize, it was the day he would invite Renee to add meaning to his miserable excuse for a life. But when? How? Certainly not while sitting across from her nostril-ogling dad.

Tyler did his best to remain enthusiastic while enduring the rest of his meal. As soon as he finished, Renee scooped a second serving onto his plate. He wanted to say, "No more, thank you. I'm stuffed!" But her beautiful eyes won the moment. He took another bite.

"Oh," she said. "I nearly forgot to tell you, Smitty called today while you were napping."

He had been "napping" much of the past two days.

"He asked if you could drop by tomorrow afternoon."

Not a chance, Tyler thought. The last place he wanted to be right now was the police station. He didn't need another reminder of his ineptitude or another sniggering glare from the likes of Kory Sanders.

"I said you'd be there around two o'clock."

"You said what?"

"Come on, babe. It'll do you good. You need to get out."

He swallowed back a protest. Renee was probably right. Nothing good would come of another day moping around the house. Besides, Smitty had been kind. He had refused to let Tyler own the blame for Judge Santiago's death. "You were right about Matthew Adams," Smitty had insisted. "The guy was no assassin."

So who was? There were countless possibilities. Unlikely as it seemed, the letters from Matthew Adams were an uncanny coincidence. He'd happened to write a series of benign letters at the same time someone else was planning an assassination. Someone, perhaps, with more to gain than Matthew. Or more to lose.

"I don't know," Tyler objected weakly. "I'm not sure I'm ready to—"

"You're ready," Renee interrupted. "And you're good at what you do."

He looked away, wishing he could agree. Then he felt Renee's hand on his jaw forcing his gaze in her direction.

"Do you hear me?" she said. "You're a very good detective. That's what Smitty thinks, anyway."

It took five seconds for the comment to sink in. "What?"

"He told me you followed the evidence where it led and that every detective on his team would have reached the exact same conclusions you did."

"He said that?"

"He did. I bet he wants to talk to you about a job."

"Unlikely." Tyler knew better. The force was still over budget. Smitty needed to cut rather than add positions.

"Or maybe he has another case for you to solve."

The possibility sounded good to Tyler. He certainly had no appetite for another House of Delights stakeout.

"OK," he relented. "I'll go."

Renee grinned with satisfaction while taking another bite.

Tyler couldn't help smiling back.

Gerry chose that moment to enter the conversation. "Dog-gone it," he said. "When do you plan to stop pussyfooting around and make an honest woman out of my daughter?"

"Daddy!" Renee shouted with a blush while Katherine looked up in apparent delight.

"Well," Gerry continued, "it's obvious neither one of you is going anywhere. Why not make it official?"

Tyler said nothing at first. A few days earlier he would have assumed Renee had orchestrated the moment. But the look on her face said she was equally surprised, equally embarrassed.

What none of the others could know was that Smitty had raised the same point two days before. "You should marry Re-nee," he had said after asking about their relationship. "She deserves to be happy. So do you."

Smitty had come to see marriage as a gift rather than a burden; a source of happiness rather than stress. He'd even invited Tyler to meet with a pastor from his church. "Premarital counseling would help you get off on the right foot," he had suggested.

Renee looked at Tyler. She appeared unsettled. "I'm sorry," she whispered toward his ear. "Daddy shouldn't have said that."

"You're right," Tyler whispered back. "He shouldn't have said it."

Then Tyler stood up from the table.

"Come on, Tyler, don't be upset," Gerry began. But Tyler raised his hand to silence the old man.

"No," he said insistently. "I have every right to be upset. And I am. I'm very upset."

Renee looked distraught, as if her father had ruined their otherwise perfect evening.

"I'm upset at myself for letting you beat me to the punch," Tyler continued. Then he bent down on one knee in front of Renee, who seemed uncertain how to respond. Was she pro-tecting herself from thinking what was happening was actually happening? "Renee," Tyler said after kissing her hand, "I have a question to ask you that's long overdue."

Tears of uncertain joy began forming in her eyes.

"Will you marry me?" he asked.

A flood of emotion released as Renee nodded breathlessly.

Tyler accepted her kiss while Gerry and Katherine reached for one another's hand.

"Oh, wait!" Tyler said suddenly as if realizing he had made a big mistake. "I take it back."

"What?" Gerry said. "Take it back?"

"I need twenty-four hours."

"What for?" Katherine asked timidly.

"I need a ring to do this properly," he said to Renee's obvious relief. Then he stood. "Can I ask you again tomorrow?"

"Yes. Yes. Yes," she shouted through tears with an even more vigorous nod.

Tyler returned to his seat, proud of his own courageous act. Reckless? Perhaps. But he knew it felt right. Knew it *was* right.

Renee accepted a hug from her mother while Tyler stabbed his fork into another bite of food. He raised it mindlessly to his mouth and began chewing. The flavor, he suddenly realized, was starting to grow on him.

CHAPTER FORTY-NINE

Matthew rubbed the patch of irritated skin that had formed beneath the metal bracelet he had been forced to wear around his ankle. The tracking device was gone. But the itchy reminder of his virtual incarceration made him boil with a fury he couldn't have suppressed even if he'd wanted to. And he didn't want to. He had every right to be angry, every reason to hate. But hate whom? Everyone!

He hated Maria Davidson. He would have given anything to make her happy. But she'd lied to him. Betrayed him. Pretended he had a chance with her. It was all a lie!

He hated Tyler Cain. The detective had said he believed Matthew. So why hadn't he let him off the hook? Why suggest the police arrest him for sending a few harmless letters?

He hated the police. They knew full well Matthew hadn't murdered the judge. Why force him to wear a digital dog leash until they got to the bottom of the case? They had already asked him every possible question. He had no more answers to give: no idea who might have written the final letter, why the person had used Matthew's pen name, or how the person had mimicked his earlier letters to near-perfection.

He hated whoever had written those letters.

And Matthew hated his professor. The detective had said Thomas Vincent had helped them connect the dots to Matthew's interest in Manichean philosophy. Dr. Vincent was no priest, and certainly no saint. But he still should have kept their conversations confidential.

Matthew had even decided to hate Judge Santiago. Why hadn't he issued a favorable opinion on the NEXT appeal? If he had done so sooner all would have been well. The judge would still have been alive and Matthew would have been able to access the money in his mother's estate. Money that rightfully belonged to him!

The sound of Reverend Grandpa's stupid bell rang again in Matthew's ears. He had been ignoring the sound for five minutes. Let the old man get his own dinner for once! Or go hungry. Maybe then he'd think twice before poking fun at matters he was too muddleheaded to grasp.

"Such a tragedy," Reverend Grandpa had said while watching the news about Judge Santiago's demise.

Matthew had looked in the old man's direction, at first holding his tongue. But that didn't last. He was in no mood for passivity. He needed to win at something. Why not demolish the Bible-thumping fool in a head-to-head debate? "It's not a tragedy. Death is freedom, the spirit's escape from a decaying body."

His anger boiled again at the recollection of words his former mentor had taught. But the words were still true, even if the man teaching them wasn't.

"Nonsense!" Reverend Grandpa retorted. "The body is every bit as sacred as the spirit. Human beings aren't ghosts. We're embodied spirits."

"You should have thought of that before you drove your car

into a ditch," Matthew said. "Now look at you. A worthless body that's nothing but a burden…on you and everyone else. The real tragedy is you taking up space and using up money that could help Marissa, Isabelle, and Peter."

Matthew could tell the old man felt the sting of rebuke. He wanted him to. Matthew hated Reverend Grandpa.

The bell continued ringing. Matthew finally got up with a huff and walked into the room where he had left the old man fifteen minutes before.

"What?"

"I don't think this is going to work out any longer."

"What are you talking about?"

The old man shifted uncomfortably in his chair. "I think we need to end your contract."

The old man was firing him? It figured. Why not add CANNED to Matthew's growing list of the week's calamities, right after DUMPED, FRAMED, and ARRESTED?

He wouldn't give Reverend Grandpa the satisfaction.

"Fine. I quit!" Matthew shouted while turning toward his room.

"I didn't mean right this second," the old man said with alarm. "I meant we should pick an end date and—"

"I don't care what you meant," Matthew said, walking back toward his client. "I'm telling you that I quit. Today. Right now! Consider this your ten-minute warning. Find some other bump-on-a-log babysitter."

Matthew went to his room to pack a bag of his most important items. He would return for the rest of his things once he got settled in, where? Who knew? Someplace. Anyplace that wasn't here.

Screw the police! He was innocent. They had no right to know where he went.

Screw Maria and Professor Vincent! They no longer deserved his admiration.

And screw Reverend Grandpa! He could find someone else to fix meals and change oxygen tanks.

Matthew heard a loud thud coming from the other room. His first impulse was to rush toward the sound. He instead spent several more minutes throwing socks and T-shirts into an open travel case and stuffing his toothbrush and shaver into the side pocket. He checked the bag. Then he checked it again. It appeared he had everything needed to make a dramatic, immediate exit.

As he moved back down the hallway Matthew heard panicked wheezing. He let the bag fall to the floor, then rounded the corner. That's when he saw Reverend Grandpa on the floor reaching desperately in Matthew's direction. His hand held the detached portion of an air tube that must have been damaged when the old man tried lunging toward a walker sitting three or four feet beyond.

No sound of escaping air came from the oxygen tank. The time Matthew had been packing would have been more than enough for it to empty itself.

The old man pointed frantically down the hall. Matthew remembered the extra tank stored in the bedroom closet. But he hesitated, giving himself two seconds for an uncommon sense of clarity.

Why prolong the inevitable? The old man should end his misery.

The family needed his dwindling resources.

Every reasonable person would call Reverend Grandpa a debit, someone who should volunteer for the greater good.

For Marissa's good.

Who needed a clinic or transition form? The old man's death, no matter how achieved, would bring the same result.

A reduced burden on society.

And a spirit free to thrive.

Matthew looked back toward a man afraid to do what was right. He needed Matthew's help. Matthew's courage.

He thought of the questions that would be asked. Why hadn't Matthew been around to prevent the accident? Simple. The old man had fired him. He'd left at the client's insistence.

He wondered how Marissa would react to the discovery. Would she suspect him of neglect? Worse? Perhaps. But she would be too relieved, too grateful, to contradict Matthew's explanation.

Then he thought of the kids. What if the boy or Isabelle found the body rather than Marissa? Would little Pete ever speak another word? He forced the question out of his mind. A greater good often comes at a price. Peter would be fine. In time.

Matthew retrieved his bag and walked quickly toward the door. He did his best to ignore the sounds of tortured suffocation. A transition would have been so much easier. Swift. Painless. Dignified. But the old man had made his choice.

Then Matthew made his exit.

As the door closed behind him Matthew stood on the front porch. In the sudden stillness he inhaled deeply, the fresh evening air offering a measure of calm to his rapidly beating heart. He instinctively turned back, his fingers wrapping themselves around the handle. He paused. This was a defining moment of belief. Walking away was right. It was compassionate. If by some small chance he was wrong, Reverend Grandpa's God could intervene. He was a God, the old man had said, who had cared enough about physical bodies to assume one. A God of miracles who could prevent his demise, or even raise him from the dead.

He released the handle, his heart racing even faster. He recalled a similar moment from a year before when he had lent his mother courage she didn't possess. When he had watched her take her final breath. He felt the rage of resentment rising within. Her transition, while setting her free, had brought him none of the promised results.

No college fund.

No Maria Davidson.

No real hope of a teaching career.

If the Supreme Being cared about his creation, loved his children, why hadn't he done anything for Matthew's mom? Or for Matthew? Or for the old man suffocating on the floor within?

He took a step off the porch and looked into the evening sky. Then he added one more name to his growing list.

Matthew Adams hated God.

CHAPTER FIFTY

"Pleased to meet you, Beth," Troy said after standing to greet the woman who was apologizing for running behind schedule. Julia smiled warmly from her chair while joining thirty seconds of polite but meaningless small talk about the traffic and warm temperatures.

Austin Tozer and his partner, the woman Amanda had called Hen, appeared to resent Beth's presence, rolling their eyes impatiently in reaction to the ritual of social etiquette. A cold glance suggested this wasn't the first time the couple had met the child welfare agent.

Troy returned to his wife's side at a kitchen table that retained a sticky residue. Julia imagined the couple hastily clearing away dishes in reaction to the doorbell. It would have been much better to meet in Troy's office. More professional and more like home turf. But she had eagerly accepted the demand they meet at Austin's home. Julia was just glad the couple had agreed to get together, no matter how reluctantly.

As Beth Morris settled into her chair, Austin made a preemptive strike. "I don't want to lose Amanda."

It was what Julia had feared after three calls in the prior two days. During the first conversation Austin had loved the thought of getting rid of Amanda so that he and Gwen could live a normal life, whatever that meant. By the second call his posture had softened considerably from that of a fed-up guardian stuck watching a she-brat to that of a sentimental brother inseparably linked to his precious little sister. He had suggested postponing the conversation but backed down when Beth Morris sent a message insisting they proceed as scheduled.

"We've grown very close," Austin continued. He shot a glance toward his partner as if hoping she would mouth his next lines. "I love Amanda, and so does Gwen." Austin took Gwen's hand clumsily as if realizing he had omitted the scripted gesture. "She's like our daughter. She needs us." He seemed to cringe as Gwen's fingers squeezed firmly. "And we need her," he added.

Julia couldn't believe her ears and didn't believe Austin's words. She glanced at Beth, who was jotting notes onto a tablet. Then she looked at Troy, who winked reassuringly in her direction.

Troy had been remarkably receptive to what Julia now feared had been an impulsive idea. She should have given him more time to grieve the disheartening news of their infertility. And that's exactly how she described it. Not *his* infertility. *Their* infertility.

"I can't get pregnant," was all she had said. It wasn't a lie. But the whole truth, she feared, would destroy her husband. Right or wrong, she couldn't allow that. So they held each other and cried themselves to sleep. Julia waited until morning to mention fostering. She waited until lunch to say anything about Amanda Tozer, a name Troy didn't recall from her dark zones story.

"I changed her name in the feature," Julia reminded him. "She needs a real family. She needs a daddy."

Now, two days later, they found themselves sitting across the table from two conniving opportunists. Austin and Gwen must have done some research on Troy's and Julia's past successes before crafting a scheme to make money off of Amanda's departure.

"I understand how you must feel," Troy said in response to Austin's prepared speech.

Julia wanted to call Austin's bluff. But she held her tongue, trusting her husband's instincts.

Troy continued, "It must be difficult to contemplate losing your sister so soon after saying goodbye to your mother."

It clearly hadn't occurred to Austin to connect the two losses. "Yes. Yes it is."

"Very difficult," Gwen added while wiping an invisible tear from her cheek. "She's a wonderful girl."

Beth Morris looked up from her pad. "Where is the wonderful girl?" she asked. "I thought she was supposed to join us. I'd like to get her perspective since she's old enough to speak into this decision."

"She's still at school," Austin said uncomfortably.

Beth glanced at the time. "The school day ended an hour ago."

"She rarely comes straight home," he said. "Besides, I don't think it would be wise to include her just yet. I mean, we are discussing sending her away from her home."

"Are we?" Beth asked abruptly. "I thought you said you had changed your mind."

Austin sent a panicked look to Gwen. "Well, that's not exactly what I meant."

Beth looked back at her notes. "You said, and I quote, 'I don't want to lose Amanda.'"

"That is what you said," Troy added.

"What he meant to say," Gwen interjected, "is that losing Amanda will be more difficult than we realized at first."

Julia fumed quietly at the lie. They wouldn't miss her in the least!

"So you are open to the idea?" Beth asked.

"Well, yes," Austin replied. "But we were sort of hoping to reach an agreement of some kind."

Gwen's eyes became daggers pointed toward her partner's loose tongue.

"An agreement of some kind?" Beth asked. "Could you be a bit more specific?"

"You know," Austin said hesitantly, clearly in unscripted territory.

"No, Mr. Tozer, I don't know. Please enlighten me."

"My mother's transition instructions placed Amanda's share of the money in trust. We receive interest on that investment to cover the cost of raising her. When she's old enough we are supposed to use the principal as a college fund."

"How much will she receive?"

"Um, well, it's not *quite* that simple," Austin stammered. "Our expenses have been much higher than anticipated and my employment history has been less lucrative than we had hoped. So—"

"So you borrowed against Amanda's share of the money," Julia finally said, no longer able to restrain herself.

Beth's head shot in Austin's direction. "Is that true, Mr. Tozer?"

Austin squirmed uneasily.

"Do you have any idea what it costs to raise a girl like Amanda?" Gwen interjected in her partner's defense. Then her eyes zeroed in on Julia. "I realize our bills would be pocket change to some people. But they keep us pretty stressed."

Julia started to react, but Troy stepped in.

"I'm sure it's been very expensive," he said. "But those expenses will only rise the longer Amanda stays with you. Won't you let us help?"

Austin's eyes brightened as if Troy had finally caught his skillfully concealed hints. "Help? Help how?"

"What was the total value of Amanda's share of the inheritance?"

"Fifty thousand dollars," Gwen said without delay, a number far higher than the meager sum Austin had implied during his interview with Julia.

Troy appeared momentarily surprised by the sum, then continued setting the trap. "As you know, Mr. Tozer, my wife is writing a feature story about people in dire economic circumstances thanks to the financial meltdown."

Austin nodded.

"I read the portion about you, although your name isn't used. I told her I thought the story would be much more powerful if it included a photograph of you and Gwen."

"Really?" Austin's partner said. "You think so?"

"I do. And, of course, it would be best to use your real name."

"Of course," Gwen agreed.

Troy looked back at Austin. "Mr. Tozer, what if I paid you a lump sum for permission to use your real name and photograph in that story?"

It took Julia a moment to follow Troy's lead, wondering where on earth he planned to get that kind of cash. Then she understood.

"That'd be perfect," she added enthusiastically. "The syndicate always prefers real names and photos when possible."

"I suppose we could do that," Austin answered warily. "How much?"

"Mr. Simmons," Beth said in an effort to take control of a conversation clearly moving out of bounds, "I don't think it prudent to continue this—"

"Please, Ms. Morris, just one thing more," he interrupted. "Julia, tell him what you found."

Julia reached into her shoulder bag to retrieve a tablet.

"What?" Austin asked. "What did you find?"

"I believe you know a private investigator named Tyler Cain. Is that right?"

Austin squirmed in his chair while receiving a threatening glower from Gwen who, Julia recalled, had been furious after Austin hired Tyler to spy on her.

"Well, he provided me with some information he thought might prove useful to my story."

"What sort of information?" Gwen asked.

"Apparently you subscribe to several rather graphic pornography services."

Austin blushed in Beth's direction. Julia looked at Gwen. She appeared unfazed by the revelation.

"And?" he asked defiantly.

"And your preference options include early adolescent girls."

Austin swallowed nervously while Beth looked disapprovingly in his direction.

"And that you've selected hair color and body styles remarkably similar to Amanda's."

"Let me see that," Beth ordered while reaching toward Julia's tablet.

"Now wait just a minute," Austin said while getting up from the table. "My entertainment options are nobody's business but my own!" He glanced sheepishly in Gwen's direction. "It's perfectly legal material."

"It may be legal, Mr. Tozer," Beth said sternly. "But these preference options raise very serious questions about your suitability as a guardian for a child who matches your parameters."

Austin cursed. He grabbed a bunched-up napkin from the

kitchen counter and threw it furiously toward the wall. It fell limply onto the floor.

"Take her then," he finally said. "Who needs her anyway?"

A moment passed before Beth Morris broke the silence. "Mr. Tozer, are you saying you will not protest the Simmons's request to pursue foster adoption of Amanda?"

He looked toward Gwen. Her eyes threatened. He no longer cared.

"Yes. That's what I'm saying."

His shoulders sank in defeat as he began leaving the room.

"Mr. Tozer. Can I ask one last question?" Julia asked.

He nodded, his face still looking toward the door.

"Where can we find Amanda?"

CHAPTER FIFTY-ONE

The car pulled close to a dying playground blemished by over-grown weeds and discolored monkey bars. Julia recognized Amanda fifty yards in the distance. She was sitting alone on a rusting swing that rocked to and fro without intent, a girl lost in solitary thought.

"Do you want me to go with you?" Troy asked.

"Give us a minute alone first. It might be better that way."

He nodded in agreement before kissing Julia on the cheek.

"Are you sure this is a good idea?" she asked. "I mean, we haven't even been married a year. Are we ready to become instant parents of an adolescent girl we barely know?"

"Correction," he said with a smile. "You barely know her. I've never met her."

She sighed at the truth of it.

"I can't explain it," he added. "But I have a strong feeling this is right for us. As if..." He hesitated.

"As if God is leading us?" she asked, giving him permission to take the conversation places she had too often resisted going.

A nod. "Yeah. Something like that."

"I'm sorry, Troy."

"Sorry for what?"

"I don't know. For dragging my feet about motherhood. And for making you feel…"

Words failed her. But the gentle touch of Troy's masculine fingers against the softness of her cheek told her he understood.

"Go on." He nudged her toward the car door. "We'll be fine."

Julia made it as far as the monkey bars when Amanda noticed her approaching form. Ten more steps and she suddenly realized who it was.

"Ms. Davidson!" Amanda said enthusiastically. "Is that you? Remember me? Amanda Tozer?"

Julia laughed. "Of course I remember you, Amanda. I came to see you."

The girl looked confused. "Me? Not Austin?"

"I already spoke to your brother. He told me you might be here."

"My half brother," she insisted. "He sent me a message saying to hang out here until he calls. Said I couldn't come home right away. Not that I wanted to anyway. He was meeting with you?"

"He was," Julia answered, reaching toward Amanda's disheveled head of hair.

"I know. Bad hair day again," she said. "I wish I had straight hair like you. It's so pretty. You're so pretty."

Julia moved toward the swing beside Amanda's. "Mind if I join you?"

"Really?"

"I'd like to chat. Then I'd like to introduce you to someone."

She looked toward the vehicle in the distance. "Your husband?"

"Yes. Troy."

"Really? Cool!"

Julia started pumping her legs back and forth. "I think I remember how to do this."

"Easy as pie!" Amanda said, pumping her legs to demonstrate for a novice.

They swung in delightful silence for a few moments while Julia tried to put herself in Amanda's shoes. A near-stranger was about to ask if she wanted to leave the home of her deceased mother, the only home the girl had ever known. How to approach the subject?

"Amanda," Julia began, "I met with your brother because I want to ask you something."

"Me? Really? What?"

Both swings eased themselves toward stillness. Julia turned toward the girl to meet her eyes.

"Do you remember when you said you wanted to call the Foster family?" Julia laughed at the recollection.

Amanda nodded. "Sure do."

"Well, I made some phone calls to get information on how you could move in with a foster family."

A series of rapid-fire questions shot in Julia's direction. "Really? You did? For me? Wow! What'd you find out?"

"If the right family comes along, and if your brother—"

"My half brother!"

"Right, sorry. If Austin doesn't oppose the arrangement, the process can move fairly quickly."

"How quickly?"

"Depends on how fast the family can complete applications, get a home study done, attend training, that sort of thing."

Amanda sat listening intently to every word.

Julia swallowed hard. "So, I was wondering—"

She didn't finish the question. Amanda's arms flew around Julia's neck. "Yes, yes, yes!" she shouted as they tilted off balance, sending both bodies to a worn patch of gravel below.

Tears flooded Julia's eyes as the girl planted her cheeks with six or seven kisses.

"I get to live with you?" she shouted between pecks. "And with your husband? Like a real family?"

Julia sat up with some effort. Then she patted the ground beside her to offer Amanda an adjoining spot.

"Everything's already in progress," she finally said. "So if you'll have us, we'd be honored to have you."

"You'll be my foster family?"

"For a while," Julia answered. "Until we qualify for full adoption."

That's when emotion filled Amanda's eyes. "You mean it?" she managed to say after a long silence.

Julia nodded decisively. "I mean it."

They sat on the gravel for several minutes while Julia explained the why, what, how, and when of a process she didn't fully grasp herself. "I'm not quite sure of all the details," she said. "But we'll figure them out as we go. Right now, there's a man over there who can't wait to meet you."

They stood. Then Amanda intertwined her fingers with Julia's as they began to walk.

Troy opened the car door in the distance. Then he stood beside the vehicle, the look on his face reminding Julia of the day he'd asked her on their first date. But he seemed less anxious, more resolute, as if about to accept an adventure neither he nor Julia could begin to comprehend.

Their eyes met. He winked as if never more proud of his friend, his lover, and his partner in the task of becoming a bright spot in Amanda's darkening world.

ABOUT THE AUTHORS

Dr. James Dobson is the Founder and President of Family Talk, a nonprofit organization that produces his radio program, "Family Talk with Dr. James Dobson." He is the author of more than thirty books dedicated to the preservation of the family. He has been active in governmental affairs and has advised three U.S. presidents on family matters. Dr. Dobson is married to Shirley and they have two grown children, Danae and Ryan, and two grandchildren. The Dobsons reside in Colorado Springs, CO.

Kurt Bruner serves as Pastor of Spiritual Formation at Lake Pointe Church and on the adjunct faculty of Dallas Theological Seminary. A graduate of Talbot Seminary and former Vice President with Focus on the Family, Kurt led the teams creating films, magazines, books, and radio drama. As President of HomePointe Inc., he helps local church leaders create an ongoing culture of intentional families. Kurt is the best-selling author of more than a dozen books. Kurt and his wife, Olivia, have four children and live in Rockwall, Texas.

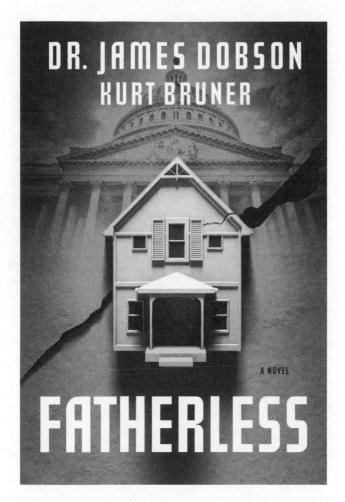

A NOVEL

FATHERLESS

Start at the Beginning

Available Now

DR. JAMES DOBSON

Dr. Dobson wasn't ready to retire when he left Focus on the Family in February 2010. He knew that God had given him a mission and a message many years ago, and that God had not yet lifted that assignment from him.

Dr. Dobson felt God directing him to start a new ministry, which he did in March 2010, to continue the important work of strengthening families, speaking to the culture, and spreading the gospel of Jesus Christ. He called the new organization Dr. James Dobson's Family Talk.

Dr. Dobson has filmed *Building a Family Legacy*, a new series, and *Your Legacy*, a documentary. Both combine new and relevant material with some of the classic presentations from his original 1978 film series seen by over 80 million people worldwide. LifeWay Christian Resources is producing small-group and personal study curricula based on these timeless resources and also sponsoring a nationwide simulcast premiering in October 2014. Dr. Dobson's new book, *Your Legacy: The Greatest Gift*, will be published in September 2014.

DR.JAMES DOBSON'S familytalk™

The voice you trust
for the family you love

www.DrJamesDobson.org

P9-DNF-016

THE ENDURING VISION

A History of the American People

Volume II: Since 1865

THE ENDURING VISION

A History of the American People

Volume II: Since 1865

EIGHTH EDITION

Paul S. Boyer
University of Wisconsin

Clifford E. Clark, Jr.
Carleton College

Karen Halttunen
University of Southern California

Joseph F. Kett
University of Virginia

Neal Salisbury
Smith College

Harvard Sitkoff
University of New Hampshire

Nancy Woloch
Barnard College

CENGAGE
Learning·

Australia • Brazil • Mexico • Singapore • United Kingdom • United States

Advantage Books: The Enduring Vision: A History of the American People, Volume II: Since 1865, Eighth Edition
Paul S. Boyer, Clifford E. Clark, Jr., Karen Halttunen, Joseph F. Kett, Neal Salisbury, Harvard Sitkoff, and Nancy Woloch

Product Director: Suzanne Jeans

Product Manager: Ann West

Content Developer: Megan Chrisman

Product Assistant: Liz Fraser

Media Developer: Kate MacLean

Executive Brand Manager: Melissa Larmon

Rights Acquisitions Specialist: Jennifer Meyer Dare

Manufacturing Planner: Sandee Milewski

Art and Design Direction, Production Management, and Composition: PreMediaGlobal

Cover Image: MICHAEL S. YAMASHITA/National Geographic Stock

For product information and technology assistance, contact us at **Cengage Learning Customer & Sales Support, 1-800-354-9706.**

For permission to use material from this text or product, submit all requests online at **www.cengage.com/permissions**. Further permissions questions can be emailed to **permissionrequest@cengage.com**.

Preassigned Control Number is on record at the Library of Congress

Student Edition:

ISBN-13: 978-1-285-19340-3

ISBN-10: 1-285-19340-7

Cengage Learning
200 First Stamford Place, 4th Floor
Stamford, CT 06902
USA

Cengage Learning is a leading provider of customized learning solutions with office locations around the globe, including Singapore, the United Kingdom, Australia, Mexico, Brazil, and Japan. Locate your local office at **international.cengage.com/region.**

Cengage Learning products are represented in Canada by Nelson Education, Ltd.

For your course and learning solutions, visit **www.cengage.com.**

Purchase any of our products at your local college store or at our preferred online store **www.cengagebrain.com.**

Instructors: Please visit **login.cengage.com** and log in to access instructor-specific resources.

Printed in the United States of America
3 4 5 6 7 17 16

In March 2012, shortly after completing his revisions to The Enduring Vision, *our colleague Paul Boyer died, leaving both the text's authors and the editors at Cengage Learning deeply regretting our loss. Paul was a distinguished cultural and intellectual historian of the twentieth-century United States who served as a quiet leader on* The Enduring Vision *team ever since its inception more than 25 years ago. For every successive edition, he worked tirelessly to bring the textbook up to date, not only by adding recent events, but often overhauling the final chapters of the text from the new perspective generated by those recent events. He was a gentle and generous colleague, and we dedicate this Eighth Edition to him with gratitude and affection.*

Brief Contents

Contents

Special Features

List of Maps

Preface

The history of the United States has been shaped by an *enduring vision,* a shared commitment to a set of beliefs and values—including individual freedom, social equality, the rule of law, and openness to diversity—that run like threads through the lives of the American people. Those powerful beliefs and values express the people's collective determination to give meaning to America. Over the course of U.S. history, even when those values have been violated, that central vision of America has endured. *The Enduring Vision,* Eighth Edition, continues its authors' commitment, first undertaken more than 25 years ago, to convey the strength of that enduring vision over centuries of often destabilizing change.

Over the past 50 years, the discipline of history itself has changed dramatically, moving from an earlier focus on national political narrative toward a rich and complex array of approaches—such as social, cultural, environmental, and global history. *The Enduring Vision* aims to integrate the best recent scholarship in all fields of American history without abandoning a clear political and chronological framework. In keeping with our central theme, our primary emphasis from the First Edition to this new Eighth Edition has been social and cultural history, the fields that have shaped the authors' own teaching and scholarship. We are attentive to the lived historical experiences of women, African Americans, Hispanic Americans, Asian Americans, and American Indians—that is, of men and women of all ethnic groups, regions, and social classes who make up the American mosaic. It was in their daily lives, their lived experience of American history, that the enduring vision of America was articulated—and it was their actions that put those visionary values to the test.

The Enduring Vision is designed for both college classrooms and Advanced Placement courses in U.S. history. Though it offers an appropriately complex treatment of the American past, it requires no prerequisite knowledge from students. Our approach is not only comprehensive, but readable, lively, and illuminating. *The Enduring Vision* is also attentive to the process of historical learning. Recent research on history education has emphasized the crucial importance of teaching students the fundamental skills of historical thinking, such as addressing both continuity and change over time, using evidence to construct and test their own hypotheses, understanding past events in their own contexts, and coming to terms with the contingency of history. *The Enduring Vision* is especially effective in helping students understand the connections between particular historical events and larger trends and developments.

NEWER APPROACHES TO THE AMERICAN PAST

This new Eighth Edition of *The Enduring Vision* sustains the emphasis on social and cultural history that was established in the First Edition. Religious history remains an important focus, from the spiritual values of pre-Columbian communities to the political activism of contemporary conservative Christian groups. Family history and the history of education receive serious attention. Visual culture—paintings, photographs, cartoons, and other illustrations—is investigated through all chapters in the volume.

Environmental History   From the first edition on, *The Enduring Vision* has also paid close attention to the environmental history of America's past, because it is clear that geography, land, and landscape have played an important role throughout human history. Our extensive coverage of environmental history, the land, and the West is fully integrated into the narrative and treated analytically—not simply "tacked on" to a traditional account. We seek to encourage students' spatial thinking about historical developments by offering a **map program** rich in information, easy to read, and visually appealing. And our primary source feature, **Going to the Source** (described in more detail later), offers a number of primary sources involving the land, including excerpts from Meriwether Lewis's Journal and a Dust Bowl diary.

Global History   In response to newer developments in the history discipline, recent editions of *The Enduring Vision* have underscored the global context of American history. We continue to engage with new literature on global history throughout the narrative, and in the special feature **Beyond America—Global Interactions** first introduced in the Sixth Edition. From the origins of agriculture ten millennia ago to the global impact of environmental changes today, we have emphasized how all facets of our historical experience emerge with fresh new clarity when viewed within a broader world framework.

Histories of Technology and Medicine   Students show a particular fascination with the histories of technology and medicine. In our popular **Technology & Culture** feature, and throughout the text, we continue to highlight the historical importance of new inventions and technological innovations. In addition to discussing the applications of science and technology, we note the often unanticipated cultural, social, and political consequences of such innovations —from new hunting implements developed by Paleo-Indians to contemporary breakthroughs in information processing. Medicine and disease receive extensive coverage, and we look at the epidemics brought by European explorers and settlers as well as today's AIDS crisis, bioethics debates, and controversies over health-care financing.

ORGANIZATION AND SPECIAL FEATURES OF *THE ENDURING VISION*

The general organization of the text is chronological, with individual chapters conforming to important historical periods. In keeping with our emphasis on social and cultural history, some chapters take a more thematic approach, overlapping chronologically with those that precede and follow them, thus introducing students to a more sophisticated understanding of the different levels—political, cultural, economic, social—of historical periodization.

Pedagogical Structure   Within each chapter, we offer a number of features designed to help students grasp its structure and purpose. The chapter opener includes an **outline** that lists the major headings of the chapter. **Chronologies** appear near the end of each chapter to provide an overview of key events. The chapter **conclusion** provides students with an opportunity to review what they've read.

As a further pedagogical aid, each chapter includes **key terms** that appear in boldface in the text where first introduced. Key terms also appear in boldface in the index and are defined in an alphabetical glossary on *The Enduring Vision* website.

Special Features   **Beyond America—Global Interactions** offers provocative, in-depth discussions of America's place in world history, focusing on such global developments as the origins and spread of agriculture, slave emancipation in the Atlantic World, and global climate change. **Technology & Culture** provides fascinating insight into such subjects as sugar production in the Americas, guns and gun culture, and the interstate highway system. Both features address important developments in U.S. history from the perspective of major new approaches to the past, with an intensity of detail geared to engaging students' curiosity and analytic engagement.

The Enduring Vision also includes a primary source feature, **Going to the Source**, first introduced in the Seventh Edition. Its pedagogical purpose is not only to bring history alive for our students, but to offer opportunities for their direct engagement in historical interpretation and analysis. **Going to the Source** offers a rich selection of primary sources, drawing on speeches, diaries, letters, and other materials created by Americans who lived through and helped shape the great events and historical changes of successive periods. In selecting documents, we focused especially, but not exclusively, on environmental themes. A brief introduction places each selection in context, and focus questions suggest assignment and discussion possibilities. The voices captured in **Going to the Source** include both prominent historical figures (from Anne Hutchinson to Al Gore) and lesser-known men and women (such as North Dakota farm girl Anna Marie Low, who endured the terrible dust storms of the 1930s).

NEW TO THE EIGHTH EDITION OF *THE ENDURING VISION*

This edition of *The Enduring Vision* brings the work fully up to date, incorporating major developments and scholarship since the Seventh Edition went to press. In our chapter revisions, we have introduced new material and new visual images, tightened and clarified lines of argument, and responded to reviewers' suggestions for strengthening our work.

For the Eighth Edition of *The Enduring Vision*, we have carefully assessed the coverage, interpretations, and analytic framework of each chapter to incorporate the latest scholarship and emerging themes. This process is reflected both in our textual revisions and in the new works of scholarship cited in the end-of-chapter bibliographies. A chapter-by-chapter glimpse of some of the changes highlights new content and up-to-the-minute scholarship.

Chapter 1 elaborates on recently uncovered evidence pertaining to the earliest known humans in the Americas. **Chapter 2** provides a stronger emphasis on the Atlantic world as central to the major developments discussed there. In **Chapter 3**, the discussion of the transition from indentured servitude to slavery has been refined. The chapter also clarifies the distinctiveness of the Middle Colonies as a colonial region. **Chapter 4** offers added discussion of the rise of the Comanches as the dominant power challenging Spain on the southern Plains and in the Southwest, and new details on the War of Jenkins' Ear.

Chapter 5 now includes reference to the French uprising against Spanish rule in Louisiana, offers new details on the Sugar Act, and elaborates on the involvement of women in resistance to the British. **Chapter 6** provides additional information on the motives, backgrounds, and postwar fates of Loyalists. **Chapter 7** provides new material on the impact in the United States of the black uprising in Saint Domingue, which resulted in the overthrow of French rule and the independence of the Republic of Haiti.

Chapter 8 sharpens the distinction between mainstream National Republicans and strict Jeffersonians or Old Republicans. **Chapter 9** has been fully revised for clarity and condensed in length. **Chapter 10** clarifies the rise of the Whig opposition, explains the grassroots origins of the woman's rights movement, and offers a new **Going to the Source** feature: "The Declaration of Sentiments" issued by the Seneca Falls Convention in 1848. **Chapter 11** sharpens the distinction between the cultures of classicism and romanticism and explains the link between the romantic view of nature and the environmental devastation brought by the commercial and industrial revolutions.

Chapter 12 has been fully revised for clarity and includes a new **Going to the Source** feature: former slave Henry Bibb's account of slave religion and resistance and his decision to escape to freedom. **Chapter 14** now explains why the Lower South seceded from the Union before Lincoln was placed in office. **Chapter 15** revisits Lincoln's stance on slavery and explores the British response to the Civil War.

Chapter 17 includes new material on Chinese prostitution and Chinese laborers. **Chapter 18** elaborates on the treatment of child labor and offers new discussion of discrimination against the physically disabled. **Chapter 19** now explores the connection between intercollegiate sports and business leadership and provides new treatment of women writers. **Chapter 20** expands its coverage of racial lynching and the emergence of Black Populism. **Chapter 21** now defines "Social Gospel," expands its treatment of the 1912 Socialist party platform, explains in a more nuanced fashion the relationship between Progressivism and the New Deal, and offers a new **Going to the Source** feature about violence at a shirtwaist workers' strike.

Chapter 22 expands on the larger significance of U.S. involvements in Latin America and the effects of World War I on African-American expectations of equality and includes a new **Going to the Source** feature describing the effects of the 1918 influenza epidemic. **Chapter 23** enhances the treatment of women voting in 1920, the rise of African-American political consciousness in the 1920s, and the international protest over the Sacco-Vanzetti case. It also offers a new **Going to the Source** feature: a memoir of a young woman's movie-going memories from the 1920s. **Chapter 24** clarifies the overall themes of the New Deal; underscores the role of the Civilian Conservation Corps in heightening environmental awareness; and emphasizes the interconnectedness of political, social, and cultural history in the 1930s. **Chapter 25** expands discussion of the dropping of the A-bombs in Japan.

Chapter 26 now includes sections on demobilization, the GI Bill of Rights, and the beginnings of the postwar economic boom. **Chapters 27 and 28** offer expanded discussions of the civil-rights movement. **Chapter 29** expands the treatment of feminism and Martin Luther King's concept of "a revolution of values."

Chapter 30 offers updated statistics on welfare and unemployment; more nuanced treatment of the term "conservative revolution"; and a brand new, more interpretive conclusion.

Chapter 31 brings *The Enduring Vision* up to date with new material on the Obama presidency; health-care reform; economic recession; congressional gridlock; the Tea Party and Occupy Wall Street movements; the presidential campaign of 2012; and recent developments in Afghanistan, Pakistan, and Iran.

SUPPLEMENTARY RESOURCES FOR *THE ENDURING VISION*, EIGHTH EDITION

The Enduring Vision, Eighth Edition, offers a wide array of supplements to help students master the material and to guide instructors in setting up and managing their courses. For more information on viewing or ordering these materials, please consult your sales representative.

For Students:

- **Companion Website for *The Enduring Vision*, Eighth Edition,** features an assortment of resources and tools to help students master the subject matter. The Companion Website includes a glossary, flashcards, tutorial quizzes, and additional suggested readings.

- Cengage Learning's **History CourseMate** brings course concepts to life with interactive learning, study, and exam preparation tools that support the textbook. History CourseMate includes an integrated eBook; interactive teaching and learning tools, including quizzes, flashcards, and videos; as well as EngagementTracker, a first-of-its-kind tool that monitors student engagement in the course. Learn more at www.cengagebrain.com.

- The interactive multimedia **CL eBook** links out to rich media assets such as video and MP3 chapter summaries. Through this eBook, students can also access self-test quizzes, chapter outlines, focus questions, chronology exercises, essay questions (for which the answers can be e-mailed to their instructors), primary source documents with critical thinking questions, and interactive (zoomable) maps. Available at www.cengagebrain.com.

For Instructors:

- **Companion Website for *The Enduring Vision*, Eighth Edition,** offers instructors access to all of the features of the **Student Companion Website,** plus access to all the instructor resources, including the **Instructor's Resource Manual** as well as **PowerPoint® slides for lecture—and testing materials.** The IRM includes chapter themes, lecture suggestions, instructional suggestions, print and nonprint resources, and document set activities.

- **PowerLecture** with **ExamView** and **JoinIn** for *The Enduring Vision,* Eighth Edition [ISBN: 9781285056678]. This dual-platform, all-in-one multimedia resource includes the **Instructor's Resource Manual; Test Bank** (with short answer, multiple-choice, and essay questions); **Microsoft® PowerPoint®** slides of lecture outlines and images and maps from the text that can be used as offered, or customized by importing personal lecture slides or other material; and **JoinIn® PowerPoint®** slides with clicker content. Also included is **ExamView**, an easy-to-use assessment and tutorial system that allows instructors to create, deliver, and customize tests in minutes. Instructors can build tests with as many as 250 questions using up to 12 question types, and using ExamView's complete word-processing capabilities, they can enter an unlimited number of new questions or edit existing ones.

Additional Supplements

- *Rand McNally Atlas of American History,* 2/e [ISBN: 9780618842018], is available for packaging with this text. This comprehensive atlas features more than 80 maps, with new content covering global perspectives, including events in the Middle East from 1945 to 2005, as well as population trends in the United States and around the world. Additional maps document voyages of discovery; the settling of the colonies; major U.S. military engagements, including the American Revolution and World Wars I and II; and sources of immigrations, ethnic populations, and patterns of economic change.

- Aplia™ is an online interactive learning solution that improves comprehension and outcomes by increasing student effort and engagement. Founded by a professor to enhance his own courses, Aplia provides automatically graded assignments with detailed, immediate explanations on every question. The interactive assignments have been developed to address the major concepts covered in *The Enduring Vision* and are designed to promote critical thinking and engage students more fully in their learning. Question types include questions built around animated maps, primary sources such as newspaper extracts, or imagined scenarios—like engaging in a conversation with Benjamin Franklin or finding a diary and being asked to fill in some blank words; more in-depth primary source question sets that address a major topic with a number of related primary sources, and questions that promote deeper analysis of historical evidence. Images, video clips, and audio clips are incorporated in many of the questions. Students get immediate feedback on their work (not only what they got right or wrong, but why), and they can choose to see another set of related questions if they want to practice further. A searchable eBook is available inside the course as well so that students can easily reference it as they are working. Map-reading and writing tutorials are available as well to get students off to a good start. Aplia's simple-to-use course management interface allows instructors to post announcements, upload course materials, host student discussions, e-mail students, and manage the gradebook; personalized support from a knowledgeable and friendly support team also offers assistance in customizing assignments to the instructor's course schedule. To learn more, ask your Cengage Learning sales representative to provide a demo—or view a specific demo for this book, at www.aplia.com.

- **CourseReader** is an online collection of primary and secondary sources that lets you create a customized electronic reader in minutes. With an easy-to-use interface and assessment tool, you can choose exactly what your students will be assigned—simply search or browse Cengage Learning's extensive document database to preview and select your customized collection of readings. In addition to print sources of all types (letters, diary entries, speeches, newspaper accounts, etc.), the collection includes a growing number of images and video and audio clips. Each primary source document includes a descriptive headnote that puts the reading into context and is further supported by both critical thinking and multiple-choice questions designed to reinforce key points. For more information visit www.cengage.com/coursereader.

- *Enduring Voices* **Document Set.** A two-volume document collection, *Enduring Voices,* can be packaged with the text. [Volume 1 ISBN: 9780395960844; Volume 2 ISBN: 9780395960868].

- **Other U.S. History Readers.** Cengage Learning, publishes a wide variety of primary and secondary source readers that could be used to complement this text. These include collections focusing on cultural history, political documents, social history essays, biography, and readers with specific methods of primary source analysis. Contact your Cengage Learning sales representative for more details about the readers that would work best for you and your students.

Acknowledgments

In undertaking this major revision of our textbook, we have drawn on our own scholarly work and teaching experience. We have also kept abreast of new work of historical interpretation, as reported by our U.S. history colleagues in their books, scholarly articles, and papers at historical meetings. We list much of this new work in the Additional Bibliographies on *The Enduring Vision* website. We are much indebted to all these colleagues.

We have also benefited from the comments and suggestions of instructors who have adopted *The Enduring Vision;* from colleagues and students who have written us about specific details; and from the following scholars and teachers who offered systematic evaluations of specific chapters. Their perceptive comments have been most helpful in the revision process.

Robert Berta, *Northern Kentucky University*
Troy Bickham, *Texas A&M University*
Michael Brattain, *Georgia State University*
Kim Brinck-Johnsen, *University of New Hampshire*
Roger Bromert, *Southwestern Oklahoma State University*
Michael Colomaio, *Alfred State College*
Scott Cook, *Motlow State Community College*
Frank Delao, *Midland College*
Kristen Foster, *Marquette University*
Frederick B. Gates, *Southwestern Oklahoma State University*
Gary Henkel, *St. Petersburg College*
Stephanie Holyfield, *University of Delaware*

George Jarrett, *Cerritos College*
Steven Kite, *Fort Hays State University*
Michael Krenn, *Appalachian State University*
Lisa Lane, *MiraCosta College*
John Leiby, *Paradise Valley Community College*
Mary Linehan, *University of Texas at Tyler*
Edith MacDonald, *University of Central Florida*
Archie McDonald, *Stephen F. Austin State University*
Steven Miller, *Goshen College*
Rick Moser, *Texas A&M University—Commerce*
Earl Mulderink, *Southern Utah University*
Son Nguyen, *Los Angeles Harbor College*
Uraina Pack, *Clarion University*
Christopher Phelps, *Ohio State University*
Gerald Pierce, *Southern Polytechnic State University*
Steven Reiss, *Northeastern Illinois University*
Donald Rogers, *Central Connecticut State University*
Michael Smith, *Ithaca College*
Steve Stein, *University of Memphis*
Patricia Thompson, *University of Texas at San Antonio*
John Ulloa, *City College of San Francisco and Skyline College*
Paul Vandermeer, *Arizona State University*
Keith Volanto, *Collin County Community College*
William Whisenhunt, *College of DuPage*
Paul C. Young, *Utica College*
Michael Zartler, *Suffolk County Community College*

In addition, Clifford Clark would like to acknowledge the research assistance of David B. Hirsch.

Finally, we salute the skilled professionals at Cengage Learning whose expertise and enthusiastic commitment to this new Eighth Edition guided us through every stage and helped sustain our own determination to make this the best book we could possibly write. Ann West, Senior Sponsoring Editor, presided over our initial planning meeting with good nature and wise suggestions, and has been a reassuring presence throughout. Development Editor Tonya Lobato managed the day-to-day challenges of keeping us all on track. Pembroke Herbert brought her creative skills to bear in seeking out fresh and powerful visual images for the work. Senior Content Project Manager Jane Lee ably shepherded the work through the crucial stages of production, while Assistant Editor Megan Chrisman oversaw the increasingly important Web-based resources. Charlotte Miller brought a wealth of cartographic experience to upgrading the *Enduring Vision*'s map program.

Paul S. Boyer
Clifford E. Clark, Jr.
Karen Halttunen
Joseph F. Kett
Neal Salisbury
Harvard Sitkoff
Nancy Woloch

About the Authors

PAUL S. BOYER was the Merle Curti Professor of History at the University of Wisconsin, Madison. He earned his Ph.D. from Harvard University. He was also a visiting professor at the University of California, Los Angeles; Northwestern University; and the College of William and Mary. An editor of *Notable American Women, 1607–1950* (1971), he also co-authored *Salem Possessed: The Social Origins of Witchcraft* (1974), for which, with Stephen Nissenbaum, he received the John H. Dunning Prize of the American Historical Association. His other works include *Urban Masses and Moral Order in America, 1820–1920* (1978), *By The Bomb's Early Light: American Thought and Culture at the Dawn of the Atomic Age* (1985), *When Time Shall Be No More: Prophecy Belief in Modern American Culture* (1992), and *Promises to Keep: The United States Since World War II* (third edition, 2005). He was also editor-in-chief of the *Oxford Companion to United States History* (2001). His articles and essays appeared in the *American Quarterly, New Republic,* and other journals.

CLIFFORD E. CLARK, Jr., M.A. and A.D. Hulings Professor of American Studies and professor of history at Carleton College, earned his Ph.D. from Harvard University. He has served as both the chair of the History Department and director of the American Studies program at Carleton. Clark is the author of *Henry Ward Beecher: Spokesman for a Middle-Class America* (1978), *The American Family Home, 1800–1960* (1986), *The Intellectual and Cultural History of Anglo-America Since 1789* in the *General History of the Americas Series,* and, with Carol Zellie, *Northfield: The History and Architecture of a Community* (1997). He also has edited and contributed to *Minnesota in a Century of Change: The State and Its People Since 1900* (1989). A past member of the Council of the American Studies Association, Clark is active in the fields of material culture studies and historic preservation, and he serves on the Northfield, Minnesota, Historical Preservation Commission.

KAREN HALTTUNEN, professor of history at the University of Southern California, earned her Ph.D. from Yale University. Her works include *Confidence Men and Painted Women: A Study of Middle-Class Culture in America, 1830–1870* (1982) and *Murder Most Foul: The Killer and the American Gothic Imagination* (1998). She edited *The Blackwell Companion to American Cultural History* (2008) and co-edited, with Lewis Perry, *Moral Problems in American Life: New Essays on Cultural History* (1998). As president of the American Studies Association and as vice-president of the Teaching Division of the American Historical Association, she has actively promoted K–16 collaboration in teaching history. She has held fellowships from the Guggenheim and Mellon Foundations, the National Endowment for the Humanities, the Huntington Library, and the National Humanities Center and has been principal investigator on several Teaching American History grants from the Department of Education.

JOSEPH F. KETT, James Madison Professor of History at the University of Virginia, received his Ph.D. from Harvard University. His works include *The Formation of the American Medical Profession: The Role of Institutions, 1780–1860* (1968), *Rites of Passage: Adolescence in America, 1790–Present* (1977), *The Pursuit of Knowledge under Difficulties: From Self-Improvement to Adult Education in America, 1750–1990* (1994), and *The New Dictionary of Cultural Literacy* (2002), of which he is co-author. His book, *Merit: The History of a Founding Ideal from the American Revolution to the Twenty-First Century,* was published in December 2012. As the former History Department chair at Virginia, he also has participated on the Panel on Youth of the President's Science Advisory Committee, has served on the Board of Editors of the *History of Education Quarterly,* and is a past member of the Council of the American Studies Association.

NEAL SALISBURY, Barbara Richmond 1940 Professor Emeritus in the Social Sciences (History), at Smith College, received his Ph.D. from the University of California, Los Angeles. He is the author of *Manitou and Providence: Indians, Europeans, and the Making of New England, 1500–1643* (1982), editor of *The Sovereignty and Goodness of God,* by Mary Rowlandson (1997), and co-editor, with Philip J. Deloria, of *The Companion to American Indian History* (2002). With R. David Edmunds and Frederick E. Hoxie, he has written *The People: A History of Native America* (2007). He has contributed numerous articles to journals and edited collections and co-edits a book series, *Cambridge Studies in North American Indian History.* He is active in the fields of colonial and Native American history and has served as president of the American Society for Ethnohistory and on the Council of the Omohundro Institute of Early American History and Culture.

HARVARD SITKOFF, Emeritus Professor of History at the University of New Hampshire, earned his Ph.D. from Columbia University. He is the author of *A New Deal for Blacks* (Thirtieth Anniversary Edition, 2009), *The Struggle for Black Equality* (Twenty-Fifth Anniversary Edition, 2008), *King: Pilgrimage to the Mountaintop* (2008), *Toward Freedom Land, The Long Struggle for Racial Equality in America* (2010), and *Postwar America: A Student Companion* (2000); co-author of the National Park Service's *Racial Desegregation in Public Education in the United States* (2000), and *The World War II Homefront* (2003); and editor of *Fifty Years Later: The New Deal Reevaluated* (1984), *A History of Our Time* (2012), and *Perspectives on Modern America: Making Sense of the Twentieth Century* (2001). His articles have appeared in the *American Quarterly, Journal of American History,* and *Journal of Southern History,* among others. A frequent lecturer at universities abroad, he has been awarded the Fulbright Commission's John Adams Professorship of American Civilization in the Netherlands and the Mary Ball Washington Professorship of American History in Ireland.

NANCY WOLOCH received her Ph.D. from Indiana University. She is the author of *Women and the American Experience* (fifth edition, 2011), editor of *Early American Women: A Documentary History, 1600–1900* (third edition, 2013), and co-author, with Walter LaFeber and Richard Polenberg, of *The American Century: A History of the United States Since the 1890s* (seventh edition, 2013). She is also the author of *Muller v. Oregon: A Brief History with Documents* (1996). She teaches American History and American Studies at Barnard College, Columbia University.

16

RECONSTRUCTION AND RESISTANCE, 1865–1877

CHAPTER OUTLINE

- Reconstruction Politics, 1865–1868 • Reconstruction Governments
- The Impact of Emancipation • New Concerns in the North, 1868–1876
- Reconstruction Abandoned, 1876–1877

RECONSTRUCTION POLITICS, 1865–1868

At the end of the Civil War, President Johnson might have exiled, imprisoned, or executed Confederate leaders and imposed martial law indefinitely. Demobilized Confederate soldiers might have continued armed resistance to federal occupation forces. Freed slaves might have taken revenge on former owners and other white southerners. But none of this occurred. Instead, intense *political* conflict dominated the immediate postwar years. National politics produced new constitutional amendments, a presidential impeachment, and some of the most ambitious domestic legislation ever enacted by Congress, the Reconstruction Acts of 1867–1868. The major outcome of Reconstruction politics was the enfranchisement of black men, a development that few—black or white—had expected when Lee surrendered.

In 1865, only a small group of politicians supported black suffrage. All were Radical Republicans, a minority faction that had emerged during the war. Led by Senator **Charles Sumner** of Massachusetts and Congressman **Thaddeus Stevens** of Pennsylvania, the Radicals had clamored for the abolition of slavery and a demanding reconstruction policy. But the Radicals, outnumbered in Congress by other Republicans and opposed by the Democratic minority, faced long odds. Still, they managed to win broad Republican support for parts of their Reconstruction program, including black male enfranchisement. Just as civil war had led to emancipation, a goal once supported by only a minority of Americans, so Reconstruction policy became bound to black suffrage, a momentous change that originally had only narrow political backing.

Lincoln's Plan   Conflict over Reconstruction began even before the war ended. In December 1863, President Lincoln issued the Proclamation of Amnesty and Reconstruction, which enabled southern states to rejoin the Union if at least 10 percent of those who had cast ballots in the election of 1860 would take an oath of allegiance to the Union and accept emancipation. This minority could then create a loyal state government. Lincoln's plan excluded some southerners from oath-taking, such as Confederate officials and military officers; they would have to apply for presidential pardons. Also excluded were blacks, who had not been voters in 1860. Lincoln hoped to undermine the Confederacy by fostering pro-Union governments within it and to build a southern Republican Party.

Radical Republicans in Congress, however, envisioned a slower readmission process that would bar even more ex-Confederates from political life. The Wade-Davis bill, passed by Congress in July 1864, provided that a military governor would rule each former Confederate state; after at least half the eligible voters took an oath of allegiance to the Union, delegates could be elected to a state convention that would repeal secession and abolish slavery. To qualify as a voter or delegate, a southerner would have to take a second, "ironclad" oath, swearing that he had never voluntarily supported the Confederacy. Like the 10 percent plan, the congressional plan did not provide for black suffrage, a measure then supported by only some Radicals. Unlike Lincoln's plan, however, the Wade-Davis scheme would have delayed the readmission process almost indefinitely.

Claiming he did not want to bind himself to any single restoration policy, Lincoln pocket-vetoed the Wade-Davis bill (failed to sign the bill within ten days of the adjournment of Congress). The bill's sponsors, Senator Benjamin Wade of Ohio and Congressman Henry Winter Davis of Maryland, blasted Lincoln's act. By the war's end, the president and Congress had reached an impasse. Arkansas, Louisiana, Tennessee, and parts of Virginia under Union army control moved toward readmission under variants of Lincoln's plan. But Congress refused to seat their delegates, as it had a right to do. What Lincoln's ultimate policy would have been remains unknown. But after his assassination, on April 14, 1865, Radical Republicans turned with hope toward his successor, **Andrew Johnson** of Tennessee.

Presidential   The only southern senator to remain in Congress when his
Reconstruction   state seceded, Andrew Johnson had served as military governor of Tennessee from 1862 to 1864. Defying the Confederate stand, he had declared that "treason is a crime and must be made odious." Above all, Johnson had long sought the destruction of the planter aristocracy. A self-educated man of humble North Carolina origins, Johnson had moved to Greenville, Tennessee, in 1826. He had entered politics in the 1830s as a spokesman for non-slave-owning whites and rose rapidly from local official to congressman to governor to senator. Once the owner of eight slaves, Johnson reversed his position on slavery during the war. When emancipation became Union policy, he supported it. But Johnson neither adopted abolitionist ideals nor challenged racist sentiments. He hoped mainly that the fall of slavery would injure southern aristocrats. Johnson, in short, had his own political agenda, which, as Republicans would soon learn, did not duplicate theirs. Moreover, he was a lifelong Democrat who had been added to the Republican, or

National Union, ticket in 1864 to broaden its appeal and who had become president by accident.

In May 1865, with Congress out of session, Johnson shocked Republicans by announcing his own program to bring back into the Union the seven southern states still without reconstruction governments—Alabama, Florida, Georgia, Mississippi, North Carolina, South Carolina, and Texas. Almost all southerners who took an oath of allegiance would receive a pardon and amnesty; all their property except slaves would be restored. Oath takers could elect delegates to state conventions, which would provide for regular elections. Each state convention, Johnson later added, would have to proclaim secession illegal, repudiate state debts incurred under the Confederacy, and ratify the Thirteenth Amendment, which abolished slavery. (Proposed by an enthusiastic wartime Congress early in 1865, the amendment would be ratified in December of that year.) As under Lincoln's plan, Confederate civil and military officers would still be disqualified, as would well-off ex-Confederates—those with taxable property worth $20,000 or more. This purge of the plantation aristocracy, Johnson said, would benefit "humble men, the peasantry and yeomen of the South, who have been decoyed ... into rebellion." Poorer whites would now be in control.

Presidential Reconstruction took effect in the summer of 1865, but with unforeseen consequences. Disqualified Southerners applied in droves for pardons, which Johnson handed out liberally—some thirteen thousand of them. Johnson also dropped plans to punish treason. By the end of 1865, all seven states had created new civil governments that, in effect, restored the status quo from before the war. Confederate army officers and large planters assumed state offices. Former Confederate generals and officials—including Alexander Stephens of Georgia, the former Confederate vice president—won election to Congress. Some states refused to ratify the Thirteenth Amendment or to repudiate their Confederate debts.

Most infuriating to Radical Republicans, all seven states took steps to ensure a landless, dependent black labor force: they passed **"black codes"** to replace the slave codes, state laws that had regulated slavery. Because Johnson's plan assured the ratification of the Thirteenth Amendment, all states guaranteed the freedmen some basic rights—to marry, own property, make contracts, and testify in court against other blacks—but the codes harshly restricted freedmen's behavior. Some established racial segregation in public places; most prohibited racial intermarriage, jury service by blacks, and court testimony by blacks against whites. All codes included provisions that effectively barred former slaves from leaving the plantations. South Carolina required special licenses for blacks who wished to enter nonagricultural employment. Mississippi prohibited blacks from buying and selling farmland. Most states required annual contracts between landowners and black agricultural workers; blacks without contracts risked arrest as vagrants and involuntary servitude.

The black codes left freedmen no longer slaves but not really liberated either. In practice, many clauses in the codes never took effect: the Union army and federal agents suspended the enforcement of racially discriminatory provisions of the new laws. But the black codes revealed white southern intentions. They showed what "home rule" would have been like without federal interference.

Many northerners denounced what they saw as southern defiance. "What can be hatched from such an egg but another rebellion?" asked a Boston newspaper. Republicans in Congress agreed. When Congress convened in December 1865, it refused to seat delegates of ex-Confederate states. Establishing the Joint (House-Senate) Committee on Reconstruction, Republicans prepared to dismantle the black codes and lock ex-Confederates out of power.

Congress Versus Johnson   Southern blacks' status now became the major issue in Congress. Radical Republicans like Congressman Thaddeus Stevens—who hoped to impose black suffrage on the former Confederacy and delay southern readmission—were still a minority in Congress. Conservative Republicans, who favored Johnson's plan, formed a minority too, as did the Democrats, who also supported the president. Moderate Republicans, the largest congressional bloc, agreed with Radicals that Johnson's plan was too feeble, but they wanted to avoid a dispute with the president. None of the four congressional blocs could claim the two-thirds majority needed to overturn a presidential veto. But ineptly, Johnson alienated a majority of moderates and pushed them into the Radicals' arms.

Two proposals to invalidate the black codes, drafted by a moderate Republican, Senator Lyman Trumbull of Illinois, won wide Republican support. Congress first voted to continue the Freedmen's Bureau, started in March 1865, whose term was ending. This federal agency, headed by former Union general O.O. Howard and staffed mainly by army officers, provided relief, rations, and medical care; built schools for freed blacks; put them to work on abandoned or confiscated lands; and tried to protect their rights as laborers. Congress extended the bureau's life for three years and gave it new power to run special military courts, to settle labor disputes, and to invalidate labor contracts forced on freedmen by the black codes. In February 1866, Johnson vetoed the Supplementary Freedmen's Bureau bill. The Constitution, he declared, did not sanction military trials of civilians in peacetime, nor did it support a system to care for "indigent persons."

In March 1866, Congress passed a second measure proposed by Trumbull, a bill that made blacks U.S. citizens with the same civil rights as other citizens and authorized federal intervention in the states to ensure black rights in court. Johnson vetoed the civil rights bill also. He argued that it would "operate in favor of the colored and against the white race." In April, Congress overrode his veto; the **Civil Rights Act of 1866** was the first major law ever passed over a presidential veto. In July, Congress enacted the Supplementary Freedmen's Bureau Act over Johnson's veto as well. Johnson's vetoes puzzled many Republicans because the new laws did not undercut presidential Reconstruction. The president insisted, however, that both bills were illegitimate because southerners had been shut out of the Congress that passed them. Johnson won support in the South and from northern Democrats. But he had alienated moderate Republicans, who now joined Radicals to oppose him. Johnson had lost "every friend he has," one moderate declared.

Some historians view Andrew Johnson as a political incompetent who, at this crucial juncture, bungled both his readmission scheme and his political future. Others contend he was merely trying to forge a centrist coalition. In either case, Johnson underestimated the possibility of Republican unity. Once united, the Republicans took their next step: the passage of a constitutional amendment to prevent the Supreme Court from invalidating the new Civil Rights Act and block Democrats in Congress from repealing it.

The Fourteenth Amendment, 1866

In April 1866, Congress adopted the **Fourteenth Amendment,** proposed by the Joint Committee on Reconstruction. To protect blacks' rights, the amendment declared in its first clause that all persons born or naturalized in the United States were citizens of the nation and of their states and that no state could abridge their rights without due process of law or deny them equal protection of the law. This section nullified the *Dred Scott* decision of 1857, which had denied that blacks were citizens. Second, the amendment guaranteed that if a state denied suffrage to any of its male citizens, its representation in Congress would be proportionally reduced. This clause did not ensure black suffrage, but it threatened to deprive southern states of some legislators if black men were denied the vote. This was the first time that the word *male* was written into the Constitution; to the women's rights advocates, woman suffrage seemed a yet more distant prospect. Third, the amendment disqualified from state and national office *all* prewar officeholders—civil and military, state and federal—who had supported the Confederacy, unless Congress removed their disqualifications by a two-thirds vote. In so providing, Congress sought to invalidate Johnson's wholesale distribution of amnesties and pardons. Finally, the amendment repudiated the Confederate debt and maintained the validity of the federal debt.

The most ambitious step Congress had yet taken, the Fourteenth Amendment revealed growing Republican receptivity to Radical demands, including black male enfranchisement. The amendment's passage created a firestorm. Abolitionists decried the second clause as a "swindle" because it did not explicitly ensure black suffrage. Southerners and northern Democrats condemned the third clause as vengeful. Southern legislatures, except for Tennessee's, refused to ratify the amendment, and President Johnson denounced it. His defiance solidified the new alliance between moderate and Radical Republicans, and turned the congressional elections of 1866 into a referendum on the Fourteenth Amendment.

Over the summer, Johnson set off on a whistlestop train tour from Washington to St. Louis and Chicago and back. But this innovative campaign tactic—the "swing around the circle," as Johnson called it—failed. Humorless and defensive, the president made fresh enemies and doomed his hope of sinking the Fourteenth Amendment, which Moderate and Radical Republicans defended.

Republicans carried the congressional elections of 1866 in a landslide, winning almost two-thirds of the House and four-fifths of the Senate. They had secured a mandate for the Fourteenth Amendment and their own Reconstruction program, even if the president vetoed every part of it.

Congressional Reconstruction, 1866–1867

Congressional debate over reconstructing the South began in December 1866 and lasted three months. Radical Republican leaders called for black suffrage, federal support for public schools, confiscation of Confederate estates, and an extended period of military occupation in the South. Moderate Republicans accepted parts of the plan. In February 1867, after complex legislative maneuvers, Congress passed the **Reconstruction Act of 1867.** Johnson vetoed the law, and on March 2, Congress passed it over his veto. Later that year and in 1868, Congress passed three further Reconstruction acts, all enacted over presidential vetoes, to refine and enforce the first.

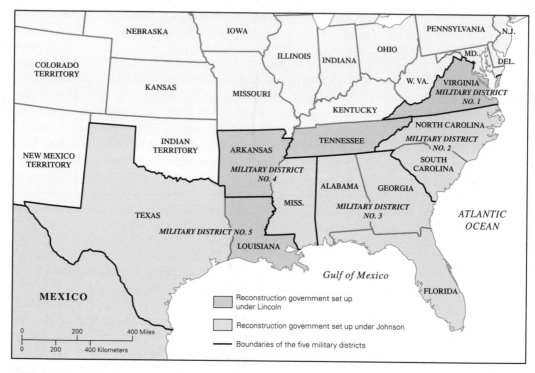

MAP 16.1   The Reconstruction of the South

The Reconstruction Act of 1867 divided the former Confederate states, except Tennessee, into five military districts and set forth the steps by which new state governments could be created.

Source: © Cengage Learning. All rights reserved. No distribution allowed without express authorization.

The Reconstruction Act of 1867 invalidated the state governments formed under the Lincoln and Johnson plans. Only Tennessee, which had ratified the Fourteenth Amendment and had been readmitted to the Union, escaped further reconstruction. The new law divided the other ten former Confederate states into five temporary military districts, each run by a Union general. Voters—all black men, plus those white men who had not been disqualified by the Fourteenth Amendment—could elect delegates to a state convention that would write a new state constitution granting black suffrage. When eligible voters ratified the new constitution, elections could be held for state officers. Once Congress approved the state constitution, once the state legislature ratified the Fourteenth Amendment, and once the amendment became part of the federal Constitution, Congress would readmit the state into the Union.

The Reconstruction Act of 1867 was far more radical than the Johnson program because it enfranchised blacks and disfranchised many ex-Confederates. It fulfilled a central goal of the Radical Republicans: to delay the readmission of former Confederate states until Republican governments could be established and thereby prevent an immediate rebel resurgence. But the new law was not as harsh toward ex-Confederates as it might have been. It provided for only temporary military rule; it did not prosecute Confederate leaders for treason, permanently bar them from politics, or provide for confiscation or redistribution of property.

During the congressional debates, Radical Republican congressman Thaddeus Stevens had argued for the confiscation of large Confederate estates to "humble the proud traitors" and to provide for former slaves. He had proposed subdividing such confiscated property into forty-acre tracts to be distributed among the freedmen and selling the rest, some 90 percent of it, to pay off war debts. Stevens's land-reform bill won Radical support but never made progress; most Republicans held property rights sacred. Tampering with such rights in the South, they feared, would jeopardize those rights in the North. Moreover, Stevens's proposal would alienate southern ex-Whigs, aggrieve other white southerners and thereby endanger the rest of Reconstruction. Thus land reform never came about. The "radical" Reconstruction acts were a compromise.

Congressional Reconstruction took effect in the spring of 1867, but Johnson, as Commander in Chief, impeded its enforcement by replacing pro-Radical military officers with conservative ones. Republicans seethed. More suspicious than ever, congressional moderates and Radicals again joined forces to block Johnson from further obstructing Reconstruction.

The Impeachment Crisis, 1867–1868　In March 1867, Republicans in Congress passed two laws to curb presidential power. The **Tenure of Office Act** barred the president from removing civil officers without Senate consent. Cabinet members, the law stated, were to hold office "during the term of the president by whom they may have been appointed" and could be fired only with the Senate's approval. The goal was to bar Johnson from dismissing Secretary of War Edwin M. Stanton, a Radical ally. The other law, a rider to an army appropriations bill, barred the president from issuing military orders except through the commanding general, Ulysses S. Grant, who could not be removed without the Senate's consent.

The Radicals' enmity toward Johnson, however, went further: they now sought grounds on which to impeach him. The House Judiciary Committee could at first find no valid charges against Johnson. But the president again rescued his foes by providing the charges they needed.

In August 1867, with Congress out of session, Johnson suspended Secretary of War Stanton and replaced him with General Grant. In early 1868, the reconvened Senate refused to approve Stanton's suspension, and Grant, sensing the Republican mood, vacated the office. Johnson then removed Stanton and replaced him with another general. Johnson's defiance forced Republican moderates, who had at first resisted impeachment, into yet another alliance with the Radicals: the president had "thrown down the gauntlet," a moderate charged. The House approved eleven charges of impeachment, nine based on violation of the Tenure of Office Act. The other charges accused Johnson of ignoring "the high duties of office," seeking to disgrace Congress, and not enforcing the Reconstruction acts.

Johnson's trial in the Senate, which began in March 1868, riveted public attention for eleven weeks. Seven congressmen, including leading Radical Republicans, served as prosecutors or "managers." Johnson's lawyers maintained that he was merely seeking a court test by violating the Tenure of Office Act, which he thought was unconstitutional. They also contended, somewhat inconsistently, that the law did not protect Secretary Stanton, an appointee of Lincoln, not Johnson. Finally, they asserted, Johnson was guilty of no crime indictable in a regular court.

The congressional "managers" countered that impeachment was a political process, not a criminal trial, and that Johnson's "abuse of discretionary power" constituted an impeachable offense. Although Senate opinion split along party lines, some Republicans wavered, fearful that removal of a president would destroy the balance of power among the three branches of the federal government. They also distrusted Radical Republican Benjamin Wade, the president pro tempore of the Senate, who, because there was no vice president, would become president if Johnson were thrown out.

Late in May 1868, the Senate voted against Johnson 35 to 19, one vote short of the two-thirds majority needed for conviction. Despite intense pressure, seven Republicans had risked political suicide and sided with the twelve Senate Democrats against removal. In so doing, they set a precedent: their vote discouraged impeachment on political grounds for decades to come. But the anti-Johnson forces had also achieved their goal: Andrew Johnson had no future as president. Serving out the rest of his term, Johnson returned to Tennessee, where he was reelected to the Senate five years later. Republicans in Congress, meanwhile, pursued their last major Reconstruction objective: to guarantee black male suffrage.

The Fifteenth Amendment and the Question of Woman Suffrage, 1869–1870
Black suffrage was the linchpin of congressional Reconstruction. Only with the black vote could Republicans secure control of the ex-Confederate states. The Reconstruction Act of 1867 had forced southern states to enfranchise black men in order to reenter the Union, but much of the North rejected black suffrage. Congressional Republicans therefore had two aims. The **Fifteenth Amendment,** proposed by Congress in 1869, sought to protect black suffrage in the South against future repeal by Congress or the states and to enfranchise northern and border-state blacks, who would presumably vote Republican. The amendment prohibited the denial of suffrage by the states to any citizen on account of "race, color, or previous condition of servitude."

Democrats argued that the proposed amendment violated states' rights by denying each state leverage over who would vote. But Democrats did not control enough states to defeat the amendment, and it was ratified in 1870. Four ex-Confederate states—Mississippi, Virginia, Georgia, and Texas—that had delayed the Reconstruction process were therefore forced to approve the Fifteenth Amendment, as well as the Fourteenth, in order to rejoin the Union. Some southerners appreciated the new amendment's omissions: as a Richmond newspaper pointed out, it had "loopholes through which a coach and four horses can be driven." What were these loopholes? The Fifteenth Amendment neither guaranteed black office holding nor prohibited voting restrictions such as property requirements and literacy tests. Such restrictions might be used—and ultimately were used—to deny blacks the vote.

The debate over black suffrage drew new participants into the political fray. In 1866, when Congress debated the Fourteenth Amendment, women's rights advocates tried to join forces with abolitionist allies in the American Equal Rights Association, which (they hoped) would promote both black suffrage and woman suffrage. Most Radical Republicans, however, did not want to be saddled with the woman-suffrage plank; they feared it would impede their primary goal, black enfranchisement.

Anthony and Stanton, CA. 1870 *Women's rights advocates Susan B. Anthony (left) and Elizabeth Cady Stanton began to promote woman suffrage when the issue of black suffrage arose in 1866. They subsequently assailed the proposed Fifteenth Amendment for excluding women. "[I]n proportion as you multiply the rulers, the condition of the politically estranged is more hopeless and degraded," Stanton declared at a woman suffrage convention. By the end of the 1860s, activists had formed two competing suffragist organizations.*

This defection provoked disputes among women's rights advocates. Some argued that black suffrage would pave the way for the women's vote and that black men deserved priority. "If the elective franchise is not extended to the Negro, he is dead," explained Frederick Douglass, a longtime women's rights supporter. "Woman has a thousand ways by which she can attach herself to the ruling power of the land that we have not." But women's rights leaders Elizabeth Cady Stanton and **Susan B. Anthony** disagreed. In their view, the Fourteenth Amendment had disabled women by including the word *male*, and the Fifteenth Amendment failed to remedy this injustice. Instead, Stanton contended, the amendment established an "aristocracy of sex" and increased women's disadvantages.

The battle over black suffrage and the Fifteenth Amendment split women's rights advocates into two rival suffrage associations, formed in 1869. The Boston-based American Woman Suffrage Association, endorsed by reformers such as Julia Ward Howe and Lucy Stone, retained an alliance with male abolitionists and campaigned for woman suffrage in the states. The New York–based and more radical National Woman Suffrage Association, led by Stanton and Anthony, condemned its former male allies and promoted a federal woman suffrage amendment.

Throughout the 1870s, the rival woman suffrage associations vied for constituents. In 1869 and 1870, independent of the suffrage movement, two territories, Wyoming and Utah, enfranchised women. But suffragists failed to sway legislators elsewhere. When Susan B. Anthony mobilized about seventy women to vote nationwide in 1872, she was indicted, convicted, and fined. One woman who tried to vote, Missouri suffragist Virginia Minor, brought suit with her husband against the registrar who had excluded her. The Minors claimed that the Fourteenth Amendment enfranchised women. In *Minor* v. *Happersett* (1875), however, the Supreme Court declared that a state could constitutionally deny women the vote. Divided and rebuffed, woman suffrage advocates braced for a long struggle.

By 1870, when the Fifteenth Amendment was ratified, Congress could look back on five years of achievement. Since the start of 1865, three constitutional amendments had strengthened American democracy: the Thirteenth Amendment abolished slavery, the Fourteenth expanded civil rights, and the Fifteenth barred the denial of suffrage on the basis of race. Congress had also readmitted the former Confederate states into the Union. But after 1868, congressional momentum slowed, and the theater of action shifted to the South, where tumultuous change occurred.

RECONSTRUCTION GOVERNMENTS

During the unstable years of Presidential Reconstruction, 1865–1867, the southern states had to create new governments, revive the war-torn economy, and face the impact of emancipation. Crises abounded. War costs had devastated southern wealth, cities and factories lay in rubble, plantation labor systems disintegrated, and racial tensions flared. Beginning in 1865, freedmen organized black conventions, political meetings at which they protested ill treatment and demanded equal rights. A climate of violence prevailed. Race riots erupted in major southern cities, such as Memphis in May 1866 and New Orleans two months later. Even when Congress imposed military rule, ex-Confederates did not feel defeated. "Having reached bottom, there is hope now that we may rise again," a South Carolina planter wrote in his diary.

Congressional Reconstruction, supervised by federal troops, took effect in the spring of 1867. The Johnson regimes were dismantled, state constitutional conventions met, and voters elected new state governments, which Republicans dominated. In 1868, most former Confederate states rejoined the Union, and two years later, the last four states—Virginia, Mississippi, Georgia, and Texas—followed.

But Republican rule was very brief, lasting less than a decade in all southern states, far less in most of them, and on average under five years. Opposition from southern Democrats, the landowning elite, thousands of vigilantes, and, indeed, most white voters proved insurmountable. Still, the governments formed under Congressional Reconstruction were unique, because black men, including exslaves, participated in them. In no other society where slaves had been liberated—neither Haiti, where slaves had revolted in the 1790s, nor the British Caribbean islands, where Parliament had ended slavery in 1833—had freedmen gained democratic political rights.

A New Electorate   The Reconstruction laws of 1867–1868 transformed the southern electorate by temporarily disfranchising 10 to 15 percent of potential white voters and by enfranchising more than seven hundred thousand freedmen. Outnumbering white voters by one hundred thousand, blacks held voting majorities in five states.

The new electorate provided a base for the Republican Party, which had never existed in the South. To scornful Democrats, southern Republicans comprised three types of scoundrels: northern "carpetbaggers," who had allegedly come south seeking wealth and power (with so few possessions that they could be stuffed into traveling bags made of carpet material); southern "scalawags," predominantly poor and ignorant whites, who sought to profit from Republican rule; and hordes of uneducated freedmen, who were ready prey for Republican manipulators. Although the "carpetbag" and "scalawag" labels were derogatory and the stereotypes they conveyed inaccurate, they remain in use as a form of shorthand. Crossing class and racial lines, the hastily established Republican Party was in fact a loose coalition of diverse factions with often contradictory goals.

To northerners who moved south after the Civil War, the former Confederacy was an undeveloped region, ripe with possibility. The carpetbaggers' ranks included many former Union soldiers who hoped to buy land, open factories, build railroads, or simply enjoy the warmer climate. Albion Tourgee, a young lawyer who had served with the New York and Ohio volunteers, for example, relocated in North Carolina after the war to improve his health; there he worked as a journalist, politician, and Republican judge. Perhaps no more than twenty thousand northern migrants like Tourgee— including veterans, missionaries, teachers, and Freedmen's Bureau agents—headed south immediately after the war, and many soon returned north. But those who remained held almost one out of three state offices and wielded disproportionate political power.

Scalawags, white southerners who supported the Republicans, included some entrepreneurs who applauded party policies such as the national banking system and high protective tariffs as well as some prosperous planters, former Whigs who had opposed secession. Their numbers included a few prominent politicians, among them James Orr of South Carolina and Mississippi's governor James Alcorn, who became Republicans in order to retain influence and limit Republican radicalism. Most scalawags, however, were small farmers from the mountain regions of North Carolina, Georgia, Alabama, and Arkansas. Former Unionists who had owned no slaves and felt no loyalty toward the landowning elite, they sought to improve their economic position. Unlike carpetbaggers, they lacked commitment to black rights or black suffrage; most came from regions with few blacks and cared little whether blacks voted or not. Scalawags held the most political offices during Reconstruction, but they proved the least stable element of the southern Republican coalition: eventually, many drifted back to the Democratic fold.

Freedmen, the backbone of southern Republicanism, provided eight out of ten Republican votes. Republican rule lasted longest in states with the largest black populations—South Carolina, Mississippi, Alabama, and Louisiana. Introduced to politics in the black conventions of 1865–1867, the freedmen sought land, education, civil rights, and political equality, and they remained loyal Republicans. As an elderly freedman announced at a Georgia political convention in 1867, "We know our friends." Although Reconstruction governments depended on African American votes, freedmen held at most one in five political offices. Blacks served in all southern legislatures but constituted a majority only in the legislature of South Carolina, whose population was more than 60 percent black. In the House of Representatives, a mere 6 percent of southern members were black, and almost half of these came from South Carolina. No blacks became governor, and only two—Hiram Revels and Blanche K. Bruce, both of Mississippi—served in the U.S. Senate. (Still, the same number of African Americans served in the Senate throughout the entire twentieth century.)

RADICAL · MEMBERS
OF THE Sº. Cᴬ. LEGISLATURE.

Museum of the Confederacy

Republicans in the South Carolina Legislature, CA. 1868 *Only in South Carolina did blacks comprise a majority in the legislature and dominate the legislative process during Reconstruction. This photographic collage of "Radical" legislators, black and white, suggests the extent of black representation. "Now is the black man's day," declared a black politician. "[N]ow is our time." A northern reporter, in contrast, saw in the legislature "the spectacle of a society suddenly turned upside down." In 1874, African Americans won the majority of seats in South Carolina's state senate as well.*

Black officeholders on the state level formed a political elite. They often differed from black voters in background, education, and wealth. A disproportionate number were literate blacks who had been free before the Civil War. In the South Carolina legislature, most black members, unlike their constituents, came from large towns and cities; many had spent time in the North; and some were well-off property owners or even former slave owners. Color differences were evident, too: 43 percent of South Carolina's black state legislators were mulattos (mixed race), compared to only 7 percent of the state's black population.

Black officials and black voters often had different priorities. Most freedmen cared mainly about their economic future, especially about acquiring land; black officeholders cared most about attaining equal rights. Still, both groups shared high expectations and prized enfranchisement. "We'd walk fifteen miles in wartime to find out about the battle," a Georgia freedman declared. "We can walk fifteen miles and more to find how to vote."

Republican Rule   Large numbers of blacks participated in American government for the first time in the state constitutional conventions of 1867–1868. The South Carolina convention had a black majority, and in Louisiana half the delegates were freedmen. The conventions forged democratic changes in their state constitutions. Delegates abolished property qualifications for office holding, made many appointive offices elective, and redistricted state legislatures more equitably. All states established universal manhood suffrage.

But no state instituted land reform. When proposals for land confiscation and redistribution arose at the state conventions, they fell to defeat, as they had in Congress. Hoping to attract northern investment to the reconstructed South, southern Republicans hesitated to threaten property rights or to adopt land-reform measures that northern Republicans had rejected. South Carolina did set up a commission to buy land and make it available to freedmen, and several states changed their tax structures to force uncultivated land onto the market, but in no case was ex-Confederate land confiscated.

Once civil power shifted from the federal army to the new state governments, Republican regimes began ambitious programs of public works. They built roads, bridges, and public buildings; approved railroad bonds; and funded institutions to care for orphans, the insane, and the disabled. They also expanded state bureaucracies, raised pay for state employees, and formed state militia, in which blacks were often heavily represented. Finally, they created public-school systems, almost nonexistent in the South until then.

These changes cost millions, and taxes skyrocketed. State legislatures increased poll taxes or "head" taxes (levies on individuals); enacted luxury, sales, and occupation taxes; and imposed new property taxes. Before the war, southern states had taxed property in slaves but had barely taxed landed property. Now state governments assessed even small farmers' holdings; propertied planters felt overburdened. Although northern tax rates still exceeded southern rates, southern landowners resented the new levies. In their view, Reconstruction punished the propertied, already beset by labor problems and falling land values, in order to finance the vast expenditures of Republican legislators.

To Reconstruction's foes, Republican rule was wasteful and corrupt, the "most stupendous system of organized robbery in history." A state like Mississippi, which had an honest government, provided little basis for such charges. But critics could justifiably point to Louisiana, where the governor pocketed thousands of dollars of state funds and corruption permeated all government transactions (as indeed it had before the war). Or they could cite South Carolina, where bribery ran rampant. Besides government officials who took bribes, postwar profiteers included the railroad promoters who doled them out. Not all were Republicans. Nor did the Republican regimes in the South hold a monopoly on corruption. After the war, bribery pervaded government transactions North and South, and far more money changed hands in the North. But critics assailed Republican rule for additional reasons.

Counterattacks   Ex-Confederates spoke with dread about black enfranchisement and the "horror of Negro domination." As soon as congressional Reconstruction took effect, former Confederates campaigned to undermine it. Democratic newspapers assailed delegates to North Carolina's constitutional convention as an "Ethiopian minstrelsy" and called Louisiana's constitution "the work of ignorant Negroes cooperating with a gang of white adventurers."

Democrats delayed mobilization until southern states were readmitted to the Union and then swung into action. At first, they sought to win black votes; but when that failed, they tried other tactics. In 1868–1869, Georgia Democrats challenged the eligibility of black legislators and expelled them from office. In response, the federal government reestablished military rule in Georgia, but determined Democrats still undercut Republican power. In every southern state, they contested elections, backed dissident Republican factions, elected some Democratic legislators, and lured scalawags away from the Republican Party.

Vigilante efforts to reduce black votes bolstered the Democrats' campaigns to win white ones. Antagonism toward free blacks, long a motif in southern life, resurged after the war. In 1865, Freedmen's Bureau agents itemized outrages against blacks, including shooting, murder, rape, arson, and "inhuman beating." Vigilante groups sprang up spontaneously in all parts of the former Confederacy under names like moderators, regulators, and, in Louisiana, Knights of the White Camelia. One group rose to dominance. In the spring of 1866, six young Confederate war veterans in Tennessee formed a social club, the **Ku Klux Klan,** distinguished by elaborate rituals, hooded costumes, and secret passwords. By the election of 1868, when black men could first vote, Klan dens had spread to all southern states. Klansmen embarked on night raids to intimidate black voters. No longer a social club, the Ku Klux Klan was now a terrorist movement and a violent arm of the Democratic Party.

The Klan sought to suppress black voting, reestablish white supremacy, and topple Reconstruction governments. Its members attacked Freedmen's Bureau officials, white Republicans, black militia units, economically successful blacks, and black voters. Concentrated in areas where black and white populations were most evenly balanced and racial tensions greatest, Klan dens adapted their tactics and timing to local conditions. In Mississippi, the Klan targeted black schools; in Alabama, it concentrated on Republican officeholders. In Arkansas, terror reigned in 1868; in Georgia and Florida, Klan strength surged in 1870. Some Democrats denounced Klan members as "cutthroats and riff-raff." But Klansmen included prominent ex-Confederates, among them General Nathan Bedford Forrest, the leader of the 1864 Fort Pillow massacre, in which Confederate troops who captured a Union garrison in Tennessee murdered black soldiers who had surrendered. Vigilantism united southern whites of different social classes and drew on Confederate veterans' energy. In areas where the Klan was inactive, other vigilante groups took its place.

Republican legislatures passed laws to outlaw vigilantism, but as state militia could not enforce them, state officials sought federal help. Between May 1870 and February 1871, Congress passed three **Enforcement Acts,** each progressively more stringent. The First Enforcement Act protected black voters, but witnesses to violations were afraid to testify against vigilantes, and local juries refused to convict them. The Second Enforcement Act provided for federal supervision of southern

The Ku Klux Klan *Disguised in long white robes and hoods, Ku Klux Klansmen sometimes claimed to be the ghosts of Confederate soldiers. The Klan, which spread rapidly after 1867, sought to end Republican rule, restore white supremacy, and obliterate, in one southern editor's words, "the preposterous and wicked dogma of Negro equality."*

elections, and the Third Enforcement Act, or Ku Klux Klan Act, strengthened punishments for those who prevented blacks from voting. It also empowered the president to use federal troops to enforce the law and to suspend the writ of *habeas corpus* in areas that he declared in insurrection. (The writ of *habeas corpus* is a court order requiring that the detainer of a prisoner bring that person to court and show cause for his or her detention.) The Ku Klux Klan Act generated thousands of arrests; most terrorists, however, escaped conviction.

By 1872, the federal government had effectively suppressed the Klan, but vigilantism had served its purpose. Only a large military presence in the South could have protected black rights, and the government in Washington never provided it. Instead, federal power in the former Confederacy diminished. President Grant steadily reduced troop levels in the South; Congress allowed the Freedmen's Bureau to die in 1869; and the Enforcement acts became dead letters. White southerners, a Georgia politician told congressional investigators in 1871, could not discard "a feeling of bitterness, a feeling that the Negro is a sort of instinctual enemy of ours." The battle over Reconstruction was in essence a battle over the implications of emancipation, and it had begun as soon as the war ended.

THE IMPACT OF EMANCIPATION

"The master he says we are all free," a South Carolina slave declared in 1865. "But it don't mean we is white. And it don't mean we is equal." Emancipated slaves faced daunting handicaps. They had no property, tools, or capital; they possessed meager skills; and more than 95 percent were illiterate. Still, the exhilaration of freedom was overwhelming, as slaves realized, "Now I am for myself" and "All that I make is my own." Emancipation gave them the right to their own labor and a new sense of autonomy. Under Reconstruction, they sought to cast off white control and shed the vestiges of slavery.

Confronting Freedom　　For former slaves, liberty meant mobility. Some moved out of slave quarters and set up dwellings elsewhere on their plantations; others left their plantations entirely. Landowners found that one freed slave after another vanished, with house servants and artisans leading the way. "I have never in my life met with such ingratitude," one South Carolina mistress exclaimed when a former slave ran off. Field workers, who had less contact with whites, were more likely to stay behind. Still, flight remained tempting. "The moment they see an opportunity to improve themselves, they will move on," diarist Mary Chesnut observed.

Emancipation stirred waves of migration within the former Confederacy. Some freed slaves left the Upper South for the Deep South and the Southwest—Florida, Mississippi, Arkansas, and Texas—where planters desperately needed labor and paid higher wages. More left the countryside for towns and cities. Urban black populations sometimes doubled or tripled after emancipation; the number of blacks in small rural towns grew as well. Many migrants eventually returned to their old locales, but they tended to settle on neighboring plantations rather than with former owners. Freedom was the major goal. "I's wants to be a free man ... and nobody say nuffin to me, nor order me roun,' " an Alabama freedman told a northern journalist.

Efforts to find lost family members prompted much movement. "They had a passion, not so much for wandering as for getting together," a Freedmen's Bureau official commented. Parents sought children who had been sold; husbands and wives who had been separated by sale, or who lived on different plantations, reunited; and family members sought extended networks of kin. The Freedmen's Bureau helped former slaves get information about missing relatives and travel to find them. Bureau agents also tried to resolve conflicts that arose when spouses who had been separated under slavery married other people.

Reunification efforts often failed. Some fugitive slaves had died during the war or were untraceable. Other exslaves had formed new relationships and could not revive old ones. Still, success stories abounded. "I'se hunted an' hunted till I track you up here," one freedman told his wife, whom he found in a refugee camp twenty years after their separation by sale. Once reunited, freed blacks quickly legalized unions formed under slavery, sometimes in mass ceremonies of up to seventy couples. Legal marriage affected family life. Men asserted themselves as household heads; wives of able-bodied men often withdrew from the labor force to care for homes and families. "When I married my wife, I married her to wait on me and she has got all she can do right here for me and the children," a Tennessee freedman explained.

Black women's desire for domestic life caused labor shortages. Before the war, at least half of field workers had been women; in 1866, a southern journal claimed, men performed almost all the field labor. Still, by Reconstruction's end, many black women had returned to agricultural work as part of sharecropper families. Others took paid work in cities, as laundresses, cooks, and domestic servants. (White women often sought employment, too, because the war had incapacitated many white breadwinners, reduced the supply of future husbands, and left families impoverished.) However, former slaves continued to view stable, independent domestic life—especially the right to bring up their own children—as a major blessing of freedom. In 1870, eight out of ten black families in the cotton-producing South were two-parent families, about the same proportion as among whites.

African American Institutions   Freed blacks' desire for independence also fostered growth of black churches. In the late 1860s, some freedmen congregated at churches operated by northern missionaries; others withdrew from white-run churches and formed their own. The African Methodist Episcopal church, founded by Philadelphia blacks in the 1790s, gained thousands of new southern members. Negro Baptist churches sprouted everywhere, often growing out of plantation "praise meetings," religious gatherings organized by slaves.

Black churches offered a fervent, participatory experience. They also provided relief, raised funds for schools, and supported Republican policies. Black ministers assumed leading political roles, first in the black conventions of 1865–1866 and later in Reconstruction governments. After southern Democrats excluded most freedmen from political life at Reconstruction's end, ministers remained the main pillars of authority in black communities.

Black schools played a crucial role for freedmen, too; exslaves eagerly sought literacy for themselves and, above all, for their children. At emancipation, blacks organized their own schools, which the Freedmen's Bureau soon supervised. Northern philanthropic societies paid the wages of instructors, about half of them women. "Our work is just as much missionary work as if we were in India or China," a Sea Islands teacher commented. In 1869, the bureau reported more than four thousand black schools in the former Confederacy. Within three years, each southern state had a public school system, at least in principle, generally with separate schools for blacks and whites. Advanced schools for blacks opened to train tradespeople, teachers, and ministers. The Freedmen's Bureau and northern organizations like the American Missionary Association helped found Howard, Atlanta, and Fisk universities (1866–1867) and Hampton Institute (1868).

However, black education remained limited. Few rural blacks could reach freedmen's schools located in towns. Underfunded black public schools, similarly inaccessible to most rural black children, held classes only for short seasons and sometimes drew vigilante attacks. At the end of Reconstruction, more than 80 percent of the black population was still illiterate, though literacy rose steadily among youngsters.

Archival and Museum Collection, Hampton University

Hampton Institute *Founded in 1868, Hampton Institute in southeastern Virginia welcomed newly freed African Americans to vocational programs in agriculture, teacher training, and homemaking. These students, photographed at the school's entrance around 1870, were among Hampton's first classes.*

School segregation and other forms of racial separation were taken for granted. Some black codes of 1865–1866 had segregated public-transportation and public accommodations. Even after the invalidation of the codes, the custom of segregation continued on streetcars, steamboats, and trains as well as in churches, theaters, inns, and restaurants. In 1870, Senator Charles Sumner of Massachusetts, a steadfast Radical, began promoting a bill to desegregate schools, transportation facilities, juries, and public accommodations. After Sumner's death in 1874, Congress honored him by a new law, the **Civil Rights Act of 1875,** which included his proposals, save for the controversial school-integration provision. But in 1883, in the *Civil Rights Cases,* the Supreme Court invalidated the law; the Fourteenth Amendment did not prohibit discrimination by individuals, the Court ruled, only that perpetrated by the state.

White southerners rejected the prospect of racial integration, which they insisted would lead to racial amalgamation. "If we have social equality, we shall have intermarriage," one white southerner contended, "and if we have intermarriage, we shall degenerate." Urban blacks sometimes challenged segregation practices; black legislators promoted bills to desegregate public transit; and some black officeholders decried all forms of racial separatism. "The sooner we as a people forget our sable complexion," said a Mobile official, "the better it will be for us as a race." But most freed blacks were less interested in "social equality," in the sense of interracial mingling, than in black liberty and community. The new postwar elite—teachers, ministers, and politicians—served black constituencies and therefore had a vested interest in separate black institutions. Rural blacks, too, widely preferred all-black institutions. They had little desire to mix with whites. On the contrary, they sought freedom from white control. Above all, they wanted to secure personal independence by acquiring land.

Land, Labor, and Sharecropping   "The sole ambition of the freedman," a New Englander wrote from South Carolina in 1865, "appears to be to become the owner of a little piece of land, there to erect a humble home, and to dwell in peace and security, at his own free will and pleasure." Indeed, to freed blacks everywhere, landownership signified economic independence; "forty acres and a mule" (a phrase that originated in 1864 when Union general William T. Sherman set aside land on the South Carolina Sea Islands for black settlement) promised emancipation from plantation labor, white domination, and cotton, the "slave crop."

But freedmen's visions of landownership failed to materialize, for, as we have seen, neither Congress nor the southern states imposed large-scale land reform. Some freedmen obtained land with the help of the Union army or the Freedmen's Bureau, and black soldiers sometimes pooled resources to buy land, as on the Sea Islands of South Carolina and Georgia. In 1866, Congress passed the Southern Homestead Act, which set aside 44 million acres of public land in five southern states for freedmen and loyal whites. This acreage contained poor soil, and few former slaves had the resources to survive even until their first harvest. About four thousand blacks resettled on homesteads under the law, but most were unable to establish farms (poor whites fared little better.) By Reconstruction's end, only a small minority of former slaves owned working farms. In Georgia in 1876, for instance, blacks controlled a mere 1.3 percent of total acreage. Without large-scale land reform, obstacles to black landownership remained overwhelming.

What were these obstacles? First, most freedmen lacked the capital to buy land and the equipment needed to work it. Furthermore, white southerners generally opposed selling land to blacks. Most important, planters sought to preserve a black labor force. Freedmen, they insisted, would work only under coercion, and not at all if the possibility of landownership arose. As soon as the war ended, the white South took steps to ensure that black labor would remain available on plantations.

During Presidential Reconstruction, southern state legislatures had tried to curb black mobility and preserve a captive labor force through the black codes. Under labor contracts in effect in 1865–1866, freedmen received wages, housing, food, and clothing in exchange for fieldwork. With cash scarce, wages usually took the form of a very small share of the crop, often one-eighth or less, divided among the entire plantation work force. Freedmen's Bureau agents promoted the new labor system; they saw black wage labor as an interim arrangement that would lead to economic independence. "You must begin at the bottom of the ladder and climb up," Freedmen's Bureau head O.O. Howard exhorted a group of Louisiana freedmen in 1865.

But freedmen disliked the new wage system, especially the use of gang labor, which resembled the work pattern under slavery. Planters had complaints, too. In some regions the black labor force had shrunk to half its prewar size or less, due to the migration of freedmen and to black women's withdrawal from fieldwork. Once united in defense of slavery, planters now competed for black workers. But the freedmen, whom planters often scorned as lazy or inefficient, did not intend to work as long or as hard as they had labored under slavery. One planter claimed that workers accomplished only "two-fifths of what they did under the old system." As productivity fell, so did land values. Plummeting cotton prices and poor harvests compounded planters' woes. By 1867, an agricultural impasse had been reached: landowners lacked labor, and freedmen lacked land. But free blacks, unlike slaves, had the right to enter into contracts—or to refuse to do so—and thereby gained some leverage.

Planters and freedmen began experimenting with new labor schemes, including the division of plantations into small tenancies. **Sharecropping,** the most widespread arrangement, evolved as a compromise. Under the sharecropping system, landowners subdivided large plantations into farms of thirty to fifty acres, which they rented to freedmen under annual leases for a share of the crop, usually half. Freedmen preferred sharecropping to wage labor because it represented a step toward independence. Household heads could use the labor of family members. Moreover, a half-share of the crop far exceeded the fraction that freedmen had received as wages under the black codes. Planters often spoke of sharecropping as a concession, but they benefited, too. They retained power over tenants, because annual leases did not have to be renewed; they could expel undesirable tenants at the end of the year. Planters also shared the risk of planting with tenants: if a crop failed, both suffered the loss. Most important, planters retained control of their land and in some cases extended their holdings. The most productive land, therefore, remained in the hands of a small group of owners, as before the war. Sharecropping forced planters to relinquish daily control over the labor of freedmen but helped to preserve the planter elite.

Sharecropping arrangements varied widely. On sugar and rice plantations, the wage system continued; strong markets for those crops enabled planters to pay workers in cash—cash that cotton planters lacked. Some freedmen remained independent renters. Some landowners leased areas to white tenants, who then subcontracted with black labor. But by the end of the 1860s, sharecropping prevailed in the cotton South, and continued to expand. A severe depression in 1873 drove many black renters into sharecropping. Thousands of independent white farmers became sharecroppers as well. Stung by wartime losses and by the dismal postwar economy, they sank into debt and lost their land to creditors. Many backcountry residents, no longer able to get by on subsistence farming, shifted to cash crops like cotton and suffered the same fate. At Reconstruction's end, one-third of white farmers in Mississippi, for instance, were sharecroppers.

By 1880, 80 percent of the land in the cotton-producing states had been subdivided into tenancies, most of it farmed by sharecroppers, white and black. Indeed, white sharecroppers now outnumbered black ones, although a higher proportion of southern blacks, about 75 percent, were involved in the system. Changes in marketing and finance, meanwhile, made the sharecroppers' lot increasingly precarious.

Toward a Crop-Lien Economy

Before the Civil War, planters had depended on factors, or middlemen, who sold them supplies, extended credit, and marketed their crops through urban merchants. These long-distance credit arrangements were backed by the high value and liquidity of slave property. When slavery ended, the factorage system collapsed. The postwar South, with hundreds of thousands of tenants and sharecroppers, needed a far more localized credit network.

Into the gap stepped the rural merchants (often themselves planters), who advanced supplies to tenants and sharecroppers on credit and sold their crops to wholesalers or textile manufacturers. Because renters had no property to use as collateral, the merchants secured their loans with a lien, or claim, on each farmer's next crop. Exorbitant interest rates of 50 percent or more quickly forced many tenants and sharecroppers into a cycle of indebtedness. Owing part of the crop to a landowner for rent, a sharecropper also owed a rural merchant a large sum (perhaps amounting to the rest of his crop, or more) for supplies. Illiterate tenants who lost track of their financial arrangements often fell prey to unscrupulous merchants. "A man that didn't know how to count would always lose," an Arkansas freedman later explained. Once a tenant's debts or alleged debts exceeded the value of his crop, he was tied to the land, to cotton, and to sharecropping.

By Reconstruction's end, sharecropping and crop liens had transformed southern agriculture. They bound the region to staple production and prevented crop diversification. Despite plunging cotton prices, creditors—landowners and merchants—insisted that tenants raise only easily marketable cash crops. Short of capital, planters could no longer invest in new equipment or improve their land by crop rotation and

© Collection of the New York Historical Society

Sharecroppers during Reconstruction *By the end of the 1870s, about three out of four African Americans in the cotton-producing states had become sharecroppers. Here, sharecroppers pick cotton in Aiken, South Carolina.*

contour plowing. Soil depletion, land erosion, and agricultural backwardness soon locked much of the South into a cycle of poverty.

Trapped in perpetual debt, tenant farmers became the chief victims of the new agricultural order. Raising cotton for distant markets, for prices over which they had no control, remained the only survival route open to poor farmers, regardless of race. But low income from cotton locked them into sharecropping and crop liens, from which escape was difficult. African American tenants saw their political rights dwindle, too. As one southern regime after another returned to Democratic control, freedmen could look for protection to neither state governments nor the federal government; northern politicians were preoccupied with their own problems.

New Concerns in the North, 1868–1876

The nomination of Ulysses S. Grant for president in 1868 launched a chaotic era in national politics. Grant's two terms in office saw political scandals, a party revolt, massive depression, and steady retreat from Reconstruction policies. By the mid-1870s, northern voters cared more about the economic climate, unemployment, labor unrest, and currency problems than about the "southern question." Responsive to the shift in popular mood, Republicans became eager to end sectional conflict and turned their backs on the freedmen of the South.

Grantism   Republicans had good reason to bypass party leaders and nominate the popular Grant. A war hero, Grant was endorsed by Union veterans and widely admired throughout the North. To oppose Grant, the Democrats nominated New York governor Horatio Seymour, arch-critic of the Lincoln administration in wartime and now a foe of Reconstruction. Grant ran on personal popularity more than issues. Although he carried all but eight states, the popular vote was close; in the South, newly enfranchised freedmen provided Grant's margin of victory.

A strong leader in war, Grant proved a passive president. Although he lacked Johnson's instinct for disaster, he had little political skill. Many of his cabinet appointees were mediocre if not unscrupulous; scandals plagued his administration. In 1869, financier Jay Gould and his partner Jim Fisk tried to corner the gold market with the help of Grant's brother-in-law, a New York speculator. When gold prices tumbled, investors were ruined and Grant's reputation suffered. Then, before the president's first term ended, his vice president, Schuyler Colfax, was found to be linked to the Crédit Mobilier, a fraudulent scheme to skim off the profits of the Union Pacific Railroad. Discredited, Colfax was dropped from the Grant ticket in 1872.

More trouble lay ahead. Grant's private secretary, Orville Babcock, was unmasked in 1875 after taking money from the "whiskey ring," distillers who bribed federal agents to avoid paying millions in taxes. In 1876, voters learned that Grant's secretary of war, William E. Belknap, had taken bribes to sell lucrative Indian trading posts in Oklahoma. Impeached and disgraced, Belknap resigned.

Although uninvolved in the scandals, Grant defended his subordinates. To his critics, "Grantism" came to stand for fraud, bribery, and political corruption—evils that spread far beyond Washington. In Pennsylvania, for example, the Standard Oil Company and the Pennsylvania Railroad controlled the legislature. Urban politics also provided rich opportunities for graft and swindles. The New York City press revealed in 1872 that Democratic boss William M. Tweed, the leader of Tammany Hall, led a ring that had looted the city treasury and collected millions in kickbacks and payoffs. When Mark Twain and coauthor Charles Dudley Warner published their satiric novel *The Gilded Age* (1873), readers recognized the book's speculators, self-promoters, and opportunists as familiar types in public life. (The term "Gilded Age" was subsequently used to refer to the decades from the 1870s to the 1890s.)

Grant had some success in foreign policy. In 1872, his administration engineered the settlement of the *Alabama* claims with Britain. To compensate for damage done by Confederate-owned but British-built ships, an international tribunal awarded the United States $15.5 million. But Grant's administration faltered when it tried to add nonadjacent territory to the United States. In 1867, Johnson's secretary of state, William H. Seward, had negotiated a treaty in which the United States bought Alaska from Russia at the bargain price of $7.2 million. Although the press mocked "Seward's Ice Box," the purchase kindled expansionists' hopes. In 1870, Grant decided to annex the eastern half of the Caribbean island of Santo Domingo (today called the Dominican Republic); the territory had been passed back and forth since the late eighteenth century among France, Spain, and Haiti. Annexation, Grant believed, would promote Caribbean trade and provide a haven for persecuted southern blacks. American speculators anticipated windfalls from land sales, commerce, and mining. But Congress disliked Grant's plan. Senator Charles Sumner denounced it as an imperialist "dance of blood." The Senate rejected the annexation treaty and further diminished Grant's reputation.

As the 1872 election approached, dissident Republicans voiced fears that "Grantism" at home and abroad would ruin the party. The dissidents took action. Led by a combination of former Radicals and other Republicans left out of Grant's "Great Barbecue" (a disparaging reference to profiteers who feasted at the public trough), the president's critics formed their own party, the **Liberal Republicans.**

The Liberals' Revolt   The Liberal Republican revolt split the Republican Party and undermined support for Republican southern policy. (The label "liberal" then meant support for economic doctrines such as free trade, the gold standard, and the law of supply and demand.) Denouncing "Grantism" and "spoilsmen" (political hacks who gained party office), Liberals urged civil service reform to bring the "best men" into government. Rejecting the "regular" Republicans' high-tariff policy, they espoused free trade. Most important, Liberals decried "bayonet rule" in the South. Even some one-time Radicals claimed that Reconstruction had achieved its goal: blacks had been enfranchised and could now fend for themselves. Corruption in government, North and South, posed greater danger than Confederate resurgence, Liberals claimed. In the South, they said, corrupt Republican regimes remained in power because the "best men"—the most capable politicians—were ex-Confederates barred from office holding.

For president, the new party nominated *New York Tribune* editor Horace Greeley, who had inconsistently supported both a stringent reconstruction policy and leniency toward former rebels. The Democrats endorsed Greeley, too; their slogan was "Anything to Beat Grant." Horace Greeley campaigned so diligently that he worked himself to death making speeches from the back of a train, and died a few weeks after the election.

Grant, who won 56 percent of the popular vote, carried all the northern states and most of the sixteen southern and border states. But division among Republicans affected Reconstruction. To deprive the Liberals of a campaign issue, Grant Republicans in Congress, the "regulars," passed the Amnesty Act, which allowed most ex-Confederate officials to hold office. A flood of private amnesty acts followed. In Grant's second term, Republican desires to discard the "southern question" mounted as depression gripped the nation.

The Panic of 1873   The postwar years brought accelerated industrialization, rapid economic growth, and frantic speculation. Investors rushed to profit from rising prices, new markets, high tariffs, and seemingly boundless opportunities. Railroads led the speculative boom. In May 1869, railroad executives drove a golden spike into the ground at Promontory Point, Utah, joining the Union Pacific and Central Pacific lines. By 1873, almost four hundred railroad corporations crisscrossed the Northeast, consuming tons of coal and miles of steel rail from the mines and mills of Pennsylvania and neighboring states. Transforming the economy, the railroad boom led entrepreneurs to overspeculate, with drastic results.

Philadelphia banker Jay Cooke, who had helped finance the Union effort with his wartime bond campaign, had taken over a new transcontinental line, the Northern Pacific, in 1869. Northern Pacific securities sold briskly for several years, but in 1873 the line's construction costs outran bond sales. In September, Cooke defaulted on his obligations, and his bank, the largest in the nation, shut down. A financial panic began; other firms collapsed, as did the stock market. The Panic of 1873 triggered a five-year depression. Banks closed, farm prices plummeted, steel furnaces stood idle, and one out of four railroads failed. Within two years, eighteen thousand businesses went bankrupt; 3 million were unemployed by 1878. Wage cuts struck those still employed; labor protests mounted; and industrial violence spread. The depression of the 1870s revealed that conflicts born of industrialization had replaced sectional divisions.

The depression also fed a dispute over currency that had begun in 1865. During the Civil War, Americans had used greenbacks, a paper currency not backed by a specific weight in gold. To stabilize the postwar currency, "sound money" supporters demanded withdrawal of greenbacks from circulation. Their opponents, "easy money" advocates, such as farmers and manufacturers dependent on easy credit, wanted an expanding currency (more greenbacks). Once depression began, demands for such "easy money" rose. The issue divided both major parties and was compounded by another one: how to repay the federal debt.

In wartime, the Union government had borrowed what were then astronomical sums, mainly by selling war bonds. Bondholders wanted repayment in coin, gold or silver, even though many had paid for bonds in greenbacks. To pacify bondholders, Senator John Sherman of Ohio and other Republicans pressed for the Public Credit Act of 1869, which promised repayment in coin. With investors reassured, Sherman guided legislation through Congress that swapped the old short-term bonds for new ones payable over the next generation. In 1872, another bill in effect defined "coin" as "gold coin" by dropping the silver dollar from the official coinage. Through a feat of compromise, which placated investors and debtors, Sherman preserved the public credit and Republican unity. His Specie Resumption Act of 1875 promised to put the nation on the gold standard in 1879.

But Sherman's measures did not satisfy the Democrats, who gained control of the House in 1875. Many Democrats and some Republicans demanded restoration of the silver dollar in order to expand the currency and relieve the depression. These "free-silver" advocates secured passage of the Bland-Allison Act of 1878, which partially restored silver coinage. In 1876, other expansionists formed the **Greenback Party,** which adopted the debtors' cause and fought to keep greenbacks in circulation, though with little success. As the depression receded in 1879, the clamor for "easy money" subsided, only to resurge in the 1890s. The controversial "money question" of the 1870s, never resolved, gave politicians and voters another reason to forget about the South.

Reconstruction and the Constitution   The Supreme Court of the 1870s also played a role in weakening northern support for Reconstruction. In wartime, few cases of note had reached the Court. After the war, however, constitutional questions arose.

First, would the Court support congressional laws to protect freedmen's rights? The decision in *Ex parte* Milligan (1866) suggested not. In *Milligan*, the Court declared that a military commission established by the president or Congress could not try civilians in areas remote from war where the civil courts were functioning. Thus, special military courts to enforce the Supplementary Freedmen's Bureau Act were doomed. Second, would the Court sabotage the congressional Reconstruction plan, as Republicans feared? In *Texas* v. *White* (1869), the Court ruled that although the Union was indissoluble and secession was legally impossible, the process of Reconstruction was still constitutional. It was grounded in Congress's power to ensure each state a republican form of government and to recognize the legitimate government in any state.

But in the 1870s, the Court backed away from Reconstruction. In the **slaughterhouse cases** of 1873, the Supreme Court chipped away at the Fourteenth Amendment. The cases involved a business monopoly, not freedmen's rights, but provided an opportunity to interpret the amendment narrowly. In 1869, the Louisiana legislature had granted a monopoly over the New Orleans slaughterhouse business to one firm and closed down all other slaughterhouses in the interest of public health. The excluded butchers brought suit. The state had deprived them of their lawful occupation without due process of law, they claimed; such action violated the Fourteenth Amendment, which guaranteed that no state could "abridge the privileges or immunities" of U.S. citizens. The Supreme Court upheld the Louisiana legislature by issuing a doctrine of "dual citizenship." The Fourteenth Amendment, declared the Court, protected only the rights of *national* citizenship, such as the right of interstate travel, but not those rights that fell to citizens through *state* citizenship. The *Slaughterhouse* decision vitiated the intent of the Fourteenth Amendment—to secure freedmen's rights against state encroachment.

The Supreme Court again backed away from Reconstruction in two cases in 1876 involving the Enforcement Act of 1870, enacted to protect black suffrage.

In *United States* v. *Reese* and *United States* v. *Cruikshank*, the Supreme Court undercut the act's effectiveness. Continuing its retreat from Reconstruction, the Supreme Court in 1883 invalidated both the Civil Rights Act of 1875 and the Ku Klux Klan Act of 1871. These decisions cumulatively dismantled the Reconstruction policies that Republicans had sponsored after the war and confirmed rising northern sentiment that Reconstruction's egalitarian goals could not be enforced.

Republicans in Retreat   The Republicans did not reject Reconstruction suddenly but rather disengaged from it gradually, a process that began with Grant's election to the presidency in 1868. Not an architect of Reconstruction policy, Grant defended it. But he believed in decentralized government and hesitated to assert federal authority in local and state affairs.

In the 1870s, as northern military force shrank in the South, Republican idealism waned in the North. The Liberal Republican revolt of 1872 eroded what remained of radicalism. Among "regular" Republicans, who backed Grant, many held ambivalent views. Commercial and industrial interests now dominated both wings of the party, and few Republicans wished to rekindle sectional strife. After the Democrats won the House in 1874, support for Reconstruction became a political liability.

By 1875, the Radical Republicans, so prominent in the 1860s, had vanished. Chase, Stevens, and Sumner were dead. Other Radicals had lost office or conviction. "Waving the Bloody Shirt"—defaming Democratic opponents by reviving wartime animosity—now seemed counterproductive. Republican leaders reported that voters were "sick of carpetbag government" and tiring of both the "southern question" and the "Negro question." It seemed pointless to continue the unpopular and expensive policy of military intervention in the South to prop up Republican regimes that even President Grant found corrupt. Finally, few Republicans shared the egalitarian spirit that had animated Stevens and Sumner. Politics aside, Republican leaders and voters generally agreed with southern Democrats that blacks, although worthy of freedom, were inferior to whites. To insist on black equality would be thankless, divisive, politically suicidal—and would quash any hope of reunion between the regions. The Republicans' retreat from Reconstruction set the stage for its demise in 1877.

RECONSTRUCTION ABANDONED, 1876–1877

"We are in a very hot political contest just now," a Mississippi planter wrote to his daughter in 1875, "with a good prospect of turning out the carpetbag thieves by whom we have been robbed for the past six to ten years." Similar contests raged through the South in the 1870s, as the white resentment grew and Democratic influence surged. By the end of 1872, the Democrats had regained power in Tennessee, Virginia, Georgia, and North Carolina. Within three years, they won control in Texas, Alabama, Arkansas, and Mississippi. By 1876, Republican rule survived in only three states—South Carolina, Florida, and Louisiana. Democratic victories in state elections of 1876 and political bargaining in Washington in 1877 abruptly ended what little remained of Reconstruction.

"Redeeming" the South   Republican collapse in the South accelerated after 1872. Congressional amnesty enabled ex-Confederate officials to regain office; divisions among the Republicans weakened their party's grip on the southern electorate; and attrition diminished Republican ranks. Carpetbaggers returned North or became Democrats. Scalawags deserted in even larger numbers. Tired of northern interference and finding "home rule" by Democrats a possibility, Scalawags concluded that staying Republican meant going down with a sinking ship. Scalawag defections ruined Republican prospects. Unable to win new white votes or retain the old ones, the always-fragile Republican coalition crumbled.

Meanwhile, Democrats mobilized once-apathetic white voters. The resurrected southern Democratic Party was divided: businessmen who envisioned an industrialized "New South" opposed an agrarian faction called the Bourbons—the old planter elite. But Democrats shared one goal: to oust Republicans from office. Tactics varied by state. Alabama Democrats won by promising to cut taxes and by getting out the white vote. In Louisiana, the "White League," a vigilante organization formed in 1874, undermined Republicans. Intimidation also proved effective in Mississippi, where violent incidents—like the 1874 slaughter in Vicksburg of about three hundred blacks by rampaging whites—terrorized black voters. In 1875, the "Mississippi plan" took effect: local Democratic clubs armed their members, who dispersed Republican meetings, patrolled voter-registration places, and marched through black areas. "The Republicans are paralyzed through fear and will not act," the anguished carpetbag governor of Mississippi wrote to his wife. "Why should I fight a hopeless battle?" In 1876, South Carolina's "Rifle Clubs" and "Red Shirts," armed groups that threatened Republicans, continued the scare tactics that had worked so well in Mississippi.

Intimidation did not completely squelch black voting, but Democrats deprived Republicans of enough black votes to win state elections. In some counties, they encouraged freedmen to vote Democratic at supervised polls where voters publicly placed a card with a party label in a box. In other instances, economic pressure impeded black suffrage. Labor contracts included clauses barring attendance at political meetings; planters used eviction threats to keep sharecroppers in line. Together, intimidation and economic pressure succeeded.

"Redemption," the word Democrats used to describe their return to power, brought sweeping changes. Some states called constitutional conventions to reverse Republican policies. All cut back expenses, wiped out social programs, lowered taxes, and revised their tax systems to relieve landowners of large burdens. State courts limited the rights of tenants and sharecroppers. Most important, the Democrats, or "redeemers," used the law to ensure a stable black labor force. Legislatures restored vagrancy laws, revised crop-lien statutes to make landowners' claims superior to those of merchants, and rewrote criminal law. Local ordinances in heavily black counties often restricted hunting, fishing, gun carrying, and ownership of dogs and thereby curtailed freedmen's everyday activities. States passed severe laws against trespassing and theft; stealing livestock or wrongly taking part of a crop became grand larceny with a penalty of up to five years at hard labor. By Reconstruction's end, black convict labor was commonplace.

For the freedmen, whose aspirations rose under Republican rule, redemption was devastating. The new laws, Tennessee blacks contended at an 1875 convention, would impose "a condition of servitude scarcely less degrading than that endured before the late civil war." In the late 1870s, as the political climate grew more oppressive, an "exodus" movement spread through Mississippi, Tennessee, Texas, and Louisiana. Some African Americans became homesteaders in Kansas. After an outbreak of "Kansas fever" in 1879, four thousand **exodusters** from Mississippi and Louisiana joined about ten thousand who had reached Kansas earlier in the decade. But the vast majority of freedmen, devoid of resources, had no migration options or escape route. Mass movement of southern blacks to the North and Midwest would not gain momentum until the twentieth century.

The Election of 1876   By the autumn of 1876, with redemption almost complete, both parties sought to discard the heritage of animosity left by the war and Reconstruction. Republicans nominated Rutherford B. Hayes, three times Ohio's governor, for president. Untainted by the Grant-era scandals and popular with all factions in his party, Hayes presented himself as a "moderate" on southern policy. He favored "home rule" in the South and a guarantee of civil and political rights for all—two contradictory goals. The Democrats nominated Governor Samuel J. Tilden of New York, a millionaire corporate lawyer and political reformer, known for his assaults on the Tweed Ring that had plundered New York City's treasury. Both candidates favored sound money, endorsed civil-service reform, and decried corruption, an irony since the 1876 election would be extremely corrupt.

Tilden won the popular vote by a 3 percent margin and seemed destined to capture the 185 electoral votes needed for victory. But the Republicans challenged the pro-Tilden returns from South Carolina, Florida, and Louisiana. If they could deprive the Democrats of these nineteen electoral votes, Hayes would triumph. The Democrats,

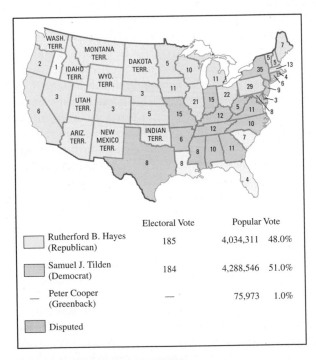

	Electoral Vote	Popular Vote	
Rutherford B. Hayes (Republican)	185	4,034,311	48.0%
Samuel J. Tilden (Democrat)	184	4,288,546	51.0%
Peter Cooper (Greenback)	—	75,973	1.0%
Disputed			

MAP 16.2 The Disputed Election of 1876

Congress resolved the contested electoral vote of 1876 in favor of Republican Rutherford B. Hayes.

who needed only one of the disputed electoral votes for victory, challenged (on a technicality) the validity of Oregon's single electoral vote, which the Republicans had won. Twenty electoral votes, therefore, were in contention. But Republicans still controlled the electoral machinery in the three unredeemed southern states, where they threw out enough Democratic ballots to declare Hayes the winner.

The nation now faced an unprecedented dilemma. Each party claimed victory in the contested states, and each accused the other of fraud. In fact, both sets of southern results involved fraud: the Republicans had discarded legitimate Democratic ballots, and the Democrats had illegally prevented freedmen from voting. In January 1877, Congress created a special electoral commission—seven Democrats, seven Republicans, and one independent—to decide which party would get the contested electoral votes. When the independent resigned, Congress replaced him with a Republican, and the commission gave Hayes the election by a vote of 8 to 7.

Congress now had to certify the new electoral vote. But Democrats controlled the House, and some threatened to obstruct debate and delay approval of the electoral vote. Had they done so, the nation would have lacked a president on inauguration day, March 4. Room for compromise remained, for many southern Democrats accepted Hayes's election: former scalawags with commercial interests still favored Republican financial policies; railroad investors expected Republican support for a southern transcontinental line. Other southerners did not mind conceding the presidency as long as the new Republican administration would leave the South alone. Republican leaders, although sure of eventual triumph, were willing to bargain as well, for candidate Hayes desired not merely victory but southern approval.

Informal negotiations ensued, at which politicians exchanged promises. Ohio Republicans and southern Democrats, who met at a Washington hotel, agreed that if Hayes won the election, he would remove federal troops from South Carolina and Louisiana, and Democrats could gain control of those states. In other bargaining sessions, southern politicians asked for federal patronage, federal aid to railroads, and federal support for internal improvements. In return, they promised to drop the filibuster, to accept Hayes as president, and to treat freedmen fairly. With the threatened filibuster broken, Congress ratified Hayes's election. Once in office, Hayes fulfilled some of the promises his Republican colleagues had made. He appointed a former Confederate as postmaster general and ordered federal troops who guarded the South Carolina and Louisiana statehouses back to their barracks. Federal soldiers remained in the South after 1877 but no longer served a political function. Democrats, meanwhile, took over state governments in Louisiana, South Carolina, and Florida. When Republican rule toppled in these states, the era of Reconstruction finally ended.

But some of the bargains struck in the **Compromise of 1877,** such as Democratic promises to treat southern blacks fairly, were forgotten, as were Hayes's pledges to ensure freedmen's rights. "When you turned us loose, you turned us loose to the sky, to the storm, to the whirlwind, and worst of all ... to the wrath of our infuriated masters," Frederick Douglass had charged at the Republican convention in 1876. "The question now is, do you mean to make good to us the promises in your Constitution?" The answer provided by the 1876 election and the 1877 Compromise was "No."

CHRONOLOGY
1863–1879

1863	President Abraham Lincoln issues Proclamation of Amnesty and Reconstruction.
1864	Wade-Davis bill passed by Congress and pocket-vetoed by Lincoln.
1865	Freedmen's Bureau established.
	Civil War ends.
	Lincoln assassinated.
	Andrew Johnson becomes president.
	Johnson issues Proclamation of Amnesty and Reconstruction.
	Ex-Confederate states hold constitutional conventions (May–December).
	Black conventions begin in the ex-Confederate states.
	Thirteenth Amendment added to the Constitution.
	Presidential Reconstruction completed.
1866	Congress enacts the Civil Rights Act of 1866 and the Supplementary Freedmen's Bureau Act over Johnson's vetoes.
	Ku Klux Klan founded in Tennessee.
	Tennessee readmitted to the Union.
	Race riots in southern cities.
	Republicans win congressional elections.
	American Equal Rights Association formed.
1867	Reconstruction Act of 1867.
	William Seward negotiates the purchase of Alaska.
	Constitutional conventions meet in the ex-Confederate states.
	Howard University founded.
1868	President Johnson is impeached, tried, and acquitted. Omnibus Act.
	Fourteenth Amendment added to the Constitution.
	Ulysses S. Grant elected president.
1869	Transcontinental railroad completed.
1870	Congress readmits the four remaining southern states to the Union.
	Fifteenth Amendment added to the Constitution.
	Enforcement Act of 1870.
1871	Second Enforcement Act.
	Ku Klux Klan Act.

1872	Liberal Republican Party formed.
	Amnesty Act.
	Alabama claims settled.
	Grant reelected president.
1873	Panic of 1873 begins (September–October), setting off a five-year depression.
1874	Democrats gain control of the House of Representatives.
1875	Civil Rights Act of 1875. Specie Resumption Act.
1876	Disputed presidential election: Rutherford B. Hayes versus Samuel J. Tilden.
1877	Electoral commission decides election in favor of Hayes.
	The last Republican-controlled governments overthrown in Florida, Louisiana, and South Carolina.
1879	"Exodus" movement spreads through several southern states.

CONCLUSION

Between 1865 and 1877, the nation experienced a series of political crises. In Washington, conflict between President Johnson and Congress led to a stringent Republican plan for restoring the South, a plan that included the radical provision of black male enfranchisement. President Johnson ineptly abetted the triumph of his foes by his defiant stance, which drove moderate Republicans into an alliance against him with Radical Republicans. In the ex-Confederate states, Republicans took over and reorganized state governments. A new electorate, in which recently freed African Americans were prominent, endorsed Republican policies. Rebuilding the South cost millions, and state expenditures soared. Objections to taxes, resentment of black suffrage, and fear of "Negro domination" spurred counterattacks on African Americans by former Confederates.

Emancipation reshaped black communities where former slaves sought new identities as free people. African Americans reconstituted their families; created black institutions, such as churches and schools; and participated in government for the first time in American history. They also took part in the transformation of southern agriculture. By Reconstruction's end, a new labor system, sharecropping, replaced slavery. Begun as a compromise between freedmen and landowners, sharecropping soon trapped African Americans and other tenant farmers in a cycle of debt; black political rights waned as well as Republicans lost control of the southern states.

The North, meanwhile, hurtled headlong into an era of industrial growth, labor unrest, and financial crises. The political scandals of the Grant administration and the impact of depression after the Panic of 1873 diverted northern attention from the South. By the mid-1870s, northern politicians were ready to discard the Reconstruction policies that Congress had imposed a decade before. Simultaneously, the southern states returned to Democratic rule, as Republican regimes toppled one by one. Reconstruction's final collapse in 1877 reflected not only a waning of northern resolve but a successful ex-Confederate campaign of violence, intimidation, and protest that had started in the 1860s. By 1877, resistance had trumped Reconstruction.

Reconstruction's end gratified both political parties. Although unable to retain a southern constituency, the Republican Party no longer faced the unpopular "southern question." The Democrats, now empowered in the former Confederacy, remained entrenched there for over a century. To be sure, the South was tied to sharecropping and economic backwardness as securely as it had once been tied to slavery. But "home rule" was firmly in place. Reconstruction's end also signified a triumph for nationalism and reunion. As the nation applauded reconciliation of South and North, Reconstruction's reputation sank. Looking back on the 1860s and 1870s, most late nineteenth-century Americans dismissed the congressional effort to reconstruct the South as a fiasco—a tragic interlude of "radical rule" or "black reconstruction" fashioned by carpetbaggers, scalawags, and Radical Republicans.

With the hindsight of a century, historians continued to regard Reconstruction as a failure, though of a different kind. No longer viewed as a misguided scheme that collapsed because of radical excess, Reconstruction is now widely seen as a democratic experiment that did not go far enough. Historians cite two main causes. First, Congress did not promote freedmen's independence through land reform; without property of their own, southern blacks lacked the economic power to defend their interests as free citizens. Property ownership, however, does not necessarily ensure political rights nor invariably provide economic security. Considering the depressed state of postwar southern agriculture, the freedmen's fate as independent farmers would likely have been perilous. Thus the land-reform question remains a subject of debate. A second cause of Reconstruction's collapse evokes less dispute: the federal government neglected to back congressional Reconstruction with military force. Given the choice between protecting blacks' rights at whatever cost and promoting reunion, the government opted for reunion. As a result, the nation's adjustment to the consequences of emancipation would continue into the twentieth century.

The Reconstruction era left some significant legacies, including the Fourteenth and Fifteenth amendments. Although neither amendment would be used to protect minority rights for almost a century, they remain monuments to the democratic zeal that swept Congress in the 1860s. The aspirations and achievements of Reconstruction also left an indelible mark on black citizens. After Reconstruction, many Americans turned to their economic futures—to railroads, factories, and mills, and to the exploitation of the country's bountiful natural resources.

17

THE TRANSFORMATION OF THE TRANS-MISSISSIPPI WEST, 1860–1900

CHAPTER OUTLINE

- Native Americans and the Trans-Mississippi West • Re-Settling the West • Southwestern Lands • Exploiting the Western Landscape
- The West of Myth and Legend

NATIVE AMERICANS AND THE TRANS-MISSISSIPPI WEST

No aspect of the transformation of the West was more visible and dramatic than the destruction of traditional Indian ways of life. Even before the newcomers poured onto the Great Plains at midcentury, Indian life in the trans-Mississippi West had changed considerably. In the Southwest, the Navajos had gradually given up migratory life in favor of settled agriculture. To the north, the Cheyenne and the Lakota Sioux, pushed out of the Great Lakes region by white settlement, had moved onto the Great Plains and had driven their enemies, the Pawnees and the Crows, farther west. These and other nomadic warrior tribes, dispersed in small bands, had followed the bison herds.

When whites invaded their territory at midcentury, these Indians resisted. Caught between a stampede of miners and settlers who took their land and the federal government that sought to force them onto reservations, Native Americans fought back. By the 1890s, confinement on reservations had become the fate of almost every Indian nation. Undaunted, Native Americans struggled to preserve their customs and rebuild their numbers.

The Plains Indians The Indians of the Great Plains inhabited three major subregions. The northern Plains, from the Dakotas and Montana southward to Nebraska, were home to large tribes, most notably the Lakota, as well as Flatheads, Blackfeet, Assiniboins, northern Cheyennes,

Arapahos, Crows, Hidatsas, and Mandans. Some of these were allies, but others were bitter enemies frequently at war. In the Central Plains, the so-called Five Civilized Tribes, driven there from the Southeast in the 1830s, pursued an agricultural life in the Indian Territory (present-day Oklahoma). Farther west, the Pawnees of Nebraska maintained the older, more settled tradition characteristic of Plains river valley culture before the introduction of horses. On the southern Plains of western Kansas, Colorado, eastern New Mexico, and Texas, the Comanches, Kiowas, Cheyennes, southern Arapahos, and Apaches maintained a migratory life appropriate to the arid environment.

Considerable diversity flourished among the Plains peoples, and customs varied even within subdivisions of the same tribe. For example, the easternmost branch of the great Sioux Nation, the Dakota Sioux of Minnesota who inhabited the wooded edge of the prairie, led a semisedentary life based on small-scale agriculture and bison hunting. In contrast, many Plains tribes—not only the Lakota Sioux, but also the Blackfeet, Crows, and Cheyennes—using horses obtained from the Spanish, roamed the High Plains to the west, and followed the bison migrations.

For all the **Plains Indians,** life revolved around extended family ties and tribal cooperation. Children were raised without physical punishment and were taught to treat each adult clan member with the respect accorded to relatives. Families and clans joined forces to hunt and farm and reached decisions by consensus.

Sioux religion, which provided the cement for village and camp life, was complex. The Lakota Sioux thought of life as a series of circles. Living within the daily cycles of the sun and moon, Lakotas were born into a circle of relatives, which broadened to the band, the tribe, the Sioux Nation, and on to animals and plants. The Lakotas also believed in a hierarchy of spirits whose help could be invoked in ceremonies like the Sun Dance. To gain access to spiritual power, or to fulfill vows made on behalf of their relatives' well-being, young men would "sacrifice" themselves by forgoing food and water, dancing until exhausted, and suffering self-torture. For example, some suspended themselves from poles or cut pieces of their flesh and placed them at the foot of the Sun Dance pole. Painter George Catlin, who recorded Great Plains Indian life before the Civil War, described such a ceremony: "Several of them, seeing me making sketches, beckoned me to look at their faces, which I watched through all this horrid operation, without being able to detect anything but the pleasantest smiles as they looked me in the eye, while I could hear the knife rip through the flesh."

On the semiarid High Plains, where rainfall averaged less than twenty inches a year, both the bison and the Native peoples adapted to the environment. The huge bison herds, which at their peak contained an estimated 30 million animals, broke into small groups in the winter and dispersed into river valleys. In the summer, they returned to the High Plains to mate and feed on the nutritious short grasses. Like the bison, the Indians dispersed across the landscape to minimize their impact on the land, wintering in the river valleys and returning to the High Plains in summer. When their horses consumed the grasses near their camps, they moved. Hunting bison not only supplied the Native peoples with food, clothing, and tipi covers, but also created a valuable trading commodity, buffalo robes. To benefit from this trade, Indians themselves, as the nineteenth century progressed, increased their harvest of animals.

The movement of miners and settlers onto the eastern High Plains in the 1850s eroded the habitat and threatened the Native American way of life. Pioneers

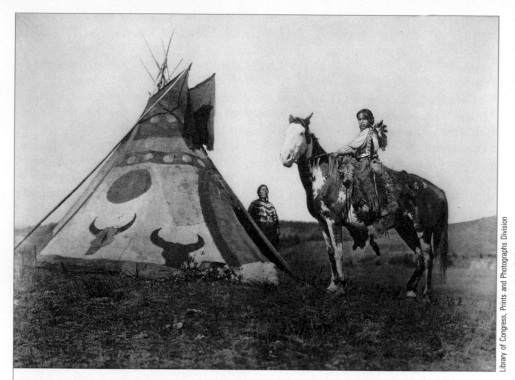

Indian Mother and Son, CA. 1890s *Indian children were taught to ride horses at an early age. Horses were a form of wealth for migratory Plains peoples and made hunting buffalo (depicted on the tipi) considerably easier.*

occupied the river valley sites, where the buffalo had wintered, and exhausted the grasses. In the 1860s, the whites began systematically to hunt the animals, often with Indian help, to supply eastern markets with carriage robes and industrial belting. **William F. "Buffalo Bill" Cody,** a famous scout, killed thousands of bison in 1867–1868 to feed railroad construction crews. Army commanders also encouraged the slaughter of buffalo to undermine Indian resistance. Inconceivable carnage resulted. Between 1872 and 1875, hunters killed 9 million buffalo, taking only the skin and leaving the carcasses to rot. By the 1880s, the once-thundering herds had been reduced to a few thousand animals, and the Native American way of life dependent on the buffalo had been ruined.

The Assault on Nomadic Indian Life

In the 1850s, Indians faced the onslaught of thousands of miners lured by the discovery of gold and silver in the Rocky Mountains. To remove the Indians, the federal government abandoned its previous position, which had treated much of the West as a vast Indian reserve, and introduced a system of smaller tribal reservations where the Indians were to be concentrated, by force if necessary.

Some Native Americans, like the Pueblos of the Southwest (who had adapted to Spanish colonial life), the Crows of Montana, and the Hidatsas of North Dakota, adjusted peacefully. Others, among them the Navajos of Arizona and New Mexico and the eastern Dakota Sioux, opposed the new policy to no avail. By 1860, eight western reservations had been established.

Significant segments of the remaining tribes on the Great Plains, more than a hundred thousand people, fought against removal. Between 1860 and 1890, the western Sioux, Cheyennes, Arapahos, Kiowas, and Comanches on the Great Plains; the Nez Percés and Bannocks in the northern Rockies; and the Apaches in the Southwest—faced the U.S. army in a series of final battles for the West.

Misunderstandings, unfulfilled promises, brutality, and butchery marked the conflict. Near Sand Creek, Colorado, in 1864, soldiers from the local militia destroyed Cheyenne and Arapaho camps. The Indians retaliated with a flurry of attacks on travelers. The governor, in a panic, authorized Colorado's white citizenry to seek out and kill hostile Indians on sight. He then activated a regiment of troops under Colonel John M. Chivington, a Methodist minister. At dawn on

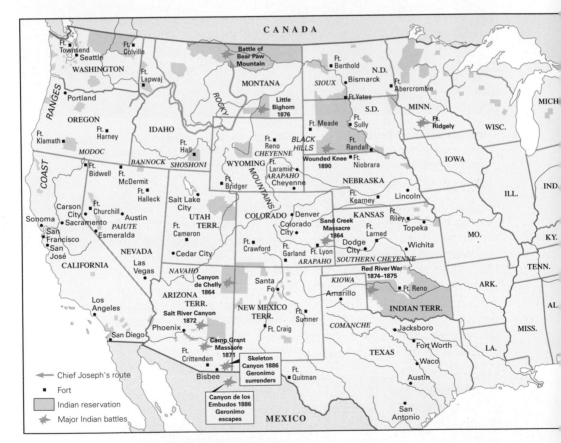

MAP 17.1 Major Indian Battles in the West

Although they were never recognized as such in the popular press, the battles between the Native Americans and the U.S. army on the Great Plains amounted to an undeclared war.

Source: © Cengage Learning. All rights reserved. No distribution allowed without express authorization.

November 29, under orders to "remember the murdered women and children on the Platte [River]," Chivington's troops massacred a peaceful band of Indians, including terrified women and children, camped at Sand Creek.

This massacre and others rekindled public debate over federal Indian policy. In response, in 1867 Congress sent a peace commission to end the fighting and set aside two large land reserves—one north of Nebraska, the other south of Kansas. There, it was hoped, the tribes would take up farming and convert to Christianity. Behind the federal government's persuasion lay the threat of force. Any Native Americans who refused to relocate, warned Commissioner of Indian Affairs Ely S. Parker, himself a Seneca Indian, "would be subject wholly to the control and supervision of military authorities, [and] ... treated as friendly or hostile as circumstances might justify."

At first, the plan appeared to work. Representatives of sixty-eight thousand southern Kiowas, Comanches, Cheyennes, and Arapahos signed the Medicine Lodge Treaty of 1867 and pledged to live in present-day Oklahoma. The following year, scattered bands of Sioux, representing nearly fifty-four thousand northern Plains Indians, signed the **Fort Laramie Treaty** and agreed to move to reservations on the so-called Great Sioux Reserve in the western part of what is now South Dakota in return for money and provisions.

But Indian dissatisfaction with the treaties ran deep. As a Sioux chief, Spotted Tail, told the commissioners, "We do not want to live like the white man.... The

Detroit Public Library, Burton Historical Collection

Buffalo Skulls at the Michigan Carbon Works, 1895 *Once the vast herds of bison had been decimated, resourceful entrepreneurs, such as those pictured here, collected the skulls and sold them for industrial use. In all, nearly 2 million tons of bones were processed.*

Great Spirit gave us hunting grounds, gave us the buffalo, the elk, the deer, and the antelope. Our fathers have taught us to hunt and live on the Plains, and we are contented." Rejecting the new system, many bands of Indians refused to move to the reservations or to remain on them once there.

In August 1868, war parties of defiant Cheyennes, Arapahos, and Sioux raided settlements in Kansas and Colorado, burning homes and killing whites. In retaliation, army troops attacked Indians, even peaceful ones, who refused confinement. That autumn, Lieutenant Colonel George Armstrong Custer's raiding party struck a sleeping Cheyenne village, killing more than a hundred warriors, shooting more than eight hundred horses, and taking fifty-three women and children prisoner. Other hostile Cheyennes and Arapahos were pursued, captured, and returned to the reservations.

In 1869, spurred on by Christian reformers, Congress established a Board of Indian Commissioners drawn from the major Protestant denominations to reform reservation abuses. But the new and inexperienced church-appointed Indian agents quickly encountered problems. Indians left the reservations in large numbers and agents were unable to restrain scheming whites who fraudulently purchased reservation lands from those who remained. Frustrated by the manipulation of Indian treaties and irritated by the ineptness of the Indian agents, Congress in 1871 abolished treaty making and replaced treaties with executive orders and acts of Congress. In the 1880s, the federal government ignored the churches' nominations for Indian agents and made its own appointments.

Caught in the sticky web of an ambiguous and deceptive federal policy, defiant Native Americans struck back in the 1870s. On the southern Plains, Kiowa, Comanche, and Cheyenne raids in the Texas Panhandle in 1874 set off the so-called Red River War. In a fierce winter campaign, regular army troops slaughtered Cheyenne fugitives near the Sappa River in Kansas. The exile of seventy-four "ringleaders" to reservations in Florida thus ended Native American independence on the southern Plains. In the Southwest, in present-day Arizona and New Mexico, the Apaches fought an intermittent guerrilla war until their leader, Geronimo, surrendered in 1886.

Custer's Last Stand, 1876   Of all the acts of Indian resistance against the new reservation policy, none aroused more passion or caused more bloodshed than the battles waged by the western Sioux tribes in the Dakotas, Montana, and Wyoming. The 1868 Treaty of Fort Laramie had set aside the Great Sioux Reserve "in perpetuity." But not all the Sioux bands had signed the treaty.

By 1873, Chief Red Cloud's Oglala band and Chief Spotted Tail's Brulé band had managed to remain on their traditional lands. To protect their hunting grounds, they raided encroaching non-Indian settlements in Nebraska and Wyoming, intimidated federal agents and harassed anyone who ventured onto their lands.

Nontreaty Sioux found a powerful leader in the Lakota Sioux chief and holy man **Sitting Bull.** Broad-shouldered and powerfully built, Sitting Bull led by example and had considerable fighting experience. "You are fools," he told the reservation Indians, "to make yourselves slaves to a piece of fat bacon, some hard-tack, and a little sugar and coffee."

Pressured by would-be settlers and developers, General William Tecumseh Sherman in 1874 sent a force under Colonel George Armstrong Custer into the Black Hills of South Dakota, near the western edge of the Great Sioux Reserve.

Lean and mustachioed, the thirty-four-year-old Custer had been a celebrity since his days as an impetuous young Civil War officer.

Custer's mission was to extract concessions from the Sioux. In November 1875, negotiations to buy the Black Hills had broken down because the Indians' asking price was deemed too high. Custer now sought to drive the Indians out of the Black Hills. Indians still outside the reservations after January 31, 1876, the government announced, would be hunted down and taken in by force.

In June 1876, leading 600 troops of the Seventh Cavalry, Custer proceeded to the Little Bighorn River area of present-day Montana, a hub of Indian resistance. On the morning of June 25, underestimating the Indian enemy and unwisely dividing his force, Custer, with 209 men, recklessly advanced against Cheyenne and Sioux warriors led by Chief Sitting Bull, who had encamped along the Little Bighorn. Custer and his outnumbered troops were wiped out.

Americans reeled from this unexpected Indian victory. Newspaper columnists groped to assess the meaning of "Custer's last stand." Some questioned the wisdom of current federal policy toward the Indians. Most, however, endorsed the federal government's determination to quash the Native American rebellion. "It is inconsistent with our civilization and with common sense," trumpeted a writer in the *New York Herald*, "to allow the Indian to roam over a country as fine as that around the Black Hills, preventing its development in order that he may shoot game and scalp his neighbors. That can never be."

Defeat at Little Bighorn made the army more determined. In Montana, troops harassed various Sioux bands for more than five years, attacking Indian camps in the dead of winter and destroying all supplies. Even Sitting Bull, who had led his band to Canada to escape the army, surrendered in 1881 for lack of provisions. The slaughter of the buffalo had wiped out his tribe's major food source.

Similar measures were used elsewhere in the West. Chief Dull Knife led some 150 survivors, including men, women, and children, north in September 1878 to join the Sioux. But the army chased them down and imprisoned them in Fort Robinson, Nebraska. When the army denied their request to stay nearer to their traditional northern lands, tribal leaders refused to cooperate. The post commander then withheld all food, water, and fuel. On a frigid night in January 1879, Dull Knife and his followers, in a desperate escape attempt, shot the guards and broke for freedom. Soldiers chased the Indians and gunned down half of them in the snow, including women and children as well as Dull Knife himself. The *Atlanta Constitution* condemned the incident as "a dastardly outrage upon humanity and a lasting disgrace to our boasted civilization." Although sporadic Indian resistance continued until the end of the century, these brutal tactics had sapped the Indians' will to resist.

"Saving" the Indians   A growing number of Americans were outraged by the federal government's flagrant violation of its Indian treaties. The Women's National Indian Rights Association, founded in 1883, and other groups took up the cause. **Helen Hunt Jackson** published *A Century of Dishonor* in 1881 to rally public opinion against the government's broken treaty obligations. "It makes little difference ... where one opens the record of the history of the Indians," she wrote; "every page and every year has its dark stain."

To encourage Indians to abandon nomadic life, reformers like Jackson advocated the creation of Indian boarding schools, much like those established for emancipated slaves. Richard Henry Pratt, a retired military officer, opened such a school in Carlisle, Pennsylvania, in 1879. Pratt believed that the Indians' customs and languages had halted their progress toward white civilization. His motto therefore became "Kill the Indian and save the man." Modeled after Carlisle, other Indian boarding schools taught farming, carpentry, dressmaking, and nursing.

Despite the reformers' best efforts, the attempt to stamp out Indian identity in the boarding schools often backfired. Forming friendships with Indians from many different tribes, boarding school students forged their own sense of Indian identity. As Mitch Walking Elk, a Cheyenne-Arapaho-Hopi student at the Phoenix Indian School, put it, "They put me in the boarding school and they cut off all my hair, gave me an education, but the Apache's still in there."

In addition to their advocacy of boarding schools, well-intentioned humanitarians concluded that the Indians' interests would be best served by breaking up the reservations, ending recognition of tribal governments, and gradually giving them the rights of citizens. In short, they proposed to eliminate the "Indian problem" by eliminating the Indians as a culturally distinct entity. Inspired by this vision, they supported the **Dawes Severalty Act,** passed in 1887.

The Dawes Act sought to turn Indians into landowners and farmers. The law emphasized severalty, or the treatment of Indians as individuals rather than as tribal members, and called for the distribution of 160 acres of reservation land for farming, or 320 acres for grazing, to each head of an Indian family who accepted the law's provisions. The remaining reservation lands were to be sold to speculators and settlers. To prevent unscrupulous people taking the lands granted to individual Indians, the government would hold each tribal member's property in trust for twenty-five years and make them U.S. citizens.

The Dawes Act did not specify a timetable for the breakup of the reservations. Few allotments were made to the Indians until the 1890s. The act proved to be a boon to speculators, who evaded its safeguards and obtained the Indians' best land. Much of what remained in Indian hands was too dry and gravelly for farming. In the twentieth century, ironically, periodic droughts and the fragile, arid High Plains landscape would push many white farmers back off the land.

Although some Native Americans who received land under the Dawes Act prospered enough to expand their holdings, countless others struggled just to survive. Hunting restrictions on the former reservation lands prevented many Indians from supplementing their limited farm yields. Alcoholism, a continuing problem exacerbated by the prevalence of whiskey as a trade item (and by the boredom that resulted from the disruption of hunting and other traditional pursuits), became more prevalent as Native Americans strove to adapt to the constraints of reservation life.

The Ghost Dance and the End of Indian Resistance on the Great Plains, 1890

Living conditions for the Sioux worsened in the late 1880s. The federal government reduced their meat rations and restricted hunting. When disease killed a third of their cattle, they became desperate. The Sioux, who still numbered almost twenty-five thousand, turned to Wovoka, a new visionary prophet popular among the Great Basin Indians in Nevada. Wovoka foresaw a

The Board of Indian Commissioners and the Dawes Act

From 1869, the Christian reformers who served on the Board of Indian Commissioners sought to improve Indian life. They persistently supported the goal, later written into the General Allotment Act (The Dawes Act, 1887), of breaking up the reservations, allotting 160 acres to each head of family, and making Indians landowner citizens of the United States. The Dawes Act corrected a glaring problem: the inability of Indians, who were not citizens, to contest in U.S. courts the fraudulent seizure of their lands. Nevertheless, by 1934, the Dawes Act had reduced Indian landholdings by nearly 65 percent.

One of the difficulties we have steadily encountered is the want of titles to land in severalty. No white man nor Indian can be expected to devote his energies to the improvement and cultivation of land to which he has no valid and sure title.... The Board, painfully conscious of this truth, has spared no labors to correct the evil, by urging the bestowment of titles to homesteads with a proper limitation of the right of alienation, to such Indians as desire to avail themselves of this privilege....

In many cases the government has failed to protect Indians even in the exclusive occupancy of lands, pledged to them under treaty stipulations. Gradually have these sacred barriers been broken down, until the onward sweeping tide of emigration has overrun them altogether, despoiling them of their homes and possessions. If this inevitable fate awaits them, let at least partial justice be done by the conferring of titles to a portion of the land which has been solemnly set apart for their use under existing treaties....

Colorado is rapidly filling up with a busy, active, and enterprising population. It is as evident to every reflecting mind that civilization and barbarism cannot long live side by side as it was to President Lincoln that the country could not long remain "half slave and half free." There is the same "irrepressible conflict" between civilization and barbarism as between freedom and slavery. Barbarism must yield to and accept civilization, flee before it, or sooner or later be overborne by it. As friends of the Indians, our efforts are directed to induce them to accept civilization while as loyal citizens we use what influence we have to induce the government to be just, patient, kind, and even generous to this weak and ignorant race....

We may moralize over the natural rights of the Indian as much as we please, but after all they have their limit. His right to the soil is only possessory. He has no title in fee. If he will cultivate it and use it as civilized men use their possessions, it will or should be well with him; but it is evident that no 12,000,000 acres of the public domain, whose hills are full of ores, and whose valleys are waiting for diligent hands to "dress and keep them," in obedience to the divine command, can long be kept simply as a park, in which wild beasts are hunted by wilder men. This Anglo-Saxon race will not allow the car of civilization to stop long at any line of latitude or longitude on our broad domain. If the Indian in his wildness plants himself on the track, he must inevitably be crushed by it. But when he sets his face and his heart towards civilization, ... then it becomes alike the interest and the duty both of the government and the people to afford all needed aid.

Questions

1. *Why did reformers draw a parallel between the treatment of slaves and Indians?*

2. *Why did the Indian Commissioners link the rights of citizenship to the reduction of tribal lands?*

Source: Eleventh Annual Report of the Board of Indian Commissioners, 1879 *(Washington, DC: U.S. Government Printing Office, 1880), pp. 5, 11, 12.*

catastrophic event that would bring the return of dead relatives, the restoration of the bison herds, and the renewal of traditional life. Some versions of his vision included the destruction of European Americans and their removal from Indian lands. To bring on this new day, the prophet preached a return to traditional ethics, and taught his followers a cycle of ritual songs and dance steps known as the **Ghost Dance.**

In the fall of 1890, as the Ghost Dance movement spread among the Sioux in the Dakota Territory, Indian officials grew alarmed. The local reservation agent decided that Chief Sitting Bull, whose cabin on the reservation had become a rallying point for the Ghost Dance movement, must be arrested. On a freezing, drizzly December morning, he dispatched Indian policemen from the agency to take Sitting Bull into custody. When the chief was pulled from his cabin, shots rang out, and Sitting Bull was mortally wounded. As bullets whizzed by, Sitting Bull's horse began to perform the tricks it remembered from its days in the Wild West show. Observers were terrified, convinced that the spirit of the dead chief had entered his horse.

Two weeks later, one of the bloodiest episodes of Indian–white strife on the Plains occurred. On December 29, as the Seventh Cavalry was rounding up 340 starving and freezing Sioux at **Wounded Knee,** South Dakota, a shot was fired. The soldiers responded with cannon fire. Within minutes three hundred Indians, including seven infants, were slaughtered. Three days later, a baby who had miraculously

Wounded Knee, Pine Ridge Reservation, South Dakota, 1890 *Thrown into an open trench, the frozen bodies of the Sioux slaughtered at Wounded Knee were a grim reminder that the U.S. army would brook no opposition to its control of Indian reservations.*

Denver Public Library, Western History Division

survived was found wrapped in a blanket under the snow. She wore a buckskin cap on which a beadwork American flag had been embroidered. Brigadier General L.W. Colby, who adopted the baby, named her Marguerite, but the Indians called her Lost Bird.

As the frozen corpses at Wounded Knee were dumped into mass graves, a generation of Indian–white conflict on the Great Plains shuddered to a close. Lost Bird, with her poignantly patriotic beadwork cap, highlights the irony of the Plains Indians' response to white expansion. Many Natives did try to adapt to non-Indian ways, and some succeeded fully. Goodbird, the son of Buffalo Bird Woman, became a Congregational minister, a prosperous farmer, and a leader of the Hidatsa tribe. He carefully blended his traditional Indian religious beliefs with Christianity. Others struggled with poverty. Driven onto reservations, many Indians became dependent on governmental support. By 1900, the Plains Indian population had shrunk from nearly a quarter-million to just over a hundred thousand. Nevertheless, the population began to increase slowly after 1900. Against overwhelming odds, the pride, religious traditions, and cultural identities of the Plains Indians survived all efforts at eradication.

Unlike the nomadic western Sioux, the more settled Navajos of the Southwest adjusted more successfully to the reservation system, preserving traditional ways and adapting to their new locations. By 1900, the Navajos had tripled their reservation land, dramatically increased their numbers and their herds, and carved out for themselves a distinct place in Arizona and New Mexico.

In the name of civilization and progress, whites after the Civil War had forced Indians off their lands in an effort that involved a mixture of sincere (if misguided) benevolence, coercion wrapped in an aura of legality, and outbursts of naked violence. Many Americans felt only contempt for Indians and greed for their land. Others had tried to uplift and Christianize the natives. Both groups, however, were blind to the value of Native American life and traditions. And both were unsuccessful in their attempts to shatter proud peoples and their ancient cultures.

RE-SETTLING THE WEST

The successive defeats of the Native Americans and their removal to reservations opened a vast territory for settlement. In the 1840s, when nearly a quarter-million Americans had trudged overland to Oregon and California, they had typically endured a six- to eight-month trip in ox-drawn wagons. After 1870, railroad expansion made the trip faster and considerably easier. In the next three decades, more land was parceled out into farms than in the previous 250 years of American history combined, and agricultural production doubled.

The First Trans-continental Railroad Passed in 1862, the Pacific Railroad Act authorized the construction of a new transcontinental link. The act provided grants of land and other subsidies to the railroads for each mile of track laid, which made them the largest landholders in the West. More than any other factor, the expansion of these railroads accelerated the transformation of everyday life west of the Mississippi.

Building the railroad took backbreaking work. Searching for inexpensive labor, the railroads turned to immigrants. The Central Pacific employed Chinese workers to chip and blast rail bed out of solid rock in the Sierra Nevada. The railroad preferred the Chinese because they worked hard for low wages, did not drink, and furnished their own food and tents. Nearly twelve thousand Chinese graded the roadbed while Irish, Mexican American, and black workers put down the track.

On May 10, 1869, Americans celebrated the completion of the first railroad spanning North America. As the two sets of tracks—the Union Pacific's, stretching westward from Omaha, Nebraska, and the Central Pacific's, reaching eastward from Sacramento, California—met at Promontory Point, Utah, beaming officials drove in a final ceremonial golden spike. The nation's vast midsection was now far more accessible than it had ever been.

The railroads sped up western development. In the battles against Native Americans, the army shipped horses and men west in the dead of winter to attack the Indians when they were most vulnerable. From the same trains, hunters gained quick access to the bison ranges and increased their harvest of the animals. Once Indian resistance had been crushed, the railroads hastened the arrival of new settlers and later shipped their cattle and grain to eastern urban markets. Railroads even supplied special detectives to support local police in towns along their lines.

Settlers and the Railroad   During the decade after the passage of the Pacific Railroad Act, Congress awarded the railroads 170 million acres, worth more than half a billion dollars. By 1893, Minnesota and Washington had also deeded to railroad companies a quarter of their state lands. As mighty landowners, the railroads had a unique opportunity to shape settlement in the region—and to reap enormous profits.

The railroads set up land sales offices and sent agents to the East Coast to recruit settlers. While the agents glorified the West as a new Garden of Eden, the land bureaus offered prospective buyers long-term loans and free transportation. Acknowledging that life on the Great Plains could be lonely, the promoters advised young men to bring their wives (because "maidens are scarce") and to emigrate as entire families and with friends.

One unintended consequence of these land promotions was to make land available to single women, or "girl homesteaders" as they were known at the time. In Wyoming, single women made up more than 18 percent of the claimants. Women filed 10 to 20 percent of the claims in Colorado, sometimes as individuals and sometimes to add to family holdings.

In addition to the millions of American migrants, the railroads helped bring nearly 2.2 million foreign-born settlers to the trans-Mississippi West between 1870 and 1900. Some agents recruited whole villages of Germans to relocate to the North Dakota plains. Irish laborers hired to lay track could be found in every town along the rail lines. By 1905, the Santa Fe Railroad alone had transported sixty thousand Russian Mennonites to the fertile Kansas plains where black pioneers called exodusters had preceded them in the 1870s (see Chapter 16).

The railroads influenced agriculture as well. To ensure repayment of money owed to them, the railroads urged farmers to specialize in cash crops—wheat on the northern Plains, corn in Iowa and Kansas, cotton in Texas. Although these crops initially brought in high revenues, many farmers grew dependent on income from a single crop and became vulnerable to fluctuating market forces.

Homesteading on the Great Plains   Liberalized land laws pulled settlers westward. The 1862 Homestead Act reflected the Republican Party's belief that free land would promote economic opportunity. It offered 160 acres of land to anyone who would pay a ten-dollar registration fee, live on the land for five years, and cultivate it. Although nearly four hundred thousand families claimed land under its provisions between 1860 and 1900, the law did not function as Congress had envisioned. Unscrupulous speculators filed false claims for the choicest locations, and railroads acquired huge landholdings. Only one acre in every nine went to the pioneers for whom it was intended.

The 160-acre limit specified by the Homestead Act created a second problem. On the rich soils of Iowa or in the fertile lands in Oregon, and Washington, a 160-acre farm was ample, but in the drier areas west of the hundredth meridian, a farmer needed more land. In 1873, to rectify this problem, Congress passed the Timber Culture Act, which gave homesteaders an additional 160 acres if they planted trees on 40 acres. Congress enacted the Desert Land Act in 1877, which made 640 acres available at $1.25 an acre, and the Timber and Stone Act of 1878, which permitted the purchase of up to 160 acres of forest land for $2.50 an acre. However, these measures were abused by grasping speculators, lumber-company representatives, and cattle ranchers. Yet, even though families did not receive as much land as Congress had intended, federal laws kept alive the dream of the West as a place for new beginnings.

In addition to problems caused by insufficient rainfall in many regions, almost all settlers faced difficult psychological adjustments to frontier life. The first years of settlement were the most difficult. Toiling to build a house, plant the first crop, and dig a well, the pioneers put in an average of sixty-eight hours of backbreaking work a week in isolated surroundings. Howard Ruede, a Pennsylvania printer who migrated to Kansas to farm, wrote home in 1877 complaining about the mosquitoes and bedbugs infesting his house, which was cut out of thick grass sod and dug into the ground. He and countless others saw their shining vision of idyllic farm life quickly dim. For blacks who emigrated from the South to Kansas and other parts of the Plains after the Civil War, prejudice compounded the burdens of adjusting to a different life.

Many women found adaptation to Plains frontier life especially difficult. At least initially, some were enchanted by the landscape. But far more were struck by the "horrible tribes of Mosquitoes," the violent drenching summer thunderstorms with hailstones as "big as hen's eggs" and blinding winter blizzards, and the crude sod huts that served as their early homes because of the scarcity of timber. One woman burst into tears upon first seeing her new sod house. The young bride angrily informed her husband that her father had built a better house for his hogs.

The high transience rate on the Great Plains in these years reflected the difficulty that newcomers faced in adjusting. Nearly half of those who staked homestead claims in Kansas between 1862 and 1890 gave up and moved on. However, in places like Minnesota and the Pacific Northwest that were populated by Germans, Norwegians, and other immigrants with a tradition of family prosperity tied to continuous landownership, the persistence rate (or percentage of people staying for a decade or more) could be considerably higher.

Many who weathered the lean early years came to identify deeply with the land. Within a decade, the typical Plains family that had "stuck it out" had moved into a new wood-framed house and had fixed up the front parlor. Women worked particularly hard on these farms and took pride in their accomplishments. "Just done the chores," wrote one woman to a friend. "I went fence mending and getting out cattle ... and came in after sundown. I fed my White Leghorns [chickens] and then sat on the step to read over your letter. I forgot my wet feet and shoes full of gravel and giggled joyously."

New Farms, New Markets   Farmers on the Plains took advantage of advances in farm mechanization and the development of improved strains of wheat and corn to boost production dramatically. Efficient steel plows; specially designed wheat planters; and improved grain binders, threshers, and windmills enabled the typical Great Plains farmer of the late nineteenth century to increase the land's yield tenfold.

Barbed wire, patented in 1874, was another crucial invention that permitted farmers to keep roving livestock out of their crops. But fencing the land touched off violent clashes between farmers and cattle ranchers, who demanded the right to let their herds roam freely until the roundup. Generally, the farmers won.

New machinery together with increased demand for wheat, milk, and other farm products created the impression that farming was entering a period of unparalleled prosperity. But few fully understood the perils of pursuing agriculture as a livelihood. The cost of the land, horses, machinery, and seed needed to start up a farm could exceed twelve hundred dollars, far more than the annual earnings of the average industrial worker. Faced with substantial mortgage payments, many farmers had to specialize in a crop such as wheat or corn that would fetch high prices. This specialization made them dependent on the railroads for shipping and put them at the mercy of the international grain market's shifting prices.

Far from being an independent producer, the western grain grower competed in a complex world market economy. High demand could bring prosperity, but when world overproduction forced grain prices down, the heavily indebted grower faced ruin. Confronted with these realities, many Plains farmers quickly abandoned the illusion of frontier independence and easy wealth.

Unpredictable rainfall and weather conditions further exacerbated homesteaders' difficulties west of the hundredth meridian, where rainfall averaged less than twenty inches a year. Farmers compensated through "dry farming"—plowing deeply to stimulate the capillary action of the soils and harrowing lightly to raise a covering of dirt that would retain precious moisture after a rainfall. They also built windmills and diverted creeks for irrigation. But the onset of unusually dry years in the 1870s, together with grasshopper infestations and the major economic depression that struck the United States between 1873 and 1878 (see Chapter 16), made the plight of some midwesterners desperate.

Building a Society and Achieving Statehood

Despite the hardships, many remote farm settlements blossomed into thriving communities. Churches and Sunday schools became humming centers of social activity as well as of worship. Neighbors readily lent a hand to the farmer whose barn had burned or whose family was sick. Cooperation was a practical necessity and a form of insurance in a rugged environment where everyone was vulnerable to instant misfortune or even disaster.

When the population increased, local boosters lobbied to turn the territory into a state. Achieving statehood required the residents of the territory to petition Congress to pass an enabling act and then to elect delegates for a state constitutional convention. Once the state constitution had been drawn up and ratified by popular vote, the territory applied to Congress for admission as a state.

Under these procedures, Kansas entered the Union in 1861, followed by Nevada in 1864, Nebraska in 1867, and Colorado in 1876. Not until 1889 did

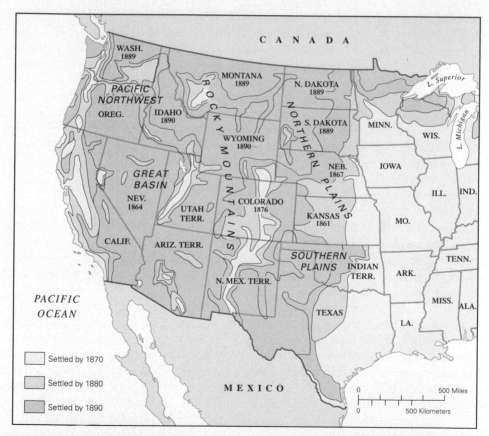

MAP 17.2   The Settlement of the Trans-Mississippi West, 1860–1890

The West was not settled by a movement of peoples gradually creeping westward from the East. Rather, settlers first occupied California and the Midwest and then filled up the nation's vast interior.

Source: © Cengage Learning. All rights reserved. No distribution allowed without express authorization.

North Dakota, South Dakota, Montana, and Washington gain statehood. Wyoming and Idaho followed the next year, and Utah in 1896. Oklahoma's admission in 1907 and Arizona's and New Mexico's in 1912 completed the process of creating states in the trans-Mississippi West.

Although generally socially conservative, the new state governments supported woman suffrage. As territories became states, pioneer women battled for the vote. Seven western states held referenda on this issue between 1870 and 1910. Success came first in the Wyoming Territory, where men outnumbered women six to one. The tiny legislature enfranchised women in 1869 in the hope that it would attract women, families, and economic growth. The Utah Territory followed in 1870 and reaffirmed its support for woman suffrage when it became a state. Nebraska in 1867 and Colorado in 1876 permitted women to vote in school elections. Although these successes were significant, by 1910 only four states—Idaho, Wyoming, Utah, and Colorado—had granted women full voting rights.

The Spread of Mormonism   In 1847, members of the Church of Jesus Christ of Latter-day Saints—known as Mormons—had escaped persecution by moving to the Great Salt Lake Valley. Led by Brigham Young, their prophet-president, and a Council of Twelve Apostles, they sought to create the independent country of Deseret. Their faith emphasized self-sufficiency and commitment to family. In the next two decades, recruitment in Great Britain and the Scandinavian countries boosted their numbers to more than 100,000. These Mormon communities increasingly conflicted with non-Mormons and with the U.S. government, which disapproved of the church's involvement in politics, its communal business practices, and its support of polygamy or plural marriage.

The Mormons tried to be economically independent. In 1869, they developed their own railroad branches connecting Salt Lake City and Ogden to the Central Pacific Railroad and set up Zion's Cooperative Mercantile Institution to control wholesale and retail activities. They asked all Mormons to abstain from coffee, tea, and alcohol, and established their own People's Party to mobilize the Mormon vote.

But a series of federal acts and court decisions, starting with the Morrill Anti-Bigamy Act in 1862, challenged the authority of their church and their practice of polygamy. In *United States* v. *Reynolds* (1879), the Supreme Court declared plural marriages unlawful and held that freedom of religion did not protect religious practices. Then, in 1887, the **Edmunds-Tucker Act** dissolved the church corporation, limited the church's assets to $50,000, abolished women's right to vote, and put its properties and funds into receivership (control by the courts).

In response, in 1890 the church president publicly announced the official end of polygamy. A year later, the Mormons dissolved their People's Party. The church supported the application for statehood, which was granted in 1896. Confiscated church properties were returned, voting rights were restored, and jailed polygamists were pardoned, but the balance between sacred and secular had permanently shifted. Mormon settlements would continue in the twentieth century to draw new members and influence development in western communities.

SOUTHWESTERN LANDS

The annexation of Texas in 1845 and the Treaty of Guadalupe Hidalgo that had ended the Mexican-American War in 1848 ceded to the United States an immense territory, part of which became Texas, California, Arizona, and New Mexico. At the time, Mexicans had controlled vast expanses of the Southwest, maintaining their own churches, large ranching operations, and trade with the Indians. Although the United States had pledged to protect the property of Mexicans who remained on American soil, over the next three decades American ranchers and settlers forced much of the Spanish-speaking population off the land. Mexicans who stayed in the region adapted to the new Anglo society with varying degrees of success.

In Texas, the struggle for independence from Mexico had left a legacy of bitterness and misunderstanding. After 1848, Texas cotton planters confiscated Mexican lands and began a racist campaign that labeled Mexicans as nonwhite. Angered by their loss of land and discriminatory treatment, Mexican bandits retaliated by raiding American communities. Tensions peaked in 1859 when Juan Cortina, a Mexican rancher, attacked the Anglo border community of Brownsville, Texas, and freed all the prisoners in jail. Cortina battled the U.S. army for years until the Mexican government, fearing a U.S. invasion, imprisoned him in 1875.

Mexican Americans in California in the 1850s and 1860s faced similar pressures. A cycle of flood and drought, together with a slumping cattle industry, had ruined many of the large southern California ranches owned by the *californios*, Spanish-speaking descendants of the original Spanish settlers. The collapse of the ranch economy forced many of them to retreat into segregated urban neighborhoods called barrios. Spanish-surnamed citizens made up nearly half the 2,640 residents of Santa Barbara, California, in 1870; ten years later, after an influx of new settlers, they comprised barely a quarter of the population.

In many western states, Mexicans, Native Americans, and Chinese experienced similar patterns of racial discrimination, manipulation, and exclusion. At first, the number of new "Anglos" was small. As the number of whites increased, they identified minority racial, cultural, and language differences as marks of inferiority. White state legislators passed laws that made ownership of property difficult for non-Anglos. Relegated to a migratory labor force, non-Anglos were tagged as shiftless and irresponsible. Yet their labor made possible increased prosperity for the farmers, railroads, and households that hired them.

The cultural adaptation of Spanish-speaking Americans to Anglo society initially unfolded more smoothly in Arizona and New Mexico, where Spanish settlement had been sparse and a small class of wealthy Mexican landowners had long dominated a poor, illiterate peasantry. Moreover, since the 1820s, well-to-do Mexicans in Tucson, Arizona, had educated their children in the United States and formed trading partnerships and business alliances with Americans. One of the most successful was Estevan Ochoa, who began a long-distance freight business in 1859 with a U.S. partner and then expanded it into a lucrative merchandising, mining, and sheep-raising operation.

The success of men such as Ochoa, who became mayor of Tucson, helped moderate American settlers' antagonistic attitudes. So, too, did the work of popular writers like Helen Hunt Jackson, who sentimentalized the colonial Spanish past. Jackson's 1884 romance *Ramona*, a tale of the doomed love of a Hispanicized mixed-blood (Irish-Indian) woman set on a California ranch overwhelmed by the onrushing tide of Anglo civilization, was enormously popular. Jackson's novel also appealed to upper-class Mexican Americans known as *Nuevomexicanos* who traced their lineage back to the Spanish conquest.

Still, conflicts over property persisted in Arizona and New Mexico. In the 1880s, Mexican American ranchers organized themselves into a self-protection vigilante group called Las Gorras Blancas (the **White Caps**). In 1888, they tore up railroad tracks and attacked both Anglo newcomers and those upper-class Hispanics who had fenced acreage previously considered public grazing land. But this vigilante action did not stop the Anglo-dominated corporate ranchers from steadily increasing their land holdings. In towns and cities, discrimination limited the economic opportunities for Mexican American businessmen and the Spanish-speaking population as a whole became more impoverished. Even in Tucson, where the Mexican American elite enjoyed considerable economic and political success, 80 percent of the Mexican Americans in the work force were laborers in 1880, taking jobs as butchers, barbers, cowboys, and railroad workers.

As increasing numbers of Mexican American men were forced to search for seasonal migrant work, women took responsibility for holding families and communities together. Women managed the households and fostered group identification by maintaining traditional customs, kinship ties, and allegiance to the Catholic Church. They tended garden plots and traded food, soap, and produce with other women, generally stabilizing the community in times of drought or persecution by Anglos.

Violence and discrimination against Spanish-speaking citizens of the Southwest escalated in the 1890s, a time of rising racism in the United States. Rioters in Beeville and Laredo, Texas, in 1894 and 1899 attacked and beat up Mexican Americans. Whites increasingly labeled Mexican Americans as violent and lazy. For Spanish-speaking citizens, the battle for fair treatment and respect would continue into the twentieth century.

EXPLOITING THE WESTERN LANDSCAPE

The displacement of Mexican American and Native peoples from their lands opened the way for the exploitation of the natural environment in the trans-Mississippi West. Between 1860 and 1900, a generation of Americans sought to strike it rich. Although the mining, ranching, and farming "bonanzas" promised unheard-of wealth, they set in motion a boom-and-bust economy in which some succeeded but others went bankrupt or barely survived.

The Mining Frontier   In the half-century that began with the California gold rush in 1849, a series of mining booms swept from the Southwest northward into Canada and Alaska. In 1853, Henry Comstock, an illiterate prospector, stumbled on the rich **Comstock Lode** along Nevada's Carson River. Later in the same decade, prospectors swarmed into the

Rocky Mountains and uncovered deep veins of gold and silver near present-day Denver. Over the next five decades, gold was discovered in Idaho, Montana, Wyoming, South Dakota, and, in 1896, in the Canadian Klondike. Although the popular press clearly exaggerated reports of miners scooping up gold by the panful, by 1900 more than a billion dollars' worth of gold had been mined in California alone.

The early discoveries of "placer" gold, panned from streams, attracted a young male population thirsting for wealth and reinforced the myth of mining country as "a poor man's paradise." In contrast to the Great Plains, where ethnic groups recreated their own ethnic enclaves, western mining camps became ethnic melting pots. In the California census of 1860, more than thirty-three thousand Irish and thirty-four thousand Chinese had staked out early claims.

Although a few prospectors became fabulously wealthy, the experience of Henry Comstock, who sold out one claim for eleven thousand dollars and another for two mules, was more typical. Because the larger gold and silver deposits lay embedded in veins of quartz deep within the earth, extracting them required huge investments in expensive equipment. Deep shafts had to be blasted into the rock. Once lifted to the surface, the rock had to be crushed and flushed with mercury or cyanide to collect the silver, which was then smelted into ingots. No sooner had the major discoveries been made, therefore, than large mining companies backed by eastern or British capital bought them out and took them over.

Life in the new mining towns was vibrant but unpredictable. Men outnumbered women three to one. Money quickly earned was even more rapidly lost. During the heyday of the Comstock Lode in the 1860s and 1870s, Virginia City, Nevada, erupted in an orgy of speculation and building. Started as a shantytown in 1859, it swelled by 1873 into a thriving metropolis of twenty thousand people complete with elaborate mansions, a six-story hotel, an opera house, 131 saloons, four banks, its own Chinatown, and uncounted brothels. Of the 138 prostitutes noted in the 1870 census, 43 were Chinese women who worked as sexual slaves.

The boom-and-bust cycle evident in Virginia City was repeated in towns across the West. Mark Twain captured the thrill of the mining "stampedes" in *Roughing It* (1872). "Every few days," wrote Twain, "news would come of the discovery of a brand-new mining region: immediately the papers would teem with accounts of its richness, and away the surplus population would scamper to take possession. By the time I was fairly inoculated with the disease, 'Esmeralda' had just had a run and 'Humboldt' was beginning to shriek for attention. 'Humboldt! Humboldt!' was the new cry, and straightway Humboldt, the newest of the new, the richest of the rich, the most marvelous of the marvelous discoveries in silver-land, was occupying two columns of the public prints to 'Esmeralda's' one."

The gold rush mania also spurred the growth of settlement in Alaska. Small strikes there in 1869, two years after the United States had purchased the territory from Russia, brought the first prospectors. More miners arrived in the 1880s. But it was the discovery of gold in the Canadian Klondike in 1897 that brought thousands of prospectors into the area and eventually enabled Alaska to establish its own territorial government in 1912.

Word of new ore deposits like the ones in Alaska lured transient populations salivating to get rich. Miners typically earned about $2,000 a year at a time when teachers made $450 to $650 and domestic help $250 to $350. But the work was extremely dangerous. One journalist commented that "no premature explosion of blasts, crushing in of timbers, caving of earth or rock—no accident of any kind is so much feared ... or is more terrible than a great fire in a large mine. It is hell...." One out of eighty miners died annually in the 1870s. Most prospectors earned only enough to go elsewhere, perhaps buy some land, and try again. Nevertheless, the production of millions of ounces of gold and silver stimulated the economy, lured foreign investors, and helped usher the United States into the mainstream of the world economy.

Progress came at a high cost to the environment. Hydraulic mining—which used water cannons to dislodge minerals—polluted rivers, turned creeks brown, and flushed millions of tons of silt into valleys. The scarred landscape that remained was littered with rock and gravel filled with traces of mercury and cyanide, and nothing would grow on it. Smelters spewed dense smoke containing lead, arsenic, and other carcinogenic chemicals, often sickening those who lived nearby. The devastation is still evident today.

Cowboys and the Cattle Frontier   The feverish growth of open-range cattle ranching paralleled the expansion of the mining frontier during the 1860s and 1870s. In this case, astute businessmen and railroad entrepreneurs, eager to fund their new investments in miles of track, promoted cattle herding as the new route to fame and fortune. The cowboy, once scorned as a ne'er-do-well and drifter, was now glorified as a man of rough-hewn integrity and self-reliant strength.

In 1868, Joseph G. McCoy, a young cattle dealer from Springfield, Illinois, shrewdly combined organizational and promotional skills to turn the cattle industry into a new money-maker. With the forced relocation of the Plains Indians onto reservations and the extension of the railroads into Kansas after the Civil War, McCoy realized that cattle dealers could now amass enormous fortunes by raising steers cheaply in Texas and bringing them north for shipment to eastern urban markets.

McCoy built a new stockyard in Abilene, Kansas. By guaranteeing to transport his steers in railcars to hungry eastern markets, he obtained a five-dollar kickback from the railroads on each cattle car shipped. To make the overland cattle drives from Texas to Abilene easier, McCoy also helped survey and shorten the Chisholm Trail in Kansas. Finally, in a clever feat of showmanship, he organized the first Wild West show, sending four Texas cowboys to St. Louis and Chicago, where they staged roping and riding exhibitions that attracted enthusiastic crowds. At the end of his first year in business, thirty-five thousand steers were sold in Abilene; the following year the number more than doubled.

The great **cattle drives** of the 1860s and 1870s turned into a bonanza for herd owners. Steers purchased in Texas at nine dollars a head could be sold in Abilene, after deducting four dollars in trail expenses, for twenty-eight dollars. A herd of two thousand head could thus bring a tidy thirty-thousand-dollar profit. But the cattlemen, like the grain growers farther north on the Great Plains, lived at the mercy of high interest rates and an unstable market. During the financial panic of 1873, cattle drovers fell into bankruptcy by the hundreds.

Little of the money made by the large-scale cattle ranchers found its way into the pockets of the cowboys themselves. The typical cowpunchers who drove herds through the dirt and dust from southern Texas to Abilene earned a mere thirty dollars a month, about the same as common laborers. They also braved the gangs of cattle thieves that operated along the trails. The most notorious of the cattle rustlers, William H. Bonney, better known as Billy the Kid, may have murdered as many as eleven men before he was killed by a sheriff in 1881 at the age of twenty-one. The long hours, low pay, and hazardous work discouraged older ranch hands from applying. Most cowboys were men in their teens and twenties who worked for a year or two and then pursued different livelihoods.

Of the estimated 35,000 to 55,000 men who rode the trails in these years, nearly one-fifth were black or Mexican. Barred by discrimination from many other trades, blacks enjoyed the freedom of life on the trail. Although they were excluded from the position of trail boss, they distinguished themselves as resourceful and shrewd cowpunchers. **Nat Love,** the son of Tennessee slaves, left for Kansas after the Civil War to work for Texas cattle companies. As chief brander, he moved through Texas and Arizona "dancing, drinking, and shooting up the town." On July 4, 1876, when the Black Hills gold rush was in full swing, Love delivered three thousand head of cattle to a point near the hills and rode into Deadwood to celebrate. Local miners and gamblers had raised prize money for roping and shooting contests, and Nat Love won both, as well as a new title, Deadwood Dick.

Close relationships sometimes developed between black and white cowboys. Shortly before Charles Goodnight, a white pioneer trailblazer, died in 1929, he recalled of the black cowboy Bose Ikard, a former slave, that "he was my detective, banker, and everything else in Colorado, New Mexico, and the other wild country I was in. The nearest and only bank was at Denver, and when we carried money I gave it to Bose." Goodnight revealed much about the economic situation of blacks on the Plains, however, when he added that "a thief would … never think of looking in a Negro's bed for money."

The cattle bonanza, which peaked between 1880 and 1885, produced more than 4.5 million head of cattle for eastern markets. Prices began to sag as early as 1882, however, and many ranchers plunged heavily into debt. In 1885 and 1886, two of the coldest and snowiest winters on record combined with summer droughts and Texas fever to destroy nearly 90 percent of the cattle in some regions, pushing thousands of ranchers into bankruptcy. The cattle industry lived on, but railroad expansion brought the days of the open range and the great cattle drives to an end. As had the mining frontier, the cattle frontier left behind memories of individual daring, towering fortunes for some, and hard times for many.

Cattle Towns and Prostitutes   One legacy of the cattle boom was the growth of cities like Abilene, Kansas, which shipped steers to Chicago and eastern markets. Like other cattle towns, Abilene went through an early period of violence that saw cowboys pulling down the walls of the jail as it was being built. But the town quickly established a police force to maintain law and order. City ordinances forbade carrying firearms and regulated saloons, gambling, and prostitution. James B. "Wild Bill" Hickok served as town marshal in

1871. Dime novelists described him as "a veritable terror to bad men on the border," but during his term as Abilene's lawman, Hickok killed just two men, one of them by mistake. Transient, unruly types certainly gave a distinctive flavor to cattle towns like Abilene, Wichita, and Dodge City, but the overall homicide rates there were not unusually high.

If cattle towns were neither as violent nor as lawless as legend would have it, they did still experience a lively business in prostitution, as did most cities at this time. Given the large numbers of unattached young men and numerous saloons (Abilene, in the 1870s, with a permanent population of five hundred, had thirty-two drinking establishments), prostitution thrived. Prostitutes came from all social classes and from as far away as China, Ireland, Germany, and Mexico. Some became prostitutes as an escape from domestic violence or because of economic hardship. Others, like the Chinese, were forced into the trade. All prostitutes risked venereal disease, physical abuse, and drug and alcohol addiction.

As western towns became more settled, the numbers of women in other occupations increased. Some found work as cooks or laundresses on ranches. Others married merchants, doctors, and businessmen. Although few of the first generation rode the range, their daughters became increasingly involved in the everyday work of ranching and became proficient riders themselves.

Bonanza Farms   Like the gold rushes and cattle bonanzas, the wheat boom of the 1870s and 1880s started small but rapidly attracted large capital investments that produced the nation's first agribusinesses. The boom in the Dakota Territory began during the Panic of 1873, when the Northern Pacific Railroad began exchanging land for its depreciated bonds. Speculators purchased more than three hundred thousand acres in the fertile Red River Valley of North Dakota for between fifty cents and a dollar an acre.

Operating singly or in groups, the speculators established factory-like ten-thousand-acre farms, each run by a hired manager, and invested heavily in labor and equipment. On the Cass-Cheney-Dalrymple farm near Fargo, North Dakota, fifty or sixty plows rumbled across the flat landscape on a typical spring day. Northern Pacific president George W. Cass, who had invested fifty thousand dollars for land and equipment, paid all his expenses plus the cost of the ten thousand acres with his first harvest alone.

The publicity generated by the tremendous success of a few large investors like Cass led to an unprecedented wheat boom in the Red River Valley in 1880. Eastern banking syndicates and small farmers alike rushed to buy land. North Dakota's population tripled in the 1880s. Wheat production skyrocketed to almost 29 million bushels by the end of the decade. But the profits soon evaporated. By 1890, some Red River Valley farmers were destitute.

The wheat boom collapsed for a variety of reasons. Overproduction, high investment costs, too little or too much rain, excessive reliance on one crop, and depressed grain prices on the international market all undercut farmers' earnings. Large-scale farmers who had invested in hopes of getting rich felt lucky just to survive. Oliver Dalrymple lamented in 1889 that "it seems as if the time has come when there is no money in wheat raising."

Large-scale farms proved most successful in California's Central Valley. Using canals and other irrigation systems to water their crops, farmers by the mid-1880s were growing higher-priced specialty crops and had created new cooperative marketing associations for cherries, apricots, grapes, and oranges. By 1900, led by California citrus growers, who used the "Sunkist" trademark for their oranges, large-scale agribusinesses in California were shipping a variety of fruits and vegetables in refrigerated train cars to midwestern and eastern markets.

The Oklahoma Land Rush, 1889   As farmers in the Dakotas and Minnesota were enduring poor harvests and falling prices, would-be homesteaders greedily eyed the Indian Territory, as present-day Oklahoma was then known. The federal government, considering much of this land virtually worthless, had reserved it for the Five Civilized Tribes since the 1830s. These tribes (except for some Cherokees) had sided with the Confederacy during the Civil War. Although Washington had already punished them by settling other tribes on lands in the western part of the territory, land-hungry whites demanded even more land.

In 1889, over the Native Americans' protests, Congress transferred to the federally owned public domain nearly 2 million acres in the central part of the Oklahoma Territory that had not been specifically assigned to any Indian tribe. At noon on April 22, 1889, thousands of men stampeded into the new lands to stake out homesteads. (Other settlers, the so-called Sooners, had illegally arrived earlier and were already plowing the fields.) Before nightfall, tent communities had risen at Oklahoma City and Guthrie near stations on the Santa Fe Railroad. Nine weeks later, six thousand homestead claims had been filed. In the next decade, the Dawes Severalty Act broke up the Indian reservations into individual allotments and opened the surplus to non-Indian settlement. The **Curtis Act** in 1898 dissolved the Indian Territory and abolished tribal governments.

The Oklahoma land rush demonstrated the continuing power of the frontier myth, which tied "free" land to the ideal of economic opportunity. Most Oklahoma farmers survived because they had obtained fertile land in an area where the normal rainfall was thirty inches, ten inches more than in the semiarid regions farther west. Still, within two generations a combination of exploitative farming, poor land management, and sporadic drought would place Oklahoma at the desolate center of the dust bowl in the 1930s (covered in Chapter 24).

THE WEST OF MYTH AND LEGEND

In 1893, four years after the last major tract of western Indian land, the Oklahoma Territory, was opened to non-Indian settlement, a young Wisconsin historian, Frederick Jackson Turner, delivered a lecture entitled "The Significance of the Frontier in American History." "[T]he frontier has gone," declared Turner, "and with its going has closed the first period of American history." Although Turner's assertion that the frontier was closed was based on a Census Bureau announcement, it was inaccurate (more western land would be settled in the twentieth century than in the nineteenth). But his linking of economic opportunity

with the transformation of the trans-Mississippi West caught the popular imagination and launched a new school of historical inquiry into the effects of the
frontier on U.S. history.

Scholars now recognize that many parts of Turner's "frontier thesis," particularly its ethnocentric omission of Native Americans' claims to the land, were
inaccurate. Yet his idealized view of the West did reflect ideas popular among
his contemporaries in the 1890s. A legendary West had taken deep root in the
American imagination. In the nineteenth century, this mythic West was a product
of novels, songs, and paintings. In the twentieth century, it would be perpetuated
by movies, radio programs, and television shows. The legend merits attention, for
its evolution is fascinating and its influence has been far-reaching.

The American Adam and the Dime-Novel Hero

Late nineteenth-century writers presented the frontiersman as
a kind of mythic American Adam—simple, virtuous, and
innocent—untainted by a corrupt social order. For example,
at the end of Mark Twain's *Huckleberry Finn*, Huck rejects
the constraints of settled society as represented by Aunt
Sally and heads west with the declaration, "I reckon I got to light out for the territory ahead of the rest, because Aunt Sally she's going to adopt me and sivilize me,
and I can't stand it. I been there before." In this version of the legend, the West is a
place of adventure where one can escape from society and its pressures.

But even as this conception of the myth was being popularized, another powerful theme had emerged as well. The authors of the dime novels of the 1860s and
1870s offered the image of the western frontiersman as a new masculine ideal, the
tough guy who fights for truth and honor. In *Buffalo Bill: King of the Border Men*
(1869), a dime novel loosely based on real-life William F. "Buffalo Bill" Cody,
Edward Judson (who published under the name Ned Buntline) created an idealized
hero who is a powerful moral force as he drives off treacherous Indians and rounds
up villainous cattle rustlers.

Cody himself, playing upon the public fascination with cowboys, organized
his own **Wild West Show** in 1883. In the show, which toured the East Coast and
Europe, cowboys engaged in mock battles with Indians, reinforcing the dime-
novel image of the West as an arena of moral encounter where virtue always
triumphed.

Revitalizing the Frontier Legend

Eastern writers and artists eagerly embraced both versions
of the myth—the West as a place of escape from society and
the West as a stage on which the moral conflicts confront-
ing society were played out. Three young members of the eastern establishment,
Theodore Roosevelt, Frederic Remington, and Owen Wister, spent much time in the
West in the 1880s, and each was intensely affected by the adventure.

Each man found precisely what he was looking for. The frontier that Roosevelt
glorified in such books as *The Winning of the West* (four volumes, 1889–1896),
and that Remington portrayed in his statues and paintings, was a stark physical
and moral environment that stripped away all social artifice and tested each individual's character. Drawing on a popular version of English scientist Charles

Darwin's evolutionary theory, which characterized life as a struggle in which only the fittest survived, Roosevelt and Remington exalted the disappearing frontier as the proving ground for a new kind of virile manhood and the last outpost of an honest and true social order.

This version of the frontier myth reached its apogee in **Owen Wister's** popular novel *The Virginian* (1902). In Wister's tale, the elemental environment of the Great Plains produces individuals like his unnamed cowboy hero, "the Virginian," an honest, strong, and compassionate man, quick to help the weak and fight the wicked. The Virginian sums up his own moral code in describing his view of God's justice: "He plays a square game with us." For Wister, as for Roosevelt and Remington, the cowboy was the Christian knight on the Plains, indifferent to material gain as he pursued justice and attacked evil.

Needless to say, the western myth was far removed from the reality of the West. Critics delighted in pointing out that not one scene in *The Virginian* showed the hard physical labor of the cattle range. The idealized version of the West also glossed over the darker underside of frontier expansion—the brutalities of Indian warfare, the racist discrimination against Mexican Americans and blacks, the risks of commercial agriculture and cattle-raising, and the boom-and-bust mentality rooted in the exploitation of natural resources.

Further, the myth obscured the complex links between the settlement of the frontier and the emergence of the United States as a major industrialized nation increasingly tied to a global economy. Eastern and foreign capitalists controlled large-scale mining, cattle, and agricultural operations in the West. The technical know-how of industrial America underlay the marvels of western agricultural productivity. Without the railroad, that quintessential symbol of the new industrial order, the transformation of the West would have been far slower.

| Beginning a National Parks Movement | Despite its one-sided and idealized vision, Owen Wister's celebration of the western experience reinforced a growing recognition that many unique features of the western landscape were being threatened by overeager entrepreneurs. |

One important byproduct of the western legend was a surge of public support for creating national parks and the beginning of an organized conservation movement.

Those who went west in the 1860s and 1870s to map its rugged terrain were often awed by the natural beauty of the landscape. Major **John Wesley Powell,** the one-armed veteran of the Civil War who charted the Colorado River through the Grand Canyon in 1869, waxed euphoric about its towering rock formations and powerful cataracts. "The river turns sharply to the east, and seems enclosed by a wall, set with a million brilliant gems ... On coming nearer, we find fountains bursting from the rock, high overhead, and the spray in the sunshine forms the gems which bedeck the way."

In his important study, *Report on the Lands of the Arid Regions of the United States* (1878), Powell argued that settlers needed to readjust their expectations about the use of water in the dry terrain west of the hundredth meridian. He urged Congress to establish governmental control of watersheds, irrigation, and public lands, a request that went largely unheeded.

Around the time Powell was educating Congress about the arid nature of the far West, a group of adventurers led by General Henry D. Washburn visited the hot springs and geysers near the Yellowstone River in northwestern Wyoming and eastern Montana. They were stunned by what they saw. Wrote one of the party, "[A]mid the canyon and falls, the boiling springs and sulphur mountain, and, above all, the mud volcano and the geysers of the Yellowstone, your memory becomes filled and clogged with objects new in experience, wonderful in extent, and possessing unlimited grandeur and beauty." Overwhelmed by the view, the Washburn explorers abandoned their plan to claim the area for the Northern Pacific Railroad and instead petitioned Congress to protect it from settlement, occupancy, and sale. Congress responded in 1872 by creating **Yellowstone National Park** to "provide for the preservation ... for all time, [of] mineral deposits, natural curiosities, or wonders within said park ... in their natural condition." In doing so, they excluded the Native Americans who had long considered the area a prime hunting range.

These first steps to conserve a few of the West's unique natural sites reflected the beginning of a changed awareness of the environment. In his influential study *Man and Nature* in 1864, **George Perkins Marsh,** an architect and politician from Vermont, attacked the view that nature existed to be tamed and conquered. Cautioning Americans to curb their destructive use of the landscape, he warned the public to change its ways. "Man," he wrote, "is everywhere a disturbing agent. Wherever he plants his foot, the harmonies of nature are turned to discords."

Marsh's plea for conservation found its most eloquent support in the work of **John Muir,** a Scottish immigrant who had grown up in Wisconsin. In 1869, Muir traveled to San Francisco and quickly fell in love with the redwood forests. For the next forty years, he tramped the rugged mountains of the West and campaigned for their preservation. A romantic at heart, he struggled to experience the wilderness at its most elemental level. Once trekking high in the Rockies during a summer storm, he climbed the tallest pine he could find and swayed back and forth in the raging wind.

Muir became the late nineteenth century's most articulate publicist for wilderness protection. "Climb the mountains and get their good tidings," he advised city dwellers. "Nature's peace will flow into you as the sunshine into the trees." Muir's spirited campaign to protect the wilderness contributed strongly to the establishment of Yosemite National Park in 1890. Two years later, he became president of the Sierra Club, an organization created to encourage the enjoyment and protection of the wilderness in the mountain regions of the Pacific coast.

The precedent established by the creation of Yellowstone National Park remained ambiguous well into the twentieth century. Other parks that preserved the high rugged landforms of the West were often chosen because Congress viewed the sites as worthless for other purposes. Awareness of the need for biological conservation would not emerge until later in the twentieth century (as discussed in Chapter 21).

Ironically, despite the crusades of Muir, Powell, and Marsh to educate the public about conservation, the campaign for wilderness preservation reaffirmed the image of the West as a unique region whose magnificent landscape produced tough individuals of superior ability. Overlooking the senseless violence and ruthless exploitation of the land, contemporary writers, historians, and publicists proclaimed that the settlement of the final frontier marked a new stage in the history of civilization, and they kept alive the legend of the western frontier as a seedbed of American virtues.

CHRONOLOGY
1860–1900

1862	Homestead Act.
	Morrill Anti-Bigamy Act.
	Pacific Railroad Act.
1864	Nevada admitted to the Union.
	Massacre of Cheyennes at Sand Creek, Colorado.
	George Perkins Marsh, *Man and Nature.*
1867	Joseph McCoy organizes cattle drives to Abilene, Kansas.
	New Indian policy of smaller reservations adopted.
	Medicine Lodge Treaty.
	Purchase of Alaska.
1868	Fort Laramie Treaty.
1869	Board of Indian Commissioners established to reform Indian reservation life.
	Wyoming gives women the vote.
1872	Yellowstone National Park established.
1873	Panic allows speculators to purchase thousands of acres in the Red River valley of North Dakota cheaply.
	Timber Culture Act.
	Biggest strike on Nevada's Comstock Lode.
1874	Invention of barbed wire.
	Gold discovered in the Black Hills of South Dakota.
	Red River War.
1875	John Wesley Powell, *The Exploration of the Colorado River.*
1876	Colorado admitted to the Union, gives women the right to vote in school elections.
	Little Bighorn massacre.
1877	Desert Land Act.
1878	Timber and Stone Act.
	John Wesley Powell, *Report on the Lands of the Arid Regions of the United States.*
1879	*United States* v. *Reynolds.*

1881	Helen Hunt Jackson, *A Century of Dishonor*.
1883	Women's National Indian Rights Association founded.
	William ("Buffalo Bill") Cody organizes Wild West Show.
1884	Helen Hunt Jackson, *Ramona*.
1886	Severe drought on the Plains destroys cattle and grain.
1887	Dawes Severalty Act.
	Edmunds-Tucker Act.
1888	White Caps raid ranches in northern New Mexico.
1889	Oklahoma Territory opened for settlement.
1890	Ghost Dance movement spreads to the Black Hills.
	Massacre of Teton Sioux at Wounded Knee, South Dakota.
1892	John Muir organizes Sierra Club.
1898	Curtis Act.

CONCLUSION

The image of the mythic West has long obscured the transformation of people and landscape that took place there in the second half of the nineteenth century. Precisely because industrialization, urbanization, and immigration were altering the rest of the nation in unsettling ways (covered in Chapters 18 and 19), many Americans embraced the legend of the West as a visionary, uncomplicated, untainted Eden of social simplicity and moral clarity. The mythic West represented what the entire society had once been like (or so Americans chose to believe), before the advent of cities, factories, and masses of immigrants.

But the mythic view of the frontier West obscured the dark side of expansion onto the Great Plains and beyond. Under the banner of economic opportunity and individual achievement, nineteenth-century Americans used the army to subdue the Indians, undermine their traditional way of life, and drive them onto reservations. They also ruthlessly exploited the region's vast natural resources. In less than three decades, they killed off the enormous buffalo herds, tore up the prairie sod, and littered parts of the landscape with mining debris.

Despite the promise of the Homestead Act, which offered 160 acres of free land to those who would settle on it for five years, much of the best land in the West had been given to railroads to encourage their expansion. Speculators purchased other prime locations. Homesteaders were often forced to settle on poorer-quality tracts in areas where rainfall was marginal. In many places, large business enterprises in mining, ranching, and agribusiness, financed by eastern and European bankers, shoved aside the small entrepreneur and took control of the choicest natural resources.

Nevertheless, the settlement of the vast continental interior did reinforce the popular image of the United States as a land of unprecedented economic opportunity and as a seedbed for democracy. The founding of new towns, the creation of new territorial and state governments, and the interaction of peoples of different races and ethnicities tested these ideas and, with time, forced their rethinking. The exclusion of blacks, Indians, and Spanish-speaking Americans belied the voiced commitment to an open society, but the increasing willingness to give women the vote in many of the new western states would spread within the next two decades.

Although the persisting mythic view of the West hid the more ruthless and destructive features of western expansionism, settling the interior territories and exploiting their extensive physical resources gave birth to the conservation movement and a reassessment of traditional American views of the environment. By the turn of the century, the West's thriving farms, ranches, mines, and cities would help make the United States into one of the world's most prosperous nations.

18

THE RISE OF INDUSTRIAL AMERICA, 1865–1900

CHAPTER OUTLINE

• The Rise of Corporate America • Stimulating Economic Growth • The New South • Factories and the Work Force • Labor Unions and Industrial Conflict

---

THE RISE OF CORPORATE AMERICA

In the early nineteenth century, the corporate form of business organization had been used to raise large amounts of start-up capital for transportation enterprises such as turnpikes and canals. By selling stocks and bonds to raise money, the corporation separated the company's managers, who guided its day-to-day operation, from its owners. After the Civil War, American business leaders pioneered new forms of corporate organization that combined innovative technologies, creative management structures, and limited liability should the enterprise fail. The rise of the giant corporation is a story of risk-taking and innovation as well as of conspiracy and corruption.

The Character of Industrial Change   Six features dominated the world of large-scale manufacturing after the Civil War: (1) the exploitation of immense coal deposits as a source of cheap energy; (2) the rapid spread of technological innovation in transportation, communication, and factory systems; (3) the demand for workers who could be driven and controlled; (4) the constant pressure on firms to compete tooth-and-nail by cutting costs, eliminating rivals, and creating monopolies; (5) the relentless drop in prices (a stark contrast to the inflation of other eras); and (6) the failure of the money supply to keep pace with productivity, a development that drove up interest rates and restricted the availability of credit.

All six factors were closely related. The great coal deposits in Pennsylvania, West Virginia, and Kentucky provided cheap energy to fuel railroad and factory growth. New technologies stimulated productivity and catalyzed breathtaking industrial expansion. Technological innovation enabled manufacturers to cut costs and hire unskilled labor. Cost cutting enabled firms to undersell one another, destroy weaker competitors, and consolidate themselves into more efficient and more ruthless firms. At least until the mid-1890s, cheap energy, immigrant labor, new technology, and fierce competition forced down overall price levels.

But almost everyone struggled terribly during the depression years, when the government did nothing to relieve distress. "The sufferings of the working classes are daily increasing," wrote a Philadelphia worker in 1874. "Famine has broken into the home of many of us, and is at the door of all." Above all, business leaders' unflagging drive to reduce costs both created colossal fortunes at the top of the economic ladder and forced millions of wage earners to live near the subsistence level.

Out of the new industrial system poured clouds of haze and soot, as well as the first tantalizing trickle of what would become an avalanche of consumer goods. In turn, mounting demands for consumer goods stimulated heavy industry's production of capital goods—machines to boost farm and factory output even further. Together with the railroads, the corporations that manufactured capital goods, refined petroleum, and made steel became driving forces in the nation's economic growth.

Railroad Innovations   Competition among the capitalists who headed American heavy industry was most intense among the nation's railroads. By 1900, 193,000 miles of railroad track crisscrossed the United States—more than in all of Europe including Russia. Taking advantage of enormous government land subsidies, these rail lines connected every state in the Union, opened up an immense new internal market, and pioneered new forms of

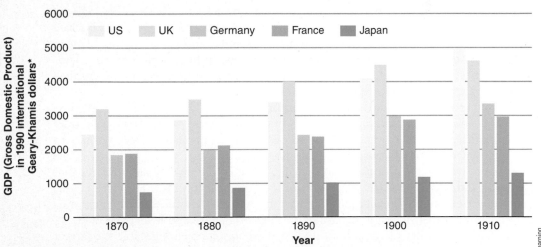

*1990 international Geary-Khamis dollars represent the monetary values of the output of the final goods and services produced in a country in one year converted into 1990 dollars at the exchange rate which would pertain if the goods and services had the same prices in all countries (purchasing power parity). See the statistical definition at the UN site: http://unstats.un.org/unsd/methods/icp/ipc7_htm.htm

© Cengage Learning

FIGURE 18.1   Late Nineteenth-Century Economic Growth in Global Perspective

large-scale corporate enterprise. They created national distribution systems, and perfected new management structures.

Railroad entrepreneurs such as Collis P. Huntington of the Central Pacific Railroad, **Jay Gould** of the Union Pacific, and James J. Hill of the Northern Pacific faced enormous financial and organizational problems. To raise the staggering sums necessary for laying track and building engines, railroads obtained generous land and loan subsidies from federal, state, and local governments (see Chapter 17). At the same time, they borrowed heavily by selling stocks and bonds to the public. Bond holders earned a fixed rate of interest; stockholders received dividends only when the company earned a profit. By 1900, the yearly interest repayments required by the combined debt of all U.S. railroads (which stood at an astounding $5.1 billion— nearly five times that of the federal government) cut heavily into their earnings.

In addition to raising substantial capital, the railroads created new systems for collecting and using information. To coordinate the complex flow of cars across the country, they relied on the magnetic telegraph, invented in 1837. To improve efficiency, they set up clearly defined, hierarchical organizational structures and divided their lines into separate divisions, each with its own superintendent. Elaborate accounting systems documented the cost of every operation for each division, from coal consumption to the repair of engines and cars. Using these reports, railroad officials could set rates and accurately predict profits as early as the 1860s, a time when most businesses had no idea of their total profit until they closed their books at year's end. Railroad management innovations thus became a model for many other businesses seeking a national market.

Consolidating the Railroad Industry   The expansion and consolidation of railroading reflected both the ingenuity and the dishonesty flourishing on the corporate management scene. Despite their organizational innovations, the industry remained chaotic in the 1870s. Hundreds of small companies used different standards for track width and engine size. Financed by large eastern and British banks, Huntington, Gould, and others devoured these smaller lines to create large, integrated track networks. In the Northeast, four major trunk lines were completed. West of the Mississippi, five great companies controlled most of the track by 1893.

Huntington, Gould, and the other corporate leaders who reorganized and expanded the railroad industry in the 1870s and 1880s often were depicted by their contemporaries as villains and robber barons who manipulated stock markets to line their own pockets. Newspaper publisher Joseph Pulitzer called Jay Gould, the short, secretive president of the Union Pacific, "one of the most sinister figures that have ever flitted batlike across the vision of the American people." Historians agree that many were indeed corrupt pirates, but note that others were shrewd innovators. Indeed, some of their ideas were startling in their originality and inventiveness.

The massive railroad systems created by these entrepreneurs became the largest business enterprises in the world. As they consolidated small railroads into a few interlocking systems, these masterminds standardized all basic equipment and facilities, from engines and cars to automatic couplers, air brakes, and signal systems. In 1883, independently of the federal government, the railroads corrected scheduling problems by dividing the country into four time zones. In May 1886, all railroads shifted simultaneously to the new standard 4′8½″ gauge track. Finally, cooperative billing arrangements enabled the railroads to ship cars from other roads at uniform rates nationwide.

But the systemization and consolidation of the railroads had its costs. Heavy indebtedness, overextended systems, and crooked business practices forced the railroads to compete recklessly with each other for traffic. They cut rates for large shippers, showered free passes on politicians, and granted substantial rebates and kickbacks to favored clients while ignoring worker safety. None of these tactics, however, shored up the railroads' precarious financial position. Ruthless competition and fraudulent business practices drove some overbuilt lines into bankruptcy.

Stung by exorbitant rates and secret kickbacks, farmers and small business owners turned to state governments for help. In the 1870s, midwestern state legislatures responded by outlawing rate discrimination. Initially upheld by the Supreme Court, these and other decisions were negated in the 1880s when the Court ruled that states could not regulate interstate commerce. In response in 1887, Congress passed the **Interstate Commerce Act.** A five-member Interstate Commerce Commission (ICC) was established to oversee the practices of interstate railroads. The law banned monopolistic activity like pooling, rebates, and discriminatory short-distance rates.

The railroads challenged the commission's rulings in the federal courts. Of the sixteen cases brought to the Supreme Court before 1905, the justices found in favor of the railroads in all but one, essentially nullifying the ICC's regulatory clout. The Hepburn Act (covered in Chapter 21), passed in 1906, strengthened the ICC by finally empowering it to set rates.

The railroads' vicious competition weakened in 1893 when a national depression forced a number of roads into the hands of **J. Pierpont Morgan** and other investment bankers. Morgan, a massively built man with piercing eyes and a commanding presence, took over the weakened systems, reorganized their administration, refinanced their debts, and built intersystem alliances. By 1906, under the bankers' centralized management, seven giant networks controlled two-thirds of the nation's rail mileage.

Applying the Lessons of the Railroads to Steel   The close connections between railroad expansion, which absorbed millions of tons of steel for tracks, and the growth of corporate organization and management are well illustrated in the career of **Andrew Carnegie.** Born in Scotland, Carnegie immigrated to America in 1848 at the age of twelve. His first job as a bobbin boy in a Pittsburgh textile mill paid only $1.20 a week. The following year, Carnegie became a Western Union messenger boy. Taking over when the telegraph operators wanted a break, he soon became the city's fastest telegraph operator and gained an insider's view of the operations of every major Pittsburgh business.

Carnegie's big break came in 1852 when Tom Scott, superintendent of the Pennsylvania Railroad's western division, hired him as his secretary and personal telegrapher. Later promoted to division chief, Carnegie cut costs while more than doubling the road's mileage. Having invested his earnings in the railroads, by 1868 Carnegie was earning more than $56,000 a year from his investments, a substantial fortune in that era.

In the early 1870s, Carnegie built his own steel mill to produce high-grade steel rails using a new technology named after its English inventor, Henry Bessemer, which shot a blast of air through an enormous crucible of molten iron to burn off carbon and impurities. Combining this new technology with the cost-analysis approach learned from his railroad experience, Carnegie became the first steel-maker to know the actual production cost of each ton of steel.

Carnegie's philosophy was deceptively simple: "Watch the costs, and the profits will take care of themselves." Using rigorous cost accounting and limiting wage increases to his workers, he lowered his production costs and prices below those of his competitors. When these tactics did not drive them out of business, he asked for favors from his railroad-president friends and gave "commissions" to railroad purchasing agents to win business.

As output climbed, Carnegie discovered the benefits of **vertical integration,** that is, controlling all aspects of manufacturing from the mining and smelting of ore to the selling of steel rails. Carnegie Steel thus became the classic example of how sophisticated new technology could be combined with innovative management (and brutally low wages) to create a mass-production system that could dramatically increase production and slash consumer prices.

The management of daily operations by his close associates left Carnegie free to pursue philanthropic activities. While still in his early thirties, Carnegie donated money to charitable projects. In his lifetime, he gave more than $300 million to libraries, universities, and international-peace causes.

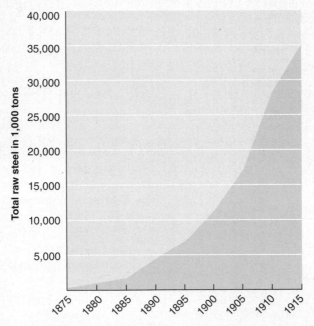

FIGURE 18.2 Iron and Steel Production, 1875–1915

New technologies, improved plant organization, economies of scale, and the vertical integration of production brought a dramatic spurt in iron and steel production.

Note: short ton=2,000 pounds.

Source: Historical Statistics of the United States.

By 1900, Carnegie Steel, employing twenty thousand people, had become the world's largest industrial corporation. Carnegie's competitors, worried about his domination of the market, decided to buy him out. In 1901, J. Pierpont Morgan purchased Carn egie's companies and set up the United States Steel Corporation, the first business capitalized at more than $1 billion. The corporation, made up of two hundred member companies employing 168,000 people, marked a new scale in industrial enterprise.

A systematic self-publicist, Carnegie portrayed his success as the result of self-discipline and hard work. The full story was more complex. Carnegie did not mention his uncanny ability to see the larger picture, his cleverness in hiring talented associates who would drive themselves (and the company's factory workers) mercilessly, his ingenuity in transferring organizational systems and cost accounting methods from railroads to steel, and his callousness in keeping wages as low as possible. To a public unaware of corporate management techniques, however, Carnegie's success gave credence to the idea that anyone might rise from rags to riches.

The Trust: Creating New Forms of Corporate Organization
Between 1870 and 1900, the same fierce competition that had stimulated consolidation in the railroad and steel industries also swept the oil, salt, sugar, tobacco, and meat-packing industries. Like steel, these highly competitive businesses required large capital investments. Entrepreneurs in each industry therefore raced to reduce costs, lower prices, and drive their rivals out of the market.

The evolution of the oil industry illustrates the process by which new corporate structures evolved. After Edwin L. Drake drilled the first successful petroleum (or "crude-oil") well in 1859 near Titusville, Pennsylvania, competitors rushed into the business. Petroleum was distilled into oil, which soon replaced animal tallow as the major lubricant, and into kerosene, which became the leading fuel for household and public lighting.

By the 1870s, the landscape near Pittsburgh and Cleveland, the sites of the first discoveries, was littered with rickety drilling rigs, assorted collection tanks, and ramshackle refineries. Oil spills were a constant problem. "So much oil is produced," reported one Pennsylvania newspaper in 1861, "that it is impossible to care for it, and thousands of barrels are running into the creek; the surface of the river is covered with oil for miles."

In this rush for riches, **John D. Rockefeller,** a young Cleveland merchant, gradually achieved dominance. Like Andrew Carnegie, the solemn Rockefeller had a passion for cost cutting and efficiency. In one case, he insisted a manager find 750 missing barrel stoppers. He realized that in a mass-production enterprise, small changes could save thousands of dollars.

Rockefeller resembled Carnegie, too, in his ability to understand the inner workings of an entire industry and the benefits of vertical integration. The firm that controlled the shipment of oil between the well and the refinery and between the refinery and the retailers, he realized, could dominate the industry. In 1872, he purchased his own tanker cars and obtained not only a 10 percent rebate from the railroads for hauling his oil but also a kickback on his competitors' shipments. When new pipeline technology became available, Rockefeller set up his own massive interregional pipeline network.

Like Carnegie, Rockefeller aggressively forced out his competitors. If local refineries rejected his offers to buy them out, he priced his products below cost and strangled their businesses. When rival firms teamed up against him, Rockefeller set up a pool—an agreement among several companies—that established production quotas and fixed prices. By 1879, Rockefeller had seized control of 90 percent of the country's oil-refining capacity.

In 1882, Rockefeller decided to eliminate competition by establishing a new form of corporate organization, the **Standard Oil Trust.** In place of the "pool" or verbal agreement among companies to control prices and markets, which lacked legal status, the trust created an umbrella corporation that ran them all. To implement his trust, Rockefeller and his associates persuaded the stockholders of forty companies to exchange their stock for trust certificates. Under this arrangement, stockholders retained their share of the trust's profits while enabling the trust to control production. Within three years, the Standard Oil Trust had consolidated crude-oil buying throughout its member firms and slashed the number of refineries in half. In this way, Rockefeller integrated the petroleum industry both vertically, by controlling every function from production to local retailing, and horizontally, by merging the competing oil companies into one giant system.

While Standard Oil justified its trust organization by pointing to the public usefulness of inexpensive heating and cooking fuels, other monopolies did not provide such benefits. James B. "Buck" Duke's American Tobacco trust, for example, targeted youths with trading cards and prizes to persuade them to smoke cigarettes. For addictive products such as cigarettes, targeting children became a means for ensuring continuous use. To gain access to even bigger markets, Duke purchased controlling interests in tobacco companies in England and Japan.

Taking a leaf from Duke and Rockefeller's book, companies in the copper, sugar, whiskey, lead, and other industries established their own trust arrangements. By limiting the number of competitors, the trusts created an *oligopoly*, the market condition that exists when a small number of sellers can greatly influence prices. But their unscrupulous tactics, semimonopolistic control, and sky-high earnings provoked a public outcry. Both major political parties denounced them in the presidential election of 1888.

Fearful that the trusts would stamp out all competition, Congress, under the leadership of Senator John Sherman of Ohio, passed the **Sherman Anti-Trust Act** in 1890. The Sherman Act outlawed trusts and any other monopolies that fixed prices in restraint of trade and slapped violators with fines of up to $5,000 and a year in jail. But the act failed to define clearly either *trust* or *restraint of trade*. The government prosecuted only eighteen antitrust suits between 1890 and 1904. When Standard Oil's structure was challenged in 1892, its lawyers simply reorganized the trust as an enormous holding company. Unlike a trust, which literally owned other businesses, a holding company simply owned a controlling share of the stock of one or more firms. The new board of directors for Standard Oil (New Jersey), the new holding company, made more money than ever.

The Supreme Court further hamstrung congressional antitrust efforts by interpreting the Sherman Act in ways sympathetic to big business. In 1895, for example,

Baseball Trading Card *To encourage boys and young men to smoke cigarettes, the American Tobacco Company included in the cigarette package collectable cards with pictures of baseball heroes such as Ty Cobb.*

COBB, DETROIT

the federal government brought suit against the sugar trust in *United States* v. *E.C. Knight Company*, arguing that by controlling more than 90 percent of all U.S. sugar refining, it operated in illegal restraint of trade. Asserting that manufacturing was not interstate commerce and ignoring the company's vast distribution network that enabled it to dominate the market, the Court threw out the suit. Thus vindicated, corporate mergers and consolidations surged ahead at the turn of the century. By 1900, these mammoth firms accounted for nearly two-fifths of the capital invested in the nation's manufacturing sector.

STIMULATING ECONOMIC GROWTH

Large-scale corporate enterprise did not alone account for the colossal growth of the U.S. economy in the late nineteenth century. Other factors proved equally important, including new inventions, specialty production, and innovations in advertising and marketing. In fact, the resourcefulness of small enterprises, which combined innovative technology with new methods of advertising and merchandising, enabled many sectors of the economy to grow dramatically by adapting quickly to changing fashions and consumer preferences.

The Triumph of Technology   New inventions not only streamlined the manufacture of traditional products but also stimulated consumer demand by creating entirely new product lines. The development of a safe, practical way to generate electricity, for example, made possible a vast number of electrical motors, household appliances, and lighting systems.

Many of the major inventions that stimulated industrial output and underlay mass production in these years were largely hidden from public view. Few Americans had heard of the improved technologies that facilitated bottle making and glassmaking, canning, flour milling, match production, and petroleum refining. Fewer still knew much about the refrigerated railcars that enabled Gustavus Swift's company to slaughter beef in Chicago and ship it east.

The inventions people did see were the ones that changed the patterns of everyday life: the sewing machine, mass-produced by the Singer Sewing Machine Company beginning in the 1860s; the telephone, developed by Alexander Graham Bell in 1876; and the light bulb, perfected by **Thomas A. Edison** in 1879.

These new inventions eased household drudgery and reshaped social interactions. The sewing machine, which relieved the tedium of sewing apparel by hand, expanded personal wardrobes. The spread of telephones—by 1900, the Bell Telephone Company had installed almost eight hundred thousand in the United States—not only transformed communication but also undermined social conventions for polite behavior that had been premised on face-to-face or written exchanges. The light bulb, by freeing people from dependence on daylight, made it possible to shop after work.

In the eyes of many, Thomas A. Edison epitomized the inventive impulse and the capacity for creating new consumer products. Born in 1847 in Milan, Ohio, Edison, like Andrew Carnegie, had little formal education and worked in the telegraphic industry. A born salesman and self-promoter, Edison shared Carnegie's vision of a large, interconnected industrial system resting on a foundation of technological innovation.

Edison's first major invention, a stock-quotation printer, in 1868 earned enough money to finance Edison's first "invention factory" in Newark, New Jersey, a research facility he moved to nearby Menlo Park in 1876. Assembling a staff that included university-trained scientists, Edison boastfully predicted "a minor invention every ten days, and a big one every six months."

Buoyed by the success and popularity of his invention in 1877 of a phonograph, or "sound writer" (*phono*: "sound"; *graph*: "writer"), Edison set out to develop a new filament for incandescent light bulbs. Characteristically, he announced his plans for an electricity-generation process before he perfected his inventions and then worked feverishly, testing hundreds of materials before he found a carbon filament that would glow dependably in a vacuum.

Edison realized that practical electrical lighting had to be part of a complete system containing generators, voltage regulators, electric meters, and insulated wiring and that the system needed to be easy to install and repair. It also had to be cheaper and more convenient than kerosene or natural gas lighting, its main competitors. In 1882, having built this system with the support of banker J. Pierpont Morgan, the Edison Illuminating Company opened a power plant in the heart of New York City's financial district, furnishing lighting for eighty-five buildings.

In the following years, Edison and his researchers pumped out invention after invention, including the mimeograph machine, the microphone, the motion picture camera and film, and the storage battery. By the time of his death in 1931, he had patented 1,093 inventions and amassed an estate worth more than $6 million. Yet Edison's greatest achievement remained his laboratory at Menlo Park. A model for the industrial research labs later established by Kodak, General Electric, and Du Pont, Edison's laboratory demonstrated that the systematic use of science in support of industrial technology paid large dividends. Invention had become big business.

Specialized Production
Along with inventors, manufacturers of custom and specialized products such as machinery, jewelry, furniture, and women's clothes dramatically expanded economic output. Using skilled labor, these companies crafted one-of-a-kind or small batches of articles that ranged in size from large steam engines and machine tools to silverware, furniture, and custom-made dresses. Keenly attuned to innovations in technology and design, they constantly created new products tailored to the needs of individual buyers.

Small dressmaking shops run by women were typical of flexible specialization displayed by small batch processors. Until the turn of the twentieth century, when ready-to-wear clothes came to dominate the market, most women's apparel was custom produced in small shops run by female proprietors. Unlike the tenement sweatshops that produced men's shirts and pants, dressmakers and milliners (a term derived from fancy goods vendors in sixteenth- and seventeenth-century Milan, Italy) paid good wages to highly skilled seamstresses. The small size of the shops together with the skill of the workers enabled them to shift styles quickly to follow the latest fashions.

Thus, alongside of the increasingly rationalized and bureaucratic big businesses like steel and oil in the late nineteenth century, American productivity was also stimulated by small producers who provided a variety of goods that supplemented the bulk-manufactured staples of everyday life.

Advertising and Marketing
As small and large factories alike spewed out an amazing array of new products, business leaders often discovered that their output exceeded what the market could absorb. This was particularly true for mass-produced consumer goods such as matches, flour, soap, and canned foods. Not surprisingly, these industries were trailblazers in developing advertising and marketing techniques. Strategies for whetting consumer demand and for differentiating one product from another represented a critical component of industrial expansion in the post–Civil War era.

TECHNOLOGY & CULTURE

Electricity

Of all the technological achievements of the nineteenth century, none seemed more inspiring or mysterious than the ability to generate electricity. Using Alessandro Volta's discovery that chemical reactions in batteries produced a weak electric current, Samuel F.B. Morse had used batteries to power his telegraph in 1837. Alexander Graham Bell followed suit with his telephone in 1876. But higher voltages were needed to run lighting systems and motors. Michael Faraday in England and Joseph Henry in America discovered in 1831 that a rotating magnet surrounded by a conducting wire would produce a continuous flow of electric current. After the Civil War, American inventors used this discovery to develop powerful generators to run incandescent lights (1879), to power motors to run trolley cars (1888), and to drive machines in factories. For many Americans, the ability to harness electricity marked the subjugation of nature and indicated the progress of American civilization.

Nowhere did the knowledge of electricity seem more impressive than its promise to reveal the secrets of the human body. X-rays, discovered in 1895 by the German physicist Wilhelm Roentgen and developed into a practical hospital machine a year later by Thomas Edison, enabled doctors to see inside the body. Physicians discovered that the workings of the nervous system and the brain itself depended on electrical impulses. It was no accident that Edison was known as the "wizard of Menlo Park," where his research laboratory was located.

The spread of electric lighting illustrates how technological advances pushed innovation. Thomas Edison's vision went far beyond the development of a practical light bulb. He conceived of an interrelated system of power plants, transmission lines, and light fixtures, all to be produced by companies he had established. Edison's system of direct current lighting (DC—which flowed in only one direction in the wires) required that users be located near power plants. But in 1886, George Westinghouse set up a competing company that used the Italian inventor Nikola Tesla's discovery that alternating current (AC—which cycled back and forth within the wires) could send high voltage electricity efficiently over long distances. Competition between the two systems was finally resolved in 1896 when Edison's successor company, General Electric, agreed to share its patents with the Westinghouse Company. With electric current now standardized as 110 volts AC at 60 Hertz (60 cycles per second), dozens of other inventors developed electric motors, spotlights, electric signs, water pumps, elevators, and household appliances—all drawing power from the same power grid. Only twenty years after the first power station had been built, electrification had started to transform everyday life.

By 1898, when the city of London had sixty-two different utilities that produced thirty-two different voltage levels, American companies had created a unified national electrical system with standardized voltages, and the United States had established itself as a world leader in electrical technology. The remarkable achievements of the American electrical industry resulted from a combination of factors. Skilled inventors such as Edison, Westinghouse, and Frank Sprague, who developed electric motors for trolley and subway cars, were critical. But the efforts might never have made it out of the laboratories without financiers, such as J. P. Morgan and Henry Villard, who funded the enormous investment in electric generators, power plants, and transmission lines. A third factor was the independence of large corporations like General Electric and Westinghouse, which were able to operate

THE
NIAGARA FALLS
POWER CO.

11000 VOLTS 3-PHASE

POWER-HOUSE

DYNAMO

C

DIRECT CURRENT
550 VOLTS

NIAGARA RAILWAYS

MOTORS REPLACE
ENGINES FOR DRIVING
DYNAMOS FOR ARC AND
INCANDESCENT LIGHTING

LIGHTING STATION

CANAL

CARBORUNDUM CO.

ALTERNATING CURRENT
100 TO 250 VOLTS

DIRECT CURRENT
160 VOLTS

PITTSBURGH REDUCTION CO.

TURBINE

NIAGARA ELECTRO-CHEMICAL CO.

DIRECT CURRENT
125 TO 165 VOLTS

TUNNEL

CARBIDE COMPANY

ALTERNATING CURRENT
100 VOLTS

C—CONVERTER OR
TRANSFORMER

MATHIESON ALKALI CO.

DIRECT CURRENT
170 TO 230 VOLTS

R—ROTARY FOR RECEIV-
ING ALTERNATING AND
DELIVERING DIRECT
CURRENT

ALTERNATING CURRENT
MOTORS IN VARIOUS
FACTORIES

V—REGULATOR FOR
CHANGING VOLTAGE

INCANDESCENT LIGHTING IN
FACTORIES AND RESIDENCES

BUFFALO

DIRECT CURRENT
550 VOLTS

11000 VOLTS 3-PHASE

2200 VOLTS 2-PHASE

From Adams, Niagara Power

The Niagara Falls Power Company *As this diagram of the power station at Niagara Falls reveals, the early transmission of electric power was closely tied to large manufacturers who had the funds to support large investments in generating equipment and power lines.*

nationally and avoid conflicting state regulations. Operating as regional monopolies, these corporations standardized voltage, alternating current, and electrical fixtures nationwide. Finally, the pooling of patents was crucial. The American patent system, by granting inventors property rights in their inventions and by publicly identifying how the discoveries worked, stimulated technological innovation in general.

At first, electricity was very expensive, and the general public could not afford the cost of wiring homes. Still, even confined to the public sphere, the establishment of a national electrical system was one of the greatest technological innovations of the century. Electric streetcars and subways, public lighting systems, and electric elevators transformed urban America, allowing the construction of skyscrapers and the quick transportation of millions of people. The electrification of factories extended the workday into the night and made work safer. In the following decades, electrification made possible the invention of lighting systems, fans, washing machines, and a host of other devices to ease the drudgery of everyday life.

In the twentieth century, some short-comings in Americans' love affair with electricity became obvious. In the early years, urban electrification accentuated the differences between city and country life. After World War II, massive power failures showed that the centralization of power distribution systems, first constructed as private monopolies between 1880 and 1932, made them vulnerable to failure when a subsystem problem cascaded throughout the network. The private ownership of power companies, now called utility companies, has enabled them at times to inflate energy prices for their own profit. Most electrical power in the United States today is produced from coal, a nonrenewable resource that also produces acid rain and air pollution. Nevertheless, the creation of a national system of electrical power generation paved the way for remarkable innovations—from lighting to televisions and computers—that remain today closely tied to America's sense of progress and material advancement.

Questions for Analysis

1. *Why did the early electrical inventions seem to mark the subjugation of nature?*

2. *What technological breakthroughs paved the way for the widespread use of electricity for street lighting and transportation?*

3. *Why did the standardization and consolidation of the electric industry take place more quickly in the United States than in England?*

Through the use of brand names, trademarks, guarantees, slogans, endorsements, and other gimmicks, manufacturers built demand for their products and won enduring consumer loyalty. Americans bought Ivory Soap, first made in 1879 by Procter and Gamble of Cincinnati, because of the absurdly precise but impressive pledge that it was "99 and 44/100ths percent pure."

Other manufacturers won consumer loyalty through the development of unique products. In the 1880s, George Eastman developed a paper-based photographic film as an alternative to the fragile glass plates then in use and sold this film loaded into an inexpensive camera. Consumers returned the camera to his Rochester factory where, for a charge of ten dollars, the film was developed and printed, the camera reloaded, and everything shipped back. In marketing a new technology, Eastman had revolutionized an industry and democratized a visual medium previously confined to a few.

Social and Environmental Costs and Benefits

By 1900, the chaos of early industrial competition, when thousands of companies had struggled to enter a national market, had given way to the most productive economy in the world, supported by a legion of small, specialized companies and dominated by a few enormous ones. An industrial transformation that had originated in railroading and expanded to steel and petroleum had spread to every nook and cranny of American business and raised the United States to a position of world leadership.

The vast expansion of economic output brought social benefits in the form of labor-saving products, lower prices, and advances in transportation and communications. The benefits and liabilities sometimes seemed inextricably interconnected. The sewing machine, for example, created thousands of new factory jobs, made available a wider variety of clothing, and eased the lives of millions of housewives. At the same time, it encouraged avaricious entrepreneurs to operate sweatshops in which the immigrant poor—often vulnerable young women—toiled long hours for pitifully low wages (discussed further in Chapter 21).

For those who fell by the wayside in this era of spectacular economic growth, the cost could be measured in bankrupted companies and shattered dreams. John D. Rockefeller put things with characteristic bluntness when he said he wanted "only the big ones, only those who have already proved they can do a big business" in the Standard Oil Trust. "As for the others, unfortunately they will have to die."

The cost was high, too, for millions of American workers, immigrant and native-born alike. The vast expansion of new products was built on the backs of an army of laborers who were paid subsistence wages and who could be fired on a moment's notice when hard times or new technologies made them expendable.

Industrial growth often devastated the environment as well. Rivers fouled by oil or chemical waste, skies filled with clouds of soot, and a landscape littered with reeking garbage and toxic materials bore mute witness to the relentless drive for efficiency and profit.

Whatever the final balance sheet of social gains and costs, one thing was clear: the United States had muscled its way onto the world stage as an industrial titan. The ambition and drive of countless inventors, financiers, managerial innovators, and marketing wizards had combined to lay the groundwork for a new social and economic order in the twentieth century.

THE NEW SOUTH

The South entered the industrial era far more slowly than the Northeast. As late as 1900, total southern cotton-mill output, for example, remained little more than half that of the mills within a thirty-mile radius of Providence, Rhode Island. Moreover, the South's $509 average per capita income was less than half that of northerners.

The reasons for the South's late economic blossoming are not hard to discern. The Civil War's physical devastation, racism, the scarcity of southern towns and cities, lack of capital, illiteracy, northern control of financial markets and patents, and a low rate of technological innovation crippled efforts by southern business leaders to promote industrialization. Economic progress was also impeded by the myth of the Lost Cause, which, through its nostalgic portrayal of pre–Civil War society, perpetuated an image of the South as traditional and unchanging. As a result, southern industrialization inched forward haltingly and was shaped in distinctive ways.

Obstacles to Economic Development

Much of the South's difficulty in industrializing arose from its lack of capital and the devastation of the Civil War. So many southern banks failed during the Civil War that by 1865 the South, with more than a quarter of the nation's population, possessed just 2 percent of its banks. The federal government policies added to the banking problem by requiring anyone wishing to start a bank to have $50,000 in capital. Few southerners could meet this standard.

With banks in short supply, country merchants and storekeepers became bankers by default, lending supplies rather than cash to local farmers in return for a lien, or mortgage, on their crops (see Chapter 16). The burden of paying these liens trapped farmers on their own land and created a shortage of the labor needed for industrial expansion.

The shift from planting corn to specializing in either cotton or tobacco made small southern farmers particularly vulnerable to the fluctuations of commercial agriculture. When the price of cotton tumbled in national and international markets from eleven cents per pound in 1875 to less than five cents in 1894, well under the cost of production, many southern farmers grew desperate.

The South's chronic shortage of funds affected the economy in indirect ways as well, by limiting the resources available for education. During Reconstruction, northern philanthropists together with the Freedmen's Bureau, the American Missionary Association, and other relief agencies had begun a modest expansion of public schooling for both blacks and whites. But Georgia and many other southern states operated segregated schools and refused to tax property for school support until 1889. As a result, school attendance remained low, severely limiting the number of educated people able to staff technical and managerial positions in business and industry.

Southern states, like those in the North, often contributed the modest funds they had to war veterans' pensions. In this way, southern state governments built a white patronage system for Confederate veterans and helped reinforce southerners' idealization of the old Confederacy—the South's Lost Cause. As late as 1911, veterans' pensions in Georgia ate up 22 percent of the state's entire budget, leaving little for economic or educational development.

The New South Creed and Southern Industrialization

Despite these obstacles, energetic southern newspaper editors such as **Henry W. Grady** of the *Atlanta Constitution* and Henry Watterson of the *Louisville Courier Journal* championed the doctrine that became known as the New South creed. The South's rich coal and timber resources and cheap labor, they proclaimed in their papers, made it a natural site for industrial development.

The movement to industrialize the South gained momentum in the 1880s. To attract northern capital, southern states offered tax exemptions for new businesses, set up industrial and agricultural expositions, and leased prison convicts to serve as cheap labor. Florida, Texas, and other states gave huge tracts of lands to railroads, whose expansion in turn stimulated the birth of new towns and villages. Other states sold forest and mineral rights on nearly 6 million acres of federal lands to speculators, mostly from the North, who significantly expanded the production of iron, sulfur, coal, and lumber.

Following the lead of their northern counterparts, the southern iron and steel industries expanded as well. Birmingham, Alabama, founded in 1871 in a region blessed with rich deposits of coal, limestone, and iron ore, grew in less than three decades to a bustling city with noisy railroad yards and roaring blast furnaces. By 1900, it was the nation's largest pig-iron shipper. In these same years, Chattanooga, Tennessee, housed nine furnaces, seventeen foundries, and numerous machine shops.

As large-scale recruiters of black workers, the southern iron and steel mills contributed to the migration of blacks to the cities. By 1900, 20 percent of the southern black population was urban. Many urban blacks toiled as domestics or in similar menial capacities, but others entered the industrial work force. Southern industry reflected the patterns of racial segregation in southern life. Tobacco companies used black workers, particularly women, to clean the tobacco leaves while white women, at a different location, ran the machines that made cigarettes. The burgeoning textile mills were lilywhite. In the iron and steel industry, blacks, who comprised 60 percent of the unskilled work force by 1900, had practically no chance of advancement. Nevertheless, in a rare reversal of the usual pattern, southern blacks in the iron and steel industry had a higher skill level and on average earned more than did southern white textile workers.

Black miners were also recruited by the West Virginia coal industry that lured them with free transportation, high wages, and company housing. The coal boom at first forced companies to pay similar wages to blacks and whites, and they initially joined biracial labor unions. But the depression of 1893 weakened the unions and workers became increasingly confined to separate jobs.

Southern segregation, while restricting black employment in many ways, opened up new opportunities for black barbers, doctors, and businessmen to work with black customers. Nevertheless, economic opportunities for blacks remained severely limited. In lumbering, which was the South's largest industry, large numbers of blacks worked in the turpentine industry, collecting sap from trees. In good times, wages could be better than those offered to farm laborers, but during economic downturns workers were laid off or confined to work camps by vagrancy laws and armed guards.

| The Southern | Unlike the urban-based southern iron and steel industry, the |

The Southern Mill Economy   Unlike the urban-based southern iron and steel industry, the textile mills that mushroomed in the southern countryside in the 1880s often became catalysts for the formation of new towns and villages. In these mill towns, country ways and values suffused the new industrial workplace.

The cotton-mill economy grew largely in the Piedmont, the highland country stretching from central Virginia to northern Georgia and Alabama. The Piedmont had long been the South's backcountry, a land of subsistence farming and limited roads. But postwar railroad construction sparked a period of intense town building and textile-mill expansion. By 1920, the South was the nation's leading textile-mill center. Augusta, Georgia, with 2,800 mill workers, became known as the Lowell of the South, named after the mill town in Massachusetts where industrialization had flourished earlier. The expansion of the textile industry nurtured promoters' visions of a new, more prosperous, industrialized South.

Sharecroppers and tenant farmers at first hailed the new cotton mills as a way out of rural poverty. But appearances were deceptive. The chief cotton-mill promoters were drawn from the same ranks of merchants, lawyers, doctors, and bankers who had profited from the commercialization of southern agriculture (and from the misfortunes of poor black and white tenant farmers and sharecroppers trapped in the new system). Cotton-mill entrepreneurs shamelessly exploited their workers, paying just seven to eleven cents an hour, 30 percent to 50 percent less than what comparable mill workers in New England were paid.

The mills dominated most Piedmont textile communities. The mill operator not only built and owned the workers' housing and the company store but also supported the village church, financed the local elementary school, and pried into the morals and behavior of the mill hands. To prevent workers from moving from one mill to another, the mill owner usually paid them just once a month, often in scrip—a certificate redeemable only in goods from the company store. Since few families had enough money to get through a month, they often overspent and fell behind in their payments. The charges were deducted from workers' wages the following month. In this way, the mill drew workers and their families into a cycle of indebtedness very much like that faced by sharecroppers and tenant farmers.

To help make ends meet, mill workers kept their own garden patches and raised chickens, cows, and pigs. Southern mill hands thus brought communal farm values, long associated with large farm families and nurtured through cooperative planting and harvesting, into the mills themselves. Although they had to adapt to machine-paced work and received barely enough pay to live on, the working poor in the mill districts, like their prewar counterparts in the North, eased the shift from rural to village-industrial life by embracing a cooperative country ethic.

As northern cotton mills did before the Civil War, southern textile companies exploited the cheap rural labor around them, settling transplanted farm people in paternalistic company-run villages. Using these tactics, the industry underwent a period of steady growth.

The Southern Industrial Lag   Industrialization progressed at a slower rate in the South than in the North and depended on outside financing, technology, and expertise. The late nineteenth-century southern economy remained essentially in a colonial status, dominated by northern industries and financial syndicates. U.S. Steel, for example, controlled the Birmingham foundries and in 1900 priced Birmingham steel according to the "Pittsburgh plus" formula based on the price of Pittsburgh steel, plus the freight costs of shipping from Pittsburgh. As a result, southerners paid higher prices for steel than northerners, despite cheaper production costs.

An array of factors thus combined to retard industrialization in the South. Banking regulations requiring large reserves, scarce capital, wartime debts, lack of industrial experience, a segregated labor force, discrimination against blacks, and control by profit-hungry northern enterprises all hampered the region's economic development. Dragged down by a poorly educated white population and by a largely unskilled black population, southern industry languished. Not until after the turn of the century did southern industry undergo the restructuring and consolidation that had occurred in northern business enterprise two decades earlier.

As in the North, industrialization brought significant environmental damage, including polluted rivers and streams, decimated forests, grimy coal-mining towns, and soot-infested steel-making cities. Although Henry Grady's vision of a New

South may have inspired many southerners to work toward industrialization, economic growth in the South, limited as it was by outside forces, progressed in its own distinctly regional way.

FACTORIES AND THE WORK FORCE

Industrialization proceeded unevenly nationwide, and most late nineteenth-century Americans still worked in small shops. But as the century unfolded, large factories with armies of workers sprang onto the industrial scene. The pattern of change was evident. Between 1860 and 1900, the number of industrial workers jumped from 885,000 to 3.2 million, and the trend toward large-scale production became unmistakable.

From Workshop to Factory
The transition to a factory economy came not as an earthquake but rather as a series of seismic jolts varying in strength and duration. Whether they occurred quickly or slowly, however, the changes in factory production had a profound impact on artisans and unskilled laborers alike, because they involved a fundamental restructuring of work habits and a new emphasis on workplace discipline. The impact of these changes can be seen by examining the boot and shoe industry. As late as the 1840s, most shoes were custom-made by skilled artisans who worked in small, independent shops. Shoemakers were aristocrats in the world of labor. Taught in an apprentice system, they took pride in their work and controlled the quality of their products.

A distinctive working-class culture subdivided along ethnic lines evolved among these shoemakers. Foreign-born English, German, and Irish workers set up ethnic trade organizations and joined affiliated benevolent associations. Bound together by religious and ethnic ties, they observed weddings and funerals according to old-country traditions, relaxed together at the local saloon after work, and helped one another weather accidents or sicknesses.

As early as the 1850s, even before the widespread use of machinery, changes in the ready-made shoe trade had eroded the status of skilled labor. The manufacturing process was broken down into a sequence of repetitive, easily mastered tasks. Thus, instead of crafting a pair of shoes from start to finish, each team member specialized in only one part of the process, such as attaching the heel or polishing the leather.

In the 1880s, shoe factories became larger and more mechanized, and traditional skills largely vanished. Shoe companies replaced skilled operatives with lower-paid, less-skilled women and children. By 1890, women made up more than 35 percent of the work force. Like the laborer whose machine nailed heels on forty-eight hundred shoes a day, even "skilled" workers in the new factories found themselves performing numbingly repetitive tasks.

The Hardships of Industrial Labor
The expansion of the factory system spawned an unprecedented demand for unskilled labor. By the 1880s, nearly one-third of the 750,000 workers employed in the railroad and steel industries, for example, were common laborers.

In the construction trades and the garment-making industries, unskilled laborers were hired under the so-called contract system by a subcontractor who took responsibility for employee relations. These common workers were seasonal help, hired in times of need and laid off in slack periods. The steel industry employed them to shovel ore in the yards and to move ingots inside the mills. The foremen drove the gangs hard; in the Pittsburgh area, the workers called the foremen "pushers."

Notoriously transient, unskilled laborers drifted from city to city and from industry to industry. In the late 1870s, unskilled laborers earned $1.30 a day, while bricklayers and blacksmiths earned more than $3. Only unskilled southern mill workers, whose wages averaged a meager eighty-four cents a day, earned less.

Unskilled and skilled workers alike worked up to twelve-hour shifts and faced grave hazards to their health and safety. Children were the most vulnerable. In the coal mines and cotton mills, child laborers typically entered the work force at age eight or nine. In the cotton mills, children could be injured by the unprotected pulley belts that powered the machines or develop brown lung disease, a crippling illness caused by breathing in cotton dust. In the coal industry, where children were commonly employed to remove pieces of slate from the conveyor belts, the cloud of coal dust that swirled around them gave them black lung disease—a disorder that leads to emphysema and heart failure.

In addition to facing these workplace hazards, working children often fell behind in their schooling. Pressured by families that needed additional income and by the desire to have some spending money of their own, many children forged work permits and their birth certificates to avoid the compulsory schooling laws (see Chapter 19) to enter the mills and the mines. This lack of education, plus the physical trauma to their bodies, would often exclude them from better-paying jobs as adults.

For adult workers, the railroad industry was one of the most perilous. In 1889, the first year the Interstate Commerce Commission compiled reliable statistics, almost two thousand rail workers were killed on the job and more than twenty thousand injured.

Those who were maimed and disfigured by industrial accidents were further ostracized when San Francisco, Chicago, and other cities passed ordinances in the 1880s that removed "unsightly beggars" from the streets. The overall effect of these laws was to make those handicapped by industrial accidents invisible to the general population at large and to hamstring efforts to force companies to adopt more effective safety regulations.

Disabled workers and widows received minimal financial aid from employers. Until the 1890s, the courts considered employer negligence one of the normal risks borne by employees. Railroad and factory owners fought the adoption of state safety and health standards on the grounds that the cost would be excessive. For sickness and accident benefits, workers joined fraternal organizations and ethnic clubs, part of whose monthly dues benefited those in need. But in most cases, the amounts set aside were too low to be of much help. When a worker was killed or maimed in an accident, the family had to rely on relatives or friends for support.

Immigrant Labor   As we shall see in more detail in Chapter 19, factory owners turned to unskilled immigrants for the muscle they needed in dangerous and undesirable jobs. Poverty-stricken French Canadians filled the most menial positions in northeastern textile mills. On the West Coast, Chinese immigrants performed the dirtiest and most physically demanding jobs in mining, canning, and railroad construction.

Writing home in the 1890s, eastern European immigrants described the hazardous and draining work in the steel mills. "Wherever the heat is most insupportable, the flames most scorching, the smoke and soot most choking, there we are certain to find compatriots bent and wasted in toil," reported one Hungarian. Yet those immigrants disposed to live frugally in a boardinghouse and to work an eighty-four-hour week could save fifteen dollars a month, far more than they could have earned in their homeland.

Although most immigrants worked hard, few adjusted easily to the fast pace of the factory. Factory operations were relentless, dictated by the unvarying speed of the machines. A brochure used by the International Harvester Corporation to teach English to its Polish workers promoted the "proper" values. Lesson I read:

> *I hear the whistle. I must hurry.*
> *I hear the five minute whistle.*
> *It is time to go into the shop.*
> *I take my check from the gate board and hang it on the department*
>   *board.*
> *I change my clothes and get ready to work.*
> *The starting whistle blows.*
> *I eat my lunch.*
> *It is forbidden to eat until then.*
> *The whistle blows at five minutes of starting time.*
> *I get ready to go to work.*
> *I work until the whistle blows to quit.*
> *I leave my place nice and clean.*
> *I put all my clothes in the locker.*
> *I must go home.*

As this "lesson" reveals, factory work tied the immigrants to a rigid timetable very different from the pace of farm life.

When immigrant workers resisted the tempo of factory work, drank on the job, or took unexcused absences, employers used a variety of tactics to enforce discipline. Some sponsored temperance societies and Sunday schools to teach punctuality and sobriety. Others cut wages and put workers on the piecework system, paying them only for the items produced. Employers sometimes also provided low-cost housing to gain leverage against work stoppages; if workers went on strike, the boss could simply evict them.

In the case of immigrants from southern Europe whose skin colors were often darker than northern Europeans', employers asserted that the workers were non-white and thus did not deserve the same compensation as native-born Americans. Because the concept of "whiteness" in the United States bestowed a sense of privilege and the automatic extension of the rights of citizenship, Irish, Greek, Italian, Jewish, and a host of other immigrants, although of the Caucasian race,

Library of Congress, Prints and Photographs Division

Textile Workers *Young children like this one often were used in the textile mills because their small fingers could tie together broken threads more easily than those of adults.*

were also considered nonwhite. Rather than a fixed category based on biological differences, the concept of race was thus used to justify the harsh treatment of foreign-born labor.

Women and Work in Industrial America   Women's work experiences, like those of men, were shaped by marital status, social class, and race. Upper-class white married women widely accepted an ideology of "separate spheres" (as discussed in Chapter 19) and remained at home, raised children, and looked after the household. The well-to-do hired maids and cooks to ease their burdens.

Working-class married women, in contrast, often had to contribute to the financial support of the family. In fact, working for wages at home by sewing, button-making, taking in boarders, or doing laundry had predated industrialization. In the late nineteenth century, unscrupulous urban entrepreneurs exploited this captive work force. In the clothing industry, manufacturers hired out finishing tasks to lower-class married women and their children, who labored long hours in crowded apartments.

Young, working-class single women often viewed factory work as an opportunity. In 1870, 13 percent of all women worked outside the home, the majority as cooks, maids, cleaning ladies, and laundresses. But most working women intensely disliked the long hours, low pay, and social stigma of being a "servant." When jobs in industry expanded in the last quarter of the century, growing numbers of single white women abandoned domestic employment for better-paying work in the textile, food-processing, and garment industries. Discrimination barred black working women from following this path. Between 1870 and 1900, the number of women of all races working outside the home nearly tripled. By the turn of the century, women made up 17 percent of the country's labor force.

A variety of factors propelled the rise in the employment of single women. Changes in agriculture prompted many young farmwomen to seek employment in the industrial sector (discussed further in Chapter 19), and immigrant parents often sent their daughters to the factories to supplement meager family incomes. Plant managers welcomed young immigrant women as a ready source of inexpensive unskilled labor. But factory owners treated them as temporary help and kept their wages low. In 1890, young women operating sewing machines earned as little as four dollars for seventy hours of work while their male counterparts made eight.

Despite their paltry wages, long hours, and often unpleasant working conditions, many young women relished earning their own income and joined the work force in increasing numbers. Although the financial support these working women contributed to their families was significant, few working women were paid enough to provide homes for themselves. Rather than fostering their independence, industrial work tied them more deeply to a family economy that depended on their earnings.

Chicago Historical Society

Women in the Workplace *The women in this photograph are testing their typing skills at a civil service exam in Chicago in the 1890s. The expansion of banking, insurance, and a variety of other businesses opened up new career opportunities for women as secretaries, stenographers, and typists.*

When the typewriter and the telephone came into general use in the 1890s, office work provided new employment opportunities, and women with high school educations moved into clerical and secretarial jobs earlier filled by men. They were attracted by the clean, safe working conditions and relatively good pay. First-rate typists could earn six to eight dollars a week, which compared favorably with factory wages. Office work carried higher prestige and generally was steadier than work in the factory or shop.

Despite the growing number of women workers, the late nineteenth-century popular press portrayed women's work outside the home as temporary. Few people even considered the possibility that a woman could attain local or even national prominence in the emerging corporate order.

Hard Work and the Gospel of Success   Although women were generally excluded from the equation, influential opinion molders in these years preached that any man could achieve success in the new industrial era. In *Ragged Dick* (1867) and scores of later tales, **Horatio Alger,** a Unitarian minister turned dime novelist, recounted the adventures of poor but honest lads who rose through initiative and self-discipline.

Some critics did not accept this belief. In an 1871 essay, Mark Twain chided the public for its naïveté and suggested that business success was more likely to come to those who lied and cheated. In testimony given in 1883 before a Senate committee investigating labor conditions, a New Yorker named Thomas B. McGuire dolefully recounted how he had been forced out of the horse-cart business by larger, better financed concerns. Declared McGuire, "I live in a tenement house, three stories up, where the water comes in through the roof, and I cannot better myself.... Why? Simply because this present system ... is all for the privileged classes, nothing for the man who produces the wealth." Only with starting capital of $10,000—then a large sum—said McGuire, could the independent entrepreneur hope to compete with the large companies.

What are the facts? Studies of nearly two hundred of the largest corporations reveal that few workers rose from poverty to colossal wealth. Ninety-five percent of the industrial leaders came from middle- and upper-class backgrounds. The best chance for native-born working-class Americans to get ahead was to master a skill and to rise to the top in a small company. Although only a few reaped immense fortunes, many improved their standard of living.

The different fates of immigrant workers in San Francisco show the possibilities and perils of moving up within the working class. In the 1860s, the Irish-born Donahue brothers grew wealthy from the Union Iron Works they had founded, where six hundred men built heavy equipment for the mining industry. In contrast, the nearly fifteen thousand Chinese workers who returned to the city after the Central Pacific's rail line was completed in 1869 were consigned by prejudice to work in cigar, textile, and other light-industry factories. Even successful Chinese entrepreneurs faced discrimination. When a Chinese merchant, Mr. Yung, refused to sell out to the wealthy Charles Crocker, a dry-goods merchant turned railroad entrepreneur who was building a mansion on Nob Hill, Crocker built a thirty-foot-high "spite fence" around Yung's house so that it would be completely sealed from view.

Thus, while some skilled workers became owners of their own companies, the opportunities for advancement for unskilled immigrant workers were considerably more limited. Some did move to semiskilled or skilled positions. Yet most immigrants, particularly the Irish, Italians, and Chinese, moved far more slowly than the sons of middle- and upper-class Americans who began with greater educational advantages and family financial backing. The upward mobility possible for such unskilled workers was generally mobility within the working class. Immigrants who got ahead in the late nineteenth century went from rags to respectability, not rags to riches.

One positive economic trend in these years was the rise in real wages, representing gains in actual buying power. Average real wages climbed 31 percent for unskilled workers and 74 percent for skilled workers between 1860 and 1900. Overall gains in purchasing power, however, often were undercut by injuries and unemployment during slack times or economic slumps. The position of unskilled immigrant laborers was particularly shaky. Even during a prosperous year like 1890, one out of every five nonagricultural workers was unemployed at least one month of the year. During the depressions of the 1870s and 1890s, wage cuts, extended layoffs, and irregular employment pushed those at the bottom of the industrial work force to the brink of starvation.

Thus, the overall picture of late nineteenth-century economic mobility is complex. At the top of the scale, a mere 10 percent of American families owned 73 percent of the nation's wealth in 1890, while less than half of industrial laborers earned more than the five-hundred dollar poverty line annually. In between the very rich and the very poor, skilled immigrants and small shopkeepers improved their economic position significantly. So although the standard of living for millions of Americans rose, the gap between the poor and the well-off remained a yawning abyss.

Labor Unions and Industrial Conflict

Aware that the growth of large corporations gave industrial leaders unprecedented power to control the workplace, labor leaders searched for ways to create broad-based, national organizations that could protect their members. But this drive to create a nationwide labor movement faced many problems. Employers deliberately accentuated ethnic and racial divisions within the work force to hamper unionizing efforts. Skilled crafts workers, moreover, felt little kinship with low-paid common laborers. Divided into different trades, they often saw little reason to work together. Thus, unionization efforts moved forward slowly and experienced setbacks.

Two groups, the National Labor Union and the Knights of Labor, struggled to build a mass labor movement that would unite skilled and unskilled workers regardless of their specialties. After impressive initial growth, however, both efforts collapsed. Far more effective was the American Federation of Labor (AFL), which represented skilled workers in powerful independent craft unions. The AFL survived and grew, but it represented only a small portion of the total labor force.

With unions weak, labor unrest during economic downturns reached crisis proportions. When pay rates were cut or working conditions became intolerable, laborers walked off the job without union authorization. These actions, called **wildcat strikes,** often exploded into violence. The labor crisis of the 1890s, with its strikes and bloodshed, would reshape the legal environment, increase the demand for state regulation, and eventually contribute to a movement for progressive reform.

Organizing Workers
From the eighteenth century on, skilled workers had organized local trade unions to fight wage reductions and provide benefits for their members in times of illness or accident. But the effectiveness of these organizations was limited. The challenge that labor leaders faced in the postwar period was how to boost the unions' clout. Some believed this goal could be achieved by forming one big association that would transcend craft lines and pull in the mass of unskilled workers.

Inspired by this vision of a nationwide labor association, William H. Sylvis, president of the Iron Molders' International Union, an organization of iron-foundry workers, in 1866 called a convention in Baltimore to form a new organization, the **National Labor Union** (NLU). Reflecting the pre–Civil War idealism, the NLU endorsed the eight-hour-day movement, which insisted that labor deserved eight hours for work, eight hours for sleep, and eight hours for personal affairs. Leaders also called for an end to convict labor, for the establishment of a federal department of labor, and for currency and banking reform. To push wage scales higher, they endorsed immigration restriction, especially of Chinese migrants, whom native-born workers blamed for undercutting prevailing wage levels. The NLU under Sylvis's leadership supported the cause of working women and elected a woman as one of its national officers. It urged black workers to organize as well, though in racially separate unions.

When Sylvis's own union failed to win a strike in 1867 to improve wages, Sylvis turned to national political reform. He invited a number of reformers to the 1868 NLU convention, including woman suffrage advocates Susan B. Anthony and Elizabeth Cady Stanton, who, according to a reporter, made "no mean impression on the bearded delegates." But when Sylvis suddenly died in 1869, the NLU faded quickly. After a brief incarnation in 1872 as the National Labor Reform Party, it vanished from the scene.

The dream of a labor movement that combined skilled and unskilled workers lived on in a new organization, the Noble and Holy Order of the **Knights of Labor,** founded in 1869. Led by Uriah H. Stephens, head of the Garment Cutters of Philadelphia, the Knights welcomed all wage earners. The Knights demanded equal pay for women, an end to child labor and convict labor, and the cooperative employer–employee ownership of factories, mines, and other businesses. At a time when no federal income tax existed, they called for a progressive tax on all earnings, graduated so that higher-income earners would pay more.

The Knights grew slowly at first. But membership rocketed in the 1880s after the eloquent Terence V. Powderly replaced Stephens as the organization's head. In the early 1880s, the Knights of Labor reflected both its idealistic origins and Powderly's collaborative vision. Powderly opposed strikes, which he considered "a relic of barbarism," and organized producer and consumer cooperatives. A teetotaler, he also urged temperance upon the membership. Powderly advocated the admission of blacks into local Knights of Labor assemblies, although he recognized the strength of racism and allowed southern local assemblies to be segregated. Under his leadership, the Knights welcomed women members; by 1886, women organizers had recruited thousands of workers, and women made up an estimated 10 percent of the union's membership.

Powderly supported restrictions on immigration and a total ban on Chinese immigration. In 1877, San Francisco workers demonstrating for an eight-hour workday, destroyed twenty-five Chinese-run laundries and terrorized the local Chinese population. In 1880, both major party platforms included anti-Chinese immigration plans. Two years later, Congress passed the Chinese Exclusion Act, placing a ten-year moratorium on Chinese immigration. The ban was extended in 1902 and not repealed until 1943.

Powderly's greatest triumph came in 1885. In that year, when Jay Gould tried to get rid of the Knights of Labor on his Wabash railroad by firing active union members, Powderly and his executive board instructed all Knights on the Wabash line to walk off the job. This action crippled the Wabash's operations. To the nation's amazement, Gould met with Powderly and canceled his campaign against the Knights of Labor. "The Wabash victory is with the Knights," declared a St. Louis newspaper; "no such victory has ever before been secured in this or any other country."

Membership in the Knights of Labor soared. By 1886, more than seven hundred thousand workers were organized in nearly six thousand locals. Turning to political action that fall, the Knights mounted campaigns in nearly two hundred towns and cities nationwide, electing several mayors and judges (Powderly himself had served as mayor of Scranton since 1878). They secured passage of state laws banning convict labor and federal laws against the importation of foreign contract labor. Business executives warned that the Knights could cripple the economy and take over the country if they chose.

But the organization's strength soon waned. Workers became disillusioned when a series of unauthorized strikes failed in 1886. By the late 1880s, the Knights of Labor was a shadow of its former self.

As the Knights of Labor declined, another national labor organization, pursuing more immediate and practical goals, was gaining strength. The skilled craft unions had long been uncomfortable with labor organizations like the Knights that welcomed skilled and unskilled alike. They were also concerned that the Knights' broad reform goals would undercut their own commitment to better wages and protecting the interests of their particular crafts. The break came in May 1886 when the craft unions left the Knights of Labor to form the **American Federation of Labor** (AFL).

The AFL replaced the Knights' grand visions with practical tactics aimed at bread-and-butter issues. **Samuel Gompers,** the immigrant cigar maker who became head of the AFL in 1886 and led it until his death in 1924, believed in "trade unionism, pure and simple." For Gompers, higher wages were the necessary base to enable working class families to live decently, with respect and dignity. The stocky, mustachioed labor leader argued that labor, to stand up to the corporations, would have to harness the bargaining power of skilled workers, whom employers could not easily replace, and concentrate on the practical goals of raising wages and reducing hours.

A master tactician, Gompers believed the trend toward large-scale industrial organization necessitated a comparable degree of organization by labor. He also recognized, however, that the skilled craft unions that made up the AFL retained a strong sense of independence. To persuade crafts workers from the various trades to join forces without violating their sense of craft autonomy, Gompers organized the AFL as a federation of trade unions, each retaining control of its own members but all linked by an executive council that coordinated strategy during boycotts and strike actions. "We want to make the trade union movement under the AFL as distinct as the billows, yet one as the sea," he told a national convention.

Focusing the federation's efforts on short-term improvements in wages and hours, Gompers at first sidestepped divisive political issues. The new organization's platform did, however, demand an eight-hour workday, employers' liability for workers' injuries, and mine safety laws. Although women participated in many craft unions, the AFL did little to recruit women workers after 1894 because Gompers and others believed that women workers undercut men's wages. By 1904, under Gompers's careful tutelage, the AFL had grown to more than 1.6 million strong.

Although the unions held up an ideal toward which many might strive, labor organizations before 1900 remained weak. Less than 5 percent of the work force joined union ranks. Split between skilled artisans and common laborers, separated along ethnic and religious lines, and divided over tactics, the unions battled with only occasional effectiveness against the growing power of corporate enterprise. Lacking financial resources, they typically watched from the sidelines when unorganized workers launched wildcat strikes that sometimes turned violent.

Strikes and Labor Unrest   Americans lived with a high level of violence from the nation's beginnings, and the nineteenth century—with its international and civil wars, urban riots, and Indian-white conflict—was no exception. Terrible labor clashes toward the end of the century were part of this continuing pattern, but they nevertheless shocked and dismayed contemporaries. From 1881 to 1905, close to thirty-seven thousand strikes erupted, in which nearly 7 million workers participated.

The first major wave of strikes began in 1873 when a Wall Street crash triggered a stock-market panic and a major depression. Six thousand businesses closed the following year, and many more cut wages and laid off workers. Striking Pennsylvania coal miners were fired and evicted from their homes. The tension turned deadly in 1877 during a wildcat railroad strike. Ignited by wage reductions on the Baltimore and Ohio Railroad in July, the strike exploded up and down the railroad lines, spreading to New York, Pittsburgh, St. Louis, Kansas City, Chicago, and San Francisco. Rioters in Pittsburgh torched Union Depot. By the time newly installed president Rutherford B. Hayes had called out the troops and quelled the strike two weeks later, nearly one hundred people had died, and two-thirds of the nation's railroads stood idle.

The railroad strike stunned middle-class America. The religious press responded hysterically. "If the club of the policeman, knocking out the brains of the rioter, will answer, then well and good," declared one Congregationalist journal, "[but if not] then bullets and bayonets ... constitute the one remedy." The same middle-class Americans who worried about Jay Gould and the corporate abuse of power grew terrified of mob violence.

Ethnic and Racial Hatred *Conservative business owners used racist advertising such as this trade card stigmatizing Chinese laundry workers to promote their own products and to associate their company with patriotism.*

Employers capitalized on the public hysteria to crack down on labor. Many required their workers to sign "yellow dog" contracts in which they promised not to strike or join a union. Some hired Pinkerton agents, a private police force, to defend their factories and, when necessary, turned to the federal government and the U.S. army to suppress labor unrest.

Although the economy recovered, more strikes and violence followed in the 1880s. On May 1, 1886, 340,000 workers walked off their jobs in support of the campaign for an eight-hour workday. Three days later, Chicago police shot and killed four strikers at the McCormick Harvester plant. At a protest rally the next evening in the city's Haymarket Square, someone threw a bomb, killing or fatally wounding seven policemen. In response, the police fired wildly into the crowd and killed four demonstrators.

Public reaction was immediate. Business leaders and middle-class citizens lashed out at labor activists and particularly at the sponsors of the Haymarket meeting, most of whom were associated with a German-language anarchist newspaper that advocated the violent overthrow of capitalism. Eight men were arrested. Although no evidence connected them directly to the bomb throwing, all were convicted of murder, and four were executed. One committed suicide in prison. In Haymarket's aftermath, still more Americans became convinced that the nation was in the grip of a deadly foreign conspiracy, and animosity toward labor unions intensified.

Confrontations between capital and labor became particularly violent in the West. When the Mine Owners' Protective Association cut wages at work sites along Idaho's Coeur d'Alene River in 1892, the miners, who were skilled dynamiters, blew up a mill and captured the guards sent to defend it. Mine owners responded by mustering the Idaho National Guard to round up the men and cripple their union.

Back east that same year, armed conflict broke out during the **Homestead Strike** at the Carnegie Steel Company plant in Homestead, Pennsylvania. To destroy the union, managers had cut wages and locked out the workers. When workers fired on the armed men from the Pinkerton Detective Agency who came to protect the plant, a battle broke out. Seven union members and three Pinkertons died. A week later the governor sent National Guardsmen to restore order. The union crushed, the mills resumed full operation a month later.

The most systematic use of troops to smash union power came in 1894 during a strike against the Pullman Palace Car Company. In 1880 George Pullman, a manufacturer of elegant dining and sleeping cars for the nation's railroads, had constructed a factory and town, called Pullman, ten miles south of Chicago. The carefully planned community provided solid brick houses for the workers, beautiful parks and playgrounds, and even its own sewage-treatment plant. Pullman also closely policed workers' activities, outlawed saloons, and insisted that his properties turn a profit.

When the depression of 1893 hit, Pullman slashed workers' wages without reducing their rents. In reaction, thousands of workers joined the newly formed American Railway Union and went on strike. They were led by a fiery young organizer, **Eugene V. Debs,** who vowed "to strip the mask of hypocrisy from the pretended philanthropist and show him to the world as an oppressor of labor." Union members working for the nation's largest railroads refused to switch Pullman cars, paralyzing rail traffic in and out of Chicago, one of the nation's premier rail hubs.

In response, the General Managers' Association, an organization of top railroad executives, set out to break the union. The General Managers imported strikebreakers from among jobless easterners and asked U.S. Attorney General Richard Olney, who sat on the board of directors of three major railroad networks, for a federal injunction (court order) against the strikers for allegedly refusing to move railroad cars carrying U.S. mail.

In fact, union members had volunteered to switch mail cars onto any trains that did not carry Pullman cars, and it was the railroads' managers who were delaying the mail by refusing to send their trains without the full complement of cars. Nevertheless, Olney, supported by President Grover Cleveland and citing the Sherman Anti-Trust Act, secured an injunction against the leaders of the American Railway

Union for restraint of commerce. When the union refused to order its members back to work, Debs was arrested, and federal troops poured in. During the ensuing riot, workers burned seven hundred freight cars, thirteen people died, and fifty-three were wounded. By July 18, the strike had been crushed.

By playing upon a popular identification of strikers with anarchism and violence, crafty corporate leaders persuaded state and federal officials to cripple organized labor's ability to bargain with business. When the Supreme Court (in the 1895 case *In re Debs*) upheld Debs's prison sentence and legalized the use of injunctions against labor unions, the judicial system gave business a potent new weapon with which to restrain labor organizers.

Yet organizers persisted. In 1897, the feisty Irish-born Mary Harris Jones, known as **Mother Jones,** persuaded coal miners in Pennsylvania to join the United Mine Workers of America, a union founded seven years earlier. She staged parades of children, invited workers' wives to stockpile food, and dramatized the importance of militant mothers fighting for their families. Her efforts were successful. Wage reductions were restored because no large companies dominated the industry and the owners needed to restore production.

Despite the achievements of the United Mine Workers, whose members had climbed to three hundred thousand by 1900, the successive attempts by the National Labor Union, Knights of Labor, American Federation of Labor, and American Railway Union to build a national working class labor movement achieved only limited success. Aggressive employer associations and conservative state and local officials hamstrung their efforts. In sharp contrast to Great Britain and Germany, where state officials often mediated disputes between labor and capital, federal and state officials in the United States increasingly sided with manufacturers. Ineffective in the political arena, blocked by state officials, divided by ethnic differences, harassed by employers, and frustrated by court decisions, American unions failed to expand their base of support. Post–Civil War labor turmoil had sapped the vitality of organized labor and given it a negative public image that it would not shed until the 1930s.

Social Thinkers Probe for Alternatives   Widespread industrial violence was particularly unsettling when examined in the context of working-class poverty. In 1879, after observing three men rummaging through garbage to find food, the poet and journalist Walt Whitman wrote, "If the United States, like the countries of the Old World, are also to grow vast crops of poor, desperate, dissatisfied, nomadic, miserably-waged populations, such as we see looming upon us of late years ... then our republican experiment, notwithstanding all its surface-successes, is at heart an unhealthy failure." Whitman's bleak speculation was part of a general public debate over the social meaning of the new industrial order. At stake was a larger issue: should government become the mechanism for helping the poor and regulating big business?

Defenders of capitalism preached the laissez-faire ("hands-off") argument, insisting that government should never attempt to control business. They buttressed their case by citing Scottish economist Adam Smith, who had argued in *The Wealth of Nations* (1776) that self-interest acted as an "invisible hand" in the marketplace, automatically regulating the supply of and demand for goods and services.

In "The Gospel of Wealth," an influential essay published in 1889, Andrew Carnegie justified laissez-faire by applying the evolutionary theories of British social scientist Herbert Spencer to human society. "The law of competition," Carnegie argued, "may be sometimes hard for the individual, [but] it is best for the race, because it insures the survival of the fittest in every department."

Tough-minded Yale professor **William Graham Sumner** shared Carnegie's disapproval of government interference. His combative book *What Social Classes Owe to Each Other* (1883) applied the evolutionary theories of British naturalist Charles Darwin to human society. In an early statement of what became known as **Social Darwinism,** Sumner asserted that inexorable natural laws controlled the social order: "A drunkard in the gutter is just where he ought to be ... The law of survival of the fittest was not made by man, and it cannot be abrogated by man. We can only, by interfering with it, produce the survival of the unfittest." The state, declared Sumner, owed its citizens nothing but law, order, and basic political rights.

Sumner's argument did not go unchallenged. In *Dynamic Sociology* (1883), Lester Frank Ward, a geologist, argued that contrary to Sumner's claim, the supposed "laws" of nature could be circumvented by human will. Just as scientists had applied their knowledge to breeding superior livestock, government experts could use the power of the state to regulate big business, protect society's weaker members, and prevent the heedless exploitation of natural resources.

Other social theorists offered more utopian solutions to the problems of poverty and social unrest. Henry George, a self-taught San Francisco newspaper editor and economic theorist, proposed to solve the nation's uneven distribution of wealth through what he called the single tax. In *Progress and Poverty* (1879), he noted that speculators reaped huge profits from the rising price of land that they neither developed nor improved. By taxing this "unearned increment," the government could obtain the funds necessary to ameliorate the misery caused by industrialization. The result would bring the benefits of socialism—a state controlled economic system that distributed resources according to need—without socialism's great disadvantage, the stifling of individual initiative. George's program was so popular that he lectured around the country and only narrowly missed being elected mayor of New York in 1886.

The vision of a harmonious industrialized society was vividly expressed in the utopian novel *Looking Backward* (1888) by Massachusetts newspaper editor Edward Bellamy. Cast as a glimpse into the future, Bellamy's novel tells of Julian West, who falls asleep in 1888 and awakens in the year 2000 to find a nation without poverty or strife. In this future world, West learns, a completely centralized, state-run economy and a new religion of solidarity have combined to create a society in which everyone works for the common welfare. Bellamy's vision of a conflict-free society where all share equally in industrialization's benefits so inspired middle-class Americans fearful of corporate power and working-class violence that nearly five hundred local Bellamyite organizations, called Nationalist clubs, sprang up to try to turn his dream into reality.

Ward, George, and Bellamy did not deny the benefits of the existing industrial order; they simply sought to humanize it. These utopian reformers envisioned a harmonious society whose members all worked together.

Marxist socialists advanced a different view. Elaborated by German philosopher and radical agitator Karl Marx (1818–1883) in *Das Kapital* (1867) and other works, **Marxism** rested on the labor theory of value: a proposition (which

Adam Smith had also accepted) that the labor required to produce a commodity was the only true measure of that commodity's value. Any profit made by the capitalist employer was "surplus value" appropriated from the exploited workers. As competition among capitalists increased, Marx predicted, wages would decline to starvation levels, and more and more capitalists would be driven out of business. Society would be divided between a shrinking bourgeoisie (capitalists, merchants, and middle-class professionals) and an impoverished proletariat (the workers). The proletariat would then revolt and seize control of the state and of the economy. Although Marx viewed class struggle as the essence of modern history, his eyes were also fixed on the shining vision of the communist millennium that the revolution would eventually usher in—a classless utopia in which the state would "wither away" and all exploitation would cease. To lead the working class in its showdown with capitalism, Marx and his collaborator Friedrich Engels helped found socialist parties in Europe, whose strength grew steadily, beginning in the 1870s.

Despite Marx's keen interest in the United States, Marxism proved to have little appeal in late nineteenth-century America other than for a tiny group of primarily German-born immigrants. The Marxist-oriented Socialist Labor Party (1877) had attracted only about fifteen hundred members by 1890. More alarming to the public at large was the handful of anarchists, again mostly immigrants, who rejected Marxist discipline and preached the destruction of capitalism, the violent overthrow of the state, and the immediate introduction of a stateless utopia. In 1892, Alexander Berkman, a Russian immigrant anarchist, attempted to assassinate Henry Clay Frick, the manager of Andrew Carnegie's Homestead Steel Works. Entering Frick's office with a pistol, Berkman shot him in the neck and then tried to stab him. A carpenter working in Frick's office overpowered the assailant. Rather than igniting a workers' insurrection that would usher in a new social order as he had hoped, Berkman came away with a long prison sentence. His act confirmed the business stereotype of "labor agitators" as lawless and violent.

CHRONOLOGY
1865–1900

1859	First oil well drilled in Titusville, Pennsylvania.
1866	National Labor Union founded.
1869	Transcontinental railroad completed.
	Knights of Labor organized.
1870	John D. Rockefeller establishes Standard Oil Company.
1873	Panic of 1873 triggers a depression lasting until 1879.
1876	Alexander Graham Bell patents the telephone.
1877	Edison invents phonograph.
	Railway workers stage first nationwide strike.
1879	Henry George, *Progress and Poverty*.
	Edison perfects incandescent lamp.

1882	Standard Oil Trust established.
	Edison opens first electric power station in New York City.
	Chinese Exclusion Act.
1883	William Graham Sumner, *What Social Classes Owe to Each Other.*
	Lester Frank Ward, *Dynamic Sociology.*
1886	American Federation of Labor (AFL) formed.
	Haymarket riot in Chicago.
1887	Interstate Commerce Act establishes Interstate Commerce Commission.
1888	Edward Bellamy, *Looking Backward.*
1889	Andrew Carnegie, "The Gospel of Wealth."
1890	Sherman Anti-Trust Act.
	United Mine Workers formed.
1892	Standard Oil of New Jersey and General Electric formed.
	Homestead Strike.
	Columbian Exposition in Chicago.
	Miners strike at Coeur d'Alene, Idaho.
1893	Panic of 1893 triggers a depression lasting until 1897.
1894	Pullman Palace Car workers strike.
1901	J. Pierpont Morgan organizes United States Steel.

CONCLUSION

By 1900, industrialization had propelled the United States into the forefront of the world's major powers, lowered the cost of goods through mass production, generated thousands of jobs, and produced a wide range of new consumer products. Using accounting systems first developed by the railroads and sophisticated new technologies, national corporations had pioneered innovative systems for distributing and marketing their goods. In the steel and oil industries, Andrew Carnegie and John D. Rockefeller had vertically integrated their companies, controlling production from the raw materials to the finished product. Through systematic cost cutting and ruthless underselling of their competitors, they had gained control of most of their industry and lowered prices.

Despite these advantages, most Americans recognized that industrialization's cost was high. The rise of the giant corporations had been achieved through savage competition, exploited workers, shady business practices, polluted factory sites, and the collapse of an economic order built on craft skills. In the South in particular, the devastation of the Civil War and the control of banking and raw materials by northern capitalists encouraged industrialists to adopt a paternalistic, family-oriented approach in the cotton mills and to pay exceedingly low wages.

Outbursts of labor violence, the growth of urban slums, and grinding poverty showed starkly that all was not well in industrial America. Although the Knights of Labor and the American Federation of Labor attempted to organize workers nationally, the labor movement could not control spontaneous wildcat strikes and violence. In response, company owners appealed to government authorities to arrest strikers, obtain court injunctions against union actions, and cripple the ability of labor leaders to expand their organizations.

As a result, Americans remained profoundly ambivalent about the new industrial order. Caught between their desire for the higher standard of living that industrialization made possible and their fears of capitalist power and social chaos, Americans of the 1880s and 1890s sought strategies that would preserve the benefits while eliminating corruption. Efforts to regulate railroads at the state level and such national measures as the Interstate Commerce Act and the Sherman Anti-Trust Act, as well as the fervor with which the ideas of a utopian theorist like Edward Bellamy were embraced, represented early manifestations of this impulse. In the Progressive Era of the early twentieth century, Americans would redouble their efforts to formulate political and social responses to the nation's economic transformation after the Civil War.

19

IMMIGRATION, URBANIZATION, AND EVERYDAY LIFE, 1860–1900

CHAPTER OUTLINE

• The New American City • Middle- and Upper-Class Society and Culture • Reforming the Working Class • Working-Class Leisure in the Immigrant City • Cultures in Conflict

---

THE NEW AMERICAN CITY

Everyday life was transformed most visibly in cities. During the late nineteenth century, American cities grew spectacularly. Between 1870 and 1900, New Orleans's population increased by nearly 50 percent, Buffalo's tripled, and Chicago's increased more than fivefold. At the start of the new century, Philadelphia, New York, and Chicago all had more than a million residents, and 40 percent of all Americans lived in cities. (In the census, cities were defined as having more than twenty-five hundred inhabitants.) In 1900, New York's 3.4 million inhabitants almost equaled the nation's entire 1850 urban population.

This spectacular urban growth, fueled by migration from the countryside and the arrival of nearly 11 million immigrants between 1870 and 1900, stimulated economic development. Like the frontier, the city symbolized opportunity for all comers.

The city's unprecedented scale and diversity threatened traditional expectations about community life and social stability. Rural America had been a place of face-to-face personal relations. In contrast, the city was a seething caldron where immigrant groups contended with one another and with native-born Americans for jobs, power, and influence. Moreover, the same rapid growth that energized manufacturing and production strained city services, generated terrible housing and sanitation problems, and accentuated class differences.

Native-born Americans complained about the noise, stench, and congestion of this transformed cityscape. They fretted about the newcomers' squalid tenements, fondness for drink, and strange customs. When native-born reformers set about cleaning up the city, they sought not only to improve the physical environment but also to destroy the distinctive customs that made immigrant culture different from their own. The late nineteenth century thus witnessed an intense struggle to control the city and benefit from its economic and cultural potential. The stakes were high, for America was increasingly becoming an urban nation.

Migrants and Immigrants   The concentration of urban industries produced demands for thousands of new workers. The promise of good wages and a broad range of jobs (labeled by historians as "pull factors") drew men and women from the countryside. So great was the migration from rural areas, especially New England, that some farm communities vanished from the map.

Young farmwomen led the exodus to the cities. With the growing mechanization of farming in the late nineteenth century, farming was increasingly male work. Rising sales of factory-produced goods through nationally distributed mail-order catalogs reduced the need for rural women's labor. So young farmwomen flocked to the cities, where they competed for jobs with immigrant, black, and city-born white women.

From 1860 to 1890, the prospect of a better life also attracted nearly 10 million northern European immigrants to American cities. Their numbers included nearly 3 million Germans, 2 million English, Scottish, and Welsh immigrants, and almost 1.5 million Irish. By 1900 more than eight hundred thousand French-Canadians had entered the New England mills, and close to a million Scandinavian newcomers had put down roots in the rich farmlands of Wisconsin and Minnesota. On the West Coast, despite the Chinese Exclusion Act of 1882 (see Chapter 18), more than eighty-one thousand Chinese remained in California and nearby states in 1900.

In the 1890s, these earlier immigrants from northern and western Europe were joined by swelling numbers of **"new immigrants"**—Italians, Slavs, Greeks, and Jews from southern and eastern Europe, Armenians from the Middle East, and in Hawaii, Japanese from Asia. In the next three decades, these new immigrants, many from peasant backgrounds, would boost America's foreign-born population by more than 18 million.

The overwhelming majority of immigrants settled in cities in the northeastern and north-central states, with the Irish predominating in New England and the Germans in the Midwest. The effect of their numbers was staggering. In 1890, New York City (including Brooklyn, still a legally separate municipality) contained twice as many Irish as Dublin, as many Germans as Hamburg, half as many Italians as Naples, and 2½ times the Jewish population of Warsaw. That same year, four out of five people living in New York had been born abroad or were children of foreign-born parents.

Overpopulation, crop failure, famine, religious persecution, violence, or industrial depression drove some of these immigrants from their homelands. (Historians call these reasons for immigration "push factors.") At the same time, the promise of high wages (a "pull factor") lured more than one hundred thousand Japanese laborers to Hawaii in the 1890s to work on sugar plantations.

A large number of immigrants were single young men. Birger Osland, an eighteen-year-old Norwegian, explained his reasons for leaving to a friend: "as I now probably have a foundation upon which I can build my own further

MAP 19.1 Percent of Foreign-born Whites and Native Whites of Foreign or Mixed Parentage in Total Population, by Counties, 1910

As this map indicates, new immigrants rarely settled in the South.

75% and over
50–75%
35–50%
25–35%
15–25%
10–15%
5–10%
Less than 5%

Source: D. W. Meinig, The Shaping of America—A Geographical Perspective of 500 Years of History. Yale University Press, Volume 3. © Cengage Learning. All rights reserved. No distribution allowed without express authorization.

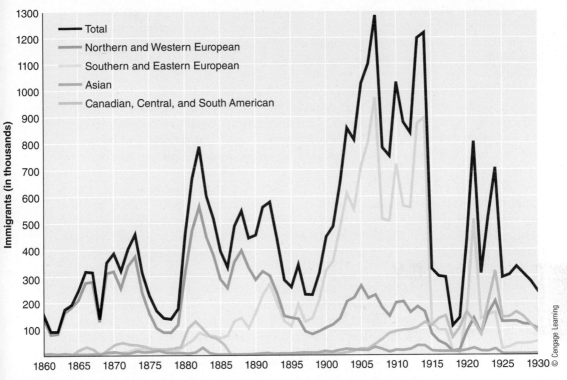

FIGURE 19.1   The Changing Face of U.S. Immigration, 1860–1930

Between 1865 and 1895, the majority of newcomers to America hailed from northern and western Europe. But the early twentieth century witnessed a surge of immigration from southern and eastern Europe.

education, I have come to feel that the most sensible thing I can do is to emigrate to America." Although significant numbers of young men remained in the United States after they had become successful, large numbers, especially Italians and Chinese, returned home as well.

Single women were less likely to come on their own, but Irish women often did so and sent their earnings back home. Most commonly, wives and children waited in the old country until the family breadwinner had secured a job and saved enough money to pay for their passage to America. They then endured a cramped steamship journey noted for its poor food, lack of privacy, and rudimentary sanitary facilities. Immigrants arrived tired, fearful, and in some cases sick.

Further complications awaited the travelers when they reached their destination, most often New York City or San Francisco. Customs officials inspected the newcomers for physical handicaps and contagious diseases. After 1892, those with "loathsome" infections such as leprosy, trachoma (a contagious viral disease of the eye), or sexually transmitted diseases were refused admittance and deported. Immigrants who passed the physical examination then had their names recorded. If a customs inspector had difficulty pronouncing a foreign name, he often Anglicized it. One German Jew became flustered when asked for his name and mumbled, "Schon vergessen [already forgotten]," meaning that he could not recall it. The inspector, who did not understand German, wrote "Sean Ferguson" on the man's roster. In this manner, many immigrants ended up with Americanized names.

In 1892, the federal government built a new immigration facility on **Ellis Island** in New York harbor. Angel Island in San Francisco Bay on the West Coast served a similar purpose after 1910. At the immigrant processing centers, America's newest residents exchanged foreign currency for U.S. dollars and purchased railroad tickets. Outside the facility, immigrants were hounded by tavernkeepers, peddlers, and porters who tried to exploit them. "When you land in America," wrote one Swedish resident to friends back home, "you will find many who will offer their services, but beware of them because there are so many rascals who make it their business to cheat the immigrants."

Those who arrived with sufficient cash, including many German artisans and Scandinavian farmers, commonly traveled west to Chicago and the rolling prairies beyond. Most of the Irish, and later the Italians remained in eastern cities like Boston, New York, and Philadelphia. The Irish and Italians who did go west typically made the trip in stages, moving from job to job on the railroad and canal systems.

Adjusting to an Urban Society   In the cities, immigrants clustered together with compatriots who had arrived earlier to ease the stress of adjusting to a new life. (Historians call this tendency "chain migration.") If a map of New York City's streets and neighborhoods were colored in by nationality, Jacob Riis observed in 1890, it "would show more stripes than on the skin of a zebra, and more colors than any rainbow." Between the West Side Irish and the East Side German neighborhoods, the streets of Manhattan teemed with Poles, Hungarians, Russians, Italians, and Chinese.

Within the cities, some immigrant groups adjusted more easily than others. Ethnic groups that formed a substantial percentage of a city's population had a major advantage. The Irish, for example, who by the 1880s made up nearly 16 percent of New York's population, 8 percent of Chicago's, and 17 percent of Boston's, facilitated Irish immigrants' entry into the American mainstream by dominating Democratic Party politics and controlling the hierarchy of the Catholic church in all three cities.

The domination of urban institutions by one immigrant group, however, often made adjustment to American society more difficult for others. In cities like Milwaukee, Germans excluded Poles from desirable jobs. Elsewhere, English and German dominance of the building trades enabled those nationalities to limit the numbers of Italians hired.

The experience of being discriminated against helped create a common ethnic identity for many groups. Groups of immigrants forged a sense of ethnic distinctiveness as Irish Americans, German Americans, or Jewish Americans that helped them compete for political power and move into mainstream society.

Not all immigrants intended to remain in the United States. Expecting only a brief stay, some made little effort to learn English or understand American customs. Of the Italians who immigrated to New York before 1914, nearly 50 percent went back to Italy. Although the rate of return migration was greatest among Chinese and Italians, significant numbers of other nationalities returned to their homelands as well.

As the number of foreigners in U.S. cities ballooned toward the turn of the century, all immigrant groups faced increasing hostility from white native-born

Picture Research Consultants & Archives

Chinatown, San Francisco *As evident in this photograph at the turn of the century, Chinese immigrants often lived in separate enclaves called "chinatowns."*

Americans who disliked the newcomers' social customs and worried about their growing influence. Fearing the loss of the privileges and status that were associated with their white skin color, native-born whites often stigmatized immigrants as racially different and inferior. Only gradually, and with much effort, did Irish, Jews, Slavs, and Italians come to be considered "white."

Slums and Ghettos   Every major city had its share of rundown, overcrowded slum neighborhoods. Generally clustered within walking distance of manufacturing districts, slums developed when landlords subdivided long, narrow buildings with few windows, called tenements, and packed in many residents. The poorer the renters, the worse the slum. Slums became ghettos when laws, prejudice, and community pressure prevented the tenement inhabitants from renting elsewhere. During the 1890s, Italians in New York, blacks in Philadelphia and Chicago, Mexican Americans in Los Angeles, and Chinese in San Francisco increasingly became locked in segregated ghettos.

Life in the slums was particularly difficult for children. Whooping cough (pertussis), measles, and scarlet fever took a fearful toll, and infant mortality skyrocketed. In one immigrant ward in Chicago in 1900, 20 percent of infants died in their first year of life.

Because tenements often bordered industrial districts, residents had to put up with the noise, pollution, and foul odors of tanneries, foundries, factories, and packing houses. Coal-fired steam engines and apartment house furnaces produced vast quantities of soot and dust that tinged the atmosphere a hazy gray and coated buildings with a grimy patina.

Most immigrants stayed in the shabbiest tenements only until they could afford better housing. Blacks, in contrast, were trapped in segregated districts. Driven out of the skilled trades and excluded from most factory work, blacks took menial jobs whose low pay left them little income for housing (see Chapter 18). Racist city-dwellers used high rents, real-estate covenants (agreements not to rent or sell to blacks), and neighborhood pressure to exclude them from areas inhabited by whites. Because the numbers of northern urban blacks in 1890 remained relatively small—for example, they composed only 1.2 percent of Cleveland's population and 1.3 percent of Chicago's—they could not overcome whites' campaigns to shut them out. Instead, wealthy black entrepreneurs established their own churches and charitable organizations in the black neighborhoods where they lived.

Fashionable Avenues and Suburbs
The same cities that harbored slums, filth, suffering, and violence also boasted of neighborhoods of dazzling opulence with the latest lighting and plumbing technologies. The wealthy built monumental residences along thoroughfares radiating from the city centers, among them Commonwealth Avenue in Boston, Euclid Avenue in Cleveland, and Summit Avenue in St. Paul.

In the 1870s and 1880s, city-dwellers began moving to nearby suburbs. Promoters of the suburban ideal contrasted the rolling lawns and stately houses on the city's periphery with the teeming streets, noisy saloons, and mounds of garbage and horse excrement downtown. Soon, most major cities could boast of their own stylish suburbs.

Middle-class city-dwellers followed the precedents set by the wealthy. Skilled artisans, shopkeepers, clerks, accountants, and sales personnel moved either to new developments at the city's edge or to outlying suburban communities (although those at the lower fringe of the middle class typically rented apartments in neighborhoods closer to the city center). Lawyers, doctors, small businessmen, and other professionals moved farther out along the main thoroughfares served by the street railway, where they purchased homes on large lots.

In time, a pattern of informal residential segregation by income took shape in the cities and suburbs. Built for families of a particular income level, certain neighborhoods and suburbs developed remarkably similar standards for lot size and house design. Two-story houses with front porches, set back thirty feet from the sidewalk, became the norm in many suburbs. Commuters who rode the new street railways out from the city center could identify the social class of the suburban dwellers along the way as readily as a geologist might distinguish different strata on a washed-out riverbank.

By 1900, whirring trolley cars and hissing steam powered trains had burst the boundaries of the compact midcentury city. As they expanded, cities often annexed contingent suburbs. Within this enlarged city, sharp dissimilarities in building height and neighborhood quality set off business sectors from fashionable residential avenues and differentiated squalid manufacturing districts from parklike suburban subdivisions. Musing about urban America in 1902, James F. Muirhead, a popular Scottish guidebook author, wrote that New York and other U.S. cities reminded him of "a lady in a ball costume, with diamonds in her ears, and her toes out at her boots." To Muirhead, urban America had become a "land of contrasts" in which the separation of various social groups and the increasingly dissimilar living conditions for rich and poor had heightened ethnic, racial, and class divisions. Along with the physical change in American cities, in short, had come a new awareness of class and cultural disparities.

MIDDLE- AND UPPER-CLASS SOCIETY AND CULTURE

Spared the struggle for survival that confronted most Americans after the Civil War, society's middle and upper ranks faced a different challenge: how to rationalize their enjoyment of the products of the emerging consumer society. To justify the position of society's wealthier members, ministers such as Brooklyn preacher Henry Ward Beecher and advice-book writers appealed to **Victorian morality**, a set of social ideas embraced by the privileged classes of England and America during the long reign (1837–1901) of Britain's Queen Victoria.

E.L. Godkin, the editor of *The Nation*, Phillips Brooks, minister to Boston's Trinity Church, and other proponents of Victorian morality argued that the financial success of the middle and upper classes arose from their superior talent, intelligence, morality, and self-control. They also extended the antebellum ideal of separate spheres by arguing that women were the driving force for moral improvement. While men were expected to engage in self-disciplined, "manly" dedication to the new industrial order, women would provide the gentle, elevating influence that would lead society in its upward march. A network of institutions, from elegant department stores and hotels to elite colleges and universities, reinforced the privileged position of these groups.

Manners and Morals   Several fundamental assumptions shaped the Victorian worldview. First, human nature was malleable: people could improve themselves. Second, work had social value: working hard not only developed self-discipline but also helped advance the progress of the nation. Finally, good manners and the cultivation of literature and art ennobled society. Although these genteel assumptions were sometimes ignored, they were held up as universal standards.

Victorian morality stressed the importance of manners and social rituals. Middle- and upper-class families in the 1870s and 1880s increasingly defined their own social standing in terms not only of income but also of behavior. Good manners, including knowledge of dining and entertaining etiquette, and good posture became important marks of status.

TECHNOLOGY & CULTURE

Flush Toilets and the Invention of the Nineteenth-Century Bathroom

The development of a system of indoor plumbing was typical of the technological breakthroughs that simplified everyday life in the late nineteenth century. In the 1860s, only about 5 percent of American houses had running water. Most Americans used chamber pots or outhouses that emptied into slimy, smelly cesspools. Two decades later, indoor plumbing standards had been established in most major U.S. cities, and wealthier urban Americans used flush toilets connected to municipal sewer systems.

The driving force for change came from outbreaks of cholera, typhoid, and yellow fever, diseases spread by polluted water, that periodically terrorized American cities. Building on the discovery of germs by Louis Pasteur and Robert Koch, sanitary reformers established stringent metropolitan health laws, created state boards of health, and mandated the licensing of plumbers and the inspection of their work. By the turn of the century, George E. Waring, Jr., a prominent sanitary engineer, could confidently declare that "Plumbing, as we know it, is essentially and almost exclusively an American Institution."

The decision to adopt a water-based system for the removal of human wastes depended on a series of inventions. First, municipal water systems had to be built with reservoirs, pumps, and water towers to provide water to the pipes that supplied buildings. A sewage system of interconnected pipes was also necessary to remove and process wastes. Machines to manufacture lead, cast-iron, and glazed stoneware pipes had to be created, as did a uniform system of pipe threads and

melted lead joints to create a reliable standardized system for connecting them. Finally, a porcelain toilet with a built-in gas trap was needed because the bacteria in feces produce methane or sewer gas. (A trap is a U-shaped joint in which the water at the low part of the U prevents gas from seeping back into the bathroom. The gas vents through a pipe in the roof.)

Despite its usefulness, the new technology was not rapidly adopted. In 1890, only 24 percent of American dwellings had running water. As late as 1897, more than 90 percent of the families in tenements had no baths and had to wash in hallway sinks or courtyard hydrants. By 1920, 80 percent of American houses, particularly those in rural areas, still lacked indoor flush toilets. The reason was simple: indoor plumbing was expensive and depended on the availability of water and sewer systems. Adding indoor plumbing increased the price of a new house by 20 percent.

Advertisers did their best to increase demand. They skillfully used the findings of science to advocate new standards of cleanliness or "hygiene," as it was called, which they associated with upper-class principles of respectability and decorum. Bathing and hand washing were touted as symbols of upper-class refinement.

Indoor plumbing not only reinforced higher standards for personal hygiene; it also enmeshed the homeowner in a web of local and state regulations. As sewage and water systems expanded to cover larger constituencies, political control moved from local to state and sometimes national arenas. Once largely

DIAGRAM SHOWING PROPER ARRANGEMENT OF WASTE PIPES, TRAPS, &C., IN AN ORDINARY THREE STORY AND BASEMENT CITY DWELLING. FOR FORM OF PLUMBING SPECIFICATION SEE OTHER PAGE.

KITCHEN PLAN.

Avery Architectural and Fine Arts Library, Columbia University

Plumbing Design *An architectural design shows the proper arrangement of waste pipes and traps in a three-story and basement city dwelling.*

independent, the homeowner now had to deal with water and power companies that often functioned regionally.

The adoption of strict sanitation systems and the use of indoor plumbing did achieve their intended result: they dramatically reduced the spread of disease. But the advances had unintended consequences. Indoor plumbing encouraged the phenomenal waste of water. A single faulty toilet could easily leak a hundred gallons of water a day. Not until the 1990s with the development of new low-water-usage toilets, which could save between 18,000 and 26,400 gallons of water a year, would new standards be established to reduce the use of water, an increasingly precious natural resource.

Question for Analysis

1. *Why does the successful introduction of new technologies often involve a system of inventions rather than a single invention?*

In her popular advice book, *The American Woman's Home* (1869), Catharine Beecher (the sister of Henry Ward Beecher) displayed the typical Victorian self-consciousness about proper manners. The following dinner-table behaviors, she said, should be avoided by those of "good breeding":

> *Reaching over another person's plate; standing up to reach distant articles, instead of asking to have them passed ... using the table-cloth instead of napkins; eating fast, and in a noisy manner; putting large pieces in the mouth; ... [and] picking the teeth at the table.*

For Beecher and other molders of manners, meals became important rituals that differentiated the social classes. The elaborate china and silver that wealthy families exclusively possessed also provided telltale clues to a family's level of refinement and sophistication.

The Victorian code—with its emphasis on morals, manners, and proper behavior—thus heightened the sense of class differences and created visible distinctions among social groups. Victorian Americans made bold claims about their interest in helping others improve themselves. More often than not, however, their self-righteous, intensely moralistic outlook simply widened the gap that income disparities had already opened.

The Cult of Domesticity

Victorian views on morality and culture, coupled with the need to make decisions about a mountain of domestic products, had a subtle but important effect on middle-class expectations about women's role within the home. From the 1840s on, architects, clergymen, and other promoters of the so-called cult of domesticity had idealized the home as "the woman's sphere." They praised the home as a protected retreat where women could express their maternal gifts, including sensitivity toward children and an aptitude for religion. "The home is the wife's province," asserted one writer; "it is her natural field of labor ... to govern and direct its interior management."

During the 1880s and 1890s, Victorian advocates of the cult of domesticity added a new obligation to foster an artistic environment that would nurture her family's cultural improvement. Houses became statements of cultural aspiration with front parlors cluttered with artwork and curiosities. Excluded from the world of business and commerce, many middle- and upper-class women directed their energies to decorating their homes, seeking to make the home, as one advice book suggested, "a place of repose, a refuge from the excitement and distractions of outside ... provided with every attainable means of rest and recreation."

Not all middle-class women pursued this domestic ideal. For some, housework and family responsibilities overwhelmed the concern for artistic accomplishment. For others, the artistic ideal was not to their taste. Sixteen-year-old Mary Putnam complained privately to a friend that she played the piano because of "an abstract general idea ... of a father coming home regularly tired at night (from the plow, I believe the usual legend runs), and being solaced by the brilliant yet touching performance of a sweet only daughter upon the piano." She then confessed that she detested the piano. In the 1880s and 1890s, as middle- and upper-class women sought other outlets for their creative energies in settlement-house work, social reform, and women's club activities, the older domestic ideal began to unravel.

**Department
Stores**   Although Victorian social thought justified the privileges of the well-to-do, many people found it difficult to shake the thriftiness of their early years and accept the new preoccupation with accumulation and display. To lure these consumers, merchandisers in the 1880s stressed the high quality and low cost of the objects they sold, encouraging Americans to loosen their purse strings and enjoy prosperity without reservations. This argument particularly appealed to women who, to provide for their families, now had to shop for soap, canned foods, and other products formerly made at home.

Department stores set the standard for consumption. In the final quarter of the nineteenth century, Rowland H. Macy in New York, John Wanamaker in Philadelphia, and Marshall Field in Chicago built giant department stores that transformed the shopping experience for their middle- and upper-class patrons. The stores advertised "rock-bottom" prices and engaged in price wars. To avoid keeping their stock too long, they held giant end-of-the-season sales at drastically marked-down prices.

Department stores made shopping an exciting activity. Rapid turnover of merchandise created a sense of constant novelty. With stained-glass skylights, marble staircases, sparkling chandeliers, and plush carpets, the large urban department store functioned as a workplace for the lower classes and as a social club for comfortably fixed women. For those who could afford it, shopping became an adventure, a form of entertainment, and a way to affirm their place in society.

**The Transformation
of Higher
Education**   At a time when relatively few Americans had even a high school education and only 4 percent of the nation's eighteen- to twenty-one-year-olds were enrolled in institutions of higher learning, colleges and universities represented another stronghold of the business and professional elite.

Wealthy capitalists gained status and a measure of immortality by endowing colleges and universities. Leland Stanford and his wife, Jane Lathrop Stanford, launched Stanford University in 1885 with a bequest of $24 million; John D. Rockefeller donated $34 million to the University of Chicago in 1891. Industrialists and businessmen dominated the boards of trustees of most educational institutions.

Not only the classroom experience but also social contacts and athletic activities—especially football—prepared affluent young men for later responsibilities in business and the professions. Adapted by American college students in the 1860s from English rugby, football became an elite sport played by college teams. But the game, initially played without pads or helmets, was marred by violence. In 1905, eighteen students died of playing-field injuries. Many college presidents dismissed football as a dangerous waste of time and money. In 1873, when the University of Michigan challenged Cornell to a game in Ann Arbor, Cornell's president Andrew D. White huffily telegraphed back, "I will not permit thirty men to travel four hundred miles merely to agitate a bag of wind."

But eager alumni and coaches strongly defended the new sport. Some—among them Henry Lee Higginson, the Civil War veteran and Boston banker who gave Harvard "Soldiers' Field" stadium as a memorial to those who had died in battle—praised football as a character-building sport. Others, including famed Yale coach Walter Camp, insisted that football could function as a surrogate frontier experience in an increasingly urbanized society. By 1900, collegiate football had become a popular fall ritual, and team captains were campus heroes. At a time when businesses stressed teamwork and played down individuality, football suggested that intercollegiate sports forged manhood by emphasizing vision, integrity, and leadership.

More than 150 new colleges and universities were founded between 1880 and 1900, and enrollments more than doubled. While wealthy capitalists endowed some institutions, others, such as the state universities in the South and Midwest, were financed largely through public funds generated from public land sales under the Morrill Land Grant Act (1862). Many colleges were also founded and funded by religious denominations.

Following the precedent set by Oberlin College in 1836, coeducational private colleges and public universities in the Midwest enrolled increasing numbers of women. In the East, Columbia, Brown, and Harvard universities admitted women to the affiliated but separate institutions of Barnard (1889), Pembroke (1891), and Radcliffe (1894), respectively. Some colleges—Mount Holyoke (1837), Vassar (1865), Wellesley and Smith (1875), and Bryn Mawr (1884)—were founded solely for women. The generation of women educated at female institutions in the late nineteenth century developed the self-confidence to break with the Victorian ideal of passive womanhood and to compete with men by displaying strength, aggressiveness, and intelligence—popularly considered male attributes. Nationally, the percentage of colleges admitting women jumped from 30 percent to 71 percent between 1880 and 1900. By the turn of the century, women made up more than one-third of the total college-student population.

At the university level, innovative presidents such as Cornell's Andrew D. White and Harvard's Charles W. Eliot, influenced by new discoveries in science and medicine, shifted the focus of higher education. In the 1850s, most physicians had attended medical school for only two sixteen-week terms. They typically received their degrees without ever having visited a hospital or examined a patient. The Civil War exposed the abysmal state of American medical knowledge. Twice as many soldiers died from infections as from wounds. Doctors were so poorly trained and ignorant about sanitation that they often infected soldiers' injuries when they probed wounds with hands wiped on pus-stained aprons. "The ignorance and general incompetency of the average graduate of American medical schools, at the time when he receives the degree which turns him loose upon the community," wrote Eliot in 1870, "is something horrible to contemplate."

In the 1880s and 1890s, leading medical professors, many of whom had studied in France and Germany, began restructuring American medical education. Using the experimental method developed by German scientists, they insisted that all medical students be trained in biology, chemistry, and physics, including working in a laboratory. Although medical school reform improved health care in some areas, it also effectively shut out African American and poor women who could not afford the tuition. New educational and professional standards, similarly, were established for architects, engineers, and lawyers.

These changes were part of a larger transformation in higher education, the rise of a new kind of institution, the **research university.** Unlike the best of the mid-nineteenth-century colleges, which focused on teaching Latin and Greek, theology, logic, and mathematics, the new research universities offered courses in a wide variety of subject areas, established professional schools, and encouraged faculty members to pursue basic research. At Cornell University, President Andrew D. White's objective was to create an environment "where any person can find instruction in any study." At Cornell, the University of Wisconsin at Madison, Johns Hopkins, Harvard, and other institutions, this new conception of higher education laid the groundwork for the central role that America's universities would play in the intellectual, cultural, and scientific life of the twentieth century.

REFORMING THE WORKING CLASS

The contrast between the affluent world of the college educated middle and upper classes and the gritty lives of the working class was most graphically on display in the nation's growing urban centers, where immigrant newcomers reshaped political and social institutions to meet their own needs. If fancy department stores and elegant hotels furnished new social spaces for the middle and upper classes, saloons became the poor man's club, and dance halls became single women's home away from home. While the rich and the wellborn looked suspiciously at lower-class recreational activities and sought to force the poor to change their ways, working-class Americans, the immigrant newcomers in particular, fought to preserve their own distinctive way of life. Indeed, the late nineteenth century witnessed an ongoing battle to eradicate social drinking and curb lower-class recreational activities.

Battling Poverty   Stunned by the levels of poverty and suffering in the expanding industrial cities, middle-class city leaders sought comprehensive solutions for relieving poverty. Jacob Riis and the first generation of reformers believed that immigrants' lack of self-discipline and their unsanitary living conditions caused their problems. Consequently, Riis and his peers focused on moral improvement and exposing squalid tenement housing. Only later would Jane Addams, Florence Kelley, and other settlement-house workers examine the crippling impact of low wages and dangerous working conditions. Although many reformers genuinely sympathized with the suffering of the lower classes, the humanitarians often turned their campaigns to help the destitute into missions to Americanize the immigrants and eliminate customs that they perceived as offensive and self-destructive.

Poverty-relief workers first targeted their efforts at the young, who were thought to be most malleable. Energized by the religious revivals of the 1830s and 1840s, Protestant reformers started charitable societies to help transient youths and abandoned street children. In 1843, Robert M. Hartley, a former employee of the New York Temperance Society, organized the New York Association for Improving the Condition of the Poor to help poor families.

Hartley's voluntaristic approach was supplemented by the more coercive tactics of Charles Loring Brace, who founded the New York Children's Aid Society in 1853. Brace admired "these little traders of the city ... battling for a hard living in the snow and mud of the street" but worried that they might join the city's "dangerous classes." Brace established dormitories, reading rooms, and workshops where the boys could learn practical skills; he also swept orphaned children off the streets, shipped them to the country, and placed them with families to work as farm hands.

Where Brace's Children's Aid Society gave adolescents an alternative to living in the slums, the Young Men's Christian Association (YMCA), founded in England in 1841 and exported to America ten years later, provided housing and wholesome recreation for country boys who had migrated to the city. The Young Women's Christian Association (YWCA) similarly provided housing and a day nursery for young women and their children. Both organizations subjected their members to curfews and expelled them for drinking and other forbidden behavior.

By 1900, more than fifteen hundred YMCAs and YWCAs served as havens for nearly a quarter-million young men and women. But YMCA and YWCA leaders reached only a small portion of the young adult population. Although charity workers made some progress in their efforts to aid youth, the strategy was too narrowly focused to stem the rising tide of urban problems.

New Approaches to Social Reform   The inability of the Children's Aid Society, YMCA, YWCA, and other relief organizations to cope with the explosive growth of the urban poor in the 1870s and 1880s convinced reformers to search for new allies in the fight against poverty. One effective agency was the **Salvation Army.** A church established along pseudomilitary lines in England in 1865 by Methodist minister "General" William Booth, the Salvation Army sent uniformed volunteers to the United States in 1880 to provide food, shelter, and temporary employment for families. Its members ran soup kitchens and day nurseries and dispatched its "slum brigades" to carry the message of morality to the immigrant poor. The army's strategy was simple. Attract the poor with marching bands and lively preaching; follow up with offers of food, assistance, and employment; and then teach them the solid middle-class virtues of temperance, hard work, and self-discipline.

The New York Charity Organization Society (COS), founded in 1882 by **Josephine Shaw Lowell,** implemented a similar approach to poor relief. To make aid to the poor more efficient, Lowell and the COS leaders divided New York City into districts, compiled files on all aid recipients, and sent "friendly visitors," who were trained, salaried women, into the tenements to counsel families on how to improve their lives. Convinced that moral deficiencies lay at the root of poverty and that the "promiscuous charity" of overlapping church welfare agencies undermined the desire to work, the COS tried to foster self-sufficiency in its charges. In 1891, Lowell helped found the Consumers' League of New York, which encouraged women to buy only from manufacturers who paid fair wages and maintained decent working conditions.

Although the COS did coordinate relief efforts and developed helpful statistics on the extent of poverty, critics justly accused the society of seeking more to control the poor than to alleviate their suffering. One of the manuals, for example, stressed the importance of introducing "messy housekeepers" to the "pleasures of a cheery, well-ordered home." Unable to see slum problems from the vantage point of the poor, they failed, for the most part, in their underlying objective: to convert the poor to their own standards of morality and decorum.

The Moral-Purity Campaign   While Josephine Shaw Lowell and other like-minded social disciplinarians worked to eradicate urban poverty, other reformers pushed for tougher measures against sin and immorality. In 1872, **Anthony Comstock**, a pious young dry-goods clerk, founded the New York Society for the Suppression of Vice. The organization demanded that municipal authorities close down gambling and lottery operations and censor obscene publications.

Nothing symbolized the contested terrain between middle- and lower-class culture better than the fight over prostitution. Considered socially degenerate by some and a source of recreation by others, prostitution both exploited women and offered them a steady income and a measure of personal freedom. After the Civil War, the number of brothels expanded rapidly. In the 1880s, saloons and cabarets hired prostitutes of their own. Even though immigrant women do not appear to have made up the majority of big-city prostitutes, reformers often labeled them as the major source of the problem.

In 1892, brothels, along with gambling dens and saloons, became targets for the reform efforts of New York Presbyterian minister Charles Parkhurst. Blaming the "slimy, oozy soil of Tammany Hall" (the Democratic organization that dominated New York City politics, discussed in the next chapter) and the New York City police—"the dirtiest, crookedest, and ugliest lot of men ever combined in semi-military array outside of Japan and Turkey"—for the city's rampant evils, he organized the City Vigilance League to clean up the city. Two years later, a nonpartisan Committee of Seventy elected a new mayor who pressured city officials to enforce the laws against prostitution, gambling, and Sunday liquor sales.

The purity campaign lasted scarcely three years. The reform coalition quickly fell apart. New York City's population was too large, and its ethnic constituencies too diverse, for middle- and upper-class reformers to curb all the illegal activities flourishing within the sprawling metropolis.

The Social Gospel   In the 1870s and 1880s, a handful of Protestant ministers took a different approach to helping impoverished city dwellers. Led by William S. Rainsford, the Irish-born minister of New York City's Saint George's Episcopal Church, they pioneered the development of the so-called institutional church movement by insisting that large downtown churches in once-elite districts that had been overrun by immigrants provide their new neighbors with social services as well as a place to worship. With the financial help of J. Pierpont Morgan, a warden of his church, Rainsford organized a boys' club, built church recreational facilities for the destitute on the Lower East Side, and established an industrial training program.

Other Protestant ministers, led by Washington Gladden, a Congregational clergyman in Columbus, Ohio, launched the **Social Gospel** movement in the 1870s. Gladden insisted that true Christianity commits men and women to fight social injustice wherever it exists. Thus, in response to the wave of violent strikes in 1877, he urged church leaders to mediate the conflict between business and labor. Their attempt to do so was unsuccessful.

If Gladden set the tone for the Social Gospel, Walter Rauschenbusch, a minister at a German Baptist church in New York's notorious "Hell's Kitchen" neighborhood, articulated the movement's central philosophy. Educated in Germany, Rauschenbusch argued that a truly Christian society would unite all churches, reorganize the industrial system, and work for international peace. Rauschenbusch's appeal for Christian unity led to the formation of the Federal Council of Churches in 1908, but his other goals were never achieved. Although the Social Gospel attracted only a handful of Protestants, their earnest voices blended with a growing chorus of critics bemoaning the nation's urban woes.

The Settlement-House Movement
In the 1880s, a younger generation of charity workers led by **Jane Addams** developed a new weapon against destitution: the settlement house. Like the Social Gospelers, these reformers recognized that the hardships of slum life were often beyond the individual's control. Living in the poor neighborhoods where they worked, they could see firsthand "the struggle for existence, which is so much harsher among people near the edge of pauperism."

The youngest daughter of a successful Illinois businessman, Jane Addams purchased a dilapidated mansion on Chicago's south side in 1889 and opened it as Hull House. Putting the middle-class ideal of true womanhood into action, Addams turned Hull House into a social center for immigrants. She invited them to plays; sponsored art projects; held classes in English, civics, cooking, and dressmaking; and encouraged them to preserve their traditional crafts. She set up a kindergarten, a laundry, an employment bureau, and a day nursery for working mothers. Hull House also sponsored recreational and athletic programs and dispensed legal aid and health care.

In the hope of upgrading the filthy and overcrowded housing in its environs, Addams and her coworkers conducted surveys of city housing conditions and pressured politicians to enforce sanitation regulations. For a time, demonstrating her principle of direct engagement with the lives of the poor, Addams even served as garbage inspector for her local ward.

By 1895, at least fifty settlement houses had opened in cities around the nation. Settlement-house leaders trained a generation of young college students, mostly women, many of whom would later serve as state and local government officials. **Florence Kelley**, for example, who had worked at Hull House, became the chief factory inspector for Illinois in 1893. For Kelley as for other female settlement workers, settlement houses functioned as a supportive sisterhood of reform. Many settlement-house veterans would later draw on their experience to play an influential role in the regulatory movements of the Progressive Era (covered in Chapter 21). Through their sympathetic attitudes toward the immigrants and their systematic publication of data about factory and slum conditions, settlement-house workers gave Americans renewed hope that urban problems could be overcome.

In their attempt to promote class cooperation and social harmony, however, settlement houses had mixed success. Although many immigrants appreciated the settlement houses' resources and activities, they believed that the reformers had little interest in helping them gain political power. Settlement-house workers did tend to overlook immigrant organizations and their leaders. In 1894, Hull House attracted two thousand visitors per week, but this was only a fraction of the more than seventy thousand people who lived within six blocks of the building. "They're like the rest," complained one immigrant, "a bunch of people planning for us and deciding what is good for us without consulting us or taking us into their confidence."

WORKING-CLASS LEISURE IN THE IMMIGRANT CITY

In colonial America, preachers had warned against leisure and idleness as temptations to sin. In the rural culture of the early nineteenth century, the unremitting routines of farm labor left little time for relaxation. Family picnics, horse races, county fairs, revival meetings, and Fourth of July and Christmas celebrations had provided occasional permissible diversions. But most Americans continued to view leisure activities skeptically. Henry Clay Work's popular song "My Grandfather's Clock" (1876), which praised the ancient timepiece for "wasting no time" and working "ninety years, without slumbering," bore witness to the tenacity of this deep-seated reverence for work and suspicion of play.

As urban populations shot up after the Civil War, striking new patterns of leisure and amusement emerged, most notably among the urban working class. After spending long hours in factories, in mills, behind department-store counters, or as domestic servants in the homes of the wealthy, working-class Americans craved

Chicago Historical Society

Garbage Box, First Ward, Chicago, CA. 1900 *Lacking space for recreation, immigrant children played atop garbage boxes in crowded alleys. Concerned for their health, Jane Addams wrote that "this slaughter of the innocents, this infliction of suffering on the newborn, is so gratuitous and so unfair, that it is only a question of time until an outraged sense of justice shall be aroused on behalf of these children."*

relaxation and diversion. They thronged the streets, patronized saloons and dance halls, cheered at boxing matches and baseball games, and organized group picnics and holiday celebrations. As amusement parks, vaudeville theaters, sporting clubs, and racetracks provided further outlets for workers' need for entertainment, leisure became a big business catering to a mass public rather than to a wealthy elite.

For millions of working-class Americans, leisure time took on increasing importance as factory work became routinized and impersonal. Although many recreational activities involved both men and women, others attracted one gender in particular. Saloons offered an intensely male environment where patrons could share good stories, discuss and bet on sporting events, and momentarily put aside pressures of job and family. Young working women preferred to share confidences with friends in informal social clubs, tried out new fashions in street promenading, and found excitement in neighborhood dance halls and amusement parks.

Streets, Saloons, and Boxing Matches   No segment of the population had a greater need for amusement and recreation than the urban working class. Hours of tedious, highly disciplined, and physically exhausting labor left workers tired and thirsting for excitement and escape from their cramped housing quarters. In 1889, a banner carried by a carpenters' union summed up their wishes: "EIGHT HOURS FOR WORK, EIGHT HOURS FOR REST, AND EIGHT HOURS FOR WHAT WE WILL."

City streets provided recreation that anyone could afford. Relaxing after a day's work, shop girls and laborers clustered on busy corners, watching shouting pushcart peddlers and listening to organ grinders and street musicians play familiar melodies. For a penny or a nickel, they could buy bagels, baked potatoes, soda, and other foods and drinks. In the summer, when the heat and humidity in tenement apartments reached unbearable levels, the streets became a hive of neighborhood social life. One immigrant fondly recalled his boyhood on the streets of New York's Lower East Side: "Something was always happening, and our attention was continually being shifted from one excitement to another."

The streets were open to all, but other leisure institutions drew mainly a male clientele. For example, in cities with a strong German immigrant presence like Baltimore, Milwaukee, and Cincinnati, gymnastic clubs (called *Turnverein*) and singing societies (*Gesangverein*) provided both companionship and the opportunity to perpetuate old-world cultural traditions.

For workmen of all ethnic backgrounds, saloons offered companionship, conviviality, and five-cent beer, often with a free lunch thrown in. New York City had an estimated ten thousand saloons by 1900 and Denver nearly five hundred. As neighborhood gathering places, saloons reinforced group identity and became centers for immigrant politics. Saloonkeepers, who often doubled as local ward bosses and turned out the vote in their neighborhoods, performed small services for their patrons, including finding jobs and writing letters for illiterate immigrants. Sports memorabilia and pictures of prominent prizefighters adorned saloon walls. With their rich mahogany bars, etched glass, shiny brass rails, and elegant mirrors, saloons provided patrons with a taste of luxury. Although working-class women rarely joined their husbands at the saloon, they might send a son or daughter to the corner pub to fetch a "growler"—a large tin pail of beer.

The conventions of saloon culture thus stood in marked contrast to both the socially isolating routines of factory labor and the increasingly private and family-centered social life of the middle class. Nevertheless, it would be a mistake to view the old-time saloon through a haze of sentimental nostalgia. Prostitution and crime flourished in the rougher saloons. Moreover, drunken husbands sometimes beat their wives and children, squandered their limited income, and lost their jobs. The pervasiveness of alcoholism was devastating. Temperance reformers, in their attack on saloons, targeted a widespread social problem.

The Rise of Professional Sports

Contrary to the prevailing myth, schoolboy Abner Doubleday did not invent baseball in Cooperstown, New York, in 1839. As an English game called rounders, the pastime had existed in one form or another since the seventeenth century. If Americans did not create baseball, they did turn it into a major professional sport. In 1845, the first organized baseball team, the New York Knickerbockers, was formed. In the 1860s, rules were codified and the sport assumed its modern form. Overhand pitches replaced underhand tosses. Fielders wore gloves, games were standardized at nine innings, and bases were spaced ninety feet apart.

In that same decade, promoters organized professional clubs and began to charge admission and compete for players. The Cincinnati Red Stockings, the first team to put its players under contract for the whole season, gained fame in 1869 by touring the country and ending the season with fifty-seven wins and no losses. Team owners organized the National League in 1876, took control from the players by requiring them to sign contracts that barred them from playing for rival organizations, and limited each city to one professional team. Soon the owners were filling baseball parks with crowds of ten to twelve thousand fans and earning enormous profits. By the 1890s, baseball had become big business.

Although baseball attracted a national following from all social levels, the working class particularly took the sport to heart. The most profitable teams were those in major industrial cities with a large working-class population. Workers avidly followed their team's progress. Many saloons reported scores on blackboards and an estimated 50 percent of players worked in saloons in the off-season or became saloon owners when they retired from the game.

If baseball helped build solidarity among some ethnic groups, it also fostered discrimination against blacks. Although at least fifty-five blacks played on integrated teams between 1883 and 1898, the refusal of the Chicago White Stockings in 1887 to play a team with George Stovey, a star black pitcher, marked a turning point. That same year, Colored baseball clubs opened in six cities. Increasingly thereafter, blacks were banned from playing on professional teams.

Newspapers thrived on baseball. Joseph Pulitzer introduced the first separate sports page when he bought the *New York World* in 1883, and much of the sporting news in the *World* and other papers was devoted to baseball. Fans who cheered the hometown team provided cities with a shared sports loyalty that reduced ethnic, class, and religious differences, but drinking and gambling continued to plague the game.

Although no organized sport attracted as large a following as baseball, horse racing and boxing contests drew big crowds of spectators and bettors. Louisville's Kentucky Derby became an important social event for the rich, but professional

Library of Congress, Prints and Photographs Division

Baltimore, 1897 *An overflow crowd watches the Baltimore Orioles play the Boston Beaneaters. Nestled in among the row houses, urban stadiums like this one drew huge crowds.*

boxing aroused more passionate devotion among laborers. Bare-knuckled prize-fighting became a testing ground where men could demonstrate their toughness and physical prowess.

For many working-class Americans, heavyweight fighter **John L. Sullivan,** "the Boston Strong Boy," personified these traits. Of Irish immigrant stock, Sullivan began boxing in 1877 at the age of nineteen. His first professional fight came in 1880 when he knocked out John Donaldson, "the Champion of the West," in a Cincinnati beer hall. With his massive physique, handlebar mustache, and arrogant swagger, Sullivan was enormously popular among immigrants. Barnstorming across the country, he vanquished a succession of local strongmen, invariably wearing his trademark green tights with an American flag wrapped around his middle. Yet, Sullivan refused to fight blacks, supposedly in deference to the wishes of his fans. This policy conveniently allowed him to avoid facing the finest boxer of the 1880s, the Australian black, Peter Jackson.

Sullivan loved drink and high living, and by the end of the 1880s he was sadly out of shape. But when the editor of the *Police Gazette*, a sensational tabloid, designed a new heavyweight championship belt—allegedly containing two hundred ounces of silver and encrusted with diamonds and pure gold—and awarded it to Sullivan's rival Jake Kilrain, the champion had to defend himself. The two met on a sweltering, hundred-degree day in New Orleans in July 1889 for the last bare-knuckles championship match. After seventy-five short but grueling rounds, Kilrain's managers threw in the towel. Newspapers around the nation banner-headlined the story. Contemptuously returning the championship belt to the *Police*

Gazette after having had it appraised at $175, Sullivan went on the road to star in a melodrama written specifically for him. Playing the role of a blacksmith, he (in the words of a recent historian of bare-knuckles boxing) "pounded an anvil, beat a bully, and mutilated his lines." But his fans did not care; he was one of them, and they adored him. As one admirer wrote,

> *His colors are the Stars and Stripes,*
> *He also wears the green,*
> *And he's the grandest slugger that*
> *The ring has ever seen.*

Vaudeville, Amusement Parks, and Dance Halls

In contrast to the male preserve of saloons and prize-fights, the world of vaudeville, amusement parks, and neighborhood dance halls welcomed all comers regardless of gender. Some of them proved particularly congenial to working-class women.

Vaudeville evolved out of antebellum minstrel shows that featured white singers made up as blacks. The shows typically opened with a trained animal routine or a dance number, followed by a musical interlude. Comic skits then ridiculed the trials of urban life, satirizing police and municipal ineptitude, poking fun at immigrant accents, and mining a rich vein of broad ethnic humor and stereotypes. Blackface skits were sometimes included. After a highbrow operatic aria and acts by ventriloquists, pantomimes, and magicians, the program ended with a "flash" finale such as flying-trapeze artists swinging against a black background. By the 1880s, vaudeville was drawing larger crowds than any other form of theater.

The white working class's fascination with vaudeville's blackface acts has been the subject of considerable recent scrutiny by historians. Some have interpreted it as a way for the white working class to mock middle-class ideals. By pretending to act like the popular stereotypes of blacks, white working-class youths could challenge traditional family structures, the virtue of sexual self-denial, and adult expectations about working hard. In this view, popular culture was making fun of the ideals of thrift and propriety being promoted in marketplace and domestic ideology. Other historians have argued that blackface buffoonery, with its grotesque, demeaning caricatures of African Americans, reinforced prejudice against blacks and restricted their escape from lower-class status. Paradoxically, therefore, the popularity of blackface vaudeville acts reinforced white racial solidarity and strengthened the expanding wall separating whites and African Americans.

Where vaudeville offered psychological escape from the stresses of working-class life, amusement parks provided physical escape. New York's Coney Island, a section of Brooklyn's oceanfront, evolved into a resort for the masses in the 1870s. At Coney Island, young couples went dancing, rode through the dark Tunnel of Love, sped down the dizzying roller coaster in Steeplechase Park, or watched belly dancers in the carnival sideshows. Customers were encouraged to surrender to the spirit of play, forget the demands of the industrial world, and lose themselves in fantasy.

By the end of the nineteenth century, New York City had well over three hundred thousand female wage earners, most of them young, unmarried women working as seamstresses, laundresses, typists, domestic servants, and department-store clerks. For this army of low-paid young working women and their counterparts in other cities, amusement parks exerted a powerful lure. Here, they could meet friends, spend time with young men beyond the watchful eyes of their parents, show off their new dresses, and try out the latest dance steps. As a twenty-year-old German immigrant woman who worked as a servant in a wealthy household observed,

> *I have heard some of the high people with whom I have been living say that Coney Island is not tony. The trouble is that these high people don't know how to dance. I have to laugh when I see them at their balls and parties. If only I could get out on the floor and show them how—they would be astonished.*

For such women, the brightly decorated dance pavilion, the exciting music, and the spell of a warm summer night could seem a magical release from the drudgery of daily life.

Ragtime   Nothing could illustrate more sharply the differences between middle- and working-class culture than the contrasting styles of popular music they favored. The middle class preferred hymns or songs that conveyed a moral lesson. The working class delighted in ragtime, which originated in the 1880s with black musicians in the saloons and brothels of the South and Midwest and was played strictly for entertainment.

Ragtime developed out of the rich tradition of sacred and secular songs through which African Americans had long eased the burdens of their lives. Like spirituals, ragtime used syncopated rhythms and complex harmonies, but it blended these with marching-band musical structures to create a distinctive style. A favorite of "honky-tonk" piano players, ragtime was introduced to the broader public in the 1890s and became a national sensation.

The reasons for the sudden ragtime craze were complex. Inventive, playful, with catchy syncopations and an infectious rhythm in the bass clef, the music displayed an originality that had an appeal all its own. Part of ragtime's popularity also came from its origin in brothels and its association with blacks, who were widely stereotyped in the 1890s as sexual, sensual, and uninhibited by the rigid Victorian social conventions that restricted whites. The "wild" and complex rhythms of ragtime were widely interpreted to be a freer and more "natural" expression of elemental feelings about love and sex.

Ragtime's great popularity proved a mixed blessing for blacks. It testified to the achievements of brilliant composers like **Scott Joplin**, composer of the "Maple Leaf Rag," helped break down the barriers faced by blacks in the music industry, and contributed to a spreading rebellion against the repressiveness of Victorian standards. But ragtime simply confirmed some whites' stereotype of blacks as primitive and sensual, a bias that underlay the racism of the period and helped justify segregation and discrimination.

CULTURES IN CONFLICT

Even within the elite and middle classes, Victorian morality and genteel cultural standards were never totally accepted. As the century ended, increasing numbers of people questioned these beliefs. Women stood at the center of the era's cultural turbulence. Thwarted by a restrictive code of feminine propriety, they made their dissatisfactions heard. The rise of women's clubs, the growth of women's colleges, and even the 1890s bicycle fad testified to the emergence of what some began to call the "new woman."

At the same time, a widening chasm divided the well-to-do from urban working-class immigrants. In no period of American history have class conflicts—cultural as well as economic—been more open and raw. As middle-class leaders nervously eyed the sometimes disorderly culture of city streets, saloons, boxing clubs, dance halls, and amusement parks, they saw a challenge to their own cultural and social values. Some middle-class reformers promoted the public school as a way to impose middle-class values on the urban masses. Others battled urban "vice" and "immorality." But ultimately it was the polite mores of the middle class, not urban working-class culture, that proved more vulnerable. By 1900, the Victorian social and moral ethos was crumbling on every front.

The Genteel Tradition and Its Critics   What was this genteel culture that aroused such opposition? In the 1870s and 1880s, a group of upper-class writers and magazine editors, led by Harvard art history professor Charles Eliot Norton and New York editors Richard Watson Gilder of *The Century* magazine and E.L. Godkin of *The Nation*, codified Victorian standards for literature and the arts. They campaigned to improve American taste in interior furnishings, textiles, ceramics, wallpaper, and books. By fashioning rigorous criteria for excellence in writing and design, they hoped to create a coherent national artistic culture. Nevertheless, at the start, they relied on women writers such as Helen Hunt Jackson (see Chapter 17), who often questioned their patriarchal views.

In the 1880s, Norton, Godkin, and Gilder, joined by the editors of other highbrow periodicals such as the *Atlantic Monthly* and *North American Review*, set up new guidelines for serious literature. They lectured the middle class about the value of high culture and the insights to be gained from painting and music. They censored their own publications to remove all sexual allusions, disrespectful treatments of Christianity, and unhappy endings. Expanding their combined circulation to nearly two hundred thousand copies, Godkin and the other editors of "quality" periodicals created an important forum for serious writing. Novelists Henry James, who published virtually all of his work in the *Atlantic*, and William Dean Howells, who served as editor of the same magazine, helped lead this elite literary establishment. James believed that "it is art that makes life.... [There is] no substitute whatever for [its] force and beauty ..."

This interest in art for art's sake paralleled a broader crusade called the "aesthetic movement," led in England by William Morris, Oscar Wilde, and other art critics, who sought to bring art into every facet of life. In America, Candace Wheeler and other reformers made its influence felt through the work of architects, jewelers, and interior decorators.

Although the magazines initially provided an important forum for new writers, their editors' elitism and desire to control the nation's literary standards soon aroused opposition. Samuel Langhorne Clemens, better known as **Mark Twain**, spoke for many young writers when he declared that he was through with "literature and all that bosh." Attacking aristocratic literary conventions, Twain and other authors who shared his concerns explored new forms of fiction and worked to broaden its appeal to the general public.

These efforts to chart new directions for American literature rested on fundamental changes taking place in the publishing industry. To compete with elite periodicals costing twenty-five to thirty-five cents, new magazines like *Ladies' Home Journal, Cosmopolitan,* and *McClure's* lowered their prices to a dime or fifteen cents and tripled or quadrupled their circulation. Supporting themselves through advertising, these magazines encouraged new trends in fiction while mass-marketing new products. Their editors sought writers who could provide accurate depictions of the "whirlpool of real life" and create a new civic consciousness to heal the class divisions of American society.

Some of these authors have been called regionalists because they captured the distinctive dialect and details of local life in their environs. In *The Country of the Pointed Firs* (1896), for example, Sarah Orne Jewett wrote of the New England village life that she knew in South Berwick, Maine. Others, most notably William Dean Howells, have been called realists because of their focus on the truthful depiction of the commonplace, especially in urban areas. Still others have been categorized as naturalists because their novels and stories deny free will and stress the ways in which life's outcomes are determined by economic and psychological forces. Stephen Crane's *Maggie: A Girl of the Streets* (1892), a bleak story of an innocent girl's exploitation and ultimate suicide in an urban slum, is generally considered the first naturalistic American novel. Yet, in practice, these categories are imprecise and often overlap. What many of these writers shared was a skepticism about literary conventions and an intense desire to understand the society around them and portray it in words.

The careers of Mark Twain and Theodore Dreiser highlight the changes in the publishing industry and the evolution of new forms of writing. Both authors grew up in the Midwest, outside the East Coast literary establishment. Twain was born near Hannibal, Missouri, in 1835, and Dreiser in Terre Haute, Indiana, in 1871. As young men, both worked as newspaper reporters and traveled widely. Both learned from direct and sometimes bitter experience about the greed, speculation, and fraud that figured centrally in Gilded Age life.

Of the two, Twain more incessantly sought a mass-market audience. With his drooping mustache, white hair, and white suits, Twain turned himself into a media personality, lecturing from coast to coast, founding his own publishing house, and using door-to-door salesmen to sell his books. The name Mark Twain became his trademark, identifying him to readers as a literary celebrity much as the labels Coca-Cola and Ivory Soap won instant consumer recognition. Although Dreiser possessed neither Twain's flamboyant personality nor his instinct for salesmanship, he, too, learned to crank out articles.

Drawing on their own experiences, Twain and Dreiser wrote about the human impact of the wrenching social changes taking place around them: the flow of people to the cities and the relentless scramble for power, wealth, and fame. In *The Adventures of Huckleberry Finn* (1884), Twain tells a story of two runaways, the rebellious Huck and the slave Jim, drifting down the Mississippi in search of freedom. Their physical journey, which contrasts idyllic life on the raft with the tawdry, fraudulent world of small riverfront towns, is a journey of identity that brings with it a deeper understanding of contemporary American society.

Dreiser's *Sister Carrie* (1900) also tells of a journey. In this case, the main character, Carrie Meeber, an innocent girl on her way from her Wisconsin farm home to Chicago, is seduced by a traveling salesman and then moves in with the married proprietor of a fancy saloon. Driven by her desire for expensive department-store clothes and lavish entertainment, Carrie is an opportunist incapable of feeling guilt. She follows her married lover to New York, knowing that he has stolen the receipts from his saloon, abandons him when his money runs out, and pursues her own career in the theater.

Twain and Dreiser broke decisively with the genteel tradition's emphasis on manners and decorum. *Century* magazine readers complained that *Huckleberry Finn* was coarse and "destitute of a single redeeming quality." The publisher of *Sister Carrie* was so repelled by Dreiser's novel that he printed only a thousand copies (to fulfill the legal terms of his contract) and then stored them in a warehouse, refusing to promote them.

Growing numbers of scholars and critics similarly challenged the self-serving certitudes of Victorian mores, including assumptions that moral worth and economic standing were closely linked and that the status quo of the 1870s and 1880s represented a social order decreed by God and nature alike. Whereas Henry George, Lester Ward, and Edward Bellamy elaborated their visions of a cooperative and harmonious society (see Chapter 18), economist Thorstein Veblen in *The Theory of the Leisure Class* (1899) offered a caustic critique of the lifestyles of the new capitalist elite. Raised in a Norwegian farm community in Minnesota, Veblen looked at the captains of industry and their families with a jaundiced eye, documenting their "conspicuous consumption" of expensive products and lamenting the widening gap between "those who worked without profit" and "those who profited without working."

Within the new discipline of sociology, Annie MacLean exposed the exploitation of department-store clerks, Walter Wyckoff uncovered the hand-to-mouth existence of unskilled laborers, and W.E.B. Du Bois documented the suffering and hardships faced by blacks in Philadelphia. The publication of these social scientists' writings, coupled with the economic depression and seething labor agitation of the 1890s, made it increasingly difficult for turn-of-the-century middle-class Americans to accept the smug, self-satisfied belief in progress and gentility that had been a hallmark of the Victorian outlook.

Modernism in Architecture and Painting   The challenge to the genteel tradition also found strong support among architects and painters. By the 1890s Chicago architects William Holabird, John Wellborn Root, and others had tired of copying European designs. Breaking with established architects such as Richard Morris Hunt, the designer of French châteaux for New York's Fifth Avenue, these Chicago architects followed the lead of Louis Sullivan, who argued that a building's form should follow its function. In their view, banks should look like the financial institutions they were, not like Greek temples. Striving to create functional American design standards, the Chicago architects looked for inspiration to the future—to **modernism**—not to the past.

The Chicago architect **Frank Lloyd Wright** designed "prairie-school" houses that represented a typical modernist break with past styles. Wright scorned the three-story Victorian house with its large attic and basement. His designs, which featured broad, sheltering roofs and horizontal silhouettes, used interconnecting rooms to create a sense of spaciousness.

The call of modernism, with its rejection of Victorian refinement, influenced late nineteenth-century American painting as well. The watercolors of Winslow Homer, a magazine illustrator during the Civil War, revealed nature as brutally tough and unsentimental. In Homer's grim, elemental seascapes, lone men struggle against massive waves that constantly threaten to overwhelm them. Thomas Eakins's canvases of swimmers, boxers, and rowers (such as his well-known *Champion Single Sculls*, painted in 1871) similarly captured moments of vigorous physical exertion in everyday life. While Mary Cassatt shared Eakins's interest in everyday life, she often took as her subject the bond between mother and child, as in her painting *The Bath* (ca. 1891). After studying at the Pennsylvania Academy of Fine Arts, she moved to Paris in 1874, where she worked closely with French Impressionist painters such as Monet and Degas.

The revolt by architects and painters against Victorian standards was symptomatic of a larger shift in middle-class thought. This shift resulted from fundamental economic changes that had spawned a far more complex social environment than that of the past. As Protestant minister Josiah Strong perceptively observed in 1898, the transition from muscle to mechanical power had "separated, as by an impassable gulf, the simple, homespun, individualistic world of the ... past, from the complex, closely associated life of the present." The increasingly evident gap between rural or small-town life—a world of quiet parlors and flickering kerosene lamps—and life in the big, glittering, electrified cities of iron and glass made nineteenth-century Americans acutely aware of differences in upbringing and wealth. Given the disparities between rich and poor, between rural and urban, and between native-born Americans and recent immigrants, it is no wonder that pious Victorian platitudes about proper manners and graceful arts seemed out of touch with the new social realities.

Distrusting the idealistic Victorian assumptions about social progress, middle-class journalists, novelists, artists, and politicians nevertheless remained divided over how to replace them. Not until the Progressive Era would social reformers draw on a new expertise in social research and an enlarged conception of the federal government's regulatory power to break sharply with their Victorian predecessors' social outlook.

From Victorian Lady to New Woman

Although middle-class women figured importantly in the revolt against Victorian refinement, their role was complex and ambiguous. Dissatisfaction with the cult of domesticity did not necessarily lead to open rebellion. Many women, although chafing against the constraints of deference and the assumption that they should limit their activities to the home, remained committed to playing a nurturing role within the family. In fact, early advocates of a "widened sphere" for women often fused the traditional Victorian ideal of womanhood with a firm commitment to political action.

The career of temperance leader **Frances Willard** illustrates how the cult of domesticity, with its celebration of special female virtues, could evolve into a broader view of women's social and political responsibilities. Like many of her contemporaries, Willard believed that women were compassionate and nurturing by nature. She was also convinced that drinking encouraged thriftlessness and profoundly threatened family life. Resigning as dean of women and professor of English at Northwestern University in 1874, Willard devoted her energies full-time to the temperance cause. Five years later she was elected president of the newly formed Woman's Christian Temperance Union (WCTU).

Willard took the traditional belief that women had unique moral virtues and transformed it into a rationale for political action. The domestication of politics, she asserted, would protect the family and improve public morality. Choosing as the union's badge a bow of white ribbon, symbolizing the purity of the home, she launched a crusade in 1880 to win the franchise for women so that they could vote to outlaw liquor. Willard soon expanded WCTU activities to include welfare work, prison reform, labor arbitration, and public health. Under her leadership, the WCTU—with a membership of nearly 150,000 by 1890—became the nation's first mass organization of women. Through it, women gained experience as lobbyists, organizers, and lecturers, in the process undercutting the assumption of "separate spheres."

An expanding network of women's clubs offered another means by which middle- and upper-class women could hone their skills in civic affairs, public speaking, and intellectual analysis. In the 1870s, many well-to-do women met weekly to study topics of mutual interest. These clubwomen soon became involved in social-welfare projects, public library expansion, and tenement reform. By 1892, the General Federation of Women's Clubs, an umbrella organization established that year, boasted 495 affiliates and a hundred thousand members. Middle-class black women, excluded from many white clubs, formed their own National Association of Colored Women's Clubs in 1900.

While older women eroded the Victorian constraints placed on them by social conventions by joining women's clubs, younger women challenged social conventions by joining the bicycling craze that swept urban America at the turn of the century. The fascination with bicycle riding developed as part of a new interest in health and physical fitness. Middle- and upper-class Americans explored various ways to improve their vigor. Some used health products such as cod liver oil and sarsaparilla for "weak blood." Others played basketball, invented in 1891 by a physical education instructor at Springfield College in Massachusetts to keep students in shape during the winter months. But bicycling, which could be done individually or in groups, quickly became the most popular sport for those who wished to combine exercise with recreation.

Bicycles of various designs had been manufactured since the 1870s, but bicycling did not become a national craze until the invention in the 1880s of the so-called safety bicycle, with smaller wheels, ball-bearing axles, and air-filled tires. By the 1890s, more than a million Americans owned bicycles.

Bicycling especially appealed to young women who had chafed under the restrictive Victorian attitudes about female exercise, which held that proper young ladies must never sweat and that the female body must be fully covered at all times.

Pedaling along in a shirtwaist or "split" skirt, a woman bicyclist made an implicit feminist statement suggesting that she had broken with genteel conventions and wanted to explore new activities beyond the traditional sphere.

Changing attitudes about femininity and women's proper role also found expression in gradually shifting ideas about marriage. **Charlotte Perkins Gilman**, a writer, suffrage advocate, and speaker for women's rights, asserted that women would make an effective contribution to society only when they won economic independence from men through work outside the home (see Chapter 21). One very tangible indicator of women's changing relationship to men was the substantial rise in the divorce rate between 1880 and 1900. In 1880, one in every twenty-one marriages ended in divorce. By 1900, the rate had climbed to one in twelve. Women who brought suit for divorce increasingly cited their husbands' failure to act responsibly and to respect their autonomy. Accepting such arguments, courts frequently awarded the wife alimony, a monetary settlement payable by the ex-husband to support her and their children.

Women writers generally welcomed the new female commitment to independence and self-sufficiency. In the short stories of Mary Wilkins Freeman, for example, women's expanding role is implicitly compared to the frontier ideal of freedom. Feminist **Kate Chopin** pushed the debate to the extreme by having Edna Pontellier, the married heroine of her controversial 1899 novel *The Awakening*, violate social conventions. First Edna falls in love with another man; then she takes her own life when his ideas about women prove as narrow and traditional as those of her husband.

Despite the efforts of these and other champions of the new woman, attitudes changed slowly. The enlarged conception of women's role in society exerted its greatest influence on college-educated, middle-class women who had leisure time and could reasonably hope for success in journalism, social work, or nursing. For female immigrant factory workers and for shop girls who worked sixty hours a week to try to make ends meet, however, the ideal remained a more distant goal. Although many women were seeking more independence and control over their lives, most still viewed the home as their primary responsibility.

Public Education as an Arena of Class Conflict   While the debate over women's proper role remained largely confined to the middle class, a very different controversy, over the scope and function of public education, engaged Americans of all socioeconomic levels. This debate starkly highlighted the class and cultural divisions in late nineteenth-century society. From the 1870s on, viewing the public schools as an instrument for indoctrinating and controlling the lower ranks of society, middle-class educators and civic leaders campaigned to expand public schooling and bring it under centralized control. Not surprisingly, the reformers' efforts aroused considerable opposition from ethnic and religious groups whose outlook and interests differed sharply from theirs.

Thanks to the crusade for universal public education started by Horace Mann and other antebellum educational reformers, most states had public school systems by the Civil War, and more than half the nation's children were receiving some formal education. But most attended school for only three or four years, and few went on to high school.

Concerned that many Americans lacked sufficient knowledge to participate wisely in public affairs or function effectively in the labor force, reformers such as William Torrey Harris worked to increase the number of years that children spent in school. First as superintendent of the St. Louis public schools in the 1870s and later as the federal commissioner of education, Harris urged teachers to instill in their students a sense of order, decorum, self-discipline, and civic loyalty. Believing that modern industrial society depended on citizens' conforming to the timetables of the factory and the train, he envisioned the schools as models of punctuality and precise scheduling: "The pupil must have his lessons ready at the appointed time, must rise at the tap of the bell, move to the line, return; in short, go through all the evolutions with equal precision."

To achieve these goals and to wrest control of the schools from neighborhood leaders and ward politicians, reform-minded educators like Harris elaborated a philosophy of public education stressing punctuality, centralized administration, compulsory-attendance laws, and a tenure system to insulate teachers from political favoritism and parental pressure. By 1900, thirty-one states required school attendance of all children from eight to fourteen years of age.

The steamroller methods used by Harris and likeminded administrators to systematize public education quickly prompted protests. New York pediatrician Joseph Mayer Rice, who toured thirty-six cities and interviewed twelve hundred teachers in 1892, scornfully criticized an educational establishment that stressed singsong memorization and prisonlike discipline.

Rice's biting attack on public education overlooked the real advances in reading and mathematics made in the previous two decades. Nationally, despite the influx of immigrants, the illiteracy rate in English for individuals ten years and older dropped from 17 percent in 1880 to 13 percent in 1890, largely because of the expansion of urban educational facilities. American high schools were also coeducational, and girls made up the majority of the students by 1900. But Rice was on target in assailing many teachers' rigid emphasis on silence, docility, and unquestioning obedience to the rules. When a Chicago school inspector found a thirteen-year-old boy huddled in the basement of a stockyard building and ordered him back to school, the weeping boy blurted out, "[T]hey hits ye if yer don't learn, and they hits ye if ye whisper, and they hits ye if ye have string in yer pocket, and they hits ye if yer seat squeaks, and they hits ye if ye don't stan' up in time, and they hits ye if yer late, and they hits ye if ye ferget the page."

By the 1880s, several different groups found themselves in opposition to centralized urban public school bureaucracies. Although many working-class families valued education, those who depended on their children's meager wages for survival resisted the attempt to force their sons and daughters to attend school past the elementary grades. Although some immigrant families made great sacrifices to enable their children to get an education, many withdrew their offspring from school as soon as they had learned the rudiments of reading and writing, and sent them to work.

Furthermore, Catholic immigrants objected to the overwhelmingly Protestant orientation of the public schools. Distressed by the use of the King James translation of the Bible and by the schools' failure to observe saints' days, Catholics set up separate parochial school systems. In response, Republican politicians, resentful of Catholic immigrants' overwhelming preference for the Democratic Party, tried unsuccessfully to pass a constitutional amendment cutting off all public aid to church-related schools in 1875. Catholics in turn denounced federal aid to public schools as intended "to suppress Catholic education, gradually extinguish Catholicity in this country, and to form one homogeneous American people after the New England Evangelical type."

At the other end of the social scale, upper-class parents who did not wish to send their children to immigrant-thronged public schools enrolled their daughters in female seminaries such as Chatham Hall in Chatham, Virginia, and their sons in private academies and boarding schools like St. Paul's in Concord, New Hampshire. The proliferation of private and parochial schools, together with the controversies over compulsory education, school funding, and classroom decorum, reveals the extent to which public education had become mired in ethnic and class differences. Unlike Germany and Japan, which created national education systems in the late nineteenth century, the United States, reflecting its social heterogeneity, maintained a system of locally run public and private institutions that allowed each segment of society to retain some influence over the schools attended by its own children. Amid the disputes, school enrollments dramatically expanded. In 1870, fewer than seventy-two thousand students were attending the nation's 1,026 high schools. By 1900, the number of high schools had jumped to more than five thousand and the number of students to more than half a million.

CHRONOLOGY
1860–1900

1865	Vassar College founded.
1869	First intercollegiate football game.
1872	Anthony Comstock founds New York Society for the Suppression of Vice.
1873	John Wanamaker opens his Philadelphia department store.
1875	Smith and Wellesley colleges founded.
1876	National League of baseball organized.
1880	William Booth's followers establish an American branch of the Salvation Army.
1881	Josephine Shaw Lowell founds New York Charity Organization Society (COS).
1884	Mark Twain, *Huckleberry Finn*.
1885	Stanford University founded.
1889	Jane Addams and Ellen Gates Starr open Hull House.
1891	University of Chicago founded.
	Basketball invented at Springfield College, Massachusetts.
1892	Ellis Island Immigration Center opened.
	General Federation of Women's Clubs organized.
1895	Coney Island amusement parks open in Brooklyn, New York.

1899	Scott Joplin, "Maple Leaf Rag."
	Kate Chopin, *The Awakening*.
	Thorstein Veblen, *The Theory of the Leisure Class*.
1900	Theodore Dreiser, *Sister Carrie*.
	National Association of Colored Women's Clubs organized.
1910	Angel Island Immigration Center opens in San Francisco.

CONCLUSION

By the 1890s, class conflict was evident in practically every area of city life, from mealtime manners to popular entertainment and recreation. As new immigrants flooded the tenements and spilled out onto neighborhood streets, it became impossible for native-born Americans to ignore their strange religious and social customs. Ethnic differences were compounded by class differences. Often poor and from peasant or working-class backgrounds, the immigrants from southern and eastern Europe took unskilled jobs and worked for subsistence-level wages. The slums and tenements in which they lived had high rates of disease. Middle- and upper-class Americans often responded by moving to fashionable avenues or suburbs and by stigmatizing them as nonwhite and racially inferior.

To distinguish themselves from these newcomers, native-born Americans stressed their commitment to Victorian morality, with its emphasis on manners, decorum, and self-control. Although never fully accepted even among the well-to-do, these Victorian ideals were meant to apply new standards for society. Lavish department stores and artistically designed houses reflected the middle- and upper-class faith that the consumption of material goods indicated good taste.

To raise standards, the prosperous classes expanded the number of high schools and created a new research university system for training educators, lawyers, doctors, and other professionals. As defenders of the new Victorian morality, educated middle- and upper-class women were expected to become the protectors of the home. Some members of the upper classes also tried to address the problems of poverty and congestion in the inner city. While Jacob Riis, Jane Addams, and other reformers worked to improve overcrowded housing and dangerous working conditions, Anthony Comstock and less sympathetic reformers attacked immigrant values and cultures in an effort to uplift and Americanize them.

Nowhere was the conflict between the social classes more evident than in the controversy over leisure entertainment. Caught up in the material benefits of a prospering industrial society, middle- and upper-class Americans battled against what they deemed "indecent" lower-class behavior in all its forms, from dancing to ragtime, gambling, and prizefighting to playing baseball on Sunday and visiting bawdy boardwalk sideshows. Even public parks became arenas of class conflict. Whereas the elite favored large, impeccably groomed urban parks that would serve as models of orderliness and propriety, working people fought for parks where they could picnic, play ball, drink beer, and escape the stifling heat of tenement apartments.

Although the well-to-do classes often appeared to have the upper hand in these clashes, significant disagreements about moral standards surfaced early within their own ranks. Critics, among them Charlotte Perkins Gilman, faulted middle-class society for its obsession with polite manners, empty social rituals, and restrictions on the occupations open to women.

By 1900, the contest for power between the elite classes and the largely immigrant working class was heading toward a partial resolution. As Victorian morality eroded, undermined by dissension from within and opposition from without, new standards emerged that blended elements of earlier positions. For example, new rules regulated behavior in the boxing ring and on the baseball field. Still, it was immigrant heroes who captured the popular imagination. The elite vision of sport as a vehicle for instilling self-discipline and self-control was transformed into a new commitment to sports as spectacle and entertainment. Sports had become big business and an important part of the new consumerism.

Similar patterns of compromise and change took place in other arenas. Vaudeville houses, attacked by the affluent for their risqué performances, evolved into the nation's first movie theaters. Ragtime music, with its syncopated rhythms, gave rise to jazz. In short, the dashing, disreputable, and raucous working-class culture of the late nineteenth-century city can be seen as the seedbed of twentieth-century mass culture. And everywhere popular culture became increasingly dominated by commercial interests that capitalized on the disposable income created by the nation's explosive urban and industrial growth.

20

POLITICS AND EXPANSION IN AN INDUSTRIALIZING AGE, 1877–1900

CHAPTER OUTLINE

• Party Politics in an Era of Upheaval, 1877–1884 • Politics of Privilege, Politics of Exclusion, 1884–1892 • The 1890s: Politics in a Depression Decade • Expansionist Stirrings and War with Spain, 1878–1901

PARTY POLITICS IN AN ERA OF UPHEAVAL, 1877–1884

Between 1877 and 1894, four presidents squeezed into office by the narrowest of margins, control of the House of Representatives changed hands five times, and seven new western states were admitted into the Union. Competition between political parties was intense. No one party could muster a working majority.

To meet these challenges, party leaders sought desperately to cement the loyalty of their followers. While the Democrats rebuilt their strength in the South, Republicans struggled to maintain the loyalties of the working class and to increase their support from business. At the municipal level, political machines worked to recruit immigrants and other newcomers in the rapidly expanding cities.

Contested Political Visions   In the late nineteenth century, more than 80 percent of eligible white males often voted, and in hard-fought elections, the percentage rose to 95 percent. Voter participation a century later would equal scarcely half that level.

Higher voter turnout resulted in part from the attempts of the major parties to navigate the stormy economy created by postwar industrial and geographic expansion, the influx of millions of immigrants, and the explosive growth of cities. As voter turnout shot up, however, political parties sidestepped issues such as taxation of corporations, support for those injured in factory accidents, and poverty relief. Nor was the American labor movement, unlike its counterpart in Europe, able to organize itself effectively as a political force. Except for the Interstate Commerce Act of 1887 and the largely symbolic Sherman Anti-Trust Act of 1890, Washington generally ignored the social consequences of industrialization.

How can we explain this refusal to address economic concerns and, at the same time, account for the enormous popular support for parties? The answer lies in the political ideology of the period and the three major symbolic and economic issues that preoccupied lawmakers nationally: the tariff, the money supply, and civil-service reform.

Political parties in the late nineteenth century energized voters not only by appealing to economic self interest, as was evident in support for industrialization and pensions for Civil War veterans and their widows but also by linking their pro-grams to deeply held beliefs about the nature of the family and the proper role of government. Republicans justified their support for the tariff and defended their commitment to Union widows' pensions as a protection for the family home. Democrats countered, using metaphors of the seduction and rape of white women by outsiders and labeling Republican programs as classic examples of the perils of using excessive government force. High tariffs imperiled the family and threatened economic disaster. With respect to both parties, men, in particular, associated loy-alty to party with a sense of masculinity.

Despite their differences over the tariff and monetary policy, neither Republicans nor Democrats believed that the national government had any right to regulate corporations or to protect the social welfare of workers. Neither party therefore courted the labor union vote. Many members of both parties embraced the doctrine of **laissez-faire**—the belief that unregulated competition represented the best path to progress. According to this view, the federal government should promote economic development but not regulate industry.

Rather than looking to Washington, people turned to local or state authorities. On the Great Plains, angry farmers demanded that their state legislatures regulate railroad rates. In the cities, immigrant groups, organized by political bosses, battled for control of municipal governments and local contracts. In response, native-born reformers attempted to oust the organizations in power and clean up corruption. Meanwhile, city and state governments vied with each other for control. Cities often could not change their system of government, alter their tax structure, or regu-late municipal utilities without state approval. When Chicago wanted to issue per-mits to street popcorn vendors, for example, the Illinois legislature had to pass a special act.

Both parties, in the North and the South, practiced fraud by rigging elections, throwing out opposition votes, and paying for "floaters" who moved from precinct to precinct to vote. Each also expressed moral outrage at the other's illegal behavior.

By linking economic policy to family values, both parties reinforced the appeal of their platforms and encouraged the participation of women in the political pro-cess. Although most women could not vote, they played an active role in politics. Frances Willard and her followers in the Woman's Christian Temperance Union (WCTU), for example, helped create a Prohibition and Home Protection Party in the 1880s. A decade later, western women Populists won full suffrage in Colorado, Idaho, and Utah.

Patterns of Party Strength   In the 1870s and 1880s, each party had its own ideological appeal and centers of regional strength. The Democrats ruled the South, southern sections of border states like Ohio, and northern cities with large immigrant populations. They campaigned for minimal government expenditures, opposed tariff increases, and generally attacked what they considered to be "governmental interference in the economy." In addition, Democrats staunchly defended their immigrant followers. On the state and local levels, they fiercely opposed prohibition, supported parochial schools, and rejected requirements that immigrant children attend only those schools that taught in English.

The Republicans reigned in rural and small town New England, Pennsylvania, and the upper Midwest and drew support from the **Grand Army of the Republic** (GAR), a social and political lobbying organization of northern Civil War veterans. They often "waved the bloody shirt," reminding voters that their party had led the nation during the Civil War. "The Democratic Party," wrote one Republican, "may be described as a common sewer and loathsome receptacle, into which is emptied every element of treason North and South." To emphasize their patriotism, the Republicans ran a series of former Union army generals for president and voted generous veterans' benefits.

State and local party leaders managed campaigns. They chose the candidates, raised money, organized rallies, and—if their candidate won—distributed public jobs to party workers. Bosses like the former saloonkeepers "Big Jim" Pendergast of Kansas City, a Democrat, and George B. Cox of Cincinnati, a Republican, turned out the vote by taking care of constituents, handing out municipal jobs, and financing campaigns with "contributions" extracted from city employees.

Although issues of governmental authority dominated on the federal level, family tradition, ethnic ties, religious affiliation, and local issues often determined an individual's vote. Outside the South, ethnicity and religion were the most reliable predictors of party affiliation. Catholics, especially Irish Catholics, and Americans of German ancestry tended to vote Democratic. Old-stock Protestant northerners, in contrast, voted Republican. Among immigrant groups, most British-born Protestants and 80 percent of Swedish and Norwegian Lutherans voted Republican, as did African Americans, North and South. Although intolerant of racial differences, the Democrats were generally more accepting of religious diversity than were the Republicans.

Political battles often centered on cultural differences, most notably, prohibition. Irish whiskey drinkers, German beer drinkers, and Italian wine drinkers were equally outraged by antiliquor legislation. State and local prohibition proposals always aroused passionate voter interest.

Political Bosses and Machine Politics   The swelling numbers of urban dwellers gave rise to a new kind of politician, the "boss," who listened to his urban constituents and lobbied on their behalf. The boss presided over the city's "machine"—an unofficial political organization designed to keep a particular party or faction in office. Whether officially serving as mayor or not, the boss, assisted by local ward or precinct captains, wielded enormous influence in city government. Often a former saloonkeeper or labor leader, the boss knew his constituents well.

For better or worse, the **political machine** was America's unique contribution to municipal government in an era of pell-mell urban growth. Typified by Tammany Hall, the Democratic organization that dominated New York City politics from the 1830s to the 1930s, machines emerged in Baltimore, Philadelphia, Atlanta, San Francisco, and a host of other cities after the Civil War.

By the turn of the century, many cities had experienced machine rule. Working through the local ward captains to turn out voters, the machine rode herd on the tangle of municipal bureaucracies, controlling who was hired for the police and fire departments. It rewarded its friends and punished its enemies through its control of taxes, licenses, and inspections. The machine gave tax breaks to favored contractors in return for large payoffs and slipped them insider information about upcoming street and sewer projects.

At the neighborhood level, the ward boss often acted as a welfare agent, helping the needy. To spend three dollars to pay a fine for a juvenile offense meant a lot to the poor, but it was small change to a boss who raked in millions from public-utility contracts and land deals. While the machine helped alleviate some suffering, it entangled urban social services with corrupt politics and often prevented city government from responding to the real problems of the city's neediest inhabitants.

Under New York City's boss, **William "Magear" Tweed,** the Tammany Hall machine revealed the slimy depths to which extortion and contract padding could sink. Between 1869 and 1871, Tweed gave $50,000 to the poor and $2,250,000 to schools, orphanages, and hospitals. In these same years, his machine dispensed sixty thousand patronage positions and pumped up the city's debt by $70 million through graft.

By the turn of the century, the bosses were facing well-organized assaults on their power, led by an urban elite whose members sought to restore "good government." In this atmosphere, the bosses increasingly forged alliances with civic organizations and reform leagues. The results, although never entirely satisfactory to anyone involved, paved the way for new sewage and transportation systems, expanded parklands, and improved public services—a record of considerable accomplishment, given the magnitude of the problems created by urban growth.

Regulating the Money Supply

In the 1870s, the debate over monetary policy—the question of how much money should be in circulation—was part of a larger struggle over how wealth and power should be distributed in post–Civil War America. The debate was shaped by Americans' almost superstitious reverence for gold and silver. Many believed that only gold or silver, or certificates exchangeable for these metals, were trustworthy. Reflecting this notion, all the federally issued currency in circulation in 1860 consisted of gold or silver coins or U.S. Treasury notes redeemable for gold or silver. (Currency from some sixteen hundred state banks also circulated, worsening a chaotic monetary situation.) During the Civil War, the federal government issued "greenbacks," paper money not backed by gold or silver.

Bankers and creditors also believed that economic stability required a strictly limited currency supply. Debtors, in contrast, favored expanding the money supply to make it easier for them to pay off their debts. The monetary debate thus focused on a specific question: should the Civil War paper "greenbacks" currently in circulation be retained or eliminated, leaving only a currency backed by gold? The hard times associated with the Panic of 1873 sharpened this dispute.

The Greenback Party (founded 1877) advocated an expanded money supply and other measures to benefit workers and farmers. In the 1878 midterm elections, with the support of labor organizations angered by the government's hostility toward the labor unrest of 1877, Greenback candidates won fourteen seats in Congress.

As prosperity returned and the Greenback party faded, the debate became focused on the controversy over the coinage of silver. In 1873, Congress instructed the U.S. mint to cease making silver coins. Silver had been "demonetized." But new discoveries in Nevada (see Chapter 17) vastly increased the silver supply, and debtor groups, hoping to lower interest rates on borrowed money, now demanded that the government resume the coinage of silver.

Backed by the silver-mine owners, silver forces won a partial victory in 1878, when Congress required the treasury to buy and mint up to $4 million worth of silver each month. But the treasury, dominated by monetary conservatives, sabotaged the law's intent by refusing to circulate the silver dollars that it minted.

Frustrated silver advocates tried a new approach in the **Sherman Silver Purchase Act** of 1890. This measure instructed the treasury to buy 4.5 million ounces of silver monthly and issue treasury notes, redeemable in gold or silver, equivalent to the cost of these purchases. The monetary supply slightly increased, but the government paid far less for its monthly purchases and therefore issued fewer treasury notes. The controversy over silver dragged on.

Civil-Service Reform   A parallel controversy to the debate over the distribution of wealth and power raged over political appointments. For decades, successful candidates in national, state, and local elections had rewarded supporters with jobs ranging from cabinet seats to lowly municipal posts. Defenders claimed that this system was a democratic means of filling government positions. Critics called it a corrupt spoils system after the old expression, "To the victor belong the spoils."

For years, a small but influential group of upper-class reformers, including Missouri senator Carl Schurz and editor E.L. Godkin of *The Nation*, had campaigned for a professional civil service based on merit. Well-educated and wealthy, these reformers favored a civil service staffed by "gentlemen." The reformers had a point. A professional civil service was needed to remove corruption and manage complex government affairs.

Elected through the compromise that ended Reconstruction (see Chapter 16), Republican president Rutherford B. Hayes cautiously embraced the civil-service cause. In 1877, he launched an investigation of the corruption-riddled New York City customs office and fired two high officials. One, Chester A. Arthur, had played a key role in passing out jobs.

When Congressman James A. Garfield won the 1880 Republican presidential nomination, the delegates, to appease the opposing New York faction, chose Chester A. Arthur, the loyalist Hayes had recently fired, as Garfield's running mate. Because Garfield enjoyed excellent health, the choice of the totally unqualified Arthur seemed safe.

The Democrats nominated a career army officer from Pennsylvania, Winfield Scott Hancock, and the Greenbackers gave the nod to Congressman James B. Weaver of Iowa. Garfield's managers stressed his Civil War record and his log-cabin birth. By a razor-thin margin, Garfield edged out Hancock; Weaver trailed far behind.

Garfield's assassination in 1881 by the crazed office-seeker Charles Guiteau brought to the White House Vice President Arthur, the very symbol of patronage corruption, and gave a powerful emotional thrust to the reform cause. Civil-service reformers portrayed the fallen president as a spoils-system martyr. In 1883, Congress enacted a civil-service law introduced by Senator George Pendleton of Ohio (Garfield's home state) and drafted by the Civil Service Reform League that had been created two years earlier. The **Pendleton Civil Service Act** set up a com-mission to prepare competitive examinations and establish standards of merit for a variety of federal jobs; it also forbade political candidates to solicit contributions from government workers.

Although the Pendleton Act initially covered only about 12 percent of federal employees, subsequent presidents gradually expanded the number of positions. By the 1890s, the act had opened up new positions for women, who now held nearly a third of the jobs as federal clerks in government agencies. The creation of a pro-fessional civil service thus helped bring the federal government in step with the modernizing trends transforming society.

"Where Is the Difference?" 1894 *By equating criminal payoffs to the police with corporate contributions to senators, this cartoon in* Puck *magazine suggests that corruption pervades society and needs to be stopped.*

As for Chester A. Arthur, his performance surprised those who had expected an utter disaster. Arthur supported civil-service reform and proved quite independent. Fed up with the feuding Republicans, in 1882 the voters gave the Democrats a strong majority in the House of Representatives. In 1884, for the first time since 1856, they would put a Democrat in the White House: Grover Cleveland.

POLITICS OF PRIVILEGE, POLITICS OF EXCLUSION, 1884–1892

The stalemate between the two major parties in their battle to control the standards for economic growth continued under President Cleveland, a Democrat, and President Harrison, a Republican. Both presidents challenged powerful interests and faced stiff opposition. Cleveland alienated strong lobbies by calling for cuts in the tariff and in veterans' pensions. In 1888, business and veterans' groups rallied to defeat Cleveland and elect Benjamin Harrison of Indiana, a former Civil War general, in one of the most corrupt campaigns in American history. Harrison alienated voters by passing a high tariff and an expanded pension law that increased the number of pensioners by 43 percent.

Responding to major party fraud and inattention to the needs of rural Americans, farmers mounted protests and began to organize. While the Grange and Farmers' Alliance movements condemned the monopolistic practices of grain and cotton buyers in the post-Reconstruction South, the white majority consolidated their political power by denying the region's black citizens their most basic rights.

A Democrat in the White House: Grover Cleveland, 1885–1889	At a tumultuous Chicago convention in 1884, the Republicans nominated their best-known leader, James G. Blaine. A gifted orator, Blaine spoke for the younger, more dynamic wing of the Republican Party eager to promote economic development and reinvigorate foreign policy.

But Blaine had been stained by the revelation that he, as Speaker of the House, had offered political favors to a railroad company in exchange for stock. For reformers, Blaine epitomized the hated patronage system. To E.L. Godkin, he "wallowed in spoils like a rhinoceros in an African pool."

Sensing Blaine's vulnerability, the Democrats chose a sharply contrasting nominee, Grover Cleveland of New York. In a meteoric rise from reform mayor of Buffalo to governor, Cleveland had fought the bosses and spoils men. The shrewdness of the Democrats' choice became apparent when Godkin, Carl Schurz, and other Republican reformers bolted to Cleveland. They were promptly nicknamed **Mugwumps,** an Algonquian term for a renegade chief.

Unfortunately, Cleveland as a youth had fathered an illegitimate child. Although he admitted the indiscretion, Republicans still jeered at rallies: "Ma, Ma, where's my pa?" Cleveland also faced opposition from Tammany Hall, the New York City Democratic machine that he had fought as governor. If Tammany's immigrant voters stayed home on election day, Cleveland could lose his own state. But, in October, a New York City clergyman denounced the Democrats as the party of "Rum, Romanism, and Rebellion." Blaine failed to immediately repudiate the remark. The Cleveland campaign managers widely publicized this triple insult to

Catholics, to patriotic Democrats, and to drinkers. This blunder and the Mugwumps' defection allowed Cleveland to carry New York State by twelve hundred votes, and with it the election.

Once in office, Cleveland embraced the belief that government must not meddle in the economy and opposed any public regulation of corporations. He also rejected providing any governmental help for those in need. Vetoing a bill that would have given seeds to drought stricken farmers in Texas, he warned that people should not expect the government to solve their problems.

One public matter did arouse Cleveland's energies: the tariff. Because it brought in revenue in the era before a federal income tax, the tariff functioned as a protection for special interests and a source of government income. But which imported goods should be subject to duties, and how much? Opinions differed radically. Producers of such commodities as coal, hides, timber, and wool demanded tariff protection against foreign competition as did many manufacturers. Other businesses, however, while seeking protection for their finished products, wanted low tariffs on the raw materials they required. Massachusetts shoe manufacturers, for example, urged high duties on imported shoes but low duties on imported hides. Most farmers, by contrast, hated all tariffs for making it hard to sell American farm products abroad.

Cleveland's call for lower tariffs arose from his concern that high tariffs created huge federal budget surpluses, which tempted legislators to distribute the money in the form of veterans' pensions or expensive public-works programs in their home districts, commonly called pork-barrel projects. With his horror of paternalistic government, Cleveland viewed the budget surplus as a corrupting influence. Although the Democratic campaign of 1888 gave little attention to the issue, Cleveland's talk of lowering the tariff angered many corporate leaders.

Cleveland stirred up another hornet's nest by opposing the routine payment of veterans' disability pensions. No one opposed pensions for the deserving, but fraudulent claims had proliferated. Unlike his predecessors, Cleveland investigated these claims and rejected many of them. He also vetoed a bill that would have pensioned all disabled veterans whether or not their injuries occurred in military service. The pension list should be an honor roll, he stressed, not a refuge for fraud.

Big Business Strikes Back; Benjamin Harrison, 1889–1893

By 1888, influential interest groups had concluded that Cleveland must go. The Republicans turned to Benjamin Harrison of Indiana. A corporation lawyer and former senator, Harrison was so aloof that some ridiculed him as the human iceberg. To avoid alienating voters, Harrison argued that a high tariff would ensure business prosperity, decent wages for workers, and a healthy home market for farmers.

The Republicans amassed a $4 million campaign fund from worried business leaders to purchase posters, buttons, and votes. Despite voter fraud, Cleveland received almost a hundred thousand more votes than Harrison. But Harrison carried the key states of Indiana and New York and won the Electoral College vote. The Republicans held the Senate and regained the House. Once in office, Harrison swiftly rewarded his supporters. He appointed as commissioner of pensions a GAR official who, on taking office, declared "God help the surplus!" The pension rolls soon ballooned from 676,000 to nearly a million. This massive pension system (which was coupled with medical care in a network of veterans' hospitals) became America's first large-scale public welfare program. In 1890, the triumphant Republicans also enacted the McKinley Tariff, which pushed rates to an all-time high.

Rarely has the federal government been so subservient to entrenched economic interests and so out of touch with the plight of the disadvantaged as during the 1880s. But inaction bred discontent. In the election of 1890, the Democrats gained sixty-six congressional seats and won control of the House of Representatives. Farmers, too, turned to politics and swung into action.

Agrarian Protest and the Rise of the People's Party   Great Plains farming had long been a risky venture. Between 1873 and 1877, terrible grasshopper infestations had consumed nearly half the midwestern wheat crop. As production rose, prices fell. Wheat tumbled from $2.95 a bushel in 1866 to $1.06 in 1880. Farmers who had borrowed heavily to finance homesteads went bankrupt or barely survived. One struggling Minnesota farmer wrote the governor in 1874, "[W]e can see nothing but starvation in the future if relief does not come."

Midwestern farmers in 1867, under the leadership of Oliver H. Kelley, a Department of Agriculture clerk, formed the **Grange,** or "Patrons of Husbandry." In the next decade, membership soared to more than 1.5 million. Offering information, emotional support, and fellowship, the Grange urged farmers to "buy less and

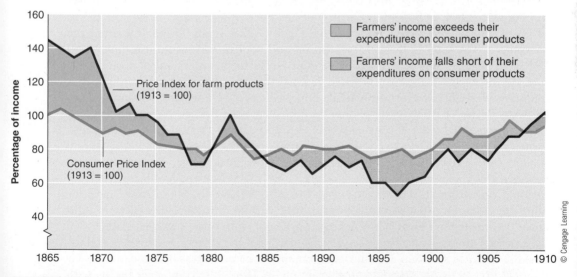

FIGURE 20.1 Consumer Prices and Farm-product Prices, 1865–1913

From 1865 to 1895, the prices that farmers received for their crops gradually declined. Even when they increased after 1895, farmers had difficulty making ends meet. As cycles of drought and debt battered Great Plains wheat growers, a Kansas farmer wrote, "At the age of 52, after a long life of toil, economy, and self-denial, I find myself and family virtually paupers."

produce more, in order to make our farms more self-sustaining." They negotiated special discounts with farm-machinery dealers and set up "cash-only" cooperative stores and grain-storage elevators to cut out the "middlemen"—the bankers, grain brokers, and merchants who made money at the farmers' expense.

Grangers focused their wrath on railroads, which routinely gave discounts to large shippers, bribed state legislators, and charged higher rates for short runs than for long hauls. Stung by these practices, Grangers in Illinois, Wisconsin, Minnesota, and Iowa lobbied state legislatures in 1874 to pass laws fixing maximum rates for freight shipments.

The railroads appealed these "Granger laws" to the Supreme Court, but in *Munn* v. *Illinois* (1877) the Court rejected the railroads' appeal and upheld an Illinois law setting maximum grain storage rates. The regulation of grain elevators, declared the Court's majority, was legitimate under the federal Constitution's acknowledgment of the right of states to exercise police powers. When the Court in *Wabash* v. *Illinois* (1886) modified this position by prohibiting states from regulating interstate railroad rates, Congress passed the Interstate Commerce Act (1887), reaffirming the federal government's power to oversee railroad activities and establishing a new agency, the Interstate Commerce Commission (ICC), to do just that. Although the commission failed to curb the railroads' monopolistic practices, it did establish the principle of federal regulation of interstate transportation.

Despite promising beginnings, the Grange movement soon faltered. In 1878, the railroads, which had lost their battle on the national level, lobbied state legislatures and won repeal of most of the state-regulation laws. The cash-only cooperative stores closed because most farmers had little cash. The Grange ideal of financial independence from banks and merchants proved unrealistic because conditions on the Plains made it impossible to farm without borrowing money. When the prices of corn, wheat, and cotton briefly revived after 1878, many farmers deserted the movement. The Grange lived on as a social and educational institution, but it had lost its appeal because it was unable to improve its members' financial position.

The problems that drove farmers to form the Grange prompted southern and midwestern farmers to form the alliance movement. The **Farmers' Alliance** began in Texas in the 1870s as small planters, trapped by the crop lien system, mortgaged future harvests to cover current expenses. Mired in debt, about a third of southern farmers gave up their land and became tenants or sharecroppers by 1900.

In 1887, Texan Charles W. Macune, a self-trained lawyer and a physician, assumed leadership of the Alliance movement. By 1889, Macune had merged several regional organizations into the National Farmers' Alliance and Industrial Union, or Southern Alliance. A parallel black organization, the National Colored Farmers' Alliance, had meanwhile emerged in Arkansas and spread to other southern states.

As they attended alliance rallies and picnics, read the alliance newspaper, and listened to alliance speakers, hard-hit farm families became increasingly aware of their political potential. An Arkansas member wrote in 1889, "Reform never begins with the leaders, it comes from the people." By 1890, the Southern Alliance claimed 3 million members. An additional 1.2 million joined the National Colored Farmers' Alliance.

Meanwhile, Alliance fever had spread to the Great Plains. In the drought-plagued years of 1880 and 1881, alliances sprang up in Kansas, Nebraska, Iowa, and Minnesota. Membership grew when insects destroyed much of the wheat crop and increases in world production drove down prices for agricultural products. Under these conditions, many settlers returned East. "In God we trusted, in Kansas we busted," some scrawled on their wagons. Western Kansas lost 50 percent of its population between 1888 and 1892. Others hung on, and the Northwestern Alliance grew rapidly. By 1890, the Kansas Alliance claimed 130,000 members, followed closely by alliances in Nebraska, the Dakotas, and Minnesota. What had begun as a desperate attempt to save their farms had now turned into a massive political campaign to change the American political and economic system.

Alliance members at first tried to create a biracial movement. Southern Alliance leaders Tom Watson of Georgia and Leonidas Polk of North Carolina urged southern farmers, black and white, to act together. For a time, this message of racial cooperation in the interest of reform offered promise. But Alliance members also shared the "separate but equal" philosophy of their "New South" counterparts that combined progressive reform with the separation of races (see Chapter 18).

Women joined the alliance leadership as well. Mary E. Lease, a Wichita lawyer, burst on the scene in 1890 as a fiery alliance orator. Other women, veterans of the Granger or prohibition cause, founded the National Women's Alliance (NWA) in 1891. Declared the NWA, "Put 1,000 women lecturers in the field and revolution is here." By no coincidence, a strong feminist strain pervades Ignatius Donnelly's *The Golden Bottle* (1892), a novel portraying the agrarian reformers' social vision.

As the movement swelled, the opposition turned nasty. When Jerry Simpson, an Alliance rancher from Kansas, mentioned the silk stockings of a conservative politician in his district and noted that he had no such finery, a hostile newspaper editor labeled him "Sockless Jerry" Simpson, the nickname he carried to his grave. When Mary Lease advised Kansas to "raise less corn and more hell," another editor sneered: "[Kansas] has started to raise hell, as Mrs. Lease advised, and [the state] seems to have an overproduction. But that doesn't matter. Kansas never did believe in diversified crops."

All this activity helped shape a new political agenda. In 1889, the Southern and Northwestern Alliances loosely merged and lined up candidates in the 1890 midterm elections. Alliance candidates focused on government action on behalf of farmers and workers, including tariff reduction, a graduated income tax, public ownership of the railroads, federal funding for irrigation research, a ban on landownership by foreigners, and "the free and unlimited coinage of silver."

The 1890 elections revealed the strength of agrarian protest. Southern Democrats who endorsed alliance goals won four governorships and control of eight state legislatures. On the Great Plains, alliance-endorsed candidates controlled the Kansas and Nebraska legislatures and gained the balance of power in Minnesota and South Dakota. Three alliance-backed senators, together with some fifty congressmen (including Watson and Simpson), went to Washington as angry winds from the hinterlands buffeted the political system.

Shared economic grievances soon overcame the regional differences, which had threatened to divide the movement. Southern Alliance leaders who initially opposed endorsing a third party, fearing it would weaken the southern Democratic Party, the bastion of white supremacy, eventually adopted the third-party idea. In February 1892, alliance leaders organized the People's Party of the United States, generally called the **Populist Party.** At the party convention in Omaha, Nebraska,

GOING TO THE SOURCE

Women in Politics

In this article, written for the *Arena* magazine in 1892, Annie L. Diggs, a Populist orator and editor from Kansas, identifies twenty-five prominent women speakers and editors who played important roles nationally in the Farmers' Alliance and the Populist Party. In 1892, the Populists in Kansas elected the governor and a majority in the state senate only to be stymied by a Republican majority in the state house.

Farm life for women is a treadmill.... The worn and weary treadmillers are anxious, troubled.... Instead of mythologic lore, they read "Seven Financial Conspiracies," "Looking Backward," "Progress and Poverty." Alas! Of this last word they know much and fear more – fear for their children's future. The [women] ... turn with all the fierceness of their primal mother-nature to protect their younglings from devouring, devastating plutocracy.

The great political victory of the people of Kansas would not have been won without the help of the women of the Alliance. Women who never dreamed of becoming public speakers grew eloquent in their zeal and fervor....

Before this question of the salvation of the imperiled homes of the nation, all other questions, whether of "prohibition" or "suffrage" pale into relative inconsequence. For where shall temperance or high thought of franchise be taught to children, by whose breath the world is saved, if sacred hearth fires shall go out? The overtopping, all-embracing moral question of the age is this for which the Alliance came. Upon such great ethical foundations is the labor movement today building itself. How could women do otherwise than be in it?

Easily first among Kansas women who rose to prominence as a platform speaker for the political party which grew out of the Alliance is Mrs. Mary E. Lease....

Seldom, if ever, was a woman so vilified and so misrepresented by malignant newspaper attacks. A woman of other quality would have sunk under the avalanche. She was quite competent to cope with all that was visited upon her. Indeed, the abuse did her much service. The people loved her for the enemies she made.

Already the story of the wondrous part she has played in the people's struggle for justice has reached other countries....

In the to-be-written history of this great epoch, Mrs. Mary E. Lease will have a most conspicuous place.

Consider this Kansas record, oh supercilious sneerer at "strong-minded" women. Most of these women have opened their mouths and spake before many people.... All these heretical things they have done, and yet are the womanliest, gentlest of women, the best of homekeepers, the loyalist of wives, the carefulest of mothers....

Thus splendidly do the *facts* about women in politics refute the frivolous *theories* of timorous or hostile objectors. The women prominent as active, responsible factors in the political arena are those who are characterized by strong common sense, high ideals, and lofty patriotism. When such as these cast ballot throughout the nation,

"Then shall their voice of sovereign choice
Swell the deep bass of duty done,
And strike the key of time to be
When God and man shall speak as one."

Questions

1. How does Diggs justify women's participation in politics?

2. What roles do traditional ideas about women's responsibilities play in her argument?

3. What ideals shaped Populist religiosity?

Source: Annie L. Diggs, "The Women in the Alliance Movement," *The Arena*, July 1892, No. XXXII, pp. 160–180.

that August, cheering delegates nominated for president the former Civil War general and Greenback nominee James B. Weaver of Iowa. Courting the South, they chose as Weaver's running mate the Virginian James Field, who had lost a leg fighting for the Confederacy.

The Populist platform called for the direct popular election of senators and other electoral reforms. It also endorsed a **subtreasury plan** devised by alliance leader Charles Macune by which farmers could store their nonperishable commodities in government warehouses, receive low-interest loans using the crops as collateral, and then sell the stored commodities when market prices rose. Their model was the postal service, an efficient, centralized, large-scale organization that worked for the public good. Ignatius Donnelly's ringing preamble pronounced the nation on "the verge of moral, political, and material ruin" and called for a return of the government "to the hands of 'the plain people' with which class it originated."

African Americans After Reconstruction   As the Populists organized, a group of citizens with profound grievances suffered renewed oppression. With the end of Reconstruction in 1877 and the restoration of power to white elites (see Chapter 16), southern white opinion demanded an end to the hated "Negro rule," and local Democratic Party officials pursued this objective. Suppressing the black vote became a major goal. Intimidation, terror, and vote fraud kept blacks from the polls or forced them to vote Democratic. Mississippi amended its state constitution in 1890 to exclude most black voters, and other southern states soon followed suit.

Because the Fifteenth Amendment (1870) guaranteed all male citizens' right to vote, white southerners used indirect means such as literacy tests (a test of the ability to read), poll taxes (a tax paid to vote), and property requirements (which restricted the right to vote to those who owned property) to disfranchise blacks. To protect illiterate whites, the so-called grandfather clause exempted from these electoral requirements anyone with an ancestor who had voted in 1860. Although black disfranchisement proceeded erratically over the South, by the early twentieth century it was essentially complete.

Disfranchisement was only one part of the system of white supremacy. In a parallel development, state after state passed laws imposing strict racial segregation in many realms of life (to be discussed in Chapter 21). African American caterers, barbers, bricklayers, and other artisans lost their white clientele. Blacks who went to prison—sometimes for minor offenses—faced the convict-lease system, which cotton planters, railroad builders, and other employers used to "lease" prison gangs and force them to work under slave-labor conditions.

The convict-lease system enforced the racial hierarchy and played an important economic role as industrialization and agricultural change came to the South. The system brought income to hard-pressed state governments and provided factories, railroads, and large-scale farms with predictable, controllable, cheap labor. The system also intimidated free laborers and discouraged foreign immigrants from going South. Thousands died under this brutal convict-labor system, which continued into the early decades of the twentieth century.

Lynching became the ultimate enforcer of southern white supremacy. Through the 1880s and 1890s, about a hundred blacks were lynched annually in the United States, mainly in the South. The stated reasons, often the rape of a white woman, frequently arose from rumor and unsubstantiated accusations. The charge of "attempted rape," as the black journalist Ida B. Wells pointed out to a national audience, could cover a wide range of behaviors unacceptable to whites, such as questioning authority or talking back.

The lynch mob demonstrated whites' absolute power. In the South, more than 80 percent of the lynchings involved black victims. Lynchings most commonly occurred in the Cotton Belt, and they tended to rise at times of economic distress. By no coincidence, lynching peaked in 1892 as many poor blacks embraced the Colored Farmers' Alliance and rallied to the Populist Party banner. Fifteen black Populists were killed in Georgia alone, it has been estimated, during that year's bitter campaign. Ironically, the photographs that reinforced racial terror and flaunted the disregard for law became the basis for reformers' proof of the brutality of the tactic.

The relationship between southern agrarian protest and white racism was complex. African American farm organizations had developed independently from their white counterparts. Some Populists, like Georgia's Tom Watson, sought to build an interracial movement with them. Watson denounced lynching and the convict-lease system. When a black Populist leader pursued by a lynch mob took refuge in his house during the 1892 campaign, Watson summoned two thousand armed white Populists to defend him. But most white Populists clung to racism. The white ruling elite, eager to drive a wedge in the protest movement, inflamed lower-class white racism.

On balance, the rise of southern agrarian protest deepened racial hatred and ultimately worsened blacks' situation. Meanwhile, the federal government stood aside. A generation of northern politicians paid lip service to egalitarian principles but failed to apply them to African Americans.

The Supreme Court similarly abandoned African Americans. The Court ripped gaping holes in the Fourteenth Amendment (1868), which granted blacks citizenship and the equal protection of the law, and in the Civil Rights Act of 1875, which outlawed racial discrimination on juries, in public places, and on railroads and streetcars. In the *Civil Rights Cases* (1883), the Court declared the Civil Rights Act of 1875 unconstitutional. The Fourteenth Amendment protected citizens only from governmental infringement of their civil rights, the justices ruled, not from acts by private citizens such as railroad conductors. In **Plessy v. Ferguson (1896),** the justices upheld a Louisiana law requiring segregated railroad cars. Racial segregation was constitutional, the Court held, if equal facilities were made available to each race. With the Supreme Court's blessing, the South segregated its public school system, ignoring the caveat that such separate facilities must be equal. White children studied in nicer buildings, used newer equipment, and were taught by better-paid teachers. Not until 1954 did the Court overturn the "separate but equal" doctrine. Rounding out their dismal record, in 1898 the justices upheld the poll tax and literacy tests by which southern states had disfranchised blacks.

Few northerners protested the South's white supremacist society. Until the North condemned lynching outright, declared the aged abolitionist Frederick Douglass in

Lynching at Clanton, Alabama, August 1891 *Reprinted in Ida B. Wells's* A Red Record, *this photograph is typical of many taken where the white audience faces the camera near the body of the victim. Such photographs were meant to intimidate any blacks who challenged white supremacy.*

Chicago Historical Society

1892, "it will remain equally involved with the South in this common crime." The restoration of sectional harmony, in short, came at a high price: acquiescence by the North in the utter debasement of the South's African American citizenry. Further, the separatist principle endorsed in *Plessy* had a negative impact, affecting blacks nationwide, Mexicans in Texas, Asians in California, and other groups.

Blacks responded to their plight in various ways. The nation's foremost black leader from the 1890s to his death in 1915 was **Booker T. Washington.** Born in slavery in Virginia in 1856, Washington attended a freedman's school in Hampton, Virginia, and in 1881 organized a black state vocational school in Alabama that eventually became Tuskegee University. Although Washington secretly contributed to lawyers who challenged segregation, he publicly urged accommodation to a racist society. In a widely publicized address in Atlanta in 1895, he insisted that the first task of America's blacks must be to acquire useful skills such as farming and carpentry. Once blacks proved their economic value, he predicted, racism would fade; meanwhile, they must patiently accept their lot. This was a position later challenged by W.E.B. Du Bois (covered in Chapter 21). Washington lectured widely, and his autobiography, *Up from Slavery* (1901), recounted his rise from poverty thanks to honesty, hard work, and kindly patrons—themes familiar to a generation reared on Horatio Alger's self-help books.

Other blacks responded resourcefully to racism. Black churches provided emotional support, as did black fraternal lodges like the Knights of Pythias. Some African Americans started businesses to serve their community. Two black-owned banks, in Richmond and Washington, DC, were chartered in 1888. The North Carolina Mutual Insurance Company, organized in 1898 by John Merrick, a prosperous Durham barber, evolved into a major enterprise. Bishop Henry M. Turner of the African Methodist Episcopal church urged blacks to return to Africa and build a great Christian nation.

Meanwhile, African American protest never wholly died out. Frederick Douglass urged that blacks press for full equality. Blacks should meet violence with violence, insisted militant New York black leader T. Thomas Fortune. But for others, the solution was to leave the South. In 1879, several thousand moved to Kansas (see Chapter 16). Some ten thousand migrated to Chicago between 1870 and 1890. Blacks who moved north, however, soon found that public opinion sanctioned many forms of de facto discrimination.

The rise of the so-called solid South, firmly established on racist foundations, had important political implications. For one thing, it made a mockery of the two-party system. For years, the only meaningful election south of the Potomac was the Democratic primary. Only in the 1960s, in the wake of sweeping social and economic changes, would a genuine two-party system emerge there. The large bloc of southern Democrats selected to Congress each year, accumulating seniority and power, exerted a great and often reactionary influence on public policy. Finally, southern Democrats wielded enormous clout in the national party. No Democratic contender for national office who was unacceptable to them stood a chance.

Above all, the caste system that evolved in the post-Reconstruction South shaped the consciousness of those caught up in it, white and black alike. White novelist Lillian Smith described her girlhood in turn-of-the-century Florida and Georgia: "From the day I was born, I began to learn my lessons.... I learned it is possible to be a Christian and a white southerner simultaneously; to be a gentle-woman and an arrogant callous creature at the same moment; to pray at night and ride a Jim Crow car the next morning; ... to glow when the word democracy was used, and to practice slavery from morning to night."

THE 1890s: POLITICS IN A DEPRESSION DECADE

Discontent with the major parties, which had smoldered during the 1870s and 1880s, burst into flames in the 1890s. As banks failed and railroads went bankrupt, the nation slid into a grinding depression. The crises of the 1890s laid bare the paralysis of the federal government—dominated by a business elite—when confronted by the new social realities of factories, urban slums, immigrant workers, and desperate farmers. In response, irate farmers, laborers, and their supporters joined a new party, the Populists, to change the system. But in 1896, in the aftermath of the massive depression, the Republicans built a coalition strong enough to control Congress and the presidency for the next fifteen years.

1892: Populists Challenge the Status Quo

In July 1892, the same month that the Populists adopted their party platform, thirteen people died in a gun battle between strikers and strikebreakers at the Homestead steel plant near Pittsburgh, and President Harrison sent federal troops to Coeur d'Alene, Idaho, where a silver-mine strike had turned violent. Events seemed to justify the platform's warnings of chaos ahead.

Ignoring the escalating unrest, both major parties launched campaigns for the White House that replayed the1888 contest. The Republicans renominated Harrison. The Democrats turned again to Grover Cleveland, who in four years out of office had made clear his growing conservatism and his opposition to the Populists. But this time Cleveland won by more than 360,000 votes, a decisive margin in this era of close elections. A public reaction against labor violence and the McKinley Tariff hurt Harrison, while Cleveland's support for the gold standard won business support.

Meanwhile, a solid showing by Populist candidates sparked great hopes for the future. James B. Weaver got more than a million votes—8.5 percent of the total—and the Populists elected five senators, ten congressmen, and three governors. The new party carried Kansas and registered some appeal in the West and in Georgia, Alabama, and Texas, where the alliance movement had taken deep root. But the party's strength was spotty. It made no dent in New England, the urban East, or the traditionally Republican farm regions of the Midwest. It even failed to show broad strength in the upper Great Plains. "Beaten! Whipped! Smashed!" moaned Minnesota Populist Ignatius Donnelly in his diary.

Throughout most of the South, racism, ingrained Democratic loyalty, distaste for a ticket headed by a former Union general, and widespread voter fraud kept the Populist vote under 25 percent. This failure killed the prospects for interracial agrarian reform. After 1892, as Populism began to revive in the South and Midwest, many southern politicians seeking to appeal to poor whites—including a disillusioned Tom Watson—stayed within the Democratic fold and laced their populism with racism.

Capitalism in Crisis: The Depression of 1893–1897

Cleveland soon confronted a major crisis, an economic collapse in the railroad industry that quickly spread. Trouble flared up in February 1893 when the Philadelphia and Reading Railroad failed. This bankruptcy came at a time of weakened confidence in the gold standard, the government's pledge to redeem paper money for gold on demand.

Confidence had ebbed when, in response to the collapse of a leading London investment bank in 1890, British investors had sold millions of dollars' worth of stock in American railroads and converted their dollars to gold, draining U.S. gold reserves. Moreover, Congress's lavish veterans' benefits during the Harrison administration had reduced government resources just as tariff revenues were dropping because of the high McKinley Tariff. Finally, the 1890 Sherman Silver Purchase Act's requirement that the government pay for its monthly silver purchases with treasury certificates redeemable for either silver or gold had further drained gold reserves.

Between January 1892 and March 1893, when Cleveland took office, the gold reserve had fallen sharply to around $100 million, the minimum considered necessary to support the dollar. This decline alarmed those who viewed the gold standard as the only sure evidence of the government's financial stability.

The collapse of a railroad thus triggered the **Panic of 1893.** Fear fed on itself as alarmed investors converted their stock holdings to gold. Stock prices fell in May and June; gold reserves sank; by the end of the year, seventy-four railroads and more than fifteen thousand commercial institutions, including six hundred banks, had failed. Just as the railroad boom had spurred the industrial prosperity of the 1880s, so had the railroad crisis of the early 1890s battered the entire economy. The Panic of 1893 started a full-scale depression and set off four years of hard times.

The crisis took a heavy human toll. Industrial unemployment soared into the 20 to 25 percent range, leaving millions of factory workers with no money to feed their families and heat their homes. Recent immigrants faced disaster. Jobless men tramped the streets and rode freight trains from city to city seeking work.

The unusually harsh winters of 1893 and 1894 made matters worse. In New York City, where the crisis quickly swamped local relief agencies, a minister reported actual starvation. Rural America, already hard-hit by declining agricultural prices, faced ruin. Farm prices dropped by more than 20 percent between 1890 and 1896. Corn plummeted from fifty cents to twenty-one cents a bushel; wheat, from eighty-four cents to fifty-one cents. Cotton sold for five cents a pound in 1894.

Some desperate Americans turned to protest. In Chicago, workers at the Pullman factory reacted to successive wage cuts by walking off the job in June 1894 (see Chapter 18). In Massillon, Ohio, self-taught monetary expert Jacob Coxey proposed as a solution to unemployment a $500 million public-works program funded with paper money not backed by gold but simply designated "legal tender" (just as it is today). A man of action as well as ideas, Coxey organized a march on Washington to lobby for his scheme. Thousands joined him en route, and several hundred reached Washington in late April 1894. Police arrested Coxey and other leaders when they attempted to enter the Capitol grounds, and his "army" broke up. Although some considered Coxey eccentric, his proposal closely resembled programs that the government would adopt during the depression of the 1930s.

As unrest intensified, fear clutched middle-class Americans. A church magazine demanded that troops put "a pitiless stop" to outbreaks of unrest. To some observers, a bloody upheaval seemed imminent.

Business Leaders Respond   In the face of suffering and turmoil, Cleveland refused to intervene. Boom-and-bust economic cycles were inevitable, he insisted. The government could do nothing. Missing the larger picture, Cleveland focused on a single issue: the gold standard. In August 1893 he persuaded Congress to repeal the Sherman Silver Purchase Act, which he blamed for the run on gold.

Nevertheless, the gold drain continued. In early 1895, with the gold reserve down to $41 million, Cleveland turned to Wall Street. Bankers J.P. Morgan and August Belmont agreed to lend the government $62 million in exchange for U.S. bonds at a special discount. With this loan, the government purchased gold to replenish its reserve. Meanwhile, Morgan and Belmont resold the bonds for

Coxey's Army

Detractors characterized Coxey's "army" of unemployed as "never do wells," but this photograph of Jacob Coxey's "Commonwealth of Christ Army" entering Washington, DC, in 1894 indicates that it was led by more well-to-do Americans making a statement about the government's responsibility to help those hurt by the depression.

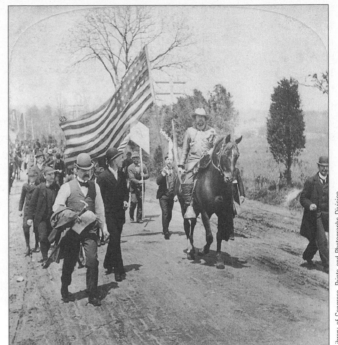

Library of Congress, Prints and Photographs Division

a substantial profit. This deal with the bankers did help restore confidence in the government's economic stability but it confirmed radicals' suspicions of an unholy alliance between Washington and Wall Street.

As the battle over the tariff made clear, corporate interests held the whip hand. Although Cleveland favored tariff reform, the Congress of 1893–1895 (despite its Democratic majorities) generally yielded to high-tariff lobbyists. The Wilson-Gorman Tariff of 1894 lowered duties somewhat, but made so many concessions to protectionist interests that Cleveland disgustedly allowed it to become law without his signature.

Hinting at changes ahead, the Wilson-Gorman Tariff imposed a modest income tax of 2 percent on all income over $4,000 (about $40,000 in purchasing power today). But in *Pollock* v. *Farmers' Loan & Trust Co.* (1895), the Supreme Court narrowly ruled the law unconstitutional, arguing that the federal government could impose such a direct tax on personal property only if it were apportioned according to the population of each state. Whether one looked at the executive, the legislature, or the judiciary, Washington's subordination to financial interests seemed absolute.

Cleveland's policies split the Democratic Party. Farm leaders and silver Democrats condemned his opposition to the Sherman Silver Purchase Act. This split in the Democratic ranks affected the elections of 1894 and 1896 and reshaped politics as the century ended.

The depression also helped reorient social thought. Middle-class charitable workers, long convinced that individual character flaws caused poverty, now realized—as socialists proclaimed and as the poor well knew—that even sober and hardworking people could succumb to economic forces beyond their control. Laissez-faire ideology weakened too, as many depression-worn Americans adopted a broadened view of the government's role in dealing with the social consequences of industrialization. The depression, in short, not only brought suffering; it also taught lessons.

Silver Advocates Capture the Democratic Party   Republican gains in the 1894 midterm election revealed the depth of revulsion against Cleveland and the Democrats, who were blamed for the hard times. The Republicans gained control of Congress and several key states. Populist candidates won nearly 1.5 million votes, 40 percent more than their 1892 total. Most Populist gains occurred in the South.

The serious economic divisions that split Americans in the mid-1890s focused on a symbolic issue: free silver. Cleveland's rigid defense of the gold standard forced his opponents into an equally exaggerated obsession with silver, obscuring the genuine issues that divided rich and poor, creditor and debtor, and farmer and city dweller. Conservatives tirelessly upheld the gold standard while agrarian radicals, urged on and sometimes financed by western silver-mine owners, extolled silver as a universal cure-all.

Each side had a point. Gold advocates recognized that a nation's paper money must be based on more than a government's ability to run printing presses and that uncontrolled inflation could be catastrophic. The silver advocates knew from experience how tight-money policies depressed prices and devastated farmers. Unfortunately, these underlying realities were rarely expressed clearly.

At the 1896 Democratic convention in Chicago, western and southern delegates adopted a platform including a demand for the free and unlimited coinage of silver at the ratio to gold of sixteen to one, in effect repudiating the Cleveland administration. **William Jennings Bryan** of Nebraska, an ardent advocate of free silver, captured the nomination. Only thirty-six years old, the young lawyer had already served two terms in Congress championing western agrarian interests.

Joining Christian imagery with economic analysis, Bryan delivered his major convention speech in the debate over the platform. With his booming voice carrying his words to the upper gallery of the convention hall, Bryan praised farmers as the nation's bedrock. The wildly cheering delegates had identified their candidate even before he reached his rousing conclusion—"You shall not press down upon the brow of labor this crown of thorns, you shall not crucify mankind upon a cross of gold!"

The silverites' capture of the Democratic Party presented a dilemma to the Populists. They, too, advocated free silver, but only as one reform among many. To back Bryan would be to abandon the broad Populist program. Furthermore, fusion with the Democrats could destroy their influence as a third party. Yet the Populist leaders recognized that a separate Populist ticket would likely siphon votes from Bryan and ensure a Republican victory. Reluctantly, the Populists endorsed Bryan, while preserving a shred of independence (and confusing voters) by naming their own vice-presidential candidate, Tom Watson of Georgia. The

Populists were learning the difficulty of organizing an independent political movement in a nation wedded to the two-party system.

The Republicans, meanwhile, had nominated former governor William McKinley, who as an Ohio congressman had given his name to the McKinley Tariff of 1890. The Republican platform embraced the high protective tariff and endorsed the gold standard.

1896: Republicans Triumphant   Bryan tried to sustain the momentum of the Chicago convention. Crisscrossing the nation by train, he delivered his free-silver campaign speech to hundreds of audiences in twenty-nine states. One skeptical editor compared him to Nebraska's notoriously shallow Platte River: six inches deep and a mile wide at the mouth.

McKinley's campaign was shrewdly managed by Mark Hanna, a Cleveland industrialist. Dignified and aloof, McKinley could not match Bryan's popular touch. Accordingly, Hanna built the campaign not around the candidate but around posters, pamphlets, and newspaper editorials. These publications warned of the dangers of free silver, caricatured Bryan as a rabid radical, and portrayed McKinley and the gold standard as twin pillars of prosperity.

Drawing on an enormous war chest, Hanna spent lavishly. J.P. Morgan and John D. Rockefeller together contributed half a million dollars, far more than Bryan's total campaign contributions. Like Benjamin Harrison in 1888, McKinley stayed home in Canton, Ohio, emerging from time to time to read speeches to visiting delegations. Carefully orchestrated by Hanna, McKinley's deceptively bucolic "front-porch" campaign involved elaborate organization. All told, 750,000 people trekked to Canton that summer.

On election day, McKinley beat Bryan by more than six hundred thousand votes. He swept the Northeast and the Midwest and even carried three farm states beyond the Mississippi—Iowa, Minnesota, and North Dakota—as well as California and Oregon. Bryan's strength was limited to the South and the sparsely settled Great Plains and mountain states. The Republicans retained control of Congress.

Why did Bryan lose despite the depression and the protest spirit abroad in the land? Certainly, Republicans' cash reserves, influence on the East Coast press, and scare tactics played a role. But Bryan's candidacy carried its own liabilities. His core constituency, while passionately loyal, was limited. Seduced by free silver and Bryan's oratory, the Democrats had upheld a platform and a candidate with little appeal for factory workers, the urban middle class, or the settled family farmers of the midwestern corn belt. Urban voters, realizing that higher farm prices, a major free-silver goal, also meant higher food prices, went heavily for McKinley. Bryan's weakness in urban America reflected cultural differences as well. To urban Catholics and Jews, this moralistic, teetotaling Nebraskan thundering like a Protestant revival preacher seemed utterly alien.

The McKinley administration quickly translated its conservative platform into law. The Dingley Tariff (1897) pushed rates to all-time high levels, and the Currency Act of 1900 officially committed the United States to the gold standard. With

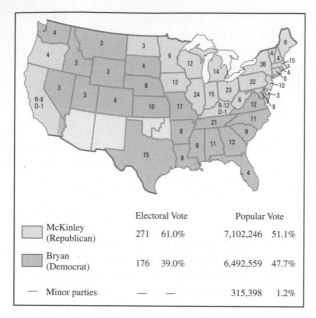

	Electoral Vote		Popular Vote	
McKinley (Republican)	271	61.0%	7,102,246	51.1%
Bryan (Democrat)	176	39.0%	6,492,559	47.7%
— Minor parties	—	—	315,398	1.2%

MAP 20.1   The Election of 1896

Republicans won the election by carrying the urban vote.

Source: © Cengage Learning. All rights reserved. No distribution allowed without express authorization.

returning prosperity, rising farm prices after 1897, and the discovery of gold in Alaska and elsewhere, these measures aroused little protest. Bryan won renomination in 1900, but the fervor of 1896 was missing. The Republican campaign theme of prosperity easily won McKinley a second term.

The elections of 1894 and 1896 produced a Republican majority that, except for Woodrow Wilson's two presidential terms (1913–1921), would dominate national politics until the election of Franklin D. Roosevelt in 1932. Bryan's defeat and the Republicans' emergence as the party of prosperity killed the Populist Party and drove the Democrats back to their regional base in the South. But although populism collapsed, a new reform movement called progressivism was emerging. Many of the Populists' reform proposals would be enacted into law in the progressive years.

EXPANSIONIST STIRRINGS AND WAR WITH SPAIN, 1878–1901

The same corporate elite that dominated late nineteenth-century domestic politics influenced U.S. foreign policy as well, contributing to surging expansionist pressures. Not only business leaders but politicians, statesmen, and editorial writers insisted that national greatness required that America match Europe's imperial expansion. Fanned by sensationalistic newspaper coverage of a Cuban struggle for independence and by elite calls for greater American international assertiveness, war between the United States and Spain broke out in 1898.

Roots of Expansionist Sentiment

Ever since the first European settlers colonized North America's Atlantic coast, the newcomers had been an expansionist people. By the 1840s, the push westward had acquired a name: Manifest Destiny. Directed inward after 1865 toward the re-settlement of the trans-Mississippi West (see Chapter 17), this impulse turned outward in the 1880s as Americans followed the example set by Great Britain, France, Belgium, Italy, Germany, and Japan, which were busily collecting colonies from North Africa to the Pacific islands. National greatness, it appeared, demanded an empire.

Many business leaders believed that continued domestic prosperity required overseas markets. As American industrial capacity expanded, foreign markets offered a safety valve for potentially explosive pressures in the U.S. economy. Secretary of State James Blaine warned in 1890 that U.S. productivity was outrunning "the demands of the home market" and insisted that American business must look abroad.

Advocates of a stronger navy further fueled the expansionist mood. In *The Influence of Sea Power upon History* (1890), **Alfred Thayer Mahan** equated sea power with national greatness and urged a U.S. naval buildup. Because a strong navy required bases abroad, Mahan and other naval advocates supported the movement to acquire foreign territories, especially Pacific islands with good harbors. Military strategy, in this case and others, often masked the desire for access to new markets.

Religious leaders proclaimed America's mission to spread Christianity. This expansionist argument sometimes took on a racist tinge. As Josiah Strong put it in his 1885 work *Our Country*, "God is training the Anglo-Saxon race for its mission"—a mission of Christianizing and civilizing the world's "weaker races."

A group of Republican expansionists, led by Senator Henry Cabot Lodge of Massachusetts, diplomat John Hay, and Theodore Roosevelt of New York, preached imperial greatness and military might. "I should welcome almost any war," declared Roosevelt in 1897; "... this country needs one." Advocates of expansionism, like Roosevelt and Lodge, built upon the Social Darwinist rhetoric of the day and argued that war, as a vehicle for natural selection, would test and refurbish American manhood, restore chivalry and honor, and create a new generation of civic-minded Americans. This gendered appeal to renew American masculinity both counterbalanced concerns about women's political activism and helped forge the disparate arguments for expansionism into a simpler, more visceral plea for international engagement that had a broad appeal.

A series of diplomatic skirmishes between 1885 and 1895 revealed the newly assertive American mood and paved the way for the war that Roosevelt desired. In the mid-1880s, quarrels between the United States and Great Britain over fishing rights in the North Atlantic and in the Bering Sea off Alaska reawakened Americans' latent anti-British feelings as well as the old dream of acquiring Canada. A poem published in the *Detroit News* (adapted from an English music-hall song) supplied the nickname that critics would apply to the promoters of expansion—jingoists:

We do not want to fight,
But, by jingo, if we do,
We'll scoop in all the fishing grounds
And the whole dominion too!

The fishing-rights dispute was resolved in 1898, but by then attention had shifted to Latin America. In 1891, as civil war raged in Chile, U.S. officials seized a Chilean vessel that was attempting to buy guns in San Diego. Soon after, a mob in Valparaiso, Chile, killed two unarmed sailors on shore leave. President Harrison practically called for war. Only when Chile apologized and paid an indemnity was the incident closed.

Another Latin American conflict arose from a boundary dispute between Venezuela and British Guiana in 1895. The disagreement worsened after gold was discovered in the contested territory. When the British rejected a U.S. arbitration offer and condescendingly insisted that America's revered Monroe Doctrine had no standing in international law, a livid Grover Cleveland asked Congress to set up a commission to settle the disputed boundary even without Britain's approval. As patriotic fervor pulsed through the nation, the British in 1897 accepted the commission's findings.

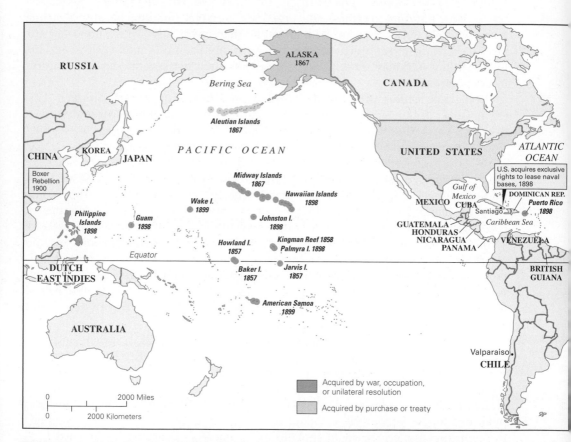

MAP 20.2 U.S. Territorial Expansion in the Late Nineteenth Century

The major U.S. territorial expansion abroad came in a short burst of activity in the late 1890s, when newspapers and some politicians urged Americans to acquire strategic ports and coaling stations abroad.

Pacific
Expansion

Meanwhile, the U.S. navy focused on the Samoan Islands in the South Pacific, where it sought access to the port of Pago Pago as a refueling station. Britain and Germany had ambitions in Samoa as well, and in March 1889 the United States and Germany narrowly avoided a naval clash when a hurricane wrecked both fleets. Secretary of State Blaine's wife wrote to one of their children, "Your father is now looking up Samoa on the map." Once he found it, negotiations began, and the United States, Great Britain, and Germany established a three-way "protectorate" over the islands.

Attention had by that time shifted to the Hawaiian Islands, which had both strategic and economic significance for the United States. New England trading vessels had visited **Hawai'i** as early as the 1790s, and Yankee missionaries had come in the 1820s. By the 1860s American-owned sugar plantations worked by Chinese and Japanese laborers dotted the islands. Under an 1887 treaty (negotiated after the planters had forcibly imposed a new constitution on Hawai'i's native ruler, Kala-kaua), the United States built a naval base at Pearl Harbor, near Honolulu. American economic dominance and the influx of foreigners angered Hawaiians. In 1891, they welcomed Liliuokalani, a strong-willed woman hostile to Americans, to the Hawaiian throne.

Meanwhile, in 1890, the framers of the McKinley Tariff, pressured by domestic sugar growers, eliminated the duty-free status enjoyed by Hawaiian sugar. In January 1893, facing ruin as Hawai'i's wholesale sugar prices plunged 40 percent, the planters deposed Queen Liliuokalani, proclaimed the independent Republic of Hawai'i, and requested U.S. annexation. The U.S. State Department's representative in Hawai'i cabled Washington, "The Hawaiian pear is now fully ripe, and this is the golden hour for the United States to pluck it." But the grab for Hawai'i troubled Grover Cleveland, who sent a representative to investigate the situation. This representative's report questioned whether the Hawaiian people actually desired annexation.

Cleveland's scruples infuriated expansionists. When William McKinley succeeded Cleveland in 1897, the acquisition of Hawai'i was pushed forward by sugar companies that had similar investments in Cuba. In 1898, Congress proclaimed Hawai'i an American territory. Sixty-one years later, it joined the Union as the fiftieth state.

Crisis over
Cuba

Many of the same expansionists who had argued for the annexation of Hawai'i turned their attention in 1898 to the Spanish colony of Cuba, ninety miles off Florida, where in 1895 an anti-Spanish rebellion had broken out. This revolt, organized by the Cuban writer José Martí and other Cuban exiles in New York City, won little support from U.S. business, which had $50 million invested in Cuba and annually imported $100 million worth of sugar and other products from the island. Nor did the rebels initially secure the backing of Washington, which urged Spain to grant Cuba a degree of autonomy.

But the rebels' cause aroused popular sympathy in the United States. This support increased with revelations that the Spanish commander in Cuba, Valeriano Weyler, was herding vast numbers of Cubans into squalid camps. Malnutrition and disease turned these camps into hellholes in which perhaps two hundred thousand Cubans died.

Fueling American anger was the sensationalized reporting of two competing New York City newspapers, William Randolph Hearst's *Journal* and Joseph Pulitzer's *World*. The *Journal*'s color comic strip, "The Yellow Kid," provided a name for Hearst's debased editorial approach: yellow journalism. The Hungarian immigrant Pulitzer normally had higher standards, but in the cutthroat battle for readers, Pulitzer's *World* matched the *Journal*'s sensationalism. Both editors exploited the Cuban crisis. Headlines turned rumor into fact, and feature stories detailed "Butcher" Weyler's atrocities. When a young Cuban woman was jailed for resisting a rape attempt by a Spanish officer, a Hearst reporter helped the woman escape and brought her triumphantly to New York.

In 1897, a new, more liberal Spanish government sought a peaceful resolution of the Cuban crisis. But Hearst and Pulitzer continued to inflame the public. On February 8, 1898, Hearst's *Journal* published a private letter by Spain's minister to the United States that described McKinley as "weak" and "a bidder for the admiration of the crowd." Irritation over this incident turned to outrage when on February 15 an explosion sank the U.S. battleship *Maine* in Havana harbor and killed 266 crewmen. Scholarly opinion about what caused the explosion is still divided, but a careful review of the evidence in 1998 concluded that a mine most likely set off the ammunition explosion that sank the ship. Newspaper headlines at the time blamed the same cause and war spirit flared high.

Despite further Spanish concessions, McKinley sent a war message to Congress on April 11, and legislators enacted a joint resolution recognizing Cuba's independence and authorizing force to expel the Spanish. The Teller Amendment, introduced by Senator Henry M. Teller of Colorado, renounced any U.S. interest in "sovereignty, jurisdiction, or control" in Cuba and pledged that America would leave the island alone once independence was assured.

The Spanish-American War, 1898   The war with Spain involved only a few days of actual combat. The first action came on May 1, 1898, when a U.S. fleet commanded by George Dewey steamed into Manila Bay in the Philippines and destroyed or captured all ten Spanish ships anchored there, at the cost of 1 American and 381 Spanish lives. In mid-August, U.S. troops occupied the capital, Manila.

In Cuba, the fighting centered on the military stronghold of Santiago on the southeastern coast. On May 19, a Spanish battle fleet of seven aging vessels sailed into the Santiago harbor, where five U.S. battleships and two cruisers blockaded them. On July 1, in the war's only significant land action, American troops seized three strongly defended Spanish garrisons overlooking Santiago on El Caney Hill, Kettleman's Hill, and San Juan Hill. Theodore Roosevelt led the volunteer "Rough Riders" unit in the capture of San Juan Hill and became a war hero. Emphasizing his toughness and sense of honor, Roosevelt would later use his war experience to reaffirm the aptitude of men like himself for political leadership.

On July 3, the Spanish attempted to break through the American blockade to the open sea. The U.S. navy fired and sank their archaic vessels. Spain lost 474 men in this gallant but doomed defense. Americans might have found a cautionary lesson in this sorry end to four hundred years of Spanish rule in the New World, but few had time for somber musings. The *Washington Post* observed, "A new consciousness seems to have come upon us—the consciousness of strength—and with it a new appetite, the yearning to show our strength." Secretary of State John Hay was more succinct. It had been, he wrote Roosevelt, "a splendid little war."

Many who served in Cuba found the war far from splendid. Ill-trained and poorly equipped, the troops went into summer combat wearing heavy woolen uniforms. The army also lacked adequate medical support. When **Clara Barton,** president of the American Association for Red Cross, visited Santiago, she found wounded soldiers lying in the rain, unable to eat the hardtack rations. Under her leadership, 1,000 trained nurses worked with the medical corps. Despite the efforts of these nurses and doctors, 379 American soldiers died in combat and more than 5,000 succumbed to food poisoning, yellow fever, malaria, and other diseases during and after the war.

Several thousand black troops fought in Cuba. Some, such as the Twenty-fourth Infantry and Tenth Cavalry, were seasoned regular army "buffalo soldiers" transferred from bases in the West. Others were volunteers from various states. At assembly points in Georgia, and then at the embarkation port of Tampa, Florida, these troops encountered the racism of a Jim Crow society. Tampa restaurants and bars refused them service; Tampa whites disparaged them. On June 6, after weeks of racist treatment, some black troops exploded in riotous rage, storming into restaurants, bars, and other establishments that had barred them. White troops from Georgia restored order. Although white and black troops sailed to Cuba on the same transport ships (actually, hastily converted freighters), the ships themselves were segregated, with black troops often confined to the lowest quarters in the stifling heat, denied permission to mingle on deck with the other units, and in other ways discriminated against.

Despite the racism, African Americans served with distinction once they reached Cuba. Black troops played key roles in the taking of both San Juan Hill and El Caney Hill. Of the total U.S. troops involved in the latter action, some 15 percent were black.

The Spanish sought an armistice on July 17. In the peace treaty signed that December in Paris, Spain recognized Cuba's independence and, after a U.S. payment of $20 million, ceded the Philippines, Puerto Rico, and the Pacific island of Guam to the United States. Americans now possessed an island empire stretching from the Caribbean to the Pacific.

From 1898 to 1902, the U.S. army governed Cuba under the command of General Leonard Wood. Wood's administration improved public health, education, and sanitation but nevertheless violated the spirit of the 1898 Teller Amendment. The troops eventually withdrew, though under conditions that limited Cuban sovereignty. The 1901 **Platt Amendment,** attached to an army appropriations bill offered by a Connecticut senator at the request of the War Department, authorized American withdrawal only after Cuba agreed not to make any treaty with a foreign power limiting its independence and not to borrow beyond its means. The United States also reserved the right to intervene in Cuba when it saw fit and to maintain a naval base there, a policy resented by the Cubans. With U.S. troops still occupying the island, the Cuban constitutional convention of 1901 accepted the Platt

National Archives and Records Administration

African American Soldiers of the Tenth U.S. Cavalry in Cuba, July 1898
These men posed shortly after the capture of San Juan Hill. Black troops, known as buffalo soldiers, played an important role in the Spanish-American War, but they were subject to harassment and discrimination.

Amendment, which remained in force until 1934. Under its terms the United States established a naval base at Guantánamo Bay, near Santiago de Cuba, which it still maintains. U.S. investments in Cuba, some $50 million in 1898, soared to half a billion dollars by 1920.

Critics of Empire   Some Americans, who had opposed imperialism for more than a decade, were dismayed by the victories of the expansionists in Cuba and the Philippines. Although few in number, the critics, like the Mugwumps who had challenged the spoils system, were influential. Indeed, some of them, like Carl Schurz and E.L. Godkin, were former Mugwumps. Other anti-imperialists included William Jennings Bryan, settlement-house founder Jane Addams, novelist Mark Twain, and Harvard philosopher William James. Steel king Andrew Carnegie gave thousands of dollars to the cause. In 1898, these critics of empire formed the **Anti-Imperialist League.**

For the United States to rule other peoples, the anti-imperialists believed, was to violate the principles of the Declaration of Independence and the Constitution. As one of them wrote, "Dewey took Manila with the loss of one man—and all our institutions." The military fever that accompanied expansionism also dismayed the anti-imperialists. Some labor leaders feared that imperial expansion would lead to competition from cheap foreign labor and products.

In February 1899, the anti-imperialists failed by one vote to prevent Senate ratification of the peace treaty with Spain. McKinley's overwhelming reelection victory in 1900 and the defeat of expansionist critic William Jennings Bryan eroded the anti-imperialists' cause. Nevertheless, at a time of jingoistic rhetoric and militaristic posturing, they had upheld an older and more traditional vision of America.

Guerrilla War in the Philippines, 1898–1902

Events in the Philippines confirmed the worst fears of the anti-imperialists. When the war ended, President McKinley was faced with the urgent problem of what to do about this group of Pacific islands that had a population of more than 5 million people. At the war's outset, few Americans knew that the Philippines belonged to Spain or even where they were. Without a map, McKinley later confessed, "I could not have told where those darn islands were within two thousand miles."

But the victory over Spain whetted the appetite for expansion. To the U.S. business community, the Philippines offered a steppingstone to the China market. McKinley, reflecting the prevailing mood as always, reasoned that the Filipinos were unready for self-government and would be gobbled up if set adrift in a world of imperial rivalries. McKinley further persuaded himself that American rule would enormously benefit the Filipinos, whom he called "our little brown brothers." A devout Methodist, he explained that America's mission was "to educate the Filipinos, and to uplift and civilize and Christianize them, and by God's grace do the very best we could by them." (In fact, most Filipinos were already Catholic, a legacy of centuries of Spanish rule.) Having prayerfully reached his decision, McKinley instructed the American peace negotiators in Paris to insist on U.S. acquisition of the Philippines.

"Uplifting" the Filipinos required a struggle. In 1896 young **Emilio Aguinaldo** had organized a Filipino independence movement to drive out Spain. In 1898, with arms supplied by George Dewey, Aguinaldo's forces had captured most of Luzon, the Philippines' main island. When the Spanish surrendered, Aguinaldo proclaimed Filipino independence and drafted a democratic constitution. Feeling betrayed when the peace treaty ceded his country to the United States, Aguinaldo ordered his rebel force to attack Manila, the American base of operations. Seventy thousand more U.S. troops were shipped to the Philippines; by the end of 1899, the initial Filipino resistance had been crushed.

These hostilities became the opening phase of a long guerrilla conflict. Before it ended, more than 125,000 American men had served in the Philippines, and four thousand had been killed. As many as twenty thousand Filipino independence fighters died. As in the later Vietnam and Iraq wars, casualties and suffering ravaged the civilian population as well. Historians estimate that at least 200,000 civilians died in the conflict. Aguinaldo was captured in March 1901, but large-scale guerrilla fighting continued through the summer of 1902.

In 1902, a special Senate committee heard testimony from veterans of the Philippines war about the execution of prisoners, the torture of suspects, and the burning of villages. The humanitarian mood of 1898, when Americans had rushed to save Cuba from the cruel Spaniards, seemed remote indeed. In retrospect, the American troops' ambivalent attitudes about the peoples of the Philippines, while deplorable, are not hard to understand. Despite America's self-image as a beacon of liberty and a savior of the world's peoples, many Americans in the 1880s and

1890s had been deeply troubled by the new immigrants from southern and eastern Europe and had expressed concerns over "backward" and "useless" races. As American nationalism was reformulated in this cauldron of immigration, imperialism, and the "winning of the West," racist attitudes about Native peoples and foreigners intermixed with rhetorical pleas for supervision and stewardship. In the process, as was evident in the treatment of American Indians (see Chapter 17), well-meaning paternalism often degenerated into deadly domination.

The subjugation of the Philippines followed years of expansionism that proclaimed America's debut on the world stage and underscored the global reach of U.S. capitalism. Nevertheless, most Americans remained ambivalent about the acquisition of territory. While anti-imperialist Mark Twain could acidly condemn "the Blessings of Civilization Trust," labor leader Samuel Gompers warned that "an inundation of Mongolians" might steal jobs from white labor. From the debate over the annexation of Hawai'i in 1898 to the end of the war against Philippine independence in 1902, white Americans recoiled from making these "barbarian peoples" a part of the United States. Not fit to manage their own affairs, Cuban, Puerto Rican, Hawaiian, and Filipino peoples were placed in a protective status that denied their independence and kept them under U.S. control.

To stabilize relations in the Philippines, Congress passed the Philippine Government Act in 1902, which vested authority in a governor general to be appointed by the president. The act also provided for an elected Filipino assembly and promised eventual self-government. Progress toward this goal inched forward, with intervals of semi military rule. In 1946, nearly half a century after Admiral Dewey's guns had boomed in Manila Bay, independence finally came to the Philippines.

CHRONOLOGY
1877–1902

1869	Boss William M. Tweed gains control of New York's Tammany Hall political machine.
1878	Congress requires U.S. Treasury to purchase silver.
1880	James Garfield elected president.
1881	Assassination of Garfield; Chester A. Arthur becomes president.
1883	Pendleton Civil Service Act.
1884	Grover Cleveland elected president.
1886	*Wabash* v. *Illinois*.
1887	Interstate Commerce Act.
1888	Benjamin Harrison elected president.
1889	National Farmers' Alliance formed.
1890	Sherman Silver Purchase Act.
	Sherman Anti-Trust Act.
	McKinley Tariff pushes tariffs to all-time high.

1893	Panic of 1893; depression of 1893–1897 begins.
	Repeal of the Sherman Silver Purchase Act.
1894	Coxey's "army" marches on Washington. Pullman strike. Wilson-Gorman Tariff.
1895	Supreme Court declares federal income tax unconstitutional.
1896	Free-silver forces capture Democratic Party and nominate William Jennings Bryan.
	William McKinley elected president.
1898	Acquisition of Hawai'i.
	Spanish-American War.
1898–1902	Guerrilla uprising in Philippines.
1900	Currency Act officially places United States on gold standard.
1901	Platt Amendment retains U.S. role in Cuba. Regular Army Nursing Corps founded.
1902	Philippine Government Act.

Conclusion

By 1900 immigration, the settlement of the frontier West, and rapid industrial expansion had pushed America to the forefront of the world economy and had sparked a major realignment in American politics. After nearly two decades of hard-fought elections in which political control had seesawed back and forth between the major parties, the Republicans now held power.

It had been difficult to achieve political dominance. The dynamic growth of the American economy, together with rapid urbanization and a massive influx of immigrants, had strained the political process. As the parties struggled to define their vision of the proper role of government in stimulating economic development, they were forced to deal with ethnic, cultural, and racial issues that included prohibition, church schools, and segregation. All this was further complicated by the Democratic Party's attempt to throw off the limits imposed by Reconstruction and gain political control of the South.

On the national level, both parties built a loyal following by linking their positions to deeply held beliefs about the family and the proper role of government. Republicans justified their support for the tariff and soldiers' pensions in terms of patriotic protection of the family. Democrats countered that a high-tariff policy was indicative of precisely the kind of excessive governmental force that would destroy family life. On the local level, both parties secured loyal voters by stressing ethnic and cultural issues. Democrats, often as political bosses and urban machines, courted the new immigrants, while Republicans catered to rural and small-town native-born Americans in the Northeast and Midwest. Political bosses gave immigrants a foothold in the political process but their participation often came at the high cost of inflated contracts and corruption that siphoned millions of dollars from the public treasury.

In the competition for new voters, the needs of rural Americans were often overlooked. Caught between declining prices for grain and cotton, and high railroad and bank rates, farmers struggled to survive. Their precarious position was further strained by years of drought, insect infestation, and overspecialization in one crop. In desperation, farmers turned first to the Grange and Farmers' Alliance movements and then to the Populist Party for help. In the South, after first courting black farmers, members of the Farmers' Alliance and later the Populists joined with Democrats to disfranchise black voters. Using lynching and intimidation, Democrats seized control of southern politics.

In the face of these threats, the Republican Party in 1896 raised huge sums from big business to turn back the Populist challenge and take control of national politics. The fusion of the Populists and Democrats behind William Jennings Bryan and the silver issue created problems of its own. Although he carried the South and almost all the Midwest, the teetotaling Bryan had little appeal for urban workers and the middle class, who believed that a monetary policy based on free silver promised only inflation and higher prices. McKinley won by playing down moral reforms such as prohibition and emphasizing patriotism and fiscal responsibility. Republicans won over the urban-industrial core of the nation—the Northeast and much of the Midwest. They would control the House of Representatives for twenty-eight out of the thirty-six years from 1894 to 1930.

McKinley's administration was drawn by events in Cuba and jingoistic advocates within his own party into the Spanish-American War and the subsequent acquisition of Hawai'i, Samoa, Guam, the Philippines, and Cuba. Although the Republicans preferred the term "expansionism" to "imperialism," the move to acquire new bases for access to global markets fit the party's probusiness stance. But expansion into the Pacific created its own obstacles when the United States became involved in a guerrilla war with Philippine nationalists. Facing mounting criticism at home, the expansionists adopted the Teller and Platt amendments, which foreshadowed eventual disengagement from the acquisition of foreign territory.

Notwithstanding these foreign interventions, the fundamental question of late nineteenth-century American politics persisted: could a government designed for the needs of a small agrarian society serve an industrialized nation of factories and immigrant-crowded cities? The answer was by no means clear. Although issues such as patronage, the tariff, veterans' benefits, and monetary policy had enabled the industrial system to grow dramatically, the needs of farmers, workers, and immigrant Americans had largely been ignored. The Republicans successfully carried the field in 1896, but Populists and other critics who argued that government should play an assertive role in solving social and economic problems would help shape the political environment of the progressive movement.

21

THE PROGRESSIVE ERA, 1900–1917

CHAPTER OUTLINE

• Progressives and Their Ideas • Grassroots Progressivism • Progressivism and Social Control • Blacks, Women, and Workers Organize • National Progressivism, Phase I: Roosevelt and Taft, 1901–1913 • National Progressivism, Phase II: Woodrow Wilson, 1913–1917

PROGRESSIVES AND THEIR IDEAS

As the twentieth century dawned, groups across the nation grappled with the problems of the new urban-industrial order. Workers protested unsafe and exhausting jobs. Experts investigated social conditions. Women's clubs embraced reform. Intellectuals challenged the ideological foundations of a business-dominated social order, and journalists exposed municipal corruption and industrialism's human toll. Throughout America, activists worked to make government more democratic, improve conditions in cities and factories, and curb corporate power.

Historians have grouped all these efforts under a single label: "the progressive movement." In fact, "progressivism" was less a single movement than a spirit of discontent with the status quo and an exciting sense of new social possibilities. International in scope, this spirit found many outlets and addressed many issues.

The Many Faces of Progressivism   Who were the progressives, and what reforms did they pursue? The social changes of the era provide clues to the answers. Along with immigration, a growing middle class transformed U.S. cities. From the men and women of this class—mostly white, native-born Protestants—came many of the progressive movement's leaders and supporters.

From 1900 to 1920, the white-collar work force jumped from 5.1 million to 10.5 million—more than double the growth rate of the labor force as a whole. This burgeoning white-collar class included corporate executives and small-business owners; secretaries, accountants, and sales clerks; civil engineers and people in advertising; and professionals such as lawyers, physicians, and teachers. New

Brown Brothers

The Triangle Fire *The bodies of Triangle Shirtwaist factory workers lie on the sidewalk after they jumped from the burning building.*

professional groups arose, from the American Association of University Professors (1915) to the American Association of Advertising Agencies (1917). For many middle-class Americans, membership in a national professional society provided a sense of identity that might earlier have come from neighborhood, church, or political party. Ambitious, well educated, and valuing social stability, the members of this new middle class were eager to make their influence felt.

For middle-class women, the city offered both opportunities and frustrations. Young unmarried women often became schoolteachers, secretaries, typists, clerks, and telephone operators. The number of women in such white-collar jobs, as well as the ranks of college-educated women, more than tripled from 1900 to 1920.

But for middle-class married women caring for homes and children, city life could bring stress and loneliness. The divorce rate rose from one in twelve marriages in 1900 to one in nine by 1916. As we shall see, middle-class women joined female white-collar workers and college graduates in leading a revived women's movement. Cultural commentators wrote nervously of the "New Woman."

This urban middle class rallied to the banner of reform. The initial reform impetus came not from political parties but from women's clubs, settlement houses, and groups with names like the Playground Association of America, the National Child Labor Committee, and the American League for Civic Improvement. In this era of organizations, the reform movement, too, drew strength from organized interest groups.

The native-born middle class, while central to progressivism, sometimes found allies in promoting reform. On issues affecting factory workers and slum dwellers, the urban-immigrant political machines—and workers themselves—often took the initiative. After a fire broke out at the Triangle Shirtwaist factory in 1911, in which 141 garment workers lost their lives, New York's machine politicians joined with middle-class reformers and union officials to push for protective legislation. (Many deaths in the Triangle fire were caused by doors that opened inward, a fire-law violation.) Some corporate leaders promoted business regulations that served their interests.

What, then, was progressivism? Fundamentally, it was a broad-based response to industrialization and its social byproducts: immigration, urban growth, growing corporate power, and widening class divisions. In contrast to populism, it enlisted many more city-dwellers, journalists, academics, and social theorists. Finally, most progressives were *reformers,* not radicals. They wished to make the new urban-industrial order more humane, not overturn it entirely.

But what specific remedies were required? Reaching different answers to this key question, progressive reformers embraced causes that sometimes overlapped, sometimes diverged. Many demanded stricter business regulation, from local transit companies to the almighty trusts. Others focused on protecting workers and the urban poor. Still others championed reform of municipal government. Some, fearful of urban disorder, favored immigration restriction or social-control strategies to regulate city-dwellers' behavior. All this contributed to the mosaic of progressive reform.

Progressives believed that most social problems could be solved through study and organized effort. They respected science and expert knowledge. Scientific and technological expertise had produced the new industrial order, so such expertise could surely also correct the social problems spawned by industrialism. Progressives marshaled research data, surveys, and statistics to support their various causes.

Some historians have portrayed progressivism as an organizational stage that all modernizing societies pass through. This perspective is useful, provided we remember that it was not an automatic process unfolding independently of human will. Persistent journalists, activist workers, and passionate reformers all played a role. Human emotion—whether indignation over child labor, suspicion of corporate power, or raw political ambition—drove the movement forward.

Intellectuals Offer New Social Views   A group of innovative social thinkers provided progressivism's underlying ideas. As we have seen, some Gilded Age intellectuals had argued that Charles Darwin's theory of evolution justified unrestrained economic competition. In the 1880s and 1890s, sociologist Lester Ward, utopian novelist Edward Bellamy, and Social Gospel advocates (a liberal religious movement that advocated applying Christian principles to the problems of the new urban-industrial order) had all attacked this harsh version of Social Darwinism (see Chapters 18 and 19). This attack intensified after 1900.

Economist Thorstein Veblen, a Norwegian American from Minnesota, satirized America's newly rich capitalists in *The Theory of the Leisure Class* (1899). Dissecting their lifestyle the way an anthropologist might study an exotic tribe, he argued that they built mansions, threw elaborate parties, and otherwise engaged in "conspicuous consumption" to flaunt their wealth and assert their claims to superiority.

The Harvard philosopher William James argued in *Pragmatism* (1907) that truth emerges not from abstract theorizing but from the experience of coping with life's realities through practical action. James's philosophy of pragmatism deepened reformers' skepticism toward the older generation's entrenched ideas and strength-ened their belief in the necessity of social change.

Herbert Croly, the son of reform-minded New York journalists, shared this faith that new ideas could transform society. In *The Promise of American Life* (1909), Croly called for an activist government of the kind advocated by Alexander Hamilton, the first secretary of the treasury. But rather than serving the interests of the business class, as Hamilton had proposed, he argued that government should promote the welfare of all. In 1914, Croly founded the *New Republic* magazine to promote progressive ideas.

The settlement-house leader Jane Addams, in *Democracy and Social Ethics* (1902) and other books, rejected the claim that unrestrained competition ensured social progress. Instead, she argued, in a complex industrial society, each indivi-dual's well-being depends on the well-being of all. Addams urged middle-class Americans to recognize their common interests with the laboring masses and to demand better conditions in factories and immigrant slums. Teaching by example, Addams made her Chicago social settlement, Hull House, a center of social activism and legislative-reform initiatives.

With public-school enrollments growing rapidly, the educational reformer John Dewey saw schools as potent engines of social change. In his model school at the University of Chicago, Dewey encouraged pupils to work collaboratively and to interact with one another. The ideal school, he said in *Democracy and Education* (1916), would be an "embryonic community" where children would learn to live as members of a social group.

Oliver Wendell Holmes, Jr., a law professor, focused on changing judicial thinking. In *The Common Law* (1881), Holmes had criticized judges who inter-preted the law rigidly to protect corporate interests and had insisted that law must evolve as society changes. Appointed to the U.S. Supreme Court in 1902, Holmes often dissented from the conservative Court majority. As the new social thinking took hold, the courts slowly grew more open to reform legislation.

Novelists, Journalists, and Artists Spotlight Social Problems   While reform-minded intellectuals reoriented American social thought, novelists and journalists chronicled cor-porate wrongdoing, municipal corruption, slum condi-tions, and industrial abuses.

In his novel *The Octopus* (1901), Frank Norris of San Francisco portrayed the struggle between California railroad barons and the state's wheat growers. Though writing fiction, Norris accurately described the railroad owners' bribery, intimida-tion, rate manipulation, and other tactics.

Theodore Dreiser's novel *The Financier* (1912) featured a hard-driving business tycoon lacking a social conscience. Dreiser modeled his story on the scandal-ridden career of an actual railway financier. Such works encouraged skepticism toward the industrial elite and stimulated pressures for tougher business regulation.

Mass magazines such as *McClure's* and *Collier's* stirred reform energies with articles exposing urban political corruption and corporate wrongdoing. President Theodore Roosevelt criticized the authors as **"muckrakers"** publicizing the worst in American life, but the label became a badge of honor. Journalist Lincoln Steffens began the exposé vogue in 1902 with a *McClure's* article documenting municipal corruption in St. Louis.

Some investigative journalists worked as factory laborers or lived in slum tenements. One described her experiences working in a Massachusetts shoe factory where the caustic dyes rotted workers' fingernails. The British immigrant John Spargo researched his 1906 book about child labor, *The Bitter Cry of the Children,* by visiting mines in Pennsylvania and West Virginia and attempting to do the work that young boys performed for ten hours a day, picking out slate and other refuse from coal in cramped workspaces filled with choking coal dust.

The muckrakers awakened middle-class readers to conditions in industrial America. Some magazine exposés later appeared as books, including Lincoln Steffens's *The Shame of the Cities* (1904), Ida Tarbell's damning *History of the Standard Oil Company* (1904), and David Graham Phillips's *The Treason of the Senate* (1906).

Artists and photographers played a role as well. A group of New York painters dubbed the Ashcan School portrayed the harshness as well as the vitality of slum life. The photographer Lewis Hine, working for the National Child Labor Committee, captured haunting images of child workers with stunted bodies and worn expressions.

GRASSROOTS PROGRESSIVISM

Middle-class citizens not only read about the problems of urban-industrial America, they observed these problems firsthand in their own communities. In fact, the progressive movement began with grassroots campaigns to end urban political corruption, regulate corporate behavior, and improve conditions in factories and slums. Eventually, these local efforts came together in a powerful national movement.

Reforming Local Politics   Beginning in the 1890s, middle-class reformers battled corrupt city governments that provided services and jobs to immigrants, but often at the price of graft and rigged elections (see Chapter 19). In New York City, Protestant clergy battled Tammany Hall, the city's entrenched Democratic organization.

In San Francisco, a courageous newspaper editor led a 1907 crusade against the city's corrupt boss. When the original prosecutor was gunned down in court, attorney Hiram Johnson took his place, winning convictions against the boss and his cronies. Full of reform zeal—one observer called him "a volcano in perpetual eruption"—Johnson rode his newly won fame to the California governorship and the U.S. Senate.

In Toledo, Ohio, a colorful figure named Samuel M. ("Golden Rule") Jones led the reform crusade. A businessman converted to the Social Gospel, Jones introduced profit sharing in his factory, and as mayor he established playgrounds, free kindergartens, and lodging houses for homeless transients.

Urban political reformers soon began to probe the roots of municipal misgovernment, including the private monopolies that ran municipal water, gas, electricity, and transit systems. Reformers passed laws regulating the rates these utilities could charge and curbing their political influence. (Some even advocated public ownership of these companies.)

Reflecting the Progressive Era's regard for expertise and efficiency, some municipal reformers advocated substituting professional city managers for mayors, and councils chosen in citywide elections for aldermen elected on a ward-by-ward basis. Dayton, Ohio, adopted a city-manager system after a ruinous flood in 1913.

Supposedly above politics, these experts were expected to run the city like an efficient business. Milwaukee set up a Citizens' Bureau of Municipal Efficiency to streamline city-government operations.

Municipal reform attracted different groups, depending on the issue. The native-born middle class, led by clergymen, editors, and other opinion molders, provided the initial impetus and core support. Business interests often pushed for city-wide elections and the city-manager system, because these changes reduced immigrants' political clout and increased the influence of the corporate elite. Reforms that promised improved services or better conditions for ordinary city-dwellers won support from immigrants and political bosses who realized that the old, informal system of patronage could no longer meet constituents' needs.

The electoral-reform movement soon spread to the state level. By 1910, for example, all states had replaced the old system of voting, involving preprinted ballots bearing the names of specific candidates, with the secret ballot, which made it harder to rig elections. The direct primary, introduced in Wisconsin in 1903, enabled rank-and-file voters, rather than party bosses, to select their parties' candidates for public office.

Hoping to trim the political power of corporate interests, some western states inaugurated the *initiative, referendum,* and *recall.* By an initiative, voters can instruct the legislature to consider a specific bill. In a referendum, citizens can actually enact a law or express their views on a proposed measure. By a recall petition, voters can remove a public official from office if they muster enough signatures to trigger a special election.

While these reforms aimed to democratize voting, party leaders and interest groups soon learned to manipulate the new electoral machinery. Ironically, the new procedures may have weakened party loyalty and reduced voter interest. Voter-participation rates dropped steeply in these years, while political activity by organized interest groups increased.

Regulating Business, Protecting Workers

The corporate consolidation that produced giants like Carnegie Steel and Standard Oil (see Chapter 18) continued after 1900. The United States Steel Company created by J.P. Morgan in 1901 controlled 80 percent of all U.S. steel production. A year later, Morgan combined six competing companies into the International Harvester Company, which dominated the farm-implement business. The General Motors Company, formed in 1908 by William C. Durant with backing from the DuPont Corporation, brought various independent automobile manufacturers, from the inexpensive Chevrolet to the luxury Cadillac, under one corporate umbrella.

Many workers benefited from this corporate growth. Industrial workers' average annual real wages (defined in terms of actual purchasing power) rose from $487 in 1900 to $687 by 1915. In railroading and other unionized industries, wages climbed still higher. But even with the cost of living far lower than today, such wages barely supported a family and provided little cushion for emergencies.

To survive, entire families went to work. Two-thirds of young immigrant women entered the labor force in the early 1900s, working as factory help or domestics or in small business establishments.

Even children worked. In 1910, the nonfarm labor force included some 1.6 million children aged ten to fifteen employed in factories, mills, tenement sweatshops, and street trades such as shoe shining and newspaper vending. The total may have been higher, because many "women workers" listed in the census were in fact young girls. One investigator found a girl of five working nights in a South Carolina textile mill.

Work was long and hazardous. Despite the eight-hour movement of the 1880s, in 1900 the average worker still toiled 9½ hours a day. Some southern textile mills required workdays of twelve or thirteen hours. In one typical year (1907), 4,534 railroad workers and more than 3,000 miners were killed on the job. Few workers enjoyed vacations or retirement benefits.

Workers accustomed to the rhythms of farm labor faced the discipline of the factory. Efficiency experts used time-and-motion studies to increase production. In *Principles of Scientific Management* (1911), Frederick W. Taylor explained how to increase output by standardizing job routines and rewarding the fastest workers. "Efficiency" became a popular catchword, but workers resented the pressures to speed up.

Americans concerned about the social implications of industrialization deplored unregulated corporate power and the hazards facing industrial workers. The drive to regulate big business, inherited from the populists, became an important component of progressivism. Because corporations had benefited from government policies such as high protective tariffs and railroad subsidies, reformers reasoned, they should also be subject to government regulation.

Wisconsin, under Governor **Robert** ("Fighting Bob") **La Follette,** took the lead in regulating railroads, mines, and other businesses. As a Republican congressman, La Follette had feuded with the state's conservative party leadership, and in 1900 he won the governorship as an independent. Challenging powerful corporate interests, La Follette and his administration adopted the direct-primary system, set up a railroad regulatory commission, increased corporate taxes, and limited campaign spending. Reflecting progressivism's faith in experts, La Follette consulted reform-minded professors at the University of Wisconsin and set up a legislative reference library to help lawmakers draft bills. La Follette's reforms gained national attention as the "Wisconsin Idea."

If electoral reform and corporate regulation represented the brain of progressivism, the impulse to improve conditions for workers represented its heart. This movement, too, began at the local and state level. By 1907, for example, thirty states had outlawed child labor. A 1903 Oregon law limited women in industry to a ten-hour workday.

Campaigns for industrial safety and better working conditions won support from some big-city political bosses. A leader of Tammany Hall, New York City's Democratic organization, headed the Triangle fire investigation. Thanks to his committee's efforts, New York passed fifty-six worker-protection laws, including required fire-safety inspections. By 1914, twenty-five states had made employers liable for job-related injuries or deaths.

Florence Kelley of Hull House, the daughter of a conservative Republican congressman, spearheaded the drive to remedy industrial abuses. In 1893, after investigating conditions in factories and sweatshops, Kelley persuaded the Illinois legislature to outlaw child labor and limit working hours for women. In 1899, she became head of the National Consumers' League, which mobilized consumer pressure for improved factory conditions. Campaigning for a federal child-labor law,

Kelley asked, "Why are ... wild game in the national parks, buffalo, [and] migratory birds all found suitable for federal protection, but not children?"

Like many progressive reforms, the crusade for workplace safety relied on expert research. The bacteriologist Alice Hamilton, a pioneer in the new field of "industrial hygiene," reported on lead poisoning among industrial workers in 1910. Later, as an investigator for the U.S. Bureau of Labor, Hamilton publicized other work-related medical hazards.

Workers themselves, who well understood the hazards of their jobs, provided further pressure for reform. For example, when the granite industry introduced new power drills that created a fine dust that workers inhaled, the *Granite Cutters' Journal* called them "widow makers." Sure enough, investigators soon linked the dust to a deadly lung disease, silicosis.

Making Cities More Livable   By 1920, the U.S. urban population passed the 50 percent mark, and sixty-eight cities boasted more than a hundred thousand inhabitants. New York City grew by 2.2 million from 1900 to 1920, Chicago by 1 million. America had become an urban nation.

Political corruption was only one of many urban problems. As factories and businesses attracted a tide of immigrants and job-seekers from rural and small-town America, many cities became congested human warehouses, lacking adequate parks, public-health resources, recreational facilities, and basic municipal services. As the reform spirit spread, the urban crisis loomed large.

Extending the achievements of Frederick Law Olmsted and others (see Chapter 19), reformers campaigned for parks, boulevards, and street lights; opposed unsightly billboards and overhead electrical wires; and advocated city planning and beautification projects. Daniel Burnham, chief architect of the 1893 Chicago world's fair, led a successful 1906 effort to revive a plan for Washington, DC, first proposed in 1791.

Burnham's 1909 *Plan of Chicago* offered a vision of a city both more efficient and more beautiful. He recommended wide boulevards, lakefront parks and museum, statuary and fountains, and a majestic domed city hall and vast civic plaza. Chicago spent more than $300 million on projects reflecting his ideas. Many urban planners shared Burnham's faith that more beautiful cities and imposing public buildings would produce orderly, law-abiding citizens.

The municipal reform impulse also included such practical goals as decent housing and better garbage collection and street cleaning. Providing a model for other cities and states, the New York legislature imposed strict health and safety regulations on tenements in 1911.

With the discovery in the 1880s that germs cause cholera, typhoid fever, and other diseases, municipal hygiene became a high priority. Reformers distributed public-health information, promoted school vaccination programs, and called for safer water and sewer systems and the regulation of food and milk suppliers. When Mary Mallon, an Irish-immigrant cook in New York, was found to be a healthy carrier of the typhoid bacillus in 1907, she was confined by the city health authorities and demonized in the press as "Typhoid Mary."

These efforts bore fruit. From 1900 to 1920, U.S. infant mortality (defined as death in the first year of life), as well as death rates from tuberculosis, typhoid fever, and other infectious or communicable diseases, all fell sharply.

© Bettmann/Corbis

The Price of Industrialization *Smoke and pollutants pour from a Pittsburgh steel mill in 1890. "Hell with the lid off" was one observer's description of the city in these years.*

Urban reformers shared the era's heightened environmental consciousness (see Chapter 17). Factory chimneys belching smoke had once inspired pride, but by the early 1900s physicians had linked factory smoke to respiratory problems, and civic reformers were deploring the soot and smoke spewing from coal-fueled factory steam boilers.

The antismoke campaign combined expertise with activism. Civil engineers formed the Smoke Prevention Association in 1906, and researchers at the University of Pittsburgh—one of the nation's smokiest cities with its steel mills—documented the hazards and costs of air pollution. Chicago merchant Marshall Field declared that the "soot tax" he paid to clean his buildings' exteriors exceeded his real-estate taxes. As women's clubs and other civic groups embraced the cause, many cities passed smoke-abatement laws.

Success proved elusive, however, as railroads and corporations fought back in the courts. With coal still providing 70 percent of the nation's energy as late as

1920, cities remained smoky. Not until years later, with the shift to other energy sources, did municipal air pollution significantly diminish.

PROGRESSIVISM AND SOCIAL CONTROL

The reform zeal of white, native-born, middle-class progressives sprang from their confidence that they knew what was best for society. While municipal corruption, unsafe factories, and corporate abuses captured their attention, so, too, did issues of personal behavior, particularly immigrant behavior. The problems they addressed deserved attention, but their moralistic rhetoric and coercive remedies also betrayed an impulse to impose their own moral standards by force of law.

Urban Amusements; Urban Moral Control   Despite the slums, dangerous factories, and other problems, early twentieth-century cities also offered fun and diversion with their department stores, vaudeville, music halls, and amusement parks (see Chapter 19). While some vaudeville owners sought respectability, bawdy routines full of sexual innuendo delighted working-class audiences.

Amusement parks offered families escape from tenements, and gave female workers an opportunity to socialize with friends, meet young men, and show off new outfits. New York City's amusement park, Coney Island, a subway ride from the city, attracted several million visitors a year by 1914.

With electrification, streetcar rides and evening strolls on well-lit downtown streets became leisure activities in themselves. Orville and Wilbur Wright's successful airplane flight in 1903 and the introduction of Henry Ford's Model T in 1908, transforming the automobile from a toy of the rich to a vehicle for the masses, foretold exciting changes ahead, with cities central to the action.

Jaunty music-hall songs added to the vibrancy of city life. The blues, rooted in the chants of southern black sharecroppers, reached a broader public with such songs as W.C. Handy's classic "St. Louis Blues" (1914). Ragtime, another import from the black South (see Chapter 19), enjoyed great popularity in early twentieth-century urban America. Both the black composer Scott Joplin, with such works as "Maple Leaf Rag" (1899), and the white composer Irving Berlin, with his hit tune "Alexander's Rag-Time Band" (1911), contributed to this vogue.

These years also brought a new entertainment medium—the movies. Initially a part of vaudeville shows, movies soon migrated to five-cent halls called "nickelodeons" in immigrant neighborhoods. At first featuring brief comic sequences like *The Sneeze* or *The Kiss*, movies began to tell stories with *The Great Train Robbery* (1903). *A Fool There Was* (1914), with its daring line, "Kiss me, my fool!," made Theda Bara (really Theodosia Goodman of Cincinnati) the first female star. The British music-hall performer Charlie Chaplin immigrated to America and appeared in some sixty short comedies between 1914 and 1917. Like amusement parks, the movies allowed immigrant youth to briefly escape parental supervision. As a New York garment worker recalled, "The one place I was allowed to go by myself was the movies. My parents wouldn't let me go anywhere else."

The diversions that eased city life for the poor worried middle-class reformers. Fearful of immorality and disorder, they campaigned to regulate amusement parks, dance halls, and the darkened nickelodeons, which they saw as moral hazards. Several states and cities set up film censorship boards, and the Supreme Court upheld such measures in 1915.

Building on the moral-purity crusade of the Woman's Christian Temperance Union (WCTU) and other groups (see Chapter 19), reformers also targeted prostitution, a major urban problem. Male procurers lured young women into prostitution and then took a share of their income. Women's paltry wages for factory work or domestic service made this more-lucrative occupation tempting. Why "get up at 6:30 ... and work in a close stuffy room ... until dark for $6 or $7 a week," reasoned one prostitute, when an afternoon with a man could bring in more.

Adopting the usual progressive approach, investigators gathered statistics on what they called "the social evil." The American Social Hygiene Association (1914), financed by John D. Rockefeller, Jr., sponsored research on sexually transmitted diseases, paid for "vice investigations" in major cities, and drafted antiprostitution laws.

As prostitution came to symbolize urban America's larger moral dangers, a "white slave" hysteria took hold. Novels, films, and magazine articles warned of kidnapped farm girls forced into urban brothels. The Mann Act (1910) made it illegal to transport a woman across a state line "for immoral purposes." Amid much fanfare, reformers shut down the red-light districts of New Orleans, Chicago, and other cities.

Racism, anti-immigrant prejudice, and anxieties about changing sexual mores all fueled the antiprostitution crusade. Authorities employed the new legislation to pry into private sexual behavior. Blackmailers entrapped men into Mann Act violations. In 1913, the African American boxer Jack Johnson, the heavyweight champion, was convicted under the Mann Act for crossing a state line with a (white) woman for "immoral purposes." Johnson went abroad to escape imprisonment.

Battling Alcohol and Drugs   Temperance had long been part of America's reform agenda, but reformers' objectives changed in the Progressive Era. Earlier campaigns had urged individuals to give up drink. By contrast, the **Anti-Saloon League** (ASL), founded in 1895, called for a total ban on the sale of alcoholic beverages. In typical Progressive fashion, full-time professionals ran the ASL, with Protestant ministers staffing state committees. ASL publications offered statistics documenting alcohol's role in many social problems. As churches and temperance groups worked for prohibition at the municipal, county, and state levels, the ASL moved to its larger goal: national prohibition.

Alcohol abuse did indeed contribute to domestic violence, health problems, and workplace injuries. But like the antiprostitution crusade, the prohibition campaign became a symbolic battleground pitting native-born citizens against immigrants. The ASL embodied Protestant America's impulse to control the immigrant city.

Reformers also targeted drug abuse—and for good reason. Physicians, patent-medicine peddlers, and legitimate drug companies freely prescribed or sold opium (derived from poppies) and its derivatives morphine and heroin. Cocaine, extracted from coca leaves, was an ingredient of Coca-Cola until about 1900.

Amid mounting reform pressure, Congress passed the Harrison Act in 1914, banning the distribution of heroin, morphine, cocaine, and other addictive drugs except by licensed physicians or pharmacists. Like progressives' environmental concerns, this campaign anticipated an issue that remains important today. But this reform, too, had racist undertones. Antidrug crusaders luridly described Chinese "opium dens" and warned that "drug-crazed Negroes" imperiled white womanhood.

Immigration Restriction and Eugenics   While many new city-dwellers came from farms and small towns, immigration remained the main source of urban growth. More than 17 million newcomers arrived from 1900 to 1917 (many passing through New York's immigration center, Ellis Island), and most settled in cities. As in the 1890s (see Chapter 19), the influx came mainly from southern and eastern Europe, but more than two hundred thousand Japanese arrived between 1900 and 1920. An estimated forty thousand Chinese entered in these years, despite the 1882 Chinese Exclusion Act (see Chapter 18), which remained in force until 1943. Thousands of Mexicans came as well, many seeking railroad work.

The dismay that middle-class Americans felt about urban slum conditions stimulated support not only for protective legislation but also for immigration restriction. If the immigrant city bred social problems, some concluded, immigrants should be excluded. Prominent Bostonians formed the Immigration Restriction League in 1894. The American Federation of Labor, fearing job competition, also endorsed restriction.

Like most Progressive Era reformers, immigration-restriction advocates tried to document their case. A 1911 congressional report allegedly proved the new immigrants' innate degeneracy. One prominent sociologist described the newcomers as "low-browed, big-faced persons of obviously low mentality."

Led by Massachusetts senator Henry Cabot Lodge, Congress passed literacy-test bills in 1896, 1913, and 1915, only to see them vetoed. These measures would have excluded immigrants over sixteen years old who could not read either English or their native language, thus discriminating against persons lacking formal education. In 1917, Lodge's bill became law over President Woodrow Wilson's veto.

Anti-immigrant fears helped fuel the eugenics movement. Eugenics is the control of reproduction to alter a plant or animal species, and some U.S. eugenicists believed that human society could be improved by this means. Leading eugenicists urged immigration restriction to protect America from "inferior" genetic stock.

In *The Passing of the Great Race* (1916), Madison Grant, a prominent progressive and eugenics advocate, used bogus data to denounce immigrants from southern and eastern Europe, especially Jews. He also viewed African Americans as inferior. Anticipating the program of Adolf Hitler in the 1930s (covered in Chapter 25), Grant called for racial segregation, immigration restriction, and the forced sterilization of the "unfit," including "worthless race types." The vogue of eugenics gave "scientific" respectability to racism and anti-immigrant sentiment.

Inspired by eugenics, many states legalized the sterilization of criminals, sex offenders, and persons adjudged mentally deficient. In the 1927 case *Buck* v. *Bell,* the Supreme Court upheld such laws.

Racism and Progressivism   Progressivism arose at a time of intense racism in America as well of major African American population movements. These realities are crucial to understanding the movement.

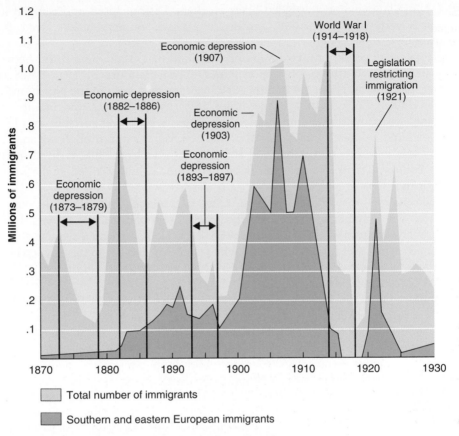

FIGURE 21.1   Immigration to the United States, 1870–1930

With the end of the depression of the 1890s, immigrants from southern and eastern Europe filled American cities, spurring an immigration-restriction movement, urban moral-purity campaigns, and efforts to improve the physical and social conditions of immigrant life.

Sources: Statistical History of the United States from Colonial Times to the Present (*Stamford, Conn.: Fairfield Publishers,* 1965)*; and report presented by Senator William P. Dillingham, Senate document 742, 61st Congress, 3rd session, December 5, 1910: Abstracts of Reports to the Immigration Commission.*

In 1900, the nation's 10 million blacks lived mostly in the rural South as share-croppers and tenant farmers. As devastating floods and the cotton boll weevil, which spread from Mexico in the 1890s, worsened their lot, many southern blacks left the land. By 1910, more than 20 percent of blacks lived in cities, mostly in the South, but many in the North. Black men in the cities took jobs in factories, docks, and railroads or became carpenters, plasterers, or bricklayers. Many black women became domestic servants, seamstresses, or workers in laundries and tobacco facto-ries. By 1910, 54 percent of America's black women held jobs.

Across the South, legally enforced racism peaked after 1900. Local "Jim Crow" laws segregated streetcars, schools, parks, and even cemeteries. The facilities for blacks, including the schools, were invariably inferior. Many southern cities imposed residential segregation by law until the Supreme Court restricted it in

1917. Most labor unions excluded black workers. Disfranchised and trapped in a cycle of poverty, poor education, and discrimination, southern blacks faced bleak prospects.

Fleeing such conditions, two hundred thousand blacks migrated north between 1890 and 1910. Wartime job opportunities drew still more in 1917–1918 (see Chapter 22), and by 1920, 1.4 million African Americans lived in the North, mostly in cities. Here, too, racism worsened after 1890 as hard times and immigration heightened social tensions. (Immigrants, competing with blacks for jobs and housing, sometimes exhibited intense racial prejudice.) Segregation, though not imposed by law, was enforced by custom and sometimes by violence. Blacks lived in run-down "colored districts," attended dilapidated schools, and worked at the lowest-paying jobs.

Their ballots—usually cast for the party of Lincoln—brought little political influence. The only black politicians tolerated by Republican Party leaders distributed low-level patronage jobs and otherwise kept silent. African Americans in the segregated army faced hostility from white soldiers and from nearby civilians. Even the movies preached racism. D.W. Griffith's *The Birth of a Nation* (1915) disparaged blacks and glorified the Ku Klux Klan.

Smoldering racism sometimes exploded in violence. Antiblack rioters in Atlanta in 1906 murdered twenty-five blacks and burned many black homes. From 1900 to 1920, an average of about seventy-five lynchings occurred yearly. Blacks whose assertive behavior or economic aspirations angered whites were especially vulnerable. Some lynchings involved brutal sadism, with large crowds on hand, mutilated bodies, and graphic photo postcards sold later. Authorities rarely intervened. At a 1916 lynching in Texas, the mayor warned the mob not to damage the hanging tree, on city property.

In such times, African Americans developed strong institutions. Black churches proved a bulwark of support. Working mothers, drawing on strategies dating to slavery days, relied on relatives and neighbors for child care. A handful of black higher-education institutions carried on against heavy odds. John Hope, who became president of Atlanta's Morehouse College in 1906, assembled a distinguished faculty, championed African American education, and fought segregation. His sister Jane (Hope) Lyons was dean of women at nearby Spelman College.

Urban black communities included black-owned insurance companies and banks, and a small elite of entrepreneurs, teachers, and ministers. Although major-league baseball excluded blacks, a thriving Negro League attracted African American fans.

In this racist age, progressives compiled a mixed racial record. Lillian Wald, director of a New York City settlement house, protested racial injustice. Muckraker Ray Stannard Baker documented racism in *Following the Color Line* (1908). Settlement-house worker Mary White Ovington helped found the National Association for the Advancement of Colored People (discussed in the next section) and wrote *Half a Man* (1911), which discussed racism's psychological toll.

But most progressives viewed African Americans, like immigrants, not as potential allies but as part of the problem. They generally supported or tolerated segregated schools and housing; restrictions on black voting rights; moral oversight of black communities; and, at best, paternalistic efforts to "uplift" this supposedly childlike people. Viciously racist southern politicians like Mississippi governor James K. Vardaman and South Carolina senator Ben Tillman also supported progressive reforms. Southern woman-suffrage leaders argued that enfranchising women would strengthen white supremacy.

At the national level, President Theodore Roosevelt's racial record was marginally better than that of other politicians in this racist age. He appointed a black to head the Charleston customs house, despite white opposition, and closed a Mississippi post office rather than yield to demands to dismiss the black postmistress. In a symbolically important gesture, he dined with Booker T. Washington at the White House. In 1906, however, he approved the dishonorable discharge of an entire regiment of black soldiers in Brownsville, Texas, because some members of the unit, goaded by racist taunts, had killed a local civilian. The "Brownsville Incident" incensed African Americans. (In 1972, after most of the men were dead, Congress reversed the dishonorable discharges.)

Under President Woodrow Wilson, racism became rampant in Washington. A southerner, Wilson displayed at best a patronizing attitude toward blacks, praised the racist movie *The Birth of a Nation,* and allowed southerners in his cabinet and in Congress to impose rigid segregation on all levels of the government.

Blacks, Women, and Workers Organize

Progressivism's organizational strategy also proved useful for groups facing discrimination or exploitation. African Americans, middle-class women, and wage workers all organized to address their grievances and improve their situation.

African American Leaders Organize Against Racism
With racism on the rise, Booker T. Washington's self-help message (see Chapter 20) seemed increasingly unrealistic, particularly to northern blacks. Washington's themes would appeal to later generations of African Americans, but in the early twentieth century, blacks confronting segregation, lynching, and blatant racism tired of his cautious approach. In 1902, William Monroe Trotter, editor of the *Boston Guardian,* a black newspaper, called Washington's go-slow policies "a fatal blow ... to the Negro's political rights and liberty."

Another opponent was the black activist **Ida Wells-Barnett.** Moving to Chicago from Memphis in 1892 after a white mob destroyed her offices, Wells-Barnett mounted a national antilynching campaign, in contrast to Booker T. Washington's public silence on the subject. Documenting the grim facts in *A Red Record* (1895), she toured the United States and Great Britain lecturing against lynching and other racial abuses.

Booker T. Washington's principal black critic was **W.E.B. Du Bois** (1868–1963). After earning a Ph.D. in history from Harvard in 1895, Du Bois taught at Ohio's Wilberforce College, the University of Pennsylvania, and Atlanta University. In *The Souls of Black Folk* (1903), Du Bois rejected Washington's call for patience and his exclusive emphasis on manual skills. Instead, Du Bois demanded full racial equality, including equal educational opportunities, and urged resistance to all forms of racism.

A New Black Leadership *Ida Wells-Barnett, Chicago-based crusader against lynching, and W.E.B. Du Bois, outspoken critic of Booker T. Washington and author of the classic* The Souls of Black Folk. *The challenge, wrote Du Bois, was to find a way "to be both a Negro and an American."*

In 1905, under Du Bois's leadership, blacks committed to battling racism held a conference at Niagara Falls. For the next few years, participants in the "Niagara Movement" met annually. Meanwhile, white reformers led by newspaper publisher Oswald Garrison Villard, grandson of abolitionist William Lloyd Garrison, had also grown dissatisfied with Washington's cautiousness. In 1909, Villard and his allies joined with Du Bois and other blacks from the Niagara Movement to form the **National Association for the Advancement of Colored People** (NAACP). This new organization called for sustained activism, including legal challenges, to achieve political equality for blacks and full integration into American life. Attracting the urban black middle class, the NAACP by 1914 had six thousand members in fifty branches.

Revival of the Woman-Suffrage Movement

As late as 1910, women could vote in only four western states: Wyoming, Utah, Colorado, and Idaho. But women's active role in progressive reform movements revitalized the suffrage cause. A vigorous suffrage movement in Great Britain reverberated in America as well. Like progressivism itself, this revived campaign had grassroots origins. A 1915 suffrage campaign in New York State, though unsuccessful, underscored the new momentum.

Developments in California illustrate both the movement's new momentum and its limitations. In the early 1900s, California's women's clubs shifted from their earlier cultural and domestic focus to reform, especially on city-government and public-school issues. In the process, many women activists concluded that full citizenship meant the right to vote. While working with labor leaders and male

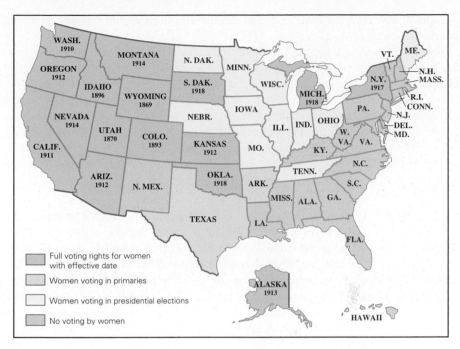

MAP 21.1 Woman Suffrage Before the Nineteenth Amendment

Beginning with Wyoming in 1869, woman suffrage made steady gains in western states before 1920. Farther east, key victories came in New York (1917) and Michigan (1918). But much of the East remained an anti-woman-suffrage bastion throughout the period.

Sources: © Cengage Learning. All rights reserved. No distribution allowed without express authorization.

progressives, they nevertheless insisted on the unique role of "organized woman-hood" in building a better society. Success came in 1911 when California voters approved woman suffrage.

But "organized womanhood" had its limits. Elite and middle-class women, mainly based in Los Angeles and San Francisco, led the campaign. Working-class and farm women played a small role, while African American, Mexican American, and Asian American women were almost totally excluded.

New leaders translated the state-level momentum into a revitalized national movement. In 1900, **Carrie Chapman Catt** of Iowa succeeded Susan B. Anthony as president of the National American Woman Suffrage Association (NAWSA). Under Catt, NAWSA adopted the so-called Winning Plan: grassroots organization with tight central coordination, focused on state-level campaigns.

Emulating the new urban consumer culture, suffragists ran newspaper ads, festooned posters and banners with catchy slogans, paraded in open cars, arranged photo opportunities for the media, and distributed fans and other items emblazoned with the suffrage message. Gradually, state after state fell into the suffrage column.

As in California (and like progressive organizations generally), NAWSA's membership remained largely white, native-born, and middle-class. Some upper-class women opposed the reform. Women already enjoyed behind-the-scenes influence, they argued; invading the male realm of electoral politics would tarnish their moral and spiritual role.

Not all suffragists accepted Catt's strategy. Alice Paul, influenced by the British suffragists' militant tactics, rejected NAWSA's state-by-state approach. In 1913, Paul founded the Congressional Union for Woman Suffrage, renamed the National Woman's Party in 1917, to pressure Congress to enact a woman-suffrage constitutional amendment. Targeting "the party in power"—in this case, the Democrats— Paul and her followers in the 1916 election opposed President Woodrow Wilson and congressional Democrats who had failed to endorse a suffrage amendment. In 1917– 1918, with the United States at war, the suffrage cause prevailed in New York and Michigan and advanced toward final success (further discussed in Chapter 22).

Enlarging the "Woman's Sphere"   The suffrage cause did not exhaust women's energies in the Progressive Era. Women's clubs, settlement-house residents, and individual activists like Florence Kelley, Alice Hamilton, and Ida Wells-Barnett promoted an array of reforms. These included the campaigns to bring playgrounds and day nurseries to the slums, abolish child labor, and ban unsafe foods and quack remedies. As Jane Addams observed, women's concern for their own families' welfare could also draw them into political activism in an industrial age when hazards came from outside the home as well as inside.

Cultural assumptions about "woman's sphere" weakened as women invaded many fronts. Katherine Bement Davis served as New York City's commissioner of corrections. Emma Goldman crisscrossed the country lecturing on politics, feminism, and modern drama while coediting a radical monthly, *Mother Earth*. A vanguard of women in higher education included the chemist Ellen Richards of the Massachusetts Institute of Technology and Marion Talbot, first dean of women at the University of Chicago.

In *Women and Economics* (1898) and other works, Charlotte Perkins Gilman explored the cultural roots of gender roles and linked women's subordinate status to their economic dependence on men. Confining women to the domestic sphere, Gilman argued, was an evolutionary throwback that had become outdated and inefficient. She advocated gender equality in the workplace; the collectivization of cooking and other domestic tasks; and state-run child-care centers. In the utopian novel *Herland* (1915), Gilman wittily critiqued patriarchal assumptions by injecting three naïve young men into an exclusively female society.

Some reformers challenged laws banning the distribution of contraceptives and birth-control information. Although countless women, particularly the poor, suffered from frequent pregnancies, artificial contraception was widely denounced as immoral. In 1914, **Margaret Sanger** of New York, whose mother had died after bearing eleven children, began her crusade for birth control, a term she coined. When her journal *The Woman Rebel* faced prosecution on obscenity charges, Sanger fled to England. Returning in 1916, she opened the nation's first birth-control clinic in Brooklyn; launched *The Birth Control Review*; and founded the American Birth Control League, forerunner of today's Planned Parenthood Federation.

Meanwhile, another New Yorker, Mary Ware Dennett, had also emerged as an advocate of birth control and sex education. While Sanger championed direct action to promote the cause, Dennett urged lobbying efforts to change the law. Sanger insisted that only physicians should supply contraceptives; Dennett argued for widespread distribution. These differences, plus personal rivalries, divided the movement.

The birth-control and sex-education movements stand as important legacies of progressivism. At the time, however, conservatives and religious leaders bitterly opposed them. Dennett's frank 1919 informational pamphlet for youth, *The Sex Side of Life,* was long banned as obscene. Not until 1965 did the Supreme Court fully legalize the dissemination of contraceptive materials and information.

Workers Organize; Socialism Advances

In this age of organization, labor unions continued to expand. In 1900–1920, the American Federation of Labor (AFL) grew from 625,000 to 4 million members. This still represented only about 20 percent of the industrial work force. With recent immigrants hungry for jobs, union activities posed risks. The boss could always fire an "agitator" and hire a newcomer. Judicial hostility also retarded unionization. In the 1908 *Danbury Hatters* case, for example, the Supreme Court ruled that boycotts in support of strikes were a "conspiracy in restraint of trade," and thus a violation of the Sherman Anti-Trust Act. The AFL's strength remained in the traditional skilled trades, not in the factories, mills, and sweatshops where most immigrants and women worked.

A few unions did try to reach these laborers. The International Ladies' Garment Workers' Union (ILGWU), founded in 1900 by immigrant workers in New York City's needle trades, conducted successful strikes in 1909 and after the 1911 Triangle fire. The 1909 strike began when young Clara Lemlich jumped up as speechmaking droned on at a union meeting and passionately called for a strike. Some picketers lost their jobs or endured police beatings, but the strikers did win higher wages and improved working conditions.

Another union that targeted the most exploited workers was the **Industrial Workers of the World** (IWW), nicknamed the Wobblies, founded in Chicago in 1905. The IWW's leader was William "Big Bill" Haywood, a Utah-born miner who in 1905 was acquitted of complicity in the assassination of an antilabor former governor of Idaho. IWW membership peaked at around thirty thousand, mostly western miners, lumbermen, fruit pickers, and itinerant laborers. It captured the imagination of young cultural rebels in New York City's Greenwich Village, where Haywood, a compelling orator, often visited.

The IWW led strikes of Nevada gold miners, Minnesota iron miners, and timber workers in the Northwest. Its victory in a bitter 1912 textile strike in Massachusetts owed much to Elizabeth Gurley Flynn, a fiery Irish American orator who publicized the cause. With an exaggerated reputation for violence, the IWW faced government harassment, especially during World War I, and by 1920 its strength was broken.

Other workers, along with some middle-class Americans, turned to socialism. All socialists foresaw capitalism's collapse and advocated public ownership of factories, utilities, railroads, and communications systems, but they differed on how to achieve these goals. The revolutionary ideology of German social theorist Karl Marx won a few converts, but the vision of democratic socialism achieved at the ballot box proved more appealing. In 1900 democratic socialists formed the Socialist Party of America (SPA). Members included Morris Hillquit, a New York City labor organizer; Victor Berger, leader of Milwaukee's German socialists; and **Eugene V. Debs,**

GOING TO THE SOURCE

A Violent Encounter at a 1909 Shirtwaist Workers' Strike

Before the tragic 1911 fire at the Triangle shirtwaist factory in New York, shirtwaist workers had organized a union and gone on strike for better wages and working conditions. This vivid account describes a confrontation between strikers and special police hired by the factory owners.

POLICE MISHANDLE GIRL STRIKE PICKETS
New York Times, December 10, 1909
Officers of the striking Shirt Waist Makers' Union are anxious to obtain a judicial interpretation of the rights of pickets.... The representatives of the union believe that pickets have the right to approach strikebreakers and persuade them peacefully to stop work. The agents of the employers, and as the girls say, the police...prevent the strikers from accosting the workers.

Miss Henrietta Mercy of 58 West 115th Street called at THE TIMES office last night to relate her experiences as a picket yesterday. Miss Mercy is not herself a striker, but the private secretary of a woman of wealth. She is a sister of Dr. Anna Mercy of 182 West Houston Street, and is herself a graduate of the Normal College. She wore a tailor-made coat with a fur turban and stole. She showed a TIMES reporter a torn sleeve in her waist which she said had been ripped by the roughness of policemen.

[S]aid Miss Mercy last night, "I am deeply interested in the girl workers of the east side. As secretary of the East Side Equal Rights League, I went out yesterday afternoon as a volunteer picket with Lena Cohen...a striker.

"There were about a dozen of us picketing a shirt waist factory at Greene and Grand Streets. We girls walked peacefully up and down in pairs.... We had no intention of creating any violence. All we wished to do was to speak to the [strikebreaking] girls kindly....

"As the girls got ready to come out of the factory [that is, the workers who had

the Indiana labor leader. Debs, a popular orator, ran for president five times between 1900 and 1920. Many Greenwich Village cultural rebels embraced socialism and supported the radical magazine *The Masses,* founded in 1911.

By 1912, SPA membership stood at 118,000, but many more voted the Socialist ticket. Debs received more than 900,000 votes for president that year, and the Socialists elected a congressman (Berger) and many municipal officials (see also the later section, "The Four-Way Election of 1912"). The party published more than three hundred newspapers, including foreign-languages papers targeting immigrants.

NATIONAL PROGRESSIVISM, PHASE I: ROOSEVELT AND TAFT, 1901–1913

By around 1905, local and state reform activities were coalescing into a national movement. In 1906, Wisconsin governor Robert La Follette was elected a U.S. senator. Five years earlier, progressivism had found its first national leader, **Theodore Roosevelt,** nicknamed "TR."

not joined the strike], between twenty and thirty special policemen employed by the factory as guards for the workers, formed a double line on the sidewalk.... They hurled themselves upon us and threw us off the sidewalk onto the pavement.... [S]ome of the girls fell on the stones. We tried to get back on the sidewalk and they shoved, elbowed and even kicked some of us to keep us in the street.

"I managed to break through the line. A uniformed policeman picked me up and pinned me against the wall.... The special policemen seized the other girls and pinned them against the wall till the strike-breakers had passed by. I said to the policeman who held me: 'You are supposed to be impartial. All we want to do is talk to these girls and you have no right to hold us against our will. It's our privilege to talk to them if they want to.' He replied: 'You can walk and talk all you want to, after they're gone. But keep still now, or I'll run you in.'

"I got free after the girls [from the factory] got away and started to run after them.... One of the special policemen seized me and threw me against a hydrant. I narrowly missed having my skull fractured.

I picked myself up, and managed to reach the uptown stairs [of the elevated train station], where several of the strike-breakers had gone.

"The special policemen followed and nearly pulled the clothes off me to keep me from going up the stairs. They called me the most vile and insulting names, and finally dragged me from the stairs. I was weak from struggling and mad with shame when I reached my sister's office in Houston Street with my clothing all disarranged and my waist torn. I believe that I should have been badly injured if a crowd had not gathered and shamed the men."

Questions

1. *The strikers wanted to persuade the non-strikers to join them. What arguments might each side have used if the police had permitted them to talk to each other?*
2. *Why, do you think, did the* New York Times *reporter provide so much information about Henrietta Mercy's education, expensive clothing, and employment by "a woman of wealth"?*

Source: The New York Times, December 10, 1909.

Self-righteous, jingoistic, verbose—but also brilliant, politically savvy, and endlessly interesting—Roosevelt became president in 1901 and made the White House a cauldron of activism. Orchestrating public opinion, Roosevelt pursued his goals—labor mediation, consumer protection, corporate regulation, natural-resource conservation, and engagement abroad.

TR's activist approach permanently enlarged the powers of the presidency. His handpicked successor, William Howard Taft, proved politically inept, however, and controversy marked his administration. With the Republicans divided, the Democrat Woodrow Wilson, espousing a somewhat different reform vision, won the presidency in 1912.

Roosevelt's Path to the White House

On September 6, 1901, in Buffalo, anarchist Leon Czolgosz shot William McKinley. At first recovery seemed likely, and Vice President Theodore Roosevelt continued a hiking trip in New York's Adirondack Mountains. But on September 14, McKinley died. At age forty-two, Theodore Roosevelt became president.

Many Republican leaders shuddered at the thought of what one called "that damned cowboy" in the White House. Roosevelt did, indeed, display traits associated with the West. The son of an aristocratic New York family of Dutch origins, he overcame a sickly childhood through bodybuilding exercises and summers in Wyoming to become a model of physical fitness. When his young wife died in 1884, he stoically carried on. Two years on a Dakota ranch deepened his enthusiasm for what he termed "the strenuous life."

Although his social peers scorned politics, Roosevelt served as a state assemblyman, New York City police commissioner, and a U.S. civil-service commissioner. In 1898, fresh from his Cuban exploits, he was elected New York's governor. Two years later, the state's Republican boss, eager to be rid of him, arranged for Roosevelt's nomination as vice president.

As with everything he did, TR found the presidency energizing. "I have been President emphatically...," he boasted. "I believe in a strong executive." He enjoyed public life and loved the limelight. "When Theodore attends a wedding he wants to be the bride," his daughter observed, "and when he attends a funeral he wants to be the corpse." With his toothy grin, machine-gun speech, and amazing energy, he dominated the political landscape. When he refused to shoot a bear cub on a hunting trip, a shrewd toy maker marketed a cuddly new product, the Teddy Bear.

Labor Disputes, Trustbusting, Railroad Regulation   Events soon tested the new president's political skills. In May 1902, the United Mine Workers Union (UMW) called a strike to gain not only higher wages and shorter hours but also recognition as a union. The mine owners resisted, and in October, with winter looming, TR acted. Summoning the two sides to the White House and threatening to seize the mines, he forced them to accept arbitration. The arbitration commission granted the miners a 10 percent wage increase and reduced their working day from ten to nine hours.

TR's approach to labor disputes differed from that of his predecessors, who typically sided with management, sometimes using troops as strikebreakers. Though not consistently prolabor, he defended workers' right to organize. When a mine owner insisted that the miners' welfare should be left to those "whom God in his infinite wisdom has given control of the [country's] property interests," Roosevelt derided such "arrogant stupidity."

With his elite background, TR neither feared nor much liked business tycoons. The prospect of spending time with "big-money men," he once wrote, "fills me with frank horror." While believing that corporations contributed to national greatness, he also embraced the progressive conviction that they must be regulated. A strict moralist, he held corporations, like individuals, to a high standard.

Yet as a political realist, Roosevelt also understood that many Washington politicians abhorred his views—among them Senator Nelson Aldrich of Rhode Island, a wily defender of business interests. Roosevelt's progressive impulses thus remained in tension with his grasp of power realities in capitalist America.

Another test came when J.P. Morgan in 1901 formed the United States Steel Company, the nation's first billion-dollar business. As public distrust of big corporations deepened, TR dashed to the head of the parade. His 1902 State of the Union message called for breaking up business monopolies, or "trustbusting." Roosevelt's attorney general soon sued the Northern Securities Company, a giant holding company recently created by Morgan and other tycoons to control railroading in the Northwest, for violating the Sherman Anti-Trust Act. On a speaking tour in the summer of 1902, TR called for a "square deal" for all Americans and denounced special treatment for capitalists. "We don't wish to destroy corporations," he said, "but we do wish to make them ... serve the public good." In 1904, a divided Supreme Court ordered the Northern Securities Company dissolved.

The Roosevelt administration filed more than forty antitrust lawsuits. In two key rulings in 1911, the Supreme Court ordered the breakup of the Standard Oil Company and the reorganization of the American Tobacco Company to make it less monopolistic.

As the 1904 election neared, Roosevelt made peace with Morgan and other business magnates. The GOP convention that nominated Roosevelt adopted a pro-business platform, stimulating $2 million in corporate contributions. The Democrats, meanwhile, eager to erase the taint of radicalism lingering from the 1890s, embraced the gold standard and nominated a conservative New York judge.

Winning easily, Roosevelt turned to a major goal: railroad regulation. He now saw corporate regulation as more effective than trustbusting, and this shift underlay the 1906 **Hepburn Act.** This law empowered the Interstate Commerce Commission to set maximum railroad rates and to examine railroads' financial records. It also curtailed the railroads' practice of distributing free passes to ministers and other shapers of public opinion.

The Hepburn Act displayed TR's political skills. In a key compromise with Senator Aldrich and other conservatives, he agreed to delay tariff reform in return for railroad regulation. Although failing to fully satisfy reformers, the Hepburn Act did expand the government's regulatory powers.

Consumer Protection   Of all progressive reforms, the campaign against unsafe food, drugs, and medicine proved especially popular. Upton Sinclair's *The Jungle* (1906) graphically described conditions in some meatpacking plants. Wrote Sinclair in one vivid passage, "[A] man could run his hand over these piles of meat and sweep off handfuls of dried dung of rats. These rats were nuisances, and the packers would put poisoned bread out for them, they would die, and then rats, bread, and meat would go into the hoppers together." (The socialist Sinclair also detailed the exploitation of immigrant workers, but this message proved less potent. "I aimed at the nation's heart, but hit it in the stomach," he later lamented.) As women's organizations and consumer groups rallied public opinion, an Agriculture Department chemist, Harvey W. Wiley, helped shape the proposed legislation. Other muckrakers exposed useless or dangerous patent medicines laced with cocaine, opium, or alcohol. One tonic "for treatment of the alcohol habit" contained 26.5 percent alcohol. Peddlers of these nostrums freely claimed that they could cure cancer, grow hair, and restore sexual vigor.

Sensing the public mood, Roosevelt supported the **Pure Food and Drug Act** and the Meat Inspection Act, both passed in 1906. The former outlawed the sale of adulterated foods or drugs and required accurate ingredient labels; the latter imposed strict sanitary rules on meatpackers and set up a federal meat-inspection system. Reputable food processors, meatpackers, and medicinal companies, eager to regain public confidence, supported these measures.

Environmental-
ism: Progres-
sive Style
Environmental concerns loomed large for Theodore Roosevelt. Describing conservation in his first State of the Union message as America's "most vital internal question," he highlighted an issue that still reverberates.

By 1900, decades of expansion and urban-industrial growth had taken a heavy toll on the land. In the West, mining and timber interests, farmers, ranchers, sheep growers, and preservationists advanced competing land-use claims. While business interests and boosters preached exploitation of the West's resources, and agricultural groups sought government aid for irrigation projects, John Muir's Sierra Club (founded in San Francisco in 1892) urged wilderness preservation. Under a law passed in 1891, Presidents Harrison and Cleveland had set aside some 35 million acres of public lands as national forests.

In the early twentieth century, amid spreading cities and factories, a wilderness vogue swept America. Popular writers evoked the tang of the campfire and the lure of the primitive. Summer camps, as well as the Boy Scouts (founded in 1910) and Girl Scouts (1912), gave city children a taste of wilderness living. Socially prominent easterners embraced the cause.

Between the wilderness enthusiasts and the developers stood government experts like Gifford Pinchot who saw the public domain as a resource to be managed wisely. Appointed by TR in 1905 to head the new U.S. Forest Service, Pinchot stressed not preservation but conservation—the planned use of forest lands for public and commercial purposes.

Wilderness advocates welcomed Pinchot's opposition to mindless exploitation, but worried that the multiple-use approach would despoil wilderness areas. "[T]rees are for human use," conceded a Sierra Club member, but added that these uses included "the spiritual wealth of us all, as well as ... the material wealth of some."

At heart Roosevelt was a preservationist. In 1903, he spent a blissful few days camping in Yosemite National Park with John Muir. He once compared "the destruction of a species" to the loss of "all the works of some great writer." But TR the politician backed the conservationists' call for planned development. He supported the **National Reclamation Act** (1902), which designated the money from public-land sales for water management in arid western regions, and set up the Reclamation Service to construct dams and irrigation projects.

This measure (also known as the **Newlands Act** for its sponsor, a Nevada congressman) ranks with the Northwest Ordinance of 1787 for promoting the settlement and productivity of a vast continental region—this one between the Rockies and the Pacific. Arizona's Roosevelt Dam spurred the growth of Phoenix; dams and waterways in Idaho's Snake River Valley stimulated the production of potatoes and other commodities on hitherto barren acres. The law required farmers who benefited from these projects to repay the construction costs, creating a federal fund for further projects. The Newlands Act and other measures of these years transformed the West from a series of isolated "island settlements" into a thriving, interconnected region.

The competition for scarce water resources in the West sparked bitter political battles. The Los Angeles basin, for example, with 40 percent of California's population in 1900, found itself with only 2 percent of the state's surface water. In 1907, the city derailed a Reclamation Service project intended for the farmers of California's Owens Valley, more than 230 miles to the north, and diverted the precious water to Los Angeles.

Meanwhile, President Roosevelt, embracing Pinchot's multiple-use land-management program, set aside 200 million acres of public land (85 million of them in Alaska) as national forests, mineral reserves, and waterpower sites. But the national-forest provisions provoked corporate opposition, and in 1907 Congress revoked the president's authority to create national forests in six timber-rich western states. Before signing the bill, Roosevelt designated 16 million more acres in the six states as national forests. TR also created fifty-three wildlife reserves, sixteen national monuments, and five new national parks. Congress established the National Park Service in 1916 to manage them.

In 1908, Gifford Pinchot organized a White House conservation conference for the nation's governors. There, experts discussed the utilitarian benefits of resource management. John Muir and other wilderness preservationists were not invited. But the struggle between wilderness purists and multiple-use advocates went on. Rallying support through magazine articles, preservationist groups and women's organizations saved a large grove of California's giant redwoods and a lovely stretch of the Maine coastline from logging.

The Sierra Club lost a battle to save the Hetch Hetchy Valley in Yosemite National Park when Congress in 1913 approved a dam on the Tuolumne River to provide water and hydroelectric power for San Francisco, 150 miles away. (Other opponents of the dam were less interested in preserving Hetch Hetchy as a wilderness than in developing it for tourism.) While the preservationists lost this battle, the controversy focused attention on environmental issues, as Americans for the first time weighed the aesthetic implications of a major public-works project.

Taft in the White House, 1909–1913   Roosevelt had pledged not to seek a third term, and as the 1908 election approached, the Republican Party's most conservative leaders regained control. They nominated TR's choice, Secretary of War **William Howard Taft,** for president but selected a conservative vice-presidential nominee and adopted a deeply conservative platform. The Democrats, meanwhile, nominated William Jennings Bryan for a third time. The Democratic platform called for a lower tariff, denounced the trusts, and embraced the cause of labor.

With Roosevelt's endorsement, Taft coasted to victory. But Bryan bested the Democrats' 1904 vote total by 1.3 million, and progressive Republican state candidates outran the national ticket. Overall, the outcome suggested a lull in the reform movement, not its end.

Republican conservatives welcomed Roosevelt's departure to hunt big game in Africa. Quipped Senator Aldrich, "Let every lion do its duty." But even an ocean away, TR's presence remained vivid. "When I am addressed as 'Mr. President,'" Taft wrote him, "I turn to see whether you are not at my elbow."

Taft, from a prominent Ohio political family, differed from TR in many respects. Whereas TR kept in fighting trim, Taft was obese. Roosevelt had installed a boxing ring in the White House; Taft preferred golf. TR loved speechmaking and battling evildoers; Taft disliked controversy. His happiest days would come later, as chief justice of the United States.

Pledged to support TR's program, Taft backed the Mann-Elkins Act (1910), which beefed up the Interstate Commerce Commission's regulatory authority and extended it to telephone and telegraph companies. Taft's administration actually prosecuted more antitrust cases than had Roosevelt's, but with little publicity. To the public, TR remained the mighty trustbuster.

The reform spotlight, meanwhile, shifted to Congress, where a group of reform-minded Republicans, nicknamed the Insurgents, including Senators La Follette and Albert Beveridge of Indiana and Congressman George Norris of Nebraska, had challenged their party's conservative congressional leadership. In 1909, the Insurgents and Taft fought a bruising battle over the tariff. Taft first backed the Insurgents' call for a lower tariff. But when high-tariff advocates in Congress pushed through a measure raising duties on hundreds of items, Taft not only signed it but praised it extravagantly, infuriating the Insurgents.

The Insurgents next set their sights on House Speaker Joseph G. Cannon of Illinois, a reactionary Republican who prevented most reform bills from even reaching a vote. In March 1910, the Insurgents joined with the Democrats to trim Cannon's power by removing him from the pivotal Rules Committee. This directly challenged Taft, who supported Cannon.

The so-called Ballinger-Pinchot controversy widened the rift. Taft's interior secretary, Richard Ballinger, was a Seattle lawyer who favored unregulated private development of natural resources. In one of several decisions galling to conservationists, Ballinger in 1909 approved the sale of several million acres of coal-rich public lands in Alaska to a Seattle business consortium that promptly resold it to J.P. Morgan and other financiers. When an Interior Department official protested, he was fired. In true muckraking style, he went public, blasting Ballinger in a *Collier's* magazine article. When Gifford Pinchot of the Forest Service also criticized Ballinger, he too got the ax. TR's supporters seethed.

Upon Roosevelt's return to America in June 1910, Pinchot met the boat. Openly breaking with Taft, Roosevelt campaigned for Insurgent candidates in that year's midterm elections. On August 31, in a speech at Osawatomie, Kansas, before a cheering throng of 30,000, Roosevelt borrowed a term from Herbert Croly's *The Promise of American Life,* and proposed a "New Nationalism" that would powerfully engage the federal government in reform. Declared the former president: "This new Nationalism regards the executive power as the steward of public welfare. It demands of the judiciary that it shall be interested primarily in human welfare rather than in property, just as it demands that the representative body shall represent all the people rather than any one class or section of the people." Particularly alarming conservatives, he endorsed the radical idea of reversing by popular vote judicial rulings that struck down reform laws favored by progressives.[1]

---

[1] More than a century later, in December 2011, President Barack Obama deliberately chose Osawatomie, with its echoes of Theodore Roosevelt's "New Nationalism" address, for a major speech outlining the themes of his 2012 presidential campaign.

The Yosemite Museum, Yosemite National Park

President Theodore Roosevelt and Friends Commune with Nature, 1903
*Dwarfed by an ancient sequoia, the Grizzly Giant, in the Mariposa Grove of California's
Yosemite National Park, TR's party includes California governor George Pardee (third from
left), the naturalist and Sierra Club founder John Muir (fourth from right) and the presidents
of Columbia University (third from right) and the University of California (far right). The Grizzly
Giant still stands and remains a favorite with tourists.*

The Democrats captured the House in 1910, a coalition of Democrats and
Insurgent Republicans controlled the Senate, and TR increasingly sounded like a
presidential candidate.

The Four-Way   In February 1912, Roosevelt announced his candidacy for
Election of 1912   the Republican nomination. But Taft wanted a second term.
                       Roosevelt generally walloped Taft in the Republican state
primaries and conventions. Taft controlled the party machinery, however, and the
Republican convention in Chicago disqualified many of Roosevelt's hard-won delegates. Outraged, TR's backers walked out and formed the **Progressive Party.** What
had been a general term for a broad reform movement now became the official
name of a political party. Riding an emotional high, the cheering delegates nominated their hero, with California senator Hiram Johnson as his running mate.

"I feel fit as a bull moose," Roosevelt trumpeted, giving his organization its
nickname, the Bull Moose Party. The convention platform endorsed most reform
causes of the day, including lower tariffs, woman suffrage, business regulation, the
abolition of child labor, the eight-hour workday, workers' compensation, the direct
primary, and the popular election of senators. The new party attracted a diverse
following, united mainly by affection for Roosevelt.

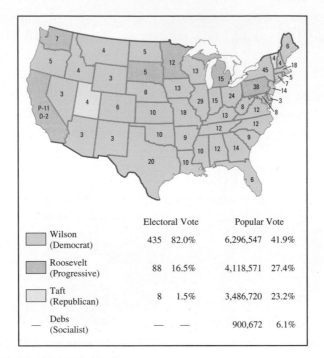

		Electoral Vote		Popular Vote	
▦	Wilson (Democrat)	435	82.0%	6,296,547	41.9%
▦	Roosevelt (Progressive)	88	16.5%	4,118,571	27.4%
▢	Taft (Republican)	8	1.5%	3,486,720	23.2%
—	Debs (Socialist)	—	—	900,672	6.1%

MAP 21.2 The Election of 1912

Meanwhile, the reform spirit had also infused the Democratic Party. In New Jersey in 1910, voters had elected a political novice, **Woodrow Wilson,** as governor. A "Wilson for President" boom soon arose, and at the Democratic convention in Baltimore, Wilson won the nomination, defeating several established party leaders.

In the campaign, Taft more or less gave up, satisfied to have denied Roosevelt the nomination and kept his party safe for conservatism. The Socialist candidate Eugene Debs proposed the "collective ownership and democratic control" of large industries, major financial institutions, and transportation and communications systems. The Socialist platform included many other reforms, some of which would later be realized, including woman suffrage, a shorter work week, a graduated income tax, and a federal "bureau of health." TR preached his New Nationalism: corporations must be regulated in the public interest, the welfare of workers and consumers safeguarded, and the environment protected.

Wilson, by contrast, called his political vision the "New Freedom." Warning that corporations were choking off opportunity for ordinary Americans, he nostalgically evoked an era of small government, small businesses, and free competition. "The history of liberty," he said, "is the history of the limitation of governmental power, not the increase of it."

Roosevelt outpolled Taft by 630,000 votes, but the Republicans' split proved costly. Wilson easily won the presidency, and the Democrats took both houses of Congress. More than 900,000 voters opted for Debs and socialism.

The 1912 election linked the Democrats firmly with reform (except on the issue of race)—a link that Franklin D. Roosevelt would strengthen in the 1930s. TR's third-party campaign demonstrated the continued appeal of reform among many grassroots Republicans. Debs's nearly 1 million votes, about 6 percent of the total, revealed socialism's appeal and the depths of discontent with the status quo, particularly among urban immigrant workers.

Several recent scholars have noted how the 1912 presidential contest anticipated future political trends. It involved party primaries, continuous campaigning, celebrity endorsements, and the new mass medium: film. TR's campaign, bypassing the party establishment, focused on his personal appeal and, targeting voters directly, in some ways foreshadowed the campaigns of Jimmy Carter in 1976 and Barack Obama in 2008 (see Chapters 29 and 31). In another modern touch, as the campaign unfolded, a sports event distracted public attention: the 1912 World Series, in which the Boston Red Sox narrowly edged out the New York Giants.

NATIONAL PROGRESSIVISM, PHASE II: WOODROW WILSON, 1913–1917

The son and grandson of Presbyterian ministers, Wilson grew up in Virginia and Georgia in a churchly atmosphere that shaped his oratorical style and moral outlook. Despite a learning disability (probably dyslexia), he graduated from Princeton and earned a Ph.D. in political science from Johns Hopkins University. Joining Princeton's faculty, he became its president in 1902. A rigid unwillingness to compromise cost him faculty support, and in 1910 Wilson resigned to enter politics. Three years later, he was president of the United States.

Impressive in bearing, with piercing gray eyes, Wilson was an eloquent orator. But the idealism that inspired people could also alienate them. At his best, he excelled at political deal-making. "He can walk on dead leaves and make no more noise than a tiger," declared one awed politician. But under pressure, he could retreat into a fortress of absolute certitude. As president, all these facets of his personality would come into play.

The progressive movement gained fresh momentum in Wilson's first term. Under his leadership, Congress enacted an array of reform measures. Despite the nostalgia for simpler times in his campaign rhetoric, he proved ready to address the problems of the new corporate order.

Tariff and Banking Reform   Lowering tariff rates—long a goal of southern and agrarian Democrats—headed Wilson's agenda. Many progressives agreed that high protective tariffs increased corporate profits at the public's expense. Breaking a precedent dating from Thomas Jefferson's presidency, Wilson appeared personally before Congress in April 1913 to read his tariff message. A low-tariff bill quickly passed the House but bogged down in the Senate. Showing his flair for drama, Wilson denounced the lobbyists flooding into Washington. His censure led to a Senate investigation of lobbyists and of senators who profited from high tariffs. Stung by the publicity, the Senate slashed tariff rates even more than the House had done. The Underwood-Simmons Tariff reduced rates an average of 15 percent.

Wilson again addressed Congress in June, this time calling for banking and currency reform. The nation's banking system clearly needed overhauling. Totally decentralized, it lacked a strong central institution, a "lender of last resort" to help banks survive fiscal crises. A financial panic in 1907, when many banks had failed, remained a vivid memory.

No consensus existed on specifics, however. Many reformers wanted a publicly controlled central banking system. But the nation's bankers, whose Senate spokesman was Nelson Aldrich, favored a privately controlled central bank similar to the Bank of England. The large banks of New York City advocated a strong central bank, preferably privately owned, so they could better compete with London banks in international finance. Others, including influential Virginia congressman Carter Glass, opposed any central banking authority, public or private.

No banking expert, Wilson did insist that the monetary system ultimately be publicly controlled. As the bargaining unfolded, Wilson's behind-the-scenes role proved crucial. The result was the **Federal Reserve Act** (1913). This compromise measure created twelve regional Federal Reserve banks under mixed public/private control. Each could issue U.S. dollars, called Federal Reserve notes, to the banks in its district to make loans to corporations and individual borrowers. Overall control of the system was shared by the heads of the twelve regional banks and the members of a Washington-based Federal Reserve Board, appointed by the president for fourteen-year terms.

The Federal Reserve Act stands as Wilson's greatest legislative achievement. Initially, the Federal Reserve Board's authority was diffuse, but eventually "the Fed" grew into the strong central monetary institution it remains today, setting interest rates and adopting fiscal policies to prevent financial panics, promote economic growth, and combat inflation.

Regulating Business; Aiding Workers and Farmers   In 1914, Wilson and Congress turned to that perennial progressive cause, business regulation. The two laws that resulted sought a common goal, but embodied different approaches.

The Federal Trade Commission Act took an administrative approach. This law created a new "watchdog" agency, the **Federal Trade Commission** (FTC), with power to investigate violations of federal regulations, require regular reports from corporations, and issue cease-and-desist orders (subject to judicial review) when it found unfair methods of competition.

The Clayton Antitrust Act, by contrast, took a legal approach. It listed corporate activities that could lead to federal lawsuits. The Sherman Act of 1890, although outlawing business practices in restraint of trade, had been vague about details. The Clayton Act spelled out specific illegal practices, such as selling at a loss to undercut competitors.

Because Wilson appointed some conservatives with big-business links to the FTC, this agency initially proved ineffective. But under the Clayton Act, the Wilson administration filed antitrust suits against nearly a hundred corporations.

Leading a party long identified with workers, Wilson supported labor unions and workers' right to organize. He also endorsed a Clayton Act clause exempting strikes, boycotts, and picketing from the antitrust laws' prohibition of actions in restraint of trade.

In 1916 (an election year), Wilson and congressional Democrats enacted three important worker-protection laws. The Keating-Owen Act barred from interstate commerce products manufactured by child labor. (This law was declared unconstitutional in 1918, as was a similar law enacted in 1919.) The Adamson Act established an eight-hour day for interstate railway workers. The Workmen's Compensation Act provided accident and injury protection to federal workers. As we have seen, however, Wilson's sympathies for the underdog stopped at the color line.

Other 1916 laws helped farmers. The Federal Farm Loan Act and the Federal Warehouse Act enabled farmers, using land or crops as collateral, to get low-interest federal loans. The Federal Highway Act, providing funds for highway programs, benefited not only the new automobile industry but also farmers plagued by bad roads.

Progressivism and the Constitution   The probusiness bias of the courts weakened a bit in the Progressive Era. In *Muller* v. *Oregon* (1908), the Supreme Court upheld an Oregon law limiting female laundry and factory workers to a ten-hour workday. Defending this law's constitutionality, Boston attorney **Louis Brandeis** not only cited legal precedent, but offered economic, medical, and sociological evidence documenting the ways long hours harmed women workers. While making an exception based on gender, the Court continued to hold (as it had in the 1905 case *Lochner* v. *New York*) that in general such worker-protection laws violated the due-process clause of the Fourteenth Amendment. Nevertheless, *Muller* v. *Oregon* marked an advance in making the legal system more responsive to new social realities.

In 1916, Woodrow Wilson nominated Brandeis to the Supreme Court. Disapproving of Brandeis's innovative approach to the law, the conservative American Bar Association protested, as did Republican congressional leaders and other prominent conservative voices. Anti-Semites opposed Brandeis because he was a Jew. But Wilson stood firm, and Brandeis won Senate confirmation.

These years also produced four Constitutional amendments, the first since 1870. The Sixteenth (ratified in 1913) empowered Congress to tax incomes, thus ending a long legal battle. A Civil War income tax had been phased out in 1872. Congress had again imposed an income tax as part of an 1894 tariff act, but the Supreme Court had promptly denounced it as "communistic" and ruled it unconstitutional. With the constitutional issue resolved, Congress in 1913 imposed a graduated federal income tax with a maximum rate of 7 percent on incomes greater than five hundred thousand dollars. Income-tax revenues helped pay for the government's expanded regulatory duties under various progressive reform measures.

The Seventeenth Amendment (1913) provided for the direct election of U.S. senators by the voters, rather than their selection by state legislatures, as described in Article I of the Constitution. This reform, earlier advocated by the Populists, sought to make the Senate less subject to corporate influence and more responsive to the popular will.

The Eighteenth Amendment (1919) prohibited the manufacture, sale, or importation of "intoxicating liquors." The Nineteenth (1920) granted women the vote. This remarkable wave of amendments underscored the Progressive Movement's profound impact on the political landscape.

1916: Wilson Edges Out Hughes

As Wilson won renomination in 1916, the Republicans turned to Charles Evans Hughes, a Supreme Court justice and former New York governor. Progressive Party loyalists again courted Theodore Roosevelt. But TR, now obsessed with the war in Europe (covered in the next chapter), told them to endorse Hughes, which they did, effectively removing the Progressive Party from the contest.

With the Republicans more or less reunited, the election was extremely close. War-related issues loomed large. Wilson won the popular vote, but the Electoral College outcome remained in doubt for several weeks as the California tally see-sawed back and forth. Ultimately, Wilson carried the state by fewer than four thousand votes and, with it, the election.

The progressive movement lost momentum as attention turned from reform to war. Final success for the prohibition and woman-suffrage campaigns came in 1919–1920, and Congress enacted a few reform measures in the 1920s. But, overall, the movement faded as America marched to war in 1917.

CHRONOLOGY
1900–1917

1900	International Ladies' Garment Workers' Union (ILGWU) founded.
	Socialist Party of America organized.
	Theodore Dreiser, *Sister Carrie*.
	Carrie Chapman Catt becomes president of the National American Woman Suffrage Association (NAWSA).
1901	Assassination of McKinley; Theodore Roosevelt becomes president.
	J.P. Morgan forms United States Steel Company.
1902	Jane Addams, *Democracy and Social Ethics*.
1903	W.E.B. Du Bois, *The Souls of Black Folk*.
	Wright brothers' flight.
1904	Theodore Roosevelt elected president in his own right.
	Lincoln Steffens, *The Shame of the Cities*.
1905	Industrial Workers of the World (IWW) organized.
1906	Upton Sinclair, *The Jungle*.
1907	William James, *Pragmatism*.
1908	William Howard Taft elected president. Model T Ford introduced.
1909	Ballinger-Pinchot controversy.
	National Association for the Advancement of Colored People (NAACP) founded.

	Herbert Croly, *The Promise of American Life.*
	Daniel Burnham, *Plan of Chicago.*
1910	Insurgents curb power of House Speaker Joseph Cannon.
1911	Triangle Shirtwaist Company fire.
1912	Republican Party split; Progressive (Bull Moose) Party founded.
	Woodrow Wilson elected president.
	International Opium Treaty.
1913	Sixteenth Amendment (Congress empowered to tax incomes).
	Seventeenth Amendment (direct election of U.S. senators).
1914	American Social Hygiene Association founded.
	Narcotics Act (Harrison Act).
1915	D.W. Griffith, *The Birth of a Nation.*
1916	John Dewey, *Democracy and Education.*
	Margaret Sanger opens nation's first birth-control clinic in Brooklyn, New York.
	National Park Service created.
	Louis Brandeis appointed to Supreme Court.
1919	Eighteenth Amendment (national prohibition).
1920	Nineteenth Amendment (woman suffrage).

CONCLUSION

What we call the progressive movement began as preachers, novelists, journalists, photographers, and painters highlighted appalling conditions in America's cities and factories. Intellectuals offered ideas for reform through the creative use of government.

At the local and state level, reform-minded politicians, together with a host of reform organizations, worked to combat political corruption, make cities safer and more beautiful, regulate corporations, and improve conditions for workers.

Progressivism had its coercive side. Some reformers concentrated on regulating urban amusements and banning alcohol consumption. Racism and hostility to immigrants are part of the progressive legacy as well.

Progressivism crested as a national movement under presidents Theodore Roosevelt and Woodrow Wilson. These years saw advances in corporate regulation, environmental conservation, banking reform, and consumer and worker protection. Constitutional amendments granted Congress the power to tax incomes and provided for the direct election of senators, woman suffrage, and national prohibition of alcohol—all aspects of the progressive impulse.

Along with specific laws, progressivism's legacy included an enlarged view of government's role in society. Progressives expanded the meaning of democracy and challenged the cynical view of government as a tool of the rich and powerful. They did not seek "big government" for its own sake. Rather, they recognized that in an industrial age of great cities and concentrated corporate power, government, too, must grow to serve the public interest and protect society's more vulnerable members.

This ideal sometimes faltered in practice. Reform laws and regulatory agencies often fell short of their purpose as bureaucratic routine set in. Reforms designed to promote the public good sometimes mainly benefited special interests. Corporations proved adept at manipulating the new regulatory state to their own advantage.

Still, the Progressive Era stands as a time when American politics seriously confronted the social upheavals caused by industrialization. It was also an era when Americans learned to think of government as an arena of possibility where public issues and social problems could be thrashed out. The next great reform movement, the New Deal of the 1930s, would build on progressivism's legacy while shedding its moralistic social-control features and broadening its white, native-born, Protestant, middle-class limitations.

22

GLOBAL INVOLVEMENTS AND
WORLD WAR I, 1902–1920

DEFINING AMERICA'S WORLD ROLE, 1902–1914

The annexation of Hawaii, the Spanish-American War, the occupation of the Philippines, and other developments in the 1890s (see Chapter 20) reflected a desire to assert American power as European nations built colonial empires; to protect and extend U.S. business investments abroad, especially in Asia and Latin America; and to impose American standards of good government beyond the nation's borders. This process continued after 1900.

Both economic and ideological considerations shaped America's dealings with Asian and Latin American nations in these years. U.S. policymakers wanted to expand corporate America's access to foreign markets and raw materials. But they also believed that other societies would benefit by adopting the principles of democracy, individual freedom, and the rule of law. Sometimes economic motives predominated, sometimes ideological, and often both.

The "Open Door": Competing for the China Market As the U.S. campaign to suppress the Philippines insurrection dragged on, the China market beckoned. Proclaimed Indiana senator Albert J. Beveridge in 1898, "American factories are making more than the American people can use; American soil is producing more than they can consume ... [T]he trade of the world must and shall be ours."

Textile producers dreamed of clothing China's millions; investors envisioned railroad construction. As China's 250-year-old Manchu Qing empire faltered, U.S. business people watched carefully. In 1896, a consortium of New York capitalists formed a company to promote trade and railroad investment in China.

But other nations were also eyeing the China market. Some pressured the weak Manchu rulers to give them exclusive trading and development rights in designated regions, or "spheres of influence." In 1896, Russia won both the right to build a railway across the Chinese province of Manchuria and a long-term lease on much of the region. In 1897, Germany secured a ninety-nine-year lease on a Chinese port as well as mining and railroad rights in the adjacent province. The British won concessions as well.

In 1899, U.S. Secretary of State John Hay asked the major European powers to ensure American trading rights in China by opening the ports in their spheres of influence to all countries. The nations gave noncommittal answers, but Hay blithely announced their acceptance of the principle of an "Open Door" to American business in China.

Hay's Open Door note showed how commercial considerations were increasingly influencing American foreign policy. It reflected a form of economic expansionism historians have called "informal empire." The U.S. government did not seek Chinese territory, but it did want access to Chinese markets for American businesses.

As Hay pursued this effort, a more urgent threat emerged. For years, antiforeign feeling had simmered in China, fanned by the aged Qing Dynasty empress, who hated the West's growing influence. In 1899, an antiforeign secret society known as the Harmonious Righteous Fists (called "Boxers" by Western journalists) killed thousands of foreigners and Chinese Christians. In June 1900, the Boxers occupied Beijing (Peking), the Chinese capital, and besieged the foreign legations. Twenty-five hundred U.S. soldiers joined an international army that marched on Beijing, quashed the **Boxer Rebellion,** and rescued the threatened legations.

The Boxers' defeat further weakened China's government. Fearing that the regime's collapse would allow European powers to carve up China, Hay issued a second, more important, series of **Open Door notes** in 1900. He reaffirmed the principle of open trade in China for all nations and announced America's determination to preserve China's territorial and administrative integrity. In the 1930s, when Japanese expansionism menaced China, Hay's policy helped shape the American response.

Along with U.S. economic expansion in China came missionary activity. American Protestant missionaries had come to Hawaii in the 1820s, and by 1900 some five thousand U.S. missionaries were active in China, Africa, India, and elsewhere. While proclaiming their religious message, the missionaries also blazed the way for U.S. economic expansion. As a U.S. diplomat in China wrote in 1895: "Missionaries are the pioneers for American trade and commerce.... The missionary, inspired by holy zeal, goes everywhere, and by degrees foreign trade and commerce follow."

The Panama Canal: Hardball Diplomacy   Traders had long dreamed of a canal across the forty-mile-wide ribbon of land joining North and South America to eliminate the hazardous voyage around South America. In 1879, a French company secured permission from Colombia to build a canal across Panama, then part of Colombia. But mismanagement and

Theodore Roosevelt Collection, Harvard College Library

TR Visits the Panama Canal Construction Site, 1906 *President Theodore Roosevelt played a key role in securing the strip of land on which the canal was built. Here, he proudly poses in a steam shovel used in the construction project.*

yellow fever doomed the project, and by 1888 it was bankrupt. Seeking to recoup its losses, the French company offered its assets, including the concession from Colombia, to the United States for $109 million.

America was in an expansionist mood. In 1902, after the French lowered their price to $40 million, Congress authorized President Theodore Roosevelt to accept the offer. The following year, Secretary of State Hay signed an agreement with a Colombian diplomat granting the United States a ninety-nine-year lease on the proposed canal for a down payment of $10 million and an annual fee of $250,000. But the Colombian senate, seeking a better deal, rejected the agreement. An outraged Roosevelt privately denounced the Colombians as "greedy little anthropoids."

Determined to have his canal, Roosevelt found a willing collaborator in Philippe Bunau-Varilla, an official of the bankrupt French company. Dismayed that his company might lose its $40 million, Bunau-Varilla organized a

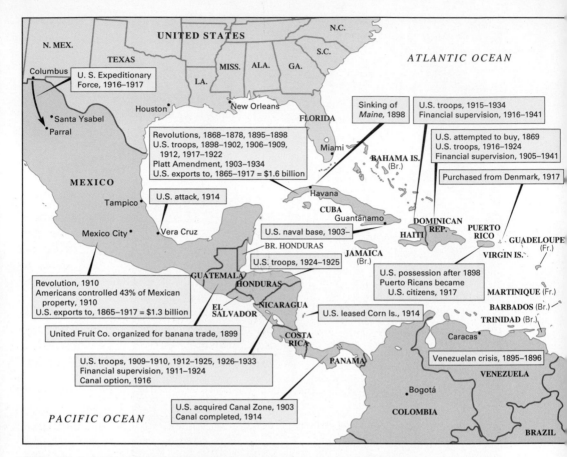

MAP 22.1   U.S. Hegemony in the Caribbean and Latin America, 1900–1941

Through many interventions, territorial acquisitions, and robust economic expansion, the United States became the predominant power in Latin America in the early twentieth century. Acting on Theodore Roosevelt's assertion of a U.S. right to combat "wrongdoing" in Latin America and the Caribbean, the United States dispatched troops to the region, where they met nationalist opposition.

Source: © Cengage Learning. All rights reserved. No distribution allowed without express authorization.

"revolution" in Panama from a New York hotel room. While his wife stitched a flag, he wrote a declaration of independence and a constitution for the new nation. When the "revolution" occurred as scheduled on November 3, 1903, a U.S. warship hovered offshore. Proclaiming Panama's independence, Bunau-Varilla appointed himself its first ambassador to the United States. John Hay quickly recognized the newly hatched nation and signed a treaty with Bunau-Varilla granting the United States a ten-mile-wide strip of land across Panama "in perpetuity" (that is, forever) on the terms earlier rejected by Colombia. Theodore Roosevelt later summed up the episode: "I took the Canal Zone, and let Congress debate, and while the debate goes on, the canal does also."

The U.S. canal builders' first challenge was the yellow fever that had haunted the French. Dr. Walter Reed of the Army Medical Corps led this effort. Earlier, in

Cuba, Reed had used volunteer U.S. experimental subjects (including himself) to prove that mosquitoes breeding in stagnant water spread the yellow fever virus. In Panama, Reed's drainage projects eradicated the disease-bearing mosquito—a remarkable public-health achievement. Construction began in 1906, and in 1914 the first ship sailed through the **Panama Canal.** In 1921, implicitly conceding the dubious methods used to acquire the Canal Zone, the U.S. Senate voted a payment of $25 million to Colombia. But the ill feeling generated by Theodore Roosevelt's actions, combined with other instances of U.S. interventionism, would long shadow U.S.-Latin American relations.

Roosevelt and Taft Assert U.S. Power in Latin America and Asia   Other, less-familiar episodes further underscored Washington's growing readiness to assert U.S. power and protect U.S. business interests in Latin America and Asia. In 1902, German, British, and Italian warships blockaded and bombarded the ports of Venezuela, which had defaulted on its debts to European investors. The standoff ended when President Theodore Roosevelt pressed all sides to settle the dispute through arbitration.

A second crisis flared in 1904 when several European nations threatened to invade the Dominican Republic, a Caribbean island nation that had also defaulted on its debts. Roosevelt reacted swiftly. If any nation intervened, he believed, it should be the United States. "Chronic wrongdoing" by any Latin American nation, he declared that December, would justify U.S. intervention.

This pronouncement has been called "the Roosevelt Corollary" to the 1823 Monroe Doctrine, which had warned European powers against meddling in Latin America. Now Roosevelt asserted that "wrongdoing" (a word he left undefined) gave the United States the right to step in. Suiting actions to words, the Roosevelt administration took over the Dominican Republic's customs service for two years and managed its foreign debt. Roosevelt once summed up his foreign-policy approach by quoting what he said was an African proverb, "Speak softly and carry a big stick."

The foreign policy of the Taft administration (1909–1913) focused on advancing American commercial interests, a policy some called "dollar diplomacy." A U.S.-backed revolution in mineral-rich Nicaragua in 1911 brought to power Adolfo Díaz, an officer of an American corporation that controlled several Nicaraguan gold mines. Washington, fearing growing British influence in Nicaragua, also worried that Germany or Japan might build a canal across Nicaragua to rival the Panama Canal. American bankers lent Díaz's government $1.5 million, in exchange for control of Nicaragua's national bank, customs service, and railroad. When a revolt against Díaz broke out in 1912, Taft sent marines to protect the bankers' investment. Except for one brief interval, they remained until 1933. Overall, these early twentieth-century U.S. involvements in Latin America served America's expanding corporate interests and warned off other foreign powers, while planting the seeds of future hostility and resentments.

In Asia, too, Roosevelt and Taft sought to project U.S. power and advance American business interests. In 1900, exploiting the turmoil caused by the Boxer uprising, Russia occupied Manchuria and began building railroads. This alarmed the Japanese, who also had designs on Manchuria and nearby Korea. Japan and

Russia went to war in 1904 after a surprise Japanese attack destroyed Russian ships in a Manchurian port. As Japan completely dominated Russia, an Asian power for the first time checked Western imperialist expansion.

Roosevelt, while pleased to see Russian expansionism challenged, believed that a Japanese victory would disrupt the Asian balance of power and threaten America's position in the Philippines. Accordingly, he invited Japan and Russia to a peace conference at Portsmouth, New Hampshire. In September 1905, the two rivals signed a peace treaty. Russia recognized Japan's rule in Korea and made other territorial concessions. After this outcome, curbing Japanese expansionism—peacefully, if possible—became America's major objective in Asia. For his role in ending the war, Roosevelt received the Nobel Peace Prize.

In 1906, U.S.-Japanese relations soured when the San Francisco school board assigned all Asian children to segregated schools. When Japan angrily protested, Roosevelt summoned the school board to Washington and persuaded them to reverse this discriminatory policy. In return, in 1908 the administration negotiated a "gentlemen's agreement" with Japan by which Tokyo voluntarily halted Japanese emigration to America. Racist attitudes and discriminatory laws against Japanese in California continued to poison U.S.-Japanese relations, however.

While Californians warned of the "yellow peril," Japanese journalists, eyeing America's military strength and involvement in Asia, spoke of a "white peril." In 1907, Roosevelt ordered sixteen gleaming U.S. battleships on a "training operation" to Japan. Although officially friendly in intent, this "Great White Fleet" underscored America's naval might.

President Taft's policies in Asia extended the focus on dollar diplomacy, which in this case meant promoting U.S. commercial interests in China—the goal Secretary of State Hay had sought with his Open Door notes. A plan for a U.S.-financed railroad in Manchuria failed, however. Not only did U.S. bankers find the project too risky, but Russia and Japan signed a treaty carving up Manchuria for commercial purposes, freezing out the Americans.

Wilson and Latin America   Taking office in 1913, Woodrow Wilson criticized his Republican predecessors' expansionist policies. The United States, he pledged, would "never again seek one additional foot of territory by conquest." But he, too, soon intervened in Latin America. In 1915, after upheavals in Haiti and the Dominican Republic (two small nations sharing the Caribbean island of Santo Domingo), Wilson sent in U.S. marines, who brutally suppressed Haitians who resisted. A Haitian constitution favorable to U.S. commercial interests was overwhelmingly ratified in a 1918 vote supervised by the marines. The marines occupied the Dominican Republic until 1924 and Haiti until 1934.

Events in Mexico triggered Wilson's most serious crisis in Latin America. Mexico had won independence from Spain in 1820, but the nation remained divided between a landowning elite and an impoverished peasantry. In 1911, rebels led by the democratic reformer Francisco Madero had ended the thirty-year rule of President Porfirio Díaz, a defender of the wealthy elite. Early in 1913, just as Wilson took office, Mexican troops loyal to General Victoriano Huerta, a full-blooded Indian, overthrew and murdered Madero.

Wilson's response focused on protecting the forty thousand U.S. citizens who had settled in Mexico under Díaz's regime and safeguarding the U.S. investors who had poured some $2 billion into Mexican oil wells and other ventures. Reversing the long-standing U.S. practice of recognizing all governments, Wilson refused to recognize Huerta's "government of butchers." Authorizing arms sales to General Venustiano Carranza, Huerta's rival, Wilson ordered the port of Veracruz blockaded to prevent a shipment of German arms from reaching Huerta. Announced Wilson: "I am going to teach the South American republics to elect good men." In April 1914, seven thousand U.S. troops occupied Veracruz and battled Huerta's forces. Sixty-five Americans and approximately five hundred Mexicans were killed or wounded. Bowing to U.S. might, Huerta abdicated; Carranza took power; and the troops withdrew.

But turmoil continued. In January 1916, a bandit chieftain in northern Mexico, Pancho Villa, murdered sixteen U.S. mining engineers. Soon after, Villa's gang burned the town of Columbus, New Mexico, and killed nineteen inhabitants. Enraged Americans demanded action. Wilson dispatched a punitive expedition under General **John J. Pershing.** When Villa eluded Pershing and brazenly staged another cross-border raid into Texas, Wilson ordered 150,000 National Guardsmen to the border— a massive response that stirred anti-American feelings among Mexico's poor, for whom Villa was a folk hero. Villa ended his raids in 1920 when the Mexican government gave him a large land grant, but he was soon assassinated.

These involvements in Asia and Latin America illuminate the basic U.S. foreign-policy goal: to achieve a global order that would embrace American political values and welcome American business. These goals reflected the worldview of the white, male, native-born foreign-policy elite. Confident of their ethnic, gender, and class status, they promoted U.S. political and corporate interests abroad, while viewing with patronizing condescension the "backward" peoples they encountered in the process.

Meanwhile, a crisis unfolding in Europe challenged Wilson's dream of an American-based world order.

WAR IN EUROPE, 1914–1917

When war engulfed Europe in 1914, most Americans wished only to remain aloof, and President Wilson proclaimed U.S. neutrality. But by April 1917, economic considerations, cultural ties, visions of a world remade in America's image, and German violations of Wilson's definition of neutral rights all combined to suck America into the maelstrom.

The Coming of War Although western Europe was at peace through much of the nineteenth century, a series of ominous developments raised warning flags. In a short, sharp war in 1870–1871, an alliance of German states handed France a humiliating defeat. In the aftermath, Germany emerged as a powerful united nation ruled by Kaiser Wilhelm II. With many Germans convinced that Germany had lagged in the race for empire, Berlin pursued modernization, expansion, and military power. Germany, Austria-Hungary, and Italy signed a military-defense treaty in 1882. France, Great Britain, and Russia signed similar treaties in 1904 and 1907.

Meanwhile, the once-powerful Ottoman Empire, centered in Turkey, was weakening, leaving in its wake such newly independent nations as Romania, Bulgaria, and Serbia. Serbian patriots dreamed of expanding their boundaries to include Serbs living in neighboring Bosnia-Herzegovina. Serbia's ally Russia supported these ambitions. The Austro-Hungarian empire, based in Vienna, had other ideas. In 1908, Austria-Hungary annexed (took over) Bosnia-Herzegovina, alarming Russia and Serbia.

In this volatile atmosphere, Archduke Franz Ferdinand of Austria visited Bosnia's capital, Sarajevo, in June 1914. As Ferdinand and his wife rode in an open car, a young Bosnian Serb gunned them down. This act pushed a continent already poised for war over the precipice. Austria declared war on Serbia. Russia, aligned with Serbia by a secret treaty, mobilized for war. Austria's ally Germany declared war on Russia and France. Great Britain, linked by treaty to Russia and France, declared war on Germany.

Thus began what contemporaries called the Great War, now known as World War I. On one side were Great Britain, Russia, and France, called the Allies. On the other were the Central Powers: Germany and Austria-Hungary. (Italy, despite its alliance with the Central Powers, joined the Allies in 1915.)

The Perils of Neutrality President Wilson urged Americans to remain neutral "in thought as well as in action." Most citizens fervently agreed. A popular song summed up the mood: "I Didn't Raise My Boy to Be a Soldier." Carrie Chapman Catt and other feminists joined Jane Addams in forming the Woman's Peace Party. In New York City, fifteen hundred women marched to protest the war.

Neutrality proved difficult, however. Many Americans had ancestral ties to England. Schoolbooks stressed the English origins of American institutions. The English language itself—the language of Shakespeare, Dickens, and the King James Bible—deepened the bond. British propaganda subtly stressed such links.

Many German Americans, by contrast, sympathized with Germany, as did some Scandinavian immigrants. Irish Americans speculated that a German victory might free Ireland from British rule. Despite these cultural and ethnic cross-currents, however, most Americans initially supported Wilson's commitment to neutrality.

Yet in 1917, America went to war. What caused this turnabout? Fundamentally, Wilson's vision of a peaceful, democratic, and capitalist world order conflicted with his neutrality. Such an international system would be impossible, he believed, if Germany won the war. Even an Allied victory would not ensure a transformed world order, Wilson became convinced, without a U.S. role in the postwar settlement. To shape the peace, America must fight the war.

These underlying ideas influenced Wilson's handling of the war's most troubling immediate challenge: neutral nations' rights. When the war began, Britain intercepted U.S. merchant ships bound for Germany, insisting that their cargo might aid Germany's war effort. Wilson protested, especially when Britain, exploiting its naval advantage, declared the North Sea a war zone; planted it with explosive mines; and blockaded all German ports, choking off Germany's imports, including food.

But Germany, not England, ultimately pushed the United States into war. If Britannia ruled the waves, Germany controlled the ocean depths with its torpedo-equipped submarines, or U-boats. In February 1915, Berlin proclaimed the waters around Great Britain a war zone and warned off all ships. Wilson quickly responded: Germany would be held to "strict accountability" for any loss of U.S. vessels or lives.

On May 1, 1915, in a small ad in U.S. newspapers, the German embassy cautioned Americans against travel on British or French vessels. Six days later, a U-boat sank the British liner *Lusitania* off Ireland, killing 1,198 people, including 128 Americans. (The *Lusitania,* historians later discovered, was secretly carrying munitions destined for England.)

In three stern notes to Germany, Wilson demanded that Berlin stop unrestricted submarine warfare and pay reparations for the U.S. deaths in the *Lusitania* sinking. Publicly, he insisted that the United States could persuade the belligerents to recognize the principle of neutral rights without going to war. "There is such a thing as a man being too proud to fight," he said.

The *Lusitania* disaster exposed deep divisions in U.S. public opinion. Many Americans, now ready for war, ridiculed Wilson's "too proud to fight" speech. Theodore Roosevelt denounced the president's "abject cowardice." The National Security League, a lobby of bankers and industrialists, promoted stepped-up U.S. arms production and organized "preparedness" parades in major cities. By late 1915, Wilson himself called for a military buildup.

Lurid British propaganda (much of it false or exaggerated) screamed of atrocities committed by "the Huns" (a derogatory term for Germans). Intercepted German messages relating to espionage in U.S. factories further discredited the German cause.

Others, however, deplored the drift toward war. Some progressives warned that war fever was eroding support for reforms. The war, Jane Addams lamented, had destroyed the international movements to reduce infant mortality and improve care for the aged. Late in 1915, automaker Henry Ford chartered a vessel to take a group of pacifists to Scandinavia to persuade the belligerents to end the war by Christmas.

Divisions surfaced even within the Wilson administration. Secretary of State William Jennings Bryan, believing Wilson's *Lusitania* notes too hostile, resigned in June 1915. Under Bryan's weak successor, Robert Lansing, Wilson himself shaped U.S. policy.

Early in 1916, some Congressmen, seeking to avoid more *Lusitania*-type crises, introduced a bill to ban Americans from sailing on belligerents' ships. President Wilson successfully opposed it, however, insisting that the principle of neutral rights must be upheld.

For a time, Wilson's conciliatory approach seemed to work. Germany ordered its U-boats to spare passenger ships and offered compensation for the Americans lost in the *Lusitania* sinking. In March 1916, however, a U-boat sank a French passenger ship in the English Channel, injuring several Americans. When Wilson threatened to break diplomatic relations—a step toward war—Berlin pledged not to attack merchant vessels without warning, provided that Great Britain, too, observed "the rules of international law." Ignoring this qualification, Wilson announced Germany's acceptance of American demands, and the crisis eased.

The Granger Collection, NYC

The Sinking of the Cunard Liner *Lusitania*, May 7, 1915, Off the Irish Coast
The destruction of the Lusitania *by a German U-boat, portrayed here in an illustration from
an English newspaper, took nearly 1,200 lives, including 128 Americans. This event outraged
U.S. public opinion and led to a build-up in military preparedness. But as President Wilson
pursued diplomatic exchanges with Germany, nearly two more years would pass before the
United States entered the war.*

Meanwhile, U.S. banks' support for the Allies eroded the principle of neutrality.
Early in the war, Secretary of State Bryan had rejected banker J.P. Morgan's request
to extend loans to France. Such loans, said Bryan, would violate "the true spirit of
neutrality." But economic considerations undermined this policy. In August
1915, Treasury Secretary William G. McAdoo warned Wilson that Allied purchases
of American munitions and farm products were essential "[t]o maintain our
prosperity." Only substantial loans to England, agreed Secretary of State Lansing,
could prevent serious domestic economic problems, including "unrest ... among the
laboring classes." The neutrality principle must not "stand in the way of our national
interests," warned Lansing.

Swayed by such arguments and personally sympathetic to the Allies, Wilson
permitted Morgan's bank to lend $500 million to the British and French govern-
ments. By April 1917, U.S. banks had lent the Allies $2.3 billion, in contrast to
$27 million to Germany.

The land war, meanwhile, had settled into a grim stalemate. A September 1914
German drive into France bogged down along the Marne River. The two sides then
dug in, constructing trenches across France from the English Channel to the Swiss
border. For more than three years, this line scarcely changed. A German offensive
in February 1916 began with the capture of two forts near the town of Verdun and
ended that June when the French recaptured the same two forts, now nothing but
rubble, at a horrendous cost in human life. Trench warfare became a nightmare of
mud, rats, artillery bursts, and random death.

The war dominated the 1916 presidential election, which pitted Wilson against Republican Charles Evans Hughes, a former New York governor. Somewhat confusingly, Hughes criticized Wilson's lack of aggressiveness while rebuking him for policies that risked war. Theodore Roosevelt campaigned more for war than for the Republican ticket. The only difference between Wilson and the bearded Hughes, Roosevelt jeered, was a shave. While Hughes did well among Irish Americans and German Americans, Wilson eked out a narrow victory, aided by women voters in western states that had adopted woman suffrage. The Democrats' winning campaign slogan, "He kept us out of war," revealed the strength of popular peace sentiment as late as November 1916.

The United States Enters the War   In February 1917, Germany resumed unrestricted submarine warfare. Even if the United States declared war as a result, German strategists believed, the U-boat campaign could bring victory before American troops reached the front.

Events now rushed forward. Wilson broke diplomatic relations on February 3. During February and March, U-boats sank five American ships. A coded telegram from German foreign secretary Arthur Zimmermann to Germany's ambassador to Mexico, intercepted by the British, promised that if Mexico declared war on the United States, Germany would help restore Mexico's "lost territories" of Texas, Arizona, and New Mexico. The "Zimmermann telegram" further inflamed the war spirit in America.

Events in Russia also helped create favorable conditions for America's entry into the war. In March 1917, Russian peasants, industrial workers, intellectuals inspired by Western liberal values, and communist revolutionaries joined in an uprising that overthrew the country's repressive czarist government. A provisional government under the liberal Alexander Kerensky briefly seemed to promise a democratic Russia, making it easier for President Wilson to portray the war as a battle for democracy.

On April 2, before a joint session of Congress, Wilson called for a declaration of war. Applause rang out as Wilson described his vision of America's role in creating a postwar international order to make the world "safe for democracy." After a short debate, the Senate voted 82 to 6 for war. The House agreed, 373 to 50. German violation of U.S. neutrality, reinforced by American ideological commitments, cultural affinities, and economic considerations had propelled the nation into the war. British propaganda and the "preparedness" campaign mounted by U.S. financial and corporate interests had played a role as well.

MOBILIZING AT HOME, FIGHTING IN FRANCE, 1917–1918

Compared to its effects on Europe, the war only grazed America. Russia suffered heavily. France, Great Britain, and Germany fought for more than four years; the United States, for nineteen months. Their armies suffered casualties of 70 percent or more; the U.S. casualty rate was 8 percent. The fighting left parts of France and Belgium brutally scarred; North America was physically untouched. Nevertheless, the war profoundly affected America. It changed not only those who participated in it directly but also the home front and the nation's government and economy.

Raising, Training, and Testing an Army   April 1917 found America's military woefully unprepared. The regular army consisted of 120,000 men, few with combat experience, and an aging officer corps, plus eighty thousand National Guard members. Ammunition reserves were paltry. The War Department was a jungle of jealous bureaucrats, one of whom hoarded thousands of typewriters as the war approached.

While army chief-of-staff Peyton C. March brought order to the bureaucracy, Wilson's secretary of war, Newton D. Baker, a former mayor of Cleveland, concentrated on raising an army. The **Selective Service Act** of May 1917 required all men between twenty-one and thirty (later expanded to eighteen through forty-five) to register with local draft boards. Mindful of the Civil War draft riots, Baker planned the draft-registration day, June 5, 1917, as a "festive and patriotic occasion."

By the war's end, more than 24 million men had registered, of whom nearly 3 million were drafted. Volunteers and National Guardsmen swelled the total to 4.3 million. Training camps gave combat instruction and introduced recruits to military discipline. Volunteer organizations built morale through shows, games, and recreational activities. The American Library Association contributed books. YMCA volunteers offered classes in literacy, French slang, and Bible study. Women volunteers in communities near military camps opened "Hostess Houses" to give homesick recruits a touch of domesticity.

The War Department closely monitored recruits' off-duty behavior. The **Commission on Training Camp Activities** presented films, lectures, and posters on the dangers of alcohol and prostitution. Any soldier disabled by venereal (sexually transmitted) disease, one poster warned, "is a Traitor!" Officers confined trainees to camp until nearby towns closed brothels and saloons.

Recruits also underwent intelligence testing. Psychologists eager to demonstrate the usefulness of their new field claimed that measuring recruits' "intelligence quotient" (IQ) could help win the war by identifying potential officers and those qualified for more specialized assignments.

When many recruits received very low scores, editorial writers reacted with alarm. In fact, the results mostly revealed recruits' lack of formal education and the tests' cultural biases. One question asked whether *mauve* was a drink, a color, a fabric, or a food. The testing also reinforced racial and ethnic stereotypes: native-born recruits of northern European origins scored highest, African Americans and recent immigrants lowest.

In short, the training camps not only turned civilians into soldiers but also reinforced the Progressive Era's moral-control campaigns (see Chapter 21) and signaled changes ahead, including a vogue for standardized testing.

Some twelve thousand Native Americans served in the **American Expeditionary Force** (AEF). While some reformers eager to preserve Indian culture argued for all-Indian units, military officials integrated Native Americans into the general army. The wartime experience, some observers predicted, would hasten Indians' assimilation into mainstream American life.

Some blacks resisted the draft, especially in the South (as discussed later in this chapter), but most followed W.E.B. Du Bois's advice urging African Americans to "close ranks" and support the war. More than 260,000 blacks volunteered or were drafted, and some 50,000 went to France. Racism pervaded the military, as it did

American society. The navy assigned blacks only to menial positions, and the marines excluded them altogether.

Black troops in some camps endured abuse. One racist senator from Mississippi warned that the sight of "arrogant, strutting" black soldiers would trigger race riots. Tensions exploded in Houston in August 1917 when black soldiers stationed at nearby Camp Logan, goaded by abuse, seized weapons, marched into town, and fatally shot sixteen whites. After court-martial trials, nineteen black soldiers were hanged and sixty-one sentenced to life imprisonment.

Organizing the Economy for War   World War I helped shape modern America. The war furthered such key later developments as an expanded government role in the economy; the growth of new professional and managerial elites; and the spread of mass production, corporate consolidation, and product standardization.

The war led to unprecedented government economic oversight and corporate regulation, long advocated by Populists and progressives. In 1916, Congress created an advisory body, the Council of National Defense, to oversee the government's military preparedness program. After war was declared, this council set up the **War Industries Board** (WIB) to coordinate military purchasing and ensure production efficiency. President Wilson reorganized the WIB in March 1918 and put the Wall Street financier Bernard Baruch in charge. Under Baruch, the WIB allocated raw materials, established production priorities, and induced competing companies to standardize and coordinate their products and processes to save scarce commodities.

With congressional authorization, Wilson set up two more new agencies, the Fuel Administration and the Food Administration. The Fuel Administration controlled coal output, regulated fuel prices and consumption, and introduced daylight-saving time— an idea first proposed by Benjamin Franklin. The Food Administration, headed by Herbert Hoover, oversaw the production and allocation of wheat, meat, and sugar to ensure supplies for the army as well as for the desperately food-short Allies. Born in poverty in Iowa, Hoover had prospered as a mining engineer in Asia. He was organizing food relief in Belgium when Wilson brought him back to Washington.

These agencies relied on voluntary cooperation, reinforced by government propaganda. Food Administration posters and ads urged Americans to conserve food. Housewives signed pledges to observe "Meatless Monday" and "Wheatless Wednesday." Slogans such as "Serve Beans by All Means" promoted substitutes for scarce commodities.

Harriot Stanton Blatch, daughter of woman's rights pioneer Elizabeth Cady Stanton, headed the Food Administration's Speakers' Bureau, which spread the administration's conservation message. Blatch also organized the Woman's Land Army, which recruited women to replace male farm workers.

In all, nearly five thousand government boards supervised home-front activities. These included the National War Labor Board, which resolved labor-management disputes that jeopardized production, and the Railroad Administration, headed by Treasury Secretary William McAdoo. When a railroad tie-up during the winter of 1917–1918 threatened the flow of supplies to Europe, the Railroad Administration stepped in and soon transformed the thousands of miles of track operated by competing companies into an efficient national system.

American business, much criticized by progressive reformers, utilized the war emergency to improve its image. Corporate executives ran regulatory agencies. Factory owners distributed prowar propaganda to workers. Trade associations coordinated war production.

The war hastened the process of corporate consolidation and economic integration. In place of trustbusting, the government now encouraged cooperation and mergers among businesses. "Instead of punishing companies for acting in concert," one magazine observed, "the government is now in some cases forcing them to unite."

Overall, the war was good for business. Despite wartime tax increases, profits soared. After-tax profits in the copper industry, for example, jumped from 12 percent in 1913 to 24 percent in 1917.

The old laissez-faire suspicion of government, already weakened, eroded further in 1917–1918. The wartime regulatory agencies disappeared quickly after the war, but their influence lingered. In the 1930s, when the nation faced a different crisis, the government activism of World War I would be remembered (as discussed in Chapter 24).

With the American Expeditionary Force in France
As the U.S. military mobilized for combat, Allied prospects looked bleak. German U-boats were battering Allied shipping. French troops mutinied in the spring of 1917 after suffering ghastly casualties. Later that year, the Italian army suffered a disastrous defeat at Caporetto near the Austrian border, and a British offensive along the French-Belgian border gained only four miles at a cost of many thousands killed and wounded. A breakthrough in military technology came in November 1917 when the British mobilized three hundred tanks along a six-mile section of the front near Cambrai, France, shattering the German defenses. Still the stalemate continued.

Russia, ill-prepared for war, had suffered devastating setbacks as well, contributing to the revolutionary upheaval. The communist faction of the revolution, the Bolsheviks (Russian for "majority"), gained strength when its top leaders, including Vladimir Lenin and Leon Trotsky, returned from exile abroad. On November 6, 1917 (October 24 by the Russian calendar), a Bolshevik coup overthrew Alexander Kerensky's provisional government and effectively removed Russia from the war. Early in 1918, the Bolsheviks signed an armistice with Germany, the Treaty of Brest-Litovsk, freeing thousands of German troops on the Russian front for fighting in France.

In these desperate circumstances, U.S. aid to the Allies initially consisted of munitions and convoys to protect Allied ships. The first U.S. troops, designated as the Allied Expeditionary Force (AEF), reached France in October 1917. Eventually about 2 million American soldiers served in France under General John J. Pershing. A West Point graduate and commander of the 1916 expedition against Pancho Villa, Pershing was an iron-willed officer with a ramrod bearing, steely eyes, and trim mustache. The death of his wife and three of their children in a fire in 1915 had further hardened him. (Ironically, Pershing was of German origin; his family name had been Pfoersching.)

Most men of the AEF at first found the war a great adventure. Plucked from towns and farms, they sailed for Europe on crowded freighters or, for a lucky few, captured German passenger liners. Once in France, railroad freight cars marked "HOMMES 40, CHEVAUX 8" (forty men, eight horses) took them to the front. Then began the routine of marching, training—and waiting.

The African Americans with the AEF worked mainly as mess-boys (mealtime aides), laborers, and stevedores (ship-cargo handlers). Although discriminatory, the latter assignments vitally aided the war effort. Sometimes working twenty-four hours nonstop, black stevedores efficiently unloaded supply ships. Some whites of the AEF pressed the French to treat African Americans as inferiors, but most ignored this advice and related to blacks without prejudice. This eye-opening experience would remain with black veterans after the war.

While most African American troops served behind the front lines, regiments of the all-black 92nd and 93rd infantry divisions saw action under French command in the Second Battle of the Marne and the Meuse-Argonne campaign near the war's end. France awarded the Croix de Guerre, a military honor, to the entire 369th infantry regiment, nicknamed the "Harlem Hellfighters," and gave several hundred black U.S. soldiers individual decorations for bravery. German propaganda leaflets described U.S. racism and urged African American soldiers to defect, but none did. Only in death was the AEF integrated, however: graves in military cemeteries were not racially segregated.

In the air, a scant fifteen years after the Wright brothers' first flight, German and Allied planes dropped bombs, reported on troop movements, and engaged in deadly aerial dogfights. Germany's legendary "Red Baron," Manfred von Richthofen, downed eighty Allied planes before his luck ran out in April 1918. As early as 1916, American volunteers joined a French air unit known as the Lafayette Escadrille (squadron). The U.S. Army's air corps was established early in 1918. America's output of planes lagged, however, despite pressure from Secretary of War Baker—a rare war-production failure.

Continuing the military's policy of close moral oversight, AEF officials warned troops of the danger of venereal disease. "A German bullet is cleaner than a whore" declared one poster. When the French government offered to provide prostitutes for the AEF (as was the French practice), Newton Baker exclaimed, "For God's sake, don't show this to the President, or he'll stop the war."

The YMCA, Red Cross, and Salvation Army, including many female volunteers, provided a touch of home. Some 16,500 U.S. women served directly in the AEF as nurses, telephone operators, canteen workers, and secretaries.

In March 1918, when Germany launched a major offensive, the Allies created a unified command under French general Ferdinand Foch. Some Americans participated in the fighting around Amiens and Armentières that slowed the German advance.

The French and British wanted to continue this pattern of absorbing the Americans into existing units. But for both military and political reasons (including ensuring a strong U.S. voice at the peace table), Pershing and his superiors in Washington insisted that the AEF fight in "distinct and separate" units. Pershing, favoring aggressive combat in traditional battle settings, abhorred the defensive mentality ingrained by three years of trench warfare.

The Germans' spring offensive resumed in May along the Aisne River, where they broke through to the Marne and faced a nearly open route to Paris, fifty miles away. On June 4, as the French government prepared to evacuate, American forces arrived in strength. Parts of three U.S. divisions and a marine brigade helped stop the Germans at the town of Château-Thierry and nearby Belleau Wood. (An AEF division at full strength consisted of twenty-seven thousand men and one thousand officers, plus twelve thousand support troops.)

The German offensive had punched several deep holes (called salients) in the Allied line. With the help of some eighty-five thousand American troops, the Allies at enormous cost halted a German attack on the cathedral city of Rheims between two of these salients. This battle proved to be the war's turning point.

American soldiers now endured the filth, vermin, and dysentery familiar to veterans of the trenches. Many would never forget the terror of combat. As shells streaked overhead, one recalled, "We simply lay and trembled from sheer nervous tension." Some collapsed emotionally and were hospitalized for "shell shock."

Deadly poison gas (first used by the Germans in 1915) often hung in the air, and rats scurried in the mud. "We are not men anymore, just savage beasts," wrote a young American. Death came in many forms, and without ceremony. Bodies, packs, rifles, photos of loved ones, and letters from home sank indiscriminately into the all-consuming mud. Worsening the horror, thousands of men on both sides died of influenza, in a pandemic that began in the war zone and quickly spread (as discussed later in this chapter).

MAP 22.2 The United States on the Western Front, 1918

American troops first saw action in the campaign to throw back Germany's spring 1918 offensive in the Somme and Aisne-Marne sectors. The next heavy American engagement came that autumn as part of the Allies' Meuse-Argonne offensive, which ended the war.

Source: © Cengage Learning. All rights reserved. No distribution allowed without express authorization.

Religious and ethical principles faded as men struggled to survive. "Love of thy neighbor is forgotten," recalled one, with "all the falsities of a sheltered civilization." The war's brutality would shape the literature of the 1920s as writers such as Ernest Hemingway stripped away the illusions obscuring the reality of mass slaughter.

Turning the Tide   The Allied counteroffensive began in July 1918. About 270,000 U.S. soldiers joined the drive to push the Germans back from the Marne. Rain pelted down as the AEF moved into position. One wrote in his diary, "Trucks, artillery, infantry columns, cavalry, wagons, caissons, mud, MUD, utter confusion." Another 100,000 AEF troops joined a parallel British counterattack in the Somme region.

In early September, as fighting continued on all fronts, Foch authorized an AEF campaign to close a German salient around the town of St. Mihiel on the Meuse River, 150 miles east of Paris. Pershing assembled nearly five hundred thousand American and one hundred thousand French soldiers. Shelling of German positions began at 1:00 A.M. on September 11. Recorded an American in his diary, "[I]n one instant the entire front ... was a sheet of flame, while the heavy artillery made the earth quake." Within four days, the salient was closed.

National Archives

The Fog of War. U.S. Troops on the Western Front, June 26, 1918 *The reality of combat differed from the idealized images offered in home-front propaganda. As the war's final stage began, these American soldiers attacked entrenched German positions in Alsace, a disputed region along the French-German border near Switzerland. They are firing a 37-mm machine gun, a weapon of deadly accuracy with a maximum range of a mile and a half.*

Although some German units had already withdrawn, St. Mihiel still cost seven thousand U.S. casualties.

In late September, 1.2 million Americans joined the struggle to drive the Germans from the Meuse River and the Argonne Forest north of Verdun. The AEF was assigned to cut the Sedan-Mezières Railroad, a vital German supply route protected by three long, heavily fortified trenches, called Stellungen. The fighting was long and fierce but the AEF at last overran the dreaded Stellungen. In early November the Sedan-Mezières Railroad was cut. The AEF had fulfilled its assignment, at a cost of 26,277 dead.

The successful Meuse-Argonne offensive ended the war. On November 11, 1918, Germany surrendered.

PROMOTING THE WAR AND SUPPRESSING DISSENT

In their own way, the war's domestic effects matched the battlefield in importance. Spurred by government propaganda, patriotic fervor gripped America. The war fever, in turn, encouraged ideological conformity and smothered dissent. Fueling the repressive spirit, government authorities and private vigilante groups hounded socialists, pacifists, and other dissidents, trampling citizens' constitutional rights.

Advertising the War   President Wilson viewed home front support as crucial to military success. "It is not an army we must shape and train for war, it is a nation," he declared. The administration drew on the new professions of advertising and public relations to pursue this goal. Treasury Secretary William McAdoo orchestrated government bond drives, called Liberty Loans, that financed about two-thirds of the war's $35.5 billion cost.

Posters exhorted citizens to "Fight or Buy Bonds." Liberty Loan parades featured flags, banners, and marching bands. Charlie Chaplin and other movie stars promoted the cause. Schoolchildren purchased "thrift stamps" convertible into war bonds.

Patriotic war songs reached millions through phonograph recordings. Beneath the ballyhoo ran a note of coercion. Only "a friend of Germany," McAdoo warned, would refuse to buy bonds.

The balance of the government's war costs came from taxes. Under authority granted by the recently ratified Sixteenth Amendment, Congress imposed wartime income taxes that reached 70 percent at the top level. War-profits taxes, excise taxes on liquor and luxuries, and increased estate taxes also helped finance the war.

Journalist George Creel headed the government's wartime propaganda agency, the **Committee on Public Information** (CPI). While claiming merely to report facts, Creel's committee in reality publicized the government's version of events and discredited all who questioned that version. One CPI division distributed posters drawn by leading illustrators. Another wrote propaganda releases that appeared in the press as "news" with no indication of their source. Popular magazines published CPI ads warning of spies, saboteurs, and anyone who "spreads pessimistic stories" or "cries for peace." Theaters screened CPI films bearing such titles as *The Kaiser: The Beast of Berlin*. All this propaganda played upon basic fears that the German enemy posed a direct threat to home, family, and cherished American values.

The CPI poured foreign-language pamphlets into immigrant neighborhoods and supplied prowar editorials to the foreign-language press. At a CPI event at Mount Vernon on July 4, 1918, an Irish-born tenor sang "The Battle Hymn of the Republic" while immigrants from thirty-three nations filed reverently past George Washington's tomb. CPI posters in factories attacked the socialists' charge that this was a capitalists' war. Samuel Gompers of the American Federation of Labor headed a prowar "Alliance for Labor and Democracy" with CPI funding. CPI volunteers called "Four-Minute Men" gave prowar pep talks to movie audiences.

Teachers, writers, editors, and religious leaders overwhelmingly supported the war. These custodians of culture saw the conflict as a struggle to defend threatened values. Historians wrote essays contrasting German brutality with the Allies' ideals. In *The Marne* (1918), expatriate American writer Edith Wharton expressed her love for France. The popular war poems of Alan Seeger, who volunteered to fight for France and died in action in 1916, portrayed the conflict as a noble crusade. An artillery barrage was for him "the magnificent orchestra of war."

Progressive reformers who had applauded Wilson's domestic program now cheered his war. Herbert Croly, Walter Lippmann, and others associated with the *New Republic* magazine zealously backed the war. In gratitude, administration officials regularly briefed them on the government's war policies.

The educator John Dewey endorsed the war in a series of *New Republic* essays. Progressive intellectuals must accept reality and shape it toward positive social goals, he wrote, not withdraw in self-righteous isolation. The war, he went on, presented exciting "social possibilities." The government's wartime activism could be channeled to reform purposes when peace returned. Internationally, America's participation in the war would transform an imperialistic struggle into a global democratic crusade.

Wartime Intolerance and Dissent   Responding to the propaganda, some Americans lashed out at all things German. Reports of sabotage by German agents, including mysterious fires at munitions plants in New Jersey and Pennsylvania, fanned the flames of fear. Libraries banished German books; towns with German names changed them. An Iowa politician charged that "90 percent of all the men and women who teach the German language are traitors." Some restaurant menus replaced hamburgers with "liberty sandwiches." The Boston Symphony Orchestra dismissed its German-born conductor. The Philadelphia Orchestra banned all German music since Brahms. A popular evangelist, Billy Sunday, proclaimed, "If you turn hell upside down you will find 'Made in Germany' stamped on the bottom."

The zealots also targeted American citizens suspected of pro-German or antiwar sentiments. Some were forced to kiss the flag or recite the Pledge of Allegiance. An Ohio woman accused of disloyalty was wrapped in a flag, marched to a bank, and compelled to buy a war bond. A Cincinnati mob horsewhipped a pacifist minister. Theodore Roosevelt branded antiwar Senator Robert La Follette "an unhung traitor." Columbia University fired two antiwar professors.

In Bisbee, Arizona, in July 1917, two thousand armed vigilantes calling themselves the Citizens Protective League forced twelve hundred striking copper miners, some of whom belonged to the antiwar Industrial Workers of the World (IWW), onto a freight train that dumped them in the New Mexico desert without food, water, or shelter. Without doubt, declared Theodore Roosevelt, "the men deported from Bisbee were bent on destruction and murder."

In Collinsville, Illinois, in April 1918, a mob lynched a German American coal miner, Robert Prager. When a jury freed the ringleaders, a jury member shouted, "Nobody can say we aren't loyal now." The *Washington Post* condemned the lynching but saw it as evidence of a "wholesome awakening" in the American heartland. President Wilson criticized Prager's murder when the German press publicized it, but the administration's strident attacks on radicals and war critics created the climate that led to such actions. In a June 1917 speech urging home-front vigilance, Wilson declared ominously: "Woe be to the man or group of men that seeks to stand in our way." A New York newspaper, advising direct action against war opponents, added: "You do not require any official authority.... [T]he only badge you need is your patriotic fervor."

Despite the persecution, many Americans persisted in opposing the war. Some had sentimental or ancestral ties to Germany. Others were religious pacifists, including Quakers, Mennonites, and Jehovah's Witnesses. Montana Congresswoman Jeannette Rankin, a pacifist and the first woman elected to Congress, opposed the declaration of war. "I want to stand by my country," she declared, "but I cannot vote for war."

Of some sixty-five thousand men who registered as conscientious objectors (COs), twenty-one thousand were drafted. Assigned to noncombat duty on military bases, these COs often experienced harsh treatment. Those who rejected this alternative went to prison. Woodrow Wilson scorned the pacifists. "[M]y heart is with them, but my mind has contempt for them," he declared; "I want peace, but I know how to get it, and they do not."

Socialist leaders such as Eugene Debs and Victor Berger denounced the war as a capitalist struggle for markets, with the soldiers as cannon fodder. The government's decision for war, they insisted, reflected Wall Street's desire to protect its loans to England and France. Other socialists supported the war, however, dividing the party.

The war split the women's movement as well. Some leaders joined Jane Addams in opposition, others endorsed the war while keeping their own goals in view. Carrie Chapman Catt, president of the National American Woman Suffrage Association (NAWSA), had helped start the Woman's Peace Party in 1915. But she supported U.S. entry into the war in 1917, sharing to some extent Wilson's vision of a more liberal postwar world order. Catt continued to fight for woman suffrage, however, as NAWSA's "number one war job." For this, some superpatriots accused her of disloyalty.

Draft resistance extended beyond the ranks of conscientious objectors. An estimated 2.4 to 3.6 million young men failed to register. Others who did register either did not appear when drafted or deserted from training camp. The rural South saw high levels of draft resistance. The urban elites who ran the draft boards were more inclined to excuse young men of their own class from service than poor farmers, white or black, fueling class resentment. In June 1918, a truck carrying soldiers pursuing draft evaders in rural Georgia crashed when a bridge collapsed, killing three. Investigators found that the bridge had been deliberately sabotaged.

African Americans had added reasons to oppose the draft. Of southern blacks who registered, one-third were drafted, in contrast to only one-quarter of whites. White draft boards justified this by arguing that black families could more easily spare a male breadwinner. As an Alabama board observed: "[I]t requires more for a white man and his wife to live than it does a negro man and his wife, due to their respective stations in life." But racial bias worked in complex ways: some southern whites, fearful of arming black men even for military service, favored drafting only whites.

One war critic, Randolph Bourne, a young journalist, rejected John Dewey's argument that reformers could direct the war to their own purposes. "If the war is too strong for you to prevent," he asked, "how is it going to be weak enough for you to … mould to your liberal purposes?" Many prowar intellectuals eventually agreed. By 1919, Dewey conceded that the war, far from promoting reform, had encouraged reaction and intolerance. Bourne did not live to see his vindication, however. He died of influenza in 1918, aged thirty-two.

Suppressing Dissent by Law   Wartime intolerance surfaced in federal laws and official actions. The **Espionage Act** of June 1917 set fines and prison sentences for a variety of loosely defined antiwar activities. The **Sedition Amendment** (May 1918) imposed stiff penalties on anyone convicted of using "disloyal, profane … or abusive language" about the government, the Constitution, the flag, or the military.

Wilson's attorney general, Thomas W. Gregory, used these laws to suppress dissent. Opponents of the war, proclaimed Gregory, should expect no mercy "from an outraged people and an avenging government." Under the federal legislation and similar state laws, authorities arrested some fifteen hundred pacifists, socialists, IWW leaders, and other war critics. One socialist, Rose Pastor Stokes, received a ten-year prison sentence (later commuted) for telling an audience, "I am for the people, and the government is for the profiteers."

Socialist leader Eugene V. Debs, arrested in June 1918 for a speech in Canton, Ohio, discussing the war's economic causes, was convicted by a jury of violating the Espionage Act and sentenced to ten years in prison. At his sentencing he declared: "[W]hile there is a lower class, I am in it; while there is a criminal element, I am of it; while there is a soul in prison, I am not free."

Under the Espionage Act, Postmaster General Albert S. Burleson banned socialist periodicals, including *The Masses*. In January 1919, Congressman-elect Victor Berger was convicted for publishing antiwar articles in his socialist newspaper, the *Milwaukee Leader*. Socialist Norman Thomas complained that Burleson "didn't know socialism from rheumatism," and Upton Sinclair protested to President Wilson that no one of Burleson's "childish ignorance" should wield such power. Still, Wilson did little to restrain the Postmaster General's excesses.

A patriotic organization called the American Protective League and local "Councils of Defense" claiming vague governmental authority further enforced ideological conformity. A group called "Boy Spies of America" recruited young patriots. The 1917 takeover in Russia by Bolsheviks who believed in a one-party state and preached the overthrow of capitalism deepened suspicion of domestic radicals. Could the United States itself fall to communism, some fearful Americans wondered.

In three 1919 decisions, the U.S. Supreme Court upheld the Espionage Act convictions of war critics despite the First Amendment guarantee of free speech. In *Schenck* v. *United States,* Justice Oliver Wendell Holmes, Jr., writing for a unanimous court, justified such repression in cases where a person's speech posed a "clear and present danger" to the nation. When the war ended, Wilson vetoed a bill repealing the Espionage Act, increasing the likelihood that the miasma of conformity and suspicion would linger into the postwar era.

ECONOMIC AND SOCIAL TRENDS IN WARTIME AMERICA

In many diverse ways, the war affected the lives of millions of Americans, including industrial workers, farmers, women, and blacks. Another of the war's byproducts, a deadly influenza pandemic, took a grievous toll. Some Progressive Era reforms advanced, but overall the war weakened the reform movement.

Boom Times in Industry and Agriculture   World War I benefited the U.S. economy. From 1914 to 1918, factory output grew by more than one-third. Even with many men in uniform, the civilian work force expanded by 1.3 million between 1916 and 1918, thanks to new jobs in shipbuilding, munitions, steel, and other war-related industries. Prices rose, but so did wages. Even unskilled workers enjoyed wartime wage increases averaging nearly 20 percent. Samuel Gompers urged a moratorium on strikes. Some IWW members and maverick AFL locals ignored this advice, but with the economy booming, most workers observed the no-strike request.

The war's social impact took many forms. Job seekers pouring into industrial centers strained housing, schools, and municipal services. Consumption of cigarettes, which soldiers and workers could carry in their shirt pockets more easily than pipes or cigars, more than tripled. Reflecting wartime prosperity, automobile production jumped from 460,000 in 1914 to 1.8 million in 1917, then dipped briefly in 1918 as steel went for military production.

Farmers profited, too. With European farm production disrupted, U.S. agricultural prices, including cotton, corn, and other commodities, more than doubled between 1913 and 1918, and farmers' real income rose significantly. This agricultural boom proved a mixed blessing, however. Farmers who borrowed heavily to expand production faced a credit squeeze when farm prices fell after the war. In the 1920s and 1930s, hard-pressed farmers would look back to the war years as a golden age of prosperity.

Blacks Migrate Northward amid New Activist Energies   An estimated half-million African Americans moved north during the war, and most settled in cities. Each day, fresh arrivals poured into Philadelphia, New York, Detroit, and Pittsburgh. Chicago's black population grew from forty-four thousand in 1910 to 110,000 in 1920, Cleveland's from eight thousand to thirty-four thousand.

With European immigration choked off by the war, booming industries hired more black workers. Some companies sent agents south to recruit black workers. African American newspapers like the *Chicago Defender* spread the word, as did letters and word-of-mouth reports. One southern black, newly settled near Chicago, wrote home, "Nothing here but money, and it is not hard to get." A Pittsburgh newcomer presented a more balanced picture: "They give you big money for what you do, but they charge you big things for what you get." As economic opportunity beckoned, impoverished southern blacks welcomed the prospect of securing jobs in a region where racism seemed less oppressive. By 1920, 1.5 million African Americans were working in northern factories and other urban-based jobs.

This vast population movement had profound social ramifications. Churches and storefront missions sprang up to serve deeply religious migrants from the South. As organizers for the National Association for the Advancement of Colored People built a national network of local branches, membership surged from 9,000 before the war to nearly 100,000 by the early 1920s. NAACP leaders pointed to African American support for the war to buttress their demand for equality.

The war profoundly affected African Americans' political consciousness as well. As Adriane Lentz-Smith argues in *Freedom Struggles: African Americans and World War I* (2009), blacks who served in the military and those who supported the war at home became convinced that their patriotic involvement would hasten the day when they would achieve full equality and the full rights of citizenship.

The struggle against racism faltered in the 1920s amid a white racist backlash, but the population movements and heightened race consciousness of the war years laid the groundwork for the civil-rights movement that lay ahead. The concentration of blacks in New York City set the stage for the Harlem Renaissance, a cultural flowering of the 1920s (covered in Chapter 23).

Still, African American newcomers in northern cities faced severe challenges. White workers resented the labor competition, and white homeowners lashed out as blacks moved into "their" neighborhoods. Tensions exploded on July 2, 1917, in East St. Louis, Illinois, home to thousands of recently arrived southern blacks. In a coordinated attack, a white mob torched black homes and shot the fleeing residents. At least thirty-nine blacks died, including a two-year-old who was shot and thrown into a burning house.

A few weeks later, an NAACP silent march down New York's Fifth Avenue protested racist violence. One banner echoed Wilson's phrase justifying U.S. involvement in the war: "Mr. President, Why Not Make AMERICA Safe for Democracy?"

Women in Wartime   From one perspective, World War I seems a uniquely male experience. Male politicians led their nations into war. Male officers ordered other men into battle. Yet war touches all of society, not just half of it. The war affected women differently, but still profoundly.

Feminist leaders like Carrie Chapman Catt hoped that the war would lead to full equality and greater opportunity for women. For a time, these goals seemed attainable. In addition to the women holding AEF clerical positions and in wartime volunteer agencies, about 1 million women worked in industry. Thousands more held other jobs, from streetcar conductors to bricklayers. "Out of … repression into opportunity is the meaning of the war to thousands of women," wrote Florence Thorne of the American Federation of Labor in 1917.

A key victory for the woman-suffrage movement came in November 1917 when New York voters amended the state constitution to permit women to vote. In Washington, members of Alice Paul's National Woman's Party (see Chapter 21) picketed the White House and posted banners criticizing President Wilson for opposing woman suffrage at home while championing democracy abroad. Several

GOING TO THE SOURCE

A U.S. Navy Admiral Copes with the Influenza Pandemic

The U.S.S. *Pittsburgh,* an armored cruiser and flagship of Rear Admiral William B. Caperton, with a crew of 829, patrolled in the South Atlantic during World War I under the command of Captain George Bradshaw. In October 1918, with the *Pittsburgh* anchored at Rio de Janeiro, Brazil, officers and crew suddenly had to cope with the influenza pandemic. Caperton's later account vividly conveys the terror of the outbreak, both on shipboard and in the city.

On the fourth of October we had noted that the so called Spanish influenza, which had passed thru Europe, had made its appearance in Brazil.... On the arrival in Rio of the SS *Dannemara* from Lisbon and Dakar, Africa, the ship reported four deaths from the disease ... [but] the local health authorities ... made no effort to quarantine the vessel.... By the seventh the *Pittsburgh* reported a few cases and the disease was incapacitating hundreds daily in Rio de Janeiro.... By the 9th, 92 cases had made their appearance on board and hundreds ashore were dying.... On the 14th of October 644 cases had been admitted to the [*Pittsburgh's*] sick list.... The Commanding Officer [Captain Bradshaw] ... and two members of my staff were sick, while the disease raged unabated in Rio where conditions defied description.

The [Navy] Department directed me to ... proceed to Bahia, ... [b]ut the prescribed cruise ... was an impossibility.... Conditions in the ship were rapidly becoming worse. More than half of the hospital corps were ill, ... [a]nd the drizzle and the rain which had set in ... continued fitfully, rendering it difficult to find room for the cots of the sick who had been kept on deck in the open, during the good weather. Ashore people died like flies, and many lay in the streets for two or three days waiting interment.... By the 18th, twelve of the 48 pneumonia cases had died in the *Pittsburgh.* Further caskets could not be obtained ashore, at any price, and the burial of our men became an urgent necessity.... On the 21st of October 16 bodies were taken from the *Pittsburgh* and landed for burial in the Sao Francisco Xavier Cemetery. Notwithstanding the previous

protesters were jailed and force-fed when they went on a hunger strike. Pressured by all wings of the suffrage movement, Wilson declared that women's war service had earned them the right to vote. In 1919, barraged by pro-suffrage petitions, the House and Senate overwhelmingly passed the **Nineteenth Amendment** granting women the vote. Ratification soon followed.

Beyond this victory, however, the war did little to better women's status permanently. Relatively few women entered the work force for the first time in 1917–1918; most simply moved to better-paying jobs. But even in these jobs, most earned less than the men they replaced. As for the women in the AEF, the War Department refused their requests for military rank and benefits.

At the war's end, many women lost their jobs to returning veterans. The New York labor federation advised, "The same patriotism which induced women to arrangement with cemetery authorities for the opening of 20 graves, the funeral cortege arrived at the cemetery and found no graves prepared ... and we were finally compelled to dig the graves for our own dead shipmates. Conditions in the cemetery beggared description. Eight hundred bodies in all states of decomposition, and lying about in the cemetery, were awaiting burial. Thousands of buzzards swarmed overhead. In the city itself there were no longer medicines, or wood for coffins and very little food. Rich and poor alike were stricken. In the big public hospital ... hundreds of naked bodies lay thrown upon each other like cord wood....

The ship had been unable to secure milk or fresh eggs and no chickens could be obtained in the market at any price.... The American women of Rio de Janeiro immediately offered their assistance and soon an adequate supply of fresh milk, eggs and chickens was available for the sick at the hospital, while sweaters and pajamas were sent off to the ship for the hundreds still in the throes of the disease. By the 24th, 654 men were on the [sick] list.... The army ... gave us one hundred beds in the hospital and the *Pittsburgh* transferred cooks and sufficient hospital corpsmen to care for the contingent ashore. The Rio Light and Power Company generously loaned us all manner of kitchen ware, glassware, ranges, mosquito netting, bed screens and other necessities for use in the hospital.... By the 31st of October there had been 58 fatal cases, but great improvement was shown throughout the ship and many men were returned to duty. Ashore, ... the streets of Rio de Janeiro, generally gay and vivid with movement and color, were deserted and motionless.... [N]ow and then some poor native with a miniature coffin on his head and followed by a sorrowful family trudged drearily to the nearest cemetery with his loved load.... [T]here was hardly a family ashore where the hand of death had not left its trace.

Questions

1. *According to Caperton's narrative, how did the influenza pandemic first reach Rio de Janeiro?*
2. *How did the U.S. women of Rio de Janeiro assist the Pittsburgh crewmen suffering from influenza?*

Source: William B. Caperton, "History of Flag Career of Rear Admiral William B. Caperton, U.S. Navy ...," pp. 377–382, National Archives and Records Administration, Washington DC, Record Group 45. Online at www.history.navy.mil/library/online /influenza_caper.htm.

enter industry during the war should induce them to vacate their positions after the war." Male streetcar workers in Cleveland went on strike to force women conductors off the job. In 1920, the percentage of U.S. women in the paid labor force was actually slightly lower than it had been in 1910.

Public-Health Crisis: The 1918 Influenza Pandemic

Along with the war's other effects, the nation in 1918 reeled under an outbreak of influenza (or "flu"), a highly contagious viral infection. The **influenza pandemic,** spread by a particularly deadly strain of the virus, killed an estimated 50 to 100 million people worldwide. Despite public-health advances, medical science had few weapons against influenza in 1918.

Originating in Africa, the virus spread from battlefields in France to U.S. military camps, striking Fort Riley, Kansas, in March 1918 and quickly advancing to other bases and the urban population. In September, a health official visiting Camp Devens in Massachusetts wrote, "I saw hundreds of young stalwart men in uniform coming into ... the hospital.... The faces wore a bluish cast, a cough brought up blood-stained sputum. In the morning, the dead bodies are stacked about the morgue like cord-wood."

The flu hit the cities hard. After a September Liberty Loan rally in Philadelphia, doctors reported 635 new influenza cases. Many cities forbade public gatherings. In the worst month, October, influenza killed 195,000 Americans. The total U.S. death toll reached about 550,000, over six times the number of AEF battle deaths in France.

The development of a flu vaccine in the 1940s and of antibiotics to control influenza's secondary infections reduced the severity of later outbreaks, but flu pandemics remain a threat. In 2004, using tissue preserved from two U.S. soldiers who had died of influenza in 1918 and from the frozen corpse of another victim buried in the Alaska tundra, scientists successfully synthesized the 1918 virus for research purposes.

The War and Progressivism   The war had mixed effects on Progressive Era reform movements. It strengthened progressivism's coercive, moral-control aspect, including the drive to prohibit alcohol consumption. Pointing out the German origins of large breweries such as Pabst, Schlitz, and Anheuser-Busch, prohibitionists hinted that beer was a German plot to undermine American fitness. With food conservation a high priority, they stressed the wastefulness of using grain to make liquor. The **Eighteenth Amendment** establishing national prohibition, which passed Congress in December 1917, was widely seen as a war measure. Ratified in 1919, it went into effect on January 1, 1920.

As we have seen, the war also strengthened the Progressive Era antiprostitution campaign. Congress appropriated $4 million to combat venereal disease among soldiers and war workers. The War Department closed red-light districts near military bases, including New Orleans's famed Storyville. (As Storyville's jazz musicians moved northward, jazz reached a national audience.) In San Antonio, a major military hub, an antiprostitution leader reflected the war mood when he declared, "We propose to fight vice ... with the cold steel of the law, and to drive in the steel from the point to the hilt until the law's supremacy is acknowledged."

In the wartime climate of "vigilance," the antiprostitution drive expanded to a broader policing of morals. Female lecturers for the Commission on Training Camp Activities urged unmarried young women to practice chastity. "Do Your Bit to Keep Him Fit" one pamphlet advised. Wartime "protective bureaus" in major cities monitored women's behavior. In Boston, female social workers hid in the Common after dark to apprehend young women dating soldiers from nearby bases.

All this moral-reform activity convinced some that traditional codes of sexual behavior, weakening before the war, had been restored. One antiprostitution crusader exulted, "Young men of today ... are nearer perfection in conduct, morals, and ideals than any similar generation.... Their minds have been raised to ideals that would never have been attained save by the heroism of ... the World War."

Labor reforms advanced as well. The Railroad Administration and the **War Labor Board** (WLB), spurred by progressives, encouraged workers to join unions and guaranteed unions' right to bargain with management. The WLB also pressured factory owners to introduce the eight-hour workday, end child labor, and open their plants to safety and sanitation inspectors. Under these favorable conditions, union membership rose from 2.7 million in 1916 to more than 5 million by 1920. Several state legislatures, eager to advance the war effort, passed wage-and-hour laws and other measures benefiting factory workers.

The **Bureau of War Risk Insurance** (BWRI), created in 1917 to aid soldiers' families, established a precedent of government help for families at risk. As Julia Lathrop, head of the Federal Children's Bureau, observed, "The least a democratic nation can do, which sends men into war, is to … [care for] the families." By the war's end, more than two million families were receiving regular BWRI checks.

Overall, however, at least in the short run, the war weakened the Progressive Era's powerful social-justice impulse. While the war brought stricter regulation of the economy—a key progressive goal—business interests often dominated the regulatory agencies, and these agencies were quickly dismantled after the war. The government's repression of radicals and antiwar dissenters fractured the fragile coalition of left-leaning progressives, women's groups, trade unionists, socialists, and politicians that had supported the prewar reforms, and ushered in a decade of reaction. The 1918 midterm election signaled the shift, as the Democrats lost both houses of Congress to a deeply conservative Republican Party.

Nevertheless, taking a longer view, reform energies, after diminishing in the 1920s, would reemerge in the depression decade of the 1930s (covered in Chapter 24). As Franklin D. Roosevelt's New Deal took shape, the memory of such World War I agencies as the War Industries Board, the War Labor Board, and the Bureau of War Risk Insurance provided ideas and inspiration.

JOYOUS ARMISTICE, BITTER AFTERMATH, 1918–1920

The euphoria that greeted the November 1918 armistice proved short lived. Having defined America's war aims in lofty terms, Woodrow Wilson dominated the 1919 peace conference but failed in his most cherished objective—American membership in the League of Nations. Amid a sour climate of racism and intolerance, the voters in 1920 repudiated Wilsonian idealism and internationalism and elected a conservative Republican as president.

Wilson's Fourteen Points; The Armistice   President Wilson took America to war determined to put his personal stamp on the peace. He and his reform-minded supporters believed that U.S. participation could transform a sordid squabble for power and empire into a crusade for a transformed world order. Wilson recruited a group of advisers to translate his vision into specific war aims. The need for such a statement grew urgent after the Bolsheviks, having seized power in Russia, published the self-serving secret treaties negotiated by European powers before the war.

Addressing Congress in January 1918, Wilson summed up U.S. war aims in fourteen points. Eight of these promised the subject peoples of the Austro-Hungarian and

Ottoman empires the right of self-determination—that is, the freedom to choose their own political futures. A ninth point insisted that imperial disputes should consider the interests of the colonized peoples. The remaining five points offered Wilson's larger postwar vision: a world of free navigation, free trade, reduced armaments, openly negotiated treaties, and "a general association of nations" to resolve conflicts peacefully. The **Fourteen Points** solidified American support for the war, especially among liberals. They seemed proof that America was fighting for noble motives, not selfish aims.

In early October 1918, facing defeat, Germany proposed an armistice based on Wilson's Fourteen Points. The British and French hesitated, but when Wilson threatened to negotiate a separate peace, they agreed. Meanwhile, in Berlin, Kaiser Wilhelm II had abdicated and a German republic had been proclaimed.

In the early morning of November 11, 1918, the Allied commander Marshal Foch and his German counterparts signed an armistice ending hostilities at 11:00 A.M. Rockets burst over the front that night, not in anger but in relief and celebration. In America, cheering throngs (some wearing masks against the influenza epidemic) filled the streets. "Everything for which America has fought has been accomplished," Wilson proclaimed.

As troop ships ferried the soldiers home, Captain Harry Truman of Missouri described his feelings in a letter to his fiancée:

> I've never seen anything that looks so good as the Liberty Lady in New York Harbor ... [T]he men ... have been in so many hard places that it takes something real to give them a thrill, but when the band ... played "Home Sweet Home" there were not many dry eyes. The hardest of hard-boiled cookies even had to blow his nose a time or two.

The Versailles Peace Conference, 1919

Unwisely, Wilson decided to lead the U.S. delegation to the peace conference himself. The strain of long bargaining sessions would take its toll on his frail nerves. Wilson compounded his mistake by naming only one Republican to the delegation, an elderly diplomat with little influence in the party. Selecting more prominent Republicans might have spared Wilson future grief. The Democrats' loss of Congress in 1918 offered a further ill omen.

Nevertheless, crowds cheered and ships' whistles blared on December 4, 1918, as the *George Washington,* a converted German liner, left New York, bearing Wilson to Europe—the first sitting U.S. president to go abroad. The giddy mood continued when Wilson reached Europe. Shouts of "Voodrow Veelson" rang out as he rode up the Champs-Élysées, Paris's ceremonial boulevard. In England, children spread flowers in his path. The euphoria faded once the peace conference began at the palace of Versailles near Paris, where, 136 years before, diplomats had signed the treaty ending the Revolutionary War. Joining Wilson were the other Allied heads of state: Italy's Vittorio Orlando; France's aged and cynical Georges Clemenceau; and England's David Lloyd George, whom Wilson called "slippery as an eel." Japan participated as well.

The French and British came to the **Versailles Peace Conference** determined to punish Germany for their nations' wartime losses. Their vengeful, vindictive agenda bore little relation to Wilson's liberal vision. As Clemenceau remarked,

"God gave us the Ten Commandments and we broke them. Mr. Wilson has given us the Fourteen Points. We shall see."

Reflecting this toxic climate, the peace treaty the sullen German delegation signed was harshly punitive. Germany was disarmed, stripped of its colonies, forced to admit sole blame for the war, and saddled with staggering reparation payments. France regained border provinces lost to Germany in 1871 and took control for fifteen years of Germany's coal-rich Saar Basin. The treaty demilitarized Germany's western border and transferred a slice of eastern Germany to Poland. These provisions cost Germany one-tenth of its population and one-eighth of its territory. The treaty gave Italy a slice of Austria that contained two hundred thousand German-speaking inhabitants. These harsh terms, bitterly resented in Germany, planted the seeds of World War II.

Some provisions did reflect Wilson's themes of democracy and self-determination. Germany's former colonies went to the various Allies under a "mandate" or trusteeship system that in theory promised eventual independence. The treaty also recognized the independence of Poland and the Baltic states of Estonia, Latvia, and Lithuania (seized by Germany in its 1918 peace treaty with Bolshevik Russia). Separate treaties provided for the independence of Czechoslovakia and Yugoslavia, new nations carved from the Austro-Hungarian and Ottoman empires.

Palestine, a part of the Ottoman Empire, went to Great Britain under a mandate arrangement. In 1917, after gaining military control of Palestine, the British had issued the Balfour Declaration supporting a Jewish "national home" in the region while also acknowledging the rights of the non-Jewish Palestinians.

But the statesmen of Versailles ignored the aspirations of colonized peoples in Asia and Africa—people like Ho Chi Minh. A young Vietnamese nationalist who would later lead his nation, Ho tried unsuccessfully to secure Vietnamese independence from France.

Nor did the peacemakers come to terms with revolutionary Russia. Indeed, in August 1918 a fourteen-nation Allied army, including some seven thousand U.S. troops, had landed at Russian ports, ostensibly to protect Allied war equipment. In fact, the aim was to overthrow the new Bolshevik regime, whose communist ideology terrified European and American leaders. President Wilson, having welcomed the liberal Russian revolution of March 1917, viewed the Bolshevik coup and Russia's withdrawal from the war as a betrayal of his hopes for a democratic Russia. Not until 1933 would the United States recognize the Soviet Union.

The Fight over the League of Nations   Dismayed by the treaty's vindictive features, Wilson focused on his one shining achievement at Versailles—a treaty provision, or covenant, creating a new international organization, the **League of Nations.** The League covenant embodied Wilson's vision of a new world order of peace and justice.

But Wilson's League faced major hurdles. A warning shot came in February 1919 when thirty-nine Republican senators and senators-elect, including powerful Henry Cabot Lodge, signed a letter rejecting the League in its present form. To reject the League covenant, Wilson retorted defiantly, would destroy the Versailles treaty's "whole vital structure."

When Wilson sent the treaty to the Senate for ratification in July 1919, Lodge bottled it up in the Foreign Relations Committee. To rally popular opinion, Wilson left Washington in September for a national speaking tour. Covering more than nine thousand miles by train, Wilson defended the League before large and friendly audiences. People wept as he described his visits to American war cemeteries in France and sketched his vision of a new world order.

But the trip exhausted Wilson, and on September 25 he collapsed in Colorado. His train sped back to Washington, where on October 2, he suffered a severe stroke. Wilson spent the rest of his term mostly in bed or in a wheelchair, a reclusive invalid, his fragile emotions betraying him into tearful outbursts and irrational, self-defeating actions. He broke with close advisers, refused to see the British ambassador, and dismissed Secretary of State Lansing, accusing him of disloyalty. In January 1920, he rejected his physician's advice to resign.

Wilson's first wife had died in 1914. His strong-willed second wife, Edith Galt, played a crucial behind-the-scenes role during this crisis. She concealed Wilson's condition from the public, controlled his access to information, and decided who could see him, barring cabinet members, diplomats, and congressional leaders. When one leader seeking a meeting urged Mrs. Wilson to consider "the welfare of the country," she snapped, "I am not thinking of the country now, I am thinking of my husband." (The Twenty-fifth Amendment, addressing issues of presidential disability, was not adopted until 1967.)

Against this grim backdrop, the League drama unfolded. On September 10, 1919, the Foreign Relations Committee at last sent the treaty to the Senate, but with a series of amendments. The Senate split into three groups. First were Democrats who supported the treaty without changes, including U.S. membership in the League of Nations. Second were Republican "Irreconcilables," led by Hiram Johnson of California, Wisconsin's Robert La Follette, and Idaho's William Borah, who opposed the League absolutely. Intensely nationalistic, they feared that League membership would restrict U.S. freedom of action and entangle America with corrupt foreign powers. Finally, a group of Republican "Reservationists," led by Lodge, demanded amendments as a condition of their support. The Reservationists especially objected to Article 10 of the League covenant, which pledged each member nation to defend the independence and territorial integrity of all other members. This provision, they believed, limited America's sovereignty and infringed on Congress's constitutional power to declare war.

Had Wilson compromised, the Senate would probably have ratified the Versailles treaty, including the League covenant, with amendments. But Wilson, ill and unyielding, instructed Senate Democrats to reject the Foreign Relations Committee's version of the treaty, which now included Lodge's reservations. Although international-law specialists argued that these reservations would not prevent U.S. participation in the League, Wilson stood firm.

Despite Wilson's speaking tour, the public did not rally behind the League, thanks in part to the reactionary mood his own administration had helped create. As the *Nation* magazine observed, "If [Wilson] loses his great fight for humanity, it will be because he was deliberately silent when freedom of speech and the right of conscience were struck down in America."

On November 19, 1919, pro-League Democrats, obeying Wilson's instructions, and anti-League Irreconcilables joined forces to defeat the proposed measure that included Lodge's reservations. A second vote in March 1920 produced the same result. The United States would not join the forty-four nations who in January 1920 launched the League of Nations, the forerunner of the United Nations. What might have been Wilson's crowning achievement had turned to ashes.

Racism and Red Scare, 1919–1920

The war's strident patriotism left a bitter aftertaste. The years 1919–1920 brought new racial violence and anti-radical hysteria. Seventy-six blacks were lynched in 1919, the worst toll in fifteen years. The victims included ten veterans, several still in uniform. In Omaha, a mob inflamed by sensational newspaper stories seized a black prisoner from the courthouse, hanged him from a lamppost, dragged his body through the streets, and burned it. Henry Fonda, a future film actor, witnessed the lynching as a fourteen-year-old. "It was the most horrendous sight I'd ever seen," he later recalled.

The worst violence exploded in Chicago, where simmering racial tension erupted on a hot afternoon in July 1919. When a black youth swimming at a Lake Michigan beach drowned after whites had pelted him with stones, black neighborhoods erupted in fury. A thirteen-day reign of terror followed as white and black marauders engaged in random attacks and arson. Black gangs stabbed an Italian peddler; white gangs pulled blacks from streetcars and shot or whipped them. The outbreak left fifteen whites and twenty-three blacks dead, more than five hundred injured, and more than a thousand families, mostly black, homeless.

Wartime antiradicalism crested in a postwar Red Scare. (Communists were called "reds" because of the red flag favored by revolutionary organizations.) A rash of strikes in 1919 deepened overwrought fears of a communist takeover in America. When the IWW and other unions called a general strike in Seattle, the panicky mayor accused the strikers of seeking to "duplicate the anarchy of Russia" and called for federal troops to maintain order. Anxiety crackled again in April, when various public officials received packages containing bombs. One severely injured a senator's maid; another damaged the home of Attorney General A. Mitchell Palmer. When 350,000 steelworkers went on strike in September, mill owners ran newspaper ads denouncing the leaders as "Red agitators."

Antiradical paranoia also infected politics. In 1919, the House of Representatives refused to seat Milwaukee socialist Victor Berger, recently indicted under the Espionage Act. Milwaukee voters promptly reelected him, but the House stood firm. The New York legislature expelled several socialist members. The Justice Department set up an antiradical division under young J. Edgar Hoover, future head of the Federal Bureau of Investigation, who ordered the arrest of hundreds of suspected communists and radicals. In December 1919, the government deported 249 Russian-born aliens, including Emma Goldman, a prominent lecturer and birth-control advocate.

On January 2, 1920, in a Justice Department dragnet coordinated by Wilson's politically ambitious Attorney General, A. Mitchell Palmer, federal marshals and local police raided the homes of suspected radicals and the headquarters of radical

Chicago Race Riot, 1919 *This graphic photo vividly conveys the horrifying reality of the racial violence that struck Chicago in July 1919.*

Chicago History Museum

organizations in thirty-two cities. Without search warrants or arrest warrants, they arrested more than four thousand persons (some 550 were eventually deported) and seized a horde of papers. Boston police paraded arrested persons through the streets in handcuffs and chains and jammed them into unsanitary cells without formal charges or the opportunity to post bail.

Gripped by anticommunist hysteria, Palmer luridly described the menace he believed his raids had averted: "The blaze of revolution was sweeping over every American institution of law and order ... eating its way into the homes of the American workman, its sharp tongues of revolutionary heat ... licking at the altars of the churches, leaping into the belfry of the school bell, crawling into the sacred corners of American homes ... burning up the foundations of society."

The hysteria soon subsided. When a bomb exploded in New York City's financial district in September 1920, killing thirty-eight people, most Americans saw the deed as the work of an isolated fanatic, not evidence of approaching revolution.

The Election of 1920   As the 1920 election approached, the invalid Wilson, lost in fantasy, considered seeking a third term, but was dissuaded. Few heeded his call to make the election a "solemn referendum" on the League. "The bitterness toward Wilson is everywhere ...," wrote a Democratic campaign worker; "he hasn't a friend."

The Democratic convention in San Francisco nominated James M. Cox, the mildly progressive governor of Ohio. As Cox's running mate they chose the young assistant secretary of the navy, Franklin D. Roosevelt, who possessed a potent political name.

The confident Republicans, meeting in Chicago, nominated Senator **Warren G. Harding** of Ohio, an amiable politician of little distinction. As one GOP leader observed, "There ain't any first raters this year.... We got a lot of second raters, and Harding is the best of the second raters." For vice president, they chose Massachusetts governor Calvin Coolidge, who had won attention in 1919 with his denunciation of a Boston policemen's strike.

Harding's vacuous campaign speeches reminded one critic of "an army of pompous phrases moving over the landscape in search of an idea." But many voters welcomed his reassuring promise of a return to "normalcy," and he won in a land-slide. Nearly a million citizens defiantly voted for socialist Eugene Debs, still impri-soned for his earlier antiwar speeches.

The election dashed all hope for American entry into the League of Nations. Senator Lodge expressed grim satisfaction that the voters had ripped "Wilsonism" up by the roots. The sense of high purpose Wilson had evoked in April 1917 seemed remote indeed as Americans turned to a new president and a new era.

CHRONOLOGY
1899–1920

1899	First U.S. Open Door note seeking access to China market.
	Boxer Rebellion erupts in China.
1900	Second U.S. Open Door note.
1904	President Theodore Roosevelt proclaims "Roosevelt Corollary" to Monroe Doctrine.
1905	Roosevelt mediates the end of the Russo-Japanese War.
1906	At the request of Roosevelt, San Francisco ends segre-gation of Asian schoolchildren.
	Panama Canal construction begins.
1911	U.S.-backed revolution in Nicaragua.
1912	U.S. Marines occupy Nicaragua.
1914	U.S. troops occupy Veracruz, Mexico.
	Panama Canal opens.
	World War I begins.
	President Wilson proclaims American neutrality.
1915	U.S. Marines occupy Haiti and the Dominican Republic.
	Woman's Peace Party organized.
	British liner *Lusitania* sunk by German U-boat.
	Wilson permits U.S. bank loans to Allies.
1916	U.S. punitive expedition invades Mexico, seeking Pancho Villa.
	Germany pledges not to attack merchant ships without warning.
	Wilson reelected.

1917	U.S. troops withdraw from Mexico.
	Germany resumes unrestricted U-boat warfare; United States declares war. Selective Service Act sets up national draft.
	War Industries Board, Committee on Public Information, and Food Administration created.
	Espionage Act passed.
	War Risk Insurance Act authorizes payments to servicemen's dependents.
	NAACP march in New York City protests upsurge in lynchings.
	Bolsheviks seize power in Russia; Russia leaves the war.
	New York State passes woman-suffrage referendum.
	U.S. government operates the nation's railroads.
	Striking miners forcibly expelled from Bisbee, Arizona.
1918	Wilson outlines Fourteen Points.
	Sedition Amendment passed.
	Global influenza pandemic takes heavy toll in United States.
	National War Labor Board created.
	American forces see action at Château-Thierry, Belleau Wood, St. Mihiel, and Meuse-Argonne campaign.
	Republicans win control of both houses of Congress (November 5).
	Armistice signed (November 11).
1919	Eighteenth Amendment added to the Constitution (prohibition).
	Peace treaty, including League of Nations covenant, signed at Versailles.
	Supreme Court upholds silencing of war critics in *Schenck* v. *United States*.
	Upsurge of lynchings; racial violence in Chicago.
	Wilson suffers paralyzing stroke.
	Versailles treaty, with League covenant, rejected by Senate.
1920	"Red raids" organized by Justice Department.
	Nineteenth Amendment added to the Constitution (woman suffrage).
	Warren G. Harding elected president.

CONCLUSION

The early twentieth century saw intensifying U.S. involvement abroad. Focused initially on Latin America and Asia, this new globalism arose from a desire to export American values, promote U.S. business interests internationally, and extend the power of a newly confident, industrialized nation.

After initial neutrality, the nation's 1917 decision to enter the European war on the Allied side reflected a combination of cultural ties, economic interests, concern for neutral rights, and President Wilson's dream of a transformed world order emerging from the carnage.

By conservative estimates, World War I cost 10 million dead. Included in this toll were 112,000 American soldiers—forty-nine thousand in battle and sixty-three thousand from disease, mostly influenza. The toll of dead and injured reflected new technologies of warfare, from U-boat torpedoes and primitive aerial bombs to tanks, poison gas, and deadlier machine guns. The Allies won, but Wilson's visionary hopes, including American membership in the new League of Nations, went unrealized.

The war had far-reaching social, political, and economic effects. It advanced some reforms, notably woman suffrage and the campaigns against prostitution and alcohol. As war measures, the government expanded its regulatory power over corporations and took steps to ensure workers' well-being and right to organize. These initiatives offered models that would prove influential in the future.

But in a larger sense, the war undermined progressivism's openness to new ideas, its larger commitment to social justice, and its humanitarian concern for society's most vulnerable members. As government propaganda encouraged ideological conformity and fear of radicalism, the reform impulse withered. The reactionary climate intensified in the early postwar era.

The war at least temporarily improved the economic prospects of many workers, farmers, blacks, and women, and enhanced the standing of the corporate executives, psychologists, public-relations specialists, and other professionals who contributed their expertise to the cause. Internationally, despite the wrangles that kept America out of the League of Nations, the conflict underscored America's new status as a world power, and left the nation's businesses and financial institutions poised for global expansion.

Some of these changes endured; others proved fleeting. Cumulatively, however, their effect was profound. The nation that celebrated the armistice in November 1918 was very different from the one that Woodrow Wilson had solemnly taken into battle only nineteen months earlier.

23

COPING WITH CHANGE, 1920–1929

CHAPTER OUTLINE   • A New Economic Order • Standpat Politics in a Decade of Change • Mass Society, Mass Culture • Cultural Ferment and Creativity • A Society in Conflict • Hoover at the Helm

A NEW ECONOMIC ORDER

Fueled by new products and new ways of producing and selling goods, the economy surged in the 1920s. Not everyone benefited, and farmers suffered severe economic woes. Still, the overall picture appeared rosy. These economic changes influenced the decade's political, social, and cultural climate, as Americans confronted a changing society.

Booming Business, Ailing Agriculture
Recession struck in 1920 as Washington canceled wartime defense contracts and veterans reentered the job market. Recovery came by 1922, however, and for the next few years the nonfarm economy hummed as the gross national product (GNP) grew by 43 percent from 1922 to 1929.

New consumer goods, including electrical products, fed the prosperity. By the mid-1920s, with more than 60 percent of the nation's homes electrified, new appliances, from refrigerators to fans, filled the stores. The manufacture and marketing of such appliances, as well as the construction of hydroelectric generating plants, provided a massive economic stimulus.

The automobile helped fuel the boom. Introduced before the war (see Chapter 21), automobiles spread like wildfire in the 1920s. By 1930, some 60 percent of U.S. families owned cars. Ford Motor Company led the market until mid-decade, when General Motors (GM) spurted ahead by touting comfort and color (Ford's Model T came only in black). GM's lowest-priced car, named for French automotive designer Louis Chevrolet, proved especially popular. In 1927, **Henry Ford** introduced the stylish Model A in various colors. By the decade's end, the automobile industry accounted for about 9 percent of all manufacturing wages and had stimulated such industries as rubber, gasoline and motor oil, advertising, and highway construction.

The stock market reflected the prevailing prosperity, and then far outran it, as a speculative frenzy gripped Wall Street (covered in Chapter 24).

To supply overseas markets, Ford, GM, and other corporations built production facilities abroad. U.S. meatpackers built plants in Argentina; Anaconda Copper bought Chile's biggest copper mine; the mammoth United Fruit Company established plants across Latin America. But true economic globalization lay far ahead. Economic nationalism prevailed in the 1920s, as the industrialized nations, including the United States, erected high tariff barriers. The Fordney-McCumber Tariff (1922) and the Smoot-Hawley Tariff (1930) pushed U.S. tariffs to all-time highs, helping domestic manufacturers but stifling foreign trade.

While prosperity lifted overall wages, workers benefited unequally, reflecting regional variations and discriminatory employment practices. Unskilled workers in the South earned about 40 percent less per hour than those in the North. Textile corporations moved south seeking lower wage rates, devastating New England mill towns. African Americans, women workers, Mexican Americans, and recent immigrants clustered at the bottom of the wage scale. For farmers, wartime prosperity gave way to hard times. Grain prices plummeted as government purchases for the army dwindled and America's high tariffs depressed agricultural exports. As tractors and other new machinery boosted farm production, the resulting surpluses further weakened prices. Farmers who had bought land and equipment on credit during the war felt the squeeze as payments came due.

New Modes of Producing, Managing, and Selling
: Productivity increased in the 1920s as new assembly-line techniques boosted industrial workers' per capita output. At Ford plants near Detroit, workers stood in place and performed repetitive tasks as chains conveyed the vehicles past them.

Assembly-line work influenced employees' behavior. Managers discouraged individual initiative and even distracting conversation. Ford employees learned to speak without moving their lips and adopted an expressionless mask that some called "Fordization of the face." Job satisfaction diminished. Assembly-line labor did not foster the pride that came from farming or mastering a craft. Nor did it offer much prospect of advancement. In Muncie, Indiana, factories employing more than four thousand workers announced only ten openings for foremen in 1924–1925.

U.S. mass-production methods had a global impact. *Fordism* became a synonym worldwide for assembly-line manufacturing. In Russia, which purchased twenty-five thousand Ford tractors in the 1920s, people "ascribed a magical quality to the name of Ford," a visitor reported.

Business consolidation, spurred by the war, continued. By the late 1920s, more than a thousand companies a year vanished through merger. Corporate giants dominated the major industries. By 1930, one hundred corporations controlled nearly half the nation's business. Without actually merging, companies that made similar products formed trade associations to set prices and product specifications.

As U.S. capitalism matured, management structures evolved. Corporations set up separate divisions for product development, market research, economic forecasting, employee relations, and so on, each under a professional manager.

Hirz/Archive Photos/Getty Images

"Honey, Where Did You Park the Car?" *Hundreds of identical Fords jam Nantasket Beach near Boston on a Fourth of July in the early 1920s.*

The shift to a consumer economy affected wage policies. Rather than paying the lowest wages possible, business leaders now realized that higher wages increased consumers' buying power. Henry Ford had led the way in 1914 by paying his workers five dollars a day, well above the average for factory workers. Other companies soon followed suit.

New systems for distributing goods emerged. Automobiles reached consumers through dealer networks. By 1926, nearly ten thousand Ford dealerships dotted the nation. Chain stores accounted for about 25 percent of retail sales by 1930. The A&P grocery chain boasted 17,500 stores. Department stores grew more inviting, with remodeled interiors and attractive displays. Air-conditioning, a recent invention, made department stores (as well as movie theaters and restaurants) welcome havens on summer days.

Advertising and credit sales further stimulated the consumer economy. In 1929, corporations spent nearly $2 billion on radio, billboard, newspaper, and magazine ads, and advertising companies employed some six hundred thousand people. Advertisers used celebrity endorsements, promises of social success, and threats of social embarrassment. Beneath a picture of a sad young woman, a Listerine mouthwash ad proclaimed: "She was a beautiful girl and talented too.... Yet in the one pursuit ... foremost in the mind of every girl and woman—marriage—she was a failure." Her problem was "halitosis," or bad breath. The remedy, of course, was Listerine, and lots of it.

Portraying a fantasy world of elegance, pleasure, and limitless abundance, ads aroused desires that the advertisers promised to fulfill. One critic in 1925 described the advertisers' "dream world":

> [S]miling faces, shining teeth, schoolgirl complexions, cornless feet, perfect fitting [under-wear], distinguished collars, wrinkleless pants, odorless breath, regularized bowels, ... charging motors, punctureless tires, perfect busts, shimmering shanks, self-washing dishes, backs behind which the moon was meant to rise.

Advertisers even defined America's essential meaning in terms of its abundance of material goods. Buying more products, they claimed, fulfilled the "pursuit of happiness" promised in the Declaration of Independence and was thus the duty of all good citizens.

A few critics challenged the advertisers' cultural dominance. In *Your Money's Worth* (1927), Stuart Chase and F.J. Schlink punctured advertisers' exaggerated claims. The *Consumers' Research Bulletin*, launched by Chase and Schlink in 1929, tested products and reported the results to consumers.

Easy credit further lubricated the economy. Earlier, credit had typically involved pawnbrokers, bank loans, or informal arrangements between buyers and sellers. Now retailers routinely offered credit plans for big-ticket items such as automobiles, furniture, and refrigerators.

Business values saturated 1920s' culture. "America stands for one idea: Business," proclaimed the *Independent* magazine in 1921; "Thru business,... the human race is finally to be redeemed." Presidents Harding and Coolidge praised corporate America and magazines profiled business tycoons. A 1923 opinion poll ranked Henry Ford as a leading presidential prospect. In *The Man Nobody Knows* (1925), ad man Bruce Barton described Jesus Christ as a managerial genius who "picked up twelve men from the bottom ranks of business and forged them into an organization that conquered the world."

Although the number of working women as a proportion of the total female population held steady in the 1920s at about 24 percent, male workers dominated the auto plants and other assembly-line factories. Women who did enter the workplace faced wage discrimination. In 1929, for example, a male trimmer in the meatpacking industry received fifty-two cents an hour; a female trimmer, thirty-seven cents. Most women workers, especially recent immigrants and members of minority groups, held low-paying, unskilled positions. By 1930, however, some 2 million women were employed in corporate offices as secretaries, rarely at higher ranks. Indeed, office-space arrangements often segregated male managers and female clerks.

Nearly fifty thousand women received college degrees in 1930, almost triple the 1920 figure. Of these female graduates who joined the work force, many entered such traditional "women's professions" as nursing, librarianship, and school teaching. With medical schools limiting the number of women students to 5 percent of their total enrollment, the number of women physicians actually declined from 1910 to 1930. A handful of women, however, following the lead of Progressive

Era trailblazers, pursued postgraduate education to become faculty members in colleges and universities.

Marginalized in the workplace, women were courted as consumers. In the decade's advertising, glamorous women smiled behind the steering wheel, swooned over new appliances, and smoked cigarettes in romantic settings. (One ad man promoted cigarettes for women as "torches of freedom.") In the advertisers' dream world, housework became an exciting challenge. As one ad put it, "Men are judged ... according to their power to delegate work. Similarly the wise woman delegates to electricity all that electricity can do."

Struggling Labor Unions in a Business Age   Organized labor struggled in the 1920s. Union membership fell from 5 million to 3.4 million in the decade. Several factors underlay this decline. Despite inequities and regional variations, overall wage rates rose, reducing the incentive to join a union. Further, the movement's strength lay in traditional crafts and older industries like printing, railroading, mining, and construction, not in the new mass-production factories.

Management hostility further weakened organized labor. Henry Ford hired thugs to intimidate union organizers. In 1929, anti-union violence flared in North Carolina, where textile workers faced low wages, long hours, and appalling work conditions. In Marion, deputy sheriffs shot and killed six striking workers. In Gastonia, the communist-led National Textile Workers Union organized the strike. The mill's absentee owners refused to negotiate and evicted strikers from their company-owned homes. When armed thugs in league with the owners raided an encampment of strikers, the police chief was shot, possibly by one of his own deputies. In the end, these strikes failed, and the textile industry remained nonunion.

As wartime antiradical sentiments persisted, opponents of labor unions often smeared them with the "communist" label, whether accurate or not. The antiunion campaign took subtler forms as well. Manufacturers' associations renamed the nonunion shop the "open shop" and dubbed it the "American Plan" of labor relations. Some corporations provided cafeterias and recreational facilities. Corporate publicists praised "welfare capitalism" (the term for this anti-union strategy) as evidence of employers' benevolent concern for their workers.

The weakening of the union movement hit women workers hard. By 1929, the proportion of women workers belonging to unions fell to a minuscule 3 percent.

Black membership in labor unions stood at only about eighty-two thousand by 1929, mostly miners, dockworkers, and railroad porters. The American Federation of Labor officially prohibited racial discrimination, but most AFL unions in fact barred African Americans. Corporations often hired jobless blacks as strikebreakers, increasing organized labor's hostility toward them.

STANDPAT POLITICS IN A DECADE OF CHANGE

With Republicans in control of Congress and the White House, politics reflected the decade's business orientation. Unsettled by rapid social change, voters turned to conservative candidates who seemed to represent stability and traditional values. In this climate, would-be reformers and exploited groups had few political options.

The Evolving Presidency: Scandals and Public-Relations Manipulation While white southerners and urban immigrants remained heavily Democratic, the Republican Party continued to attract northern farmers, businesspeople, many white-collar workers and professionals, and some skilled blue-collar workers. The GOP also benefited from the antiradical mood that fueled the early postwar Red Scare (see Chapter 22) and the anti-union campaign. Exploiting such fears, the Republican-led New York legislature set up a committee to investigate "seditious activities" and required loyalty oaths of public-school teachers.

With Republican progressives having bolted to Theodore Roosevelt in 1912, GOP conservatives controlled the 1920 convention and nominated Ohio Senator **Warren G. Harding** for president. As a young newspaper editor, Harding had married the local banker's daughter, who helped manage his 1914 Senate campaign. A genial backslapper, he enjoyed good liquor, a good poker game, and at least one long-term extramarital affair. In the election, Harding swamped his Democratic opponent James M. Cox. After the stresses of war and Wilson's moralizing, voters welcomed Harding's bland oratory.

Harding made some notable cabinet selections: Henry C. Wallace, the editor of an Iowa farm periodical, as secretary of agriculture; **Charles Evans Hughes**, former New York governor and 1916 presidential candidate, secretary of state; and **Andrew Mellon**, a Pittsburgh financier, treasury secretary. **Herbert Hoover**, the wartime food czar, became secretary of commerce.

Harding also made some disastrous appointments: his political manager, Harry Daugherty, as attorney general; a Senate pal, Albert Fall of New Mexico, as secretary of the interior; a wartime draft dodger, Charles Forbes, as Veterans' Bureau head. Such men set the low ethical tone of Harding's presidency. By 1922, Washington rumor hinted at corruption in high places. "I have no trouble with my enemies," Harding told an associate; "[b]ut ... my goddamn friends ... keep me walking the floor nights." In summer 1923, vacationing in the West, Harding suffered a heart attack and died in a San Francisco hotel.

A 1924 Senate investigation exposed the scandals. Charles Forbes, convicted of stealing Veterans' Bureau funds, evaded prison by fleeing abroad. The bureau's top lawyer committed suicide, as did an aide to Attorney General Daugherty accused of influence peddling. Daugherty himself narrowly escaped conviction in two criminal trials. Interior Secretary Fall went to jail for leasing government oil reserves, one in Teapot Dome, Wyoming, to oilmen in return for a $400,000 bribe. Like "Watergate" in the 1970s, **"Teapot Dome"** became a shorthand label for a tangle of scandals.

With Harding's death, Vice President **Calvin Coolidge**, on vacation in Vermont, took the presidential oath by lantern light from his father, a local magistrate. After entering local politics in Massachusetts, Coolidge had been elected Massachusetts governor in 1918 and secured the Republican vice-presidential nomination in 1920.

Coolidge's image as "Silent Cal," a Yankee embodiment of old-fashioned virtues, was carefully crafted. The advertising executive Bruce Barton, an early master of political image-making, guided Coolidge's bid for national office in 1919–1920. Having persuaded a Boston publisher to issue a book of Coolidge's speeches, Barton sent autographed copies to key GOP convention delegates. Barton planted pro-Coolidge articles in magazines and in other ways marketed his candidate just as advertisers were marketing soap, socks, and cereal. The very name *Calvin Coolidge*, he wrote in a *Collier's* magazine article building brand recognition, "seems cut from granite; one could almost strike sparks with such a name, like a flint." Targeting newly enfranchised women, Barton composed a "Message to Women" published under Coolidge's name in *Woman's Home Companion*.

Long before Franklin D. Roosevelt's "fireside chats" of the 1930s (covered in Chapter 24), Bruce Barton understood the political potential of radio. He advised Coolidge to speak conversationally in his radio addresses, avoiding earlier politicians' spread-eagle oratory. Wrote an admirer of Barton: "No man is his equal in [analyzing] the middle-class mind and directing an appeal to it."

Republican Policy Making in a Probusiness Era   While Coolidge raised the ethical tone of the White House, the probusiness policies, symbolized by high tariffs, continued. Prodded by Treasury Secretary Mellon, Congress lowered income-tax rates for the wealthy from their high wartime levels. Lower tax rates for the well-to-do, Mellon argued, would actually increase revenues by reducing the incentive to seek tax shelters. He also contended that tax cuts for high-income earners encouraged business investment and thus benefited everyone. In the same probusiness spirit, the Supreme Court under Chief Justice William Howard Taft (appointed by Harding in 1921) overturned a federal ban on child labor passed in 1919.

While promoting corporate interests, Coolidge opposed government assistance for other Americans. This position faced a test in 1927 when torrential spring rains caused severe flooding on the Mississippi River. Soil erosion resulting from poor farming practices worsened the flood conditions, as did ill-considered engineering projects aimed at draining the river's natural floodplain for development purposes. One official described the river as "writh[ing] like an imprisoned snake" within its artificial confines. From Cairo, Illinois, to the Gulf of Mexico, water poured over towns and farms, flooding twenty-seven thousand square miles. Hundreds died, and the toll of the homeless, including many African Americans, reached several hundred thousand. Disease spread in makeshift refugee camps. Floodwaters swept over New Orleans's low-lying black neighborhoods.

President Coolidge rejected calls to aid the victims. The government had no duty to protect citizens "against the hazards of the elements," he declared. Coolidge did, however, sign the Flood Control Act of 1928 funding levee construction along the Mississippi.

Another test of Coolidge's antigovernment ideology came when hard-pressed farmers rallied behind the **McNary-Haugen Bill**, a price-support plan under which the government would purchase the surplus of six basic farm commodities—cotton, corn, rice, hogs, tobacco, and wheat—at their average price in 1909–1914 (when farm prices were high). The government would then sell these surpluses abroad at market prices and recover the difference, if any, through a tax on domestic sales of these commodities. Coolidge twice vetoed the McNary-Haugen bill, warning of "the tyranny of bureaucratic regulation and control." The government must not favor a single interest group, he argued—even though corporations had long benefited from high tariffs and other measures. These vetoes led many angry farmers to vote Democratic in 1928. In the

Special Collections Research Center, University of Chicago Library

The 1927 Mississippi River Flood *A few of the 700,000 people displaced by the raging waters of the Mississippi await rescue, their partially submerged homes in the background. President Calvin Coolidge resisted calls for federal aid.*

1930s, New Deal planners would draw upon the McNary-Haugen approach in shaping farm policy (as discussed in Chapter 24).

Independent Internationalism   The Harding and Coolidge administrations continued to oppose U.S. membership in the League of Nations. Coolidge did support U.S. membership in the new International Court of Justice (the World Court), but the Republican-controlled Congress imposed unacceptable reservations, and the United States did not join.

Backing away from Woodrow Wilson's idealistic view of America's global destiny, the Republican administrations of the 1920s pursued foreign policies that served America's economic interests—an approach historians have called "independent internationalism." Despite postwar Europe's battered economies, Washington demanded repayment of $22 billion in Allied war debts and German reparation payments. A study commission in 1924 reduced these claims, but high U.S. tariffs and Europe's economic problems, including runaway inflation in Germany, made repayment of even the lower claims unrealistic. When Adolf Hitler took power in Germany in 1933 (covered in Chapter 25), he repudiated all reparations payments.

The Republican administrations worked to protect U.S. corporate interests in Latin America. In Mexico, the U.S. State Department vigorously opposed the efforts of a new revolutionary government to regain control of oilfields earlier granted to U.S. companies and to restrict landholding by foreign interests. In Nicaragua, President Coolidge in 1926 sent U.S. Marines to put down an insurrection against the country's president, Adolfo Diàz, who had close ties to a U.S.-owned gold-mining company.

One notable diplomatic achievement was the **Washington Naval Arms Conference**. After the war ended, the United States, Great Britain, and Japan edged toward a dangerous (and costly) naval-arms race. In 1921, Secretary of State Hughes called a Washington conference to address the problem. He startled the delegates by outlining a specific ratio of warships among the world's naval powers. Great Britain, Japan, Italy, and France accepted Hughes's plan, and agreed to halt battleship construction for ten years. The United States and Japan also pledged to respect each other's territorial holdings in the Pacific. Although this treaty ultimately failed to prevent World War II, it did represent an early arms-control effort.

Another U.S. peace initiative was mainly symbolic. In 1928, the United States and France, eventually joined by sixty other nations, signed the Kellogg-Briand Pact renouncing aggression and outlawing war. Lacking enforcement mechanisms, this high-sounding document accomplished little.

Progressive Stirrings, Democratic Party Divisions

The reform spirit survived in Congress. The **Sheppard-Towner Act** (1921) funded rural prenatal and baby-care centers staffed by public-health nurses. The Federal Radio Commission, created by Congress in 1927, extended the regulatory principle to this new industry. A reform-minded Nebraska senator, George Norris, prevented the Coolidge administration from selling a wartime federal hydroelectric plant to Henry Ford at bargain prices. In the 1930s, this Alabama plant would become part of the Tennessee Valley Authority, a key New Deal agency.

In the 1922 midterm election, labor and farm groups joined forces to defeat some conservative Republicans. In 1924, this alliance revived the Progressive Party and nominated Senator Robert La Follette for president. The Socialist Party and the American Federation of Labor endorsed La Follette.

The 1924 Democratic convention in New York City split between urban and rural wings. By one vote, the delegates defeated a resolution condemning the **Ku Klux Klan** (discussed later in this chapter). While the party's Protestant southern wing favored former Treasury Secretary William G. McAdoo, the big-city delegates championed New York's Catholic governor **Alfred E. Smith**, of Irish, German, and Italian immigrant origins. This split mirrored deep divisions in the nation. After 102 ballots, the exhausted delegates nominated an obscure New York corporation lawyer, John W. Davis.

Calvin Coolidge, aided by media adviser Barton, easily won the Republican nomination. The GOP platform praised the high protective tariff and urged tax cuts and reduced government spending. Amid general prosperity, Coolidge polled about twice Davis's total. La Follette's 4.8 million votes cut into the Democratic total, contributing to Coolidge's landslide victory.

Women and Politics in the 1920s: Achievements and Setbacks

With the ratification of the Nineteenth Amendment in August 1920, the long struggle for women's suffrage succeeded at last, and women streamed to the polls for the first time in a national election that November. (Charlotte Woodward, a youthful signer of the "Declaration of Sentiments" at the 1848 Women's

Rights Convention in Seneca Falls, New York, survived to see women vote in 1920.) Suffrage advocates had long predicted that this reform would transform politics, and this hope survived briefly after the war. Polling places shifted from saloons to schools and churches. Carrie Chapman Catt and other suffrage leaders founded the nonpartisan **League of Women Voters** in 1920 to educate voters on issues and research civic issues. The 1920 major-party platforms endorsed several measures proposed by the League. The **Women's Joint Congressional Committee** (WJCC), a coalition of activist groups, lobbied for child-labor laws, protection of women workers, maternal health care, and federal support for education. The WJCC played a key role in passage of the Sheppard-Towner Act and in congressional enactment of a constitutional amendment banning child labor in 1924.

As former suffragists scattered across the political spectrum, however, the movement lost focus. The League of Women Voters, drawing mainly white middle-class and professional women, played a role in the formation of the WJCC, but otherwise gradually abandoned feminist activism. Alice Paul's National Woman's Party proposed a constitutional amendment guaranteeing women equal rights, but other reformers argued that it could jeopardize laws protecting women workers. Politically active African American women battled racial discrimination rather than addressing feminist issues; Hispanic women in the Southwest focused on labor-union organizing.

The reactionary political climate intensified this retreat from feminist activism. Patriotic groups accused Jane Addams and other woman's-rights leaders of communist sympathies. Younger women, bombarded by ads defining liberation in terms of consumption, rejected the prewar feminists' civic engagement. One in 1927 criticized earlier suffragists' lack of "feminine charm" and their "constant clamor about equal rights."

The reforms backed by women's groups proved short-lived. The Supreme Court struck down child-labor and women's-protective laws. Few states ratified the constitutional amendment banning child labor, as critics accused its supporters, including the WJCC, of undermining the free-enterprise system. The Sheppard-Towner Act, denounced by the American Medical Association for weakening physicians' monopoly of health care, expired in 1929.

MASS SOCIETY, MASS CULTURE

Amid this conservative political climate, major transformations were reshaping society. Assembly lines, advertising, new consumer products, and innovations in mass entertainment and corporate organization all fueled the ferment. While some welcomed these changes, others recoiled in fear.

Cities, Cars, Consumer Goods   In the 1920 census, the urban population (defined as persons living in communities of twenty-five hundred or more) surpassed the rural. The United States had become an urban nation.

Urbanization affected different groups in different ways. African Americans migrated cityward in massive numbers, especially after the 1927 Mississippi River floods. By 1930, more than 40 percent of the nation's 12 million blacks lived in cities, 2 million of them in urban centers of the North and West. The first black congressman since Reconstruction, Oscar De Priest of Chicago, won election in 1928.

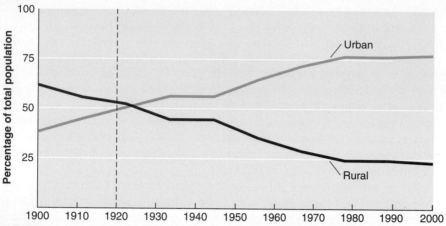

FIGURE 23.1   The Urban and Rural Population of the United States, 1900–2000

The urbanization of America in the twentieth century had profound political, economic, and social consequences.

Source: Census Bureau, Historical Statistics of the United States, *updated by relevant* Statistical Abstracts of the United States, and U.S. Department of Transportation, Federal Highway Administration.

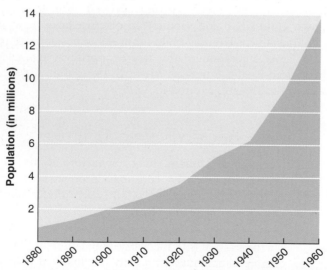

FIGURE 23.2   The African American Urban Population, 1880–1960 (in millions)

The increase in America's urban black population from under 1 million in 1880 to nearly 14 million by 1960 represents one of the great rural-urban migrations of modern history.

Source: Historical Statistics of the United States, Colonial Times to 1970 (Washington, DC: Bureau of the Census, 1975), vol. I, p. 12.

For many women, city life meant eased housework thanks to laborsaving appliances. Store-bought clothes replaced hand-sewn apparel. Home baking and canning declined as bakeries and supermarkets proliferated.

For social impact, nothing matched the automobile. In *Middletown* (1929), a study of Muncie, Indiana, Robert and Helen Lynd reported one resident's comment: "Why ... do you need to study what's changing this country? I can tell you ... in just four letters: A-U-T-O."

The A-U-T-O's social impact proved decidedly mixed, including traffic jams, parking problems, and highway fatalities (more than twenty-six thousand in 1924). In some ways, the automobile brought families together. As family vacations became more common, tourist cabins and roadside restaurants sprang up. But the automobile also eroded family cohesion and parental authority. Young people could borrow the car to catch a movie, attend a distant dance, or park in a secluded lovers' lane.

Middle- and upper-class women welcomed the automobile. They could now drive to work, attend meetings, visit friends, and gain a sense of independence. Stereotypes of feminine delicacy faded as women mastered this new technology. As an automotive magazine editorialized in 1927, "[E]very time a woman learns to drive, ... it is a threat to yesterday's order of things."

Automobiles offered farm families easier access to neighbors and to the city, lessening rural isolation. The automobile's country cousin, the tractor, increased productivity and reduced the physical demands of farming. Yet increased productivity did not always mean increased profits. And as farmers bought automobiles, tractors, and other mechanized equipment on credit, the rural debt crisis worsened.

Ads celebrated the freedom automobiles offered, in contrast to the fixed routes and schedules of trains and streetcars. Yet the automobile and other forms of motor transport also further standardized American life. Buses carried children to consolidated schools. Neighborhood grocery stores declined as people drove to supermarkets served by trucks bringing commercial foods from distant facilities. With the automobile came the first suburban shopping center (in Kansas City) and the first fast-food chain (A & W Root Beer).

Even at $300 or $400, and despite a thriving used-car market, automobiles remained too expensive for many. The "automobile suburbs" that sprang up beyond the streetcar lines attracted mainly the well-to-do, widening class divisions in American society.

Soaring Energy Consumption and Environmental Threats   Electrification and the spread of motorized vehicles impacted America's natural resources and the environment. Electrical generating plants consumed growing quantities of coal. In 1929, U.S. refineries used more than a billion barrels of petroleum to meet the gasoline and oil demands of the nation's 20 million cars.

Rising gasoline consumption underlay Washington's efforts to ensure U.S. access to Mexican oil and triggered feverish competition in the oilfields of Texas and Oklahoma. The natural gas found with petroleum seemed so abundant that it was simply burned off. In short, heavy fossil-fuel consumption, though small by later standards, already characterized America in the 1920s.

The wilderness that had inspired nineteenth-century artists and writers became more accessible as cars and improved roads gave easier access to national parks and once-pristine regions. While this development broadened the constituency for wilderness preservation, it also subjected the nation's parks and wilderness areas to heavy pressures as vacationers came to expect service stations, restaurants, hotels, and other amenities. Worried by such contradictions, Secretary of Commerce Herbert Hoover in 1924 called a National Conference on Outdoor Recreation to consider ways to balance wilderness preservation and the decade's vacation-minded leisure culture.

The Sierra Club and other groups battled to protect wilderness and wildlife. In 1923, the Izaak Walton League, serving fishing enthusiasts, persuaded Congress to halt a development scheme to drain wetlands on the upper Mississippi. Instead, Congress declared this beautiful waterway a wildlife preserve. For too long, wrote preservationist Aldo Leopold in 1925, "a stump was our symbol of progress." However, few Americans in the expansive 1920s worried about the environmental issues that would occupy future generations.

Mass-Produced Entertainment   Prosperity and workplace drudgery stimulated leisure activities in the 1920s. In their free hours, Americans sought the fulfillment their jobs often failed to provide.

Mass-circulation magazines proliferated. By 1922, ten U.S. magazines boasted circulation of more than 2.5 million. The *Saturday Evening Post,* with its Norman Rockwell covers and fiction featuring small-town life, specialized in nostalgia. *Reader's Digest,* founded in 1921 by DeWitt and Lila Wallace, offered condensed versions of articles first published elsewhere. A journalistic equivalent of the Model T, the *Digest* offered standardized fare for mass consumption.

Book publishers expanded their market by selling through department stores or directly to the public via the Book-of-the-Month Club (founded 1926). While some criticized such mass-market ventures for debasing literary taste, they did help sustain a common national culture in an increasingly diverse society.

Radio and the movies similarly offered standardized cultural fare. The radio era began on November 2, 1920, when Pittsburgh station KDKA reported Warren Harding's election. In 1922, New York's WEAF began a regular news program, and a Newark station broadcast the World Series (the New York Giants beat the Yankees). Hundreds of new stations soon began operations, as radio fever gripped America.

In 1926, three corporations—General Electric, Westinghouse, and the Radio Corporation of America—formed the first radio network, the National Broadcasting Company (NBC). The Columbia Broadcasting System (CBS) soon followed. Testing popular taste through market research, the networks soon ruled broadcasting. Americans everywhere laughed at the same jokes, heard the same news, and absorbed the same commercials.

Some public-policy commentators advocated preserving radio as an educational and cultural medium, free of advertising, but commercial sponsorship soon won out. The first network comedy show, *Amos 'n Andy* (1928), enriched its sponsor, Pepsodent toothpaste. White actors played the black characters on the program, which softened the realities of a racist society with stereotyped caricatures of African American life.

The movies migrated from the nickelodeons of the immigrant wards to elegant uptown pleasure palaces and reached all social classes. Los Angeles and its nearby suburb Hollywood, with abundant sunlight ideal for filming, replaced New York as the nation's film capital. In 1922, facing protests about sexually suggestive movies, industry moguls named Postmaster General Will Hays, a former head of the Republican National Committee, to police movie morals. While enforcing a code of standards, Hays also promoted Hollywood films.

Despite charges of immorality, movies often reinforced conservative values. *The Ten Commandments* (1923), directed by Cecil B. De Mille (the son of an Episcopal clergyman), cautioned against breaking moral taboos. "America's sweetheart," Mary Pickford, with her look of frail vulnerability, played innocent girls in need of protection, reinforcing traditional gender stereotypes that many young women were challenging. (Pickford herself sometimes played plucky young women facing danger courageously, and in real life she shrewdly managed her career and financial interests.)

Technical innovations kept moviegoers coming. Al Jolson's *The Jazz Singer* (1927) introduced sound. Walt Disney's cartoon *Steamboat Willy* (1928) not only introduced Mickey Mouse but also showed the potential of animation. By 1930, with weekly attendance approaching 80 million, the corporate giants Metro-Goldwyn-Mayer,

Billie Dove, Silent-Movie Star. *This scene is from Dove's 1928 film* Night Watch *with Donald Reed, the same year she made* Adoration *with Antonio Moreno, mentioned by the young women whose movie memories appear in Going to the Source. Such torrid scenes help explain why moralists and religious leaders of the 1920s found the movies so alarming.*

John Springer Collection/Corbis

GOING TO THE SOURCE

A College Student Recalls Her Movie-Going Experiences in the 1920s

In the early 1930s, sociologist Herbert Blumer asked more than 1,500 young people to write their "motion-picture auto-biographies." Here are excerpts from the recollections of a twenty-two year old young woman.

[T]he first time that I went to a movie ... must have been when I was very young, because I cannot recall the event.... At fifteen I liked the stories of modern youth; the gorgeous clothes and settings fascinated me. My first favorite was Norma Talmadge ... in a picture where she wore ruffly hoop-skirts which greatly attracted me.... I like Joan Crawford because she is so modern, so young, and so vivacious! Billie Dove is so beautifully beautiful that she just gets under your skin.... Sue Carol is cute 'n' peppy. Louise Brooks has her assets, those being

legs and a clever hair-cut. Norma Shearer wears the kind of clothes I like and is a clever actress.

The day-dreams instigated by the movies consist of clothes, ideas on furnishings, and manners. I don't day-dream much, ... [but] it is hard for any girl not to imagine herself cuddled up in some voluptuous ermine wrap, etc.

I'm always at the mercy of the actor at a movie. I feel nearly every emotion he portrays.... Movies do change my moods, but they never last long. I'm off on something else before I know it. If I see a dull or morose show, it sort of deadens me and the vim and vigor dies out 'til the movie is forgotten....

Goodness knows, you learn plenty about love from the movies.... You meet the flapper, the good girl, 'n' all the feminine types and their little tricks of the trade. We pick up their snappy comebacks which

Warner Brothers, and Columbia, relying on formulaic plots and typecast stars, produced most films. As U.S. business expanded abroad, Hollywood, too, sought overseas markets.

Like advertising, the movies created a dream world only loosely tethered to reality. One ad promised "all the adventure, ... romance, ... [and] excitement you lack in your daily life." These mass-produced fantasies shaped behavior and values, especially of the young. Hollywood, observed novelist John Dos Passos, offered a "great bargain sale of five-and-ten-cent lusts and dreams." Along with department stores, mass magazines, and advertising, the movies, too, stimulated consumption with alluring images of the good life, opening new vistas of consumer abundance.

The 1920s mass culture was a byproduct of urbanization. Even when advertisers, radio programmers, filmmakers, and magazine editors nostalgically evoked rural or small-town life, they did so from big-city offices and studios.

For all its influence, the new mass culture penetrated society unevenly. It had less impact in rural America and met resistance among evangelical Christians suspicious of worldly amusements. Mexican Americans preserved traditional festivals and leisure activities despite the "Americanization" efforts of non-Hispanic priests and well-intentioned outsiders. Working-class African Americans flocked to concerts by performers outside the mass-culture mainstream like blues singers Bessie are most handy when dispensing with an unwanted suitor, a too ardent one, too backward one, etc....

I can remember when we all nudged one another and giggled at the last close-up in a movie. I recall [one] ... close-up when the boyfriend squeezes your arm and looks soulfully at you. Oh, it's lotsa fun! No, I never fell in love with my movie idol ... [or wrote] them idiotic letters as some girls I've known do. I have imagined playing with a movie hero many times, though, ... while I'm watching the picture. I forget about it when I'm outside the theater. Buddy Rodgers and Rudy Valentino have kissed me oodles of times, but they don't know it. God bless 'em!"

Yes, love scenes have thrilled me and have made me more receptive to love. I was going with a fellow whom I liked as a playmate, so to speak; he was a little younger than me and he liked me a great deal. We went to the movie [*Adoration*, 1928]—Billie Dove in it ... , Antonio Moreno was the lead, and there were some lovely scenes which just got me all hot 'n' bothered. After the movie we went for a ride 'n' parked along the lake; it was a gorgeous night. Well, I just melted (as it were) in his arms, making him believe I loved him, which I didn't. I sort of came to, but I promised to go steady with him. I went with him till I couldn't bear the sight of him.... I've wished many times that we'd never seen that movie. Another thing not exactly on the subject, but important, I began smoking after watching Dolores Costello, I believe it was, smoke, which hasn't added any joy to my parents' lives.

Questions

1. *As this young woman discusses her favorite film actresses, what traits does she single out for admiration?*
2. *On the basis of this memoir, in what ways did the movies most significantly influence young people's behavior and values in the 1920s?*

Source: Herbert Blumer, *Movies and Conduct* (New York, 1933), excerpts in Robert Sklar, ed., *The Plastic Age, 1917–1930* (New York, 1970), pp. 44–47.

Smith and Gertrude "Ma" Rainey. Black-oriented "race records" catered to this specialized market.

Along with network shows, radio stations also broadcast farm reports, local news, church services, community announcements, and ethnic or regional music. Similarly, neighborhood movie theaters provided opportunities for socializing and for exuberant responses to the film. The *Chicago Defender,* voice of the city's black middle class, deplored the raucousness of movie theaters in black neighborhoods, where "during a death scene ... you are likely to hear the orchestra jazzing away." Despite the new mass culture, cultural diversity survived in the 1920s.

Celebrity Culture   Professional sports and media-promoted spectacles provided diversion as well. In 1921, Atlantic City promoters launched a bathing-beauty contest they grandly called the Miss America Pageant. Celebrities dominated professional sports: Babe Ruth of the New York Yankees, who hit sixty home runs in 1927; Ty Cobb, the Detroit Tigers' manager, whose earlier record of 4,191 hits still inspired awe; prizefighters Jack Dempsey and Gene Tunney, whose two heavyweight fights drew massive radio audiences. Ruth was a coarse, heavy-drinking womanizer; Cobb, a foul-tempered racist. Yet the alchemy of publicity transformed them into heroes with contrived nicknames: "the Sultan of Swat" (Ruth) and "the Georgia Peach" (Cobb).

This celebrity culture illuminates the stresses facing ordinary Americans in these years of social change. For young women uncertain about society's shifting expectations, beauty pageants offered one ideal to which they could aspire. For men confronting unsettling developments from feminism to Fordism, the exploits of sports heroes like Dempsey or Ruth could restore damaged self-esteem.

Celebrity worship crested in the response to **Charles Lindbergh**, a daredevil stunt pilot who flew solo across the Atlantic in his small single-engine plane, *The Spirit of St. Louis,* on May 20–21, 1927. A Minnesotan of Swedish ancestry, Lindbergh had entered a $25,000 prize competition offered by a New York hotel for the first nonstop New York-to-Paris flight. His success gripped the public's imagination. In New York, thousands cheered a ticker-tape parade. Radio, newspapers, magazines, and movie newsreels offered saturation coverage.

An instant celebrity, Lindbergh became a blank screen onto which people projected their hopes, fears, and ideologies. President Coolidge praised the flight as a triumph of U.S. business and corporate technology. Many editorial writers, by contrast, saw Lindbergh as proof that despite standardization and mechanization, the individual still counted. Others praised this native-born midwesterner of Scandinavian roots as more authentically American than the recent immigrants crowding the cities.

Overall, the new mass media had mixed social effects. Certainly, they promoted cultural standardization and uniformity of thought. But mass magazines, radio, and movies also helped forge a national culture and introduced new viewpoints and ways of behaving. Implicitly they conveyed a potent message: a person's immediate surroundings need not limit his or her horizons. If the larger world they opened for Americans was often superficial or tawdry, it could also be exciting and liberating.

CULTURAL FERMENT AND CREATIVITY

American life in the 1920s involved more than politics, assembly lines, and celebrity worship. Young people savored the postwar moment as engrained pieties and traditional ways faced challenges. As writers, artists, and musicians embraced the modernist spirit of cultural innovation, African Americans created a cultural flowering known as the Harlem Renaissance.

The Jazz Age and the Postwar Crisis of Values   The war's disillusioned aftermath sharpened the cultural restlessness already bubbling in prewar America. The year 1918, wrote Randolph Bourne, marked "a sudden ... stop at the end of an intellectual era." Poet Ezra Pound hammered the same point in 1920. America had marched to war, he wrote, to save "a botched civilization; ... an old bitch gone in the teeth."

The postwar cultural ferment, summed up in the phrase "the Jazz Age," took many forms. Some young people—especially affluent college students— boisterously assailed middle-class standards of behavior. Grabbing the freedom offered by the automobile, they threw parties, drank bootleg liquor, and flocked to jazz clubs. Asked her favorite activity, a California college student replied, "I adore dancing; who doesn't?" Urged by advertisers, many young women defied prevailing taboos and took up cigarettes. For some, smoking became a feminist issue. As one female college student reasonably asked, "Why [should] men ... be permitted to smoke while girls are expelled for doing it?"

Young people also discussed sex more freely. Sigmund Freud, the Viennese physician who explored the sexual aspects of human psychology, enjoyed a popular vogue in the 1920s. Despite much talk about sex and charges of rampant immorality, however, the 1920s' "sexual revolution" is hard to pin down. Premarital intercourse remained exceptional and widely disapproved, especially for women.

What *can* be documented are changing courtship patterns. "Courting" had once been a formal prelude to marriage. The 1920s brought the more casual practice of "dating," whereby young people gained social confidence and a degree of sexual experience without necessarily contemplating marriage. Wrote novelist F. Scott Fitzgerald, "None of the Victorian mothers had any idea how casually their daughters were accustomed to be kissed." A Methodist bishop denounced new dances that brought "the bodies of men and women in unusual relation to each other." The 1920s saw greater erotic freedom, but within bounds, as most young people drew a clear line between permissible and taboo behavior.

For women, these changes in some ways proved liberating. Female sexuality was more openly acknowledged. Skirt lengths crept up; makeup became more acceptable; and the elaborate armor of petticoats and corsets fell away. The awesome matronly bosom mysteriously deflated as a more boyish figure became the fashion ideal.

An enduring twenties stereotype is "the flapper," the sophisticated, pleasure-mad young woman. (The term originated with a magazine illustration of a fashionable young lady whose rubber rain boots were open and flapping.) In the nineteenth century, the idealized woman on her moral pedestal had symbolized an elaborate complex of cultural ideals. The flapper, with her bobbed hair, defiant cigarette, lipstick, and short skirt, although a journalistic creation, similarly epitomized youthful rejection of entrenched stereotypes.

In some ways, however, 1920s' mass culture thwarted full gender equality nearly as effectively as had earlier Victorian stereotypes. Many young women, while rejecting older taboos, now molded their appearance according to standards dictated by fashion magazines. Advertisers and movies encouraged women to pursue a "glamorous" lifestyle by purchasing new fashions, cosmetics, silk stockings, and other consumer accessories. Further, the traditional double standard, which held women to a stricter behavior code, remained in force. Young men could boast of sexual exploits, but young women who "went all the way" or were reputed to be "fast" risked damaged reputations.

Around 1922, according to F. Scott Fitzgerald, adults embraced the rebelliousness of the young. As middle-aged Americans "discovered that young liquor will take the place of young blood," he wrote, "the orgy began." But such sweeping cultural generalizations can mislead. During the years of Fitzgerald's alleged national orgy, the divorce rate remained constant, and many conservative, religious Americans clung to traditional standards, rejecting alcohol and wild parties. Many farmers, industrial workers, blacks, Hispanics, and recent immigrants found economic concerns more pressing than the latest fads.

F. Scott Fitzgerald and His Wife Zelda

While Fitzgerald chronicled the 1920s in his fiction, he and Zelda lived the high life in New York, Paris, and the French Riviera.

Stock Montage

The "Jazz Age" was partially a media and literary creation. Fitzgerald's romanticized novel about affluent postwar youth, *This Side of Paradise* (1920), spawned many imitators. With his movie-idol good looks, Fitzgerald not only wrote about the Jazz Age but lived it. Yet if the Jazz Age stereotype obscured the complexity of the 1920s, it did capture a part of the postwar scene, especially the raucous new mass culture and the hedonism and materialism of the well-to-do as they basked in the era's prosperity.

Alienated Writers   Like Fitzgerald, many young writers found the decade's cultural turbulence energizing. Rejecting the old order's moralistic pieties, they also disliked the business pieties of the new order. In *Main Street* (1920), novelist Sinclair Lewis satirized the smugness and cultural barrenness of Gopher Prairie, a fictional midwestern town based on his native Sauk Centre, Minnesota. In *Babbitt* (1922), Lewis skewered a mythic larger city, Zenith, and the protagonist George F. Babbitt, a real-estate agent trapped in middle-class conformity.

H.L. Mencken, a journalist and critic, in 1924 launched the iconoclastic *American Mercury* magazine, an instant success with alienated intellectuals and college youth. Mencken championed writers like Lewis and Theodore Dreiser while ridiculing politicians, small-town America, Protestant fundamentalism, and the middle-class "Booboisie." His essays on Harding, Coolidge, and Bryan remain classics of political satire. Asked why he stayed in America, Mencken replied, "Why do people visit zoos?"

For the novelist Ernest Hemingway, seriously wounded in 1918 while a Red Cross volunteer on the Italian front, World War I was a watershed experience. In 1926, now an expatriate in Paris, Hemingway published *The Sun Also Rises*, portraying a group of American and English young people, variously damaged by the war, as they drift around Spain. His *A Farewell to Arms* (1929), loosely based on his own experiences, depicts the war's futility and politicians' empty rhetoric. In one passage, the narrator says,

> *I was always embarrassed by the words sacred, glorious, and sacrifice and the expression in vain. We ... had read them, on proclamations that were slapped up ... over other proclamations, now for a long time, and I had seen nothing sacred, and the things that were glorious had no glory and the sacrifices were like the stockyards at Chicago if nothing was done with the meat except to bury it.*

Although writers like Hemingway and Lewis blasted wartime hypocrisy and postwar vulgarity, they remained American at heart, striving to create a more authentic national culture. Even Fitzgerald, himself caught up in Jazz Age excesses, was fundamentally a moralist. His masterpiece, *The Great Gatsby* (1925), portrayed not only the party-filled lives of the decade's moneyed class, but also their superficiality, selfishness, and heedless disregard for the less fortunate.

Architects, Painters, and Musicians Confront Modern America   A burst of architectural creativity transformed the urban skyline in the 1920s. By 1930, New York City boasted four buildings more than fifty stories tall. Work on the 102-story Empire State Building, long the world's tallest building, began that year. The skyscraper, proclaimed one writer, "epitomizes ... American civilization." Cultural critic Lewis Mumford, by contrast, in *Sticks and Stones* (1924) and other works, deplored urban America's skyscrapers and automobile-clogged streets. Mumford preferred smaller communities and regional cultures to the congested cities and mass culture of 1920s' America.

The decade's leading painters took America—real or imagined—as their subject. While Thomas Hart Benton evoked a past of cowboys, pioneers, and riverboat gamblers, Edward Hopper portrayed faded towns and lonely cities of the present. Hopper's painting *Sunday* (1926), picturing a man slumped on the curb of an empty street of abandoned stores, conveyed both the bleakness and potential beauty of urban America.

The painter and photographer Charles Sheeler found inspiration in factories, including Henry Ford's plant near Detroit. The Italian immigrant Joseph Stella captured New York's vitality in such paintings as *The Bridge* (1926), an abstract representation of the Brooklyn Bridge. Wisconsin's Georgia O'Keeffe, who moved to New York City in 1918, evoked the allure of the metropolis in her paintings of the later 1920s.

The decade's creative ferment inspired composers as well. Ruth Crawford Seeger arranged American folksongs for the poet Carl Sandburg's *American Song-bag* (1927). Carl Ruggles set a Walt Whitman poem to music in 1923. And

Frederick Converse's ambitious 1927 tone poem about the automobile, "Flivver Ten Million," featured such episodes as "May Night by the Roadside" and "The Collision."

Of all the musical innovations, jazz best captured the modernist spirit. The Original Dixieland Jass Band—white musicians imitating New Orleans' black jazz bands—had debuted in New York City in 1917, launching a vogue that spread by live performances, radio, and recordings. The white bandleader Paul Whiteman offered watered-down "jazz" versions of standard tunes, and white composers embraced jazz as well. George Gershwin's *Rhapsody in Blue* (1924) and *An American in Paris* (1928) revealed strong jazz influences.

Meanwhile, black musicians preserved authentic jazz and explored its potential. The 1920s recordings of trumpeter Louis Armstrong and his band decisively influenced the future of jazz. While the composer and bandleader Duke Ellington mesmerized audiences at Harlem's Cotton Club, Fletcher Henderson's band, featuring singer Ethel Waters and saxophonist Coleman Hawkins, held forth at New York's Roseland Ballroom. Pianists Fats Waller, Ferdinand "Jelly Roll" Morton, and Earl Hines demonstrated that instrument's jazz potential. Although much of 1920s' popular culture faded quickly, jazz endured.

The Harlem Renaissance   Jazz was only one of many black contributions to 1920s' American culture. The social upheavals of these years energized African American cultural life, especially in New York City's Harlem. Once an elite white suburb, Harlem attracted many African Americans during and after World War I, and by 1930 most of New York's 327,000 blacks lived within its boundaries. This concentration, plus the proximity of Broadway theaters, record companies, book publishers, and the NAACP's national headquarters, all contributed to the Harlem Renaissance.

This cultural flowering took varied forms. The Mississippi-born black composer William Grant Still, moving to Harlem in 1922, produced many works, including *Afro American Symphony* (1931). Painter Aaron Douglas and sculptor Augusta Savage explored the visual arts. Savage, moving from Florida to Harlem in 1921, opened a studio and later an art school.

The 1921 Broadway hit *Shuffle Along* launched a series of popular all-black musicals. Film-maker Oscar Micheaux featured black actors and black story lines. The multi-talented Paul Robeson gave vocal concerts; made films; and appeared on Broadway in Eugene O'Neill's *The Emperor Jones* and other plays.

Poet Langston Hughes incorporated African themes and southern black traditions in *The Weary Blues* (1926), and the Jamaican-born poet and novelist Claude McKay evoked Harlem's vibrant, sometimes sinister, nightlife in *Home to Harlem* (1928). In *Cane* (1923), Jean Toomer used poetry, drama, and fictional vignettes to convey the world of the rural black South. Novelist Nella Larsen, from the Danish West Indies, told of a mulatto woman's struggles in *Quicksand* (1928). In *The New Negro* (1925), Alain Locke, a philosophy professor at Howard University, assembled essays, poems, short stories, and artworks to document Harlem's cultural riches.

The white cultural establishment took notice. Book publishers and magazine editors courted black writers. Broadway producers mounted black shows. Whites jammed Harlem's jazz clubs. The 1929 Hollywood film *Hallelujah,* featuring an

Langston Hughes, Poet of the Harlem Renaissance. *Hughes was part of the African American cultural and political awakening of the 1920s that foreshadowed changes ahead.*

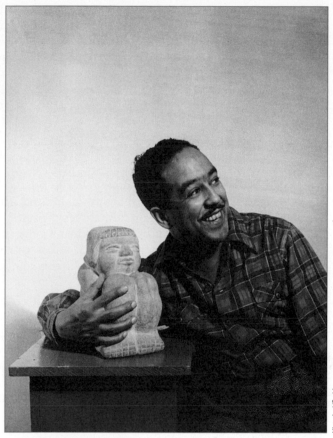

Historical/Corbis

all-black cast, romanticized plantation life and dramatized the city's dangers. DuBose Heyward's 1925 novel *Porgy* (adapted for the stage by Heyward and his wife Dorothy) drew inspiration from Charleston's African American community. George Gershwin's musical version, *Porgy and Bess,* premiered in 1935.

The Harlem Renaissance resonated internationally. Jazz won fans in Europe. Langston Hughes and Claude McKay found readers in Africa, Latin America, and Europe. The dancer and singer Josephine Baker, after debuting in Harlem, moved to Paris in 1925, where her highly erotic performances created a sensation.

With white support came misunderstanding and attempts at control. Rebellious young whites romanticized Harlem nightlife, ignoring the community's social problems. Some whites idealized black culture for its spiritual or "primitive" qualities. When Langston Hughes's poems addressed the gritty realities of black life in America, his wealthy white patron angrily withdrew her support. Wrote Hughes: "[S]he felt that [Negroes] were America's great link with the primitive.... But unfortunately I did not feel the rhythms of the primitive surging through me ... I was not Africa. I was Chicago and Kansas City and Broadway and Harlem."

The exuberance of the Harlem Renaissance faded as hard times hit in the 1930s. Nevertheless, future black writers, artists, musicians, and performers would owe a great debt to their predecessors of the 1920s. With this cultural awakening came a heightened political consciousness, mobilized by such groups as the National Association for the Advancement of Colored People, the National Urban League, and the National Association of Colored Women. As historian Clare Corbould argues in *Becoming African Americans: Black Public Life in Harlem, 1919–1939* (2009), .this sharpened political awareness involved tensions between integrationist and separatist impulses—tensions that W.E.B. Du Bois had expressed in a famous essay in *The Souls of Black Folk* (1903) on the "double consciousness" of African Americans.

A SOCIETY IN CONFLICT

The social changes and tensions of the 1920s produced a fierce backlash. While Congress restricted immigration, highly publicized trials in Massachusetts and Tennessee cast a harsh spotlight on the nation's divisions. Millions of whites embraced the bigotry of a revived Ku Klux Klan, and many newly urbanized African Americans rallied to Marcus Garvey, a magnetic black leader with a riveting message of racial pride. Prohibition stirred further controversy in this conflict-ridden decade.

Immigration Restriction   Fed by wartime super-patriotism and xenophobia, the impulse to remake America into a nation of like-minded, culturally homogeneous people revived in the 1920s.

The **National Origins Act** (1924) restricted annual immigration from any foreign country to 2 percent of the number of persons of that "national origin" in the United States in 1890. The great influx of southern and eastern Europeans had come later, so this provision clearly aimed to reduce immigration from these regions. As Calvin Coolidge observed on signing the law, "America must be kept American."

In 1929, Congress changed the base year for determining "national origins" to 1920, but even under this formula, Poland's annual quota stood at a mere 6,524; Italy's at 5,802; and Hungary's, 869. This quota system, which survived to 1965, represented a counterattack by native-born Protestant America against the immigrant cities. Total immigration fell from 1.2 million in 1914 to 280,000 in 1929. The law excluded Asians and South Asians entirely.

Court rulings underscored the nativist message. In *Ozawa* v. *United States* (1922), the U.S. Supreme Court denied citizenship to a Japanese-born university student. In 1923, the Supreme Court upheld a California law limiting Japanese immigrants' right to own or lease farmland.

Needed Workers/ Unwelcome Aliens: Hispanic Newcomers   Extremely restrictive otherwise, the 1924 law did not limit immigration from the Western Hemisphere. Accordingly, immigration from Latin America (as well as from French Canada) soared. Poverty and political turmoil propelled thousands of Mexicans northward. By 1930, at least 2 million Mexican-born immigrants lived in the United States, mostly in the Southwest. California's Mexican American population surged from 90,000 to nearly 360,000 in the 1920s.

Many of these immigrants worked in low-paid migratory agricultural jobs. Mexican labor sustained California's citrus industry. Cooperatives such as the

Southern California Fruit Growers Exchange (which used the brand name "Sunkist") hired itinerant workers on a seasonal basis, provided substandard housing in isolated settlements, and fought the migrants' attempts to form labor unions.

Other Mexican immigrants settled in cities. Migrants to the Midwest worked not only in agriculture but also in the automobile, steel, and railroad industries. Retaining deep ties to "México Lindo" (Beautiful Mexico), they formed local support networks and cultural institutions. The Mexican American community was divided, however, between recent arrivals and earlier immigrants who had become U.S. citizens. The strongest Mexican American organization in the 1920s, the League of United Latin-American Citizens, ignored the migrant laborers of the Southwest.

Though deeply religious, Mexican Americans found little support from the U.S. Catholic Church. Earlier, European Catholic immigrants had attended ethnic parishes and worshiped in their own languages, but church policy had changed by the 1920s. In parishes with non-Hispanic priests, Spanish-speaking Mexican new-comers encountered pressure to abandon their language and traditions.

In the larger society, Mexican immigrants faced ambivalent attitudes. Their labor was needed, but their presence angered nativists eager to preserve a "white" and Protestant nation. Would-be immigrants confronted strict literacy and financial tests, and in 1929 Congress made it a criminal offense to cross the border without following required immigration procedures. The flow continued, however, as an estimated one hundred thousand Mexicans arrived annually, legally and clandestinely, to fill the U.S. labor market's pressing demands.

Nativism, Antiradicalism, and the Sacco-Vanzetti Case   The anti-immigration movement reflected deep ethnic, racial, and religious prejudice in 1920s' America. Anti-Semitic propaganda filled Henry Ford's weekly newspaper, the *Dearborn Independent*, distributed through Ford dealerships and mailed free to schools and libraries. The anti-Semitic articles were reprinted in pamphlets called *The International Jew*. Sued for defamation by a Jewish attorney, Ford in 1927 issued an evasive apology blaming subordinates.

Ethnic and antiradical prejudices pervaded the **Sacco-Vanzetti Case**, a Massachusetts murder case that began in April 1920, when robbers shot and killed a paymaster and guard at a South Braintree, Massachusetts, shoe factory. In 1921, a jury convicted two Italian immigrants, Nicola Sacco and Bartolomeo Vanzetti, of the crime. After many appeals and a review by a blue-ribbon panel of notables, they were electrocuted on August 23, 1927.

These bare facts hardly convey the passions the case aroused. Sacco and Vanzetti were anarchists, and the prosecution harped on their radicalism. The judge barely concealed his hostility to the pair, whom he privately called "those anarchist bastards." While conservatives supported the verdict, liberals and socialists protested. On the night of the electrocution, novelist John Dos Passos wrote a bitter poem that ended: *All right you have won you will kill the brave men our friends tonight … all right we are two nations.*

Later research on Boston's anarchist community and ballistics tests on Sacco's gun pointed to their guilt. But the prejudices that tainted the trial remain indisputable, as does the case's symbolic importance in exposing the deep fault lines in

1920s' American society. Indeed, the case stirred global protests, as radical groups in Europe and elsewhere made it an international cause célèbre.

Fundamental-ism and the Scopes Trial   An equally famous case in Tennessee highlighted another front in the decade's cultural wars: the growing prestige of science. While "individually powerless," wrote the Harvard philosopher Alfred North Whitehead in *Science and the Modern World* (1925), scientists were "ultimately the rulers of the world." Many Americans welcomed the advance of science, but some religious believers found it threatening. Their fears had deepened as scholars had subjected the Bible to critical scrutiny, psychologists and sociologists had studied supernatural belief systems as expressions of human emotional needs, and biologists had embraced the naturalistic explanation for the variety of life forms on earth advanced in Charles Darwin's *Origin of Species* (1859).

While liberal Protestants had generally accepted these findings, evangelical believers had resisted. This gave rise to a movement called **fundamentalism**, after *The Fundamentals,* a series of tracts published in 1909–1914. Fundamentalists insisted on the Bible's inerrancy and literal truth, including the Genesis account of Creation.

In the early 1920s, fundamentalists targeted Darwin's theory of evolution. Many state legislatures considered barring public schools from teaching evolution, and several southern states enacted such laws. Texas governor Miriam "Ma" Ferguson personally censored textbooks that discussed evolution. "I am a Christian mother," she declared, "and I am not going to let that kind of rot go into Texas textbooks." Former Democratic presidential candidate William Jennings Bryan endorsed the anti-evolution cause.

In 1925, when Tennessee's legislature outlawed the teaching of evolution in the state's public schools, the American Civil Liberties Union (ACLU) offered to defend any teacher willing to challenge this law. A high-school teacher in Dayton, Tennessee, John T. Scopes, encouraged by local businessmen and civic boosters, accepted the offer. After summarizing Darwin's theory to a science class, Scopes was arrested. Famed criminal lawyer Clarence Darrow headed the defense, while Bryan assisted the prosecution. Journalists poured into Dayton; a Chicago radio station broadcast the proceedings; and the **Scopes Trial** became a media sensation.

Cross-examined by Darrow, Bryan embraced the biblical version of creation and dismissed evolutionary theory. Although the jury found Scopes guilty (in a decision later reversed on a technicality), the trial exposed Fundamentalism to ridicule. When Bryan died of a heart attack soon after, H.L. Mencken wrote a scathing column contemptuously dismissing him and his fundamentalist admirers.

The Scopes Trial exposed the anxieties felt by many Americans. Bryan shrewdly appealed to citizens fearful of cultural forces beyond their control. Let parents and local communities decide what children are taught, he pled, evoking memories of his 1896 populist campaign defending common folk against the rich and powerful (see Chapter 20). Despite the setback in Dayton, Fundamentalism survived. Mainstream Protestant denominations grew more liberal, but many local congregations, radio preachers, Bible schools, new denominations, and flamboyant evangelists like Billy Sunday upheld the traditional faith. Southern and western states continued to pass antievolution laws, and textbook publishers modified their treatment of evolution to appease local school boards.

In Los Angeles, the charismatic Aimee Semple McPherson filled her cavernous Angelus Temple and reached thousands more by radio. Her followers, mainly transplanted midwesterners, embraced her fundamentalist theology while enjoying her theatrical sermons. (She once used a gigantic electric scoreboard to illustrate the triumph of good over evil.) At her death in 1944, her International Church of the Foursquare Gospel had more than six hundred branches in the United States and abroad.

The Ku Klux Klan   The tensions gripping American society of the 1920s also bubbled up in the form of a resurrected Ku Klux Klan (KKK). The original Klan of the Reconstruction South had eventually faded (see Chapter 16), but in 1915 hooded men gathered at Stone Mountain, Georgia, revived it. D.W. Griffith's glorification of the original Klan in his 1915 movie *The Birth of a Nation* provided further fuel.

In 1920, two Atlanta entrepreneurs plotted a national campaign to profit from the appeal of the Klan's ritual and its nativist, white-supremacist ideology. Their wildly successful scheme involved a ten-dollar membership fee divided among the salesman (called the Kleagle), the local sales manager (King Kleagle), the district sales manager (Grand Goblin), the state leader (Grand Dragon), and national leader (Imperial Wizard)—with a rake-off to themselves. The sale of Klan robes, masks, horse blankets, and bottled Chattahoochee River water (used in initiation rites) added to the take.

Preaching "100 percent Americanism," the Klan demonized blacks, Catholics, Jews, aliens, and, in some cases, women suspected of violating sexual taboos. Membership estimates for the KKK and its women's auxiliary in the early 1920s range as high as 5 million. From its southern base, the Klan spread through the Midwest and across the country from Long Island to the West Coast. The white working class and lower middle class in cities with native-born Protestant majorities proved especially receptive. In 1922, Imperial Wizard Hiram Wesley Evans admitted the Klan's image as a haven of "hicks" and "rubes" and urged college graduates to support the great cause.

Although the Klan was basically a money-making scam riddled with corrupt and cynical leaders, observers commented on the ordinariness of the typical members. (Evans, a Texas dentist, called himself "the most average man in America.") The Klan's litany of enemies and its promise to restore the nation's lost purity—racial, ethnic, religious, and moral—appealed to economically marginal Protestants disoriented by a new social order of giant corporations, mass media, rebellious youth, and immigrant-filled cities. The rituals, parades, and night-time cross burnings added a jolt of drama and excitement to life's everyday routines.

But if individual Klan members seemed more needy than sinister, the Klan as a mass movement was menacing. Some KKK groups employed threats, beatings, and lynching in their quest to purify America. In several states, the Klan won political power. Oklahoma's Klan-controlled legislature impeached and removed an anti-Klan governor. The Oregon Klan elected a governor and enacted legislation requiring all children to attend public school, an attempt to destroy the state's Catholic schools.

The Klan collapsed with shocking suddenness. In March 1925, Indiana's Grand Dragon, David Stephenson, brutally raped his young secretary, who swallowed poison and died several weeks later. In prison, Stephenson revealed sordid details of political corruption. Its moral pretensions in shreds, the KKK faded. When civil-rights activism surged in the 1950s, however, the Klan would again rear its head.

The Garvey Movement   Among African Americans who had fled southern rural poverty and racism only to experience discrimination and racism in the urban North, the 1920s produced a different kind of mass movement, led by **Marcus Garvey** and his Universal Negro Improvement Association (UNIA). Born in Jamaica in 1887, the son of a stonemason, Garvey founded UNIA in 1914 and soon after moved to Harlem. In a white-dominated society, Garvey glorified all things black. Urging black economic solidarity and capitalist enterprise as the lever of racial advance, he founded UNIA grocery stores and other businesses. Summoning blacks to return to "Motherland Africa," he established the Black Star Steamship Line to help them get there.

An estimated eighty thousand blacks joined UNIA, and thousands more felt the lure of Garvey's oratory, the excitement of UNIA parades and uniforms, and the appeal of economic self-sufficiency and a glorious future in Africa. Although centered in New York and other northern cities, the movement had chapters across the South as well. Garvey's popularity unsettled established black church leaders and roused opposition from the NAACP, which saw the African American future in America, not Africa, and advocated racial integration rather than separation. W.E.B. Du Bois was among Garvey's sharpest critics.

The movement also highlighted social tensions in Harlem, where two streams of the African diaspora, one from the Caribbean, the other from the American South, converged. The resulting economic and political rivalry sharpened resistance to the UNIA, with its Jamaican founder and Caribbean leadership.

In 1923, a federal court convicted Garvey of fraud in the management of his Black Star Steamship Line. He was deported in 1927, and the UNIA collapsed. But this first mass movement in black America had revealed the social aspirations and activist potential of African Americans in the urban North. "In a world where black is despised," commented an African American newspaper after Garvey's fall, "he taught his followers that black is beautiful." Garvey is honored in his native island as a heroic forerunner of Jamaican independence from British Colonial rule.

The NAACP, meanwhile, remained active even in a decade of rampant racism. In some 300 branches nationwide, members kept the civil-rights cause alive and patiently laid the groundwork for legal challenges to segregation.

Prohibition: Cultures in Conflict   A bitter controversy over alcohol deepened the fissures in American society. As noted in Chapter 21, the Progressive Era **prohibition** campaign was both a legitimate effort to address social problems associated with alcohol abuse and a symbolic crusade by native-born Protestants to control the immigrant cities.

These tensions persisted in the 1920s. When the Eighteenth Amendment took effect in 1920, prohibitionists rejoiced. Saloons closed, liquor advertising vanished, and arrests for drunkenness declined. Yet prohibition gradually lost support, and in 1933 it ended.

What went wrong? Essentially, prohibition's failure illustrates the difficulty in a democracy of enforcing a widely opposed law. The Volstead Act, the 1919 prohibition law, was underfunded and weakly enforced, especially in antiprohibition areas. New York, for example, repealed its prohibition-enforcement law as early as 1923. Would-be drinkers grew bolder as enforcement faltered. For many young people, alcohol's illegality increased its appeal. Challenging prohibition, declared one college student, represented "the natural reaction of youth to rules and regulations."

Rum-runners smuggled liquor from Canada and the West Indies, and every city harbored speakeasies selling alcoholic drinks. People concocted home brew, shady entrepreneurs sold flavored industrial-grade alcohol, and sacramental wine sales soared. By 1929, alcohol consumption reached about 70 percent of prewar levels.

Organized crime helped circumvent the law. Chicago, where gangsters battled to control the liquor business, witnessed 550 gangland killings in the 1920s. Speakeasies controlled by Chicago gangster Al Capone generated annual profits of $60 million. Although not typical, Chicago's crime wave underscored prohibition's failure. A reform designed to improve public morality was turning citizens into lawbreakers and mobsters into celebrities.

Prohibition, too, became a battleground in the decade's cultural wars. The "drys"—usually native-born Protestants—praised it. The "wets"—liberals, Jazz Age rebels, big-city immigrants—condemned it as moralistic meddling. At one college, the student newspaper suggested a campus distillery as the senior class gift.

Prohibition influenced the 1928 presidential campaign. While Democratic candidate Al Smith advocated repeal of the Eighteenth Amendment, Republican Herbert Hoover praised it as "a great social and economic experiment, noble in motive and far-reaching in purpose." Once elected, Hoover appointed a commission to study the issue. Its confusing 1931 report admitted prohibition's failure, but urged its retention. A journalist parodied the findings:

> Prohibition is an awful flop.
> We like it.
> It can't stop what it's meant to stop.
> We like it.
> It's left a trail of graft and slime,
> It's filled our land with vice and crime,
> It don't prohibit worth a dime,
> Nevertheless we're for it.

The Eighteenth Amendment was finally repealed in 1933, a relic of another age.

HOOVER AT THE HELM

Herbert Hoover, elected president in 1928, appeared well fitted to sustain the nation's prosperity. No standpat conservative like Harding and Coolidge, he brought to the White House a social and political philosophy that reflected his engineering background. He seemed the ideal president for the new technological age.

The Election of 1928   A Hollywood casting agent could not have chosen two individuals who better personified America's divisions than the 1928 presidential candidates, Al Smith and Herbert Hoover.

The Democratic Party's urban-immigrant wing had gained strength since the deadlocked 1924 convention, and New York governor Al Smith easily won the nomination. A Catholic and a wet, Smith exuded the flavor of immigrant New York. Originally a machine politician and basically conservative, he had impressed reformers by backing social-welfare measures. His key advisers included several reform-minded women, notably Frances Perkins, head of the state industrial board.

Herbert Hoover won the Republican nomination after Coolidge chose not to run. Some conservative party leaders mistrusted the brilliant but aloof Hoover, who had never held elective office and had spent much of his adult life abroad. Born in Iowa and orphaned in boyhood, Hoover had put himself through Stanford University and made a fortune as a mining engineer in China and Australia. After his tour as wartime food administrator, he had served as secretary of commerce since 1921.

Disdaining conventional campaigning, Hoover instead issued "tons of reports on dull subjects" (as H.L. Mencken complained) and read radio speeches in a droning monotone that obscured the originality of his ideas. (Some Hoover strategists did make use of sound film to promote his cause.) Smith, by contrast, campaigned spiritedly across the nation. This may have hurt him, however, because his big-city wisecracking and New York accent put off many voters.

The effect of Smith's Catholicism remains debatable. Hoover urged tolerance, and Smith himself denied any conflict between his religion and the duties of the presidency. His candidacy energized Catholic voters, but anti-Catholic prejudice also played a role. Rumors circulated that Smith would follow the Vatican's orders if he won. (A postelection joke had Smith sending the pope a one-word telegram, "Unpack."). The decisive issue was probably not popery but prosperity. Republican orators pointed to the booming economy and warned of "soup kitchens instead of busy factories" if Smith won. In his nomination-acceptance speech, Hoover grandly predicted "the final triumph over poverty."

Hoover won in a landslide, grabbing 58 percent of the vote and even making deep inroads in the Democratic South. However, the outcome also hinted at an emerging political realignment. Smith did well among hard-pressed midwestern farmers angered by Coolidge's insensitivity to their plight. In northern cities, Catholic and Jewish wards voted heavily Democratic. Smith carried the nation's twelve largest cities, all of which had gone Republican in 1924. Should prosperity falter, the Republican Party faced trouble.

Herbert Hoover's Social Thought   Admirers dubbed Hoover "the Great Engineer." Although a self-made man, he did not uncritically praise the capitalist system. His Quaker background, humanitarian activities, engineering experience, and Republican loyalties combined to produce a unique social outlook, summed up in his 1922 book *American Individualism*.

Like Theodore Roosevelt (whom he had supported in 1912), Hoover opposed untrammeled free-market competition. Rational economic development, he insisted, demanded corporate cooperation in resource allocation, product standardization, and other areas. The economy, in short, should operate like an efficient machine.

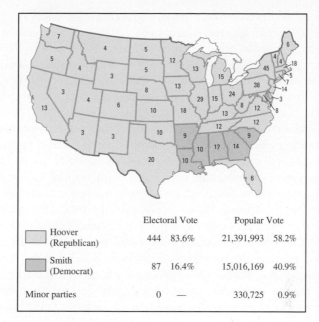

	Electoral Vote	Popular Vote
Hoover (Republican)	444 83.6%	21,391,993 58.2%
Smith (Democrat)	87 16.4%	15,016,169 40.9%
Minor parties	0 —	330,725 0.9%

MAP 23.1 The Election of 1928

Although Hoover won every state but Massachusetts and six Deep South states, Smith's 1928 vote in the midwestern farm belt and the nation's largest cities showed significant gains for the Democratic Party over 1924.

Source: © Cengage Learning. All rights reserved. No distribution allowed without express authorization.

Believing in ethical business behavior, Hoover welcomed the growth of welfare capitalism. But above all, he advocated *voluntarism*. The efficient, socially responsible economic order he envisioned must arise from the voluntary action of capitalist leaders, not government coercion or labor-management power struggles.

TABLE 23.1 | PRESIDENTIAL VOTING BY SELECTED GROUPS IN CHICAGO, 1924, 1928, AND 1932

	Percent Democratic		
	1924	1928	1932
Blacks	10	23	21
Czechoslovaks	40	73	83
Germans	14	58	69
Italians	31	63	64
Jews	19	60	77
Lithuanians	48	77	84
Poles	35	71	80
Swedes	15	34	51
Yugoslavs	20	54	67

Source: John M. Allswang, A *House for All Peoples: Ethnic Politics in Chicago, 1890–1936* (Lexington: University Press of Kentucky, 1971).

Putting his philosophy into practice, Hoover as secretary of commerce had convened more than 250 conferences where business leaders discussed issues of common concern. He urged higher wages to increase consumer purchasing power, and in 1923 he persuaded the steel industry to adopt an eight-hour workday as an efficiency measure. During the 1927 Mississippi River floods, as President Coolidge did nothing, Hoover had visited the stricken area to mobilize private relief efforts.

A conservationist, Hoover as secretary of commerce had pushed for planned use of water resources and programs to combat the pollution of rivers and lakes. In 1922, he negotiated a compact among western states to share Colorado River water. This agreement opened the way for a dam on the Colorado to provide hydroelectric power, control flooding, and supply water for irrigation. Construction of Hoover Dam began in 1930. (In an act of petty politics, Democrats changed the name to Boulder Dam in 1933, but Congress later restored the original name.)

Hoover's ideology had limitations. He showed more enthusiasm for cooperation among capitalists than among consumers or workers. His belief that capitalists would voluntarily embrace ethical behavior and pursue the general good reflected an exaggerated faith in the power of altruism in business decision making. His opposition to government economic intervention would prove disastrous when such intervention became urgently necessary.

Still, Hoover's presidency began promisingly. He created various commissions to gather data on recent social trends. At his urging, Congress created a Federal Farm Board to promote cooperative marketing. This, he hoped, would raise farm prices while preserving the voluntarist principle. Meanwhile, however, an economic crisis was approaching that would overwhelm and ultimately destroy his presidency.

CHRONOLOGY
1920–1929

1920–1921	Postwar recession.
1920	Warren G. Harding elected president.
	League of Women Voters founded.
	Radio station KDKA, Pittsburgh, broadcasts election returns.
	Sinclair Lewis, *Main Street*.
1921	Economic boom begins; agriculture remains depressed.
	Sheppard-Towner Act.
	Shuffle Along, all-black musical review.
1921–1922	Washington Naval Arms Conference.
1922	Supreme Court declares child-labor law unconstitutional.
	Fordney-McCumber Tariff restores high rates.
	Herbert Hoover, *American Individualism*.

1923
Harding dies; Calvin Coolidge becomes president.

Teapot Dome scandals investigated.

National Origins Act (immigration restriction).

1924
Calvin Coolidge elected president.

1925
Scopes Trial.

Ku Klux Klan scandal in Indiana.

Alain Locke, *The New Negro*.

DuBose Heyward, *Porgy*.

F. Scott Fitzgerald, *The Great Gatsby*.

1926
Book-of-the-Month Club founded.

National Broadcasting Company founded.

Langston Hughes, *The Weary Blues*.

U.S. Marines intervene in Nicaragua.

1927
The Jazz Singer, first sound movie.

Coolidge vetoes the McNary-Haugen farm bill.

Henry Ford introduces the Model A.

Ford apologizes for anti-Semitic publications.

Execution of Sacco and Vanzetti.

Charles A. Lindbergh's transatlantic flight.

Marcus Garvey deported.

Mississippi River flood.

1928
Herbert Hoover elected president.

1929
Federal Farm Board created.

Sheppard-Towner program terminated.

Textile strike in Gastonia, North Carolina.

Ernest Hemingway, *A Farewell to Arms*.

Claude McKay, *Home to Harlem*.

CONCLUSION

Repudiating the Wilsonian vision of America's postwar world role, the Republican administrations of the 1920s pursued a nationalistic foreign policy aimed at collecting war debts and protecting U.S. corporate interests in Latin America. The 1921 Washington Naval Arms Conference, though ultimately unsuccessful, represents the one diplomatic initiative of note in these years.

At home, the 1920s brought new entertainment media, consumer products, marketing strategies, and mass-production techniques. While enjoying widespread (if uneven) prosperity, Americans grappled with massive technological and social changes. Like jet-lagged travelers, they struggled to adapt to the new order. Skyscrapers, radio, automobiles, movies, and electrical appliances—all familiar today—were exciting novelties for this generation.

While the Harding and Coolidge administrations celebrated the corporate order and pursued probusiness policies, society seethed in ferment. Ironically, the same stresses that sparked social conflict also stimulated cultural creativity. Jazz Age youth; Mexican immigrants seeking a better life; native-born advocates of immigration restriction, prohibition, and Fundamentalism; white Protestant KKK members; blacks who rallied to Marcus Garvey; the artists and writers of the Harlem Renaissance; and the musicians, painters, and novelists who revitalized American culture were all, in their different ways, responding to the promise and uncertainties of modernity.

24

THE GREAT DEPRESSION AND THE NEW DEAL, 1929–1939

CHAPTER OUTLINE

• Crash and Depression, 1929–1932 • The New Deal Takes Shape, 1933–1935 • The New Deal Changes Course, 1935–1936 • The New Deal's End Stage, 1937–1939 • Social Change and Social Action in the 1930s • The American Cultural Scene in the 1930s

---

CRASH AND DEPRESSION, 1929–1932

The prosperity of the 1920s ended in October 1929 with the stock market collapse. The Wall Street crash, and the economic problems that underlay it, launched a depression that hit every household. President Hoover struggled to respond, but his commitment to private initiative and his horror of direct federal intervention limited his effectiveness. In November 1932, voters turned to the Democratic Party and its leader, **Franklin Delano Roosevelt**. This set the stage for a vast federal response to the economic and social crisis.

Black Thursday and the Onset of the Depression — Stock prices had risen through much of the 1920s, but 1928–1929 brought a frenzied upsurge as speculators plunged into the market. In 1925, the market value of all stocks had stood at about $27 billion; by October 1929, it hit $87 billion. With stockbrokers lending buyers up to 75 percent of a stock's cost, credit or "margin" buying spread. The income-tax cuts promoted by Treasury Secretary Andrew Mellon had increased the flow of money into the market. Upbeat statements also fed the boom. In March 1929, former president Calvin Coolidge declared stocks "cheap at current prices." "Investment trusts," akin to today's mutual funds, lured novices into the market. The construction industry faltered in 1928–1929, signaling a decline in the housing market and in business expansion.

The Federal Reserve Board tried to dampen speculation by raising interest rates and urging member banks to restrain their lending. But with speculators paying up to 20 percent interest to buy more stock, lending institutions continued to loan money freely—equivalent to dumping gasoline on a raging fire.

The collapse came on October 24, 1929—"Black Thursday." As prices fell, some stocks found no buyers at all: they had become worthless. In the ensuing weeks, feeble upswings alternated with further plunges.

President Hoover, in the first of many optimistic statements, pronounced the economy "sound and prosperous." After a weak upswing early in 1930, the economy went into a long tailspin, producing a full-scale depression.

Economists probing the depression's underlying causes focus on structural problems that made 1920s' prosperity highly unstable. Agriculture remained depressed throughout the decade. In the industrial sector, wage increases lagged behind factory output, reducing consumer purchasing power. At the same time, assembly-line methods encouraged overproduction. By summer 1929, not only housing but also the automobile, textile, tire, and other industries were seriously overextended. Further, key industries such as railroads, steel, and textiles lagged technologically in the 1930s and could not attract the investment needed to stimulate recovery.

Some economists, called monetarists, also blame the Federal Reserve System's tight-money policies in the early 1930s. This policy, they argue, strangled any hope of recovery by reducing the capital available to businesses for investment and growth.

All analysts link the U.S. depression to a global economic crisis. European economies, struggling with war-debt payments and a severe trade imbalance with the United States, collapsed in 1931, crippling the U.S. export market.

The worsening depression devastated the U.S. economy. From 1929 to 1932, the gross national product dropped from $104 billion to $59 billion. Farm prices, already low, fell by nearly 60 percent. By early 1933 more than fifty-five hundred banks had closed, and unemployment stood at 25 percent, or nearly 13 million workers. In some cities, the jobless rate surged far higher. Many who still had jobs faced cuts in pay and hours.

Hoover's Response   Historically, Americans had viewed depressions as similar to natural disasters: little could be done other than ride out the storm. President Hoover disagreed. Drawing upon his experience as U.S. food administrator in World War I and as secretary of commerce, Hoover initially responded boldly. But his belief in private initiative limited his options.

Viewing unemployment as a local issue, Hoover advised city and state officials to create public-works projects. In October 1930, he set up an Emergency Committee for Employment to coordinate voluntary relief efforts. In 1931, he persuaded the nation's largest banks to create a private lending agency to help smaller banks make business loans.

Despite these initiatives, public opinion turned against Hoover. In the 1930 midterm election, the Republicans lost the House of Representatives and gave up eight Senate seats. In 1931, dreading a budget deficit, Hoover called for a tax increase, further angering hard-pressed Americans. That same year, U.S. Steel and

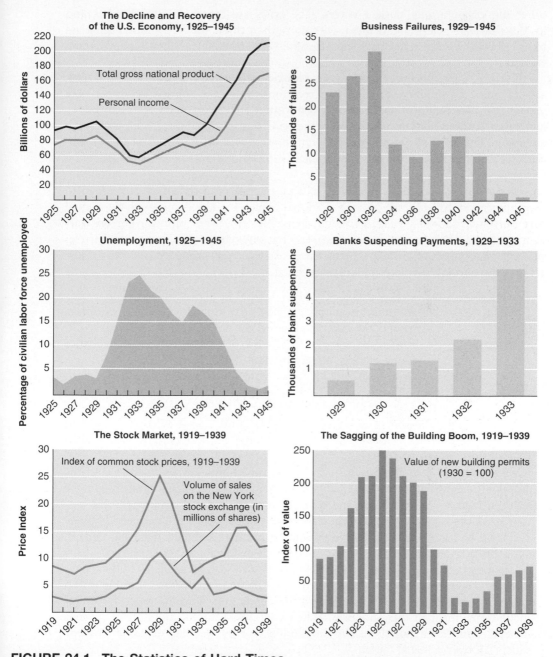

FIGURE 24.1   The Statistics of Hard Times

Figures on the gross national product, personal income, unemployment, the stock market, and business failures all show the depression's shattering impact, with gradual and uneven improvement as the 1930s wore on.

Sources: Thomas C. Cochran, *The Great Depression and World War II: 1929–1945* (Glenview, Ill.: Scott, Foresman, 1968); *Historical Statistics of the United States, Colonial Times to 1970* (Washington, D.C.: U.S. Government Printing Office, 1975).

other big corporations slashed wages. The crisis swamped private charities and local welfare agencies. Philadelphia, with more than three hundred thousand jobless by 1932, cut weekly relief payments to $4.23 per family and then stopped them entirely.

In 1932, a presidential election year, Hoover swallowed his principles and took a bold step. In January, at Hoover's recommendation, Congress set up a new agency, the **Reconstruction Finance Corporation** (RFC), to make loans to banks and other lending institutions. By July, the RFC had pumped $1.2 billion into the economy. The RFC also granted $2 billion to state and local governments for job-creating public-works programs, and allocated $750 million for loans to struggling businesses.

Hoover supported these measures reluctantly, warning that they could lead to "socialism and collectivism." Blaming global forces for the depression, he argued that only international measures would help. His call for a moratorium on war-debt and reparations payments by European nations made sense, but seemed irrelevant to the plight of ordinary Americans. As Hoover predicted recovery "just around the corner," his unpopularity deepened.

Mounting
Discontent
and Protest

An ominous mood spread as the jobless waited in breadlines, trudged the streets, and rode freight trains seeking work. Americans reared on the ethic of hard work and self-reliance found chronic unemployment deeply demoralizing.

The *New York Times* described "Hoover Valley"—a section of Central Park where jobless men lived in boxes and packing crates, keeping warm with layers of newspapers they bitterly called Hoover blankets. The suicide rate soared. In Youngstown, Ohio, a jobless father of ten whose family faced eviction jumped to his death from a bridge. Violence threatened in some cities when landlords evicted families unable to pay their rent.

Many farmers lost their lands because of tax delinquency, with Iowa and the Dakotas especially hard hit. At some forced farm auctions, neighbors bought the foreclosed farm for a trivial sum and returned it to the evicted family.

In 1931, midwestern farmers organized a movement called the Farmers' Holiday Association to force prices up by withholding grain and livestock from the market. Dairy farmers angered by low prices dumped milk in Iowa and Wisconsin.

The most alarming protest came from World War I veterans. In 1924, Congress had voted veterans a bonus stretched over a twenty-year period. In June 1932, some ten thousand veterans, many jobless, descended on Washington to lobby for immediate payment of these bonuses. When Congress refused, most of the "bonus marchers" went home, but about two thousand stayed on, building makeshift shelters. President Hoover called in the army.

On July 28, troops commanded by General Douglas MacArthur and armed with tear gas, tanks, and machine guns drove the veterans from their camp and burned their shelters. A journalist described the scene:

[The veterans and their families] wandered from street to street or sat in ragged groups, the men exhausted, the women with wet handkerchiefs laid over their smarting eyes, the children waking from sleep to cough and whimper from the tear gas in their lungs.

Burning Shanties of Bonus Marchers, Washington, DC, July 1932 *When President Herbert Hoover ordered the army to evict jobless veterans who had come to Washington seeking early payment of promised bonuses, it reinforced his public image as aloof and uncaring amid a worsening depression.*

... Their shanties and tents had been burned, their personal property destroyed, except for the few belongings they could carry on their backs.

To many Americans, this action symbolized the administration's heartlessness.

American writers shared the despairing mood. In *The 42nd Parallel* (1930), John Dos Passos drew a grim picture of a depression-wracked nation. Says one character: "Everything you've wanted crumbles in your fingers as you grasp it." In *Young Lonigan* (1932), James T. Farrell portrayed the empty existence of a jobless Irish-immigrant youth in Chicago. Betrayed by the American dream, he aimlessly wanders the streets.

Some radical novelists openly attacked the capitalist system. The Communist Party encouraged such fiction through writers' clubs and contests for working-class writers. Jack Conroy's *The Disinherited* (1933) dealt with life in the Missouri coal fields, where his own father and brother had died in a mine disaster.

The Election of 1932   A gloomy 1932 Republican convention renominated Hoover. The Democrats gathered in Chicago, by contrast, scented victory. Their platform, crafted to erase the party divisions of the 1920s, appealed to urban voters with a call for repeal of prohibition, to farmers with support for aid programs, and to fiscal conservatives with demands for a balanced budget and spending cuts. Rejecting Al Smith, the party's 1928 candidate, the delegates nominated New York governor Franklin D. Roosevelt for president.

Despite a rousing acceptance speech pledging "a new deal for the American people," Roosevelt's campaign offered few specifics. He called for "bold persistent experimentation" and compassion for "the forgotten man at the bottom of the economic pyramid," yet he also attacked Hoover's "reckless" spending and insisted that "only as a last resort" should Washington play a larger depression-fighting role.

But Roosevelt exuded confidence, and above all he was not Hoover. On November 8, FDR and his running mate, Texas congressman John Nance Garner, received nearly 23 million votes, while Hoover received fewer than 16 million. Roosevelt carried every state but Pennsylvania and four in New England. Both houses of Congress went heavily Democratic.

How would Roosevelt use this impressive mandate? The nation waited.

THE NEW DEAL TAKES SHAPE, 1933–1935

The Roosevelt years began in a whirl of activity. An array of emergency measures reflected three basic goals: industrial recovery through business—government cooperation and pump-priming federal spending; agricultural recovery through crop reduction; and short-term emergency relief. These programs conveyed the sense of an activist government addressing urgent national problems. Hovering over the bustle loomed a confident Franklin Roosevelt, cigarette holder jauntily tilted upward, a symbol of hope. By 1935, however, the New Deal faced problems, and opposition was building.

Roosevelt and His Circle   FDR's inaugural address exuded confidence and hope. "The only thing we have to fear," he intoned, "is fear itself." In an outpouring of support, half a million letters deluged the White House.

Roosevelt seemed an unlikely popular hero. Like his distant cousin Theodore, FDR was of the social elite, with merchants and landowners among his Dutch-immigrant ancestors. He attended Harvard College and Columbia Law School. But as a state senator and governor, he had backed the Democratic Party's urban-immigrant wing. When the depression hit, he had introduced innovative measures in New York, including unemployment insurance and a public-works program. Intent on promoting recovery while preserving capitalism and democracy, Roosevelt encouraged competing proposals, compromised (or papered over) differences, and then backed the measures he sensed that Congress and the public would support.

Roosevelt brought to Washington a circle of advisers nicknamed the brain trust. It included Columbia University professor Rexford G. Tugwell and lawyer Adolph A. Berle. Shaped by the progressive reform tradition, Tugwell and Berle advocated federal economic planning and corporate regulation. But no single ideology or inner circle controlled the New Deal, for FDR sought a broad range of opinions.

Eleanor Roosevelt played a key role. A niece of Theodore Roosevelt, she had been active in settlement-house work and in Florence Kelley's National Consumers' League. Through her, FDR met reformers, social workers, and advocates of minority rights. Recalled Rexford Tugwell: "No one who ever saw Eleanor Roosevelt sit down facing her husband, and holding his eyes firmly, say to him 'Franklin, I think you should ...,' or 'Franklin, surely you will not ...' will ever forget the experience." Traveling ceaselessly, she was an astute observer for her wheelchair-bound husband. (A Washington newspaper once headlined "MRS. ROOSEVELT SPENDS NIGHT AT WHITE HOUSE.") In 1935, she began a newspaper column, "My Day."

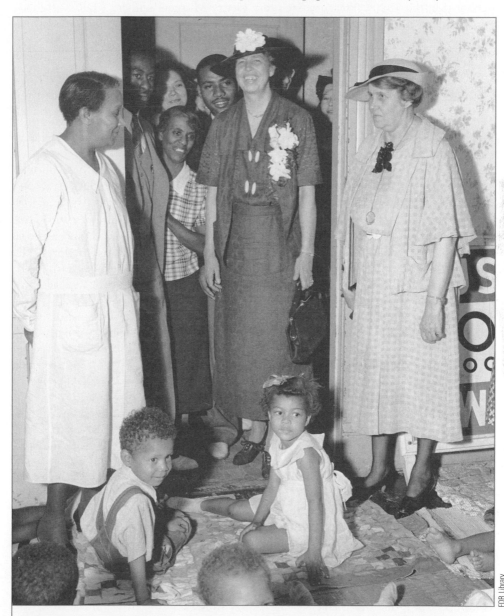

FDR Library

Eleanor Roosevelt Visits a Nursery School in Des Moines Operated by the Works Progress Administration, June 1936 *Intensely shy as a young woman, Mrs. Roosevelt played an active, influential, and highly visible role during her years as First Lady.*

Roosevelt's cabinet reflected the New Deal's diversity. Postmaster General James Farley distributed patronage jobs, managed his campaigns, and dealt with state and local Democratic leaders. Secretary of Labor **Frances Perkins,** the first woman cabinet member, had served as industrial commissioner of New York. Interior Secretary **Harold Ickes** had organized liberal Republicans for Roosevelt in 1932. Secretary of Agriculture Henry A. Wallace held the same post his father had occupied in the 1920s. Treasury Secretary Henry Morgenthau, Jr., FDR's neighbor and political ally, though a fiscal conservative, tolerated the spending necessary to finance New Deal antidepression programs.

Newcomers poured into Washington in 1933—former progressives, liberal-minded professors, bright young lawyers. They drafted bills, staffed government agencies, and debated recovery strategies. From this pressure-cooker environment emerged the laws, programs, and agencies gathered under a catch-all label: the New Deal.

While the "alphabet soup" of New Deal agencies can seem intimidating, it is important to keep the larger picture in mind. Reflecting a variety of approaches and shifting emphases, these programs, extending from 1933 to 1938, represented a remarkable and unprecedented level of government intervention in the economy, aimed at stimulating recovery, regulating the financial industry, reducing glaring economic inequities, and helping those most hurt by the crisis.

The Hundred Days   Between March and June 1933, a period labeled the "Hundred Days," Congress enacted more than a dozen key measures. Drawing upon precedents from the Progressive Era, World War I, and the Hoover presidency, these measures expanded Washington's involvement in America's economic life.

FDR first addressed the banking crisis. As borrowers defaulted, depositors withdrew savings, and homeowners missed mortgage payments, thousands of banks had failed, undermining confidence in the system. On March 5, Roosevelt ordered all banks to close for four days. At the end of this so-called bank holiday, he proposed an Emergency Banking Act. This law and a later one permitted healthy banks to reopen, set up procedures for managing failed banks, increased government oversight of banking, and required banks to separate savings deposits from investment funds. Congress also created the Federal Deposit Insurance Corporation (FDIC) to insure bank deposits up to five thousand dollars. Launching a series of radio talks, the president assured Americans that they could again trust their banks.

Other measures addressed the urgent problem of relief for Americans struggling to survive. Two new agencies assisted those who were losing their homes. The Home Owners Loan Corporation (HOLC) helped city-dwellers refinance their mortgages. The Farm Credit Administration provided loans to rural Americans.

Another early relief program, the **Civilian Conservation Corps** (CCC), employed jobless youths in government projects such as reforestation, park maintenance, and erosion control. By 1935, half a million young men were earning thirty-five dollars a month in CCC camps—a godsend to desperate families. As Neil M. Maher argues in *Nature's New Deal: The Civilian Conservation Corps and the Roots of the American Environmental Movement* (2008), the CCC introduced many city youth to the American wilderness and helped keep environmental awareness alive in the 1930s (see also the later section "The Environment and the West").

The principal relief measure of the Hundred Days, the **Federal Emergency Relief Act,** appropriated $500 million for financially strapped state and local relief agencies. To head this program, FDR chose **Harry Hopkins,** the relief administrator in New York State, who soon emerged as a powerful New Deal figure.

While supplying immediate relief, the early New Deal also faced the larger challenge of promoting agricultural and industrial recovery. To push up low farm prices, the government advocated reduced production. As a first step, the government paid southern cotton planters to plow under much of their crop and midwestern farmers to slaughter some 6 million piglets and pregnant sows. Destroying crops and killing pigs amid widespread hunger proved a public-relations nightmare. Pursuing the same goal more systematically, in May 1933 Congress passed the Agricultural Adjustment Act. This law gave payments, called subsidies, to producers of the major farm commodities—including hogs, wheat, corn, cotton, and dairy products—in return for cutting production. A tax on grain mills and other food processors (a tax ultimately passed on to consumers) financed these subsidies. A new agency, the **Agricultural Adjustment Administration** (AAA), supervised the program.

The other key recovery measure of the Hundred Days, the National Industrial Recovery Act, appropriated $3.3 billion for large-scale public-works projects to provide jobs and stimulate the economy. The **Public Works Administration** (PWA), headed by Interior Secretary Harold Ickes, ran this program.

This law also created the **National Recovery Administration** (NRA). The NRA brought together business leaders to draft codes of "fair competition" for their industries. These codes set production limits, prescribed wages and working conditions, and forbade price cutting and unfair competitive practices. The aim was to promote recovery by breaking the cycle of wage cuts, falling prices, and layoffs. This approach revived the trade associations promoted by Washington during World War I (see Chapter 22). Indeed, the NRA's head, Hugh Johnson, had served with the War Industries Board of 1917–1918.

Dependent on voluntary support by business and the public, NRA officials used parades, billboards, magazine ads, and celebrity events to persuade people to patronize companies that subscribed to an NRA code. Such companies displayed the NRA symbol, a blue eagle, and its slogan, "We Do Our Part."

While the NRA sought economic recovery, some New Dealers also saw its reform potential. Pressured by Labor Secretary Frances Perkins, the NRA's textile-industry code banned child labor. And thanks to New York senator Robert Wagner, Section 7a of the National Industrial Recovery Act affirmed workers' right to organize unions.

The Reconstruction Finance Corporation, dating from the Hoover years, remained active, lending large sums to banks, insurance companies, and even new business ventures. The early New Deal thus had a strong probusiness tone. In his speeches of 1933–1935, FDR always included business in the "all-American team" working for recovery.

A few early measures, however, took a tougher approach to business. A post–1929 antibusiness mood deepened when a Senate investigation revealed that none of the twenty partners of the powerful Morgan Bank had paid any income tax in 1931 or 1932. People jeered when the head of the New York Stock Exchange told a Senate committee considering regulatory measures, "You gentlemen are making a big mistake. The Exchange is a perfect institution."

Reflecting public support for tougher regulation, the Federal Securities Act of 1933 required corporations to inform the government fully on all stock offerings. This law also made executives personally liable for any misrepresentation of securities their companies issued.

The most innovative program of the Hundred Days, the **Tennessee Valley Authority** (TVA), had its origins in a government-built hydroelectric plant on the Tennessee River in Alabama that had powered a World War I munitions factory. In the 1920s, Senator George Norris of Nebraska had urged the use of this facility to supply electricity to nearby farmers.

Expanding Norris's idea, TVA advanced the economic and social development of the poverty-stricken Tennessee River Valley. While creating construction jobs, TVA dams brought electricity to the region, provided recreational facilities, and reduced flooding and soil erosion. Under director David Lilienthal, TVA proved one of the New Deal's most popular and enduring achievements.

The outpouring of laws and new agencies during the Hundred Days suggests both the dynamism and the confusion of the New Deal. How all these new programs would work in practice remained to be seen.

Problems and Controversies Plague the Early New Deal
As the depression persisted, several early New Deal programs, including the NRA and the AAA, faltered. The NRA's problems related partly to the personality of the hard-driving, hard-drinking Hugh Johnson, who left in 1934. But the trouble went deeper. As the unity spirit of the Hundred Days faded, corporate America resisted NRA regulation. Code violations increased. Small businesses complained as corporate trade associations used the codes to stifle competition and fix prices. The agency itself, meanwhile, became bogged down in drafting trivial codes. The shoulder-pad industry, for example, had its own code.

In May 1935, the Supreme Court unanimously ruled the NRA unconstitutional. The Court cited two reasons: first, the law gave the president regulatory powers that constitutionally belonged to Congress; second, the NRA regulated commerce inside states, violating the constitutional provision limiting federal regulation to *interstate* commerce. Few mourned. As a recovery measure, the NRA had failed.

The AAA, too, faced controversy. Farm prices did rise as production fell, and by 1937 overall farm income increased by 50 percent. But the AAA did not help farm laborers or migrant workers; indeed, its crop-reduction payments actually hurt southern tenants and sharecroppers, who faced eviction as cotton planters removed acreage from production.

Some victims of this process resisted. In 1934, the interracial Southern Tenant Farmers' Union, led by the Socialist Party, emerged in Arkansas. Declared one black sharecropper at the organizing meeting: "The same chain that holds my people holds your people too.... [We should] get together and stay together." The landowners struck back, harassing union organizers.

While some New Dealers focused on raising total agricultural income, others took a more class-based approach and urged attention to the poorest farmers.

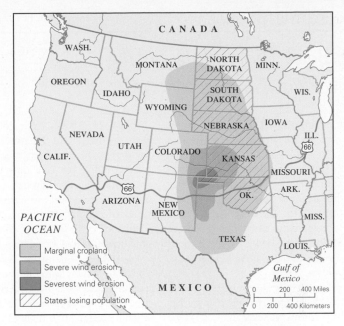

MAP 24.1 The Dust Bowl

From the Dakotas southward to the Mexican border, farmers in the Great Plains suffered from a lack of rainfall and severe soil erosion in the 1930s, worsening the hardships of the Great Depression.

Source: © Cengage Learning. All rights reserved. No distribution allowed without express authorization.

Their cause was strengthened as a parching drought turned much of the Great Plains into a dust bowl. The rains failed in 1930, devastating wheat and livestock. In 1934, dust clouds darkened the skies over East Coast cities. As a dense dust cloud passed over Washington, DC, one legislator commented: "There goes Oklahoma." Through 1939, each summer brought a new scourge of dust.

Even night brought no relief. Recalled a Kansas woman, "A trip for water to rinse the grit from our lips, and then back to bed with washcloths over our noses. We try to lie still, because every turn stirs the dust on the blankets." Folk singer Woody Guthrie recalled his 1930s' boyhood in Oklahoma and Texas in a song called "The Great Dust Storm."

Battered by debt and drought, many families gave up. Nearly 3.5 million people left the Great Plains in the 1930s. Some migrated to nearby cities, further swamping relief rolls. Others packed their belongings into old cars and headed west. Though from various states, they all bore a derisive nickname, Okies. The plight of dust-bowl migrants further complicated New Deal agricultural planning.

Policy differences also plagued New Deal relief. Harry Hopkins argued for direct federal relief programs, rather than channeling funds through state and local agencies. Late in 1933, FDR named Hopkins to head a temporary agency, the Civil Works Administration (CWA). Through the winter the CWA funded short-term work projects for the jobless, but when spring came, FDR abolished it. Like his

GOING TO THE SOURCE

Dust Bowl Diary: Life on the Great Plains in the 1930s

The dust storms of the 1930s on the Great Plains, one of the twentieth century's major ecological disasters, resulted from a severe drought plus decades of farming practices that had destroyed the prairie grasses holding the soil in place. These excerpts from the diary of Ann Marie Low, a young schoolteacher, convey the reality of the Dust Bowl as she experienced it on her parents' farm near Kensal, North Dakota.

April 25, 1934. Last weekend was the worst dust storm we ever had.... [T]he air is just full of dirt coming, literally, for hundreds of miles. It sifts into everything. After we wash the dishes and put them away, so much dust sifts into the cupboard we must wash them again before the next meal. Clothes in the closets are covered with dust.... Newspapers say the deaths of many babies and old people are attributed to breathing in so much dirt.

May 21, 1934.... Saturday Dad, Bud [her brother], and I planted an acre of potatoes. There was so much dirt in the air I couldn't see Bud only a few feet in front of me.... The newspapers report that on May 10 ... [an] estimated 12,000,000 tons of Plains soil was dumped on [Chicago].

May 30, 1934 [returning home after a week away]. The mess was incredible! Dirt had blown into the house all week and lay inches deep on everything. Every towel and curtain was just black. There wasn't a clean dish or cooking utensil.... The cupboards had to be washed out to have a clean place to put them.... [E]very towel, curtain, piece of bedding, and garment had to be taken outdoors to have as much dust as possible shaken out before washing. The cistern is dry, so I had to carry all the water we needed from the well.... That evening Cap [her boyfriend] came to take me to the movie, as usual.

---

conservative critics, FDR feared creating a permanent welfare underclass. As local relief agencies ran out of money, however, further federal programs became inevitable.

Hopkins and Harold Ickes, head of the Public Works Administration, competed to control federal relief policy. Large-scale PWA projects did promote recovery, but the cautious Ickes micro-managed every proposal, leaving funds stalled in the pipeline. Hopkins, by contrast, wanted to put people to work, even at make-work projects like raking leaves and collecting litter, and get money circulating. Given the urgent crisis, Hopkins's approach proved more influential.

Despite problems and rivalries, the public works programs of the PWA and WPA not only created jobs but reshaped the nation's infrastructure and promoted economic development. With projects throughout the nation, these agencies built dams, public buildings, airports, highways, bridges, viaducts, dams, water utilities, and sewage-treatment plants. The military factories and war-workers' housing construction of World War II and the public housing and interstate highway system of the postwar era would all reflect the legacy of these New Deal agencies.

Ixnay [No]. I'm sorry I snapped at Cap. It isn't his fault, or anyone's fault, but I was tired and cross. Life in what the newspapers call "the Dust Bowl" is becoming a gritty nightmare.

July 9, 1934 [After a movie, Ann and Cap talk of marriage, but the discussion soon turns to their bleak economic prospects.] [Cap] is really a handsome man, ... [but] suddenly I seemed to see what his face will be someday—a tombstone on which is written an epitaph of dead dreams. I shivered. [Cap said] "Oh sweetheart, you are cold.... I'll take you home." I didn't tell him I wasn't shivering from cold.

August 1, 1934. As far as one can see are brown pastures and fields which, in the wind, just rise up and fill the air with dirt. It tortures animals and humans, makes housekeeping an everlasting drudgery, and ruins machinery. The crops are long since ruined.... [A]ll subsoil moisture is gone. Fifteen feet down the ground is dry as dust. Trees are dying by the thousands. Cattle and horses are dying, some from starvation and some from dirt they eat on the grass.

July 11, 1936. Yesterday was 110° with a hot wind blowing. Today is the same. I'm writing this lying on the living room floor, dripping sweat and watching the dirt drift in the windows and across the floor. I've dusted this whole house twice today and won't do it again.

August 1, 1936. This is the worst summer yet. The fields are nothing but grasshoppers and dried-up Russian thistle.... There is one dust storm after another. It is the most disheartening situation I have seen yet. Livestock and humans are really suffering. I don't know how we keep going....

Questions

1. Along with their economic toll, what does this diary reveal about the dust storms' emotional and psychological impact?

2. What was Ann Marie Low's basic source of information for events outside her immediate community?

Source: Reprinted from Dust Bowl Diary *by Ann Marie Low by permission of the University of Nebraska Press. Copyright 1984 by the University of Nebraska Press.*

1934–1935: Challenges from Right and Left
Despite the New Deal's initiatives, hard times persisted. In 1934 national income rose about 25 percent above 1933 levels but remained far below that of 1929. Millions had been jobless for years. Rising frustration exploded in 1934 in nearly two thousand strikes, some communist-led. Conservatives, meanwhile, attacked the New Deal as socialistic. In 1934, several business leaders, joined by an embittered Al Smith, formed the anti–New Deal American Liberty League. Anti-Roosevelt jokes circulated among the rich, many of whom denounced him as a traitor to his class.

But the New Deal remained broadly popular, reflecting both its promise and FDR's political skills, enhanced by speechwriters and publicists. Pursuing his "national unity" theme, he exhorted Americans to join the battle for economic recovery just as they had united for war in 1917. Although Republican newspaper publishers remained hostile, FDR enjoyed good relations with the working press, and journalists responded with favorable stories.

Unlike Hoover, Roosevelt loved public appearances and took naturally to radio. Frances Perkins described his radio talks, nicknamed "fireside chats": "His head would nod and his hands would move in simple, natural, comfortable gestures. His face would smile and light up as though he were actually sitting … with [his listeners]."

The 1934 midterm election ratified the New Deal's popularity. Reversing the usual pattern, the Democrats increased their congressional majorities. As for FDR, Kansas journalist William Allen White observed, "He's been all but crowned by the people."

Yet the political scene remained unstable. While conservatives criticized the New Deal for going too far, critics on the left attacked it for not going far enough and ridiculed Roosevelt's efforts to include big business in his "all-American team."

In 1934, socialist Upton Sinclair, famed for his 1906 muckraking exposé of the meatpacking industry, *The Jungle,* won the Democratic nomination for governor of California. Sinclair's End Poverty in California (EPIC) program proposed to take over idle factories and run them cooperatively. Despite a barrage of vicious attack ads that anticipated a later era of U.S. politics, Sinclair garnered 37 percent of the vote.

Demagogues peddled various nostrums. The Detroit Catholic priest and radio spellbinder Charles Coughlin viciously attacked FDR, made anti-Semitic allusions, and called for nationalization of the banks. For a time, Coughlin's National Union of Social Justice attracted considerable support, mainly from the lower middle class.

Meanwhile, California doctor Francis Townsend proposed that the government pay all retired citizens two hundred dollars a month, requiring them to spend it within thirty days. This plan, Townsend insisted, would help the elderly, stimulate the economy, and create jobs by encouraging retirement. The scheme would have bankrupted the nation, but many older citizens rallied to Townsend's banner.

FDR's wiliest rival was Louisiana's Huey Long. A country lawyer elected governor in 1928, Long built highways, schools, and public housing while tolerating graft and political corruption. He roared into Washington as a senator in 1933, preaching his "Share Our Wealth" program: a 100 percent tax on all income over $1 million and appropriation of all fortunes over $5 million. Once this money was redistributed, Long promised, every family could live in comfort. By 1935, he boasted 7.5 million supporters. His 1935 book, *My First Days in the White House,* made clear his ultimate goal. Long was assassinated that September, but his organization survived.

Battling back, Roosevelt regained the political high ground in 1935 with a fresh surge of legislation that rivaled that of the Hundred Days.

THE NEW DEAL CHANGES COURSE, 1935–1936

As the 1936 election neared, Roosevelt shelved the unity theme and championed the poor and the working class. His 1935 State of the Union address outlined six initiatives: expanded public-works programs, assistance to the rural poor, support for organized labor, benefits for retired workers and other at-risk groups, tougher business regulation, and heavier taxes on the well-to-do. These priorities translated into a bundle of reform measures some called "the Second New Deal." FDR's landslide victory in 1936 solidified a new Democratic coalition. The New Deal also addressed environmental issues and launched public-works and power projects that stimulated economic development in the American West.

Expanding Federal Relief   With unemployment still high, Congress passed the $5 billion Emergency Relief Appropriation Act in April 1935. Roosevelt swiftly set up the **Works Progress Administration** (WPA) under Harry Hopkins to funnel assistance directly to the jobless. Roosevelt insisted that the WPA provide work, not handouts. Over its eight-year life, the WPA employed more than 8 million Americans and constructed or improved vast numbers of bridges, roads, post offices, and other public facilities.

The WPA also assisted writers, performers, and artists. The Federal Writers' Project (FWP) employed jobless writers nationwide to produce state and city guides and histories of ethnic and immigrant groups. In the South, research teams recorded the reminiscences of former slaves. Sterling Brown, the FWP's "Negro Affairs editor," worked to include African American history and voices in FWP publications.

Under the WPA's Federal Music Project, unemployed musicians gave free concerts, often featuring American composers. Artists working for the Federal Arts Project designed posters, offered courses, and painted murals on public buildings.

The Federal Theatre Project (FTP) employed actors. One FTP project, the Living Newspaper, which dramatized current social issues, was criticized as New Deal propaganda. Nervous WPA officials canceled one FTP production, Marc Blitzstein's radical musical *The Cradle Will Rock* (1937), before the opening-night performance. The cast and audience defiantly walked to another theater, and the show went on.

Harold Ickes's Public Works Administration, after a slow start, eventually completed some thirty-four thousand major construction projects, from New York City's Lincoln Tunnel to the awesome Grand Coulee Dam on the Columbia River. The PWA employed thousands of jobless workers.

All this relief spending generated large federal budget deficits, cresting at $4.4 billion in 1936. According to British economist John Maynard Keynes, governments should deliberately use deficit spending during depressions to fund public-works programs, thereby increasing purchasing power and stimulating recovery. The New Deal approach, however, was not Keynesian. Because every dollar spent on relief programs was counterbalanced by taxation or government borrowing, the stimulus effect was nil. FDR saw deficits as an unwelcome necessity, not a positive good.

The New Deal's second phase more frankly targeted workers, the poor, and the disadvantaged. Social-justice advocates like Frances Perkins and Eleanor Roosevelt encouraged this class-based emphasis, but so did political calculations. Looking to 1936, FDR's political advisers feared that the followers of Coughlin, Townsend, and Long could siphon off enough votes to cost him the election.

The Second New Deal's agricultural policy addressed the plight of sharecroppers (a plight the AAA had helped create) and other poor farmers. The Resettlement Administration (1935) made loans to help tenant farmers buy their own farms and to enable displaced sharecroppers, tenants, and dust-bowl migrants to move to more productive areas.

The Resettlement Administration also funded two documentary films directed by Pare Lorenz. *The Plow That Broke the Plains* (1936) explained the farming practices that led to the dust bowl. *The River* (1938) dealt with the devastating effects of Mississippi River flooding, and the promise of New Deal flood-control projects. Lorenz's films rank among the outstanding cultural productions of the 1930s.

The Rural Electrification Administration, also started in 1935, made low-interest loans to utility companies and farmers' cooperatives to extend electricity to the 90 percent of rural America that still lacked it. By 1941, 40 percent of U.S. farms enjoyed electric power.

The agricultural-recovery program suffered a setback in January 1936 when the Supreme Court declared the Agricultural Adjustment Act unconstitutional. The processing tax that funded the AAA's subsidies, the Court held, was an illegal use of the government's tax power. To replace the AAA, Congress passed a soil-conservation act that paid farmers to plant grasses and legumes instead of soil-depleting crops such as wheat and cotton (which also happened to be the major surplus commodities).

Organized labor won a key victory in 1935, thanks to Senator Robert Wagner. During the New Deal's national-unity phase, FDR had criticized Wagner's campaign for a prolabor law as "special interest" legislation. But in 1935, when the Supreme Court outlawed the NIRA, including Section 7a protecting union members' rights, as unconstitutional, FDR called for a labor law that would survive court scrutiny. The **National Labor Relations Act** of July 1935 (the **Wagner Act**) guaranteed collective-bargaining rights and outlawed such management tactics as blacklisting union organizers. The law created the National Labor Relations Board (NLRB) to enforce the law and supervise shop elections. A wave of unionization soon followed (discussed later in this chapter).

The Second New Deal's more class-conscious thrust shaped other 1935 measures as well. The Banking Act strengthened the Federal Reserve Board's control over the nation's financial system. The Public Utilities Holding Company Act, targeting the sprawling public-utility empires of the 1920s, restricted gas and electric companies to one geographic region.

In 1935, too, Roosevelt called for steeper taxes on the rich to combat the "unjust concentration of wealth and economic power." Congress responded with a revenue act, also called the Wealth Tax Act, raising taxes on corporations and on the well-to-do. With its many loopholes, this law was not quite the "soak the rich" measure some believed, but it did express the Second New Deal's more radical spirit.

The Social Security Act of 1935; End of the Second New Deal

The **Social Security Act** of 1935 stands out for its long-range significance. Drafted by a committee chaired by Frances Perkins, this measure drew upon Progressive Era ideas and European social-welfare programs. It established a mixed federal-state system of workers' pensions, unemployment insurance, survivors' benefits for victims of industrial accidents, and aid for disabled persons and dependent mothers with children.

Taxes paid partly by employers and partly by workers (in the form of sums withheld from their paychecks) helped fund the program. This cut in take-home pay contributed to a recession in 1937. But it made sense politically because workers would resist any threat to a pension plan they had contributed to. As FDR put it, "With those taxes in there, no damned politician can ever scrap my social security program."

The Social Security Act bypassed farmers, domestic workers, and the self-employed. But it established the principle of federal responsibility for social welfare and laid the foundation for future welfare programs.

As 1935 ended, the Second New Deal was complete. Although conservatives called it "anti-business," FDR insisted that he had saved capitalism through prudent reform. In earlier eras, the business class had dominated government, marginalizing other groups. Business interests remained influential in the 1930s, but the evolving New Deal also responded to other organized interest groups, including labor. And in 1935, with an election looming, New Deal strategists reached farther still, crafting legislation to aid sharecroppers, migrant workers, the disabled, the elderly, and others largely ignored by politicians of the past.

In the process, the New Deal enlarged the government's role in American life, as well as the power of the presidency. Building on precedents set by Theodore Roosevelt, FDR so dominated 1930s' politics that Americans now expected presidents to offer programs, address national issues, and shape the public debate. This decisively altered the power balance between the White House and Congress. Along with specific programs, the New Deal's importance thus also lay in how it enlarged the scope of the presidency and the social role of the state.

The 1936 Roosevelt Landslide and the New Democratic Coalition

FDR confidently faced the 1936 campaign. "There's one issue," he told an aide; "it's myself, and people must be either for me or against me."

The Republican candidate, Kansas governor Alfred Landon, a moderate fiscal conservative, proved an inept campaigner. ("Wherever I have gone in this country, I have found Americans," he revealed in one speech.) FDR, by contrast, responded zestfully when Republicans lambasted his alleged dictatorial ambitions or charged that the social security law would require all workers to wear metal dog tags. The forces of "selfishness and greed … are united in their hatred for me," he declared at a tumultuous election-eve rally in New York City, "and I welcome their hatred."

In the greatest landslide since 1820, FDR carried every state but Maine and Vermont. Landon even lost Kansas. Pennsylvania went Democratic for the first time since 1856. The Democrats increased their majorities in Congress. Socialist Norman Thomas received less than 200,000 votes, the Communist Party's presidential candidate only about 80,000. The Union Party, a coalition of Coughlinites, Townsendites, and Huey Long supporters, seemingly so formidable in 1935, polled less than 900,000 votes.

The 1936 election signaled the emergence of a new Democratic coalition. Since Reconstruction, the Democrats had enjoyed three bases of support: the white South, parts of the West, and urban white ethnic voters. FDR retained these centers of strength. He rarely challenged state or local party leaders who produced the votes, whether or not they supported the New Deal.

Building on Al Smith's urban gains in 1928, FDR carried the nation's twelve largest cities in 1936. Aided by New Deal relief programs, many city-dwellers idolized Roosevelt. Cheering throngs greeted his visits to New York, Boston, or other cities. In filling New Deal positions, FDR often turned to the newer urban-immigrant groups, including Catholics and Jews.

Expanding the Democratic base, FDR also courted farmers and union members. Republican midwestern farmers, won over by the New Deal's agricultural program, voted accordingly. FDR decisively carried Iowa, a GOP bastion, in 1936. Union members, too, joined the Roosevelt bandwagon that year, and unions pumped money into Roosevelt's campaign chest (though far less than business gave the Republicans). Despite his early criticism of the Wagner bill, FDR's reputation as a "friend of labor" proved unassailable.

African Americans came aboard as well. Although most southern blacks remained disfranchised, northern blacks could vote, and as late as 1932, two-thirds of them voted Republican, the party of Lincoln. The New Deal caused a historic shift. In 1936, 76 percent of black voters supported FDR.

Economically, this shift made sense. New Deal relief programs greatly aided blacks. On racial-justice issues, however, the New Deal's record was mixed at best. Some NRA codes included racially discriminatory clauses, causing black activists to deride the agency as "Negroes Ruined Again." TVA and other New Deal agencies tolerated racial bias. Lynchings increased in the 1930s as some whites translated economic worries into racial violence, but Roosevelt kept aloof from an NAACP campaign to make lynching a federal crime. When southern Democratic senators killed such a bill in 1935, FDR, concerned about other legislative initiatives, did little. "[T]he Roosevelt administration [has] nothing for [blacks]," the NAACP concluded bitterly.

In limited ways, FDR did address racial issues. He cautiously tried to rid New Deal agencies of blatant racism. He appointed more than a hundred blacks to policy-level and judicial positions, including Eleanor Roosevelt's friend Mary McLeod Bethune as director of minority affairs in the National Youth Administration. Bethune, a Florida educator, led the so-called black cabinet that linked the administration and black organizations. Roosevelt's Supreme Court appointees opposed racial discrimination in cases involving housing, voting rights, and other issues.

The New Deal also supported racial justice in symbolic ways. In 1938, when the participants in a conference in Birmingham, Alabama, were segregated in compliance with local statutes, Mrs. Roosevelt placed her chair halfway between the white and black delegates. In 1939, when the Daughters of the American Revolution barred black contralto Marian Anderson from performing in Washington's Constitution Hall, Mrs. Roosevelt and Harold Ickes arranged an Easter concert by Anderson at the Lincoln Memorial. Even symbolic gestures outraged many southern whites. When a black minister delivered the invocation at the 1936 Democratic convention, a South Carolina senator noisily stalked out.

Led by Molly Dewson, head of the Democratic Party's women's division, the New Deal also courted women voters. In the 1936 campaign, fifteen thousand women volunteers distributed flyers describing New Deal programs. "[W]e did not make the old-fashioned plea that our nominee was charming," she recalled; "We appealed to [women's] intelligence."

Dewson did not promote a specifically feminist agenda. The New Deal's economic programs, she argued, benefited both sexes. FDR did, however, appoint the first woman cabinet member, the first woman ambassador, and a number of female federal judges. Through Dewson's efforts, the 1936 Democratic platform committee reflected a fifty-fifty gender balance.

Despite the New Deal's symbolic gestures and appointment of a few blacks and women, racial and gender discrimination pervaded U.S. society in the 1930s, and Roosevelt, grappling with the depression, did relatively little to change things. That challenge would await a later time.

The Environment and the West   Environmental issues loomed large in the New Deal. While still in the New York Senate, FDR had sought logging regulation to protect wildlife. As president, he strongly supported the Civilian Conservation Corps' program of planting trees, thinning forests, and building hiking trails.

Soil conservation had high priority. The 1930s' dust storms resulted not only from drought, but from overgrazing and poor farming practices. For decades, Great Plains' wheat farmers had used tractors, combines, and heavy-duty plows called "sodbusters" to uproot the native prairie grasses that anchored the soil. When the rains failed, as they do in this drought-prone region, little remained to hold the soil in place, and parching winds whipped up devastating dust storms. By the 1930s, 9 million acres of farmland had been lost to erosion in the Great Plains, the South, and elsewhere.

In response, the Department of Agriculture's Soil Conservation Service promoted contour plowing, crop rotation, and soil-strengthening grasses. The Taylor Grazing Act of 1934 restricted the grazing on public lands that had exacerbated the problem. TVA dams helped control the floods that worsened erosion in the Tennessee valley.

New Deal planners also promoted national-park development, including Olympic National Park in Washington, Virginia's Shenandoah National Park, and Kings Canyon National Park in California. The administration also created some 160 new national wildlife refuges. FDR even closed a Utah artillery range near a nesting site of the endangered trumpeter swan!

The wilderness-preservation movement gained momentum in the 1930s, supported by such groups as the Wilderness Society (1935), started by environmentalist Aldo Leopold and others, and the National Wildlife Federation (1936), funded by firearms makers eager to preserve hunting areas. Pressured by such groups, Congress began to set aside protected wilderness areas. Building on these beginnings, the United States by 2008 had 704 officially designated national wilderness areas, comprising 107 million acres.

By later standards, the New Deal's environmental record was spotty. The decade's massive hydroelectric projects, while providing rural families with electricity, had serious ecological consequences. The Grand Coulee Dam, for example, destroyed salmon spawning on much of the Columbia River's tributary system. Other dams disrupted fragile ecosystems and the livelihoods of local residents, particularly Native American communities, who depended on them.

Viewed in context, however, the New Deal's environmental record remains impressive. While coping with the depression, the Roosevelt administration also focused a level of attention on environmental issues that had not been seen since the Progressive Era and would not be seen again for a generation.

The New Deal's impact on the West was profound, especially because the federal government owned a third or more of the land in eleven western states and much more in some states. New Deal agencies and laws such as the Soil Conservation Service, the Taylor Grazing Act, and the Farm Security Administration (discussed shortly) set new rules for western agriculture, from prairie wheat fields and cattle ranges to California citrus groves and truck farms dependent on migrant labor.

The PWA and WPA built many large projects in the West, including thousands of public buildings, from courthouses and post offices to tourist facilities such as beautiful Timberline Lodge on Oregon's Mount Hood. Federal assistance also upgraded the highways linking the West to the rest of America, such as Route 66 from Chicago to Los Angeles.

Above all, the PWA in the West built dams—not only Grand Coulee, but also Shasta on the Sacramento River, Bonneville on the Columbia, Glen Canyon on the Colorado, and others. The PWA completed Hoover Dam on the Colorado, authorized by Congress in 1928 (see Chapter 23), well ahead of schedule. Despite their ecological downside, these great undertakings—among the largest engineering projects in history—supplied electricity to vast regions while contributing to flood control, irrigation, and soil conservation. (Las Vegas owed its post–World War II emergence as a gambling and entertainment mecca to power from nearby Hoover Dam.)

A New Deal initiative especially important for the West was Harold Ickes's National Planning Board, later renamed the National Resources Planning Board. This agency, which extended Herbert Hoover's promotion of multi-state water-resource planning in the West, facilitated state and regional management of water, soil, timber, and minerals.

THE NEW DEAL'S END STAGE, 1937–1939

Buoyed by his 1936 victory, Roosevelt proposed a controversial restructuring of the Supreme Court. After losing this fight, FDR confronted a stubborn recession and resurgent conservative opposition. With a few measures in 1937–1938, the New Deal ended.

FDR and the Supreme Court   In 1937, four of the Supreme Court's nine elderly justices were archconservatives who abhorred the New Deal. Joined by more moderate colleagues, these conservatives had struck down the NRA, the AAA, and progressive state laws. Roosevelt feared that the Social Security Act, the Wagner Act, and other key measures would meet a similar fate. Indeed, some corporate lawyers, convinced that the Social Security Act would be ruled unconstitutional, advised their clients to ignore it.

In February 1937, FDR proposed a bill that would have allowed him to appoint an additional Supreme Court member for each justice over age seventy, up to a total of six. Roosevelt blandly insisted that this would ease aging justices' heavy workload, but his political motivation was obvious.

Despite FDR's popularity, the press and public reacted with hostility. The Supreme Court's size, although unspecified in the Constitution, had held steady at nine since 1869, and thus seemed almost sacrosanct. Conservatives blasted FDR's "court-packing" scheme as a dangerous power grab. Even many Democrats disapproved. When the Senate voted down the scheme in July, FDR quietly dropped it.

But was this a defeat? Roosevelt's challenge to the Court, plus his 1936 electoral victory, sent powerful political signals that the justices heeded. In spring 1937, the Court upheld several New Deal measures, including the Wagner Act and a state minimum-wage law. Four conservative justices soon retired, enabling FDR to nominate successors of his choice and to create a judicial legacy that would long endure.

Overall, the New Deal era saw a fundamental shift in the Supreme Court's constitutional views. For decades, the court had interpreted very narrowly the Constitution's Commerce Clause (Article I, Sec. 8), which empowers the government to regulate business. After the 1930s, the court interpreted the Commerce Clause more broadly and proved much more receptive to business regulation and to the protection of individual rights as well as property rights.

The Roosevelt Recession   After a partial recovery, the economy dipped ominously in August 1937. Industrial production slumped. Unemployment again dominated the headlines. Federal policies that reduced consumer income contributed to this "Roosevelt recession." Social-security payroll taxes withdrew some $2 billion from circulation. The Federal Reserve Board had raised interest rates to forestall inflation, further contracting the money supply. FDR, meanwhile, concerned about mounting deficits, had cut back the New Deal relief programs.

Echoing Hoover, FDR assured his cabinet, "Everything will work out ... if we just sit tight." Meanwhile, however, some advisers had embraced John Maynard Keynes's advocacy of deficit spending as the key to recovery. Aware that political rather than economic arguments carried more weight with FDR, they warned of a political backlash if conditions worsened. Convinced, FDR in April 1938 authorized new relief spending. By late 1938, unemployment had declined and industrial output increased. As late as 1939, however, more than 17 percent of the labor force remained jobless.

Final Measures; Growing Opposition   Preoccupied by the Supreme Court fight, the recession, and events abroad (covered in Chapter 25), FDR offered few domestic initiatives after 1936. Congress, however, enacted several significant measures.

In 1937, Congress created the **Farm Security Administration** (FSA), replacing the under-funded Resettlement Administration. The FSA made low-interest loans to help tenant farmers and sharecroppers become farm owners. However, the FSA often rejected the poorest farmers' loan applications as too risky, weakening the program's impact.

The FSA operated camps offering shelter and medical services to impoverished migrant farm workers. FSA nurses and home economists provided practical advice on hygiene and house-keeping to poor farm families. The FSA also commissioned photographers to record the lives of migrant workers, tenant farmers, and dust-bowl refugees. These FSA photographs, published in various periodicals, helped shape a gritty documentary style that pervaded 1930s' popular culture, including movies and Henry Luce's photo magazine *Life,* launched in 1936. Today, they comprise a haunting album of depression-era images.

Other measures set precedents for the future. The 1937 Housing Act appropriated $500 million for slum-clearance and public-housing projects that would vastly expand in the 1950s. The **Fair Labor Standards Act** of 1938 banned child labor and set a national minimum wage (initially forty cents an hour) and a maximum workweek of forty hours. This measure reflected not only humanitarianism but also some northern legislators' desire to undermine the competitive edge of the low-wage South. Despite many loopholes, the law helped exploited workers and underscored the government's role in regulating abusive workplace conditions.

In a final stab at raising farm income, the 1938 Agricultural Adjustment Act created a mechanism by which the government, in years of big harvests and low prices, would make loans to farmers and warehouse their surplus crops. When prices rose, farmers could sell these commodities and repay their loans. This complicated system set the framework of federal farm price support for decades.

Overall, New Deal farm policy produced mixed results. Large-scale growers benefited from government payments, but the cumbersome price-support mechanisms created many problems. The FSA assisted some tenants, sharecroppers, and small farmers (though often not the neediest), but did little to slow the long-term

Library of Congress, Prints and Photographs Division

A Camera's-Eye View of Depression-Era America *This 1937 image by Dorothea Lange, a photographer with the Farm Security Administration, pictures migrants from the Texas dust bowl gathered at a roadside camp near Calipatria in southern California.*

decline of family farms and the rise of agribusinesses. In reality, many small farmers dreamed of becoming large-scale commercial operators. Most did not succeed, however, and gradually left the land.

The New Deal's slower pace after 1935 also reflected the rise of an anti–New Deal congressional coalition of Republicans and conservative southern Democrats. In 1937, this coalition rejected FDR's proposal to reorganize the executive branch. The plan made administrative sense, but critics again warned darkly of FDR's dictatorial ambitions.

In 1938–1939, conservative legislators slashed relief appropriations, cut corporate taxes, and killed the WPA's Federal Theatre Project for its alleged radicalism. Meanwhile, the House Un-American Activities Committee (created in 1937) investigated New Deal agencies for communist infiltration. The 1939 Hatch Act, barring federal employees from electoral campaigning, reflected conservatives' suspicions that WPA staff members were doubling as campaign workers. Indeed, Harry Hopkins and other public-works officials well understood these programs' electoral value, and political calculations influenced the allocation of PWA and WPA funds.

Although FDR campaigned in the 1938 midterm elections, the Republicans gained in the House and Senate and won a net of thirteen governorships. In the Democratic primaries, Roosevelt opposed several anti–New Deal Democratic senators, but most defeated their pro–New Deal primary challengers and went on to win in November. Highlighting foreign affairs in his January 1939 State of the Union message, FDR proposed no new domestic measures and merely noted the need to "preserve our reforms." The New Deal was over.

SOCIAL CHANGE AND SOCIAL ACTION IN THE 1930S

American life in the 1930s involved more than politics. The depression affected everyone, including the jobless and their families; working women; and all age groups. For industrial workers, African Americans, Hispanics, and Native Americans, the crisis brought hard times but also encouraged organized resistance to exploitation and brought new legislative initiatives.

In organizing our treatment of the 1930s, we have separated the decade's political developments and its social/cultural trends. In reality, of course, all these realities unfolded together. The social crisis and labor activism added urgency to the New Deal and helped drive its shifts of emphasis. New Deal agencies influenced the decade's culture, while the era's cultural products, in turn, shaped public perceptions of the meaning of the Depression and the New Deal for America.

The Depression's Psychological and Social Impact   The depression marked all who lived through it. Despite the New Deal, unemployment never fell below about 14 percent in the 1930s and was often considerably higher. A quarter of all farm families sought public or private assistance during the 1930s. Even the employed often had to take jobs below their level of training: college alumni pumped gas; business-school graduates sold furniture; a retired navy captain became a movie theater usher.

Psychologists described "unemployment shock": jobless persons who walked the streets seeking work and then lay awake at night worrying. When shoe soles wore out, cardboard or folded newspapers had to serve. Advertisements for mouthwashes, deodorants, and correspondence courses exploited feelings of shame and failure. Women's magazines described low-cost meals and other budget-trimming strategies. Habits of scrimping and saving acquired in the 1930s often survived into more affluent times. As Caroline Bird wrote in *The Invisible Scar* (1966), a social history of the 1930s, the depression for many boiled down to "a dull misery in the bones."

New York senator Robert Wagner called the working woman in the depression "the first orphan in the storm." Indeed, for the 25 percent of U.S. women employed in 1930, the depression brought difficult times. The female jobless rate exceeded 20 percent for much of the decade. Working women often took lower-paying jobs. Laid-off factory workers became waitresses. Jobless men competed with women even for such traditional "women's work" as library posts and school teaching.

Married women workers endured harsh criticism. Although most worked because of economic necessity, critics accused them of stealing men's jobs. Even Labor Secretary Frances Perkins urged married women to leave the labor market so more men could work. School boards fired married women teachers.

Women workers faced wage discrimination. In 1939, women teachers earned nearly 20 percent less than male teachers with comparable experience. Some NRA codes authorized lower pay for women. The minimum-wage provision of the Fair Labor Standards Act did not include the more than 2 million women who worked for wages in private households.

The late 1930s' unionization drive had mixed effects on women workers. Women employed in mass-production industries benefited, but the heavily female sectors of the labor force—textiles, sales, clerical and service work—resisted unionization. Male managers and even male union leaders opposed a campaign to unionize female clerical workers.

Despite the criticism, the percentage of married women in the work force increased in the 1930s from under 12 percent to nearly 16 percent. The depression may actually have hastened the long-term movement of women into the workplace as married women took jobs out of necessity. When her husband stopped looking for work in 1932, one working wife explained, "[At] twenty-eight, with two little girls, ... I took a job as a salesclerk ..., and worked through the Depression."

As this story suggests, the depression affected family life. The birthrate fell in the early thirties as married couples postponed a family, and as birth-control devices became more readily available. The U.S. population in the 1930s grew by only 7 percent, in contrast to an average of 20 percent per decade from 1900 to 1930.

Family survival posed major challenges. Parents patched clothes, stretched food resources, and sought public assistance when necessary. In homes with a tradition of strong male authority, the husband's loss of a job could prove devastating. "I would rather turn on the gas and put an end to the whole family than let my wife support me," one man told a social investigator. Desertions increased, and the divorce rate spiked, hitting a then all-time high by 1940.

The depression spared neither old nor young. Bank failures wiped out the savings of older Americans. By 1935, a million citizens over sixty-five were on relief.

One observer compared young people to runners waiting for a starting gun that never sounded. High-school enrollment increased as many youths, lacking job prospects, stayed in school. The marriage rate declined as anxious young people postponed this step. Commented Eleanor Roosevelt in 1934, "I have moments of real terror when I think we might be losing this generation."

Children found vacation plans canceled, birthdays with few presents, and mealtimes tense with anxious discussions. Depression-era children wrote sad letters to Eleanor Roosevelt. A Michigan high-school senior described her shame at lacking a graduation dress. "I give all I earn for food for the family," she explained. A thirteen-year-old Arkansas girl wrote, "I have to stay out of school because I have no books or clothes to ware."

Rediscovering traditional skills, depression-era families canned fruit and vegetables, painted their houses, and repaired their own cars. Many would later recall the 1930s as a time of simple, inexpensive pleasures and neighborly sharing of scant resources.

For the neediest—among them blacks, Hispanics, and southern sharecroppers—the depression imposed added misery on poverty-blighted lives. In *Native Son* (1940), novelist Richard Wright portrayed the desperate conditions in Chicago's black slums. Yet hope survived. Emotional resilience, habits of mutual aid, and survival skills honed over the years helped poor families cope. In New York's Harlem, a charismatic black religious leader calling himself Father Divine institutionalized this cooperative spirit by organizing kitchens that distributed free meals to the needy.

Industrial Workers Unionize

Of America's 7.7 million factory workers in 1930, most remained unorganized. Major industries such as steel, automobiles, and textiles had resisted workers' attempts to unionize. The conservative mood of the 1920s had further weakened the labor movement.

But with hard times and a favorable government climate, labor militancy surged in the 1930s. The Wagner Act's guarantee of workers' right to organize jolted the U.S. labor movement. The nation's major labor organization, the American Federation of Labor (AFL), had historically organized unions of skilled craftsmen rather than of all workers in a given industry (see Chapter 18). In the 1930s, that pattern changed. In November 1935, John L. Lewis of the United Mine Workers and Sidney Hillman of the Amalgamated Clothing Workers, frustrated by the AFL's slowness in organizing factory workers, started the Committee for Industrial Organization (CIO) within the AFL. CIO activists preached unionization in Pittsburgh steel mills, Detroit auto plants, Akron rubber factories, and southern textile mills. Unlike the narrowly restrictive AFL unions, CIO unions welcomed all workers in a particular industry, regardless of race, gender, or skill level.

In 1936 a CIO-sponsored organizing committee announced a strike to unionize the steel industry. (In fact, John L. Lewis had already secretly negotiated a settlement with the head of U.S. Steel.) In March 1937, U.S. Steel recognized the union, raised wages, and introduced a forty-hour workweek. Other big steel companies followed suit, and soon four hundred thousand steelworkers were union members.

Other CIO organizers targeted General Motors, an anti-union stronghold. Their leader was a redheaded young autoworker and labor activist, Walter Reuther.

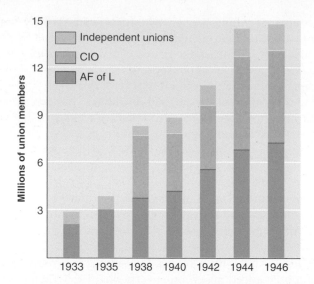

FIGURE 24.2 The Growth of Labor Union Membership, 1933–1946

The CIO's industrial unions grew rapidly with passage of the pro-union National Labor Relations Act in 1935. Union membership increased still more as war plants hired workers in the early 1940s.

Source: Historical Statistics of the United States, Colonial Times to 1970 (1975), 176–177.

Reuther's German American father was a committed socialist, and when the depression hit, young Reuther rediscovered his radical roots. On December 30, 1936, employees at GM's plants in Flint, Michigan, stopped work and peacefully occupied the factories. This "sit-down" strategy (adopted so GM could not hire strikebreakers to keep the plants operating) paralyzed GM's production.

Although women workers did not participate in the plant occupation (to avoid gossip that might discredit the strike), they picketed outside. A Women's Auxiliary led by strikers' families provided meals, set up a speakers' bureau, and organized marches.

GM sent spies to union meetings, called in police to harass the strikers, and threatened to fire them. A showdown with the police led to the formation of the Women's Emergency Brigade, whose members remained on twenty-four-hour alert for picket duty or to surround the plants in case of police raids.

GM asked President Roosevelt and Michigan's governor to send troops to expel the strikers, as Herbert Hoover had done with the bonus marchers. Both declined, however. Although the sit-down tactic troubled FDR, he refused to intervene.

On February 11, 1937, GM signed a contract recognizing the United Automobile Workers (UAW). Bearded workers who had vowed not to shave until victory was won streamed out of the plants. As Chrysler fell into line also, the UAW boasted more than four hundred thousand members. Unionization of the electrical and rubber industries advanced as well.

In 1938, the Committee for Industrial Organization broke with the AFL to become the **Congress of Industrial Organizations,** a 2-million-member association of industrial unions. In response, the AFL, too, began to adapt to the changed nature of the labor force. Overall, U.S. union membership shot from fewer than 3 million in 1933 to more than 8 million in 1941.

Some big corporations resisted. Henry Ford hated unions, and his tough lieutenant Harry Bennett organized a squad of union-busting thugs to fight the UAW. In 1937, Bennett's men viciously beat Walter Reuther and other UAW officials outside Ford's plant near Detroit. Not until 1941 did Ford finally yield to the union's pressure.

The Republic Steel Company, headed by a union hater named Tom Girdler, dug in as well. Even after the major steelmakers signed with the CIO, Republic and other smaller companies known collectively as "Little Steel" resisted. In May 1937, workers in twenty-seven Little Steel plants, including Republic's factory in Chicago, walked off the job. Anticipating the strike, Girdler had assembled an arsenal of guns and tear gas. On May 30, Memorial Day, a group of strikers approached more than 250 police guarding the factory. When someone threw a large stick at the police, they responded with gunfire that left four strikers dead and scores wounded. An investigative committee condemned the killings as "clearly avoidable." In 1941, under growing pressure, the Little Steel companies, including Republic, finally accepted the CIO union.

Another holdout was the textile industry, with more than six hundred thousand low-paid workers, mostly in the South and 40 percent female. A unionizing effort in the 1920s had failed owing to mill owners' hostility (see Chapter 23). In 1934, the AFL affiliated United Textile Workers launched a new drive. Some four hundred thousand textile workers went on strike, but again the mill owners fought back. Anti-union southern governors mobilized the National Guard. Several strikers were killed and thousands arrested. The strike failed, and the textile industry remained mostly nonunion as the decade ended.

Indeed, despite the unionization surge, more than three-quarters of the nonfarm labor force remained unorganized in 1940, including low-paid manual laborers; domestic workers; and employees in department stores, offices, restaurants, and laundries—categories that included many women, blacks, and recent immigrants. Nevertheless, the unionization of many industrial workers ranks among the decade's memorable developments.

Why did powerful corporations yield to unionization after years of resistance? Workers' militancy and union organizers' tactical skill were crucial. But so was a changed government climate. Historically, the government had helped corporations break strikes. Although this still happened in the 1930s, as in the textile-industry strike, the Roosevelt administration and state officials generally refused to play the role of strikebreaker. New Deal labor laws made clear that Washington would no longer automatically back management in labor disputes. Once corporate managers realized this, unionization often followed.

Organized labor's successes in the later 1930s concealed some complex tensions. A core of activists, including communists and socialists, led the unionizing drive. Most rank-and-file workers were not political radicals, but once the CIO's militant minority showed the effectiveness of picket lines and sit-down strikes, workers signed up by the thousands. As they did, the radical organizers lost influence, and the unions became more conservative.

Black and Hispanic Americans Resist Racism and Exploitation
The depression stirred activism within the African American and Hispanic communities. Although black migration northward slowed in the 1930s, four hundred thousand southern blacks moved to northern cities in the decade. By 1940, nearly one-quarter of America's 12 million blacks lived in the urban North.

Rural or urban, life was hard. Black tenant farmers and sharecroppers often faced eviction. Although some black industrial workers benefited from the CIO's nondiscriminatory policy, workplace racism remained a fact of life.

More than one hundred blacks died by lynching in the 1930s, and other miscarriages of justice continued, especially in the South. In 1931, an all-white jury in Scottsboro, Alabama, sentenced eight black youths to death on highly suspect rape charges. In 1935, after heavy publicity and an aggressive defense, the Supreme Court ordered a new trial for the "Scottsboro Boys" because they had been denied legal counsel and blacks had been excluded from the jury. Five of the group were again convicted, however, and served long prison terms.

But rising activism signaled changes ahead. The NAACP battled in courts and legislatures for voting rights and against lynching and segregation. Under the banner "Don't Shop Where You Can't Work," black protesters picketed businesses that refused to hire blacks, particularly in black neighborhoods. In March 1935, hostility toward discriminatory white-owned businesses in Harlem, intensified by anger over racism and joblessness, ignited a riot that caused heavy property damage and left three dead.

The Communist Party publicized lynchings and racial discrimination, and supplied lawyers for the "Scottsboro Boys," as part of a depression-era recruitment effort in the black community. But despite a few notable recruits (including the novelist Richard Wright), few blacks joined the party.

Other groups also faced discrimination. California continued to restrict landownership by Japanese Americans. In 1934, Congress limited annual immigration from the Philippines to fifty, and offered free travel "home" for Filipinos long settled in the United States.

The more than 2 million Hispanic Americans confronted difficulties as well. Some were citizens with ancestral roots in the Southwest, but most were recent arrivals from Mexico or Caribbean islands such as Cuba and Puerto Rico (a U.S. holding whose residents are American citizens). While the Caribbean immigrants settled in East Coast cities, most Mexican newcomers worked as migratory agricultural laborers in the Southwest and elsewhere or in midwestern steel or meatpacking plants.

As the depression deepened, Mexican-born residents endured rising hostility. "Okies" fleeing the dust bowl competed for jobs with Hispanic farm workers. By 1937, more than half of Arizona's cotton workers were out-of-staters who had supplanted Mexican-born laborers. With their migratory work patterns disrupted, Mexican Americans poured into the barrios (Hispanic neighborhoods) of southwestern cities. Lacking work, half a million returned to Mexico in the 1930s. Many did so voluntarily, but immigration officials and local authorities repatriated others. Los Angeles welfare officials announced free one-way transportation to

Mexico. The savings in relief payments, they calculated, would more than offset the cost of sending *repatriados* to Mexico. Though the plan was "voluntary," those who remained were denied relief payments or jobs with New Deal work programs. Under federal and local pressure, an estimated seventy thousand Mexicans left Los Angeles in 1931 alone.

Mexican American farm workers who remained endured appalling conditions and near-starvation wages. A wave of strikes (some led by Communist organizers) swept California. A labor organization called the Confederación de Uniones de Campesinos y Obreros Mexicanos (Confederation of Unions of Mexican Workers and Farm Laborers) emerged from a 1933 grape workers' strike. More strikes erupted in 1935–1936 from the celery fields and citrus groves around Los Angeles to the lettuce fields of the Salinas Valley.

Organizations like the citrus-growers' marketing cooperative Sunkist fought the unions, sometimes with violence. In October 1933, bullets ripped into a cotton pickers' union hall in Pixley, California, killing two men and wounding others. Resisting intimidation, the strikers won a 20 percent pay increase. Striking cotton pickers and other Mexican American farm workers gained hard-fought victories as well. These strikes awakened at least some Americans to the plight of one of the nation's most exploited groups.

A New Deal for Native Americans The 1930s also focused attention on the nation's 330,000 Native Americans, most of whom endured poverty, scant education, and poor health care. The 1887 Dawes Act (see Chapter 17) had dissolved the tribes as legal entities, allocated some tribal lands to individual Indians, and offered the rest for sale. By the 1930s, non-Indians held about two-thirds of the land that Indians had possessed in 1887. Indians had gained voting rights in 1924, but this did little to improve their lot.

In 1923, the reformer John Collier, who had lived among New Mexico's Pueblo Indians, founded the American Indian Defense Association to reverse the Dawes Act approach and to revitalize traditional Indian life. The National Council of American Indians, headed by Gertrude Bonnin, a Yankton Dakota Sioux, also pressed for reform.

Appointed commissioner of Indian affairs in 1933, Collier gathered funds from various New Deal agencies to construct schools, hospitals, and irrigation systems on reservations, and to preserve sites of cultural importance. The Civilian Conservation Corps employed twelve thousand Indian youths on projects on Indian lands.

Pursuing his vision, Collier drafted a bill to halt tribal land sales and restore the remaining unallocated lands to tribal control. Collier's bill also gave broad powers to tribal councils and required Indian schools to teach Native American history and handicrafts. Some Indian leaders criticized it as a plan to transform reservations into living museums and to isolate Native Americans from modern life. Some Indian property owners and entrepreneurs rejected the bill's tribalist assumptions. The bill did, indeed, reflect the idealism of well-meaning outsiders rather than the views of the nation's diverse Native American groups.

The **Indian Reorganization Act** of 1934, a compromise measure, halted tribal land sales and enabled tribes to regain title to unallocated lands. But Congress scaled back Collier's proposals for tribal self-government and dropped his proposals for renewing traditional tribal culture.

Of 258 tribes that voted on the law (a requirement for it to go into effect), 181 favored it, while 77 did not. America's largest tribal group, the 40,000-strong Navajo, voted no, largely because the law, to promote soil conservation, restricted grazing rights.

Indian policy remained contentious. But the law did recognize Indian interests and the value of cultural diversity. The restoration of tribes as legal entities laid the groundwork for later tribal business ventures as well as legal efforts to enforce long-ignored treaty rights (to be discussed in Chapter 30).

THE AMERICAN CULTURAL SCENE IN THE 1930S

Radio and the movies offered escapist fare amid the hard times of the 1930s, though some films addressed depression-era realities. Novelists, artists, playwrights, and photographers tended toward a highly critical view of capitalist America when the depression first struck, as we have seen. As the decade went on, however, a more positive view of America emerged, reflecting both optimism about the New Deal and apprehension about events abroad.

Avenues of Escape: Radio and the Movies   The standardization of mass culture continued in the 1930s. Each evening, Americans turned to their radios for network news, musical programs, and comedy shows. Radio humor flourished as Americans battled hard times. Comedians like Jack Benny and the husband-and-wife team George Burns and Gracie Allen attracted millions.

So, too, did the fifteen-minute afternoon domestic dramas known as soap operas (for the soap companies that sponsored them). Despite their assembly-line quality, these programs won a devoted audience, consisting mostly of housewives. Identifying with the radio heroines' troubles, female listeners gained temporary escape from their own difficulties. As one put it, "I can get through the day better when I hear they have sorrows, too."

The movies, with their low-priced tickets, remained extremely popular. In 1939, 65 percent of Americans went to the movies at least once a week.

Films of the early 1930s like *I Am a Fugitive from a Chain Gang* (1932) captured the grimness of the early depression. The popular Marx Brothers movies reflected the uncertainty of the Hoover years, when the economy and the social order itself seemed on the verge of collapse. In comedies like *Animal Crackers* (1930) and *Duck Soup* (1933), these vaudeville troupers of German Jewish immigrant origins ridiculed authority and satirized the established order.

After Roosevelt took office, Warner Brothers studio (with close ties to the administration) made several topical films that presented the New Deal in a favorable light. These included *Wild Boys of the Road* (1933), about unemployed youth; *Massacre* (1934), on the mistreatment of Indians; and *Black Fury* (1935), dealing with striking coal miners.

Early thirties' gangster movies, inspired by real-life criminals like Al Capone, presented a different style of film realism. Films like *Little Caesar* (1930) and *The Public Enemy* (1931) offered gritty images of depression America: menacing streets, forbidding industrial sites, gunfights between rival gangs. (When civic groups protested the glorification of crime, Hollywood made the police and "G-men"—FBI agents—the heroes, while retaining the violence.) The movie gangsters played by Edward G. Robinson and James Cagney, variants of the Horatio Alger hero battling adversity, appealed to depression-era moviegoers.

Above all, Hollywood offered escape from depression-era realities. The publicist who claimed that the movies "literally laughed the big bad wolf of the depression out of the public mind" exaggerated, but cinema's escapist function in the 1930s is clear. Musicals such as *Gold Diggers of 1933* (with its theme song, "We're in the Money") offered dancing, music, and cheerful plots involving the triumph of pluck over adversity. In Frank Capra's *Mr. Deeds Goes to Town* (1936) and *Mr. Smith Goes to Washington* (1939), virtuous heroes representing "the people" vanquish entrenched interests. When color movies arrived in the late 1930s, they seemed an omen of better times ahead.

African Americans appeared in 1930s' movies, if at all, mostly as stereotypes: the scatterbrained maid in *Gone with the Wind* (1939); the indulgent house servant played by tap dancer Bill Robinson and patronized by child star Shirley Temple in *The Little Colonel* (1935); the slow-witted "Stepin Fetchit" played in many movies by black actor Lincoln Perry.

In representing women, Hollywood offered mixed messages. While some 1930s' movie heroines found fulfillment in marriage and domesticity, other films challenged the stereotype. Joan Bennett played a strong-willed professional in *The Wedding Present* (1936). Katharine Hepburn portrayed independent-minded women in such films as *Spitfire* (1934) and *A Woman Rebels* (1936). Mae West, brassy and openly sexual, mocked conventional stereotypes in *I'm No Angel* (1933) and other 1930s hits.

The Later 1930s: Opposing Fascism; Reaffirming Traditional Values

The 1930s ended on a cautiously upbeat note. America had survived the depression. The social fabric remained whole; revolution had not come. As other societies collapsed into dictatorships, U.S. democracy endured. Writers, composers, and other cultural creators reflected the changed mood.

International developments and a domestic political movement known as the **Popular Front** influenced this shift. In the early 1930s, the U.S. Communist Party attacked Roosevelt and the New Deal. But in 1935, Russian dictator Joseph Stalin, fearing attack by Nazi Germany, called for a worldwide alliance, or Popular Front, against Adolf Hitler and his Italian fascist ally, Benito Mussolini. (Fascism is a form of government involving one-party rule, extreme nationalism, hostility to minority groups, and the suppression of dissent.) Parroting the new Soviet line, U.S. communists now praised FDR and summoned writers and intellectuals to the antifascist cause. Many noncommunists, alarmed by developments in Europe, responded.

The Spanish Civil War was the Popular Front's high-water mark. In July 1936, Spanish fascist general Francisco Franco began a military revolt against Spain's legally elected government, a coalition of left-wing parties. With aid from Hitler and Mussolini, Franco won backing from Spanish monarchists, landowners, industrialists, and the Catholic Church.

The Spanish Loyalists (that is, those loyal to Spain's elected government) won support from U.S. writers, artists, and intellectuals who backed the Popular Front, including the writer Ernest Hemingway, who visited Spain in 1936–1937. In contrast to his antiwar novels of the 1920s (see Chapter 23), Hemingway's *For Whom the Bell Tolls* (1940) told of a young American volunteer who dies while fighting with the Loyalists. For Hemingway, the Spanish Civil War offered a cause "in which you felt an absolute brotherhood with the others who were engaged in it."

The Popular Front collapsed in August 1939 when Stalin and Hitler signed a nonaggression pact. Overnight, enthusiasm for joining with communists under the "antifascism" banner faded. But while it lasted, the Popular Front influenced U.S. culture and alerted Americans to threatening events abroad.

The New Deal's programs for writers, artists, and musicians, as well as its turn leftward in 1935–1936, also contributed to the late 1930s' cultural shift. More positive views now replaced the cynical tone of the 1920s and early 1930s. In John Steinbeck's best-selling novel *The Grapes of Wrath* (1939), an uprooted dust-bowl family, the Joads, make their difficult way from Oklahoma to California along Route 66. Steinbeck stressed ordinary Americans' endurance, cooperation, and mutual support. As Ma Joad tells her son Tom, "They ain't gonna wipe us out. Why, we're the people—we go on." Made into a movie starring Henry Fonda, *The Grapes of Wrath* stands as a memorable cultural document of the later 1930s.

In 1936, journalist James Agee and photographer Walker Evans lived with Alabama sharecropper families while researching a magazine article. From this experience came Agee's masterpiece, *Let Us Now Praise Famous Men* (1941). Enhanced by Evans's photographs, Agee's work evoked the strength and decency of depression-era Americans.

On the stage, Thornton Wilder's *Our Town* (1938) lovingly portrayed early-twentieth-century life a New England town. William Saroyan's *The Time of Your Life* (1939) celebrated the foibles and virtues of a colorful group of patrons gathered in a San Francisco waterfront bar.

Composers, too, caught the spirit of cultural nationalism. In such works as *Billy the Kid* (1938), Aaron Copland drew upon American legends and folk melodies. George Gershwin's 1935 musical *Porgy and Bess,* based on DuBose and Dorothy Heyward's 1920s' novel and play (see Chapter 23), brought this portrayal of black life in Charleston, South Carolina, to a larger audience.

Jazz gained popularity thanks to swing, a danceable style originated by pianist Fletcher Henderson and popularized by the bands of Count Basie, Benny Goodman, Duke Ellington, and others. The Basie band started at Kansas City's Reno Club, where, as Basie later recalled, "We played from nine o'clock in the evening to five or six the next morning.... [T]he boys in the band got eighteen dollars a week and I got twenty one." Moving to New York in 1936, Basie helped launch the swing era.

Benny Goodman, of a Chicago immigrant family, had played the clarinet as a boy at Jane Addams's Hull House. Challenging racial prejudices, Goodman included black musicians in his orchestra. The Goodman band's 1938 performance at New York's Carnegie Hall, a citadel of high culture, underscored jazz's growing cultural influence.

The later 1930s also saw a heightened interest in regional literature, painting, and folk art. Zora Neale Hurston's novel *Their Eyes Were Watching God* (1937) portrayed a black woman's search for fulfillment in rural Florida. William Faulkner's *Absalom, Absalom!* (1936) continued the saga of his mythic Yoknapatawpha County in Mississippi. Painters Thomas Hart Benton of Missouri (descended from a nineteenth-century senator of the same name), John Steuart Curry of Kansas, and Iowa's Grant Wood explored traditional and regional themes in their work.

Galleries displayed folk paintings, Amish quilts, and New England weather vanes. A 1938 show at New York's Museum of Modern Art introduced Horace Pippin, a black Philadelphia laborer partially disabled in World War I. In such paintings as *John Brown Going to His Hanging,* Pippin revealed a genuine, if untutored, talent. In 1939, the same museum featured seventy-nine-year-old Anna "Grandma" Moses of Hoosick Falls, New York, whose memory paintings of her farm girlhood enjoyed great popularity.

The surge of cultural nationalism heightened interest in American history. Visitors flocked to historical re-creations such as Henry Ford's Greenfield Village near Detroit and Colonial Williamsburg in Virginia, restored by John D. Rockefeller, Jr. Texans restored the Alamo in San Antonio, the "Cradle of Texas Liberty." Historical novels like Margaret Mitchell's Civil War epic *Gone with the Wind* (1936) became best sellers. These restorations and fictions often distorted history. Colonial Williamsburg and Mitchell's novel downplayed or romanticized slavery. "Texas Liberty" resonated differently for the state's Hispanic, African American, and Indian peoples than it did for the white patriotic organizations that venerated the Alamo.

Streamlining and a World's Fair: Corporate America's Utopian Vision   A design style called streamlining also shaped the visual culture of the late 1930s. This style originated in the 1920s when industrial designers, inspired by the airplane, introduced flowing curves into the design of commercial products. Consumers loved streamlining—a vital business consideration during the depression. When Sears Roebuck streamlined its Coldspot refrigerators, sales surged. As products ranging from house trailers to pencil sharpeners and cigarette lighters emerged in sleek new forms, streamlining helped corporate America rebuild its image and present itself as the shaper of a better future.

Under the theme "The World of Tomorrow," the 1939 New York World's Fair represented the high point of the streamlining vogue and of corporate America's public-relations blitz. The Trylon and Perisphere, a soaring tapered tower and a globe that seemed to float on water symbolized the fair's futuristic theme. Inside the Perisphere, visitors found "Democracity," a revolving diorama portraying an idealized city of the future.

At Futurama, the General Motors exhibit, visitors entered a darkened auditorium where, amid piped-in music and a resonant recorded narration, a vision of America in the distant year 1960 slowly unfolded. A multilane highway network complete with cloverleaf exits and stacked interchanges dominated the imagined landscape. A brilliant public-relations investment, Futurama built support for the interstate highway system that would soon become a reality. Forget the depression and the bitter auto-workers' strike, GM's exhibit seemed to whisper; behold the exciting future we are preparing for you.

Also featuring such wonders as television and automatic dishwashers, the World's Fair portrayed "The World of Tomorrow" as a technological utopia created by America's corporations. A visit to the fair, a business magazine editorialized, "should convince [any doubters] that American business has been the vehicle which carried the discoveries of science and the benefits of machine production to ... American consumers." The fair epitomized corporate America's version of the patriotism and hopefulness stirring in America as the 1930s ended.

But the hopefulness was tinged with fear, as danger loomed beyond the seas. The anxiety triggered by the menacing world situation surfaced on October 31, 1938, when CBS radio aired an adaptation of H.G. Wells's science-fiction story *War of the Worlds* directed by Orson Welles. In realistic detail, the broadcast reported the landing of a spaceship in New Jersey and aliens with ray guns advancing toward New York City. The show sparked a panic. Some terrified listeners jumped in their cars and sped off into the night. Others prayed. A few attempted suicide. Beneath the terror lay a more well-founded fear: of approaching war. For a decade, as America had battled the depression, the international situation had steadily worsened. By October 1938, another European war loomed on the horizon.

The panic triggered by Orson Welles's Halloween prank quickly faded, but the anxieties aroused by the all-too-real dangers abroad only escalated. By the time the New York World's Fair offered its hopeful vision of the future, the actual world of 1939 looked bleak indeed.

CHRONOLOGY
1929–1939

1929	Stock market crash; onset of depression.
1932	Reconstruction Finance Corporation.
	Veterans' bonus march.
	Franklin D. Roosevelt elected president.
1933	Repeal of Eighteenth Amendment.
	Civilian Conservation Corps (CCC).
	Federal Emergency Relief Act (FERA).
	Tennessee Valley Authority (TVA).
	Agricultural Adjustment Administration (AAA).
	National Recovery Administration (NRA).
	Public Works Administration (PWA).
1934	Securities and Exchange Commission (SEC).
	Taylor Grazing Act.
	Indian Reorganization Act.

1934–1936	Strikes by Mexican American agricultural workers in the West.
1935	Supreme Court declares NIRA unconstitutional.
	Works Progress Administration (WPA).
	Resettlement Administration.
	National Labor Relations Act (Wagner Act).
	Social Security Act.
	NAACP campaign for federal antilynching law.
	Huey Long assassinated.
	Revenue Act raises taxes on corporations and the wealthy.
	Supreme Court reverses conviction of the "Scottsboro Boys."
	Harlem protests and riot.
1935–1939	Era of the Popular Front.
1936	Supreme Court declares AAA unconstitutional.
	Roosevelt wins landslide reelection victory.
	Autoworkers' sit-down strike against General Motors begins (December).
1937	Roosevelt's "court-packing" plan defeated.
	Farm Security Administration.
	GM, U.S. Steel, and Chrysler sign union contracts.
1934	Securities and Exchange Commission (SEC).
	Taylor Grazing Act.
	Indian Reorganization Act.
1937–1938	The "Roosevelt recession."
1938	Fair Labor Standards Act.
	Republicans gain heavily in midterm elections.
	Congress of Industrial Organizations (CIO) formed.
	Carnegie Hall concert by Benny Goodman Orchestra.
	Orson Welles's "War of the Worlds" radio broadcast.
1939	Hatch Act.
	Marian Anderson concert at Lincoln Memorial.
	John Steinbeck, *The Grapes of Wrath*.
1940	Ernest Hemingway, *For Whom the Bell Tolls*.

Conclusion

The stock-market crash and the Great Depression exposed major weaknesses in the U.S. and world economies. These ranged from chronically low farm prices and uneven income distribution to trade barriers, a glut of consumer goods, and a constricted money supply. As the crisis deepened, President Hoover struggled to respond. In 1932, with Hoover discredited, Franklin D. Roosevelt and his promised "New Deal" brought a surge of hope.

Initially focusing on immediate economic relief and recovery, Roosevelt welcomed big business in his depression-fighting coalition. By 1935, however, the New Deal adopted a more class-based approach. FDR now addressed the plight of the poor, including sharecroppers and migrants; pursued business regulation and higher taxes for the wealthy; and championed such fundamental reforms as Social Security, centerpiece of the welfare state, and the Wagner Act, guaranteeing workers' right to unionize. His smashing reelection victory in 1936 solidified FDR's Democratic coalition, including the white South, farmers, urban ethnics, union members, and African Americans. By 1938, facing conservative opposition and menaces abroad, the New Deal's reformist energies faded.

The depression and the New Deal affected different groups in different ways. For citizens across the West and in the region served by TVA, public-works projects brought hydroelectric power and economic growth, while the New Deal also renewed attention to conservation and environmental issues. Women were told to stay home so jobless men could find work. Many resisted, however, and the female labor force expanded. For industrial workers, the decade's spirit of militance and favorable legislation brought a wave of strikes and unionization campaigns.

While African Americans benefited from New Deal relief programs, the Roosevelt administration failed to address lynching and racial discrimination. Mexican-born farm laborers, facing deportation threats, organized strikes demanding better wages and working conditions. For Native Americans, New Deal legislation restored tribes' legal status, laying the groundwork for future enterprises and treaty claims.

American culture in the 1930s reflected the decade's economic and social realities. While movies and radio offered diversion, writers, painters, and other cultural creators initially expressed disillusionment over capitalism's failure. But as New Deal programs inspired hope, and as foreign threats loomed, the later 1930s brought a more upbeat and affirmative cultural climate.

The New Deal has its downside. Some programs failed, and recovery proved elusive. Only in 1943, as war plants boomed, did full employment return. On racial issues, symbolic gestures substituted for genuine engagement. But the New Deal's achievements remain impressive, reflecting an unprecedented level of governmental engagement with social and economic issues. FDR and his administration reshaped the role of the presidency, the Supreme Court, the nation's political agenda, and citizens' expectations of government's role in meeting urgent public needs.

When a severe economic recession hit the United States in 2008, thoughts turned back to the Great Depression, seventy-five years earlier. The economic policies of the New Deal, and their relevance to the current crisis, were debated with fresh intensity, underscoring how profoundly the 1930s reshaped American thought about the role of government in the economy.

Looming over the decade is the larger-than-life image of Franklin D. Roosevelt. Neither saint nor superman, FDR could be devious, superficial, and cavalier about details. But for most Americans of the 1930s—and most historians since—his strengths outweighed his liabilities. His experimental approach served a suffering nation well. He once compared himself to a football quarterback, deciding which play to call after seeing how the last one worked out.

Above all, Roosevelt's optimism inspired a demoralized people. "We Americans of today ..." he told an audience of young people in 1939, "are characters in the living book of democracy. But we are also its author. It falls upon us now to say whether the chapters ... to come will tell a story of retreat or a story of continued advance."

25

AMERICANS AND A WORLD IN CRISIS, 1933–1945

THE UNITED STATES IN A MENACING WORLD, 1933–1939

Apart from improving relations with Latin America, the early administration of President Franklin D. Roosevelt (FDR) remained largely aloof from the crises in the world. Americans reacted ambivalently as Italy, Germany, and Japan grew more aggressive. Millions of Americans, determined not to stumble into war again, supported neutrality. Only a minority wanted the United States to help embattled democracies abroad. All the while, the world slid toward the precipice.

Nationalism and the Good Neighbor
President Roosevelt at first put American economic interests above all else and showed little interest in international cooperation. He did, however, extend the internationalist approach of his predecessor in Latin America, where bitterness over "Yankee imperialism" ran high. FDR declared a **"Good Neighbor" policy,** renouncing any nation's right to intervene in the affairs of another. To that end, Roosevelt withdrew the last U.S. troops from Haiti and the Dominican Republic and terminated the Platt Amendment, which had given the United States its right to intervene in Cuba since 1901.

An economic crisis in Cuba in 1933 brought to power a leftist regime that the United States opposed. Instead of sending in the marines, as earlier administrations might have done, the United States provided indirect aid to a conservative revolt led by Fulgencio Batista in 1934 that overthrew the radical government. American economic assistance would then allow Batista to retain power until his overthrow by Fidel Castro in 1959. In Mexico, a reform government came to power in 1936 and promptly nationalized several oil companies owned by U.S. and British corporations. While insisting on fair compensation, the United States refrained from military intervention. The better relations fostered by FDR would help the United States achieve hemispheric solidarity in World War II, as well as later in the Cold War.

The Rise of Aggressive States in Europe and Asia   Meanwhile, powerful forces raged across much of the world. As early as 1922, economic and social unrest in Italy enabled **Benito Mussolini** to seize power. Dictator until 1943, Mussolini suppressed dissent, imposed one-party fascist rule, adopted anti-Semitic laws, and, hoping to recreate a Roman empire, invaded Ethiopia in 1935.

Borrowing the straight-armed Roman salute from Mussolini, **Adolf Hitler** and his National Socialist (Nazi) party in Germany gained broad support as a result of the depression, fear of communism, and resentment of the harsh Versailles treaty. In 1933, Hitler became Germany's chancellor. Crushing opponents and rivals, Hitler imposed a brutal dictatorship on Germany and began the pursuit of world domination he had proclaimed in his book *Mein Kampf* (*My Struggle*) (1923). He also instituted a program to purify the fatherland of Jews—whom he considered an "inferior race" responsible for Germany's defeat in World War I.

Violating the Versailles treaty, Hitler began rearming Germany in 1935. A year later, German troops reoccupied the Rhineland, a region between the Rhine River and France specifically demilitarized by the Versailles treaty. In 1938, as German tanks rolled into Vienna, Hitler proclaimed an *anschluss* (union) between Austria and Germany. London, Paris, and Washington murmured disapproval but took no action. An emboldened Hitler then claimed Germany's right to the Sudetenland, a part of neighboring Czechoslovakia containing 3 million ethnic Germans. British prime minister Neville Chamberlain and his French counterpart, insisting that their countries could not endure another war like that of 1914–1918, yielded to Hitler's demands in return for his assurance that Germany had no further territorial ambitions—a policy dubbed **appeasement**—at a conference in Munich in September 1938.

In Japan, meanwhile, militarists gained control of the government and launched a fateful course of expansion, sending troops into the northern Chinese province of Manchuria in 1931. Japan then initiated a full-scale war against China in 1937 and soon controlled key parts of that nation.

The American Mood: No More War   The feeble American response reflected the people's belief that the decision to go to war in 1917 had been a mistake. This conviction was rooted in the nation's isolationist tradition—its wish to avoid military and political entanglements in Old World quarrels—as well as in its desire to have the government focus on the problems of the depression, not foreign affairs. Numerous popular books concluded that banking and corporate interests had dragged the United States into World War I. So did a 1934–1936 Senate investigation headed by Republican Gerald P. Nye of North Dakota, which maintained that war profiteers, whom it called "merchants of death," had tricked the United States into war for financial gain. A January 1937 poll showed that 70 percent of the people believed that the United States should have stayed out of the war.

By the mid-1930s, an overwhelming majority of Americans thought that the "mistake" of intervention must not be repeated. In 1935–1937, a series of **Neutrality Acts** echoed the longing for peace. To prevent a repetition of 1917, these measures outlawed arms sales and loans to nations at war and forbade Americans to travel on the ships of belligerent powers. With the public firmly isolationist and some American companies, like IBM, with large financial investments in German industry, confrontation with fascism came solely in sports. At the 1936 Olympics in Berlin, African American track star Jesse Owens made a mockery of Nazi theories of racial superiority by winning four gold medals. In 1938, in a boxing match laden with symbolism, the black American Joe Louis knocked out German fighter Max Schmeling in the first round of their world heavyweight championship fight. Americans cheered—but still opposed any policies that might involve them in war.

The Gathering Storm: 1938–1939   On March 15, 1939, Nazi troops overran the rest of Czechoslovakia, violating the Munich accords. Five months after that, Hitler reached an agreement with Soviet premier **Joseph Stalin** in the German-Soviet Nonaggression Pact that their nations would not fight one another and that they would divide Poland after Germany invaded it. No longer worried about waging war on two fronts, Hitler's troops attacked Poland. As expected, Britain and France declared war on Germany. World War II had begun.

Although isolationist sentiment remained strong in the United States, opinion began to shift. After the fall of Czechoslovakia, Roosevelt called for actions "short of war" to check fascism and asked Hitler and Mussolini to pledge no further aggression. A jeering Hitler ridiculed FDR's message, while in Rome Mussolini mocked Roosevelt's physical disability, joking that the president's paralysis must have reached his brain. Roosevelt, however, did more than send messages. In October 1938, he asked Congress for a $300 million military appropriation; in November, he instructed the Army Air Corps to plan for an annual production of 20,000 planes; in January 1939, he submitted a $1.3 billion defense budget. Hitler and Mussolini, he said, were "two madmen" who "respect force and force alone."

America and the Jewish Refugees   Hitler and the Nazis had translated their hatred of Jews into official policy. The Nuremberg Laws of 1935 stripped Jews of the rights of German citizenship and increased restrictions on Jews in all spheres of German educational, social, and economic life. This campaign of hatred reached a violent crescendo on November 9–10, 1938, when the Nazis unleashed *Kristallnacht* (Night of the Broken Glass), a frenzy of arson, destruction, and looting against Jews throughout Germany.

No longer could anyone mistake Hitler's malignant intent. Jews, who had been leaving Germany since 1933, streamed out by the hundreds of thousands, seeking haven. Between 1933 and 1938, sixty thousand fled to the United States. Most Americans condemned the Jews' persecution, but only a minority favored admitting more refugees. Congress rejected all efforts to liberalize the immigration law, with its discriminatory quotas, and FDR did little to translate his sympathy for the Jews into effective policies.

The consequences of such attitudes became clear in June 1939, when the *St. Louis*, a German liner jammed with 950 Jewish refugees, asked permission to put its passengers ashore at Fort Lauderdale, Florida. Immigration officials refused this request and a Coast Guard cutter stood by to prevent possible attempts by refugees to jump off and swim ashore. The *St. Louis* turned slowly away from the lights of America and sailed back to Europe, where most of its passengers would die from Nazi brutality.

Into the Storm, 1939–1941

Following the lightning German victories in Western Europe in spring 1940, President Roosevelt's policy of neutrality to keep America out of war gave way to a policy of economic intervention. He knew that extending increasing amounts of aid to those resisting aggression by the so-called Rome-Berlin-Tokyo Axis, as well as his toughening conduct toward Germany and Japan, could, as he said, "push" the United States into the crisis of worldwide war. Japan's attack on the U.S. fleet at Pearl Harbor would provide the push.

The European War   The war in Europe began on September 1, 1939, as Nazi armies poured into Poland and the *Luftwaffe* (German air force) devastated Polish cities. Two days later, Britain and France, honoring commitments to Poland, declared war on Germany. Although FDR invoked the Neutrality Acts, he would not ask Americans to be impartial in thought and deed.

Isolationism Versus Interventionism *In front of the White House in 1941, an American soldier grabs a sign from an isolationist picketing against the United States entering the war in Europe. A diverse group, isolationists ran the gamut from pacifists who opposed all wars, to progressives who feared the growth of business and centralized power that a war would bring, to ultra-rightists who sympathized with fascism and/or shared Hitler's anti-Semitism.*

Thomas McAvoy/TimeLife Pictures/Getty Images

Tailoring his actions to the public mood, which favored both preventing a Nazi victory and staying out of war, FDR persuaded Congress in November to amend the Neutrality Acts to allow the belligerents to purchase weapons from the United States if they paid cash and carried the arms away in their own ships. But "cash-and-carry" did not stop the Nazis. In spring 1940, Hitler unleashed a *blitzkrieg* (lightning war) against Denmark, Norway, the Netherlands, Belgium, and Luxembourg. The Nazi *wehrmacht* (war machine) swept all the way to the English Channel in a scant two months. In early June, the British evacuated most of their army at Dunkirk, and on June 22, France surrendered.

Hitler then took aim against Great Britain, terror-bombing British cities in hopes of forcing a surrender or, failing that, preparing the ground for a cross-channel invasion. With thousands of civilians killed or wounded and much of London in smoking ruins, British prime minister **Winston Churchill** pleaded for American aid. Many Americans, shocked at the use of German air power against British civilians, favored such aid. But a large minority opposed it as wasteful of materials needed for U.S. defenses or as a ruse to lure Americans into war.

From Isolation to Intervention   In the United States in 1940, news of the "Battle of Britain" competed with speculation about whether FDR would break with tradition and run for an unprecedented third term. Not until the eve of the Democrats' July convention did he reveal that, given the world crisis, he would consent to a "draft" from his party. The Axis threat clinched his renomination and similarly led the Republicans to nominate Wendell Willkie of Indiana, an all-out internationalist who championed greater aid to Britain.

Adroitly playing the role of a national leader too busy with defense and diplomacy to engage in partisan politics, Roosevelt appointed republicans Henry Stimson and Frank Knox as secretaries of war and the navy, respectively; signed the Selective Service and Training Act, the first peacetime draft in U.S. history; approved a dramatic increase in defense funding; and, in September, engineered a "destroyers-for-bases" swap with England, sending fifty vintage American ships to Britain in exchange for leases on British air and naval bases in the Western Hemisphere.

These moves infuriated isolationists, particularly the America First Committee. Largely financed by Henry Ford, and featuring Charles Lindbergh as its most popular speaker, the AFC insisted "Fortress America" could stand alone. But 55 percent of Americans, reassured by the president's promise never to "send an American boy to fight in a foreign war," voted him into a third term.

Roosevelt now called on the United States to become "the arsenal of democracy." He proposed a **"lend-lease"** program to allow the U.S. to lend or lease war materiel to any nation vital to America's security. While Roosevelt likened the plan to loaning a garden hose to a neighbor whose house was on fire, isolationist Senator Robert Taft compared it to chewing gum: after a neighbor uses it, "you don't want it back." Congress, however, approved lend-lease in March 1941, and supplies began to flow across the Atlantic. When Hitler's armies invaded the Soviet Union in June 1941, FDR dispatched supplies to the Soviets, despite American hostility toward communism. To defeat Hitler, FDR said, "I would hold hands with the Devil."

To counter the menace of German submarines that threatened to choke the transatlantic supply line, Roosevelt in mid-1941 authorized the U.S. Navy to convoy British ships, with orders to destroy enemy ships if necessary. In August, he met with Churchill aboard a warship off Newfoundland. They issued a statement, known as the **Atlantic Charter,** that condemned aggression, affirmed national self-determination, and endorsed the principles of collective security, free trade, and disarmament. After a German submarine fired at an American destroyer in September, Roosevelt authorized naval patrols to shoot on sight all Axis vessels operating in the western Atlantic. Now on a collision course with Germany, Roosevelt persuaded Congress in November to permit the arming of merchant ships and to allow the transport of lend-lease supplies to belligerent ports in war zones. Unprepared for a major war, America was nevertheless fighting a limited one, and full-scale war seemed imminent.

Pearl Harbor and the Coming of War
Hitler's triumphs in western Europe encouraged Japan to expand farther into Asia. Seeing Germany as America's primary threat, Roosevelt tried to apply enough pressure to deter Japanese aggression without provoking Tokyo to war before the United States had built the "two-ocean navy" authorized by Congress in 1940. "I simply have not got enough navy to go around," he told Harold Ickes in mid-1941, "and every episode in the Pacific means fewer ships in the Atlantic."

The Japanese, too, hoped to avoid war but would not compromise their desire to create the Greater East Asia Co-Prosperity Sphere (an empire embracing much of China, Southeast Asia, and the western Pacific). Japan saw the United States as blocking its legitimate rise to power, while Americans viewed Japan's talk of national aspirations as a smokescreen to cloak aggression. Decades of "yellow-peril" propaganda had hardened U.S. attitudes toward Japan, and even those who were isolationist toward Europe tended to be interventionist toward Asia.

The two nations became locked in a deadly dance. In 1940, believing that economic coercion would force the Japanese out of China, the United States ended a long-standing trade treaty with Japan and banned the sale of aviation fuel and scrap metal to the Japanese. Tokyo responded by occupying northern Indochina, a French colony, and signing the Tripartite Pact with Germany and Italy in September, creating a military alliance, the Berlin-Rome-Tokyo Axis, that required each government to help the others in the event of a U.S. attack.

When the Japanese then overran the rest of Indochina in July 1941, Roosevelt froze all Japanese assets in the United States and clamped a total embargo on trade with Japan. Tokyo had two choices: submit to the United States to gain a resumption of trade for vital resources or conquer new lands to obtain them. In October, expansionist war minister General Hideki Tojo became Japan's prime minister. Tojo set the first week in December as the deadline for a preemptive strike if the United States did not yield. By late November, U.S. intelligence—deciphering Japan's top diplomatic code—alerted the Roosevelt administration that war was imminent. Eleventh-hour negotiations under way in Washington made no headway, and warnings went out to all commanders in the Pacific advising that a Japanese attack was imminent. U.S. officials believed the Japanese would strike British or Dutch possessions or even the Philippines—but the Japanese gambled on a knock-out punch, hoping to destroy the U.S. Pacific Fleet at Pearl Harbor and compel Roosevelt, preoccupied with Germany, to seek accommodation with Japan.

Waves of Japanese dive-bombers and torpedo planes thundered across Hawaii's island of Oahu Sunday morning, December 7, 1941, bombing ships at anchor in Pearl Harbor and strafing planes parked wingtip to wingtip at nearby air bases. In less than three hours, eight battleships, three light cruisers, and two destroyers had been sunk or crippled, and 360 aircraft destroyed or damaged. The attack killed more than twenty-four hundred Americans and opened the way for Japan's advance toward Australia. Americans had underestimated the resourcefulness, skill, and daring of the Japanese. At the same time, Japanese leaders erred in counting on a paralyzing blow at Pearl Harbor. That miscalculation assured an aroused and united nation determined to avenge the attack.

Roosevelt called December 7 a "date which will live in infamy." On December 8, Congress declared war on Japan. (The sole dissenter was Montana's Jeannette Rankin, who had also cast a nay vote against U.S. entry into World War I.) Three days later, Hitler declared war on the "half Judaized and the other half Negrified" Americans, and Mussolini followed suit. Congress immediately reciprocated without a dissenting vote. America faced a global war that it was not ready to fight.

After Pearl Harbor, U-boats wreaked havoc in the North Atlantic and prowled the Caribbean and the East Coast of the United States. Every twenty-four hours, five more Allied vessels went to the bottom. By the end of 1942, U-boat "wolf packs" had destroyed more than a thousand Allied ships, offsetting the pace of American ship production. The United States was losing the battle of the Atlantic.

Additionally, the war news from Europe and Africa was, as Roosevelt admitted, "all bad." Hitler's rule covered an enormous swath of territory, from the outskirts of Moscow and Leningrad—a thousand miles deep into Russia—to the Pyrenees on the French-Spanish border, and from northern Norway to the Libyan desert. In North Africa, the German Afrika Korps swept toward the Suez Canal, the British oil lifeline. It seemed as if the Mediterranean would become an Axis sea and that Hitler would soon be in India to greet Tojo marching across Asia before the United States was ready to fight.

The Japanese inflicted defeat after defeat on Allied Pacific forces. Tojo followed Pearl Harbor with a rampage across the Pacific that put Guam, Wake Island, Hong Kong, Singapore, Burma, and the Netherlands East Indies under Japan's control by the end of April 1942. American forces in the Philippines, besieged for months on the island of Bataan, surrendered in May. Japan's rising sun flag blazed over hundreds of islands in the central and western Pacific and over the entire eastern perimeter of the Asian mainland from the border of Siberia to the border of India.

AMERICA MOBILIZES FOR WAR

In December 1941, American armed forces numbered just 1.6 million, and war production accounted for only 15 percent of U.S. industrial output. Pearl Harbor changed everything. Congress passed a War Powers Act, granting the president unprecedented authority over all aspects of the war. Volunteers and draftees swelled the armed forces; by war's end, some 15 million men and nearly 350,000 women would serve. More would work in defense industries. Mobilization required unprecedented coordination of the American government, economy, and military. In 1942, those responsible for managing America's growing war machine moved into the world's largest building, the newly constructed Pentagon. Like the Pentagon, which was intended to house civilian agencies after the war, far-reaching domestic changes would also outlast the war and significantly alter American attitudes, behavior, and institutions.

Organizing for Victory   To direct the military engine, Roosevelt formed the Joint Chiefs of Staff, made up of representatives of the army, navy, and army air force. (Only a minor "corps" within the army as late as June 1941, the air force would grow more dramatically than any other branch of the service, achieve virtual autonomy, and play a vital role in combat strategy.) The changing nature of modern warfare also led to the creation of the Office of Strategic Services (OSS), forerunner of the Central Intelligence Agency, to conduct the espionage required for strategic planning.

Roosevelt established the **War Production Board** (WPB) to allocate materials, limit the production of civilian goods, and distribute contracts. The newly created War Manpower Commission (WMC) supervised the mobilization of men and women for the military, war industry, and agriculture; the National War Labor Board (NWLB) mediated disputes between management and labor; and the **Office of Price Administration** (OPA) imposed strict price controls to check inflation.

Although a Nazi commander had jeered, "The Americans can't build planes, only electric iceboxes and razor blades," the United States achieved a miracle of war production in 1942. Car makers retooled to produce planes and tanks; a pinball-machine maker converted to armor-piercing shells. By late 1942, 33 percent of the economy was committed to war production. Whole new industries appeared virtually overnight. With almost all of the nation's crude-rubber supply now in Japanese-controlled territory, the government built some fifty new synthetic-rubber plants. By the end of the war, the United States had become the world's largest exporter of synthetic rubber.

America also became the world's greatest weapons manufacturer, producing more war materiel by 1944 than its Axis enemies combined: 300,000 military aircraft, 86,000 tanks, 2.6 million machine guns, and 6 million tons of bombs. "To American production," Stalin would toast FDR and Churchill, "without which the war would have been lost." The United States also built more than five thousand cargo ships and eighty-six thousand warships. Henry J. Kaiser, who had supervised the construction of the Boulder Dam, introduced prefabrication to cut the time needed to build ships. In 1941, the construction of a Liberty-class merchant ship took six months; in 1943, less than two weeks. By 1945, Kaiser, dubbed "Sir Launchalot," was completing a cargo ship every day.

Such breakneck production had costs. The size and powers of the government expanded as defense spending zoomed from 9 percent of gross national product (GNP) in 1940 to 46 percent in 1945; the federal budget soared from $9 billion to $98 billion. Federal civilian employees mushroomed from 1.1 million to 3.8 million. The executive branch, directing the war effort, grew the most, and an alliance formed between the defense industry and the military. (A generation later, Americans would call these concentrations of power the "imperial presidency" and the "military-industrial complex.")

"Dr. New Deal," in FDR's words, gave way to "Dr. Win the War." Because the government sought the maximum production in the shortest time, it guaranteed profits, provided generous tax write-offs and subsidies, and suspended antitrust prosecutions. "If you are going to try to go to war in a capitalist country," said Secretary of War Stimson, "you have to let business make money out of the process or business won't work." Two-thirds of all war-production dollars went to the hundred largest firms, greatly accelerating trends toward economic concentration.

The War Economy   The United States spent more than $360 billion ($250 million a day) to defeat the Axis, ten times the cost of World War I. Wartime spending stimulated an industrial boom that transformed the nation from economic paralysis to record-shattering productivity and prosperity. It doubled U.S. industrial output and the per capita GNP, created 17 million new jobs, increased corporate after-tax profits by 70 percent, and raised the real wages or purchasing power of industrial workers by 50 percent.

The federal government poured $40 billion into the West, making it an economic powerhouse, the center of massive aircraft and shipbuilding industries. California alone secured more than 10 percent of all federal funds; by 1945, nearly half the personal income in the state came from the federal government.

A dynamic Sun Belt, stretching from the coastal Southeast to the coastal Southwest, was the recipient of billions spent on military bases and the needs of the armed forces. The South's industrial capacity increased by 40 percent, and per capita income tripled. Boom times enabled hundreds of thousands of sharecroppers and farm tenants to leave the land for better-paying industrial jobs. While the South's farm population decreased by 20 percent in the 1940s, its urban population grew 36 percent.

Full employment, a longer workweek, larger paychecks, and the increased hiring of minorities, women, and the elderly brought a middle-class standard of living to millions of families. In California, the demand for workers in the shipyards and aircraft factories opened opportunities for thousands of Chinese Americans previously confined to menial jobs within their own communities. In San Diego, 40 percent of retirees returned to work. Deafening factories hired the hearing-impaired, and aircraft plants employed dwarfs as inspectors because of their ability to crawl inside small spaces.

The war years produced the only significant shift toward greater equality in the distribution of income in the twentieth century. The earnings of the bottom fifth of all workers rose 68 percent, and those of the middle class doubled. The richest 5 percent, conversely, saw their share of total disposable income drop from 23 to 17 percent.

Large-scale commercial farmers prospered, benefiting from higher consumer prices and increased productivity thanks to improved fertilizers and more mechanization. As sharecroppers, tenants, and small farmers left the land for better-paying industrial jobs, the overall agricultural population fell by 17 percent. Farming became "agribusiness," and organized agriculture wielded power alongside organized labor, big government, and big business.

Organized labor grew mightier as union membership rose from 9 million to 14.8 million workers. Although the National War Labor Board attempted to limit wage increases to restrain inflation, salaries and wages more than doubled during the war, and unions negotiated unprecedented fringe benefits for workers, including paid vacation time and health and pension plans. Because most workers honored

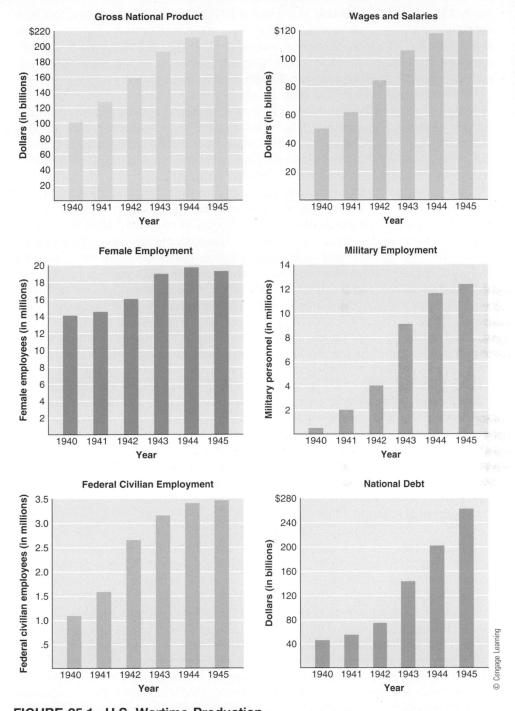

FIGURE 25.1   U.S. Wartime Production

Between 1941 and 1945, the economy grew at a remarkable pace.

the "no-strike" pledge that they had given immediately after Pearl Harbor, less than one-tenth of 1 percent of wartime working hours was lost to wildcat strikes. Those strikes, however, cost the union movement: in 1943, Congress passed, over Roosevelt's veto, the Smith-Connally War Labor Disputes act, empowering the president to take over any facility where strikes threatened war production.

Far more than strikes, inflation threatened the wartime economy. The OPA constantly battled inflation—fueled by greater spending power combined with a scarcity of goods. Throughout 1942, prices climbed at a 2-percent-per-month clip, and at the year's end, Congress gave the president authority to freeze wages, prices, and rents. As the OPA clamped down, inflation slowed dramatically: consumer prices went up only 8 percent in the war's last two years.

The OPA also instituted rationing to combat inflation and conserve scarce materials. Under the slogan "Use it up, wear it out, make it do, or do without," the OPA rationed gasoline, coffee, sugar, butter, cheese, and meat. Americans endured "meatless Tuesdays" and cuffless trousers, ate sherbet instead of ice cream, and put up with imitation chocolate that tasted like soap and imitation soap that did not lather. Most Americans cheerfully formed carpools, planted victory gardens, and recycled paper and fats, while their children, known as "Uncle Sam's Scrappers" and "Tin-Can Colonels," scoured their neighborhoods for scrap metal.

Buying war bonds—"bullets in the bellies of Hitler's hordes!" said the Treasury Department—further curtailed inflation by decreasing consumer purchasing power, while giving civilians a sense of involvement in the distant war. Small investors bought $40 billion in "E" bonds, and wealthy individuals and corporations invested nearly twice that amount. Bond sales raised almost half the money needed to finance the war. Roosevelt sought to raise the rest by drastically increasing taxes. Congress refused the president much of what he sought. Still, the Revenue Act of 1942 raised the top income-tax rate from 60 percent to 94 percent and imposed income taxes on middle- and lower-income Americans for the first time. Beginning in 1943, the payroll-deduction system automatically withheld income taxes from wages and salaries. In 1945, the federal government collected nearly twenty times the tax revenue it had in 1940.

"A Wizard War"   Recognizing wartime scientific and technological developments, Winston Churchill dubbed World War II "a wizard war." Mathematicians went to work deciphering enemy codes, psychologists devised propaganda, and, as never before, the major combatants mobilized scientists into virtual armies of invention. In 1941, FDR created the Office of Scientific Research and Development (OSRD) for the development of new weapons and medicines. The OSRD spent more than $1 billion to produce improved radar and sonar, rocket weapons, and proximity fuses for mines and artillery shells. It also funded the development of jet aircraft and high-altitude bombsights. Other OSRD research hastened the development of the laser and insecticides, contributed to improved blood transfusions, and produced "miracle drugs," such as penicillin.

The demand for greater accuracy in artillery required the kind of rapid, detailed calculations that only computing machines could supply. By 1944, navy personnel in the basement of Harvard's physics laboratory were operating IBM's Mark I, a cumbersome device fifty-one feet long and eight feet high that weighed five tons and contained 760,000 parts. A second-generation computer, ENIAC (electronic numerical integrator and computer), soon reduced the time to multiply two tenth-place numbers from Mark I's three seconds to less than three-thousandths of a second.

Nothing saved the lives of more wounded servicemen than improvements in battlefield medical care. Military needs led to advances in heart and lung surgery and to the use of synthetic antimalarial drugs to substitute for scarce quinine. So-called miracle drugs, antibiotics to combat infections (which were a rarity on the eve of war), would be copiously produced. The use of DDT cleared many islands of malaria-carrying mosquitoes. Along with innovations like the Mobile Auxiliary Surgical Hospital (MASH), science helped save tens of thousands of soldiers' lives and improved the health of the nation as well. Life expectancy rose by three years during the war.

The atomic bomb project began in August 1939 when Albert Einstein, a Jewish refugee and Nobel Prize–winning physicist, warned Roosevelt that Nazi scientists were seeking to use atomic physics to construct an extraordinarily destructive weapon. In 1941, FDR launched a massive Anglo-American secret program—the Soviets were excluded—to construct an atomic bomb. The next year, the participating physicists, both Americans and Europeans, achieved a controlled chain reaction under the University of Chicago football stadium and acquired the basic knowledge necessary to develop the bomb. By July 1945, this program—code-named the **Manhattan Project**—had employed more than 120,000 people and spent nearly $2 billion.

Just before dawn on July 16, 1945, a blinding fireball with "the brightness of several suns at midday" rose over the desert at Alamogordo, New Mexico, followed by a billowing mushroom cloud. Equivalent to twenty thousand tons of TNT, the blast from this first atomic explosion was felt a hundred miles away. "A few people laughed, a few people cried," recalled J. Robert Oppenheimer, the Manhattan Project's scientific director. "Most people were silent. I remembered the line from the Hindu scripture, the Bhagavad-Gita: 'Now I am become Death, the destroyer of worlds.'" The atomic age had dawned.

Propaganda and Politics   People as well as science and machinery had to be mobilized. To sustain a spirit of unity, the Roosevelt administration carefully managed public opinion. The Office of Censorship, established in December 1941, examined all letters going overseas and worked with publishers and broadcasters to suppress information that might damage the war effort, such as details of troop movements. Fearful of demoralizing the public, the government banned, until late 1943, the publication of any pictures of American war dead; then, worried about an overconfident public, it prodded the media to show American servicemen killed by the enemy.

To shape public opinion, FDR created the Office of War Information (OWI) in June 1942. The OWI employed more than four thousand writers, artists, and advertising specialists to explain the war and to counter enemy propaganda. The OWI depicted the war as a moral struggle between good and evil—the enemy had to be destroyed, not merely defeated. Hollywood films highlighted the heroism and unity of the American forces, while inciting hatred of the enemy. Films about the war portrayed the Japanese, in particular, as treacherous and cruel, as beasts in the jungle, as "slant-eyed rats," while jukeboxes blared songs like "We're Gonna Have to Slap the Dirty Little Jap."

While the Roosevelt administration concentrated on the war, Republican critics seized the initiative in domestic politics. Full employment and high wages undermined the Democrats' class appeal, and many of the urban and working-class voters essential to the Roosevelt coalition were serving in the armed forces and did not vote in the 1942 elections. Republicans gained nine seats in the Senate and forty-six in the House. A coalition of conservative Republicans and southern Democrats held power and, resentful of the wartime expansion of executive authority and determined to curb labor unions and welfare spending, it abolished the CCC and the WPA and rebuffed attempts to extend the New Deal.

Despite the strength of the conservative coalition, the war expanded governmental and executive power enormously. As never before, Washington managed the economy, molded public opinion, funded scientific research, and influenced people's daily lives.

THE BATTLEFRONT, 1942–1944

America's industrial might and Soviet manpower turned the tide of war, and diplomacy followed in its wake. Allied unity diminished as the Axis weakened; increasingly, the United States, Britain, and the Soviet Union each sought wartime strategies and postwar arrangements best suited to its own interests.

Liberating Europe   After Pearl Harbor, British and American officials agreed to concentrate on defeating Germany first and then Japan. But they differed on where to mount an attack. Stalin demanded a second front, an invasion of western Europe to force Hitler to transfer troops west and thus relieve pressure on the Russians, who faced the full fury of the Nazi armies. Churchill insisted on clearing the Mediterranean before invading France, and he wanted American aid in North Africa to protect the Suez Canal. Despite Soviet protests, Roosevelt gave in to Churchill, and American troops under General Dwight D. Eisenhower landed in Morocco and Algeria in November 1942 as part of "Operation Torch." Pushing eastward, they trapped the German and Italian armies being driven westward by the British, and in May 1943 some 260,000 German–Italian troops surrendered.

Left alone to face two-thirds of the Nazi force, the Soviet Union hung on and, in the turning point of the European war, halted the German advance in the protracted Battle of Stalingrad (August 1942–January 1943). As the Russian snow turned red with blood (costing each side more battle deaths in half a year than the United States suffered in the entire war), and its hills became "white fields," strewn with human bones, Soviet forces saved Stalingrad, defended Moscow, and relieved besieged Leningrad (now St. Petersburg). The Red Army then went on the offensive along a thousand-mile front.

Although Stalin renewed his plea for a second front, Churchill again objected, and Roosevelt again agreed to a British plan: the invasion of Sicily. In summer 1943, Anglo-American forces overran Sicily in less than a month, leading the Italian

MAP 25.1   World War II in Europe and Africa

The momentous German defeats at Stalingrad and in Tunisia in early 1943 marked the turning point in the war against the Axis. By 1945, Allied conquest of Hitler's "thousand-year" Reich was imminent.

military to depose, and then execute, Mussolini, and to surrender to the Allies on September 8. As Allied forces moved up the Italian peninsula, German troops poured into Italy. Facing elite Nazi divisions in strong defensive positions, the Allies spent eight months inching their way 150 miles to Rome, and were still battling through northern Italy when the war in Europe ended in May 1945.

In 1943 and 1944, the United States and Britain turned the tide in the Atlantic and sent thousands of bombers over Germany. British and American air forces began round-the-clock bombardment, raining thousands of tons of bombs on German cities. In raids on Hamburg in July 1943, Allied planes dropping incendiary bombs created terrible firestorms, killing more than thirty-five thousand people and leveling the city, much as they had done earlier at Cologne and would do in February 1945 to Dresden, where some sixty thousand people died.

Meanwhile, in July 1943, the Red Army, eating U.S. rations, marching in American-made boots, and driving Dodge and Ford trucks, engaged the Germans at Kursk. With a million men actively engaged on each side in the largest pitched battle of the war, Soviet soldiers won decisively and forced a German retreat. Advancing swiftly, they drove the Germans out of Soviet territory by mid-1944 and plunged into Poland, where the Soviets set up a puppet government. Late summer and early fall saw Soviet troops seize Romania and Bulgaria and aid communist guerillas under Josip Broz Tito in liberating Yugoslavia.

As the Soviets swept across eastern Europe, Allied forces opened the long-promised second front. On June 6, 1944—D-Day—nearly 200,000 Allied troops in the largest armada ever assembled landed in Normandy in northwestern France. Within six weeks, another million Allied troops had crossed the channel and waded ashore. Under General Eisenhower, the Allies liberated Paris in August and reached the German border by the end of summer.

In mid-December, as the Allies prepared for a full-scale assault on the German heartland, Hitler desperately threw his last reserves against American positions. The **Battle of the Bulge**—named for the "bulge" eighty miles long and fifty miles wide that Hitler's troops drove into the Allies' line—raged for nearly a month, and when it ended American troops stood on the banks of the Rhine. It had cost the United States 55,000 soldiers dead or wounded and 18,000 taken prisoner. But the way to Germany lay open, and the end of the European war was in sight.

War in the Pacific

The day after the Philippines fell to Japan in mid-May 1942, U.S. and Japanese fleets confronted each other in the Coral Sea off northeastern Australia, the first naval battle fought entirely from aircraft carriers. Both sides took heavy losses, but the Battle of the Coral Sea stopped the Japanese advance on Australia. Less than a month later, a Japanese armada turned toward Midway Island, the crucial American outpost between Hawaii and Japan. Because the U.S. Signal Corps had broken the Japanese naval code, Japan's plans were known. The Americans won a decisive victory, sinking four Japanese carriers and hundreds of enemy planes. The stunned Japanese could now only try to hold what they had already won.

On the offensive, U.S. marines waded ashore at Guadalcanal in the Solomon Islands in August 1942. Facing fierce resistance as well as tropical diseases like malaria, the Americans needed six months to take the island, a bitter preview of the battles to come. As the British moved from India to retake Burma, the United States began a two-pronged advance toward Japan in 1943. The army, under General Douglas MacArthur, advanced north on the islands between Australia and the Philippines, and the navy and marines, under Admiral Chester Nimitz, "island-hopped" across the central Pacific to seize strategic bases and put Tokyo in range of American bombers. In fall 1944 the navy annihilated what remained of the Japanese fleet at the battles of the Philippine Sea and Leyte Gulf, giving the United States control of Japan's air and shipping lanes and leaving the Japanese home islands open to invasion.

The Grand Alliance

President Roosevelt had two main goals for the war: the total defeat of the Axis at the least possible cost in American lives, and the establishment of a world order strong enough to

MAP 25.2 World War II in the Pacific

Source: © Cengage Learning. All rights reserved. No distribution allowed without express authorization.

American ships and planes stemmed the Japanese offensive at the battles of the Coral Sea and Midway Island. Thereafter, the Japanese were on the defensive against American amphibious assaults and air strikes.

ensure peace, open trade, and national self-determination in the postwar era. Aware that only a common enemy fused the Grand Alliance together, Roosevelt tried to promote harmony by concentrating on military victory and postponing divisive postwar matters.

Churchill and Stalin had other goals. Britain wanted to remain a world power and retain its imperial possessions. As Churchill said, he had "not become the King's First Minister to preside over the liquidation of the British Empire." The Soviet Union wanted a permanently weakened Germany and a sphere of influence (a region whose governments can be counted on to do a great power's bidding) in eastern Europe. To hold together this fragile alliance, FDR relied on personal diplomacy to mediate conflicts.

The first president to travel by plane while in office, Roosevelt arrived in Casablanca, Morocco's main port, in January 1943, where he and Churchill resolved to attack Italy before invading France and proclaimed that the war would continue until the "unconditional surrender" of the Axis. By so doing, they sought to reduce Soviet mistrust of the West, which had deepened with the postponement of the second front. Ten months later, in Cairo, Roosevelt met with Churchill and Jiang Jieshi (Chiang Kaishek), the anticommunist head of the Chinese government. To keep China in the war, FDR promised the return of Manchuria and Taiwan to China and a "free and independent Korea." From Cairo, FDR and Churchill continued on to Tehran, Iran's capital, to meet with Stalin. Here they set the invasion of France for June 1944, and agreed to divide Germany into zones of occupation and to impose reparations on the Reich. Most importantly to Roosevelt, Stalin pledged to enter the war against Japan after Hitler's defeat.

Roosevelt then turned his attention to domestic politics. Increasing conservative sentiment in the nation led him to drop the liberal Henry A. Wallace from the ticket and accept Harry S. Truman as his vice presidential candidate. A moderate senator from Missouri, now dubbed "the new Missouri Compromise," Truman restored a semblance of unity to the Democrats for the 1944 campaign. To compete, the Republicans nominated moderate and noncontroversial New York governor Thomas E. Dewey. The campaign focused more on personalities than on issues, and the still-popular FDR defeated his dull GOP opponent, but with the narrowest margin since 1916—winning only 53 percent of the popular vote. A weary Roosevelt, secretly suffering from hypertension and heart disease, now directed his waning energies toward defeating the Axis and constructing an international peacekeeping system.

War and American Society

The crisis of war altered the most basic patterns of American life. Few families went untouched: more than 15 million Americans served in the armed forces (three out of every four men aged eighteen to thirty-two), an equal number moved to find jobs, and millions of women went to work outside the home. As well, the war opened some doors of opportunity for African Americans and other minorities, although many remained closed. It heightened minority aspirations and widened cracks in the wall of white racist attitudes and policy, while maintaining much of America's racial caste system, thereby tilling the ground for future crises.

The GIs' War   Most servicemen griped about regimentation and were more interested in dry socks than in ideology. They knew little of the big strategies, and cared less. They fought because they were told to and wanted to stay alive. Reluctant recruits rather than professional warriors, most had few aims beyond returning to a safe, familiar United States.

But the GIs' war dragged on for almost four years, transforming them in the process. Millions who had never been far from home traveled to unfamiliar cities and remote lands, shedding their parochialism. Sharing tents and foxholes with men of different religions, ethnicities, and classes, they experienced a "melting pot" effect that freed them from some prewar prejudices.

Besides serving with people they had never previously encountered, more than a million GIs married overseas, broadening personal horizons and sowing the seeds of a more tolerant and diverse national culture. At the same time, many GIs became evermore distrustful of foreigners and outsiders and returned home obsessed with the flag as a symbol of patriotism.

Physical misery, chronic exhaustion, and, especially, intense combat took a heavy toll, leaving lasting psychological as well as physical wounds. Both American and Japanese troops saw the other in racist images, as animals to be exterminated, and brutality became as much the rule as the exception in "a war without mercy." Both sides machine-gunned hostile flyers in parachutes; both tortured and killed prisoners in cold blood; both mutilated enemy dead for souvenirs. In the fight against Germany, cruelties and atrocities also occurred, although on a lesser scale. A battalion of the second armored division calling itself "Roosevelt's Butchers" boasted that it shot all the German soldiers it captured. Some who served became cynical about human life; others, haunted by nightmares about the war, would long languish in veterans' hospitals.

The Home Front   Nothing transformed the social topography more than the vast internal migration of an already mobile people. About 15 million men moved because of military service, often accompanied by family members. Many other Americans moved to secure new economic opportunities, especially in the Pacific Coast states. Nearly a quarter of a million found jobs in the shipyards of the Bay area and at least as many in the aircraft industry that arose in the orange groves of southern California. More than one hundred thousand worked in the Puget Sound shipyards of Washington State and half as many in the nearby Boeing airplane plants. Others flocked to the world's largest magnesium plant in Henderson, Nevada, and to the Rocky Mountain Arsenal and Remington Rand arms plant outside Denver.

At least 6 million people left farms to work in urban areas, including several million southern blacks and whites. They doubled Albuquerque's population and increased San Diego's some 90 percent. This mass uprooting of people from familiar settings made Americans both more cosmopolitan and lonelier. Some who moved far from their hometowns left behind their traditional values. Housing shortages left millions living in converted garages and trailer camps, even in cars. Some workers in Seattle lived in chicken coops. The swarms of migrants to Mobile, Alabama, attracted by a new aluminum plant, two massive shipyards, an air base, and an army supply depot, transformed a sleepy fishing village into a symbol of urban disorder.

Overcrowding and wartime separations strained family and community life. High rates of divorce, mental illness, family violence, and juvenile delinquency

GOING TO THE SOURCE

Women War Workers of Color

African American Fanny Christina Hill moved from Texas to Los Angeles in 1940, and found work as a live-in domestic, cleaning and cooking for a white family. In 1943, while her husband served in the military, she took a job with North American Aviation for sixty cents an hour.

Sometimes even if you're good, you just don't get the breaks if the color's not right. I could see where they made a difference in placing you in certain jobs. They had fifteen or twenty departments, but all the Negroes went to Department 17 because there was nothing but shooting and bucking rivets. You stood on one side of the panel and your partners stood on this side, and he would shoot the rivets with a gun and you'd buck them with the bar. That was about the size of it. I just didn't like it. I didn't think I could stay there with all this shooting and a'bucking

and a'jumping and a'bumping. I stayed in it about two or three weeks and then I just decided I did *not* like that. I went and told my foreman and he didn't do anything about it, so I decided to leave.... I went over to the union and they told me what to do. I went back inside and they sent me to another department where you did bench work and I liked that much better....

I must have stayed there nearly a year, and then they put me over in another department, "Plastics." ... I worked over there until the end of the war. Well, not quite the end, because I got pregnant, and while I was off having the baby the war was over....

When North American called me back, was I a happy soul! ... So, from sixty cents an hour, when I first hired in there, up to one dollar. That wasn't traveling fast, but it was better than anything else because you had hours to work by and you had

reflected the disruptions caused in part by the lack of privacy, the sense of impermanence, the absence of familiar settings, and the competition for scarce facilities. Few boom communities had the resources to supply their swollen populations with transportation, recreation, and social services. Urban blight and conflicts between newcomers and old-timers accelerated.

While military culture fostered a sexist mentality, emphasizing the differences between "femininity" and "masculinity," millions of American women donned pants, put their hair in bandannas, and went to work in defense plants. The government that previously had discouraged women from employment now proclaimed it was their "patriotic duty" to join the war effort. More than 6.5 million women entered the labor force during the war, increasing the number of employed women to 19 million. Less than a quarter of the labor force in 1940, women constituted well over a third of all workers in 1945.

Before the war, most female wage earners had been young and single. By contrast, 75 percent of the new women workers were married, 60 percent were over thirty-five, and more than 33 percent had children under the age of fourteen. They tended blast furnaces, operated cranes, greased locomotives, drove taxis, welded hulls, loaded shells, and worked in coke plants and rolling mills. On the Pacific Coast, more than one-third of all workers in aircraft and shipbuilding were benefits and you come home at night with your family. So it was a good deal.

It made me live better. I really did. We always say that Lincoln took the bale off of the Negroes.… Well, my sister always said— that's why you can't interview her because she's so radical—"Hitler was the one that got us out of the white folks' kitchen."

Born in Mexico, Beatrice Morales Clifton was a married mother of four children when, over her husband's strenuous objections, she accepted a job offer from Lockheed in Los Angeles. Like Hill, she encountered resistance from male co-workers yet worked her way up to increasingly more skilled positions.

I felt proud of myself and felt good being that I had never done anything like that. I felt good that I could do something, and being that it was war, I felt that I was doing my part.

I went from 65 cents to $1.05. That was top pay. It felt good and, besides, it was my own money. I could do whatever I wanted with it because my husband, whatever he was giving to the house, he kept on paying it. I used to buy clothes for the kids; buy little things that they needed. I had a bank account and I had a little saving at home where I could get ahold of the money right away if I needed it. Julio never asked about it. He knew how much I made; I showed him. If there was something that had to be paid and I had the money and he didn't, well, I used some of my money.

Questions

1. *What effects did wartime employment have on these women's sense of themselves?*

2. *How might their wartime experiences have helped generate the civil rights and women's movements of the postwar era?*

Source: From Sherna Berger Gluck, Rose the Riveter: Women, the War, and Social Change, Twayne Publishers, 1987, pp. 37–42, 208–211. Reprinted by permission of the author.

women. **"Rosie the Riveter,"** holding a pneumatic gun in arms bulging with muscles, became the symbol of the woman war worker; she was, in the words of a popular song, "making history working for victory".

Yet traditional attitudes and gender discrimination existed throughout the war. Many women workers were clustered in "women only" jobs, and women in manufacturing earned just 65 percent of what men earned for the same work. One popular advertisement pictured a woman in overalls about to leave for work. Her daughter asks, "Mother, when will you stay home again?" The woman responds: "Some jubilant day, mother will stay home again doing the job she likes—making a home for you and daddy when he gets back."

The stigma attached to working mothers also shaped government resistance to establishing child-care centers for women employed in defense. "A mother's primary duty is to her home and children," the Labor Department's Children's Bureau stated. "This duty is one she cannot lay aside, no matter what the emergency." Funds for federal child-care centers covered fewer than 10 percent of defense workers' children, and the young suffered. Terms like "eight-hour orphans" and "latch-key children" described unsupervised children forced to take care of themselves. Fueling fears that the employment of women outside the home would cause the family to disintegrate, juvenile delinquency increased fivefold, and the divorce rate zoomed from 16 per 100 marriages in 1940 to 27 per 100 in 1944.

The impact of war on women and the family proved multifaceted and even contradictory. As the divorce rate soared, so did marriage rates and birthrates. Although some women remained content to roll bandages for the Red Cross, more than three hundred thousand joined the armed forces and, for the first time in American history, were given regular military status and served in positions other than that of nurse. As members of the Women's Army Corps (WACs) and the Navy's Women Appointed for Volunteer Emergency Service (WAVES) they replaced men in such noncombat jobs as mechanics and radio operators and served as mapmakers and ferry pilots. About a thousand women became civilian pilots with the WASPs (Women's Airforce Service Pilots).

Overall, women gained a new sense of their potential. The war proved their capabilities and widened their world. Recalled one war wife whose returning husband did not like her independence, "He had left a shrinking violet and come home to a very strong oak tree." Some of these women were among the 350,000 teachers who took better-paying war work or joined the armed services, leaving schools badly understaffed. Students, too, abandoned school in record numbers. High school enrollments sank as the full-time employment of teenagers rose from 900,000 in 1940 to 3 million in 1944.

The loss of students to war production and the armed services forced colleges to admit large numbers of women and to contract themselves out to the armed forces. Nearly a million servicemen took college classes in science, engineering, and foreign languages. Harvard University awarded four military-training certificates for every academic degree it conferred. The chancellor of one branch of the University of California announced that his school was "no longer an academic tent with military sideshows. It is a military tent with academic sideshows." Higher education became more dependent on the federal government, and most universities sought increased federal contracts and subsidies. The universities in the West received some $100 billion from the Office of Scientific Research and Development, more money than had been spent on scientific research by all the western universities since their founding.

The war profoundly affected American culture. Spending on books and theater entertainment doubled. More than sixty million people (in a population of 135 million) attended movies weekly, and the film industry reached its zenith in 1945–1946. But as the war dragged on, people grew tired of war films, and Hollywood reemphasized romance and nostalgia with such stars as Katharine Hepburn and Judy Garland.

Similarly, popular music went from "Goodbye, Mama, I'm Off to Yokohama," the first hit of 1942, to songs of lost love and loneliness, like "They're Either Too Young or Too Old." By 1945, bitterness pervaded lyrics, and songs like "Saturday Night Is the Loneliest Night of the Week" revealed impatience for the war's end.

In bookstores, nonfiction ruled the roost, and every newsmagazine increased its circulation. The Government Printing Office published Armed Services Editions, paperback reprints of classics and new releases; the nearly 350 million copies distributed free to soldiers sped up the American acceptance of quality paperbacks, which were introduced in 1939 by the Pocket Book Company. Wendell Willkie's *One World* (1943) became the fastest-selling title in publishing history to that time, with 1 million copies snapped up in two months. A vision of a world without military alliances and spheres of influence, this brief volume expressed hope that an

Al Palmer/Historical/Corbis

African American Women War Workers *Unlike the situation during the Great Depression, when women were expected to step aside in the job market to make way for unemployed men, the war brought increased opportunities for women in munitions plants and on assembly lines. Some 400,000 African American women left domestic work as servants in private homes for work in defense plants. "Hitler was the one," recalled one such defense worker, "that got us out of the white folk's kitchen."*

international organization would extend peace and democracy through the postwar world. Most startlingly, Willkie attacked "our imperialisms at home." Unless the United States ended its own racism, he concluded, nonwhites around the globe would rebuff its claim to world leadership.

An avid interest in wartime news also spurred the major radio networks to increase their news programs from 4 percent to nearly 30 percent of broadcasting time, and enticed Americans to listen to the radio an average of 4½ hours a day. Daytime radio serials, like those featuring Dick Tracy tracking down Axis spies, reached the height of their popularity, as did juvenile comic books in which a platoon of new superheroes, including Captain America and Captain Marvel, saw action on the battlefield. Even Bugs Bunny donned a uniform to combat America's foes.

Racism and New Opportunities

Recognizing that the government needed the loyalty and labor of a united people, black leaders entered World War II determined to secure equal rights. In 1942, civil rights spokesmen insisted that African American support of the war hinged on America's commitment to racial justice. They demanded a *"Double V"* campaign to gain victory over racial discrimination at home as well as over the Axis abroad. Membership in the NAACP multiplied nearly ten times, reaching half a million in 1945. The association pressed for legislation outlawing the poll tax and lynching, decried discrimination in defense industries and the armed services, and sought to end black disfranchisement. Its campaign for voting rights gained momentum when the Supreme Court, in *Smith* v. *Allwright* (1944), ruled the Texas all-white primary unconstitutional. The decision eliminated a bar that had existed in eight southern states, although these states promptly resorted to other devices to minimize voting by blacks.

A new civil-rights organization, the Congress of Racial Equality (CORE), was founded in 1942. Employing the same forms of nonviolent direct action that Mohandas Gandhi used in his campaign for India's independence, CORE sought to desegregate public facilities in northern cities.

Also proposing nonviolent direct action, **A. Philip Randolph,** president of the Brotherhood of Sleeping Car Porters, in 1941 called for a "thundering march" of one hundred thousand blacks on Washington if the president did not end discrimination in the armed services and the defense industry. FDR agreed to compromise.

© Bettmann/Corbis

Tuskegee Airmen *Although the great majority of African Americans in the army served in menial labor, noncombat, segregated units, black units performed admirably in combat when given the opportunity. The 99th Air Force Fighter squadron, known as the Tuskegee Airmen, gained high marks in action against the* Luftwaffe *and became one of the most highly respected fighter groups in the Army Air Corps.*

In June 1941, Roosevelt issued Executive Order 8802, the first presidential directive on race since Reconstruction. It prohibited discriminatory employment practices by federal agencies and by all unions and companies engaged in war-related work and established the Fair Employment Practices Commission (FEPC) to monitor compliance. Although the FEPC lacked effective enforcement powers, booming war production and a labor supply depleted by military service resulted in the employment of some 2 million African Americans in industry and two hundred thousand in the federal civil service. Between 1942 and 1945, the proportion of blacks in war production work rose from 3 to 9 percent. Black membership in labor unions doubled to 1.25 million, and the number of skilled and semiskilled black workers tripled. Formerly mired in low-paying domestic and farm jobs, nearly half a million black women found work in factories and the civil service. Overall, the average wage for African Americans increased from $457 to $1,976 a year, compared with a gain from $1,064 to $2,600 for whites.

About 1 million African Americans served in the armed forces. Wartime needs forced the military to end the policies of excluding blacks from the marines and coast guard, restricting them to jobs as mess boys in the navy, and confining them to noncombatant units in the army. From just five in 1940—three of them chaplains—the number of black officers grew to over seven thousand in 1945, including the Tuskegee Air Corps. The first class of five African American pilots, trained in Tuskegee, graduated in March 1942. They, and those that followed, manned both fighter planes and bombers. Their 332nd Fighter Group, commanded by West Point graduate Lt. Col. Ben Davis, Jr., the son of America's first black general, eventually flew more than fifteen hundred missions over Italy and the Mediterranean, earning numerous awards and making it a special source of pride for African Americans.

The great majority of blacks, however, served throughout the war in segregated service units commanded by white officers. This indignity, made worse by the failure of military authorities to protect black servicemen off the post and by the use of white military police to keep blacks "in their place," sparked rioting on army bases. At least fifty black soldiers died in racial conflicts during the war. "I used to sing gospel songs until I joined the Army," recalled blues-guitar great B.B. King, "then I sang the blues."

Violence within the military mirrored growing racial tensions on the home front. As blacks protested against discrimination, many whites resisted blacks' efforts to improve their economic and social status. Race riots erupted in 1943 in Harlem, Mobile, and Beaumont, Texas. The bloodiest melee exploded in Detroit that year when white mobs assaulted blacks caught riding on trolleys or sitting in movie theaters and blacks smashed and looted white-owned stores and shops. After thirty hours of racial beatings, shootings, and burning, twenty-five African Americans and nine whites lay dead, more than seven hundred had been injured, and more than $2 million of property had been destroyed. The fear of continued violence led to a greater emphasis on racial tolerance by liberal whites and to a reduction in the militancy of African American leaders.

Yet the war jolted the racial status quo in ways that laid the foundation for an eventual successful drive for black civil rights. The migration of hundreds of thousands of rural southern either to cities in the South or to the North and West transformed race into a national concern. It created a new attitude of independence in African Americans freed from the constraints of caste. As the growing numbers of blacks in northern cities began to vote, moreover, African Americans could hold a balance of power in close elections. This prompted politicians in both major parties to extend greater recognition to blacks and to pay more attention to civil-rights issues.

African American expectations of greater government concern for their rights also resulted from the new prominence of the United States as a major power in a predominantly nonwhite world. As Japanese propaganda appeals to the peoples of Asia and Latin America emphasized lynchings and race riots in the United States, Americans had to confront the peril that white racism posed to their national security. In addition, the horrors of Nazi racism discredited America's own white-supremacist attitudes and practices. A pluralist vision of American society now became part of official rhetoric—and of the liberal-left agenda. The contradiction between American ideals of freedom and equality and the actual state of African Americans became manifest. Swedish economist Gunnar Myrdal, in his massive study of race problems, *An American Dilemma* (1944), concluded that "not since Reconstruction had there been more reason to anticipate fundamental changes in American race relations ... there is bound to be a redefinition of the Negro's status as a result of this War." Returning black veterans, and African Americans who had served the nation on the home front, soon expected to gain all the rights enjoyed by whites.

War and   Wartime winds of change also brought new opportunities
Diversity   and difficulties to other minorities. More than twenty-five
                     thousand Native Americans served in the armed forces,
including 400 Navajo "code talkers" who confounded the Japanese by using their complex native language to relay messages between U.S. command centers. "Were it not for the Navajos, the Marines would never have taken Iwo Jima," one Signal Corps officer declared.

Another fifty thousand Indians left the reservation to work in defense industries, mainly on the West Coast. The Rosebud Reservation in South Dakota lost more than a quarter of its population to migration during the war. It was the first time most had lived in a non-Indian world, and the average income of Native American households tripled during the war. Such economic improvement encouraged many Indians to remain outside the reservation and to try to assimilate into mainstream life. But anti-Indian discrimination, particularly in smaller towns near reservations, such as Gallup, New Mexico, and Billings, Montana, forced many Native Americans back to their reservations, which had suffered severely from budget cuts during the war. Prodded by those who coveted Indian lands, lawmakers demanded that Indians be taken off the backs of the taxpayers and "freed from the reservations" to fend for themselves." To mobilize against the campaign to end all reservations and trust protections, Native Americans organized the National Congress of American Indians in 1944.

To relieve labor shortages in agriculture, caused by conscription and the movement of rural workers to city factories, the U.S. government negotiated an agreement with Mexico in July 1942 to import *braceros*, or temporary workers.

Classified as foreign laborers rather than as immigrants, an estimated two hundred thousand **braceros,** half of them in California, received short-term contracts promising adequate wages, medical care, and decent living conditions. But farm owners frequently violated the terms of these contracts and also encouraged an influx of illegal migrants from Mexico desperate for employment. Unable to complain about their working conditions without risking arrest and deportation, hundreds of thousands of Mexicans were exploited by agribusinesses in Arizona, California, and Texas. At the same time, tens of thousands of Chicanos left agricultural work for jobs in factories, shipbuilding yards, and steel mills. By 1943, about half a million Chicanos were living in Los Angeles County, 10 percent of the total population. In New Mexico nearly 20 percent of Mexican American farm laborers escaped from rural poverty to urban jobs. Even as their occupational status and material conditions improved, most Mexican Americans remained in communities (*colonias*), segregated from the larger society and frequently harassed by the police.

Much of the hostility toward Mexican Americans focused on young gang members who wore "zoot suits"—a fashion that originated in Harlem and emphasized long, broad-shouldered jackets and pleated trousers tightly pegged at the ankles. Known as *pachucos*, zoot-suited Mexican Americans aroused the ire of servicemen stationed or on leave in Los Angeles who saw them as delinquents and draft dodgers. After a luridly publicized trial arising from a Mexican American gang fight at a swimming hole called Sleepy Lagoon, and newspaper headlines of a Chicano "crime wave," bands of sailors and soldiers rampaged through Los Angeles in early June 1943, stripping *pachucos*, cutting their long hair, and beating them. Military authorities looked the other way. City police intervened only to arrest Mexican Americans, and the city council made the wearing of a zoot suit a misdemeanor. Nothing was done about the substandard housing, disease, and racism Hispanics had to endure.

Unlike African Americans, however, more than 350,000 Mexican Americans served in the armed forces without segregation, and in all combat units. They volunteered in higher numbers than warranted by their percentage of the population and earned a disproportionate number of citations for distinguished service as well as seventeen Medals of Honor. Returning Mexican American GIs joined established antidiscrimination groups, like the League of United Latin American Citizens (LULAC), and organized their own associations, like the American GI Forum, to press for equal rights.

Thousands of gay men and lesbians who served in the armed forces also found new wartime opportunities. The military officially barred those they defined as "sexual perverts," but owing to the urgency of building a massive armed forces, just four to five thousand men out of eighteen million examined for induction were excluded because of homosexuality. For the vast majority of gays not excluded, being emancipated from traditional expectations and the close scrutiny of family and neighbors, and living in overwhelmingly all-male or all-female environments, brought freedom to meet like-minded gay men and women. Like other minorities, many gays saw the war as a chance to prove their worth under fire. Yet some suspected of being gay were dishonorably discharged, sent to psychiatric hospitals, or imprisoned in so-called queer stockades. In 1945, gay veterans established the Veteran's Benevolent Association, the first organization in the United States to combat discrimination against homosexuals.

The Internment of Japanese Americans   Far more than any other minority in the United States, Japanese Americans suffered grievously during the war. About thirty-seven thousand first-generation Japanese immigrants (Issei) and nearly seventy-five thousand native-born Japanese American citizens (Nisei) were interned in "relocation centers" guarded by military police—a tragic reminder of the fragility of civil liberties in wartime.

The **internment of Japanese Americans** reflected forty years of anti-Japanese sentiment on the West Coast, rooted in racial prejudice and economic rivalry. Nativist politicians and farmers who wanted Japanese American land had long decried the "yellow peril." Following the attack on Pearl Harbor they whipped up the rage of white Californians, aided by a government report falsely blaming Japanese Americans in Hawaii for aiding the Japanese naval force. Patriotic associations and many newspapers clamored for evacuating the Japanese Americans, as did the army general in charge of the Western Defense Command, who proclaimed, "A Jap is a Jap is a Jap. It makes no difference whether he is an American citizen or not.... I don't want any of them."

In February 1942, President Roosevelt gave in to the pressure and issued Executive Order 9066, authorizing the removal from military areas of anyone deemed a threat. Although not a single Japanese American was apprehended for espionage or sedition and neither the FBI nor military intelligence uncovered any evidence of disloyal behavior by Japanese Americans, the military ordered the eviction of all Nisei and Issei from the West Coast. Only Hawaii was excepted. Despite the far larger number of Hawaiians of Japanese ancestry, as well as of Japanese living in Hawaii, no internment policy was implemented there, and no sabotage occurred.

Forced to sell all they owned at whatever prices they could obtain, Japanese Americans lost an estimated $2 billion in property and possessions. Tagged with numbers rather than names, they were herded into barbed-wire-encircled detention camps in the most desolate parts of the West and Great Plains—places, wrote one historian, "where nobody had lived before and no one has lived since." Few protested the incarceration. Stating that it would not question government claims of military necessity during time of war, the Supreme Court upheld the constitutionality of the evacuation in the *Korematsu* case (1944). By then the hysteria had subsided, and the government had begun a program of gradual release, allowing some Nisei to attend college or take factory jobs (but not on the West Coast); about eighteen thousand served in the military. The 442nd regimental combat team, entirely Japanese American, became the most decorated unit in the military.

In 1982, a special government commission concluded in its report, *Personal Justice Denied*, that internment "was not justified by military necessity." It blamed the Roosevelt administration's action on "race prejudice, war hysteria, and a failure of political leadership" and apologized to Japanese Americans for "a grave injustice." In 1988, Congress voted to pay twenty thousand dollars in compensation to each of the nearly sixty-two thousand surviving internees; in 1998, President Bill Clinton further apologized for the injustice by giving the nation's highest civilian honor, the Presidential Medal of Freedom, to Fred Korematsu, who had protested the evacuation decree all the way to the Supreme Court.

National Archives

Young Nisei evacuees at the Turlock Assembly Center *Awaiting their turn for baggage inspection on May 2, 1942, these children would be interned in remote "relocation centers" along with 37,000 first-generation Japanese immigrants (Issei) and some 75,000 native-born Japanese American (Nisei) citizens of the United States. Hastily uprooted from their homes, farms, and stores, most lost all their property and personal possessions and spent the war under armed guard.*

TRIUMPH AND TRAGEDY, 1945

Spring and summer 1945 brought stunning changes and new crises. In Europe, a new balance of power emerged after the collapse of the Third Reich. In Asia, continued Japanese reluctance to surrender led to the use of atomic bombs. And in the United States, a new president, Harry S. Truman, presided over both the end of World War II and the beginning of the Cold War and the nuclear age.

The Yalta Conference   By the time Roosevelt, Churchill, and Stalin met in the Soviet city of Yalta in February 1945, the military situation favored the Soviet Union. The Red Army had overrun Poland, Romania, and Bulgaria; driven the Nazis out of Yugoslavia; penetrated Austria, Hungary, and Czechoslovakia; and was massed just fifty miles from Berlin. American forces, in contrast, were still recovering from the Battle of the

Bulge and facing stiff resistance on the route to Japan. The Joint Chiefs of Staff, contemplating the awesome cost in American casualties of invading Japan, insisted that Stalin's help was worth almost any price. And Stalin was in a position to make demands. The Soviet Union had suffered most in the war against Germany, it already dominated eastern Europe, and, knowing that the United States did not want to fight a prolonged war against Japan, Stalin had the luxury of deciding whether and when to enter the Pacific war.

The **Yalta accords** reflected these realities. Stalin again vowed to declare war on Japan "two or three months" after Germany's surrender, and in return Churchill and Roosevelt reneged on their arrangement with Jiang Jieshi and promised the Soviet Union concessions in Manchuria and the territories it had lost in the Russo-Japanese War (1904) (see Chapter 22). The Big Three delegated a final settlement of the German reparations issue to a postwar commission and left vague the matter of partitioning Germany and its eventual reunification. The conference also vaguely called for interim governments in eastern Europe "broadly representative of all democratic elements" and for eventual freely elected permanent governments. On the matter dearest to FDR's heart, the negotiators accepted a plan for a new international organization and agreed to a founding conference of the new United Nations in San Francisco in April 1945.

Stalin proved adamant about the nature of the postwar Polish government. Twice in the twentieth century German troops had used Poland as a springboard for invading Russia. Stalin would not expose his land again, and after the Red Army had captured Warsaw in January 1945, he installed a procommunist regime and brutally subdued the anticommunist Poles. Conservative critics would later charge that FDR "gave away" Eastern Europe. Actually, the Soviet Union gained little it did not already control, and short of going to war against the Soviets while still battling Germany and Japan, FDR could only hope that Stalin would keep his word.

Victory in Europe   As the Soviets prepared for their assault on Berlin, American troops crossed the Rhine at Remagen in March 1945 and encircled the Ruhr Valley, Germany's industrial heartland. Churchill now proposed a rapid thrust to Berlin. But Eisenhower and Roosevelt saw no point in risking high casualties to rush to an area of Germany already designated as the Soviet occupation zone. So Eisenhower advanced methodically along a broad front until the Americans met the Russians at the Elbe River on April 25. By then, the Red Army had taken Vienna and reached the suburbs of Berlin. On April 30, as Soviet troops approached his headquarters, Hitler committed suicide. Berlin fell to the Soviets on May 2, and on May 8 a new German government surrendered unconditionally.

Jubilant Americans celebrated Victory in Europe (V-E) Day less than a month after they had mourned the death of their president. On April 12, an exhausted President Roosevelt had abruptly clutched his head, moaned that he had a "terrific headache," and fell unconscious. A cerebral hemorrhage ended his life. As the nation grieved, Roosevelt's unprepared successor assumed the burden of ending the war and dealing with the Soviet Union.

"I don't know whether you fellows ever had a load of hay or a bull fall on you," Harry Truman told reporters on his first full day in office, "but last night the moon, the stars, and all the planets fell on me." An unpretentious politician awed by his new responsibilities, Truman struggled to continue FDR's policies. But Roosevelt had made no effort to familiarize his vice president with world affairs. Perhaps sensing his own inadequacies, Truman adopted a tough pose toward adversaries. In office less than two weeks, he lashed out at Soviet ambassador V.M. Molotov that the United States was tired of waiting for the Russians to allow free elections in Poland, and he threatened to cut off lend-lease aid if the Soviet Union did not cooperate. The Truman administration then reduced U.S. economic assistance to the Soviets and stalled on their request for a $1 billion reconstruction loan. Simultaneously, Stalin strengthened his grip on eastern Europe, ignoring the promises he had made at Yalta.

The United States neither conceded the Soviet sphere of influence in eastern Europe nor tried to end it. Although Truman still sought Stalin's cooperation in establishing the United Nations and in defeating Japan, Soviet–American relations deteriorated. By June 1945, when the Allied countries succeeded in framing the United Nations Charter, hopes for a new international order had dimmed, and the United Nations emerged as a diplomatic battleground. Truman, Churchill, and Stalin met at Potsdam, Germany, from July 16 to August 2 to complete the postwar arrangements begun at Yalta. But the Allied leaders could barely agree to demilitarize Germany and to punish Nazi war criminals. Given the diplomatic impasse, only military power remained to determine the contours of the postwar world.

The Holocaust   When news of the **Holocaust**—the term later given to the Nazis' extermination of European Jewry—first leaked out in early 1942, many Americans discounted the reports. Not until November did the State Department admit knowledge of the massacres. A month later, the American broadcaster Edward R. Murrow, listened to nationwide, reported on the systematic killing of millions of Jews, "It is a picture of mass murder and moral depravity unequalled in the history of the world. It is a horror beyond what imagination can grasp. ... There are no longer 'concentration camps'—we must speak now only of 'extermination camps.' "

Most Americans considered the annihilation of Europe's 6 million Jews beyond belief. There were no photographs to prove it, and, some argued, the atrocities attributed to the Germans in World War I had turned out to be false. So few took issue with the military's view that the way to liberate those enslaved by Hitler was by speedily winning the war. Pleas by American Jews for the Allies to bomb the death camps and the railroad tracks leading to them fell on deaf ears. In fall 1944, U.S. planes flying over Auschwitz in southern Poland bombed nearby factories but left the gas chambers and crematoria intact, in order, American officials explained, not to divert air power from more vital raids elsewhere. "How could it be," historian David Wyman has asked, "that Government officials knew that a place existed where 2,000 helpless human beings could be killed in less than an hour, knew that this occurred over and over again, and yet did not feel driven to search for some way to wipe such a scourge from the earth?"

How much could have been done remains uncertain. Still, the U.S. government never seriously considered rescue schemes or searched for a way to curtail the Nazis' "final solution" to the "Jewish question." Its feeble response was due to its overwhelming focus on winning the war as quickly as possible, congressional and public fears of an influx of destitute Jews into the United States, Britain's wish to placate the Arabs by keeping Jewish settlers out of Palestine, and the fear of some Jewish American leaders that pressing the issue would increase anti-Semitism at home. Accordingly, the State Department assisted in saving the lives of just two hundred thousand Jews, while 6 million other Jews—75 percent of the European Jewish population—were gassed, shot, and incinerated. The internal investigation of its inaction was appropriately entitled "Report to the Secretary on the Acquiescence of This Government in the Murder of the Jews."

"The things I saw beggar description," wrote General Eisenhower after visiting the first death camp liberated by the U.S. army. He sent immediately for a delegation of congressional leaders and newspaper editors to make sure Americans would never forget the gas chambers and human ovens. Only after viewing the photographs and newsreels of corpses stacked like cordwood, boxcars heaped with the bones of dead prisoners, bulldozers shoving emaciated bodies into hastily dug ditches, and liberated, barely-alive living skeletons lying in their own filth, their vacant, sunken eyes staring through barbed wire, did most Americans see that the Holocaust was no myth.

The Atomic Bombs Meanwhile, the war with Japan ground on. Early in 1945, an assault force of marines invaded Iwo Jima, 700 miles from Japan. In places termed the "Meat Grinder" and "Bloody Gorge," the marines savagely battled thousands of Japanese soldiers hidden in tunnels and behind concrete bunkers and pillboxes. Securing the five-square-mile island would cost the marines nearly twenty-seven thousand casualties—and one-third of all the marines killed in the Pacific. In June, American troops waded ashore on Okinawa, 350 miles from Japan and a key staging area for the planned U.S. invasion of the Japanese home islands. Death and destruction engulfed Okinawa as waves of Americans attacked nearly impregnable Japanese defenses head-on, repeating the bloody strategy of World War I. After eighty-three days of fighting on land and sea, twelve thousand Americans lay dead and three times as many wounded, a 35 percent casualty rate, higher than at Normandy.

The appalling rate of loss on Iwo Jima and Okinawa weighed on the minds of American strategists. The Japanese Cabinet showed no willingness to give up the war despite Japan's being blockaded and bombed daily (on March 9–10 a fleet of B-29s dropped napalm-and-magnesium bombs on Tokyo, burning sixteen square miles of the city to the ground and killing some eighty-four thousand). Japanese military leaders insisted on fighting to the bitter end; surrender was unthinkable. Japan possessed an army of more than 2 million—plus up to 4 million reservists and five thousand kamikaze aircraft—and the U.S. Joint Chiefs initially feared it might take eighteen more months of battle and more than a hundred thousand American casualties before victory could be achieved.

The successful detonation of history's first nuclear explosion at Alamagordo in mid-July gave Truman an alternative. On July 25, while meeting with Stalin and Churchill in Potsdam, Truman ordered the use of an atomic bomb if Japan did not surrender before August 3. The next day, in the **Potsdam Declaration,** he warned Japan to surrender unconditionally or face "prompt and utter destruction." Japan refused, and on August 6, a B-29 bomber named *Enola Gay* took off from the Marianas island of Tinian and dropped a uranium bomb on Hiroshima. It plunged the city into what Japanese novelist Masuji Ibuse termed "a hell of unspeakable torments." The 300,000-degree centigrade fireball incinerated houses and vaporized people. More than sixty thousand died immediately from the blast, and another seventy-five thousand died from burns and radiation poisoning by late 1945. On August 8, Stalin declared war on Japan, and U.S. planes dropped leaflets on Japan warning that another bomb would be dropped if it did not surrender. Japan's military leaders still preferred death to surrender. The next day, at high noon, the *Bock's Car* flattened Nagasaki with a plutonium bomb, killing thirty-six thousand, and injuring more than sixty thousand. On August 14, Japan accepted the American terms of surrender, which implicitly permitted the emperor to retain his throne but subordinated him to the U.S. commander of the occupation forces. General MacArthur received Japan's surrender on the battleship *Missouri* on September 2, 1945. The war was over.

While Americans at the time overwhelmingly backed the atomic bombings of Japan as the necessary way to end the war with the least cost in U.S. lives, many historians have subsequently questioned the necessity of using such a terrible weapon of mass destruction. Some believe that racist American attitudes toward the Japanese motivated the decision to drop the bombs. As war correspondent Ernie Pyle wrote, "The Japanese are looked upon as something inhuman and squirmy—like some people feel about cockroaches or mice." However, those involved in the Manhattan Project had regarded Germany as the target, and considering the ferocity of the Allied bombings of Hamburg and Dresden—which claimed more victims than Hiroshima and Nagasaki—there is little reason to assume that the Allies would not have dropped atomic bombs on Germany had they been available. By 1945, the Allies as well as the Axis had abandoned restraints on attacking civilians.

Other critics maintain that demonstrating the bomb's terrible destructiveness on an uninhabited island would have moved Japan to surrender. We will never know for sure. American scientists rejected a demonstration bombing because the United States had an atomic arsenal of only two bombs and they did not know whether the mechanism for detonating them in the air would work. Still others are persuaded that the president, aware of worsening relations between the United States and the USSR, ordered the atomic attack to scare the Russians into submission and end the Pacific war before Stalin could enter it and share in the postwar occupation of Japan. Referring to the Soviets, President Truman noted just before the atomic test at Alamogordo, "If it explodes, as I think it will, I'll certainly have a hammer on those boys." Truman's new secretary of state, James Byrnes, thought that the bomb would "make Russia more manageable" and would "put us in a position to dictate our own terms at the end of the war." Citing a U.S. intelligence survey that concluded that "Japan would have surrendered even if the atomic bombs had not been dropped, even if Russia had not entered the war, and even if no invasion had been planned or contemplated," critics charge that the bomb was used primarily to intimidate the Soviet Union rather than to secure victory over Japan.

In fact, no military or political leader advising Truman debated *not* using the bomb. The momentum behind the Manhattan Project was such that no one in power questioned the assumption that, once developed, the atomic weapon would be used. Secretary of War Stimson considered it "as legitimate as any other of the deadly explosive weapons of modern war." And given the ferocious Japanese resistance at Okinawa and Iwo Jima, and the likelihood of still greater bloodshed if an invasion of Japan became necessary, Truman saw no reason not to save American lives. As throughout the war, American leaders relied on production and technology to win the war with the minimum loss of American life. Every new weapon was put to use, the concept of "total war" easily accommodated the bombing of civilians, and the atomic bomb was one more item in an arsenal that had already wreaked enormous destruction on the Axis. In "Operation Thunderclap," the Allies had obliterated miles of German and Japanese cities, making no pretense of distinguishing military and civilian targets. The rules of war that had once stayed the use of weapons of mass destruction against enemy civilians no longer prevailed. Before Hiroshima, the United States had already crossed the callous threshold into mass murder from the air.

No member of the committee formed to advise Truman on the use of the bomb counseled that the United States should sacrifice American servicemen to lessen death and destruction in Japan, the nation that had unleashed a wanton, brutal attack on Pearl Harbor, or not use a weapon developed with $2 billion in taxpayer money, or not drop bombs that might force Stalin to be more reasonable. There seemed no good reason not to drop the bombs. To the vast majority of Americans, the atomic bomb was, in Churchill's words, simply "a miracle of deliverance" that saved Allied lives. So E.B. Sledge and his comrades in the First Marine Division, slated to take part in the first wave of the invasion of Japan's home islands, breathed "an indescribable sense of relief." Hearing the news of the atomic bombs and Japan's surrender, Sledge wrote, they sat in stunned silence:

> We remembered our dead. So many dead. So many maimed. So many bright futures consigned to the ashes of the past. So many dreams lost in the madness that engulfed us. Except for a few widely scattered shouts of joy, the survivors of the abyss sat hollow-eyed and silent, trying to comprehend a world without war.

The atomic bombs ended the deadliest war in history. A truly global conflict, involving over half the world's peoples and some fifty nations, with armies ranging over continents and navies fighting on every ocean, the war affected women, men, and children as victims of civilian bombing campaigns, as war workers, as slave laborers and comfort women. Neither side gave much quarter in seeking to destroy the other's will and resources. Perhaps 60 million died—more than half of them civilians. The Soviet Union lost roughly 20 million people, China 15 million, Poland 6 million, Germany 4 million, and Japan 2 million. Much of Asia and Europe was rubble. Some three hundred thousand Americans died in combat, and, although physically unscathed, the United States had changed profoundly—for better and worse.

CHRONOLOGY
1933–1945

1931–1932	Japan invades Manchuria and creates a puppet government.
1933	Adolf Hitler becomes chancellor of Germany and assumes dictatorial powers.
1934–1936	Nye Committee investigations.
1935–1937	Neutrality Acts.
1937	Japan invades China.
1938	Germany annexes Austria; Munich Pact gives Sudetenland to Germany.
	Kristallnacht, night of Nazi terror against German and Austrian Jews.
1939	Nazi-Soviet Pact.
	Germany invades Poland; World War II begins.
1940	Germany conquers the Netherlands, Belgium, France, Denmark, Norway, and Luxembourg.
	Germany, Italy, and Japan sign the Tripartite Pact.
	Selective Service Act.
	Franklin Roosevelt elected to an unprecedented third term.
1941	Lend-Lease Act.
	Roosevelt establishes the Fair Employment Practices Commission (FEPC).
	Germany invades the Soviet Union.
	Japan attacks Pearl Harbor; the United States enters World War II.
	War Powers Act.
1942	Battles of Coral Sea and Midway halt Japanese offensive.
	Internment of Japanese Americans.
	Revenue Act expands graduated income-tax system.
	Allies invade North Africa (Operation TORCH).
	First successful atomic chain reaction.
	CORE founded.
1943	Soviet victory in Battle of Stalingrad.
	Coal miners strike; Smith-Connally War Labor Disputes Act.
	Detroit and Los Angeles race riots.

	Allied invasion of Italy.
	Roosevelt, Churchill, and Stalin meet in Tehran.
1944	Allied invasion of France (Operation Overlord).
	U.S. forces invade the Philippines.
	Roosevelt wins fourth term.
	Battle of the Bulge.
1945	Yalta Conference.
	Battles of Iwo Jima and Okinawa.
	Roosevelt dies; Harry S. Truman becomes president.
	Germany surrenders.
	Truman, Churchill, and Stalin meet in Potsdam.
	United States drops atomic bombs on Hiroshima and Nagasaki; Japan surrenders.

CONCLUSION

Most Americans, and their government, initially responded to the war clouds over Asia and Europe by reaffirming their isolationism. As one senator proclaimed, prior to the vote that defeated Roosevelt's effort to have the United States join the World Court, "To hell with Europe and the rest of those nations!" Not till the Japanese attack on the American fleet at Pearl Harbor, more than two years after the war in Europe had begun, did the United States enter the fray, and even then it waited until Hitler and Mussolini declared war on it before joining the armed struggle engulfing the world. Once engaged, the Americans rapidly went on a war footing. Mobilization transformed the scope and authority of the federal government, vastly expanding presidential powers. It ended the unemployment of the depression and made American industry more productive than it had ever been—and made most Americans more prosperous than they had ever been. It tilted the national economic balance toward the South Atlantic, Gulf, and Pacific coasts. It accelerated trends toward bigness in business, agriculture, and labor. It involved the military in the economy and education as never before.

To achieve an unconditional victory, with the least possible cost in American lives, Roosevelt concentrated on defeating Germany first yet delaying a second front in Europe until Soviet forces had routed the German army in eastern Europe. Meanwhile, half a world away, a two-pronged American offensive, across the central Pacific and north from Australia, brought Japan to the brink of defeat. On the home front, the war catalyzed vital changes in racial and social relations, causing fundamental challenges to long-held assumptions about the "place" for women and blacks. Both arenas intensified prejudices against minorities and women and also broadened educational and employment opportunities that widened their public spheres and heightened their expectations. Fighting and winning the greatest war in history, moreover, restored American faith in capitalism and democratic institutions. It was a vital coming-of-age experience for an entire generation that did much to give postwar American society a confident, "can-do" spirit, optimistic for the "American Century" that they knew lay ahead.

The awesome development and use of an atomic bomb bolstered that spirit and enabled the United States to defeat Japan promptly, to try to force the Soviets to be more manageable, and to avoid an invasion of the Japanese home islands costing untold thousands of American casualties. The mass destruction of the war and total defeat of the Axis, however, brought new crises to cloud the bright dawn of peace. The world's two superpowers—the United States and the USSR—soon squared off in a Cold War that would see the United States play a role in global affairs inconceivable to most Americans just five years before.

26

▬▬◆▬▬

THE COLD WAR ABROAD AND AT HOME, 1945–1960

CHAPTER OUTLINE

• Anticommunism and Containment, 1946–1953 • The Truman Administration at Home, 1945–1952 • The Politics of Anticommunism • The Cold War Continues

---

ANTICOMMUNISM AND CONTAINMENT, 1946–1953

The "shotgun wedding" that joined the United States and the USSR in an alliance to defeat Hitler dissolved at war's end into a struggle to fill the power vacuums left by the defeat of the Axis, the exhaustion and bankruptcy of Western Europe, and the crumbling of colonial empires in Asia and Africa. As the two powers sought greater security, each feeding the other's fears, a cycle of misperception and misunderstanding, of distrust and animosity, resulted in the Cold War.

Polarization and Cold War The destiny of Eastern Europe, especially Poland, stood at the heart of the strife between the United States and the USSR. Wanting to end the Soviet Union's vulnerability to invasions from the West, Stalin insisted on a demilitarized Germany and a buffer zone of nations friendly to Russia along its western flank. He considered a Soviet sphere of influence in Eastern Europe essential to Russian security, a just reward for bearing the brunt of the war against Germany, and no different than the American spheres of influence in Western Europe, Japan, and Latin America. Stalin also believed that Roosevelt and Churchill had implicitly accepted a Soviet zone in Eastern Europe at the Yalta Conference.

With the Red Army occupying half of Europe at war's end, Stalin installed pro-Soviet puppet governments in Bulgaria, Hungary, and Romania and supported the establishment of communist regimes independent of Moscow in Albania and

Yugoslavia. Ignoring the Yalta Declaration of Liberated Europe, Stalin barred free elections in Poland and brutally suppressed Polish democratic parties. Poland, he said, was "not only a question of honor for Russia, but one of life and death."

Stalin's insistence on dominance in Eastern Europe collided with Truman's unwillingness to concede Soviet supremacy beyond Russia's borders. What Stalin saw as critical to Russian security Truman viewed as a violation of national self-determination, a betrayal of democracy, and a cover for communist aggression. He believed that accepting the "enforced sovietization" of Eastern Europe would betray American war aims and that appeasement of dictators only fed their appetite for aggressive expansion. Domestic political considerations also shaped Truman's response to Stalin. The chief executive feared that the Democrats would invite political disaster if he reneged on the Yalta agreements. The Democrats counted on winning most of the votes of the 6 million Polish Americans and millions of other Americans of Eastern European origin, who remained keenly interested in the fates of their homelands. The president resolved not to appear "soft on communism."

Combativeness fit the temperament of the feisty Truman. Eager to demonstrate his command, the president matched Stalin's intransigence on controlling Poland with his own demands for Polish democracy. Emboldened by America's monopoly of atomic weapons and its position as the world's economic superpower, he believed the United States could control the terms of the postwar settlement.

The Iron Curtain Descends   Truman's assertiveness inflamed Stalin's mistrust of the West and deepened Soviet obsession with its own security. The Soviet Union stepped up its confiscation of materials and factories from occupied territories and forced its satellite nations (countries under Soviet control) to close their doors to American trade and influence. In a February 1946 speech that the White House considered a "declaration of World War III," Stalin asserted that there could be no lasting peace with capitalism and vowed to overcome the American edge in weapons.

Two weeks later, **George F. Kennan,** an American diplomat in Moscow and leading student of Russian affairs, wired a telegram to the State Department describing Soviet expansionism as "like a toy automobile, wound up and headed in a given direction, stopping only when it meets some unanswerable force." The only way to deal with Soviet aggressiveness, Kennan asserted, was a "long-term, patient but firm and vigilant containment of Russian expansive tendencies." Truman, who had already insisted the time had come "to stop babying the Soviets" and "to get tough with Russia," accepted Kennan's advice. **Containment**—a policy uniting military, economic, and diplomatic strategies to curb, or "contain," any further Soviet communist expansion—became Washington gospel.

In early March 1946, Truman accompanied Winston Churchill to Westminster College in Missouri, where the former British prime minister warned of a new threat to democracy. Stalin, he said, had drawn an "iron curtain" across the eastern half of Europe. To meet the threat of further Soviet aggression, Churchill called for an alliance of the English-speaking peoples and the maintenance of an Anglo-American monopoly of atomic weapons: "There is nothing the Communists admire so much as strength and nothing for which they have less respect than for military weakness."

As mutual hostility escalated, the Soviets and Americans rushed to develop doomsday weapons. In June, Truman submitted to the United Nations a plan for the United States to destroy its atomic arsenal if the Soviet Union stopped its work on nuclear weapons and submitted to UN inspections. As expected, the Soviets rejected the American proposal, and Congress established the Atomic Energy Commission (AEC) to spur both nuclear energy and, especially, nuclear weaponry. By 1950, one AEC adviser reckoned, the United States "had a stockpile capable of somewhat more than reproducing World War II in a single day."

Thus, less than a year after American and Soviet soldiers had jubilantly met at the Elbe River to celebrate Hitler's defeat, a Cold War emerged. It would be waged by economic pressure, nuclear intimidation, propaganda, subversion, and proxy wars (fought by governments and peoples allied to the principals rather than directly by the principals themselves). It would affect American life as decisively as any military engagement the nation had fought.

Containing Communism   On February 21, 1947, Britain informed the United States that it could no longer afford to assist Greece and Turkey in their struggles against communist insurgents in the eastern Mediterranean. The harsh European winter, the most severe in memory, heightened the sense of urgency in Washington. The economies of Western Europe had come to a near halt. Famine and tuberculosis plagued the continent. European colonies in Africa and Asia had risen in revolt. Cigarettes and candy bars circulated as currency in Germany, and the communist parties in France and Italy appeared ready to topple democratic coalition governments. Truman resolved to meet the challenge. But congressional leaders balked, agreeing to support the president only if he could "scare hell out of the country" to gain popular backing for meeting the Soviet threat.

Truman could and did. On March 12, 1947, addressing a joint session of Congress, he asked for $400 million in military assistance to Greece and Turkey while announcing the **Truman Doctrine.** Instead of mentioning that the aid would go to a right-wing, military-dominated Greek regime and an autocratic Turkey, the Truman Doctrine pictured the matter as a global struggle "between alternative ways of life," a holy war between God-fearing democracy and an atheistic communism that relied on "terror and oppression." Accordingly, the policy of the United States would be to support any free people "resisting attempted subjugation by armed minorities or by outside pressures." The Truman Doctrine and the funds appropriated by Congress helped the Greek monarchy to defeat the rebel movement and Turkey to stay out of the Soviet orbit. Moreover, this unilateral declaration proclaimed the nation's intention to be a global policeman—everywhere on guard against advances by the Soviet Union and its allies—and laid the foundation for American foreign policy for much of the next four decades.

To back up the new international initiative, Congress passed the **National Security Act of 1947,** unifying the armed forces under a single Department of Defense, creating the National Security Council (NSC) to advise the president on strategic matters, and establishing the Central Intelligence Agency (CIA) to gather information abroad and engage in covert activities in support of the nation's security. Congress also approved the administration's proposal for massive U.S.

assistance for European recovery in 1947. Advocated by Secretary of State George C. Marshall, and thus called the **Marshall Plan,** the European Recovery Plan (ERP) aimed to combat the "hunger, poverty, desperation" that spawned communism. Truman correctly guessed that the Soviet Union and its satellites would refuse to take part in the plan, because of the controls linked to it, and accurately foresaw that Western European economic recovery would expand sales of American goods abroad and promote prosperity in the United States.

Although denounced by the Left as a "Martial Plan" and by the Right as a "Share-the-American-Wealth Plan," the Marshall Plan helped Western Europe revive, prosper, and achieve an unprecedented unity. By 1952, industrial production had risen 200 percent in Western Europe, and the economic and social chaos that communists had exploited had been overcome in the sixteen nations that shared the $17 billion in aid. Not coincidentally, Western Europe had also become a major center of American trade and investment.

Confrontation in Germany The Soviet Union reacted to the Truman Doctrine and the Marshall Plan by tightening its grip on Eastern Europe. Communist takeovers added Hungary and Czechoslovakia to the Soviet bloc in 1947 and 1948, and Stalin set his sights on Germany. The 1945 Potsdam Agreement had divided Germany into four separate zones (administered by France, Great Britain, the Soviet Union, and the United States) and created a joint four-power administration for Germany's capital, Berlin, which lay 110 miles within the Soviet-occupied eastern zone. As the Cold War intensified, the Western powers moved toward uniting their zones into an anti-Soviet West German state. Stalin responded in June 1948 by blocking all rail and highway traffic into Berlin.

Truman resolved neither to abandon Berlin nor to shoot his way into the city and possibly trigger World War III. Instead, he ordered a massive airlift of supplies to the city (the **Berlin airlift**). American cargo planes landed in West Berlin every three minutes around the clock, bringing the mountain of food and fuel necessary to provide the blockaded city with a precarious lifeline. In May 1949, the Soviets ended the blockade. Stalin's gambit had failed. The airlift highlighted American determination and technological prowess, revealed Stalin's readiness to use innocent people as pawns, and dramatically heightened anti-Soviet feeling in the West. Continuing fears of a Soviet attack on Western Europe and public support for "firmness and increased 'toughness' in relations with Russia" then led Truman to push for a rearmed West German state and an Atlantic collective security alliance.

In May 1949, the United States, Britain, and France ended their occupation of Germany and approved the creation of the Federal Republic of Germany (West Germany). A month earlier, ten Western Europe nations had signed the North Atlantic Treaty, establishing a military alliance with the United States and Canada in which "an armed attack against one or more of them ... shall be considered an attack against them all." After overwhelming Senate approval, the United States officially joined the **North Atlantic Treaty Organization** (NATO), marking the formal end of America's long tradition of avoiding entangling alliances abroad.

Truman believed that if NATO had been in existence in 1914 and 1939, the world would have been spared two disastrous wars. Accordingly, he spurred Congress to authorize the deployment of U.S. troops in Europe and $1.3 billion

© Bettmann/Corbis

The Berlin Airlift, 1948 *German children watching an American plane in "Operation Vittles" bring food and supplies to their beleaguered city. The airlift kept a city of 2 million people alive for nearly a year and made West Berlin a symbol of the West's resolve to contain the spread of Soviet communism.*

for military assistance to NATO nations. The Soviet Union responded by creating the German Democratic Republic (East Germany) in 1949, exploding its own atomic bomb that same year, and forming in 1955 an Eastern bloc military alliance—the Warsaw Pact. The United States and Soviet Union had divided Europe into two armed camps.

The Cold War in Asia   Moscow–Washington hostility also carved Asia into contending camps. The Russians created a sphere of influence in Manchuria, the Americans denied Moscow a role in postwar Japan, and the two superpowers partitioned a helpless Korea.

As head of the U.S. occupation forces in Japan, General Douglas MacArthur oversaw that nation's transformation from an empire in ruins into a prosperous democracy. In 1952, the occupation ended, but a military security treaty allowed the United States to retain its Japanese bases and brought Japan under the American "nuclear umbrella." In further pursuit of containment, the United States helped crush a procommunist insurgency in the Philippines and aided French efforts to reestablish colonial rule in Indochina (Vietnam, Laos, and Cambodia), despite American declarations in favor of national self-determination and against imperialism.

In China, however, U.S. efforts to block communism failed. The Truman administration first tried to mediate the civil war between the nationalist government of Jiang Jieshi and the communist forces of **Mao Zedong.** Between 1945 and 1949, it also sent nearly $3 billion in aid to the nationalists. But American dollars

MAP 26.1 The Postwar Division of Europe, 1945–1989

The wartime dispute between the Soviet Union and the Western Allies over Poland's future hardened after World War II into a Cold War that split Europe into competing American and Russian spheres of influence. Across an "iron curtain," NATO countries faced the Warsaw Pact nations.

could not prevent the surrender of Jiang's armies to Mao's forces or the collapse of the nationalists' corrupt regime, whose remnants fled to the island of Taiwan.

Mao's establishment of the communist People's Republic of China (PRC) shocked Americans. The most populous nation in the world, seen as a counterforce to communism and a market for American goods, had become "Red China." Although Truman blamed Jiang's defeat on his failure to reform China, most Americans were unconvinced. China's "fall" especially embittered conservatives who believed that America's interests lay in Asia, not Europe. Their pressure influenced the administration's refusal to recognize the PRC, block its admission to the United Nations, and proclaim Jiang's nationalist regime in Taiwan the legitimate government of China.

In September 1949, as the "Who lost China" debate raged, the president announced that the Soviet Union had exploded an atomic bomb. The loss of its nuclear monopoly shattered American illusions of invincibility. Combined with Mao's victory, it spawned an anticommunist hysteria and led to irrational searches for scapegoats and subversives to explain American setbacks in world affairs.

Ordinary Americans sought safety in civil defense. Public schools held air-raid drills, teaching students to "duck and cover"—dive under their desks and shield their eyes against atomic blasts. "We took the drills seriously," recalled novelist Annie Dillard; "surely Pittsburgh, which had the nation's steel, coke, and aluminum, would be the enemy's first target." Four million Americans volunteered to be Sky Watchers, looking for Soviet planes. More than a million purchased or constructed their own family bomb shelters. Those who could not afford a bomb shelter were advised by the Federal Civil Defense Administration to "jump in any handy ditch or gutter ... bury your face in your arms ... never lose your head."

In January 1950, stung by charges that he was "soft on communism," Truman ordered the development of a fusion-based hydrogen bomb (H-bomb), a thousand times more destructive than an atomic bomb. In November 1952, the United States exploded its first H-bomb, completely vaporizing one of the Marshall Islands in the Pacific, carving a mile-long, 175-foot-deep crater in the ocean floor, and spilling radioactive dust over thousands of square miles. "You would swear the whole world was on fire," a sailor wrote home. Nine months later, the Soviets detonated their own H-bomb. The balance of terror escalated.

So, too, did nuclear-generated environmental and health problems. Nuclear tests left minimally protected U.S. soldiers and South Pacific islanders exposed to radiation, and radioactive debris from atomic tests contaminated vast areas of Colorado, Utah, Nevada, and Washington. Although the AEC insisted the fallout was harmless, many people exposed to radiation, as well as unborn children, would pay the cost of an out of control arms race poisoning the atmosphere.

In April 1950, a committee appointed by the president issued a sweeping analysis of U.S. defense policy. **National Security Paper 68 (NSC-68)** emphasized the Soviet Union's aggressive intentions, territorial greed, and military strength. To counter the Soviets' "design for world domination," NSC-68 urged massive increases in America's nuclear arsenal, vigorous covert action by the CIA, and open-ended increases in the defense budget to resist Communist expansion anywhere and everywhere. Secretary of State Acheson characterized NSC-68 as "the fundamental paper" defining American foreign policy into the foreseeable future. The United States now approached the Cold War as a military confrontation. By the end of 1950, Congress had tripled the defense budget of the self-proclaimed "world policeman."

The Korean War, 1950–1953

After World War II, the United States and Soviet Union temporarily divided Korea, which had been controlled by Japan since the Russo-Japanese War of 1904, at the thirty-eighth parallel. This line then solidified into a de facto border between the Soviet-backed Democratic People's Republic of Korea in the north and the American-supported Republic of Korea, or South Korea, each claiming the sole right to rule all of Korea.

On June 25, 1950, North Korean troops swept across the thirty-eighth parallel to attack South Korea. Truman decided to fight back, viewing the assault as Stalin's test of U.S. will and containment policy. "Korea is the Greece of the Far East," Truman maintained. "If we are tough enough now, if we stand up to them like we did in Greece ... they won't take any next steps." Mindful of the failure of appeasement at Munich in 1938, he believed the communists were doing in Korea exactly what Hitler

MAP 26.2　The Korean War, 1950–1953

The experience of fighting an undeclared war for the limited objective of containing communism confused the generation of Americans who had just fought an all-out war for the total defeat of the Axis. General MacArthur spoke for the many who were frustrated by the Korean conflict's mounting costs in blood and dollars: "There is no substitute for victory."

and the Japanese had done in the 1930s: "If this was allowed to go unchallenged," Truman observed, "it would mean a third world war."

Without consulting Congress, Truman ordered air and naval forces to Korea on June 27. That same day, he asked the United Nations to authorize action to repel the invasion. Because the Soviets were boycotting the Security Council to protest the UN's unwillingness to seat Mao's China, and could not use their veto power, Truman gained approval for a UN "police action" to restore South Korea's border. The Cold War had turned hot.

North Korean forces initially routed the outnumbered American and South Korean troops. Then, in mid-September, with UN forces cornered on the southeastern tip of the Korean peninsula, struggling to avoid being pushed into the sea, General Douglas MacArthur, the commander of the UN forces, executed a brilliant amphibious maneuver, landing his troops at Inchon, 150 miles behind North Korean lines. Within two weeks, UN forces drove the North Koreans back across the thirty-eighth parallel. Basking in victory, MacArthur persuaded Truman to let him go beyond the UN mandate to repel aggression and to cross the border to liberate all of Korea from communism.

As UN troops approached the Yalu River—the boundary between Korea and China—the Chinese, fearful of America's commitment to "liberate" China and return Jiang Jieshi to control, warned that they would not "sit back with folded hands and let the Americans come to the border." Dismissing the threat as "hot air," MacArthur deployed his forces in a thin line below the river. On November 25, thirty-three Chinese divisions (about 300,000 men) counterattacked, driving MacArthur's forces back below the thirty-eighth parallel in what *Time* magazine called "the worst military setback the United States has ever suffered." By March 1951, the fighting had deadlocked at roughly the original dividing line between the two Koreas. "We were eyeball to eyeball," recalled Bev Scott, one of the first black lieutenants to head a racially integrated infantry squad.

> *Just 20 meters of no man's land between us. We couldn't move at all in the daytime without getting shot at.... It was like World War I. We lived in a maze of bunkers and deep trenches.... There were bodies strewn all over the place. Hundreds of bodies frozen in the snow. We could see the arms and legs sticking up. Nobody could get their dead out of there.*

Stalemated, Truman reversed course and sought a negotiated peace based on the original objective of restoring the integrity of South Korea. MacArthur rocked the boat, however, urging that he be allowed to seek total victory even at the risk of an all-out war with China. Truman refused: "We are trying to prevent a world war— not to start one." He sought a limited war for a limited objective: to hold the line in Korea. But MacArthur would not accept a stalemate. When he bluntly and repeatedly criticized Truman's limited war—the "appeasement of Communism"—the president fired the general to protect civilian control of the military. Public opinion, however, backed the general. To Americans accustomed to unconditional victory, the very idea of limited war was baffling. Mounting casualties for no apparent purpose at places named Heartbreak Ridge or Pork Chop Hill added anger to the mix. Despite warnings from the chairman of the Joint Chiefs of Staff that MacArthur's proposals would result in "the wrong war at the wrong place in the wrong time and with the wrong enemy," a growing number of Americans agreed with MacArthur that "There is no substitute for victory," and listened sympathetically to Republican charges that communist agents controlled American policy.

Truman, meanwhile, found himself bogged down in Korea, unable to win a victory or craft a peace. After two more years of fighting, the two sides reached an armistice in July 1953 that left Korea divided. The "limited" conflict cost the United

© Bettmann/Corbis

A Racially Integrated Unit in the Korean War *The Korean War was the first war in U.S. history in which most soldiers fought in racially integrated units. President Truman ordered the integration of the armed forces in 1948, despite the opposition of many military officers, and the successful performance of African Americans in Korea accelerated acceptance of military integration.*

States 54,246 lives (about 33,700 of them battlefield deaths), another 103,284 wounded, and some $54 billion. The Chinese lost 900,000 men, and the two Korean armies lost 800,000. As in World War II, massive U.S. "carpet bombing" killed at least a million civilians and left North Korea looking like a moonscape.

The **Korean War** had major consequences. It accelerated implementation of NSC-68 and the expansion of the containment doctrine into a global commitment. From 1950 to 1953, defense spending zoomed from $13 billion to $60 billion—from one-third to two-thirds of the entire federal budget—the U.S. army grew from half a million men to 3.6 million, and the American atomic stockpile mushroomed from 150 to 750 nuclear warheads. The United States acquired new bases around the world, committed itself to rearm West Germany, and joined a mutual-defense pact with Australia and New Zealand. Increased military aid flowed to Jiang Jieshi on Taiwan and to France's fight against communist insurgents in Indochina.

Truman's intervention in Korea preserved a precarious balance of power in Asia and stepped up the administration's commitment to the anticommunist struggle. Containment, originally advanced to justify U.S. aid to Greece and Turkey, had become the ideological foundation for a major war in Korea and, ominously, for a deepening U.S. involvement in Vietnam. Truman's actions enhanced the powers of an already powerful presidency and set a precedent for future undeclared wars. They also augmented an economic boom, accelerated the desegregation of the armed forces, and brought to fever pitch a period of xenophobia that rivaled the Red Scare of 1919.

THE TRUMAN ADMINISTRATION AT HOME, 1945–1952

The Cold War profoundly changed the United States for better and for worse. It weakened the nation's commitment to civil liberties while propelling research in medicine and science that, for the most part, made lives longer and better. It spurred more than a quarter of a century of economic growth and prosperity, the longest such period in American history. That, along with a vast expansion of higher education, enabled many Americans to become middle class, diminishing support for the expansion of the welfare state.

Demobilization and Reconversion　When the war ended, GIs and civilians alike wanted those who had served overseas "home alive in '45." Troops demanding transport ships barraged Congress with threats of "no boats, no votes." On a single day in December 1945, sixty thousand postcards flooded the White House with the message "Bring the Boys Home by Christmas." Truman bowed to popular demand, and by 1948, American military strength had dropped from 12 million to just 1.5 million.

Returning veterans faced readjustment problems intensified by a soaring divorce rate and a drastic housing shortage. Many feared the return of mass unemployment and economic depression as war plants closed. Defense spending dropped from $76 billion in 1945 to under $20 billion in 1946, and more than a million defense jobs vanished.

Yet by the end of the decade, more women were working outside the home than during World War II. Most took jobs in traditional women's fields, especially office work and sales, to pay for family needs. Although the postwar economy created new openings for women in the labor market, many public figures urged women to seek fulfillment at home. Popular culture romanticized married bliss and demonized career women as a threat to social stability.

The GI Bill of Rights　The Servicemen's Readjustment Act of 1944, commonly called the GI Bill of Rights or **GI Bill,** was designed to forestall the expected recession by easing veterans back into the work force and to reward the "soldier boys" for their wartime service. The GI Bill gave veterans priority for many jobs, occupational guidance, and if need be, fifty-two weeks of unemployment benefits. It also provided low-interest government loans to some 4 million returning GIs who were starting businesses or buying homes, helping to fuel a baby boom, suburbanization, and a record demand for new goods and services.

The government also promised to pay up to four years of further education or job training for veterans. Some Americans opposed it as opening the door to socialism, and some university administrators, fearing the influx of riffraff, echoed the complaint of the University of Chicago president that their colleges would become "educational hobo jungles." Yet, by 1946, flush with stipends of $65 a month—$90 for those with dependents—and up to $500 a year for tuition and books, 1.5 million veterans were attending college, spurring the creation of many new state and community colleges. By 1947, veterans made up more than half of all college students. Often married and the fathers of young children, they were generally less interested in knowledge than in a degree and a higher-paying job. Accommodating them, colleges offered accelerated programs and more vocational or career-oriented courses.

To make room for the millions of GIs pursuing higher education after the war, many colleges limited the percentage of women admitted or barred students from out of state. The percentage of female college graduates dropped from 40 percent in 1949 to 25 percent in 1950. By then, most women who might have been students were the working wives of the veterans who took advantage of the GI Bill to go college.

The GI Bill democratized higher education. By 1956, nearly 10 million veterans had used the GI Bill to enroll in vocational training programs and colleges (most the first in their families to do so). No longer a citadel of privilege, universities awarded twice as many degrees in 1950 as in 1940, propelling millions of veterans into the middle class. Two decades later, these more affluent and educated veterans expected their children to follow suit. Higher education became an accepted part of the American Dream.

| **The Economic Boom Begins** | In addition to the assistance given returning servicemen, a 1945 tax cut of $6 billion spurred corporate investment in new facto- |

ries and equipment and helped produce an economic boom. Wartime savings and a pent-up demand for consumer goods further kindled postwar growth and prosperity. The men and women who had endured the Great Depression and Second World War craved the "good life" and had $140 billion in bank accounts and government bonds to purchase the advertised "all-electrified kitchen-of-the-future." Sales of homes, cars, and appliances skyrocketed. Scores of new products—televisions, high-fidelity phonographs, filter cigarettes, automatic transmissions, freezers, and air conditioners—became hallmarks of the middle-class lifestyle.

The Bretton Woods Agreement (1944) among the Allies had set the stage for the United States to become economic leader of the noncommunist world. It created several institutions to oversee international trade and finance: the International Monetary Fund (IMF) to stabilize exchange rates by valuing ("pegging") other currencies in relation to the U.S. dollar, the International Bank for Reconstruction and Development (World Bank) to help rebuild war-battered Asia and Europe, and the 1947 General Agreement on Tariffs and Trade (GATT) to break up closed trading blocs and expand international trade. Because Americans largely controlled and funded these economic institutions, they gave the United States an especially favorable position on the world stage.

With many nations in ruins, American firms could import raw materials cheaply; with little competition from other industrial countries, they could increase exports to record levels. U.S. economic dominance also resulted from wartime advances in science and technology, which significantly increased the productivity of American workers and led to revolutionary developments in such industries as electronics and plastics.

| **Truman's Domestic Program** | Americans' hunger for the fruits of affluence left them with little appetite for extending the New Deal. Truman agreed. "I don't want any experiments," he confided. "The American people have been through a lot of experiments and they want |

a rest." His only major domestic accomplishment in the Seventy-ninth Congress was the **Employment Act of 1946.** It committed the federal government to ensuring economic growth and established the Council of Economic Advisers to confer with the president and formulate policies for maintaining employment, production, and purchasing power. Congress, however, gutted both the goal of full employment and the enhanced executive powers to achieve that objective.

Congressional eagerness to dismantle wartime controls worsened the nation's chief economic problem: inflation. Consumer demand outran the supply of goods, intensifying the pressure on prices. The Office of Price Administration (OPA) sought to hold the line by enforcing price controls, but food producers, manufacturers, and retailers opposed continuing wartime controls. While some consumers favored the OPA, others deplored it as an irksome relic of wartime regulations. In June 1946, Truman vetoed a bill that would have extended the OPA's life but deprived it of power, effectively ending all price controls. Food costs rose 16 percent within a week and the price of beef doubled. "PRICES SOAR, BUYERS SORE, STEERS JUMP OVER THE MOON," headlined the *New York Daily News*.

Congress then passed, and Truman signed, a second bill extending price controls in weakened form. Protesting any price controls, however, farmers and meat producers threatened to withhold food from the market. Knowing that "meatless voters are opposition voters," Truman lifted controls on food prices just before the 1946 midterm elections. When Democrats fared poorly anyway, Truman ended all price controls. By then, the consumer price index had jumped nearly 25 percent since the end of the war.

Sharp price rises and shrinking paychecks shorn of overtime goaded organized labor to demand higher wages. In 1946 alone, more than 4.5 million workers went on strike. When a United Mine Workers walkout paralyzed the economy for forty days, Truman ordered an army seizure of the mines. A week later, after Truman had pressured owners to grant most of the union's demands, the miners returned to work, only to walk out again six months later. Meanwhile, on the heels of the first mine workers settlement, railway engineers and trainmen announced they would shut down the nation's railroad system for the first time in history. "If you think I'm going to sit here and let you tie up this whole country," Truman shouted at the heads of the two unions, "you're crazy as hell." In May, he asked Congress for authority to draft workers who struck vital industries. Before he could finish his speech, the rail unions gave in, leaving the Senate to reject the president's proposal. Still, Truman's threat alienated labor leaders.

By the fall of 1946, Truman had angered most major interest groups. Less than a third of Americans polled approved of his performance. "To err is Truman," some gibed. Summing up the public discontent, Republicans asked, "Had enough?" In the 1946 elections, they captured twenty-five governorships and, for the first time since 1928, won control of Congress.

The public mood reflected more than just economic discontent. Under the surface, laughter at stores advertising atomic sales or bartenders mixing atomic cocktails ran a deep current of fear. An NBC radio program depicted a nuclear attack on Chicago in which most people died instantly. "Those few who escaped the blast, but not the gamma rays, died slowly after they had left the ruined city," intoned the narrator. "No attempt at identification of the bodies or burial ever took place. Chicago was simply closed." Schoolchildren wore dog tags in order to be identified after an atomic attack and practiced crawling under their desks and putting their hands over their heads to protect themselves from the bomb. There was much talk of urban dispersal—resettling people in small communities in the country's vast open spaces—and of how to protect oneself in a nuclear attack. The end of World War II had brought an uneasy peace.

The Eightieth Congress, 1947–1948   In 1946, Republicans won control of Congress for the first time since 1930. Many Republicans interpreted the election as a mandate to reverse the New Deal. As "Mr. Republican," Senator Robert A. Taft of Ohio, declared, "We have got to break with the corrupting idea that we can legislate prosperity, legislate equality, legislate opportunity." The Republican-controlled Congress defeated Democratic bills to raise the minimum wage and to provide federal funds for education and housing. Capitalizing on the national consensus for curbing labor union power generated by the waves of postwar strikes, Congress passed the **Taft-Hartley Act** (Labor-Management Relations Act) in 1947. It barred the closed shop—a workplace where all employees had to join the union; outlawed secondary boycotts—strikes against suppliers of a targeted business; required union officials to sign anticommunist loyalty oaths; and permitted the president to call a cooling-off period to delay strikes that might endanger national safety or health. The act weakened organizing drives in the nonunion South and West, hastening the relocation of labor-intensive industries, such as textiles, from the Northeast and Midwest to the Sunbelt, and it drove leftist leaders out of the CIO, weakening organized labor as a force for social justice.

Truman gave in to union demands that he veto the "slave labor bill." Although Congress easily overrode the veto, Truman had taken a major step toward regaining organized labor's support and reforging FDR's New Deal coalition. Now playing the role of a staunch liberal New Dealer, Truman urged Congress to repeal Taft-Hartley and to provide federal aid to education and housing, national health insurance, and high farm-price supports. To woo ethnic voters of Eastern European descent, Truman railed against Soviet communism; and to court Jewish American voters, as well as express his deep sympathy toward Holocaust survivors, he overrode the objections of the State Department, which feared alienating the oil-rich Arab world, and extended diplomatic recognition to the new state of Israel within hours of its establishment in May 1948.

Still, Truman's chances for victory dimmed as southern segregationists, alarmed by the president's support in 1948 for antilynching and anti-poll tax bills, bolted the Democrats and nominated Governor Strom Thurmond of South Carolina as the candidate of the States' Rights ("Dixiecrat") party, a significant step toward the eventual breakup of the Democratic political coalition of southern conservatives and northern liberals. Further diminishing Truman's chances, leftwing Democrats joined with communists to launch a new Progressive Party headed by former vice president Henry A. Wallace. To capitalize on Democratic divisions, Republicans tried to play it safe, nominating the moderate governor of New York, Thomas E. Dewey, for president, and Californian Earl Warren for vice president. Confident of victory, Dewey ran a complacent campaign designed to offend the fewest people. Truman, in contrast, campaigned aggressively, blasting the "no-good, do-nothing"

Republicans as "gluttons of privilege." To shouts of "Give 'em hell, Harry," the president hammered away at the Republican-controlled Congress. Pollsters applauded Truman's spunk but predicted a Dewey victory.

Instead, the president won the biggest electoral upset in U.S. history. The Progressives and Dixiecrats, ironically, helped Truman. Their extremism kept most moderates safely in the Democratic fold. Most importantly, Truman succeeded as the defender of the New Deal against the party of Herbert Hoover and the depression. The Roosevelt coalition—organized labor, farmers, urban ethnics, blacks, and most white southerners—had held together one more time.

The Fair Deal   Despite his slim victory, Truman proposed in 1949 a vast liberal agenda—the **Fair Deal**—that included civil rights, national health-care legislation, and federal aid to education. Unlike New Deal liberalism, the Fair Deal counted on continual economic growth. An expanding economic pie would mean a bigger piece for most Americans (so they would not resent helping those left behind) and more tax revenue for the government (so it would have the funds to pay for more social-welfare programs).

With increasing prosperity sapping public enthusiasm for liberal initiatives, the bipartisan conservative coalition of northern Republicans and southern Democrats, which had largely controlled Congress since 1938, rejected the Fair Deal. While extending some existing programs, such as the minimum wage and social security, and authorizing the construction of 800,000 units of low-income housing, Congress would go no further. Special interest groups, such as the American Medical Association and the National Association of Manufacturers, lobbied extensively against what they called "creeping socialism," and by 1950, Truman again subordinated domestic issues to foreign policy.

THE POLITICS OF ANTICOMMUNISM

As the Cold War worsened, some Americans concluded that the roots of the nation's difficulties abroad lay in domestic treason and subversion. How else could the communists have taken China and built an atomic bomb? Millions of fearful Americans enlisted in a crusade that equated dissent with disloyalty and blamed scapegoats for the nation's problems.

Similar intolerance had prevailed in the Red Scare of 1919–1920 (see Chapter 22), but the Second Red Scare lasted longer, affected more people, and had greater consequences. It took root in the creation of the House Committee on Un-American Activities—later called the House Un-American Activities Committee (HUAC)—in 1938 to ferret out fascists, but it quickly became a platform for right-wing denunciations of the New Deal as a communist plot. After World War II, mounting numbers of conservative Democrats and Republicans found it popular to climb aboard the anti-Red bandwagon.

The **Second Red Scare** influenced both governmental and personal actions. Millions of Americans were subjected to security investigations and loyalty oaths. Anticommunist extremism destroyed the Left, undermined labor militancy, and discredited liberalism. Any and all progressive initiatives—from health insurance to child-care centers to proposals for civil rights—were denounced as socialist or "soft on communism." Foreign and domestic anticommunist policies reinforced each other, spawning a "silent generation" of college students and prohibiting any dissent from America's cold war against the USSR.

Loyalty and Security   The U.S. Communist Party had claimed eighty thousand members during the Second World War, and no one knew how many occupied sensitive government positions. In mid-1945, a raid on the offices of a procommunist magazine revealed that classified documents had been given to it by government employees. Ten months later, the Canadian government exposed a spy network that had passed American military information and atomic secrets to the Soviets during the war. Moreover, recently disclosed Soviet documents, declassified after the fall of communism, revealed that the Russians had spies in the scientific community working on the atom bomb as well as highly placed communists operating undercover in the federal government.

Republicans accused the Democratic administration of being "soft on communism," and in March 1947, a week after his Truman Doctrine speech defining the Cold War as a holy crusade between good and evil, the president issued Executive Order 9835 establishing the Federal Employee Loyalty Program to root out subversives in the government. It authorized the attorney general to prepare a list of "subversive" organizations and made association with such groups grounds for dismissal. The drive for security overran civil liberties because those suspected could neither face their accusers nor require investigators to reveal sources.

Mere criticism of American foreign policy could result in an accusation of disloyalty. People lost jobs because they liked foreign films, associated with radical friends, or favored the unionization of federal workers. "Of course the fact that a person believes in racial equality doesn't prove he's a communist," mused an Interior Department Loyalty Board chairman, "but it certainly makes you look twice, doesn't it?" Of the 4.7 million jobholders and applicants who underwent loyalty checks by 1952, 560 were fired or denied jobs, and several thousand resigned or withdrew their applications. Although Loyalty Board probes uncovered no evidence of espionage or subversion, it spread fear among government employees. The effect on free political debate was chilling. "If communists like apple pie and I do," claimed one federal worker, "I see no reason why I should stop eating it. But I would."

The Anticommunist Crusade   The very existence of a federal loyalty probe fed fears of domestic subversion. It promoted hysteria about communist infiltrators and legitimated a witch-hunt for subversives. College administrators cooperated with the FBI in spying on students and faculty, universities banned controversial speakers, and popular magazines featured articles like "Reds Are After Your Child." By the end of Truman's term, thirty-nine states had created loyalty programs. Few had any procedural safeguards. Schoolteachers, college professors, and state and city employees throughout the nation had to sign loyalty oaths or lose their jobs. No one knows how many were dismissed, denied tenure, or drifted away, leaving behind colleagues too frightened to speak out.

GOING TO THE SOURCE

Remembering the Hollywood Blacklist

In 1947, attorney Bartley Crum helped represent the Hollywood Ten before HUAC. In 1997, Crum's daughter, Patricia Bosworth, wrote to the *New York Times* about her memories of the subsequent blacklist and its effects on the people involved. Bosworth emphasizes the chilling hardships that HUAC's assault on civil liberties brought down on individuals.

I first learned about the Hollywood blacklist on Nov. 24, 1947. I remember the exact moment. I was standing with my father, Bartley Crum, by a phone booth near Union Square in San Francisco, feeding him nickels and dimes while he made a series of intense phone calls to Dore Schary, who was the head of MGM.

If you're wondering why he had to make calls from a pay phone, it's because our house was bugged by the F.B.I. At that point I was too young to quite grasp the bugged calls, but I did know that my father had been one of six lawyers who had just defended the "Hollywood 10" in front of the House Un-American Activities Committee (HUAC) in Washington.

These were the writers, directors, and producers who had been subpoenaed to testify about their political beliefs. But they stood on their First Amendment rights and refused to reveal whether they were Communists. After the hearings, in October, the Hollywood 10 were indicted for contempt, sent to jail, and "blacklisted" from working in Hollywood.

On that foggy afternoon in San Francisco so long ago, my father stopped making phone calls and turned to me to try to explain why the Hollywood 10 would have to be sacrificed to appease HUAC. It was the start of the Red Scare and America's paranoia about Russia and Communism.

Today, almost nobody I know has anything but the vaguest memories of the Hollywood blacklist. Nobody remembers that HUAC continued its investigations into the film community well into 1956 and that hundreds of witnesses were called to testify and to inform on colleagues to prove their loyalty and their patriotism.

Back in the 50s, there wasn't any talk of selling out when blacklisted writers, just out

---

In 1947, blurring distinctions between dissent and disloyalty, between radicalism and subversion, the **House Un-American Activities Committee** (HUAC) held hearings to expose communist influence in American life. When some prominent film directors and screenwriters, dubbed the Hollywood Ten, refused to testify about past political associations, claiming the free-speech protections of the First Amendment, HUAC had them cited for contempt of Congress and sent to federal prison. The president of the Motion Picture Association announced that no one would be hired who failed to cooperate with HUAC. Blacklists in the motion picture industry and in radio broadcasting quickly followed. They barred the employment of those with a questionable past or those who had associated, however remotely, with others deemed "subversive" or "un-American". They silenced many talented people and prompted the entertainment media either to shun controversial issues or to tilt politically to the right.

of jail, huddled in our living room. Instead, my father's conversations with them focused on the meaning of loyalty and questions about censorship and how one could survive in the writers' black market. All the best writers had been blacklisted, and everyone was writing under pseudonyms and being paid in cash; it was hard to open a bank account, impossible to get life insurance. Nobody had enough money. Everyone was being hounded by the F.B.I.

My father was being hounded too. Because he had defended the Hollywood 10 and taken on numerous loyalty cases as well, he was labeled subversive. He was followed relentlessly by the F.B.I., and our phones remained tapped. My father was even put on the F.B.I. security index, which meant that in the event of an "emergency" he would be put in a concentration camp. He lost most of his clients. Close to bankruptcy and in despair, my father informed on two colleagues already known to be Communists. In 1959, he committed suicide.

The cold war lasted until 1991. During much of the time between the 1950's and then HUAC was still active in various forms. Many movie executives were afraid to stand up for anything, least

of all blacklisted writers. And nobody wanted to seem soft on Communism.

Today there are still threats to our freedom of expression, many of them the work of self-appointed guardians of decency. We can put them in historical context by remembering the blacklist of the 1950's.

Questions

1. *What were some of the consequences of defying the House Un-American Activities Committee?*

2. *In what ways does the postwar assault on domestic radicalism shed light on developments in American life today? How is it similar? How does it differ?*

Source: Patricia Bosworth's books include biographies of Marlon Brando and the photographer Diane Arbus as well as the memoir, *Anything Your Little Heart Desires—An American Family Story.* It's the story of her father Bartley Crum, but it's also a cultural history of the 1940s and 1950s about the fall of liberalism and the dawn of the Cold War and the political turmoil that ensued, which created an environment of anticommunist hysteria that ruined many lives full of promise. This letter first appeared in the *New York Times*, April 20, 1997. Copyright © 1997 by Patricia Bosworth. Reprinted with permission.

HUAC also frightened the labor movement into expelling communists and avoiding progressive causes. Fearful of appearing "red," or even "pink," most unions shunned politics to focus on securing better pay and benefits for their members.

The 1948 presidential election campaign also fed national anxieties. Truman lambasted Henry Wallace as a Stalinist dupe, and the GOP dubbed the Democrats "the party of treason." The rising Republican star, Richard M. Nixon of California, charged that the Democrats bore responsibility for "the unimpeded growth of the communist conspiracy." To blunt such accusations, Truman's Justice Department prosecuted eleven top leaders of the American Communist Party under the Smith Act of 1940, which outlawed any conspiracy advocating the overthrow of the government. The Supreme Court upheld the Smith Act's constitutionality (*Dennis* v. *United States*, 1951), declaring that Congress could curtail freedom of speech if national security required such restriction. Ironically, the Communist Party was fading into obscurity at the very time politicians magnified its threat. By 1950, its membership had shrunk to less than thirty thousand.

McCarthyism   Nothing set off more alarms of a diabolic Red conspiracy than the matter of **Alger Hiss and Whittaker Chambers**. In 1948 Chambers, a repentant ex-communist, identified Hiss, president of the Carnegie Endowment for International Peace, as an underground member of a secret "communist cell" operating in Washington in the 1930s. Hiss was eventually found guilty of perjury, although one could not tell truth from lies in the trial testimony, and the documents that convicted him seemed insignificant. That an eminent official such as Hiss had been disloyal intensified the widespread fears of a communist underground in the government. Then, a month after Hiss's perjury conviction, another spy case shocked Americans. In February 1950, the British arrested Klaus Fuchs, a German-born scientist involved in the Manhattan Project, for passing atomic secrets to the Soviets in 1944–1945. His confession led to the arrest of an American who then named his brother-in-law and sister, **Julius and Ethel Rosenberg,** as co-conspirators in the wartime spy network. The Rosenbergs insisted they were victims of anti-Semitism being prosecuted for their leftist beliefs. But in March 1951, a jury found them guilty of conspiring to commit espionage, and in June 1953 they each died in the electric chair—the first American civilians to lose their lives for espionage.

The release of classified Soviet documents in the 1990s confirm that Hiss did pass secret information to the Soviets and that Julius Rosenberg, who described himself as a "soldier of Stalin," was part of a spy ring that gave the USSR data on America's atomic bomb project. Ethel Rosenberg, however, appears to have been merely "a lever" to pressure Julius into naming other spies.

By 1950, many Americans could not separate fact from fantasy regarding the communist threat. Only a conspiracy, it seemed, could explain U.S. setbacks. Frustrated by unexpected failure in the 1948 election, Republicans eagerly exploited the fearful mood, accusing the "Commiecrats" of selling out America.

In February 1950, Republican senator **Joseph R. McCarthy** of Wisconsin, desperate for an issue on which to run for reelection in 1952, boldly told a West Virginia audience that communists working in the State Department had betrayed America. "I have in my hand 205 cases of individuals," he asserted as he waved a laundry list, "who would appear to be either card carrying members or certainly loyal to the Communist Party, but who nevertheless are still helping to shape our foreign policy." Although McCarthy never released any names or proof, his senatorial stature and brazen style gave him a national forum. A Senate committee found McCarthy's accusations "a fraud and a hoax," but he persisted. "McCarthyism" became a synonym for personal attacks on individuals by means of indiscriminate allegations and unsubstantiated charges.

As the Korean War dragged on, McCarthy's efforts to "root out the skunks" escalated. He ridiculed Secretary of State Dean Acheson as the "Red Dean" and charged George Marshall with having "aided and abetted a communist conspiracy so immense as to dwarf any previous such venture in the history of man." McCarthyism especially appealed to midwestern Republicans opposed to Democratic internationalism and restrictions on business. For them, anticommunism was a weapon of revenge against liberals—a means to regain the dominance that conservatism had once held. McCarthy also won a devoted following among blue-collar workers who felt that all true Americans detested "communists and queers" and among Catholic ethnics, who sought acceptance as "100 percent Americans" through a show of anticommunist zeal. Countless Americans also shared McCarthy's scorn for State Department liberals as the "bright young men who are born with silver spoons in their mouths." And McCarthy's conspiracy theory offered a simple answer to the perplexing questions of the Cold War: the fault is in Washington.

McCarthy's political power rested on both the Republican establishment and Democratic fears of antagonizing him. In the 1950 elections, when he helped Republicans defeat Democrats who had denounced him, McCarthy appeared invincible.

Over Truman's veto, Congress in 1950 adopted the **McCarran Internal Security Act,** which required organizations deemed communist by the attorney general to register with the Department of Justice. It also authorized the arrest and detention during a national emergency of "any person as to whom there is reason to believe might engage in acts of espionage or sabotage." The McCarran-Walter Immigration and Nationality Act of 1952, also adopted over Truman's veto, maintained the quota system that severely restricted immigration from southern and eastern Europe and from Asia, but did end Asian exclusion. The new law also strengthened the attorney general's authority to exclude or deport "undesirable" aliens suspected of homosexuality or communism.

| The Election of 1952 | In 1952, public apprehension about the loyalty of government employees combined with frustration over the Korean stalemate to sink Democratic hopes to their lowest level since the |

1920s. Truman's approval rating plummeted to 23 percent, the lowest ever recorded by a president. Popular resentment of Truman's handling of the Korean War and revelations of bribery by his political associates gave the GOP ammunition for charging the Democrats with "plunder at home, and blunder abroad." Republicans campaigned on the "K1 C2" slogan—"Korea, Communism, and Corruption."

With Truman too unpopular to run for reelection, dispirited Democrats drafted Governor Adlai Stevenson of Illinois and, to appease southern white voters, nominated segregationist Senator John A. Sparkman of Alabama for vice president. But Stevenson could neither dissociate himself from Truman nor overcome the sentiment that twenty years of Democratic rule was enough.

Compounding Democratic woes, the GOP nominated the hugely popular war hero **Dwight D. Eisenhower** and chose as his running mate Richard Nixon, who had won a seat in the Senate in 1950 by red-baiting his opponent, Helen Gahagan Douglas, as "pink right down to her underwear."

Eisenhower and Nixon proved unbeatable. With a captivating grin and an unimpeachable record of public service, Eisenhower projected both personal warmth and the vigorous authority associated with military command. At the same time, Nixon kept public apprehensions at the boiling point. Accusing the Democrats of treason, he charged that the election of "Adlai the appeaser ... who got a Ph.D. from Dean Acheson's College of Cowardly Communist Containment" would bring "more Alger Hisses, more atomic spies."

Less than two weeks before the election, Eisenhower dramatically pledged to "go to Korea" to end the stalemated war. It worked: 62.7 percent of those eligible to vote (compared to just 51.5 percent in 1948) turned out in 1952 and gave the Republican ticket 55 percent of the ballots. Ike cracked the Solid South, carrying thirty-nine states (and 442 electoral votes). Enough Republicans rode his coattails to give the GOP narrow control of both houses of Congress.

The Downfall of Joseph McCarthy

Although he despised Joseph McCarthy, Eisenhower thought it beneath his dignity to "get into the gutter with that guy." He also understood the usefulness of anticommunism as a GOP campaign issue. So Ike allowed McCarthy to grab plenty of rope in hopes that the demagogue would hang himself. He did.

In 1954, McCarthy accused Army officials of harboring communist spies; the military retaliated by charging McCarthy with using his influence to get preferential treatment for an aide who had been drafted. The resulting Army–McCarthy hearings— the first Senate hearings broadcast on the new medium of television—brought McCarthy down. Millions witnessed McCarthy's boorish behavior on television. His contemptuous combativeness repelled viewers. He behaved like the bad guy in a TV western, observed novelist John Steinbeck: "He had a stubble of a beard, he leered, he sneered, he had a nasty laugh. He bullied and shouted. He looked evil." When the hearings ended in June, the spell of the inquisitor had been broken. That December, the Senate voted 67 to 22 to censure McCarthy for contemptuous behavior. This powerful rebuke demolished McCarthy as a political force. In 1957, he died from an alcohol-related illness, ignored by the media that had made him powerful. But the fears he exploited lingered. Congress annually funded HUAC into the 1960s, and local governments continued to require loyalty oaths from teachers. Just to be safe, the Cincinnati Reds renamed their baseball team the "Redlegs."

McCarthyism also remained a rallying call of conservatives disenchanted with the postwar consensus. Young conservatives like William F. Buckley, Jr., and groups like the Christian Anti-Communist Crusade continued to claim that domestic communism was a major subversive threat. The John Birch Society denounced Eisenhower as a conscious agent of communism and equated liberalism with treason. Although few saw the conspiratorial dangers that the John Birch Society did, Barry Goldwater, George Wallace, and Ronald Reagan, among others, used its anticommunist, antigovernment rhetoric to advantage. Stressing victory over communism, rather than its containment, the "new conservatives" (or radical Right, as their opponents called them) criticized the "creeping socialism" of Eisenhower, advocated a return to traditional moral standards, and condemned the liberal rulings of the Supreme Court.

"Modern Republicanism"

Most Americans in the 1950s did not venture that far right. They voted for a president who would steer a moderate course, and they got what they wanted. Rarely in history has a president better fit the national mood than "Ike." Exhausted by a quarter-century of upheaval, Americans craved stability and peace. And Eisenhower delivered. He gave a people weary of partisanship a sense of unity; he set a quieter, less angry national mood; and he inspired confidence and comforted people in an anxious, demanding age.

Born on October 14, 1890, in Denison, Texas, Eisenhower grew up in Abilene, Kansas, in a poor, religious family. More athletic than studious, he graduated from the U.S. Military Academy at West Point in 1915. In directing the Allied invasion of North Africa in 1942 and of western Europe in 1944, he proved to be a skillful war planner and diplomatic executive. His approach to the presidency reflected his wartime leadership style. He concentrated on major matters, delegated authority, and worked to reconcile contending factions. His restrained view of presidential authority and his low-key style, combined with frequent fishing and golfing vacations, led Democrats to scoff at Eisenhower as a leader who "reigned but did not rule."

The image of passivity masked a "hidden-hand" presidency that enabled him to work successfully behind the scenes. More pragmatic than ideological, the president wished to reduce taxes, contain inflation, and when necessary, check downturns by stimulating the economy. After the Democrats retook Congress in 1954, Eisenhower supported extending social-security benefits, raising the minimum wage, adding 4 million workers to those eligible for unemployment benefits, and providing federally financed public housing for low-income families. He also approved construction of the St. Lawrence Seaway, linking the Great Lakes and the Atlantic Ocean, and creation of the Department of Health, Education, and Welfare. In 1956, Eisenhower backed the largest and most expensive public-works program in American history: the Interstate Highway Act, authorizing construction of a 41,000-mile system of expressways that would soon snake across America, accelerating suburban growth, heightening dependence on imported oil, and contributing to urban decay and air pollution.

Republicans renominated Ike by acclamation in 1956, and voters gave him a landslide victory over Democrat Adlai Stevenson. With the GOP crowing, "Everything's booming but the guns," the president won by the greatest popular majority since FDR's victory in 1936.

The Cold War Continues

Eisenhower essentially maintained Truman's containment policy. Stalin's death in 1953 and Eisenhower's veiled threat to use nuclear weapons broke the Korean stalemate. The armistice signed in July 1953 set the boundary between North and South Korea once again at the thirty-eighth parallel. Some Americans claimed that communist aggression had been thwarted and containment vindicated; others condemned the truce as peace without honor.

Ike and Dulles   Eager to ease Cold War hostilities, Eisenhower first had to quiet the GOP right wing's clamor to roll back the Red tide. To do so, he chose as his secretary of state **John Foster Dulles,** a rigid, humorless Presbyterian who advocated a holy war against "atheistic communism," including "instant, massive retaliation" with nuclear weapons. Dulles called for "liberation" of the captive peoples of Eastern Europe and for unleashing Jiang Jieshi against communist China. Believing that the Soviet Union understood only force, Dulles insisted on the necessity of "brinksmanship," the art of never backing down in a crisis—even at the risk of war.

Such saber rattling pleased the Right, but Eisenhower preferred conciliation, partly to keep the cost of containment at a manageable level and partly because he feared a nuclear war—the Soviet Union had tested its own hydrogen bomb in 1953. Eisenhower refused to translate Dulles's rhetoric into action. Aware of the limits of American power, the United States did nothing to check the Soviet interventions that crushed uprisings in East Germany (1953) and Hungary (1956). There would be no rolling back Red power in Eastern Europe.

As multimegaton thermonuclear weapons replaced atomic bombs in U.S. and Soviet arsenals, and both nations developed intercontinental ballistic missiles

(ICBMs) to deliver such bombs, Eisenhower worked to reduce the probability of mutual annihilation. He proposed "atoms for peace," whereby both superpowers would contribute fissionable materials to a new UN agency for use in industrial projects. In the absence of a positive Soviet response, the government constructed an electronic air defense system to provide early warning of a missile attack.

Work also began on commercial nuclear plants in the mid-1950s, promising electricity "too cheap to meter." However, most money continued to go for military nuclear research. Radioactive fallout from atomic tests, especially the 1954 U.S. tests that spread strontium-90 over a wide area, heightened world concern about the nuclear-arms race. In 1955, Eisenhower and Soviet leaders met in Geneva for the first East–West conference since World War II. Discussions produced no concrete plan for arms control, but mutual talk of "peaceful coexistence" led reporters to hail the "spirit of Geneva." In March 1958, Moscow suspended atmospheric tests of nuclear weapons, and the United States followed suit.

But the Cold War continued. Dulles negotiated mutual-defense pacts with forty-three nations and created SEATO in 1954, extending collective security agreements between the United States and Australia, New Zealand, Pakistan, the Philippines, and Thailand. Rather than trying to match the communists "man for man, gun for gun," Eisenhower's "New Look" defense program reduced conventional forces and emphasized nuclear weapons. Promising "more bang for the buck," it succeeded in reducing the defense budget yet spurred the Soviets to seek "more rubble for the ruble" by enlarging their nuclear stockpile.

Meanwhile, the focus of the Cold War shifted from Europe to the Third World, the largely nonwhite developing nations. There, the two superpowers waged war by proxy, using local guerrillas and military juntas. There, too, the CIA fought covert wars against those thought to imperil American interests.

CIA Covert Actions

Established in 1947 to conduct foreign intelligence gathering, the CIA soon began to carry out undercover operations to topple regimes friendly to communism. By 1957, half its personnel and 80 percent of its budget were devoted to "covert action." To woo influential foreign thinkers away from communism, the CIA also sponsored intellectual conferences and jazz concerts. It bankrolled anticommunist cultural events, subsidized magazines to publish articles supporting the United States, and recruited college students and businessmen traveling abroad as "fronts" in clandestine CIA activities.

In 1953, the CIA orchestrated a coup to overthrow the government of Iran. Fearing that the prime minister, who had nationalized the oil fields, might open oil-rich Iran to the Soviets, the CIA replaced him with the pro-American Shah Reza Pahlavi. The United States gained a loyal ally on the Soviet border, and Western oil companies prospered when the Shah made low-priced oil available to them. But Iranian hatred of America took root—a hostility that would haunt the United States into the twenty-first century.

The CIA also intervened in Philippine elections in 1953 to ensure a pro-American government. The following year, a CIA-supported band of mercenaries in Guatemala overthrew the elected communist-influenced regime, which had seized land from the American-owned United Fruit Company. The new pro-American government restored United Fruit's properties and trampled political opposition.

"Our traditional ideas of international sportsmanship," Eisenhower noted privately in 1955, "are scarcely applicable in the morass in which the world now flounders."

Troubles in the   In Indochina, viewed as a Cold War battleground, Eisenhower
Third World   first followed Truman's course of providing France with large-
                          scale military assistance to fight Vietnamese insurgents. When
that failed, he pinned his hopes on the CIA-installed President Ngo Dinh Diem to keep South Vietnam an independent anticommunist nation tied to the United States. That policy, too, appeared to be faltering as he left office (to be further discussed in Chapter 28).

Eisenhower faced his greatest crisis, however, in the Middle East. In 1954, Gamal Abdel Nasser came to power in Egypt, determined to modernize his nation. To woo him, the United States offered financing for a dam at Aswan to harness the Nile River. But when Nasser purchased arms from Czechoslovakia, John Foster Dulles canceled the loan. Nasser retaliated by nationalizing the British-controlled Suez Canal.

Viewing the canal as the lifeline of its empire, Britain, in alliance with France, which feared Arab nationalism in their Algerian colony, and with Israel, which feared the Egyptian arms buildup, attacked Egypt in October 1956. Angered that America's three closest allies had not consulted him, and fearful that such military action would drive the Arab world and its precious oil to the Russians, Eisenhower forced his allies to withdraw their troops.

The **Suez crisis** had major consequences. It swelled Third World anti-Western sentiment, and the United States replaced Britain and France as the protector of Western interests in the Middle East. Determined to guarantee the flow of oil to the West, the president announced the **Eisenhower Doctrine** in 1957—a proclamation that the United States would send military aid and, if necessary, troops to any Middle Eastern nation threatened by "Communist aggression."

Such interventions intensified anti-American feelings in Third World nations. Angry crowds in Peru and Venezuela spat at Vice President Nixon and stoned his car in 1958. In 1959, Fidel Castro overturned a dictatorial regime in Cuba and confiscated American properties without compensation. He then established close economic and military ties with the Soviet Union. If the United States dared intervene, Soviet premier Nikita Khrushchev warned, he would defend Cuba with nuclear weapons. "The Monroe Doctrine has outlived its time," Khrushchev said.

A tougher blow came on May 1, 1960, two weeks before a scheduled summit conference between Eisenhower and Khrushchev, when Soviet air defenses shot down a U.S. spy plane far inside their border. Khrushchev displayed the captured CIA pilot and the photos taken of Soviet missile sites. Eisenhower refused to apologize, and the summit collapsed.

The Eisenhower   Just before leaving office, Eisenhower offered Americans a
Legacy   farewell and a warning. The demands of national security,
                          he stated, had produced the "conjunction of an immense military establishment and a large arms industry." Swollen defense budgets had yoked American economic health to military expenditures, and military contracts had become the staff of life for research scholars, politicians, and America's largest corporations. This combination of interests, Eisenhower believed, exerted enormous

leverage and threatened the traditional subordination of the military in American life. "We must guard against the acquisition of unwarranted influence ... by the **military-industrial complex**. The potential for the disastrous rise of misplaced power exists and will persist."

The president concluded that he had avoided war but that lasting peace was not in sight. Most scholars agreed. Eisenhower ended the Korean War, avoided direct intervention in Vietnam, initiated relaxing tensions with the Soviet Union, and suspended atmospheric nuclear testing. At the same time, he presided over an accelerating nuclear-arms race and a Cold War that encircled the globe. His domestic record was mixed as well. His acceptance of some progressive social-welfare measures angered the Republican Right, and liberal Democrats faulted his passivity toward McCarthyism. Still, Ike had given the majority of Americans what they most wanted—prosperity, reassurance, and a breathing spell in which to relish the comforts of life.

CHRONOLOGY
1945–1960

1946	George Kennan's "long telegram."
	Winston Churchill's "iron curtain" speech.
	Republicans win control of Congress.
1947	Truman Doctrine.
	Federal Employee Loyalty Program.
	Taft-Hartley Act.
	National Security Act.
	HUAC holds hearings on Hollywood.
1948	State of Israel founded.
	Berlin airlift.
	Congress approves Marshall Plan to aid Europe.
	Communist leaders put on trial under the Smith Act.
	Truman elected president.
1949	North Atlantic Treaty Organization (NATO) established.
	East and West Germany founded as separate nations.
	Communist victory in China; People's Republic of China established.
	Soviet Union detonates an atomic bomb.
1950	Soviet spy ring at Los Alamos uncovered.
	Joseph McCarthy launches anticommunist crusade.
	Korean War begins.
	McCarran Internal Security Act.
	Truman accepts NSC-68.

1951	Julius and Ethel Rosenberg convicted of espionage.
1952	First hydrogen bomb exploded.
	Dwight D. Eisenhower elected president.
1953	Korean War truce signed.
1954	Army-McCarthy hearings.
1956	Suez crisis.
	Eisenhower reelected.
1957	Eisenhower Doctrine announced.
1959	Fidel Castro comes to power in Cuba.
1960	U-2 incident.

CONCLUSION

After nearly two decades of depression and war, the end of World War II meant the beginning of a new era of hope for most Americans. At the same time, an assertive United States, eager to protect and expand its influence and power in the world, sought to contain a Soviet Union obsessed with its own security and self-interest. Stalin's aggressive posture toward Eastern Europe and the Persian Gulf was met by an American policy of containment, in whose name the United States aided Greece and Turkey, established the Marshall Plan, airlifted supplies into Berlin for a year, approved the creation of the Federal Republic of Germany (West Germany), established NATO, implemented NSC-68, financed France's war in Vietnam, and went to war in Korea. The resulting stalemate would last for four decades, define American politics and society, transform the U.S. economy, and condition the thinking of a generation.

The Cold War obsession with communism, as well as postwar prosperity, weakened the appeal of liberal reform. In a political climate far more conservative than that of the 1930s, New Deal measures remained in place, but Truman's Fair Deal to assist the disadvantaged with new initiatives in education, health insurance, and civil rights failed. Anticommunist hysteria squashed the Left and narrowed the range of politically acceptable ideas. Most importantly, Truman's actions at home and abroad fed America's fear of communism, which grew with the president's responses to the Soviet detonation of an atomic bomb, the fall of China to the communists, the invasion of South Korea, and Truman's own loyalty probe to root out subversive government workers. Witch-hunts for communism in American life and the discovery of a Soviet atomic spy ring added to the paranoia. In this atmosphere, Truman's actions encouraged others to seek scapegoats for American failures abroad and legitimated conservative accusations that equated dissent with disloyalty.

As the Cold War continued throughout the 1950s, continuity would also mark the domestic and foreign policies of Truman's successor. Dwight Eisenhower, in the main, pursued a centrist course in domestic affairs. While tilting to the right in favoring private corporations, the Eisenhower administration left New Deal reforms in place, expanded existing social-welfare benefits, and employed Keynesian deficit spending to curtail economic recessions. The president made no effort to hamper labor unionization and proposed construction of a vast interstate highway system.

Eisenhower also followed Truman in his determination to contain communism abroad, while putting new emphasis on the need to avoid nuclear war and to fight communism in the Third World. Gaining short-term victories in local conflicts, often by clandestine means, Ike and Secretary of State Dulles largely ignored the nationalist yearnings and socioeconomic deprivations of local peoples and increasingly allied the United States with reactionary, repressive regimes.

27

AMERICA AT MIDCENTURY, 1945–1961

CHAPTER OUTLINE

- Postwar Jitters • The Affluent Society • Prosperity and the Suburbs
- The Other America • The Civil Rights Movement • Seeds of Disquiet

---

POSTWAR JITTERS

The immediate concerns of most Americans following V-J Day centered on "bringing the boys home" and avoiding a return to the Great Depression. The steep decline in defense spending and factory jobs caused many to fear demobilization and the reconversion to a peacetime economy. Strife between labor and management, as well as inflation and shortages, intensified the anxiety. But by 1947, consumer spending and the Cold War had begun to spur a quarter-century of economic growth and prosperity, the longest such period in American history.

THE AFFLUENT SOCIETY

In 1958, the economist John Kenneth Galbraith published *The Affluent Society*, a study of postwar America whose title reflected the broad-based prosperity that made the 1950s seem the fulfillment of the American Dream. By the end of the decade, about 60 percent of American families owned homes; 75 percent, cars; and 87 percent, at least one TV. The economy perfectly matched Eisenhower's pursuit of moderation. Government spending, a huge upsurge in productivity, and steadily increasing consumer demand pushed the gross national product (GNP) up 50 percent. The United States achieved the world's highest living standard ever. By 1960, the average worker's income, adjusted for inflation, was 35 percent higher than in 1945. With just 6 percent of the world's population, the United States produced and consumed nearly half of everything made and sold on Earth.

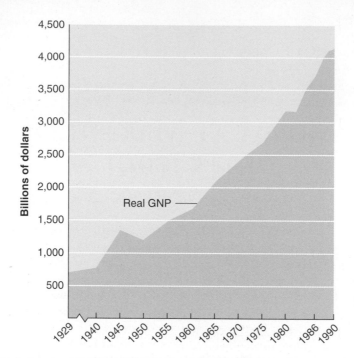

FIGURE 27.1   Gross National Product, 1929–1990

Following World War II, the United States achieved the highest living standard in world history. Between 1950 and 1970, the real GNP, which factors out inflation and reveals the actual amount of goods and services produced, steadily increased. However, in 1972, 1974–1975, 1980, and 1982, the real GNP declined.

Sources: National Agricultural Statistics Service, U.S. Department of Agriculture; U.S. Bureau of the Census, *Statistical Abstract of the United States, 1991, 1992, 2001* (Washington, D.C.).
Note: Data shown in 1982 dollars.

The New Industrial Society

Federal spending constituted a major source of economic growth, nearly doubling in the 1950s to $180 billion. Just 1 percent of the GNP in 1929, federal expenditures reached 17 percent by the mid-1950s. These funds built roads and airports, financed home mortgages, supported farm prices, and provided stipends for education. More than half the federal budget—10 percent of the GNP—went to defense spending. These expenditures made the federal government the nation's main financier of scientific and technological research and development (R&D).

For the West, especially, it was as if World War II never ended. Politicians from both parties in California sought contracts for Lockheed, those from Texas labored for General Dynamics, and those from Washington State kept defense funds flowing to Boeing. By the late 1950s, California alone received half the space budget and a quarter of all major military contracts. By then, Denver had the largest number of federal employees outside Washington, DC; Albuquerque boasted more Ph.D. degrees per capita than any other U.S. city; and more than a third of workers in Los Angeles depended on defense industries. Utah, once the Mormon dream of an agricultural utopia, received the nation's highest per capita expenditures on space and defense research. Government spending transformed the mythic West of rugged individualists into a West of bureaucrats, defense contractors, and scientists dependent on federal funds.

Science became a ward of the state, and government funding and control transformed both the U.S. military and industry. Financed by the Atomic Energy Commission (AEC) and utilizing navy scientists, the nation's first nuclear-power plant came on line in 1957. The chemical industry continued its wartime growth. As pesticides contaminated ground water supplies and plastics reduced landfill space, Americans— unaware of the hidden perils—marveled at vegetables covered with Saran Wrap and delighted in their Dacron suits, Acrilan socks, and Teflon-coated pans.

Electricity consumption tripled in the 1950s, and electronics became the fifth-largest American industry, as factories automated and consumers purchased all manner of electric appliances. Domestic oil production and foreign imports rose steeply, and by 1960 oil had replaced coal as the nation's main energy source. Hardly anyone paid attention when a physicist warned in 1953 that "adding 6 billion tons of carbon dioxide to the atmosphere each year is warming up the Earth."

Plentiful, cheap gasoline fed the growth of the automobile and aircraft industries. The nation's third-largest industry in the 1950s, aerospace depended on defense spending and on federally funded research. The automobile industry, still the nation's industrial titan, also utilized technological R&D. Between 1945 and 1960, the industry halved the number of hours and workers required to produce a car.

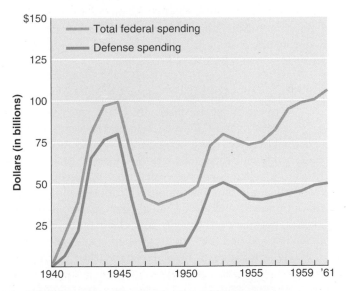

FIGURE 27.2 National Defense Spending, 1941–1960

In 1950, the defense budget was $13 billion, less than a third of the total federal outlay. In 1961, defense spending reached $47 billion, fully half of the federal budget and almost 10 percent of the gross national product.

Source: Adapted from U.S. Bureau of the Census, Current Censuses, 1930–1970 (Washington, D.C.: U.S. Government Printing Office).

The Age of Computers   The computer was key to technological revolution. To decipher secret Axis codes, International Business Machines (IBM) in 1944 produced the Mark I calculator, a cumbersome device with five hundred miles of wiring. In late 1945, to improve artillery accuracy, the military devised ENIAC, the first electronic computer. Still unwieldy, with eighteen thousand vacuum tubes, ENIAC could perform five thousand calculations per second. Next came the development of operating instructions, or programs, that could be stored inside the computer's memory; the substitution of printed circuits for wires; and in 1948, at Bell Labs, the invention of tiny solid-state transistors that ended reliance on radio tubes.

Sales of electronic computers to industry rose from twenty in 1954 to more than a thousand in 1957 and more than two thousand in 1960. Major manufacturers used them to monitor production lines, track inventory, and ensure quality control. In government, computers were as indispensable to Pentagon strategists playing war games as they were to the Census Bureau and the Internal Revenue Service. By the mid-1960s, more than thirty thousand mainframe computers would be used by banks, hospitals, and universities. Further developments led to the first integrated circuits and to what would ultimately become the Internet.

The development of the high-technology complex known as Silicon Valley began in 1951 as Stanford University utilized its science and engineering faculties to design and produce products for the Fairchild Semiconductor and Hewlett-Packard companies. This relationship between universities and corporations became a model followed by other high-tech firms. Soon apricot and cherry orchards throughout the Santa Clara Valley gave way to industrial parks filled with computer firms and pharmaceutical laboratories. Similar developments would follow the military-fueled research complexes along Boston's Route 128, near Austin, Texas, and in North Carolina's Research Triangle.

The Costs of Bigness   Rapid technological advances accelerated the growth and power of big business. In 1950, twenty-two U.S. firms had assets of more than $1 billion; ten years later more than fifty did. By then, one-half of 1 percent of all companies earned more than half the total corporate income in the United States. The wealthiest became oligopolies, swallowing up weak competitors. Three television networks monopolized the nation's airwaves; three automobile and three aluminum companies produced more than 90 percent of America's cars and aluminum; and a handful of firms controlled the lion's share of assets and sales in steel, petroleum, chemicals, and electrical machinery. Corporations acquired overseas facilities to become "multinational" enterprises and formed "conglomerates" by merging companies in unrelated industries: International Telephone and Telegraph (ITT) branched out from communications into car rental, home building, motel chains, insurance, and more. Growth and consolidation meant greater bureaucratization. "Executives" replaced "capitalists." Success required conformity not creativity, teamwork not individuality. According to sociologist David Riesman's *The Lonely Crowd* (1950), the new "company people" were "other-directed," eager to follow the cues from their peers and not think innovatively or act independently. In the old nursery rhyme "This Little Pig Went to Market," Riesman noted, each pig went his own way. "Today, however, all little pigs go to market; none stay home; all have roast beef, if any do; and all say 'we-we.' "

Production Line at Douglas Aircraft Company *The Cold War stimulated an enormous boom in defense spending. By midcentury, more than half the federal budget, about 10 percent of the GNP, went to defense contractors like Douglas Aircraft, which helped the economy of the South and the West to flourish.*

Changes in American agriculture paralleled those in industry. Farming grew increasingly scientific and mechanized. Technology halved the work hours necessary to grow crops between 1945 and 1960, causing many farm families to migrate to cities. In 1956 alone, one-eleventh of the farm population left the land. Meanwhile, heavily capitalized farm businesses, running "factories in the field," prospered by using more machines and chemicals.

Until the publication of Rachel Carson's *Silent Spring* in 1962, few Americans understood the extent to which fertilizers, herbicides, and pesticides poisoned the environment. Carson, a former researcher for the Fish and Wildlife Service, dramatized the problems caused by use of the insecticide DDT and its spread through the food chain. Her depiction of a "silent spring" caused by the death of songbirds from DDT toxicity led many states to ban its use. The federal government followed suit. But the incentives for cultivating more land, and more marginal land, led to further ravages.

Blue-Collar Blues   Consolidation also transformed the labor movement. In 1955, the merger of the AFL and CIO brought 85 percent of union members into a single federation. Although labor leadership promised aggressive unionism, organized labor fell victim to its success

ENIAC, the Electronic Numerical Integrator and Computer *The co-conceiver and designer of ENIAC, Dr. John W. Mauchly of the University of Pennsylvania's School of Electrical Engineering, publicly unveiled the first general-purpose electronic computer in February 1946.*

at the bargaining table. Higher wages, shorter workweeks, paid vacations, health-care coverage, and automatic wage hikes tied to the cost of living led most workers to view themselves as middle class rather than the proletariat.

Further sapping labor militancy, by 1956, for the first time in U.S. history, white-collar employees outnumbered blue-collar workers. The office with hundreds of little cubicles superseded the assembly line as the dominant image of the American work-place. Employees in ties or skirts replaced those in blue-collar work shirts. Although most service jobs were as routinized as any factory job, few unions sought to woo white-collar workers. The percentage of the unionized labor force dropped from a high of 36 percent in 1953 to 31 percent in 1960, and kept falling.

Prosperity and the Suburbs

As real income (adjusted for inflation) rose, Americans spent less of their income on necessities and more on powered lawnmowers and air conditioners. They heaped their shopping carts with frozen, dehydrated, and fortified foods. When they lacked cash, they borrowed. In 1950, Diner's Club issued the first credit card; American

Express followed in 1958. Installment buying, home mortgages, and auto loans tripled Americans' private indebtedness in the 1950s. In its effort to convince people to buy what they did not need, business spent more on advertising than the nation did on public schools.

Suburban America

Urged to "Buy Now, Pay Later," Americans purchased 58 million new cars during the 1950s. Manufacturers enticed people to trade in and up by offering flashier models, two-tone color, tail fins, and extra-powerful engines—like Pontiac's 1955 "Sensational Strato-Streak V-8," which could go more than twice as fast as any speed limit. Seat belts remained an unadvertised extra-cost option. The consequences were increases in highway deaths, air pollution, oil consumption, and "autosclerosis"—clogged urban arteries.

Government policy as well as "auto mania" spurred white Americans' exodus to the suburbs. Federal spending on highways skyrocketed from $79 million in 1946 to $2.6 billion in 1960, putting once-remote areas within "commuting distance" for city workers. The income-tax code stimulated home sales by allowing deductions for home-mortgage interest payments and for property taxes. The Federal Housing Administration (FHA) and Veterans Administration (VA) offered low-interest loans; and both continued to deny loans to blacks who sought to buy homes in white neighborhoods. In 1960, suburbia was 98 percent white.

In 1947, some thirty miles from midtown Manhattan on Long Island, Alfred and William Levitt used the mass-production construction techniques they perfected during the war to construct standardized 720-square-foot houses as quickly as possible. All 17,000 looked alike. Deeds to the property prohibited picket fences, mandated regular lawn mowing, and specified when the wash could be hung to

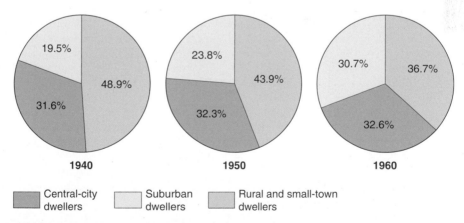

FIGURE 27.3   Urban, Suburban, and Rural Americans, 1940–1960

In the fifteen years following World War II, more than 40 million Americans migrated to the suburbs, where, as one father put it, "a kid could grow up with grass stains on his pants." Over the same period, fourteen of the fifteen largest U.S. cities lost population.

Source: Adapted from U.S. Bureau of the Census, Current Censuses, 1930–1970 (Washington, DC: U.S. Government Printing Office).

TECHNOLOGY & CULTURE

The Interstate Highway System

As a young captain after World War I, Dwight Eisenhower had been given the task of accompanying a convoy of army trucks across the country. The woefully inadequate state of the roads for military transport dismayed him then as much as he would later be impressed by the German autobahns that allowed Hitler to deploy troops around Germany with incredible speed. Not surprisingly, when he became president, he sought a transportation system that would facilitate the rapid movement of the military, as well as increase road safety and aid commerce. The arms race with the Soviet Union, moreover, necessitated a network of highways for evacuating cities in case of a nuclear attack—a change, according to the *Bulletin of the Atomic Scientists*, from "Duck and Cover" to "Run Like Hell."

In 1954, Eisenhower set up a high-powered commission to recommend a highway program that would cost as much as a war. He appointed an army general to head it to emphasize the connection between highways, national defense, and the concerns Americans had about their security. The next year, with the entire federal budget at $71 billion, Eisenhower asked Congress for a $40 billion, forty-one-thousand-mile construction project, to be financed by government bonds. Conservative Republicans, fearful of increasing the federal debt, balked. So Ike switched to a financing plan based on new gasoline, tire, bus, and trucking taxes. The federal government would use the taxes to pay 90 percent of the construction costs in any state willing to come up with the other 10 percent.

Millions of suburbanites commuting to central cities loved the idea of new multi-lane highways. So did motorists dreaming of summer travel; the powerful coalition of automobile manufacturers, oil companies, asphalt firms, and truckers, who stood to benefit financially the most; and the many special interests in virtually every congressional district, including real-estate developers, shopping mall entrepreneurs, engineers, and construction industries. Indeed, the interstate highway bill promised something to almost everybody except the inner-city poor. It sailed through Congress in 1956, winning by voice vote in the House and by an 89 to 1 margin in the Senate.

The largest and most expensive public-works scheme in American history, the interstate highway system was designed and built as a single project for the entire country, unlike the haphazard development of the canal and railroad networks. It required taking more land by eminent domain than had been taken in the entire history of road building in the United States. Expected increases in highway use, speed of travel, and weight of loads necessitated drastic changes in road engineering and materials. Utilizing the technological advances that had produced high-quality concrete and asphalt, diesel-powered roadbed graders, reinforced

dry in the backyard. All the town streets curved at the same angle. A tree was planted every twenty-eight feet. The Levitts then built a second, larger Levittown in Bucks County, Pennsylvania, and a third in Willingboro, New Jersey.

Other contractors followed suit, and 85 percent of the 13 million new homes built in the 1950s were in the suburbs. In the greatest internal migration in the nation's history, some 20 million Americans moved to the suburbs in the steel, and safely controlled explosives, construction crews built superhighways with standardized twelve-foot-wide lanes, ten-foot shoulders, and median strips of at least thirty-six feet in rural areas. Terrain in which a dirt trail was difficult to blaze was laced with cloverleaf intersections and some sixteen thousand exits and entrances. More than fifty thousand bridges, tunnels, and overpasses traversed swamps, rivers, and mountains. Road curves were banked for speeds of seventy miles per hour, with grades no greater than 3 percent and minimum sight distances of six hundred feet. The massive amounts of concrete poured, Ike later boasted, could have made "six sidewalks to the moon" or sixty Panama Canals.

The network of four-to-eight-lane roads linking cities and suburbs made it possible to drive from New York to San Francisco without encountering a stoplight. It more than fulfilled the initial hopes of most of its backers, enormously speeding the movement of goods and people across the country, invigorating the tourist industry, providing steady work for construction firms, enriching those who lived near the interstates and sold their lands to developers, and hastening suburban development.

The freeways that helped unify Americans by increasing the accessibility of once-distant regions also helped homogenize the nation with interchangeable shopping malls, motels, and fast-food chains. In 1955, Ray Kroc, who supplied the Multimixers for milk shakes to the original McDonald's drive-in in San Bernardino, California, began to franchise similar family restaurants beside highways, each serving the same standardized foods under the instantly recognizable logo of the golden arches. By century's end, McDonald's would be the world's largest private real-estate enterprise, as well as the largest food provider, serving more than 40 million meals daily in a hundred countries.

Moreover, the expressways boosted the interstate trucking business and hastened the decline of the nation's railroad lines and urban mass-transportation systems. The highways built to speed commuters into the central cities—"white men's roads through black men's bedrooms," said the National Urban League—often bulldozed minority neighborhoods out of existence or served as barriers between black and white neighborhoods. The beltways that lured increasingly more residents and businesses to suburbia eroded city tax bases, which in turn accelerated urban decay, triggering the urban crisis that then furthered suburban sprawl. The interstates had locked the United States into an ever-increasing reliance on cars and trucks, drastically increasing air pollution and American dependence on a constant supply of cheap and plentiful gasoline.

Questions for Analysis

1. *Why did Congress authorize the construction of an interstate highway system?*

2. *Describe some of the unintended consequences of the new highway system.*

decade—making the suburban population equal to that of the central cities. Many critics followed Lewis Mumford in decrying the "multitude of uniform, unidentifiable houses, lined up inflexibly, at uniform distances, on uniform roads, in a treeless, communal wasteland, inhabited by people of the same class, the same income, the same age group." Yet suburbia remained the American dream for most families longing for their own home, good schools, safe streets, and neighbors like themselves.

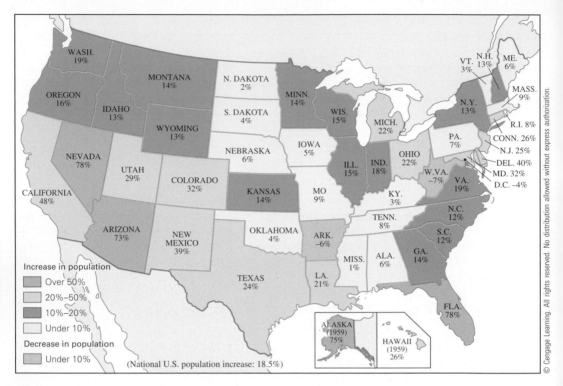

MAP 27.1   The Growth of the Sunbelt, 1950–1960

The years after the Second World War saw a continuation of the migration of Americans to the Sunbelt states of the Southwest and the West Coast.

Americans also moved South and West, into the Sunbelt, lured by job opportunities, the climate, and the pace of life. California, where the population went from 9 to 19 million between 1945 and 1964, supplanted New York as the most populous state. Los Angeles boasted the highest per capita ownership of private homes and cars of any city. Initially designed to lure shoppers downtown, the highway system instead had become the road to a home in the suburbs.

Industry, too, headed south and west, drawn by low taxes, low energy costs, and anti-union right-to-work laws. Senior citizens headed to the easier climate. Both brought a conservative outlook. By 1980, the population of the **Sunbelt,** which stretched from the old Confederacy across Texas to southern California, exceeded that of the North and East. The political power of the Republican Party rose accordingly.

Consensus and Conservatism   Not everyone embraced the conformity of 1950s consumer culture. Intellectuals found an audience for their attack on "organization men" bent on getting ahead by going along and on "status seekers" pursuing external rewards to compensate for inner insecurities. Others, like Riesman, took aim at "other-directed" conformists and "an America of mass housing, mass markets, massive corporations, massive government, mass media, and massive boredom." Riesman described modern Americans as shaped by the opinions of their peers rather than by their own consciences. Some took aim at the consumerist middle class: "all items in a national supermarket—categorized, processed, labeled, priced, and readied for merchandising."

This criticism oversimplified reality. It ignored ethnic and class diversity, the acquisitiveness and conformity of earlier generations, and the currents of dissent swirling beneath the surface. But it rightly spotlighted the elevation of comfort over challenge, and of private pleasures over public affairs. It was, in the main, a time of political passivity and preoccupation with personal gain.

Togetherness, the Baby Boom, and Domesticity   After years of separation and loss, Americans yearned for emotional security as well as material success, and looked to family for stability in an insecure world. In 1954, *McCall's* magazine coined the term *togetherness* to celebrate the "ideal" couple: the man and woman who centered their lives on home and children. Confident in continued economic prosperity, Americans in the 1950s tended to marry young, to have babies quickly, and to have more of them. The fertility rate (the number of births per thousand women), eighty in 1940, peaked at 123 in 1957, when an American baby was born every seven seconds. That year, the number of children per family had risen to 3.2, from 2.4 in 1945, and one-third of the population was under the age of 15.

New antibiotics subdued diphtheria and whooping cough, streptomycin drastically reduced tuberculosis, and the Salk and Sabin vaccines ended the dread of polio. The decline in childhood mortality helped raise American life expectancy from 65.9 years in 1945 to 70.9 years in 1970. Coupled with the "baby boom," it led to a 19 percent population spurt during the 1950s—a larger jump than in any previous decade.

The sheer size of the **baby-boom generation** (the 76 million Americans born between 1946 and 1964) ensured its impact and historical importance. Its needs and expectations at each stage of life would be as contorting as the digestion of a pig by a boa constrictor. First came the bulge in baby carriages; in the 1950s, school construction boomed; and in the 1960s, college enrollments soared. Then in the 1970s—as the baby boomers had their own families—home construction peaked. The 1980s and 1990s brought a surge in retirement investments, and the twenty-first century a preoccupation with health matters. In the 1950s, the baby boom also made child rearing a foremost concern, reinforcing the idea that women's place was in the home. No one did more to emphasize the necessity for women to be full-time mothers than **Dr. Benjamin Spock.** Only the Bible outsold his *Common Sense Book of Baby and Child Care* (1946) in the 1950s. Spock urged mothers not to work outside the home in order to create an atmosphere of warmth and intimacy for their children. Crying babies were to be comforted; breast-feeding came back into vogue.

The postwar emphasis on family togetherness renewed the ideal of domesticity in defining—and constraining—the role of women. Popular culture glorified marriage and parenthood, emphasizing a woman's role as a helpmate to her husband

and a full-time mother to her children. Television mostly pictured women as at-home mothers, and Hollywood perpetuated the stereotype of career women as neurotic.

Education reinforced these notions. Girls were encouraged to study typing and cooking and cautioned not to "miss the boat" of marriage by pursuing higher education. "Men are not interested in college degrees but in the warmth and humanness of the girls they marry," stressed a textbook on the family. More men than women went to college in the 1950s, and only one-third of college women completed a degree.

Profound changes, however, were under way. By 1952, 2 million more women worked outside the home than had during the war; and by 1960, twice as many did as in 1940. In 1960, one-third of the labor force was female, and one out of three married women worked outside the home. Of all women workers that year, 60 percent were married, while 40 percent had school-age children.

Most women worked to augment family income, not to challenge stereotypes. Most held so-called "pink-collar" jobs in the service industry—secretary or clerk, waitress or hairdresser. Their median wage was less than half that for men. Yet many women, as during World War II, developed a heightened sense of expectations and empowerment as a result of employment. Transmitted to their daughters, their experience would fuel a feminist resurgence in the late 1960s.

Religion and Education   "Today in the U.S.," *Time* claimed in 1954, "the Christian faith is back in the center of things." Evangelist **Billy Graham,** Roman Catholic Bishop Fulton J. Sheen, and Protestant minister Norman Vincent Peale all had syndicated newspaper columns, best-selling books, and radio and television programs. Each promoted a potent mixture of religious salvation and aggressive anticommunism. Hollywood religious extravaganzas were the biggest box-office hits of the 1950s, while television pronounced that "the family that prays together stays together." Congress added "under God" to the Pledge of Allegiance and required "IN GOD WE TRUST" to be put on all U.S. currency. While church membership doubled to 114 million between 1945 and 1960, the *intensity* of faith diminished for some, as mainstream churches downplayed sin and evil and preached Americanism and fellowship. Yet millions of others, alienated by the rapidity of social change and appalled at the secular hedonism of modern life, embraced evangelical fundamentalism, becoming "born again" Christians—a trend that would swell in the coming decades.

Similarly, education swelled in the 1950s yet seemed to many to be less rigorous than in earlier decades. The baby boom inflated primary school enrollment by 10 million (compared with 1 million in the 1940s). California opened a new school every week throughout the decade and still faced a classroom shortage. The proportion of college-age Americans in higher education climbed from 15 percent in 1940 to more than 40 percent by the early 1960s. "Progressive" educators promoted sociability and self-expression over science and history. The "well-rounded" student became more prized than the highly skilled or intelligent student. Surveys of college students found them conservative, conformist, and careerist—a "silent generation" seeking security and comfort.

Few university faculty challenged the reigning thought of the day or addressed the problems of those in need. Historians downplayed class conflicts and highlighted the pragmatism of most Americans. Consensus—the widely shared agreement on most matters of importance, especially respect for private property and equal opportunity—was frequently depicted as central to America's history and greatness.

Postwar Culture   American culture reflected both the spirit of prosperity and Cold War anxiety. Enjoying more leisure time and fatter paychecks, Americans spent one-seventh of the GNP on entertainment. Spectator sports boomed, new symphony halls opened, and book sales doubled.

With the opening of a major exhibit of abstract expressionists by the Museum of Modern Art in 1951, New York replaced Paris as the capital of the art world. Like the abstract canvases of Jackson Pollock and the cool jazz of trumpeter Miles Davis, introspection and improvisation characterized the major novels of the era. Popular writers, like J.D. Salinger and John Updike, presented characters vaguely dissatisfied with jobs and home, longing for a more vital and authentic existence but incapable of decisive action. Southern, African American, and Jewish American writers turned out the decade's most vital fiction. William Faulkner continued his dense saga of Yoknapatawpha County, Mississippi, while Eudora Welty evoked southern small-town life in *The Ponder Heart* (1954). The black experience found memorable expression in James Baldwin's *Go Tell It on the Mountain* (1953) and Ralph Ellison's *Invisible Man* (1951). Bernard Malamud's *The Assistant* (1957) explored the Jewish immigrant world, and Philip Roth's *Goodbye Columbus* (1959) dissected the very different world of upwardly mobile Jews.

Hollywood reflected the diminished interest in political issues, churning out westerns, musicals, and costume spectacles. Most films about contemporary life portrayed Americans as one happy white, middle-class family. Minorities and the poor remained invisible, and women appeared largely as "dumb blondes" or cute helpmates. As TV viewing soared, movie attendance dropped 50 percent, and a fifth of the nation's theaters became bowling alleys or supermarkets by 1960.

The Television Culture   No cultural medium ever grew so huge so quickly as television. In 1946, one in 18,000 households had a TV set; by 1960, nine of ten households had at least one TV, and more Americans had televisions than had bathrooms.

Business capitalized on the phenomenon. The three main radio networks—ABC, CBS, and NBC—gobbled up virtually every TV station in the country and, just as in radio, they profited by selling time to advertisers who wanted to reach the largest possible audiences. *TV Guide* soon outsold all other periodicals. First marketed in 1954, the TV dinner altered the nation's eating habits. When Walt Disney produced a show on Davy Crockett in 1955, stores could not keep up with the massive demand for "King of the Wild Frontier" coonskin caps. TV could sell anything.

Initially, TV showcased talent and creativity. Opera performances appeared in prime time, as did sophisticated dramas and political documentaries. Early situation comedies featured ethnic working-class families. But as the price of TV sets came down and the chill of McCarthyism spread, the networks' caution and appetite for

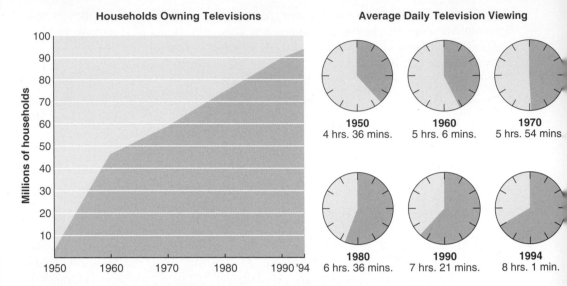

FIGURE 27.4   The Television Revolution, 1950–1994

As televisions became commonplace in the 1950s, TV viewing altered the nature of American culture and politics.

a mass audience transformed TV into a celebration of conformity and consumerism. Controversy went off the air. Most situation comedies portrayed perfectly coiffed moms who loved to vacuum in high heels, frisky yet obedient kids, and all-knowing dads. Even Lucille Ball and Desi Arnaz in *I Love Lucy*—which no network initially wanted because its all-American redhead was married to a Cuban— had a baby and left New York for suburbia.

Decrying TV's mediocrity in 1961, the head of the Federal Communications Commission called it "a vast wasteland." A steady parade of soaps, unsophisticated comedies, and violent westerns led others to call TV the "idiot box."

Measuring television's impact is difficult. Different people read the "texts" of TV (or of movies or books) in their own way and so receive their own messages from the medium. While TV bound some to the status quo, it raised expectations of others. It functioned both as a conservator and as a spur to change. In the main, however, television reflected existing values and institutions. It stimulated the desire to be included in American society, not to transform it. It spawned mass fads for Barbie dolls and hula hoops and spread the message of consumerism. It reinforced gender and racial stereotypes, rarely showing African Americans and Latinos—except in servile roles or prison scenes. It extolled male violence in fighting evil; it portrayed women as either zany madcaps or self-effacing moms.

Television also changed political life. Politicians could effectively appeal to the voters over the heads of party leaders, and appearance mattered more than content. At least 20 million watched Senator Joseph McCarthy bully and demean witnesses. Richard Nixon reached 58 million and saved his political career with his appeal in the "Checkers" speech, answering charges that he had received gifts and money from California businessmen. Eisenhower's pioneering use of brief "spot advertisements" clinched his smashing presidential victories. And in 1960, John F. Kennedy's "telegenic" image played a major role in his winning the presidency.

Overall, television helped produce a more national, homogenized culture, diminishing provincialism and regional differences. It vastly increased the cost of political campaigning while decreasing the content level of political discussion. And its overwhelming portrayal of a contented citizenry reinforced complacency and hid the reality of "the other America."

THE OTHER AMERICA

"I am an invisible man," declared the African American narrator of Ralph Ellison's *Invisible Man*; "I am invisible, understand, simply because people refuse to see me." Indeed, few middle-class white Americans perceived the extent of social injustice in the United States. "White flight" from cities to suburbs physically separated races and classes. New expressways walled off ghettos and rural poverty from middle-class motorists speeding by. Popular culture focused on affluent Americans enjoying the "good life." But poverty and racial discrimination were rife and dire, and the struggles for social justice intensified.

Poverty and Urban Blight   Although the percentage of poor families (defined as a family of four with a yearly income of less than $3,000) declined from 34 percent in 1947 to 22 percent in 1960, 35 million Americans remained below the "poverty line." Eight million elderly had yearly incomes of less than $1,000. A third of the poor lived in depressed rural areas, where 2 million migrant farm workers experienced the most abject poverty. Observing a Texas migratory-labor camp in 1955, a journalist reported that 96 percent of the children had consumed no milk in the previous six months; eight out of ten adults had eaten no meat; and most slept "on the ground, in a cave, under a tree, or in a chicken house."

The bulk of the poor huddled in decaying inner-city slums. Displaced southern blacks and Appalachian whites, Native Americans forced off reservations, and newly arrived Hispanics strained cities' inadequate facilities. Nearly two hundred thousand Mexican Americans were herded into San Antonio's Westside barrio. A local newspaper described them as living like cattle in a stockyard. As described by Michael Harrington in *The Other America: Poverty in the United States* (1962), the poor lived trapped in a vicious cycle of want and a culture of deprivation. Unable to afford good housing, a nutritious diet, and doctors, the poor got sick more often and for longer than more affluent Americans. Losing wages and finding it hard to hold steady jobs, they could not pay for the decent housing, good food, or doctors that would keep them from getting and staying sick. Children of the poor started school disadvantaged, quickly fell behind, and, lacking encouragement or expectation of success, dropped out. Living with neither hopes nor skills, the poor bequeathed a similar legacy to their children.

The pressing need for low-cost housing went unanswered. "Slum clearance" generally meant "Negro clearance," and "urban renewal" meant "poor removal," as developers razed low-income neighborhoods to put up parking garages and

National Archives

In a Kentucky Mining Town *Life was not the "nifty fifties" for many Americans. Nearly one in four lived below the poverty line, which was calculated by the federal government to be $2,973 for a family of four in 1959. The bottom 20 percent of Americans then owned only 0.05 percent of the nation's wealth.*

expensive housing. Bulldozers razed the Los Angeles barrio of Chavez Ravine to make way for Dodger Stadium. Landlords, realtors, and bankers deliberately excluded nonwhites from decent housing. Half of the housing in New York's Harlem predated 1900. A dozen people might share a tiny apartment with broken windows, faulty plumbing, and gaping holes in the walls. Harlem's rates of illegitimate births, infant deaths, narcotics use, and crime soared above the averages for the city and the nation. "Where flies and maggots breed, where the plumbing is stopped up and not repaired, where rats bite helpless infants," black social psychologist Kenneth Clark observed, "the conditions of life are brutal and inhuman."

Latinos and Latinas

High unemployment on the Caribbean island and the advent of direct air service to New York in 1945 brought a steady stream of Puerto Ricans to the city, where they could earn four times the average wage on the island. From seventy thousand in 1940 to a quarter of a million in 1950 and then nearly a million in 1960, El Barrio in New

York City's East Harlem had a larger Puerto Rican population and more bodegas than San Juan.

In New York, Puerto Ricans suffered from inadequate housing, employment, and schools and from police harassment. Like countless earlier immigrants, they gained greater personal freedom in the United States while losing the security of a strong cultural tradition. Family frictions flared in the transition to unaccustomed ways. Parents felt upstaged by children who learned English and obtained jobs that were closed to older Puerto Ricans. The relationship between husbands and wives changed as women found readier access to jobs than did men. Yet, however much they tried to embrace American ways, many could not enjoy the promise of the American Dream because of their skin color and language. Increasingly, they turned to organizations like Antonia Pantoja's Puerto Rican Association for Community Affairs (PRACA), which sought to end discrimination against Puerto Ricans and *Nuyoricans*—their children born in New York City.

Mexican Americans suffered the same indignities. Most were underpaid and segregated from mainstream American life. The presence of countless "undocumented aliens" compounded their woes.

After World War II, new irrigation systems added 7.5 million acres to the agricultural lands of the Southwest, stimulating demand for cheap Mexican labor. In 1951, to stem the resulting tide of illegal Mexican immigrants, Congress reintroduced the wartime "temporary worker" program that brought in seasonal farm laborers (*braceros*). Many stayed without authorization, joining a growing number of Latinos who entered the country illegally.

During the 1953–1955 recession, the U.S. government deported some 3 million allegedly undocumented entrants during the Eisenhower administration's "Operation Wetback" (*wetback* being a term of derision for illegal Mexican immigrants who supposedly swam across the Rio Grande to enter the United States). Periodic roundups, however, did not stop the millions of Mexicans who continued to cross the poorly guarded border. The **bracero program** itself peaked in 1959, admitting 450,000 workers. Neither the *Asociación Nacional México-Americana* (founded in 1950) nor the older League of United Latin American Citizens (LULAC) could stop the exploitation or widespread violations of the rights of Mexican American citizens.

The Mexican American population of Los Angeles County doubled to more than six hundred thousand, and the *colonias* of Denver, El Paso, Phoenix, and San Antonio grew proportionately as large. The most rural of all major ethnic groups in 1940, 85 percent of Mexican Americans lived in urban areas by 1970. As service in World War II gave Hispanics an increased sense of their own American identity and of their claim on the rights of American citizens, urbanization provided better educational and employment opportunities. Unions like the United Cannery, Agricultural, Packing and Allied Workers of America brought higher wages and better working conditions for their Mexican American members. Middle-class organizations included LULAC, the Unity League, and the GI Forum (established in 1949 after a funeral parlor in Texas refused to bury a deceased Chicano veteran). These groups campaigned to end discrimination and segregation and won important court decisions that declared school segregation of Mexican Americans unconstitutional

(*Mendez*, 1947, and *Delgado*, 1948) and ended their exclusion from Texas jury lists (*Hernandez,* 1954).

The mobilization of Hispanic voters led to the election of the first Mexican American mayor, in El Paso, in 1958. Latinos also took pride in baseball star Roberto Clemente and their growing numbers in the major leagues, in Nobel Prize winners like biologist Severo Ochoa, and in Anthony Quinn and other Hollywood stars. But the existence of millions of undocumented aliens and the continuation of the *bracero* program stigmatized all Hispanics. Their median income was less than two-thirds that of Anglos. At least a third lived in poverty.

Native Americans

Native Americans remained the poorest minority, with a death rate three times the national average. Unemployment rates on reservations during the 1950s reached a staggering 70 to 86 percent for some tribes. Congress again changed course, moving away from New Deal efforts to reassert Indian sovereignty and cultural autonomy and

Mexican Farm Laborers Being Deported Back to Mexico *Following World War II, the U.S government continued to use the* bracero *program when it needed inexpensive laborers to do the arduous work in the hot agricultural fields of the Sunbelt and then deported millions of Mexicans when it no longer needed them, as in this photo taken during "Operation Wetback" in the recession of 1953–1955.*

back toward the goal of assimilation. Between 1954 and 1962, Congress terminated treaties and withdrew financial support from sixty-one reservations. Proponents claimed such measures would increase "Indian self-sufficiency," but this termination policy, which reduced federal services, sold off tribal lands, and pushed Indians off the reservations, was disastrous. First applied to the Menominees of Wisconsin and the Klamaths of Oregon, who owned valuable timberlands, it further impoverished the tribes and transferred more than 500,000 acres of Native American lands to non-Indians.

To lure Indians off the reservations and into urban areas, and to speed the sale of Indian lands to developers, the government established the Voluntary Relocation Program. It provided Native Americans with moving costs, assistance in finding housing and jobs, and living expenses until they obtained work. "We're like wheat," said one Hopi woman who went to the city. "The wind blows, we bend over.... You can't stand up when there's wind."

By 1960, about sixty thousand Indians had been relocated to cities. Some became middle class, generally losing their Indian identity in the process; some ended up on state welfare rolls, living in rundown shantytowns and addicted to alcohol; and nearly a third returned to their reservations. The National Congress of American Indians vigorously opposed termination, and most tribal politicians advocated Indian sovereignty, treaty rights, federal trusteeship, and the special status of Indians.

THE CIVIL RIGHTS MOVEMENT

The integration of baseball in 1947, spearheaded by the brilliant **Jackie Robinson,** symbolized a new robustness in the fight against racial discrimination and segregation in the postwar era. The war had heightened African American expectations for racial equality, and demands included a permanent Fair Employment Practices Commission (FEPC), the outlawing of lynching, and the right to vote.

The Politics of Race   Fearful of black assertiveness in seeking the vote and in mobilizing grassroots forces, as during the war, white racists accelerated their repression and violence. In 1946, whites killed several black veterans in Georgia for daring to vote and blinded a black soldier for failing to sit in the rear of a bus in South Carolina. In Columbia, Tennessee, also in 1946, a white riot against blacks who were insisting on their rights led to the arrest of seventy African Americans and the jailhouse lynching of two of the prisoners.

These events horrified President Truman. Aware of the importance to the Democratic party of the growing African American vote, Truman also realized how much white racism damaged U.S. relations with much of the world. Genuinely believing that every American should enjoy the full rights of citizenship, Truman established the **President's Committee on Civil Rights** in late 1946 to investigate race relations. The committee's report, *To Secure These Rights,* published in 1947, called for the eradication of racial discrimination and segregation and proposed antilynching and antipoll tax legislation and enactment of a permanent FEPC.

Boldly, Truman sent a special message to Congress in February 1948 urging law-makers to enact most of the committee's proposals. Although Truman's subsequent actions would fall short of his rhetoric, the president insisted on closing the gap between the nation's ideals and its racist practices, and he issued executive orders barring discrimination in federal employment and creating a committee to ensure "equality of treatment and opportunity" for all persons in the armed services.

Jim Crow in Court   During the Truman presidency, moreover, the Supreme Court declared segregation in interstate bus transportation unconstitutional (*Morgan* v. *Virginia*, 1946) and outlawed restrictive housing covenants that forbade the sale or rental of property to minorities (*Shelley* v. *Kraemer*, 1948). Soon thereafter, reflecting the growing determination of black Americans to demand their rights, the NAACP's chief attorney, Thurgood Marshall, abandoned the call for greater equality within "separate but equal" under which, for example, a county in South Carolina with segregated schools could, and did, provide $179 in public funds per white student but only $43 per black student. Instead, Marshall undertook a direct attack on segregation itself. He pursued a strategy built on an earlier federal court ruling that had prohibited the segregation of Mexican American children in California schools as well as on decisions in 1950 in which the Supreme Court significantly narrowed the possibility of separate law school and graduate education ever being constitutional.

In May 1954, the new Chief Justice appointed by Eisenhower, **Earl Warren** (1953), speaking for a unanimous Court, reversed the "separate but equal" doctrine of *Plessy* v. *Ferguson* (see Chapter 20) in the landmark case of **Brown v. Board of Education of Topeka.** Overturning more than sixty years of legal segregation, the Supreme Court ruled that separate educational facilities for blacks and whites were "inherently unequal," denying black children the "equal protection of the laws" guaranteed by the Fourteenth Amendment, and thereby unconstitutional. A year later, however, the Court decreed that school desegregation should proceed "with all deliberate speed"—an oxymoron that implied gradualism.

In the border states, some African American and white students sat side by side for the first time in history. But in the South, where segregation was deeply entrenched in law and custom, politicians vowed resistance, and President Eisenhower refused to press them to comply: "I don't believe you can change the hearts of men with laws or decisions." Although not personally racist, Ike never publicly endorsed the *Brown* decision. He privately called his appointment of Earl Warren "the biggest damn fool mistake I ever made" and later told an aide that *Brown* had "set back progress in the south at least fifteen years."

Encouraged by the president's indecisiveness, White Citizens' Councils organized to defend segregation, and the Ku Klux Klan revived. Declaring *Brown* "null, void, and of no effect," southern legislatures adopted a strategy of "massive resistance" to thwart compliance with the law. They closed down or denied state aid to school systems that desegregated and enacted pupil-placement laws that permitted school boards to assign black and white children to different schools. In 1956, more than a hundred members of Congress signed the **Southern Manifesto,** denouncing *Brown*, and that year not a single African American attended school with whites in the Deep South, and few did so in the Upper South.

The Laws of the Land   Southern resistance reached a climax in September 1957. Although the Little Rock school board had accepted a federal court order to desegregate Central High School, Arkansas governor Orval E. Faubus mobilized the state's National Guard to block enforcement and bar nine African American students from entering the school. After another court order forced Faubus to withdraw the guardsmen, an angry mob of whites blocked the black students' entry.

Eisenhower, believing he had to uphold federal authority, nationalized the Arkansas National Guard, augmented by a thousand federal troops, to protect the African American students for the rest of the academic year. He thus became, albeit

Will Counts, The Arkansas Democrat-Gazette, Inc., courtesy Vivian Counts and Indiana University Archives

Little Rock, 1957 *Elizabeth Eckford, age fifteen, one of the nine black students to desegregate Central High School, endures abuse on her way to school, September 4, 1957. Such scenes of angry whites jeering, screaming, and threatening African American students were televised to the nation, showing the human suffering caused by racist hatred in the South. By so doing, television made Americans aware of the stark consequences of racism. Forty years later, the young white woman shouting insults in this picture asked for forgiveness.*

reluctantly, the first president since Reconstruction to use federal troops to enforce the rights of blacks. Local authorities, however, shut down Little Rock's public schools the next year, and by decade's end, fewer than 1 percent of African American students in the Deep South attended desegregated schools.

Clearly, court victories alone would not end Jim Crow. Nor would weak legislation. The Civil Rights Act of 1957, the first since Reconstruction, established a permanent commission on civil rights with broad investigatory powers, but did little to guarantee the ballot to blacks, and the Civil Rights Act of 1960 only slightly strengthened the first measure's enforcement provisions. At best, these bills implied a changing view of race relations by the federal government, which further encouraged blacks to fight for their rights.

Mass Protest in Montgomery   To sweep away the separate but rarely equal Jim Crow facilities in the South, a grassroots insurgency of African Americans turned to new tactics, organizations, and leaders. As never

Rosa Parks Being Booked *Rosa Parks's arrest for refusing to give up her seat to a white man and move to the back of the bus inspired Montgomery's black leaders to strike a blow for freedom—to call for a boycott of the city bus system in protest. The massive response by the city's black community sparked the nonviolent civil disobedience phase of the struggle against white supremacy.*

before, ordinary blacks acted in extraordinary ways to challenge the system of segregation. Often sparked by local actions and grounded in daily struggles that took place over a generation, they utilized nonviolent direct-action protest to engage large numbers of blacks in the freedom struggle and to arouse white America's conscience.

In the 1950s, racism still touched even the smallest details of daily life. In Montgomery, Alabama, black bus riders had to surrender their seats so that no white rider would stand. Although they were more than three-quarters of all passengers, African Americans had to pay their fares at the front of the bus, leave, and reenter through the back door, sit only in the rear, and then give up their seats to any standing white passengers.

On December 1, 1955, **Rosa Parks,** for many years an officer of the Montgomery NAACP and a veteran of protests in the 1930s and 1940s to secure dignity and proper treatment of black folks, refused to get up so that a white man could sit. "I was not tired physically," she later wrote. "No, the only tired I was, was tired of giving in." Her arrest sparked Jo Ann Robinson of the Women's Political Council, and other blacks who had been engaged in the freedom struggle in Montgomery, to propose a boycott of the buses—the beginning of the mass phase of the civil-rights movement. They founded the Montgomery Improvement Association (MIA) to organize the protest, and elected **Martin Luther King, Jr.,** a twenty-seven-year-old preacher, to lead the boycott. "There comes a time when people get tired," declared King, articulating the anger of Montgomery blacks, "tired of being segregated and humiliated; tired of being kicked about by the brutal feet of oppression." The time had come, he continued, to cease being patient "with anything less than freedom and justice." "My soul has been tired for a long time," an old woman told a minister who had stopped his car to offer her a ride; "now my feet are tired, and my soul is resting." Montgomery African Americans—inspired by earlier protests and by *Brown*—trudged the streets, organized car pools, and raised thousands of dollars to carry on the fight, and when city leaders would not budge, blacks persisted for more than a year until the Supreme Court ordered the buses desegregated.

The Montgomery bus boycott demonstrated African American strength and determination. It shattered the myth that African Americans approved of segregation and that only outside agitators opposed Jim Crow. It affirmed the possibility of social change and inspired further protests elsewhere in the South. It vaulted Dr. King, whose oratory simultaneously inspired black activism and touched white consciences, into the national spotlight. As no one before, King presented the case for black rights in a vocabulary that echoed both the Bible and the Founding Fathers.

King's philosophy of civil disobedience fused the spirit of Christianity with the strategy of achieving racial justice by nonviolent resistance. Casting aside the legalistic strategies of the NAACP, direct action gave every African American an opportunity to demonstrate the moral evil of racial discrimination. King's insistence on nonviolence also diminished the likelihood of bloodshed. Preaching that blacks must lay their bodies on the line to provoke crises that would force whites to confront their racism, King urged his followers to love their enemies. By so doing, he believed, blacks would convert their oppressors and bring "redemption and reconciliation." In 1957, King and a group of black ministers formed the Southern Christian Leadership Conference (SCLC) "to carry on nonviolent crusades against the evils of second-class citizenship." Yet more than on leaders, the movement's triumphs in the decade ahead would depend on the thousands of African Americans who marched, rallied, and demonstrated courageously in grassroots protest movements.

New Tactics for a New Decade   Foreshadowing the massive grassroots activism to come, four black college students in Greensboro, North Carolina, entered the local Woolworth's on February 1, 1960, and sat down at the whites-only lunch counter, defying segregation. "We don't serve colored here," the waitress replied when the freshmen ordered coffee and doughnuts. The blacks remained seated. They would not be moved.

Impatient yet hopeful, taught by teachers who urged them to believe in themselves and stand up for their rights, the students would not accept the inequality their parents had endured. They vowed to sit-in until they were served. Six months later, after prolonged sit-ins, boycotts, and demonstrations by hundreds of students, and after violent white resistance, Greensboro's civic leaders grudgingly allowed blacks to sit down at hitherto segregated restaurants and be served.

The courageous example of the Greensboro "coffee party" catalyzed similar sit-ins throughout the border states and Upper South. Black students confronted humiliations and violence: they endured beatings, cigarette-burnings, tear-gassing, and jailing in their sit-ins to desegregate eating facilities, as well as in their "kneel-ins" in churches, "sleep-ins" in motel lobbies, "wade-ins" on restricted beaches, "read-ins" at public libraries, "play-ins" at city parks, and "watch-ins" at segregated movie theaters. Yet they stayed true to nonviolent principles and refused to retaliate.

The determination of the students transformed the struggle for racial equality. Their activism and commitment emboldened black adults and other youths to act. Their assertiveness desegregated facilities and generated a sense of self-esteem and strength. "I myself desegregated a lunch counter, not somebody else, not some big man, some powerful man, but little me," claimed a student. By year's end, nearly fifty thousand people had participated in demonstrations, desegregating lunch counters and other public facilities in 126 southern cities. Each victory convinced others that "nothing can stop us now."

Newly encouraged and emboldened, the Congress of Racial Equality (CORE), which had been founded in World War II, organized a "freedom ride" through the Deep South in spring 1961 to dramatize the flouting of federal court decisions banning segregation in interstate transportation facilities. It aroused white wrath. Mobs beat the Freedom Riders in Anniston, Alabama, burning their bus, and they mauled the protestors in Birmingham, making the **Freedom Rides** front-page news. A week later, scores of racist southerners in Montgomery beat Freedom Riders with bats and iron chains, generating international publicity and indignation, which ultimately forced the Interstate Commerce Commission to require the desegregation of all interstate carriers and terminals.

Many of the Freedom Riders were members of the **Student Nonviolent Coordinating Committee** (SNCC). Brought together by Ella Baker of SCLC, they followed her advice to form their own independent organization in April 1960, and to strive for "more than a hamburger," more than a seat in a restaurant, more than a place in the bus. SNCC (known as "Snick") stressed both nonviolent civil disobedience and the need to stimulate local activism and leadership. Within months, SNCC volunteers spread out into Mississippi, organizing voting-rights campaigns and sit-ins; in fall 1961, it chose Albany, Georgia, as the site of a campaign to desegregate public facilities and secure the vote. There, wily local authorities avoided the overt violence that had won the Freedom Riders national sympathy. The Albany movement collapsed; but the lesson of Albany, and of the Freedom Rides, had been learned: only the provocation of cruel, vicious white violence generated national publicity and forced the federal government to intervene to protect the rights of African Americans. The young activists who learned that lesson and how to use the media skillfully would chart the course of the 1960s.

SEEDS OF DISQUIET

Late in the 1950s, apprehension ruffled the calm surface of American life. Questions about the nation's values and goals, periodic recessions, rising unemployment, and the growing national debt made Khrushchev's boast that "your grandchildren will live under communism" ring in American ears. The growing alienation of American youth and a technological breakthrough by the Soviet Union further diminished national pride.

Sputnik   On October 4, 1957, the Soviet Union launched the first artificial satellite, **Sputnik** ("Little Traveler"). Weighing 184 pounds and only twenty-two inches in diameter, *Sputnik* dashed the American myth of unquestioned technological superiority. When *Sputnik II*, carrying a dog, went into a more distant orbit on November 3, Democrats charged that Eisenhower had allowed a "technological Pearl Harbor."

The Eisenhower administration disparaged the Soviet achievement, but behind the scenes pushed to have the American Vanguard missile launch a satellite. On December 6, with millions watching on TV, Vanguard rose six feet in the air and exploded. Newspapers ridiculed America's "Flopnik."

Eisenhower did not laugh. He more than doubled the funds for missile development and established the Science Advisory Committee, whose recommendations led to the creation of the National Aeronautics and Space Administration (NASA) in July 1958. By decade's end, the United States had launched several space probes and successfully tested the Atlas intercontinental ballistic missile (ICBM).

Spurred by *Sputnik*, Americans embarked on a crash program to improve American education. The National Defense Education Act (1958) for the first time provided direct federal funding to higher education, especially to improve the teaching of the sciences, mathematics, and foreign languages. Far more funds went to university research to ensure national security. By 1960, the U.S. government was funneling $1.5 billion to universities, a hundred-fold increase over 1940, and nearly a third of scientists and engineers on university faculties worked full-time on government research, primarily defense projects. Some observers dubbed it the "military-industrial-educational complex."

A Different Beat   Few adults considered the implications of affluence for the young, or the consequences of having a teenage generation stay in school instead of working. Few pondered how the young would respond to growing up in an age when traditional values like thrift and self-denial had declining relevance or to maturing when young people had the leisure and money to shape their own subculture. Little attention was paid to the decline in the age of menarche (first menstruation) or the ways that the relatively new institution of junior high school affected the behavior of youth. Despite talk of family togetherness, busy fathers paid little attention to their children, and mothers sometimes spent more time chauffeuring their young than listening to them. Much of what adults knew about teenagers (a noun that first appeared in the 1940s but was not commonly used until the 1950s) they learned from the mass media, which focused on the sensational and the superficial.

Accounts of juvenile delinquency abounded, portraying high schools as war zones, city streets as jungles, and teenagers as zip-gun-armed hoodlums. In truth, teenage crime had barely increased. But male teenagers sporting black-leather motorcycle jackets, their hair slicked into "ducktails," aroused adult alarm.

As dismaying to parents, young Americans embraced rock-and-roll. In 1952, Cleveland radio host Alan Freed, having observed white teenagers dancing to rhythm-and-blues records by such black performers as Chuck Berry and Bo Diddley, started a new radio program, "Moondog's Rock and Roll Party," to play "race music." In 1954, Freed took the program to New York, creating a national craze for "rock-and-roll," the very term that had been used in blues songs for sexual intercourse.

Just as white musicians in the 1920s and 1930s had adapted black jazz for white audiences, white performers in the 1950s transformed the heavy beat and suggestive lyrics of rhythm-and-blues into "Top Ten" rock-and-roll. In 1954, Bill Haley and the Comets dropped the sexual allusions from Joe Turner's "Shake, Rattle, and Roll," added country-and-western guitar riffs, and had the first major white rock-and-roll hit. When Haley performed "Rock Around the Clock" in *The Blackboard Jungle*, a 1955 film about juvenile delinquency, many parents linked rock-and-roll with crime. Red hunters saw it as a communist plot to corrupt youth. Segregationists claimed it was a ploy "to mix the races." Psychiatrists feared it was "a communicable disease." Churches condemned it as the "devil's music."

"If I could find a white man who had the Negro sound and the Negro feel," said Sam Phillips, the owner of Sun Records in Memphis, "I could make a million dollars." He made it by finding **Elvis Presley.** Born in Tupelo, Mississippi, Elvis melded the Pentecostal music of his boyhood with the powerful beat and sexual energy of rhythm-and-blues. In songs like "Hound Dog" and "All Shook Up" he transformed the bland pop music that youth found wanting into a proclamation of teenage "separateness." Presley's gyrating pelvis and bucking hips—exuding sexuality—shocked middle-class adults, but the more adults condemned rock-and-roll, the more teenagers relished its assault on mainstream values. Record sales tripled between 1954 and 1960, and Dick Clark's *American Bandstand* became the decade's biggest TV hit. The songs for black artists written by the

Jewish songwriters Jerry Leiber and Mike Stoller, the rocking versions of Mexican folk music by East Los Angeles' Richie Valens (Valenzuela), and Little Richard dancing on his piano nourished the roots of the coming youth revolt.

Portents of Change Teens cherished rock-and-roll for defying adult propriety. They elevated characters like James Dean in *Rebel Without a Cause* (1955) to cult status for rejecting society's mores. They delighted in *Mad* magazine's ridiculing of the phony and pretentious in middle-class America. They customized their cars to reject Detroit's standards. All were signs of their distinctiveness from the adult world.

Nonconformist writers known as the **Beats** expressed a more fundamental revolt against middle-class society. In Allen Ginsberg's *Howl* (1956) and Jack Kerouac's *On the Road* (1957), the Beats scorned the conformity, religion, family values, and materialism of "square" America. They romanticized society's outcasts—the mad ones, wrote Kerouac, "the ones who never yawn or say a commonplace thing, but burn, burn, burn like fabulous yellow roman candles exploding like spiders across the stars." They glorified uninhibited sexuality and spontaneity in the search for "It," the ultimate authentic experience.

The mass media scorned the Beats, as they did all dissenters. But some college youth admired their rejection of conformity. They read poetry and listened to jazz; some even protested capital punishment and demonstrated against the continuing investigations of the House Un-American Activities Committee. Others decried the nuclear-arms race. In 1958 and 1959, thousands participated in Youth Marches for Integrated Schools in Washington. Together with the Beats and rock music, this vocal minority of the "silent generation" revealed the currents of agitation just beneath the surface calm of centrist conformity. They heralded a youth movement that would explode in the 1960s.

CHRONOLOGY
1944–1961

1944	Servicemen's Readjustment Act (GI Bill).
1946	ENIAC, the first electronic computer, begins operation.
1947	Levittown, New York, development started.
	Jackie Robinson breaks Major League Baseball's color line.
	President's Committee on Civil Rights issues *To Secure These Rights*.
1948	Bell Labs develops the transistor.
1950	*Asociación Nacional México-Americana* established.
1953	Earl Warren appointed chief justice.
	Operation Wetback begins.

1954	*Brown* v. *Board of Education of Topeka.*
	Father Knows Best begins on TV.
1955	Salk polio vaccine developed.
	AFL-CIO merger.
	Elvis Presley ignites rock-n-roll.
	James Dean stars in *Rebel Without a Cause.*
	Montgomery bus boycott begins.
1956	Interstate Highway Act.
1957	Little Rock school-desegregation crisis.
	Soviet Union launches *Sputnik.*
	Peak of baby boom (4.3 million births).
	Southern Christian Leadership Conference founded.
1958	National Defense Education Act.
	National Aeronautics and Space Administration (NASA) founded.
1960	Sit-ins begin.
	Suburban population almost equals that of central city.
1961	Freedom Rides begin.

Conclusion

A far more complex era than that implied in the stereotype of the "nifty fifties," the decade encompassed contradictions. Although mightier than any nation had ever been and basking in a level of material comfort previously unknown in world history, many Americans felt uneasiness as the Cold War continued and prosperity brought unsettling changes.

The postwar era was one of unparalleled affluence for most Americans. New technologies that increased productivity and high levels of government spending spurred an economic boom. Prosperity further enriched the rich, transformed the working class into the middle class, and left the poor isolated on a remote island of deprivation and powerlessness in "the other America."

Overall, the postwar United States, with its burgeoning suburbia and cornucopia of consumerism, seemed the very model of contentment and complacency—what Americans considered the good life. Despite the criticism by the Beats and intellectuals of conservatism and conformity, despite the alienation and rebelliousness of young people questioning their parents' embrace of the status quo, most middle-class whites ignored the seeds of disquiet along with the inequities in American society. Enjoying their private pleasures, they rejected radicalism, condoned the income disparity and persistent prejudice minorities encountered, extolled a benign and optimistic religion, lauded mass culture, and idealized traditional gender roles, domesticity, and togetherness. Busy working and consuming, they left for a future decade the festering problems of hidden poverty, urban decay, and racial injustice.

Still, the cracks in the picture of a placid people widened. Unrest competed with consensus. Although racism remained omnipresent, the seeds of struggle, planted in the 1930s and World War II, flowered in new campaigns to end racial discrimination and segregation. In the courts, the NAACP ceased requesting that separate facilities be equal and instead insisted that true equality required desegregation. And in the streets, Martin Luther King, Jr., SNCC, and CORE employed the techniques of nonviolent civil disobedience to attack Jim Crow, bringing some gains and stimulating an insurgency that spurred further challenges to make the nation live up to its ideals.

28

LIBERALISM, CIVIL RIGHTS, AND WAR IN VIETNAM, 1960–1975

THE KENNEDY PRESIDENCY, 1961–1963

Projecting an image of youthful vigor, **John F. Kennedy** personified the self-confident liberal who believed that an activist state could improve life at home and confront the communist challenge abroad. His wealthy father, Joseph P. Kennedy, seethed with ambition and instilled in his sons a passion to excel and to rule. Despite a severe back injury, John Kennedy served in the navy in World War II and came home a war hero. He then used his charm and his father's connections to win election in 1946 to the House of Representatives from a Boston district where he had never lived. Although Kennedy earned no distinction in Congress, Massachusetts voters sent him to the Senate in 1952 and overwhelmingly reelected him in 1958.

By then, Kennedy had a beautiful wife, Jacqueline, and a Pulitzer Prize for *Profiles in Courage* (1956), written largely by a staff member. Despite the obstacle of his Roman Catholic faith, he won a first-ballot victory at the 1960 Democratic convention. Just forty-two years old, he sounded the theme of a "New Frontier," to "get this country moving again."

A New Beginning   "All at once you had something exciting," recalled a University of Nebraska student. "You had a guy who had little kids and who liked to play football on his front lawn. Kennedy was talking about pumping new life into the nation and steering it in new directions." But most voters, middle aged and middle class, wanted the stability and security of Eisenhower's "middle way" promised by the Republican candidate,

Vice President Richard M. Nixon. Although scorned by liberals for his McCarthyism, Nixon was better known and more experienced than Kennedy, identified with the still-popular Ike, and a Protestant.

Nixon fumbled his opportunity, agreeing to meet his challenger in televised debates. More than 70 million tuned in to the first televised debate between presidential candidates, a broadcast that secured the dominance of television in American politics. Nixon, sweating visibly, appeared haggard and insecure; in striking contrast, the tanned, telegenic Kennedy radiated confidence. Radio listeners judged the debate a draw, but the far more numerous television viewers declared Kennedy the victor. He shot up in the polls, and Nixon never recovered.

Kennedy also benefited from an economic recession in 1960 and from his choice of a southern Protestant, Senate Majority Leader Lyndon B. Johnson, as his running mate. Still, the election was the closest since 1884. Only 120,000 votes separated the two candidates. Kennedy's religion cost him millions of popular votes, but his capture of 80 percent of the Catholic vote in the closely contested midwestern and northeastern states delivered crucial Electoral College votes, enabling him to squeak to victory.

Kennedy's inauguration set the tone of a new era: "the torch has been passed to a new generation of Americans." In sharp contrast to Eisenhower's reliance on businessmen (see Chapter 27), Kennedy surrounded himself with liberal intellectuals. He seemed more a celebrity than a politician. He adorned his presidency with the trappings of culture and excellence, inviting distinguished artists to perform at the White House and studding his speeches with quotations from Emerson. Awed by his grace and taste—and his wit and wealth—the media extolled him as a vibrant leader and adoring husband. The public knew nothing of his fragile health, use of mood-altering drugs to alleviate pain, and extramarital affairs.

Kennedy's Domestic Record   Media images obscured Kennedy's lackluster domestic record. The conservative coalition of Republicans and southern Democrats that had stifled Truman's Fair Deal similarly doomed the New Frontier. Lacking the votes, JFK rarely pressed Congress for social legislation.

Pressing for higher defense expenditures and investment incentives for private enterprise, JFK made stimulating economic growth his domestic priority. In 1961, he persuaded Congress to boost the defense budget by 20 percent. He vastly increased America's nuclear stockpile, strengthened the military's conventional forces, and established the Special Forces ("Green Berets") to engage in guerrilla warfare. By 1963, the defense budget reached its highest level as a percentage of total federal expenditures in the entire Cold War era. Kennedy also persuaded Congress to finance a "race to the moon," which Americans would win in 1969 at a cost of more than $25 billion. Most importantly, Kennedy took his liberal advisers' Keynesian advice to call for a huge cut in corporate taxes, which would greatly increase the deficit but would presumably provide capital for business to invest, stimulating the economy and thus increasing tax revenues.

When the Kennedy presidency ended tragically in November 1963, the proposed tax cut was bottled up in Congress. But Kennedy's spending on technology and the military had already doubled the 1960 rate of economic growth, and decreased inflation and unemployment, triggering the United States' longest uninterrupted economic expansion.

The boom would both cause further ecological damage and provide the affluence that enabled Americans to care about the environment. A growing concern for the environment would build on an older conservation movement, emphasizing the efficient use of resources, a preservation movement (focusing on preserving "wilderness"), and the fallout scare of the 1950s, which had raised questions about the biological well-being of the planet. The publication in 1962 of Rachel Carson's *Silent Spring* (see Chapter 27), documenting the hazards of pesticides, intensified concern. Additionally, postwar prosperity made many Americans less interested in increased production and more with the quality of life. In 1963, Congress passed a Clean Air Act, regulating automotive and industrial emissions. After decades of heedless pollution, Washington hesitantly began to address environmental problems.

| Cold War Activism | Proclaiming in his inaugural address that "we shall pay any price, bear any burden, meet any hardship," to assure the "success of liberty," Kennedy launched a major military |

buildup and surrounded himself with Cold Warriors who shared his belief that American security depended on superior force and the willingness to use it. He also increased economic assistance to Third World countries to counter the appeal of communism. The Peace Corps, created in 1961, exemplified the New Frontier's liberal anticommunism. By 1963, five thousand Peace Corps volunteers were serving two-year stints as teachers, sanitation engineers, crop specialists, and health workers in more than forty Third World nations.

In early 1961, a crisis flared in Laos, a tiny nation in Southeast Asia where a civil war between American-supported forces and Pathet Lao rebels seemed headed toward a communist triumph. In July 1962, Kennedy agreed to a face-saving compromise that restored a neutralist government but left communist forces dominant in the countryside.

Spring 1961 brought Kennedy's first major foreign-policy crisis. To turn back communism in the hemisphere, he approved a CIA plan, drawn up in the Eisenhower administration, to invade Cuba. In April, fifteen hundred anti-Castro exiles, "La Brigada," stormed Cuba's Bay of Pigs, expecting their arrival to trigger a general uprising to overthrow Fidel Castro. It was a fiasco. Deprived of air cover by Kennedy's desire to conceal U.S. involvement, the invaders had no chance against Castro's superior forces.

In July 1961, on the heels of the Bay of Pigs failure, Kennedy met with Soviet premier Nikita Khrushchev, who threatened war unless the West retreated from Berlin (see Chapter 26). A shaken Kennedy returned to the United States and declared the defense of West Berlin essential to the Free World. He doubled draft calls, mobilized reservists, and called for increased defense spending. The threat of nuclear war escalated until mid-August, when the Soviets constructed a wall to seal off East Berlin and end the exodus of brains and talent to the West. The Berlin Wall became a concrete symbol of communism's denial of personal freedom until it fell in 1989.

**To the Brink of
Nuclear War**   In mid-October 1962, aerial photographs revealed that the Soviet Union had built bases for intermediate-range ballistic missiles (IRBMs) in Cuba, capable of striking U.S. soil. Smarting from the Bay of Pigs disaster, and believing his credibility at stake, Kennedy

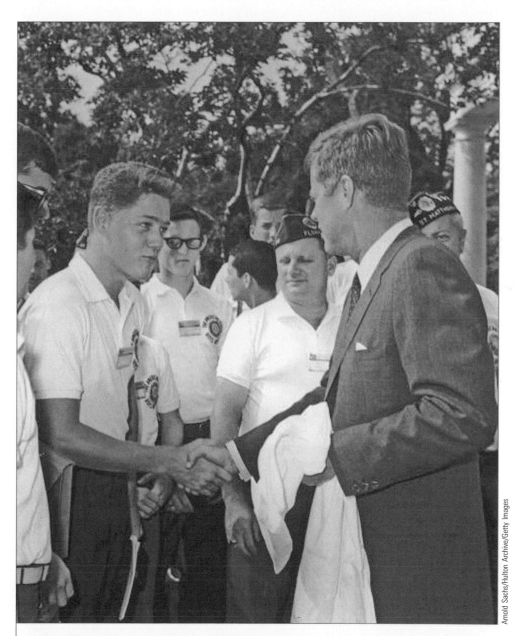

Arnold Sachs/Hulton Archive/Getty Images

A President Greets a Future President *At the White House on January 1, 1963, President John F. Kennedy greets a group of student leaders that includes a young Bill Clinton.*

responded forcefully. He announced that the United States would "quarantine" Cuba—impose a naval blockade—to prevent delivery of more missiles and would dismantle by force the missiles already in Cuba if the Soviets did not do so.

The world held its breath. The two superpowers appeared on a collision course toward nuclear war. Soviet technicians worked feverishly to complete the missile launch pads, and Soviet missile-carrying ships steamed toward the blockade. U.S. B-52s armed with nuclear bombs took to the air, and nearly a quarter-million troops assembled in Florida to invade Cuba. Secretary of State Dean Rusk gulped, "We're eyeball to eyeball."

"I think the other fellow just blinked," a relieved Rusk remarked on October 25. Kennedy received a message from Khrushchev promising to remove the missiles if the United States pledged never to invade Cuba. As Kennedy prepared to respond positively, a second, more belligerent message arrived from Khrushchev insisting that American missiles be withdrawn from Turkey as part of the deal. Hours later, an American U-2 reconnaissance plane was shot down over Cuba. Robert Kennedy then persuaded his brother to accept the first message and ignore the second one. The next morning Khrushchev pledged to remove the missiles in return for Kennedy's noninvasion promise. Less publicly, Kennedy subsequently removed U.S. missiles from Turkey.

Only after the end of the Cold War did the Russians disclose that Soviet forces in Cuba had possessed thirty-six nuclear warheads as well as nine tactical nuclear weapons for battlefield use and that Soviet field commanders had independent authority to use these weapons. Speaking in 1992, former secretary of defense Robert McNamara stated: "No one should believe that U.S. troops could have been attacked by tactical nuclear warheads without the U.S.'s responding with nuclear warheads.... And where would it have ended? In utter disaster."

Chastened by coming to the brink of nuclear war, Kennedy and Khrushchev installed a telephone "hot line" so that the two sides could communicate instantly in future crises and then agreed to a treaty outlawing atmospheric and undersea nuclear testing. These efforts signaled a new phase of the Cold War, later called détente, in which the superpowers moved from confrontation to negotiation. Concurrently, the **Cuban missile crisis** escalated the arms race by convincing both sides of the need for nuclear superiority.

The Thousand-Day Presidency On November 22, 1963, during a trip to Texas to shore up the president's reelection chances, John and Jackie Kennedy rode in an open car along Dallas streets lined with cheering crowds. Shots rang out. The president slumped, dying, his skull and throat shattered. Soon after, aboard Air Force One, Lyndon B. Johnson was sworn in as president.

Grief and disbelief numbed the nation, as most Americans spent the next four days in front of TV sets staring at replays of the murder of accused assassin Lee Harvey Oswald; at the somber state funeral, with the small boy saluting his father's casket; at the grieving family lighting an eternal flame at Arlington National Cemetery. Few who watched would forget. Kennedy had helped make television central to American politics; now, in death, it made him the fallen hero-king of Camelot.

More admired in death than in life, JFK ranked as one of the very few "great" presidents, in the view of a public that associated him with a spirit of energy and innovation, with new beginnings. While Kennedy loyalists continue to stress his intelligence and ability to change, his detractors point to his lack of achievements, the discrepancy between his public image and his private philandering, his aggressive Cold War tactics, and his vast expansion of presidential powers.

Kennedy's rhetoric expressed the new liberalism, but he frequently compromised with conservatives and segregationists in Congress; economic expansion came from spending on missiles and the space race, not on social welfare. Partly because his own personal behavior made him beholden to FBI director J. Edgar Hoover, JFK allowed the agency to infringe on civil liberties, even as the CIA plotted with the Mafia to assassinate Fidel Castro. (Scholars are still trying to untangle the plots and policies that enmeshed the Kennedy brothers, Hoover, organized crime, and the national security agencies.)

Internationally, Kennedy left a mixed record. He signed the world's first nuclear-test-ban treaty, yet initiated a massive arms buildup. He compromised on Laos but deepened U.S. involvement in Vietnam. He came to question the need for confronting the Soviet Union, yet insisted on U.S. global superiority and aggressively prosecuted the Cold War. However, JFK inspired Americans to expect greatness, aroused the poor and the powerless, and stimulated the young to activism. Dying during the calm before the storm, he left his successor soaring expectations at home and a deteriorating entanglement in Vietnam.

THE CONTINUING STRUGGLE FOR BLACK EQUALITY, 1961–1968

Following the lunch-counter sit-ins and Freedom Rides, civil-rights activists eager to climb the next steps of racial justice pressed Kennedy to act. Yet the president continued to stall. Viewing civil rights as a thorny thicket to avoid, not as a moral issue, Kennedy feared it would split the Democratic Party, immobilize Congress in filibusters, and jeopardize his reelection. Yet the movement persisted until it had achieved de jure, or legal, equality; made protest respectable; and become an inspiration and model of activism for aggrieved others.

The African American Revolution

As television coverage of the struggle for racial equality brought mounting numbers of African Americans into the movement, civil-rights leaders beseeched Kennedy to intervene. They realized it would take decades of blood and bravery to dismantle segregation piecemeal; only comprehensive national legislation, backed by the power of the federal government, could guarantee full citizenship for African Americans. To achieve this goal, they needed a crisis that would outrage the conscience of the white majority and force the president's hand.

Determined to expose the violent extremism of southern racism and provoke a crisis, Martin Luther King, Jr., launched nonviolent marches, sit-ins, and pray-ins in Birmingham, Alabama. In the most rigidly segregated big city in America, nicknamed "Bombingham" for the many past acts of violence against civil-rights protestors, few doubted Police Commissioner Eugene "Bull" Connor's pledge that "blood would run in the streets of Birmingham before it would be integrated."

When jailed for instigating a march that a local court had prohibited, King penned the "Letter from Birmingham Jail." It detailed the humiliations of racial discrimination and segregation, vindicated the nonviolent struggle against Jim Crow, and justified civil disobedience to protest unjust laws.

In May, thousands of schoolchildren, some only six years old, joined King's crusade. Connor lost his temper. He unleashed his men—armed with electric cattle prods, high-pressure water hoses, and snarling attack dogs—on the nonviolent youthful demonstrators. The ferocity of Connor's attacks, caught on camera and television, horrified the world.

"The civil-rights movement should thank God for Bull Connor," JFK remarked. "He's helped it as much as Abraham Lincoln." Connor's vicious tactics seared the nation's conscience and pushed Kennedy to help negotiate a settlement that ended the demonstrations in return for desegregating stores and hiring black workers. By mid-1963, the rallying cry "Freedom Now!" reverberated across the nation as the protests grew. Increasingly concerned about America's image abroad as well as the "fires of frustration and discord" raging at home, Kennedy feared that if the government did not act, blacks would turn to violence. When Governor George Wallace refused to allow two black students to enter the University of Alabama in June 1963, Kennedy forced Wallace—who had pledged "Segregation now! Segregation tomorrow! Segregation forever!"—to capitulate to a court desegregation order.

On June 11, the president went on television to define civil rights as "a moral issue" and to declare that "race has no place in American life or law." A week later, Kennedy proposed a bill outlawing segregation in public facilities and authorizing the federal government to withhold funds from programs that discriminated.

Birmingham, 1963

The ferocious attempts by local authorities, led by Eugene "Bull" Connor, to repel nonviolent black protesters with fire hoses (capable of 100 pounds of water pressure per square inch), electric cattle prods, and snarling, biting police dogs— shown nightly on TV— made white supremacy an object of revulsion throughout most of the country and forced the Kennedy administration to intervene to end the crisis.

AP Photo/Bill Hudson

As the bill bogged down in Congress, civil-rights adherents planned to march on Washington to muster support for the legislation.

The March on Washington, 1963   The idea for a March on Washington had originally been proposed by A. Philip Randolph in 1941 to protest discrimination against blacks in the defense mobilization (see Chapter 25). Twenty-two years later, a quarter of a million people, including fifty thousand whites, converged on Washington, DC. After a long, sweltering day of speeches and songs, Martin Luther King, Jr., took the podium to remind Americans that the hopes generated by the Emancipation Proclamation had still not been fulfilled and to reiterate his dream of true brotherhood, in which blacks would be an integral, equal part of American society, not embittered opponents of it.

With one of the greatest American speeches ever, King turned a political rally into a historic event. But not even that quelled the rage of white racists. In September, the Ku Klux Klan bombing of a black church in Birmingham killed four girls attending Sunday school. (Not until 2002 was the last of the four main suspects brought to justice.) And southern obstructionism still kept the civil-rights bill stymied in Congress.

Civil Rights at High Tide   Kennedy's assassination, however, brought to the White House a southerner, Lyndon Johnson, who knew he had to prove himself on the race issue or the liberals "would get me.... I had to produce a civil rights bill that was even stronger than the one they'd have gotten if Kennedy had lived."

The resulting **Civil Rights Act of 1964**—the most significant civil-rights law in U.S. history—banned racial discrimination and segregation in public accommodations, outlawed bias in federally funded programs, granted the federal government new powers to fight school segregation, and created the Equal Employment Opportunity Commission (EEOC) to enforce the ban on job discrimination.

The Civil Rights Act did not, however, address the right to vote. So CORE and SNCC activists, believing the ballot held the key to power for southern blacks, mounted a major campaign to register black voters. They organized the Mississippi Freedom Summer Project of 1964 to focus on the state most hostile to black rights. Although 42 percent of Mississippi's population, blacks comprised only 5 percent of the registered voters. A thousand college-student volunteers assisted blacks in registering to vote and in organizing "Freedom Schools" that taught black history and emphasized African American self-worth. Harassed by Mississippi law-enforcement officials and Ku Klux Klansmen, the volunteers endured the firebombing of black churches and of movement headquarters, as well as arrests and even murders.

To show that blacks wanted to vote, the civil-rights workers enrolled nearly sixty thousand disfranchised African Americans in the Mississippi Freedom Democratic Party (MFDP). In August 1964, they took their case to the national Democratic convention, seeking to be seated as the proper delegation. "I was beaten till I was exhausted," Fannie Lou Hamer, the twentieth child of poor sharecroppers,

The Black Freedom Movement

Most often discussed as an event in African American history and as a catalyst for other social movements in the United States, the Black Freedom Movement, in its origins and consequences, was a global phenomenon. It owed much to the ideological battle of the Cold War, when race became a national security issue, threatening to undermine U.S. claims of the superiority of democracy over communism. Although the Cold War led civil rights proponents to shrink from a broader critique of the American economic and political system, they counted on America's need to appeal to people of color in Africa, Asia, and Latin America to gain governmental support for black rights. In turn, Washington was eager to counter Communist propaganda that emphasized American racism and keen to maintain its stature as the "leader of the free world." The federal government began to view civil rights for African Americans as integral to its foreign policy mission.

For example, America's alleged mission to de-nazify and democratize West Germany took place amid separate, substandard accommodations for African American soldiers, commanded almost exclusively by white officers, in the former heartland of Aryanism. Embarrassed, the Truman administration desegregated the military and broke precedent by submitting friend of the court briefs on behalf of the African American plaintiffs in the momentous *Brown* v. *Board of Education* cases. John Kennedy reversed course and submitted a civil-rights bill to Congress after Bull Connors's televised fire-hosing of demonstrators in Birmingham prompted international condemnation. Similarly, the criticism from abroad following violence against demonstrators in Selma helped push Lyndon Johnson to propose voting-rights legislation far sooner than he wished.

The movement also owed much to India's independence activist Mohandas Gandhi and to Africans struggling for their freedom and independence. Various African American leaders had avidly followed Gandhi's struggle against British colonialism, and Martin Luther King, Jr., as he led the Montgomery Bus Boycott, promoted the techniques and philosophy of Gandhian nonviolent civil disobedience. Often referred to in the press as "the American Gandhi," King made the strategy of nonviolent direct action his own, rooting his own Southern Christian Leadership Conference in Gandhian precepts of love, nonviolence, and reconciliation. His lead prompted activists in SNCC and CORE to apply Gandhian tactics in their own endeavors to end southern racism.

King had closely followed South African Albert Lutuli's efforts to make Gandhian nonviolence the keynote of the African National Congress struggle against apartheid, and like other African Americans, he had been persuaded by African anticolonialists such as Kenya's Tom Mboya and Ghana's Kwame Nkrumah that they were all part of a worldwide struggle by black people to control their own destiny. Seventeen African nations achieved independence between January and November 1960, and another seventeen freed themselves from colonial bondage by 1963. It was an embarrassment to some: "All of Africa will be free before we can get a lousy cup of coffee," sneered black author James Baldwin. It was an inspiration to others: "We could hardly miss the lesson for ourselves," said SNCC's John Lewis. "They were getting their freedom, and we still didn't have ours in what we believed was a free country."

Soon after, it would be the black freedom struggle in the United States that would inspire the oppressed around the globe. In South Africa, Steve Biko's Students' Organization patterned itself on SNCC, Bishop Desmond Tutu repeatedly quoted Martin Luther King, Jr., and the Black Consciousness movement owed much to the American Black Power movement. To protest discrimination, Australian aborigines conducted Freedom Rides, and called them that. The leaders who freed Surinam from Dutch rule in 1975 credited the African American civil-rights campaigns for their tactics and motivation. The New Beginning Movement in Trinidad adopted the ideology and language of late-1960s African American militancy.

Trinidad, and most other Caribbean nations, also appropriated the protest music of African Americans. Songs such as the Impressions' "Keep on Pushing," Nina Simone's "Mississippi Goddam," and James Brown's "Say It Loud I'm Black and I'm Proud," along with many others, carried specifically African American notions of dissent and self-esteem.

In Canada, the civil rights movement to the south raised the awareness and sense of liberation among that nation's 100,000 blacks. They too railed against the term "Negro" and condemned the disparities in income, health, occupation, and education between white and black Canadians. Young Native Canadian militants, criticizing the "Uncle Tomahawks" among their own people, assumed the leadership of organizations like the National Indian Brotherhood to promote the betterment of Indians and the recognition of aboriginal rights.

Much like the segregation of buses in Montgomery, a specific local irritant spawned a more pervasive movement in Northern Ireland. In May 1963—when the black struggle in the United States was headline news around the world—a group of young Catholic housewives in Dungannon organized to protest discrimination in the allocation of public housing. Amid talk of a march on the town like the proposed March on Washington, the local Catholic newspaper insisted that the Catholic minority in Northern Ireland were "white negroes."

Catholic protests against similar discrimination in the Springtown area of Derry led to sit-ins at the local council chamber. The demonstrators sang American civil rights songs and vowed to fight for their rights "as the Blacks in America were fighting." The Derry civil rights protests attracted new participants, particularly youths, who supplied unsuspected reservoirs of energy and initiative. In 1964 some university students set up the Working Committee on Civil Rights in Northern Ireland, the first Irish organization to use the term "civil rights" in its name. The various protest organizations soon engaged together in direct-action civil disobedience to protest discrimination and demand constitutional equality.

By 1968, the banners at mass protests in Northern Ireland invariably included "Civil Rights," the sit-ins included singing "We Shall Overcome," and police reaction included violence that inevitably fueled the discontent. In October 1968, a Belfast to Derry march modeled on the Selma to Montgomery march produced a baton charge by the Royal Ulster Constabulary analogous to the Alabama State Police charge on black marchers.

Moreover, as in the United States, the endless television replays of police attacking peaceful demonstrators sparked dissatisfaction with the slow pace of reform. Increasingly, the Catholic minority engaged in provocative street marches likely to bring violence in full view of the media. And as in the United States, it worked. The Northern Ireland and United Kingdom governments implemented a series of reforms, including universal adult suffrage for local council elections and a Fair Employment Act and Equal Opportunities Commission.

The civil-rights movement in Northern Ireland had brought change—but not enough. And again as in the United States, that shortcoming triggered a generational and ideological conflict. Young Irish militants, like their African American counterparts, demanded a far more radical transformation than their moderate elders. As one, Bernadette Devlin, admitted in her autobiography: "What we really wanted to do was pull the carpet off the floor to show the dirt that was under it." Yet as increasingly combative, less politically sophisticated youths joined the protests, mounting mayhem brought a backlash. Unlike in the United States, however, in Northern Ireland, "the troubles" became a conflict of murder and terror that would last for decades.

Questions for Analysis

1. How did the Cold War affect the U.S. civil rights movement?
2. How did the U.S. civil rights movement affect protest movements in other countries?

told the convention. "All of this on account we wanted to register, to become first class citizens. If the Freedom Democratic party is not seated now, I question America." Despite her testimony, the MFDP was not seated. The disillusioned members of the MFDP, rejecting Johnson's compromise offer of two open delegate seats as a "token" gesture, then walked out of the convention.

Still determined to win a strong voting-rights law, however, King and the SCLC organized mass protests in Selma, Alabama, in March 1965. Blacks were half the population of Dallas County, where Selma was located, but only 1 percent were registered to vote.

King knew he again had to create a crisis to pressure Congress to act. He masterfully provoked Selma's county sheriff, Jim Clark, into brutally beating and arresting thousands of black protestors.

When civil-rights activists sought to march from Selma to Montgomery, to petition Governor George Wallace, Alabama state police stormed into the defenseless marchers, who were clubbed, shocked with cattle prods, and tear-gassed. Showcased on TV, the spectacle provoked national outrage and support for a voting rights bill.

Signed by the president in August 1965, the **Voting Rights Act** invalidated the use of any test or device to deny the vote and authorized federal examiners to register voters in states that had disfranchised blacks. The law dramatically expanded black suffrage, boosting the number of registered black voters in the South from 1 million in 1964 to 3.1 million in 1968, and transformed southern politics.

The number of blacks holding office in the South swelled from fewer than two dozen in 1964 to nearly twelve hundred in 1972, including half the seats on Selma's city council and the first two African Americans elected to Congress from the former Confederacy since the nineteenth century. Electoral success brought jobs for African Americans, contracts for black businesses, and improvements in facilities and services in black neighborhoods. Most importantly, as Fannie Lou Hamer recalled, when African Americans could not vote, "white folks would drive past your house in a pickup truck with guns hanging up on the back and give you hate stares.... Those same people now call me Mrs. Hamer."

Fire in the Streets   The civil-rights movement changed, but did not revolutionize race relations. It ended de jure racial discrimination and segregation, broke the white monopoly on political power in the South, and galvanized a new black sense of self-esteem. It raised hopes for the possibility of greater change and legitimated protest. But its inability to move beyond opportunity to achievement, to gain equality as a result, not just a right, underscored the limitations of liberal change, especially in the urban ghetto. The movement did little to change the deplorable economic conditions of many African Americans, and the anger bubbling below the surface boiled over.

On August 11, 1965, five days after the signing of the Voting Rights Act, a scuffle between white police and blacks in Watts, the largest African American

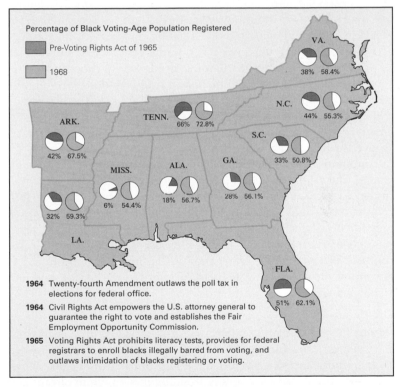

MAP 28.1 Voter Registration of African Americans in the South, 1960–1968

As blacks overwhelmingly registered to vote as Democrats, some former segregationist politicians, among them George Wallace, started to court the black vote, and many southern whites began to cast their ballots for Republicans, inaugurating an era of real two-party competition in the South.

Source: © Cengage Learning. All rights reserved. No distribution allowed without express authorization.

district in Los Angeles, ignited the most destructive race riot in decades. For six days, blacks looted shops, firebombed white-owned businesses, and sniped at police officers and firefighters, leaving in their wake thirty-four dead, nine hundred injured, and four thousand arrested.

Watts proved to be just a prelude to a succession of "long hot summers." In 1966, rioting erupted in more than a score of northern ghettos, forcing whites to heed the squalor of the slums and the brutal behavior of police in the ghetto—problems the civil-rights movement had ignored. Frustrated by the allure of America's wealth portrayed on TV and by what seemed the empty promise of civil-rights laws, black mobs stoned passing motorists, ransacked stores, torched white-owned buildings, and hurled bricks at the troops sent to quell the disorder.

The following summer, black rage at oppressive conditions and impatience with liberal change erupted in 150 racial skirmishes and forty riots—the most intense and destructive period of racial violence in U.S. history. In Newark, New Jersey, twenty-seven people died and more than eleven hundred were injured. The following week, Detroit went up in smoke in the decade's worst riot. By the time the Michigan National Guard and U.S. army paratroopers quelled the riot, forty-three people had died, two thousand were injured, and seven thousand had been arrested. Then in 1968, following the assassination of Martin Luther King, Jr., (discussed in Chapter 29), black uprisings flared in the ghettos of a hundred cities. The 1964–1968 riot toll included two hundred dead, seven thousand injured, forty thousand arrested, and at least $500 million in property destroyed—mostly white-owned stores and tenements that exemplified exploitation in the ghetto.

A frightened, bewildered nation asked why rioting occurred just when blacks achieved many of their goals. Militant blacks saw the uprisings as revolutionary violence to overthrow a racist, reactionary society. The Far Right thought them evidence of a communist plot. Conservatives described them as senseless outbursts by troublemakers. The administration's National Advisory Commission on Civil Disorders (known as the Kerner Commission) indicted white racism for fostering an "explosive mixture" of poverty, slum housing, poor education, and police brutality. The commission recommended increased federal spending to create new jobs for urban blacks, construct additional public housing, and end de facto (existing in practice, but not in law) school segregation in the North. Johnson and Congress, however, aware of the swelling white backlash, ignored the advice, and most whites approved their inaction.

"Black Power"   For many young African Americans, liberalism's response to racial inequality proved "too little, too late." The demand for **Black Power** sounded in 1966 paralleled the fury of the urban riots. More a cry of rage than a systematic doctrine, it sprang from decades of white intransigence, from poverty in its rawest form, and from the growing sense that whites never conceded to black demands except through coercion.

Derived from a long tradition of black nationalism, autonomy, and race pride, Black Power owed much to the charismatic leadership of Malcolm X. A former drug addict and street hustler, Malcolm X had converted to the Nation of Islam, or the Black Muslim faith, while in prison. Founded in Detroit in 1931 by Elijah

Malcolm X and Muhammad Ali *The Black Muslim minister, Malcolm X, who preached a message of black nationalism, self-help, and racial separation, was a charismatic figure to many young black men, including boxer Cassius Clay, who joined the Nation of Islam in 1964 and then took the name Muhammad Ali. More than any other African American leader of his day, Malcolm X's celebration of the African heritage and black self-sufficiency pointed the way to a new black consciousness.*

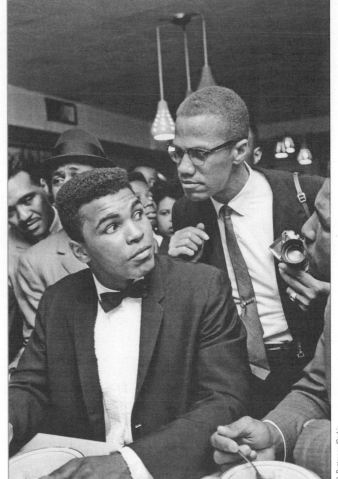

© Bettmann/Corbis

Poole (who took the Islamic name Elijah Muhammad), the Black Muslims insisted that blacks practice self-discipline and self-respect, and they rejected integration. Malcolm X accordingly urged African Americans to separate themselves from the "white devil" and to relish their African roots and their blackness. Blacks, he asserted, had to rely on armed self-defense and seize their freedom "by any means necessary." "If ballots won't work, bullets will," he said. Malcolm X's assassination by members of the Nation of Islam in February 1965, after he had broken with Elijah Muhammad, did not still his voice. *The Autobiography of Malcolm X* (1965) became the main text for the rising Black Power movement.

Two days after winning the world heavyweight championship in 1964, boxer Cassius Clay shocked the sports world by announcing his conversion to the Nation of Islam and his new name, Muhammad Ali. Refusing induction into the armed services on religious grounds, Ali was found guilty of draft evasion, stripped of his title, and exiled from boxing for three and a half years during his athletic prime.

Inspired by the examples of Ali and Malcolm X—and bitter at the failure of the established civil-rights organizations to achieve a fundamental distribution of wealth and power—young, urban African Americans abandoned nonviolence and reform. In 1966, CORE and SNCC changed from interracial organizations committed to achieving integration nonviolently to all-black groups advocating racial separatism and Black Power "by any means necessary."

The Black Panther Party for Self-Defense, founded in Oakland, California, in 1966 by Huey P. Newton and Bobby Seale, urged blacks to become "panthers—striking by night and sparing no one." Despite sponsoring community centers and school breakfast programs, the Panthers attained national notoriety from their paramilitary style and shootouts with the police. A violent and often illegal campaign of repression by federal, state, and local authorities left some Black Panthers dead and more in prison, further splintering the black–white civil-rights alliance and contributing to the rightward turn in politics.

The Black Power movement failed to alleviate the poverty and racism afflicting African Americans, and the concept remained amorphous—ranging from notions of black capitalism to local control of schools to revolutionary schemes to overthrow the American system. But Black Power celebrated black pride and stressed the importance of black self-determination as no mass movement had done before. Scores of new community self-help groups and self-reliant black institutions exemplified it, as did the establishment of black studies programs at colleges, the mobilization of black voters to elect black candidates, and the encouragement of racial self-esteem—"black is beautiful." As never before, African Americans rejected skin bleaches, gave their children Islamic names, and gloried in soul music. "I may have lost hope," SCLC leader Jesse Jackson had students repeating with him, "but I am ... somebody ... I am ... black ... beautiful ... proud ... I must be respected." This message, and Black Power's critique of American society, resonated with other marginalized groups, and helped shape their protests.

The Struggle Goes On   As a result of civil-rights activism, millions of blacks experienced significant upward mobility. In 1965, black students accounted for less than 5 percent of total college enrollment; by 1990, the figure had risen to 12 percent, close to their proportion in the general population. By 1990, some 46 percent of black workers held white-collar jobs. TV's *Cosby Show*, a late-1980s comedy in which Bill Cosby played a doctor married to a lawyer, portrayed this upwardly mobile world.

Outside this world lay the inner-city slums, inhabited by perhaps a third of the black population. Here, up to half the young people never finished high school, and the jobless rate soared as high as 60 percent, owing to suburbanization and deindustrialization. In 1980, the poverty rate among African Americans stood at 32 percent, three times the rate for non-Hispanic whites.

Cocaine and other drugs pervaded the inner cities. Some black children recruited as lookouts for drug dealers eventually became dealers themselves. With drugs came violence. In the 1980s, a young black male was six times as likely to be murdered as a young white male. Drug abuse affected all social levels, including yuppies and show-business celebrities, but drug use and trafficking particularly devastated the inner cities. Serious social problems among those left behind in the inner cities, as well as upward mobility and educational advances by African Americans, would continue into the twenty-first century (as discussed in Chapter 31).

To compensate for past racial discrimination in employment and education, some cities set aside a percentage of building contracts for minority businesses, industries adopted hiring goals and recruitment training program, and many educational institutions reserved slots for minority applicants. These so-called **affirmative action** programs faced court challenges, however. In *University of California Regents* v. *Bakke* (1978), the Supreme Court declared racial quotas unconstitutional, yet also held that universities might consider race as a factor in admission "to remedy disadvantages cast on minorities by past racial prejudice."

THE EXPANDING MOVEMENT FOR EQUALITY

Native Americans, Hispanic Americans, and Asian Americans were similarly affected by liberalism. They, too, were inspired by Kennedy's rhetoric, by Johnson's actions, and by the assertive outlook of Black Power. Each followed the black lead in challenging the status quo, demanding full and equal citizenship rights, and emphasizing group identity and pride. And like blacks, each group saw its younger members push for ever more radical action.

Native American Activism   In 1961, representatives of sixty-seven tribes drew up a Declaration of Purposes criticizing the termination policy of the 1950s (see Chapter 27), and in 1964 hundreds of Indians lobbied in Washington for inclusion in the War on Poverty (covered later in this chapter). Indians suffered the worst poverty and the highest disease and death rates of any American group. President Johnson responded by establishing the National Council on Indian Opportunity in 1965, which funneled more federal funds onto reservations than any previous program. Promising to erase "old attitudes of paternalism," Johnson advocated Indian self-determination, "the right of the First Americans to remain Indians while exercising their rights as Americans."

Militant Native Americans, meanwhile, began to organize. By 1968, younger Indian activists, calling themselves "Native Americans," demanded "Red Power." They protested the lack of protection for Indian land and water rights and the desecration of Indian sacred sites. They established reservation cultural programs to reawaken spiritual beliefs and teach native languages. The Navajo and Hopi protested strip-mining in the Southwest, the Taos Pueblo organized to reclaim the Blue Lake sacred site in northern New Mexico, and the Puyallup held "fish-ins" to assert old treaty rights to fish in the Columbia River and Puget Sound.

The most militant group, the **American Indian Movement** (AIM), founded in 1968 by Chippewas, Sioux, and Ojibwa living in Minnesota, sought to stop police harassment of Indians in urban "red ghettos." In November 1969, AIM occupied Alcatraz Island in San Francisco Bay and held it for nineteen months. As one participant glowed, "we got back our worth, our pride, our dignity, our humanity." AIM's militancy helped foster a new sense of identity among American Indians and aroused other Native Americans to be proud of their heritage. Their members "had a new look about them, not that hangdog reservation look I was used to," Mary Crow Dog remembered, and they "loosened a sort of earthquake inside me." Many of the eight hundred thousand who identified themselves as Indians in the 1970 census did so for the first time and by 1990 their number had soared to 1.7 million.

Hispanic Americans Organize

As earlier in American history, immigration swelled the ranks of minority groups in the second half of the twentieth century. Of enormous significance, President Johnson proposed and Congress enacted the **Immigration Act of 1965,** abolishing the national-origins quotas of the 1920s. Annual legal immigration began an increase from 250,000 to well over a million, and the vast majority of new immigrants came from Asia and Latin America. The Latino, or Hispanic American, population increased from 4.5 percent in 1970 to nearly 12 percent in 2000. Less than 1 percent of the U.S. population in 1960, Asian Americans (discussed in the next section) comprised more than 4 percent in 2000. During the 1960s, these groups contributed to the general spirit of activism.

Like Native Americans, Latinos—the fastest-growing minority—became impatient with their establishment organizations, which had been unable to better their dismal conditions: a median annual wage half the poverty level, a functional illiteracy rate of 40 percent among Mexican American adults, and de facto segregation common throughout the Southwest. As they turned to the more militant tactics of the civil-rights movement, Latinos found a charismatic leader in **César Estrada Chávez.**

Born on an Arizona farm first cultivated in the 1880s by his grandfather, Chávez grew up a migrant farm worker, joined the U.S. navy in World War II, and then devoted himself to gaining union recognition and improved working conditions for the mostly Mexican American farm laborers in California. A magnetic leader who, like Martin Luther King, Jr., blended religion with nonviolent resistance to fight for social change, Chávez led his followers in the Delano vineyards of the San Joaquin Valley to strike in 1965. He and United Farm Workers (UFW) cofounder Dolores Huerta organized consumer boycotts of table grapes to dramatize the farm workers' struggle, often referred to as La Causa.

Chavez and Huerta made La Causa part of the struggle of the entire Mexican American community and of the larger national civil-rights movement. For the first time, farm workers gained the right to unionize to secure better wages; by mid-1970, two-thirds of California grapes were grown under UFW contracts. Just as the UFW flag featured an Aztec eagle and the Virgin of Guadalupe, Chávez combined religion, labor militancy, and Mexican heritage to stimulate ethnic pride and politicization.

Also in the mid-1960s, young Hispanic activists began using the formerly pejorative terms **Chicano and Chicana** to express a militant collective identity. "Our main goal is to orient the Chicano to *think* Chicano so as to achieve equal status with other groups, not to emulate the Anglo." Rejecting assimilation, Chicano student organizations came together in 1967 in *El Movimiento Estudiantil Chicano de Aztlan*

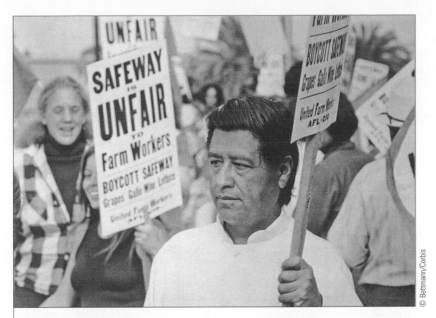

César Chávez *César Chávez, from a farm worker family, founded the United Farm Workers to help migrant Mexican farm hands, who worked long hours for meager pay. Utilizing nonviolent protests, consumer boycotts, and personal hunger strikes, Chávez and his followers won the enactment in 1975 of a California law requiring growers to bargain collectively with the elected representatives of the farm workers.*

(MEChA). MEChA demanded bilingual education and more Latino teachers in high schools as well as Chicano studies programs and organizations at colleges.

Similar zeal led poet Rodolfo "Corky" Gonzales to found the Crusade for Justice in Colorado in 1965 to fight police brutality and foster Chicano culture. It led Reies Lopez Tijerina to form the *Alianza Federal de Mercedes* in New Mexico to reclaim land usurped by whites in the 1848 Treaty of Guadalupe Hidalgo. It also led Jose Angel Gutierrez and others in Texas to create an alternative political party in 1967, *La Raza Unida,* to elect Latinos and instill cultural pride. Across the West, Hispanic American activists created the "brown is beautiful" vogue and the paramilitary Brown Berets, with conceptual roots in the Black Panthers.

Similarly inspired, Puerto Ricans in New York City founded the Young Lords. Modeled on the Black Panthers, the Young Lords published a newspaper, started drug treatment programs, and even hijacked ambulances and occupied a hospital to demand better medical services in the South Bronx.

Meanwhile, a steady influx of immigrants, both legal and illegal, continued to arrive in the United States. Where most had once come from Europe, some 45 percent now came from the Western Hemisphere and 30 percent from Asia. As in the past, economic need drew these newcomers. Mexico's chronic poverty forced many to seek jobs in the north. But life in the United States was often harsh. In 1980, some 26 percent of persons of Hispanic origin in the United States lived in poverty, twice the national rate. Despite adversity, Hispanic newcomers preserved their language and traditions, influencing U.S. culture in the process.

Millions of Hispanic immigrants lacked official documentation. Many sweated in the garment trades, cleaned houses, held low-paying service-sector jobs, and labored in agricultural fields. The **Immigration Reform and Control Act of 1986,** an update of the 1965 Immigration Act, outlawed the hiring of undocumented immigrants but offered legal status to aliens who had lived in the United States for five years.

Asian American Activism   Like their counterparts, young activists with roots in East Asia rejected the term *Oriental* in favor of *Asian American,* to signify a new ethnic consciousness. Formed at the University of California in 1968, the **Asian American Political Alliance** encouraged Asian Americans to claim their own cultural identity and, in racial solidarity with their "Asian brothers and sisters," to protest against the U.S. war in Vietnam.

Asian American students marched, sat in, and went on strike to gain courses on Asian American studies or to protest repressive dictatorships in their homeland. Others worked to improve housing and working conditions for Asian Americans in need. The Redress and Reparations Movement agitated to force the government to make restitution for the wartime internment of Japanese Americans.

None of these movements for ethnic pride and power, in later decades, would sustain the fervent activism and media attention they attracted in the late 1960s. But by elevating the consciousness and nurturing the confidence of the younger generation, each contributed to the empowerment of its respective group and to the politics of identity that would continue to grow in importance.

Liberalism Ascendant, 1963–1968

Although a New Dealer in the 1930s, **Lyndon Baines Johnson** came to be distrusted by liberals as "a Machiavelli in a Stetson" and regarded as a usurper by Kennedy loyalists. He had become the 36th president of the United States through the assassination of a popular president in his home state. Though just nine years older than JFK, he seemed a relic of the past, a back-room wheeler-dealer, as crude as Kennedy was smooth.

Yet Johnson had substantial political assets. He had served in Washington almost continuously since 1932, accruing enormous experience and a close association with the Capitol Hill power brokers. He excelled at wooing allies, neutralizing opponents, forging coalitions, and achieving results.

Demonstrating his determination to prove himself to liberals, Johnson deftly handled the transition of power, won a landslide victory in 1964, and guided through Congress the greatest array of liberal legislation in U.S. history, surpassing the New Deal. Needing to outdo JFK, even FDR, LBJ had both great talents and glaring flaws. His swollen yet fragile ego could not abide the sniping of Kennedy loyalists—and the press. Wondering aloud, "Why don't people like me?" Johnson labored to make the American Dream a reality for everyone and to vanquish all

The LBJ Treatment

Not content unless he could wholly dominate friend as well as foe, Lyndon Johnson used his body as well as his voice to bend others to his will and gain his objectives.

Lyndon B. Johnson Presidential Library

foes at home and abroad. Ironically, in seeking consensus and adoration, Johnson divided the nation and left office repudiated.

Johnson Takes Over   Calling for quick passage of the tax-cut and civil-rights bills as a memorial to JFK, Johnson used his skills to win passage of the Civil Rights Act of 1964 and a $10 billion tax-reduction bill, which produced a surge in capital investment and personal consumption that further spurred economic growth and shrank the budget deficit. More boldly, Johnson declared "unconditional **war on poverty** in America."

Largely invisible in an affluent America, according to Michael Harrington's *The Other America* (1962), some 40 million people lived in a "culture of poverty," lacking the education, medical care, and employment opportunities that most Americans took for granted. To be poor, Harrington asserted, "is to be an internal alien, to grow up in a culture that is radically different from the one that dominates the society."

LBJ championed a campaign to bring these "internal exiles" into the mainstream. Designed to offer a "hand up, not a handout," the Economic Opportunity Act established the Office of Economic Opportunity to fund and coordinate such programs as a job corps to train young people in marketable skills; VISTA (Volunteers in Service to America), a domestic peace corps; Project Head Start, to provide compensatory education for preschoolers from disadvantaged families; an assortment of public-works and training programs; and a Community Action Program to encourage the "maximum feasible participation" of the poor in decisions that affected them.

Summing up his goals in 1964, Johnson offered his vision of the **Great Society,** a place of "abundance and liberty for all. It demands an end to poverty and racial injustice," yet is more concerned with "the quality of goals than the quantity of goods." It serves not merely "the demands of commerce but the desire for beauty and hunger for community."

The 1964 Election   Johnson's Great Society horrified the "new conservatives," such as William F. Buckley and the college students of Young Americans for Freedom (YAF). The most persuasive criticism came from Arizona Senator **Barry Goldwater.** A western outsider fighting the power of Washington and a fervent anticommunist, Goldwater advocated as little federal governmental intervention in the economy as possible and opposed government efforts to expand and protect civil rights and liberties.

Johnson's jibe that civil-rights leaders would have to wear sneakers to keep up with him evoked no laughter from southern segregationists or from blue-collar workers in northern cities who dreaded the integration of their neighborhoods, schools, and workplaces. Their support of Alabama's segregationist governor George Wallace in the spring 1964 Democratic presidential primaries heralded a "white backlash" against the civil-rights movement.

Buoyed by this backlash, right-wing Republicans gained control of the GOP in 1964. They nominated Barry Goldwater for the presidency and adopted a platform totally opposed to liberalism. Determined to offer the nation "a choice not an echo," Goldwater lauded his opposition to civil-rights legislation, denounced the War on Poverty, and accused the Democrats of a "no-win" strategy in the Cold War, hinting that he might use nuclear weapons against Cuba and North Vietnam. His stance appealed most to those angered by the Cold War stalemate, by the erosion of traditional moral values, and by the increasing militancy of African Americans. But his charge that the Democrats had not pursued total victory in Vietnam allowed Johnson to appear the apostle of restraint: "We are not going to send American boys nine or ten thousand miles from home to do what Asian boys ought to be doing for themselves."

LBJ won a landslide victory, 43 million votes to Goldwater's 27 million. The GOP lost thirty-eight House and two Senate seats. Many proclaimed the death of Republican conservatism. But Goldwater's coalition of economic, social, and religious conservatives, and anti-integrationist whites, presaged the Right's future triumph. It transformed the Republicans from a moderate, eastern-dominated party to one decidedly conservative, southern, and western. It built a national base of financial support for conservative candidates; catalyzed the creation of new conservative publications and think-tanks; energized volunteers like Phyllis Schlafly to campaign for Goldwater and stay involved in politics; and mobilized future leaders of the party, like Ronald Reagan. But in the short run, the liberals controlled all three branches of government.

The Great Society   "Hurry, boys, hurry," LBJ urged his aides. "Get that legislation up to the hill and out. Eighteen months from now ol' Landslide Lyndon will be Lame-Duck Lyndon." Johnson flooded Congress with liberal proposals. The results were astounding, outpacing even the dazzling array of legislation enacted in the first two years of the New Deal.

The Eighty-ninth Congress expanded the War on Poverty and passed the Voting Rights Act. It enacted **Medicare** to provide health insurance for the aged under social security and a **Medicaid** health plan for the poor. By 1975, the two programs would be serving 47 million people and account for a quarter of the nation's health-care expenditures. The legislators also appropriated funds for public education and housing and for aid to Appalachia and inner-city neighborhoods. They created new cabinet departments of transportation and of housing and urban development as well as the National Endowments for the Arts and the Humanities. The first president to send a special message on the environment to Congress, Johnson won the enactment of measures to control air and water pollution, protect endangered species, set aside millions of acres of wilderness, and preserve the natural beauty of the American landscape. As noted, Congress enacted the Immigration Act of 1965, abandoning the quota system enacted in the 1920s that had discriminated against Asians and southern and eastern Europeans and transforming America's racial and ethnic kaleidoscope.

The Great Society improved the lives of millions. The proportion of the poor in the population dropped from 22 percent in 1960 to 13 percent in 1969, infant mortality declined, and African American family income rose from 54 percent to 61 percent of white family income. The percentage of blacks living below the poverty line plummeted from 40 percent to 20 percent. Great Society programs gave those on the bottom reason to hope and a sense of entitlement to a fair share of the American Dream. But because Johnson oversold the Great Society and Congress underfunded it, rising expectations outdistanced results.

For many in need, the Great Society remained more a dream than a reality. The war against poverty, Martin Luther King, Jr., asserted, was "shot down on the battlefields of Vietnam." The Asian war diverted LBJ's attention from liberal reforms and devoured tax dollars that might have gone to the Great Society. Yet the perceived liberality of federal spending and the "ungratefulness" of rioting blacks, as well as the intrusive rulings of the Supreme Court, alienated many middle- and working-class whites. The Democrats' loss of forty-seven House seats in 1966 ended the sway of congressional liberalism.

The Liberalism of the Warren Court   The Supreme Court, led by Chief Justice Earl Warren, far more liberal than public opinion or Congress, supported an activist government to protect the disadvantaged and accused criminals and expanded individual rights to a greater extent than ever before in American history.

In landmark cases, the Court prohibited Bible reading and prayer in public schools, limited local power to censor books and films, and overturned state bans on contraceptives. It ordered states to apportion legislatures on the principle of "one person, one vote," increasing the representation of urban minorities.

The Court's upholding of the rights of the accused in criminal cases, at a time of soaring crime rates, particularly incensed many Americans. Criticism of the Supreme Court reached a climax in 1966 when it ruled in **Miranda v. Arizona** that police must advise suspects of their right to remain silent and to have counsel during questioning. In 1968, presidential candidates Richard Nixon and George Wallace would win favor by promising to appoint judges who emphasized "law and order" over individual liberties.

THE VIETNAM CRUSADE, 1961–1975

The activist liberals who boldly tried to uplift the downtrodden also went to war to contain communism in Vietnam. The nation's longest war, and most controversial, would shatter the liberal consensus and divide the United States as nothing had since the Civil War.

Origins and Causes   American involvement in Vietnam grew out of the containment policy to stop the spread of communism. First as a means of strengthening our anti-Soviet ally France, President Truman authorized U.S. aid for French efforts to reestablish its colonial rule in Indochina. After the outbreak of war in Korea, with all of Asia now viewed as a Cold War battleground, Truman ordered vastly increased assistance for the French army fighting the Vietminh, a broad-based Vietnamese nationalist coalition led by the communist Ho Chi Minh. By 1954, the United States was paying three-quarters of the French war costs in Vietnam.

But the French were losing. In early 1954, the Vietminh besieged twelve thousand French troops in the valley of Dienbienphu. France appealed for U.S. intervention, and some American officials toyed with the idea of a nuclear strike, which President Eisenhower flatly rejected. In May, the French surrendered at Dienbienphu. An international conference in Geneva arranged a cease-fire and divided Vietnam at the seventeenth parallel, pending elections in 1956 to choose the government of a unified nation.

Although unwilling to go to war, Eisenhower would not accept a communist takeover of Vietnam. In what became known as the **domino theory,** Eisenhower warned that, if Vietnam fell to the communists, then Thailand, Burma, Indonesia, and ultimately all of Asia would follow. The United States refused to sign the Geneva Peace Accords and in late 1954 created the Southeast Asia Treaty Organization (SEATO), a military alliance patterned on NATO (see Chapter 26).

In June 1954, the CIA installed Ngo Dinh Diem, a fiercely anticommunist Catholic, as premier and then president of an independent South Vietnam. CIA agents helped him eliminate political opposition and block the election to reunify

Vietnam specified by the Geneva agreements. As Eisenhower later admitted, "Possibly 80 percent of the population would have voted for the communist Ho Chi Minh as their leader." Washington pinned its hopes on Diem to maintain a noncommunist South Vietnam with American dollars rather than American lives.

But the autocratic Diem's Catholicism alienated the predominantly Buddhist population, and his refusal to institute land reform and end corruption spurred opposition. In December 1960, opponents of Diem coalesced in the communist-led **National Liberation Front** (NLF). Backed by North Vietnam, the insurgency soon controlled half of South Vietnam.

Kennedy and Vietnam   Following the 1962 compromise settlement in Laos, President Kennedy, resolved not to give further ground in Southeast Asia, stepped up clandestine operations against the North, ordered massive shipments of weaponry to South Vietnam, and increased the number of American forces there from less than seven hundred in 1960 to more than sixteen thousand by late 1963. Like Eisenhower, he believed that letting "aggression" go unchecked would lead to wider wars (the Munich analogy); thought that the communist takeover of one nation would lead to others going communist (the domino theory); and viewed international communism as a monolithic force, a single global entity controlled by Moscow and Beijing. He wanted to prove that the United States was not the "paper tiger" that Mao Zedong (Mao Tse-tung) mocked.

To counter Vietcong, or NLF gains in the countryside, the United States used both chemical defoliants, which destroyed vegetation and deprived the Vietcong of natural cover, and napalm bombs, whose petroleum jelly burned at 1,000 degrees and clung to whatever it touched, including human flesh. It also forcibly uprooted Vietnamese peasants and moved them into fortified villages, or "strategic hamlets," to prevent infiltration by the Vietcong. But South Vietnamese President Diem rejected American pressure to gain popular support through reform measures, instead crushing demonstrations by students and Buddhists. By mid-1963, Buddhist monks were setting themselves on fire to protest Diem's repression, and Diem's own generals were plotting a coup.

Frustrated American policymakers concluded that only a new government could prevent a Vietcong victory and secretly encouraged the coup to overthrow Diem. On November 1, South Vietnamese military leaders captured and murdered Diem and his brother, the head of the secret police. Although the United States promptly recognized the new government (the first of nine South Vietnamese regimes in the next five years), it too made little headway against the Vietcong. JFK now faced two unpalatable alternatives: increase the combat involvement of American forces or withdraw and seek a negotiated settlement.

What Kennedy would have done remains unknown. Less than a month after Diem's death, John Kennedy himself fell to an assassin's bullet. His admirers contend that by late 1963 he favored the withdrawal of American forces after the 1964 election. "It is their war ... it is their people and their government who have to win or lose the struggle," he proclaimed. Yet the president then restated the domino theory and promised that America would not withdraw from the conflict. Virtually all his closest advisers held that an American victory in Vietnam was essential to check communism in Asia. National Security Adviser McGeorge

Bundy, Secretary of Defense Robert McNamara, and Secretary of State Dean Rusk would counsel Kennedy's successor accordingly.

Lyndon Johnson's Endless War

Now President Johnson had to choose between intervening decisively or withdrawing from a conflict that three previous presidents had insisted the communists must not win. Privately describing Vietnam as "a raggedy-ass fourth-rate

MAP 28.2 The Vietnam War, to 1968

Wishing to guarantee an independent, noncommunist government in South Vietnam, Lyndon Johnson remarked in 1965, "We fight because we must fight if we are to live in a world where every country can shape its own destiny. To withdraw from one battlefield means only to prepare for the next."

country" undeserving of American blood and dollars, LBJ feared that an all-out American military effort might lead to World War III and foresaw that full-scale engagement in "that bitch of a war" would destroy "the woman I really loved— the Great Society." Yet Johnson also accepted the domino theory and Munich analogy and saw both the nation's and his own credibility as on the line. He worried that a pullout would make him appear cowardly, threaten his liberal agenda, and leave him vulnerable to conservative attack.

Trapped between unacceptable alternatives, feeling like "a catfish who had just grabbed a big juicy worm with a right sharp hook in the middle of it," Johnson escalated a Vietnamese civil war into America's war, hoping that U.S. firepower would force Ho Chi Minh to the bargaining table. But the North Vietnamese and NLF calculated that they could gain more by outlasting the United States than by negotiating. In 1964, Johnson took steps to impress North Vietnam with American resolve and to block his opponent, Barry Goldwater, from capitalizing on Vietnam in the presidential campaign. He ordered the Pentagon to prepare for air strikes against North Vietnam; appointed General Maxwell Taylor, an advocate of escalation, as ambassador to Saigon; and had his advisers draft a congressional resolution authorizing an escalation of American military action. In early August, North Vietnamese patrol boats allegedly clashed with two U.S. destroyers in the Gulf of Tonkin. Privately surmising that the "navy might have been shooting at whales out there," Johnson publicly announced that Americans had been victims of Hanoi's "open aggression on the high sea." Never admitting that the U.S. ships took part in covert raids against North Vietnam, Johnson ordered retaliatory air strikes on North Vietnamese naval bases and asked Congress to pass the prepared resolution giving him the authority to "take all necessary measures to repel any armed attack" on American forces "and to prevent further aggression." Assured that this meant no "extension of the present conflict," the Senate passed the Gulf of Tonkin Resolution 88 to 2, and the House 416 to 0.

Privately, LBJ called the resolution "grandma's nightshirt—it covered everything." Although it was initially designed to deflect Goldwater's charge that he was weak on communism, Johnson also considered the resolution a blank check to commit U.S. forces if that became necessary. Yet he assured the public during the 1964 campaign that he would neither deploy American troops to fight in Vietnam nor extend the war by bombing North Vietnam.

Both assurances were short-lived. Early in 1965, Johnson ordered "Operation Rolling Thunder," the sustained bombing of North Vietnam. It would lead to the dropping of eight hundred tons of bombs a day on North Vietnam between 1965 and 1968, three times the tonnage dropped by all the combatants in World War II. Yet it neither forced Hanoi to negotiate nor stopped the flow of soldiers and supplies coming from North Vietnam via the so-called Ho Chi Minh Trail.

Unable to turn the tide by bombing, Johnson committed U.S. combat troops. Adopting a "meat-grinder" or attrition strategy, Johnson sought to inflict unacceptable casualties on the communists to force them to the peace table. Johnson sent 485,000 troops (a greater military force than the U.S. had deployed in Korea) to Vietnam by the end of 1967. But superiority in numbers and weaponry did not defeat an enemy that could choose when and where to attack and then melt back into the jungle. Determined to battle until the United States lost the will to fight, Hanoi matched each American troop increase with its own. No end was in sight.

First among pacifists and socialists, then on college campuses, and lastly in the wider society, a growing number of Americans opposed the war. In March 1965, students and faculty at the University of Michigan staged the first teach-in to raise questions about U.S. intervention. Later that spring, twenty-five thousand people, mainly students, rallied in Washington to protest the escalation. In 1966, large-scale campus antiwar protests erupted. Students demonstrated against the draft and university research for the Pentagon. They proved only a prelude to 1967's massive Spring Mobilization to End the War in Vietnam protests in New York and San Francisco, which drew half a million participants, and the October demonstrations at the Pentagon by another hundred thousand.

Intellectuals and clergy joined the chorus of opposition to the war. Some decried the massive bombing of an underdeveloped nation; some doubted the United States could win at any reasonable cost; some feared the demise of the Great Society and liberalism. In 1967, prominent critics, including Senator Robert Kennedy and Martin Luther King, Jr., spurred hundreds of thousands to participate in antiwar protests.

Critics also noted that the war's toll fell most heavily on the poor. Owing to college deferments, the use of influence, and a military-assignment system that shunted the better-educated to desk jobs, lower-class youths were twice as likely to be drafted and, when drafted, twice as likely to see combat duty as middle-class youths. About 80 percent of the enlisted men who fought in Vietnam came from poor and working-class families; only two of the twelve hundred men in Harvard's class of 1970 served in Vietnam.

TV coverage of the war further eroded support. Scenes of children maimed by U.S. bombs and of dying Americans, replayed nightly, laid bare the horror of war and undercut the optimistic reports of government officials. Americans shuddered as they watched U.S. troops, supposedly winning the hearts and minds of the Vietnamese, burn villages and leave thousands of civilians mutilated or dead.

Yet for every protestor shouting "Hell No, We Won't Go!" many more war supporters affixed bumper stickers reading "America, Love It or Leave It!" Until 1968, most Americans either supported the war or remained undecided. "I want to get out, but I don't want to give up" expressed a widespread view. They were not prepared to accept a communist victory over the United States.

Equally disturbing was how polarized the nation had grown. **"Hawks"** would accept little short of total victory, whereas **"doves"** insisted on negotiating, not fighting. Civility vanished. As Johnson termed his critics "nervous Nellies" and refused to de-escalate, demonstrators paraded past the White House chanting, "Hey, hey, LBJ, how many kids did you kill today?" By 1968, the president had become a virtual prisoner in the White House, unable to speak in public without being shouted down. So ended an era of hope and liberalism.

The Tet Offensive and a Shaken President   In January 1968, liberal Democratic senator **Eugene McCarthy** of Minnesota, a Vietnam War critic, announced he would challenge LBJ for the presidential nomination. Pundits scoffed that McCarthy had no chance of unseating

Johnson, who had won the presidency in 1964 by the largest margin in U.S. history. The last time such an insurgency had been attempted, in 1912, even the wildly popular Teddy Roosevelt had failed. Yet McCarthy persisted, determined that at least one Democrat should enter the primaries on an antiwar platform.

Suddenly, on January 31—the first day of Tet, the Vietnamese New Year—America's hopes for victory in Vietnam sank, and with them LBJ's political fortunes. NLF and North Vietnamese forces mounted a huge offensive, attacking more than a hundred South Vietnamese cities and towns, and even the U.S. embassy in Saigon. U.S. and South Vietnamese troops repulsed the offensive, inflicting a major military defeat on the communists, who failed to unleash a general uprising against the government in Saigon or to hold any South Vietnamese city. With the Viet Cong largely decimated, the brunt of the fighting now had to be borne by North Vietnamese troops.

Victory, however, came at an enormous psychological cost. The dramatic initial reports of the media, highlighting communist success and the immense scope of the Tet offensive, undercut Johnson administration claims of imminent victory, of "light at the end of the tunnel." They deepened the growing mood of gloom about the war and intensified doubts that the United States could win at an acceptable cost. Public approval of the president's conduct of the war fell to just 26 percent in the immediate aftermath of Tet.

After Tet, moreover, McCarthy's criticism of the war won many new sympathizers. *Time, Newsweek,* and influential newspapers published editorials urging a negotiated settlement. The nation's premier newscaster, Walter Cronkite of CBS, observed that, at best, the war would end in a stalemate. "If I've lost Walter," LBJ sighed, "then it's over. I've lost Mr. Average Citizen." The number of Americans who described themselves as prowar "hawks" slipped from 62 percent in January to 41 percent in March, while the antiwar "doves" jumped from 22 percent to 42 percent.

Beleaguered, Johnson pondered a change in American policy. When the Joint Chiefs of Staff sought 206,000 additional troops, he turned to old friends for advice. Former secretary of state and venerable Cold Warrior Dean Acheson told him, "The Joint Chiefs of Staff don't know what they're talking about." Clark Clifford, once a hawk and now secretary of defense, concluded "that the military course we were pursuing was not only endless but hopeless."

Meanwhile, nearly five thousand college students had swarmed to New Hampshire to stuff envelopes and ring doorbells for Eugene McCarthy in the nation's first primary contest. "Clean for Gene," they cut their long hair and dressed conservatively so as not to alienate potential supporters. McCarthy astonished the experts by winning nearly half the popular vote in a state usually regarded as conservative.

After this upset, twice as many students converged on Wisconsin to canvass its more liberal voters. Expecting Johnson to lose, Senator **Robert Kennedy,** also promising to end the war, entered the Democratic contest. Projecting the family's glamour and magnetism, Kennedy was the one candidate who Johnson feared could deny him renomination. Indeed, millions viewed Kennedy as the rightful heir to the White House. Appealing to minorities, the poor, and working-class ethnic whites, Kennedy became, according to a columnist, "our first politician for the pariahs, our great national outsider."

On March 31, Johnson surprised a television audience by announcing a halt to the bombing in North Vietnam. Adding that he wanted to devote all his efforts to the search for peace, LBJ then announced startlingly, "I shall not seek, and I will not accept, the nomination of my party for another term as your president." Embittered by the personal abuse he had endured and reluctant to polarize the nation further, LBJ inaugurated peace negotiations and called it quits. Both physically and emotionally spent, LBJ lamented, "The only difference between the [John F.] Kennedy assassination and mine is that I am alive and it has been more torturous." Two days later, pounding the final nail into Johnson's political coffin, McCarthy trounced the president in the Wisconsin primary.

Ignored and often forgotten in retirement, Johnson died of a heart attack in January 1973—on the same day the Paris Peace Accords ended America's combat role in Vietnam. In many ways a tragic figure, he had carried out Vietnam policies shaped by his predecessors and received little acclaim for his enduring domestic achievements, especially in civil rights and reducing poverty. Although he often displayed high idealism and generosity of spirit, the enduring image of LBJ remained that of a crude, overbearing politician with an outsized ego that masked deep insecurities.

Nixon's War

Following his election in 1968, President Richard Nixon plotted a strategy of détente—reduced tensions—with the USSR and China that hinged on ending the Vietnam War. The war had sapped American military strength, worsened inflation, and devastated Lyndon Johnson. "I'm not going to end up like LBJ, holed up in the White House afraid to show my face on the street. I'm going to stop the war. Fast."

The Nixon Doctrine, announced in August 1969, redefined America's role in the Third World as that of a helpful partner rather than a military protector. It reflected the war weariness of both the electorate and U.S. troops in Vietnam. Johnson's decision to negotiate rather than escalate had left American troops with the sense that little mattered except survival. Morale plummeted. Discipline collapsed. Racial conflict became commonplace and drug use soared. The army reported hundreds of cases of "fragging"—enlisted men killing officers. By war's end, 20 percent of the Americans who served in Vietnam, nearly 500,000, had received less-than-honorable discharges.

The toll of atrocities against the Vietnamese also mounted. Instances of Americans dismembering enemy bodies, torturing captives, and murdering civilians came to light. In March 1968, an army unit led by an inexperienced lieutenant, William Calley, massacred several hundred defenseless civilians in My Lai. Soldiers gang-raped girls, lined up women and children in ditches and shot them, and then burned the village. Revelations of such incidents, and the increasing number of returned soldiers who joined Vietnam Veterans Against the War, undercut the already-diminished support for the war.

Despite pressure to end the war, Nixon would not sacrifice America's prestige. Seeking "peace with honor," he acted on three fronts. First: "Vietnamization," which would replace American troops with South Vietnamese. By 1972, U.S. forces had been cut from half a million to thirty thousand. Second: bypassing South Vietnamese leaders, Nixon sent Kissinger to negotiate directly, and secretly,

The My Lai Massacre *Under the command of First Lieutenant William Calley, the men of Charlie Company entered the small village of My Lai in March 1968 to attack the Vietcong believed to be there. Instead, they found unarmed civilians, mostly women and children, and massacred them. The military kept the incident secret for a year, but when news of the incident surfaced late in 1969, it became symbolic of the war's brutality and the futility of the U.S. effort in the Vietnam War.*

with North Vietnam's foreign minister, Le Duc Tho. Third: to force the communists to compromise despite the U.S. troop withdrawal, Nixon escalated the bombing of North Vietnam and secretly ordered air strikes on Cambodia and Laos. He told an aide,

> *I want the North Vietnamese to believe I've reached the point where I might do any-thing to stop the war. We'll just slip the word to them that "for God's sake, you know Nixon is obsessed about communism. We can't restrain him when he's angry—and he has his hand on the nuclear button"—and Ho Chi Minh himself will be in Paris in two days begging for peace.*

The secret B-52 raids neither made Hanoi beg for peace nor disrupted communist supply bases. They did, however, undermine the stability of Cambodia, and increase North Vietnam infiltration of troops into that tiny republic. Nixon ordered a joint U.S.–South Vietnamese incursion into Cambodia at the end of April 1970. The invaders seized large caches of arms and bought time for Vietnamization. But the costs were high. It ended Cambodia's neutrality, widened the war throughout Indochina, and provoked massive American protests, culminating in student deaths at Kent State University and Jackson State (discussed in Chapter 29).

In February 1971, Nixon had South Vietnamese troops invade Laos to destroy communist bases there. The South Vietnamese were routed. Emboldened, North Vietnam mounted a major campaign in April 1972—the Easter Offensive—their largest since 1968. Nixon retaliated by mining North Vietnam's harbors and unleashing B-52s on its major cities, vowing: "The bastards have never been bombed like they are going to be bombed this time."

America's Longest War Ends   The 1972 bombing helped break the impasse in the Paris peace talks, stalemated since 1968. Just days before the 1972 presidential election, Kissinger announced that "peace is at hand." The cease-fire agreement he had secretly negotiated with Le Duc Tho required the withdrawal of all U.S. troops, provided for the return of American prisoners of war, and allowed North Vietnamese troops to remain in South Vietnam.

Kissinger's negotiation sealed Nixon's reelection, but South Vietnam's President Thieu refused to sign a cease-fire permitting North Vietnamese troops to remain in the South. An angry Le Duc Tho then pressed Kissinger for additional concessions, and Nixon retaliated with massive B-52 raids. The 1972 Christmas bombing of Hanoi and Haiphong, the most destructive of the war, roused fierce domestic opposition but broke the deadlock.

The Paris Accords, signed in late January 1973, essentially restated the terms of the earlier truce. It ended hostilities between the United States and North Vietnam, but left unresolved the differences between North and South Vietnam, guaranteeing that Vietnam's future would yet be settled on the battlefield. After the "decent interval" that Kissinger and Nixon had insisted upon, North Vietnamese troops in the spring of 1975 overran South Vietnam, took control of Saigon, and forced American helicopters to airlift the last remaining officials out of the besieged U.S. embassy.

America's longest war had ended in defeat. It had left fifty-eight thousand American dead and three hundred thousand wounded. The expenditure of at least $150 billion (more than $700 billion in 2009 dollars) had damaged the economy, diverted resources from reform, and triggered huge budget deficits and inflation. It shattered the liberal consensus and inflamed dissent. "No more Vietnams" decided many in the military: the U.S. should not fight abroad unless its national security was clearly at stake, there was demonstrable public support, and it had the necessary means to accomplish the goal.

Virtually all who survived, wrote one marine veteran, returned "as immigrants to a new world. For the culture we had known dissolved while we were in Vietnam, and the culture of combat we lived in so intensely ... made us aliens when we returned." Beyond media attention on the psychological difficulties of readjusting to civilian life, which principally fostered an image of them as disturbed and dangerous, the nation paid little heed to its Vietnam veterans—reminders of a war that Americans wished to forget.

Even fewer gave much thought to the 2 million Vietnamese casualties, or to the suffering in Laos, or the price paid by Cambodia. In 1975, the fanatical Khmer Rouge (Cambodian communists), led by Pol Pot, took power and turned Cambodia into a genocidal "killing field," murdering some 2 million, an estimated third of the population.

"We've adjusted too well," complained Tim O'Brien, a veteran and novelist of the war. "Too many of us have lost touch with the horror of war.... It would seem that the memories of soldiers should serve, at least in a modest way, as a restraint on national bellicosity. But time and distance erode memory. We adjust, we lose the intensity. I fear that we are back where we started. I wish we were more troubled."

CHRONOLOGY
1960–1975

1960	John F. Kennedy elected president.
1961	Peace Corps and Alliance for Progress created.
	Bay of Pigs invasion.
	Berlin Wall erected.
1962	Cuban missile crisis.
1963	Civil-rights demonstrations in Birmingham.
	March on Washington.
	Test-Ban Treaty between the Soviet Union and the United States.
	Kennedy assassinated; Lyndon B. Johnson becomes president.
1964	Freedom Summer in Mississippi.
	Civil Rights Act.
	Gulf of Tonkin incident and resolution.
	Economic Opportunity Act initiates War on Poverty.
	Johnson elected president.
	Bombing of North Vietnam and Americanization of the war begin.
1965	Assassination of Malcolm X.
	Civil-rights march from Selma to Montgomery.
	César Chávez's United Farm Workers strike in California.
	Teach-ins to question U.S. involvement in war in Vietnam begin.
	Voting Rights Act.
	Watts riot in Los Angeles.
1966	SNCC and CORE call for Black Power.
	Black Panthers formed.
	Massive antiwar demonstrations.

1967	Race riots in Newark, Detroit, and other cities.
1968	Vietnam peace talks open in Paris.
	Richard Nixon elected president.
1970	United States invades Cambodia.
1971	United States and South Vietnam invade Laos.
1973	Vietnamese cease-fire agreement signed.
1974	Indian Self-Determination Act.
1975	South Vietnam surrenders following North Vietnam's capture of Saigon.

CONCLUSION

Kennedy's liberal rhetoric captivated the media and obscured a so-so domestic record. Stymied by the conservative coalition in Congress, Kennedy did more to stimulate hope than to achieve change. Others would force changes from the bottom up, and the next president, Lyndon Johnson, would persuade Congress to make a reality of the liberal ideal of an activist government promoting a fairer life for all Americans.

Fed up with the more legalistic, cautious strategy of the civil-rights movement in the past, young African Americans in the 1960s initiated a new direct action phase in black America's struggle for equal rights. Their activism, bubbling up from the local level, and Martin Luther King Jr.,'s stirring oratory and leadership, led to the landmark Civil Rights and Voting Rights Acts, which ended the legality of racial discrimination and black disfranchisement, provided greater equality of opportunity for African Americans, and nurtured the self-esteem of blacks. However, the laws left untouched the maladies of the urban black ghetto. There, unfulfilled expectations and frustrated hopes exploded into rioting, which helped trigger a white backlash that undermined support for the liberal agenda.

For Kennedy's successor, Lyndon Johnson, that agenda meant Great Society legislation promoting health, education, voting rights, urban renewal, immigration reform, federal support for the arts and humanities, protection of the environment, and a war against poverty—the most sweeping liberal measures since the New Deal, and a significant enlargement in the role of the federal government in the lives of most Americans. Although the aggressiveness and violence of some blacks, and the Great Society's vast expansion of governmental powers and expenditures, helped shatter the liberal consensus, many liberal programs endured. Most Americans still supported Social Security and Medicare, favored a safety net of benefits for those truly in need, and did not want an unmanaged economy or a polluted environment.

Still, in the riot-torn streets of the "long hot summers," and, above all, the rice paddies of Vietnam, the liberal consensus exploded. To prevent South Vietnam from being taken over by the communists, Kennedy significantly increased the number and fighting role of American advisers in Vietnam and gave the green light for a coup to overthrow Diem, the unpopular head of the government in Saigon. Inheriting a deteriorating limited war from Kennedy, LBJ also chose to escalate America's involvement, hoping to force North Vietnam to negotiate a compromise. Three years later, a half-million American troops were stationed in Vietnam, and the United States was dropping more bombs on Vietnam than had been dropped in World War II. Still, the United States was no closer to achieving its objective, and Richard Nixon would fare no better. Although the nation had not been so deeply divided since the Civil War, Nixon's determination to prevent the United States from appearing a "pitiful helpless giant," kept the war dragging on for four more years, with increasing American casualties and destruction in Indochina, until he accepted the limitations of U.S. power and bowed to the resolution of the North Vietnamese. Yet, the bitterness engendered by the war, and its unprecedented— and, for many, humiliating—defeat, would linger, and the liberal idealism articulated by King would remain a dream.

29

A TIME OF UPHEAVAL, 1961–1980

COMING APART

By the 1960s, the number of American students pursuing higher education had risen from 1 million in 1940 to 8 million. More than half the U.S. population was then under age thirty. Their sheer numbers gave the young a collective identity and guaranteed that their actions would have impact. And not just in the United States. Major student demonstrations shook the governments of Japan, Korea, Turkey, and Venezuela in 1960, and many more would follow.

Most baby boomers followed conventional paths. They sought a secure place in the system, not its overthrow. They preferred beer to drugs and football to political demonstrations. They joined fraternities and sororities and majored in subjects that would equip them for the job market. Whether or not they went to college—and fewer than half did—the vast majority had their eyes fixed primarily on a good salary.

Many politically engaged young people mobilized on the right, joining organizations like Young Americans for Freedom (YAF), which by 1970 boasted fifty thousand members—far more than any other student group. Rather than John Kennedy, these youths idolized Barry Goldwater, who embodied the traditional values and muscular anticommunism they cherished. YAF would be the seedbed of a new generation of conservatives who later gained control of the GOP, yet it was overshadowed in the 1960s by young activists in the New Left.

Toward a New Left Although a tiny minority of youth, an insurgent band of leftist students got the lion's share of attention. Most, comfortably middle-class, took economic security for granted, and felt "free" to criticize the shortcomings of the consumer society. Hopeful, they welcomed the idealism of the civil-rights movement, admired the mavericks and outsiders of the fifties, and answered the inspiring call of President Kennedy "to make a difference" and serve the nation.

In June 1962, some sixty students adopted the Port Huron Statement, a broad critique of American society and a call for more genuine human relationships. Proclaiming themselves "a new left," they organized the **Students for a Democratic Society** (SDS), which envisioned a nonviolent youth movement transforming the United States into a "participatory democracy" in which individuals would control the decisions that affected their lives. They pledged to revitalize American democracy and to end consumerism, militarism, and racism.

The generation of activists who found their agenda in the Port Huron Statement had their eyes opened by the police dogs in Birmingham, the assassination of President Kennedy, and the escalating war in Vietnam. Most never joined SDS but associated with what they vaguely called "the Movement" or "the New Left." Unlike the Leftists of the 1930s, they rejected Marxist ideology and emulated SNCC's style. Many became radicalized by the rigidity of campus administrators and mainstream liberalism's inability to achieve swift, fundamental change. Only a radical rejection of the liberal consensus, they presumed, could restructure society and create a genuinely democratic nation.

From Protest to Resistance   Returning from the Mississippi Freedom Summer to the Berkeley campus of the University of California in fall 1964, Mario Savio and other student activists tried to solicit funds and recruit volunteers near the campus gate, a spot traditionally open to political activities. Prodded by local conservatives, university administrators suddenly banned such practices; but when police arrested one of the activists, students surrounded the police car and kept it from moving. Savio then founded the **Berkeley Free Speech Movement** (FSM), a coalition of student groups insisting on the right to campus political activity. Likening the university to an impersonal machine, and its students to interchangeable machine parts, Savio insisted that "when the operation of the machine becomes so odious, makes you so sick to heart, you've got to put your bodies upon the gears and upon the wheels ... and you've got to make the machine stop until we're free." More than a thousand students then sat-in on the administrative "gears." Their arrests led to more demonstrations and a strike by nearly 70 percent of the student body.

The conservative former movie star Ronald Reagan, running for governor in 1966, vowed to "clean up the mess at Berkeley," with its "Beatniks, radicals and filthy speech advocates" and its "sexual orgies so vile I cannot describe them." But the demands and tactics of the FSM reverberated on campuses nationwide. Students disenchanted with filing into impersonal buildings to endure lectures from remote professors initiated a wave of protests seeking greater involvement in university affairs. Their objectives changed the character of American higher education: curricular reform, the end of rules regulating dormitory life, and the admission of more minority students.

The escalation of the war in Vietnam, and the abolition of automatic student deferments from the draft in January 1966, transformed campus protests into a *mass* social movement. Initially buoyed with hope, activists set out to stop the war with peaceful protests. Popularizing the slogan "Make Love—Not War," SDS organized some two hundred new chapters and harassed campus recruiters for the Dow Chemical Company, the chief producer of flesh-burning napalm and the defoliant Agent Orange used on Vietnam forests. The futility of such protests alienated young antiwar protestors, and in 1967, SDS—urging a shift "From Protest to Resistance"—supported draft resistance and civil disobedience in selective service centers. By 1968, it claimed one hundred thousand members on three hundred campuses and attracted a half-million antiwar protesters to its spring Mobilization to End the War in Vietnam. With no end in sight, they chanted, "Burn cards, not people" (meaning draft cards) and "Hell no, we won't go!"

That spring, at least forty thousand students on a hundred campuses demonstrated against war and racism. In April, the SDS chapter at Columbia University demanded the university end all its military research projects, and the Students' Afro-American Society insisted it stop the construction of a new gymnasium, claiming that it encroached on the Harlem community. Shouting "Gym Crow must go," a thousand students barricaded themselves inside five campus buildings, declaring them "revolutionary communes" and holding them for six days. "Up against the wall, motherfucker," SDS's leader told the Columbia president. "This is a stickup."

Outraged by the brutality of the police who retook the buildings by storm, the moderate majority of Columbia students joined a sympathy boycott of classes that shut down the university for the rest of the semester. Similar scenarios recurred throughout the country, and elsewhere. Students in Czechoslovakia, France, Germany, Ireland, Italy, Japan, Mexico, and South Korea expressed their own revolutionary bombast. Their protests far exceeded in size and ferocity anything that occurred in the United States. In part, the turbulence of the young reflected the sheer numbers of the postwar baby boom in many nations, which produced a heightened sense of the power of youth, higher levels of expectations and impatience, and a huge number of university students attracted to nonconformity and even rebellion. Satellite technology and new portable video cameras now made it easy to instantly transmit student uprisings in one nation to students around the globe.

The year 1969 saw the high point of the Movement with the New Mobilization, a series of huge antiwar demonstrations culminating in mid-November with a March Against Death. Three hundred thousand protestors descended on Washington to march in a candle-lit parade, carrying signs with the names of soldiers killed or villages destroyed in Vietnam. By 1972, antiwar sentiment would be nationwide. In contrast to the apolitical students of the 1950s, youth in the 1960s proved themselves able to challenge the authorities and inequities of American society.

**Kent State and
Jackson State**

Although revulsion against the war continued to grow after Richard Nixon assumed office in 1969, his periodic announcements of troop withdrawals from Vietnam brought a lull in campus demonstrations. On April 30, 1970, however, the U.S. invasion of Cambodia jolted a war-weary nation and reawakened student protest.

At Kent State University in Ohio, as elsewhere, antiwar students broke windows and torched the ROTC building. Nixon branded them "bums," his vice president compared them to Nazi storm troopers, and the Ohio governor slapped martial law on the university. Three thousand National Guardsmen in full battle gear rolled onto the campus in armored personnel carriers. On May 4, as six hundred Kent State students demonstrated, Guardsmen in

John Filo

"My God, They're Killing Us" *Following President Nixon's announcement of the military incursion into Cambodia, a formally neutral nation, many colleges exploded in anger. To quell the protests at Kent State University, where more than a thousand students clashed with local police, Ohio National Guardsmen fired on students, killing four. News of the shootings outraged many students nationwide, touching off yet another round of campus protests, which led hundreds of colleges to cancel final exams and shut down for the semester.*

Troop G, poorly trained in crowd control, opened fire on students retreating from tear gas, leaving four dead and eleven wounded. None had broken a law or was a campus radical.

Ten days later, Mississippi state patrolmen, responding to a campus protest, unleashed a barrage of gunfire at a women's dormitory at a black college, Jackson State, killing two students and wounding a dozen. Nationwide, students exploded in anger against the violence, the war, and the president. More than four hundred colleges and universities, many of which had seen no previous unrest, shut down as students boycotted classes. The war had come home.

The nation was polarized. Most students blamed Nixon for widening the war, yet more Americans blamed the victims for the campus violence and criticized students for undermining U.S. foreign policy. Patriotism, class resentment against privileged college students, and a fear of social chaos underlay the condemnation of protesters. Many Kent townspeople shared the view of a local merchant that the guard had "made only one mistake—they should have fired sooner and longer." A local ditty promised, "The score is four, and next time more."

Legacy of Student Frenzy   The campus disorders after the invasion of Cambodia were the final spasm of a tumultuous, now fragmenting, movement. SDS shattered into desperate splinter groups, each seeking to prove itself more radical than the others. Endorsing terrorist violence, the "Weathermen" (Bob Dylan's "You Don't Need a Weatherman to Tell You Which Way the Wind Blows") launched the "Days of Rage" in Chicago, merely justifying the government's repression of the remnants of the antiwar movement. When a bomb planted by antiwar radicals destroyed a science building at the University of Wisconsin in summer 1970, killing a graduate student, most deplored the tactic. With the resumption of classes in the fall, the fad of "streaking"—racing across campus in the nude—more reminiscent of the 1920s than the 1960s, heralded a change in the student mood. By then, Nixon had significantly reduced the draft calls, and the entire conscription system was soon to be ended. Some antiwar activists turned to other causes, or to communes, careers, and parenthood.

The consequences of campus upheavals outlived the New Left. Student radicalism provoked a massive backlash from Americans who insisted that law and order was the basis of a civilized society. It spurred the resentment of millions of Americans, shattering the liberal consensus and propelling Republicans like Ronald Reagan to prominence. "If it takes a bloodbath, let's get it over with," he declared of militants in 1966. "No more appeasement!"

At the same time, the New Left helped mobilize campuses into a force that the government could not ignore, and it made continued U.S. involvement in Vietnam difficult. The Movement also liberalized many facets of campus life and made university governance less authoritarian: virtually ending dress codes and curfews, making ROTC an elective rather than a requirement, and forcing the increased recruitment of minority students and the proliferation of Black Studies programs. Such changes, however, fell short of the New Left vision of remaking society and politics. While masses of students could be mobilized in the short run for a particular cause, only a few made long-term commitments to Movement activism. The generation that the New Left had hoped would be the vanguard of radical change preferred pot to politics, and rock to revolution.

THE COUNTERCULTURAL REBELLION

The alienation and hunger for change that drew some youths into radical politics led others to cultural rebellion, to personal rather than political change, to discarding middle-class conformity, careerism, and sexual repression. A San Francisco journalist termed these young people **"hippies."** They disdained consumerism, preferring to make what they needed and share it with others. They donned simple garments and let their hair grow long. Love, cooperation, and immediate gratification became their mantra.

Many hippies joined communes and tribes that glorified personal liberation, helped bring ecology and alternative medicine into the mainstream, and disdained decorum. In urban areas such as San Francisco's Haight Ashbury or Chicago's Old Town—"places where you could take a trip without a ticket"—communards experimented with drugs, mysticism, and uninhibited sexuality. Historian Theodore Roszack called them "a **'counter culture'** ... a culture so radically disaffiliated from the mainstream assumptions of our society that it scarcely looks to many as a culture at all, but takes on the alarming appearance of a barbarian intrusion."

Hippies and Drugs   Illustrative of the gap between the two cultures, one saw marijuana as a "killer weed," a menace to health and life, and the other thought it a harmless social relaxant. At least half the college students in the late sixties tried marijuana, and a minority used mind-altering drugs, particularly LSD. The high priest of LSD, Timothy Leary, preached "Tune in, turn on, drop out." On the West Coast, novelist Ken Kesey and his followers, the Merry Pranksters, conducted "acid tests" (distributing free tablets of LSD in orange juice) and created the "psychedelic" craze of Day-Glo-painted bodies gyrating to electrified rock music under flashing strobe lights.

Many youths distanced themselves from middle-class respectability, flaunting outrageous personal styles ("do your own thing") and shaggy beards; expressing contempt for consumerism by wearing surplus military clothing or torn jeans; and expanding the language to include *bummer, far-out,* and *groovy.* Typical of the generation that had been schooled in the deprivation and duty of the 1930s and 1940s, newly elected Governor Ronald Reagan of California responded by defining a hippie as one "who looked like Tarzan, walked like Jane, and smelled like Cheetah."

Musical Revolution   "This the dawning of the age of Aquarius," sang the cast of 1968's *Hair*, and the nation pulsed with music that both echoed and developed a separate generational identity, a distinct youth culture. In the early 1960s, the revived popularity of folk music mirrored youth's search for an "authentic" alternative to what they considered an artificial consumer culture. Expressing their idealism in protesting war and racism, Bob Dylan sang hopefully of changes "blowin' in the wind" and indignantly of changes that would "shake your windows and rattle your walls."

"Beatlemania" swept the country in 1964. The Beatles would soon be joined by Motown rhythm-and-blues black performers and eardrum-shattering acid rockers—extolling "sex, drugs, and rock-and-roll" for a generation at war.

In August 1969, 400,000 young people gathered for the **Woodstock festival** in New York's Catskill Mountains to celebrate their vision of freedom and harmony. For one long weekend, they reveled in rock music and openly shared drugs and sexual partners. One magazine claimed it "the model of how good we will all feel after the revolution." Many heralded Woodstock as the dawning of an era of love and peace—the Age of Aquarius.

Its luster had already dimmed. "Freedom's just another word for nothing left to lose," sang Janis Joplin, one of a number of rock stars who would soon die of drug addiction. The pilgrimage of "flower children" to the Haight and to New York's East Village in the mid-sixties had brought in their wake a train of rapists and organized-crime dope peddlers. In August 1969, hippie Charles Manson and his "family" of runaways ritually murdered a pregnant movie actress and four of her friends, and the Rolling Stones hired the Hell's Angels motorcycle gang to guard them at their rock concert at the Altamont Raceway near San Francisco. While the Stones snarled "Street Fighting Man," the Hell's Angels terrorized spectators and stabbed and stomped a young black man to death. In 1970, the Beatles disbanded. John Lennon sang, "The dream is over."

Advertisers awoke to the economic potential of the youth culture, using "revolution" to sell cars and jeans. Rock groups, commanding huge fees, became big business. Although the counterculture's quest for personal liberation undoubtedly sapped the forces of protest, it exerted a lasting influence on attitudes toward family life and sex. Self-fulfillment remained a popular goal, and the questioning of conventional values and authority became commonplace.

The Sexual Revolution   The counterculture's "if it feels good, do it" approach fit the hedonistic and permissive ethic of the 1960s, leading to a revolution in sexual norms. Although the AIDS epidemic and the graying of the baby boomers in the late 1980s chilled the ardor of promiscuity, liberalized sexual mores were more publicly accepted than ever before, making full gender equality and gay liberation realizable goals.

Many commentators linked the increase in sexual permissiveness to "the Pill"—an oral contraceptive that freed women from the threat of pregnancy. It became available in 1960, and by 1970, 10 million women were taking it. Still other women used the intrauterine device (IUD, later banned as unsafe) or the diaphragm. Many universities ended their rules on dormitory visits and living off campus, allowing more women to explore and enjoy their sexuality, but also increasing pressures from men for women to have sex lest they be labeled "frigid" and unliberated. Some states legalized abortion. In New York, one fetus was legally aborted for every two babies born in 1970. The Supreme Court's **Roe v. Wade** (1973) decision struck down all remaining state laws infringing on a woman's constitutional right to abortion during the first trimester (three months) of pregnancy.

The Supreme Court also threw out most laws restricting any "sexually explicit" art with "redeeming social importance." Mass culture exploited the new permissiveness. *Playboy* featured ever-more-explicit erotica, and women's periodicals encouraged readers to enjoy recreational sex. *The Joy of Sex* (1972)—a "Gourmet Guide to Love Making"—became a fixture in middle-class bedrooms. Hollywood filled movie screens with scenes of couples having sex; Broadway presented plays featuring full-frontal nudity and mock orgies; and even television presented dramas about, and frank discussions of, once-forbidden topics. Attitudinal changes brought behavioral changes, and vice versa. Cohabitation— living together without marriage—became thinkable to average middle-class Americans. Some marital counselors even touted "open marriage" (in which spouses are free to have sex with other partners) and "swinging" (sexual sharing with other couples) as cures for stale relationships. By the mid-1970s break-throughs had clearly occurred—especially among college-educated young women—in attitudes toward premarital sex, homosexual relations between consenting adults, and abortion.

Influenced by changing norms of personal freedom and self-fulfillment, the institutions of marriage and family would be fundamentally altered. Freer social behavior and language spread throughout much of American society. But what some hailed as liberation others bemoaned as moral decay. Offended by open sexuality and its preferences, and by "topless" bars and X-rated theaters, many Americans applauded politicians who promised a war on immorality. The public association of the counterculture and the sexual revolution with student radicalism and ghetto riots swelled the tide of conservatism in the 1970s.

FEMINISM AND A VALUES REVOLUTION

The rising tempo of social activism also stirred a new spirit of self-awareness and dissatisfaction among educated women, catalyzing the Second wave of Feminism, which would outlast the other social movements and profoundly alter the economic and legal status of women, as well as attitudes about gender roles and sexual relationships.

A Second Feminist Wave   Several events fanned the embers of women's discontent into flames. Unprecedented numbers of women were going to college and employed outside the home. In 1963, the report of John Kennedy's Presidential Commission on the Status of Women documented occupational inequities similar to those endured by minorities. Women received less pay than men for comparable work, and they made up only 7 percent of the nation's doctors and less than 4 percent of its lawyers. The women who served on the presidential commission successfully urged that the Civil Rights Act of 1964 prohibit gender-based as well as racial discrimination in employment.

Dismayed by the Equal Employment Opportunity Commission's failure to act on complaints of sex discrimination, a group of activists formed the **National Organization for Women** (NOW) in 1966. A civil-rights group for women, NOW labored "to bring women into full participation in the mainstream of American society." It lobbied for equal opportunity, filed lawsuits against gender discrimination, and mobilized public opinion against sexism.

NOW's prominence owed much to the publication of journalist Betty Friedan's critique of domesticity, *The Feminine Mystique* (1963), Friedan decried "the problem that has no name"—the discontent of educated, middle-class wives and mothers who, told that "they could desire no greater destiny than to glory in their own feminity," had subordinated their own aspirations to the needs of men. Friedan urged women, imprisoned in a "comfortable concentration camp," to escape by pursuing careers that would establish their own independent identity and would "fulfill their potentialities as human beings."

Still another catalyst for feminism came from the involvement of younger women in the civil-rights and anti–Vietnam War movements. These activists had acquired confidence in their own potential, an ideology to understand oppression, and experience in the strategy and tactics of organized protest. They also became conscious of their own second-class status, as they were sexually exploited and relegated to menial jobs by male activists. In the words of the civil rights movement's Casey Hayden: the "assumptions of male superiority are as widespread and deep-rooted and every much as crippling to the woman as the assumptions of white supremacy are to the Negro."

Although small in number, young women who shared such thoughts would soon create a women's liberation movement more critical of sexual inequality than NOW.

Women's Liberation   In 1968, militant feminists adopted "consciousness-raising" as a recruitment device and a means of transforming women's perceptions of themselves and society. Tens of thousands of women assembled in supportive groups to share experiences and air grievances. They learned that others felt dissatisfaction similar to their own: "When I saw that what I always felt were my own personal hangups was as true for every other woman in that room as it was for me! Well, that's when my consciousness was raised." Women came to understand that their personal, individual problems were in fact shared problems with social causes and political solutions—"the personal is political." This new consciousness opened eyes and minds and begot a sense that "sisterhood is powerful."

Women's liberation groups employed a variety of publicity-generating, confrontational tactics. In 1968, radical feminists crowned a sheep Miss America to dramatize their belief that beauty pageants enslaved women "in high-heeled, low-status roles" and set up "freedom trash cans" in which women could discard girdles, make-up, and other "women-garbage." They demanded inclusion in the Boston Marathon, no longer accepting the excuse that "it is unhealthy for women to run long distances." Overcoming male condescension, they established health collectives and shelters for abused women, created day-care centers and rape crisis centers, founded abortion-counseling services and women's studies programs. Publishing nearly five hundred new feminist publications, they fought negative portrayals of women in the media and advertising. Terms like *male chauvinist pig* entered the vocabulary and those like *chicks* exited.

In August 1970, feminists joined in the largest women's rights demonstration ever. Commemorating the fiftieth anniversary of woman suffrage, the Women's Strike for Equality brought out tens of thousands of women to parade for the right to equal employment and safe, legal abortions. By then, the women's movement had already ended newspapers' practice of listing employment opportunities under separate "Male" and "Female" headings and pressured banks to issue credit to women in their own name.

In the 1970s, feminists focused especially on three issues: equal treatment in education and employment, access to abortion, and passage of the **Equal Rights Amendment** (ERA) barring discrimination on the basis of sex. In 1972, Title IX of the Education Amendments Act prohibited educational institutions that received federal funds from discriminating on the basis of sex. Women gained entry to the U.S. military academies in 1976; and at the state and local levels, they won laws expanding what constituted rape as well as greater protection for victims of domestic violence and more effective prosecution of abusers. Many single-sex colleges became coeducational. The percentage of female students in medical schools rose from 8 to 24 percent and in law schools from 5 percent to 40 percent in the 1970s. By century's end, women would constitute about 20 percent of all state and federal legislators.

The right to control their own sexuality and to make the decisions regarding having children became feminist rallying cries. In addition to using "the Pill," some women challenged demeaning obstetrical practices. Others explored alternatives to hospital births and popularized alternatives to radical mastectomy for breast cancer. And many, aware of the dangers of illegal abortions, pushed for their legalization, achieved in *Roe* v. *Wade*. Perhaps the most controversial ruling of the century, *Roe* v. *Wade* and the subsequent doubling of abortions, to 1.5 million by 1980, triggered an enormous backlash from social conservatives and from Catholics and Protestants, many of whom believed abortion to be the moral equivalent of murder. Abortion opponents would seek a "right to life" amendment to the Constitution and simultaneously energize Phyllis Schlafly's "STOP ERA" campaign.

In 1972, both houses of Congress passed the ERA with little opposition and, within a year, twenty-eight of the necessary thirty-eight states approved the proposed amendment. Its ultimate adoption seemed self-evident. Then Schlafly, a Republican organizer and working woman herself, took up the fight. Her monthly newsletter, *The Phyllis Schlafly Report*, added antifeminism to its traditional attacks on communism and federal social programs. Her affirmation of traditional gender roles struck a responsive chord with many men as well as with working-class women who felt estranged from the largely upper-middle-class feminist movement. Schlafly charged that the ERA would force women into combat roles in the military, necessitate "unisex toilets," and promote lesbianism. Her relentless assault helped kill the amendment. Selling millions of records, country artist Tammy Wynette sang "Don't Liberate Me, Love Me."

While the number of women working outside the home leaped from under 20 million in 1960 to nearly 60 million by 1990, women's wages still lagged behind

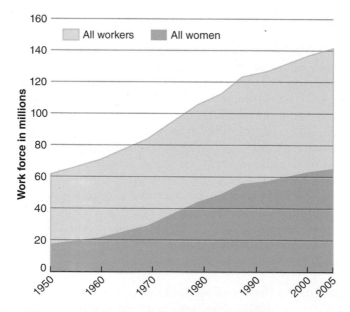

FIGURE 29.1   Women in the Work Force, 1950–2005

After 1960, the numbers of American women who were wage earners surged upward. Both the women's movement and economic pressures encouraged this trend.

Source: U.S. Department of Labor, Bureau of Labor Statistics (www.blo.gov).

those of men, the workplace remained gender segregated, and the "glass ceiling" that limited their ability to rise beyond a certain corporate level remained in place. As divorce and out-of-wedlock births became more common, the number of women heading families increased; by 1980, only 15 percent of American families with children had a father who worked and a mother who stayed at home. Children now constituted the bulk of the poor, and sociologists wrote about the "feminization of poverty."

Evidenced by the rising divorce rate in the 1970s, from one-third to one-half of the marriages occurring annually, complex issues of role-sharing befuddled middle-class families too. Women who worked still bore primary responsibility for their homes and family. Yet day-care centers for working women became commonplace; grown women were no longer "girls," gender-neutral terms (for example, *firefighter* in place of *fireman*) came into vogue, and the ideal male changed from swashbuckler to one more "in touch with his feelings." Few pined for the era when child care, housework, and volunteerism had defined "women's sphere." American women had learned, according to historian Gerda Lerner:

> *that they belong to a subordinate group; that they have suffered wrongs as a group; that their condition of subordination is not natural, but societally determined; that they must join with other women to remedy these wrongs; and finally, that they must and can provide an alternative vision of societal organization in which women as well as men will enjoy autonomy and self-determination.*

Gay Liberation   Like feminists, gay men and women were emboldened by the new sexual openness to assert their values, and stimulated by the other protest movements in the sixties, **gay liberation** emerged publicly in 1969. During a routine raid by New York City police, the homosexual patrons of the Stonewall Inn, a gay bar in Greenwich Village, unexpectedly fought back fiercely. The furor triggered a surge of "gay pride," a new sense of identity and self-acceptance, and widespread activism. As the Gay Liberation Front asserted, "We are going to be who we are."

By 1973, some eight hundred openly gay groups campaigned for equal rights, for incorporating lesbianism into the women's movement, and for removing the stigma of immorality and depravity attached to being gay. That year, the American Psychiatric Association officially ended its classification of homosexuality as a mental disorder.

In 1977, "Gay Pride" parades drew seventy-five thousand marchers in New York City and three hundred thousand in San Francisco. More taboos fell: Elaine Noble, an avowed lesbian, won a seat in the Massachusetts legislature in 1974, and Harvey Milk, an openly gay candidate, was elected to the San Francisco board of supervisors in 1977. In 1987, Massachusetts congressman Barney Frank publicly acknowledged his homosexuality. Many states and cities repealed laws against same-sex relations between consenting adults and, like the U.S. Civil

Service Commission in 1975, barred job discrimination on the basis of sexual orientation.

Environmental   Building on the concerns raised in the early sixties,
Activism   environmentalists also carried the tide of reform into
                      the 1970s. Following the first Earth Day in April 1970,
which attracted some 20 million participants, large numbers of Americans began to focus on ecology and the interaction of humans with their environment. For the first time, the media began to highlight acid rain, global warming, nuclear waste disposal, and other human-caused environmental hazards. Well-publicized disasters greatly furthered concern. Cleveland's Cuyahoga River burst into flames, and Lake Erie "died," both contaminated by decades of toxic chemical dumping. A huge oil spill fouled the coast of Santa Barbara, and many Americans choked on the air they breathed while dead fish floated in local rivers and beaches closed owing to sewage contamination.

Environmental advocacy groups gained many fresh recruits. Older organizations such as the Sierra Club and the Audubon Society continued their efforts to preserve natural areas for habitat protection and the recreational and aesthetic pleasures of future generations. Newer groups such as Greenpeace and Friends of the Earth worked against threats to ecological balance. Founded in 1971 when Canadian activists protested a planned U.S. nuclear test on an island in the Bering Sea, Greenpeace established its U.S. branch a year later, working to preserve old-growth forests and protect the world's oceans. By 2000, it had 250,000 U.S. members. The Save the Whales campaign, launched by the Animal Welfare Institute in 1971, opposed the slaughter of the world's largest mammals by fleets of floating processing factories that made dog-and-cat food.

Environmentalists also targeted the nuclear-power industry, adopting techniques from the civil-rights and antiwar campaigns to protest at planned nuclear facilities. The movement crested in 1979 when a partial meltdown crippled the **Three Mile Island** nuclear-power plant in Pennsylvania. A movie released at the same time, *China Syndrome*, portrayed a fictitious but plausible nuclear-power disaster caused by a California earthquake. Deepening public concerns about nuclear power encouraged citizen groups like the Clamshell Alliance in New England to stop new atomic power plants from going online.

However, at a time of concern over an energy crisis, and of rising unemployment, Americans divided over environmental issues like construction of the Trans-Alaska Pipeline in 1973 and whether or not to abandon atomic power, offshore oil drilling, and restrictions on logging. A popular bumper sticker read: "If You're Hungry and Out of Work, Eat An Environmentalist." Yet other Americans sought a healthy lifestyle that promoted less consumption. Cigarette smoking declined. Organic food consumption increased. A jogging craze swept the middle class.

The "Me Decade"   Whatever political views Americans held, personal pursuits and self-fulfillment largely shaped 1970s American society. Journalist Tom Wolfe dubbed this turn from the public sphere the "Me Decade," and many citizens—reacting to defeat in Vietnam, an economic downturn, and the corruption of public officials—retreated inward, following the advice of Robert Ringer's best-seller *Looking Out for Number One.*

Highly individualistic pet causes flourished, as did new faiths. Some young people practiced Transcendental Meditation or joined the Reverend Sun Myung Moon's Unification Church. Others embraced the International Society for Krishna Consciousness, whose shaved-head, saffron-robed followers added an exotic note in airports and on college campuses. Several thousand rural communes arose as some counterculture veterans sought to escape the urban-corporate world, practice organic farming, revive old technologies, and live in harmony with nature. Most communes proved short-lived.

Journalists discovered the "Yuppie" (young urban professional), preoccupied—often obsessed—with physical fitness and consumer goods. Yuppies jogged and bicycled; ate pesticide-free natural foods; and in a process known as gentrification, purchased and restored rundown inner-city apartments, often displacing poor and elderly residents in the process. Self-indulgence appeared to be their hallmark, and many identified with conservatism's priority on, above all, individual rights.

As baby boomers sang "We want the world, and we want it now!" the 1970s saw the rise of punk rock, an aggressively anti-establishment genre promoted by groups like the Sex Pistols. Tejano music spread from Texas to win national popularity thanks to performers such as Selena Quintanilla. Rap or hip-hop, whose free-form improvised recitations had roots in Jamaican reggae music and West African storytelling traditions, emerged from poor black New York City neighborhoods. And disco music spotlighted the desire to dance on one's own and to pursue individual rather than societal goals.

In the cultural arena, much but not all reflected the era's malaise. Along with films featuring the madness of the war in Vietnam and corruption in high places, blockbuster movies like *Star Wars* (1977) offered escapist fare. *Happy Days*, the top TV show of 1976–1977, evoked nostalgia for the 1950s. The TV series *Dallas*, chronicling the steamy affairs of a Texas oil family, captivated millions, as did numerous other hit programs featuring characters that defied traditional morality. And beginning in 1971 and gaining popularity throughout the decade, *All in the Family* featured a blue-collar working stiff, Archie Bunker, raging against "girls with skirts up to here" and "men with hair down to there," as well as just about everything else associated with the 1960s. Whether those who laughed were rejecting Archie's bigoted politics or endorsing his tirades against big government and social disorder may never be known. But the character his creator meant to be a cultural and political dinosaur actually forecast a shift to the right, a backlash against "the sixties."

A DIVIDED NATION

By 1968, the combined stresses and strains in American society had produced the most tumultuous era in the United States since the Civil War. The tensions that year resulted in riots, fiery demonstrations, two stunning assassinations, Lyndon Johnson's retreat in Vietnam and from politics, and an election that heralded a realignment in American politics—the first since the New Deal—and the demise of liberalism.

Assassinations and Turmoil   Three days after the Wisconsin primary, a bullet from a sniper's high-powered rifle killed Martin Luther King, Jr., in Memphis, Tennessee, where he had gone to support striking sanitation workers. The presumed assassin, James Earl Ray, a white escaped convict, would confess, be found guilty, and then recant, leaving aspects of the killing unclear. As in the assassination of John F. Kennedy, it seemed unworthy that one misfit was alone responsible.

As the news spread, black ghettos burst into violence in more than a hundred cities. Twenty blocks of Chicago's West Side went up in flames, and Mayor Richard Daley ordered police to shoot to kill arsonists. In Washington, DC, under night skies illuminated by seven hundred fires, army units in combat gear set up machine-gun nests outside the Capitol and White House. It would take seventy-five thousand troops to quell the riots, which left forty-six dead, three thousand injured, and nearly twenty-seven thousand in jail.

Entering the race as the favorite of the party bosses and labor chieftains, LBJ's vice president, **Hubert Humphrey,** turned the contest for the nomination into a three-cornered scramble. **Eugene McCarthy** remained the candidate of the "new politics"—a moral crusade against war and injustice directed to affluent, educated liberals. **Robert Kennedy** campaigned as the tribune of the less privileged, the sole candidate who appealed to both the white ethnic working class and the minority poor. In early June, after his victory in the California primary, the brother of the murdered president was himself assassinated by a Palestinian refugee, Sirhan Sirhan, who loathed Kennedy's pro-Israel views.

The deaths of King and Kennedy frustrated untold Americans. The murders denied them a fundamental democratic right, the right to choose their own leaders. "I won't vote," a youth said. "Every good man we get, they kill." Although Kennedy's death cleared the way for Humphrey's nomination, increasing numbers of Democrats turned to third-party candidate George Wallace's thinly veiled appeal for white supremacy or to the GOP nominee Richard M. Nixon. The Republican, appealing to those disgusted with inner-city riots and antiwar demonstrations, promised to end the war in Vietnam with honor and to restore "law and order." Nixon also said he would heed "the voice of the great majority of Americans, the forgotten Americans, the non-shouters, the non-demonstrators, those who do not break the law, people who pay their taxes and go to work, who send their children to school, who go to their churches, ... who love this country." Tapping the same wellsprings of anger and frustration, Wallace pitched his message to southern segregationists and blue-collar workers fed up with anti-war demonstrators and black militants. Wallace vowed, if elected, to crack down on "long-hair, pot-smoking, draft-card-burning youth."

In August 1968, violence outside the Democratic National Convention in Chicago reinforced the appeal of both Wallace and Nixon. Determined to avoid the rioting that wracked Chicago after King's assassination, Mayor Richard Daley had turned the city into a virtual fortress, denying demonstrators permits to march or engage in meaningful protest and giving police a green light to attack "the hippies, the **yippies,** and the flippies." On August 28, as a huge national television audience looked on and protesters chanted "The whole world is watching," Daley's bluecoats took off their badges and clubbed demonstrators, tossed tear gas at bystanders, and bloodied reporters and photographers. The police's brutal response—termed a "police riot" by the official commission that investigated—tore the Democrats apart and created an image of them as the party of dissent and disorder. Some 70 percent of Americans supported the police violence against the protestors. Hubert Humphrey, who for years had dreamed of becoming president, had received a nomination that appeared worthless.

Conservative Resurgence   Nixon capitalized on the tumult. Portraying himself as the candidate of the Silent Majority, he criticized the Supreme Court for safeguarding criminals and radicals; promised to crack down on "pot, pornography, protest, and permissiveness"; and asserted that "our schools are for education—not integration."

George Wallace, meanwhile, stoked the fury of the working class against "bearded anarchists, smart-aleck editorial writers, and pointy-headed professors looking down their noses at us." He vowed that "if any demonstrator ever lays down in front of my car, it'll be the last car he'll ever lie down in front of." Nearly 14 percent of the electorate—primarily young, lower-middle-class, small-town workers—cast their votes for Wallace.

In a narrow outcome with large consequences, Nixon and Humphrey split the rest of the vote almost evenly. But with Humphrey receiving just 38 percent of the white vote and not even close to half the labor vote, the long-dominant New Deal coalition was shattered. The election spelled clear-cut defeat for those who had dreamed of a society committed to social justice and economic equality. The liberal era had ended.

The 57 percent of the electorate who chose Nixon or Wallace would dominate American politics into the next century. While the Democratic Party fractured into a welter of contending groups, the Republicans attracted a new majority, many of whom lived in the suburbs and the Sunbelt—the southern states of the Old Confederacy, the desert Southwest, and populous southern California—and who regarded the federal government as wasteful, blamed protestors and hippies for lawlessness, and objected to special efforts to assist minorities and those on welfare.

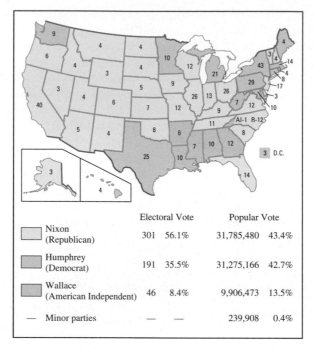

		Electoral Vote		Popular Vote	
	Nixon (Republican)	301	56.1%	31,785,480	43.4%
	Humphrey (Democrat)	191	35.5%	31,275,166	42.7%
	Wallace (American Independent)	46	8.4%	9,906,473	13.5%
—	Minor parties	—	—	239,908	0.4%

MAP 29.1   The Election of 1968

A Matter of Character

A Californian of Quaker roots, Richard Milhous Nixon was elected to Congress as a navy veteran in 1946. He won prominence for his role in the HUAC investigation of Alger Hiss (see Chapter 26) and advanced to the Senate in 1950 by accusing his Democratic opponent of disloyalty. He served two terms as Eisenhower's vice president but lost the presidential race to Kennedy in 1960 and a run for the California governorship in 1962. Ignoring what seemed a political death sentence, Nixon campaigned vigorously for GOP candidates in 1966 and won his party's nomination and the presidency in 1968.

Nixon yearned to be remembered as an international statesman, but domestic affairs kept intruding. He tried to reform the welfare system and solve complex economic problems. But the underside of Nixon's personality appealed to the darker recesses of the nation and intensified the fears and divisions among Americans.

Although highly intelligent, he displayed the rigid self-control of a man monitoring his own every move. When the private Nixon emerged, he was suspicious, insecure, seeking vengeance. His conviction that enemies lurked everywhere, waiting to destroy him, verged on paranoia. He sought to annihilate his Democratic opponents, to "get them on the ground ... stick our heels in, step on them hard ... crush them, show them no mercy."

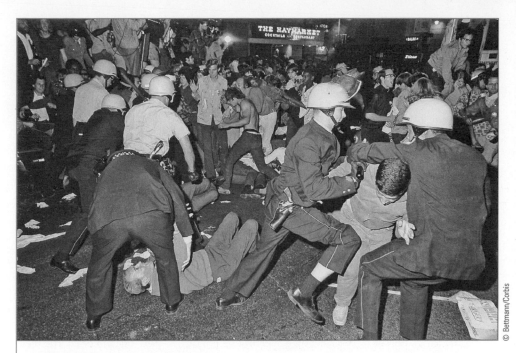

"The Whole World Is Watching" *Photographs and televised pictures of Chicago police beating and gassing antiwar protesters and innocent bystanders at the Democratic convention in 1968 linked Democrats in the public mind with violence and mayhem. The scenes made Republican Richard Nixon a reassuring presence to those he would term "the silent majority."*

© Bettmann/Corbis

The classic outsider, reared in pinched surroundings, physically awkward, unable to relate easily to others, Nixon remained fearful that he would never be accepted. At the beginning of his administration, however, his strengths stood out. He spoke of national reconciliation, took bold initiatives internationally, and dealt with domestic problems responsibly.

Symbolic of his positive start, the nation celebrated the first successful manned mission to the moon. In July 1969, the Apollo 11 lunar module, named *Eagle,* descended to the Sea of Tranquility. As millions watched on television, astronaut **Neil Armstrong** walked on the moon's surface and proclaimed, "That's one small step for man, one giant leap for mankind." Five more lunar expeditions followed, and in 1975 the space race essentially ended with the United States and the Soviet Union engaging in cooperative efforts to explore the rest of the universe.

The first newly elected president since 1849 whose party controlled neither house of Congress, Nixon cooperated with the Democrats to increase social-security benefits, build subsidized housing, expand the Job Corps, and grant the vote to eighteen-year-olds. He especially sought measures to protect the environment and signed bills for cleaner air and water, for reducing toxic wastes, and for the further protection of endangered species and wilderness. He also approved legislation creating the Occupational Safety and Health Administration (OSHA), which enforced health and safety standards in the workplace, and the Environmental Protection Agency (EPA), which required federal agencies to prepare an environmental-impact analysis for all proposed projects.

Conservatives grumbled as government grew larger and more intrusive and as race-conscious employment policies, including affirmative-action quotas, were mandated for all federal contractors. Conservatives grew still angrier when Nixon unveiled the Family Assistance Plan (FAP) in 1969. A bold effort to overhaul the welfare system, FAP proposed a guaranteed minimum annual income for all Americans. Caught between liberals who thought the income inadequate and conservatives who disliked it on principle, FAP died in the Senate.

A Troubled Economy   Nixon inherited the fiscal consequences of President Johnson's effort to wage the Vietnam War and finance the Great Society by deficit financing—to have both "guns and butter." Facing a "whopping" budget deficit of $25 billion in 1969 and an inflation rate of 5 percent, Nixon cut government spending and encouraged the Federal Reserve Board to raise interest rates. The result was a combination of inflation and recession that economists called "stagflation" and Democrats termed "Nixonomics."

Accelerating inflation lowered the standard of living of many families and sparked a wave of strikes as workers sought wage hikes to keep up with the cost of living. It encouraged the wealthy to invest in art and real estate rather than technology and factories. More plants shut down, industrial jobs dwindled, and many displaced workers lost their savings, their health and pension benefits, and their homes.

Throughout 1971, Nixon lurched from policy to policy. Declaring "I am now a Keynesian," he increased deficit spending to stimulate the private sector, which resulted in the largest budget deficit since World War II. Then, Nixon devalued the dollar to correct the balance-of-payment deficit. Finally, he froze wages, prices, and rents for ninety days, a short-term fix that worked until after the 1972 election. Then Nixon again reversed course, replacing controls with voluntary—and ineffective—guidelines. Inflation zoomed as the **Organization of Petroleum Exporting Countries** (OPEC), a group of Third World nations that had joined together to set production levels and prices, launched an embargo that raised the price of crude oil, and sluggish growth dogged the economy throughout the decade.

Law and Order   Despite his public appeals for unity, Nixon hoped to divide the American people in ways that would create a new Republican majority coalition. His "southern strategy" sought to attract Dixie's

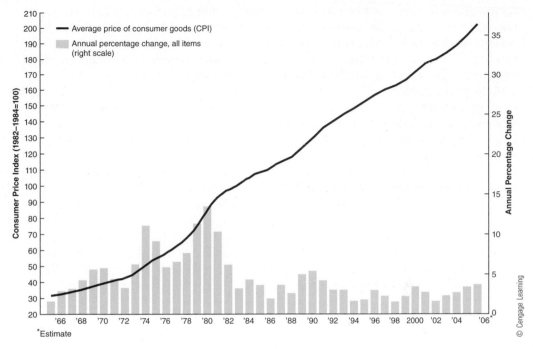

FIGURE 29.2   Inflation, 1965–2006

Inflation, which had been moderate during the two decades following World War II, began to soar with the escalation of the war in Vietnam in the mid-1960s. In 1979 and 1980, the nation experienced double-digit inflation in two consecutive years for the first time since World War I.

white Democrats into the GOP fold, while his stands on crime, drugs, and protestors wooed blue-collar laborers and suburbanites—voters whom political strategist Kevin Phillips described as "in motion between a Democratic past and a Republican future."

To combat the militants he despised, Nixon used the full resources of the federal government. He had the IRS audit their tax returns, the Small Business Administration deny them loans, and the National Security Agency illegally wiretap them. The FBI worked with local officials to disrupt and immobilize the Black Panthers, the CIA illegally investigated and compiled dossiers on thousands of American citizens, and the Justice Department prosecuted antiwar activists and black radicals in highly publicized trials. Nixon's aides also drew up an "enemies list" of adversaries to be harassed by the government.

In 1970, Nixon widened his offensive against the antiwar movement by approving the Huston Plan, which would use the CIA and FBI in various illegal activities. The plan called for wiretapping and electronic surveillance, break-ins to gather or plant evidence of illegal activity, and a new agency to centralize domestic covert operations under White House supervision. But FBI chief J. Edgar Hoover opposed the plan as a threat to the bureau's independence. Blocked, Nixon secretly created his own White House unit to discredit his opposition and ensure executive secrecy. Nicknamed **"the plumbers"** because of their assignment to plug government leaks, the team was headed by former FBI agent G. Gordon Liddy and former CIA operative E. Howard Hunt.

The plumbers first targeted Daniel Ellsberg, a former Defense Department analyst who had given the press the **Pentagon Papers,** a secret chronicle of U.S. involvement in Vietnam. On June 13, the *New York Times* began publishing the *Pentagon Papers,* revealing a long history of White House lies to Congress, foreign leaders, and the American people. Although the papers contained nothing about his administration, Nixon, fearing that they would undermine trust in government and establish a precedent for publishing classified material, sought to bar their publication. The Supreme Court, however, ruled that publication of the *Pentagon Papers* was protected by the First Amendment. Livid, Nixon directed the Justice Department to indict Ellsberg for theft and ordered the plumbers to break into the office of Ellsberg's psychiatrist in search of information to discredit the man who had become a hero to the antiwar movement.

The Southern Strategy   Nixon especially courted whites upset by the drive for racial equality. The administration opposed extension of the Voting Rights Act of 1965, sought to cripple enforcement of the Fair Housing Act of 1968, pleaded for the postponement of desegregation in Mississippi's schools, and filed suits to prohibit busing children to desegregate schools.

The strategy of wooing angry and fearful whites also dictated Nixon's Supreme Court nominations. To reverse the Warren court's liberalism, he sought strict constructionists—judges who would not "meddle" in social issues or be "soft" on criminals. In 1969, he appointed Warren Burger as chief justice. Although the Senate then twice rejected southern conservatives nominated by Nixon, the president succeeded in appointing Harry Blackmun of Minnesota, Lewis Powell of Virginia, and William Rehnquist of Arizona. Along with Burger, they steered the Court in a centrist direction, ruling liberally in most cases involving abortion, desegregation, and the death penalty, while shifting to the right on civil liberties, community censorship, and police power.

As the 1970 congressional elections neared, Nixon's vice president, Spiro T. Agnew, assailed the Democrats as "sniveling hand-wringers" and the news media as "nattering nabobs of negativism." Liberals deplored Agnew's alarming alliterative allegations, but the 1970 elections proved a draw, with the GOP losing just nine House seats and winning two Senate seats.

SUCCESSES ABROAD, CRISES AT HOME

Above all else, Nixon focused on foreign affairs. Considering himself a master of *realpolitik*—a pragmatic approach stressing national interest rather than ethical goals; he sought to check Soviet expansionism and to limit the nuclear-arms race and reduce superpower conflict. To achieve a new era of **détente**—reduced tensions—with the communist world, Nixon chose **Henry Kissinger,** a refugee from Hitler's Germany and professor of international relations, who shared Nixon's penchant for secrecy and for the concentration of decision-making power in the White House, as his chief foreign policy advisor.

In his second inaugural, Nixon pledged "to make the next four years the best four years in America's history." Ironically, they would rank among its sorriest. His vice president would resign in disgrace, his closest aides would go to jail, and he would serve barely a year and a half of his second term before resigning to avoid impeachment.

Détente   Having entered into negotiations to end the war in Vietnam (see Chapter 28), Nixon pursued détente with the Soviet Union and a turnabout in Chinese–American affairs. These developments, the most significant shift in U.S. foreign policy since the start of the Cold War, created a new relationship among the United States, the Soviet Union, and China.

Presidents from Truman to Johnson had refused to recognize the People's Republic of China, to allow its admission to the United Nations, and to permit American allies to trade with it. But by 1969, a widening Sino-Soviet split made the prospect of improved relations with both nations attractive to Nixon, who hoped to have "closer relations with each side than they did with each other." In June 1971, Kissinger began secret negotiations with Beijing, laying the groundwork for Nixon's historic February 1972 trip to China "to seek the normalization of relations." The first visit ever by a sitting American president to the largest nation in the world, it ended more than twenty years of Chinese–American hostility. Full diplomatic recognition followed in 1979.

Equally significant, Nixon went to Moscow in May 1972 to sign agreements with the Soviets on trade, technological cooperation, and the limitation of nuclear weapons. The **Strategic Arms Limitation Treaty** (SALT I) froze each side's offensive nuclear missiles for five years and committed both countries to strategic equality rather than nuclear superiority; and the Anti-Ballistic Missile (ABM) Treaty restricted the deployment by both sides of nationwide missile-defense systems. Although they did not end the arms race, the treaties moved both countries toward "peaceful coexistence" and, in an election year, enhanced Nixon's stature.

Shuttle Diplomacy   Not even better relations with China and the Soviet Union ensured global stability. In 1967, Israel, fearing an imminent Arab attack, launched a preemptive strike on its neighbors, routing them in six days and seizing Sinai and the Gaza Strip from Egypt, the West Bank and East Jerusalem from Jordan, and Syria's Golan Heights. Israel promised to give up the occupied lands in exchange for a negotiated peace, but the Arab states refused to negotiate with Israel or to recognize its right to exist. Palestinians, many of them refugees since the creation of Israel in

1948, turned to the Palestine Liberation Organization (PLO), which demanded Israel's destruction.

War exploded again in 1973 when Egypt and Syria attacked Israel on the Jewish high holy day of Yom Kippur. Only massive shipments of military supplies from the United States enabled a reeling Israel to stop the assault. In retaliation, the Arab states embargoed shipments of crude oil to the United States and its allies. The five-month embargo dramatized U.S. dependence on foreign energy sources and, following a spike in oil prices, sharply intensified inflation.

The dual shocks of the energy crisis at home and rising Soviet influence in the Arab world spurred Kissinger to engage in "shuttle diplomacy." Flying from one Middle East capital to another for two years, he negotiated a cease-fire, pressed Israel to cede some captured territory, and persuaded the Arabs to end the oil embargo. Although Kissinger's diplomacy left the Palestinian issue festering, it successfully excluded the Soviets from a major role in Middle Eastern affairs.

Nixon–Kissinger *realpolitik* based American aid on a nation's willingness to oppose communism, not on the nature of its government. Thus the Nixon administration liberally supplied arms and assistance to the shah of Iran, the white supremacist regime of South Africa, and President Ferdinand Marcos in the Philippines, as well as furnishing aid to antidemocratic regimes in Argentina, Brazil, South Korea, and Portuguese colonial authorities in Angola.

When Chileans elected a Marxist, Salvador Allende, president in 1970, Nixon secretly funded the CIA to support opponents of the leftist regime and cut off economic aid to Chile. In 1973, a military junta overthrew the Chilean government and killed Allende. Nixon quickly recognized the new dictatorship, and economic aid and investment again flowed to Chile.

The Election of 1972   Nixon's reelection appeared certain. He faced a deeply divided Democratic Party and counted on his diplomatic successes and the winding down of the Vietnam War to win over moderate voters. He expected his southern strategy and law-and-order posture to attract conservative voters. Nixon's only possible worry, another third-party candidacy by Wallace, vanished on May 15, 1972, when Wallace was shot during a campaign stop. Paralyzed from the waist down, Wallace withdrew from the race, leaving Nixon a monopoly on the white backlash.

The Senate's most outspoken dove, **George McGovern** of South Dakota, capitalizing on antiwar sentiment, blitzed the Democratic primaries. He gained additional support from new party rules requiring state delegations to include minority, female, and youthful delegates in approximate proportion to their numbers. Actress Shirley MacLaine approvingly described California's delegation as "looking like a couple of high schools, a grape boycott, a Black Panther rally, and four or five politicians who walked in the wrong door." A disapproving labor leader complained about "too much hair and not enough cigars at this convention," but McGovern won the nomination.

Perceptions of McGovern as inept and radical drove away all but the most committed supporters. McGovern dropped his vice-presidential running mate, Thomas Eagleton, when it became known that Eagleton had received electric-shock therapy for depression. Subsequently, several prominent Democrats publicly declined to run with him. McGovern's endorsement of decriminalization of marijuana, immediate withdrawal from Vietnam, and pardons for those who had fled the United States to avoid the draft exposed him to GOP ridicule as the candidate of the radical fringe.

Remembering his narrow loss to Kennedy in 1960 and too-slim victory in 1968, Nixon left no stone unturned. To do whatever was necessary to win, he appointed his attorney general, John Mitchell, to head the Committee to Re-Elect the President (CREEP). Millions of dollars in campaign contributions financed "dirty tricks" against Democrats and paid for an espionage unit, led by Liddy and Hunt, to spy on the opposition. In 1972, it received Mitchell's approval to wiretap telephones at the Democratic National Committee headquarters in Washington's Watergate apartment and office complex. However, a security guard foiled the break-in to install bugs in June 1972. Arrested were James McCord, a retired CIA officer and the security coordinator of CREEP, and several other Liddy and Hunt associates.

Dirty tricks went from a scandal to a constitutional crisis when Nixon abused the power of his office to cover up wrongdoing and hinder criminal investigations. Asserting that "no one in the White House staff, no one in this administration, presently employed, was involved in this bizarre incident," Nixon coached associates on what they should tell investigators, authorized the payment of hush money and hints of a presidential pardon to buy the silence of those arrested, and directed the CIA to halt the FBI's investigation on the pretext that it would damage national security.

With the McGovern campaign a shambles and Watergate seemingly contained, Nixon amassed nearly 61 percent of the popular vote and an overwhelming 520 electoral votes. Supported primarily by minorities and low-income voters, McGovern carried just Massachusetts and the District of Columbia. The election solidified the 1968 realignment. Nevertheless, the GOP gained only twelve seats in the House and lost two in the Senate, demonstrating the growing difficulty of unseating incumbents, the rise in ticket-splitting, and the decline of both party loyalty and voter turnout. Only 55.7 percent of eligible voters went to the polls (down from 63.8 percent in 1960).

The Watergate Upheaval   The scheme to conceal links between the White House and the accused Watergate burglars had succeeded during the 1972 campaign. But after the election, federal judge "Maximum John" Sirica, known for his tough treatment of criminals, used the threat of heavy sentences to pressure one burglar into confessing that the White House knew in advance of the break-in and that the defendants had committed perjury during the trial. Two *Washington Post* reporters, Carl Bernstein and Bob Woodward, following clues furnished by a secret informant named **"Deep Throat"**—identified in 2005 as Mark Felt, second in command at the FBI—wrote a succession of front-page stories tying the break-in to illegal contributions and "dirty tricks" by CREEP.

In February 1973, the Senate established the Special Committee on Presidential Campaign Activities to investigate, and stunning evidence of scandal revealed the existence of a White House "enemies list," the president's use of government agencies to harass opponents, and administration favoritism in return for illegal campaign donations. Both the president's special counsel and the acting head of the FBI testified to the involvement of the White House in the Watergate break-in, forcing Nixon to announce the resignation of his principal aides and the appointment of a special Watergate prosecutor with broad powers of investigation and subpoena. Then the most dramatic bombshell, the disclosure that Nixon taped every conversation in the Oval Office, meant there was an incontrovertible record of "what the president knew and when he knew it."

When the special prosecutor insisted on access to the tapes, Nixon ordered the attorney general to fire him. The attorney general and the number-two man in the Justice Department refused and were dismissed in what became known as the "Saturday night massacre." More than 150,000 telegrams poured into the White House, and eighty-four members of Congress sponsored sixteen different bills of impeachment. The House Judiciary Committee began impeachment proceedings, and Congress went to the Supreme Court to demand access to the original tapes.

Adding to Nixon's woes, Vice President Agnew pleaded no contest—"the full equivalent to a plea of guilty," according to the trial judge—to charges of income tax evasion and solicitation of bribes, both as governor of Maryland and as vice president. Agnew left office in October 1973 with a fine and suspended sentence, and was replaced, under provisions of the Twenty-fifth Amendment, by House Minority Leader Gerald R. Ford of Michigan.

A President Disgraced   In late July 1974, the Supreme Court ruled unanimously in *United States* v. *Nixon* that the unedited tapes must be turned over to Congress. The tapes produced the "smoking gun," proving beyond doubt that Nixon had ordered the cover-up, engaged in a criminal conspiracy to hinder the investigation of the break-in, and lied about his role for more than two years. The House Judiciary Committee adopted three articles of impeachment, charging Nixon with obstruction of justice, abusing the powers of the presidency by using federal agencies to harass citizens and deprive them of their rights, and contempt of Congress for refusing to obey a congressional subpoena for the tapes. Checkmated, Nixon surrendered the subpoenaed tapes.

In trying to explain Watergate, some historians point to the increasing expansion of presidential power, "the imperial presidency," stretching back several decades. Others argue that Nixon simply got caught and that his liberal foes forced him to pay a higher price for his misdeeds than had other presidents. Most focus on Nixon himself and his obsession to destroy his hated adversaries. Whatever the cause, Richard Nixon, certain the Senate would vote to convict him once impeached, became the first president to resign—and Gerald Ford took office as the nation's first chief executive who had not been elected either president or vice president.

A TROUBLED NATION AND PRESIDENCY

In the aftermath of the Vietnam debacle and Richard Nixon's disgrace, presidents **Gerald Ford** and **Jimmy Carter** grappled with inflation, recession, and industrial stagnation. They faced humiliations abroad, and, for Carter, an especially maddening hostage crisis. The confident 1950s and early 1960s, when prosperous America had savored its role as the Free World's leader, now seemed remote. A nation convinced that it was immune to the historical forces that constrained other societies seemed prey to forces beyond its control—particularly significant foreign competition and an energy crisis.

Panic at the Pump   In 1973–1974, Americans sat in their cars and waited in long lines to buy gasoline at skyrocketing prices. Angry and frustrated, motorists fought each other and battled with police. At one service station with no gas to sell, a driver threatened the attendant, "You are going to give me gas or I will kill you." The nation had long taken cheap, abundant energy for granted, yet remained heavily dependent on the third of its oil it imported. This vulnerability became apparent when Arab nations, angered by Nixon's support of Israel during the 1973 war, cut off the supply of oil to the West. Then, the seven Arab members of OPEC quadrupled the cost of a barrel of oil from $3 to $12 in 1976. OPEC would almost triple it again, to $34 in 1979, pushing the price of a gallon of gas over $1 for the first time, a price barrier many had thought unreachable. Overall, consumer prices would more than double in the 1970s, with inflation soaring to 14 percent. It battered American families and turned hard-pressed taxpayers against the welfare programs adopted during past Democratic administrations.

Disturbing economic developments forced millions of Americans in the 1970s to, according to a magazine, "Learn to Live with Less": less energy and jobs, less possibilities and power. Unemployment ranged between 6 and 10 percent, nearly twice the usual postwar level, and the federal deficit soared from $8.7 billion in 1970 to $72.7 billion in 1980. Federal borrowing to cover the deficit increased the costs of all businesses that had to borrow, which worsened the rising price spiral and the galloping inflation rate that had resulted from President Johnson's attempt to fund both the Vietnam War and the Great Society without raising taxes. Moreover, in 1971 the dollar, long the strongest currency in the world, fell to its lowest level since 1949, and the United States posted its first trade deficit—importing more than it exported—in almost a century.

Most acutely, higher costs and greater foreign competition ravaged the manufacturing regions of the Midwest and Northeast, soon to be called the "Rust Belt." The automobile industry was especially hard hit by soaring gasoline prices that boosted sales of more fuel-efficient foreign imports, mainly from Japan. U.S. purchases of foreign cars grew from 2 million in 1970 to 4 million in 1989. Chrysler, the third largest automaker, was saved from bankruptcy only by a $1.2 billion federal loan guarantee. Facing severe production cutbacks, the Big Three carmakers eliminated the jobs of one in three autoworkers between 1978 and 1982.

Long-term sources of industrial decline included aging machinery, inefficient production methods, complacent management, and fierce competition from foreign companies paying lower wages, especially in the countries of the Pacific Rim. In 1979–1983, 11.5 million U.S. workers lost jobs because of plant closings and cutbacks. Although new employment opportunities opened in the so-called knowledge-based industries (and would lead to an uneven economic revival later in the century), many industrial workers lacked the skills to fill these jobs.

With the loss of industrial jobs, the union movement weakened. In 1960, 31 percent of U.S. workers belonged to unions; thirty years later, that figure had been virtually halved to 16 percent, with further declines ahead. Some workers did join unions in these years, mainly teachers, public employees, and service workers, many of whom were female. Service-sector unionization, however, only slowed, but did not reverse, the overall decline of union membership.

Gerald Ford, Caretaker   Former Michigan congressman Gerald Ford became president after Nixon's resignation, August 9, 1974. Acknowledging he was "a Ford not a Lincoln," he urged Americans to move beyond the "long national nightmare" of Watergate. The honeymoon quickly ended, however, when Ford pardoned Nixon for "any and all crimes" committed while in office, meaning that Nixon would neither have to assume responsibility nor face prosecution for his actions.

Economic problems, particularly inflation, dogged Ford's presidency. In October 1974, Ford unveiled a program of voluntary price restraint dubbed "Whip Inflation Now" (WIN), but prices continued upward. When the Federal Reserve Board tried to cool the economy by raising interest rates, a severe recession resulted. Unemployment approached 11 percent by 1975. Then Ford tried tax cuts to stimulate business activity. They made inflation worse and did little to promote employment. As oil and gas prices soared, Americans for the first time since World War II struggled to curb energy consumption. Congress set fuel-efficiency standards for automobiles in 1975 and imposed a national speed limit of fifty-five miles per hour.

National morale sank further in late April 1975 when the South Vietnamese government fell, and television chronicled desperate helicopter evacuations from the U.S. embassy in Saigon (soon renamed Ho Chi Minh City). A few weeks later, Cambodia seized a U.S. merchant ship, the *Mayagüez*. Ford ordered a military rescue, which freed the thirty-nine *Mayagüez* crew members but cost the lives of forty-one U.S. servicemen. As the nation entered the election year 1976—also the bicentennial of the Declaration of Independence—Americans found little reason for optimism.

Jimmy Carter, Outsider   Gerald Ford won the 1976 Republican nomination, turning back a strong challenge from former California governor Ronald Reagan, who opposed détente. Jimmy Carter—a Georgia peanut grower, graduate of the naval academy, and former governor—effectively used the media to bypass party machines and sweep the Democratic primaries by stressing his honesty, his evangelical Christian faith, and his status as a Washington outsider who would bring the virtue and morality of small-town America to government.

With his running mate, Minnesota senator Walter Mondale, Carter squeaked to victory with 51 percent of the vote. Underscoring his rejection of Nixon's "imperial presidency," Carter walked with his wife Rosalyn in the inaugural parade, and in an echo of Roosevelt's fireside radio chats, he delivered some TV speeches wearing a sweater and seated by a fireplace.

Despite the populist symbolism and huge Democratic majorities in Congress, Carter never shaped a liberal agenda. Lacking both Washington experience and the inclination to deal with the capitol's key political players, he distanced himself from congressional Democrats and could not break the legislative gridlock. At heart a fiscal conservative, he favored cutting federal spending. "Government cannot solve our problems," he asserted in his second State of the Union address. "It cannot eliminate poverty, or provide a bountiful economy, or reduce inflation, or save our cities, or cure illiteracy, or provide energy." Accordingly, Carter left unresolved the major economic and social problems of the 1970s, especially, **"stagflation"**—economic stagnation combined with price inflation—which topped 20 percent in 1979.

Carter further disappointed liberals by pushing for deregulation—the removal of government controls on the airline, railroad, and trucking industries, as well as on oil and natural gas prices—and by failing to adopt an effective energy policy. Angered by rising gasoline prices and increasing dependence on foreign oil—more than 40 percent by 1980—Americans wanted energy self-sufficiency. Yet, on the central domestic policy issue of his time, Carter proposed a program that barely reduced oil consumption, grandiosely calling it the "moral equivalent of war"; most Americans sneered at it as MEOW. His failures contributed immensely to the destruction of what remained of the liberal coalition and enormously boosted the fortunes of political conservatism.

In Niagara Falls, New York, where for years the Hooker Chemical and Plastics Corporation had dumped tons of waste in a district known as Love Canal, Carter confronted a major environmental crisis. In 1953, Hooker had covered the landfill with earth and sold it to the city. Homes and schools sprang up, but residents complained of odors and strange substances oozing from the soil. In the late 1970s, tests confirmed that toxic chemicals, including deadly dioxin, were seeping into

GOING TO THE SOURCE

Carter and Stockman on Energy

In his first presidential speech on energy, Jimmy Carter sought to win the support of the American people for conservation and for governmental solutions. In response, Congressman David Stockman (R-MI) argued against federal intervention and for allowing unfettered global markets to provide abundant energy.

Carter on energy: Our national energy plan is based on 10 fundamental principles. The first principle is that we can have an effective and comprehensive energy policy only if the Government takes responsibility for it and if the people understand the seriousness of the challenge and are willing to make sacrifices....

The third principle is that we must reduce our vulnerability to potentially devastating embargoes. We can protect ourselves from uncertain supplies by reducing our demand for oil, by making the most of our abundant resources such as coal, and by developing a strategic petroleum reserve....

The fifth principle is that we must be fair. Our solutions must ask equal sacrifices from every region, every class of people, and every interest group. Industry will have to do its part to conserve just as consumers will. The energy producers deserve fair treatment, but we will not let the oil companies profiteer.

The sixth principle, and the cornerstone of our policy, is to reduce demand through conservation.... Conservation is the quickest, cheapest, most practical source of energy. Conservation is the only way we can buy a barrel of oil for about $2. It costs about $13 to waste it.

The seventh principle is that prices should generally reflect the true replacement cost of energy. We are only cheating ourselves if we make energy artificially cheap and use more than we can really afford....

The ninth principle is that we must conserve the fuels that are scarcest and make the most of those that are plentiful. We can't continue to use oil and gas for 75 percent of our consumption, as we do now, when they only make up 7 percent of our domestic reserves. We need to shift to plentiful coal, while taking care to protect the environment, and to apply stricter safety standards to nuclear energy.

---

buildings, polluting the air, and discharging into the Niagara River. Medical researchers found elevated levels of cancer, miscarriages, and birth defects among Love Canal residents.

In 1978, President Carter authorized federal funds to relocate Love Canal families, and in 1980 he declared the situation a national emergency, freeing more federal money for relocation and clean-up. As his presidency ended, Carter signed legislation creating a federal "Superfund" to clean up the nation's most polluted sites. In addition, the **Alaska Lands Act** set aside more than 100 million acres of public land for parks, wildlife refuges, and national forests and added twenty-six rivers to the nation's Wild and Scenic River System. These two bills proved to be Carter's rare successes.

Carter's foreign-policy record proved mixed. He spoke out for human rights, pushed through a Panama Canal Treaty that transferred full control over the canal

The tenth and last principle is that we must start now to develop the new, unconventional sources of energy that we will rely on in the next century.

Stockman's response: At bottom, the notion that "home grown energy is better" implies a radical rejection of the global trading system and the law of comparative advantage [that some nations can more efficiently produce certain commodities, such as oil] on which it is premised.... The result would be substantial, unnecessary loss in national output, and an artificially high domestic-energy-cost structure which would reduce the competitiveness of our exports and increase the cost-advantage of imports....

Overall, the planet's accessible natural hydrocarbon reserves readily exceed 20 trillion barrels. This is the equivalent of five centuries of consumption at current rates.... The case for fossil-fuel exhaustion simply cannot rest on physical scarcity or the stinginess of the planet.

... It is time to discard our medieval energy maps. There is no region filled with lurking dragons and other perils on the far side of the ocean. So rather than institute a politically imposed and bureaucratically managed and enforced regime of domestic-energy autarky [a policy based on authoritarian power], we need do little more than decontrol domestic energy prices, dismantle the energy bureaucracy, and allow the U.S. economy to equilibrate at the world level. Energy supply and demand will take care of itself ... and by thus encouraging full integration of the U.S. economy into the world marketplace's search for the least-cost-development sequence of our planet's prodigious remaining energy resources, we will produce the highest possible level of domestic economic growth and welfare.

Questions

1. *How do the two men differ on the causes and solution of the energy crisis?*

2. *Explain how the goals of Carter's energy proposals might conflict with his economic and environmental goals?*

Source: Jimmy Carter, "The Energy Problem," April 18, 1977, Public Papers of the Presidents of the United States: Jimmy Carter, 1977–1981; and David Stockman, "The Wrong War? The Case Against a National Energy Policy," Public Interest, 53 (Fall 1978).

to Panama by 2000, and brought together Egyptian President Anwar Sadat and Israeli Premier Menachem Begin at Camp David—refusing to let them leave until they agreed to make peace. However, the other Arab states rejected the **Camp David Accords;** Israel continued to build Jewish settlements in the occupied territories; Islamic fundamentalists assassinated Sadat in 1981. Peace in the Middle East remained as elusive as ever.

Toward the Soviet Union, Carter first showed conciliation, but toughness ultimately won out. In 1979, Carter and the Soviet leader Leonid Brezhnev signed the SALT II treaty, limiting each side's nuclear arsenals. Senate ratification stalled when Cold Warriors who had never accepted détente attacked the treaty for allegedly favoring the Soviets. Support dissolved entirely in late December 1979 when the Soviets invaded Afghanistan. Carter revived registration for the military draft, boycotted the 1980 Summer Olympics in Moscow, and embargoed grain shipments to Russia.

Iran   The low point of Carter's presidency involved Iran. Protests against a repressive regime headed by the shah of Iran, a long-time American ally, who had come to power in 1953 with CIA help (see Chapter 26), swelled in 1979. In November, after Carter admitted the shah to the United States for cancer treatment, the Islamic militant supporters of Ayatollah Khomeini stormed the U.S. embassy in Tehran and seized sixty-six American hostages, demanding the return of the shah in exchange for the captured Americans. Thus began a 444-day ordeal that virtually paralyzed the Carter administration. Night after night, TV images of blindfolded hostages, anti-American mobs, and U.S. flags being burned rubbed American nerves raw. A botched rescue attempt in April 1980, in which several U.S. helicopters malfunctioned and eight GIs died, added to the nation's humiliation—and to the public's view of Carter as an ineffective bumbler. Not until January 20, 1981, the day Ronald Reagan took office as the new president, did the Iranian authorities release the hostages.

As with Herbert Hoover in the early 1930s, Americans turned against the remote figure in the White House. When Carter's approval rating sagged to 26 percent in mid-1979 (lower than Nixon's when he resigned as a result of Watergate), he retreated to Camp David, where he delivered a TV address blaming the American people's "crisis of confidence" for the nation's troubles. When a cabinet reshuffle was all that followed, most Americans thought the helpless Carter was the problem. The 1980 Democratic convention glumly renominated Carter, but defeat in November loomed. A successful post-presidential career of public service would do much to restore Carter's reputation and bring him the Nobel Peace Prize in 2002. But in 1980, most Americans hungered for a new president and changed policies.

CHRONOLOGY
1961–1980

1964	Berkeley Free Speech Movement (FSM).
	The Beatles arrive in the United States.
1965	Ken Kesey and Merry Pranksters stage first "acid test."
1966	Abolition of automatic student deferments from the draft.
1967	March on the Pentagon.
	Israeli–Arab Six-Day War.
1968	Tet offensive.
	Martin Luther King, Jr., assassinated; race riots sweep nation.
	Students take over buildings at Columbia University.
	Robert F. Kennedy assassinated.
	Violence mars Democratic convention in Chicago.
	Vietnam peace talks open in Paris. Richard Nixon elected president.

1969	Apollo 11 lands first Americans on the moon.
	Nixon begins withdrawal of U.S. troops from Vietnam.
	Woodstock festival.
1970	United States invades Cambodia.
	Students killed at Kent State and Jackson State Universities.
	Beatles disband.
	Earth Day first celebrated.
1971	*Swann* v. *Charlotte-Mecklenburg Board of Education.*
	New York Times publishes *Pentagon Papers.*
	Nixon institutes wage-and-price freeze.
	South Vietnam invades Laos with the help of U.S. air support.
1972	Nixon visits China and the Soviet Union.
	SALT I agreement approved.
	Break-in at Democratic National Committee headquarters in Watergate complex.
	Nixon reelected president.
1973	Vietnam cease-fire agreement signed.
	Senate establishes special committee to investigate Watergate.
	President Salvador Allende ousted and murdered in Chile.
	Vice President Spiro Agnew resigns; Gerald Ford appointed vice president.
	Roe v. *Wade.*
	Yom Kippur War; OPEC begins embargo of oil to the West.
	Saturday Night Massacre.
1974	House Judiciary Committee votes to impeach Nixon.
	Nixon resigns; Ford becomes president.
1975	South Vietnamese government falls.
	Mayagüez incident.
1976	Jimmy Carter elected president.
1977	Panama Canal treaties ratified.
	Introduction of Apple II computer.
	Gay Pride parades in New York and San Francisco.
1978	Carter authorizes federal funds to relocate Love Canal residents.

1979	Menachem Begin and Anwar el-Sadat sign peace treaty at White House.
	Second round of OPEC price increases.
	Accident at Three Mile Island nuclear plant.
	Carter establishes full diplomatic relations with the People's Republic of China.
	Iran hostage crisis begins.

CONCLUSION

Baby boomers took material comfort and their own importance for granted. Longing for meaning in their lives, as well as personal liberty, they sought a more humane democracy, a less racist and consumerist society, and an end to the war in Vietnam. Failing to get what they wanted quickly, the New Left became increasingly radical and violent. Most of the young, however, were more interested in "sex, drugs, and rock-and-roll." Ultimately, the student movement and counterculture helped prod the United States into becoming a more tolerant, diverse, and permissive society. They helped pave the way for the environmental movement and spurred an end to America's longest war—which had cost the nation dearly in lives and dollars, in turning Americans against one another and in diverting society from pressing needs.

The youth rebellion, racial rioting, and the Tet offensive in Vietnam brought politics to a boil in 1968. The year of assassinations and turmoil cost Democrats the White House and triggered a conservative resurgence and major political realignment. Pursuing the national interest by *realpolitik*, President Richard Nixon and Henry Kissinger undertook secret negotiations with North Vietnam to end hostilities. At the same time, they opened the way for reduced tensions with China and the Soviet Union, enhancing the world outlook for peace, while also giving economic and military assistance to anticommunist dictatorships.

Equally vital to his political success, Nixon wooed whites upset by civil strife and by hippies and radicals. He emphasized law and order to attract the silent majority concerned with the upsurge of criminality and breakdown of traditional values, and he played upon middle-class resentment of rising taxes to pay for the federal largess going to minorities and the poor. Following a "southern strategy," he nominated conservatives for the Supreme Court, opposed extension of the Voting Rights Act and school busing for racial integration, and cracked down on militant blacks and young radicals.

In 1972, the secret schemes Nixon had put in place to spy upon and destroy those who opposed his Vietnam policies began to unravel. His obsession for secrecy and his paranoia about opponents brought his downfall. The arrest of the Watergate burglars and the subsequent attempted cover-up of White House involvement led to revelations of a host of "dirty tricks" and criminal acts, the indictment of nearly fifty Nixon administration officials and the jailing of a score of his associates, and a House Judiciary Committee vote to impeach the president. To avoid certain conviction, a disgraced Nixon resigned on August 9, 1974. Neither his successor, Gerald Ford, nor Jimmy Carter restored confidence in the White House. The national government seemed helpless as the plague of inflation, energy crisis, recession, and deindustrialization swept the land. The deepening public disenchantment with politicians and disillusionment with government, which had led millions to turn inward, would last throughout the 1970s and into the next century.

30

A CONSERVATIVE REVIVAL AND THE END OF THE COLD WAR, 1980–2000

CHAPTER OUTLINE

• A Conservative Shift in Culture and Politics • Domestic Drift and a New World Order • Domestic and Global Issues at Century's End • Tobacco Wars, White House Scandal, Disputed Election, 1996–2000 • Economic and Cultural Trends at Century's End

---

A CONSERVATIVE SHIFT IN CULTURE AND POLITICS

Ronald Reagan won the presidency in 1980 riding the conservative tide that had been building for years. Domestically, Reagan and his congressional allies enacted tax cuts and deregulatory measures reflecting their free-market, small-government ideology. The Reagan era began with a recession and ended with a stock-market crash. In between, though, inflation eased and the overall economy improved. Reagan's policies produced mounting federal deficits, however, while economic inequities, inner-city problems, and stubborn unemployment persisted.

An avid Cold Warrior, Reagan boosted military spending and adopted a tough stance toward Russia. The administration's secretive efforts to overthrow a leftist regime in Latin America triggered a constitutional crisis in Reagan's second term. But a dramatic easing of Cold War tensions ended his presidency on a high note.

Roots of the Conservative Turn   Post-1945 U.S. conservatism, an unstable blend of antigovernment libertarianism, anticommunism, and nostalgia for a premodern past, found a champion in William F. Buckley, who launched the *National Review* magazine in 1955; founded Young Americans for Freedom (1960); and started a conservative TV talk show, *Firing Line*, in 1966. Barry Goldwater's 1964 presidential campaign, though unsuccessful, gave evidence of conservatism's latent strength.

While the 1960s' counterculture and antiwar protests drew media attention, many Americans deplored what they saw as the decade's radical excesses. As we saw in Chapter 29, Richard Nixon exploited this disaffection to win the White House in 1968. Think tanks like the Heritage Foundation (1973), founded by Colorado beer baron Joseph Coors, promoted the conservative cause.

In local communities in the fast-growing South and West, conservatives came together and mobilized politically. Southern California's Orange County, recently transformed from citrus groves to suburban developments, illustrates this process. Orange County conservatives—mostly upwardly mobile, white evangelical Protestants—were intensely anticommunist, dismayed by 1960s' radicals, and suspicious of the "liberal elites" dominating the media and national politics. Recognizing their common agenda, these conservatives organized locally. Foreshadowing changes ahead nationally, Orange County helped elect Ronald Reagan governor of California in 1966 and in 1978 rallied behind Proposition 13, a state referendum mandating deep cuts in property taxes.

Conservatives mobilized around specific issues, especially abortion. As noted in Chapter 29, in the wake of *Roe* v. *Wade*, "right to life" activists pressed for a constitutional amendment outlawing abortion. Led by Roman Catholic and conservative Protestant activists, "pro-life" advocates rallied, signed petitions, and picketed abortion clinics and pregnancy-counseling centers.

Feeling the pressure, Congress in 1976 ended Medicaid funding for most abortions, effectively denying this procedure to the poor. Handing conservatives another victory, President Nixon in 1972 had vetoed a bill funding day-care centers, criticizing its "communal approach to child-rearing." The Equal Rights Amendment, denounced by Phyllis Schlafly and other conservatives, died in 1982—three states short of ratification.

To religious conservatives, gay and lesbian activism foretold society's moral collapse. "God ... destroyed the cities of Sodom and Gomorrah because of this terrible sin," thundered TV evangelist Jerry Falwell. In 1977, singer Anita Bryant led a successful campaign against a Miami ordinance protecting homosexuals' civil rights. "God created Adam and Eve, not Adam and Bruce," she pointed out. Soon after, *Good Housekeeping* magazine readers voted Bryant America's "most admired woman." Other cities, too, reversed earlier measures protecting gay rights.

In 1978, as the backlash intensified, a member of the San Francisco board of supervisors fatally shot gay activist and board member Harvey Milk and Milk's political ally, Mayor George Moscone. When the killer received a light sentence, riots erupted in the city. (Thirty years later, actor Sean Penn won an Academy Award for his starring role in a film celebrating Milk's career.)

The conservative movement gained strength from the political mobilization of evangelical Protestants, with their emphasis on strict morality, biblical authority, and a "born again" conversion experience. Evangelical denominations such as the Southern Baptist Convention grew explosively in the 1970s and 1980s, as did independent suburban megachurches. Meanwhile, liberal churches whose ministers had rallied behind the civil-rights and antiwar movements lost members.

Evangelicals had supported antislavery and other social reform before the Civil War. Their modern-day successors also preached reform, but of a conservative variety. Jerry Farwell's Moral Majority, founded in 1979 as a "pro-life, pro-family, pro-moral, and pro-America" crusade, supported conservative candidates. So did Pat Robertson, founder of the Christian Broadcasting Network. Tim LaHaye of San Diego, another politicized evangelical, was also active in mobilizing support for conservative causes. In 1981, LaHaye founded the Council for National Policy, a secretive political lobby.

While battling abortion, homosexuality, and pornography, often in alliance with conservative Catholics, evangelicals also attacked the Supreme Court's 1962 *Engel* v. *Vitale* decision banning organized prayer in public schools on First Amendment grounds. They advocated home schooling and private Christian schools to shield children from what they saw as the public schools' permissiveness and secularist (nonreligious) values.

Christian bookstores, religious radio stations, and TV evangelists fueled the revival. Falwell's *Old Time Gospel Hour*, Robertson's *700 Club*, and other luminaries of the so-called electronic church attracted a loyal following. In a world of change, evangelicals found certitude and a sense of community in their shared faith. In the process, they profoundly influenced late twentieth-century American life.

Not all evangelicals were political conservatives. Most African American evangelicals remained in the Democratic Party. Some white evangelicals resisted the rightward political turn. In general, however, newly politicized evangelicals helped propel the conservative tide that carried Ronald Reagan to the White House in 1980.

Conservatism Triumphant: The 1980 Election   Reagan grew up in Dixon, Illinois, the son of an alcoholic father and a devout mother. In 1937, after a stint as a radio sports announcer, he went to Hollywood. His fifty-four films proved forgettable, but he gained political experience as president of the Screen Actors' Guild. A New Dealer in the 1930s, Reagan moved rightward in the 1950s, and in 1954 became the General Electric Company's corporate spokesperson. In a 1964 TV speech for Barry Goldwater, he lauded American individualism and the free-enterprise system. As governor of California (1967–1975), he espoused conservative ideas and denounced campus demonstrators, but also proved open to compromise.

In the 1980 Republican primaries, Reagan bested his principal opponent, George H.W. Bush (father of the later President George W. Bush), whom he then chose as his running mate. Belying his sixty-nine years, he campaigned vigorously against President Jimmy Carter, seeking a second term. In the election, Reagan garnered 51 percent of the vote to 41 percent for the Carter–Mondale ticket. (An independent candidate, liberal Republican John Anderson, collected most of the balance.)

Republicans gained eleven Senate seats, winning a majority for the first time since 1955, and narrowed the Democrats' majority in the House of Representatives. The Republican successes revealed the power of conservative political action committees (PACs) whose computerized mass mailings focused on emotional issues like abortion and gun control.

Benefiting from the continuing erosion of Democratic strength in the South fostered by Richard Nixon, Reagan carried every southern state except Carter's Georgia. He also swept every state west of the Mississippi except Minnesota and Hawaii. More than half of white blue-collar workers, once solidly Democratic, voted Republican. Of FDR's New Deal coalition, only black voters remained solidly Democratic.

Jerry Falwell's pro-Reagan Moral Majority registered an estimated 2 million new voters in 1980 and 1984. The organization disbanded after 1984, but Pat Robertson's Christian Coalition took its place, mobilizing evangelicals to elect candidates to local office as a stepping stone to expanded national influence.

Population changes contributed to Reagan's success. While urban Democratic strongholds in the Northeast and Midwest lost population in the 1970s, Texas, California, Florida, and other more conservative Sunbelt states grew.

Voters frightened by stagflation welcomed Reagan's promise that tax cuts would bring recovery. His antigovernment rhetoric and dismissal of social-welfare programs like Johnson's War on Poverty resonated with white middle-class and blue-collar Americans. Like his one-time political hero Franklin Roosevelt, Reagan promised a new deal. But unlike FDR's, Reagan's new deal meant individualism, smaller government, lower taxes, and untrammeled free enterprise.

Reagan, a seasoned actor and public speaker, wrapped these themes into an appealing message of moral affirmation and support for "traditional values." At a time of national malaise, he exuded confidence. His unabashed patriotism, calls for military strength, and praise of America's greatness soothed the battered psyche of a nation traumatized by Vietnam and the frustrations of the seventies. Some found Reagan's core ideology negative and mean-spirited. But in 1980, most voters embraced his hopeful message.

Enacting the Conservative Economic and Political Agenda   While Reagan rhetorically endorsed the religious conservatives' cultural agenda, he mostly ignored it once in office. By contrast, he actively promoted his economic and political program, with broad—though far from universal—public support.

Reagan's economic plan, dubbed "Reaganomics" by the media, boiled down to the belief that the U.S. economy, if freed from taxes and regulations, would achieve wonders of productivity. Reagan proposed a 30 percent cut in federal income taxes over three years. Trimming this proposal slightly, Congress voted a 25 percent cut: 5 percent in 1981, 10 percent in 1982 and 1983.

To partially counterbalance the lost revenues, Congress slashed more than $40 billion from domestic spending. Economists still warned that the tax cut would produce huge federal deficits, but Reagan insisted that lower tax rates would stimulate economic growth, pushing up tax revenues. In the Republican primaries, George H.W. Bush had ridiculed Reagan's rosy predictions as "voodoo economics," but as vice president he tactfully remained silent.

Business deregulation had begun under Carter, but Reagan pushed it into new areas such as banking, the savings-and-loan industry, and communications. Transportation regulations aimed at improving air quality and fuel economy were trimmed back. Interior Secretary James Watt of Wyoming opened federal wilderness areas, forest lands, and coastal waters to oil, gas, and timber companies and cut back on environmental and endangered species protections. Watt earlier spearheaded the so-called Sagebrush Rebellion, a campaign by ranchers, farmers, and mineowners to shift federal lands in the West to state and county control. Environmental groups protested Watt's policies and demanded his ouster. After various public-relations gaffes, Watt resigned in 1983.

Reagan had little sympathy for organized labor. In 1981, when the Professional Air Traffic Controllers Organization (PATCO) went on strike, Reagan invoked the 1947 Taft-Hartley law against strikes by federal employees and ordered them back to work. When more than eleven thousand PATCO members defied the order, Reagan fired them and barred them permanently from federal employment. Reagan acted within the law, but his action struck many as unduly harsh.

To combat continuing inflation (see Chapter 29), the Federal Reserve Board pushed up interest rates. This medicine, coupled with falling oil prices, did lower inflation, but high interest rates also brought on a recession. By late 1982, unemployment stood at 10 percent. Reagan's cuts in social programs worsened the plight of the poor, including inner-city blacks and Hispanics. The Fed's policy also hurt U.S. exports. As foreign investors bought Treasury bonds to earn high U.S. interest rates, the dollar rose in value, making U.S. export goods more expensive. With U.S. imports of cars, TVs, and other goods from Japan and elsewhere soaring, the trade deficit surged to $111 billion in 1984.

Facing a recession and rising federal deficits, Reagan in 1982–1983 slowed military spending, approved emergency job programs, restored some spending on social programs, and authorized tax increases disguised as "revenue-enhancement measures." Nevertheless, the recession hurt Reagan's popularity, and Democrats made gains in the 1982 midterm elections.

By 1983, with the economy rebounding, the stock market surged. Money managers like Ivan Boesky, an apparent genius at stock transactions, became celebrities. E.F. Hutton and other brokerage firms lured new investors. Corporate mergers proliferated. Savings-and-loan (S&L) companies, newly deregulated and flush with deposits from eager investors, ladled out billions to developers planning shopping malls, condominiums, and retirement villages.

The Wall Street frenzy had an unsavory underside. In 1985, E.F. Hutton officials pled guilty to illegal fund manipulation. Ivan Boesky went to prison after a 1986 conviction for insider trading (profiting through advance knowledge of corporate actions). The high-flying S&L industry would collapse in 1988 (as detailed later in this chapter). The 1987 film *Wall Street* captured the decade's darker side. As protagonist Gordon Gekko, a hard-driving speculator played by Michael Douglas, puts it: "Greed, for lack of a better word, is good. Greed is right, greed works. Greed ... captures the essence of the evolutionary spirit."

On October 19, 1987, the stock market crashed, reducing the paper value of the nation's stocks by 20 percent overnight. The market soon recovered, but the collapse had a sobering effect on giddy investors.

Even during the boom, systemic economic problems persisted. Federal budget deficits—the predictable consequence of Reagan's tax cuts and military spending spree—surpassed $200 billion in 1985 and 1986. Budget deficits, the trade deficit, widening economic disparities amid the boom times, and a savings-and-loan crisis related to deregulation must rank among Reagan's economic legacies.

Reagan also shaped the Supreme Court. His 1981 selection of Sandra Day O'Connor as the first woman Supreme Court justice won praise. He nudged the high court in a conservative direction in 1986 by elevating William Rehnquist, a Nixon appointee, to the chief justiceship upon Warren Burger's retirement, and nominating Antonin Scalia to replace him. Scalia would prove a leader of the Court's conservative wing, defending the powers of the executive branch, opposing abortion rights, and upholding the view that the "original intent" of the Constitution's eighteenth-century framers must guide any governmental responses to changing social realities.

When another vacancy opened in 1987, Reagan nominated Robert Bork, a judge and legal scholar whose abrasive personality and rigid views led the Senate to reject him. After a second failed nomination, Reagan's third choice, Anthony Kennedy, a conservative California jurist, won quick confirmation.

The Cold War Heats Up   The late 1970s' deterioration in U.S.–Soviet relations worsened during Reagan's first term. Addressing a convention of evangelicals, the president demonized the Soviet Union as an "evil empire." Anti-Soviet fury exploded in September 1983 when the Russians shot down a Korean passenger plane that strayed into their airspace, killing all 269 aboard.

Insisting that post-Vietnam America had grown dangerously weak, Reagan launched a military expansion. The Pentagon's budget nearly doubled, reaching more than $300 billion by 1985. The buildup included nuclear weapons. Secretary of State Alexander Haig spoke of using "nuclear warning shots" in a conventional war; other officials mused about the "winnability" of nuclear war. Despite protests across Europe, the administration deployed 572 nuclear missiles in Western Europe in 1983, fulfilling a NATO decision to match Soviet missiles in Eastern Europe. In an echo of the 1950s, the administration issued a nuclear-war defense plan whereby city-dwellers would flee to nearby small towns, and a Defense Department official proposed backyard shelters as adequate protection in a nuclear war.

Spooked by all the talk of nuclear war, many Americans rallied to a campaign for a multinational freeze on the manufacture and deployment of nuclear weapons. Antinuclear protesters packed New York's Central Park in June 1982. That November, voters in nine states, including California and Wisconsin, approved nuclear-freeze referenda.

To counter the freeze campaign, Reagan in March 1983 proposed the **Strategic Defense Initiative** (SDI), a computerized antimissile system involving space based lasers and other high-tech components. Critics quickly dubbed the scheme "Star Wars." Experts warned of monumental technical hurdles and the danger of further

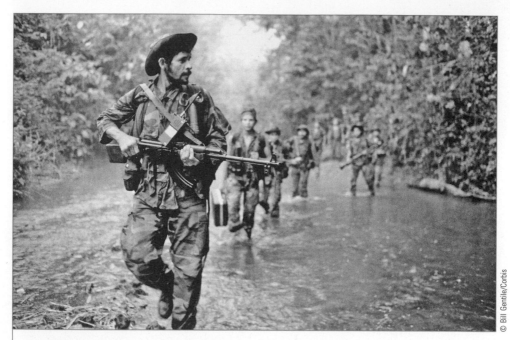

Anti-Sandinista Contras on Patrol in Nicaragua, 1987 *Under Reagan, the CIA recruited, financed, and equipped an army to overthrow Nicaragua's leftist Sandinista regime. This support continued clandestinely despite congressional prohibitions, leading to the so-called Iran-contra scandal.*

escalating the nuclear-arms race. Nevertheless, Reagan prevailed, and Congress authorized a costly SDI research program.

Fearing communist gains in Latin America, the administration backed El Salvador's military junta in its brutal suppression of a leftist insurgency supported by Fidel Castro's Cuba. In Nicaragua, Reagan vigorously opposed the Sandinista insurgents who overthrew dictator Anastasio Somoza in 1979. The Sandinistas, Reagan claimed, were turning Nicaragua into a communist state like Cuba. In 1982, the CIA organized and financed an anti-Sandinista guerrilla army, called the contras, based in neighboring Honduras and Costa Rica. The contras, with links to the hated Somoza regime, conducted raids and sabotage in Nicaragua that killed many civilians.

Fearing another Vietnam, Congress late in 1982 voted a year-long halt in U.S. military aid to the contras, and in 1984 imposed a two-year ban. Ignoring these prohibitions, the White House secretly continued to funnel money to the contras, resulting in a major scandal in Reagan's second term.

Reagan's one success in Latin America involved the tiny island of Grenada, where a 1983 coup had installed a pro-Castro government. In October 1983, two thousand U.S. troops invaded Grenada and substituted a pro-U.S. government.

Extending its anticommunist campaign to Afghanistan, the Reagan administration (expanding a policy started by President Carter) secretly funneled funds and

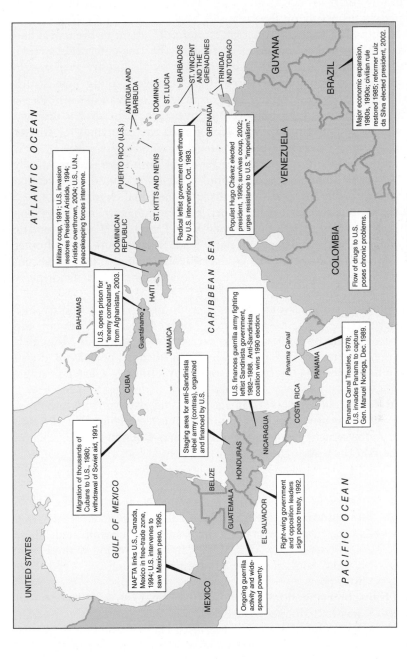

MAP 30.1 The United States in Central America and the Caribbean, 1978–2006

Plagued by poverty population pressures, repressive regimes, and drug trafficking, this region has experienced turmoil and conflict—but also hopeful developments—in recent decades.

Source: © Cengage Learning. All rights reserved. No distribution allowed without express authorization.

The following labels appear on the map:

UNITED STATES

ATLANTIC OCEAN

GULF OF MEXICO

Migration of thousands of Cubans to U.S., 1980; withdrawal of Soviet aid, 1991.

U.S. opens prison for "enemy combatants" from Afghanistan, 2003.

Military coup, 1991; U.S. invasion restores President Aristide, 1994; Aristide overthrown, 2004; U.S., U.N., peacekeeping forces intervene.

BAHAMAS

Guantánamo

HAITI

DOMINICAN REPUBLIC

PUERTO RICO (U.S.)

ST. KITTS AND NEVIS

ANTIGUA AND BARBUDA

DOMINICA

ST. LUCIA

BARBADOS

ST. VINCENT AND THE GRENADINES

TRINIDAD AND TOBAGO

GUYANA

Radical leftist government overthrown by U.S. intervention, Oct. 1983.

GRENADA

BRAZIL

Major economic expansion, 1980s, 1990s; civilian rule restored 1985; reformer Luiz da Silva elected president, 2002.

Staging area for anti-Sandinista rebel army (contras), organized and financed by U.S.

U.S. finances guerrilla army fighting leftist Sandinista government, 1982–1988. Anti-Sandinista coalition wins 1990 election.

CUBA

JAMAICA

CARIBBEAN SEA

Populist Hugo Chávez elected president, 1998; survives coup, 2002; urges resistance to U.S. "imperialism."

VENEZUELA

COLOMBIA

Flow of drugs to U.S. poses chronic problems.

Panama Canal

Panama Canal Treaties, 1978; U.S. invades Panama to capture Gen. Manuel Noriega, Dec. 1989.

PANAMA

COSTA RICA

NICARAGUA

HONDURAS

BELIZE

EL SALVADOR

Right-wing government and opposition leaders sign peace treaty, 1992.

GUATEMALA

Ongoing guerrilla activity and widespread poverty.

NAFTA links U.S., Canada, Mexico in free-trade zone, 1994; U.S. intervenes to save Mexican peso, 1995.

MEXICO

PACIFIC OCEAN

equipment to Islamic fighters, called *mujahadeen*, battling to expel Russian troops that had invaded Afghanistan in 1979 to prop up an unpopular pro-Russian regime. Ironically, young **Osama bin Laden,** a wealthy Saudi Arabian who would later become a deadly foe of America, was also financing the mujahadeen, putting him and the United States briefly on the same side.

Reagan's determination to make America "stand tall" again in the world had broad appeal, as did his tax cuts and celebration of the free-enterprise system. Americans also liked Reagan's upbeat style, typified by his jaunty response in March 1981 when a ricocheting bullet fired by a deranged young man struck him in the chest. Rushed to the hospital, Reagan insisted on walking in. "Please tell me you're all Republicans," he quipped to physicians. (The attack disabled Reagan's press secretary, James Brady, who later joined the campaign for stricter gun control.)

With the recession fading, Reagan and Vice President Bush were enthusiastically renominated at the 1984 Republican convention. Staged for TV, the convention accented themes of patriotism, prosperity, and Reagan's personal charm.

In the Democratic primaries, civil-rights leader Jesse Jackson garnered 3.5 million votes and won five southern states. But former Vice President Walter Mondale captured the nomination with backing from party leaders, labor unions, and other traditional Democratic constituencies. His vice-presidential choice, New York congresswoman Geraldine Ferraro, became the first woman to run on a major-party presidential ticket.

Reagan's ideological and personal appeal, combined with prosperity and the continued support of "Reagan Democrats," proved decisive. Reagan and Bush won 59 percent of the popular vote and carried every state but Mondale's Minnesota plus the District of Columbia. The Republicans' post-1968 dominance of the White House—interrupted only by Jimmy Carter's single term—continued.

In 1985, frustrated by the Democrats' image as a "big government" and "tax-and-spend" party, Arkansas governor Bill Clinton, Tennessee senator Al Gore, and others formed the more centrist **Democratic Leadership Council** (DLC). Clinton would later use the DLC as a springboard for a presidential bid.

The Iran-Contra Scandal and a Thaw in U.S.–Soviet Relations

Reagan's second-term achievements included the 1986 Immigration Reform and Control Act (see Chapter 29) and a tax-reform law making the system less complicated. These were overshadowed, however, first by a major White House scandal and then by a dramatic easing of Cold War hostilities.

The so-called **Iran-contra scandal,** began obscurely in 1986 with reports that in 1985 the United States had shipped, via Israel, 508 antitank missiles to Iran, America's avowed enemy. Admitting the sale, Reagan claimed the goal had been to encourage "moderate elements" in Tehran and to gain the release of U.S. hostages held in Lebanon by pro-Iranian groups. In February 1987, a presidentially appointed investigative panel blamed Reagan's chief of staff, Donald Regan, who resigned.

Next came the revelation that Oliver North, a National Security Council aide, had secretly diverted profits from the Iran arms sales to the Nicaraguan contras despite Congress's ban on such aid. To hide this crime, North and his secretary had altered and destroyed incriminating documents.

In May 1987 congressional hearings on the scandal were opened. North, in his U.S. marine uniform, boasted of his patriotism, and National Security Adviser John Poindexter testified that he had deliberately concealed the scheme from President Reagan. The congressional investigative committee found no proof that Reagan knew of illegalities, but criticized the lax management and contempt for the law that pervaded the White House. In 1989, North was convicted of obstructing a congressional inquiry and destroying and falsifying official documents. (The conviction was later reversed on a technicality.) Although less damaging than Watergate, the Iran-contra scandal took its toll in public trust of government.

Attorney General Edwin Meese resigned in 1988 amid charges of using his influence to promote ventures from which he hoped to profit. In 1989 came revelations that former interior secretary James Watt and other prominent Republicans had collected hundreds of thousands of dollars for using their influence to help housing developers seeking federal subsidies. Reagan's popularity seemed unaffected; some dubbed him the Teflon president—nothing stuck to him.

Improved U.S.–Soviet relations highlighted Reagan's second term. At meetings in Europe in 1985 and 1986, Reagan and Soviet premier Mikhail Gorbachev revived the stalled arms-control process. Beset by economic problems and by unrest in Eastern Europe, Gorbachev worked to reduce superpower tensions while restructuring Russia's economy, loosening Moscow's grip in Eastern Europe, and bringing more openness to Russia's government.

In 1987, in Washington, Reagan and Gorbachev signed the **Intermediate-range Nuclear Forces** (INF) **Treaty,** eliminating twenty-five hundred U.S. and Soviet missiles from Europe. This, in turn, led to Reagan's historic May 1988 visit to Moscow, where the two leaders strolled in Red Square.

Some Reaganites protested as their hero embraced the world's top communist. But Reagan cheerfully pointed to Gorbachev's reforms and argued that the "evil empire" was becoming more benign. Most Americans welcomed improved relations with Moscow.

The INF treaty and Reagan's trip to Moscow marked a significant thaw in the Cold War. While historians still debate the relative importance of Reagan's military buildup versus the Soviet Union's internal weaknesses in producing this outcome, the fact that one of America's most dedicated Cold Warriors presided over the early stages of the Cold War's end remains a striking irony of recent U.S. history.

Conflict and Terrorism in the Middle East and Beyond   Although the Cold War conflict eased, the Reagan administration faced serious challenges abroad. In 1980, and under strongman Saddam Hussein, Iraq invaded its neighbor Iran. The incoming Reagan administration, hoping to slow the spread of the anti-American Islamic fundamentalism fomented by Iran's Ayatollah Khomeini, backed Iraq in what became an eight-year war. (Two decades later, the United States would invade Iraq to overthrow Saddam Hussein, covered in Chapter 31.)

As the administration confronted the ongoing conflict among Israel, the Palestinians, and Israel's Arab foes, it faced conflicting interests. The United States gave its ally Israel large annual grants in military aid and other assistance, while also providing aid to Egypt and the Palestinians and importing oil from Saudi Arabia and other Arab states.

In June 1982, when extremists linked to the Palestinian Liberation Organization (PLO) shot and critically wounded Israel's ambassador to Great Britain, Israeli troops under Defense Minister Ariel Sharon attacked PLO bases in southern Lebanon and forced its leaders to evacuate the country. As part of this operation, a Lebanese Christian militia, with Sharon's approval, invaded two Palestinian refugee camps thought to harbor PLO terrorists, where they massacred hundreds of residents, including women and children. In September 1982, Reagan ordered two thousand marines to Lebanon as part of a multinational force to keep peace among the country's religious and political factions. On October 23, 1983, a Shiite Muslim crashed an explosives-filled truck into a U.S. barracks, killing 239 marines. Reagan had never made clear how the deployment served U.S. interests, and early in 1984 he withdrew the surviving marines.

In 1987, Palestinians launched an *intifada,* or uprising, against Israeli occupation of Gaza and the West Bank, territories occupied by Israel since the 1967 war. In response, Secretary of State George Shultz (who had replaced Alexander Haig) proposed negotiations leading to an independent Palestinian state. Israel refused to negotiate until the *intifada* ended, however, and the Palestinians rejected Shultz's proposals for not assuring Palestinian interests. Over U.S. objections, Jewish settlement continued in the occupied territories.

A deadly byproduct of the Middle East conflict was a series of bombings, assassinations, hijackings, and hostage-takings by anti-Israel and anti-American terrorists. At the 1972 Summer Olympics in Munich, Palestinian gunmen killed eleven Israeli athletes. In 1985, terrorists bombed the Vienna and Rome airports and hijacked a TWA flight en route from Athens to Rome, holding the crew and passengers hostage for seventeen days and killing one passenger, a U.S. sailor. That same year, armed men demanding the release of Palestinians held by Israel hijacked an Italian cruise ship, dumping a wheelchair-bound Jewish American passenger into the sea.

A 1986 bombing of a Berlin club popular with Americans killed two GIs. Accusing Libyan strongman Muammar al-Qaddafi of this and other attacks, Reagan ordered the bombing of Libyan military sites. But the attacks continued. In December 1988, a bomb detonated aboard Pan Am flight 103, en route from London to New York. It crashed near Lockerbie, Scotland, killing all 259 aboard, including many Americans. In 1991, U.S. and British authorities indicted two Libyan officials in the attack. In 1999, Qaddafi released the two for trial. A Scottish court acquitted one, but convicted the other and imposed a life sentence.

The stationing of U.S. troops in Saudi Arabia, site of Islam's holiest shrines, as well as expanding Jewish settlements in the Palestinian territories, fed the anger that fueled terrorist attacks. So did deep religious and political divisions. Hatred of Israel, and even denial of its right to exist, gripped parts of the Muslim world. Radical Islamic clerics called for *jihad* (holy war in defense of Islam) against a Christian (or secular) West that seemed increasingly dominant militarily, economically, and culturally.

The Reagan Years: A Summing Up Despite nerve-wracking terrorist attacks, many Americans felt confident about the nation's prospects as Reagan's term ended. After Nixon's disgrace, Ford's caretaker presidency, and Carter's rocky tenure, Reagan's two terms restored a sense of stability to U.S. politics. Domestically, Reagan compiled a mixed record. Inflation eased, and the economy improved after 1982. But the federal deficit soared, and the antiregulatory spirit planted the seeds of future problems. Despite Reagan's antigovernment rhetoric, on his watch the federal budget and bureaucracy continued to grow. Reagan himself proved pragmatically ready to compromise when circumstances dictated.

Building on Nixon's strategy, Reagan exploited the anxieties of middle-class white voters. He dismissed 1960s-style social activism, criticized affirmative-action programs, and ridiculed the welfare system by recounting urban legends about Cadillac-driving "welfare queens."

To his critics, Reagan's celebration of individual freedom could readily morph into self-centered materialism. Apart from individualism, anticommunism, and content-free patriotism, they contended, Reagan offered no social vision or common goals around which all Americans could rally.

In 1988, former chief of staff Donald Regan, still smarting over his forced resignation, published a memoir that portrayed Reagan as little more than an automaton: "Every moment of every public appearance was scheduled, every word was scripted, every place where Reagan was expected to stand was chalked with toe marks."

Reagan's admirers praised him for reasserting the values of self-reliance, criticizing government excesses, and restoring national pride. The 1984 Summer Olympics in Los Angeles, they suggested, when exuberant American fans had waved flags and chanted "USA, USA," captured this revived confidence. Reagan's fierce anticommunism and military build-up, they contended, hastened America's Cold War victory. Alzheimer's disease darkened Reagan's post-presidential years, but aspiring Republican politicians still seek to recapture the Reagan magic.

DOMESTIC DRIFT AND A NEW WORLD ORDER

George H.W. Bush was a patrician in politics. Son of a Connecticut senator, Yale graduate, and World War II bomber pilot, he entered the Texas oil business, served in Congress, and was a U.N. ambassador and CIA director before becoming

Reagan's running mate in 1980. Elected president in 1988, Bush reacted decisively to a foreign crisis, but proved less impressive on domestic issues.

1988: The Conservative Momentum Continues Easily winning the 1988 Republican presidential nomination, Bush in a Reagan-esque acceptance speech pledged, "Read my lips: no new taxes." As his running mate, he selected Indiana senator Dan Quayle, son of a newspaper publisher.

On the Democratic side, Jesse Jackson again did well in the primaries, but Massachusetts governor Michael Dukakis captured the nomination, choosing Texas senator Lloyd Bentsen to fill out the ticket.

In the campaign, Bush emphasized prosperity and improved Soviet relations, while distancing himself from the Iran-contra scandal. A TV commercial aired by Bush supporters played on racist stereotypes in criticizing a Massachusetts prisoner-furlough program supported by Dukakis.

Dukakis emphasized his managerial skills, pointed to holes in the "Swiss-cheese" Reagan economy, and urged "Reagan Democrats" to return to the fold. But Dukakis's focus on competence rather than ideology offered no compelling political vision. Both candidates relied on sound bites and TV photo opportunities. Bush visited flag factories and military plants. Dukakis proved his toughness on defense by posing in a tank. Editorial writers deplored the "junk-food" campaign.

Bush won, carrying forty states and garnering 54 percent of the vote. Dukakis prevailed in only ten states plus the District of Columbia. The Democrats, however, retained control of Congress.

The Cold War Ends; Global Challenges Persist The Soviet Union's collapse, heralded by the opening of the Berlin Wall, proceeded with breathtaking rapidity. In 1989, guards opened the gates of the wall that was built by the Russians in 1961. East Berliners joyously poured through and West Berliners greeted them with with flowers, tears, and shouts of welcome. East Germany's communist regime imploded. The Baltic republics annexed by Moscow in 1940—Estonia, Latvia, and Lithuania—declared independence. The other Soviet republics moved toward autonomy as well.

In July 1991, President Bush and Mikhail Gorbachev signed a treaty reducing their nuclear arsenals by 25 percent. Secretary of Defense Dick Cheney proposed a 25 percent reduction in U.S. military forces over five years. NATO announced major troop reductions.

That August, die-hard communists tried to overthrow Gorbachev. But thousands of Muscovites, rallied by Boris Yeltsin, president of the Russian Republic, protectively surrounded Moscow's parliament building, and the coup failed. Gorbachev, overwhelmed by forces he himself had unleashed, soon resigned, and Boris Yeltsin filled the power vacuum.

The Cold War was over. Speaking at Pearl Harbor on December 7, 1991, fifty years after the attack that propelled the United States into World War II, President Bush proclaimed: "[N]ow we stand triumphant—for a third time this century—this time in the wake of the Cold War. As in 1919 and 1945, we face no enemy menacing our security."

But even as Americans savored the moment, new problems arose, some of them a byproduct of the Cold War's end. As the Soviet Union fragmented, Secretary of State James Baker, a Bush family friend, worked to ensure the security of nuclear missiles based in Russia and in newly independent Ukraine, Belarus, and Kazakhstan, and to prevent rogue states or terrorists from acquiring nuclear materials or know-how from these countries.

For decades, the superpowers had backed client states and rebel insurgencies around the world. As the Cold War ended, some local disputes faded as well. In Nicaragua, Bush abandoned Reagan's proxy war against the leftist Sandinista government. In the Philippines, a former U.S. colony and long-time military ally, the United States closed two naval bases under pressure from the Philippines legislature.

Meanwhile, South Africa's policy of racial segregation—apartheid—provoked worldwide protests, supported by U.S. black leaders and campus activists. In 1986, over Reagan's veto, Congress had joined other nations in imposing economic sanctions against white-ruled South Africa, including a ban on U.S. corporate investment. Yielding to these pressures and to domestic anti-apartheid campaigners, the South African government in 1990 released black leader Nelson Mandela after years in prison. When South Africa scrapped its apartheid policy in 1991, President Bush lifted the sanctions. In 1994, Mandela was elected president and his party, the African National Congress, assumed power.

In 1989, Chinese troops brutally crushed a pro-democracy demonstration in Beijing's Tiananmen Square, killing several hundred students and workers. The Bush administration curtailed diplomatic contacts, but Bush, committed to expanding U.S. trade, did not break diplomatic relations or cancel trade agreements with Beijing.

The Persian Gulf War, 1991   On August 2, 1990, Iraq invaded neighboring Kuwait. Iraq's dictator, Saddam Hussein, viewed Kuwait's ruling sheiks as Western puppets and asserted Iraq's historic claims to Kuwait's vast oil fields.

The United States had backed Iraq in its war with Iran. But now, confronted by Iraq's invasion of a vital, oil-producing nation, Bush responded decisively, assembling a force of more than five hundred thousand U.S. troops. A multination coalition, including Persian Gulf states, contributed additional troops and logistics.

When Saddam ignored a UN resolution demanding Iraq's withdrawal by January 15, 1991, both houses of Congress endorsed military action. Most Democrats voted against war, however, favoring economic sanctions. Vietnam memories stirred as America debated another war.

Beginning January 16, U.S. bombers pounded Iraqi troops, supply depots, and command centers in Iraq's capital, Baghdad. In retaliation, Saddam fired Soviet-made Scud missiles against Tel Aviv and other Israeli cities, as well as against Riyadh, the capital of Saudi Arabia, which backed the U.S.-led war. As TV viewers watched distant explosions filmed through aircraft bombsights, and interceptor missiles streaking off to attack incoming Scuds, the war seemed unreal, almost like a video game.

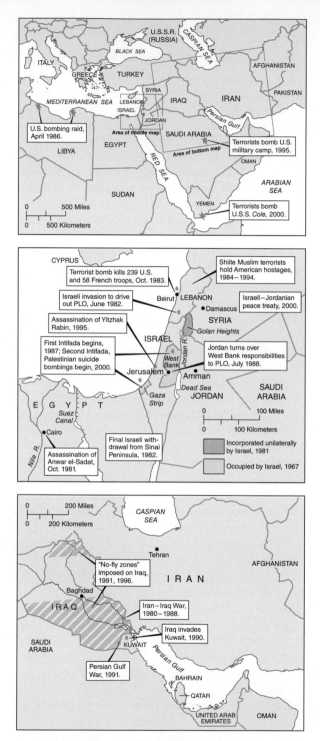

MAP 30.2 The Mideast Crisis, 1980–2000

With terrorist attacks, the Iran–Iraq War, the Persian Gulf War, and the ongoing struggle between Israel and the Palestinians, the Middle East saw almost unending violence and conflict in these years.

On February 23, two hundred thousand U.S. troops moved across the desert toward Kuwait. Thousands of Iraqi soldiers fled or surrendered. U.S. forces destroyed thirty-seven hundred Iraqi tanks while losing only three. With Iraqi resistance crushed, President Bush declared a cease-fire, and Kuwait's ruling family returned to power. U.S. casualties numbered 148 dead—including thirty-five killed inadvertently by U.S. firepower—and 467 wounded. Iraqi military casualties were estimated at twenty-five thousand to sixty-five thousand.

For President Bush, the **Persian Gulf War** proved that Americans were prepared to use force to pursue national interests. "By God, we've kicked the Vietnam syndrome once and for all," he declared.

Bush and his top advisers rebuffed some who urged invading Iraq itself and overthrowing Saddam Hussein. Such an invasion, they feared, could lead to an extended occupation. The UN did impose "no-fly zones" on Iraqi aircraft, and a somewhat chastened Saddam granted UN inspectors access to his weapons-production facilities. Nevertheless, Saddam's army brutally suppressed antigovernment uprisings by Iraq's Shiite Muslims and ethnic Kurds.

Troubles at Home: Economic Woes, Racial Tensions, Environmental Threats

At home, a rare accomplishment for Bush was the **Americans with Disabilities Act** of 1990. Supported by Bush, this law barred discrimination against disabled persons in hiring or education. As in the earlier civil-rights movement, Congress acted following demonstrations and lobbying by the disabled and their advocates. Thanks to this law, job opportunities for handicapped persons increased and public schools enrolled more physically or developmentally impaired children.

Otherwise, the Bush years saw more problems than achievements on the home front. By the early 1990s, the impact of Reagan-era tax cuts and deregulation began to hit home. First came the collapse of the savings-and-loan (S&L) industry, provider of home loans and a modest but secure return to depositors. In the late 1970s, as inflation had pushed up interest rates, the S&Ls had offered higher interest to retain investors, even though the S&L's assets were mostly in fixed-rate mortgages. Following the Reagan tax cuts, money flowed into S&Ls with their attractive rates. Meanwhile, in the deregulatory fervor, Congress eased the rules governing S&Ls, enabling them to make loans on risky real-estate ventures. Amid a glut of commercial development, many of these investments went bad. In 1988–1990, nearly six hundred S&Ls failed, especially in the Southwest, wiping out depositors' savings.

Because the government insures S&L deposits, the Bush administration in 1989 set up a program to repay depositors and sell hundreds of foreclosed office towers and apartment buildings in a depressed market. Estimates of the bailout's cost topped $400 billion.

Meanwhile, the federal deficits mounted, thanks in part to Reagan's tax cuts and military spending. In 1990, Bush agreed to a deficit-reduction plan involving spending cuts and tax increases. Bush's retreat from his "no new taxes" pledge angered voters. Despite this plan, the 1992 deficit neared $300 billion, thanks to the Persian Gulf War, S&L bailout, and soaring welfare and Medicare payments.

Making matters worse, another recession had struck in 1990. Retail sales slumped; housing starts fell. General Motors, battered by Japanese imports, laid off thousands of workers—a foretaste of worse to come. By 1992, the jobless rate exceeded 7 percent and the ranks of Americans living in poverty had risen alarmingly. If 1984 was "morning in America," wrote a columnist, quoting a Reagan campaign slogan, this was "the morning after."

The recession worsened inner-city poverty and despair. In April 1992, an outbreak of arson and looting in Watts, the predominantly black district of Los Angeles and scene of rioting in 1965 (see Chapter 28), left forty persons dead and millions in property damage. The immediate cause was outrage over a jury's acquittal of white police officers whose brutal beating of a black motorist had been captured on videotape.

Underlying the outbreak, too, was tension between local residents and Korean American shopkeepers. The black filmmaker Spike Lee anticipated such a scenario in his 1989 movie *Do the Right Thing,* set in a mainly black district of Brooklyn. In the film, a dispute between the Italian American owner of a pizza restaurant and a local black youth escalates into a full-scale riot that the police combat with heavy-handed brutality.

Environmental worries increased during Bush's presidency. In March 1989, a giant oil tanker, the *Exxon Valdez,* ran aground in Alaska's Prince William Sound, spilling more than 10 million gallons of oil. The accident fouled coastal habitats, killed thousands of sea otters and shore birds, and jeopardized Alaska's fisheries. Bush deplored the spill, but insisted that America's energy-hungry economy required ever more oil, coal, and natural gas.

That summer, air pollution in many U.S. cities exceeded federal standards. A 1991 Environmental Protection Agency study found that pollutants were eroding the atmosphere's ozone layer, which reduces cancer-causing solar radiation. Growing numbers of scientists also warned of global climate change related to increasing levels of carbon dioxide in the atmosphere and the role of human activity in causing it.

Squeezed between environmental concern and his party's free-market ideology and links to the energy industries, Bush signed a stricter Clean Air Act passed by the Democratic Congress in 1990, but otherwise backed oil exploration in Alaskan wilderness preserves, proposed to open protected wetlands to developers, and largely ignored a 1992 UN conference addressing environmental issues.

Of President Bush's two Supreme Court nominations, David Souter, a New Hampshire judge of moderate views, won easy confirmation. With Clarence Thomas, however, Bush continued Reagan's effort to push the court to the right. Bush nominated Thomas in 1991 to replace Thurgood Marshall, a black who as an NAACP lawyer had helped win the historic *Brown* school desegregation case (see Chapter 27). Thomas, an African American with limited judicial experience or qualifications, supported right-wing causes and, as head of the Equal Employment Opportunity Commission (EEOC) under Reagan, had opposed affirmative-action programs.

In the Senate confirmation hearings, a former EEOC staff member, Anita Hill, accused Thomas of sexual harassment. Thomas narrowly won confirmation,

Aftermath of the *Exxon Valdez* Disaster *An oil-soaked cormorant after the 1989 oil spill in Alaska's Prince William Sound.*

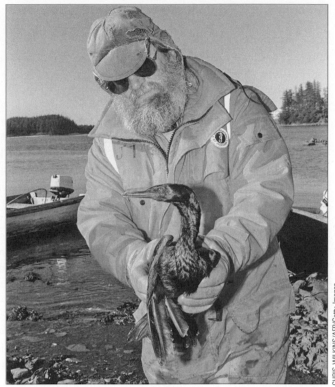

CHRIS WILKINS/AFP/Getty Images

but Republican efforts to discredit Hill angered many women, and this may have played a role in the 1992 elections, when women candidates did particularly well.

On the Court, Thomas allied with other Republican-appointed justices who supported expanded executive power and a strict interpretation of the Constitution. Sometimes joined by moderates Sandra Day O'Connor or Anthony Kennedy, the conservative bloc narrowed the rights of arrested persons; curbed death-penalty appeals; cut back affirmative-action programs; and, in *Planned Parenthood* v. *Casey* (1992), upheld a Pennsylvania law imposing restrictions on abortion providers.

1992: America's Voters Choose a New Course   Given President Bush's popularity after the Persian Gulf War, many top Democrats opted out of the 1992 presidential race. But Arkansas Governor **William Jefferson (Bill) Clinton** took the plunge. Fending off reports of marital infidelity, Clinton won the nomination. As his running mate, he chose Tennessee senator **Albert (Al) Gore, Jr**.

President Bush quashed a primary challenge by conservative columnist Pat Buchanan, but at the Republican convention, underscoring the party's rightward turn, Buchanan and evangelist Pat Robertson gave hard-line speeches on divisive cultural issues. A third-party candidate, H. Ross Perot, founder of a Texas data-processing firm, insisted that the nation's economic problems could easily be solved by remedies that voters would ratify through electronic "town meetings." Perot's popularity neared 40 percent at one point, but his eccentricities and thin-skinned response to criticism cost him support.

While Bush promised more attention to domestic issues in a second term, Clinton hammered on the recession and the problems of the middle class. Clinton won 43 percent of the vote to Bush's 38 percent. Perot's 19 percent was the best for a third-party candidate since Teddy Roosevelt in 1912. Clinton did well in the South, carried Ohio and other swing states, and lured back many blue-collar and suburban "Reagan Democrats." The recession, Bush's lackluster domestic record, and the divisive Perot campaign all helped Clinton. With Democrats now in control of Congress and the White House, Clinton's presidential prospects looked promising.

Thirty-eight African Americans and seventeen Hispanics won congressional seats. The new Senate included six women and the House forty-seven. California became the first state with two women senators, Barbara Boxer and Dianne Feinstein. Illinois elected the first African American woman senator, Carol Moseley Braun.

Apart from the Persian Gulf War, President Bush's single term proved unmemorable. A *New York Times* editorial, judging him "shrewd and energetic in foreign policy ..., clumsy and irresolute at home," went on: "The domestic Bush flops like a fish, leaving the impression that he doesn't know what he thinks or doesn't much care, apart from the political gains to be extracted from an issue."

DOMESTIC AND GLOBAL ISSUES AT CENTURY'S END

Clinton's presidency soon met setbacks, notably the failure of an ambitious national health-care plan and the 1994 midterm election produced a Republican landslide. Energized congressional Republicans pursued their conservative agenda, including—with Clinton's cooperation—sweeping welfare reform.

Clinton preferred domestic issues, but world events intruded. Abroad, four key challenges loomed: instability in the former Soviet Union, Israeli–Palestinian relations, security threats posed by nuclear proliferation and Islamic terrorism, and U.S. trade and investment interests in an evolving global economy (covered in this chapter's last section).

Trade, Gay Rights, Health Care: Clinton's Mixed Record   Born in Arkansas in 1946, Bill Clinton was part of the baby-boom generation that admired Elvis and came of age in the era of JFK, Vietnam, and the Beatles. After college and a fellowship at Oxford University, he attended Yale Law School where he met his future wife, Hillary Rodham. Returning to Arkansas, he was elected governor at age thirty-two. Now, at forty-six, he was president.

As a founder of the New Democratic Coalition—moderates eager to shed the party's "ultraliberal" reputation—Clinton in his campaign stressed middle-class

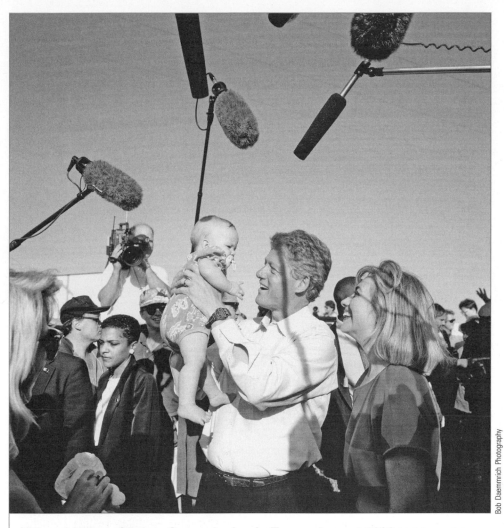

Bill and Hillary Clinton Campaigning in Texas, August 1992 *Holding a future voter as microphones record the moment, Bill Clinton demonstrates the popular appeal that helped him win the presidency. Hillary Clinton would soon emerge as a powerful political figure in her own right.*

concerns and muted the party's traditional attention to the poor and social-justice issues. Seeking middle ground on abortion, he said it should be "safe, legal, and rare." He endorsed environmental protection; indeed, his running mate, Al Gore, in 1992 published an environmental manifesto, *Earth in the Balance.*

Clinton named women to head several cabinet departments and advisory panels. To fill a Supreme Court vacancy in 1993, he nominated Judge Ruth Bader Ginsberg. (When a second vacancy arose in 1994, Clinton chose moderate liberal Stephen G. Breyer.) In 1996, he named Madeleine K. Albright as secretary of state—the highest U.S. government office ever held by a woman.

GOING TO THE SOURCE

Al Gore Reflects on Our Relation to Nature

In 1992, the year he was elected vice president, Al Gore published *Earth in the Balance: Ecology and the Human Spirit.* While this best-selling work mostly discussed specific environmental hazards and proposed remedies, Gore here reflects more broadly on modern society's relationship to the natural world.

Civilization has become astonishingly complex, but as it grows ever more elaborate, we feel increasingly distant from our roots in the earth. In one sense, civilization itself has been on a journey from its foundations in the world of nature to an ever more contrived, controlled, and manufactured world... [T]he price has been high. At some point during this journey we lost our feeling of connectedness to the rest of nature. We now dare to wonder: Are we so unique and powerful as to be essentially separate from the earth?

Many of us act–and think–as if the answer is yes. It is now all too easy to regard the earth as a collection of "resources" having an intrinsic value no larger than their usefulness at the moment. Thanks in part to the scientific revolution, we organize our knowledge of the natural world into smaller and smaller segments and assume that the connection between these separate compartments aren't really important. In our fascination with the parts of nature, we forget to see the whole.

The ecological perspective begins with a view of the whole, an understanding of how the various parts of nature interact in patterns that tend toward balance and persist over time. But ... we are part of the whole too, and looking at it ultimately means looking at ourselves. And if we do not see that the human part of nature has an increasingly powerful influence over the whole of nature–that we are, in effect, a natural force just like the winds and the tides–then we will not be able to see how dangerously we are threatening to push the earth out of balance...

Even though it is sometimes hard to see their meaning, we have by now all witnessed surprising experiences that signal the damage from our assault on the environment... But our response to these signals is puzzling. Why haven't we launched a massive effort to save our environment? ... Why do some images startle us into immediate action ... [while] other images, though sometimes equally dramatic, produce instead a kind of paralysis?...

Now that our relationship to the earth has changed so utterly, we have to see that change and understand its implications... [T]he startling images of environmental destruction now occurring all over the world ... are symptoms of an underlying problem broader in scope and more serious than any we have ever faced. Global warming, ozone depletion, the loss of living species, deforestation–they all have a common cause: the new relationship between human civilization and the earth's natural balance...

[T]he faith that is so essential to restore the balance now missing in our relationship to the earth is the faith that we do have a future. We can believe in that future and work to achieve it and preserve it, or we can whirl blindly on, behaving as if one day there will be no children to inherit our legacy. The choice is ours; the earth is in the balance.

Questions

1. *In Gore's view, how have science and technology altered the way we view nature?*

2. *Considering economic, political, and cultural factors, how would you answer Gore's rhetorical question: "Why haven't we launched a massive effort to save our environment?"*

To reduce the budget deficit and combat the recession, Clinton proposed military spending cuts, tax increases, and programs to stimulate job creation. Congress adopted the spending cuts and tax increases, but with the economy improving, shelved the stimulus package.

With Clinton's support, Congress in 1993 ratified the **North American Free Trade Agreement** (NAFTA), negotiated by the Bush administration. This pact admitted Mexico to the U.S.–Canadian free-trade zone created earlier. While Ross Perot and others warned that U.S. jobs would flee to Mexico, NAFTA backers, including most economists, predicted a net job gain as Mexican markets opened to U.S. products. (After twenty years the debate continues, with economists finding both positive and negative economic effects within the NAFTA trading bloc, including the United States.)

Other early Clinton initiatives faltered. Fulfilling a campaign pledge to gay-rights organizations, Clinton proposed to end the ban on gays in the military. When religious conservatives and some military leaders protested, he backed off and embraced a compromise summed up in the phrase "Don't ask, don't tell." The ban continued, but officers were barred from querying service members about their sexual orientation.

Health-care reform proved an even greater minefield. With Medicare costs exploding, and millions of citizens lacking health insurance, this issue stood high on Clinton's "to do" list. Working in secret, a task force headed by **Hillary Rodham Clinton** devised a plan for universal health insurance. Cost-containment provisions included health-care purchasing cooperatives, caps on insurance premiums, and limits on Medicare/Medicaid payments to physicians. Higher tobacco taxes would cover start-up expenses.

Lobbyists for physicians, insurance and tobacco companies, and other special interests rallied the opposition. By fall 1994, the ambitious plan was dead. But soaring costs and dissatisfaction with the status quo guaranteed that this issue would remain on the political agenda.

Jolted by these setbacks, Clinton in 1994 turned to issues with broad appeal: crime fighting and welfare reform. His anticrime bill included a ban on assault weapons and funds for more prisons and police officers. After partisan maneuvering, Congress enacted a bill similar to Clinton's proposal.

Clinton's welfare-reform bill put a two-year limit on payments from the federal welfare program, Aid to Families with Dependent Children (AFDC). After that, able-bodied recipients would have to find work, in a public-service job if necessary. The bill included job training and child-care provisions, measures to force absent fathers ("deadbeat dads") to support their offspring, and procedures to bar unmarried welfare mothers who had more babies from automatically receiving increased payments. In 1995, having regained control of Congress, Republicans shaped their own, even tougher bill (discussed shortly).

The approaching midterm election found the administration mired in problems. Republican critics publicized the Clintons' earlier involvement in a murky Arkansas real-estate speculation. The 1993 suicide of an assistant White House counsel, a Clinton insider, attracted conspiracy theorists. In 1994, Paula Jones, an Arkansas state employee, sued Clinton for alleged sexual harassment during his governorship.

Radio commentator Rush Limbaugh won fans for his jeering attacks on the Clintons and liberals in general. The religious Right remained a potent political force. Pat Robertson's **Christian Coalition,** with hundreds of chapters nationwide, controlled several state Republican parties.

Favorable economic news helped Clinton somewhat. Nevertheless, although the inflation and unemployment rates were falling, an ominous 58 percent of Americans told pollsters in October 1994 that they felt no better off despite the economic upturn.

Conservative Resurgence and Welfare Reform: 1994–1996

Bill Clinton had run as a "new Democrat," but by 1994 Republicans tarred him as an old Democrat of the big-government, "tax-and-spend" variety, beholden to gays, feminists, and other "special interests." The failed health-care plan, they charged, simply perpetuated the New Deal/Great Society style of top-down reform.

A network of conservative organizations, from the Christian Coalition to the National Rifle Association, sustained the rightward swing in U.S. politics. Direct-mail campaigns and conservative radio commentators tirelessly hammered such hot-button issues as abortion, gun control, gay rights, school prayer, "radical feminism," sex education, and an alleged erosion of "family values."

Georgia congressman **Newt Gingrich** mobilized the discontent. In September 1994, about three hundred Republican congressional candidates signed Gingrich's "Contract with America," pledging to support tax cuts, tougher crime laws, antipornography measures, a balanced-budget amendment, and other reforms. The Contract nationalized the midterm election, normally fought on local issues.

In November, voters gave the GOP control of both houses of Congress for the first time since 1954. In Texas, George W. Bush, son and namesake of the former president, defeated a popular Democratic governor. Evangelicals again turned out in large numbers, mostly to vote Republican.

In the Senate, North Carolina's reactionary Jesse Helms became chairman of the Foreign Relations Committee, and ninety-two-year-old Strom Thurmond of South Carolina, presidential candidate of the segregationist States' Rights Party in 1948, headed the Armed Services Committee. In the House of Representatives, a jubilant horde of 230 Republicans, seventy-three of them newly elected, chose Newt Gingrich as Speaker, made Rush Limbaugh an "honorary member," and set about enacting the Contract with America. A constitutional amendment requiring a balanced federal budget passed the House but narrowly failed in the Senate. House Republicans also targeted the Public Broadcasting System and the National Endowment for the Arts, suspected of a liberal bias. Fulfilling the anti-pornography pledge, Congress passed a Communications Decency Act strengthening the government's censorship powers. (In 1997, the Supreme Court ruled it unconstitutional.)

The torrent of bills, hearings, and press releases recalled the heady days of the early New Deal. Now, however, the activist energy came from the conservative side of the political spectrum.

The architect of this revolution, Newt Gingrich, stumbled in 1995 when he accepted, then returned, a $4.5 million advance from a publishing house owned by Rupert Murdoch, a conservative media tycoon with interests in federal legislation. Gingrich's network of political action groups, dubbed "Newt, Inc.," funded by corporations and conservative foundations, also drew critical scrutiny.

Turning to welfare reform, congressional Republicans criticized the system on both economic and public-policy grounds. AFDC, with 14.2 million women and children on its rolls, cost about $125 billion in 1994, including direct payments, food stamps, and Medicaid benefits, up sharply from 1989. Though dwarfed by the benefits enjoyed by the middle class through social security, Medicare, farm subsidies, and various tax loopholes, this was still a substantial sum. On public-policy grounds, the critics contended that the welfare system encouraged irresponsible social behavior and trapped recipients in a multi-generational cycle of dependence. Many linked the soaring rate of out-of-wedlock births to AFDC policies that paid mothers higher benefits for each child.

As a consensus emerged on the system's flaws, debate focused on how to change it. While Clinton favored federally funded child-care and job-training programs to ease the transition from welfare to work, Republicans argued that

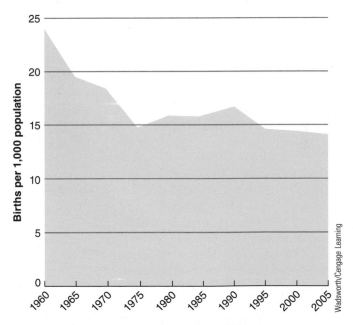

FIGURE 30.1 The American Birthrate, 1960–2005

Families of five or six children or more were once common in the United States, and the birthrate remained high in the baby-boom years of the later 1940s and the 1950s. (The nearly 80 million children of the baby boomers, born between 1982 and 1995, were dubbed "echo boomers.") The U.S. birthrate fell dramatically from 1960 to the mid-1970s, rose slightly, and then resumed its downward trend after 1990.

Source: National Center for Health Statistics, U.S. Dept. of Health and Human Services.

businesses, the states, and private agencies could best provide these services. Clinton vetoed two bills lacking the safeguards he thought essential.

At last, Clinton signed the **Welfare Reform Act of 1996**. Modifying sixty years of welfare policy, the law replaced AFDC with block grants to states to develop their own temporary-assistance programs within funding limits and guidelines restricting recipients to two years of continuous coverage, with a five-year lifetime total.

Advocates for the poor warned of the effects on inner-city children whose mothers lacked education or job skills, but many observers rated welfare reform at least a qualified success. From 1996 to 2005, the number of families on welfare fell by 57 percent, and the out-of-wedlock birthrate leveled off. The percentage of unmarried mothers in the work force rose from around 48 percent in 1996 to around 65 percent in 2000, although many held low-paying, unskilled jobs, and changed jobs frequently. In 2009, as an economic recession hit home (see Chapter 31), the number of families receiving cash-assistance welfare benefits rose, as did the number receiving food stamps. The totals remained far below pre-1996 levels, however.

Clinton Confronts the Post–Cold War World

As we have seen, global crises persisted despit—and some-times as a direct consequences of—the Cold War's end. In Yugoslavia, an unstable nation comprised of Serbia, Bosnia, Croatia, and other enclaves, the ruling communist party collapsed in 1990. As Yugoslavia broke apart, Serbian forces incited by Serbia's president Slobodan Milosevic launched a campaign of "ethnic cleansing" in neighboring Bosnia. Supported by Bosnia's ethnic Serbs, they killed or drove out Muslims and Croats. In August 1995, after UN peacekeepers failed to stop the killing, a joint U.S. and NATO operation launched air strikes against Bosnian Serb targets.

Later in 1995, the Clinton administration flew the leaders of Bosnia's warring factions to Dayton, Ohio, for talks. The resulting Dayton Accords imposed a cease-fire and created a governing framework for Bosnia. Clinton committed twenty thousand U.S. troops to a NATO operation to enforce the cease-fire.

In 1998, when Serbian forces attacked Muslims in Serbia's southern province, Kosovo, Clinton approved U.S. bombing of Serbian facilities in Kosovo and in Serbia itself, including Belgrade, the capital, as part of a NATO response. As Serb forces withdrew from Kosovo, U.S. troops joined a NATO occupying force, and refugees slowly returned. In 2001, a new Serbian government, eager for Western aid, delivered Slobodan Milosevic to a war-crimes tribunal at The Hague. The trial ended inconclusively with Milosevic's death in 2006.

In Russia, meanwhile, President Boris Yeltsin's position weakened amid hard times and corruption linked to Russia's hasty conversion to a free-market economy. Moscow's costly 1995 invasion of the breakaway Islamic republic of Chechnya further undermined Yeltsin.

Despite Yeltsin's fading popularity, the Clinton administration continued to support him, and used diplomacy, economic aid, and technical assistance to ensure the safe disposal of deactivated nuclear weapons throughout the former Soviet Union. In 1999, the administration backed Russia's admission to the Group of Seven (G-7), the world's leading industrialized nations. In the same year, however, over Russia's protests, the United States supported NATO's decision to admit three new members from the former Soviet bloc—Hungary, Poland, and the Czech Republic. With Yeltsin's resignation in December 1999, Prime Minister Vladimir Putin, a former agent of the KGB, the Soviet secret police, succeeded him as president, opening a new chapter in the tortured history of U.S.–Russian relations.

In the Israeli–Palestinian conflict, of vital U.S. concern, prospects brightened in 1993 when negotiators from the two sides meeting in Norway agreed on a framework for peace providing for a Palestinian state, the return of Israeli-held land in the West Bank and Gaza, and further talks on Palestinian refugees' claims and the final status of Jerusalem. In 1994, President Clinton presided as Israeli Prime Minister Yitzhak Rabin and the PLO's Yasir Arafat signed the agreement at the White House.

After hopeful beginnings, however, this initiative failed. In 1995, a young Israeli opposed to the Oslo Accords assassinated Rabin. Israel's next election brought to power Benjamin Netanyahu of the hard-line Likud Party. Suicide bombings in Israel by Palestinian extremists in 1996–1997 triggered retaliatory attacks. Under U.S. pressure, Netanyahu withdrew some Israeli forces from the West Bank. But as attacks continued, Netanyahu halted the withdrawal. By 2000, the West Bank and Gaza had an estimated two hundred thousand Jewish settlers, with accompanying checkpoints, security forces, and limited-access highways making existence difficult for Palestinians.

In July 2000, Clinton invited Arafat and Israel's new prime minister, Ehud Barak, of the more moderate Labour Party, for talks at Camp David. Barak made major concessions, reportedly including acceptance of a Palestinian state; Israeli withdrawal from most of the West Bank and all of Gaza; and the transfer of Jerusalem's Temple Mount, sacred to both Muslims and Jews, to a vaguely defined "religious authority." In return, the PLO would end hostilities and give up further claims on Israel.

Arafat rejected Barak's offer, however, and the summit failed. The Palestinians launched a new *intifada*, and in 2001 Israelis elected the hard-liner Ariel Sharon prime minister. As Clinton left office, the conflict raged on.

In 1997, when Iraq's Saddam Hussein barred UN inspectors from facilities suspected of research on chemical and nuclear weapons, Clinton dispatched ships, bombers, and troops to the Persian Gulf and sought support for a multinational military strike. But France, Russia, and various Arab states resisted, and the standoff continued.

Other nations, too, posed threats of nuclear proliferation. Neither India nor Pakistan, at odds over the disputed region of Kashmir, had signed the 1968 Nuclear Nonproliferation Treaty (NPT). In 1988, India tested a "nuclear device" and Pakistan soon followed. Both the Bush and Clinton administrations imposed sanctions on the two countries, but the threat of nuclear confrontation in this volatile region remained urgent.

North Korea, despite having signed the NPT, used nuclear-weapons development and missile testing as a bargaining chip to secure economic aid from the United States and other nations. In 1994, facing UN economic sanctions and the loss of international assistance, North Korea pledged to halt its nuclear-weapons program. In 1999, wracked by famine, North Korea agreed to suspended missile testing in return for economic and diplomatic concessions. The secretive nation's nuclear intentions remained opaque and worrisome as Clinton's term ended.

Terrorism: "The War of the Future"

Attacks by anti-American Islamic extremists continued. A February 1993 bomb blast beneath one of the towers of New York's World Trade Center killed six persons and injured hundreds. Five Islamic militants were arrested, and three, including the alleged mastermind, a blind Egyptian cleric known for his hatred of America, were convicted of murder and given life sentences.

The terrorist threat extended to Africa. In 1992, President Bush committed twenty-six thousand U.S. troops to a UN humanitarian mission in Somalia, a predominantly Muslim East African nation beset by civil war and famine. As the warring factions battled, forty-four Americans were killed, including eighteen in Mogadishu, Somalia's capital. President Clinton withdrew the U.S. force in 1994. Later evidence implicated Osama bin Laden in the killings. Son of a wealthy Saudi contractor, bin Laden had been expelled from Saudi Arabia in 1991 and settled in Sudan, where he financed construction and agricultural projects but also plotted anti-Western terrorist activities.

On August 7, 1998, simultaneous bombings of the U.S. embassies in Nairobi; Kenya; and Dar es-Salaam, Tanzania, killed 220—including twelve Americans. U.S. intelligence again pinpointed bin Laden, by now organizing terrorist training camps in Afghanistan. Clinton ordered cruise-missile strikes on one of these Afghan camps as well as on a suspected chemical-weapons factory in Sudan allegedly financed by bin Laden. A U.S. grand jury charged bin Laden with complicity in the embassy attacks and the earlier killing of GIs in Somalia.

Declared Secretary of State Albright: "We are involved here in a long-term struggle ..., This is, unfortunately, the war of the future." Underscoring Albright's grim assessment, on October 12, 2000, a bomb aboard a small boat in the harbor of Aden, Yemen, ripped a gaping hole in the U.S. destroyer *Cole*, killing seventeen sailors.

Defining America's Role amid Global Changes

As the century ended, the peaceful post–Cold War era that many had anticipated seemed a cruel mirage. The Soviet adversary had collapsed, but crises flared around the world. Like firefighters battling many small blazes rather than a single conflagration, policy makers now wrestled with a baffling tangle of issues.

Some larger trends could be discerned. Economic and cultural **globalization** played an ever greater role. International trade and finance increasingly shaped

America's foreign-policy interests. U.S. movies, popular music, and TV programs (including the sermons of televangelists) reached a worldwide audience in an age of communications satellites.

Along with globalization, however, came a widening chasm that divided the prosperous, comparatively stable industrialized world from societies marked by poverty, disease, illiteracy, and explosive population growth. This vast gulf helped spawn resentment, hatred, and terrorism.

Ancient ethnic hatreds re-ignited as the bipolar Cold War world fragmented. The lethal conflict in the former Yugoslavia was far from unique. Similar clashes erupted in many regions. In the African nation of Rwanda, as many as a million people perished in 1994 in genocidal violence between two hostile ethnic groups, the Hutu and the Tutsi. Thousands more fled in panic, creating a refugee crisis. (The 2004 film, *Hotel Rwanda,* about a courageous Rwandan hotel manager who sheltered over a thousand Tutsi refugees, conveyed the horror of the genocide.) Traumatized by the Somalia fiasco, President Clinton did not intervene.

Religious fundamentalism intensified the global unrest. As Muslim fundamentalists denounced Western liberalism and secularism, a lethal minority—often drawn from an impoverished urban underclass—embraced violence as a religious duty. In India, violence erupted in 1992 when Hindu fundamentalists destroyed an ancient Muslim mosque they claimed had been built on an even more ancient Hindu shrine. Meanwhile, some ultra-religious Israeli Jews (supported by U.S. Christian fundamentalists) claimed a divine right to the West Bank and Jerusalem's Temple Mount, the basis of ancient biblical texts.

Confronting such complexities, some U.S. citizens simply gave up. In a 1997 poll, only 20 percent of Americans said they followed foreign news, down sharply from the 1980s, with the biggest drop among young people. TV coverage of events abroad fell by more than 50 percent from 1989 to 1995.

Newt Gingrich's 1994 Contract with America largely ignored foreign policy, and key Republican legislators pushed isolationist views. Jesse Helms, as chair of the Senate Foreign Relations Committee, denounced the United Nations and criticized environmental treaties. Congressional Republicans refused to pay $1 billion in past UN dues. Bending to such pressures (and to Pentagon objections), Clinton in 1998 declined to sign a multinational treaty banning land mines, even though these mines remain deadly for years, often killing or maiming children.

Nevertheless, opinion polls indicated that most Americans supported internationalist approaches to global problems and envisioned a positive role for America in the world. The U.S. part in negotiating the Dayton Accords that brought peace to Bosnia offered a noteworthy instance of this role. Another came in 1998 when former Democratic senator George Mitchell, appointed by President Clinton as a special envoy to Northern Ireland, helped to negotiate a peace treaty between Catholics favoring independence and Protestants advocating continued ties to Great Britain.

With the Cold War's end, some hoped that the United Nations, long hostage to the superpowers' conflict, could fulfill the role its supporters had envisioned in

1945. Indeed, by 2010, nearly one hundred thousand UN peacekeepers were deployed in fifteen world trouble spots. A complex network of UN agencies addressed global environmental, nutritional, public-health, and human-rights issues. The UN-sponsored International Court of Justice at The Hague adjudicated disputes between nations and tried perpetrators of mass violence in Bosnia, Rwanda, Liberia, and elsewhere.

TOBACCO WARS, WHITE HOUSE SCANDAL, DISPUTED ELECTION, 1996–2000

Straddling the political center, Bill Clinton won reelection in 1996. Along with sending U.S. forces to Kosovo and the final stab at resolving the Israeli–Palestinian dispute, his second term saw a battle over tobacco-industry regulation and a sex scandal that led to his impeachment. A disputed presidential election in 2000 deepened the nation's divisions.

Clinton Battles Big Tobacco and Woos Political Moderates   Chastened by his party's defeat in the 1994 midterm election, President Clinton fought back. In a 1995 budget battle, Clinton outmaneuvered House Speaker Newt Gingrich, who annoyed voters by twice allowing a partial government shutdown.

Kansas senator Bob Dole, a partially disabled World War II veteran, won the 1996 Republican presidential nomination after General Colin Powell, the popular former chairman of the Joint Chiefs of Staff, declined to run. Fundraising scandals marred Clinton's reelection campaign. After an event at a Los Angeles Buddhist temple attended by Vice President Al Gore, priests and nuns sworn to poverty contributed over a hundred thousand dollars to the Democratic cause, apparently from Asian businessmen currying favor with the administration. But Dole ran a lackluster campaign, and Clinton won with 49 percent of the vote to Dole's 41 percent. (Ross Perot garnered 8 percent.) The Republicans retained control of Congress but proved more subdued than after their 1994 triumph.

Tobacco regulation, a major public-health issue, loomed large as Clinton's second term began. In 1997, facing lawsuits by former smokers and by states saddled with medical costs linked to smoking-related diseases, the tobacco industry agreed to pay some $368 billion in settlement. The agreement limited tobacco advertising, especially when directed at young people.

Because the agreement required government approval, the debate shifted to Washington. Legislators from tobacco states defended the industry, but the Clinton administration backed a bill imposing tougher penalties, higher cigarette taxes, and stronger antismoking measures. The bill's supporters documented the industry's manipulation of nicotine levels and targeting of children. The industry struck back with a $40 million lobbying campaign and heavy contributions to key politicians, killing the bill. The Republican Party, commented Arizona Republican senator John McCain, appeared to be "in the pocket of the tobacco companies."

In 1998, the tobacco industry and most states reached a new settlement, scaled back to $206 billion.

Pursuing his middle-of-the-road strategy, Clinton in his January 1998 State of the Union address offered some initiatives to help the poor, such as enrolling the nation's 3 million uninsured children in Medicaid, but mostly highlighted proposals attractive to the middle class (college-tuition tax credits; extending Medicare to early retirees) and fiscal conservatives (reducing the national debt; shoring up social security). Some liberals dismissed the speech as "Progressivism Lite," but it had broad appeal.

Further, Clinton's economic policies contributed to the decade's prosperity and in 1998 produced the first federal budget surplus in nearly thirty years. Under normal circumstances, Clinton's record would have assured that his presidency, despite early missteps, would end in a glow of success.

Scandal Grips the White House   But conditions were not normal. Even as Clinton spoke, scandal swirled around his presidency. Adultery charges had long clung to Clinton, and now he faced Paula Jones's sexual-harassment suit, dating from his days as Arkansas governor.

Seeking to prove a pattern of sexual harassment, Jones's lawyers quizzed Clinton about rumors linking him to a young White House intern, Monica Lewinsky. Under oath, Clinton and Lewinsky denied everything. As the rumors became public, Hillary Clinton blamed "a vast right-wing conspiracy." Clinton settled Paula Jones's suit by paying her $850,000, but problems remained. In telephone conversations illegally taped by her "friend" Linda Tripp, Lewinsky had described a White House affair with Clinton. Tripp passed the tapes to Kenneth Starr, an independent counsel investigating the Clintons' Arkansas real-estate dealings. Fitting Tripp with a recording device, the FBI secured further Lewinsky evidence.

Starr's inquiry now shifted to whether Clinton had committed perjury in his Paula Jones testimony and persuaded Lewinsky to lie. In August, after a promise of immunity, Lewinsky admitted the affair to a grand jury. As the scandal unfolded in tabloid headlines, late-night television jokes, and Internet humor, Clinton in a brief TV address conceded "inappropriate" behavior but attacked Starr as politically motivated.

In a September 1998 report to the House Judiciary Committee, Starr recommended Clinton's impeachment for perjury, influencing others to commit perjury, and obstructing justice by coaching his secretary on his version of events. The Judiciary Committee, on a party-line vote, forwarded four articles of impeachment to the House of Representatives. In a similarly partisan vote, the House approved and sent to the Senate two articles of impeachment: perjury and obstruction of justice.

The public, however, sent the Republicans an ominous message: Clinton's approval ratings rose, and the Democrats gained five House seats in the 1998 midterm elections. Few believed the president's actions met the Constitution's "high crimes and misdemeanors" standard for removal from office. With the economy booming and Clinton's political program generally popular, voters appeared willing to tolerate his personal flaws. Further, many saw him as the target of Republican zealots.

The trial began in January 1999. With Chief Justice William Rehnquist presiding, House Republicans presented their case. White House lawyers dismissed the charges as a "witches' brew of speculation." On February 12, the Senate rejected both charges, and the trial ended. In November, Newt Gingrich, a leader of the impeachment effort but now embroiled in his own ethical and personal controversies, resigned as Speaker and left Congress.

While the impeachment failed, the scandal tarnished Clinton's reputation. Still facing legal liability as he left office in January 2001, the president admitted to perjury, paid a $25,000 fine, and lost his law license for five years.

| 2000: Divided Nation, Disputed Election | At their 2000 convention, the Democrats nominated Vice President Al Gore for the top job. He chose as his running mate Connecticut senator Joseph Lieberman, who had denounced Clinton's behavior in the Lewinsky affair. |

In the Republican contest, Arizona's somewhat maverick senator John McCain, a Vietnam-era prisoner of war, made a strong bid. But Texas governor **George W. Bush,** with powerful backers, a familiar name, and a folksy manner, won the nomination. His running mate, Dick Cheney, had been defense secretary in the first Bush administration. The environmentally minded Green Party nominated consumer advocate Ralph Nader.

Both Gore and Bush courted the center while trying to hold their bases. For Bush, this included energy companies, religious conservatives, and so-called Reagan Democrats in the white middle class and blue-collar ranks. Gore's base included liberals, many academics and professionals, union members, environmentalists, feminists, and African Americans. The Hispanic vote remained divided.

Gore boasted of the nation's prosperity and pledged to extend health-care coverage and protect social security. In TV debates, Gore proved more informed and articulate, but some found him pompous. Perhaps unwisely, Gore kept Clinton at arm's length, despite the president's popularity.

Bush was widely seen as a lightweight, dependent on family influence. As Texas's former Democratic governor Ann Richards quipped, "George was born on third base and thought he had hit a home run." Calling himself a "compassionate conservative," Bush subtly reminded voters of Clinton's misdeeds by promising to restore dignity to the White House. Polls showed that most voters agreed with Gore on the issues, but preferred Bush as a person.

On election day, Gore won the popular vote by more than 500,000. But the all-important Electoral College outcome came down to Florida, where a handful of votes separated the two candidates.

Flaws in Florida's voting process quickly emerged. In Palm Beach County, a poorly designed ballot led several thousand Gore supporters to vote for Pat Buchanan, running on Ross Perot's Reform Party ticket. In counties with many black voters, antiquated

The Florida Election Dispute *A Fort Lauderdale judge scrutinizes a partially punched-out ballot in late November 2000.*

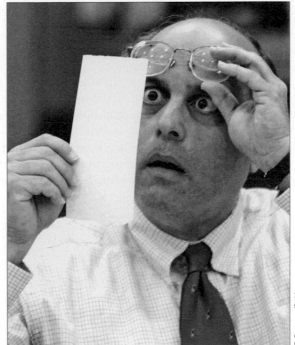

© Bettmann/Corbis

voting machines rejected thousands of ballots in which the paper tabs, called "chads," were not fully punched out. When election officials began a hand count of rejected ballots, Bush's lawyers sued to prevent it.

On November 21, the Florida Supreme Court, with a preponderance of Democrats, unanimously ruled that the ongoing recount should constitute the official result. Bush's legal team appealed to the U.S. Supreme Court. Despite a long-established precedent leaving electoral disputes to the states, the justices accepted the case. On November 26, Florida's secretary of state, Katherine Harris, certified the original, contested Florida vote, awarding Bush the state. (Harris, a political ally of Florida governor Jeb Bush, the candidate's brother, had co-chaired George W. Bush's Florida campaign.)

After further legal maneuvering, the Supreme Court on December 12, by a 5-to-4 vote, halted the recount and let Harris's ruling stand. Gore conceded the next day. Five Supreme Court justices (all Republican appointees) had made George W. Bush president. Had the nearly 100,000 Floridians who voted for third-party candidate Ralph Nader not had that option, Gore would almost certainly have won the state and the presidency.

The election produced an evenly divided Senate, giving Vice President Cheney the deciding vote. Hillary Rodham Clinton, the first presidential spouse to pursue an independent political career, won election as senator from New York. The Republicans narrowly held the House of Representatives.

ECONOMIC AND CULTURAL TRENDS AT CENTURY'S END

The Clinton years saw sustained economic growth, increased productivity, falling unemployment, low inflation, and the first federal budget surplus in years. Economic globalization fueled U.S. economic growth, but when foreign economies faltered, the American economy stumbled as well.

As corporate profits surged and the stock market soared, America exuded a glow of abundance amid leisure-time diversions. But real wages lagged, many workers lacked the skills valued by the emerging knowledge-based economy, and the gap between the super wealthy and most Americans widened. A continuing AIDS epidemic, outbursts of mass violence, and acrimonious cultural disagreements also characterized American society as the twentieth century ended.

An Uneven Prosperity   From 1992 to 2000, the jobless rate fell from 7.5 percent to 4 percent. The gross domestic product, a key economic indicator, rose nearly 40 percent in the decade. Leisure pursuits and consumer spending burgeoned. In 2000, Americans spent $105 billion on new cars and $107 billion on video, audio, and computer equipment. Attendance at the Disney theme parks in Florida and California neared 30 million in 2000. Crucial to the boom was a revolution in information technology.

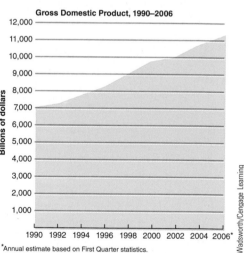

Unemployment Rate, 1990–2006 — Percentage of civilian labor force unemployed

Gross Domestic Product, 1990–2006 — Billions of dollars

*First Quarter

*Annual estimate based on First Quarter statistics.

Wadsworth/Cengage Learning

FIGURE 30.2 The U.S. Economy, 1990–2006

The unemployment rate fell, and the gross domestic product rose during the boom years of the 1990s. As recession hit in 2001, however, the jobless rate increased and the GDP flattened.

Source: Unemployment Rate chart: Bureau of Labor Statistics, U.S. Department of Labor; GDP: U.S. Department of Commerce. http://www.bea.gov/bea/dn/gdplev.xls. *The GDP figures are in constant dollars, adjusted for inflation.*

Wall Street stock prices far outran many companies' actual earnings prospects. From under 3,000 in 1991, the Dow Jones Industrial Average approached 12,000 by early 2001. By 1998, nearly half of U.S. families owned stock directly or through their pension plans. In 1996, Federal Reserve Board chairman Alan Greenspan warned of "irrational exuberance" in the stock market, but with little effect.

Information technology (IT) stocks fed the boom. The NASDAQ index, loaded with technology stocks, shot up from under 500 in 1991 to over 5,000 by early 2000. Some stock offerings by unknown IT start-up companies hit fantastic levels, turning young entrepreneurs into paper millionaires. Corporate mergers and acquisitions in the media industry proliferated. In 2000, communications giant Viacom swallowed CBS for $41 billion. In one super-merger, Internet company America Online (AOL) acquired Time Warner (the product of earlier mergers) for $182 billion.

The prosperity was spotty, however. From 1979 to 1996, the share of the total national income going to the wealthiest 20 percent of Americans increased by 13 percent, while the share going to the poorest 20 percent *dropped* by 22 percent. Commented economist Richard Freeman in 1998: "The U.S. has the most unequal distribution of income among advanced countries—and the degree of inequality has increased more here than in any comparable country." This disparity would widen in the years ahead (see Chapter 31).

Adjusted for inflation, the buying power of the average worker's paycheck fell or remained flat from 1986 to 2000. As corporations maintained profits by downsizing, cost cutting, and exporting jobs overseas, workers faced uncertain times. The growing service sector included not only white-collar positions, but also low-paying jobs in fast-food outlets, custodial work, car washes, telemarketing, and so forth. Only 13.5 percent of the labor force was unionized in 2000, eroding this means by which workers had historically bettered their wages and job conditions. As unions grew weaker, protests by labor leaders failed to prevent Congress's ratification of the 1993 NAFTA treaty.

Job market success increasingly required special skills, posing problems for displaced industrial workers and those lacking advanced education. Overall employment statistics also obscured racial and ethnic variables. In 2000, the jobless rate for blacks and Hispanics remained significantly higher than the rate for whites. As shifting immigration patterns created an increasingly diverse American population (see Chapter 31), newcomers with needed skills found well-paying positions, but many took low-paying jobs with few benefits or long-term prospects. In short, while many Americans prospered during these boom years, millions more experienced minimal gains or none at all.

As the economy boomed and banks passed out credit cards like candy, consumer debt soared alarmingly. Unscrupulous finance companies offered would-be homeowners mortgages they could ill afford, often at low "teaser" rates that rose sharply after a year or two. The deregulation of business and banking that began in the late 1970s and continued through the Clinton years (and beyond) encouraged these dangerous trends. Credit buying and the deregulation mania gave the economy a glow of prosperity, but also laid the groundwork for unwelcome economic consequences (see Chapter 31).

America and the World Economy   As the NAFTA agreement showed, trade issues ranked high on Clinton's agenda. When the U.S. trade deficit hit $133 billion in 1993, including a $59 billion trade gap with Japan, Clinton, like his predecessor, pressured the Japanese to buy more U.S. goods.

Global economic considerations increasingly shaped U.S. foreign policy. Despite China's human rights abuses and one-party rule, Clinton welcomed Chinese president Jiang Zemin in 1997 and visited China in 1998. This reflected economic realities. In 2000, U.S. imports from China surpassed $100 billion, making it America's fourth largest trading partner, after Canada, Mexico, and Japan.

In 1997–1998, a banking and credit crisis threatened the booming export economies of Thailand, South Korea, Indonesia, and other Asian nations and indirectly jeopardized the U.S. economy. The International Monetary Fund, a Washington-based agency to which the United States is the largest contributor, put together a $40 billion bailout package to stabilize the situation. As the crisis spread to Japan, the Clinton administration pressed that country to undertake economic reforms. U.S. prosperity and well-being increasingly depended on developments in a complex global economy.

Affluence and a Search for Heroes   As Wall Street and Silicon Valley spawned thousands of youthful millionaires, *Vanity Fair* magazine in 1997 described New York as "the champagne city, making the brash consumption of the 1980s look like the depression." Elegant restaurants offered absurdly expensive cigars and wines; exclusive shops sold $13,000 handbags. The sales of gas guzzling sport-utility vehicles (SUVs) soared. When a White House press secretary was asked in 2001 if people should reduce consumption to conserve energy, he replied, "[I]t should be the goal of policy makers to protect the American way of life—the American way of life is a blesséd one."

The boom encouraged a hard-edged "winner take all" mentality like that of the Gilded Age, when the rich turned their backs on the rest of society. In *Bowling Alone: The Collapse and Revival of American Community* (2000), political scientist Robert Putnam found diminished civic engagement; weakened interest in public affairs; and a more self-absorbed, individualistic society. *The Prayer of Jabez* (2000), a best-selling motivational book, cited a shepherd's prayer recorded in the Bible ("Bless me indeed, and enlarge my territory") as a key to success. "If Jabez had worked on Wall Street," wrote the author, "he might have prayed 'Lord, increase the value of my investment portfolio.'"

The mass culture offered escapist fare. The 1997 film *Titanic* grossed $600 million. The top-rated TV show of 1999–2000, *Who Wants to Be a Millionaire?*, celebrated raw greed. So-called reality shows like *Survivor* offered viewers a risk-free taste of challenges that contemporary American life itself often lacked, at least for the privileged.

Millions followed TV coverage of the 1995 trial of O.J. Simpson, a former football star accused of killing his former wife and her friend. The 1996 murder of

The McMansion: Domestic Architecture as Conspicuous Consumption *As some Americans grew rich in the boom years of the 1980s and 1990s, ostentatious and pretentious houses, nicknamed McMansions, sprang up across the country.*

a six-year-old Colorado girl whose parents had pushed her into child beauty pageants similarly mesmerized the public. The Clinton sex scandals often seemed little more than another media diversion in a sensation-hungry decade.

But the popular culture also offered evidence of more complex social crosscurrents. Some critics interpreted *Titanic*, which sided with its working-class hero in steerage against the rich snobs in first class, as a comment on America's widening class differences. One even called the movie "an exercise in class hatred." Dissatisfaction with a materialistic culture and money-driven politics, some suggested, found expression in bestselling books about past heroes and more heroic times, such as Stephen Ambrose's *Eisenhower* (1991); David McCullough's *Truman* (1993); and Tom Brokaw's *The Greatest Generation* (1998), about the GIs who fought in World War II.

The 2001 film *Pearl Harbor*, argued critic Frank Rich, reflected a longing "for what is missing in our national life: some cause larger than ourselves." Concluded Rich: "Even those Americans who are ... foggy about World War II ... know intuitively that it was fought over something more blessed than the right to guzzle gas."

The AIDS Epidemic Rages On; Outbursts of Violence Stir Concern

Beneath the prosperity, darker currents stirred. The AIDS crisis continued its deadly course. By 2000, U.S. deaths surpassed 458,000, with more new cases of AIDS and HIV, an infection that often precedes full-blown AIDS, diagnosed each year. Tony Kushner's play *Angels in America* (1991–1992), and the long-running rock musical *Rent* (1996), an update of the opera *La Bohème,* explored the human and cultural impact of AIDS. As knowledge about preventive measures spread and HIV treatments advanced, the U.S. crisis abated somewhat by the early twenty-first century—but the worldwide epidemic continued, with sub-Saharan Africa particularly hard hit.

A popular 1999 film, *American Beauty,* and TV's *The Sopranos,* an HBO series about a mobster and his family, explored a violent substratum in American life. True, overall crime rates fell nearly 20 percent between 1992 and 2000—a decline experts attributed to prosperity, a drop in the young male population, the waning crack cocaine epidemic, and tougher sentencing rules. (The prison population approached 2 million by 2000.) But violent outbursts punctuated the decade. Gun deaths exceeded twenty-eight thousand in 2000. In April 1999, two students at Columbine High School near Denver fatally shot twelve students and a teacher before committing suicide. After this massacre, President Clinton called for stricter gun-control laws, but the National Rifle Association fought such efforts.

The culture wars sometimes spurred violence. In 1998, two youths tortured and murdered a gay student at the University of Wyoming, Matthew Shepard, because of his sexual orientation. In the 1990s, at least five physicians who performed abortions or staff members at clinics providing this service were murdered, and other clinics were bombed.

On April 19, 1995, in the decade's worst incident of mass violence, explosives concealed in a truck demolished a federal office building in Oklahoma City, killing 168, including nineteen children in a day-care center. Police soon arrested Timothy McVeigh, a Gulf War veteran obsessed with conspiracy theories. McVeigh, convicted of murder, was executed in 2001. A co-conspirator, Terry Nichols, received a life sentence.

The **Oklahoma City bombing** came precisely two years after a government raid on the Waco, Texas, compound of the Branch Davidians, a heavily armed apocalyptic religious sect led by David Koresh. An earlier confrontation at Waco had left four government agents and six Davidians dead. The April 1993 raid ended tragically when fires inside the compound, probably set by Koresh and others, killed some eighty Davidians as federal tanks moved in. Timothy McVeigh boasted that his Oklahoma City attack represented retaliation for Waco.

Culture Wars: A Broader View

While the 1990s' culture wars typically did not descend into violence, they did involve fierce contests that some viewed as a struggle for the nation's soul. During the Cold War, the ideological menace had centered in Moscow. Now, many Americans projected the same black-and-white worldview onto the home-front culture and searched for the enemy within.

The struggle unfolded on many fronts, from televangelists' programs, bookstore shelves, and radio talk shows to school-board protests and demonstrations at family-planning clinics. Some endorsed a constitutional amendment permitting prayer in public school classrooms; others criticized history textbooks as insufficiently patriotic or excessively multicultural. The Southern Baptist Convention, America's largest Protestant denomination, urged a boycott of Disney World for unofficially sponsoring "Gay Pride" days. In 1995, the Smithsonian Institution canceled a planned exhibit marking the fiftieth anniversary of the U.S. atomic bombing of Japan when politicians and veterans' organizations criticized it for graphically documenting the bombs' human toll and for presenting differing contemporary views of the bombings.

Politicized evangelical groups denounced the nation's alleged moral decline. In 1997, thousands of men representing a conservative Protestant movement called Promise Keepers rallied in Washington, DC, for a day of prayer, hymn singing, and pledges to reclaim leadership of their families. Activists complained about Republican politicians who courted their votes but ignored their agenda once in power.

Pat Robertson's *The New World Order* (1991) interpreted world history as a vast conspiracy that will soon end in the rule of the Antichrist. The best-selling *Left Behind* series of novels (1995–2004), coauthored by the conservative activist Tim LaHaye, described an approaching end time when satanic forces will take over America and the world.

But did the apocalyptic culture warriors speak for most Americans? Was the nation as polarized as the overheated rhetoric, amplified by the mass media, sometimes suggested? In *One Nation After All* (1998), sociologist Alan Wolfe found most contemporary Americans surprisingly tolerant of diverse views and lifestyles. "[T]here is little truth to the charge that middle-class Americans, divided by a culture war, have split into two hostile camps," Wolfe concluded. "Middle-class Americans, in their heart of hearts, are desperate that we once again become one nation."

CHRONOLOGY
1980–2000

1980	Ronald Reagan elected president.
1981	Major cuts in taxes and domestic spending.
	Large increases in military budget.
1982	Equal Rights Amendment dies.
	CIA funds contra war against Nicaragua's Sandinistas.
	Central Park rally for nuclear weapons freeze.

1983	239 U.S. marines die in Beirut terrorist attack.
	U.S. deploys Pershing II and cruise missiles in Europe.
	Reagan proposes Strategic Defense Initiative (Star Wars).
	U.S. invasion of Grenada.
1984	Reagan defeats Walter Mondale to win second presidential term.
1984–1986	Congress bars military aid to contras.
1985	Rash of airline hijackings and other terrorist acts.
1986	Congress passes South African sanctions.
	Immigration Reform and Control Act.
1987	Congressional hearings on Iran-contra scandal.
	Stock-market crash.
1988	Reagan trip to Moscow.
	George H.W. Bush elected president.
1989	Massive Alaskan oil spill by *Exxon Valdez*.
	Supreme Court, in several 5-to-4 decisions, restricts civil-rights laws.
	China's rulers crush prodemocracy movement.
	Berlin Wall is torn down.
1990	Federal Clean Air Act strengthened.
	Americans with Disabilities Act passed.
	Iraq invades Kuwait.
	Recession (1990–1993).
	Germany reunified; Soviet troops start withdrawal from Eastern Europe.
1991	Persian Gulf War (Operation Desert Storm).
	Hearings on Clarence Thomas's Supreme Court nomination.
	Collapse of Soviet Union.
1992	Supreme Court in *Planned Parenthood* v. *Casey* approves abortion restrictions but upholds *Roe* v. *Wade*.
	President Bush commits U.S. troops in Somalia.
	Bill Clinton elected president.
1993	Congress approves NAFTA treaty.
	Economy expands, stock market surges (1993–2000).

	Clinton health-care reform plan fails (1993–1994).
	Eighty Branch Davidians die in fire as federal agents raid compound in Waco, Texas.
	World Trade Center bombing kills six.
1994	Christian Coalition gains control of Republican Party in several states.
	Yasir Arafat and Yitzhak Rabin sign Oslo Accords at White House.
	Clinton withdraws U.S. forces from Somalia.
	United States joins the World Trade Organization (WTO).
	Republicans proclaim "Contract with America" and win control of House and Senate; Newt Gingrich becomes Speaker.
1995	Oklahoma City federal building bombed.
	Dayton Accords achieve cease-fire in Bosnia; Clinton commits U.S. troops to enforce agreement.
1996	Welfare Reform Act.
	Clinton defeats Robert Dole to win second presidential term.
1997	Congressional battle over tobacco industry regulation.
1998	Clinton impeached by House of Representatives in sex scandal.
1999	Senate dismisses impeachment charges.
	Columbine High School shootings.
	U.S. and NATO forces intervene in Kosovo.
2000	George W. Bush wins presidency when Supreme Court ends Florida election dispute.

CONCLUSION

What broad themes emerge from the turbulent American scene as the twentieth-century closed—so recent, yet already fading in memory? Certainly the conservative political and cultural turn, symbolized by Ronald Reagan's presidency, looms large. Indeed, some see Reagan as a "transformational president" comparable to Franklin D. Roosevelt. Reagan, a master politician who wrapped his ideological message in a sunny vision of America's past greatness and future promise, unquestionably dominates the era's political landscape.

Yet Reagan did not accomplish the conservative turn single-handedly. He benefited from currents in American public life decades in the making, including an initially muted but ultimately influential repudiation by conservative ideologists of New Deal liberalism in favor of small-government, free-market economic ideas. Underlying Reagan's success, too, was the resentment of blue-collar and middle-class whites against the civil-rights movement and Lyndon Johnson's social programs, a backlash against the antiwar activism and counterculture of the 1960s, and the political mobilization of religious conservatives.

The latter process is particularly interesting. Many of the trends that troubled religious conservatives—secularization, hedonism, the alleged erosion of "family values"—had little to do with politics. They were byproducts of long-term social changes and of contemporary mass culture and a consumption-driven economy driven by television, the movies, and the ceaseless marketing of consumer goods.

Yet from the 1970s onward, prominent leaders and organizations politicized evangelicals' cultural uneasiness, demonizing the Democratic Party as the source of the moral crisis, and the Republican Party as the savior. A great irony of the period is that while evangelicals flocked to the Republican banner, most GOP politicians, including Reagan, gave little more than lip service to their cultural and moral agenda. Instead, they used their power to enact an economic program—tax cuts that particularly benefited corporations and upper-income groups, business deregulation, cuts in social programs—that was quite contrary to the economic interests of their culturally conservative supporters, often drawn from society's blue-collar and lower-middle-class ranks.

Another striking characteristic of Reagan's presidency is his pragmatic willingness to shift positions in light of changing circumstances, despite his ideological commitments. This pragmatism, sometimes on display on domestic policy issues, emerged most dramatically in his welcoming response to the most important global development of his presidency: the transformations in Russia that presaged the end of the Cold War.

In assessing this period, it is tempting to overstate both the completeness of the "conservative revolution" and the pervasiveness of the culture wars. In fact, liberal resistance to the conservative economic agenda remained vigorous and articulate. The federal government that Reagan rhetorically belittled actually grew during his presidency, and the landmark achievements of the New-Deal/Great Society reforms remained in place. In the larger society, major changes, already under way, continued. Race relations, though far from utopian, were vastly different than a generation earlier. Women continued to enter many fields once largely closed to them. Acceptance of gays and lesbians advanced markedly despite the fulminations of cultural warriors.

Where does President Clinton fit in? Opportunistic, accommodating to shifting political currents, Clinton clearly moved the Democratic Party to a more centrist position than that of, say, George McGovern, the party's 1968 presidential candidate. Yet he resisted the harsher approaches of some welfare reformers; battled Big

Tobacco's lobbying forces; and, though his health-care reform failed, placed the issue squarely on the national agenda.

From a longer perspective, the era's most notable trends may well be ones little related to political battles or culture wars. The computer revolution, climate change, the rise of a globalized economy, and social/political ferment in the Muslim world all seemed likely to shape America's future in profound ways.

31

A CHANGING NATION CONFRONTS
HOME-FRONT CRISES AND
NEW GLOBAL REALITIES,
2001 TO THE PRESENT

AMERICA UNDER ATTACK: SEPTEMBER 11, 2001, AND ITS AFTERMATH

On September 11, 2001, a devastating attack horrified the nation. President George W. Bush mobilized a multinational coalition to invade Afghanistan, stronghold of al Qaeda, the organization responsible. Bush also secured new laws and reorganized federal agencies to tighten homeland security. Accusing Iraq's dictator Saddam Hussein of complicity in the 9/11 attacks, Bush launched an invasion of Iraq as well.

A New Administration, a Day of Horror   Assuming the presidency in January 2001, George W. Bush named General **Colin Powell** as secretary of state, making him the highest-ranking African American to serve in a presidential administration. **Condoleezza Rice,** a Russian specialist at Stanford University, also African American, became national security adviser.

Other appointees, like Vice President **Richard (Dick) Cheney** and Secretary of Defense **Donald Rumsfeld,** were veterans of earlier Republican administrations with corporate ties. Ultraconservative John Ashcroft became attorney general.

Bush proposed education reforms, tax cuts favoring the wealthy, an energy bill shaped by the energy industries, and initiatives welcomed by his conservative Christian base. With Bush attentive mainly to his core supporters, his approval ratings fell. This changed dramatically on **September 11, 2001,** a day of horror that energized the administration and dominated Bush's remaining years in office.

On that morning, three commercial airliners hijacked by terrorists slammed into the Pentagon and the twin towers of New York's World Trade Center. As the blazing towers collapsed, 2,752 men and women met their deaths, including nearly 350 firefighters and 23 police officers. The Pentagon attack left 245 dead on the ground. A fourth plane crashed in Pennsylvania when heroic passengers overpowered the hijackers. Nearly 250 passengers and crew in the four planes perished. When investigators identified the nineteen hijackers as Muslims from the Middle East, President Bush urged Americans to distinguish between a few terrorists and the world's 1.2 billion Muslims, including some 6 million in the United States. Islamic leaders worldwide repudiated the attacks, although demonstrators in some Arab cities and Palestinian refugee camps celebrated.

As the nation mourned, political divisions faded. The World War II anthem "God Bless America" enjoyed renewed popularity. "United We Stand" proclaimed billboards and bumper stickers. The airline and hospitality industries reeled as jittery travelers canceled trips. Anxiety increased in October, when letters containing deadly anthrax spores appeared in the offices of NBC News, two senators, and a tabloid newspaper. Five persons, including two postal workers, died from anthrax-tainted mail. In 2008, a researcher at an army biological research laboratory committed suicide after the FBI identified him as the likely perpetrator.

Confronting al Qaeda in Afghanistan   President Bush declared the attacks an "act of war," and the Senate unanimously authorized Bush to use "all necessary and appropriate force" to retaliate and to prevent future terrorist attacks. The president's approval ratings neared 90 percent. On September 20, before a joint session of Congress, Bush blamed **al Qaeda** ("the base"), an organization headed by Osama bin Laden in Afghanistan. Bin Laden, already under indictment for the 1998 attack on U.S. embassies in Africa, had long denounced America for supporting Israel and for stationing "infidel" troops on Saudi soil.

Bush also targeted the Taliban, a Pakistan-based Muslim fundamentalist movement that had controlled Afghanistan since 1996. This U.S. effort enjoyed NATO backing and broad international support. Pakistan's military government endorsed Bush's decision to invade, despite Taliban enclaves in Pakistan's border regions. On October 7, a U.S.-led coalition of forces launched the attack.

A Day of Horror: September 11, 2001
Smoke billows from the World Trade Center's north tower moments after a commercial aircraft hijacked by terrorists crashed into it.

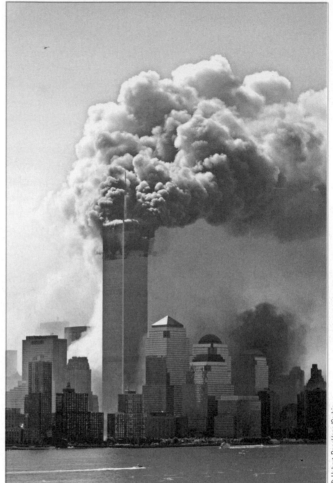

© Hubert Boesl/epa/Corbis

The Taliban soon surrendered Kabul, the Afghan capital, and by mid-December, the U.S.-led coalition claimed victory. Hundreds of captured prisoners were sent to the U.S. base in **Guantánamo Bay,** Cuba. With U.S. support, Afghan tribal leaders named an interim prime minister, Hamid Karzai. However, Osama bin Laden, Taliban leader Mullah Omar, and many al Qaeda loyalists escaped capture.

Tightening Home-Front Security   Congress late in 2001 created the Transportation Security Administration to oversee an expanded force of airport security personnel. Over the protests of civil liberties advocates, the Justice Department rounded up hundreds of Middle Easterners in the United States, some for minor visa violations, and held them without filing charges.

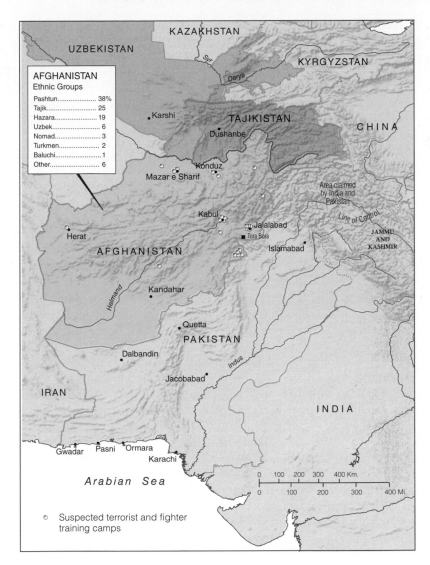

MAP 31.1 Afghanistan and Pakistan

After the attacks of September 11, 2001, U.S. and NATO forces attacked the terrorist organization al Qaeda, based in Afghanistan. The country's radical Islamist Taliban regime was overthrown, but many fighters retreated to the mountains along the Afghanistan–Pakistan border. Afghanistan remained violent and unsettled, and al Qaeda leader Osama bin Laden was still at large.

Source: © Cengage Learning. All rights reserved. No distribution allowed without express authorization.

The **USA-Patriot Act,** the administration's sweeping antiterrorist bill passed by Congress in October 2001, granted the government authority to monitor telephone and e-mail communications. Civil libertarians and others protested this expansion of federal power. (Congress renewed the Patriot Act in 2005, adding some civil-liberties safeguards.)

The media soon reported missed clues before the 9/11 attack. Through the summer of 2001, President Bush's daily security briefings included warnings of an al Qaeda plot to hijack a U.S. airliner. In August 2001, the FBI bungled a Minnesota flight school's warning of a suspicious person seeking to enroll. (Later linked to the 9/11 plot, he was tried and given a life sentence.)

In November 2002, Congress created a new **Department of Homeland Security,** which absorbed the Federal Emergency Management Agency (FEMA) and other agencies.

In 2005, Bush appointed a Director of National Intelligence to coordinate the government's fifteen different intelligence agencies. Whether such bureaucratic reshufflings actually increased security remained unclear.

War in Iraq, 2003–2004   Although Afghanistan remained unstable and Osama bin Laden uncaptured, the administration's attention shifted elsewhere. In his January 2002 State of the Union address, President Bush especially targeted Iraq's ruler, Saddam Hussein, weakened but still in power following the 1991 Persian Gulf War. In coordinated speeches and interviews, Cheney, Rumsfeld, Rice, and other officials accused Saddam of complicity in the 9/11 attacks and of developing nuclear, chemical, and biological weapons.

This focus on Iraq was orchestrated by a close-knit group of Republican **neoconservatives,** including Cheney, Rumsfeld, and their key aides. (The term, meaning "new conservatives," originally applied to Democrats who switched to the Republican Party when the Democratic Party moved leftward in the 1960s.)

Throughout the Cold War, some hardliners rejected negotiation, advocating instead a policy of overwhelming U.S. military superiority and aggressive challenges to Soviet power. With the Soviet Union's collapse, neoconservatives continued to promote the aggressive projection of U.S. power worldwide. Any actual or potential threat to America's global interests, they insisted, must be resisted by all available means, including preemptive military action. For neoconservatives, the traditional foreign policy goal of resolving conflict by compromise conveyed weakness. The point was not to negotiate with adversaries, but to defeat them.

With George W. Bush's election, neoconservatives gained the opportunity to put their ideology into practice. Although Cheney, Rumsfeld, and their top aides were its real architects, Bush was its public spokesperson, clothing it with an aura of religious certitude. America must "rid the world of evil" he proclaimed after 9/11. "The liberty we prize," he added in his 2003 State of the Union address, "is not America's gift to the world, it is God's gift to humanity." The administration's proposed military intervention in Iraq proved controversial from the outset. Critics challenged the administration to prove its claims. A preemptive war would violate U.S. principles, they charged, and could drag on for years, outrage the Muslim world, and divert attention from Afghanistan. British prime minister Tony Blair backed the administration, but other NATO allies, along with most Arab leaders, objected.

Nevertheless, in October 2002, Congress authorized President Bush to "defend the national security ... against the continuing threat posed by Iraq." While Republicans supported the resolution, Democrats were divided, with some fearful of opposing a resolution Bush called vital to American security. As Lyndon Johnson had cited the Gulf of Tonkin Resolution to justify his Vietnam War escalation, so President Bush used this resolution to justify invading Iraq.

Bolstered by the 2002 midterm elections, in which Republicans regained control of the Senate and increased their House majority, the administration pushed its Iraq invasion plans. In a February 2003 UN speech, Secretary of State Colin Powell, relying on CIA evidence, insisted that Saddam Hussein was developing weapons of mass destruction (WMDs).

On March 19, 2003, U.S. cruise missiles hit Baghdad. Two days later, U.S. and British troops invaded southern Iraq, populated by anti-Sadaam Shi'ite Muslims. Securing the region's oil fields, the invaders moved north. In early

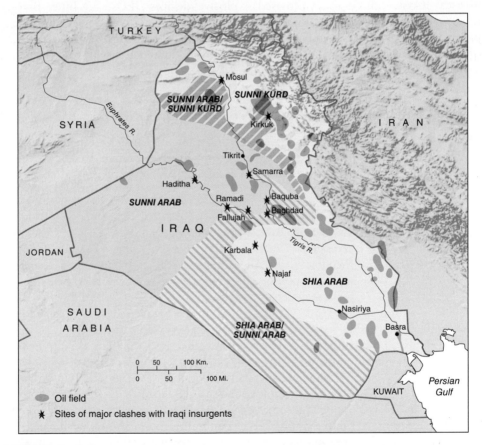

MAP 31.2 Iraq

With Saddam Hussein's overthrow by U.S.-led forces in 2003, violence erupted among Iraq's ethnic and religious groups, including the majority Shia Muslims concentrated in the southeast and the minority Sunni Muslims, who ruled the country under Saddam.

Source: © Cengage Learning. All rights reserved. No distribution allowed without express authorization.

April, U.S. troops occupied Baghdad and toppled a large statue of Saddam. As the regime fell and Saddam fled, basic municipal services collapsed and widespread looting erupted.

On May 1, aboard the aircraft carrier *Abraham Lincoln* off San Diego, President Bush declared: "[M]ajor combat operations in Iraq have ended." A banner behind him proclaimed "Mission Accomplished." Bush named Paul Bremer, a Foreign Service officer, to administer affairs in Iraq. In December, Saddam was captured. After conviction by special tribunal of Iraqi judges of human-rights and genocidal abuses, he was hanged in December 2006. Iraq's Sunni Muslims, though a minority, long dominated Iraqi politics. Resenting their loss of power, they mobilized to expel the invaders. Radical Muslim fighters from outside Iraq added to the unrest. So did a young anti-American Shi'ite cleric, Moqtada al-Sadr, popular among Baghdad's poor.

Conditions worsened through 2004, with kidnappings, suicide bombings, and highway blasts caused by improvised explosive devices (IEDs). In June, Bremer transferred power to a provisional Iraqi government, but little changed. The campaign the Bush team had launched so confidently seemed bogged down. Secretary of State Powell, who privately opposed the war, resigned in November. Bush named Condoleezza Rice to replace him.

POLITICS AND THE ECONOMY AS A NEW CENTURY BEGINS

While pursuing the post–9/11 "war on terror," the early Bush administration also proposed tax cuts and other measures reflecting its conservative ideology. Meanwhile, the nation endured a recession and a cascade of bankruptcies and corporate scandals.

Economic Reverses and Corporate Scandals

George W. Bush's presidency began with a short but sharp recession. The high-flying Silicon Valley IT companies led the downturn. An estimated 250 such businesses collapsed in a few months. The market value of the surviving companies plummeted.

The recession soon spread. The stock market fell by 24 percent. Industrial production dropped; unemployment rose. The Bush administration, having inherited a budget surplus, now projected years of deficits. To stimulate recovery, the Federal Reserve Board cut interest rates to a forty-year low.

A wave of corporate bankruptcies and scandals in the energy and telecommunications fields further eroded investor confidence. Houston's Enron Corporation, with close ties to the administration, was an early casualty. A marketer of electric power that had moved into utilities and telecommunications, Enron in 2000 ranked seventh among America's corporations. The end came with brutal swiftness in 2001 when Enron filed for bankruptcy and admitted to falsifying profit reports. More than five thousand jobless Enron workers also lost their retirement funds, consisting mostly of Enron stock. Shortly before the collapse, the company's top officials sold their Enron stock, profiting handsomely. In 2006, a Houston jury convicted Enron

President George W. Bush, May 1, 2003 *Wearing a flight suit, a confident Bush prepares to fly to the aircraft carrier* USS Abraham Lincoln *anchored off San Diego, to proclaim victory in Iraq.*

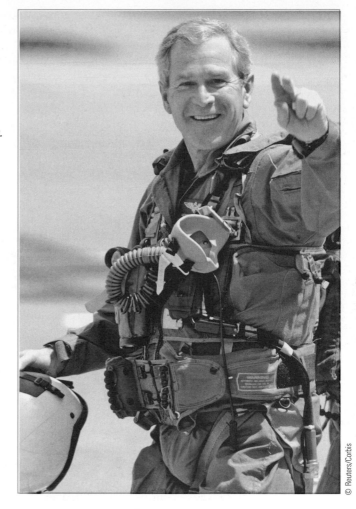

© Reuters/Corbis

founder Kenneth Lay and the company's CEO Jeffrey Skilling on multiple counts of fraud and conspiracy.

In 2002, America's second-largest telecommunications company, World-Com, admitted to falsifying its annual reports, filed for bankruptcy, and fired seventeen thousand employees. WorldCom's CEO, convicted of securities fraud, received a twenty-five-year prison sentence. Also in 2002, the CEO of Tyco, an industrial-products company, was indicted for looting the company of $600 million, including $2 million for his wife's birthday party on a Mediterranean island. Along with a prison sentence, he was fined $70 million and ordered to repay Tyco $134 million.

Declared a Wall Street investment banker: "I cannot think of a time when business ... has been held in less repute." The University of Maryland business school organized field trips to penitentiaries where imprisoned executives lectured students on honesty. Responding to public anger, Congress in July 2002 imposed stricter financial reporting rules on corporations and toughened criminal penalties for business fraud.

Recovery began in 2003, stimulated by consumer spending (much of it on credit) and a housing boom. But prosperity was spotty. While the average real income of the nation's richest 1 percent increased by more than 12 percent in 2004, that of the remaining 99 percent grew by only 1.5 percent. Observed economist Paul Krugman: "It's a great economy if you're a high-level corporate executive or someone who owns a lot of stock. For most other Americans, economic growth is a spectator sport." By mid-2006, even this uneven recovery faltered, and the jittery stock market again sank. The worst recession since the 1930s lay ahead.

The Republican Domestic Agenda   In February 2001, President Bush proposed $1.6 trillion in income-tax cuts over a ten-year period, with wealthy taxpayers receiving the highest percentage reduction. The cuts would stimulate investment, Bush argued. Democrats attacked the bill for favoring the rich and warned that such deep cuts would produce even larger federal deficits.

In May, Congress passed a $1.35 trillion tax cut somewhat less slanted toward the rich. Mounting budget deficits predictably followed, erasing the surplus Clinton had achieved. Nevertheless, the Republican-led Congress cut taxes further in 2003 and 2005.

The administration's 2001 energy bill emerged from secret meetings of oil and gas executives with Vice President Cheney (a former energy company head). Enron's Kenneth Lay, a major GOP contributor, played a key role. The bill eased environmental regulations on energy companies and provided tax incentives to expand coal, oil, nuclear power, and natural gas production, including drilling in Alaska's **Arctic National Wildlife Refuge** (ANWR), strongly opposed by environmentalists.

The bill Congress passed in 2005 included most of these provisions, though. Congress did reject drilling in ANWR and offered tax credits for purchasing hybrid vehicles and energy-efficient appliances and incentives for research on renewable and cleaner energy sources. Despite lobbying by environmental groups, Congress did not tighten vehicle fuel-efficiency requirements. Overall, the law pleased the energy companies that helped draft it.

Bush's education program, labeled **No Child Left Behind,** passed by Congress in 2001, required states to administer standardized reading and math tests in grades four and eight. Schools that failed to raise test scores even after required remedial programs faced the loss of federal funds and other penalties. Critics worried that teachers would focus too exclusively on the tested subjects. Others warned of federal intrusion in public education, traditionally a local matter. As test data accumulated, results proved mixed.

Reflecting Republicans' preference for private-sector solutions to social problems, the administration also supported school vouchers, by which children in poorly performing public schools could receive grants to enroll in private schools, mostly church-sponsored. While many supported the voucher idea, others, including the teachers' unions, criticized vouchers for draining tax dollars from the public schools and allowing private schools to "cherry pick" the most promising applicants. Congressional Democrats rejected Bush's call for a federally funded voucher program.

Some education reformers also supported charter schools, which gain exemption from many regulations governing public schools in exchange for agreeing to contracts mandating specific student achievement goals. By 2011, some 5,600 charter schools across the nation enrolled an estimated 2 million students. This attention to school reform suggested that the nation's public education system did, indeed, need strengthening—particularly in a globalizing economy and an information-based job market.

Rewarding his conservative religious base, Bush created an Office of Faith-Based and Community Initiatives to funnel tax dollars to church-run social programs. Grants went to antiabortion groups, organizations promoting teenage sexual abstinence, and evangelical prison ministries.

President Bush pleased abortion opponents by restricting stem-cell research. Stem cells are produced during an early stage of human embryo development, and fertility clinics often have "surplus" fertilized embryos. Because stem cells can develop into more specialized human cells, they are valuable for medical research. In 2001, Bush barred federal funding for research involving stem cells harvested from human embryos in the future.

Committed to a free-market ideology, Bush's appointees throughout the federal bureaucracy reduced regulatory oversight of business and finance and weakened environmental and consumer protection laws.

Campaign Finance Reform and the 2004 Election   Citizens who deplored the ever-growing role of money in politics targeted so-called soft-money contributions to political parties that then flowed on to specific candidates. In the 2000 election, soft-money contributions reached $400 million. Big contributors ranged from (mostly Republican) business lobbies, anti-abortion groups, and the National Rifle Association to (mostly Democratic) labor unions, trial lawyers, and teachers' unions.

In 2002, President Bush signed a campaign finance reform bill cosponsored by Arizona Republican senator John McCain and Wisconsin Democrat Russell Feingold. It banned soft-money contributions and restricted TV "issue ads" designed to influence elections. In a 2010 decision, however, discussed later in this chapter, the U.S. Supreme Court largely negated such efforts to limit the role of outside money in campaigns. As the 2004 election approached, Howard Dean, a former Vermont governor, emerged as the early frontrunner for the Democratic presidential nomination. Criticizing the Iraq War, Dean built a following via the Internet, especially on college campuses. His campaign faded, however, as senators **John Kerry** of Massachusetts and John Edwards of North Carolina gained momentum. Nevertheless, Dean tapped into growing opposition to the Iraq War and demonstrated the Internet's political potential.

Kerry won the nomination and chose Edwards as his running mate. Democratic strategists hoped Kerry's distinguished Vietnam War record would neutralize charges of Democratic weakness on defense while underscoring Bush's avoidance of service in Vietnam. Bush and Cheney, raising some $150 million from corporations and wealthy individual donors, again headed the Republican ticket.

Although Kerry had voted for the Patriot Act and initially supported the Iraq War, he now accused Bush of misleading the nation and criticized parts of the Patriot Act as threats to civil liberties. He also called for stricter environmental laws, tougher fuel-efficiency standards, and support for renewable energy.

President Bush defended both the Iraq War and the Patriot Act. Citing Kerry's changing positions, Republicans accused him of "flip-flopping." Anti-Kerry TV commercials, funded by a shadowy group supposedly independent of the Republican campaign, questioned his Vietnam record.

Cultural issues such as abortion, the death penalty, gun control, and gay rights loomed large in the campaign. In 2004, San Francisco's mayor challenged California law by marrying same-sex couples, and the Massachusetts Supreme Court ruled that banning same-sex marriage violated the state constitution's equal rights clause. Outraged religious conservatives applauded Bush's call for a constitutional amendment banning gay marriage. Antigay marriage referenda, on the ballot in eleven states, passed in all eleven. Bush carried nine of the eleven, including Ohio, a key swing state.

Bush, a tax-cutting president seen as a leader in the "war on terror" and a defender of embattled conservative cultural values, eked out a razor-thin victory, garnering 50.7 percent of the popular vote. Republicans gained a net of four Senate seats and four House seats.

Democrats took heart from the fact that Kerry won 55 percent of voters under thirty, a growing cohort. In Illinois, a young African American Democratic state legislator, Barack Obama, won election to the U.S. Senate.

The election highlighted the Internet's political role. During the campaign and after, *MoveOn.org*, a website initially launched to oppose President Clinton's impeachment and later devoted to resisting the Iraq War, raised funds and mobilized e-mails and telephone calls on behalf of liberal candidates and causes. While conservative organizations had long built support through magazines, direct mail, and talk radio, liberals appeared to have the edge in Internet-based activism, especially among young people.

Conservative political and religious groups remained active. But so did progressive organizations such as People for the American Way, Planned Parenthood, and the Sierra Club. Even among evangelical Christians, support for Bush was not unanimous. Jim Wallis of the evangelical Sojourners movement espoused social justice and the search for peace in his books and *Sojourners* magazine.

DEBATING IRAQ AND CONFRONTING OTHER GLOBAL CHALLENGES

As the Iraq conflict dragged on, home-front support eroded. Revelations of prisoner abuse, illegal spying on U.S. citizens, and distortions in the administration's case for invading Iraq sapped Bush's standing at home and abroad. The Israeli–Palestinian struggle, nuclear proliferation threats, and concern about climate change posed further challenges.

The Continuing Struggle in Iraq As Bush's second term began, conditions in Iraq worsened. Sunni insurgents in Baghdad and in strongholds north of the capital battled to prevent a Shi'ite-dominated government. A November 2004 anti-insurgent operation in Fallujah involved approximately ten thousand U.S. and Iraqi forces. Typically, however, the insurgents returned after the troops withdrew. Followers of the radical Shi'ite cleric Moqtada al-Sadr attacked Sunnis, GIs, journalists, and foreign contractors alike. Muslim militants from elsewhere, attracted by the U.S. presence, added to the unrest.

Reconstruction lagged, and basic municipal services faltered. A subsidiary of the Halliburton Company, once headed by Vice President Cheney, with $3.6 billion in no-bid reconstruction contracts, faced accusations of fraud. Iraq's vital oil exports remained below prewar levels.

On the political front, Sunnis boycotted a January 2005 election, resulting in a Shi'ite-dominated National Assembly. Sunnis accused Shi'ite militias and Interior Ministry "death squads" of kidnapping and killing Sunni leaders and detonating car bombs in Sunni neighborhoods. In February 2006, suicide bombers destroyed a revered Shi'ite mosque in Samarrah dating to 944 C.E., triggering anti-Sunni reprisal attacks. (The Kurds in northern Iraq, hoping for an independent Kurdish state, remained aloof from the sectarian violence.)

As thousands of refugees fled Iraq or sheltered in makeshift camps, an Iraqi leader lamented: "If this is not civil war, then God knows what civil war is." As other coalition forces withdrew, the United States bore the brunt of the anti-insurgency fighting.

Sagging Support at Home Under these circumstances, U.S. public opinion turned against the war. In November 2005, Pennsylvania Democratic congressman Jack Murtha, a decorated Vietnam War veteran, urged immediate withdrawal from Iraq. Conservative writer William Buckley bluntly declared: "[T]he American objective in Iraq has failed." Michael Moore's anti-Bush satirical documentary *Fahrenheit 9/11* packed movie theaters in 2004. Singers including Bruce Springsteen, Neil Young, and the Dixie Chicks country trio expressed opposition to the administration's policies. On the other hand, conservative media voices such as radio personality Rush Limbaugh and commentators on Rupert Murdoch's Fox TV network supported the president, along with many evangelical religious leaders. In an already polarized cultural and political climate, the Iraq War further divided America.

Under critical scrutiny, the administration's arguments for invading Iraq crumbled. After the invasion, investigators found no WMDs. President Bush's claim in his 2003 State of the Union address that Iraq had imported uranium from Africa proved false, and Saddam's alleged role in the 9/11 attacks remained unproven. A Senate inquiry found that Vice President Cheney and other administration officials had pressured the CIA to link Saddam to al Qaeda while ignoring contradictory data.

Defense Secretary Rumsfeld's prewar assurances that a small U.S. force equipped with high-tech weaponry would achieve quick victory proved tragically wrong. When Army chief of staff General Eric Shineski told Congress in March 2003 that success in Iraq would require several hundred thousand troops, Rumsfeld derided this estimate. Although Shinesky's estimate proved accurate, Bush initially rejected calls for Rumsfeld's dismissal. "I am the decider, and I decide what is best," declared Bush in April 2006, "and what's best is for Don Rumsfeld to remain as secretary of defense."

Shocking evidence of prisoner mistreatment deepened home-front malaise. In 2004, photographs surfaced showing the abuse and sexual humiliation of Iraqis held by U.S. forces at Baghdad's Abu Ghraib prison. Further evidence soon revealed a broader pattern of prisoner abuse, approved at the highest level, including at Guantánamo, where more than five hundred prisoners from Afghanistan were held without trial. In a secret 2002 memo, a Justice Department lawyer argued that the Geneva Conventions protecting prisoners of war did not apply to persons the president designated as "enemy combatants." The only interrogations constituting torture, he wrote, were those causing "death, organ failure, or serious impairment of bodily functions." All else was permissible.

This "torture memo," approved by Bush's White House counsel, became public in 2004, unleashing more controversy. The International Red Cross and prisoner rights organizations denounced as torture interrogation techniques at Guantánamo, including "water boarding," in which the victim is nearly drowned. The army, however, called its interrogation techniques "safe, secure, and humane," and the administration claimed the right to hold the Guantánamo prisoners without trial as long as the open-ended "war on terrorism" continued. Evidence also surfaced that the CIA had secretly flown some detainees to an uncertain fate in Egyptian and Eastern European prisons.

In 2005, Congress passed legislation proposed by Senator John McCain forbidding "cruel, inhuman, and degrading" treatment of prisoners. McCain himself had been tortured as a POW in Vietnam. Bush signed the bill but issued a "signing statement," asserting, in effect, that he was not bound to obey it.

This was one of many such pronouncements by which the president "interpreted" bills he was signing, even though the Constitution gives presidents no authority to interpret laws as they choose. The *New York Times* editorialized in May 2006: "This president seems determined not to play by any rules other than the ones of his own making."

Americans also learned in 2005 that President Bush in 2002 had secretly authorized the National Security Agency (NSA), a government body created in 1952, to tap U.S. citizens' overseas phone calls and e-mails without securing a warrant as required by law. Evidence also surfaced that the NSA had tapped domestic as well as foreign phone calls and e-mails and that the FBI had targeted peace groups and journalists for surveillance. In defense of this warrantless surveillance, Bush and Attorney General Alberto Gonzales argued that the 2001 congressional resolution authorizing the president to use "all necessary and appropriate force" to prevent future attacks covered almost anything the administration chose to do. These invasions of privacy disturbed not only civil libertarians but many ordinary citizens as well.

In *Hamdi* v. *Rumsfeld* (2004), the Supreme Court addressed the Bush administration's claim that "enemy combatants" could be held indefinitely.

This case involved a U.S. citizen captured in Iraq in 2001 and held thereafter without trial or legal counsel. Eight of the justices agreed that the government had violated Hamdi's Fifth Amendment right to due process. Four justices went further, declaring that all alleged enemy combatants, whether U.S. citizens or not, had the right to trial.

In response to criticism, the Bush administration set up special military tribunals, not bound by the customary rules of courtroom procedure, to try the Guantánamo prisoners. In 2006, the Supreme Court ruled that such tribunals violated both the Constitution and the Geneva Conventions.

In March 2006, *Time* magazine reported that in November 2005, U.S. marines killed twenty-four unarmed Iraqi men, women, and children after a roadside IED killed one of their unit. As this and other atrocities came to light, memories of the Vietnam era massacre at My Lai stirred uneasily. Amid a cascade of disturbing news, the reputation not only of the Bush administration but of America itself suffered.

By 2011, when combat operations in Iraq finally ended, as discussed later in this chapter, U.S. military deaths neared 4,500, with more than 33,000 wounded, many severely. Figures on Iraqi civilian dead, both from combat crossfire and sectarian violence, though difficult to tally precisely, clearly mounted into the tens of thousands.

Other International Crises Loom for Bush and His Successors

Despite the open wound of the Iraq War, other urgent global issues confronted the Bush administration, including the Israeli–Palestinian conflict, nuclear weapons proliferation, and climate change. These were long-term challenges, clearly extending beyond any single presidential administration.

On the Israeli–Palestinian front, the Bush administration accomplished little. As the Palestinian *intifada* (uprising) continued, Israeli Prime Minister Ariel Sharon demanded an end to the violence before resuming talks, while Palestinian leader Yasir Arafat insisted that protests would continue so long as Israel fostered Jewish settlements in Palestinian territory. In 2002, Israel began a security barrier, partially extending into the West Bank, to control access and discourage attacks.

The Bush administration proposed a so-called road map to peace in 2003, but it did not push the initiative. In 2005, Israel withdrew Jewish settlements from Gaza, but in January 2006 Palestinian elections gave victory to the radical Hamas organization, which condoned attacks on Israel and even denied Israel's right to exist. Taking control of Gaza, Hamas rejected a call by the United States, the European Union, Russia, and the UN, collectively called the Quartet, to renounce violence and recognize Israel.

Meanwhile, Hezbollah, a militant Lebanon-based Shi'ite organization supported by Iran and Syria, killed or kidnapped several Israeli soldiers and lobbed rockets into northern Israel. In retaliation, Israel invaded Lebanon in July 2006 and bombed not only Hezbollah bases but also bridges, highways, and Beirut's airport. The Israelis soon withdrew, leaving Hezbollah intact and claiming victory.

As Hamas militants in Gaza fired rockets into border towns, Israel in December 2008 launched a full-scale air and ground assault on Gaza, jammed with 1.5 million people. More than thirteen hundred Gazans died, including forty children at two UN schools. The Israelis withdrew after three weeks, leaving Hamas in power and the underlying conflict no nearer solution.

The danger of nuclear proliferation worsened in these years. Impoverished and isolated North Korea withdrew from the Nuclear Nonproliferation Treaty and in 2006 tested both a long-range missile and a nuclear weapon. Despite stop-and-start negotiations, North Korea exploded an even more powerful bomb in May 2009 and fired more missiles, alarming neighboring nations, as well as the United States.

Iran, meanwhile, pursued a uranium-enrichment program, allegedly for nuclear power development. Under UN pressure, Iran suspended this program in 2004 but resumed it in 2006 after the election of Mahmoud Ahmadinejad, a fanatically anti-American, anti-Israeli Islamic fundamentalist, as president. Secretary of State Rice worked with the UN and European allies to induce Iran to open its program to inspection or face economic sanctions, but the stand-off continued. An Iranian long-range missile test in May 2009 deepened uneasiness about its intentions. Citing these threats, the Bush administration pursued a land-based version of President Reagan's missile-defense system (see Chapter 30). Russian president Vladimir Putin vigorously opposed the administration's plans to build radar facilities in Poland and the Czech Republic as part of this missile-defense program.

In 2006, President Bush agreed to provide fuel and parts for India's nuclear power reactors even though India refused to sign the Nuclear Nonproliferation Treaty and barred UN inspectors from its nuclear weapons facilities. Critics warned that this would encourage other nations to pursue nuclear weapons programs. Meanwhile, political instability in Pakistan, a nuclear power, intensified fears of deepening nuclear dangers stalking the world.

On the list of urgent global challenges, environmental hazards and climate change loomed large as well. Three Mile Island, Love Canal, and the *Exxon Valdez* disaster (see Chapters 29 and 30) underscored modern technology's environmental risks. A 1986 nuclear power plant explosion at Chernobyl in the Ukraine and a 1984 disaster in Bhopal, India, in which deadly gases from a U.S.-owned chemical plant killed seventeen hundred people, highlighted the global scope of these risks. Polluted water caused untold deaths in poor countries.

Environmental hazards included radioactive waste disposal. In 2002, President Bush designated Nevada's Yucca Mountain as the storage site for nuclear wastes that will remain deadly for thousands of years. But as Nevada politicians protested and scientists warned of seismic activity and water seepage in the area, the project stalled. Meanwhile, radioactive byproducts of dismantled weapons and aging nuclear power plants accumulated in temporary sites.

Above all, **climate change** loomed as a grave threat. The United States, with less than 5 percent of the world's population, accounts for 25 percent of global energy consumption, primarily from fossil fuels widely viewed as contributing to climate change. The Bush administration downplayed the environmental impact of fossil-fuel consumption. Energy conservation might be a "sign of personal virtue," said Vice President Cheney, but had little place in shaping public policy. The administration rejected calls for stricter emissions standards, weakened enforcement of existing regulations, and marginalized government scientists who questioned its policies.

Despite America's important role, climate change remained a truly global issue, with India, China, and other developing economies generating massive greenhouse gas emissions as well. (As host of the 2008 Olympic Games, China did reduce Beijing's notorious air pollution, at least temporarily.)

A 1997 UN conference on global warming held in Kyoto, Japan, set strict emission targets for industrialized nations. President Clinton signed the **Kyoto Accords** but did not submit the document for Senate ratification, fearing defeat. President Bush repudiated the agreement on the grounds that it would hurt the U.S. economy and did not include developing nations such as China and India. The Kyoto Accords, revised to meet U.S. objections, went into effect in 2005, with only the United States, Australia, India, and China remaining aloof.

As late as November 2008, in its final months, the Bush administration opened thousands of acres near fragile national park sites in Utah to oil and gas exploration. Bush's environmental record, charged the head of the EPA under President Nixon, "represents a radical rollback of environmental policy going back ... many, many years."

SOCIAL AND ECONOMIC TRENDS IN CONTEMPORARY AMERICA

As a new century began, long-term population shifts and changing immigration patterns, with other developments, brought significant changes to U.S. society. Upward mobility continued for some, but so did poverty and inequality. Economic changes benefited some but disadvantaged others, including inner-city residents and displaced industrial workers, widening the economic gap between those at the top and the rest of society.

An Increasingly Diverse People   Americans have long been a people on the move, and this mobility continues. California's population grew by nearly 7.5 million from 1990 to 2010, Maricopa County, Arizona (which includes Phoenix), by nearly 1.7 million. The South expanded rapidly in these years as well. Across the Midwest and Great Plains, by contrast, populations remained stable and even declined.

Household patterns changed as well. The proportion of "traditional" families headed by a married heterosexual couple fell from 74 percent in 1960 to under 50 percent in 2007. Commented The *New York Times*: "In modern America no type of family can really be recognized to the exclusion of all others."

Climate Change as a Worldwide Challenge

As long ago as 1957, Roger Revelle, director of the Scripps Institution of Oceanography in San Diego, coauthored a scientific paper warning of rising carbon dioxide levels in the atmosphere and attributing the increase in part to combustion of fossil fuels (coal, oil, and natural gas). Global warming could result, the article cautioned.

In the decades since, the conclusions of this farsighted paper have been verified. The Earth's average temperature rose by one degree Fahrenheit in the twentieth century, and the rate of increase shot up after 1970. The century's ten hottest years came after 1985, and 2005 was the hottest year ever recorded.

Rising carbon dioxide levels have also been documented by many studies, including ice-core sampling. In the 1990s, U.S., Russian, and French scientists extracted a two-mile-long ice core in Antarctica and measured carbon dioxide levels in trapped air bubbles over a 440,000-year span. In 2005, European researchers reported on ice cores extending back 650,000 years. Both teams found current carbon dioxide levels at an all-time high. Throughout these incredibly long time spans, carbon dioxide levels remained within a range of 180 to 300 parts per million. However, beginning around 1950, the level crept up. In 2005, it reached 380 parts per million.

The connection between carbon dioxide levels and global warming is clear as well. Just as the glass roof of a greenhouse traps the sun's heat, so carbon dioxide and other "greenhouse gases" blanketing the Earth prevent solar heat from escaping.

Further, despite some skeptics, most scientists now agree that human pursuits involving increasing use of fossil fuels in factories, homes, and motor vehicles have contributed significantly to the rising levels of atmospheric carbon dioxide. In a 2005 report, the leading scientific bodies of the United States, Canada, France, Italy, Germany, Great Britain, Japan, China, India, Russia, and Brazil attributed "most of the warming in recent decades … to human activities."

The United States is the world's major producer of carbon dioxide emissions from fossil fuels, followed by China, Russia, Japan, and India. This is clearly a global issue. Throughout the world, growing numbers of factories belching smoke and motorized vehicles spewing exhaust worsen the problem. In 2005, annual carbon dioxide emissions in the United States and Japan were about 20 percent greater than in 1990. In the same fifteen-year period, however, India's annual emissions more than doubled, and China's soared by a startling 237 percent. The burning of vast tracks of the Amazonian rain forest to create more grazing land has placed Brazil high on the list of greenhouse gas producers as well.

In moderate levels, greenhouse gases pose no threat; indeed, they are essential. Without their warming effect, the Earth would be a frozen waste. But the recent surge, now widely linked to human activity, brings serious hazards—present and potential.

Photographs transmitted by two Russian satellites launched in 2002 reveal that Antarctica's icecap is melting at a rate of thirty-six cubic miles per year, with a similar melt-off in the Greenland and Arctic Ocean icecaps. As polar ice has melted, sea levels have risen. Storm surges are destroying homes in Shishmaref, an Inupiat village in northwestern Alaska, as a protective sea-ice barrier melts. In 2002, the residents voted to move farther inland to preserve their community.

As the permafrost weakens in Alaska and northern Canada, highways buckle and cracks develop in houses. The stability of Alaska's oil pipeline from Prudhoe Bay to Valdez is threatened. In northern Iceland, vast lagoons have appeared as glaciers recede. In the Swiss and Austrian Alps, deadly avalanches, shrinking glaciers, and melting permafrost threaten the economy of a region dependent on skiers, tourists, and mountain climbers.

Beyond such immediate effects, global warming is affecting the Earth's delicate ecological balance. Examples abound:

- The mountain pine beetle, advancing northward as Alaska and western Canada grow warmer, has devastated millions of acres of spruce forest.
- Antarctica's penguin population has dramatically declined since 1950, as melting ice reduces breeding areas.
- The U.S. Interior Department placed polar bears on the endangered species list in 2008, as warming threatened their Arctic habitat.
- In 2005, amphibian disease experts documented a massive decline in rare Latin American frog species because of a spreading fungus attributed to global warming.
- Australian researchers report dying coral reefs as ocean temperatures rise.

Projections of future trends offer further cause for concern. Even with preventive measures, carbon dioxide levels are predicted to increase for years. Climatologists using computer simulations foresee continued global temperature increases for at least a century. The resulting polar melting could increase sea levels up to five feet, endangering coastal cities from Boston and New York to Mumbai and Hong Kong. In low-lying Bangladesh, flooding could displace 6 million people.

Climatic changes could radically disrupt agricultural production and extend the range of disease-causing organisms. Rising ocean temperatures could affect fisheries and generate ferocious tropical storms.

Global warming has triggered a global response. The 1997 Kyoto Accords represent a major multinational commitment to reducing greenhouse gases. Brazil in 2008 announced a bold plan to protect the Amazonian rain forest. China, India, and other developing nations are addressing the issue as well, though environmental objectives often clash with economic goals.

Many international organizations and hundreds of Internet websites publicize the issue. Al Gore's *Earth in the Balance* reached a vast audience, and his 2006 book and Academy-Award-winning film *An Inconvenient Truth* further documented the dangers of global warming. Germany's environmental minister ordered six thousand DVDs of the film for showing in German schools. Other nations took similar steps. In 2007, Gore and the UN's Intergovernmental Panel on Climate Change jointly received the Nobel Peace Prize for promoting awareness of global warming.

Research on alternative energy sources, including solar, wind, and thermal, is accelerating as is work on more fuel-efficient hybrid vehicles. The United States and many other nations have set emissions standards for factories and vehicles.

Whether this international response will match the magnitude of the challenge remains an urgent question as the global community confronts its future.

Questions for Analysis

1. *What are some possible long-term consequences of global warming?*
2. *What international responses have addressed the problem of greenhouse gas emissions?*

Heavy immigration from Asia and Latin America reversed a long decline in the proportion of foreign-born persons in the population. From a low of about 5 percent in 1970, this figure stood at 12 percent in 2010. The 2010 U.S. population of 308.7 million was about 13 percent Hispanic, 12 percent black, 4 percent Asian, and 1 percent American Indian. The nation's Hispanics—nearly 60 percent of Mexican origin, with Puerto Ricans, Cubans, and Salvadorans comprising most of the balance—are predicted to make up 25 percent of the population by 2050. Some 6 million Muslims, mainly from the Middle East and North Africa, add to the ethno-religious mix.

These demographic changes have far-reaching political, economic, and cultural implications and offer a preview of a dynamic future nation very different from that of yesterday or today.

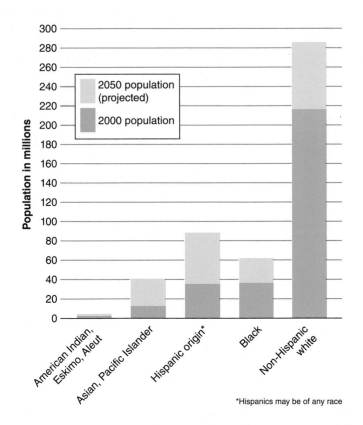

*Hispanics may be of any race

FIGURE 31.1   U.S. Population by Race and Hispanic Origin, 2000 and 2050 (Projected)

By 2050, the Census Bureau projects, non-Hispanic whites will constitute only about half the total U.S. population.

Source: U.S. Census Bureau, 2004.

Upward Mobility and Social Problems in a Multiethnic Society   African American median household income in 2007 approached $35,000. Although below the national median of around $50,700, this represented a substantial gain, in constant dollars, since 1990. (The recession that hit in 2008, discussed later in this chapter, reduced this figure to $32,584 by 2009.) College-educated blacks enjoyed significantly higher earnings, and 57 percent of black high school graduates in 2005 went on to college. TV's long-running *Cosby Show* (1984–1992), starring Bill Cosby as an obstetrician and his wife (Phylicia Rashad) as an attorney, offered a fictional version of this upwardly mobile group of African Americans.

But many inner-city blacks faced dismal job prospects, poor schools, and drug-related crime. Prison statistics for ill-educated young black males, often involving drug-related offenses, were similarly bleak.

Inner-city black women face risks of drug use, HIV/AIDS infection, and out-of-wedlock pregnancy. In 2010, 72 percent of black births were to unmarried women, almost twice the percentage in 1970. Many of these unmarried mothers were teenagers, reducing their prospects for education and employment. (Out-of-wedlock births among other groups also rose, but at a far lower rate.)

Inner-city churches and community organizations addressed the multiple social problems of their neighborhoods. In 2006, a group of big-city mayors demanded action to curb the plague of illegal guns.

Among Native Americans, renewed tribal pride and activism continued, including lawsuits to enforce long-ignored Indian treaties. Tribal gambling casinos, approved by Congress in 1988, proliferated. By 2008, about four hundred casinos generated more than $18 billion in annual income. Some tribal leaders lamented the social problems casinos sometimes brought in their wake, but casino income did fund tribal schools, museums, job training, and substance-abuse programs.

The Hispanic population resisted sweeping generalizations. While Mexican Americans concentrated in the Southwest, many lived elsewhere. Cubans, Puerto Ricans, and Haitians (mostly of African origin), resided mainly in Florida, New York, New Jersey, and Illinois.

Hispanic households' median income neared $40,000 by 2008, and unemployment among Hispanics dropped from 9 percent in 1995 to 5.6 percent in 2007. However, in 2007, 21.5 percent lived in poverty, many in troubled inner-city neighborhoods. Religion and family loom large in Hispanic culture, but stressful social conditions took their toll. In 2007, more than five thousand Hispanics held elective public office, including Los Angeles mayor Antonio Villaraigosa. Ten million Hispanics streamed to the polls in 2008, making them an increasingly important constituency. In 2009, filling a Supreme Court vacancy, President Barack Obama successfully nominated Sonia Sotomayor, a U.S. district court judge of Puerto Rican descent. Of the nation's 13 million Asian Americans in 2007, 75 percent had arrived since 1980. Prizing education and supported by family networks, many followed a trajectory of academic achievement and upward mobility. Nearly 50 percent of adult Asian Americans hold college degrees, and among high school graduates, the college enrollment rate nears 90 percent.

By 2050, demographers predict, given baby-boom mortality and comparative fertility rates, non-Hispanic whites, while still a plurality, will simply be another minority. Adding further diversity, 14.6 percent of newly married couples in 2008 married outside their racial or ethnic group, up from 6.8 percent in 1980. Recognizing these realities, the Census Bureau now permits citizens to check more than one racial category, or none at all.

With the graying of the baby-boom generation (those born between 1946 and 1964), America is also aging. The proportion of Americans over sixty-five, about 13 percent in 2009, is projected to reach 20 percent by 2050—a statistic with profound implications for health care, Social Security and Medicare funding, and other economic and social issues.

The "New Economy" and Its Mixed Effects

In the early twentieth century, industrial production replaced agriculture as America's economic engine. The century's end saw an equally profound transformation: the rise of a professional and service-based economy. Farming and manufacturing continued, of course, but with far fewer workers.

In the U.S. work force of 154 million in 2011, about 60 percent held white-collar jobs, ranging from sales clerks, office workers, and teachers to physicians, lawyers, engineers, computer programmers, and business executives. Service-sector employees in health care, custodial work, restaurants, and so forth accounted for another 16 percent. Only 23 percent worked in manual-labor fields that as recently as 1960 had dominated the labor market.

This transformation had mixed effects. Young people with education, skills, and contacts did well in the new electronics, programming, and telecommunications fields and in the corporate and financial services sectors. For others, supermarkets, car washes, fast-food outlets, and discount superstores provided entry-level jobs, but few long-term prospects.

As the computer-based information revolution continued, newspaper circulation fell significantly. Even major papers such as The *New York Times* faced hard times as Americans turned to TV or online news sources—which for some meant Jon Stewart's satirical *Daily Show* on TV's Comedy Central. The new technologies affected the music and book industries as well. CD sales fell dramatically as fans downloaded songs electronically to their laptops or iPods. Bound-book sales declined as readers turned to handheld devices. The bookstore chain Borders declared bankruptcy in 2011.

The economic transformation summed up by the term "globalization" complicated all these changes. Today's large corporations and financial institutions are all global in scope. Thanks to regional trading blocs such as NAFTA and multinational agreements administered by the **World Trade Organization** (WTO), the production and marketing of goods and the flow of capital now largely ignores national boundaries. The WTO, created in 1995 as successor to an earlier body set up in 1947, monitors and promotes trade among its 153 member nations.

The 2007 U.S. trade deficit approached $800 billion. This imbalance mainly reflected imports of oil, automobiles (mostly Japanese), and consumer goods from China. The 2007 trade deficit with China alone surged to $256 billion. Managing U.S.–Chinese economic relations proved particularly complex. U.S. manufacturers complained that China artificially manipulated its currency to make Chinese exports cheaper. However, big-box discounters, and their customers, welcomed cheap Chinese imports.

China's 2010 gross domestic product (GDP) of $8.7 trillion ranked second in the world, after the United States. Some economists predicted that China's GDP would surpass America's in twenty years. For China to sustain its growth and provide its people a higher living standard, the U.S. market was crucial. On exchange visits in 2005 and 2006, President Bush and China's leaders acknowledged their economic interdependence, while recognizing strains in the relationship, including China's repressive regime and poor human-rights record.

U.S. economic well-being increasingly depends on developments beyond the nation's borders. As imports replaced American-made products and manufacturers shifted operations overseas to cut labor costs, displaced workers faced unemployment or lower-wage service-sector jobs. Union membership by 2007 sank to only 12 percent of the labor force, leaving workers even more vulnerable.

The shifting fortunes of the U.S. auto industry typifies the pattern. After losing sales because of rising gasoline prices in the 1970s (see Chapter 30), American carmakers had returned to profitability with gas-guzzling SUVs and light trucks. But as gas prices again rose after 2000, car buyers turned to more fuel-efficient imports, particularly Japan's Toyota, Honda, and Nissan. By mid-2007, foreign carmakers had captured more than half the U.S. market—a historic first.

Foreign automakers set up U.S. production plants, mostly in the South and West, and mostly nonunion. By 2008, Toyota employed thirty-six thousand workers in fourteen U.S. plants and supported thousands more through its dealerships, parts suppliers, and advertising agencies.

At GM, a century-old icon of America's industrial might, annual losses spurted to nearly $39 billion in 2008. GM's stock price tumbled, and the company shed tens of thousands of jobs. Said one GM engineer: "This once was the premier company ... to work for. You were at the top of the heap, the major leagues.... Today, you know this company is crumbling around you."

From 2005 through mid-2008, GM, Chrysler, and Ford eliminated nearly 150,000 jobs and closed thirty-five plants, causing pain across America. The 2008 recession (discussed later in this chapter) further battered the domestic auto companies, though a government bailout helped them weather the storm. Economists continued to defend globalization as beneficial for America overall, lowering consumer prices and opening world markets for U.S. exports. But for displaced workers, this was cold comfort. In addition to the impact on U.S. industrial workers, human-rights activists charged that corporations in a "race to the bottom" open factories in poor countries where workers, often young women, live in prison-like barracks and work long hours for low wages with no benefits. Such factories often are environmental polluters as well.

Amid economic worries and a "war on terror," post–9/11 popular culture reflected crosscurrents of anxiety and escapism. Rupert Murdoch's Fox TV network, while rallying support for Bush, also offered the top-rated *American Idol* program, in which amateur vocalists competed for audience votes. Such shows, along with long-running syndicated game shows *Jeopardy* and *Wheel of Fortune* and the contrived scenarios of so-called reality programs, provided distraction from the stress of contemporary life. A longing to obliterate shadowy enemies perhaps contributed to the success of fantasy movies such as *Spider-Man 3* (2007) and *The Incredible Hulk* (2008), in which comic-book superheroes battle menacing foes.

THE BUSH ERA ENDS

Along with the ongoing Iraq War, President Bush's second term brought multiple setbacks, including soaring federal deficits, a bungled attempt at immigration reform, and an inept response to a devastating hurricane. Two Supreme Court appointments extended Bush's conservative legacy, but lobbying scandals further eroded Bush's standing as his term ended.

Mounting Deficits, Immigration Controversies, Disaster in New Orleans

In 2003, Congress enacted Bush's proposal to pay part of seniors' prescription drug expenses under the federal Medicare program. Democrats charged that the plan mainly benefited drug firms and insurance companies and would worsen a deepening federal budget deficit.

George W. Bush, leader of a party historically committed to fiscal prudence, presided over spending levels unprecedented in U.S. history. The prescription drug benefit helped push the government's share of Medicare costs to $179 billion in 2007, more than five times the 1990 figure. Medicare and social security costs, plus Bush's tax cuts, the unfunded Iraq and Afghan wars, and interest payments on the national debt, produced yawning federal deficits from 2002 on. Congress members of both parties continued the time-honored practice of quietly inserting into spending bills pet projects known as "earmarks" that benefited their districts.

Foreign investors funded the mushrooming federal debt by purchasing U.S. government bonds. China, awash in dollars—thanks to its U.S. exports—held nearly $700 billion in U.S. government bonds by 2008.

In 2005, Bush proposed a partial privatization of social security, the New Deal pension program. Under Bush's plan, people could shift some of their social security funds to private investment accounts. Although the social security system faced budgetary strains as the baby-boom generation retired, Bush's scheme failed to win acceptance. Most citizens preferred a government program to the uncertainties of the market.

The administration stumbled again over immigration policy. Of the estimated 11 million undocumented immigrants in the United States, most from Mexico or elsewhere in Latin America, many worked in a low-wage "shadow economy" as farm laborers, janitors, motel cleaners, or nursing-home attendants or in food-processing plants. In 2005, the administration proposed a bill by which these workers could eventually gain legal status. The debate that erupted revealed deep divisions in U.S. public opinion. Supporters invoked America's tradition of welcoming newcomers. Undocumented immigrants, they argued, did the essential work shunned by others. Businesses employing immigrants supported the bill. But opponents denounced it as "amnesty" for lawbreakers. Deport them, they argued, and the law of supply-and-demand would push up wages for the jobs they held, attracting U.S.-born workers. Late in 2005, the House of Representatives, with strong Republican support, defied the administration by passing a tough immigration bill criminalizing illegal aliens and requiring their deportation; strengthening the U.S.–Mexican border; and making it a felony for anyone, including ministers, priests, and health-care providers, to help undocumented immigrants.

The reaction was swift. Religious leaders denounced the bill. Protesters, supported by Spanish-language radio and TV, marched in Los Angeles and other cities. The bill's supporters mobilized as well. Radio personality Rush Limbaugh angrily denounced the marches. In the Southwest, volunteers organized a vigilante-like "Minuteman Project" to patrol the border.

With the Hispanic vote in play (some called it "the sleeping giant of American politics"), politicians proceeded cautiously. In the Senate, a bipartisan bill funded tougher border controls, but also established procedures by which undocumented immigrants could secure citizenship. Defying the White House, a bloc of Senate Republicans defeated the compromise bill.

Abandoning immigration reform, the administration took a harsh line. In 2006, Bush signed a bill to build a 700-mile reinforced fence along the U.S.–Mexican border. Federal agents raided plants employing undocumented Hispanics. Humanitarian and civil-rights groups protested, noting the impact on children and disrupted families. A 2008 film, *The Visitor*, portrayed the human consequences of rigidly enforced deportation policies. In 2008, the Supreme Court struck down an administration effort to deny deportees legal representation.

The administration took another hit in August 2005, when **Hurricane Katrina** struck the Gulf Coast, taking as many as fourteen hundred lives, inflicting heavy property damage, disrupting shipping on the Mississippi River, and smashing oil refineries and offshore oil rigs. New Orleans suffered most. Much of the city lies below sea level, protected by levees. Over the years, developers drained surrounding marshland, destroying a buffer against storm surges. As New Orleans' levees burst, rampaging water flooded the lower wards, home to many poor blacks. Many drowned or died awaiting rescue. Others lost homes and possessions. The elderly, hospitalized, and nursing home residents suffered most. Thousands poured into New Orleans's Superdome, which soon became a squalid disaster zone.

Washington's response was appallingly inadequate. Despite a local FEMA official's urgent warnings, neither President Bush nor the Homeland Security director recognized the emergency. FEMA head Michael Brown, a political appointee with no disaster experience, proved hopelessly inept. Though praised by Bush ("Heck of a job, Brownie"), he soon resigned. The distribution of emergency relief funds involved massive fraud and ineptitude. FEMA spent $900 million on twenty-six thousand mobile homes, many of which sat unused. Despite the reorganization of the national security bureaucracy after 9/11, Hurricane

© Michael Ainsworth/Dallas Morning News/Corbis News/Corbis

New Orleans in the Aftermath of Hurricane Katrina, September 1, 2005
Four days after the city's levees burst and flood waters devastated their homes, New Orleans residents await evacuation to the Superdome, which quickly became a scene of nightmarish conditions as thousands of desperate people crowded in.

Katrina revealed the same pattern of missed warnings, failed communication, and bumbling response.

Extending Republican Influence: From the Supreme Court to K Street Supreme Court justice Sandra Day O'Connor, a key swing vote in close decisions, retired in 2005. To replace her, Bush nominated federal judge John Roberts, who had held posts in the Reagan administration. When Chief Justice Rehnquist died that September, Bush elevated Roberts to the chief justiceship. He won easy Senate confirmation while revealing little about his judicial philosophy.

To fill the second vacancy, Bush first nominated his White House counsel, a longtime Texas friend. Widely criticized as unqualified, she soon withdrew. Bush next nominated Samuel Alito, Jr., who, as a federal judge, had endorsed the sweeping view of executive powers asserted by the Bush administration to justify its post–9/11 actions at home and abroad. Alito won confirmation, 58 to 42.

With Roberts and Alito joining Scalia and Thomas as a bloc of reliably conservative justices, Justice Anthony Kennedy emerged as the swing vote. Prochoice advocates feared (and abortion opponents hoped) that the increasingly conservative high court would overturn *Roe* v. *Wade,* the 1973 abortion-rights ruling. Although the issue remained contentious, opinion polls showed broad support for *Roe* v. *Wade*, with about 55 percent endorsing legal abortions with certain restrictions and 24 percent favoring no legally imposed restrictions at all. In *Gonzales* v. *Carhart* (2007), the Supreme Court, on a 5 to 4 vote, upheld a 2003 congressional ban on late-term abortions. In the decision, however, the majority cited *Roe* v. *Wade* as a precedent, thus implicitly reaffirming that ruling.

As Supreme Court politics attracted notice, so did the influence of Washington lobbyists. (This term stems from the era when individuals representing special interests would crowd the lobbies of the Capitol and state legislatures.) Long a part of U.S. politics, lobbyists' influence increased during the ascendancy of Texas Republican Congressman Tom "the Hammer" DeLay, who became House majority leader in 2003. From 2000 to 2005, the ranks of registered Washington lobbyists more than doubled, to nearly thirty-three thousand, with many more unregistered ones. Implementing a plan dubbed "the K Street project" (after the Washington street where many lobbyists had offices), DeLay extracted campaign contributions from lobbyists and pressured them to hire Republican staffers—often members of legislators' families. This reflected a broader GOP effort, originating with White House political strategist Karl Rove, to create a permanent Republican majority.

An eruption of scandals in 2005 focused attention on lobbyists and money's role in politics. In September, DeLay resigned as majority leader, and soon left Congress altogether, after a grand jury indicted him for violating Texas election laws by engineering a redistricting scheme that benefited

Republicans. In December, a federal grand jury indicted Jack Abramoff, a Washington lobbyist with ties to DeLay. Abramoff had collected millions from corporations trying to influence legislation, including $82 million from Indian tribes seeking to influence the award of casino licenses. Laundered through dummy organizations, this money paid for dinners, gifts, campaign donations, and golf junkets for Congress members—including some Democrats—while Abramoff siphoned off millions for himself.

Pleading guilty, Abramoff went to prison. Both he and DeLay had close White House connections, but President Bush denied any wrongdoing. As public disgust mounted, politicians scrambled to return tainted contributions and regulate lobbyists more strictly.

A Shifting Political Landscape: The 2006 Election and Beyond In the 2006 midterm election, voters rendered a stinging verdict on the Bush administration and the Republican-led Congress. Even President Bush admitted that his party had taken a "thumping." Democrats gained thirty-two House seats, retaking control for the first time in twelve years. The Democrat Nancy Pelosi of San Francisco became Speaker of the House, the first woman to hold that post. Democrats also narrowly won control of the Senate, 51 to 49. The number of women senators rose to sixteen, a record high. Democrats won a majority of governorships, including Massachusetts, where Deval Patrick became only the second African American elected governor since Reconstruction.

The election results also signaled deep national discontent over the Iraq War. Consequently, President Bush fired Defense Secretary Rumsfeld and named Robert Gates his successor. A former CIA director, Gates had served on a blue-ribbon Iraq Study Group whose 2006 report criticized both the decision to invade Iraq and the administration's conduct of the war. Vice President Cheney's influence diminished as well, as Secretary of State Rice and other administration officials challenged the imprisonments without trial, harsh interrogation techniques, sweeping domestic surveillance, and other policies promoted by Cheney after 9/11.

Advised by General David Petraeus, the new commander in Iraq, Bush in 2007 ordered a temporary "surge" of troops to Iraq. With additional GIs patrolling Baghdad and other trouble spots, sectarian violence declined. An uneasy cease-fire by Shi'ite militias and cooperation by Sunni clan leaders helped as well. Assassinations, suicide bombings, and IED attacks continued, but U.S. military deaths in Iraq for 2008 fell sharply from previous years. In November 2008, the Iraqi parliament ratified an agreement with Washington for the complete withdrawal of U.S. combat forces by 2012.

In December 2008, Bush made a final visit to Baghdad. At a news conference with Prime Minister Nouri al-Maliki, an Iraqi journalist hurled his shoes at the president—a gesture of contempt in Arabic societies—while shouting, "This is for widows and orphans and all those killed in Iraq!" The president shrugged off the incident. "That's what happens in free societies," he commented, "where people try to draw attention to themselves."

Despite encouraging developments, the situation, in General Petraeus's words, remained "fragile and reversible." Historically a patchwork of ethnic and religious groups ruled by successive invaders and then by British colonial administrators after World War I, Iraq had achieved independence only in 1932. Whether it could avoid fragmentation, sectarian turmoil, or renewed despotism remained unknown.

Despite Bush's claim that Saddam Hussein's overthrow justified the war, most Americans continued to view it as a disastrous mistake, diverting resources from the more vital conflict in Afghanistan. Reports of poor care in veterans' hospitals and massive fraud in the Iraq reconstruction program deepened public anger over the war.

Other controversies plagued Bush's final years in office. In March 2007, Vice President Cheney's chief of staff was convicted and imprisoned for perjury and obstruction of justice. The case arose from charges that Cheney's office had revealed to reporters the identity of a covert CIA agent, as part of a campaign to discredit her husband, a critic of the administration's prewar claims about Iraq's nuclear weapons program.

In August 2007, Attorney General Alberto Gonzales resigned amid an uproar over the hiring and firing of U.S. attorneys and Justice Department lawyers for blatantly political reasons rather than competence and experience. Gonzales's approval of the Justice Department's "torture memo" and of illegal FBI spying during his tenure as White House counsel added to the firestorm of criticism.

As Bush's presidency wound down, his approval ratings sank to around 25 percent—close to the lowest ever recorded for any president and a steep decline from their stratospheric levels after 9/11. What caused this reversal? Beyond the unpopular Iraq War and related issues of torture, unlimited detention, and violations of citizens' rights, many saw a go-it-alone approach that damaged America's standing worldwide. Critics also targeted the administration's dismissal of scientific evidence on the role of human activity in climate change, the politicization of federal agencies, the secretive power exercised by Vice President Cheney and a small circle of like-minded advisers, and the dominance of narrow partisanship and rigid ideology in shaping administration policies. To his opponents, Bush's black-and-white worldview, preference for snap decisions based on gut instincts, and reluctance to admit mistakes further limited his effectiveness.

The Economist, a respected London-based magazine that had endorsed Bush in 2000, reached a harsh judgment as his term ended: "He leaves the White House as one of the least popular and most divisive presidents in American history, ... [and] the most partisan ... in living memory.... [G]ood policy repeatedly took a back seat to Mr. Bush's overweening political ambition. Both the country and, ultimately, the Republican Party are left the worse for it."

Many Americans continued to support Bush, of course. The Iraq invasion, tax cuts, educational reforms, and free-market suspicion of government regulation all had their admirers. Bush himself defended his record, insisting that even his most controversial post–9/11 actions aimed to protect the country from terrorists. In 2008, despite Bush's personal unpopularity, 46 percent of the electorate voted Republican. Citing Harry Truman's post-presidential popularity, Bush suggested rather wistfully that he, too, would be vindicated by history.

THE OBAMA PRESIDENCY

The 2008 election represented a historic landmark in American history: the election of the first African American president, Barack Obama. Launched on a wave of hope and enthusiasm, the Obama administration pursued an ambitious agenda, headed by health-care reform. But a sharp political backlash, a stubborn recession, and chronic problems abroad portended challenges ahead.

Obama Wins in 2008   Among the 2008 Democratic presidential contenders, New York senator and former first lady **Hillary Clinton** emerged as the frontrunner; **Barack Obama,** a first-term black senator from Illinois, seemed an improbable long shot. Of an array of Republican hopefuls, Arizona senator **John McCain** outlasted the rest. A Vietnam War bomber pilot who spent six years in a Hanoi prison, McCain had built a reputation as a party maverick. As running mate, he chose Alaska governor Sarah Palin, an evangelical Christian with a populist touch who had bucked her state's Republican establishment to win the governorship after serving as a small-town mayor. After an initial buzz of excitement, Palin struck many as ill-informed and unqualified.

In the Democratic contest, Barack Obama won the Iowa primary and emerged as a formidable candidate, especially among young people attracted by his cool demeanor and inspiring speeches at rallies that attracted thousands. Energized by Internet websites, Obama backers phoned, put up posters, and rang doorbells. They also contributed millions to his campaign, far outstripping McCain's fundraising efforts. Winning the nomination after a grueling series of primaries against a determined Hillary Clinton, Obama chose as his running mate Delaware senator Joseph Biden.

McCain, downplaying his differences with the Bush administration, stressed his patriotism, called for victory in Iraq, and courted evangelical Christians despite his earlier criticism of some politicized preachers as "agents of intolerance." In TV debates, the seventy-two-year-old McCain sometimes seemed out of touch, especially on economic matters, while Obama exuded confidence. Responding to divisive pronouncements by his black minister, Obama delivered a thoughtful address on race that won favorable comment. Obama hammered the Bush administration's failures and emphasized his themes of change, hope, and overcoming partisan divisions.

Obama captured 53 percent of the popular vote and a solid Electoral College majority, carrying not only such crucial swing states of Florida, Ohio, and Pennsylvania, but also Virginia and North Carolina, long Republican strongholds. Along with overwhelming black support, he won 67 percent of the Hispanic vote, a significant increase over John Kerry's 2004 total, and nearly 70 percent of the eighteen–to–twenty-four-year old vote. The Democrats widened their majorities in both houses of Congress.

Around the world, people savored the historic moment. Nearly 150 years after the Emancipation Proclamation, and half a century beyond the civil-rights struggles of the 1950s and 1960s, an African American had won the presidency. Obama himself marveled in his inaugural address that sixty years earlier, many Washington restaurants would have denied his father service.

Barack Obama was born in Hawaii in 1961, the son of a Kenyan university student and his white wife, an anthropologist from Kansas. The couple soon separated, and Obama was reared by his mother and grandparents. After college and Harvard Law School, he worked as a community organizer in Chicago, and in 1996 won election to the Illinois legislature. His wife Michelle, also a lawyer, traced her southern ancestry to slavery days.

In his inaugural address, delivered before a vast throng in Washington and a global radio and television audience, Obama rejected what he called the "worn out dogmas" that blocked bold responses to urgent problems. Implicitly targeting the Bush administration's excesses, he said: "We reject as false the choice between our safety and our ideals.... Those ideals still light the world, and we will not give them up for expedience's sake.... [O]ur power alone cannot protect us, nor does it entitle us to do as we please." "America's "patchwork heritage" of ethnicities and national origins, of "Christians and Muslims, Jews and Hindus and nonbelievers," was no liability, he declared, but a great asset as the nation sought to restore its battered reputation in an equally diverse world.

When Obama was unexpectedly awarded the Nobel Peace prize in October 2009, after only nine months in office, it was widely viewed as a recognition of his high aspirations and an expression of hope for the future.

Early Initiatives at Home and Abroad   Obama named Hillary Clinton secretary of state, a post she would fill with great effectiveness. He ordered the Guantánamo prison closed (a policy that proved complicated to implement) and granted an interview to a popular Arabic-language television network. Obama's choice as attorney general, Eric Holder, declared in his Senate confirmation hearing that water boarding, the interrogation technique used on some Guantánamo prisoners, constituted torture and would be forbidden.

In a speech in Prague in April 2009, Obama pledged to work for a world free of nuclear weapons. North Korea's nuclear tests, Iran's secretive nuclear program, and the dangerous instability of nuclear-armed Pakistan underscored the urgency of this issue.

Obama also asked Congress to end the so-called "Don't ask, don't tell," policy requiring gays in the military to conceal their sexual orientation. After legal and political maneuvering, the policy was officially rescinded in 2011.

Obama lifted Bush's ban on stem-cell research and named Steven Chu, a Nobel laureate in physics and advocate of alternative energy sources, to lead the Department of Energy. To head the EPA, he chose an authority on environmental protection. Reversing Bush administration policy, Obama announced that by 2016 all new automobiles, light trucks, and SUVs would be required to meet the tougher fuel-efficiency standards already adopted by California and other states. Obama also urged redoubled work on alternative energy sources to reduce the nation's reliance on fossil fuels and to cut the emissions contributing to global climate change.

In April 2010, the nation faced another catastrophic oil spill when a drilling platform operated by the British-based BP energy company exploded and burned in the Gulf of Mexico, killing eleven workers and fouling large sections of the Gulf Coast's valuable fisheries industry. Obama (mindful of his predecessor's mishandling of the Katrina disaster) ordered the Coast Guard to monitor BP's clean-up efforts, imposed a temporary moratorium on deep-water drilling in the Gulf, and appointed a federal administrator to distribute damage claims from a fund established by BP.

Obama Wins a Close-Fought Victory on Health-Care Reform   Despite a gathering economic crisis, Obama pursued his top domestic goal: health-care reform to control costs while extending coverage to the uninsured. Securing cost-cutting pledges from the drug industry, health insurers, hospital associations, and other key players, Obama called on Congress to enact comprehensive health-care legislation.

Reform momentum soon slowed, however. Some critics resorted to scare tactics, conjuring visions of government "death panels" denying care to the elderly or terminally ill. As they had since President Truman's day, opponents warned of "socialized medicine" and "a government-run health care system," even though Medicare, the federal health-insurance program for the elderly, enjoyed broad popularity. The pharmaceutical and health-insurance industries, profiting handsomely under the present system, opposed any cost-control regulations beyond what they had already voluntarily pledged.

Reform proponents, by contrast, pointed to the millions of uninsured Americans, the loss of coverage that often came with unemployment, insurance companies' denial of coverage to high-risk applicants, and the spiraling costs of U.S. health care in contrast to other nations with comparable or superior medical outcomes.

Despite Obama's call for bipartisan cooperation, party divisions hardened. Even Democrats were divided. Democrats from conservative districts favored a cautious, incremental approach. Democratic liberals, by contrast, supported a "public option," a government health-insurance program, supplementing the private system, that would serve the uninsured and provide a benchmark for

President Obama Signs Health Care into Action *The Patient Protection and Affordable Care Act of 2010 mandated health insurance for most Americans, provided subsidies to poor Americans who couldn't afford it, and guaranteed health coverage for all, even those with pre-existing conditions.*

cost control. The August 2009 death of Massachusetts Democratic senator Edward Kennedy, a champion of health-care reform, inspired advocates to redoubled efforts.

In March 2010, on strictly party lines, Congress passed and Obama signed a health-care reform law, the Patient Protection and Affordable Care Act. The law extended Medicare coverage to some 32 million uninsured Americans, with the costs to be covered by Medicare savings, higher Medicare rates to upper-income earners, and tax increases on the wealthiest Americans. The law also prohibited insurance companies from denying coverage because of preexiting conditions and extended coverage to dependent children up to age twenty-six.

Recession Strikes   Even as the acrimonious health-care debate unfolded, attention increasingly turned to a recession that had begun in 2007 in the real-estate market and quickly worsened. Beginning in the late 1990s, housing prices spiked upward, especially in California, Florida, the Southwest, and Northeast. The bubble burst in 2007. As real-estate prices tumbled, homebuilding and commercial developments stalled.

The crisis soon spread, worsened by lax governmental regulation. In 1999, Congress repealed the Glass-Steagall Act, a 1933 law designed to regulate bank practices and protect depositors. Introduced by Republicans, the repeal won bipartisan support and was signed by President Clinton. Freed of regulatory constraints, investment banks could now acquire unregulated financial services companies and indulge in various forms of financial chicanery. During the real-estate boom, unscrupulous lending companies extended mortgages to home-buyers who could ill afford them. With slogans like "No credit? No problem" and low initial rates that quickly jumped higher, predatory lenders lured first-time home buyers, many of them black and Hispanic. By 2008, nearly 30 per-cent of all mortgages were rated as "subprime." These risky mortgages were then sold to Wall Street investment banks or other financial institutions that bundled or "securitized" them into stock offerings purchased by pension funds, mutual funds, and foreign banks. Decades of deregulation, driven by free-market ideology, encouraged both predatory lending and the marketing of highly risky securities.

As the real-estate market weakened, homeowners facing exorbitant mort-gage payments could neither sell their homes nor refinance their mortgages. Many defaulted, leaving behind empty, neglected houses and a sea of foreclo-sure signs. As homeowners defaulted, the value of the securities based on these mortgages collapsed. Wall Street banks and financial services companies found themselves holding securities, now relabeled "toxic assets," they could not sell, and whose actual market value no one knew.

Wall Street's largest banks faced disastrous losses, with some nearing insolvency. Giant Lehman Brothers collapsed in September 2008. Fearing further losses, the big banks stopped lending. As credit froze, the broader economy suffered. Business activity slowed; jittery consumers cut spending. The Dow Jones stock market average, after soaring above 14,000 in October 2007, sank to under 8,000 by March 2009, wiping out billions in investors' assets.

The recession hit home as Americans saw their savings, property values, and retirement funds shrivel and as companies announced layoffs. In 2008, 2.6 million workers lost their jobs, the highest rate of loss in sixty years. By September 2009, the unemployment rate stood at 9.8 percent. Even this figure did not include involuntary part-time workers or discouraged jobseekers who had stopped looking. In Michigan, home of the U.S. auto industry, the jobless rate passed 15 percent. Even the high-flying IT sector suffered, as mighty Microsoft and the giant chipmaker Intel announced layoffs. As the worst reces-sion since the Great Depression bit deeper, college students worried about their prospects. For displaced workers and unskilled youth, an already tough job market looked even grimmer.

The recession struck an economy whose benefits were already very unevenly distributed. While some had profited handsomely from the Bush tax cuts, the soaring stock market, and the boom in financial services and electronics technolo-gies, most Americans' real income remained flat through the Bush years. The surge in consumer spending was largely financed with plastic. Total consumer debt in 2008, excluding mortgages, approached $2.6 trillion. After a decade when both Washington and American consumers had plunged deeply into debt, the chickens now came home to roost. In 2009, U.S. banks wrote off $83 billion in unpaid credit-card debt.

The Bush administration in its waning months tried to grapple with the crisis. In July 2008, despite his party's free-market beliefs, President Bush signed a bill that helped homeowners refinance their mortgages, tightened mortgage-lending regulations, and strengthened federal oversight of two privately owned but government-supported home-loan agencies—nicknamed Fannie Mae and Freddie Mac—that were deeply implicated in the crisis. In late in 2008, Congress appropriated $700 billion to provide more capital to the investment banks in hopes of stimulating the economy. But as the Treasury Department ladled out the billions, it imposed few rules on what the banks should do with the money, and most simply used it to stabilize their own balance sheets rather than making loans to promote recovery.

Revelations of the bloated earnings of the financiers who had caused the crisis deepened public anger. In 2004–2007, the CEO of Countrywide Finance, a giant subprime mortgage lender, made $270 million. As late as December 2008, after fourth-quarter losses of $15 billion, Merrill Lynch's CEO doled out millions in bonuses to top executives and spent $2.2 million redecorating his office. A familiar pattern of greed and excess in the upper reaches of American capitalism as millions faced desperate times was again unfolding.

In an era of globalization, the crisis quickly spread. Banks in Europe and Asia tightened credit as the U.S. securities in their portfolios lost value. With Obama in the White House, the recession he had inherited was now his problem. Treasury Secretary Timothy Geithner, formerly president of the Federal Reserve Bank of New York, and economist Lawrence Summers, named head of the White House National Economic Council, led Obama's recession-fighting team. (Ironically, both had supported the deregulatory legislation that helped lay the groundwork for the crisis.)

In February 2009, Obama signed a $787 billion economic-stimulus bill. It channeled $120 billion to states for highways, bridges, rapid transit, and other infrastructure projects; appropriated additional billions for school construction and energy-related projects; and cut taxes for middle- and lower-income Americans while restoring higher rates for upper-income earners. Ominously, despite Obama's pleas for bipartisanship, only three Senate Republicans voted for the bill.

Obama also insisted that future distributions from the Wall Street bailout package must ensure that banks actually channeled the funds into the credit market, to promote recovery. He also called for limits on executive compensation in return for federal money. When The *New York Times* revealed that Wall Street executives had pocketed $18.4 billion in bonuses in 2008 while their banks received government bailout money, Obama denounced the news as "outrageous."

While the administration granted a multi-billion-dollar emergency bailout to the ailing U.S. auto industry, Obama created a While House task force to oversee the industry's long-term restructuring. Chrysler filed for bankruptcy, though a takeover by the Italian automaker Fiat brightened its long-term prospects. As once mighty General Motors briefly entered bankruptcy in 2009, Americans realized the depth of the crisis facing this core domestic industry. After government assistance and a court-ordered reorganization, including losses to stock- and bond-holders and concessions by unions, GM returned to profitability in 2010.

In July 2010, Obama signed a financial-services reform law, called the Dodd-Frank Act for its two principal sponsors, addressing abuses that had led to the economic meltdown. The law strengthened federal oversight of the financial-services industry and outlawed mortgage abuses and speculative bank practices that had proliferated during the mania for business deregulation.

Economists generally agreed that the Dodd-Frank law helped correct glaring abuses, and that Obama's economic recovery program, though less aggressive than it might have been, prevented the recession from becoming far worse. Further, the years 2010 and 2011 bought tantalizing signs of recovery, including a gradually reviving housing market and a stabilizing and then slowly improving employment picture. But millions of Americans still faced economic woes, and in a bitterly contentious political climate, Obama received little credit for his accomplishments and much of the blame for the slow pace of recovery. Leading Republicans fed this mood. As Senate minority leader Mitch McConnell of Kentucky candidly acknowledged in October 2010: "The single most important thing we want to achieve is for President Obama to be a one-term president."

A Tangle of Problems in Afghanistan, Pakistan, and Iran

Meanwhile, the war in Afghanistan ground on. A resurgent Taliban, allied with radical Islamist groups in Pakistan, increased attacks on U.S. troops, Afghan government forces, and the civilian population. With some 68,000 G.I.s deployed in that country, U.S. military fatalities by the end of 2011 neared two thousand, with nearly one thousand additional dead among the 38,000 NATO coalition forces. U.S. military wounded surpassed 14,000. As the Taliban regained control in parts of southern Afghanistan, they weakened the U.S.-backed government of President Hamid Karzai and destabilized neighboring Pakistan as well. Rampant government corruption, accusations of fraud in an August 2009 election, and Afghanistan's leading role in the cultivation of opium poppies (from which heroin is manufactured) further complicated the picture.

Declaring the Afghan struggle a "war of necessity" (in contrast to George W. Bush's misadventure in Iraq), Obama initially committed 30,000 more troops to the conflict. In 2011, however, as home-front support for the war eroded, particularly among his own party, Obama announced major troop withdrawals by the summer of 2012 and a complete withdrawal by 2014. As the Americans simultaneously combatted the Taliban and sought to open lines of communication with them while maintaining relations with an increasingly erratic Afghan government, the future in Afghanistan appeared deeply uncertain.

A clear Obama success came in May 2011, when U.S. special forces killed Osama bin Laden in a safe house near a major Pakistani military installation. Pakistani protests at not being consulted about this operation added to their grievances over U.S. drone aircraft raids that targeted militants in Pakistan's lawless borderlands, but sometimes killed civilians. As Washington accused elements of the Pakistani military of supporting Taliban-related groups, relations between the two countries worsened.

Meanwhile, Iran, still fiercely anti-American and anti-Israel, continued to pursue a nuclear-development program in secure underground facilities. Allegedly for peaceful purposes, the program increasingly seemed aimed at developing nuclear weapons. As the Western powers imposed ever-stricter sanctions and warned of military measures, Iran responded belligerently, even threatening to close the Straits of Hormus, a vital lifeline through which Iranian oil passed to the world market.

Washington Gridlock, Grassroots Anger, the 2010 Midterm Election

A conciliator by temperament, Obama took office confident that he and the Republican opposition could reach compromise on urgent national issues. This hope proved unrealistic. Taking advantage of a Senate rule requiring a "supermajority" of 60 percent on major bills, the Republicans thwarted Obama at every turn and spurned his conciliatory efforts. Even some Obama supporters perceived him as too deferential and too ready to give ground even before hard bargaining began. Remembering Obama the feisty, aggressive campaigner, they longed for a more feisty, aggressive president.

Adhering to their free-market ideology, the Republicans argued that tax cuts and fewer business regulations would stimulate recovery and end the recession. Insisting that the federal deficit posed the nation's most urgent problem, they demanded spending cuts in social programs to address it. The deficit was indeed a serious issue, compounded by rising social security and Medicare costs. Ironically, however, the deficit problem had been severely worsened by Bush-era tax cuts, by the unfunded prescription-drug benefit, and by the unfunded wars in Iraq and Afghanistan—conflicts for which U.S. taxpayers had made no sacrifices. Yet when Obama, in his quest for compromise, proposed modest tax increases for the very wealthiest Americans as part of a deficit-reduction package, the Republican leadership adamantly refused.

Among the electorate at large, an ugly mood spread. Some Americans formed the so-called Tea Party movement, inspired by the original Boston Tea Party of 1773 protesting British taxation. Venting their hostility to "Obamacare," taxes, big government, and federal assistance to mortgage holders who had lost their homes, they also demonized Obama personally, accusing him of being a socialist and even questioning his U.S. citizenship.

The 2010 midterm election reflected the sour national mood, worsened by the recession. The Republicans regained control of the House of Representatives, with many new Tea Party members even more rigidly anticompromise than their party leadership, ensuring continued gridlock. Several showdowns initiated by Tea Party members over raising the federal debt limit, normally a noncontroversial act to preserve the nation's credit, threatened government shutdowns.

Newly elected Republican governors and legislators in Ohio and Wisconsin pushed through harsh measures restricting the rights of public-employee unions, including teachers. (In both states, angry voters pushed back. Ohio voters repealed the anti-union law by referendum, and Wisconsin voters organized a recall campaign to force a special gubernatorial election.)

The 2010 election generated some $4 billion in campaign contributions—an all-time record for a mid-term election—much of it from outside corporate donors and other groups. Fueling this vast infusion of cash was a landmark 2010 Supreme Court decision, *Citizens United* v. *Federal Elections Commission*. This 5 to 4 ruling held that the First Amendment granted corporations, unions, or any other group the right to spend unlimited sums to influence elections. This decision effectively gutted the McCain-Feingold campaign-finance law and indeed threw into confusion a century of efforts to restrain the role of big money in politics. Encouraged by the electoral results, the Republican leadership dug in still more firmly against any Obama proposals, even blocking White House nominees for public office that, under other conditions, would have been routinely approved. Congress refused, for example, to approve Obama's choice to head the new Consumer Financial Protection Bureau, authorized by the Dodd-Frank law to protect consumers from predatory mortgage lenders, credit-card issuers, and other financial-services providers. Opponents claimed the new agency lacked sufficient congressional oversight. In 2012, taking advantage of a congressional recess, Obama appointed Richard Cordray, Ohio's attorney general and a consumer advocate, to the post.

In the face of continual gridlock, public opinion turned against Congress. In an October 2011 *New York Times*/CBS News poll, only 9 percent of Americans approved of Congress's performance, the lowest figure ever recorded. By contrast, Obama's ratings, from a low of 41 percent in September 2011, began to trend upward, though his electoral prospects clearly depended on factors beyond his control—above all the state of the economy, both domestically, and in Europe, which was struggling with a serious debt crisis in Greece and other countries.

Deepening the political malaise was a growing realization that the economic disparities between the very wealthiest Americans and the rest of the population, including the vast middle class, had widened enormously in recent decades, reaching levels not seen since the 1920s. While overall U.S. median income, corrected for inflation, has declined since 1999, that of the top 1 percent has soared. Expressing this sense of inequity, an "Occupy Wall Street" movement began in October 2011 with hundreds of protesters occupying a park near Manhattan's financial district. The movement quickly spread to other U.S. cities and beyond. While conservatives defended such vast disparities as a natural outcome of a meritocratic, free-market system, others saw serious dangers to social harmony and to the sense of common purpose characteristic of the nation at its best.

As another presidential election loomed, President Obama used the January 2012 State of the Union address to highlight his campaign themes. Pointing to signs of economic improvement, he made job creation and economic fairness his highest priorities and insisted that the richest citizens should pay their fair share of taxes. America faced a choice, he said, between a society where "a shrinking number of people do really well while a growing number of Americans barely get by," and a society "where everyone gets a fair shot, everyone does their fair share, and everyone plays by the same rules."

Sharpening the contrast between his readiness to compromise and Republican obstructionism, the president again called for an end to partisan gridlock, "Our destiny is stretched together like those fifty stars and those thirteen stripes ... ," Obama declared; "This nation is great because we built it together."

In the Republican response, Governor Mitch Daniels of Indiana insisted that his party was upholding the principles of free enterprise, frugal government, and "the dignity and capacity of the individual citizen," against Democratic big-government solutions. In contrast to the more libertarian wing of his party, however, Daniels insisted that the social safety net of social security and Medicare must be preserved and that the wealthiest American had a duty to pay their fair share toward resolving the deficit crisis.

THE 2012 PRESIDENTIAL ELECTION

Conservatism dominated the 2012 Republican presidential primaries. Several prominent moderate Republicans, including Mitch Daniels and former Florida governor Jeb Bush (brother of the 43rd president), decided not to run. Others, like Jon Huntsman, failed to gain traction and dropped out of the race early.

Ironically, it was Mitt Romney, the candidate with the weakest conservative credentials, who won the Republican nomination. As candidate for governor of Massachusetts in 2002, he supported *Roe* v. *Wade*; in office, he signed a landmark health care law that—like Obama's Affordable Care Act—mandated coverage and provided premium support for the poor. But in the Republican primaries in 2011 and 2012, he re-billed himself as "severely conservative," called for a huge tax cut and tough measures regarding illegal immigration, and opposed abortion rights and "Obamacare." This swing to the right helped Romney appeal to the Republican base.

Once he got to the general election, Romney pivoted again and adroitly moved to the center on key issues. In three televised debates, Romney embraced health-care reform on the state level and agreed with many of Obama's foreign policies, notably the president's use of economic sanctions against Iran and his promise to withdraw all U.S. troops from Afghanistan. Highlighting his success as a corporate CEO, Romney cast himself as the candidate best able to create jobs, forge bipartisan consensus, and balance a $1 trillion federal budget deficit. And Romney parried Obama's call to balance the budget with higher taxes on the wealthy by claiming that he could achieve the same result by closing unspecified tax loopholes.

At the start, Obama's reelection campaign faced strong headwinds. In 2011 and the first half of 2012, the unemployment rate hovered between 9 and 10 percent, while 4.1 million struggling homeowners received foreclosure notices. However, the "green shoots" of an economic recovery began to take hold. By the fall, Obama could point to improvements since he took office, such as a rebounded auto industry, net job growth, and falling unemployment (down to 7.8 percent by September). In a stroke of political good fortune, the recovery was especially strong in the swing state of Ohio. There, Democrats and labor unions were riding high after defeating a Republican effort in 2011 to strip collective bargaining rights from public-sector workers. The president's bailout of the automobile industry was popular in Ohio as well.

Obama's campaign also held a clear advantage with African Americans and the fast-growing Hispanic population. Since 2008, when two-thirds of Hispanics supported the president, about 4 million Hispanics were newly eligible to vote. In June 2012, Obama issued an executive order halting the deportation of thousands of young, undocumented immigrants who were attending school or serving in the military. That same month, Obama's signature legislative accomplishment, the Affordable Care Act, was saved from destruction when the Supreme Court upheld it in a 5–4 decision.

President Obama also seemed to have the advantage on foreign policy. The so-called Arab Spring revolutions of 2011 unseated dictators in Tunisia and Egypt. American warplanes helped depose a long-time foe of the United States, Libyan ruler Muammar Gaddafi. Another U.S. antagonist, Bashar al-Assad of Syria, faced a massive internal insurgency and was hanging on to power by a thread. And the crisis over Iran's nuclear program abated somewhat when U.S. sanctions crippled that country's economy. In addition, Obama pulled U.S. troops out of Iraq, ordered the raid in May 2011 that killed Osama bin Laden, and called for a withdrawal of all American troops from Afghanistan by the end of 2014. And although Obama's increasing reliance on unmanned drones sparked criticism, his support for these deadly drone attacks remained popular among U.S. voters (including Mitt Romney, who supported them). Obama's decisive response to Hurricane Sandy, which devastated the New Jersey coast just eight days before the election, also burnished his credentials as Commander in Chief.

On election day, President Obama prevailed in Ohio and won a second term. Although narrower than 2008's victory, the 2012 result illustrated the extent to which politics had been transformed by changing demographics. About 45 percent of Obama's support came from minority voters. One of ten voters was

Hispanic: 70 percent voted for the president. Obama won the youth vote by more than 20 percent.

Furthermore, Obama's support for reproductive rights and equal pay for women helped him sustain a Democratic advantage among female voters. (The 113th Congress included a record number of women elected to the House [77] and the Senate [20], including consumer advocate Elizabeth Warren, the first-ever female senator from Massachusetts.) Buoyed by these trends, Democrats maintained control of the Senate. Meanwhile, Romney's chief advantage was among older voters and white males—a shrinking share of the electorate. "A coalition of aging white men," wrote journalist Nicholas Kristof, "is a recipe for failure in a nation that increasingly looks like a rainbow."

But even as they fretted about their place in a changed political landscape, Republicans rejected the notion that Obama had received a mandate to rule without compromise. "The American people re-elected the president, and re-elected our majority in the House," said John Boehner, the Republican Speaker of the House. "If there is a mandate, it is a mandate for both parties to find common ground and take steps together to help our economy grow and create jobs, which is critical to solving our debt." As a budget crisis loomed, both sides now faced difficult choices with consequences for every American.

CHRONOLOGY
2001–2012

2001	Bush administration repudiates Kyoto protocol on emission standards.
	Congress passes $1.35 trillion tax cut bill.
	Stock market falls; wave of corporate bankruptcies and scandals.
	Congress passes No Child Left Behind Act.
	U.S. withdraws from ABM (Anti-Ballistic Missile) Treaty and pursues missile-defense system.
	Terrorist attacks on World Trade Center, Pentagon (September 11).
	U.S. and allied forces overthrow Taliban regime in Afghanistan.
	Captured fighters and others imprisoned at Guantánamo Bay, Cuba.
	USA-Patriot Act passed.
2002	McCain-Feingold Campaign Reform Act passed.
	Department of Homeland Security created.
	Bush authorizes warrantless spying by National Security Administration.
	Republicans gain in midterm elections.

2003	U.S. and coalition forces invade Iraq (March 21).
	North Korea withdraws from Nuclear Non-Proliferation Treaty.
	Prescription-drug benefits added to Medicare.
2004	Revelation of abuses at Baghdad's Abu Ghraib prison.
	George W. Bush wins second term, defeating John Kerry.
2005	Congress passes Energy Act.
	Trade deficit and budget deficit hit record levels.
	Bush names John Roberts and Samuel Alito to Supreme Court.
	Hurricane Katrina devastates New Orleans.
	Lobbyist Jack Abramoff indicted on multiple criminal charges.
2006	Tom DeLay resigns House seat.
	Widespread criticism of government response to Hurricane Katrina.
	Radical Hamas organization wins Palestinian elections.
	Iran resumes nuclear enrichment program.
	U.S. sells India nuclear fuel and reactor parts.
	Administration's immigration-reform bill fails; arrests and deportation of illegal immigrants increase.
	Democrats gain control of both houses in mid-term elections.
	Resignation of Defense Secretary Donald Rumsfeld.
2007	Bush sends more troops to Iraq; violence declines.
	Real-estate market falls; recession begins.
2008	United States and Iraq set timetable for U.S. troop withdrawals.
	Military situation in Afghanistan worsens.
	Recession deepens; major banks fail; job losses increase.
	Congress passes bank bailout legislation.
	Barack Obama, America's first African American president, is elected; Democrats make gains.
	Gaza rockets hit Israel; Israel responds with major military attack causing heavy civilian casualties.

2009	President Obama orders closing of Guantánamo prison.
	Obama reverses Bush administration on vehicle emissions, stem-cell research.
	Congress enacts broad economic stimulus package as recession worsens.
2010	Supreme Court's *Citizens United* v. *Federal Elections Commission* ruling opens door to unlimited campaign contributions.
	Catastrophic BP oil spill in Gulf of Mexico.
	Obama signs landmark health-care measure into law.
	Dodd-Frank Act regulates abuses in financial-services and mortgage industries.
	Republicans regain House of Representatives.
2011	Osama bin Laden killed by U.S. special forces in Pakistan.
	Final withdrawal of U.S. combat forces from Iraq.
	"Arab Spring" revolutions unseat dictators in Egypt, Tunisia, and Libya.
	Budget showdown nearly leads to shutdown of government.
2012	Senate rejects House budget calling for changes to Medicare, cuts in federal spending.
	U.S. Supreme Court upholds Affordable Care Act.
	Barack Obama defeats Mitt Romney and wins reelection.

Conclusion

This most recent chapter in the American story we have traced in *The Enduring Vision* clearly had its shining moments, including the election of the nation's first African American president. Even Barack Obama's political opponents recognized the symbolic significance of his election. Yet this was also a stressful time. Beginning with the devastating attacks of September 11, 2001, and continuing through a controversial war in Iraq, a mortgage crisis and deep recession that upended the lives of millions of Americans, economic challenges from emerging economies, and a period of unusual political rancor, these were years of uncertainty and anxiety.

In such times, seeking a longer historical perspective beyond the daily headlines can offer reassurance. The United States has faced many uncertain times, but the nation also has a history of overcoming challenges and discovering sources of renewal. As President Obama declared in his 2008 inaugural address, "The time has come to reaffirm our enduring spirit, to choose our better history."

What, then, is the "enduring vision" of our title? There is, of course, no single vision, but many. That is part of America's meaning. Nor is this a vision of a fore-ordained national destiny unfolding effortlessly, but rather of successive genera-tions' often-frustrating struggle to better their common life as a people. At their best, these shared aspirations are rooted in hope, not fear, in a sense of unity, not divisiveness. In 1980, Jesse de la Cruz, a Mexican American activist for California's migrant workers, summed up her philosophy: "Is America progressing toward the better? … With us, there's a saying: *La esperanza muere al ultimo.* Hope dies last. You can't lose hope. If you lose hope, that's losing everything."

Index

Irvin "Rags" Rather, Dan's
father, fishing

Dan's mother, Byrl Rather,
holding Dan in front of the
house in Wharton, 1931

Byrl Rather in front of
a neighbor's car, 1931

Irvin Rather on his way to a job interview, 1946

As a member of the William G. Love Elementary School "rhythm band," Dan (last row, second from left) played triangle

Dan, on the far left, in 3rd grade at Love Elementary School

Dan (far right, second row) at a Boy Scout gathering in Houston, 1945

Dan (center) spent his college days as the editor of *The Houstonian*, circa 1952

As a young Marine

Dan (who did play-by-play) with University of Houston football coach Harold Lahar, Rice coach Jess Neely, and color analyst Roy Hebert

At KTRH Radio,
circa 1959

Alone while covering
Hurricane Carla in
Galveston, Texas, 1961

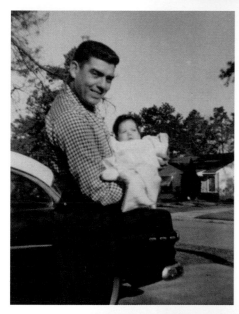

Dan with his daughter,
Robin, 1958

Dan with his
son, Danjack,
Christmas 1962

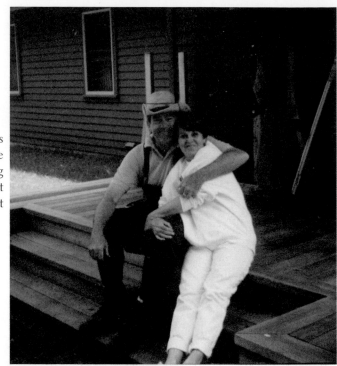

Dan with his wife, Jean, at the Beaverkill fishing lodge, just after it was built

Dan with Jean at a Christmas ball given by the Rathers for the CBS News staff, mid-1980s

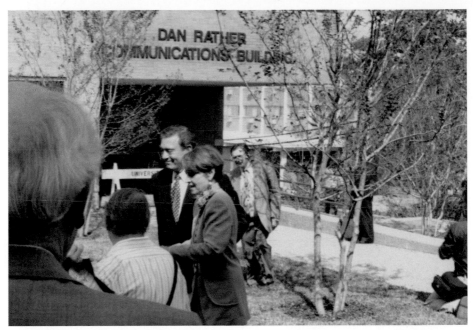

At the 1994 dedication of the Dan Rather Communications Building at Sam Houston State University, with Jean

With fellow anchors Brian Williams, Walter Cronkite, and Tom Brokaw (Evan Agostini/Getty Images Entertainment/Getty Images)

With actor George Clooney (Michael Tran/ FilmMagic/Getty Images)

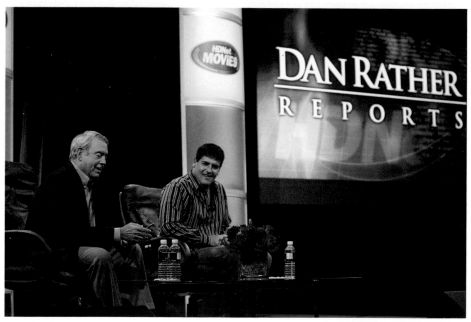

With Mark Cuban, founder of HDNet (Frederick M. Brown/Getty Images Entertainment/ Getty Images)